The Essential Turgenev

The Essential Turgenev

IVAN SERGEEVICH TURGENEV

Edited and with an Introduction by
ELIZABETH CHERESH ALLEN

Northwestern University Press · Evanston, Illinois

Northwestern University Press
Evanston, Illinois 60208-4210

"The Execution of Troppmann" from *Ivan Turgenev: Literary Reminiscences and Autobiographical Fragments*, translated by David Magarshack. Translation copyright © 1958 by Farrar, Straus and Cudahy, Inc. Reprinted by permission of Farrar, Straus and Giroux, Inc.

Turgenev's letters from *Turgenev: Letters*, volumes one and two, edited and translated by David Lowe. Translation copyright © 1983 by Ardis. Reprinted by permission of Ardis Publishers.

Introduction, Note on the Text, and translations of "Hamlet and Don Quixote," "Autobiography," and "Speech Delivered at the Dedication of the Monument to A. S. Pushkin in Moscow" copyright © 1994 by Northwestern University Press.

Printed in the United States of America

ISBN cloth 0-8101-1060-1
     paper 0-8101-1085-7

Library of Congress Cataloging-in-Publication Data
Turgenev, Ivan Sergeevich, 1818–1883.
  [Selections. English. 1994]
  The essential Turgenev / Ivan Sergeevich Turgenev ; edited and with an introduction by Elizabeth Cheresh Allen.
    p. cm.
  ISBN 0-8101-1060-1. — ISBN 0-8101-1085-7 (pbk.)
  1. Turgenev, Ivan Sergeevich, 1818–1883—Translations into English. I. Allen, Elizabeth Cheresh, 1951– . II. Title.
PG3421.A2A45 1994
891.73'3—dc20
                                               94-6719
                                                  CIP

The paper used in this publication meets the minimum requirements of the American National Standard for Information Sciences—Permanence of Paper for Printed Library Materials, ANSI Z39.48-1984.

Contents

v

Contents

Acknowledgments

A project of this magnitude is never completed without the help of many people, and I can only begin to acknowledge those who have been so generous with their assistance. Robert Louis Jackson, who first drew me into the study of Turgenev, Caryl Emerson, and Cathy Popkin each offered valuable suggestions on the works to be included, and William Mills Todd III offered his typically wise counsel regarding the introduction. My colleagues Dan E. Davidson, Christine G. Borowec, and Linda Gerstein were always willing to discuss difficult points of translation, and graciously cooperated when the demands of this project took me away from our department at Bryn Mawr. My longstanding friend and former fellow student of Russian literature Helen Gredd greatly facilitated the physical production of the manuscript, not least by introducing me to Martha Burke, typist extraordinaire, who maintained inimitable calm while producing revision upon revision in record time. Dedicated graduate students Catharine M. Cooke, Camelot Marshall, Sarah Ann Mathews, and Jeanette Owen made the correction of page proofs as enjoyable as that painstaking process can possibly be. Susan Harris, managing editor of Northwestern University Press, devoted innumerable hours to matters large and small through every phase of the publication process. And special thanks go to Shavaun K. McGinty, my departmental assistant, whose superlative administrative skills, along with her exceptional warmth and wit, enabled me to conserve sufficient time, energy, and good humor to bring this project to its close.

My husband, James Sloan Allen, displayed a tolerance for my seemingly interminable involvement with Turgenev perhaps second only to Louis Viardot's for *his* wife's fabled relationship with this author. In addition, my husband heroically endured countless consultations on the fine points of English diction and syntax, and patiently read various versions of the introduction, providing me with constant inspiration and guidance by virtue of his unswerving intelligence, objectivity, and integrity.

Gary Saul Morson, who has figured ever more prominently in my life as a teacher, mentor, and friend, steadfastly lent his support to this project from beginning to end, rendering crucial assistance to keep it going at moments when it might otherwise have come to a halt. And so it is with the deepest gratitude, admiration, and affection that I dedicate the finished product to Saul.

E. C. A.

Bryn Mawr, 1994

Introduction: Turgenev Today

It is a portrait of Ivan Turgenev—not of Fedor Dostoevsky or of Lev Tolstoy—that serves as the frontispiece for one of the earliest collections of Russian literature in English translation, Leo Wiener's *Anthology of Russian Literature: The Nineteenth Century*, published in 1903. For it was Turgenev, not his two great contemporaries, who stood at the pinnacle of Russian literature at the turn of the century and who most notably spoke for his nation to the West. Thus the choice of his likeness to open that anthology would have come as no surprise to readers at the time. But readers of today might well wonder at this choice, since nowadays Dostoevsky and Tolstoy are far more famous and widely read in the West than is Turgenev. The selection of Turgenev's portrait therefore gives rise to two questions: Why was Turgenev seen as Russian literature's emblematic figure then? And why is Turgenev not, most would agree, perceived that way now?

The first question has many answers, most of which are relatively easy to find in the artistic and social circumstances of Turgenev's times. The second question is more complicated, pointing as it does to the vagaries of literary reputation and to the attitudes, tastes, and circumstances of twentieth-century literary culture. This introduction and the extensively revised collection of Turgenev's works in English translation that follows aspire at once to shed light on this second question and to answer it anew by setting forth a Turgenev for our times, as well as to reaffirm Turgenev's stature for all time.

Born in 1818 on a rural estate south of Moscow, the son of a retired cavalry officer and a wealthy, domineering mother, Turgenev was first tutored at home, then attended universities in both Moscow and St. Petersburg, and finally received what he considered his formative education at the University of Berlin between 1838 and 1841. Soon thereafter, his life took a pivotal turn when he fell passionately, albeit chastely—as far as we know—in love with the acclaimed Spanish songstress Pauline Viardot. Although she was married, Turgenev accompanied her and her family around Europe for the rest of his life, never getting married himself. He did return periodically to his Russian family estate, Spasskoe, even as he established residences near the Viardots' in Germany and then France, where he died, with Pauline at his side, in 1883.

Whatever its costs may have been to his personal life, this enduring attachment had the professional benefit of allowing Turgenev to socialize with the eminent French authors of the day, among them Gustave Flaubert, George Sand, Eugene Sue, Emile Zola, and the brothers Goncourt; Turgenev thus became the most cosmopolitan Russian author of his generation. His perennial presence in the West also enabled Turgenev to promote assiduously the translation and publication of numerous Russian authors' works all across Europe. At the same time, he established a prominent place for himself there, as well as in Russia, by producing a constant stream of work from 1843 onward, including narrative poems, novels, novellas, short stories, plays, essays, and critical commentaries, most of which were rapidly translated into western European languages. To be sure, many of Dostoevsky's and Tolstoy's works were also promptly translated—thanks in part to Turgenev's efforts—but their prodigious density rendered them less accessible to Western readers than Turgenev's economical, lapidary prose. Hence Dostoevsky and Tolstoy did not become as widely recognized as Turgenev among readers and critics until the early decades of the twentieth century.

Of his many writings, it was the fiction, set primarily in Russia and convincingly portraying the varieties of Russian social life, that caused Turgenev to be lionized as the preeminent Russian literary figure of his era. He was hailed for possessing the genius "to render life, only life, slices of life," as Guy de Maupassant put it. Or as the French historian Ernest Renan proclaimed upon Turgenev's death, "No other man has been so much the incarnation of a whole race. A world lived in him, spoke through his lips."

This reputation as the peerless chronicler of his era in Russia earned Turgenev high honor among writers of the dominant literary movement of the mid-nineteenth century, realism. Representatives of this movement—including most of the major novelists of that time—are said to have adopted as their goal the detailed, objective depiction of historical, political, and social conditions of a particular place and moment, usually of the contemporary world. Although many authors themselves disliked being labeled "realists," Turgenev was not as consistently reluctant to identify himself as such, declaring to one correspondent in 1875 that "in the main, I am a realist, and am above all interested in the living truth of physiognomy."

So adept was Turgenev at depicting "physiognomy" that not only did contemporaries praise his realism but many leading authors of the late nineteenth and early twentieth centuries, notably William Dean Howells, Henry James, Thomas Mann, Joseph Conrad, Virginia Woolf, W. Somerset Maugham, and Ernest Hemingway, also extolled the masterly artistry that underlay this realism; Hemingway is said to have advised aspiring young writers to read a work or two by a wide range of authors but to read *all* of Turgenev.

Yet even as early-twentieth-century authors were admiring Turgenev's art and artistry, the critical tide was turning. Modernist aesthetics were moving away from the close observation of characters within social milieus presented in traditional narrative forms and were moving toward more probing psychological explorations of characters in some sort of isolation and toward greater formal experimentation. It was as if the culture were losing confidence in connections between appearance and reality, between fiction and fact—central to the realist enterprise. In 1925, the Russian poet Osip Mandelstam gently remarked this loss of confidence as it applied to Turgenev: "In my youth, I already knew that the tranquil world of Turgenev was gone, never to be recovered." And so Turgenev's reputation went into eclipse—even while Dostoevsky's and Tolstoy's reputations were rising—because Turgenev's works were increasingly regarded as inextricably bound to a bygone era, irrelevant to the complexities of the twentieth century, and of interest predominantly to students of nineteenth-century social and literary history.

Turgenev's ability to portray nineteenth-century Russia realistically is indisputable, but to read his work for this alone is to leave him needlessly rooted in the past. It is to miss his true genius, which is revealed in what he has to say to readers of the present and the future. Thus to discover that genius is to find a Turgenev for the twentieth century and beyond.

Turgenev actually has a great deal to say to present and future readers, no less, and in certain respects even more, than do Dostoevsky and Tolstoy. For unlike those two creators of numerous protagonists who probe the depths and scale the heights of human existence, Turgenev largely focuses on protagonists who conduct more ordinary lives within more ordinary psychological limits, limits familiar to readers today, even if the historical circumstances he portrays are not. In fact, these protagonists confront the same existential trials as do Dostoevsky's and Tolstoy's—trials such as physical pain, fear, sorrow, illness, and death—but Turgenev's generally meet those trials differently, often in ways that are more instructive to readers.

Many of Dostoevsky's and Tolstoy's protagonists have the psychological strength to encounter and even embrace the hardships their lives bring them. Sometimes they do this in defiance, sometimes from the desire to comprehend the universal significance of those hardships—responses at least partially born of a nineteenth-century confidence in the human capacity to surmount any and all obstacles, physical or metaphysical, in pursuit of the fundamental truths of human existence. By contrast, most Turgenevan protagonists are psychologically weaker and more equivocal: they tend to avoid confrontation with and exploration of existential difficulties; they manifest no overarching confidence in the human ability to grasp the truths of their own lives, much less of existence in general. This is not to say that they lack the intellectual or emotional capacities of Dostoevskian and Tolstoyan protagonists. But unlike Dostoevsky and Tolstoy, who represent individuals brazenly facing and even triumphing over the suffering engendered by the conflicts, the horrors, the tragedies of life, Turgenev envisions individuals seeking to evade those conflicts, horrors, and tragedies. These individuals sometimes succeed, sometimes fail, and frequently do so ambiguously—like most human beings.

This ambiguous vision of both success and failure stems from Turgenev's conception of human nature—one arguably belonging more to the twentieth century than to the nineteenth. It differs radically from the conceptions of human nature held by either Dostoevsky or Tolstoy, which envision that nature as inherently resilient. Turgenev's conception of human nature, by contrast, is rooted in a conviction that human beings are fundamentally psychologically fragile and prone to suffering; hence they are profoundly vulnerable to assaults on their emotional stability from manifold forces arrayed against them in modern life. And Turgenev locates the primary sources of that suffering in nature, other people, and the irrational.

As Turgenev represents it, nature causes suffering in two ways. First, the natural life cycle from birth to death guarantees that, sooner or later, everything organic will undergo the physical ravages of disease, degeneration, and extinction. Thus, in Turgenev's fictional universe, illness and death are virtually everywhere; few characters remain untouched by them. Second, perhaps even more severe than the physical pain nature begets directly is the psychological pain it induces through its seemingly implacable indifference to human miseries. Turgenev personifies this indifference in one of his final published works, the prose poem "Nature," in the figure of "a majestic woman wearing a flowing green robe" who responds to the narrator's plaintive question, "But aren't we human beings your favorite children?" with the reply, "All creatures are my children. . . . I care for them all equally—and I destroy them all equally. . . . I have given you life, and I will take it away and give it to others, to worms or to people . . . I don't care." Denied the opportunity to converse further, the narrator is left in despair, devastated by the dismissal of any human claim to a privileged position in the natural world. His despair is emblematic, encapsulating the emotional as well as the physical wounds nature inflicts on so many of Turgenev's characters, who consistently seek ways to avoid those wounds and who are just as consistently tormented by their inability to avoid them for long.

Even when they do temporarily elude the abuses of nature, Turgenev's characters repeatedly find themselves suffering at the hands of other people. Although human beings are almost never a cause of death in Turgenev's world, they generally do more harm than good in their relationships with others. And they do the greatest harm in the closest relationships, especially love. For Turgenev's characters, the satisfactions of love are few and brief, whereas the sorrows are manifold and lasting, because love as Turgenev portrays it usually deceives. Seeming to offer affirmation and strength, it actually deprives and weakens by seducing lovers into a demeaning, self-destructive pursuit of ephemeral or unattainable pleasures. Turgenev's renowned novella *First Love* carries a warning to all would-be lovers: "Fear that bliss, that poison." Yet when Turgenev's characters evade the "poison" of love, their relationships among family, friends, or social acquaintances generally afford them little more comfort. Almost without exception, friends are sources of criticism, families are sources of constraint and misunderstanding, and social acquaintances are sources of casual diversion at best and demoralizing discouragement at worst. For in Turgenev's works, all human relationships entail the exposure of individual vulnerabilities that others too often fail to recognize or choose to ignore. Even in solitude, though, Turgenev's characters cannot escape the most egregious adversary of all, the most dangerous source of suffering: themselves. Turgenev knows, as Bazarov tells Arkadii in *Fathers and Sons*, that people continually "go and invent all sorts of difficulties for themselves, and spoil their lives." Throughout his works, Turgenev shows that human beings "invent difficulties" and even "spoil" their lives principally as a result of their own irrationality. However carefully they protect themselves, existentially and emotionally, against the pain potentially inflicted by nature and other people, Turgenev's characters can be beset by internal, irrational forces at any moment—impulsive urges and desires can surface without warning, unexpected and therefore less susceptible to restraint. The urge to gratify instinctual appetites or to indulge selfish desires generates misery for these characters, whether they withstand or succumb. Irresistible sexual attractions, for instance, lead some to abandon satisfying lives; irrepressible fears of commitment and responsibility lead others to flee possibly fulfilling relationships. Embittered remorse invariably follows, while efforts to resist merely suppress those impulses and thereby render them all the more insidious, subversive, and uncontrollable. In the end, it is these sufferings, the ones characters bring upon themselves through their inability to comprehend and control their own emotions and actions, that lead to the cruelest torments of all in Turgenev's fictional universe.

Turgenev exhibits enduring sympathy for human vulnerability and the various torments it occasions, seeing in it not only the essence of human nature but the key to understanding human behavior. Central to his works is the illustration of people protecting themselves from their vulnerabilities by developing strategies of psychic survival, or what have commonly become known as "defense mechanisms." Turgenev understands and delineates as few other authors have done the mental machinations of self-protection—denial, projection, sublimation, and, above all, rationalization—employed by individuals to minimize the pains of human existence. Again and again he portrays characters engaged in psychological maneuvers to save themselves from suffering as they inch along what he perceives to be an extremely fine line between rational and irrational self-protective behavior. Yet while sympathizing with the needs and desires that inspire such behavior, he exposes it as regularly yielding more harm than good, rooted as it so often is in self-deception. This subtle understanding and portrayal of the triumphs, defeats, and uncertainties generated by disparate strategies of self-protection must constitute one of Turgenev's highest intellectual and artistic accomplishments.

In depicting the varieties of self-protection, Turgenev sets a single strategy above all others, one he both elucidates in his fiction and embodied in his life. It is none other than the creation of art itself. Throughout his narratives, Turgenev extols the psychological advantages of artistic creation—that is, the imposition of aesthetic order on experience. Those narratives reveal that Turgenev prizes aesthetic order—balance, harmony, restraint, coherence—not merely because of its link to a conception of beauty he admires but also as a means of transforming all experience, for his readers no less than for himself and his characters. By imposing this aesthetic order on the representation of events, Turgenev demonstrates that all individuals can render the events they encounter not only aesthetically pleasing but also psychologically manageable. For he suggests that the creative act of artfully organizing experience enables people to mold any experience, however threatening, into a controlled form, hence diminishing its power to inflict pain. Each of Turgenev's own works can consequently be read as a model for readers to emulate, since by artistically transforming the disordered, frequently hurtful raw material of human life, each work shows readers how to do the same: how to become the artists of their own lives, as it were, and thereby protect themselves from harm.

To read Turgenev well today is thus to read him less for his meticulous portrayals of nineteenth-century Russia and more for his insights into the psychological benefits of aesthetic order that these portrayals both exemplify and advocate. Readers of today also need to recognize that Turgenev's poetics, the consistent artistic practices he uses to construct his narratives, are deeply rooted in his psychology and philosophy of life. Among the most exemplary components of Turgenev's poetics are the representations of space and time, the use of language, the techniques of narration, and the modes of characterization.

In Turgenev's fictional universe, space and time are chiefly represented as inflexible boundaries, both delimited and delimiting, rather than as continuums. Characters rarely travel far, and when they do, they generally fail to return; within one area, they often move in circles; they usually live in markedly enclosed spaces; they repeatedly lament the past they cannot recapture; they recurrently see the future bearing down upon them. Many of Turgenev's characters object to limits that appear arbitrarily imposed, such as those on the length of life itself. But spatial and temporal boundaries are seldom shown to be damaging constraints; instead they are portrayed as sources of psychological protection. And those who can root their identities in willed acceptance of such boundaries are shown to have discovered a valuable mental bulwark against the vicissitudes of what would otherwise seem to be unpredictable, uncontrollable existences.

Turgenev conveys similar possibilities of protection through his use of language. Although he is renowned for his varied, precise descriptions of both characters and natural settings, his language engages many devices that help to distance individuals from threatening experiences. At distressing moments, both his characters and his narrators typically cloud perceptions with vague words, or else they fall silent, often proudly—many of the narratives close with an image of silence. These linguistic vagaries and elisions conceal the exact nature of emotional difficulties while nonetheless subtly bespeaking their presence.

Representative among the linguistic devices Turgenev favors is the rhetorical figure of the litotes, a double negative, as in the phrases "not unclear" or "not dissimilar." He frequently introduces a litotes—usually in the form "not without"—semantically to obscure and yet to signal a character's uncertainty, confusion, or conflict. For instance, in *Fathers and Sons*, upon returning home after completing his university studies, Arkadii Kirsanov listens, "not without surprise, albeit not without sympathy either," to some lines of poetry sentimentally quoted by his father. Caught between the embarrassment and the affection his father's performance arouses, Arkadii can only respond equivocally, as the two litotes indicate. In their very imprecision, these litotes at once reveal that Arkadii is conflicted and conceal the nature and extent of his conflict. Hence litotes provide a linguistic defense against conflict even as they mirror the psychological process of struggling with it.

Similar effects are achieved by Turgenev's reliance on several other forms of expression: simple negatives that specify only what is *not* the case instead of what is; imprecise qualifiers such as "somehow," "somewhat," and above all "some sort of," which dilute or obscure the semantic impact of the term they qualify; adverbs such as "slightly" and "hesitantly," which indicate attempts to constrain the manifestation of emotional disturbance; adjectives such as "strange" or "unusual," which betoken efforts to maintain psychological distance by emphasizing unfamiliarity. Only by understanding Turgenev's abundant and subtle use of linguistic devices to instill ambiguity in his narratives can readers appreciate how his artistry goes beyond verbal portraiture to erect psychological protections against the painful experiences those narratives treat and to present ways in which readers can protect themselves against similar experiences in their own lives.

Turgenev's overarching narrative techniques lead to the same ends. The most conspicuous of these is the narrative frame, a story that sets forth the circumstances under which a subsequent story takes place or has been transmitted for publication. Common in the eighteenth century, this technique was rejected by most authors of fiction in the mid-nineteenth century as an outmoded, transparent attempt to persuade readers of a narrative's veracity. Turgenev is therefore unusual among his contemporaries in insistently placing narrative frames around most of his short stories and around narrative digressions within his novels. By doing so, though, Turgenev marks his fiction as such, signaling his readers that they can remain emotionally detached from the events related, since those events cannot affect reality. At the same time, Turgenev implies that emotional detachment from actual events can also be achieved by viewing them, if not necessarily as fiction, then at least as narratives that can be framed. These events thus become experiences that can be aesthetically organized and distanced so as to insure psychological control over their impact as well.

Turgenev deftly illustrates another means to obtain this control through his narrative voices. He allows the narrative voice in virtually all his works to shift among several different points of view, from one that conveys the seemingly objective observations of an uninvolved narrator to another that implies a close identification between the narrator and some character, and then to another that expresses the narrator's own opinions. By seamlessly switching among these points of view, at times even within a single page or a single paragraph, and especially when a narrator is portraying emotionally difficult or disruptive moments, Turgenev accomplishes more than sheltering his readers from disturbing images. He additionally displays the value of altering one's own perspective on distressing experiences to avoid a single, consistent point of view that could lead to a disquietingly direct confrontation. Turgenev reveals the virtues of avoiding such confrontations most dramatically in his portraits of characters. He has been said by some critics to portray two main types of characters, the Hamletic—weak-willed, overly self-conscious, usually male protagonists incapable of decisive action—and the Quixotic—strong-willed, self-sacrificing, usually female protagonists devoted to ideals. This interpretation derives in part from Turgenev's famous essay "Hamlet and Don Quixote," in which he analyzes these two literary figures as exemplars of contrasting psychological types. But his characterizations are much more varied and subtle than a simple, dualistic typology can capture. For Turgenev's characters all struggle in different ways against the forces of unhappiness: a few of them are completely victorious; a few are completely defeated; most attain their own mixture of victory and defeat.

Those characters who are the most successful in defending themselves against unhappiness are the most self-aware and self-reliant, possessing the greatest psychological autonomy and spiritual integrity. Perhaps most fully embodying these qualities is Lukeria in "A Living Relic," one of the *Sportsman's Sketches*. Although an accident has left her badly paralyzed, she nevertheless draws upon impressive resources of will and imagination to find self-affirming pride and equanimity. At the opposite extreme are such characters as Maria Dmietrievna in *A Nest of Gentry*, the elderly princess Zasekina in *First Love*, and the sycophant Sitnikov in *Fathers and Sons*—all near-caricatures of dependence, self-deception, and discontent.

Most of Turgenev's protagonists, however, are at neither extreme. They fall somewhere in between as they only partially succeed in securing a healthy, independent self shielded against suffering caused by the forces of nature, society, and irrationality. To mention a few: Aleksei Petrovich and Maria Aleksandrovna in "A Correspondence," Petr Ivanych in *First Love*, Evgenii Bazarov and Anna Sergeevna Odintsova in *Fathers and Sons*, and Fabius in "The Song of Triumphant Love" must each battle to sustain their carefully fashioned sense of identity when subjected to impulsive desires they had never imagined having, much less acting upon. Aleksei Petrovich and Petr Ivanych ultimately lose this battle; Maria Aleksandrovna, Bazarov, and Fabius dangerously falter, although they manage to reassert their self-control; Anna Sergeevna prevails but leads a life devoid of emotional gratification. However different the outcomes, such psychological struggles largely define Turgenev's characters, shaping the contours of their personalities and the dramas of their lives.

As self-concerned as these characters inevitably become when they engage in their psychological battles, it would be a mistake to envision them waging these battles merely in pursuit of selfish psychological satisfactions. For in Turgenev's fictional universe these battles are fundamentally moral, and this is the crux of Turgenev's conception of human nature and existence. Although Turgenev's controlled style has led many commentators to perceive his works as morally neutral—"more concerned," in the words of critic Richard Freeborn, "to make man real than to make him better"—this perception misses the essence of Turgenev's art, because what appears to be his moral distance or constraint can be much better understood as his moral investment in distance and constraint. To Turgenev, the maintenance of these aesthetic and psychological qualities leads to an eminently ethical end: the creation of the best possible self. He conceives of that ideal self as the one most prepared to undergo life's difficulties with equanimity, to endure its ills with dignity and integrity, to achieve the contentment that comes only with psychological autonomy. This self will be the least dependent on other people or outside circumstances for its definition; it will be the most capable of governing itself and outside circumstances by imposing its own perceptions and interpretations on experience. As a result, it will be the least vulnerable to injury, the least susceptible to suffering.

This ideal self will therefore be notably "composed," in two senses of the term: it will be composed emotionally—calm, controlled, imperturbable in the face of any threat—and it will be composed imaginatively—artfully formed and imbued with the power to impose protective order on disordered experience. Individuals so composed will ceaselessly maintain the distance and constraint required to ward off harm most effectively, and will thereby cause only minimal pain both to themselves and to others. Thus, for Turgenev, the protection and enhancement of the self constitute not simply psychological needs but moral quests for an ideal state of being.

Yet Turgenev's works also reveal that the pursuit of this ideal can actually give rise not to self-enhancement and self-preservation but to self-denigration or even self-destruction. These undesirable ends may occur precisely because the very psychological defenses erected to protect and enhance the self can also cause harm—distance can foster the defense mechanism of denial, for instance, and rationality can induce self-deceptive rationalization. Turgenev shows that even the most well-intentioned, self-affirming acts can have the most unintentionally self-defeating consequences if vigilance is not sustained. And he demonstrates how difficult it can be to tell whether any damage to the self is caused by an individual's inability to resist uncontrollable forces or by an individual's unwillingness to exert the energy to try to oppose them; Turgenev's works are insistently, if restrainedly, infused with the dramatic tension between moral inclinations and immoral impulses, between ethical self-defense and unethical self-delusion. This tension enfolds many a character whose full motives Turgenev leaves unclear even as he makes it quite clear that among those motives is the universal desire to avoid pain.

Whatever the tangle of his characters' motives and the ambiguous consequences of their actions, then, Turgenev portrays those characters seeking in one way or another to save themselves. And he indicates throughout his works that the sole form of salvation they can achieve is one twentieth-century readers can well comprehend: secular salvation. By contrast to the conception of a redemptive deity offered by some organized religions—Turgenev evinces no faith in the divine—Turgenev's secular salvation promises redemption only in this life from the loss of psychological autonomy and moral integrity. It is a salvation gained solely through the exercise of intellect and imagination to create a strong identity capable of self-protection and self-determination.

Readers nowadays should consequently detect in Turgenev not only a voice of his times but a voice of our times as well. For he understood the complexities and conflicts, the doubts and dilemmas, encountered by all people who sense that they must impart meaning to their existences and strive to save themselves on their own. Turgenev was not just a morally neutral, dispassionate, realistic portraitist of his age, his country, and his countrymen; he was a consummate artist of the psychological and moral life, admiring of existential and ethical triumphs and sympathetic to lapses. He clearly recognized that those lapses were unavoidable, so difficult and demanding is the task of self-protection, and he tacitly forgave characters who failed even as he unswervingly condemned their failures. Hence Turgenev emerges as among the most tough-minded yet tolerant, perceptive, and humane of modern writers. And it is these qualities that should make his quiet voice resonate for readers of today and tomorrow in ways readers of the nineteenth and earlier twentieth centuries may not have been ready to hear.

*   *   *   *   *   *

The works selected for inclusion in *The Essential Turgenev* span Turgenev's career and represent the highest level of his achievements in a broad variety of fiction and nonfiction. Presented here are three of Turgenev's six novels, one of his three novellas, eight of the twenty-five *Sportsman's Sketches*, seven of his thirty-two other short stories, fifteen of his eighty-three *Poems in Prose*, and one each of his speeches, essays, biographical memoirs, and autobiographical sketches. (None of his generally somewhat less distinguished lyric and narrative poems, plays, critical reviews, libretti, or introductions to other authors' works have been incorporated.) Each work included here was chosen not only for its own distinctive merits, but also for its "essential" contribution to a complete picture of Turgenev's art and thought.

Turgenev won his greatest acclaim as a novelist. He did so during the time when the novel had attained unparalleled popularity and preeminence as a literary form, the standard for which had been set by relatively long novels, often published serially. But Turgenev achieved his acclaim without producing the lengthy fictions typical of his renowned fellow authors: Turgenev's longest novel, *Virgin Soil*, occupies fewer than 200 standard printed pages (at around 400 words per page), and his most famous novel, *Fathers and Sons*, runs to about 150 pages. By contrast, for example, Flaubert's *Madame Bovary* fills over 280 pages and his *Sentimental Education* over 400, Dickens's *Great Expectations* just under 500, Eliot's *Middlemarch* around 750, Dostoevsky's *Brothers Karamazov* approximately 900, and Tolstoy's *War and Peace* more than 1,100. The economical size of Turgenev's novels is more than an incidental feature—it reflects the values of order, constraint, and self-discipline that distinguish his aesthetic and ethical vision. Moreover, his relatively short narratives enable him to focus more on the dynamics of character and human relationships than on historical and social panoramas as he etches his characters' portraits with masterly care and conveys his moral message with understated efficacy.

But despite the relatively narrow compass of his novels and their concentration on the lives of individuals, Turgenev also indicates that his characters face uncertainties and contraditions within themselves and in their relationships with others that are akin to those the Russian nation as a whole had to confront to establish its own identity and autonomy. Every novel contains at least one earnest conversation about Russia's current condition and future fate, conversations that are invariably bound up with the characters' struggles for mastery of their own present and prospective circumstances, and Turgenev frequently implies that the conclusions they draw about Russia's destiny will parallel the conclusions they draw about their own. Thus he aligns particular characters with general social trends and embeds specific plots in broad historical issues, adhering all the while to his signal creative principles. Turgenev thereby provides his readers with novels that, although brief by nineteenth-century standards, present a full spectrum of compelling images and ideas ranging from the psychological to the political, from the artistic to the moral. As a result, his characters and their struggles are of our times as well as theirs—and of the future as well.

The three novels in this volume best exemplify Turgenev's strengths as a novelist, setting forth many of his most unforgettable characters and adeptly integrating personal dramas into social and historical contexts, all the while displaying Turgenev's ethically inspired artistry.

Turgenev's first published novel, *Rudin* (1856), centers on the morally ambiguous title character: he is either a glib manipulator of impressionable inferiors who repeatedly flees real work and real relationships out of cowardice, or he is a geniune if naive idealist who endlessly seeks the most appropriate venue to enact his noble visions. Either way, Rudin constitutes one version of an emergent Russian social phenomenon, the "superfluous man" (a term Turgenev popularized in his short story "The Diary of a Superfluous Man"). Appearing amid nineteenth-century Russian society and recognizable in such other literary figures as Aleksandr Griboedov's Chatskii, Aleksandr Pushkin's Onegin, and Mikhail Lermontov's Pechorin, the superfluous man is a solitary, socially alienated male who lacks an established social position as well as traditional emotional connections to home and family; he therefore cannot play any significant, lasting role in other people's lives or in society at large.

Through his provocative portrayal of this superfluous man, Turgenev poses questions about the nature and future of both that character type and Russia as a whole, questions as pertinent today as the day *Rudin* was published: Does Russian society have the flexibility to accommodate new ideas and new types of people? If it does have that flexibility, is it right to accommodate them? And what models should it follow in giving direction to its people and itself? Turgenev's first novel offers no definitive answers to these questions, although the sympathetic treatment afforded the title character in the novel's epilogue (which Turgenev attached only after public disappointment in the novel's original conclusion) suggests that Turgenev favored tolerance for the well-meaning if occasionally self-deceived Rudins of this world.

Rudin also exposes Turgenev's interest in another subject that he explored throughout his literary career: the essence and value of language. Turgenev depicts Rudin first easily winning over new acquaintances with eloquent discourses on truth, beauty, and humanity but later disappointing them with his inability to act upon the ideals he so passionately articulates. Turgenev thus implies that language may be insubstantial at best and deceptive at worst, a set of artificial, conventionalized forms lacking content but capable of misleading numerous individuals and even nations. In the novel's epilogue, Rudin himself bitterly summarizes his own existence as consisting of "words, just words," regretfully concluding: "There were no deeds!"

Yet Turgenev gives the novel's last words about words not to Rudin but to Rudin's friend from university days, Lezhnev, who observes, "A kind word is also a deed." Despite having previously criticized Rudin's verbal facility, in the end Lezhnev stoutly defends Rudin's expressive use of language on the grounds that he may have inspired others to take actions he himself was incapable of performing. Judging Rudin as weak rather than malicious, Lezhnev also affirms the constructive moral power of language, a power that must be respected and channelled to avoid its abuse. Through *Rudin*, then, Turgenev both affirms the power of language and cautions against its misuse, especially by intellectuals facing personal, social, and ethical uncertainties.

Turgenev's second novel, *A Nest of Gentry* (1859), focuses on a small group of characters belonging to a well-defined Russian social stratum, the landed gentry. Ranking between the titled nobility and the peasantry, typically owning both a home in a city or town and an income-generating estate in the countryside, the gentry comprised a portion of Russia's growing middle class, although it lacked much of the education, the political liberalism, and the work ethic of its Western counterparts. In depicting the residents, relations, and acquaintances of one gentry household, Turgenev explores the psychological and moral strengths and weaknesses of this class, which would play a prominent role in determining Russia's future as the nation attempted to become the social, economic, and cultural equal of its European neighbors.

Turgenev parallels Russia's challenges in deciding its future with those of the novel's two main protagonists, Liza Kalitina and Fedor Lavretskii, in deciding theirs. Both are introduced while on the verge of selecting a course for their own lives: with obvious symbolism, Liza first appears poised on the threshold of a room, just as she, at age nineteen, is poised on the threshold of adulthood; at the novel's outset, Lavretskii has just returned to begin life anew in Russia after separating from his unfaithful wife and aimlessly wandering around Europe for several years. From their entrances onward, Liza and Lavretskii contemplate different ways of life open to them, finding themselves urged in various directions by other characters, finally choosing paths they independently determine to be most compatible with their own natures and moral convictions. In making these choices, which ultimately call for profound sacrifices—the forsaking of deeply felt love, the dissolution of long-standing relationships, the admission of insecurities and inadequacies, the confrontation of ethical dilemmas—Liza and Lavretskii illustrate the possibilities and the limits, the complications and the contradictions, the benefits and the costs inherent in the pursuit of independence, whether for individuals or for nations. At the same time, Liza's and Lavretskii's lives suggest that the failure to pursue independence, whatever that pursuit entails, will thwart the formation of the identity and integrity necessary for both individuals and nations to insure viable futures.

Turgenev's fourth novel, *Fathers and Sons* (1862), is by far his most famous and, many would say, his best. Its literary values were largely ignored, though, when, upon publication, its political implications aroused a torrent of controversy. Commentators on both the extreme left and the arch-conservative right were already engaged in fierce polemics, prompted by the emancipation of the serfs in 1861, over the proper design of Russian society. Both sides railed against the novel's protagonist Bazarov, the self-styled "nihilist," for being either insufficiently or excessively radical. As a result, Turgenev found himself attacked from one side for advocating fundamental change in Russian social and political structures and from the other side for opposing such change.

To be sure, it is difficult for readers of today to see what in Bazarov could have provoked such attacks, given his relatively moderate pragmatism and even idealism in comparison to subsequent violent "nihilist" revolutionary activism. But it is not difficult to recognize in Bazarov's criticisms of mid-nineteenth-century Russia and in his differences with his elders the timeless conflicts between generations over values, beliefs, and behavior. The eternal disagreements between youth and age spread across the pages as characters debate the legitimacy of social traditions, the merits of aesthetics and religion, the meaning of happiness, and the correct course to take in the future—both for themselves and for Russia. At the novel's end, it is only the members of the two generations who can reach some accord with one another that unite to form their own "nest of gentry."

Tellingly, the novel is dominated by three characters who cannot reach such an accord: Pavel Petrovich Kirsanov, Anna Sergeevna Odintsova, and Bazarov himself. Arguably the most complex and compelling of all Turgenev's characters, these three are at once psychologically strong and yet profoundly vulnerable; they are all highly intelligent and yet limited in their capacities to comprehend themselves and the people closest to them; they are all motivated by long-held moral principles and yet morally flawed; they all struggle fiercely to preserve their sense of identity, and all pay a supremely high price for doing so. All three end up tragically frozen in isolation forever, as the present tense of the conclusion conveys— Pavel Petrovich in self-imposed exile, Anna Sergeevna in a loveless marriage of convenience, and Bazarov in his grave—permanently removed from the human affections that their forceful yet fragile personalities would not dare to trust. Indeed, in no other work does Turgenev more subtly and more movingly delineate the emotional and existential sacrifices sometimes required by choosing self-protection over self-indulgence. *Fathers and Sons* embodies as intellectually and morally sophisticated a portrayal of human experience as Turgenev was ever to offer his readers.

Although Turgenev won his greatest fame as a novelist, his literary genius is even better displayed in his novellas and short stories. In these shorter works Turgenev dwells more closely on character and human relations, often employing first-person narrators whose observations, reflections, and self-revelations flow through and shape their narratives. The limited scope of these narratives also gives Turgenev the ideal format in which to concentrate dramatic intensity while still illustrating the virtues of distance and constraint. His novellas and short stories therefore exhibit Turgenev's subtle artistry, psychological insight, and moral vision with the utmost effectiveness.

Turgenev's finest aesthetic achievement of all is arguably the novella *First Love* (1860). Superbly integrating form and content, Turgenev constructs a complex narrative depicting the vicissitudes of the first real love experienced by its three principal characters. Each discovers that love is not the pleasure anticipated, something simple, ego-gratifying, and controllable in course and intensity. Instead each finds love to be a force of nature that overwhelms individuals without regard to their needs or aspirations and forces them to face painful truths about themselves and their lives. At the same time, while revealing the torments such tumultuous discoveries cause his characters, Turgenev mitigates the emotional impact of those torments on readers by creating concentric narrative frames that, like a camera lens changing focus, can bring his characters' experiences close one moment and distance them the next. Turgenev thus provides readers a measure of protection from those experiences—including the experience of death itself, observed by the narrator hat the end of *First Love*. Nowhere does Turgenev create a more compelling model of how aesthetics can instill psychological distance and constraint.

The values of distance and constraint that Turgenev illuminates so amply in the novella *First Love* are also made manifest in his best short stories. The earliest of these, written and published individually between 1847 and 1851, then published together in 1852 under the title *A Sportsman's Sketches* (Turgenev later added "A Living Relic" [1874] and two others), present artfully restrained yet vivid depictions of peasants and their rural milieu, which allegedly so impressed Tsar Alexander II that they inspired him to abolish serfdom in 1861. As apocryphal as this claim may be, these profoundly humane sketches indisputably brought the Russian peasantry legitimacy as a subject worthy of sustained, serious literary attention; prior to Turgenev's stories, peasants had typically been rendered as minor characters or caricatures. However, with the advent of sagacious Khor and gentle Kalinych, sternly devout Kasian, musically gifted Yakov, pathetically lovelorn Akulina, nobly unselfpitying Lukeria, and the many other distinctive figures portrayed in these sketches, the stage of Russian literature was suddenly peopled with a new cast of characters that would distinctly enliven subsequent works.

A Sportsman's Sketches also afforded Turgenev a perfect vehicle for experimenting with narrative techniques. By producing a series of stories with the same narrator—the "sportsman" who encounters a variety of individuals on his hunting expeditions—Turgenev was able to place that narrator in different roles: curious interlocutor, as in "Khor and Kalinych" and "A Living Relic"; accidental participant, as in "My Neighbor Radilov" and "Lgov"; passive observer, as in "The Singers" and "The Tryst"; recorder of others' stories, as in "Death," and so on. Turgenev portrays this sportsman not merely as someone in quest of game or in search of novel experiences, but as an individual seeking a way of *narrating*, which is to say, a manner of comprehending and communicating his experiences. These diverse roles no doubt reflect Turgenev's own quest for a narrative style at the beginning of his career, but they also betoken the emphasis he would place throughout that career on the ability to change perspectives if the demands of self-protection so require. For changing from one perspective, or mode of narration, to another gives Turgenev's narrators—and, by extension, his readers—a constructive means, so important to Turgenev, of at once taking hold of experience and keeping it at a safe distance when it threatens to overwhelm.

From *A Sportsman's Sketches*, Turgenev went on to create a number of other prominent narrators altering their perspectives on life as they undergo transformative experiences. "A Journey to Polesje" (1857), which at first glance could be taken for an adjunct to *A Sportsman's Sketches*, presents a contemplative narrator who is far more absorbed in his own psychological condition and philosophical disposition than the hunter in the *Sketches* ever appears to be. This narrator struggles with the dawning awareness of his own mortality, but then reconciles himself to it as he goes through a rapid spiritual regeneration upon his discovery of a pervasive, elemental, natural harmony in existence based on aesthetic order and moral balance. By the conclusion of his journey, this narrator becomes one of the very few characters in all of Turgenev's works equitably to accept the temporal limits nature imposes on every life, an acceptance that paves the way to an emotionally tranquil existence.

In "The Diary of a Superfluous Man" (1850) and "A Correspondence" (1856), by contrast, Turgenev extensively explores the emotional travails of the character type with which Rudin has been identified—the superfluous man, an individual lacking a clearly defined social role or occupation. The diarist Chulkaturin bitterly relegates himself to this type in the journal he begins just days before his death as he documents the agonizing process he underwent in coming to recognize his social and existential irrelevance. The letters of Alexei Petrovich in "A Correspondence" further probe the psychological sufferings of the superfluous man. But, unlike Chulkaturin, Alexei Petrovich alternates between acceptance and denial of responsibility for the web of self-consciousness that has confined him to a superfluous existence, announcing at one point, "I was my own spider!" but then immediately blaming Russian temperament and society for his miseries until he, too, lies on his deathbed.

Alexei Petrovich's revelations of the superfluous man's self-defeating psychology are underscored by the contrasting psychology expressed in the letters of his correspondent, Maria Aleksandrovna, the only female character in all of Turgenev's works to serve as a primary narrator. Although she is also something of an outsider, having forged an identity for herself as an antisocial intellectual and having rejected the conventional path of marriage and motherhood, she nonetheless sees her situation clearly and remains true to her idealistic principles, even if that means further isolating herself from society. The carefully orchestrated correspondence between Maria Aleksandrovna and Alexei Petrovich therefore comprises a cautionary tale highlighting the distinction between a self-deceptive life of pathetic superfluity and a self-aware life of courageous commitment.

Three of Turgenev's late short stories, "A Strange History" (1870), "The Dream" (1877), and "The Song of Triumphant Love" (1881), treat characters struggling not so much to sustain equanimity in light of their own complex personalities and behavior as to achieve equanimity in the face of the peculiar personalities and behavior of others—and thus confronting the ambiguities of human existence. In "A Strange History," an illiterate young artisan makes images of the dead appear before the narrator, who at first dismisses them as illusions born of wine and the artisan's powers of suggestion. But when this artisan later becomes an itinerant, self-flagellating religious fanatic attended by the hitherto seemingly rational daughter of a wealthy official, the narrator is truly baffled. Unable to explain her choice of a life of deprivation and servitude, he is reduced to labeling her actions "strange." Turgenev leaves it for readers to select their own perspective from which to view these events and decide whether the artisan is a divinely inspired visionary, a charlatan, or a madman, whether the young woman is a nobly self-sacrificing worshipper, a fool, or a madwoman, and whether the narrator is an innocent and confused observer or an ignorant and shallow unbeliever.

"The Dream" and "The Song of Triumphant Love," written during the last years of Turgenev's life, extend his exploration of the peculiar farther toward the apparently inexplicable—hence their frequent classification as "supernatural tales"; these are arguably the darkest and most morally ambiguous of all Turgenev's narratives. Among their protagonists are two who share striking attributes: they are unusual-looking, malevolent males that mysteriously appear and disappear accompanied by servants of exotic origins, gratifying their physical and emotional desires at will and evidently eluding the grasp of death itself. Yet Turgenev emphasizes the uncertain nature of their possibly supernatural powers by enfolding these characters within narrative contexts that bring the reliability of their contents into question. The very title "The Dream" signals that this story may be just that, the narrator's personal nightmare, and no more; "The Song of Triumphant Love" which purports to be a sixteenth-century chronicle, has its veracity undermined from the start by its dedication to the nineteenth-century author Gustave Flaubert. Therefore even these bizarre, disturbing works can be viewed as elaborate narrative experiments, which Turgenev has cast in aesthetic forms that place their unsettling and unexplained contents at a safe psychological distance from his readers.

One other short story included here, "Enough" (1865), is often taken to be the most pessimistic and least psychologically restrained of all Turgenev's works, since many commentators read it not so much as fiction but as Turgenev's personal *cri de coeur*, issuing from his deepening belief in the meaninglessness and futility of human existence. This reading misses Turgenev's primary purpose, however, which his narrative ingenuity conveys. For as the subtitle says, "Enough" is comprised of the "notes of a dead artist."

Although Turgenev may well have identified himself with this figure at many points, he has not lost the ability to find meaning in life, as the dead artist has, because Turgenev has not lost the creative strength to impose aesthetic form on life and thereby achieve some measure of emotional balance. It is the dead artist, not Turgenev, who is irrevocably overwhelmed by the perception of intolerable, unalterable forces eternally governing human existence: "the same credulity and the same cruelty . . . the same grasping for power, the same traditions of slavishness, the same natural acceptance of false-hood—in a word, the same busy leaps of a squirrel turning the same old unreplaced wheel." Fatalistic, despair-filled laments like these bespeak a helpless mind and a thwarted imagination im-prisoned within the circularity of obsessive thoughts. To be sure, Turgenev occasionally knew such despair. But it was his achieve-ment to have continued to transcend it, and to have pointed the way for his readers to transcend it as well. That transcendence comes from cultivating the power the dead artist has lost—the power of art to transform existence into shapes that vulnerable human beings can bear to encounter. Turgenev might have feared losing that power, but he never did. So "Enough" is best read not as a veiled autobiographical statement but as a warning against sub-mitting to experience solely on its terms, and as an encouragement to maintain the aesthetic and psychological control of existence that imbues it with salutary moral meaning.

Like his fiction, Turgenev's nonfiction is not voluminous. Al-though he published works in a variety of nonfictional genres—journalistic articles, essays, literary reviews, biographical sketches, and prefaces to other authors' works—he made no more than a dozen or two contributions to each. In this way, as in his fiction, he differed from his prolific contemporaries, like Dostoevsky and Tolstoy in Russia or George Eliot and Henry James in the West, who wrote a great deal of nonfiction as well as fiction. Yet though relatively slight in quantity, Turgenev's nonfiction is also "essen-tial" to an understanding of both him and his art. For this reason, a selection of his nonfiction is included here among the fiction.

The one genre of nonfiction in which Turgenev's output did rival that of his literary contemporaries is letters—over six thousand of them have been preserved. Still, numerous as they are, these letters also set Turgenev apart from his fellow authors, for, unlike many of them, he did not regularly use letters to express his unguarded self or to explore the nature of his own art. Except for a few youthful, impassioned missives, his letters bear a striking resemblance to his fiction in their maintenance of distance and self-constraint. Although he chattily reports on recent experiences and states opinions on cultural artifacts and events, Turgenev rarely employs any of these as pretexts to engage in elaborate self-analysis, the way artists so frequently do. Only in a paragraph here, a page there, does he forsake the conversational tone that characterizes so much of his mature correspondence in order to consider his personality and his artistry in true depth—he tends to stay on the surface. It is, of course, this absence of extended self-exposure that makes them so Turgenevan. And the fact that Turgenev made Pauline Viardot promise to destroy upon his death the diary in which he had made entries for years—a promise she evidently kept, since only a few fragments remain—underscores the extent to which he avoided opening himself up to the scrutiny of others.

But if Turgenev was not a habitually probing or deliberately self-revealing letter-writer, his correspondence nonetheless both inadvertently discloses his character and punctuates the narrative of his life. The forty-two letters included in this volume touch on many of the people and subjects that interested him over the course of his lifetime while retaining much of his typical reticence about himself and his art, and they contain a number of the most significant self-analytical statements he did make. These letters have the additional feature of possessing some significant connection to the works presented here. They have thus been interspersed chronologically throughout the volume in order to exhibit their relation to the selections that precede or follow them: a sampling of Turgenev's letters reacting to criticism of *Fathers and Sons*, for instance, are placed after that novel, and his epistolary description of the preparations for the dedication of a monument to the poet Pushkin appears prior to the speech he gave on that occasion. The associations between other letters and works are more general; for example, Turgenev's description of his relationship to one woman introduces his fictional portrayal of the relationship between the male and female protagonists of "A Correspondence." The letters are therefore intended to thread the volume together both formally and thematically, allowing Turgenev's private voice to unify his public performances.

Like Turgenev's letters, his few ventures into autobiography are typical in their self-conscious reluctance to engage in profound self-revelation. In response to requests by several editors and publishers for autobiographical sketches to accompany his fiction, he composed self-portraits of remarkable brevity and impersonality. The representative example offered here (published in 1876) employs a modest four sentences to summarize his entire literary career; he prefers to elaborate on favorite teachers and memorable incidents of his youth, such as an apparently traumatic brush with death in Switzerland as a child. And it is telling that Turgenev casts this self-portrait in the third person, so that even when explicitly describing his own past, he can psychologically detach himself from that past by detaching himself from himself, as it were, treating himself as an object of description rather than as the source of that description. He thereby transforms his autobiography into more of a biography, attenuating any risks of self-revelation and demonstrating yet one more means of self-protection.

The value Turgenev places on detachment plays a dramatic role in his poignant narrative "The Execution of Troppmann" (1870), one of a collection of essays he grouped under the title "Literary and Biographical Reminiscences." In part a didactic protest against capital punishment, in part an autobiographical memoir, it narrates Turgenev's experiences as a witness to the guillotining of a then-infamous murderer, Jean Troppmann. After depicting with journalistic objectivity the hours of preparation before the execution, Turgenev describes himself abruptly turning away at the climax, unable to watch the decapitation itself. He reports focusing instead on a young sentry, whose emotions and past life Turgenev briefly, imaginatively recreates until being led away, deeply shaken. Dostoevsky would later condemn what he took to be Turgenev's combination of cowardice and elitism in refusing to observe this act of man's inhumanity to man, affirming that "man on the surface of the earth does not have the right to turn away and ignore what is taking place on earth." Dostoevsky could not accept the notion that Turgenev's refusal to watch a hideous act of human destruction was a product of Turgenev's own ethics. But to Turgenev, those who do watch such sights inevitably grow inured to their horror, and consequently become less humane, less human, and less moral. As a result, when the act of seeing entails exposure to immoral, inhumane ugliness and disorder, the act of not seeing, or of reenvisioning what is seen within new, aesthetically ordered limits, may constitute the sole morally acceptable option for individuals who seek to preserve themselves and their humanity.

In his best known nonfictional work, the essay "Hamlet and

Don Quixote" (1860), Turgenev fuses his gifts as a student of human nature and as a literary critic to analyze the psychological and moral import of two of the most famous characters in all of Western literature. Concentrating on the opposing attributes of these towering fictional figures and their creators as Turgenev conceives of them, the titanic Shakespeare and the temperate Cervantes (Turgenev's image of Shakespeare reading Cervantes is movingly memorable), Turgenev delineates two extremes of the human personality. In his view, Hamlet epitomizes cynicism, rationalization, and excessive self-consciousness, whereas Don Quixote embodies idealism, impulsiveness, and noble selflessness. No pure Hamlets or pure Don Quixotes exist, Turgenev grants, but they do represent tendencies within all human beings to greater or lesser degrees. An impressive and persuasive foray into literary psychology, "Hamlet and Don Quixote" should nevertheless not be read the way it has been by some, as a programmatic description of Turgenev's own renderings of his fictional characters; these are vastly more subtle and varied than any schematic typology can capture.

In one of his last, and perhaps inadvertently self-revealing, nonfictional works, Turgenev addresses a subject that had been a constant preoccupation throughout his career: the state of the Russian literary tradition. This had been a concern of his not only as a body of works to which he contributed but also as a cultural movement whose history he wished to understand and whose future he sought to insure. The ceremonies held in 1880 dedicating a statue of Russia's foremost poet, Aleksandr Pushkin, gave Turgenev an ideal opportunity to take up this subject. In the company of other luminaries, including Fedor Dostoevsky and Ivan Goncharov, Turgenev hails Pushkin's enormous achievement in establishing a Russian literary language and providing models of literary characters and images that would inspire generations of Russian writers to come. But Turgenev also designates Pushkin an "initiator," or founder, rather than a "completer" of the Russian literary tradition; Pushkin, who was killed in a duel at the age of thirty-seven, had launched Russian literature but had not lived to bring it to the full aesthetic and intellectual maturity required for it to claim its rightful place in world literary history. That task, Turgenev asserts, remains for "a new, still unknown, select individual" who "will surpass his teacher," Pushkin. It is possible that Turgenev secretly hoped this task was his own, but he was too self-deprecating ever to have said so explicitly.

A group of Turgenev's last literary works, however, may constitute

Turgenev's implicit claim to this task, exhibiting as they do a distinctly self-conscious relation to the Russian literary tradition: the *Poems in Prose* (1877–82). Shortly before he died, Turgenev released for publication fifty-one of these brief, lapidary pieces that he had written during the final years of his life (he withheld thirty-two, which were published posthumously). He had considered entitling the collection *Senilia*, declaring them "merely the last heavy sighs of . . . an old man." But even if his prose poems are somewhat uneven in quality, they are much more than his last artistic gasps. For one thing, they complete the circle of his literary career, which began with the lyric poems he wrote in his youth and the concise, often poetic *Sportsman's Sketches*. For another, they incorporate elements from an extremely wide variety of literary genres—myth, fairy tale, satire, romance, drama, reminiscence, horror story, eulogy, dream fantasy, legend, and extended epigram. By invoking so many genres, and hence employing markedly different modes of discourse, rapidly shifting points of view, and highly divergent topics, *Poems in Prose* impressively displays the broad range and expressive freedom that the Russian literary language had attained at this time.

It is no mere coincidence that the final prose poem Turgenev released for publication during his lifetime, "The Russian Language," treats this very subject. Although generally regarded as a somewhat overblown, sentimentalized tribute to his native language, this prose poem not only asserts but demonstrates in a distinctively Turgenevan way that the Russian language has achieved maturity and is indeed, as the first line proclaims, "great, powerful, righteous, and free." Paradoxical as it may seem, the negatively couched rejection of disbelief in its last line (essentially if not technically a litotes)—"it's impossible to believe that such a language wasn't given to a great people!"—in Turgenev's view may provide some of the best evidence that the Russian language has sufficient capacity, flexibility, and resilience to rival any other Western language in stature and autonomy. Certainly no one more avidly wanted to prove this, and no one did more to make that proof possible, than Turgenev.

It is this enduring appreciation of his mother tongue that led Turgenev to foster its potential throughout his lifetime—although fluent in several other languages, he wrote fiction only in Russian—up to the very end, when, as he tells Tolstoy in one of his last known letters, he had grown too tired to go on writing. By that time, the literary possibilities of his language that Turgenev discovered and developed had brought him surpassing celebrity in the nineteenth century. Now it remains for new generations of readers to discover in him the remarkable aesthetic and moral sensibilities, coupled with the acute understanding of human nature and modern human experience, that make him an author for the twentieth and twenty-first centuries as well.

Note on the Translations

The works of Turgenev contained here are, with three exceptions, revised versions of previously published translations. The translations of the fiction are by Constance Garnett; those of the letters are by David Lowe; that of the essay "The Execution of Troppmann" is by David Magarshack. The hitherto unpublished translations of "Hamlet and Don Quixote," the "Autobiography" of 1876, and the "Speech Delivered at the Dedication of the Monument to A. S. Pushkin in Moscow" are mine.

I have only lightly revised Lowe's and Magarshack's translations, and have not included the bulk of Lowe's scholarly annotations of the letters, although I have retained his footnotes identifying the people to whom Turgenev wrote. In contrast, I have extensively revised Garnett's translations, drawing throughout on the canonical Russian texts presented in the *Polnoe sobranie sochinenii I. S. Turgeneva*, edited by M. P. Alekseev et al., published by the U.S.S.R. Academy of Sciences between 1978 and 1986. While seeking to preserve the many virtues of Garnett's early-twentieth century British translations, especially their admirable reflections of the subtle tonalities of Turgenev's prose, I have corrected some errors and omissions, and have additionally striven to accomplish two inter-related editorial goals: to transmit the varieties and nuances of Turgenev's language with the utmost fidelity, and to render Turgenev's fiction as accessible as possible to late-twentieth-century American readers. To achieve these goals, I have revised Garnett's diction when it failed to reflect fully the precise, subtle connotations of the Russian, and when it was either markedly old-fashioned or conspicuously British. I have also changed the punctuation where Garnett adhered so faithfully to the original Russian that she sacrificed English standards of usage and clarity. Furthermore, I have rearranged or simplified syntax, especially in prepositional and adverbial phrases, and have broken up overly long sentences containing multiple clauses characteristic of Russian but not of English. In addition to these revisions, I have endeavored, more than did Garnett—as well as a number of Turgenev's other translators—to capture the informal, conversational quality typical of many of Turgenev's narratives. To this end, I have departed from Garnett's formal English in numerous dialogues and narrative passages by introducing locutions characteristic of contemporary spoken American English, including contractions. But I have revised some translations, specifically, utterances that are either highly colloquial or are spoken by relatively poorly educated characters (peasants, servants, waiters, etc.), in an opposite direction. Although quite comprehensible in the original Russian, the rhetorical idiosyncrasies of these utterances make them difficult to translate effectively. Garnett tended to translate those idiosyncrasies into British idioms of her day, resulting in some expressions that can be misleading for Americans today. My solution has been to translate these utterances in relatively straightforward English, while still attempting to reflect some portion of their distinctive vocabulary and tone.

English transliteration of Russian (i.e., the conversion of letters of the Cyrillic alphabet into letters of the English alphabet) has not been fully standardized. Where well-established English versions of Russian words do not exist, I have utilized throughout the volume, with minor exceptions, the modified Library of Congress system, which for the most part renders Russian names and other terms pronounceable in English without wholly Anglicizing them. Words and phrases in languages other than Russian (including the fractured French that Bazarov's father occasionally interjects as he speaks in *Fathers and Sons*), when left untranslated in Turgenev's original texts, have been presented untranslated here as well, since Turgenev often intended to subordinate their literal meaning to the fact that the speaker does not know or has forsaken Russian, which for Turgenev frequently indicated a morally questionable state of mind. I have also chosen not to annotate historical references, in an effort to avoid interrupting the flow of the translations with footnotes. The few editorial footnotes are numbered; Turgenev's original notes are marked with asterisks.

As every reader of Russian literature in translation knows, people's names in Russian are a chronic source of confusion. Russian full names are comprised of a formal first name, a patronymic derived from the father's formal first name, and a last name (e.g., "Fedor Ivanovich Lavretskii"); Russian women traditionally use the last names of their fathers or husbands, attaching the feminine ending "a" or "aia" to them (e.g., the formal full name of Fedor Ivanovich Lavretskii's wife is "Varvara Pavlovna Lavretskaia"). Both men and women are often referred to and addressed politely by the formal first name plus patronymic (the penultimate syllable of which is sometimes elided in men's names—e.g., "Ivanych" for "Ivanovich"), but both can also be referred to solely by their last names. Where Turgenev refers to a married woman solely by her last name with the feminine ending (e.g., "Lavretskaia"), I have chosen to use the conventional English formulation "Mrs."—Garnett used the French "Madame"—before the husband's last name without the feminine ending (e.g., "Mrs. Lavretskii"). But I have retained the feminine ending on women's last names when the complete, formal name is used.

To add to the complexity of Russian names, close friends, relatives, and children are also often referred to and addressed by a nickname derived from the formal first name (e.g., "Natasha" from Natalia, "Mitia" from Dmitrii, "Fedia" from Fedor, "Liza" from Elizaveta, "Volodia" from Vladimir, "Vasia" from Vasilii). Although some confusion may occasionally result, all the various forms of an individual's name have been retained here in order to help convey the degree of social and emotional proximity suggested by the form employed.

In revising overall, I have sought to preserve what Virginia Woolf termed the "simplicity so complex" of Turgenev's writings—the lapidary language that lucidly, yet subtly and powerfully, conveys the intellectual, aesthetic, psychological, and moral intricacies of Turgenev's vision of human experience. In this way, I hope to win new appreciation for Turgenev among American readers in particular, both those who have read him before and those who have not.

The Essential Turgenev

Letter to Bettina von Arnim.[1]

My dear lady,

When you told me yesterday about the amazing association that arose in you while you observed the flickering fire, when you then spoke of nature as something animate and living and then at the end asked me whether I understood you, I answered in the affirmative; but it's very important for me to know whether I really understand it. This intimate link between the human spirit and nature isn't the most pleasant, most beautiful, and most profound phenomenon in our lives by accident: only with a spiritual basis, with ideas, is it possible for our spirit and our thoughts to be joined so profoundly. However, in order to have the opportunity to enter into this union, one must be as ingenuous as nature itself, in order that each of nature's ideas and each of its movements be transformed in the human soul directly into conscious thoughts and spiritual images. But even a person who's still alien to truth feels that; the longing of evening, the quiet self-preoccupation of night, and the thought-filled joy of morning alternate in his breast; he's made of flesh and blood, he breathes and sees; he can't avoid nature's influence; he can't live entirely in falsehood. The more intensely a person strives for the simplicity of truth, the richer and fuller will be his relationship with nature—and how could it be otherwise, since truth is nothing other than the nature of man? If you look at it from this point of view (and many people do), then how infinitely sweet—and bitter—and joyous and at the same time painful life is! You find yourself in a constant struggle—and you can never save yourself by retreating: you must see the struggle through to the end. The profound, beautiful meaning of nature is suddenly revealed to us and then disappears; these are presentiments that, as soon as they flutter out of one's soul, immediately vanish; at times it seems that nature (and by nature I mean the whole living spirit made flesh) wants to speak, and suddenly it grows mute and lies before us dead and silent; the darkest night covers everything all around. That we don't live in the truth is so easy to recognize!!! You need only go out into the open field or the forest, and if, in

---

1. Bettina von Arnim (1785–1859) was a German writer with whom Turgenev had become acquainted in 1838 in Berlin while he was a student. This letter, in German, is an unfinished draft.

spite of the joyousness of your soul, you nonetheless feel in its hidden depths a certain constraint, an inner constraint that appears just at the instant when nature takes possession of a man—then you learn your limits, you become aware of that darkness which refuses to disappear in the bright light of self-oblivion, then you'll say to yourself: "You're still an egoist!" But that it's possible, as you said yesterday, to be freed of your own personality and find it again in the spirit to which you've surrendered (*"the more multifaceted, the more individual,"* as you say in your *Gündrode*) you proved to us yesterday—or no—you've lived it, as we observe. That you thought of Goethe while watching the wind carry the ashes away from the flame, and the *way* you thought of that wasn't, and I'm certain of this, a *comparison*: there was no disjunction between your cognition and your thought—the motion of nature was transformed directly into that thought. For just as all of nature, including its most hidden palpitations, is open to you, so is your spirit open to nature. Your thoughts grow like plants out of the earth's soil—this is the same self-revelation of the spirit, which, like an organic image here and the idea of that image there, like a sprout from the soul, reveals itself to the light. Every person ought to be like this: instead of doing as many do, for instance, on hearing a nightingale sing, surrendering to an overwhelming desire, people ought to have in their breast an inexhaustible spring of thoughts full of the feeling of love. And just as multifaceted and infinite as the focus of nature should be the focus of thoughts divine and simple, whether they be insignificant or great, like the word of nature, which is "God"—sometimes calm and restrained, like a deep valley at sunrise, sometimes unconstrained and wild, like a storm—just as rich and varied as sound. To be unified and infinitely diverse—isn't that really a miracle? Nature is a miracle and an entire world of miracles: that's the way every person should be—and is; and the fact that he is has been revealed to us by great people of every era. Could it really be in vain that we're human beings? Could it really be in vain that everything spiritual in nature has been united in a single focus, which is called "I"? What would nature be without us, what would we be without nature? Both are unthinkable! Testimony to the fact that you're blessed and will be blessed, that you're truthful and free, is in your love—your compassion for nature, which grieves because it's been abandoned by humans. That's why it was frank with you, spoke to you, revealed its whole life—and its grief—to you, like that brook to which you once called out,

"Child, why are you weeping? What do you lack?" when it was babbling so anxiously in the reeds. For that reason you've never described nature. I'd say that under your pen nature was transformed into words; what each word means, what divinity is contained in it, what art and form are called, you were the first to teach us. I don't know whether you'll believe this, but I want to be cognizant of the happiness I experience when I read you: I've been granted by heaven such capacities for self-oblivion that I can completely forget myself. I myself don't know whether what I've just written is true—I don't even want to know; happiness is speaking through my lips, and I'm giving it the freedom to speak. When I can't find a word, when it's been denied me, then even nature is denied me, because the word is the nature of the spirit and of the thought. But I experience myself on the inside: I have a premonition of blessedness, which is justified—the blessedness of truth. I've found the appropriate word: between you and nature there's no boundary; in both of you lives one and the same God, who manifests Himself in your consciousness as thought and revelation. Is He great? How can you know this or express it? Does God see Himself as great? As you said yesterday: is thought really a property or a possession? Isn't each of us a tool, and a spoken word—isn't it the speech of God, the sense of which is revealed to you with the help of a joyous miracle? Only believe that you're always right—no matter what people say; through the simple contact with truth the genuine and ideal are revealed in every relationship. What people don't wish to admit, what frightens those who are hard of heart, we must admit: "He who's righteous is good, and free, and blessed—and wise." This isn't an honor, but merely the simplest thing—and it ought to be the most ordinary and commonplace of things.

A Sportsman's Sketches

Khor and Kalinych

Anyone who has happened to cross from the Bolkhovskii district into the Zhizdrinskii district has to have been impressed by the striking difference between the type of people in the Orel province and those in the Kaluga province. The Orel peasant isn't tall, is rather stooped, sullen, and regards other people with suspicion; he lives in a wretched little hovel made of aspenwood, labors in the fields as a serf, engages in no kind of trading, is miserably fed, and wears shoes woven from rope fibers. The rent-paying Kaluga peasant lives in a roomy cottage made of pinewood; he's tall, regards other people boldly and cheerfully, is neat and clean-shaven; he trades in butter and tar, and wears boots on holidays. The typical Orel village (we're speaking now about the eastern part of the province) is usually situated in the midst of plowed fields, near a ravine that has somehow been converted into a filthy pool. Except for a few always-accommodating willows and two or three gaunt birches, you don't see any trees for a verst around; hut is huddled against hut, their roofs covered with rotting thatch.... The typical Kaluga village, by contrast, is generally surrounded by forest; the huts stand more freely, are more upright, and have boarded roofs; the gates fasten tightly, the hedges aren't dilapidated or unkempt, so there aren't any gaps to invite the visit of a passing pig.... And things are much better in the Kaluga province for the hunter. In the Orel province, the last of the woods and squares* will disappear within five years, and there's no trace of a marsh

* In the Orel province, "square" means a large, thick mass of bushes. The Orel dialect is distinguished in general by numerous unique words and turns of phrase, some of which are perfectly apt, others relatively meaningless.

left; in the Kaluga province, on the contrary, the marshes extend over tens of versts, the forest over hundreds, and a splendid bird, the grouse, hasn't fled from there; there's an abundance of the friendly, larger snipe as well, and the loudly flapping partridge thrills and startles the marksman and his dog by its abrupt upward flight.

On one hunting trip to the Zhizdrinskii district, I encountered a small landowner of the Kaluga province named Polutykin in the fields. He was an enthusiastic hunter and, it therefore follows, an excellent fellow. He was subject to a few weaknesses, it's true: for instance, he used to court every unmarried heiress in the province and, when he'd been rejected and denied entry to her house, he'd brokenheartedly confide his sorrows to all his friends and acquaintances, and would continue to shower offerings of sour peaches and other raw produce from his garden upon the young lady's parents; he was fond of repeating the same anecdote, which, in spite of Polutykin's appreciation of its merits, had certainly never amused anyone else; he admired the works of Akim Nakhimov and the novel *Pinna*; he stammered; he called his dog Astronomer; he said "howsomever" instead of "however." He'd instituted a French system of cooking in his household, the secret of which consisted, according to his cook, in a complete transformation of the natural taste of each dish: in the hands of this expert, meat assumed the flavor of fish, fish of mushrooms, macaroni of gunpowder; to make up for this, though, not a single carrot went into the soup without taking the shape of a rhombus or a trapezoid. But, with the exception of these few, insignificant failings, Polutykin was, as has already been remarked, an excellent fellow.

On the first day of my acquaintance with Polutykin, he invited me to spend the night at his house.

"It's five versts farther to my house," he added. "It's a long way to walk. Let's drop in first at Khor's." (The reader must excuse my omitting his stammer.)

"Who's Khor?"

"A peasant of mine. He lives quite nearby."

We set off in that direction. Khor's solitary homestead stood in a well-cultivated clearing in the middle of the forest. It consisted of several pinewood buildings enclosed by fences; a porch supported by slender posts ran along the front of the central building. We went in. We were met by a young, tall, good-looking youth of twenty.

"Ah, Fedia! Is Khor at home?" Polutykin asked him.

"No. Khor's gone into town," answered the young man, smiling and displaying a row of snow-white teeth. "Would you like the little cart brought around?"

"Yes, my boy, we'd like the little cart. And bring us some kvass." We went into the cottage. There wasn't a single cheap Suzdal' print pasted up on the clean boards of the walls; a lamp was burning in the corner before a heavy icon in its silver frame; the limewood table had recently been sanded and scrubbed; there were no lively beetles running about or contemplative cockroaches hiding between the timbers and in the cracks of the window-frames. The young man soon reappeared carrying a large white pitcher filled with excellent kvass, a huge loaf of wheat bread, and a dozen salted cucumbers in a wooden bowl. He put all these provisions on the table and then, leaning his back against the door, began to gaze at us with a smile.

We barely had time to finish eating our meal before the cart was already rattling at the doorstep. We went out. A curly-haired, rosy-cheeked boy of fifteen was driving the cart and was having difficulty holding back the well-fed piebald horse. Six young giants were standing around the cart, looking very much like one another and like Fedia.

"All of these are Khor's sons!" said Polutykin.

"These are all Khorkies," put in Fedia, who'd followed us onto the steps. "But these aren't all of them—Potap's in the woods, and Sidor's gone with old Khor to town.... See here, Vasia," he went on, turning to the one driving, "drive like the wind. You're driving the master. Only be careful over the ruts and go a little slower. Don't tip the cart over and upset the master's stomach!"

The other Khorkies smiled at Fedia's joke. "Lift Astronomer in!" Polutykin cried ceremoniously. Not without amusement, Fedia lifted the dog into the air as it displayed a strained smile, and laid it on the bottom of the cart. Vasia let the horse go. We rolled away.

"And here's my office," Polutykin said suddenly, pointing to a small, low-pitched house. "Shall we go in?"

"By all means."

"It's no longer in use," he observed, going in. "Still, it's worth looking at."

The office consisted of two empty rooms. The caretaker, a one-eyed old man, ran in from the backyard.

"Good day, Miniaich," said Polutykin. "Bring us some water."

The one-eyed old man disappeared, and immediately returned with a bottle of water and two glasses. "Taste it," Polutykin urged me. "It's wonderful springwater." We drank a glass each, while the old man bowed low. "Come on, I think we can go," said my new friend. "I sold the merchant Alliluev four acres of forest for a good price in that office." We took our seats in the cart, and half an hour later we reached the courtyard of the main house.

"Tell me, please," I asked Polutykin at supper, "why does Khor live apart from your other peasants?"

"Well, here's why—he's an intelligent peasant. Twenty-five years ago his cottage burned down, so he came to my late father and said, 'Nikolai Kuzmich,' says he, 'allow me to settle in your forest in the marsh. I'll pay you a good rent.' 'But what do you want to settle in the marsh for?' 'Oh, I just want to, only please, your honor, Nikolai Kuzmich, don't require any labor from me, but set the rent that you think best.' 'Fifty rubles a year!' 'All right.' 'But I don't want you in arrears, mind you!' 'Of course not, no arrears.' And so he settled in the marsh. Since then they've called him Khor."

"Well, has he gotten rich?" I inquired.

"Yes, he's gotten quite rich. Now he pays me a full hundred rubles in rent, and I'll raise it again, I suppose. I've said to him more than once, 'Buy your freedom, Khor, buy your freedom,' . . . but he declares that he can't, the rogue. Has no money, he says. . . . As though that were likely. . . ."

The next day, right after our morning tea, we started out to hunt again. As we were driving through the village, Polutykin ordered the coachman to stop at a low-pitched cottage and called out loudly, "Kalinych!" "Coming, your honor, coming," rang out a voice from the yard. "I'm tying my shoes." We proceeded on foot; outside the village a man of about forty overtook us. He was tall and thin, with a small, erectly held head. It was Kalinych. His good-humored, swarthy face, somewhat pitted with smallpox, pleased me at first glance. Kalinych (as I learned afterward) went hunting with his master every day, carried his bag and sometimes his gun as well, noted where game could be found, fetched water, built temporary shelters, gathered strawberries, and ran behind the carriage. Polutykin couldn't stir a step without him. Kalinych was a man of the most cheerful, most gentle disposition; he was constantly singing to himself in a low tone and looking around lightheartedly. He spoke in a somewhat nasal voice, while smiling, habitually squinting his light-blue eyes and tugging at his scanty, wedge-shaped beard with his hand. He didn't walk rapidly, but he took big strides, leaning lightly on a long, thin walking stick. He spoke with me more than once during the day, waiting on me without obsequiousness, but he looked after his master as if Polutykin were a child. When the unbearable heat drove us to seek shelter at midday, he took us to his apiary in the very heart of the forest. There Kalinych opened a little hut, which was decorated with bunches of dry, fragrant herbs. He made us comfortable on some dry hay and then put a kind of netted bag over his head, took a knife, a little pot, and a smoldering stick, and went out to the hives to get us some honeycomb. We drank springwater with the warm, transparent honey, and then fell asleep to the monotonous hum of the bees and the rustling murmur of the leaves.

A slight gust of wind awakened me. . . . I opened my eyes and saw Kalinych: he was sitting on the threshold of the half-open door, carving a spoon with his knife. I admired his face, as mild and clear as an evening sky, for a long while. Polutykin also woke up, but we didn't get up right away. After our long walk and deep sleep, it was pleasant to lie in the hay without moving; we felt weary and languid; our faces gave off a slightly warm glow; our eyes closed in delicious laziness. We finally got up and set off wandering again until evening. At supper, I began to talk about Khor and Kalinych again.

"Kalinych is a good peasant," Polutykin told me. "He's a helpful, diligent peasant. Howsomever, he can't farm his land properly, since I'm always taking him away from it. He goes out hunting with me every day. . . . You can judge for yourself how his farm must fare."

I agreed with him, and we went to bed.

The next day Polutykin had to go to town on some business concerning his neighbor Pichukov. This neighbor, Pichukov, had plowed over some land owned by Polutykin and had flogged a peasant woman of his on this same piece of land. I went out hunting alone, and toward evening I dropped by Khor's house. I was met on the threshold of the cottage by an elderly man—bald, short, broad-shouldered, and stout—Khor himself. I looked at the man with curiosity. The shape of his face recalled that of Socrates: he had the same high, knobby forehead, the same little eyes, the same snub nose. We went into the cottage together. The same Fedia brought me some milk and black bread. Khor sat down on a bench and, quietly stroking his curly beard, entered into conversation with me. He seemed to know his own worth; he spoke and moved slowly; from time to time a chuckle emerged from under his long moustache.

We discussed sowing, crops, the peasant's way of life.... He always seemed to agree with me, but then I'd get embarrassed.... Thus our conversation progressed somewhat strangely. Doubtlessly owing to caution, Khor expressed himself quite obliquely at times.... Here's a sample of our conversation:

"Tell me, Khor," I said to him, "why don't you buy your freedom from your master?"

"And what would I buy my freedom for? Now I know my master, and I know my rent.... We have a good master."

"It's always better to be free," I remarked. Khor gave me a dubious look.

"Surely," he agreed.

"Well then, why don't you buy your freedom?"

Khor shook his head.

"What would you have me buy it with, your honor?"

"Oh, come on, old man!"

"If Khor were thrown among free men," he continued in an undertone, as though to himself, "everyone without a beard would be superior to Khor."

"Then shave your beard."

"What's a beard? A beard is grass—one can cut it."

"Well then?"

"Then it seems Khor will become a merchant right off. Merchants lead a fine life, and they have beards."

"Why, do you do a little selling, too?" I asked him.

"We sell a little bit of butter and a little bit of tar.... Would your honor like the cart loaded?"

"You're a smart man, and you keep a tight rein on your tongue," I thought to myself.

"No," I said aloud, "I don't want the cart. I'll go on foot in the woods near your house tomorrow and, if you'll let me, I'll spend tonight in your hayloft."

"You're most welcome. But will you be comfortable in the loft? I'll tell the women to spread a sheet and give you a pillow....

Hey, women!" he cried, getting up from his seat. "Come here, women! . . . . And you, Fedia, come with them. Women, you know, are foolish folk."

A quarter of an hour later, Fedia escorted me to the barn with a lantern. I threw myself down on the fragrant hay; my dog curled up at my feet; Fedia bid me good night; the door creaked and slammed. I couldn't get to sleep for quite a while. A cow came up to the door and exhaled heavily twice; the dog growled at her with dignity; a pig passed by, grunting pensively; a horse somewhere nearby began to munch hay and snort. . . . I finally fell asleep.

Fedia awakened me at sunrise. I liked this cheerful, lively young man and, from what I could see, he was old Khor's favorite, too. They often bantered with one another in friendly fashion. The elderly man came out to meet me. Whether because I'd spent the night under his roof or for some other reason, Khor treated me far more cordially than he had the day before.

"The samovar's ready," he told me with a smile. "Let's go and have some tea."

We took our seats at the table. A robust-looking peasant woman, one of his daughters-in-law, brought in a jug of milk. All his sons came into the cottage, one after another.

"What a fine set of offspring you have!" I remarked to the elderly man.

"Yes," he said, breaking off a tiny piece of sugar with his teeth, "my old woman and I have nothing to complain about, seemingly."

"And do they all live with you?"

"Yes. They themselves choose to, and so they live here."

"And are they all married?"

"Here's one who's not married, the scamp!" he replied, pointing at Fedia, who, as before, was leaning against the door. "Vaska, he's still too young—he can wait."

"And why should I get married?" retorted Fedia. "I'm quite well off the way I am. What do I want a wife for? To squabble with, eh?"

"Now then, you . . . ah, I know you! You wear a silver ring. . . . You're always after the girls up at the manor house. . . . 'Stop it! Shame on you!'" the elderly man went on, mimicking the servant girls. "Ah, I know you, you pampered rascal!"

"But what good's a peasant woman?"

"A peasant woman's a real worker," Khor said seriously. "She's a peasant man's servant."

"And what do I want with a worker?"

"So you'd like to play with the fire and let others burn their fingers. We know the sort of person you are."

"Well, marry me off, then. Eh? Why don't you answer?"

"There, that's enough, that's enough, jokester. You can see that we're disturbing the gentleman. I'll marry you off, depend on it.... And you, your honor, don't be vexed with him. You see, he's only a baby—he hasn't had time to develop much common sense."

Fedia shook his head.

"Is Khor at home?" rang out a well-known voice, and Kalinych came into the cottage holding a bunch of wild strawberries that he'd gathered for his friend Khor. The elderly man gave him a warm welcome. I looked at Kalinych with surprise. I confess that I hadn't expected such a "delicate attention" on the part of a peasant.

I started out to hunt that day four hours later than usual, and I spent the following three days at Khor's. My new friends interested me. I don't know how I gained their confidence, but they began to talk to me unconstrainedly. The two friends weren't the least bit alike. Khor was an affirmative, practical man with a head for business, a rationalist; Kalinych, on the contrary, belonged to the ranks of idealists and romantics, of dreamy, ecstatic spirits. Khor had a grasp of reality, that is to say, he thought ahead, saved a little money, and stayed on good terms with his master and the other authorities; Kalinych wore shoes woven from rope fibers and lived from hand to mouth. Khor had reared a large family whose members were obedient and unified; Kalinych had once had a wife, whom he'd feared, and had had no children. Khor viewed Polutykin with a critical eye; Kalinych revered his master. Khor loved Kalinych and took special care of him; Kalinych loved and respected Khor. Khor said little, chuckled, and thought for himself; Kalinych expressed himself heatedly, although he didn't have the command of refined language that a glib factory worker had. But Kalinych was endowed with gifts that even Khor acknowledged: he could charm away hemorrhages, fits, madness, and could cure worms; his bees always did well; he had a light touch. In my presence, Khor asked him to bring a newly bought horse to his stable, and Kalinych carried out the old skeptic's request with scrupulous gravity. Kalinych had a greater affinity with nature; Khor, with people and society. Kalinych didn't like to argue and

believed everything blindly; Khor had adopted a cynical point of
view even toward life itself. He'd seen and experienced a great
deal, and I learned a lot from him.

For instance, I learned from his stories that every year before
mowing-time a small, peculiar-looking cart makes its appearance
in the villages. In this cart sits a man in a long coat who sells
scythes. He charges one ruble twenty-five kopecks—a ruble and a
half in notes—for cash, three rubles if he gives credit. All the
peasants, of course, get scythes from him on credit. In two or three
weeks, he reappears and asks for the money. Since each peasant's
just cut his oats, he's able to pay him, so he goes to the tavern
with the merchant and the debt is settled there. Once some landowners came up with the idea of buying the scythes themselves
for cash and letting the peasants have them on credit for the same
price, but the peasants seemed dissatisfied, even dejected: they'd
been deprived of the pleasure of tapping the scythe and listening
to the ring of the metal, of turning it over and over in their hands
and asking the devious town merchant at least twenty times, "Eh,
my friend, isn't this blade a bit weak?"

The same tricks are played with the sale of sickles, the only
difference being that the women have a hand in the business then,
and they sometimes drive the merchant himself to the point of
beating them—for their own good, of course. But women suffer
the most ill-treatment under the following circumstances: contrac-
tors who supply the material for paper factories employ a special
class of people, called "eagles" in some districts, for the purchase
of rags. Such an "eagle" receives two hundred rubles in banknotes
from the merchant and starts off in search of his prey. But, unlike
the noble bird from whom he has derived his name, he doesn't
swoop down upon it openly and boldly; on the contrary, the "eagle" is forced to resort to deceit and cunning. He leaves his cart
somewhere in a thicket near the village and goes to the backyards
and back doors alone, like someone casually passing by or simply
a tramp. The women sense his proximity and sneak out to meet
him. The bargain is hastily concluded. In return for a few copper
coins, a woman gives the "eagle" not only every useless rag she
has but often even her husband's shirt and her own petticoat.
Recently, the women have also deemed it profitable to steal from
themselves and to sell hemp, especially hemp in "home-woven"
form, the same way—a major expansion and improvement in business for the "eagles"! The peasant men have gotten more cunning

in their turn, however, and at the slightest suspicion, at the most distant rumor the approach of an "eagle," they promptly, spiritedly resort to corrective and preventive measures. And, after all, isn't it disgraceful? Selling hemp is the men's business, and they certainly do sell it—not in town (they'd have to haul it there themselves), but to traders who come for it and, lacking scales, calculate that forty handfuls equal thirty-six pounds—and you know what a Russian's hand is like and what it can hold, especially when he "tries his best"!

Since I hadn't had much experience and wasn't a "native" of the countryside (as they say in Orel), I listened to many such narratives. But Khor wasn't always the narrator; he questioned me about many things, too. He learned that I'd spent time abroad, and his curiosity was aroused.... Kalinych wasn't the less curious, but he was more attracted by descriptions of nature, mountains, waterfalls, extraordinary buildings, and great towns; Khor was interested in questions of government and administration. He considered everything methodically: "Well, is that the same among them as it is among us, or is it different?... Come, tell us, your honor, what is it like?" "Ah, Lord, thy will be done!" Kalinych would exclaim while I told my story. Khor mostly kept silent, merely lowering his bushy eyebrows and remarking from time to time, "That wouldn't do for us. Still, that's a good thing—that's real order."

I can't recount all his inquiries, nor is it necessary, but I carried one conviction away from our conversations that my readers probably won't anticipate: the conviction that Peter the Great was supremely Russian—Russian, above all, in his reforms. The Russian is so convinced of his own strength and fortitude that he isn't afraid of putting himself to the test. He takes little interest in his own past and boldly looks forward to the future. What is good, he likes; what is sensible, he wants; and where it comes from, he doesn't care.

Khor's vigorous mind eagerly ridiculed weak German theories, but, in his words, "Germans are an inquisitive people," and he was ready to learn a little from them. Thanks to his exceptional situation, his elemental independence, Khor told me a great deal that you couldn't pry or, as the peasants say, grind with a grindstone, out of any other man. He really did understand his situation. Conversing with Khor, I listened to the simple, intelligent discourse of the Russian peasant for the first time. Khor's knowledge was sufficiently broad, in his own opinion, but he couldn't read, whereas Kalinych could. "That good-for-nothing was taught to read and write," observed Khor, "and his bees never die during the winter."

"But didn't you teach your children to read?"

Khor was silent for a minute.

"Fedia can read."

"And the others?"

"The others can't."

"Why not?"

The elderly man didn't answer, and changed the subject. However intelligent he was, he had many prejudices and preconceptions. He despised women from the depths of his soul, for instance, and in lighthearted moments he amused himself by making jokes at their expense. His wife was a cross old woman who lay on the stove all day long, incessantly grumbling and scolding; her sons paid no attention to her, but she instilled the fear of God in her daughters-in-law. Tellingly, in one Russian ballad the mother-in-law sings: "What a son you are to me! What sort of head of a household! You don't beat your wife, you don't beat your young wife. . . ."

I attempted to intercede for the daughters-in-law once and sought to arouse Khor's sympathy, but he asked me tranquilly, "Why do you want to worry about such . . . trifles? Let the women fight it out. . . . If anything separates them, that only makes matters worse . . . and it's not worth getting your hands dirty."

Sometimes the spiteful old woman got down from the stove and called the yard dog out of the hay, crying, "Here, here, doggie," then she'd beat it on its thin back with a poker, or she'd stand on the porch and "snarl," as Khor expressed it, at everyone who went past. She stood in awe of her husband, though, and would return to her place on the stove at his command.

It was especially curious to hear Khor and Kalinych argue whenever the subject of Polutykin came up.

"There, Khor, let him alone," Kalinych would say.

"But why doesn't he order some boots for you?" Khor would retort.

"Eh? Boots! . . . What do I want with boots? I'm a peasant."

"Well, I'm a peasant, too, but look!"

And Khor would lift up his foot and show Kalinych a boot that looked as if it'd been cut from a mammoth's hide.

"As if you were one of us!" replied Kalinych.

"Well, at least he might pay for your woven shoes. You go out hunting with him—you must wear out a pair a day."

"He does give me something for woven shoes."

"Yes, he gave you two copper coins last year."

Kalinych turned away in frustration, but Khor was overcome by a fit of laughter, during which his little eyes completely disappeared. Kalinych sang quite pleasingly and played the balalaika a little. Khor never grew weary of listening to him; Khor would let his head fall to one side and would chime in lugubriously. He was particularly fond of the song "Ah, my fate, my fate!" Fedia never lost an opportunity to make fun of his father, saying, "What are you so unhappy about, old man?" But Khor would lean his cheek on his hand, cover his eyes, and continue to mourn his fate. . . . Yet at other times no man could be more active—he was always busy doing something: mending the cart, patching the fence, looking after the harness. He didn't insist on a very high degree of cleanliness, however, and, in response to some observation of mine, once said, "A cottage ought to smell as if it was lived in."

"Notice," I responded, "how clean it is in Kalinych's apiary."

"The bees wouldn't live there otherwise, your honor," he said with a sigh.

"Tell me," he asked me another time, "do you have an estate of your own?"

"Yes."

"Is it far from here?"

"A hundred versts or so."

"Do you live on your own land, your honor?"

"Yes."

"But you like wandering around with your gun the best, I suppose?"

"Yes, I must confess I do."

"And you're right to do so, your honor. Shoot grouse to your heart's content—just change your bailiff more often."

On the fourth day, Polutykin sent for me in the evening. I was sorry to part from the old man. I took my seat in the carriage with Kalinych.

"Well, goodbye, Khor, good health to you," I said. "Goodbye, Fedia."

"Goodbye, your honor, goodbye. Don't forget us."

We started; the first red glow of sunset had just appeared.

"It'll be a fine day tomorrow," I remarked, looking at the clear sky.

"No, it'll rain," Kalinych replied. "The ducks over there are splashing restlessly, and the smell of the grass is terribly strong." We drove off into the bushes. Kalinych began to sing in an undertone as he bounced up and down on the driver's seat, and he kept gazing at the sunset.

The next day I departed from Polutykin's hospitable home.

My Neighbor Radilov

In the autumn, woodcocks often take refuge in aged gardens of lime trees. There are a good many such gardens among us in the Orel province. Our forefathers, when they selected a site to build an estate, invariably marked out two acres of good ground for a fruit garden, its paths lined with lime trees. During the last fifty or seventy years at most, these estates—"nests of gentry," as they're called—have gradually disappeared from the face of the earth: the houses are falling to pieces or have been sold for building materials; the stone outhouses have become piles of rubbish; the apple trees have died and been turned into firewood; the hedges and fences have been pulled up. Only the lime trees remain in all their prior glory; now, with plowed fields all around them, they tell a tale to our frivolous generation about "the fathers and brothers who lived before us." Such an old lime tree is a magnificent tree. . . . Even the merciless axe of the Russian peasant spares it. Its leaves are delicate, its powerful limbs spread out in all directions, and one can always find shade under them.

Once, as I was wandering in the fields hunting partridges with Ermolai, I saw a deserted garden off to one side, and turned toward it. I'd barely crossed its border when a snipe rose up out of a bush, its wings flapping noisily. I fired my gun, and at the same instant, a few paces away from me, I heard a shriek. The frightened face of a young girl peeped out for a second from behind some trees and instantly disappeared.

Ermolai ran up to me. "Why are you shooting here? There's a landowner living here."

Before I had time to answer him, before my dog, with dignified importance, had time to bring me the bird I'd shot, I heard swift footsteps approaching, and a tall man with a moustache emerged from a thicket and came to a halt in front of me with an expression of annoyance on his face. I apologized as best I could, gave him my name, and offered him the bird that had been killed on his domain.

"Very well," he said to me with a smile. "I'll take your game, but only on one condition—that you'll stay and dine with us."

I must confess that I wasn't overly delighted at his offer, but it was impossible to refuse.

"I'm a landowner here and your neighbor, Radilov. Perhaps you've heard of me?" continued my new acquaintance. "Today is Sunday, and we'll be sure to have a decent dinner. Otherwise I wouldn't have invited you."

I made the sort of reply one does in such circumstances, and turned to follow him. A little path that had recently been cleared soon led us out of the grove of lime trees; we entered the kitchen garden. Rows of curly whitish-green cabbages grew between some old apple trees and gooseberry bushes; hops twined their tendrils around high poles; thick rows of brown twigs were tangled up with dried peas; large flat pumpkins seemed to be rolling on the ground; cucumbers shone yellow under their dusty, angular leaves; tall nettles waved alongside a hedge; in two or three places, clumps of honeysuckle, elderberry bushes, and wild roses bloomed—the remnants of former flowerbeds. A well surrounded by puddles could be seen near a small fishpond full of reddish, slimy water. Ducks were busily splashing and waddling among these puddles; a dog blinking and twitching in every limb was gnawing a bone in the meadow, where a piebald cow was lazily chewing on grass, flicking its tail across its lean back from time to time. The little path turned to one side; from behind thick willows and birch trees we caught sight of a little old gray house with a board roof and a curved porch. Radilov stopped short.

"But," he said, as he cast a good-humored glance at my face, "on second thought . . . maybe you don't care to visit us after all. In that case. . . . "

I didn't allow him to finish, but assured him that, on the contrary, it'd be a great pleasure for me to dine with him.

"Well, as you wish."

We went into the house. A young man in a long caftan of thick blue cloth met us on the steps. Radilov promptly told him to bring Ermolai some vodka; my huntsman made a respectful bow to the back of his munificent host. From the hallway, which was decorated with various multicolored pictures and checked curtains, we went into a small room—Radilov's study. I took off my hunting gear and put my gun in a corner; the young man in the long shirt busily brushed me off.

"Well, now, let's go into the drawing room," Radilov cordially suggested. "I'll introduce you to my mother."

I followed behind him. In the drawing room, an elderly woman of medium height with a thin, kindly face and a timid, mournful expression, wearing a cinnamon-colored dress and a white cap, was sitting on a sofa in the center of the room.

"Here, mother, let me introduce to you our neighbor...."

The elderly woman stood up and bowed to me without letting a fat worsted workbag that looked like a sack drop from her withered hands.

"Have you been in this vicinity a long time?" she asked in a weak, low voice, blinking her eyes.

"No, not long."

"Do you intend to remain here long?"

"Until winter, I think."

The elderly woman said nothing more.

"And this," interjected Radilov, indicating a tall, thin man whom I hadn't noticed on entering the drawing room, "is Fedor Mikheich.... Come on, Fedia, give our visitor a sample of your art. Why have you hidden yourself away in that corner?"

Fedor Mikheich immediately got up from his chair, fetched a wretched little violin from the window, picked up the bow—not by the end, as is the customary, but by the middle—put the violin to his chest, closed his eyes, and began to dance, singing a song and scraping the bow across the strings. He appeared to be about seventy; a long cloth coat flapped pathetically around his dessicated, bony limbs. He danced, leaping boldly at times, then letting his bald little head droop and stretching out his scraggy neck as if he were dying, stamping his feet on the floor, and occasionally bending his knees with obvious difficulty. His toothless mouth emitted a voice cracked with age. Radilov must have guessed from the expression on my face that Fedia's "art" didn't give me much pleasure.

"Very good, old man, that's enough," he said. "You can go and refresh yourself."

Fedor Mikheich immediately laid the violin down on the windowsill, bowed first to me as the guest, then to the elderly woman, then to Radilov, and went out.

"He was also a landowner," my new friend continued, "and a rich one, but he ruined himself—so now he lives with me. . . . But in his day he was considered the most dashing fellow in the province—he ran off with two married ladies. He used to keep singers, and sang himself, and danced like a master. . . . But won't you have some vodka? Dinner's almost ready."

A young woman, the one I'd caught a glimpse of in the garden, came into the room.

"And here's Olga!" Radilov remarked, turning his head slightly. "Let me introduce you. . . . Well, let's go in to dinner."

We went in and sat down at the table. As we were coming out of the drawing room and taking our seats, Fedor Mikheich, whose eyes were bright and nose rather red after his "refreshment," sang "Raise the cry of victory." A separate place setting for him had been arranged in one corner on a little table without a tablecloth. The poor old man couldn't boast of very nice manners, so they always kept him at a certain distance from company. He crossed himself, sighed, and began to eat like a shark. The dinner actually wasn't bad and, in honor of its being Sunday, was accompanied, naturally, by jelly and Spanish pastry.

At the table Radilov, who'd served in an infantry regiment for ten years and had been in Turkey, began to relate anecdotes. I listened to him attentively, and secretly observed Olga at the same time. She wasn't very pretty, but the tranquil, resolute expression on her face, her broad, white forehead, her thick hair, and especially her brown eyes—which weren't large, but were clear, intelligent, and animated—would have made an impression on anyone in my place. She seemed to be following every word Radilov uttered; not so much sympathy as impassioned concentration was manifest on her face. Given his age, Radilov might have been her father—he addressed her familiarly—but I immediately guessed that she wasn't his daughter. In the course of the conversation, he made reference to his deceased wife—"her sister," he added, gesturing toward Olga. She quickly blushed and looked down. Radilov paused a moment and then changed the subject.

The elderly woman didn't utter a word during the whole dinner. She hardly ate anything herself, and didn't press me to eat, either. Her features betrayed some sort of timorous, hopeless expectation, as well as the sadness of old age that it breaks one's heart to see. At the end of dinner, Fedor Mikheich was beginning to "honor" the hosts and guests, but Radilov looked at me and asked him to be quiet. The old man passed his hand across his lips, began to blink, bowed, and sat down again, but only on the very edge of his chair. After dinner, I returned to Radilov's study with him.

People who are constantly, intensely preoccupied with one idea or one passion have something in common, a kind of external similarily of manner, however different their attributes, their abilities, their position in society, and their upbringing may be. The more I watched Radilov, the more I felt that he belonged to this class of people. He spoke about husbandry, about crops, about war, about district gossip and the approaching elections. He spoke without constraint, and even with interest, but he'd suddenly sigh and collapse into a chair, running his hand across his face like a man worn out by a tedious task. His whole nature—a decent, warmhearted one—seemed saturated or steeped in one emotion. I was amazed by the fact that I couldn't discover in him a passion for food, or wine, or hunting, or Kursk nightingales, or sickly pigeons, or Russian literature, or trotting horses, or Hungarian coats, or cards and billiards, or dances, or trips to the provincial towns and the capital, or paper factories and beet-sugar refineries, or painted pavilions, or tea, or trace-horses trained to hold their heads high, or even for fat coachmen belted up to their very armpits—those magnificent coachmen whose eyes, God knows why, seem to be rolling and starting out of their heads at every movement. . . .

"What sort of landowner is this, then?" I wondered. Nonetheless, he didn't in the least pose as a gloomy individual dissatisfied with his fate. On the contrary, he seemed to be full of indiscriminate kindness, of cordial and even almost offensive readiness to become intimate with everyone he came across. Yet, in reality, at the same time, you felt that he couldn't make friends or become really intimate with anyone, not because he basically didn't need other people, but because his whole life had been turned inward upon itself for such a long time. Looking at Radilov, there was no way I could imagine him being happy, either now or at any other time. He wasn't handsome, either, but there was something mysteriously attractive in his eyes, in his smile, in his entire being—something hidden, to be precise. As a result, it seemed, one wanted to get to know him better, to learn to love him. Of course, at times the landowner and inhabitant of the steppes appeared in him, but all the same, he was a wonderful person.

We were beginning to talk about the new marshal of the district when we suddenly heard Olga's voice at the door: "Tea is ready."

We went into the drawing room. As before, Fedor Mikheich was sitting in his corner between the little window and the door, his legs curled up underneath him. Radilov's mother was knitting a stocking. A breath of autumn freshness and the scent of apples wafted through the open windows. Olga was busy pouring tea. I regarded her now with more care than I had at dinner. Like most provincial young women, she said very little, but at least I didn't observe in her any of their desire to say something impressive, accompanied by their painful consciousness of their own vacuity and helplessness; she didn't sigh as though burdened by inexplicable sensations, or roll her eyes, or smile vaguely and dreamily. Her gaze betrayed the calm indifference of someone who is becoming composed after experiencing great happiness or great distress. Her walk, her every movement, was purposeful and unconstrained. I liked her very much.

I began to converse with Radilov again. I don't recall what led us to discuss the well-known notion that the most insignificant things often produce more of an effect on people than the most significant.

"Yes," Radilov agreed, "I've experienced that myself. As you know, I was married. It wasn't for long—three years. My wife died in childbirth. I thought I wouldn't survive her. I was terribly saddened; I felt desolate, but I couldn't weep—I just wandered around like someone possessed. They dressed her carefully, as they always do, and laid her on a table—in this very room. The priest arrived, the deacons arrived, they began to sing and pray and burn incense. I bowed down to the ground, hardly shedding a tear. My heart seemed to have turned to stone—and my head, too. I felt weighted down all over. Thus the first day passed. Would you believe it?—I even slept that night. I went in to look at my wife the next morning. It was summertime, the sunshine was bathing her from head to toe, and it was very bright. Suddenly I saw . . ." (here Radilov shuddered involuntarily) "what do you think? One of her eyes wasn't quite shut, and a fly was walking across this eye. . . . I collapsed in a heap, and when I came to, I began to weep and weep . . . I couldn't stop myself. . . ."

Radilov fell silent. I looked at him, then at Olga. . . . I'll never forget the expression on her face as long as I live. The elderly woman laid the stocking down on her knees and took a handkerchief out of her workbag; she stealthily wiped away her tears. Fedor Mikheich suddenly got up, seized his violin, and began to sing a song in a savage, hoarse voice. He undoubtedly wanted to lift our spirits, but we all shuddered at his first note, and Radilov asked him to be quiet.

"Still, what's done is done," he continued. "We can't return to the past, and in the end . . . everything is for the best in this world, as I think Voltaire said," he added hurriedly.

"Yes," I replied, "of course. Besides, every misfortune can be endured, and there's no situation so terrible that it's impossible to escape from it."

"Do you think so?" said Radilov. "Well, perhaps you're right. I remember once when I was lying in a hospital in Turkey, half-dead from typhus. Our quarters were nothing to brag about—of course, it was war—and we had to thank God for what we had! Suddenly they bring in more sick men—where should they put them? The doctor checks here and there—there's no room left. So he comes up to me and asks the attendant, 'Is he alive?' He answers, 'He was alive this morning.' The doctor bends down and listens— I'm breathing. The good man couldn't help saying, 'Well, how absurd nature is. This man is dying, he's sure to die, but he keeps breathing, lingering on, taking up space for nothing, and keeping others out.' 'Well,' I thought to myself, 'it looks bad for you, Mikhail Mikhailich. . . .' But I got well after all, and am alive to this day, as you see for yourself. You're evidently right."

"I'm right in any case," I replied. "Even if you'd died, you still would have escaped your terrible situation."

"Of course, of course," he added, suddenly violently striking his fist on the table. "One merely has to make a decision. . . . What's the point of being in a terrible situation? . . . What's the use of delaying, of lingering on? . . ."

Olga quickly rose and went out into the garden.

"Well, Fedia, let's have a dance!" cried Radilov.

Fedia jumped up and started to walk around the room with that artificial, peculiar motion affected by someone who plays the well-known part of a "goat" for a tame bear, commencing the song "While at our gates. . . ."

The clatter of a racing carriage sounded at the entrance, and a few minutes later a tall, broad-shouldered, stout man, the peasant landowner Ovsianikov, entered the room.

But Ovsianikov is such a remarkable, original personage that, with the reader's permission, we'll describe him in another sketch. Now I'll only add that the next day I set off at daybreak to hunt with Ermolai and returned home after the day's shooting was over.... A week later I went back to Radilov's but didn't find either him or Olga at home, and two weeks later I learned that he'd suddenly disappeared, forsaking his mother, and had run off somewhere with his sister-in-law. The whole province got excited and discussed this event at length. Only then did I thoroughly comprehend the expression on Olga's face while Radilov was telling us his story. Her face hadn't merely exuded compassion; it had also been aflame with jealousy.

Before leaving the village, I visited Radilov's mother. I found her in the drawing room; she was playing cards with Fedor Mikheich. "Have you received any news about your son?" I eventually asked her.

The old lady began to cry. I never made any further inquiries about Radilov.

Lgov

"Let's go to Lgov," Ermolai, whom the reader already knows, suggested to me one day. "We can shoot ducks there to our heart's content."

Although wild ducks afford no special pleasure to a genuine hunter, still, due to the lack of other game at the time (it was the beginning of September, snipe hadn't begun to migrate yet, and I was tired of running across fields after partridges), I agreed to my huntsman's suggestion, and we set off for Lgov.

Lgov, a large steppe village that has a very old stone church with a single cupola and two mills, is situated on a marshy little river called the Rosota. Five versts from Lgov, this river becomes a wide, swampy pond overgrown with thick reeds at the edges and also in spots near the center. Here, in the streams, or rather pools, between the reeds, a countless multitude of all possible kinds of ducks—mallards, half-mallards, pintails, teals, divers, etc.—live and breed. Small flocks are always flying back and forth and swimming across the water; at the sound of a gunshot, they rise in such clouds that the hunter involuntarily clutches his hat with one hand and utters a prolonged "Whew!" I began to hunt alongside this pond with Ermolai, but, in the first place, the duck is a wary bird and ordinarily can't be found very close to the bank, and in the second, even when some straggling, inexperienced teal exposed itself to our shots and lost its life, our dogs weren't able to get it out of the thick reeds; in spite of their noblest efforts, they could neither swim nor walk on the bottom, and merely cut their precious noses on the sharp reeds in vain.

"No," Ermolai finally concluded, "this won't do. We have to get a boat.... Let's go back to Lgov."

We set off. We'd only gone a few paces when a rather wretched-looking setter ran out from behind a bushy willow tree to meet us, and behind him appeared a man of medium height in a blue, worn-out coat, a yellow vest, and pants of a nondescript gray color hastily tucked into high boots full of holes, with a red kerchief tied around his neck and a single-barreled gun resting on his shoulder. While our dogs engaged in the standard Chinese ceremonies typical of their species—sniffing at their new, obviously frightened acquaintance, who held its tail between its legs, let its ears droop, and kept rapidly turning around and around while displaying its teeth—the stranger approached us and bowed with extreme civility. He appeared to be about twenty-five; his long, dark hair, thoroughly saturated with kvass, stood up in stiff tufts; his small brown eyes twinkled genially; his face, bound up in a black kerchief as though he had a toothache, was all smiles.

"Allow me to introduce myself," he began in a soft, ingratiating voice. "I'm a huntsman from these parts—Vladimir.... Having heard of your presence and having learned that you proposed to visit the shores of our pond, I resolved, if it weren't displeasing to you, to offer you my services."

The huntsman Vladimir uttered those words exactly like a young provincial actor playing the lead role of the lover. I acceded to his proposition, and before we reached Lgov, I managed to learn his whole history. He was a freed house serf; he'd been taught music in his early youth, then had served as a valet. He could read and write; he'd read—as far as I could discover—a few minor books, and now existed, as many people in Russia exist, without a bit of cash, without any regular occupation, eating only manna from heaven, or something on that order. He expressed himself with extraordinary elegance, and obviously prided himself on his manners. He must have been devoted to the fair sex, too, and in all probability was popular with them—Russian young women love eloquence. Among other things, he led me to understand that he occasionally visited the neighboring landowners, that he regularly went to stay with friends in town, where he played the card game of preference, and that he was acquainted with people in the capital. His smile was always confident and yet exceedingly varied; one that especially suited him was a modest, restrained smile, which played across his lips as he listened to anyone else's conversation. He was attentive to you; he agreed with you completely; but he never lost sight of his own dignity, and seemingly sought to make you understand that he could, if the occasion arose, express convictions of his own. Ermolai, not being very refined and utterly devoid of "subtlety," began to address him familiarly. The exquisite irony with which Vladimir used "sir" in his replies was worth hearing.

"Why is your face bound up?" I inquired. "Do you have a toothache?"

"No," he answered, "it's a rather disastrous consequence of carelessness. I had a friend, a good fellow but not at all a hunter, as happens sometimes. Well, one day he says to me, 'My dear friend, take me out hunting. I'm curious to learn what this amusement consists of.' Naturally, I didn't like to refuse a comrade, so I got him a gun and took him out hunting. Well, we shot a bit in the usual fashion, and then we decided to rest. I sat down under a tree, and he began to play with his gun, occasionally pointing it at me. I asked him to stop, but in his inexperience, he didn't listen. The gun went off and I lost half my chin, plus the first finger on my right hand."

We reached Lgov. Vladimir and Ermolai had both concluded that we couldn't hunt without a boat.

"Suchok has a flatboat," remarked Vladimir, "but I don't know where he's hidden it. We'll have to go to his place."

"Whose place?" I asked.

"The man who lives here—Suchok is his nickname."

Vladimir set off for Suchok's with Ermolai. I told them I'd wait for them at the church. While I was looking at the tombstones in the churchyard, I stumbled upon a blackened, four-sided urn with the following inscription on the first side, in French: *"Ci gît Théophile-Henri, Vicomte de Blangy"*; on the second, "Under this stone is laid the body of a French subject, Count Blangy, born 1737, died 1799, in the 62d year of his life"; on the third, "Peace to his ashes"; and on the fourth:

Under this stone there lies a French emigrant.
Of high descent was he, and also of talent.
A wife and murdered family he bewailed,
And left his homeland, by tyrants cruel assailed;

The friendly shores of Russia he attained,
And hospitable shelter here obtained;
Children he taught; their parents' cares allayed;
Here, by God's will, in peace he has been laid.

The approach of Ermolai, accompanied by Vladimir and the man with the strange nickname, Suchok, interrupted my meditations.

Bare-legged, ragged, and disheveled, Suchok looked like a dismissed house serf who was about sixty years old.

"Do you have a boat?" I asked him.

"I have a boat," he replied in a hoarse, cracked voice, "but it's a very poor one."

"How so?"

"Its boards have split apart, and the fasteners have fallen off the cracks."

"That's no great disaster!" asserted Ermolai. "We can stuff them with tow."

"Of course you can," Suchok assented.

"And who are you?"

"I'm the estate's fisherman."

"How can it be, if you're a fisherman, that your boat's in such bad condition?"

"There aren't any fish in our river."

"Fish don't like slimy marshes," my huntsman observed with a dignified air.

"All right," I said to Ermolai, "go get some tow and fix the boat for us as soon as you can."

Ermolai went off.

"Well, we'll most likely sink to the bottom this way," I said to Vladimir.

"God is merciful," he responded. "Anyway, we can assume that the pond isn't deep."

"No, it isn't deep," affirmed Suchok, who spoke in a strange, faraway voice, as though he were dreaming, "and there's grass as well as mud at the bottom. It's all overgrown with grass. But there are deep holes, too."

"But if the grass is that thick," said Vladimir, "it'll be impossible to row."

"Who'd row a flatboat? You have to pole it. I'll go with you. My pole's there—or else I can use a wooden spade."

"It won't be easy with a spade. You might not touch the bottom in some places," said Vladimir.

"That's true—it won't be easy."

I sat down on a tombstone to wait for Ermolai. Vladimir moved a bit to one side, out of respect to me, and also sat down. Suchok remained standing in the same place, his head bent and his hands clasped behind his back, as was the old custom of house serfs.

"Tell me, please," I began, "have you been the fisherman here for a long time?"

"This is the seventh year," he replied, rousing himself with a start.

"And what was your previous occupation?"

"I was a coachman before this."

"Who dismissed you from the position of coachman?"

"The new mistress."

"Which mistress?"

"Oh, the one that bought us. Your honor doesn't know her. Her name's Alena Timofeevna. She's a fat lady . . . she's on the old side."

"Why did she decide to make you a fisherman?"

"God knows. She came to see us from her estate in Tambov, gave orders for the entire household to assemble, and came out to meet us. First we kissed her hand and she didn't say anything— she wasn't angry. . . . Then she began to question us one by one: 'What is your position? What duties do you have?' She came to me in turn, so she asked: 'What do you do?' I say, 'Coachman.' 'Coachman? Well, a fine coachman you are. Just look at you! You're not fit to be a coachman, so be my fisherman and shave off your beard. On the occasions of my visits, provide fish for the table, do you hear?' So since then I've been listed as a fisherman. 'And mind you, keep my pond in order.' But how can anyone keep it in order?"

"To whom did you previously belong?"

"To Sergei Sergeich Pekhterev. We came to him through his inheritance. But he didn't own us for long, only six years in all. I was his coachman, but not in town—he had others there—just in the countryside."

"And were you a coachman from your youth onward?"

"A coachman from youth? Oh, no! I became a coachman in Sergei Sergeich's time, but before that I was a cook—but not a cook in town, just in the countryside."

"Whose cook were you then?"

"Oh, my former master's, Afanasii Nefedych, Sergei Sergeich's uncle. Lgov was bought by him, by Afanasii Nefedych, but Sergei Sergeich inherited it from him."

"Whom did he buy it from?"

"From Tatiana Vasilevna."

"Which Tatiana Vasilevna was that?"

"Why, the one that died last year in Bolkhov ... that is, near Karachev, an old maid.... She'd never gotten married. Don't you know her? We came to her from her father, Vasilii Semenych. She owned us for quite a while ... about twenty years."

"Then you were a cook for her?"

"Yes, at first I was a cook, and then I was a coffee-bearer."

"A what?"

"A coffee-bearer."

"What sort of duty is that?"

"I don't know, your honor. I stood at the sideboard and was called Anton instead of Kuzma. The mistress ordered everyone to call me that."

"Your real name is Kuzma, then?"

"Yes."

"And were you a coffee-bearer all the time?"

"No, not all the time. I was an actor, too."

"Really?"

"Yes, I was.... I acted in the theater. Our mistress set up a theater of her own."

"What kind of parts did you play?"

"What did you just say?"

"What did you do in the theater?"

"Don't you know? Why, they'd take me and dress me up, and I'd walk around dressed up, or stand, or sit down, as I was told, and they'd say, 'See, this is what you have to say,' and I'd say it. Once I played a blind man.... They put little peas under each eyelid.... Yes, indeed."

"And what did you do next?"

"Next I became a cook again."

"Why did they demote you to a cook again?"

"My brother ran away."

"Well, and what did you do for the father of your first mistress?"

"I had different duties. At first I was a page. I've also been a coachman, a gardener, and a huntsman's assistant."

"A huntsman's assistant? ... Did you ride to hounds?"

"Yes, I rode to hounds, and was nearly killed. I fell off my horse, and the horse was injured. Our old master got very angry. He ordered me to be flogged and then sent to learn a trade in Moscow with a shoemaker."

"To learn a trade? But you weren't a child, I presume, when you were a huntsman's assistant?"

"I was over twenty at that time."

"But could you learn a trade at twenty?"

"I suppose I could, somehow, since the master ordered me to. But luckily he died soon after that, and they sent me back to the countryside."

"And when were you taught to cook?"

Suchok lifted his thin, yellowish little face and grinned.

"Is that something you're taught? ... Old women can cook."

"Well," I remarked, "you've seen many things in your time, Kuzma! What do you do now as a fisherman, since there aren't any fish?"

"Oh, your honor, I don't complain. And I thank God they made me a fisherman. Why, the mistress sent another old man like me— Andrei Pupyr—to the paper factory as a ladler. 'It's a sin,' she said, 'to eat bread in idleness.' And Pupyr had even counted on her favor, since his cousin's son was a clerk in the mistress's office and he'd promised to send his name to the mistress, to ask her to remember Pupyr. A fine way he asked her to remember him! ... And Pupyr had fallen at his cousin's knees before my very eyes."

"Do you have a family? Have you ever been married?"

"No, your honor, I've never been married. Tatiana Vasilevna— God rest her soul!—didn't allow anyone to get married. 'God forbid!' she said sometimes. 'Here I am, living alone! What indulgence! What do they need it for?'"

"What do you live on now? Do you get wages?"

"Wages, your honor! ... I'm given my food, thanks be to Thee, oh Lord! I'm well-contented. May God grant our mistress a long life!"

Ermolai returned.

"The boat's repaired," he announced sternly. "Go get your pole— you there!"

Suchok ran to get his pole. During my entire conversation with the poor old man, the huntsman Vladimir had been staring at him with a contemptuous smile.

"A stupid fellow," he commented when the latter had gone off. "An utterly uneducated individual—a peasant and nothing more. You can't even call him a house serf . . . and he was bragging the whole time. How could he have been an actor? Judge for yourself! You exerted yourself for nothing in talking to him."

A quarter of an hour later, we were sitting in Suchok's flatboat; we'd left the dogs at a hut in the care of my coachman. We weren't very comfortable, but hunters aren't fastidious people. Suchok stood poling at the rear, which was straight, Vladimir and I sat on planks laid across the boat, and Ermolai positioned himself in front, at the very tip. In spite of the tow in the cracks, water soon started to appear under our feet. Fortunately, the weather was calm and the pond seemed to be slumbering.

We floated along rather slowly. The old man had difficulty drawing his long pole out of the sticky mud; it came up all tangled with green stalks of water-grass; the flat, round leaves of waterlilies also hindered the progress of our boat. We finally made it to the reeds, and then the fun began. Ducks noisily flew up from the pond, scared by our unexpected appearance in their domain; shots immediately rang out after them. It was a pleasure to see these short-tailed birds turn somersaults in the air and splash heavily into the water. We couldn't get to all the ducks that we shot, of course: those that were slightly wounded swam away; some that had been killed fell into such thick reeds that even Ermolai's catlike little eyes couldn't find them; yet our boat still became filled to the brim with game to have for dinner.

To Ermolai's great satisfaction, Vladimir didn't shoot well at all. He appeared surprised after each unsuccessful shot, looked at his gun, blew into its barrels, seemed puzzled, and then explained to us why he'd missed. Ermolai, as always, shot triumphantly, whereas I, as usual, shot rather badly. Suchok watched us with the eyes of a man who's been the servant of others since youth. Now and then he cried out: "There, there, there's another little duck," and he continually scratched his back, not with his hands but with a peculiar movement of his shoulder blades. The weather was magnificent: curly, white clouds peacefully drifted high above our heads and were vividly reflected on the water; the reeds around us whispered to one another; here and there the pond sparkled like steel in the sunshine. We were preparing to return to the village when a rather unpleasant adventure suddenly befell us.

We'd been aware for a long time that water had gradually been filling our boat. Vladimir had been entrusted with the task of bailing it out by means of a ladle, which my huntsman had had the foresight to steal in case of an emergency from a peasant woman who was looking in the other direction. Everything went well as long as Vladimir didn't neglect his duty. But at the end of the hunt, the ducks, as if to say goodbye to us, rose in such flocks that we barely had time to load our guns. In the heat of the moment, we weren't paying any attention to the condition of our boat—when suddenly Ermolai, in an effort to grab a dead duck, leaned all his weight on the boat's edge. At his overeager movement, our old tub listed to one side, began to fill with water, and majestically sank to the bottom—fortunately, not in a deep place. We cried out, but it was too late; we were instantly standing in water up to our necks, surrounded by the floating carcasses of the slaughtered ducks. I can't help laughing now when I recall the scared, white faces of my companions (although my own face probably wasn't particularly rosy at that moment), but I must confess that it didn't occur to me to laugh at the time. Each of us held his gun above his head, and Suchok, no doubt from the habit of imitating his masters, lifted his pole above his. Ermolai was the first to break the silence.

"Phooey! Damn it!" he muttered, spitting into the water. "What a mess! It's all your fault, you old devil!" he added, wrathfully turning toward Suchok. "What kind of boat is this?"

"It's my fault," stammered the old man.

"Yes—and you're a fine one," continued my huntsman, turning his head in Vladimir's direction. "What were you thinking about? Why weren't you bailing? You, you. . . . ."

But Vladimir wasn't able to reply: he was shaking like a leaf, his teeth were chattering, and he was smiling away inanely. What had become of his elegant language, his feeling for refined manners, and his own dignity now!

The accursed boat rocked feebly under our feet. . . . The water seemed terribly cold to us at the moment of our immersion, but we quickly got accustomed to it. When the first shock had passed, I looked around me. The reeds rose up in a circle ten steps away from us; in the distance, the bank was visible above their tops. "It looks bad," I thought.

"What should we do?" I asked Ermolai.

"Well, we'll take a look around. We can't spend the night here," he answered. "Here, you, take my gun," he said to Vladimir. Vladimir obeyed submissively.

"I'll go and find the ford," Ermolai continued, as though there inevitably had to be a ford in every pond. He took the pole from Suchok and waded off in the direction of the bank, warily feeling for the bottom as he walked.

"Can you swim?" I asked him.

"No, I can't," his voice came back from behind the reeds.

"Then he'll drown," Suchok remarked matter-of-factly. He'd been terrified at first—not of the danger, but of our anger—and now, completely reassured, he drew a long breath from time to time and seemed to feel no need to budge from his present location.

"And he'll perish without doing any good," Vladimir added piteously.

Ermolai didn't return for over an hour. That hour seemed like an eternity to us. At first, we kept calling to him quite energetically; then his answering shouts grew less frequent; eventually he became completely silent. The bells in the village began to ring for the evening church service. We didn't converse at all; indeed, we tried not to look at one another. The ducks hovered over our heads; some seemed disposed to settle near us, but suddenly rose up into the air and flew away, quacking. We began to grow numb. Suchok shut his eyes as though he were getting ready to go to sleep.

At last, to our indescribable delight, Ermolai returned.

"Well?"

"I've been to the bank, and I've found the ford. . . . Let's go."

We wanted to set off at once, but first he took some twine out of his pocket under the water, tied the slaughtered ducks together by their legs, put both ends between his teeth, and then slowly moved forward. Vladimir followed him, I got behind Vladimir, and Suchok brought up the rear. It was about two hundred feet to the bank. Ermolai walked assuredly, without stopping (so well had he observed the path), only occasionally crying out, "More to the left—there's a hole here to the right!" or "Keep to the right— you'll sink in there to the left. . . ." Sometimes the water came up to our necks, and twice poor Suchok, who was shorter than the rest of us, got a mouthful and started to splutter. "Come on, come on!" Ermolai shouted at him roughly—and Suchok, scrambling, hopping, and skipping, managed to reach a shallower place, but even in his worst distress, he never dared to clutch at the edge of my coat. Worn out, muddy, and wet, we finally reached the bank.

Two hours later, we were all sitting in a large hay barn, as dry as circumstances would permit, preparing for supper. The coachman Iegudil, an exceedingly lethargic, heavy-footed, cautious, slow-witted individual, stood at the entrance, diligently plying Suchok with snuff (I've noticed that coachmen in Russia make friends very quickly). Suchok was taking snuff with frenzied energy, in quantities sufficient to make him ill; he was spitting, coughing, and apparently enjoying himself hugely. Vladimir had assumed a languid air; he leaned his head to one side and didn't say much. Ermolai was cleaning our guns. The dogs were wagging their tails at a great rate in hopes of getting fed some oatmeal. The horses were stamping and neighing in the shed.... The sun had set; its last rays were broken up into broad stripes of purple; golden clouds extended across the sky in ever finer threads, like washed and combed fleece.... The sound of singing floated up from the village.

Kasian from Beautiful Meadow

I was returning home from hunting in a bumpy little cart. Overcome by the stifling heat of a cloudy summer day (it's well known that the heat is often more unbearable on days like that than on bright days, especially when there's no wind), I dozed and swayed, resigning myself with sullen fortitude to attacks of the fine white dust incessantly being raised from the beaten road by the warped, creaking wheels. Suddenly my attention was aroused by the unusual agitation and anxious movements of my coachman, who until that instant had been dozing more soundly than I. He tugged at the reins, shifted uneasily on the box, and started to shout at the horses, staring in one direction the whole time. I looked around. We were riding across a wide, plowed plain; low hills, which had also been plowed, were spread across it in gently sloping, swelling waves; the eye could take in some five versts of deserted countryside; in the distance, the rounded treetops of some small birch grove were the only objects to interrupt the nearly straight line of the horizon. Narrow paths extended over the fields and disappeared into the hollows, winding around the little hills. On one of these paths, which happened to intersect our road five hundred feet ahead of us, I discerned some sort of procession. It was this procession that my coachman was staring at.

It was a funeral. In front, in a cart harnessed to one steadily plodding horse, rode the priest; beside him sat the deacon, driving; behind the cart, four bareheaded peasants carried a coffin covered with a white cloth; two women followed the coffin. The shrill, wailing voice of one of the women suddenly reached my ears. I listened: she was intoning a dirge. This chanted, monotonous, hopelessly sorrowful lament resounded dismally across the empty fields. My coachman whipped the horses; he wanted to get ahead of this procession—meeting a corpse on the road is a bad omen. And he did succeed in galloping ahead past the path before the funeral had had time to turn out of it onto the main road, but we'd barely gone a hundred feet beyond this point when our cart suddenly jolted violently, lurched to one side, and all but overturned. The coachman brought the galloping horses to a halt, leaned down from his seat, took a look, waved his hand, and spat.

"What is it?" I asked.

My coachman got down without speaking or hurrying.

"But what is it?"

"The axle is broken.... It caught fire," he replied gloomily, and suddenly rearranged the harness collar on the offside horse with such indignation that he almost pushed it over; but it stood its ground, snorted, shook itself, and tranquilly began to scratch its foreleg below the knee with its teeth.

I got out and stood on the road for a while, prey to a vague, unpleasant feeling of helplessness. The right wheel was almost completely bent under the cart and seemed to be turning its hub upward in mute despair.

"What should we do now?" I eventually inquired.

"That's what's to blame!" said my coachman, pointing his whip at the funeral procession, which had just turned onto the road and was approaching us. "I've always noticed," he went on, "that it's a true saying—'Meet a corpse . . .'—yes, indeed."

And he began to pester the offside horse again, which, perceiving his displeasure and irritation, resolved to remain perfectly quiet, contenting itself with discreetly switching its tail now and again. I walked up and down a bit, and then stopped beside the wheel again.

Meanwhile, the funeral had caught up with us. Carefully turning off the road onto the grass, the mournful procession slowly moved past us. My coachman and I took off our caps, bowed to the priest, and exchanged glances with the bearers. They walked with difficulty under their burden, their broad chests expanding from the strain. Of the two women who followed the coffin, one was very old and pale; her set face, terribly distorted by grief as it was, still maintained an expression of severe, ceremonial dignity. She walked in silence, lifting one wasted hand to her thin, drawn lips from time to time. The other, a young woman of about twenty-five, had red, moist eyes, and her whole face was swollen from crying; as she passed us, she ceased singing her dirge and hid her face in her sleeve. . . . But when the funeral had gone around us and turned back onto the road, her piteous, heart-piercing lament began again. In silence, my coachman followed the measured swaying of the coffin with his eyes. Then he turned toward me.

"It's Martin the carpenter they're burying," he said. "Martin of Riabaia."

"How do you know?"

"I recognized the women. The old one's his mother, and the young one's his wife."

"Had he been sick, then?"

"Yes . . . fever. The overseer sent for the doctor the day before yesterday, but they couldn't find him. Martin was a good carpenter. He drank a bit, but he was a good carpenter. See how upset his wife is. . . . But then, women's tears don't cost much, we know. Women's tears are only water . . . yes, indeed."

Then he bent down, crept under the offside horse's harness, and seized the wooden yoke that goes over the horses' heads with both hands.

"In any event," I remarked, "what are we going to do?"

My coachman first supported himself by putting his knees on the shaft-horse's shoulder, shook the back-strap twice, and straightened the pad; then he crept under the offside horse's harness again, giving it a blow on the nose as he passed, and went up to the wheel. Never taking his eyes off it, he slowly took a box out from beneath his coat, slowly pulled open the lid by a strap, slowly inserted two fat fingers (which barely fit) into it, rolled up some snuff, and, wrinkling his nose in anticipation, inhaled several times, each time resulting in prolonged fits of sneezing. Then, faintly blinking his runny eyes, he lapsed into profound meditation.

"Well?" I finally said.

My coachman carefully thrust the box back into his pocket, brought his hat forward onto his forehead without the aid of his hand by a single motion of his head, and pensively climbed up onto the seat.

"What are you doing?" I asked him, not without bewilderment.

"Please be seated," he replied calmly, picking up the reins.

"But how can we go on?"

"We can go on now."

"But the axle. . . ."

"Please be seated."

"But the axle's broken."

"True, it's broken, but we'll get to the settlement . . . at a walking pace, of course. Over here, beyond the grove on the right, there's a settlement. They call it Iudiny."

"And you think we can make it there?"

My coachman didn't favor me with a reply.

"I'd better walk," I said.

"As you like. . . ." And he flourished his whip. The horses started.

We did succeed in getting to the settlement, although the right front wheel was barely attached and turned in a very strange manner. It almost flew off on one hill, but my coachman shouted in a nasty voice, and we descended in safety.

The Iudiny settlement consisted of six little low-pitched huts, the walls of which had already begun to warp, although they certainly hadn't been standing for long; the yards of some of the huts weren't even fenced in by a hedge. As we drove into this settlement, we didn't meet a single living soul; there weren't any hens to be seen in the street, or even any dogs, except for one black, crop-tailed cur that, at our approach, hurriedly leaped out of a perfectly dry, empty trough, to which it must have been driven by thirst, and immediately, without barking, rushed headlong under a gate. I went up to the first hut, opened the door to the outer room, and called for the master of the house. No one answered me. I called out once more, and the hungry mewing of a cat came from behind another door. I pushed it open with my foot; a thin cat ran past me, her green eyes glittering in the dimness. I poked my head into the room and looked around; it was empty, dark, and smoky. I returned to the yard, and found no one there. . . . A calf mooed behind a fence; a lame gray goose waddled past a little way off. I crossed over to the second hut. There wasn't a soul in the second hut, either. I went into the yard. . . .

A boy was lying in the middle of the yard amid the glaring sunlight, his face resting on the ground and a cloak thrown over his head. In a thatched shed a few steps beyond him, a thin little nag wearing a broken harness was standing near a wretched little cart. The sunshine, falling in shafts through the narrow cracks in the dilapidated roof, streaked its shaggy, reddish-brown coat with short bands of light. Up above, in a high birdhouse, starlings were chattering and looking down inquisitively from their airy home. I went up to the sleeping figure and began to wake him up.

He lifted his head, saw me, and immediately jumped to his feet.... "What? What do you want? What is it?" he muttered, half asleep.

I didn't answer him at first, so struck was I by his appearance. Picture to yourself a diminutive creature approximately fifty years of age with a little, round, wrinkled face, a sharp nose, small, barely visible brown eyes, and thick, curly black hair that stood up on his tiny head like the cap on top of a mushroom. His entire body was extremely thin and frail—and it's absolutely impossible to convey in words the extraordinary strangeness of his gaze.

"What do you want?" he asked me again. I explained the problem to him. He listened, blinking slowly, without taking his eyes off me.

"So can we get a new axle?" I finally said. "I'll be glad to pay for it."

"But who are you? Hunters, eh?" he asked, surveying me from head to toe.

"Yes, hunters."

"Do you shoot the little birds of heaven, then?... The wild beasts of the forest?... And isn't it a sin to kill God's birds, to shed innocent blood?"

The strange old man spoke in a drawl. The sound of his voice also astonished me. No feebleness of advanced age could be heard in it—it was marvelously sweet, youthful, and almost feminine in its softness.

"I don't have an axle," he added after a brief silence. "That thing won't suit you." He pointed to his cart. "You have a large cart, I suppose."

"But can I get one in the village?"

"Not much of a village here!... No one has an axle.... And there's no one at home, either. They're all at work. You'll have to go on farther," he announced abruptly, and lay down on the ground again.

I hadn't expected this conclusion at all.

"Listen, old man," I said, touching him on the shoulder. "Do me a favor—help me."

"Go away, in God's name! I'm tired. I've already driven to town," he said, and drew his cloak back over his head.

"Please do me a favor," I said. "I ... I'll pay for it."

"I don't want your money."

"But please, old man. . . . "

He raised himself halfway and then sat up, crossing his little legs.

"Maybe I could take you to the clearing. Some merchants have bought the forest there—God be their judge! They're cutting down the forest, and they've built an office there—God be their judge! You might order an axle from them, or buy one ready-made."

"That's wonderful!" I cried in delight. "Wonderful! Let's go."

"An oak axle, a good one," he continued, without getting up from his place.

"Is it far to this clearing?"

"Three versts."

"That's nothing! We can ride there in your cart."

"Oh, no. . . . "

"Come on, let's go," I said. "Let's go, old man! My coachman's waiting for us in the road."

The old man reluctantly rose and followed me into the street. We found my coachman in an irritable frame of mind: he'd tried to water his horses, but the water in the well, apparently, was very limited in quantity as well as bad-tasting, and water is the first concern of coachmen. . . . However, he grinned at the sight of the old man, nodded his head, and cried, "Hello, Kasianushka! Good health to you!"

"Good health to you, Erofei, righteous man!" Kasian replied in a mournful voice.

I instantly communicated his suggestion to my coachman; Erofei expressed his approval and moved the cart into the yard. While he was busy carefully unharnessing the horses, the old man stood leaning his shoulders against the gate and looking disconsolately first at him, then at me. He seemed puzzled; he wasn't very pleased at our sudden visit, so far as I could tell.

"So they've resettled you, too?" Erofei asked him suddenly, lifting the wooden arch of the harness.

"Yes."

"Ugh!" my coachman grunted between his teeth. "You know Martin the carpenter? . . . Of course you know Martin of Riabaia."

"Yes."

"Well, he's dead. We've just encountered his funeral."

Kasian shuddered.

"Dead?" he asked, and his head sank dejectedly.

"Yes, he's dead. Why didn't you cure him, eh? You know they say you can cure diseases, that you're a doctor."

My coachman was apparently laughing and jeering at the old man. "And is this your cart, then?" he added with a shrug of his shoulders in its direction.

"Yes."

"Well, a cart's ... a cart!" he repeated, and, taking it by the shafts, almost turned it upside down. "What a cart! ... But what will you use to get it to the clearing? ... You can't harness our horses in these shafts—our horses are all too big."

"I don't know what we can use," replied Kasian. "That beast, perhaps," he added with a sigh.

"That?" Erofei echoed, and, going up to Kasian's nag, he tapped it disparagingly on the back with the third finger of his right hand. "Look," he added contemptuously, "it's asleep, the scarecrow!"

I asked Erofei to harness it as quickly as he could. I wanted to go to the clearing with Kasian myself; grouse are fond of such places. When the little cart was all ready, after my dog and I had somehow been installed in its warped shell, and Kasian, huddled into a little ball with his continually dejected expression on his face, had taken his seat in front, Erofei came up to me and whispered with a mysterious air: "You're right to go with him, your honor. He's such an odd fellow. He's a holy man, you know, and his nickname is the Flea. I don't know how you managed to understand him. ..."

I wanted to tell Erofei that, thus far, Kasian had seemed to me to be a perfectly reasonable individual, but my coachman promptly continued in the same tone: "But watch out where he takes you. And, your honor, please choose the axle yourself. Please choose a sound one. ... Well, Flea," he added aloud, "could I get a bit of bread in your house?"

"Look around—you may find some," Kasian answered. He shook the reins and we rolled away.

To my genuine astonishment, his little horse proceeded fairly rapidly. Kasian preserved an obstinate silence the whole way, or gave abrupt, reluctant answers to my questions. We quickly reached the clearing and then made our way to the office, a tall hut standing by itself near a small stream that had hastily been dammed up and converted into a pool. Inside the office, I found two young merchant's clerks with snow-white teeth, pleasant eyes, pleasant glib speeches, and pleasant wily smiles. I bought an axle from them and returned to the clearing. I'd assumed that Kasian would stay with the horse and wait for me to come back, but he suddenly approached me.

"Are you going to shoot little birds now?" he asked.

"Yes, if I come across any."

"I want to come with you. . . . May I?"

"Certainly, certainly."

So we set off. The cleared land stretched across a verst or so. I must confess that I paid more attention to Kasian than to my dog. He'd been aptly nicknamed the Flea. His small, black, uncovered head (his hair was actually as good a covering as any cap) seemed to flash here and there among the bushes. He walked extraordinarily swiftly, and always seemed to be hopping up and down as he moved. He kept stooping over to pick one kind of herb or another, thrusting what he collected into his bosom while muttering to himself, and he kept looking at me and my dog with a strange, searching gaze. Among low bushes and in clearings, one often finds little gray birds that ceaselessly flit from tree to tree and whistle as they dart away; Kasian mimicked them, answering their calls. A young quail flew up from between his feet, chirping, and he chirped in imitation; a lark began to swoop down toward him, flapping its wings while singing melodiously, and Kasian joined in its song. He didn't speak to me at all. . . .

The weather was glorious, even more so than before, but the heat hadn't diminished. The high, thin clouds barely stirred in the clear sky. They were yellowish-white, like late spring snow, flat and drawn out like unfurled sails. Their fringed edges, as soft and fluffy as cotton, slowly but perceptibly changed every moment; they were melting, these clouds, and they didn't provide any shade. I strolled around the clearing with Kasian for a long while. Young plant shoots that still hadn't had time to grow more than a few feet high surrounded low, blackened stumps with their smooth, slender stems; spongy funguses with gray edges—the same ones that are used to make tinder—clung to these stumps; strawberry plants flung their rosy tendrils over them; mushrooms thronged around them in groups. One's feet kept getting caught and entangled in the long grass that had been parched by the scorching sun; one's eyes were dazzled on all sides by the bright metallic glitter of the reddish young leaves on the trees; variegated blue clusters of peas, golden buds of buttercups, and the half-purple, half-yellow blossoms of pansies were everywhere. In some places, near little-used paths on which wheel tracks were marked by streaks on the thin, bright grass, piles of wood were stacked, blackened by wind and rain, laid in yard lengths; they cast faint shadows in slanting oblongs. There was no other shade anywhere. A light breeze would come up, then subside again; suddenly it would blow straight into one's face and seem to become playful: everything would begin to rustle merrily, nodding and stirring, the supple tops of the ferns would bow down gracefully, and one would rejoice in it all. But then the breeze would die away again, and everything would become still once more. Only the grasshoppers would continue to chirp in chorus, and this incessant, sharp, dry sound was oppressive. It's a sound appropriate to the persistent heat of midday: it seems akin to the heat, as though summoned by it out of the scorched earth.

Without having roused a single covey of game, we eventually reached another clearing. The aspen trees there had been felled quite recently, and lay stretched out mournfully on the ground, crushing the grass and undergrowth beneath them; on some, the leaves were still green, although already dead, and hung limply from the immobile branches; on others, they were crumpled and dessicated. Fresh, golden-white wood chips lay in heaps around the stumps, which were covered with bright droplets; a special, very pleasant, pungent odor arose from them. Farther away, closer to the grove, the dull blows of an axe rang out, and from time to time, as if bowing and spreading its arms wide, a leafy tree would fall to the ground slowly and majestically. . . .

I didn't find a single bird for a long time. Finally, a corncrake flew out of a thick clump of young oak trees through the wormwood growing around it. I fired; it turned over in the air and fell. At the sound of the shot, Kasian quickly covered his eyes with his hand, and he didn't stir until I'd reloaded the gun and picked up the bird. When I'd moved farther on, he went up to the place where the wounded bird had fallen, bent down to the grass, on which some drops of blood were sprinkled, shook his head, and looked at me in dismay. . . . Afterward I heard him whisper, "A sin! . . . Ah, yes, it's a sin!"

The heat ultimately forced us to enter the grove. I flung myself down under a tall bush, over which a shapely young maple gracefully stretched its delicate branches. Kasian sat down on the thick trunk of a fallen birch tree. I looked at him. The leaves faintly stirred overhead, and their slender, greenish shadows swept softly to and fro across his frail body, muffled in a dark coat, and across

his little face. He didn't raise his head. Bored by his silence, I lay
on my back and began to admire the tranquil play of the tangled
foliage against the background of the bright, distant sky.

What a marvelously enjoyable occupation it is to lie on your back
in the woods and gaze upward! You imagine that you're looking
into a bottomless sea that stretches far and wide *beneath* you, that
the trees aren't rising out of the earth but, like the roots of gigantic
weeds, are descending, falling straight down into those glassy,
limpid depths; one moment the leaves on the trees are as translucent as emeralds, the next they've condensed into golden, almost
dark verdure. Somewhere far off, at the end of a slender twig, a
single leaf hangs motionless against a blue patch of transparent
sky, and beside it another one trembles like a fish on a line, as
though it's moving of its own volition and isn't being disturbed
by the wind. Round, white clouds calmly float into sight and
calmly pass by like magical submerged islands; then suddenly, this
whole ocean—this shining air, these branches and leaves steeped
in sunlight, everything—begins to vibrate, quivering with fleeting
brilliance, and a fresh, tremulous whisper arises like the tiny, ceaseless ripples of unexpectedly bestirred eddies. You don't move; you
watch—and no words can describe what peace, what joy, what
sweetness reigns in your heart. You watch—the deep, clear blue
sky brings a smile as innocent as it is to your lips; like the clouds
moving across the sky—along with them, as it were—happy memories pass through your mind in a slow procession; it seems to you
that your gaze goes deeper and deeper, and draws you yourself
with it up into that peaceful, shining vastness, and you can't bear
to tear yourself away from that height, that depth. . . .

"Master, master!" Kasian suddenly cried in his musical voice.

I straightened up in surprise; he'd barely replied to my questions
until that moment, and now he was unexpectedly addressing me.

"What is it?" I asked.

"What did you kill the bird for?" he began, looking me straight
in the eye.

"What for? Corncrake is game. One can eat it."

"That wasn't what you killed it for, master. As though you were
going to eat it! You killed it for amusement."

"Well, but don't you yourself eat geese or chickens?"

"Those birds are provided by God for man, but the corncrake
is a wild bird of the woods. And not only that one: there are many

of them, the wild things of the woods and the fields, and the wild things of the rivers and the marshes and the meadows that fly up above or crawl down below. It's a sin to slay them. Let them live their allotted life upon the earth. Other food has been provided for man. His food is different, as is his drink—he has bread, the gift of God, and the water of heaven, and the tame beasts that have descended to us from our forefathers."

I looked at Kasian in amazement. His words flowed freely—he didn't have to search for them; he spoke with quiet inspiration and gentle dignity, occasionally closing his eyes.

"So it's sinful to kill fish, then, in your opinion?" I queried.

"Fish have cold blood," he replied with conviction. "The fish is a mute creature—it knows neither fear nor joy. The fish is a voiceless creature. The fish doesn't feel, the blood in it isn't living.... Blood," he continued after a pause, "blood is a holy thing! God's sun doesn't look upon blood, it's hidden away from the light.... It's a great sin to bring blood into the light of day, a great sin and a horror.... Ah, a great sin!"

He sighed, and his head drooped forward. I confess, I looked at the strange old man in absolute astonishment. His language didn't sound like the language of a peasant: the common people don't speak like that—nor do orators. His speech was meditative, solemn, and strange.... I'd never heard anything like it.

"Tell me please, Kasian," I began, without taking my eyes off his slightly flushed face, "what's your occupation?"

He didn't answer my question right away. His eyes strayed uneasily for an instant.

"I live as the Lord commands," he finally declared, "and as for my occupation—no, I have no occupation. I've never been very clever, from my youth onward. I work when I can. I'm not much of a workman—how could I be? I'm in poor health, and my hands are clumsy. I catch nightingales in the spring."

"You catch nightingales?... But didn't you just tell me that we shouldn't touch any of the wild things of the woods and the fields, and so on?"

"We shouldn't kill them, indeed. Death will take them on its own all the same. Look at Martin the carpenter. Martin lived, and didn't live for long, and died. Now his wife grieves for her husband, for her little children.... Neither man nor beast has any magic charm against death. Death doesn't go fast, but you can't go faster.

Still, we mustn't aid death. . . . And I don't kill nightingales—God forbid! I don't catch them to harm them, to spoil their lives, but to give pleasure to people, for their comfort and delight."

"Do you go to Kursk to catch them?"

"Yes, I go to Kursk, and farther than that sometimes. I spend nights alone in the marshes or in the fields, in the thickets. The woodcocks whistle there, and the hares call out, and the wild ducks lift up their voices. . . . In the evening I observe them, in the morning I listen to them, and at daybreak I cast my net over the bushes. . . . There are nightingales that sing such pitiful, sweet songs. . . . Yes, they're pitiful."

"And do you sell them?"

"I give them to good people."

"And what are you doing now?"

"What am I doing?"

"Yes, how are you employed?"

The old man fell silent for a moment.

"I'm not employed at all. . . . I'm a poor workman. But I can read and write."

"You can read?"

"Yes, I can read and write. I learned with the help of God and good people."

"Do you have a family?"

"No, no family."

"How so? . . . Are they dead, then?"

"No, that wasn't my task in life. For all that's in God's hands. We're all in God's hands. People should be righteous—that's all! Pleasing to God, that is."

"And you don't have any relatives?"

"Yes . . . well . . . there's. . . ."

The old man became embarrassed.

"Tell me something, please," I began. "I heard my coachman ask you why you didn't cure Martin. Can you cure diseases?"

"Your coachman is a righteous man," Kasian responded thoughtfully, "but he is not without sin. They call me a doctor. . . . Me, a doctor, indeed! And who can heal the sick? That's all a gift from God. But there are . . . yes, there are herbs, there are flowers that are of use, indeed. There are plantains, for instance, herbs that are good for people. There's marigold, too. It's not sinful to speak about them—they're pure herbs of God. Then there are others that aren't like that. They may be of use, but it's a sin to use them, and to speak about them is also a sin. Still, with prayer, perhaps.... And of course, there are certain words.... But he who has faith shall be saved," he added, lowering his voice.

"You didn't give Martin anything?" I inquired.

"I heard about it too late," the old man replied. "But what of it? Each man's destiny is written from his birth. The carpenter Martin wasn't destined to live—he wasn't meant to live upon the earth. That's already clear. No, when a man isn't meant to live upon the earth, the sunshine doesn't warm him as it does others, and bread doesn't nourish him and make him strong. It's as though something is drawing him away.... Yes, God rest his soul!"

"Have you been living among us for a long time?" I asked him after a short pause.

Kasian was startled.

"No, not for long. About four years. In the old master's day, we always lived in the same place, but the new master has transported us. Our old master was kindhearted, a man of peace—the kingdom of Heaven be his! The new master judged rightly, to be sure, since evidently it all had to happen."

"And where did you live previously?"

"I'm from Beautiful Meadow."

"Is that far from here?"

"A hundred versts or so."

"Well, were you better off there?"

"Yes ... yes, there was open countryside around there, with rivers. It was our nest. Here we're cramped and parched.... Here we're orphans. There, at home, in Beautiful Meadow, you could climb a hill, and oh, my God, what sights you could see! Streams and plains and forests, and there was a church, and then came plains again. You could see far, far away. Yes, how far you could see—you could look and look, ah, yes! The soil is better here, no doubt. It's loam—good loam, as the peasants say. For me, the corn grows well enough everywhere."

"Confess then, old man—would you like to visit your birthplace again?"

"Yes, I'd like to see it. Still, all places are good. I'm a man without a family, without neighbors. And, after all, do you gain much by staying at home? But, then, the farther you walk," he went on, raising his voice, "the lighter your heart grows, truly. And the sun shines upon you, and you're in the sight of God, and singing comes more easily. In one place, you look to see what herb is growing, you look at it and you pick it. In another place, maybe water is flowing—springwater, a source of pure holy water, so you drink it. You look at it, too. The birds of heaven sing. . . . And beyond Kursk come the steppes, such steppes—there's a marvel, there's a delight for man! There's freedom, there's a blessing from God! And that land reaches to the warm seas themselves, people say, where the sweet-voiced bird, the Gamaiun, dwells, where the leaves fall from the trees neither in autumn nor in winter, and apples of gold grow on silver branches, and everyone lives in right-eousness and contentment. And I'd willingly go there. . . . For I've journeyed far already! I've been to Romen and to Simbirsk, a glorious city, and even to Moscow of the golden domes. I've been to Oka-the-nurse, and to Tsna-the-dove, and to our mother Volga, and I've seen many people, good Christians, and I've visited noble cities. . . . Well, I'd go there . . . yes . . . and other places, too . . . and not only I, a poor sinner. . . . Many other Christians walk in woven shoes, they roam the world over, they seek the truth . . . yes! . . . For what is there at home? There's no righteousness in man—it's that which. . . . "

Kasian uttered these last words quickly, almost unintelligibly. Then he said something I couldn't catch at all, and such a strange expression passed across his face that I involuntarily recalled the epithet used by Erofei, "a holy man." He looked down, cleared his throat, and seemed to recover himself.

"What sunshine!" he murmured in a low voice. "It's a blessing, Lord! What warmth there is in the woods!"

He shrugged his shoulders and fell silent. Absently looking around, he began to sing softly. I couldn't catch all the words of his drawn-out song, but I did hear the following:

> They call me Kasian,
> But my nickname's the Flea.

"Oh," I thought, "he's making it up!" Suddenly he shivered and stopped singing, staring intently at one thick part of the forest. I turned and saw a little peasant girl of about eight wearing a blue dress with a checkered kerchief on her head, holding a woven bark basket in her small, bare, sunburned hand. She clearly hadn't expected to encounter us; she'd "stumbled onto us," as they say, and she stood stock-still in a shady recess among the thick foliage of the trees, fearfully gazing at me with her large, black eyes. I barely had time to catch a glimpse of her before she dove behind a tree.

"Annushka! Annushka! Come here, don't be afraid!" cried the old man caressingly.

"I'm afraid," her shrill voice resounded.

"Don't be afraid, don't be afraid. Come here to me."

Annushka silently left her hiding place, quietly walked toward us—her little child's feet barely making a sound on the thick grass—and emerged from the bushes near the old man. She wasn't a child of eight, as I'd thought at first from her diminutive stature, but a girl of thirteen or fourteen. Her entire body was small and thin, but very neat and graceful, and her pretty little face was strikingly similar to Kasian's, although he certainly wasn't handsome. They both had the same sharp features and the same strange expression, shrewd and yet trusting, withdrawn and yet penetrating, and made the same gestures. . . . Kasian kept his eyes trained on her; she stood by his side.

"Well, have you picked any mushrooms?" he asked.

"Yes," she answered with a shy smile.

"Did you find many?"

"Yes." (She cast a swift glance at him and smiled again.)

"Are there some white ones?"

"Yes."

"Show me, show me. . . ." (She slipped the basket off her arm and half-lifted the big burdock leaf that covered the mushrooms.)

"Ah!" said Kasian, bending over the basket. "What handsome ones! You've done well, Annushka!"

"She's your daughter, Kasian, isn't she?" I asked. (Annushka's face became faintly flushed.)

"No. Well, a relative," Kasian replied with feigned indifference. "Now, Annushka, run along," he immediately added. "Run along, and God be with you! And be careful. . . ."

"But why should she go on foot?" I interjected. "We could take her with us."

Annushka blushed as red as a poppy, grasped the handle of her basket with both hands, and looked at the old man in trepidation.

"No, she'll get there all right," he responded in the same languid, indifferent voice. "Why not? . . . She'll get there. . . . Run along!"

Annushka rapidly ran off into the forest. Kasian watched her go, then looked down and smiled to himself. In this smile, in the few words he'd spoken to Annushka, in the very sound of his voice when he'd spoken to her, there was intense, indescribable love and tenderness. He looked in the direction she'd gone once more, smiled to himself once more, and running his hand across his face, nodded his head several times.

"Why did you send her away so soon?" I asked him. "I'd have bought her mushrooms."

"Well, you can buy them there at home just the same, if you like," he replied, using the formal form of "you" for the first time in addressing me.

"She's very pretty, your girl."

"No . . . only so-so," he said with seeming reluctance, and from that moment on, he lapsed into the same taciturnity as he'd displayed at first.

Seeing that all my efforts to make him talk again were fruitless, I went off into the clearing. In the meantime, the heat had abated somewhat; but my bad luck or, as they say among us, my bad work continued, and I returned to the settlement with nothing but one corncrake and the new axle. Just as we were driving into the yard, Kasian suddenly turned to me.

"Master, master," he began, "I think I've wronged you. It was I who cast a spell to keep all the game away."

"How so?"

"Oh, I can do that. You have a well-trained dog, a good one here, but he could find nothing. When you think of it, what are people? What do they do? Here's an animal. What have they made him into?"

It would have been pointless for me to try to convince Kasian of the impossibility of "casting a spell" over game, hence I didn't respond. Meanwhile, we'd turned into the yard.

Annushka wasn't in the hut; she'd had time to get there before us and leave her basket of mushrooms. Erofei fitted the new axle in place, first subjecting it to severe and most unjust criticism. An hour later I set off, leaving a small sum of money with Kasian, which he was unwilling to accept at first, but then, after a moment's thought while holding it in his hand, he put it in his bosom. In the course of this hour, he'd hardly uttered a single word; he stood in the same pose as before, leaning against the gate. He didn't reply to the reproaches of my coachman, and said goodbye to me quite coldly.

As soon as I turned around, I could see that my worthy Erofei was in a bad mood. . . . To be sure, he hadn't found anything to eat in the village, and the only water for his horses had been foul. We drove off. Even the back of his head expressed dissatisfaction as he sat on the box, burning to begin a conversation with me. While waiting for my first question, he merely muttered under his breath, and gave some fairly caustic instructions to the horses. "A village," he grumbled. "You call that a village? You ask for a drop of kvass—not even a drop of kvass. . . . Ah, Lord! . . . And the water—absolute filth!" (He spat loudly.) "Not a cucumber, no kvass, no nothing. . . . Now, then!" he added aloud, turning to the right offside horse, "I know you, you lazybones!" (And he gave it a cut with the whip.) "That horse has started to shirk his work entirely, and yet it was willing enough before. Now, then—look alive!"

"Tell me, please, Erofei," I began, "what sort of man is Kasian?"

Erofei didn't answer me right away—he was generally a reflective, deliberate fellow—but I could immediately see that my question soothed and cheered him.

"The Flea?" he finally responded, gathering up the reins. "He's an extraordinary person, indeed, and a holy man. He's such an extraordinary person, you wouldn't find another one like him in a hurry. You know, he's just like this roan horse here: he avoids everything—avoids work, that is. But then, what sort of workman could he be? . . . He hardly has a body big enough to keep his soul in . . . but nonetheless. . . . He's been like that ever since childhood, you know. At first, he went into his uncle's business as a carter—there were three of them in the business. But then he got tired of it, you know, and he gave it up. He began to live at home, but he couldn't stay at home for long. He's too restless—just like a flea, in fact. Luckily, he happened to have a good master—one who made no demands on him. He's been wandering around ever since like a lost sheep. And then, he's so unpredictable, you can't understand him. Sometimes he'll be as silent as a post, and then he'll begin to talk, and God knows what he'll say! Is that just his manner? No, it isn't. He's an unfathomable person, yes, he is. But he sings well."

"And does he really cure diseases?"

"Cure diseases! . . . Well, how could he? A fine sort of doctor he'd be! Although he did cure me of scrofula, I must confess. . . . But how could he? He's a stupid fellow, that's what he is," he added after a moment's pause.

"Have you known him a long while?"

"Quite a while. I was his neighbor at Sychovka, in Beautiful Meadow."

"And what about that girl who met us in the forest, Annushka—what's her relation to him?"

Erofei looked at me over his shoulder and a smile spread across his face.

"Ha, ha! . . . Yes, they're related. She's an orphan—she hasn't got a mother, and it's not even known who her mother was. But she must be a relative—they're so much alike. . . . Anyway, she lives with him. She's a smart girl, there's no denying it, a good girl. And as for the old man, she's simply the apple of his eye. She's a good girl. And you know, you wouldn't believe it, but he's managed to teach Annushka to read. Oh, yes! That's just like him—he's such an unusual man, such an unpredictable man. You can't expect anything from him, really. . . . Eh! Eh! Eh!"

My coachman suddenly interrupted himself, stopped the horses, bent to one side, and began to sniff.

"Isn't there a smell of burning? There is! Why, it's that new axle. . . . I thought I'd greased it. . . . We need to get some water. Fortunately, here's a puddle."

Erofei slowly climbed down from his seat, untied a pail, went over to the puddle, and, upon coming back, listened not without satisfaction to the hissing of the wheel as the water suddenly splashed over it. . . . He had to pour water on the smoldering axle six times during the next ten versts or so, and it was well into the evening by the time we got home.

Death

I have a neighbor who's a young landowner and an avid hunter. One fine July morning, I rode over to his place with the suggestion that we go grouse hunting together. He agreed.

"Only let's go to my small piece of land at Zusha," he suggested. "I can use the opportunity to take a look at Chaplygino—you know, my oak forest. They're cutting timber there now."

"Let's go."

He ordered his horse to be saddled, put on a green coat that had bronze buttons stamped with the likeness of a boar's head, picked up an embroidered game bag and a silver flask, slung a newfangled French gun over his shoulder, turned around in front of the mirror not without satisfaction, and summoned his dog, Esperance, who was a gift from his cousin, an old maid with an extremely kind heart and no hair on her head.

We set off. My neighbor took along the village constable, Arkhip, a stout, squat peasant with a square face and a jaw of antediluvian proportions, as well as an overseer he'd recently hired from the Baltic provinces, a thin, blond, nearsighted youth of nineteen with sloping shoulders and a long neck, by the name of Gottlieb von der Kock. My neighbor had only recently inherited his estate himself. He'd inherited it from an aunt, the widow of the councillor of state Kardon-Kataev. She was an extremely fat woman who did nothing but lie in bed, sighing and groaning.

We soon reached the "small piece of land." "Wait for me here at the clearing," said Ardalion Mikhailych (my neighbor), addressing his companions.

The German bowed, got off his horse, pulled a book out of his pocket—a novel by Johanna Schopenhauer, I believe—and sat down under a bush; Arkhip remained sitting in the sun for an hour without moving a muscle. Ardalion Mikhailych and I circled among the bushes, but didn't come across a single covey of game. He then announced his intention to proceed to the forest. I myself somehow had no faith in our luck that day, so I strolled along after him. We went back to the clearing. The German marked his page, got up, put the book in his pocket, and, not without difficulty, mounted his bobtailed, broken-winded mare, who neighed and kicked at the slightest touch. Arkhip shook himself, gave a tug at both reins at the same time, swung his legs, and finally succeeded in rousing his dull-witted, dispirited nag. We departed.

I'd been familiar with Ardalion Mikhailych's forest since my childhood: I'd often strolled in Chaplygino with my French tutor, Monsieur Désiré Fleury, the kindest of men (who'd almost ruined my health for life, though, by dosing me with Leroux's elixir every evening). The entire forest consisted of some two or three hundred immense oak and ash trees. Their stately, powerful trunks stood out in majestic darkness against the transparent golden-green of the hazel and rowan trees; higher up, their wide, knotted branches were silhouetted in graceful lines against the clear blue sky, unfolding in a tent overhead; hawks, buzzards, and kestrels noisily flew under the motionless treetops; variegated woodpeckers tapped loudly against the stout bark; the blackbird's bell-like trill suddenly rang out in the thick foliage after the ever-changing notes of the orioles; robins, siskins, and peewits chirped and twittered in the bushes below; finches swiftly ran down the paths; a hare stole along the edge of the wood, hopping cautiously; a reddish-brown squirrel leaped briskly from tree to tree, then suddenly sat still, its tail arched above its head. Violets and lilies of the valley, as well as mushrooms colored russet, yellow, brown, red, and crimson, bloomed in the grass among the high anthills, beneath the delicate shade of lovely, feathery, deep-indented ferns; in patches of grass among the spreading bushes glimmered red strawberries.... And, oh, the shade in the forest! In the most stifling heat, even at midday, it was like night: there was such peace, such fragrance, such freshness....

I'd spent many happy moments in Chaplygino, and so, I must confess, it was not without a melancholy feeling that I entered the forest I knew so well. The deadly, snowless winter of 1840 hadn't spared my old friends, the oak and the ash trees. Withered, naked but for some sickly foliage here and there, they mournfully struggled to rise above the young growth that "took their place, but would never replace them."*

Some trees, still covered with leaves at the bottom, lifted their lifeless, broken branches upward, as if in reproach and despair; others thrust dry, dead branches out of the midst of foliage that was still fairly lush, although lacking the luxuriant abundance of old; the bark had fallen off others; still others had completely collapsed and lay rotting on the ground like corpses. And—who could have foreseen this?—there wasn't any shade. There was no shade to be found anywhere in Chaplygino! "Ah," I thought, looking at the dying trees, "isn't this humiliating, isn't this painful for you?" . . . Koltsov's lines came back to me:

What has become
Of the lofty voices,
The proud strength,
The royal pomp?
Where is your
Green might now? . . .

"How did it happen, Ardalion Mikhailych," I began, "that they

---

*In 1840, there were severe frosts, and no snow fell before the very end of December. All the foliage was frozen, and many splendid oak forests were destroyed by that merciless winter. It'll be hard to replace them: the productive vitality of the land is apparently diminishing, and in the "preserved" lands (ones visited by processions with icons and therefore not allowed to be touched), birches and aspens grow up by themselves instead of the noble trees of former days. Indeed, there's no other way of planting groves among us at all.

didn't cut down these trees the very next year? For now they won't be worth a tenth of what they'd have been worth before."

He merely shrugged his shoulders.

"You should have asked my aunt that. The timber merchants came, offered cash, and pursued the matter quite insistently."

"*Mein Gott! Mein Gott!*" von der Kock exclaimed at every step. "Vat a bity, vat a bity!"

"What's a bity?" my neighbor inquired with a smile.

"That is, how bitiful, I meant to tell-l-l." (It's a well-known fact that all Germans, when they've finally mastered the pronunciation of our letter *l*, emphasize it excessively.)

What particularly aroused his regret were the oaks lying on the ground—and, indeed, many millers would have paid dearly for them. But the constable Arkhip preserved an unruffled calm and didn't indulge in any lamentations. On the contrary, he actually seemed to jump over them not without satisfaction, cracking his whip at them.

We were getting near the spot where they were cutting down the trees when suddenly, following the crash of a falling tree, shouts and hurried discussions became audible. A few moments later, a young peasant dashed out of the thicket toward us, looking pale and disheveled.

"What is it? Where are you going?" Ardalion Mikhailych asked him.

He stopped immediately.

"Ah, Ardalion Mikhailych, sir, there's been an accident!"

"What happened?"

"Maksim's been crushed by a tree, sir."

"How did it happen?...Maksim the foreman?"

"That's right, the foreman, sir. We'd started cutting down an ash tree, and he was standing there watching....He stood there for a while, and then went off to the well for some water—he wanted a drink, it seems—when suddenly the ash tree began to creak and fall straight toward him. We shouted to him, 'Run, run, run!'...He should have thrown himself to one side, but he ran straight ahead....He was scared, naturally. The ash tree buried him in its top branches. But the Lord only knows why it fell so soon!...Maybe it was rotten at the core."

"And so it crushed Maksim?"

"Yes, sir."

"To death?"

"No, sir, he's still alive—but he's as good as dead. His arms and legs are smashed. I was running to get Seliverstych, to get the doctor."

Ardalion Mikhailych told the constable to gallop to the village for Seliverstych, while he himself proceeded toward the clearing at a rapid trot. . . . I followed him.

We found poor Maksim on the ground; about ten peasants were standing near him. We got off our horses. He was hardly moaning at all; he opened his eyes wide from time to time, looked around as if in astonishment, and bit his lips, which were quickly turning blue. . . . The lower part of his face was twitching; his hair was matted on his forehead; his breast heaved irregularly—he was dying. The faint shadow of a young lime tree fell softly across his face.

We bent over him. He recognized Ardalion Mikhailych.

"Please, sir," he said to him, barely comprehensibly, "send . . . for the priest . . . order . . . the Lord . . . has punished me . . . arms, legs, all smashed . . . today's . . . Sunday . . . and I . . . I . . . see . . . didn't let the boys off . . . work."

He fell silent. He gasped for breath.

"And my money . . . for my wife . . . give it to my wife . . . after deducting . . . Onisim here knows . . . who I . . . what I owe."

"We've sent for the doctor, Maksim," my neighbor observed. "Maybe you won't die yet."

He tried to open his eyes, and raised his eyebrows and eyelids with an effort.

"No, I'm dying. Here . . . here it's coming . . . here it. . . . Forgive me, boys, if in any way. . . ."

"God will forgive you, Maksim Andreich," the peasants declared hollowly, in unison, and they took off their caps. "Please forgive us!"

He suddenly shook his head despairingly, his breast heaved laboriously, and he closed his eyes again.

"We can't let him lie here and die, though," Ardalion Mikhailych cried. "Boys, fetch the mat from the cart and carry him to the hospital."

Two men ran to the cart.

"I bought a horse . . . yesterday," faltered the dying man, "off Efim . . . from Sychov . . . paid money down . . . so the horse is mine. . . . Give it . . . to my wife . . . too. . . ."

They began to move him onto the mat. . . . He trembled all over, like a wounded bird, and stiffened. . . .

"He's dead," the peasants murmured.

We mounted our horses in silence and rode away.

Poor Maksim's death started me musing. The way the Russian peasant dies is surprising! The mood in which he meets his end can't be called indifference or stolidity; he dies as though he were performing a solemn rite, coolly and simply.

A few years ago, a peasant in one village belonging to another neighbor of mine was severely burned in the drying shed where the corn is stored. (He'd have stayed in there, but a passing town-dweller plunged into a tub of water, took a running start, broke down the door under the burning eaves, and pulled him out half-dead.) I went to his hut to see him. It was dark, smoky, and stuffy in the hut. I inquired, "Where's the sick man?"

"There, sir, by the stove," a careworn peasant woman answered me in a singsong voice.

I went closer; the peasant was lying there covered with a sheep-skin, breathing heavily.

"Well, how do you feel?"

The injured man stirred in his place. Covered with burns, within sight of death as he was, he nonetheless tried to rise.

"Lie still, lie still, lie still. . . . Well, how are you?"

"In a bad way, for sure," he said.

"Are you in pain?"

No answer.

"Is there anything you need?"

No answer.

"Shouldn't I send you some tea, or something?"

"There's no need."

I moved away from him and sat down on a bench. I sat there for a quarter of an hour; I sat there for half an hour. The silence of the tomb reigned in the hut. A little girl about twelve years old eating a piece of bread crouched in a corner behind a table under the icons. Her mother shouted at her every now and then. In the outer room, the sounds of coming and going, of activity and conversation could be heard: his brother's wife was chopping cabbage.

"Hey, Aksinia," the injured man finally called out.

"What?"

"Give me some kvass."

Aksinia gave him some kvass. Silence set in again. I asked in a whisper, "Have they given him the sacrament?"

"Yes."

So, it appeared, everything was in order: he was waiting for death, and that was all. I couldn't bear it, and went away. . . .

Then again, I recall going to the hospital in the village of Krasnogorie one day to see the surgeon Kapiton, a friend of mine and an enthusiastic hunter.

This hospital consisted of what had once been the lodge of the manor house. The lady of the house had founded it herself—that is, she'd given orders for a blue board to be nailed above the door with the inscription "Krasnogorie Hospital" written in white letters, and had herself handed Kapiton a red album to record the names of the patients in. On the first page of this album, one of the obsequious parasites attached to this Lady Bountiful had inscribed the following lines:

> Dans ces beaux lieux, où règne l'allégresse
> Ce temple fut ouvert par la Beauté;
> De vos seigneurs admirez la tendresse
> Bons habitants de Krasnogorié!

while another gentleman had written below that:

> Et moi aussi j'aime la nature!
> Jean Kobyliatnikoff

The surgeon had bought six beds at his own expense, and had gratefully set to work healing God's children. In addition to him, the staff consisted of two people: an engraver, Pavel, who was subject to fits of insanity; and a one-armed peasant woman, Melikitrisa, who performed the duties of cook. Both of them mixed medicines, and dried and made herbal teas; they also controlled the patients when they became delirious. The insane engraver was sullen–looking and taciturn; at night, he'd sing a song about "lovely Venus" and besiege everyone he met with a request for permission to marry a girl named Malania, who'd long since died. The one-armed peasant woman used to beat him regularly, and made him look after the turkeys.

Well, one day I'd gone to Kapiton's. We'd begun to talk over our recent hunting experiences when a cart drawn by an exceptionally stout horse, of the sort that belong only to millers, suddenly rolled into the yard. In the cart sat a thickset peasant whose beard was streaked with gray, wearing a new overcoat.

"Ah, Vasilii Dmitrich," Kapiton shouted from the window. "Please come in. . . . The miller from Lybovshin," he whispered to me.

Groaning, the peasant climbed out of the cart, came into the surgeon's room, and after looking around for the icons, crossed himself.

"Well, Vasilii Dmitrich, any news? . . . But you must be sick. You don't look well."

"Yes, Kapiton Timofeich, something's not right."

"What's wrong with you?"

"Well, it was like this, Kapiton Timofeich. I bought some millstones in town not long ago, so I took them home, and as I went to lift them out of the cart, I strained myself or something. I felt a sort of jerk in the abdomen, as though something had been torn, and I've felt sick ever since. Today I feel worse than ever."

"Hmm," Kapiton commented, and he inhaled a pinch of snuff. "It's a hernia, no doubt. But how long has it been since this happened?"

"It's been ten days now."

"Ten days?" (The surgeon drew a long breath and shook his head.) "Let me examine you."

"Well, Vasilii Dmitrich," he declared at last, "I'm sorry for you, heartily sorry, but your situation isn't good at all—you're seriously ill. Stay here with me. I'll do everything possible on my part, although I can't answer for anything."

"Is it as bad as that?" muttered the astounded miller.

"Yes, Vasilii Dmitrich, it's that bad. If you'd come to me a day or two sooner, it would have been nothing much. I could have cured you in a snap. But now, inflammation has set in. Before we know where we are, there'll be massive infection."

"But this can't be, Kapiton Timofeich."

"I tell you, it is."

"But how is this possible?"

The surgeon shrugged his shoulders.

"And I have to die from a little thing like that?"

"I'm not saying that . . . but you should stay here."

The peasant thought for a long while, his eyes trained on the floor. Then he glanced up at us, scratched his head, and picked up his cap.

"Where are you going, Vasilii Dmitrich?"

"Where? Why, home, to be sure, if it's that bad. I have to put my affairs in order, if it's like that."

"But you'll do yourself harm, Vasilii Dmitrich, for heaven's sake. I'm surprised that you managed to get here. Stay."

"No, my friend, Kapiton Timofeich. If I have to die, I'll die at home. Why die here? I've got a home, and the Lord knows how it'll end."

"No one can tell yet, Vasilii Dmitrich, how it'll end.... Of course, there's danger, considerable danger, there's no denying it ... but for that very reason, you ought to stay here."

The peasant shook his head.

"No, Kapiton Timofeich, I won't stay ... but maybe you'll prescribe some medicine for me."

"Medicine alone won't do you any good."

"I won't stay, I tell you."

"Well, do what you want.... Just don't blame me for it afterward."

The surgeon tore a page out of the album and, writing out a prescription, gave him some advice as to what else he could do. The peasant took the sheet of paper, handed Kapiton half a ruble, left the room, and took his seat in the cart.

"Well, goodbye, Kapiton Timofeich. Don't think badly of me, and remember my orphans, if anything...."

"Oh, do stay, Vasilii!"

The peasant simply shook his head, slapped the horse with the reins, and drove out of the yard. The road was muddy and full of holes. The miller drove cautiously, unhurriedly, guiding his horse skillfully and nodding to the acquaintances he met. Four days later, he was dead.

The way Russians die is generally surprising. Many of the dead now come back to my memory. I recall you, Avenir Sorokoumov, my old friend who left the university without a degree, as the noblest, the best of men! Once again, I see your sallow, consumptive face, your thin brown hair, your gentle smile, your ecstatic gaze, your long limbs; I hear your feeble, affectionate voice. You lived at the estate of a Russian landowner named Gur Krupianikov; you taught Russian grammar, geography, and history to his children, Fofa and Zezia; you patiently endured all the ponderous jokes of Gur himself, as well as the coarse remarks of the steward and the vulgar pranks of the spiteful urchins; you complied with the capricious demands of their bored mother, not without a bitter smile, but without complaining. Yet to make up for all that, what bliss, what peace was yours in the evening, after supper, when, free at last of all duties and tasks, you sat at the window, pensively smoking a pipe or greedily turning the pages of a greasy, mutilated issue of some fat magazine brought to you from town by the land surveyor—just another poor, homeless devil like yourself! How delighted you were then with any sort of poem or novel; how readily the tears came to your eyes; with what pleasure did you laugh; what genuine love for others, what generous sympathy for everything good and beautiful filled your pure, youthful soul!

I have to concede the truth: you weren't distinguished by excessive wit; nature hadn't endowed you with either a fine memory or lofty ambition; you were regarded as one of the least promising students at the university—you dozed at lectures, you preserved a solemn silence at examinations. But who would beam with joy and be breathless with excitement at a friend's success, at a friend's triumphs? . . . Avenir! . . . Who had a blind faith in the exalted destiny of his friends? Who extolled them with pride? Who championed them with angry vehemence? Who was equally innocent of envy and of vanity? Who was prepared for the most disinterested self-sacrifice? Who readily deferred to people unworthy to untie his shoe? . . . That was you, all you, my dear Avenir!

I remember how brokenhearted you were to part from your comrades as you left in order to become a tutor in the countryside. You were haunted by a presentiment of evil. . . . And, indeed, your life in the countryside was a sad one: you had no one there to listen to with veneration, no one to admire, no one to love. . . . The neighbors—crude inhabitants of the steppes and polished landowners alike—treated you like a tutor: some rudely, others dismissively. Besides, you didn't have a prepossessing presence: you were shy, inclined to blush, perspire, and stammer. . . . Even your health didn't improve in the country air—you melted away like a candle, poor man! It's true, your room looked out over the garden; cherry, apple, and lime trees strewed their delicate blossoms across your desk, your inkstand, your books; on the wall hung a blue silk cushion to hold a clock, a parting present from a kindhearted, sentimental German governess with blond curls and little blue eyes. Sometimes an old friend from Moscow would come to visit you and render you ecstatic over someone's new poetry, or even over his own. But the loneliness, the intolerable slavery of a tutor's lot! The impossibility of escape, the endless autumns and winters, the inescapable disease! ... Poor, poor Avenir!

I paid Sorokoumov a visit not long before his death. He was barely able to walk then. The landowner, Gur Krupianikov, hadn't thrown him out of the house, but had given up paying him a salary and had hired another tutor for Zezia. ... Fofa had been sent to cadet school. Avenir was sitting near the window in an old easy chair. The weather was exquisite. A serene autumn sky of cheerful blue rose above the dark-brown outlines of the bare lime trees; a few last bright gold leaves rustled and whispered here and there. The earth had been covered with a frost that was now melting into droplets in the sun, whose ruddy rays fell slanting across the pale grass; there was a faint, crisp crackle in the air; the voices of the laborers in the garden reached us clearly and distinctly. Avenir wore an old Bokharan robe; a green scarf wrapped around his neck cast a deathly hue across his terribly sunken face. He was highly delighted to see me, held out his hand, and immediately began talking and coughing. I made him be quiet, and sat down next to him. ... On Avenir's knee lay a notebook filled with Koltsov's poems, which he'd carefully copied; he patted it with a smile.

"Here's a poet," he stammered, repressing his cough with an effort, and he began to declaim in a nearly inaudible voice:

> Can the eagle's wings
>   Be chained and fettered?
> Can the pathways of heaven
>   Be closed against him?

I stopped him—the doctor had forbidden him to talk. I knew what would please him. Sorokoumov never "kept up," as they say, with intellectual currents of the day, but he was always anxious to know what conclusions the leading scholars had reached. Sometimes he used to back an old friend into a corner and begin to question him; he'd listen and be amazed, accept every word on faith, and repeat it all later. He took a special interest in German philosophy. I began holding forth to him on Hegel (this all happened a long time ago, as you may have gathered). Avenir nodded his head approvingly, raised his eyebrows, smiled, and whispered: "I see! I see! Ah, that's fine! Fine! ... " The childish curiosity of this poor, dying, homeless outcast moved me to tears, I confess. It should be noted that Avenir, unlike most consumptives, didn't deceive himself in regard to his disease. . . . And what for? He didn't sigh or grieve; he didn't refer to his condition even once. . . .

Rallying his strength, he started to talk about Moscow, about old friends, about Pushkin, about the theater, about Russian literature. He recalled our little suppers, the heated debates among our circle of friends. He regretfully uttered the names of two or three of those friends who'd died. . . .

"Do you remember Dasha?" he went on. "Ah, there was a heart of pure gold! What a soul! And how she loved me!. . . What's happened to her now? Has she wasted away as I imagine, the poor thing?"

I didn't have the courage to disillusion the sick man, and indeed, why should he find out now that his Dasha had become broader than she was tall, that she was living under the protection of some merchants, the brothers Kondachkov, that she used powder and rouge, and that she was constantly swearing and complaining?

"Can't we get him away from here?" I wondered, looking at his wasted face. "Maybe there's still a chance of curing him."

But Avenir cut short my suggestion.

"No, thanks, my friend," he said. "It doesn't matter where one dies. I won't survive until winter, you see. . . . Why go to the trouble for nothing? I'm used to this house. It's true, the people. . . ."

"They're unkind, eh?" I interjected.

"No, they're not unkind, but they're insensitive somehow. Still, I can't complain about them. There are neighbors as well—the landowner Kasatkin has a daughter who's a cultivated, kind, charming girl . . . not at all proud. . . ."

Sorokoumov began to cough again.

"I wouldn't care about anything else," he continued after catching his breath, "if only they'd let me smoke my pipe. . . . But I'll get my pipe, or die trying!" he added with a sly wink. "Thank God, I've lived long enough! I've known so many fine people. . . ."

"But you should at least write to your relatives," I interrupted.

"Why write to them? They won't be any help. When I die, they'll find out. But why talk about it? . . . I'd rather you tell me what you saw when you were abroad."

I began to tell him about my experiences. He virtually seemed to drink in my tales. I left toward evening, and ten days later, I received the following letter from Mr. Krupianikov:

I have the honor to inform you, my dear sir, that your friend, the

student living in my house, Mr. Avenir Sorokoumov, died at two
o'clock in the afternoon four days ago, and was buried today, at my
expense, in the parish church. He asked me to send you the books
and manuscripts enclosed herewith. He was found to have twenty-
two and a half rubles that, along with the rest of his belongings, will
pass into the possession of his relatives. Your friend was fully conscious
and, I may say, equally insensitive, up to the moment of his death,
showing no signs of regret even when my entire family said a final
farewell to him. My wife, Kleopatra Aleksandrovna, sends you her
regards. The death of your friend couldn't fail to affect her nerves,
of course. As for myself, I'm in good health, thank God, and have
the honor to remain your humble servant,

G. Krupianikov.

Many more examples of death come to mind—but I can't recount
them all. I'll confine myself to one.

I was present at one old lady's deathbed. The priest had begun
to read the prayers for the dying over her, but suddenly noticing
that the patient actually seemed to be dying, he hastened to give
her the cross to kiss. The lady turned away with dissatisfaction.

"You're in too much of a hurry, father," she said in a nearly
inarticulate voice. "You'll have time. . . ."

She kissed the cross, put her hand under the pillow, and took
her last breath. Under the pillow lay a silver ruble; she'd wanted
to pay the priest for her own death service. . . .

Yes, the way Russians die is surprising!

The Singers

The small village of Kolotovka once belonged to a lady known in
its vicinity by the nickname The Skinflint—an allusion to her steely,
sharp personality (her real name has been forgotten)—but now it's
become the property of some German from Petersburg. The village
lies on the slope of a barren hill that's cut in half from top to
bottom by a tremendous ravine. It's a yawning chasm whose sides
have been hollowed out by rain and snow, and it winds along the
very center of the main village street, separating the two sides of
the poor hamlet far more definitively than a river could, for at least
a river could be crossed by a bridge. A few gaunt willow trees
cautiously creep down its sandy sides; at its very bottom, which
is dry and yellow as copper, lie huge slabs of clay-like rock. It's
a cheerless sight, there's no denying it—yet all the region's inhab-

itants know the road to Kolotovka well, and go there eagerly and often.

At the very summit of the ravine, just a few steps from the point where it starts as a narrow fissure in the earth, stands a small square hut; it stands alone, apart from all the others. It's thatched, and has a chimney. One window, like a sharp eye, keeps watch over the ravine; on winter evenings, when it's illuminated from within, it can be seen from far away through the dreary, frosty fog, and its twinkling light has provided a guiding star for more than one passing peasant. A blue board is nailed up above the door, announcing that this hut is a tavern called "The Welcome Resort."* Liquor is sold here at probably no less than the usual price, but it's frequented far more regularly than any other establishment of the same sort in the neighboring area. The reason for this is the tavernkeeper, Nikolai Ivanych.

Nikolai Ivanych—once a slender, curly-haired, rosy-cheeked youth, now an unusually stout, grizzled man with a fat face, craftily good-natured little eyes, and a shiny forehead with wrinkles that look like threads all across it—has lived in Kolotovka for more than twenty years. Nikolai Ivanych is an efficient, shrewd individual, like the majority of tavernkeepers. Although he makes no conspicuous effort to please or converse with people, he's mastered the art of attracting and keeping customers, who find it particularly enjoyable to sit at his bar under the placid and genial, albeit alert, eye of the phlegmatic host. He possesses a lot of common sense; he's thoroughly familiar with the landowner's way of life, as well as the peasant's and the merchant's. He could give sensible advice in difficult situations but, like every prudent and egotistical person, he prefers to remain aloof, at most leading his customers—and then only his favorite customers—along the path of truth by remote hints, dropped seemingly unintentionally. He's an authority on everything that's of interest or importance to a Russian: horses, cattle, timber, bricks, crockery, wool and leather, songs and dances.

When he doesn't have any customers, he usually sits on the ground in front of the door of his hut, looking like a sack, his thin legs tucked under him, exchanging a friendly greeting with every passerby. He's seen a great deal in his time; he's outlived many small landowners who used to come to him to get "the real thing"; he

---

*Any place where people eagerly gather, any shelter, is called "The Welcome Resort."

knows about everything that goes on within a hundred versts yet never gossips, never gives a sign of knowing what the most astute policeman doesn't begin to suspect. He knows how to restrain himself, even when he laughs and drinks toasts. His neighbors respect him; the civilian general Shcherpetenko, the highest-ranking landowner in the district, gives him a condescending nod whenever he rides past his little house. Nikolai Ivanych is a man of influence: he once made a notorious horse-stealer return a horse taken from the stable of one of Nikolai Ivanych's friends; he brought the peasants of a neighboring village to their senses when they refused to accept a new overseer, and so on. It shouldn't be assumed, though, that he did this out of a love of justice or a sense of devotion to his neighbors—oh, no! He simply tries to forestall everything that might in any way interfere with his peace and quiet.

Nikolai Ivanych is married, and has children. His wife, an energetic, sharp-nosed, keen-eyed woman from a merchant family, has recently grown somewhat stout, like her husband. He relies on her in everything, and she keeps the key to the cash-box. Drunken brawlers are afraid of her, and she doesn't like them—they bring little profit and make lots of noise. Drinkers who are taciturn and surly are more to her taste. Nikolai Ivanych's children are still small; the first four all died, but those who have survived resemble their parents, and it's a pleasure to look at their intelligent, healthy little faces.

It was an unbearably hot day in July when, slowly dragging my feet, I led my dog up along the Kolotovka ravine toward The Welcome Resort. The sun blazed in the sky as if it were angry, baking the parched earth relentlessly; the air was full of stifling dust. Glossy crows and ravens with gaping beaks plaintively gazed at the passersby, as though asking for sympathy. The sparrows alone didn't succumb: pluming their feathers, they twittered more vigorously than ever as they quarreled among the hedges or simultaneously rose from the dusty road and hovered over the green hemp fields in gray clouds. I was tortured by thirst. There was no water nearby: in Kolotovka, as in many other steppe villages that have no spring or well, the peasants drink some sort of thin mud out of a pond . . . for who could call that repulsive beverage water? I wanted to get a glass of beer or kvass at Nikolai Ivanych's.

It must be confessed that Kolotovka doesn't present a very joyous spectacle at any time of the year, but it has a particularly depressing effect when the relentless rays of a dazzling July sun pour down on it all: the brown, tumbledown roofs of the houses; the deep ravine; the scorched, dusty common pasture across which skinny, long-legged hens meander hopelessly; the remains of the old manor house, now a hollow, gray aspenwood frame with holes instead of windows that's been overgrown by nettles, wormwood, and grass; the black, seemingly charred pond covered with goose feathers, its banks formed by half-dried mud, and its broken-down dike, near which sheep huddle together dejectedly on the finely trodden, ashy soil, breathlessly gasping from the heat, their heads drooping as low as possible with weary patience, as though waiting for this intolerable state finally to pass. I approached Nikolai Ivanych's dwelling with weary steps, arousing the usual curiosity in the village urchins—evinced by an intense but mindless stare—and indignation in the dogs, expressed by such hoarse, furious barking that it seemed as if it were tearing out their very entrails, leaving them coughing and panting, when suddenly a tall peasant without a cap, dressed in a cloth overcoat belted below his waist with a blue scarf, appeared in the tavern doorway. He looked like a house serf; tangled, thick gray hair surrounded his withered, wrinkled face. He was calling to someone, hurriedly waving his arms, which he evidently couldn't quite control. It was obvious that he'd already been drinking.

"Come on, come on!" he stammered, raising his shaggy eyebrows with an effort. "Come on, Blinker, come on! Ah, friend, you do creep along, I swear! It's too bad, friend. They're waiting for you inside and here you just crawl along. . . . Come on."

"Well, I'm coming, I'm coming!" a rasping voice called out, and a short, fat, lame man came into sight from behind a hut. He was wearing a fairly tidy jacket he'd pulled halfway on, and a high pointed cap drawn right over his forehead that gave his round, plump face a sly, mocking expression. His little yellow eyes looked around restlessly, his thin lips wore a constant, tense smile, and his sharp, long nose jutted forward saucily, like a rudder. "I'm coming, my dear man." He hobbled toward the tavern. "Why are you calling me? . . . Who's waiting for me?"

"Why am I calling you?" the man in the cloth overcoat echoed reproachfully. "You're an amazing man, Blinker, my friend. We call you to come to the tavern, and you ask why? Good people are all waiting for you—Yashka the Turk, and the Wild Gentleman, and the street vendor from Zhizdra. Yashka's made a bet with the street vendor. The stake's a keg of beer for the one that does the best, sings the best, I mean . . . do you see?"

"Is Yashka going to sing?" the man addressed as Blinker asked with lively interest. "You aren't lying, are you, Babbler?"

"I'm not lying," Babbler replied with dignity. "But you're talking nonsense. Of course he'll sing, since he's got a bet on it, you precious innocent, you fool, Blinker!"

"Well, let's go, simpleton!" Blinker retorted.

"Well, at least give me a kiss, my dear," Babbler stammered, opening his arms wide.

"Go away, you big baby!" Blinker responded contemptuously, giving him a poke with his elbow. And then stooping, they both entered the low doorway.

The conversation I overheard greatly aroused my curiosity. Rumors about Yashka the Turk being the best singer in the vicinity had reached me more than once, and suddenly here was an opportunity to hear him in competition with another master of the art. I quickened my steps and entered the tavern.

Few of my readers have probably ever had the opportunity to get a good look at any village taverns, but we hunters go everywhere. They're constructed according to an exceedingly simple plan. They usually consist of a dark exterior porch and a white interior room divided in two by a partition that none of the customers is allowed to go behind. A wide opening above a broad oak table has been cut in this partition; wine is served at this table or bar. Sealed bottles of various sizes stand in a row on shelves across from the opening. In the front part of the room, which is devoted to the customers, there are benches, two or three empty barrels, and a corner table. For the most part, village taverns are fairly dark, and you hardly ever see any of the glaring, cheap prints few peasant dwellings fail to display on their timbered walls.

When I entered The Welcome Resort, a relatively large group had already assembled there.

In his usual place behind the bar, filling up almost the entire opening in the partition, Nikolai Ivanych stood wearing a striped cotton shirt, a lazy smile on his puffy face; he poured two glasses of wine with his plump white hand for Blinker and Babbler as they came in. Behind him, in a corner near the window, his sharp-eyed wife could be seen. Yashka the Turk, a thin, attractive individual of about twenty-three dressed in a long blue caftan, was standing in the middle of the room. He looked like an enterprising factory worker who, it appeared, didn't enjoy very good health. His hollow cheeks, large, restless gray eyes, straight nose with delicate, mobile nostrils, light-brown curls brushed back over a sloping white forehead, and full but beautiful, expressive lips—his entire face betrayed a passionate, sensitive nature. He was extremely agitated: he kept blinking his eyes, he breathed unevenly, his hands shook as though he had a fever—and he really did have a fever, that sudden fever of excitement so well known to anyone who's ever had to speak or sing in front of an audience.

Near him stood a man of about forty with broad shoulders and a broad jaw, a low forehead, narrow Tartar eyes, a short, flat nose, a square chin, and shining black hair as coarse as bristles. The expression on his face—whose swarthy complexion had some sort of leaden hue to it—and especially on his pale lips might almost have been called savage if it hadn't been so calm and thoughtful. He barely moved a muscle, and just looked around slowly, like an ox yoked to a cart. He was wearing some sort of well-worn coat with smooth brass buttons; an old black silk scarf was wound around his immense neck. He was called the Wild Gentleman.

Directly opposite him, on a bench under the icons, sat Yashka's rival, the street vendor from Zhizdra. He was a short, thickset man about thirty years old, pockmarked and curly-haired, with a blunt, turned-up nose, lively brown eyes, and a scant beard. He looked around alertly, sitting with his hands beneath him, chatting nonchalantly, and swinging his feet, which were encased in stylish boots with a colored border. He was wearing a nice, new gray cloth coat with a plush collar, which contrasted sharply with the crimson shirt under it that was buttoned tightly across the throat. In the opposite corner, to the right of the door, a peasant wearing a narrow, shabby jacket with a huge rip in one shoulder sat at the table. The sunlight fell through the dusty panes of two small windows in a thin, yellowish stream, but it seemed to struggle in vain against the habitual darkness of the room; all the objects in it were only dimly illuminated, in patches. Thus it was almost cool in there, and the stifling heat seemed to drop off my shoulders like a burden I'd unloaded as soon as I crossed the threshold.

I could see that my entrance was somewhat disconcerting to Nikolai Ivanych's customers at first, but observing that he greeted me as an acquaintance of his, they were reassured, and didn't pay any more attention to me. I asked for some beer and sat down in the corner, near the peasant with the ragged jacket.

"Well, now!" Babbler suddenly piped up, draining a glass of wine at one gulp and accompanying his exclamation with the strange gesticulations without which he seemed incapable of uttering a single word. "What are we waiting for? If we're going to begin, then begin. Hey, Yasha?"

"Begin, begin," Nikolai Ivanych chimed in approvingly.

"Let's begin, by all means," the street vendor remarked coolly, with a self-confident smile. "I'm ready."

"I'm ready, too," Yakov announced agitatedly.

"Well then, begin, lads," Blinker whined. But in spite of the unanimously expressed desire, neither one began; the street vendor didn't even get up from the bench. They all seemed to be waiting for something.

"Begin!" the Wild Gentleman commanded sharply and sullenly. Yashka shuddered. The street vendor pulled down his belt and cleared his throat.

"But who should begin?" he asked the Wild Gentleman in a slightly changed voice. The Wild Gentleman was still standing motionless in the middle of the room, his thick legs spread wide apart and his powerful arms thrust into his pants' pockets up to the elbow.

"You, you, street vendor," Babbler stammered. "You, friend."

The Wild Gentleman looked at him mistrustfully. Babbler gave a faint squeak, looked up at the ceiling in confusion, shrugged his shoulders, and didn't say another word.

"Cast lots," the Wild Gentleman called out emphatically, "and put the keg on the table."

Nikolai Ivanych bent down, picked a keg of beer up off the floor with a gasp, and set it on the table.

The Wild Gentleman glanced at Yakov and said, "Well?"

Yakov fumbled in his pockets, took out a copper coin, and marked it with his teeth. The street vendor pulled a new leather bag out from under the hem of his caftan, carefully untied the string, and shaking a quantity of small change into his hand, picked out a new copper coin. Babbler held out his dirty cap with its broken brim hanging loose; Yakov dropped in his coin, and the street vendor dropped in his.

"You have to pick one out," the Wild Gentleman declared, turning to Blinker.

Blinker smiled complacently, took the cap in both hands, and began shaking it.

For an instant, a profound silence reigned, broken only by the faint sound of coins jingling against one another. I looked around attentively: every face wore an expression of intense anticipation; the Wild Gentleman himself showed signs of uneasiness; even my neighbor, the peasant in the tattered jacket, craned his neck inquisitively. Blinker put his hand into the cap and took out the street vendor's coin; everyone drew a long breath. Yakov flushed, and the street vendor ran his hand through his hair.

"There, I said you'd begin," Babbler cried. "Didn't I say so?"

"Well, now, don't 'squawk,'"* the Wild Gentleman said contemptuously. "Begin," he went on, nodding at the street vendor.

"What song should I sing?" the street vendor inquired, starting to get nervous.

"Whatever you choose," Blinker answered. "Sing anything you can think of."

"Whatever you choose, of course," Nikolai Ivanych added, slowly rubbing his hand across his chest. "You're completely on your own in that regard. Sing what you want, only sing well. We'll make a fair decision afterward."

"A fair decision, of course," Babbler affirmed, licking the rim of his empty glass.

"Let me clear my throat a bit, friends," the street vendor requested, fingering the collar of his caftan.

"Well, come on, no fooling around—begin!" the Wild Gentleman insisted, and he looked down.

The street vendor thought for a minute, shook his head, and stepped forward. Yakov's eyes were riveted upon him. . . .

But before I embark upon a description of the contest itself, I think it wouldn't be inappropriate to say a few words about each of the characters in my story. I already knew the histories of some of them when I saw them at The Welcome Resort; I collected some facts about the others later on.

Let's begin with Babbler. His real name was Evgraf Ivanov, but no one in the whole region knew him as anything except Babbler,

---

*Hawks are said to "squawk" when they're frightened by something.

and he even referred to himself by that nickname, so well did it fit him. Indeed, nothing could have been better suited to his unprepossessing, ever-restless features. He was a dissipated, unmarried house serf whose own masters had gotten rid of him long ago, and who, without having any form of employment, without earning any money whatsoever, found ways to get drunk at other people's expense every single day. He had a great number of acquaintances who treated him to wine and tea, although they themselves didn't know why they did so, since, far from being entertaining in the company of others, he bored everyone with his meaningless chatter, his insufferable familiarity, his spasmodic gestures, and his incessant, unnatural laugh. He could neither sing nor dance; he'd never said an intelligent or even a sensible thing in his entire life. He just chattered away, telling lies about everything—a true Babbler! And yet not a single drinking party took place within forty versts without his lanky figure showing up among the guests. Thus everyone was used to him by now, and endured his presence as a necessary evil. It's true that they all treated him with contempt, but only the Wild Gentleman knew how to keep Babbler's foolish sallies in check.

Blinker didn't resemble Babbler in the least. His nickname suited him, too, although he was no more given to blinking than other people were; it's a well-known fact that Russian peasants have a talent for finding good nicknames. In spite of my efforts to obtain more detailed information about this man's past, many aspects of his life have remained obscure to me—and probably to many other people as well—episodes buried, as literary people say, in the deep haze of oblivion. I could only find out that he'd been a coachman for some childless old lady at one time and had run away, taking three horses that he was in charge of, had been gone for a whole year, and, no doubt having been convinced the hard way of the drawbacks and misfortunes of an itinerant life, had gone back of his own accord, at that point a cripple, and had flung himself at his mistress's feet. He succeeded in effacing the memory of his crime within a few years by his exemplary conduct and, gradually gaining her favor, finally won her complete confidence, was promoted to bailiff, and, at his mistress's death, ended up—how he did so never became clear—receiving his freedom. He became a member of the merchant class, rented land from his neighbors, grew rich, and was now living in ease and comfort. He was an experienced, cunning individual, more calculating than either good or evil; he'd seen something of the world, understood people, and knew how to make use of them. He was cautious and resourceful at the same time, like a fox; although he was as fond of gossip as an old woman, he never discussed his own affairs, whereas he got everyone else to talk freely about theirs. He didn't pretend to be simple-minded, though, as so many crafty men of his sort do. Indeed, it would have been difficult for him to fool anyone that way—I've never seen a more intelligent, more penetrating pair of eyes than his tiny, devious little "peepers."* They never simply looked around; they were always looking someone up and down, through and through. Blinker would occasionally ponder some apparently easy undertaking for weeks, and yet sometimes would abruptly decide to embark on some desperately bold action that might ruin him then and there.... But it'd always turn out all right; everything would always go smoothly. He was lucky, and believed in his own luck—and also believed in omens. He was exceedingly superstitious in general. He wasn't well liked, because he didn't want to have very much to do with anyone, but he was respected. His entire family consisted of one little son, whom he idolized and who, reared by such a father, was likely to go far. "Little Blinker will follow in his father's footsteps," old men already say about him in undertones as they sit on their mud walls and gossip during summer evenings. And everyone knows what that means—there's no need to say more.

As for Yashka the Turk and the street vendor, there isn't much to say about them. Yakov, nicknamed the Turk because he actually was descended from a Turkish woman taken prisoner during the war, was by nature an artist in every sense of the word, and was by calling a ladler in a paper factory belonging to a merchant. As for the street vendor, I must confess that I don't know anything about the course of his life; he struck me as an inventive, ambitious local tradesman. But the Wild Gentleman requires a more detailed description.

The first impression the sight of this man produced was of some sort of coarse and ponderous but irresistible strength. He was clumsily built, a "shambler," as they say among us, but there was an air of invincible health about him, and—strange to say—his bearlike form didn't lack a certain grace of its own, a result, perhaps, of his utterly serene confidence in his own physical prowess.

---

*Orel residents call eyes "peepers," just as they call mouths "feeders."

At first, it was hard to decide what social class this Hercules belonged to: he didn't look like a house serf, or a merchant, or an impoverished retired clerk, or a ruined small landowner who becomes a hunter or a street brawler. In fact, he was simply himself. No one knew where he'd come from or what had brought him to our district. It was rumored that he belonged to a freed peasant-proprietor family and had once been in government service somewhere, but nothing definite was known about this, and indeed, there wasn't anyone from whom one could find out—certainly not from him: no man was more silent and morose. Thus no one knew for sure how he supported himself: he plied no trade, never visited anyone, associated with virtually no one, and yet had money to spend—not much, it's true, but some. His behavior wasn't exactly shy—there wasn't anything shy about him in general—but he was subdued; he acted as though he didn't notice anyone around him and definitely didn't need anyone. The Wild Gentleman (that was the nickname he'd been given; his real surname was Perevlesov) wielded immense influence throughout the entire district; he was promptly and eagerly obeyed, although he had no right at all to give orders to anyone and didn't evince the slightest claim to authority over the people he came into casual contact with. He spoke, they submitted—strength always exerts an influence of its own. He hardly drank, had nothing to do with women, and was passionately fond of singing. There was a lot about this man that was mysterious. It seemed as though vast forces sullenly reposed inside him, knowing, as it were, that once roused, once bursting free, they were bound to crush him and everything else they came in contact with. And I'd be greatly mistaken if there hadn't been some such outburst during this man's lifetime, if it wasn't the teachings of experience, some narrow escape from disaster, that now caused him to keep himself under such a tight rein. What especially struck me was his combination of some sort of inborn natural ferocity and an equally inborn nobility—a combination I've never encountered in any other man.

In any event, the street vendor stepped forward and, half shutting his eyes, began to sing in a high falsetto. He had a fairly sweet and pleasing, albeit rather hoarse, voice; he played with that voice like a lark, bending and twisting it in continuous glissandos and trills up and down the scale, repeatedly returning to the highest notes, which he held and prolonged with special care. Then he'd break off, and suddenly resume a previous melody with some sort of reckless audacity. At times, his modulations were fairly adventuresome, at times, fairly amusing; they'd have given a connoisseur great satisfaction, and would have made a German indignant. He was a Russian *tenore di grazia, ténor léger.* He sang a song set to a lively dance tune, the words of which, to the extent that I could catch them amid the endless maze of variations, exclamations, and repetitions, were as follows:

> A tiny patch of land, young miss,
>   I'll plow for you,
> And tiny crimson flowers, young miss,
>   I'll sow for you.

Everyone paid close attention to him while he sang. He seemed to sense that he was dealing with highly knowledgeable individuals and therefore gave it everything he had, as they say. And they really do know music in our part of the country: the village of Sergievskoe on the Orel main road is praised all throughout Russia for its lovely, harmonious choral singing. The street vendor sang for a long while without evoking much enthusiasm in his audience—he lacked the support of a chorus—but eventually, after one particularly effective flourish that made even the Wild Gentleman smile, Babbler couldn't refrain from shouting with delight. Everyone became more animated. Both Babbler and Blinker began to sing along under their breath, periodically exclaiming: "Well done! ... Sing it, you rogue! ... Sing it out, you serpent! Hold it! Hold it longer! Light it up, you dog, you! May Herod confound your soul!" and so on. Behind the bar, Nikolai Ivanych nodded his head approvingly from side to side. Babbler subsequently began to swing his legs, tap his feet, and twitch his shoulder, while Yashka's eyes practically glowed like coal—he was trembling all over like a leaf and smiling nervously. Only the Wild Gentleman's face didn't change; he was standing still, in the same position as before. But his eyes, which were fastened on the street vendor, softened somewhat, although the expression on his face remained scornful.

Emboldened by these signs of general approbation, the street vendor launched into a whirl of flourishes, and began to offer such trills, to pound such rhythms with his tongue, and to make such furious sounds with his throat that when he finally uttered the last dying note, flinging his whole body backward, pale, exhausted, and bathed in hot perspiration, a collective shout violently burst forth in response. Babbler threw his arms around the street vendor's neck, starting to strangle him with his long, bony arms; a flush appeared on Nikolai Ivanych's oily face, and he seemed to have grown younger; Yashka shouted, "Bravo! Bravo!" like a madman. Even my neighbor, the peasant in the torn jacket, couldn't restrain himself, and slamming his fist on the table, he cried: "Aha! Well done, the devil take it, well done!" And he spat decisively to one side.

"Well, brother, you've given us a treat!" Babbler shouted, without releasing the exhausted street vendor from his embrace. "You've given us a treat, there's no denying it! You've won, brother, you've won! I congratulate you—the keg is yours! Yashka's miles behind you . . . I tell you—miles. . . . Take my word for it." (And he clasped the street vendor to his breast again.)

"Hey, let him alone, let him alone. No one can get rid of you . . . ," Blinker remarked with irritation. "Let him sit down on the bench. He's tired, see. . . . You're an ass, brother, a perfect ass! What are you sticking to him like a wet leaf for?"

"Well, then, let him sit down, and I'll drink to his health," Babbler said, and he went up to the bar. "At your expense, brother," he added, addressing the street vendor.

The street vendor nodded, sat down on the bench, pulled a piece of cloth out of his cap, and began to wipe his face, while Babbler emptied his glass with greedy haste, and groaning in the manner of confirmed drunkards, adopted a careworn, melancholy air.

"You sing beautifully, brother, beautifully," Nikolai Ivanych observed caressingly. "And now it's your turn, Yasha. Look out, now, don't be afraid. We'll see who's who, we'll see. . . . The street vendor does sing beautifully, though, by God, he does."

"Very beautifully," Nikolai Ivanych's wife affirmed, and she regarded Yakov with a smile.

"Beautifully, ha!" my neighbor echoed in a low voice.

"Ah, a twisted Polesjan!"* Babbler cried out suddenly, and going up to the peasant with the rip on his shoulder, he pointed his finger at that peasant while he jumped up and down and lapsed into a fit of insulting laughter. "A Polesjan! A Polesjan! Ha! Bah! Get along!† What brought you here, twisted man?" he shouted amid general laughter.

*The inhabitants of southern Polesje, a long strip of forest beginning at the borders of the Bolkhov and the Zhizdra districts, are called Polesjans. Many distinctive habits characterize their way of life, their manners, and their speech. They're referred to as "twisted" because of their suspicious, closed-minded personalities.
†Polesjans add the exclamations "Ha!" and "Bah!" to almost every word. They also say "Get along!" instead of "Go away!"

The poor peasant became embarrassed, and was just about to get up and leave as fast as he could when the Wild Gentleman's iron voice rang out abruptly: "What does that insufferable brute want?" he asked, gritting his teeth.

"I wasn't doing anything," Babbler muttered. "I didn't . . . I only. . . ."

"Well, all right, shut up!" the Wild Gentleman retorted. "Yakov, begin!"

Yakov grabbed himself by the throat.

"Well, really, friends . . . something. . . . Hmm. . . . I don't know, in fact, what. . . ."

"Well, now, that's enough, don't be shy. Shame on you! . . . Why back out? . . . Sing as well as you can, by God's grace."

And the Wild Gentleman nodded his head expectantly.

Yakov remained silent for a minute, then glanced around and covered his face with his hand. Everyone had their eyes glued on him, especially the street vendor; a slight, involuntary look of concern was visible behind his habitual expression of self-confidence and the triumphant flush of his success. He leaned back against the wall and put both hands beneath him again, but didn't swing his legs the way he had before. When Yakov finally uncovered his face, it was as pale as a corpse's, and his eyes just barely gleamed under their drooping lashes. He gave a deep sigh, and began to sing. . . . The first sound of his voice was faint and uneven, seeming not to have come from his chest but to have been wafted from somewhere far away, as though it'd floated into the room by accident. This tremulous, resonant sound had a strange effect on all of us; we glanced at one another, and Nikolai Ivanych's wife seemed to straighten up. This first note was followed by another, which was firmer and more prolonged, but was still obviously quivering like a harp string that, after suddenly being plucked by a strong finger, throbs in a final, swiftly dying waver. The second note was followed by a third, and, gradually gaining force and range, the notes joined and expanded into a pathetic melody. "Not a single little path ran across the field," he sang, and we all felt both delighted and saddened.

I've seldom heard a voice like his, I must confess: it was slightly raspy and wasn't perfectly true; there was even something sickly about it at first. But it contained genuine depth of passion, and youth, and power, and sweetness, and some sort of fascinatingly careless, pathetic sorrow. An ardent, righteous spirit, a Russian spirit, reverberated and came to life in that voice, which seemed to go straight to your heart, straight to all that was Russian in it. The song swelled and flowed. Yakov was clearly carried away by enthusiasm; he wasn't intimidated now; he'd wholly surrendered himself to the rapture of his art. His voice no longer trembled: it quavered, but only with the nearly imperceptible inward quaver of passion that pierces to the very soul of the listener like an arrow, and it constantly gained strength and steadiness and breadth.

I remember that one day, at sunset, on a flat sandy shore, when the tide was low and the sea was ominously moaning in the distance, I saw a large white seagull. It was sitting still, its silky breast turned to the crimson glow of the setting sun; it merely spread its long wings wide once in a while to greet the familiar sea, to greet the brilliant, sinking sun. I recalled this seagull as I listened to Yakov. He continued to sing, utterly oblivious to his rival and the rest of us; he was seemingly supported by our silent, impassioned attention the way a vigorous swimmer is supported by the waves. He continued to sing, and we seemed to recognize something dear to us, something immeasurably wide, in each sound of his voice, as though the well-known steppes were unfolding before our eyes and stretching out into the endless distance. I felt tears gathering in my heart and rising to my eyes; I suddenly heard dull, smothered sobs. . . . I looked around—the tavernkeeper's wife was weeping, her bosom pressed close to the window. Yakov cast a quick glance at her and sang more sweetly, more melodiously than ever; Nikolai Ivanych looked down; Blinker turned away; Babbler, thoroughly touched, stood with his mouth foolishly hanging open; the little peasant sobbed softly in the corner, shaking his head with a plaintive murmur; and a single heavy tear slowly rolled down the Wild Gentleman's steely face from under his overhanging eyebrows; the street vendor raised his clenched fist to his forehead and didn't move a muscle. . . . I don't know how the general emotional tumult would have been assuaged if Yakov hadn't suddenly come to a stop on a high, exceptionally shrill note—as though his voice had broken. No one called out or even stirred: we all seemed to be waiting to see whether or not he was going to sing any more. But he opened his eyes as though surprised at our silence, looked around at all of us with an inquisitive expression, and saw that the victory was his. . . .

"Yasha," the Wild Gentleman began, laying his hand on Yasha's shoulder—and he couldn't say anything else.

We all stood where we were, as if petrified. The street vendor rose quietly and went over to Yakov.

"You . . . yours . . . you've won," he finally conceded with an effort, and dashed out of the room.

His rapid, decisive action broke the spell, as it were; we all suddenly lapsed into noisy, elated conversation. Babbler jumped up and down, stammering and brandishing his arms like the shafts of a windmill; Blinker limped up to Yakov and began to kiss him; Nikolai Ivanych got up and solemnly announced that he'd add a second keg of beer to the prize himself; the Wild Gentleman uttered a kindly laugh of a sort I'd never have expected to hear from him; the little peasant, as he wiped his eyes, cheeks, nose, and beard on his sleeves in his corner, kept repeating, "Ah, that was fine, by God! I may be a son of a bitch, but that was fine!" Meanwhile, Nikolai Ivanych's wife, whose face was thoroughly flushed from weeping, stood up quickly and went out. Yakov enjoyed his triumph like a child: his whole face was transformed, and his eyes glowed with a special happiness. They dragged him to the bar. He beckoned to the weeping peasant, and sent the tavernkeeper's little son to look for the street vendor, who couldn't be found, however. The festivities began.

"You'll sing for us again. You're going to sing for us 'til evening," Babbler declared, waving his hands in the air.

I took one more look at Yakov and left. I didn't want to stay—I was afraid of spoiling the impression I'd received. But the heat was as unbearable as before. It seemed to hang in a thick, heavy cloud right above the earth. Tiny, bright sparks appeared to spin across the extremely fine, almost black, dust floating in the dark blue sky. Everything was silent; there was something hopeless, something oppressive in the profound silence of exhausted nature. I made my way to a hayloft and lay down on freshly cut yet already almost dry grass. I couldn't go to sleep for a long while; Yakov's compelling voice continued to ring in my ears. . . . Heat and fatigue finally gained their sway, though, and I fell into a deep sleep. When I awoke, everything was dark; the hay that was scattered about emitted a strong, slightly damp odor. Pale little stars shone faintly through the slender rafters of the half-uncovered roof. I went outside. The glow of sunset had long since died away, and its last traces just glimmered on the horizon. But amid the freshness of the night, the heat in the air that had so recently been baked by the sun was still palpable, and my lungs thirsted for a cool breeze. There wasn't any wind; there weren't any clouds; the sky all around was clear and transparently dark, glittering with innumerable but barely visible stars.

Lights were twinkling in the village; from the lamplit tavern nearby arose a vague, discordant din, amid which I thought I recognized Yakov's voice. Bursts of wild laughter sporadically came from that direction. I went up to the little window and pressed my face against the pane. I saw a cheerless, albeit varied and lively scene: everyone was drunk, beginning with Yakov. He was sitting on a bench with his chest bared, singing some street song to the melody of a dance-tune in a thick voice as he lazily fingered and strummed the strings of a guitar. His moist hair was hanging in tufts above his terribly wan face. Babbler, completely "unhinged," minus his caftan, was hopping around in the middle of the room and dancing in front of the peasant wearing the gray jacket; that peasant, for his part, was laboriously stamping and scraping his feet, grinning mindlessly through his disheveled beard. He waved one hand from time to time, as if to say, "Who cares?" Nothing could have been more ludicrous than his face: no matter how much he twitched his eyebrows, his heavy eyelids couldn't rise—they seemed to have fallen asleep across his nearly invisible, cloudy, mawkish eyes. He was enjoying the amiable frame of mind of a perfectly intoxicated man that inevitably causes every passerby who looks him in the face to say, "That's fine, friend, that's fine!" Blinker, as red as a lobster, his nostrils widely dilated, was laughing maliciously in one corner. Only Nikolai Ivanych had preserved his habitual composure, as befits a good tavernkeeper. The room was thronged with many new arrivals, but I didn't see the Wild Gentleman among them.

I turned away and rapidly began to descend the hill on which Kolotovka lies. At the foot of this hill stretches a wide plain; immersed in the misty waves of the evening haze, it seemed more vast than ever, as if it were part of the darkening sky. I was walking along the road by the ravine with long strides when a boy's clear voice suddenly called out from somewhere far off in the plain. "Antropka! Antropka-a-a!..." he shouted in persistent, tearful desperation, deliberately drawing out the last syllable.

He fell silent for a few moments, and then started shouting again. His voice carried distinctly in the motionless, lightly slumbering air. He called the name Antropka at least thirty times until all at once, from the farthest end of the plain, as though from another world, floated a barely audible reply:

"Wha-a-t?"

The boy's voice promptly shouted back with gleeful exasperation, "Come here, you devil, you wo-o-od imp!"

"What fo-or?" responded the other after a long pause.

"Because daddy wa-a-nts to thrash you!" the first voice immediately shouted back.

The second voice didn't respond any more, and the boy began shouting for Antropka again. His cries, fainter and fainter, less and less frequent, continued to reach my ears after it'd gotten completely dark and I'd reached the border of the forest that skirts my village and lies over four versts from Kolotovka....

"Antropka-a-a!" still echoed in the air, which was filled with the shadows of the night.

The Tryst

I was sitting in a birch grove in autumn, about the middle of September. A fine rain had been falling since early morning, alternating with intervals of warm sunshine—the weather was unsettled. Sometimes the sky was overcast with soft white clouds, at other times it suddenly cleared in places for an instant, and then blue sky appeared behind the parting clouds, sky as bright and tender as beautiful eyes. I sat still, watching and listening. The leaves rustled faintly above my head; one could tell what time of year it was from the sound of them alone. It wasn't the cheerful, laughing chatter of spring, or the subdued whispering, the prolonged gossip of summer, or the cold, timid stammer of late autumn, but a barely audible, drowsy murmur.

A slight breeze was just stirring the treetops. Wet from the rain, the inmost recesses of the grove were constantly changing in appearance as the sun either shone or hid behind a cloud. At one moment it was all radiant, as though everything there were suddenly smiling—the slender stems of the somewhat sparse birch trees unexpectedly took on the soft luster of white silk, the tiny leaves lying on the earth suddenly became flecked and fiery with purplish gold, and the graceful stalks of the high, curly bracken, already decorated in their autumn hue, the color of an overripe grape, seemed to intertwine in an endless, tangled web before one's eyes. Then everything suddenly became slightly bluish—the bright tints died away instantaneously, the birch trees turned lusterless and white, as white as fresh-fallen snow before the cold, capricious rays of the winter sun have caressed it. Slyly, stealthily, a very fine rain began to fall again, whispering throughout the woods.

The leaves on the birches were almost all still green, although they had paled perceptibly; single, young leaves, all red or gold, hung in just a few places, and it was wonderful to see how they gleamed in the sunlight when the sunbeams suddenly pierced through the thick network of delicate twigs freshly washed by the sparkling rain. Almost no birds could be heard: all of them were hiding and had fallen silent, except for the jeering tomtit, whose metallic, bell-like call rang out from time to time.

Before pausing in this birch grove, I had been walking through a grove of aspen trees with my dog. I confess that I have no great liking for that tree, the aspen, with its pale-lilac trunk and its grayish-green metallic leaves, which it flings as high as it can and unfolds in the air like a quivering fan; I don't care for the ceaseless quaking of its round, messy leaves, which are awkwardly attached to long stems. It's only appealing on some summer evenings when, rising alone above low undergrowth, it faces the brilliant beams of the setting sun, shining and quivering, bathed from root to peak in one unbroken yellow-purple glow, or when, on a clear, windy day, it ripples, rustles, and whispers all over, standing out against the blue sky, and every leaf seems to have been seized with a longing to break away, to fly off and soar into the distance. But as a rule, I don't care for the tree, and so, not stopping to rest in the aspen grove, I made my way to the birch grove, and nestled down under one tree whose branches started near the ground and were consequently capable of shielding me from the rain. After briefly admiring the surrounding view, I fell into the sweet, untroubled sleep known only to hunters.

I can't say how long I was asleep, but when I opened my eyes, the interior of the forest was entirely filled with sunlight, and in all directions, amid the joyously rustling leaves, there were glimpses and sparkles, as it were, of intense blue sky; the clouds had vanished, driven away by a blustery wind; the weather had cleared, and I felt the special, dry freshness in the air that fills the heart with a sense of vitality and is almost always a sure sign of a calm, bright evening after a rainy day.   ·

I was just about to get up and try my luck again when my eyes

suddenly came across a motionless human form. I looked carefully—
it was a young peasant woman. She was sitting twenty feet away
from me, her head bowed in thought and her hands lying in her
lap; in one of them, which was half-open, lay a thick bouquet of
wildflowers, which stirred quietly on her checked skirt with every
breath. A clean white blouse, buttoned at the throat and wrists,
draped her figure in short, soft folds; two rows of big yellow beads
fell from her neck to her breast. She was very pretty. Her thick,
fair hair, a lovely, almost ashen shade, was parted into two carefully
combed semicircles under a narrow crimson ribbon, which came
down almost to her ivory-white forehead; the rest of her face was
faintly tanned to the golden hue that only delicate skin can attain.
I couldn't see her eyes—she didn't raise them—but I saw her delicate, high eyebrows and her long eyelashes: they were wet, and
on one of her cheeks, the traces of quickly drying tears that streaked
right down to her slightly pale lips glistened in the sun. Her little
head was quite charming; even a rather thick snub nose didn't
spoil it. I was especially taken with the expression on her face: it
was so simple and gentle, so sad, and so full of childish wonder
at its own sadness.

She was obviously waiting for someone. Something made a faint
crackling noise in the forest; she immediately raised her head and
looked around. In the transparent shade, I caught a quick glimpse
of her eyes, which were large, clear, and frightened, like a fawn's.
She listened for a few moments, not taking her wide-open eyes off
the spot the faint sound had come from. Then she sighed, turned
her head slowly, bowed it still lower, and began sorting her flowers.
Her eyelids turned red, her lips twitched bitterly, and a fresh tear
rolled out from under her thick eyelashes, shining brightly on her
cheek.

A fairly long time passed this way. The poor young woman didn't
stir, except for a despairing movement of her hands now and then—
and she kept listening and listening. . . . A crackling noise came
from the forest again; she shivered. The noise didn't cease this
time; it grew more distinct, and came closer. Eventually, quick,
resolute footsteps could be heard. She straightened up and seemed
to become shy; her intent gaze began to waver, aglow with anticipation. The figure of a man soon emerged on the far side of the
thicket. She gazed at him, blushed suddenly, gave him a radiant,
blissful smile, tried to get up, only to drop back down immediately,

turned pale and looked confused, and merely raised her quavering, almost supplicating eyes to the approaching man when he came to a stop beside her.

I regarded him from my hiding place with curiosity. I confess that he didn't make a good impression on me. He was, to judge by external appearances, the pampered valet of some rich young gentleman. His clothes betrayed pretensions to style and dandified casualness: he wore a shortish, bronze-colored coat buttoned to the top, no doubt from his master's wardrobe, a short pink tie with lilac tips, and a black velvet cap with a gold lace border pulled down to his eyebrows. The round collar of his white shirt mercilessly propped up his ears and cut into his cheeks; his starched cuffs covered his hands down to his crooked red fingers, which were adorned with gold and silver rings sporting turquoise forget-me-nots. His ruddy, fresh, impudent face belonged to the type that, as far as I have observed, are almost always repulsive to men and, unfortunately, are very often attractive to women. He was obviously trying to impart a scornful, bored expression to his coarse features: he incessantly squinted his small, milky-gray eyes; he scowled, lowering the corners of his mouth; he pretended to yawn, and, with practiced though not perfectly natural nonchalance, pushed back his modishly curled red hair or pinched the blond whiskers sprouting on his thick upper lip. In sum, he was unbearably affected.

He began to display his affectations as soon as he caught sight of the young peasant woman waiting for him. He walked up to her slowly, with a swagger, stood for a moment shrugging his shoulders, stuffed both hands into his coat pockets, and, hardly granting the poor girl a cursory, indifferent glance, lowered himself to the ground.

"Well," he began, still gazing away from her, swinging his leg and yawning, "have you been here for a long time?"

The young woman couldn't answer right away.

"Yes, for a long time, Viktor Aleksandrych," she finally replied in a barely audible voice.

"Ah!" (He took off his cap, majestically ran his hand through his thick, stiffly curled hair, which grew almost to his eyebrows, and, looking around with dignity, carefully covered his precious head again.) "And I completely forgot about it. Besides, it rained!" (He yawned again.) "There's so much to do. I can't do everything, and he's always complaining. We're leaving tomorrow. . . ."

"Tomorrow?" echoed the young woman. She fastened her startled eyes on him.

"Yes, tomorrow.... Well, now, please!" he added hastily, with annoyance, seeing that she was shaking all over and had quietly bowed her head. "Please don't cry, Akulina. You know I can't stand that." (And he wrinkled his snub nose.) "Otherwise I'll leave right now.... How silly of you—you're sniveling!"

"Then I won't, I won't!" Akulina cried, swallowing her tears with an effort. "You're leaving tomorrow?" she added after a brief silence. "When will God grant that we see each other again, Viktor Aleksandrych?"

"We'll see each other, we'll see each other. If not next year—then after that. The master wants to enter government service in Petersburg, I believe," he went on, pronouncing his words with casual condescension, through his nose, "and maybe we'll go abroad, too."

"You'll forget me, Viktor Aleksandrych," Akulina declared sadly.

"No—why would I? I won't forget you, only do be sensible, don't be a fool, obey your father.... And I won't forget you—no-o." (He stretched placidly, yawning again.)

"Don't forget me, Viktor Aleksandrych," she went on pleadingly. "I love you so much, I've done everything for you, it seems.... You tell me to obey my father, Viktor Aleksandrych.... But how can I obey my father?..."

"Why can't you?" (He uttered these words as if they came from his stomach, lying on his back with his hands behind his head.)

"But how can I, Viktor Aleksandrych? You know yourself...."

She fell silent. Viktor toyed with his steel watch-chain.

"You're not a fool, Akulina," he responded eventually, "so don't talk nonsense. I want what's good for you—do you understand me? To be sure, you're not a fool, not altogether a peasant, so to speak, and your mother wasn't always a peasant, either. Still, you haven't had any education, so you ought to do what you're told."

"But that's terrible, Viktor Aleksandrych."

"O-oh! What nonsense, my dear—that's a funny thing to find terrible! What have you got there?" he added, moving closer to her. "Flowers?"

"Yes," Akulina answered dejectedly. "That's some wild tansy I picked," she continued, brightening up a little. "It's good for calves. And this is marigold—it works against scrofula. See what a marvelous little flower it is! I've never seen such a marvelous little flower before. These are forget-me-nots, and these are violets.... And I picked these for you," she noted, taking a small bunch of blue cornflowers tied up with a thin blade of grass out from under the yellow tansy. "Do you want them?"

Viktor languidly held out his hand, took the flowers, casually sniffed them, and began to twirl them in his fingers, looking upward with pensive self-importance. Akulina watched him.... Her mournful gaze expressed such tender devotion, adoring submissiveness, and love. She was afraid of him, and didn't dare cry. She was saying goodbye to him, admiring him for the last time, while he lay lolling like a sultan, enduring her adoration with magnanimous patience and condescension. I must confess that I glared indignantly at his red face, on which, beneath the pretense of scornful indifference, one could discern soothed, gratified vanity. Akulina was so fine at that moment: her whole soul was confidingly, passionately laid bare before him, full of longing and tenderness, while he . . . he dropped the cornflowers on the grass, pulled a round monocle with a brass rim out of the side pocket of his coat, and began trying to stick it in his eye. But however he tried to hold it in with a lowered eyebrow, an elevated cheek, and even his nose, the monocle kept popping out and falling into his hand.

"What's that?" Akulina finally asked wonderingly.

"A lorgnette," he replied with dignity.

"What's it for?"

"Why, to see better."

"Show it to me."

Viktor scowled, but handed her the monocle.

"Don't break it. Look out."

"Heavens, I won't break it." (She shyly put it to her eye.) "I can't see anything," she remarked innocently.

"You have to shut your eye," he retorted in the voice of a displeased teacher. (She closed the eye she was holding the monocle in front of.)

"Not that one, not that one, you fool! The other one!" Viktor cried, and he took the monocle away without letting her correct her mistake.

Akulina flushed slightly, gave a faint laugh, and turned away.

"It's clearly not for the likes of us," she commented.

"Indeed not!"

The poor young woman became silent for a moment and gave a deep sigh.

"Ah, Viktor Aleksandrych, it'll be so hard for me to be without you!" she said suddenly.

Victor rubbed the monocle on his coat lapel and put it back in his pocket.

"Yes, yes," he finally responded, "it'll be hard for you at first, certainly." (He patted her condescendingly on the shoulder; she silently took his hand from her shoulder and timidly kissed it.) "Yes, yes, you're a good girl, certainly," he added with a self-satisfied smile, "but what can I do? You can see for yourself! The master and I could never stay here. It'll be winter soon, and winter in the countryside—you know yourself—is simply horrible. But it's quite another matter in Petersburg! There are wonders there of the sort a silly girl like you could never see in your dreams! Such houses, such streets, and society, and culture—it's simply marvelous!...." (Akulina listened with ravenous attention, her lips slightly parted, like a child.) "But what's the use," he added, turning over on the ground, "of my telling you all this? You can't understand it!"

"Why not, Viktor Aleksandrych? I understood, I understood everything."

"What a smart girl you are!"

Akulina looked down.

"You never used to talk to me like that before, Viktor Aleksandrych," she observed without raising her eyes.

"Before?... Before!... My goodness!... Before!" he exclaimed as though insulted.

They were both silent for a moment.

"But it's time for me to go," Viktor announced, and he began to raise himself onto his elbow.

"Wait just a little while longer," Akulina urged in a supplicating voice.

"What for?... I've already said goodbye to you."

"Wait a little while," Akulina repeated.

Viktor lay down again and began to whistle. Akulina never took her eyes off him. I could see that she was gradually being overcome by agitation: her lips twitched, her pale cheeks glowed faintly....

"Viktor Aleksandrych," she finally began in a broken voice, "it's sinful of you... it's sinful of you, Viktor Aleksandrych, by God!"

"What's so sinful?" he asked, frowning, and he sat up and turned his head toward her.

"It's sinful, Viktor Aleksandrych. You might at least say one kind little word to me in parting, you might say one little word to me, a poor unfortunate orphan. . . ."

"But what should I say to you?"

"I don't know—you know that best, Viktor Aleksandrych. Here you're going away, and not one little word. . . . What have I done to deserve this?"

"You're such a strange creature! What can I do?"

"Say at least one little word. . . ."

"Goodness, she keeps going on about the same thing," he remarked in annoyance, and got up.

"Don't be angry, Viktor Aleksandrych," she added hurriedly, barely suppressing her tears.

"I'm not angry, only you're silly. . . . What do you want? You know that I can't marry you, can I? I can't, can I? What is it you want then, eh?" (He thrust his face forward as though expecting an answer, and spread his fingers apart.)

"I don't want anything . . . anything at all," she answered falteringly, and she ventured to hold her trembling hands out to him. "Just one little word, in parting."

And her tears fell in a torrent.

"Well, there she goes, now she's started crying," Viktor observed cold-bloodedly, pulling his cap down over his eyes.

"I don't want anything," she continued, sobbing and covering her face with her hands, "but what's left for me with my family? What's there for me? What will happen to me? What will become of me, poor wretch? They'll marry me off to some hateful orphan. . . . Poor little me!"

"Cry away, cry away," Viktor muttered under his breath, fidgeting impatiently as he stood there.

"And he might say one little word, just one. . . . He might say, 'Akulina . . . I. . . .'"

Sudden, heartrending sobs prevented her from finishing; she lay with her face in the grass and bitterly, bitterly wept. . . . Her whole body shook convulsively, her neck fairly heaved. . . . Her long-suppressed grief finally burst out in a torrent. Viktor stood above her, hesitated for a moment, shrugged his shoulders, turned away, and strode off.

A few moments passed. . . . She grew calmer, raised her head, jumped up, looked around, and wrung her hands. She tried to run after him, but her legs gave way under her—she fell to her knees. . . . I couldn't refrain from rushing up to her, but almost before she had time to look at me, somehow finding the strength, she got up with a faint shriek and vanished behind the trees, leaving her flowers scattered on the ground.

I stood still for a minute, then picked up the bunch of cornflowers and walked out of the grove into an open field. The sun had sunk low in the pale, clear sky, and its rays seemed to have grown pale and cold as well: they didn't shine, but spread out in an unbroken, watery light. It was within half an hour of sunset, yet there was hardly any glow of evening. A gusty wind scurried to meet me across the yellow, parched stubble; little curled-up leaves, scudding hurriedly before it, flew by across the road along the edge of the grove; the side of the grove that faced the fields like a wall was shaking all over, illuminated by tiny gleams of distinct but dull light; on each blade of the reddish grass, on the straw everywhere, innumerable threads of autumn spiderwebs sparkled and swayed. I paused . . . I felt sad; through the cheerless if fresh smile of fading nature, a dismal fear of the coming winter seemed to steal over me. A cautious raven flew high above me, sharply cleaving the air with its wings; it turned its head, looked sideways at me, soared upward, and shrieking abruptly, vanished beyond the forest; a large flock of doves playfully flew up from a threshing field and, after abruptly circling in a column, busily scattered. A sure sign of autumn! Someone came along driving an empty, rattling cart over the barren hillside. . . .

I returned home, but it was a long time before the image of poor Akulina faded from my mind, and her cornflowers, long since withered, are still in my possession. . . .

A Living Relic

O long-suffering native land,
Land of the Russian people!
—F. Tiutchev

A French proverb says: "A dry fisherman and a wet hunter are sorry sights." Never having developed any taste for fishing, I can't gauge what the fisherman's feelings are in fine, clear weather, or how much the pleasure derived from the abundance of fish in bad weather compensates for the unpleasantness of being wet. But for the hunter, rain is a real calamity. Ermolai and I experienced just such a calamity on one of our grouse-hunting expeditions in the Belevskii district. It rained nonstop from early morning on. We did everything imaginable to escape it! We put rubber capes almost on top of our heads and stood under the trees to avoid the rain-drops. . . . Still, the waterproof capes not only interfered with our shooting but actually let water leak through them shamelessly; under the trees, although the rain didn't reach us at first, it's true, eventually the water that collected on the leaves suddenly flowed down, every branch poured on us like a spigot, and cold streams made their way under our collars and trickled down our spines. . . . This was really the last straw, as Ermolai put it.

"No, Petr Petrovich," he finally cried, "we can't go on like this. . . . We can't do any hunting today. The dogs' sense of smell has been drowned. The guns misfire. . . . Ugh! What a mess!"

"What should we do?" I asked.

"Well, I'll tell you what. Let's go to Alekseevka. Maybe you don't know it—it's a settlement that belongs to your mother. It's eight versts from here. We'll spend the night there, and tomorrow. . . ."

"We'll come back here?"

"No, not here. . . . I know some places beyond Alekseevka . . . they're much better than here for grouse!"

I didn't proceed to question my faithful companion as to why he hadn't taken me to those places before, and we made our way that same day to my mother's peasant settlement, the existence of which, I must confess, I hadn't even suspected until then. There was a little lodge at this settlement, it turned out. This lodge was quite old, but because it'd never been inhabited, it was clean; I spent a fairly tranquil night in it.

I woke up fairly early the next day. The sun had just risen, and there wasn't a single cloud in the sky. Everything was glistening with a dual brilliance—that of the fresh morning sunlight and that of the previous day's downpour. While they were harnessing a cart for me, I took a stroll in a small orchard, now neglected and run wild, which surrounded the little lodge with its fragrant, luscious growth. Ah, how delightful it was in the open air, under the clear sky, where the larks were trilling—their melodious notes rained down like silvery beads! On their wings, no doubt, they carried drops of dew, and their songs seemed to be infused with dew as well. I took off my cap and drew a deep, joyful breath. . . . A beehive was visible on the slope of a shallow ravine, close to a hedge. A narrow path led up to this beehive, winding like a snake between dense walls of the high grass and nettles above which sprouted—God knows where they came from—pointed stalks of dark-green hemp.

I turned into this path; I approached the beehive. A little wattle shanty called an *amshanik*, where they put beehives for the winter, stood beside it. I peeped into the half-open door. It was quiet, dark, and dry; it smelled of mint and ointment. Some boards were fitted together in one corner, and on them, covered by a quilt, was a little figure of some sort.... I started to walk away....

"Master, master! Petr Petrovich!" I heard a faint, slow, hoarse voice that sounded like the whispering of marsh rushes.

I stopped.

"Petr Petrovich! Come in, please!" the voice repeated. It came from the corner where the boards I had noticed were lying.

I drew closer, and was struck speechless with amazement. Before me was a living human being—but what sort of being was it?

I saw an utterly withered head of a uniform coppery color, just like some very ancient icon, a nose as sharp as a keen-edged knife, lips that could barely be seen—only the teeth flashed white—and eyes; some thin wisps of blond hair straggled onto a forehead from underneath a kerchief. At chin level, where the quilt was folded, two tiny hands of the same coppery color were moving, the fingers slowly twitching like little sticks. I looked more intently: the face, far from being ugly, was positively beautiful, but strange and horrifying as well. And this face seemed even more horrifying to me because on it, across its metallic cheeks, I saw struggling ... struggling—and unable to spread fully—a smile.

"Don't you recognize me, master?" the voice whispered again. It seemed to breathe from the barely moving lips. "And indeed, how could you? I'm Lukeria. ... Do you remember, the one who used to lead the dance at your mother's, at Spasskoe? ... Do you remember, I used to lead the choir, too?"

"Lukeria!" I cried. "Is it you? Can this be?"

"Yes, it's I, master—I. I'm Lukeria."

I didn't know what to say, and gazed in stupefaction at the dark, motionless face with its clear, deathlike eyes fastened upon me. Was it possible? This mummy—Lukeria, the greatest beauty in our entire household, that tall, plump, pink-and-white, singing, laughing, dancing creature! Lukeria, our smart Lukeria, whom all our young men were courting, for whom I had heaved some secret sighs—I, a boy of sixteen!

"For heaven's sake, Lukeria!" I finally said. "What's happened to you?"

"Oh, such a misfortune befell me! But don't be put off, sir, don't let my trouble revolt you. Sit there on that little tub—a little nearer, or you won't be able to hear me.... I don't have much of a voice nowadays!... Well, I'm glad to see you! What brought you to Alekseevka?"

Lukeria spoke very softly and feebly, but unhesitatingly.

"Ermolai, the huntsman, brought me here. But tell me...."

"Tell you about my misfortune? Certainly, sir. It happened to me a long time ago now—six or seven years. I'd just gotten engaged to Vasilii Poliakov—do you remember how handsome he was, with curly hair? He waited on the table at your mother's. But you weren't in the countryside then—you'd gone off to Moscow to study. We were very much in love, Vasilii and I, and I could never get him out of my mind. It was in the spring that it all happened. Well, one night... not long before sunrise, it was... I couldn't sleep—a nightingale in the garden was singing so wonderfully sweetly!... I couldn't help getting up and going out onto the steps to listen. It trilled and trilled... and all at once, I thought that someone was calling me. It seemed like Vasia's voice was saying 'Lusha!' ever so softly... I looked around, and being half asleep, I suppose, I stumbled and fell straight from the top step right onto the ground! I thought I wasn't seriously hurt, because I immediately got up and went back to my room. Only it seems that something inside me—inside my body—was broken.... Let me get my breath... just a minute... sir."

Lukeria fell silent, and I looked at her in surprise. What particularly surprised me was that she told her story almost cheerfully, without sighs and groans, not complaining or asking for sympathy in any way.

"Ever since that happened," Lukeria continued, "I began to get thin and weak. My skin got dark, and walking became difficult for me. Then I lost the use of my legs altogether. I couldn't stand or sit, so I had to lie down all the time. And I didn't want to eat or drink. I got worse and worse. Your mother, out of the kindness of her heart, made me see a doctor and sent me to a hospital. But they couldn't cure me. Not one doctor could even say what was wrong with me. What didn't they do to me? They burned my spine with hot irons, they sat me in ice water—and all for nothing. I was quite numb by the end.... So the gentlemen decided there was no point in treating me any more, and since they couldn't keep cripples up at the manor house... well, they sent me here—because I have relatives in the area. So here's where I live, as you see."

Lukeria fell silent again, and again tried to smile.

"But this is awful—your situation!" I exclaimed ... and not knowing how to go on, I inquired, "And what happened to Vasilii Poliakov?" What a stupid question that was.

Lukeria turned her eyes a little to one side.

"What about Poliakov? He grieved, he grieved for a little while—and then he married another girl, a girl from Glinnoe. Do you know Glinnoe? It's not far from here. Her name is Agrafena. He loved me dearly, but he's a young man, you know. He couldn't remain a bachelor. And what sort of a spouse could I be? The wife he found for himself is a nice, kind woman, and they have children. He's a clerk for a neighbor. Your mama gave him a passport and let him go, and he's doing very well, praise God."

"And so you just lie here all the time?" I asked again.

"Yes, sir, I've been lying here for seven years. In the summer, I lie in this shanty, and when it gets cold, they move me into the bathhouse. Then I lie there."

"Who waits on you? Does anyone look after you?"

"Oh, there are kind folks here as well—they don't desert me. Besides, I don't need much care. As to food, I eat nothing to speak of, and water is here in the pitcher. It's always kept full of pure springwater. I can reach the pitcher myself—I still have the use of one arm. There's a little girl here, an orphan, who comes to see me now and then, the dear child. She was here just now.... You didn't run into her? Such a pretty, fair little thing. She brings me flowers. I'm a great lover of them, of flowers. There were some in the garden—but they've all disappeared. But wildflowers are nice, too. They smell even better than garden flowers. Lilies of the valley, now ... what could be sweeter?"

"But aren't you bored, aren't you miserable, my poor Lukeria?"

"Why, what can I do? I don't want to lie about it. First it was very tedious, but later on I got used to it, I got more patient. It's nothing. There are others who are still worse off."

"In what possible way?"

"Why, some people don't have a roof to shelter themselves with! And some are blind or deaf! But I have splendid vision and hear everything, thank God, everything. If a mole burrows in the ground, I can even hear that. And I can smell every scent, even the faintest one! When the buckwheat blooms in the meadow, or the lime tree blossoms in the garden, I don't need to be told about it—I'm the first to know, at least if the slightest bit of a wind is

blowing from that direction. No, why stir God's wrath? Many are
far worse off than I am. Consider this: anyone in good health may
easily commit a sin, but I'm even cut off from sin. The other day
Father Aleksei, the priest, came to give me the sacrament, and he
said: 'There's no need to hear your confession. You can't sin in
your condition, can you?' But I said to him, 'What about sinning
in thought, father?' 'Ah, well,' he said, and he himself laughed,
'that's no great sin.'

"But I'm probably no great sinner even in that way, in thought,"
Lukeria went on, "for I've trained myself not to think, and above
all, not to remember. The time goes faster."

I must confess that I was surprised. "You're always alone,
Lukeria. How can you prevent thoughts from coming into your
head? Or are you constantly asleep?"

"Oh no, sir! I can't always sleep. Even though I'm in no great
pain, I still have an ache right here inside me, and in my bones,
too. It won't let me sleep the way I should. No . . . and so I lie
here by myself. I lie here for hours and don't think. I feel that I'm
alive, I'm breathing—and all of me is here. I watch, I listen. Bees
buzz and hum in the hive, a dove sits on the roof and coos, a hen
comes along with her chicks to peck crumbs, a sparrow or a butterfly flies in—and that's a great treat for me. The year before last,
some swallows even built a nest over there in the corner and raised
their little ones in it. Oh, how interesting it was! One would fly
to the nest, press its body close, feed a young one, and fly off
again. I'd look back, and the other would already have replaced
the first. Sometimes one wouldn't fly in, but would just fly past
the open door, and the little ones would immediately begin to peep
and open their beaks. . . . I was hoping they'd come back again the
next year, but they say a hunter here shot them with his gun. What
could he have gained by that? A swallow is hardly bigger than a
beetle. . . . What evil men you are, you hunters!"

"I don't shoot swallows," I hastened to remark.

"And once," Lukeria began again, "it was so funny! A rabbit
ran in here, it really did! The hounds were after it, I suppose.
Anyway, it seemed to tumble right in the door! . . . It squatted down
quite close to me, and sat that way for a long time. It kept sniffing
with its nose and twitching its whiskers—like a regular army officer!
And it stared at me. I'm sure it understood that I was no threat
to it. It finally got up, hopped to the door, and looked around in
the doorway. How observant it was! Such a funny creature!"

Lukeria glanced at me, as much as to say, "Wasn't it funny?" To satisfy her, I laughed. She moistened her parched lips.

"In the winter, of course, I'm worse off, because it's dark. It would be a waste to burn a candle, and what for? I can read, to be sure, and was always fond of reading—but what could I read? There are no books of any kind here, and even if there were, how could I hold a book? Father Aleksei brought me a calendar once to entertain me, but he saw that it was no good, so he took it away again. And yet even though it's dark, there's always something to listen to. A cricket chirps, or a mouse begins scratching somewhere. That's when it's a good thing not to think!"

"And I repeat prayers, too," Lukeria continued, after resting a little, "only I don't know many of them—prayers, I mean. And besides, why should I bother the Lord God? What can I ask Him for? He knows better than I do what I need. He's laid a cross upon me—that means He loves me. This is the way we are commanded to understand things. I repeat the Lord's Prayer, the hymn to the Virgin, the supplication of all the afflicted, then I lie still again without any thoughts at all, and everything is all right!"

About two minutes passed. I didn't break the silence, and didn't shift on the narrow tub that was serving me as a seat. The cruel, stony immobility of the living, unfortunate creature before me communicated itself to me—I, too, seemed to have gotten numb.

"Listen, Lukeria," I finally began, "listen to the suggestion I'm going to make to you. Would you like me to arrange for them to take you to a hospital—a good hospital in town? Who knows— maybe you could still be cured. In any case, you wouldn't be alone. . . . "

Lukeria's eyebrows stirred slightly. "Oh no, sir," she responded in a troubled whisper. "Don't move me to a hospital. Don't touch me. I'll only have more agony to bear there! How could they cure me now? . . . Why, there was a doctor who came here once because he wanted to examine me. I begged him, for Christ's sake, not to disturb me. It was no use. He began turning me over, pushing and pounding my hands and legs, and pulling me in all directions. He said, 'I'm doing this for science. I'm a servant of science—a scientific man! And you really shouldn't resist me,' he said, 'because I've been given a medal for my labors, and it's for simpletons like you that I'm working so hard.' He poked me all over, told me the name of my disease—some wonderful long name—and then he left. Afterward, my poor bones ached for a week. You say that I'm all

alone, always alone. But oh, no, not always. People come to see
me. I'm quiet—I don't bother them. The peasant girls come in
and chat a bit, or a pilgrim woman will wander in and tell me
tales about Jerusalem, Kiev, and the holy cities. And I'm not afraid
of being alone. Indeed, it's better—oh, yes! Master, don't touch
me, don't take me to the hospital. . . . Thank you, you're very
kind—only don't touch me, my dear!"

"Well, whatever you want, whatever you want, Lukeria. You
know I only suggested it for your own good."

"I know that it was for my own good, master. But, master dear,
who can help someone else? Who can enter into another's soul?
Everyone must help themselves! Maybe you won't believe me, but
when I lie here all alone sometimes . . . it's as though there were
no one else in the world except me. As if I alone were alive! And
it seems to me as though something were overwhelming me. . . .
I'm carried away by visions that are really marvelous!"

"What do you envision then, Lukeria?"

"That I can't find words for, master. I can't explain. Besides, I
forget it all afterward. It's like a cloud floating past, bursting with
rain. Then it gets so fresh and lovely, but you don't know just
what happened! Only I find myself thinking that if people were
around me, none of that would happen, and I wouldn't feel anything
except my misfortune."

Lukeria heaved a painful sigh. Her breathing, like her limbs,
wasn't under her control.

"When I look at you, master," she began again, "I see that
you're very sorry for me. But you mustn't be too sorry, really! I'll
tell you one thing, for instance, sometimes, even now I. . . . Do you
remember how lively I used to be in my time? Quite an active
girl! . . . So do you know what? Even now I sing songs."

"Sing? . . . You?"

"Yes. I sing the old songs, songs for choruses, for feasts, Christ-
mas songs, all sorts! I know a lot of them, you see, and I haven't
forgotten them. Only I don't sing dance songs. In my present
condition, they don't suit me."

"How do you sing them . . . to yourself?"

"To myself, yes, and aloud, too. I can't sing loudly, but it's still
comprehensible. I told you that a little girl comes to see me—she's
a quick learner, this little orphan. So I've taught them to her. She's
learned four songs from me already. Don't you believe me? Wait
a minute, I'll show you now. . . ."

Lukeria took a breath. . . . The thought that this half-dead creature was getting ready to sing awakened an involuntary feeling of horror in me. But before I could utter a word, a long-drawn-out, barely audible, but pure, true note was quivering in my ears. . . . It was followed by a second and a third. Lukeria sang "In the Meadows." As she sang, the expression on her stony face remained unchanged, and even her eyes stayed riveted on one spot. But how touchingly that poor, struggling little voice reverberated, wavering like a thread of smoke! How she longed to pour her whole soul into it! . . . I didn't feel any horror now. My heart throbbed with inexpressible pity.

"Ah, I can't!" she declared suddenly. "I haven't got the strength. I'm so happy to see you."

She closed her eyes.

I laid my hand over her tiny, cold fingers. . . . She glanced at me, and her dark eyelids, fringed with golden lashes like an ancient statue's, closed again. An instant later, they glistened in the half-darkness. . . . They were moistened by a tear.

As before, I didn't move.

"I'm so silly!" Lukeria remarked suddenly, with unexpected strength, and opened her eyes wide. She tried to blink the tears out of them. "I ought to be ashamed! What am I doing? It's been a long time since I've been like this . . . not since the day Vasia Poliakov was here last spring. While he sat and talked with me, I was all right, but when he left—how I cried from loneliness! Where did I get the tears from? But there, we girls get our tears for free. Master," Lukeria added, "do you happen to have a handkerchief? . . . If you don't mind, wipe my eyes."

I hastened to carry out her wish, and gave her the handkerchief. She refused it at first. . . . "What can I do with such a gift?" she queried. The handkerchief was plain enough, but clean and white. Then she clutched it in her weak fingers, and didn't let go again. As I got used to the darkness in which we both were sitting, I could discern her features clearly, could perceive the delicate flush that appeared under the coppery color of her face, could even discover traces of former beauty in her face, or so it seemed to me.

"You asked me, master," Lukeria began again, "whether I sleep. I don't sleep very much, but every time I fall asleep I dream—such splendid dreams! I'm never sick in my dreams, I'm always healthy and young. . . . There's one sad thing, though. I wake up really wanting to stretch, and it's as if I were in chains. I once had

such an exquisite dream! Shall I tell it to you? Well, listen. I
dreamed I was standing in a meadow, and there was a rye field all
around me, full of tall rye as ripe as gold! . . . And I had a reddish
dog with me—a wicked dog. It kept trying to bite me. And I had
a sickle in my hands—not a simple sickle. It seemed to be the
moon itself, the moon like it is when it's the shape of a sickle.
And I had to cut all the rye with this very moon. Only I was
exhausted from the heat, and the moon blinded me, and laziness
swept over me, and cornflowers were growing all around, such big
ones, and they all turned their heads toward me! And I decided
to pick them. Vasia had promised to come, so I wanted to pick
myself a wreath first—I still had time to weave it. I began to pick
cornflowers, but they kept melting between my fingers, no matter
what I did. And I couldn't make myself a wreath. And meanwhile,
I heard someone coming toward me, quite close, calling, 'Lusha!
Lusha! . . . ' 'Ah,' I thought, 'what a pity I didn't have time to
finish! But it doesn't matter, I'll put that moon on my head instead
of cornflowers.' I put it on like a tiara, and I immediately began
to shine. I made the whole field around me light up. And behold!
Not Vasia but Christ Himself came quickly gliding toward me over
the very top of the ears of rye! And how I knew it was Christ I
can't say—they don't paint Him like that—only it was He! Beardless, tall, young, all in white—only His belt was golden. And He
held out His hand to me. 'Fear not,' He said. 'You are my bride
adorned. Follow Me. You shall lead the choral singing in the heavenly kingdom and sing the songs of Paradise.' And how I clung
to His hand! My dog started to follow at my heels . . . but then we
began to float upward! He went ahead of me. . . . His wings spread
across the whole sky—they were long, like a seagull's—and I rose
after Him! And my dog had to stay behind. Only then did I
understand that the dog was my illness, and that there was no
place for it in the heavenly kingdom."

Lukeria paused for a minute.

"And I had another dream, too," she began again. "But maybe
it was a vision. I really don't know. It seemed to me that I was
lying in this very hut, and then my dead parents, my father and
mother, came to see me and bowed low to me, but didn't say
anything. And I asked them, 'Why do you bow to me, father and
mother?' They said, 'Because you suffer so greatly in this world,
you've not only spared your own soul, but have taken a great burden
off us, too. And it's become much easier for us in the other world.

You've atoned for your own sins, and now you're expiating our sins.' And having said this, my parents bowed down to me again, and then I couldn't see them. I could only see the walls. Afterward, I was very uncertain about what had happened to me. I even told the priest about it in confession. Only he thinks it wasn't a vision, because real visions come only to members of the clerical class.

"And I'll tell you another dream," Lukeria went on. "I dreamed I was sitting on the main road, under a willow tree. I had a walking stick, a pouch on my shoulders, and my hair was tied up in a kerchief, just like a pilgrim woman! And I had to go somewhere a long, long way off, on a pilgrimage. And pilgrims kept going past me. They were walking slowly, as if against their will, all going one way. Their faces were weary, and they all looked very much alike. And I dreamed that among them was a woman who was a head taller than the rest, wearing special clothes, not like ours, not Russian. And her face was special as well—a worn, stern face. And all the others stayed away from her. But suddenly she turned and walked straight up to me. She stopped and looked at me, and her eyes were large and clear and yellow, like a falcon's. And I asked her, 'Who are you?' And she said to me, 'I'm your death.' But instead of being frightened, it was just the opposite. I was as joyful as I could be, I crossed myself! And the woman, my death, said to me: 'I'm sorry for you, Lukeria, but I can't take you with me. Farewell!' Good God! How sad I got then!... 'Take me,' I said, 'good mother, dearest one, take me!' And my death turned to me and began to speak to me.... I knew that she was telling me the hour of my death, but indistinctly, incomprehensibly. 'After St. Peter's Day,' she said.... With that I awoke.... Yes, I have such wonderful dreams!"

Lukeria turned her eyes upward . . . and sank into thought.

"The only sad thing is that sometimes a whole week will go by without my falling asleep once. Last year, a lady passing by came to see me and gave me a little bottle of medicine for sleeplessness. She told me to take ten drops at a time. It did me so much good, and I used to sleep, only the bottle was all finished a long time ago. Do you know what medicine that was, and how to get it?"

The lady had evidently given Lukeria opium. I promised to get her another bottle like it, and couldn't refrain from expressing my amazement at her patience once more.

"Ah, master!" she replied. "Why do you say that? What patience? Simeon Stylites, now, had great patience. He stood on a pillar for thirty years! And another saint had himself buried in the ground, right up to his breast, and the ants ate away his face.... And I'll tell you what I was told by a biblical student. Once there was a country that the Ishmaelites made war on, and they tortured and killed the inhabitants. And whatever they tried to do, the inhabitants couldn't get rid of them. And then a holy virgin appeared among these inhabitants. She took up a great sword, put on weighty armor, set out against the Ishmaelites, and drove them all beyond the sea. After she'd driven the enemy out, she said to them: 'Now burn me at the stake, for that was my vow, that I would die a death by fire for my people.' And the Ishmaelites took her and burned her at the stake, and the people have been free ever since then! Now that was a noble deed. But how noble am I?"

I wondered to myself whence and in what form the legend of Joan of Arc had reached her, and after a brief silence, I asked Lukeria how old she was.

"Twenty-eight ... or nine.... I won't reach thirty. But why count the years? I've got something else to tell you...."

Lukeria suddenly coughed somewhat hollowly, and groaned....

"You're talking a great deal," I observed to her. "It may be bad for you."

"It's true," she whispered, barely audibly. "It's time to end our little conversation—but what difference does it make? Now, when you leave me, I can be silent as long as I like. Anyway, I've opened my heart...."

I began to say goodbye to her. I repeated my promise to send her some medicine, and asked her once more to think it over and tell me—wasn't there anything she wanted?

"I don't want anything. I'm satisfied with everything, thank God!" she uttered with a very great effort, but also with gratitude. "God grant good health to everyone! But then, master, you might say a word to your mother. The peasants here are poor. If she could subtract the least little bit from their rent! They don't have enough land, or any comforts.... They'd pray to God for you.... But I don't want anything. I'm satisfied with everything."

I gave Lukeria my word that I'd carry out her request, and was already walking to the door.... She called me back again.

"Do you remember, master," she said, and there was a gleam of something wonderful in her eyes and on her lips, "what lovely hair I used to have? Do you remember—it hung right down to my knees! It was a long while before I could decide to. . . . What hair it was! But how could it be kept combed? In my condition!. . . So I had it cut off. . . . Yes. . . . Well, goodbye, master! I can't talk anymore. . . ."

That day, before setting off to hunt, I had a conversation with the village bailiff about Lukeria. I learned from him that they called Lukeria "the living relic" in the village, but that she gave them no trouble, that they never heard her voice any complaints or regrets. "She doesn't demand anything, but, on the contrary, is grateful for everything. A gentle soul, one must say, if ever there was one. Stricken by God," the bailiff concluded, "for her sins, one must suppose; but we don't go into that. And as for judging her, no—no, we don't judge her. Let her be!"

A few weeks later, I heard that Lukeria was dead. So her death had finally come for her . . . and "after St. Peter's Day." They told me that on the very day of her death she kept hearing the sound of bells, although it was over five versts from Alekseevka to the church, and it was a weekday. Lukeria, however, had said that the sounds didn't come from the church, but from up above! She probably didn't dare to say—from heaven.

Letter to A. A. Kraevskii[1]

Paris.
December 13, 1849.

I just received your letter this minute, dear Kraevskii, with the 300 silver rubles enclosed, and I am answering immediately. This money has positively saved me from death by starvation—and I'm intent on proving my gratitude to you. In the first place, I'm sending you a rewritten third of "The Diary," a piece long since finished, but because of my unforgivable laziness and sloth, as yet not completely recopied; I'm sending it to prove to you that this "Diary" isn't a myth; I'll work day and night on the rest of the things—and may I be a Bulgarin if with n two weeks you don't receive the conclusion, *along with a report on "Le Prophète."* As regards *The Governess*, that comedy is absolutely separate from *The Student*—and on this point I must ask your forgiveness. I'd forgotten that I'd promised you *The Student* and promised it to *The Contemporary* as well, but you won't lose anything because of this; I give you my word of honor not to send *The Student* to *The Contemporary* any earlier than I send you *The Governess*. *The Student* is up to the fourth act; *The Governess*, to the third (both comedies are in five acts). Again, I beg your pardon if any misunderstandings arise because of this. *The Party* is absolutely finished, but I don't know whether I shouldn't rewrite it, because the censor will surely maim it. That's the accurate and true "state of affairs." Supporting evidence for my activity may be found in the fact that my break with Mama is now final, and that I have to earn my daily bread. As a result of that, you won't blame me if I tell you that my price per printer's page is 200 paper rubles. I take 50 silver rubles a page from *The Contemporary*—and you know yourself the difference between your page and *The Contemporary*'s. That means that instead of owing you 610 silver rubles 85 kopecks, I subtract 28 rubles 57½ kopecks (100 rubles—25 per page)—that leaves 582 silver rubles 27½ kopecks. A decent sum—but you'll see how fast I earn it. Your advice about my returning is extraordinarily sensible—and I'm very grateful for your concern; but even without it I was firmly resolved *to return in the spring.* It's time—as you say. I'll be in your office at the beginning of May.

I thank you for your promise about *Notes of the Fatherland.* I

---

1. Andrei Aleksandrovich Kraevskii (1810–89), well-known journalist and publisher.

hope that you are well and in good spirits—I wish you all the best. I would hope that you like "The Diary"—I wrote it *con amore.*

I press your hand firmly and remain
Your devoted
I. Turgenev.

P.S. Please keep my manuscripts until I arrive. In two weeks—the conclusion of "The Diary."

The Diary of a Superfluous Man

March 20, 18—.

The doctor has just left my room. I've finally learned something definite! For all his subtlety, he had to express himself unequivocally at last. Yes, I'm going to die soon, very soon. The frozen rivers will break up, and I'll probably float away with the last traces of snow . . . where? God knows! To the ocean as well. So, what of it? Since one must die, one may as well die in the spring. But isn't it silly to begin a diary possibly a mere two weeks before one's death? What difference does it make? And are fourteen days so much less than fourteen years, or fourteen centuries? In comparison to eternity, they say, everything is trivial—yes, but in that case, eternity itself is trivial. It seems I'm lapsing into metaphysics. That's a bad sign—am I becoming cowardly? I'd better begin to describe something. It's damp and windy outside—I've been forbidden to go out. What can I describe, then? No decent man talks about his illnesses; writing stories isn't one of my specialities; reflections on elevated topics are beyond me; descriptions of the routine of life around me couldn't interest even me; I'm tired of inactivity but too lazy to read. Ah, I've got it! I'll record the story of my entire life, just for myself. An excellent idea! Prior to death, it's the proper thing to do, and it can't offend anyone. I'll start right now.

I was born thirty years ago, the son of fairly well-to-do landowners. My father was a compulsive gambler, whereas my mother was a woman of strong character . . . a highly virtuous woman. Yet I've never known a woman whose virtue brought fewer rewards. She was crushed beneath the weight of her own merits, and tormented everyone, herself above all, as a result. During the fifty years of her life, she never ever took a nap or sat with her hands folded. She was always fussing and bustling around like an ant— to absolutely no good purpose, which can't be said of an ant. The worm of restlessness gnawed at her day and night. Only once did I see her perfectly at peace, and that was the day after her death, in her coffin. As I looked at her, it actually seemed to me that her face wore an expression of subdued astonishment—its half-open lips, sunken cheeks, and meekly motionless eyes seemed to be saying, "How good it is not to move!" Yes, it's good, very good, finally to be rid of that torturous sense of life, of that persistent, worrisome consciousness of existence! But that's not the point.

I was brought up badly and unhappily. My father and mother both loved me, but that didn't make things any better for me. Even in his own house, my father didn't have the slightest authority or consequence, being someone openly devoted to a shameful, ruinous vice. He was conscious of his own degradation and, not having the strength to give up his favorite passion, he at least tried to earn the condescending forgiveness of his exemplary wife by his invariably amiable, humble demeanor and his unswerving submissiveness. My mother certainly bore her misfortune with the superb, majestic fortitude of the saintly, in which there's so much egotistical pride. She never reproached my father for anything, gave him every last bit of her money, and paid his debts without a word. He praised her highly to her face and behind her back as well, but he didn't like to be at home very much, and he caressed me in secret, as though he were afraid of contaminating me by his presence. But at those times his twisted features would express such kindness, the feverish grin on his lips would be replaced by such a touching smile, and his brown eyes, encircled by fine wrinkles, would shine with such love, that I couldn't help pressing my cheek to his, which would be warm and wet with tears. I'd wipe those tears away with my handkerchief, and they'd flow again effortlessly, like water from an overly full glass. I'd begin to cry myself and he'd comfort me, stroking my back and kissing me all over my face with his quivering lips. Even now, more than twenty years after his death, when I think about my poor father, mute sobs rise to my throat and my heart beats as hotly and bitterly, aching with as poignant a pity, as if it were going to go on beating for a long time—as if there were anything to pity!

My mother's behavior toward me, by contrast, was uniformly

kind, but cold. One often comes across such mothers, who are righteous and moralizing, in children's books. She loved me, but I didn't love her. Yes! I felt distant from my virtuous mother and passionately adored my corrupt father. But that's enough for today. It's a beginning—and as for the end, whatever it may be, I don't need to worry about it. That's for my illness to take care of.

March 21.

The weather is marvelous today—it's warm and bright. The sunshine is frolicking cheerily on the melting snow, and everything is glistening, steaming, dripping. The sparrows are chattering away like mad among the drenched, dark hedges. The moist, fresh air is irritating my chest both pleasantly and painfully. Spring, spring is coming! I'm sitting at the window, looking across the river into the open countryside. Oh nature, nature! I love you so much, yet I came forth from your womb unfit even for life. There goes a cock sparrow, hopping along with his wings outspread. He's chirping, and every note of his, every ruffled feather on his little body is exuding health and strength....

What should one conclude from that? Nothing. He's healthy, and has a right to chirp and ruffle his feathers, but I'm sick and have to die—that's all. It's not worthwhile saying any more about it. And tearful apostrophes to nature are ludicrous. Let's return to my narrative.

I was brought up, as I've said, quite badly and unhappily. I didn't have any brothers or sisters. I was educated at home. And, indeed, what would my mother have had to do if I'd been sent to a boarding school or government institution? That's what children are for—to insure that their parents don't get bored. We lived in the countryside, for the most part, and occasionally went to Moscow. I had tutors and instructors as a matter of course. One in particular has remained in my memory, a dessicated, tearful German named Rickmann, an exceptionally mournful creature cruelly maltreated by fate and fruitlessly consumed by an intense longing for his distant fatherland. At times, my unshaven attendant, Vasilii (nicknamed the Goose), would sit near the stove in the horrible mustiness of the crowded hallway filled with the sour smell of stale kvass, wearing an ancient shirt with a blue border, playing cards with the coachman, Potap, who'd be wearing a new sheepskin coat

as white as foam and boots oiled to impermeability, while in the
next room, behind a partition, Rickmann would sing:

Herz, mein Herz, warum so traurig?
Was bekümmert dich so sehr?
S'ist ja schön im fremden Lande.
Herz, mein Herz, was willst du mehr?

We moved to Moscow for good after my father's death. I was
twelve years old at the time. My father died one night from a stroke.
I'll never forget that night. I was sleeping soundly, as children generally do, but I remember that I was aware of a laborious, gasping
sound occurring at regular intervals, even in my sleep. Suddenly I
felt someone grasp my shoulder and poke me. I opened my eyes and
saw my tutor.

"What is it?"

"Get up, get up. Aleksei Mikhailych is dying...."

I jumped out of bed and ran like a madman into my father's bedroom. I looked at the bed—my father was lying there with his head
thrown back, his face red all over, gasping in agony. The servants
were crowding around the door with terrified expressions on their
faces. Someone in the hallway was asking in a thick voice, "Have
they sent for the doctor?" In the yard outside, a horse was led out
of the stable, and the gates creaked. A candle was burning on the
floor in the bedroom. My mother was there, looking terribly upset,
but she wasn't oblivious to the proprieties or to her own dignity. I
flung myself onto my father's bosom and hugged him, murmuring,
"Papa, Papa...." He was lying still, squinting strangely. I looked
at his face—unbearable horror took my breath away. I shrieked in
terror, like a captured bird. They picked me up and carried me
away. Just the evening before, as though aware that his death was at
hand, he'd caressed me so passionately, so despondently.

A sleepy, unkempt doctor reeking of vodka arrived. My father
died under his lancet, and the next day, utterly stupefied by grief,
I stood holding a candle in front of a table on which the dead man
lay, mindlessly listening to the bass chanting of the deacon, which
was periodically interrupted by the weak voice of my priest. Tears
kept streaming down my cheeks onto my lips, my collar, my shirt—
I was dissolved in tears. I watched my father's rigid face persistently, closely, as though I expected something from him, while
my mother slowly bowed down to the ground, slowly rose again,
and firmly pressed her fingers to her forehead, shoulders, and chest

as she crossed herself. I didn't have a single thought in my head, I was completely numb—but I felt that something terrible had happened to me. . . . Death had looked me in the face that day, and had noticed me.

We moved to Moscow after my father's death for a very simple reason: our estate was sold in its entirety at an auction to pay our debts—that is, in its entirety except for one little village, the one in which I'm living out my magnificent existence at this very moment. I must admit that, in spite of my youth at the time, I grieved over the sale of our home; or rather, in reality, I grieved over the loss of our garden. Virtually my sole happy memories are associated with our garden. It was there, one mild spring evening, that I buried my best friend, an old bobtailed dog with crooked paws named Trixie. It was there, hidden in the tall grass, that I used to eat apples I'd stolen—sweet, red, Novgorod apples. It was there, too, among the ripe raspberry bushes, that I saw for the first time the housemaid Klavdia who, in spite of her turned-up nose and habit of giggling while hiding her face behind her kerchief, awakened such a tender passion in me that I could barely breathe, and became faint and tongue-tied in her presence. Once, at Easter, when it was her turn to kiss my lordly hand, I almost flung myself at her feet to embrace her well-worn goatskin slippers. My God! Can all that have been twenty years ago? It seems to me it wasn't very long ago that I used to ride my shaggy chestnut pony beside the old fence of our garden and, standing up in the stirrups, used to pick the multicolored poplar leaves. While a man is living, he's unaware of his own life—it becomes audible to him, like a sound, only after a certain period of time.

Oh, my garden! Oh, the overgrown paths by my tiny pond! Oh, the sandy spot below the tumbledown dike where I used to catch little fish! And oh, you tall birch trees with your long, dangling branches, from beyond which would float a peasant's doleful song, disrupted by the uneven jolting of his cart on the village road—I send you all my final farewell! . . . As I depart from life, I stretch out my hands to you alone. Would that I might inhale the fresh, bitter fragrance of wormwood and the sweet scent of mown buckwheat in the fields of my native land one more time! Would that I might hear the muffled chime of our cracked parish church bell in the distance one more time, that I might lie for a while in the cool shade under an oak sapling on the slope of a familiar ravine one more time, that I might watch the wind flowing like a dark wave over the golden grass of our meadows one more time! ... Ah, what good is all this? I can't go on today. Until tomorrow.

March 22.

It's cold and cloudy again today. Such weather is much more suitable—it's more in harmony with my task. Yesterday quite inappropriately stirred up a multitude of useless emotions and memories inside me. This won't happen again. A sentimental outburst is like licorice: when you first suck on it, it's not bad, but it leaves a very nasty taste in your mouth afterward. I'll just start to tell the story of my life simply and serenely.

And so we moved to Moscow....

But something occurs to me: is it really worthwhile to tell the story of my life?

No, it definitely isn't.... My life hasn't been different from the lives of a multitude of other people in any respect. A parental home, the university, government service in the lower grades, retirement, a small circle of friends, respectable poverty, modest pleasures, unambitious pursuits, moderate desires—please tell me, to whom isn't all this quite familiar? And therefore I won't tell the story of my life, especially since I'm writing for my own satisfaction. And if my past doesn't afford even me any sensation of great pleasure or great pain, it means that there's nothing in it worthy of attention. I'd be better off trying to describe my own character to myself.

What kind of man am I? ... It may be remarked that no one is asking me this question—I grant that. But then again, I'm dying— by God, I'm dying—and in fact, at the point of death, it seems to me that a desire to find out what sort of odd duck one really was may be excused.

Mulling over this important question carefully and, moreover, having no need whatsoever to speak about myself too harshly, the way people firmly convinced of their meritorious qualities often do, I must admit one thing: I was an utterly superfluous man, or perhaps I should say duck, in this world. And I propose to prove this tomorrow, since I keep coughing today like an old sheep, and my nurse, Terentevna, is giving me no peace. "Lie down, your honor," she says, "and drink a little tea...." I know why she keeps after me—she wants some tea herself. Well, she's welcome to it! Why not let the poor old woman extract the utmost benefit from her master that she can at the end? . . . While there's still time.

March 23.

It's winter again. The snow is falling in large flakes. Superfluous, superfluous. . . . That's an excellent word I've hit upon. The more deeply I delve into myself and the more carefully I review my entire past, the more convinced I become of the precise accuracy of this term. Superfluous—that's just it. This term isn't applicable to other people. . . . People are good or bad, intelligent or stupid, pleasant or unpleasant, but superfluous . . . no. Understand me, though—the universe could get along without those people, too . . . no doubt about it. But uselessness isn't their fundamental characteristic, their most distinctive attribute, and when you speak about them, the word "superfluous" isn't the first one to come to your lips. But I . . . there's nothing else one can say about me—I'm superfluous, in a word. A supernumerary—that's all. Nature evidently didn't count on my appearance, and consequently treated me as an unexpected, uninvited guest. One amusing gentleman, a great devotee of the card game of preference, quite aptly said that I was the forfeit my mother had paid at the game of life. I'm speaking about myself calmly now, without any bitterness. . . . It's all over and done with!

Throughout my entire life, I kept constantly finding my place already taken, perhaps because I didn't look for that place where I should have looked. I was nervous, shy, and irritable, like all unhealthy people. Moreover, probably due either to my excessive self-consciousness or else to the generally unfortunate cast of my personality, some sort of inexplicable, incomprehensible, and utterly insuperable barrier existed between my thoughts and feelings on the one hand and the expression of those thoughts and feelings on the other. And whenever I'd make up my mind to break down this barrier by force, to overcome this obstacle, my gestures, my facial expression, my entire body would manifest the most painful constraint. I'd not only seem to be but would actually become unnatural and affected. I'd sense this myself, and would promptly withdraw into myself again. Then a terrible upheaval would occur within me. I'd analyze myself to the last shred, I'd compare myself to other people, I'd recall the slightest glances, smiles, and words of the people in front of whom I'd tried to open myself up, I'd put the worst interpretation on everything, I'd laugh vindictively at my own pretensions "to be like everyone else"—and suddenly, in the midst of my laughter, I'd collapse out of sheer misery, sink into the most ludicrous depression, and then begin the whole process again—going around and around, in fact, like a caged squirrel on its wheel. I spent whole days in this torturous, fruitless exercise. Well now, tell me, if you please, tell me yourself, to whom and for what purpose is such a man necessary? Why did this keep happening to me? What was the explanation for this petty self-torment? Who knows? Who can say?

I remember that once I was traveling away from Moscow in a carriage. Although it was a good road and the driver had harnessed four horses abreast, he'd still hitched an extra one alongside them. Such unfortunate, utterly useless fifth horses, which are always somehow fastened onto the front of the shaft by a short, stout cord that mercilessly cuts into their shoulders, forcing them to run in the most unnatural way, twisting their whole bodies into the shape of a comma, always arouse my deepest pity. I remarked to the driver that I thought we might have gotten along without the fifth horse this time. . . . He was silent for a moment, shook his head, struck that horse a dozen times across its thin back and under its distended belly with his whip, and then responded, not without a grin: "Yes, indeed—why do we drag him along with us? What the devil is he good for?"

And here I am, likewise being dragged along. . . . But, thank goodness, the way station isn't far off.

Superfluous. . . . I promised to prove the validity of my claim, and I'll fulfill my promise. I don't consider it necessary to mention the thousand trifles, the everyday incidents, the typical events that would serve as irrefutable evidence in my support—I mean, in support of my contention—in the eyes of any rational individual. I'd be better off beginning directly by reporting one rather important incident, after which no doubts about the accuracy of the term "superfluous" will likely remain. I repeat: I don't intend to indulge in minutely detailed descriptions, but I can't fail to mention one rather curious and significant fact—that is, the strange behavior of my friends (I, too, used to have friends) whenever I happened to encounter them, or even went to visit them. They used to seem ill at ease—as they came forward to greet me, they'd smile in a somehow unnatural way, look, not into my eyes or at my feet, as some people do, but rather at my cheeks, hurriedly shake my hand and hurriedly say, "Ah! How are you, Chulkaturin?" (this is the

surname that fate burdened me with) or "Ah! Here's Chulkaturin!"
immediately turn away, and then stand still for a moment, as though
trying to recall something. I used to notice all of this, for I'm not
devoid of insight or the gift of observation. On the whole, I'm not
a fool—sometimes ideas that are quite amusing and not wholly
commonplace come into my head. But since I'm a superfluous man
with a padlock on my inner self, it's extremely painful for me to
express my ideas, all the more so because I know beforehand that
I'll express them badly. It even occasionally strikes me as strange
the way people manage to talk so simply and freely. . . . It's marvelous, really, when you consider it. Although, to confess the truth,
in spite of my padlock, I too sometimes get the urge to talk. But
I actually uttered words only in my youth; in my more mature
years I almost always managed to stop myself from speaking. I'd
murmur to myself, "Come now, we'd better keep silent," and I'd
stifle myself. We Russians are all good at keeping silent, and our
women are particularly outstanding in that regard. Many a cultivated Russian young lady keeps silent so strenuously that the spectacle is calculated to produce faint shudders and cold perspiration
even in those who are prepared to face it. But that's not the point,
and it's not appropriate for me to criticize others. I should proceed
with my promised narrative.

A few years ago, owing to a combination of circumstances that
were quite insignificant in themselves but very important for me,
I had to spend six months in the district town of O——. The whole
town was constructed on a slope, and most awkwardly constructed
at that. There are estimated to be about eight hundred inhabitants
in it living in exceptional poverty. The houses are hardly worthy
of the name; in the main street by way of an excuse for pavement,
some huge white slabs of rough-hewn limestone are scattered here
and there, in consequence of which even carts drive around the
street instead of through it. A diminutive yellowish edifice with
black holes in it rises in the very center of an astonishingly filthy
main square, and men wearing large caps sit in these holes, pretending to buy and sell things. An extraordinarily high, striped
post sticks up in the air here, and a cartload of yellow hay is kept
near the post in the interests of public order, by proclamation of
the authorities. One government hen struts to and fro. In short,
existence in the town of O—— is truly unparalleled. During the
first days of my stay in this town, I nearly went out of my mind
from boredom. I should note that even though I'm indubitably a

superfluous man, I'm not that way of my own volition. I'm unhealthy myself, but I can't bear anything unhealthy.... I'm not
even averse to happiness—indeed, I've tried to approach it from
both the right and the left.... And so it's no wonder that even I
can get bored, just like any other mortal. I was staying in the town
of O—— on official business....

Terentevna has evidently sworn to finish me off. Here's a sample
of our conversation:

Terentevna. Oh—oh, your honor! Why are you always writing?
It's bad for you to keep writing.

I. But I'm bored, Terentevna.

She. Oh, have a cup of tea now and lie down. By God's mercy,
you'll sweat some and maybe doze a bit.

I. But I'm not sleepy.

She. Ah, your honor! Why do you talk like that? Lord have
mercy on you! Lie down now, lie down. It's better for you.

I. I'm going to die anyway, Terentevna!

She. Lord bless us and save us!...Well, do you want a little
tea?

I. I won't live out the week, Terentevna!

She. Eh, eh, your honor! Why do you talk like that?...Well,
I'll go heat up the samovar.

Oh decrepit, yellow, toothless creature! Is it possible I'm not
really a human being, even in your eyes?

March 24. Sharp frost.

On the very day of my arrival in the town of O——, the official
business I referred to earlier brought me into contact with a certain
Kirill Matveevich Ozhogin, one of the chief functionaries of the
district, but I only really got to know him or, as they say, become
intimately acquainted with him, two weeks later. His house was
situated on the main street and was distinguished from all the others
by its size, its painted roof, and the two lions on its gates, lions
belonging to the species that extraordinarily resembles those hideous dogs whose native home is Moscow. One might safely conclude
from those lions alone that Ozhogin was a man of property. And
so he was—he owned four hundred peasants. He entertained all
the best society in the town of O—— at his house, and had a
reputation for hospitality. Even the mayor came to his receptions
in a wide, chestnut-colored carriage drawn by a matching pair of

horses; he was an exceptionally bulky man who looked as though he'd been cut out of material that had been tossed aside.

The other local officials also used to attend Ozhogin's receptions: the assessor, a jaundiced, spiteful creature; the land surveyor, a wit of German extraction with a Tartar face; the inspector of the means of communication, a tender soul and a singer, but a scandalmonger as well; a former marshal of the district, a gentleman with dyed hair, a crumpled shirtfront, tight trousers, and that lofty expression so characteristic of men who have been on trial. Two landowners also used to attend. They were inseparable friends, both already middle-aged and even somewhat the worse for wear, the younger of whom was continually humiliating the older and causing him to fall silent with one and the same reproach: "Don't speak any more, Sergei Sergeich! What do you have to say? Why, you spell the word 'cork' with two *k*'s in it....Yes, gentlemen," he'd continue with all the fire of conviction, turning to everyone present, "Sergei Sergeich spells it 'kork,' not 'cork.'" And everyone present would laugh, although none of them was probably noted for the particular accuracy of their orthography, while the unfortunate Sergei Sergeich would hold his tongue and bow his head with a faint smile.

But I'm forgetting that my hours are numbered, and I'm letting myself lapse into excessively detailed descriptions. And so, without further ado—Ozhogin was married, he had a daughter named Elizaveta Kirillovna, and I fell in love with her.

Ozhogin himself was an ordinary individual, neither good- nor bad-looking, and his wife resembled an aged chicken, but their daughter hadn't taken after her parents. She was very pretty and had an animated, sweet disposition. Her clear, gray eyes regarded the world benignly and straightforwardly from beneath childishly arched brows. She almost always smiled, and laughed quite often as well. Her youthful voice had the loveliest ring to it; she moved easily and rapidly—and blushed cheerily. She didn't dress overly elegantly; unadorned clothing suited her. I didn't form acquaintances very quickly as a rule, and if I felt comfortable around anyone from the beginning—which hardly ever occurred, however—this said a great deal in favor of that new acquaintance, I must confess. I didn't know how to behave toward women at all, and I either scowled and donned a fierce expression in their presence, or grinned in the most idiotic way and curled my tongue inside my mouth from embarrassment. But with Elizaveta Kirillovna, by contrast, I felt at home from the very first moment. This is how it happened.

I dropped in on the Ozhogins one day before dinner and asked, "Are they at home?" I was told: "The master's at home, changing clothes. Please come into the drawing room." I went into the drawing room and beheld a girl in a white dress standing at the window with her back toward me, holding a cage in her hands. I was somewhat taken aback, as usual. I showed no sign of it, however, and merely cleared my throat out of politeness. The girl turned around quickly, so quickly that her curls lightly slapped her face, saw me, bowed, and smilingly showed me a little box half-filled with seeds. "Do you mind?" Of course, as is the custom in such instances, I first bowed my head, at the same time rapidly bending my knees and straightening them again as though someone had hit me in the legs from behind—a sure sign of good breeding and pleasant, informal manners—then smiled and raised my hand, slowly and carefully brandishing it twice in the air. The girl promptly turned away from me, took a small piece of board out of the cage, began vigorously scraping it with a knife, and suddenly, without changing her position, uttered the following words: "This is Papa's parrot. . . . Do you like parrots?"

"I prefer finches," I replied, not without some effort.

"I like finches, too, but look at him—isn't he pretty? Look, he isn't afraid." (What surprised me was that *I* wasn't afraid.)

"Come closer. His name's Popka."

I went up to her and bent over.

"Isn't he precious?"

She turned her face toward me, but we were standing so close together that she had to tip her head back slightly to regard me with her bright eyes. I gazed at her: her entire rosy, youthful face was smiling in such a friendly fashion that I smiled as well, and even nearly laughed aloud with delight. The door opened; Ozhogin came in. I immediately walked over to him and began talking to him quite unconstrainedly. I don't know how it happened, but I ended up staying for dinner and spending the whole evening with them, and the next day Ozhogin's footman, a lanky, partially blind individual, smiled upon me as a friend of the family when he helped me remove my overcoat.

To find a refuge, to build oneself even a temporary nest, to experience the comforts of daily interactions and shared habits was a happiness that I, a superfluous man with no family connections, had never known before. If anything about me had borne any resemblance to a flower, and if the comparison weren't so hackneyed, I'd dare to say that my soul blossomed from that day onward. Everything inside me and all around me was suddenly transformed! My entire life, the whole of it down to the tiniest details, was illuminated by love the way a dark, deserted room lights up when a candle has been carried into it. I went to bed, arose, got dressed, ate my breakfast, and smoked my pipe—all differently than before. I virtually skipped as I walked along, as though wings had suddenly sprouted from my shoulders. I remember that I didn't for a moment entertain the slightest uncertainty as to the feelings Elizaveta Kirillovna inspired in me. I fell passionately in love with her from the first day on, and I knew I was in love from that very first day. I saw her every day during the course of the next three weeks. Those three weeks constituted the happiest period of my life—but their memory is painful for me. I can't focus on them alone; I can't help dwelling on what happened after that—and the most intense bitterness slowly takes possession of my susceptible heart.

When an individual is very happy, his brain isn't terribly active, as is well known. A calm, joyous sensation, the sensation of contentment, pervades his whole being, and he's consumed by it. The consciousness of his own individuality vanishes within him—he's in ecstasy, as badly educated poets say. But when this "enchantment" finally ends, that individual occasionally becomes annoyed and regrets that he paid so little attention to himself in the midst of his bliss, that he didn't redouble and prolong his feelings by contemplation, by recollection . . . as though the "ecstatic" individual had so much time, and as though it were worth his while to contemplate his sensations! The happy individual is a fly basking in the sunlight.

And thus, when I recall those three weeks, it's almost impossible for me to retain any exact, specific impressions, all the more so since nothing very remarkable occurred between us during that time. . . . I remember those twenty days as something warm and young and fragrant, as a sort of ray of light in my dingy, grayish existence. My memory suddenly becomes remorselessly clear and reliable only from the moment when, to use another phrase of those badly educated writers, the blows of fate began to fall upon me.

Yes, those three weeks. . . . To be sure, they've left certain images in my mind. Sometimes, when I happen to brood over that time for a long while, random memories suddenly float up out of the darkness of the past—like stars unexpectedly appearing to eyes that strain to catch sight of them in the evening sky. One stroll through the woods beyond the town has remained especially distinct in my memory. There were four of us, old Mrs. Ozhogin, Liza, I myself, and a certain Bizmenkov, a minor official from the town of O——, a blond, good-natured, harmless personage. I'll have more to say about him later. Ozhogin himself had stayed at home; he'd gotten a headache from sleeping too much. The day was lovely—warm and calm. I should remark that pleasure gardens and social promenades don't appeal to the average Russian. You never meet a living soul at any time of the year in the so-called public gardens of district towns; at most, some old woman sits moaning and groaning on a green garden bench in the broiling sun, not far from a sickly tree—and then only if there's no greasy little plank to sit on in the gateway nearby. But if a scraggly grove of birch trees happens to be anywhere in the vicinity of a town, its tradespeople and even government officials eagerly make excursions to it on Sundays and holidays. They bring samovars, pies, and melons, set all this abundance on the dusty grass close to the road, then sit down in a circle and eat and drink tea, perspiring away until evening.

Just this sort of birch grove stood a mile and a half from the town of O—— at that time. We went there after dinner, duly drank our tea, and then all four of us began to stroll among the birches. Bizmenkov took Mrs. Ozhogin on his arm and I walked with Liza on mine. The day was already drawing toward evening. I was in the full flush of first love at that time (less than two weeks had passed since our first meeting), in that condition of passionate, concentrated adoration when your entire soul innocently and unconsciously follows every movement of your beloved, when you can never get enough of her presence or hear enough of her voice, when you smile with the look of a child recovering from an illness, and when a man with even the slightest worldly experience can't fail to recognize how you feel at one glance from a hundred yards away. I'd never had a chance to stroll with Liza on my arm until that day. We walked side by side, moving slowly across the green grass. A light breeze seemingly frolicked around us among the white trunks of the birches, blowing the ribbon on her hat into my face every now and then. I consistently looked where she looked until she finally turned toward me happily, and we smiled at one

another. The birds chirped approvingly up above us; the blue sky
peeped at us caressingly through the delicate foliage. My head was
spinning from an excess of bliss.

I hasten to note that Liza wasn't the least bit in love with me.
She liked me, and she was never shy around anyone. But it wasn't
reserved for me to trouble her childlike peace of mind—she walked
arm in arm with me as she would have walked with a brother. She
was seventeen at the time. . . . And meanwhile, that very evening,
before my eyes, began the quiet, inner ferment that precedes the
metamorphosis of a child into a woman. . . . I was a witness to that
total transformation, that guileless bewilderment, that anxious in-
trospection. I was the first to detect that sudden softness in her
gaze, that uncertain ring in her voice. And—oh, fool, oh, superfluous man!—for a whole week I had the audacity to imagine that
I, *I*, was the cause of this transformation.

This was how it happened.

We strolled for quite a long while, late into the evening, not
talking very much. I kept silent, like all inexperienced lovers, and
she probably didn't have anything to say to me. But she seemed
to be pondering something, and seriously shook her head as she
pensively nibbled on a leaf she'd picked. Sometimes she'd start to
walk straight ahead, ever so resolutely . . . then she'd suddenly stop
and wait for me, looking around with raised eyebrows and a distracted smile. The previous evening, we'd been reading *The Prisoner of the Caucasus* together—she'd listened to me with such
eagerness, her face propped on both hands and her bosom pressed
against the table! I began to talk about what we'd read; she blushed,
asked me whether I'd given the parrot any hempseed before we
left, began to hum some little song out loud, and then suddenly
fell silent again.

The birch grove ended at the edge of a rather high precipice; a
winding stream coursed below it, and beyond that, a boundless
meadow stretched into the distance, rising like waves in some
places, spreading wide like a tablecloth in others, broken here and
there by ravines. Liza and I reached the edge of the grove first;
Bizmenkov and the elderly lady lingered behind. We walked forward, stopped, and both involuntarily shielded our eyes. The sun
was setting directly across from us, looking huge and purple amid
a steamy mist. Half the sky was a fiery red; glowing rays fell
diagonally across the meadow, casting a crimson radiance even on
the sides of the ravines in the shadows, lying in streaks of flame

on the stream where it wasn't covered by overhanging bushes, and falling on the breast, as it were, of the precipice and the birch grove. We stood bathed in the blazing brilliance. I'm incapable of describing the completely overwhelming solemnity of this scene. They say that a blind person imagines the color red as the sound of a trumpet. I don't know the extent to which this comparison is justified, but there truly was something trumpetlike in the evening's gleaming light, in the incandescent glow of the earth and sky.

I uttered a cry of rapture and instantly turned toward Liza. She was looking straight at the sun. I remember that the glow of the sunset was reflected as little points of fire in her eyes. She was stunned—and profoundly moved. She didn't respond to my exclamation; she stood for a long while without stirring, her head bowed. . . . I held out my hand to her, but she turned away from me and suddenly burst into tears. I looked at her in secret, almost joyous perplexity. . . . Bizmenkov's voice became audible a few steps away. Liza quickly wiped away her tears and looked at me with a faltering smile. The elderly woman emerged from among the birches, leaning on the arm of her fair-haired escort; they admired the view in their turn. She addressed some question to Liza, and I remember that I couldn't help shuddering when her daughter's voice cracked like breaking glass as she replied. Meanwhile, the sun set and the glow began to fade. We turned back. I took Liza's arm in mine again. It was still light among the trees, and I could discern her features quite clearly. She was embarrassed, and didn't raise her eyes. The flush that had spread across her face hadn't disappeared— it was as though she were still standing in the rays of the setting sun. . . . Her hand barely touched my arm. I couldn't frame a sentence for a long while, my heart was beating so violently. The carriage could be glimpsed in the distance through the trees; the coachman was walking along the soft sand of the road to meet us.

"Elizaveta Kirillovna," I finally said, "why were you crying?"

"I don't know," she responded after a short silence. She looked at me with her gentle eyes, which were still wet with tears—her look struck me as somehow changed—and she fell silent again.

"You love nature, I see," I continued. That wasn't what I'd meant to say at all, and my tongue could barely finish forming the words. She shook her head. I couldn't utter another syllable. . . . I was waiting for something . . . not a confession—how could that have been possible? I was waiting for a trusting glance, for a question. . . . But Liza stared at the ground and remained silent. I repeated once more in a whisper, "Why?" and received no reply. I saw that she'd grown uncomfortable, almost ashamed.

A quarter of an hour later, we were sitting in the carriage, riding back to town. The horses proceeded at an even trot; we rolled along quickly through the darkening, damp evening. I suddenly began to talk, alternately addressing Bizmenkov and Mrs. Ozhogin. I didn't look at Liza, but I could see that her gaze never turned toward me as she sat musing in one corner of the carriage. She managed to rouse herself at home, but refused to read anything with me, and soon went off to bed. She'd reached a turning point, the turning point I've spoken about. She'd ceased to be a little girl, she'd also begun... like me... to wait for something. She didn't have long to wait.

But that night I went home to my lodgings in a state of absolute enchantment. The vague half-presentiment, half-suspicion that had been growing inside me had vanished. I ascribed the sudden constraint in Liza's behavior toward me to maidenly bashfulness, to timidity.... Hadn't I read a thousand times over in various books that the first appearance of love always upsets and frightens a young woman? I felt supremely happy and was already making various plans in my head....

If only someone had whispered in my ear then: "You're raving, my dear man! That's not what's ahead of you at all. What's ahead of you is to die alone in a wretched little cottage amid the insufferable grumblings of an old hag who'll impatiently await your death in order to sell your boots for a few copper coins...."

Yes, one can't help echoing a certain Russian philosopher: "How can one know what one doesn't know?"

Until tomorrow.

March 25. A white, winter day.

I reread what I wrote yesterday and nearly tore up the whole manuscript. I think my narrative is too long and too sentimental. However, since the remainder of my memories from that period of time contain nothing of a gratifying nature—except the peculiar sort of gratification Lermontov had in mind when he said that there's both pleasure and pain in irritating the scars of old wounds— why not indulge myself? But one must know where to draw the line. And so I'll continue without any sentimentality whatsoever.

During the entire week following the excursion to the grove, my situation didn't actually improve in any way, although the change in Liza became more perceptible every day. I interpreted this change, as I've already said, in the terms most favorable to me. . . . The misfortune of solitary, shy people—people who are shy due to self-consciousness—is precisely that, even though they have eyes, and even though they open them wide, they see nothing, or else they see everything in a false light, as though they were looking through tinted glasses. Their own conceptions and interpretations trip them up at every step. At the beginning of our acquaintance, Liza behaved confidingly and openly toward me, like a child; perhaps she may have even felt something more than mere childish affection for me. . . . But after this strange, almost instantaneous change had taken place in her, after a brief period of uncertainty, she began to feel constrained in my presence; she involuntarily turned away from me, and became sad and pensive at the same time. . . . She was waiting . . . for what? She herself didn't know . . . whereas I . . . I was delighted at this change, as I've said earlier. . . . Yes, by God, I was about to expire from rapture, as they say. To be sure, I'm ready to admit that anyone in my place might have been deceived. . . . Who among us has no pride? I needn't say that all this only became clear to me over the course of time, as I was forced to lower my clipped and ever-weaker wings.

The misunderstanding that had arisen between Liza and me lasted an entire week, and there's nothing surprising about that—I've witnessed misunderstandings that lasted for years and years. Who was it, by the way, who said that only truth is real? Lies have just as much life as truth, if not more so. Admittedly, I recall that even during this week I felt an uneasy gnawing sensation inside me from time to time . . . but solitary people like me, I say again, are as incapable of understanding what's occurring inside themselves as they are of comprehending what's taking place before their eyes. And besides, is love really a natural feeling? Is it typical of a human being to love? Love is a disease, and there's no law governing diseases. Granted, there was an unpleasant pang in my heart at times—but everything inside me had been turned upside down. And how can one know what's right and what's wrong, what's the cause and what's the significance of each separate symptom in such circumstances? In any event, all those misconceptions, presentiments, and hopes were shattered in the following manner.

One day—it was at around noon—I'd just entered Ozhogin's hallway when I heard an unfamiliar, resonant voice in the drawing room. The door opened and a tall, slender man of about twenty-five appeared in the doorway, escorted by the master of the house. He quickly put on a military overcoat that lay on a sideboard and cordially said goodbye to Kirill Matveich. As he brushed past me, he casually touched his cap and then disappeared with a clink of his spurs.

"Who was that?" I asked Ozhogin.

"Prince N—," he responded with a preoccupied expression, "who's been sent from Petersburg to assemble army recruits. But where are the servants?" he continued in an annoyed tone. "No one handed him his coat."

We went into the drawing room.

"Has he been here a long while?" I inquired.

"He arrived yesterday evening, they tell me. I offered him a room here, but he declined. He seems to be a very nice man, though."

"Did he visit with you for long?"

"About an hour. He asked me to introduce him to Olimpiada Nikitichna."

"And did you introduce him?"

"Naturally."

"And Elizaveta Kirillovna as well, did he...?"

"He met her, too—naturally."

I remained silent for a moment.

"Will he be staying here for long, do you know?"

"Yes, I believe he has to be here for over two weeks."

And Kirill Matveich hurried off to change clothes.

I paced around the drawing room several times. I don't recall Prince N—'s arrival making any special impression on me at the time, except by arousing the feeling of hostility that normally possesses us at the appearance of any new personage in our domestic circle. Possibly something like the envy of a shy, obscure individual from Moscow toward a brilliant officer from Petersburg was also mingled with this feeling. "The prince," I mused, "is an upstart from the capital. He'll look down on us...." I hadn't seen him for more than a minute, but I'd had time to observe that he was good-looking, suave, and self-assured. After pacing around the room for some time, I finally stopped in front of a mirror, pulled a comb out of my pocket, imparted a picturesque disorder to my hair, and, as sometimes happens, suddenly became absorbed in the contemplation of my own face. I remember that my attention anxiously centered on my nose—the soft, imprecise contours of that feature afforded me no particular satisfaction. All at once, in the dark depths of the sloping mirror that reflected virtually the entire room, I saw the door open; Liza's slender figure appeared. I don't know why, but I didn't move, maintaining the same expression on my face. Liza leaned her head forward and looked at me intently. Then, raising her eyebrows, biting her lips, and holding her breath the way someone who's glad not to be noticed does, she cautiously took one step back and quietly pulled the door toward her. The door creaked slightly. Liza shuddered and stood rooted to the spot. . . . I still didn't move. . . . She pulled the handle again, and vanished. There was no possibility of doubt: the expression on Liza's face at the sight of me, an expression in which nothing could be detected except a desire to retreat successfully, to escape an unpleasant encounter, the brief gleam of satisfaction I'd managed to catch in her eyes when she thought she'd actually be able to slip away unnoticed—it all spoke too clearly. This girl didn't love me. I couldn't take my eyes off that motionless, mute door, which had become merely a patch of white in the mirror once more, for a long, long while. I tried to smile at my own drawn face; I lowered my head, went back home, and flung myself on the sofa. I felt extraordinarily sick at heart, so much so that I couldn't cry . . . and, besides, what was there to cry about? . . . "Is it possible?" I repeated interminably, lying on my back as though I'd been murdered, my arms folded across my chest—"Is it possible?" . . . How do you like that expression, "Is it possible?"

March 26. Thaw.

The next day, when I entered the Ozhogins' familiar drawing room after much hesitation, with a sinking heart, I was no longer the same man they'd gotten to know during the previous three weeks. All my old habits, which I'd begun to overcome under the influence of a feeling I'd never known, suddenly reappeared and took possession of me, like proprietors returning to their home. People like me usually aren't guided so much by established facts as by their own impressions. I, who'd been dreaming about the "raptures of love requited" just the day before, was no less convinced of my "misfortune" that day, and was in utter despair, even though I myself couldn't find any rational basis for my despair. I couldn't be jealous of Prince N— as yet, and whatever his merits might be, his mere arrival wasn't sufficient to undermine Liza's predisposition toward me all at once. . . . But wait, had any predisposition on her part ever existed? I reviewed the past. "What about our stroll in the woods?" I asked myself. "Then what about the expression on her face in the mirror? But," I went on, "the stroll in the woods, it seems. . . . Shame on me! My God, what a wretched creature I am!" I finally exclaimed out loud. These were the sort of half-phrased, incomplete thoughts that swirled monotonously around and around in my head a thousand times. I repeat, I returned to the Ozhogins' the same hypersensitive, suspicious, constrained creature I'd been since childhood. . . .

I found the whole family in the drawing room; Bizmenkov was also sitting there in a corner. Everyone seemed to be in a good mood; Ozhogin in particular was positively beaming, and his first words informed me that Prince N— had spent the entire previous evening with them. Liza greeted me calmly. "Oh," I said to myself, "now I understand why you're in such a good mood." I confess that the prince's second visit puzzled me. I hadn't expected that. As a rule, people like me expect everything under the sun except that which is bound to occur in the natural order of things. I sulked, and adopted the air of an injured but magnanimous person. I tried to punish Liza by showing my displeasure—from which, however, one may conclude that I still wasn't completely desperate, after all. They say that in some cases, when one is truly beloved, it can be useful to torment the object of one's affections, but in my situation, it was inexpressibly stupid—Liza, in the most innocent possible way, paid no attention to me whatsoever. No one but Mrs. Ozhogin noticed my solemn silence, and she anxiously inquired as to my health. I replied with a bitter smile that I was, of course, perfectly well, thank God. Ozhogin continued to enlarge on the subject of their visitor, but, observing that I responded reluctantly, he addressed himself principally to Bizmenkov, who was listening to him with great attention when a servant suddenly came in to announce the arrival of Prince N—. Our host leaped up and rushed out to meet him. Liza, upon whom I immediately turned a sharp eye, flushed with delight and started to rise from her chair. The prince came in, attractively perfumed, cheerful, engaging. . . .

Since I'm not composing a romance for a well-disposed reader but simply writing for my own satisfaction, it stands to reason that I don't need to employ the usual literary devices favored by genteel authors. I'll say straight out, without further ado, that Liza had fallen passionately in love with the prince from the first day she'd

seen him, and that the prince had fallen in love with her, too—
partly because he had nothing else to do, partly due to a propensity
to flirt, and additionally as a result of the fact that Liza really was
a very charming creature. There was nothing surprising about their
falling in love with one another. He'd certainly never expected to
find such a pearl in such a wretched shell (I'm alluding to the
godforsaken town of O——), and never in her wildest dreams had
she seen anything even remotely resembling this distinguished,
witty, captivating aristocrat.

After the first pleasantries, Ozhogin introduced me to the prince,
who behaved most affably toward me. He was quite polite to everyone in general, and in spite of the immeasurable social distance
between him and our obscure provincial circle, he not only managed
to avoid being a source of constraint to anyone but even to appear
to be our equal, someone only living in St. Petersburg by accident,
as it were.

That first evening.... Oh, that first evening! In the happy days
of our childhood, teachers used to describe and hold up as an
example to us the manly fortitude of the young Spartan who, having
stolen a fox and hidden it under his tunic, allowed it to eat his
entrails without uttering a single shriek, thus preferring death itself
to disgrace.... I can find no better comparison to express my
unspeakable suffering during the evening when I first saw the
prince by Liza's side. My incessant, forced smile, my agonized
vigilance, my idiotic silence, my miserable and ineffectual desire
to get away—they were all quite possibly truly remarkable in their
own way. It wasn't just one wild beast that gnawed at my entrails:
jealousy, envy, a sense of my own insignificance, and helpless rage
all tortured me. I couldn't fail to admit that the prince really was
a most agreeable young man.... I devoured him with my eyes; I
believe I even forgot to blink as I stared at him. Liza wasn't the
only person he spoke to, of course, but everything he said was
actually for her alone. No doubt he considered me a terrible bore.
He probably soon guessed that he was encountering a rejected lover,
but out of sympathy for me, as well as a profound sense of my
utter innocuousness, he treated me with extraordinary benevolence.
You can imagine how this wounded me!

In the course of the evening, as I recall, I tried to smooth over
my earlier mistake. I swear to God (don't laugh at me, whoever
happens to scan these lines, especially since this was my final
illusion) ... I swear to God, in the midst of my various torments,

I suddenly imagined that Liza wanted to punish me for my deliberate coolness at the beginning of my visit, that she was angry with me, and that she was only flirting with the prince out of annoyance. . . . I seized an opportunity and went up to her with a meek but gracious smile, murmuring, "That's enough, forgive me . . . although I'm not saying this because I'm afraid"—and abruptly, without waiting for her reply, I donned an extraordinarily animated, carefree expression, laughed artificially, extended my hand above my head in the direction of the ceiling (I wanted to straighten my tie, as I recall), and was even about to pirouette on one foot, as though to say, "It's all over. I'm happy now, let's all be happy." I didn't execute this maneuver, however, because I was afraid of losing my balance as a result of some unnatural stiffness in my knees. . . . Liza thoroughly failed to comprehend me. She looked me in the face with amazement, gave me a hasty smile, as though she wanted to get rid of me as quickly as possible, and walked back over to the prince. As blind and deaf as I was, I couldn't help being inwardly aware that she wasn't the least bit angry and wasn't even annoyed with me at that moment—she simply never gave me a thought. The blow was a decisive one: my last hopes shattered with a crash, just the way a block of ice thawed by the spring sunshine suddenly crumbles into tiny pieces. I was totally defeated in the first skirmish and, like the Prussians at Jena, had lost everything all at once, in a single day. No, she wasn't angry with me! . . .

Alas, quite the contrary! She herself—I could see it—was being swept off her feet by a torrent. Like a young tree already half torn from the bank, she eagerly bent over the flood, ready to abandon the first blossom of her spring, of her entire life, to it forever. Whoever has happened to witness such a passion has lived through bitter moments, if he himself has loved and hasn't been loved in return. I'll always remember that ravenous attention, that tender merriment, that innocent self-oblivion, that gaze—still a child's and yet already a woman's—the joyous, almost blooming smile that never left her half-parted lips and glowing cheeks. . . . Everything that Liza had vaguely foreseen during our walk in the woods had now come to pass—and as she wholly gave herself over to love, she became calm and radiant at the same time, like new wine that ceases to ferment because it's reached its full maturity. . . .

I had the fortitude to sit through that first evening, and many subsequent evenings . . . all to the very end! I could entertain no

hope whatsoever. Liza and the prince became more and more attached to one another every day. . . . But I'd completely forsaken
all sense of personal dignity, and couldn't tear myself away from
the spectacle of my own misery. I remember that I tried not to go
there one day, swore to myself in the morning that I'd stay at home,
and at eight o'clock that evening (I usually left at seven) leaped
up like a madman, put on my hat, and breathlessly ran all the way
to Kirill Matveich's drawing room.

My situation was extraordinarily absurd. I remained obstinately
silent; sometimes I didn't utter a word for days at a time. As I've
already said, I was never noted for eloquence, but now every
thought I'd ever considered took flight, as it were, in the presence
of the prince, and I was stripped completely bare. Besides, when
I was alone, I made my wretched brain work so hard, painstakingly
reviewing everything I'd noticed or surmised the preceding day,
that when I returned to the Ozhogins', I barely had enough energy
left to observe anything anymore. They treated me considerately,
as though I were sick—I saw that. Every morning I adopted some
new, ultimate resolution, usually one tortuously formed during the
course of a sleepless night. Once, I made up my mind to confront
Liza, to give her friendly advice . . . but when I happened to be
alone with her, my tongue suddenly ceased to work, as if it had
frozen, and we both awaited the entrance of some third person in
great discomfort. Another time, I decided to run away—forever, of
course—leaving my beloved a letter filled with reproaches, and one
day I even began to write that letter, but a sense of justice hadn't
altogether disappeared within me as yet. I realized that I had no
right to reproach anyone for anything, and I threw what I'd written
into the fire. Still another time, I suddenly offered up my entire
self as a sacrifice and gave Liza my benediction, praying for her
happiness in love and smiling at the prince from a corner in meek,
friendly fashion. But the cruel-hearted lovers not only failed to
thank me for my self-sacrifice, they never even noticed it, and were
apparently perfectly ready to dispense with my smiles and my
benedictions. . . . Then, annoyed, I abruptly switched to the completely opposite mood. Wrapping my cloak around me like a Span-
iard, I promised myself that I'd spring from some dark corner and
stab my fortunate rival, and I imagined Liza's despair with ferocious
glee. . . . But, in the first place, there were few such corners in the
town of O——, and in the second place, the wooden fence, the
street lamp, the policeman in the distance. . . . No! It was somehow

much more suitable to sell buns and oranges in such corners than to shed human blood in them.

I must confess that, among my other means of deliverance—as I ever so vaguely put it in my conversations with myself—I considered turning to Ozhogin himself . . . calling the attention of that nobleman to his daughter's perilous situation, to the regrettable consequences of her indiscretion. . . . I even began to speak to him once about this delicate subject, but my remarks were so oblique and obscure that, after listening to me at length, he suddenly ran his hand across his face quickly and vigorously, not even sparing his nose, as if he were just waking up, gave a snort, and walked away from me. Needless to say, in resolving on this step, I'd persuaded myself that I was acting from the most disinterested motives, was desirous of the general welfare, and was doing my duty as a friend of the family. . . . But I suspect that even if Kirill Matveich hadn't cut short my outpourings, I still wouldn't have had the courage to finish my monologue. Sometimes I set to work with all the solemnity of an ancient sage, weighing the prince's merits; at other times I comforted myself with the hope that this was just a passing fancy, that Liza would come to her senses, that her love wasn't true love . . . oh, no! In short, I know of no idea over which I failed to fret at that time. There was only one possibility, I candidly admit, that never entered my head: I never once thought of taking my own life. I don't know why that didn't occur to me. . . . Perhaps even then I had a presentiment that I wouldn't have long to live in any case.

It's readily understandable that, under such unfavorable circumstances, my manner, my behavior toward people, was more unnatural and constrained than ever. Even Mrs. Ozhogin—that dull-witted creature—began to shun me, and didn't know how to treat me at times. Bizmenkov, ever polite and ready to perform any service, regularly avoided me. It even occurred to me at the time that I had a comrade in him—that he loved Liza as well. But he never responded to my hints and was generally reluctant to converse with me. The prince behaved toward him in a very friendly way— the prince respected him, one might say. Neither Bizmenkov nor I presented any obstacle to the prince and Liza, but Bizmenkov didn't distance himself from them the way I did, or look savage or injured—and readily joined them whenever they wanted. It's true that he didn't display any particular jocularity on such occasions, but his sense of humor had always been somewhat subdued.

About two weeks passed in this fashion. The prince wasn't merely handsome and intelligent—he played the piano, sang, sketched fairly well, and was a fine raconteur. His anecdotes, drawn from the highest circles of Petersburg society, always made a strong impression on his listeners, all the more so because he seemingly attached no special significance to them.....

As a result of this simple accomplishment, if you will, during his brief stay in the town of O—— the prince completely enchanted the entire population. Enchanting us poor steppe-dwellers is always an extremely easy task for anyone coming from a higher social sphere. The prince's frequent visits to the Ozhogins (he spent all his evenings there) naturally aroused the jealousy of the other worthy gentry and local officials. But the prince, like an intelligent man of the world, never neglected any of them: he called on all of them; he addressed at least one flattering phrase to every married old lady and every unmarried young lady; he let them feed him inordinately heavy meals and force him to drink horrible wines with magnificent names; he conducted himself, in short, like a model of diplomacy and tact. Prince N—— had a generally vivacious temperament, was sociable and courteous by inclination— and in these circumstances, incidentally, by calculation as well. How could he fail to succeed completely in every way?

Ever since his arrival, everyone in the house had felt time flying by with unusual speed. Everything was going beautifully. Even though Old Ozhogin pretended not to notice anything, he was doubtlessly rubbing his hands in private at the thought of such a son-in-law. The prince, for his part, was managing matters with the utmost sobriety and discretion when, all of a sudden, an unexpected incident....

Until tomorrow. I'm tired today. These memories irritate me even on the brink of the grave. Terentevna noticed today that my nose has already begun to grow sharp, and that, they say, is a bad sign.

March 27. Thaw continuing.

The situation stood as I've described it above: the prince and Liza were in love with each other; the elder Ozhogins were waiting to see what would come of it; Bizmenkov was also present at the proceedings—there was nothing else to be said about him. I was struggling like a fish on dry land, and watching out as well as I could—I remember that at the time I assigned myself the task of at least preventing Liza from falling into the snares of a seducer, and consequently began paying particular attention to the maid-servants and the fateful "back stairs"—although I nonetheless often spent entire nights dreaming about the touching magnanimity with which I'd hold out a hand to the betrayed victim one day and say to her: "That traitor has deceived you, but I'm your true friend. . . . Let's forget the past and be happy!"—when a joyous report suddenly began to circulate around the whole town: the marshal of the district intended to give a large ball on his private estate, Gornostaevka, also known as Gubniakovo, in honor of their respected guest. All the high and mighty officials in the town of O—— received invitations, from the mayor on down to the pharmacist, an extremely emaciated German with dreadful illusions about his ability to speak Russian properly, which caused him repeatedly and utterly inappropriately to employ what he took to be racy colloquialisms such as "The devil take me, I feel positively boyish today. . . . " Naturally, tremendous preparations got under way. One purveyor of cosmetics sold sixteen dark-blue jars of pomade, all of which bore the inscription *à la jesmin*. The young ladies provided themselves with close-fitting dresses, agonizingly tight at the waist and jutting out sharply over the abdomen; their mamas placed some formidable concoctions on their own heads in lieu of caps; their beleaguered papas were laid low, as they say, by all the fuss.

The longed-for day finally arrived. I was among those invited. It was about nine versts to Gornostaevka from town. Kirill Matveich offered me a seat in his carriage, but I refused. . . . Children who have been punished and want to wreak revenge on their parents refuse their favorite food at the dinner table in the same way. Besides, I felt that my presence might constrain Liza. Bizmenkov took my place. The prince went in his own carriage, and I rode in a wretched little cart I hired for an immense sum on this ceremonial occasion. I won't bother to describe that ball—everything about it was just as it should have been. There was an orchestra, including exceptionally off-key trumpets in the gallery; there were flustered country gentlemen accompanied by their inevitable families, lilac-colored ice cream, viscous lemonade, servants in worn-out boots and woven cotton gloves, provincial social lions with unpleasantly contorted faces, etc., etc. . . . And this entire little world revolved around its sun—the prince.

Lost in the crowd, unnoticed even by the forty-eight-year-old ladies with red blotches on their foreheads and blue flowers perched

on top of their hair, I incessantly stared alternately at the prince
and at Liza. She was most charmingly dressed, and looked very
pretty that evening. They only danced together twice (it's true, he
did dance the mazurka with her!), but it seemed to *me* at least that
there was some sort of secret, constant communication between
them. Even when he wasn't looking at her or speaking to her, he
still seemed to be addressing her and her alone. He was handsome,
brilliant, and charming to other people—for her sake alone. She was
evidently conscious that she was the queen of the ball and that she
was loved. Her face was beaming with childlike delight, with innocent pride, and at the same time was illuminated by some other,
deeper feeling as well. She radiated happiness. I noticed all of
this. . . . It wasn't the first time that I'd watched them. . . . At first,
this deeply wounded me, then it almost touched me, but eventually
it infuriated me. I suddenly felt extraordinarily wicked and, as I recall, was extraordinarily delighted at this new sensation—I even conceived a certain respect for myself. "We'll show them we're not
crushed yet," I said to myself.

When the first inviting notes of the mazurka sounded, I looked
around calmly and coolly, casually approached a long-faced young
lady who had a red, shiny nose, a mouth that hung open awkwardly,
as though it had become unhinged, and a sinewy neck reminiscent
of the handle on a double bass. I walked up to her and, with a
perfunctory click of my heels, invited her to join me during the
dance. She was wearing a pink dress, which looked as though it
had been sick recently and hadn't yet fully recovered; a striped,
dismal insect of some sort attached to a thick bronze pin quivered
atop her head. In general, if one may put it thus, this lady was
pierced through and through by some sort of embittered sense of
boredom and inveterate failure. She hadn't stirred from her seat
since the evening's outset; no one had even considered asking her
to dance. One blond youth of sixteen, lacking a partner, had been
on the verge of turning to this lady and had taken a step in her
direction, but had thought it over a bit, had glanced at her, and
had hurriedly dived back into the crowd. You can imagine the
joyful amazement with which she accepted my invitation! I solemnly led her across the entire ballroom, picked out two chairs,
and sat down with her among ten couples arranged in a circle for
the mazurka. We sat almost opposite the prince, who naturally had
been offered the lead position. The prince, as I've said already,
was paired with Liza.

Neither my partner nor I was disturbed by invitations to dance, and, as a result, we had plenty of time for conversation. To speak frankly, my partner wasn't distinguished by the capacity to articulate words coherently—she used her mouth primarily for the production of a strange, downward smile of a sort I'd never beheld until then, raising her eyes upward at the same time, as though some unseen force were pulling her face in different directions. But I didn't regret her lack of eloquence. Fortunately, I felt positively evil, and my partner didn't inhibit me. I started to criticize everything and everyone on earth, placing special emphasis on town-bred young men and Petersburg dandies, becoming so exercised at length that my partner gradually stopped smiling and, instead of raising her eyes upward, suddenly began to look strangely cross-eyed—from astonishment, I suppose—as though she'd just noticed for the first time that she had a nose on her face. And one of the social lions I referred to earlier, who was sitting next to me, kept glancing at me, and even turned toward me, wearing the facial expression of an actor on stage who has awakened in unfamiliar surroundings, as though to say, "Why are you here?"

While I poured forth my tirade, however, I still kept watch over Liza and the prince like a hawk, as they say. They were each repeatedly invited to dance, but I suffered less when they were both dancing, or even when they were sitting side by side and smiling the sweet smile that hardly ever leaves the faces of happy lovers as they talk to one another—even then, I wasn't so deeply tortured. But when Liza floated across the room with some dashing dandy while the prince pensively followed her with his eyes, holding her blue gauze scarf on his knees, as though he were delighting in his conquest, then, oh, then, I underwent intolerable agonies, and, in my frustration, I gave vent to such spiteful observations that the pupils of my partner's eyes became absolutely glued on her nose!

Meanwhile, the mazurka was drawing to a close. They were beginning a segment called *la confidente*. In this segment, one lady sits in the middle of a circle, chooses another lady as her confidante, and whispers in her ear the name of the gentleman with whom she wants to dance. Her partner conducts one dancer after another to her, but the lady who's been confided in refuses them until the lucky man who was chosen beforehand finally comes forth. Liza sat in the middle of the circle and chose the daughter of the host as her confidante, one of those young ladies about whom one says "God help them!"

The prince was commanded to find Liza's choice. After presenting about ten young men to her in vain (the host's daughter refused them all with the most amiable of smiles), he finally turned to me. Something unusual occurred inside me at that instant: I seemed to tremble all over and would have refused, but I stood up and stepped forward. The prince led me up to Liza . . . who didn't even look at me. The host's daughter shook her head in refusal, whereupon the prince glanced at me and, probably encouraged by the foolish expression on my face, bowed to me deeply. This sarcastic bow, the refusal transmitted to me by my triumphant rival, his casual smile, Liza's indifferent inattention—all this drove me to a frenzy. . . . I moved closer to the prince and whispered angrily, "You permit yourself to mock me, it seems?"

The prince looked at me with contemptuous surprise, took my arm again, and, pointedly conducting me back to my seat, responded coldly, "I?"

"Yes, you!" I continued in a whisper, while nonetheless obeying, that is, following him to my seat. "You. But I don't intend to allow any empty-headed Petersburg upstart. . . ."

The prince smiled tranquilly, almost condescendingly, pressed my arm, whispered, "I understand you, but this isn't the place. We'll have a word later on," turned away from me, went over to Bizmenkov, and led him up to Liza. The pale little official turned out to be the chosen partner. Liza stood up to greet him.

Sitting down beside my partner with the dismal insect on her head, I felt virtually heroic. My heart was beating violently, my breast was heaving gallantly under my starched shirt, I drew deep, rapid breaths—and I abruptly gave the social lion near me such a majestic glare that one of his feet involuntarily quivered. Having disposed of this individual, I scanned the entire circle of dancers. . . . I thought that two or three gentlemen were staring at me not without perplexity, but I concluded that my conversation with the prince hadn't been widely remarked. . . . My rival was already sitting in his chair looking perfectly composed, wearing the same smile on his face as before. Bizmenkov led Liza back to her seat. She gave him a friendly bow and immediately turned toward the prince with some alarm, it seemed to me. But he laughed in response, gracefully flourished his hand, and must have said something very pleasant to her, because she flushed with delight, lowered her eyes, and then directed them toward him again in affectionate reproach.

The heroic mood that had suddenly come over me hadn't disappeared by the end of the mazurka, but I didn't indulge in any more witticisms or criticisms. I merely occasionally glanced with glum severity at my partner, who was obviously beginning to be afraid of me and had become utterly tongue-tied. She was blinking continuously by the time I placed her under the protection of her mother, an obese woman with a red toque on her head. Having consigned the terrified young lady to her natural surroundings, I walked over to a window, folded my arms, and began to await whatever would happen. I had to wait a fairly long time. The prince was constantly surrounded by his host—surrounded just the way England is surrounded by the sea—to say nothing of the other members of the marshal's family and the rest of the guests. And besides, he could hardly go up to such an insignificant person as myself and begin to converse without arousing general surprise. This insignificance, I remember, even gave me pleasure at the time. "All right," I thought as I watched him courteously addressing first one and then another highly respected individual, each of whom was honored by his notice, even if it was only for a "fleeting moment," as the poets say. "All right, my dear sir. . . . You'll come and speak to me soon enough—for I've insulted you." Finally, somehow deftly escaping the throng of his admirers, the prince walked past me, looked somewhere between the window and my hair, started to turn away, and then stopped suddenly, as though he'd just remembered something. "Ah, yes!" he said, turning to me with a smile. "By the way, I have a small matter to discuss with you."

Two of the most persistent country gentlemen who were obstinately following the prince probably imagined that this "small matter" related to official business, and respectfully stepped backward. The prince took my arm and led me to one side. My heart was pounding against my ribs.

"You, it seems," he began, prolonging the word "you" and regarding my chin with a contemptuous expression that in a strange way was supremely becoming to his youthful, handsome face, "you said something rude to me?"

"I said what I thought," I replied, raising my voice.

"Shh . . . be quiet," he responded. "Decent people don't shout. Perhaps you'd like to fight a duel with me?"

"That's up to you," I answered, stiffening my posture.

"I'll be obliged to challenge you to one," he remarked casually, "if you don't retract your assertion. . . ."

"I don't intend to retract anything," I declared proudly.

"Really?" he retorted, not without a sardonic smile. "In that case," he continued after a brief pause, "I'll have the honor of sending my second to call on you tomorrow."

"Very well, sir," I agreed in as nonchalant a voice as possible. The prince bowed slightly.

"I can't prevent you from considering me empty-headed," he added, as he haughtily narrowed his eyelids, "but no one bearing the title of Prince N—— can be considered an upstart. Goodbye until we meet again, Mr. . . . Mr. Shtukaturin."

He quickly turned his back on me and returned to his host, who was already beginning to get worried.

Mr. Shtukaturin! . . . My name is Chulkaturin. . . . I couldn't find anything to say to him in response to this final insult, and could only glare at his back with fury. "Until tomorrow," I muttered, clenching my teeth, and I immediately started looking for an officer I was acquainted with, a cavalry captain in the Uhlans named Koloberdiaev, an incorrigible malingerer and a most genial fellow. I briefly told him about my quarrel with the prince and asked him to be my second. He promptly consented, naturally, and I went home.

I couldn't sleep all night—from excitement, not from cowardice. I'm not a coward. I actually didn't think much about the possibility of losing my life—that greatest good on earth, as the Germans assure us. I could only think about Liza, about my dashed hopes, about what I ought to do. "Should I try to kill the prince?" I asked myself. Of course, I wanted to kill him—not out of revenge, but out of my concern for Liza's welfare. "But she wouldn't survive a blow like that," I went on. "No, it'd be better to let him kill me!" I must confess that it was also pleasant to think that I, an obscure, provincial person, had forced such an important man to fight a duel with me.

Daybreak found me still absorbed in these reflections. Koloberdiaev appeared not long afterward.

"Well, where's the prince's second?" he asked, entering my room with a clatter.

"For heaven's sake," I responded with irritation, "it's seven o'clock at most. The prince is still asleep, I imagine."

"In that case," replied the undaunted cavalry officer, "order me some tea. I've had a headache since yesterday evening. . . . I haven't taken off my clothes all night. Although," he added, yawning, "I rarely take off my clothes in general."

My servant brought him some tea. He drank six glasses of tea with rum added to them, smoked four pipefuls of tobacco, told me that on the preceding day he'd bought a horse for next to nothing that some coachman refused to put in a harness, which he intended to harness with one of its forelegs tied up, and fell asleep on the sofa without undressing, his pipe dangling from his mouth. I got up and put my papers in order. I was going to put an invitation from Liza, the only note I'd ever received from her, in my breast pocket, but on second thought, I tossed it in a drawer. Koloberdiaev was snoring feebly, his head lolling on a leather pillow. . . . I scrutinized his unkempt, audacious, carefree, good-natured face for a long while, I remember. At ten o'clock, the servant announced Bizmenkov's arrival—the prince had chosen him as a second!

Together we awakened the soundly sleeping cavalry officer. He sat up, stared at us with bleary eyes, and hoarsely demanded vodka. He roused himself, and after exchanging greetings with Bizmenkov, went into the next room with him to arrange matters. The worthy seconds' consultation didn't last long. A quarter of an hour later, they both came into my bedroom. Koloberdiaev announced, "We're going to fight today at three o'clock, with pistols." I silently nodded my head to signal my approval. Bizmenkov immediately excused himself and departed. He was rather pale and inwardly agitated, like a man unaccustomed to such tasks, but was nonetheless perfectly polite and composed. I felt conscience-stricken, as it were, in his presence, and I couldn't look him in the eye. Koloberdiaev began telling me more about his horse. This conversation was most welcome to me—I was afraid that he'd mention Liza. But the good-natured cavalry officer wasn't a gossip, and moreover, he despised all women, referring to them as salad, God knows why. We had lunch at two o'clock, and by three, we'd reached the chosen spot—the very birch grove where I'd previously strolled with Liza, a few steps from the precipice.

We arrived first, but the prince and Bizmenkov didn't keep us waiting for long. It's no exaggeration to say that the prince was as fresh as a daisy. His brown eyes looked out from under the brim of his cap with extraordinary cordiality. He was smoking a cigar and, upon seeing Koloberdiaev, shook his hand warmly. He even bowed to me quite amiably. By contrast, I was conscious of being pale and of my hands trembling slightly, to my extreme vexation. . . . My throat was parched. . . . I'd never fought a duel before.

"Oh God," I thought, "if only that cynical gentleman doesn't take my agitation for fear!" I inwardly cursed my nerves, but when I finally looked straight at the prince's face and caught sight of an imperceptible smile on his lips, I suddenly became furious again, and immediately calmed down. Meanwhile, our seconds were setting up a barrier, counting out paces, and loading pistols. Koloberdiaev did most of it; Bizmenkov largely watched him. It was a glorious day—as glorious as the day of that unforgettable stroll. The intense blue of the sky shone through the golden verdure of the leaves, just as it had then. Their wind-stirred murmuring seemed to be mocking me. The prince went on smoking his cigar, leaning his shoulder against the trunk of a young lime tree. . . .

"Please take your places, gentlemen—everything's ready," Koloberdiaev eventually announced, handing us each a pistol.

The prince took a few steps away from the tree, stopped, and turning his head, asked me over his shoulder, "Do you still refuse to retract your words?"

I wanted to respond to him, but my voice failed me, and I satisfied myself with a contemptuous wave of the hand. The prince smiled again and assumed his position. We began approaching one another. I raised my pistol, was about to aim at my enemy's chest—but suddenly tilted it upward, as though someone had given my elbow a shove, and fired. The prince staggered and put his left hand up to his left temple—a thread of blood flowed down his cheek from under his white leather glove. Bizmenkov rushed over to him.

"It's nothing," he said, taking off his cap, which the bullet had pierced. "Since it's in the head and I haven't fallen down, it must be a mere scratch."

He calmly pulled a cambric handkerchief out of his pocket and pressed it against his blood-stained curls.

I stared at him as though I'd turned to stone, and didn't stir from the spot.

"Proceed to the barrier, please!" Koloberdiaev ordered sternly.

I obeyed.

"Should the duel go on?" he added, addressing Bizmenkov.

Bizmenkov didn't reply. But the prince, without taking the handkerchief away from his wound, without even giving himself the satisfaction of tormenting me at the barrier, proclaimed with a smile, "The duel is over," and fired into the air. I almost started to weep out of rage and frustration. This man had definitively trampled me in the mud, completely crushing me with his generosity of spirit. I was about to protest, to demand that he fire at me. But he came up to me and held out his hand.

"Everything between us can all be forgotten now, can't it?" he said in an amicable voice.

I looked at his pallid face, at the blood-stained handkerchief, and I squeezed his hand, thoroughly lost, ashamed, and humiliated.

"Gentlemen," he added, turning to the seconds, "I trust that all this will be kept secret?"

"Naturally!" cried Koloberdiaev. "But, Prince, allow me...."

And he himself bandaged the prince's head.

As he left, the prince bowed to me once more, but Bizmenkov didn't even glance at me. Destroyed—morally destroyed—I went home with Koloberdiaev.

"Why, what's the matter with you?" the cavalry captain asked me. "Don't worry, the wound isn't serious. He'll be able to dance by tomorrow, if he wants. Or are you sorry that you didn't kill him? You're wrong, if you are. He's a fine man."

"Why did he spare me?" I finally muttered.

"Oh, so that's it!" the cavalry captain said tranquilly.... "Oh, you authors are too much for me!"

I don't know what made him call me an author.

I absolutely refuse to describe my anguish during the evening following that unfortunate duel. My pride suffered inexpressibly. It wasn't my conscience that tortured me, it was the consciousness of my own idiocy that mortified me. "I, I alone have struck the final, conclusive blow upon myself!" I kept repeating as I strode up and down my room. "The prince, having been wounded by me and having forgiven me.... Yes, Liza belongs to him now. Nothing can save her now, nothing can hold her back at the edge of the abyss."

I knew very well that our duel couldn't be kept secret, in spite of the prince's words. In any case, it couldn't be kept secret from Liza. "The prince isn't such a fool," I mumbled in a frenzy of rage, "as to fail to make use of...." But, as it turned out, I was mistaken. The whole town found out about the duel and its true cause the very next day, of course—yet the prince hadn't bragged about it. On the contrary, when he appeared before Liza with his head bandaged and an explanation he'd prepared in advance, she'd already learned everything.... Whether Bizmenkov had given me away or the news had reached her by other means, I can't say. And indeed, can anything ever be concealed in a small town?

You can imagine how Liza welcomed him—how the entire Ozhogin family welcomed him! As for me, I suddenly became the object of universal scorn and loathing, a monster, a jealous, bloodthirsty madman. My few acquaintances shunned me as though I were a leper. The local authorities swiftly brought the prince a proposal to punish me in an appropriately severe manner. Nothing but the persistent, urgent entreaties of the prince himself averted the disaster that threatened me. That man was destined to humiliate me in every possible way. It was as if he'd fastened a coffin lid down over me by his magnanimity. Needless to say, the Ozhogins' doors were immediately closed to me. Kirill Matveich even returned a pencil I'd left at his house. In reality, he of all people had no cause to be angry with me. My "insane" (that was the term used around town) jealousy had brought out or clarified, so to speak, the prince's relationship to Liza. Not only the elder Ozhogins themselves but their fellow citizens began to look upon him as virtually engaged to her. In essence, this couldn't have been quite to his liking. But he was strongly attracted to Liza, and furthermore, he hadn't attained all his goals at that time. . . . He adjusted to his new position with all the agility of an intelligent man of the world and promptly entered into the spirit of his new role, as they say.

Whereas I . . . I renounced all of my own hopes for my future at that time. When suffering reaches the point of making one's entire being creak and groan like an overloaded cart, it ought to stop being laughable . . . but no! Laughter not only accompanies tears to the bitter end, to the point of exhaustion, when it's impossible to shed any more—it even echoes and reechoes after one's tongue has become mute and misery itself has faded away. . . . And so, in the first place, since I don't intend to make myself seem laughable, even to myself, and, in the second place, since I'm awfully tired, I'll defer the continuation and, please God, the conclusion of my story until tomorrow. . . .

March 29. A slight frost; yesterday it was thawing.

I didn't have the strength to go on with my diary yesterday. Like Poprishchin, I lay on my bed most of the time and talked to Terentevna. What a woman! Sixty years ago she lost her first fiancé during the plague, she's outlived all her children, is inexcusably old, drinks tea to her heart's content, is well fed and warmly clothed—and what do you suppose she spent all day yesterday talking to me about? I'd sent another, utterly destitute elderly woman the collar of an old, half moth-eaten jacket to put on her vest (she places strips of cloth across her chest as a vest)...and why hadn't I given it to her? "Since I'm your nurse, it seems....Oh...oh, your honor, it's sinful of you...after I've taken care of you the way I have!..." and so on. The merciless old woman completely wore me out with her reproaches....But to get back to my story.

And so I suffered like a dog whose hindquarters have been run over by a wheel. It was only then, only after my banishment from the Ozhogins' house, that I fully realized how much satisfaction a man can extract from the contemplation of his own unhappiness. Oh human beings! What a pitiful race!...But so much for philosophical reflections....I spent my days in total solitude and could only find out what was going on in the Ozhogin household and what the prince was doing by the most indirect and even humiliating methods. My servant had become acquainted with the cousin of the prince's coachman's wife. This acquaintance afforded me some relief, for my servant quickly deduced from my hints and little presents what he should talk about while pulling his master's boots off every evening. I occasionally happened to encounter some member of the Ozhogin family or Bizmenkov or the prince on the street....I bowed to the prince and to Bizmenkov, but I didn't enter into conversation with them. I saw Liza only three times: once with her mother in a dress shop; once with her father and mother and the prince in an open carriage; and once in church. Naturally, I didn't dare approach her, and merely observed her from a distance. In the shop, she was quite preoccupied, but cheerful....She was ordering something for herself, and was busily matching ribbons. Her mother was gazing at Liza with her hands in her lap and her nose in the air, smiling the foolish, devoted smile that's permissible only in doting mothers. In the carriage with the prince, Liza was...I'll never forget that encounter! The older people were sitting in the back of the carriage, the prince and Liza in the front. She was paler than usual; a patch of pink was barely visible on each of her cheeks; she was half-facing the prince. Leaning on her right arm, which was straight (she was holding a parasol in her left hand), her little head drooping languidly, she was looking directly at his face with her expressive eyes. At that instant, she was utterly surrendering herself to him, entrusting herself to him forever. I didn't have time to get a good look at his face—the carriage rolled by too rapidly—but it seemed to me that he, too, was deeply moved.

The third time I saw her was in church. Not more than ten days had passed since I'd seen her in the carriage with the prince, not more than three weeks since the day of my duel. The business on which the prince had come to O—— had already been completed, but he kept putting off his departure. In Petersburg, he was reported to be sick; in town, it was expected daily that he'd make a formal proposal to Kirill Matveich. I myself was only awaiting this final blow before going away forever—the town of O—— had grown abhorrent to me. I couldn't stay indoors, and wandered in the outlying areas from morning to night. One gray, inclement day, as I was returning from a walk that had been cut short by rain, I stopped in at a church. The evening service had just begun; very few people were there. I looked around and suddenly, near a window, glimpsed a familiar profile. I didn't recognize it at first: that pale face, that listless gaze, those sunken cheeks—could this be the same Liza I'd seen two weeks earlier? Wrapped in a cloak, bareheaded, illuminated on one side by the cold light falling from a broad white window, she was staring at the icons and seemed to be trying to pray, trying to awaken from some sort of despondent stupor. A red-cheeked, plump little servant boy with yellow squares on his jacket was standing near her, his arms crossed behind his back, watching his mistress in sleepy bewilderment. I trembled all over and started to go up to her, but stopped short. A painful sense of foreboding restrained me. Liza didn't move until the very end of the evening service. All the other people left, a deacon began to sweep the church, but she never stirred from her place. The servant boy went up to her, said something, and touched her dress; she looked around, ran her hand across her face, and went out. I followed her home at a distance, then returned to my lodgings.

"She's been vanquished!" I cried when I got to my own room.

On my honor, I don't know to this day what my sensations were at that moment. I remember that I threw myself onto the sofa with clasped hands and stared at the floor. But—I don't know—in the midst of my misery, I was seemingly pleased at something. . . . I wouldn't admit this for anything in the world if I weren't writing for myself alone. . . . To be sure, I'd been tormented by horrible, agonizing presentiments . . . and—who knows?—perhaps I'd have been deeply disconcerted if they hadn't been fulfilled. "Such is the human heart!" some middle-aged Russian pedagogue would exclaim in an expressive voice at this point while raising a fat forefinger adorned with a cornelian ring. But what difference does the opinion of a Russian pedagogue with an expressive voice and a cornelian ring on his finger make to us?

Be that as it may, my presentiments proved to be well founded. The news suddenly spread all over town that the prince had left, presumably in response to a summons from Petersburg, that he'd left without discussing any proposal of marriage with either Kirill Matveich or his wife, and that it merely remained for Liza to deplore his treachery until the end of her days. The prince's departure was utterly unexpected, because just the evening before, so my servant assured me, his coachman hadn't had the slightest suspicion as to his master's intentions. This piece of news threw me into a feverish excitement. I immediately got dressed and was about to rush off to the Ozhogins', but, on thinking the matter over, I deemed it more appropriate to wait until the next day.

I lost nothing by remaining at home, however. That very evening, a man named Pandopipopulo dropped in briefly to visit me. He was an itinerant Greek, stranded by accident in the town of O——, a scandalmonger of the first order who'd been more indignant toward me about my duel with the prince than anyone else. He didn't even give my servant time to announce his arrival—he practically burst into my room, warmly shook my hand, begged my pardon a thousand times, called me a paragon of nobility and courage, depicted the prince in the darkest colors, condemned the elder Ozhogins who, in his opinion, had been deservedly punished, made some dismissive reference to Liza in passing, and hurried off again after kissing me on the shoulder. Among other things, I learned that on the eve of his departure, in response to a delicate hint from Kirill Matveich, the prince, *en vrai grand seigneur,* had coldly replied that he had no intention of deceiving anyone and wasn't thinking of getting married, had risen, bowed in farewell— and that was all. . . .

I went to the Ozhogins' the next day. At my appearance, the partially blind footman leaped up from his bench with the speed of lightning. I sent him off to announce my arrival; he hurried away and promptly returned. "Please come in," he said. "You're cordially invited to come in." I went into Kirill Matveich's study. . . . Until tomorrow.

March 30. Frost.

And so I went into Kirill Matveich's study. I'd handsomely pay anyone who could show me right now what my face looked like at the moment when that highly respected official approached me with outstretched arms after hurriedly buttoning his jacket. I must have positively exuded self-effacing triumph, indulgent sympathy, and boundless benevolence. . . . I felt somewhat like Scipio Africanus. Ozhogin was visibly embarrassed and saddened—he avoided my gaze and continually fidgeted. I also noticed that he somehow spoke unnaturally loudly and generally expressed himself quite vaguely. He vaguely but warmly begged my forgiveness, vaguely alluded to their departed guest, vaguely added a few general remarks about deception and the inconstancy of earthly blessings, and, suddenly sensing tears in his eyes, hurriedly took a pinch of snuff, probably in an attempt to deceive me as to the cause of his tearfulness. . . . He used green Russian snuff, and it's well known that this substance forces even old men to shed tears that make the human eye look dull and senseless for several minutes.

I behaved quite circumspectly with the elderly man, naturally, inquiring about the health of his wife and daughter and then artfully turning the conversation to the fascinating subject of crop rotation. I was dressed in the usual manner, but the feelings of delicate propriety and benign condescension coursing through my veins gave me a refreshed, festive sensation, as though I were wearing a formal white vest and white tie. Only one thing disturbed me— the thought of seeing Liza. . . . Ozhogin himself finally proposed to escort me in to see his wife. This kindhearted but foolish woman was terribly embarrassed upon seeing me at first, but her brain wasn't capable of maintaining the same condition for long, so she quickly became at ease. Finally I saw Liza. . . . She entered the room. . . .

I'd expected to find her a shamefaced, penitent sinner, and had adopted a most affectionate, reassuring expression beforehand. . . . Why lie about it? I truly loved her and was thirsting for the happiness of forgiving her, of holding out my hand to her. But, to my unspeakable astonishment, she laughed coldly in response to my meaningful bow, remarked indifferently, "Oh, is that you?" and immediately turned her back on me. It's true that her laugh struck me as forced, and didn't accord with her terribly thin face in any case . . . but all the same, I hadn't expected such a reception. . . . I looked at her in astonishment. . . . What a transformation had taken place in her! There was nothing in common between the child she'd been and the woman in front of me now. She seemed to have grown up, to have become taller. All her facial features, especially her lips, seemed to have become more defined . . . her gaze had grown deeper, harder, and darker. I stayed at the Ozhogins' until dinnertime. She stood up, left the room, and reentered it several times, answering questions with composure and deliberately ignoring me. I saw that she wanted to make me feel I wasn't even worth her anger, although I'd nearly killed her lover. I finally lost my temper, and a spiteful allusion fell from my lips. . . . She shuddered, glanced at me swiftly, stood up, and, going over to the window, declared in a slightly tremulous voice, "You can say anything you please, but be aware that I love this man, and will always love him, and don't consider him to blame toward me in any way—quite the contrary. . . ." Her voice broke, she stopped. . . . She tried to control herself but failed, burst into tears, and ran out of the room. . . . The elderly couple became very upset. . . . I squeezed their hands, sighed, turned my eyes heavenward, and withdrew.

I'm too weak, I have too little time left—I'm not in a condition to describe in detail the new series of torturous reflections, firm resolutions, and other products of so-called inner conflict that manifested themselves within me after the renewal of my acquaintance with the Ozhogins. I didn't doubt that Liza still loved the prince, and would love him for a long time . . . but, as someone reconciled to the inevitable and anxious to be conciliatory, I didn't even dream of her love. I wanted only her friendship; I wanted to gain her confidence and her respect, which, we're assured by people of experience, forms the soundest basis for happiness in marriage. . . .
Unfortunately, I'd lost sight of one rather important fact, namely, that Liza had hated me ever since the day of the duel. I found this out too late.

I began to be a frequent visitor at the Ozhogins, as before. Kirill Matveich welcomed me more effusively and affably than ever. I even have reason to believe that he would have cheerfully permitted me to marry his daughter at that time, although I certainly wasn't a desirable fiancé. Public opinion was very severe toward him as well as Liza, whereas it extolled me to the skies. Liza's attitude toward me remained unchanged. For the most part, she kept silent. She obeyed when they begged her to eat, and showed no outward signs of sorrow, but nonetheless was melting away like a candle.

I must give Kirill Matveich credit by noting that he spared her in every possible way. Old Mrs. Ozhogin just ruffled up her feathers like a hen whenever she looked at her poor nestling. There was only one person Liza didn't avoid, although she didn't talk much even to him, and that was Bizmenkov. The elderly couple were rather abrupt, not to say rude, in their behavior toward him—they couldn't forgive him for having been a second at the duel. But he continued to visit them as though he didn't notice their lack of cordiality. He was very cool toward me and—strangely enough—I was almost afraid of him.

This state of affairs continued for about two weeks. Finally, after a sleepless night, I resolved to confront Liza, to open my heart to her, to tell her that in spite of the past, in spite of all the potential gossip and scandal, I'd consider myself only too happy if she'd give me her hand in marriage and restore her trust in me. I really imagined in all seriousness that I was showing what textbooks call an unparalleled example of nobility, and that she would consent from sheer amazement. In any case, I resolved to confront her and end my suspense once and for all.

There was a rather large garden behind the Ozhogins' house that ended at a little grove of neglected, overgrown lime trees. An old Chinese-style pavilion stood in the middle of this grove. A wooden fence separated the garden from a dead-end path. Liza sometimes walked in this garden for hours on end. Kirill Matveich knew this, and forbade everyone from disturbing or following her—let her grief wear itself out, he said. When they couldn't find her indoors, they merely had to ring a bell on the steps at dinnertime and she'd appear immediately, the same stubborn silence on her lips and in her eyes, with some tiny leaf crushed in her hand. Thus, noticing that she wasn't inside the house one day, I indicated my intention to leave, said goodbye to Kirill Matveich, put on my hat, went from the hallway out into the courtyard and from the courtyard out into the street, but promptly darted back through the gate with unusual rapidity and hurried past the kitchen into the garden. Luckily, no one noticed me. Not wasting any time in thought, I entered the grove with quickened steps.

Liza was standing on a little path right in front of me. My heart was pounding violently. I stopped, drew a deep breath, and was just about to go up to her, when suddenly, without turning around, she lifted her head and began to listen. . . . From behind the trees, in the direction of the dead-end path, came the distinct sound of two taps, as though someone were knocking on the fence. Liza clapped her hands together, the faint creak of a gate was audible, and Bizmenkov emerged from the grove. I hastily hid behind a tree. Liza turned toward him without speaking. . . . Without speaking either, he drew her arm under his, and the two of them started to walk slowly along the path. I watched them in astonishment. They stopped, looked around, disappeared behind some bushes, reappeared, and eventually went into the pavilion. This pavilion was a diminutive, round edifice with a door and one little window. An old, one-legged table covered with fine green moss stood in the middle of it; two discolored benches made of boards sat along the sides at a certain distance from the damp, darkened walls. They used to have tea here on exceptionally hot days, perhaps once a year or so, in earlier times. The door didn't quite shut, the window-frame had fallen out of the window a long while ago and, remaining attached just at one corner, was hanging down disconsolately, like a bird's broken wing. I snuck up to the pavilion and peered cautiously through a hole in the window. Liza was sitting on one of the benches with her head bowed. Her right hand was lying on one knee while Bizmenkov was holding her left one in both of his. He was gazing at her sympathetically.

"How are you today?" he asked in a low voice.

"The same as ever," she replied, "neither better nor worse. The emptiness, the awful emptiness!" she added, raising her eyes despondently.

Bizmenkov didn't say anything.

"What do you think?" she went on. "Will he write to me one more time?"

"I don't think so, Elizaveta Kirillovna!"

She was silent for a time.

"And after all, what would he have to say? He told me everything in his first letter. I never could have been his wife, but I've been happy . . . not for long . . . but I've been happy. . . ."

Bizmenkov looked down.

"Ah," she continued with energy, "if you only knew how I detest that Chulkaturin. . . . I always seem to see . . . his blood . . . on that man's hands." (I shuddered behind the hole.) "Although, who knows," she added thoughtfully, "maybe, if it hadn't been for that duel. . . . Ah, when I saw that he'd been wounded, I instantly felt that I was utterly his."

"Chulkaturin loves you," observed Bizmenkov.

"What difference does that make to me? Do I want anyone's love?..." She stopped and added slowly, "Except yours. Yes, my friend, I need your love. I would have perished without you. You've helped me bear some terrible moments...."

She fell silent.... Bizmenkov began stroking her hand with fatherly tenderness.

"What else can I do, what else can I do, Elizaveta Kirillovna?" he repeated several times.

"And even now," she continued in a hollow voice, "I'd die, I think, if it weren't for you. Your support alone is sustaining me. Besides, you remind me of him.... You knew all about it, you see. Do you remember how wonderful he was that day?... But forgive me. It must be hard for you...."

"Go on, go on! Nonsense! God bless you!" Bizmenkov interrupted her.

She squeezed his hand.

"You're very kind, Bizmenkov," she went on. "You're angelically kind. What can I do? I believe I'll love him until I die. I've forgiven him—I'm even grateful to him. May God grant him happiness! May God send him a wife after his own heart"—and her eyes filled with tears. "If only he won't forget me, if only he'll occasionally remember his Liza!... Let's go," she added after a brief pause.

Bizmenkov raised her hand to his lips.

"I know," she began again heatedly, "everyone's blaming me now, everyone's casting stones at me. Let them! I wouldn't exchange my misery for their happiness, anyway.... No! No!... He didn't love me for long, but he did love me! He never deceived me, he never told me I'd be his wife, and I never contemplated it myself. It was only poor Papa who hoped for that. And even now, I'm not altogether unhappy—I still have my memories, and however horrible the consequences.... I'm suffocating in here.... It was here that I saw him for the last time.... Let's go out into the fresh air."

They stood up. I barely had time to slip to one side and hide behind a thick lime tree. They came out of the pavilion and, as far as I could tell from the sound of their footsteps, went off into the grove. I don't know how long I remained standing there without stirring from the spot, enmeshed in some sort of mindless confusion, when I suddenly heard footsteps again. I shivered and cautiously peeked out from my hiding place. Bizmenkov and Liza were coming back along the same path. They both looked extremely agitated, especially Bizmenkov. He seemed to be crying. Liza stopped, looked at him, and then distinctly uttered the following words: "I accept, Bizmenkov. I never would have accepted if you were merely trying to save me, to rescue me from a horrible situation, but you do love me, you know everything—and you do love me. I'll never find a more trustworthy, true friend. I'll be your wife."

Bizmenkov kissed her hand. She smiled at him sadly and walked toward the house. Bizmenkov hurried off into the grove, and I went on my way. Since Bizmenkov had apparently said to Liza precisely what I'd intended to say to her, and since she'd given him precisely the reply I'd wanted to hear from her, there was no need for me to concern myself any further. She married him within two weeks. The elder Ozhogins were thankful to find any husband for her.

Well, tell me, aren't I a superfluous man? Didn't I play the role of a superfluous individual throughout the entire affair? The prince's role . . . there's nothing more to be said about that. Bizmenkov's role is equally comprehensible. . . . But mine? Why was I mixed up in it? . . . An idiotic fifth wheel on the cart! . . . Ah, this is bitter, this is bitter for me! . . . But then, as the barge haulers say, "One more heave, and then one more"—one more day, and then one more, and nothing will be either bitter or sweet for me any longer.

March 31.

I'm not well. I'm writing these lines in bed. There's been a sudden change in the weather since yesterday evening. It's hot today—it's almost summery. Everything is thawing, breaking apart, streaming with water. The air is filled with the odor of exposed earth—a strong, heavy, stifling odor. Steam is rising on all sides. The sun seems to be beating down so hard that it could shatter everything. I'm not well. I sense that I'm decomposing.

I wanted to write a diary, and instead of that, what did I do? I related one incident from my life. I chattered away—dormant memories awakened and distracted me. I've written without haste, in detail, as though I had years ahead of me. And now there's no time to continue. Death, death is coming. I can already hear its menacing crescendo. It's time. . . . It's time. . . .

And indeed, what difference does it make? Isn't it all the same, no matter what I write? In sight of death, the final earthly cares disappear. I feel that I'm growing calm—I'm becoming simpler and clearer. I've gotten a grip on myself too late!...It's a strange thing! I'm growing calm—I definitely am—and at the same time...I'm afraid. Yes, I'm afraid. Hanging halfway over the silent, yawning abyss, I shudder and turn away, then begin to examine everything around me with avid attention. Every object is doubly precious to me now. I can't gaze enough at my impoverished, cheerless room, saying farewell to each little spot on my walls. Drink your fill for the last time, my eyes. Life is retreating— it's receding from me smoothly and gradually, the way the shore recedes from the eyes of a sailor. My nurse's old jaundiced face tied up in a dark kerchief, the hissing samovar on the table, the geranium pot in the window, my poor dog, Tresór, the pen I'm writing these lines with, my own hand—I can see you all now...here you are, right here....Is it possible that...perhaps even today...I'll never see you again? It's hard for a living creature to part with life! Why are you fawning over me, poor dog? Why are you pressing your chest up against the bed, wagging your stumpy tail so violently and keeping your kind, doleful eyes fastened on me the whole time? Are you sorry for me? Or do you already sense that your master will be gone soon? Ah, if only I could mentally review all my memories the way I've visually reviewed all the objects in my room. I know that these memories are melancholy and inconsequential, but I have no others. "The emptiness, the awful emptiness!"—as Liza said.

Oh my God, my God! I'm dying right now....A heart capable of loving and ready to love will shortly cease to beat....And will it actually remain stilled forever, never having known happiness, never having expanded with joy? Alas! It's impossible, it's impossible, I know....If only now, at least, prior to my death—for death is nonetheless a sacred thing, elevating every living being—if some lovely, mournful, friendly voice would sing a farewell song over me, a song of my own sadness, perhaps I could become resigned to it. But to die silently, stupidly....

I think I'm beginning to rave.

Farewell, life! Farewell to you, my garden, and to you, my lime trees! When summer comes, be sure you don't forget to cover yourself with flowers from head to toe....May it be pleasant for people to lie in your fragrant shade on the new grass, under the soft murmur of your leaves as they're slightly stirred by the wind. Farewell, farewell! Farewell to everything, forever!

Farewell, Liza! I wrote those two words—and almost laughed

aloud. This exclamation seems so bookish. It's as though I were writing a sentimental novel or concluding a despairing letter. . . .
Tomorrow is April first. Will I really die tomorrow? Somehow that would be too unseemly. And yet it's appropriate for me. . . . How the doctor did chatter away today!. . .

                                                              April 1.
It's all over. . . . Life is over. I'm definitely going to die today. It's hot outside . . . almost suffocating . . . or is it that my lungs are already refusing to breathe? My little comedy has been played out. The curtain is falling.

Having been destroyed, I cease to be superfluous. . . .

Ah, how bright the sun is! Those mighty rays betoken eternity. . . .

Farewell, Terentevna! . . . This morning she was crying as she sat by the window . . . perhaps because of me . . . and perhaps because she'll have to die soon herself. I've made her promise not to destroy Tresór.

It's hard for me to write. . . . I'll put down my pen. . . . It's high time! Death is already approaching with a growing rumble, like a carriage on the pavement at night. It's here, it's wafting over me like the light breath that made the prophet's hair stand on end. . . .

I'm dying. . . . Live, you who are living!

> And around the grave
> May youthful life rejoice
> And indifferent nature
> Glow with eternal beauty.

Note from the Editor.[1] Under this final line appeared a head drawn in profile with a large tuft of hair, a moustache, eyes *en face,* and eyelashes like rays. Below the head, someone had written the following words:

> This manuscript was read
> And the Contents of It Not Approved
> Petr Zudoteshin
> M M M M
> My Dear Sir
> Petr Zudoteshin.
> My Dear Sir.

But since the handwriting of these lines wasn't the least bit like

the handwriting in which the other part of the manuscript was
written, the editor considers himself justified in concluding that
the above lines were added subsequently by some other person,
especially since he (the editor) has learned that Mr. Chulkaturin
actually did die during the night between the first and second of
April in 18—— at his native home in Sheep's Springs.

1. A fictional editor created by Turgenev.

Letter to Louis and Pauline Viardot[1]

To *Monsieur and Madame Viardot.*

St. Petersburg.
May 1, 1852.

My dear friends,

This letter will be delivered to you by a person who is leaving here in a few days . . . or else he will send it to Paris after having crossed the border, so that I may have a little talk with you frankly and without fearing the curiosity of the police.

I will begin by telling you that if I didn't leave St. Petersburg a month ago, it was entirely against my will. I am under arrest at a police station, by order of the emperor, for having had an article published, a few lines about Gogol in a Moscow journal. That was only a pretext; the article in itself was absolutely insignificant. I've been looked at askance for some time. They latched on to the first occasion that presented itself. I have no complaint with the emperor. The affair was presented to him in such a vile way that he couldn't have acted otherwise. They wanted to forbid anything's being said about Gogol's death, and they weren't sorry to put an embargo on my literary activity at the same time.

In fifteen days I'll be sent from here to the country, where I'll have to remain until a new order comes. None of this is very cheerful, as you can see; I must say, however, that I'm being treated very humanely; I have a good room, books; I can read. I was able to see people during the early days. Now that's been forbidden, because too many people were coming. Misfortune doesn't make one's friends flee, even in Russia. The *misfortune*, to tell the truth, isn't so great. The year 1852 won't have had a springtime for me, and that's all. What's saddest in all this is that I have to say a definitive farewell to any hope of taking a trip outside the country, but I never had any illusions on that score. I knew well, when I left you, that it was for a long time, if not forever. Now I have only one desire, that I be permitted to come and go inside Russia. I hope I won't be refused that.

---

1. The original of this letter is in French. Pauline Viardot (née Garcia) (1821–1910) was one of the most important singers of the nineteenth century. She married Louis Viardot in 1840. Whether Turgenev and Pauline were ever in fact lovers is a question that probably will never be answered. It is clear, however, that she was the single most important person in Turgenev's life.

The heir apparent is very kind. I've written him a letter from which I expect some good to come. You know that the emperor has left.

My papers have been sealed, or rather, they sealed the doors of my apartment, which they opened ten days later without having examined anything. It's likely that they knew they wouldn't find anything forbidden there.

I have to admit that I'm reasonably bored in this hole of mine. I'm making use of the enforced leisure by working on Polish, which I began studying six weeks ago. I have fourteen days of incarceration left. I'm counting them, believe me!

So, my dear friends, this is the news, hardly pleasant, that I have to give you. I hope the news you give me will be better. My health is good, but I've aged ridiculously. I could send you a lock of white hair—that's no exaggeration. But I'm not losing my courage. *Hunting* awaits me in the country! Then I'm going to try to put my affairs in order. I'll continue my studies of the Russian people, the strangest and most astonishing people in the world. I'll work on my novel with all the more freedom of spirit, since I won't think of its passing through the claws of censorship. My arrest is probably going to make the publication of my work in Moscow impossible. I regret that, but what can I do about it?

I beg you to write me often, my dear friends—your letters will play a large role in giving me courage during this time of trials. Your letters and the memory of days spent at Courtavenel, those are all my worldly possessions. I won't linger on this topic for fear of being too moved. You know well that my heart is with you. I can say that now, especially. . . . My life is finished, the charm in it is gone. I've eaten all my white bread; we'll chew what's left of the brown bread, and we'll pray that heaven will be "very kind," as Vivier said.

I have no need to tell you that all of this must remain a complete secret; the slightest mention, the slightest allusion in a newspaper, would be enough to do me in.

Farewell, my dear and kind friends; be happy, and your good fortune will make me as happy as I can be. Be of good health, don't forget me, write me often, and be assured that my thoughts are with you always. I kiss you all, and I send you a thousand blessings. Dear Courtavenel, I salute you as well! Write me often. I kiss you again. Farewell!

Your
Iv. Tourguéneff

Letter to O. A. Turgeneva[1]

Petersburg.
January 6, 1855.

Olga Aleksandrovna, allow me first of all to thank you for your decision to write me. I've been waiting to have a frank talk with you for a long time, but without your letter, our relations would have probably ended mutely and hollowly. I thank you for your faith and confidence—I especially thank you for giving me the opportunity to express to you those feelings of sincere admiration and heartfelt friendship with which you have inspired me and which I hope to keep forever.

You ask *my* forgiveness ... but of the two of us, Olga Aleksandrovna, of course I alone am at fault. I am older than you, it's my duty to think for both of us; I shouldn't have allowed myself to yield to an uncontrolled enthusiasm, and I especially ought not to have let you notice it until I myself realized clearly what sort of enthusiasm it was ... I shouldn't have forgotten that you were risking a lot—I, nothing at all. And nonetheless—I did all of that! At my age it's absurd to use the rashness of my first inclinations as a justification—but I can't imagine any other justification, because it's the only real one. When I became convinced that the feeling that was in me had begun to alter and grow weaker—even then I behaved badly. Instead of indulging in those idiotic, splenetic pranks you endured with such simplicity and gentleness, I should have left at once. You see that I alone am to blame—and only the feminine, moreover, only the virginal magnanimity of a pure soul could even go so far as not to reproach a person who had done all of this—and practically to blame herself!

You ask me not to *hate* you ... but I would consider myself the most worthless person if only I didn't respect you! Believe me— I'm able to appreciate your worth, and in spite of everything that happened, I still consider my acquaintance with you one of the happiest incidents of my life. Now my main duty is to avoid frequent meetings and close relations with you. We must put a stop to the rumors and gossip, the cause of which was my conduct. But I'd be sincerely grieved if you attributed my present estrangement from you to any other reason. ... On the contrary, I dare to hope that when all of this settles down, we'll grow close again—if you yourself

---

1. Olga Aleksandrovna Turgeneva (1836-72) was a distant relative of the author. Turgenev had a short flirtation with her in 1854.

desire that. Believe me—no matter what your and my future fate may be, the feeling of profound attachment to you will never die in me. Forgive me, Olga Aleksandrovna—and I'll forgive myself only when I see you surrounded by the happiness of which you are so worthy. Give me your hand, allow me to clasp it firmly— and together with my profound gratitude, please accept the expression of the sincere devotion

Of your

Iv. Turgenev.

A Correspondence

I was in Dresden a few years ago, staying at a hotel. I strolled around town from early morning until late evening, and didn't feel the need to become acquainted with my neighbors. I eventually learned by chance that another Russian was staying in the hotel— he was ill. I went to see him and found a man suffering from severe tuberculosis. I was getting tired of Dresden, so I stayed indoors with my new acquaintance. It's boring to keep a sick person company, but sometimes even boredom is pleasant. Moreover, my patient wasn't depressed and was eager to talk. We tried to pass the time all sorts of ways: we played cards, we made fun of the doctor. My compatriot used to tell this completely bald German all sorts of lies about himself, which the doctor had always "long since anticipated." He used to mimic the doctor's astonishment at any new, exceptional symptom, to throw his medicine out the window, and so forth. I observed to my friend more than once, however, that it wouldn't be a bad idea to send for a good doctor before it was too late, that his illness wasn't a joke, and so forth. But Aleksei (my new friend's name was Aleksei Petrovich S——) always rejected my advice with witty remarks about doctors in general and his own in particular.

Finally, one rainy autumn evening, he responded to my urgent entreaties with such a grim look, shook his head so sorrowfully, and smiled so strangely, that I became somewhat bewildered. Aleksei grew worse that very night, and he died the next day. Right before his death, his customary cheerfulness deserted him, he shifted in bed uneasily, sighed, looked around drearily . . . clutched at my hand, whispered with an effort, "It's hard to die, you know . . . ," let his head fall back on the pillow, and wept. I didn't know what to say to him, and sat next to his bed in silence. But

Aleksei quickly mastered these final, belated regrets.... "Listen," he said to me, "our doctor will arrive today and find me dead.... I can imagine his ugly face...." And the dying man tried to mimic him.... He asked me to send all his things to his relatives in Russia, with the exception of a small parcel that he gave me as a memento.

This parcel contained letters—a young woman's letters to Aleksei and copies of his letters to her. There were fifteen of them. Aleksei Petrovich S—— had known Maria Aleksandrovna B—— for a long time, since childhood, it appears. Aleksei Petrovich had a cousin; Maria Aleksandrovna had a sister. In those earlier times, they'd all lived in the same place, then they'd moved away and hadn't seen one another for a long while. Later on, they'd all happened to be reunited in the country one summer, and they'd fallen in love—Aleksei's cousin with Maria Aleksandrovna and Aleksei with her sister. That summer passed, the autumn came, and they parted. Aleksei, like a sensible person, soon came to the conclusion that he wasn't in love at all, and had ended his relationship with the lady most successfully. His cousin had continued writing to Maria Aleksandrovna for nearly two more years ... but he, too, finally realized that he was deceiving both her and himself in an unconscionable manner, and he fell silent as well.

I could tell you something about Maria Aleksandrovna, kind reader, but you'll find out about her yourself from her letters. Aleksei wrote his first letter to her shortly after she'd definitively ended her relationship with his cousin. Aleksei was in Petersburg at the time. He subsequently went abroad, fell ill, and died in Dresden. I decided to publish his correspondence with Maria Aleksandrovna, and hope for a bit of indulgence from the reader, since these letters aren't love letters—God forbid! Love letters are usually only read by two people (they read them a thousand times to compensate for that fact), but they're unbearable, if not ridiculous, for a third person to read.

I

From Aleksei Petrovich to Maria Aleksandrovna

St. Petersburg, March 7, 1840

Dear Maria Aleksandrovna!

It seems I've never written to you before, and here I am, writing to you now.... I've chosen a strange time to begin, haven't I? I'll tell you what gave me the idea. *Mon cousin Théodore* visited me today and . . . how shall I put it? . . . he confided to me as his greatest secret (he never tells anyone anything any other way) that he's in love with some nobleman's daughter here, that this time he firmly intends to get married, and that he's already taken the first step— he's declared his intentions! Naturally, I hastened to congratulate him on such a pleasant event—he's been longing for an opportunity to declare his intentions for quite a while . . . but inwardly, I must confess, I was rather surprised. Although I knew that everything was over between the two of you, I'd still thought. . . . In short, I was surprised. I'd made arrangements to go and visit some friends today, but I stayed home and intend to have a little chat with you. If you don't want to listen to me, toss this letter straight into the fire. I warn you that I intend to be frank, although I consider you completely justified in regarding me as rather importunate. Note, however, that I wouldn't have picked up my pen if I hadn't known that your sister wasn't there with you. She's spending the entire summer with her aunt, Mrs. B——, *Théodore* told me. May God bestow every blessing upon her!

And so this is how it all resolved itself. . . . But I'm not going to offer you my friendship, and so forth. I'm generally averse to ceremonial speeches and "heartfelt" effusions. In beginning to write this letter, I simply obeyed a momentary impulse. If there's another feeling concealed within me, let it remain under a bushel for the time being.

I'm not going to offer you any sympathy, either. In sympathizing with others, people for the most part want to rid themselves of an unpleasant feeling of involuntary, self-centered pity as quickly as possible. . . . I understand what genuine, warm sympathy is . . . but you wouldn't accept such sympathy from just anyone. . . . Please get angry with me. . . . If you get angry, you'll probably read my missive through to the end.

Yet what right do I have to write to you, to speak about my friendship, about my feelings, about consolation? None, absolutely none—I'm obliged to admit this, and can only throw myself on your mercy.

Do you know what the beginning of my letter sounds like? Here's what: Some Mr. N.N. walks into the drawing room of a lady who doesn't expect him at all and who possibly expects someone else. . . . He realizes that he's come at an awkward moment, but there's nothing he can do. . . . He sits down and begins to talk . . . God knows about what—poetry, the glories of nature, the advantages of a good education. . . . He utters the most appalling absurdities, in fact. But meanwhile, the first five minutes have gone by, he's made himself comfortable, the lady has resigned herself to the inevitable, and so Mr. N.N. regains his self-possession, takes a breath, and begins a real conversation—to the best of his ability. In spite of all this verbiage, however, I still don't feel quite comfortable. I seem to see a bewildered and even rather hostile expression on your face. I sense that it'll be almost impossible for you not to ascribe some hidden motives to me, and therefore, like a Roman who has committed some folly, I'll wrap myself regally in my toga and await your final answer in silence. . . .

The question is this: Will you give me permission to go on writing to you? I remain sincerely, warmly devoted to you,

Aleksei S——

II
From Maria Aleksandrovna to Aleksei Petrovich

Village of ——no, March 22, 1840

Dear Sir, Aleksei Petrovich,

I've received your letter, and I really don't know what to say to you. I wouldn't have answered you at all if it hadn't seemed to me that some friendly feeling is actually concealed beneath your jocular remarks. Your letter made an unpleasant impression on me. In response to your "verbiage," as you call it, let me put one question to you in turn: *What for?* What do I have in common with you, or you with me? I don't ascribe any bad motives to you . . . on the contrary, I'm grateful to you for your sympathy . . . but we're strangers to one another, and, just now at least, I don't have the slightest desire to become more intimately acquainted with anyone at all. With sincere respect, I remain, etc.,

Maria B——

III
From Aleksei Petrovich to Maria Aleksandrovna

St. Petersburg, March 30

I thank you, I thank you for your note, Maria Aleksandrovna, as stiff as it was. I've been in terrible suspense the whole time— I've thought about you and about my letter twenty times a day. You can't imagine how bitterly I've mocked myself—but now I'm in an excellent mood and am extremely pleased with myself. Maria

Aleksandrovna, I'm going to begin a correspondence with you! You must confess that this wasn't at all what you expected after your reply. I myself am surprised at my audacity. . . . Well, I don't care. Here goes! But don't worry—I don't want to talk about you, but about myself. Don't you see, it's absolutely essential for me to open myself up to someone, as the old-fashioned saying goes. I don't have the slightest right to select you as my confidante—I grant that. But do understand: I don't need any answers to my letters from you. I don't even want to know whether or not you read my "verbiage." But, in the name of all that's holy, don't send my letters back to me!

I must tell you, I'm utterly alone on earth. I led a solitary life in my youth, although as far as I can recall, I never imitated Byron. But in the first place, certain circumstances, and in the second, an aptitude for fantasizing accompanied by a love of fantasy, plus relatively cold blood, pride, indolence—in sum, a number of different factors kept me isolated from the company of other human beings. My transition from a life in dreams to a life in reality took place late . . . perhaps too late, or perhaps it hasn't fully taken place as yet. As long as I could entertain myself with my own thoughts and feelings, as long as I was capable of abandoning myself to causeless, silent ecstasies and the like, I didn't complain about my solitude. I had no companions—I had so-called friends. Sometimes I required their presence, the way an electrical machine requires a sparkplug—and that was all. As for love . . . we won't speak about that subject for the present. But now, I confess, now my solitude weighs heavily on me, and at the same time, I see no means of escape from my situation. I don't blame fate; I alone am to blame, and am being duly punished. In my youth, I was absorbed by one thing—my precious *self*. I took my inherent pride for shyness. I avoided society—and now here I am, horribly sick of myself. What should I do with myself? There's no one that I love—all my relationships with other people are somehow strained and false. I don't have any memories, either, for I can't find traces of anything but my own personality in my entire past. Save me. I haven't made passionate protestations of love to you, I've never drowned you in a flood of mindless babble. I passed you by rather coldly—and I've decided to turn to you now for precisely that reason. (I've thought about doing so before, but you weren't free then. . . .) Among all my manufactured sensations, joys, and sorrows, the one genuine feeling I had was my slight but instinctive attraction to you, which withered up at the time like a single stalk of wheat in the midst of worthless weeds. . . . Let me look into another face, into another soul, just once—my own face has become repugnant to me. I'm like a man who should have been condemned to live out his entire life in a room with mirrored walls. . . . I don't require any sort of confession from you—God, no! Give me a sister's unspoken sympathy, or at least a reader's simple curiosity. I'll entertain you, I truly will.

Meanwhile, I have the honor to be your sincere friend.

A.S.

IV

From Aleksei Petrovich to Maria Aleksandrovna

St. Petersburg, April 7

I'm writing to you again, even though I foresee that I'll fall silent shortly without your approval. I must concede that you can't fail to distrust me somewhat. Well, perhaps you're right. In earlier days, I would have announced to you triumphantly (and I probably would have believed my own words myself) that I'd "developed," that I'd made progress since the time we parted. I'd have referred to my past with condescending, almost affectionate contempt, then I'd have divulged the secrets of my current existence to you with touching conceit . . . but now, I assure you, Maria Aleksandrovna, I'm thoroughly ashamed and disgusted when I recall the superficiality and pettiness my paltry pride once led me to indulge in. Don't worry: I'm not going to impose any great truths or any profound views on you. I don't entertain any of them—these truths and views. I've become a simple, good man—it's true. I'm bored, Maria Aleksandrovna, I'm simply bored beyond all endurance. That's why I'm writing to you. . . . I really believe that we might come to be friends. . . .

But I definitely can't talk to you until you hold out your hand to me, until I get a note from you with the single word "yes" on it. Maria Aleksandrovna, will you listen to me?—that's the question.

Yours devotedly,

A.S.

V

From Maria Aleksandrovna to Aleksei Petrovich

Village of ——no, April 14

What a strange person you are! All right, then—yes!

Maria B.

VI
From Aleksei Petrovich to Maria Aleksandrovna
St. Petersburg, May 2, 1840

Hurray! Thank you, Maria Aleksandrovna, thank you! You're a supremely kind, indulgent creature.

As I promised, I'll begin by speaking about myself, and I'll speak with a pleasure verging on avidity.... Quite so. One may speak about anything on earth with fire, with enthusiasm, with ecstasy, but one only speaks about oneself with avidity.

I must tell you, a very strange thing has happened to me during the last few days. I've undertaken a complete review of my past for the first time. You have to understand: each one of us often recalls our experiences—out of regret, or irritation, or simply because there's nothing else to do. But casting a cold, clear gaze over one's entire past life—the way a traveler turns on top of a high mountain and looks at the plain he has just crossed—can only happen at a certain age... and a secret chill clutches the heart when that happens for the first time. Mine, in any case, felt a sickening pang. While we're young, *this* sort of complete review is impossible. But my youth is over, and like someone who has climbed a mountain, everything has become clearly visible to me.

Yes, my youth is gone, gone never to return!... It's lying here before me, as it were, in the palm of my hand....

It's a cheerless spectacle! I'll confess to you, Maria Aleksandrovna, that I'm very sorry for myself. My God! My God! Can it be that I myself have so utterly ruined my life, so mercilessly confused and tortured myself?... I've come to my senses now, but it's too late. Have you ever had occasion to save a fly from a spider? Have you? You remember, you put it in the sun, since its wings and legs have gotten sticky, are glued together.... How awkwardly it moves, how clumsily it tries to clean itself!... After prolonged efforts, it somehow rights itself, crawls forward, and attempts to open its wings... but it can't move easily, it can't buzz in the sunshine with careless abandon the way it did before, when it could fly into a cool room and fly out again through an open window, winging its way into the outdoor heat without constraint.... At least the fly didn't fall into that dreadful web of its own volition... but I!

I've been my own spider.

And yet I can't blame myself too much. Tell me, who is ever really to blame for anything—alone? Or, to put it better, we're all to blame, and yet we can't be blamed. Circumstances define us; they force us onto one road or another, and then they punish us for it. Each individual has his own destiny.... Wait a moment, wait a moment! An intellectually contrived and yet accurate comparison has come to mind: just as clouds first condense from the earth's moisture, rise from its depths, then separate and move away from it, ultimately bringing prosperity or ruin, in the same way— how can I put it?—a sort of element is fashioned both around each of us and out of each of us that subsequently has a redemptive or a destructive effect on us. I call this element destiny.... In other words, simply put, each individual makes his own destiny and destiny makes each individual....

Each individual makes his own destiny—yes!... But people like us care about it too much—that's what's wrong with us! Consciousness is awakened in us too soon, we begin to observe ourselves too early.... We Russians have assigned ourselves no other task in life but the cultivation of our own personalities, and when we're barely past childhood, we set to work to cultivate them, those unfortunate personalities! Receiving no specific guidance from the outside, having no real respect for anything and no strong belief in anything, we're free to make of ourselves what we choose.... It's impossible to expect everyone immediately to comprehend the sterility of a mind "seething in vain activity."... And so one more monster appears on earth, one more of those worthless creatures whose egotistical habits subvert the quest for truth, in whom ludicrous simplicity coexists with pathetic duplicity... one more of those creatures whose impotent, restless minds will never know the satisfactions of productive labor, or the pain of genuine suffering, or the triumph of genuine conviction.... Incorporating within ourselves the defects of all life's stages, we deprive every defect of its positive, redeeming side.... We're as foolish as children, but we aren't as sincere as they are. We're as cold as old people, but we possess none of the wisdom of old age.... To compensate for all this, we're psychologists. Oh, yes, we're great psychologists! But our psychology is akin to pathology, for our psychology is an intricate study of the laws of a morbid condition and a morbid development, with which healthy people have no connection.... And the worst of it is that we aren't young—even in our youth, we aren't young!

At the same time—why malign ourselves? Were we never young? Did we never know the play, the fire, the throb of life's vital forces?

We too have been in Arcadia, we too have wandered among its gleaming fields! . . . When strolling among the shrubbery, have you ever happened to come across those dark grasshoppers that leap up from under your very feet, suddenly expanding bright red wings with a whirr, fly a few paces, then drop back into the grass? That's just how our dark youth occasionally spreads its multicolored wings for a few moments, albeit not for any extended flight. . . . Do you remember the silent evening walks around your garden's borders that the four of us used to take together after some long, lively, heated conversation? Do you remember those heavenly moments? Nature would tenderly and graciously clasp us to its bosom. Swooning, we'd plunge into a flood of bliss. The sunset would glow all around us with an unexpected, soft flush; the earth and sky would seem to be bathed in light. Everything everywhere would be filled with the fresh, fiery breath of youth, with the joyous triumph of some deathless happiness. The sunset would blaze up, and our rapturous hearts would likewise burn with a silent, passionate fire, while the tiny leaves on the young trees would quiver faintly over our heads, as though in response to the inward tremor of our vague emotions and expectations. Do you remember the purity, the decency and optimism of our ideas, the generosity of our noble hopes, the silence of our overflowing hearts? Didn't we merit something better than what life had bestowed upon us even then? Why was it ordained for us to see the desired shore only at rare moments, and never to stand firmly on it, never to touch it:

> Never to weep with joy, like the first Jew
> On the threshold of the promised land?

These two lines by Fet remind me of others he wrote as well. . . . Do you remember that once, while we were standing in the road, we saw a cloud of pink dust against the setting sun stirred up in the distance by a light breeze? You began to recite "In an eddying cloud," and we all instantly fell silent in order to listen:

> In an eddying cloud
> Dust rises in the distance . . .
> A rider or a man on foot—
> One cannot tell in the dust.
> I see someone trotting
> On a gallant steed . . .
> My friend, distant friend,
> Remember me!

You stopped. . . . We each felt a shudder run through us, as though the breath of love had swept across our hearts, and each of us—I'm sure of this—felt irresistibly drawn to the distance, that unknown distance where the phantom of bliss arises and beckons through the mist. And yet note how strange this was: why, one wonders, should we have yearned for the distance? Weren't we in love with one another? Wasn't happiness "so near, so possible"? As I just asked you: why was it we didn't touch the desired shore? Because falsehood walked hand in hand with us, because it poisoned our best feelings, because everything inside us was artificial and strained, because we didn't love one another at all, but were merely endeavoring to love, imagining that we loved. . . .

But that's enough, that's enough! Why inflame one's own wounds? Besides, it's all over and done with. That which was good about our past has moved me, and, fortified by that good, I'll say goodbye to you for a while. It's time to finish this long letter. I'm going out for a breath of the May air here, in which spring is breaching the dry fortress of winter with some sort of damp, piercing warmth. Goodbye.

Your A.S.

VII
From Maria Aleksandrovna to Aleksei Petrovich

Village of ——no, May 20, 1840

I've received your letter, Aleksei Petrovich. Do you know what feeling it aroused in me? Indignation . . . yes, indignation . . . and I'll tell you why it aroused that feeling in me. It's just a shame that I'm not more skilled with a pen. I rarely write, and can't express my thoughts precisely, in a few words. But you'll come to my aid, I trust. You yourself must try to understand me, if only to find out why I'm indignant.

Tell me—you're an intelligent person—have you ever asked yourself what sort of creature a Russian woman is, what her destiny or her position in the world is—in short, what her life is all about? I don't know whether you've ever taken the time to ask yourself this question, and I can't imagine how you'd answer it. . . . Perhaps I'd be able to convey my views on this subject to you in conversation, but I'm hardly equal to the task on paper. It doesn't matter, though. The point is this: you'll probably agree with me that we women, at least those of us who aren't satisfied with the ordinary tasks of domestic life, in any case, receive our ultimate education from you men—you wield a vast, mighty influence over us. Now consider how you treat us. I'm talking about young women, especially those like me who live in remote places, of whom there are so many in Russia. Besides, I don't know the others and can't draw conclusions about them. Picture to yourself a young woman like this. Her education ends and she begins to live her life, to enjoy herself. But enjoyment alone doesn't mean much to her. She demands more from life—she reads, she dreams . . . about love. A young woman always only dreams about love, you'll say. . . . That may be true, but this word means a great deal to her. I repeat that I'm not talking about a young woman for whom thinking is burdensome or boring. . . . She looks around, waiting for the moment when the man for whom her soul yearns will arrive. . . . At last he appears and she's enthralled, she's like putty in his hands. Everything—happiness and love and ideas—everything floods over her upon his arrival. He soothes all her anxieties, resolves all her doubts. Truth itself seems to speak through his lips. She worships him, she's ashamed of her own happiness, she learns, she loves. His power over her is so great at that time! . . . If he were a hero, he'd inspire her, he'd teach her to sacrifice herself—and every sacrifice would be easy for her! But there are no heroes in our time. . . . In any event, he directs her attention wherever he pleases. She devotes herself to whatever interests him, and every word of his sinks into her soul. She still hasn't learned how worthless and empty and false a word can be, how little it costs the person who utters it, and how little it deserves belief! After these first moments of bliss and hope usually comes a parting of the ways—because of circumstances (circumstances are always to blame). They say there have been instances when two kindred souls have become irrevocably united at the very moment of their introduction to one another. I've also heard it said that things didn't always go smoothly for them as a result . . . but I won't speak about things I myself haven't witnessed. And the fact that the pettiest calculation, the most pathetic cautiousness, can coexist with the most passionate enthusiasm in a youthful heart—that fact, unfortunately, I've experienced personally. Thus the parting comes. . . . The fortunate young woman immediately realizes that everything is over and doesn't deceive herself with any expectations! But you brave, fair-minded men for the most part don't have the spirit or even the desire to tell us the truth. . . . It's less upsetting for you to deceive us. . . . However, I'm prepared to believe that you deceive yourselves as well as us. . . . Parting! To endure parting is both

difficult and easy. If only one had perfect, undiminished faith in
the person one loves, one's soul could master the anguish of
separation.... I'll say further that it's only when she's been left
alone does she discover the sweetness of solitude—not a barren
solitude, but a solitude filled with memories and ideas. It's only
then that she discovers herself, becomes her true self, and grows
strong.... She finds support for herself in the letters of a distant
friend, and in her own, perhaps for the first time, she finds complete
self-expression.... But, just as two people who set out walking
away from the source of a stream along opposite banks initially
can touch hands, then can only communicate by voice, and eventually lose sight of one another altogether, in the same way do two
natures eventually diverge after their parting. Well, what's wrong
with that, you'll say. It's clear that they weren't destined to be
together.... But herein lies the difference between a man and a
woman. For a man, it means nothing to begin a new life, to cut
himself off from his entire past. But a woman can't do that. No,
she can't cast off her past, she can't break away from her roots—
no, a thousand times no! Thus a pitiful, ludicrous spectacle
begins.... Gradually losing hope and faith in herself—you can't
even imagine how bitter that is!—she withers away as she wears
herself out in solitude, obstinately clinging to her memories and
turning away from everything that the life surrounding her has to
offer.... But he? Try to find him! Where is he? Is it worth it for
him to remain standing still? When does he have time to look
back? For it's all a thing of the past to him. Or else here's what
happens: he feels a sudden urge to meet the former object of his
affections, and even deliberately goes out of his way to do
so.... But my God! The petty conceit that leads him to do that!
Such consciousness of his superiority is manifested in his gracious
sympathy, in his would-be friendly advice, in his condescending
account of the past! It's so pleasant, so enjoyable for him to permit
himself to perceive what an intelligent person he is, what a kind
person he is, at every moment! And how little he realizes what
he's done! How can he possibly fail to guess what's taking place
in a woman's heart—and how offensively he sympathizes with her
if he does guess!...

Tell me, please, where can she find the strength to bear all this?
Remember this, too: for the most part, a young woman in whose
brain the intellect has begun to stir—to her misfortune—such a
young woman, when she begins to love and thus falls under a man's

influence, unintentionally grows distant from her family, from her acquaintances. Even before then, she wasn't satisfied with their life, although she marched in step with them, treasuring all her secret dreams in her soul.... But the distance soon becomes apparent.... They cease to comprehend her and are prepared to regard everything she does with suspicion.... This means nothing to her at first, but later, later ... when she's been left alone, when that toward which she's been striving, for which she's sacrificed everything, has disappeared, when heaven hasn't been gained and everything near, everything possible, has been lost—what can support her then? She could still somehow endure the jeers, the sly hints, the vulgar triumph of coarse common sense ... but what should she do, where can she find refuge, when an inner voice begins to whisper to her that they all were right and she was wrong, that life, whatever it may be, is better than dreams, just as health is better than sickness ... when her favorite activities, her favorite books, books from which she can't obtain happiness, become hateful to her—tell me, what can support her then? Mustn't she inevitably succumb amid such a struggle? How can she live, and go on living, in such a desert? To admit that you've been defeated, to extend your hand like a beggar to utterly indifferent people so that they'll bestow the sympathy a proud heart had once imagined it could dispense with—all that would mean nothing! But to consider yourself ludicrous at the very moment when you're shedding bitter, bitter tears.... May God spare you such suffering....

My hands are trembling, and I'm thoroughly feverish—my face is burning. It's time to stop.... I'll send off this letter quickly, before I become embarrassed by its weakness. But for God's sake, don't offer a single word—do you hear?—not a single word of sympathy in your reply, or I'll never write to you again. Understand me: I don't want you to take this letter to be the outpouring of a misunderstood, miserable soul.... Ah! I don't care! Goodbye.

M.

VIII
From Aleksei Petrovich to Maria Aleksandrovna
St. Petersburg, May 28, 1840

Maria Aleksandrovna, you're a marvelous creature! ... You ... your letter revealed the truth to me at last! Oh, my God! What suffering! An individual repeatedly thinks that he's finally achieved a condition of simplicity, that he's no longer showing off, posing,

lying ... but when you examine him more closely, you find he's become virtually worse than before. And note this fact as well: this individual himself—that is, on his own—never attains self-awareness,
try as he might. His eyes can't see his own defects, just as a type-
setter's weary eyes can't see the printing errors he makes—someone
else's fresh eye is needed to do that. Thank you, Maria Aleksandrovna.... You see, I'm speaking to you about myself; I don't dare
to speak about you.... Ah, how ridiculous my last letter seems to
me now, how rhetorically elaborate and sentimental! I earnestly
implore you, continue your confession. I'm convinced both that
you'll feel better for it and that it'll do me immense good. It's
truly said: "A woman's mind is superior to many ideas," and a
woman's heart is far and away ... by God, yes! If women knew
how much better, nobler, and more intelligent they are than men—
yes, more intelligent—they'd become conceited and spoiled. But
fortunately, they don't know it. They don't know it because their
intellects aren't in the habit of incessantly turning inward upon
themselves, as ours do. They don't think about themselves very
much—that's their weakness and their strength. That's the whole
secret—I won't say of our superiority, but of our power. They
squander the riches of their souls the way a prodigal heir spends
his father's gold, while we exact a percentage on every worthless
morsel.... How can they possibly contend with us? ... These aren't
compliments, they're simple truths, proved by experience. I implore you once more to go on writing to me, Maria
Aleksandrovna.... If only you knew what thoughts were coming
into my head! ... But I have no desire to speak now. I want to
listen to you.... My turn will come later. Write, write.

Your devoted A.S.

IX
From Maria Aleksandrovna to Aleksei Petrovich

Village of ——no, June 12, 1840

I'd barely sent you my last letter, Aleksei Petrovich, when I
regretted it, but there was nothing I could do about it then. One
thing reassures me somewhat: I'm sure that you realized it was
written under the influence of feelings long suppressed and that
you forgave me. I didn't even read through what I'd written to you
at the time. I remember that the pen shook in my fingers, my
heart was beating so violently. However, although I probably would
have expressed myself differently if I'd given myself time to reflect,

I still don't intend to disavow either my own words or the feelings that I conveyed to you as well as I could. I'm much more cold-blooded and self-possessed today.

I remember that, at the end of my letter, I spoke about the difficult position of a young woman aware of being isolated, even among her own relatives. . . . I won't elaborate on this further, but I'll give you a few examples instead. I suspect I'll bore you less that way.

In the first place, then, you should know that I'm never called anything throughout the entire region except the female philosopher. The ladies in particular honor me with that appellation. Some claim that I go to sleep wearing glasses, holding a Latin book in my hand, while others declare that I know how to derive some sort of cube roots. Not one of them doubts that I wear men's clothing in secret and that instead of saying "good morning," I abruptly blurt out, "George Sand!"—and indignation toward the female philosopher increases. We have a neighbor, a man of about forty-five, a great wit . . . at least, he's reputed to be a great wit. . . . My poor personage provides an inexhaustible source of jokes for him. He says that I can't take my eyes off the moon as soon as it rises, and he himself mimics the way I gaze at it. He asserts that I even take my coffee with moonlight rather than milk—that is, I set my cup in the moon's rays. He swears that I use phrases of the following sort: "It's easy because it's difficult, although, on the contrary, it's difficult because it's easy. . . ." He claims that I'm always searching for some special word, always striving to get "there," and inquires with comic rage, "Where is there? Where?" He's also circulated the rumor that I ride horseback up and down by the river at night, singing a Schubert serenade or simply moaning, "Beethoven, Beethoven!" "She's such a fiery old woman," he says, and so on and so forth. Of course, all this comes straight to my ears.

Perhaps this surprises you, but don't forget that four years have passed since your stay in this area. You remember how everyone frowned upon us in those days. . . . Now their turn has come. And even all of this is insignificant. I have to hear many things that wound my heart much more. I won't say anything about my poor, well-meaning mother, who has never been able to forgive me for your cousin's indifference to me. But my whole life is going up in flames, as my nursemaid used to put it. "Of course," I constantly hear, "we can't keep up with you! We're plain folks, we're guided by nothing but common sense. But still, when you think about it, what have all these meditations and books and relationships with educated people done for you?" Perhaps you remember my sister—not the one to whom you weren't indifferent at one time, but the other one, the older one, who's married. Her husband, as you may recall, is a simple, rather comical person—you regularly made fun of him in those days. But she's happy nonetheless. She's the mother of a family, she loves her husband, her husband adores her.... "I'm like everyone else," she says to me sometimes, "whereas you...?" And she's right. I envy her....

And yet I feel that I wouldn't want to change places with her for all that. Let them call me a female philosopher, an eccentric, or whatever they please—I'll remain eternally faithful... to what? To an ideal? Yes, to an ideal. Yes, I'll remain eternally faithful to that which first made my heart throb—to that which I once acknowledged and still acknowledge to be truth, to be goodness.... If only my strength doesn't fail me, if only my god doesn't turn out to be a mute, soulless idol....

If you really feel any friendship for me, if you really haven't forgotten me, you ought to help me—you ought to resolve my doubts and reinforce my convictions....

But then again, what help can you give me? "All this is trivial nonsense," my uncle said to me yesterday. I don't think you know him—he's a retired naval officer, a very sensible man. "A husband, children, a pot of cabbage soup—looking after your husband and children and keeping an eye on the pot—that's what a woman needs."... Tell me—is he right?

If he really is right, I can still make up for the past, I can still lapse into the common groove. Why should I wait any longer? What have I got to hope for? In one of your letters, you spoke about the wings of youth. They can be tied so often, for so long! And then a time comes when they fall off, and it's impossible to rise above the earth and fly toward heaven any more. Write to me.

Your M.

X
From Aleksei Petrovich to Maria Aleksandrovna
St. Petersburg, June 16, 1840

I hasten to answer your letter, dear Maria Aleksandrovna. I confess to you that if it weren't... I can't say for business, because I don't have any... if it weren't for the fact that I'm foolishly accustomed to this place, then I'd have come to see you again and talked to you to my heart's content, whereas on paper, everything comes out coldly and lifelessly. . . .

I tell you again, Maria Aleksandrovna, women are better than men, and you ought to demonstrate this in actuality. Let men like us throw away our convictions like a crust of bread or lull them into endless slumber and place a gravestone above them, as we do above the dead who were once dear to us, whom we visit at rare intervals in order to pray. Let us do all that, but you women mustn't betray yourselves. You mustn't betray your ideal. . . . That word has become ridiculous. . . . To fear the ridiculous is not to love the truth. It happens, to be sure, that the mindless laughter of a fool forces even good people to forsake a great deal . . . the defense of an absent friend, for instance. . . . I've been guilty of that myself. But, I repeat, you women are better than us men. . . . You surrender in trivial matters more quickly than we do, but you know how to look the devil in the face better than we do. I don't want to give you either advice or help—how could I? Besides, you don't need either. But I hold out my hand to you, I say to you, "Have patience, fight on to the end, and know that the consciousness of an honorably waged battle, the feeling it provides, is almost superior to the triumph of victory. . . . Victory doesn't depend on us."

Of course, your uncle is right, from a certain point of view. Family life is everything for a woman—there isn't any other life for her.

But what does that prove? None but Jesuits would maintain that all means are equally good if only they attain the desired end. That's not true! That's not true! Feet sullied with the mud of the road are unworthy to enter a holy temple. At the end of your letter is a phrase I don't like: you want to lapse into the common groove. Be careful—don't take a false step! Besides, don't forget that you can't erase the past, and however much you try, however much you force yourself, you won't turn yourself into your sister. You've become superior to her, but your spirit has been wounded, whereas hers is untouched. You can descend to her level, reduce yourself to her, but nature won't give up its rights, and the wounded spot won't heal again. . . .

You're afraid—let's speak plainly—you're afraid of becoming an old maid. You're already twenty-six, I know. Certainly, the situation old maids find themselves in is an unenviable one: everyone is so eager to laugh at them, everyone comments on their peculiarities and flaws with such ungenerous delight. But if you observe any old bachelor the least bit attentively, you can point a finger at him as well—you can find plenty in him to laugh at, too. What else can you do? You can't become happy by struggling to become happy. But we mustn't forget that human dignity, not happiness, constitutes the chief goal of life.

You describe your situation with great humor—I comprehend all its bitterness very well. One could really call your situation tragic. But you should know that you're not alone in it: there's hardly anyone alive today who couldn't find himself in it. You'll say that this doesn't make it any easier for you, but I think that suffering together with thousands of others is entirely different from suffering alone. Then it isn't a matter of individual ego, but of a sense of general inevitability.

Granted, this is all very well, you'll say . . . but unfeasible in reality. Why unfeasible? Until now I've thought—and I hope I'll never stop thinking—that everything honorable, good, and true is feasible in God's world, and will be realized sooner or later. Not only will it be realized, but it's already being realized, if only everyone holds his ground and doesn't lose patience or desire the impossible, but does everything he has the power to do. I seem to have digressed too far, though. I'll defer the continuation of my reflections until my next letter, but I can't lay down my pen without warmly, warmly shaking your hand and wishing you everything good on earth from the bottom of my heart.

Your A.S.

P.S. By the way, you say that it's useless for you to wait, that you've got nothing to hope for. How do you know that, may I ask?

XI
From Maria Aleksandrovna to Aleksei Petrovich

Village of ——no, June 30, 1840

How grateful I am to you for your letter, Aleksei Petrovich! How much good it did me! I see that you really are a kind, trustworthy man, and so I won't conceal anything from you. I believe in you. I know that you won't take advantage of my openness, and will give me some friendly advice. Here's the question.

You noticed a phrase at the end of my letter that you didn't altogether like. I'll tell you what it referred to. There's a neighbor here . . . he wasn't here when you were, and you've never met him. He . . . I could marry him if I wanted to—he's still young, he's well-educated, and he owns property. My parents have no objection.

On the contrary—I know for a fact—they desire this marriage. He's a decent man, and he loves me, I think . . . but he's so listless and narrow-minded, his aspirations are so limited, that I can't help being conscious of my superiority to him. He's aware of this and seemingly rejoices in it—that's just what has turned me against him. I can't respect him, although he has a warm heart. What should I do? Tell me! Do my thinking for me, and send me your sincere opinion.

But how grateful I am to you for your letter! . . . Do you know, at times I've been haunted by such bitter thoughts. . . . Do you know, I'd gotten to the point where I was almost ashamed of every— I won't say exalted—every affirmative feeling. I kept closing books in annoyance whenever there was anything in them about hope or happiness, I turned away from a cloudless sky, from the fresh green trees, from everyone that smiled and rejoiced. What a painful condition it was! I say "was" . . . as though it were over!

I don't know whether it's over or not. I do know that if it doesn't return, I owe that to you. Do you see how much you've done, Aleksei Petrovich, perhaps without even suspecting it yourself? By the way, do you know that I'm very sorry for you? We're currently enjoying the very peak of summer—the days are exquisite, the sky is bright blue. . . . It couldn't be lovelier even in Italy, and you're staying in a stifling, dusty town, walking along burning pavement. What's inducing you to do that? You might at least move to some summer villa outside of town. They say that there are some lovely places beyond Petersburg, on the seacoast.

I'd like to write more to you, but it's impossible. Such a sweet fragrance has wafted over from the garden that I can't stay indoors. I'm going to put on my hat and go for a walk. . . . Goodbye until another time, dear Aleksei Petrovich.

Your devoted M.B.

P.S. I forgot to tell you . . . Just imagine, that witty gentleman I wrote to you about the other day has made me a declaration of love in the most ardent terms. I thought he was making fun of me at first, but he concluded with a formal proposal! What a conclusion, after all his mockery. But he's definitely too old. Yesterday evening, to tease him, I sat down at the piano in front of the open window, in the moonlight, and played Beethoven. It was so nice to feel the cool light on my face, it was so delightful to fill the fragrant night air with the sublime music, through which one could occasionally hear a nightingale singing. It's a long time since I've been so happy. But write to me regarding the question I asked you at the beginning of my letter. It's very important.

XII
From Aleksei Petrovich to Maria Aleksandrovna

St. Petersburg, July 8, 1840

My dear Maria Aleksandrovna, here's my opinion in a few words: throw both the old bachelor and your suitor overboard! There's no need even to consider them. Neither of them is worthy of you—that's as clear as two times two is four. Perhaps your young neighbor truly is a kind person—God bless him! I'm sure that you two have nothing in common, and you can imagine how delightful it'd be for you two to live together! Besides, why be in a hurry? Is it possible that a woman like you—I don't want to pay you compliments, so I won't elaborate any further—that such a woman would never meet anyone who could appreciate her? No, Maria Aleksandrovna, listen to me, if you really believe that I'm your friend and that my advice is useful. But confess that it was enjoyable to see the old rumor-monger at your feet. . . . If I'd been in your place, I'd have forced him to sing Beethoven's "Adelaide" and gaze at the moon all night long.

That's enough about your admirers, though! I don't want to talk to you about them now. I'm in a strange, half-irritated, half-agitated state of mind today because of a letter I received yesterday. I'm enclosing a copy of it for you. This letter was written by one of my oldest friends, a colleague in government service, a kindly but rather narrow individual. He went abroad two years ago, and hasn't written to me once until now. Here's his letter. N.B.: He's very handsome.

Cher Alexis—
I'm in Naples, sitting at the window in my room on the *Chiaja*. The weather is superb. I stared at the sea for a long while, then I was suddenly overwhelmed with impatience and the brilliant idea of writing a letter to you came to mind. I've always felt an affinity for you, my dear friend—I swear to God. And so now I'm inclined to pour out my soul on your breast . . . I believe that's how one expresses it in the elevated language you favor. And here's why I'm overwhelmed with impatience. I'm waiting for a woman—we're going to Baiae together to eat oysters and oranges, to see shepherds with dark-brown skin wearing red caps dance the tarantella, to bask in the sun like

lizards—in short, to enjoy life to the utmost. My dear friend, I'm happier than I can possibly tell you. If only I could write like you— oh, what a picture I could draw before your eyes! But unfortunately, as you're well aware, I'm an illiterate person. The woman I'm waiting for, who has kept me continually flinching and looking at the door for more than an hour, loves me—and I suspect that even your eloquent pen couldn't describe the extent to which I love her.

I must tell you that it's been three months since I met her, and from the very first day of our acquaintance, my love has mounted in a constant crescendo like a chromatic scale, higher and higher, and at the present moment I'm simply in seventh heaven. I'm joking, but my devotion to this woman is actually something extraordinary, something supernatural. Imagine, I barely talk to her—I just incessantly gaze at her and laugh like a fool. I sit at her feet, feeling incredibly stupid—and happy, simply inexcusably happy. She occasionally happens to lay her hand on my head. . . . Well, then, I tell you. . . . But never mind, you can't understand all this. You're a philosopher and always were a philosopher. Her name is Nina, Ninetta, if you like. She's the daughter of a wealthy merchant here, as beautiful as any of your Raphaels, as volatile as gunpowder, full of joy, and so intelligent that it's amazing she can care for a fool like me. She sings like a bird, and her eyes. . . .

Please excuse this unintentional break. . . . I thought that the door creaked. . . . No, she still hasn't come, the cruel woman! You'll ask me—how all this is going to end, what do I intend to do with myself, and will I stay here for a long time? I don't know anything about any of this, my friend, and I don't want to know. What will be, will be. . . . Why, if one were always stopping and considering. . . .

It's she! . . . She's running up the staircase, singing. . . . Here she is. Well, goodbye, my friend. . . . I don't have any more time for you now. I'm sorry—she's splattered water across the whole letter by slapping a damp bouquet down on the paper. At first, she thought I was writing a letter to another woman, but when she found out it was to a male friend, she told me to convey her greetings and to ask you whether there are any flowers where you are, and whether they have any fragrance. Well, goodbye. . . . If only you could hear her laugh. . . .

Even silver doesn't resound like that—and there's such kindness in every note of it, you want to kiss her little feet. We're leaving, we're leaving. Please don't mind the messy smudges, and envy your devoted

M——

The letter really had been splattered with water, and smelled like orange blossoms. . . . Two white petals had stuck to the paper. This letter has upset me. . . . I recalled my own visit to Naples. . . . The weather was magnificent then, too—it was the very beginning of May. I'd recently turned twenty-two, but I didn't know any Ninetta. I strolled around alone, consumed with a thirst for bliss that was torturous and delightsome at the same time, so delightsome that it almost resembled bliss itself. . . . Ah, that's what it means to be young! . . . I remember that once I went for a boat ride in the bay. There were two of us—the boatman and I . . . what did you think I was going to say? What a night it was, what a sky, what stars! How their reflection quivered and fragmented into tiny pieces on the waves! What a delicate flame flashed and glimmered in the water beneath the oars, what a delicious fragrance floated across the entire bay! I can't describe all this, no matter how "elevated" my style may be. A French ocean liner was anchored in the harbor. Its lanterns made it glow all over, and long streaks of reddish light came through its shining windows, trembling slightly as they stretched across the dark water. The captain of the ship was giving a ball. Joyful music drifted over toward me in snatches at rare intervals. I especially recall the trill of a little flute in the midst of a deep blare of trumpets—it seemed to flit around my boat like a butterfly. I ordered the boatman to row toward the ship. He took me around it twice. . . . I caught glimpses of women's figures at the windows, gracefully borne in circles by the whirlwind of a waltz. . . . I told the boatman to row away, far away, straight into the darkness. . . . I remember that the music followed me persistently for a long while. . . . It finally died away. I stood up in the boat and stretched out my arms to the sea in a mute agony of desire. . . . Oh, how my heart ached at that moment! How oppressive my solitude was to me! With what rapture would I have utterly abandoned myself then, utterly . . . utterly, if only there'd been someone to abandon myself to! What a bitter feeling there was in my soul as I flung myself down into the hull of the boat and, like Repetilov, asked to be taken anywhere, anywhere far away!

But this friend of mine hasn't experienced anything like that. And why should he? He's managed things far more intelligently than I have. He's living . . . while I. . . . He may well dub me a philosopher. . . . It's strange! They call you a philosopher, too. . . . Why should this misfortune have befallen both of us? . . .

I'm not living. . . . But who is to blame for that? Why am I staying here, in Petersburg? What am I doing here? Why am I wasting day after day? Why don't I go to the countryside? What's wrong with our steppes? Can't one breathe freely there? Is it crowded there? Why do I have this desire to run after dreams when perhaps happiness is within reach? That does it! I'll leave, I'll leave tomorrow, if I can. I'll come home, that is, to your home. It's just the same—we live only twenty versts from one another. Why should I continue to grow stale here, after all? And why didn't this idea occur to me sooner? Dear Maria Aleksandrovna, we'll be seeing each other soon. It's extraordinary, though, that this idea never entered my head before! I should have left long ago. Goodbye until we're reunited, Maria Aleksandrovna.

July 9

I purposely gave myself twenty-four hours to reflect, and now I'm absolutely convinced that I have no reason to stay here. The dust in the streets is so invasive that it stings my eyes. I'm already beginning to pack today. I'll probably leave the day after tomorrow, and I'll have the pleasure of seeing you within ten days. I hope that you'll welcome me the way you did before. Incidentally, your sister is still staying at your aunt's, isn't she?

Maria Aleksandrovna, allow me to shake your hand warmly and say with all my heart, "Goodbye until we're reunited." I'd been preparing to leave, but that letter has quickened my resolve. Supposing that the letter proves nothing, even supposing that Ninetta wouldn't please anyone else—me, for instance—I'm still leaving. That's definite now. Until we're reunited.

Your A.S.

XIII
From Maria Aleksandrovna to Aleksei Petrovich

Village of ——no, July 16, 1840

Are you are coming here, Aleksei Petrovich? Will you really be with us soon? I won't conceal the fact that this news both delights and disturbs me. . . . What will our reunion be like? Will the spiritual tie that seems to me to have developed between us endure? Won't it be ruptured when we meet? I don't know—I feel afraid somehow. I won't respond to your last letter, although I could say a great deal. I'm putting it all off until our reunion. My mother is very pleased that you're coming. . . . She knew that I was corresponding with you. The weather is wonderful. We'll go on numerous walks, and I'll show you some new places I've discovered. . . . I especially like one long, narrow valley lying between hills that are blanketed by a forest. . . . The valley seems to be hiding in their bends. A little brook runs through it, barely appearing to move amid a mass of grass and flowers.... You'll see. Come. Perhaps you won't be bored.

M.B.

P.S. I don't think you'll encounter my sister—she's still staying at my aunt's. I think (but this is between us) that she's going to marry a very genial young man—an officer. Why did you send me that letter from Naples? Life here can't help but seem dingy and poor by contrast to all that luxury and splendor. But Mademoiselle Ninetta is wrong. Flowers do grow and have fragrance—even where we are.

XIV
From Maria Alekandrovna to Aleksei Petrovich

Village of ——no, January 1841

I've written to you several times, Aleksei Petrovich.... You haven't replied. Are you alive? Perhaps you've gotten tired of our correspondence—perhaps you've found a diversion more pleasant than the letters of a provincial young lady can afford you. You evidently remembered me simply because you had nothing better to do. If that's the case, I wish you happiness. If you don't answer me now, I won't trouble you any further. It only remains for me to regret my indiscretion in allowing myself to have been bestirred in vain, in having held out my hand to another human being and having emerged from my lonely corner, if only for a moment. Now I have to remain in it forever, I have to lock myself in—that's my allotted fate, the fate of all old maids. I have to grow accustomed to this idea. It's useless to go out into the light of day—it's pointless to long for fresh air when one's lungs can't stand it. By the way, we're completely hemmed in now by deadly drifts of snow. In the future, I'll be wiser.... No one dies from boredom, but one quite possibly could perish from misery. If I'm wrong, prove it to me. But I don't think I'm wrong. In any case, goodbye. I wish you every happiness.

M.B.

XV
From Aleksei Petrovich to Maria Aleksandrovna

Dresden, September 1842

I'm writing to you, dear Maria Aleksandrovna, and I'm writing only because I don't want to die without saying goodbye to you, without having reminded you of me. I've been condemned by the doctors . . . and I myself can feel my life ebbing away. A rose is standing in a vase on my bedside table—before it withers, I'll no longer exist. This comparison isn't an altogether apt one, however. A rose is far more interesting than I am.

As you see, I'm abroad. It's been six months since I arrived in Dresden. I received your final letters—I'm ashamed to confess— more than a year ago. I lost some of them, and never responded to you. . . . I'll tell you why in a moment. But it's apparent that you were always dear to me. I have no desire to say goodbye to anyone but you, although perhaps I have no one else to say goodbye to.

Shortly after I wrote my last letter to you (I was on the very brink of departure for your region, and had made various arrangements in advance), an incident occurred that, one may legitimately say, had a strong impact on my fate, so strong an impact that I'm dying here now thanks to that incident. It was this: I went to the theater to see a ballet. I'd never cared for ballet, and had always nourished a secret dislike for every sort of actress, singer, and dancer. . . . But it's evidently impossible to change one's fate. No one knows himself, and no one can foresee the future. Actually, only the unexpected happens in life, and we do nothing during an entire lifetime except accommodate ourselves to events. . . . But I seem to be lapsing into philosophy again. That old habit! In brief, I fell in love with a dancer.

This was all the more strange in that one couldn't even call her a beauty. It's true that she had marvelous ash-blond hair and large, bright eyes with a thoughtful and yet mischievous look in them. . . . How could I fail to know the look in those eyes? I melted and swooned in their rays for a whole year. She had a marvelous figure, and when she danced her national dance, the members of the audience would stamp their feet and shout with delight. . . . But, it seems, no one else fell in love with her except me—at least, no one fell in love with her the way I did. From the very moment I first saw her (would you believe it, I merely have to close my eyes and the theater instantly appears before me, I see the nearly empty stage intended to represent the heart of a forest, and she's running in from the righthand wing with a wreath of grape leaves on her head and a tigerskin over her shoulders), from that fatal moment on, I totally belonged to her, just the way a dog belongs to its master. And if I don't belong to her right now, as I lie here dying, it's only because she drove me away.

To tell you the truth, she never particularly cared about me. She barely noticed me, even though she was extremely good-natured about making use of my money. To her I was, as she expressed it in her broken French, *"oun Rousso, boun enfant,"* and nothing more. But I ... I couldn't live anywhere she didn't live, so I tore myself away from everything dear to me, from my country itself, once and for all, and followed that woman.

You'll think, perhaps, that she was intelligent? Not in the least! One needed merely to glance at her low forehead, merely to get a glimpse of her lazy, carefree smile to become instantly convinced as to the poverty of her intellectual gifts. And I never imagined her to be an exceptional woman. In fact, I never deceived myself about her for one moment. But that didn't help me in any way. Whatever I might have thought about her in her absence, I felt nothing but slavish adoration in her presence.... Knights often fall under this sort of enchantment in German fairy tales. I couldn't tear my eyes away from her face, I never tired of listening to her talk, of admiring her every gesture—I even breathed when she did. She was kindhearted and unconstrained, though—too unconstrained. She didn't flaunt herself the way actresses generally do. She had a lot of vitality, that is, a lot of blood, that splendid southern blood into which the sun of those parts must have poured some of its beams. She slept for nine hours a day, loved to eat, and never read a single printed line with the possible exception of newspaper articles in which she was mentioned. Virtually the only tender feeling she ever experienced was her devotion to *il signore Carlino*, a greedy little Italian who served in the capacity of her secretary, and whom she subsequently married.

How could I fall in love with such a woman—I, a man who was versed in all sorts of intellectual sophistries, a man who was already growing old? ... Who could have expected it? I, at least, didn't expect it at all. I didn't expect that I'd ever have to play such a role. I didn't expect that I'd hang around rehearsals, standing behind the scenery, bored and freezing to death, inhaling the dust and grime of the theater, becoming acquainted with all sorts of thoroughly disreputable people.... Becoming acquainted, did I say? More like fawning over them. I didn't expect that I'd carry a dancer's shawl, buy her new gloves, clean her old ones with stale bread (I even did that, alas!), carry her bouquets home, run back and forth between the offices of journalists and editors, squander my income, sing serenades, catch colds, completely exhaust myself. . . . I didn't expect that I'd eventually be given the mocking nickname *"der Kunst-barbar"* in a little German town. . . . And all of this was in vain, in the fullest sense of the term—in vain. That's exactly what it was. . . . Do you remember how we used to discuss love, debating all sorts of nuances, in our conversations and letters? But, in fact, it turns out that real love is a feeling utterly unlike the one we envisioned. Love isn't actually a feeling at all—it's an illness, a certain condition of body and soul. It doesn't develop gradually. One can't doubt its existence, and one can't outwit it, although it doesn't always manifest itself in the same form. Usually it takes possession of someone without his permission, all of a sudden, against his will—just like cholera or a fever. . . . Love seizes him, the poor creature, the way a hawk pounces on a chicken and carries it off wherever the hawk pleases, no matter how it struggles or resists. . . . There's no equality in love, there's none of that so-called free union of souls or any other such idealized notion concocted by German professors at their leisure. . . . No, in love, one person is the slave and the other is the master—and the poets are correct to speak about the chains imposed by love. Yes, love is a chain, the heaviest kind to bear. That's the conclusion I've reached, at least, and I've reached it in the course of experience. Indeed, I've bought this conviction at the cost of my life, since I'm dying as a slave.

What a fate has been meted out to me, if you think about it! In my early youth, nothing would satisfy me but to take heaven by storm. . . . Then I began to dream about the welfare of all humanity, the welfare of my country—then that passed, too. I only thought about establishing a home and a domestic life for myself . . . and then I tripped over an anthill—and fell right into my grave. . . . Ah, what masters we Russians are at ending up like this!

But it's time to turn away from all that—it's way past time! May this burden be lifted from my soul along with my life! For the last time, if only for an instant, I want to enjoy the benevolent, gentle feeling that spreads through me like a soft glow as soon as I think of you. Your image is doubly precious to me now. . . . The image of my country rises up with it in front of me; I send farewell regards both to it and to you. Live, live long and happily, and re-member one thing: whether you remain in that remote corner of the steppes, where it's been so difficult for you at times but where I so much would have liked to spend my last days, or whether you em-bark upon a different course, remember that life deceives everyone except the individual who doesn't contemplate it, the individual who demands nothing from it, the individual who serenely accepts its few gifts and serenely makes the most of them. Go forward while you can, but if your strength fails you, sit down near the road and gaze without anger or envy at those who pass by. They don't have far to go, either. I didn't tell you this before, but death will teach it to anyone. Meanwhile, who can say what constitutes life, what constitutes truth? Do you remember who it was that gave no reply to this question? . . . Farewell, Maria Aleksandrovna, farewell for the last time. Don't think badly of poor

Aleksei

Letter to E. E. Lambert[1]

Village of Spasskoe.

June 10, 1856.

Your letter from Revel, dear Countess, made me very happy and somewhat embarrassed: I feel that I don't deserve all those nice things with which it is filled, and I know (though I've only read thirty pages of your book so far) that the human heart is made such that even undeserved praise provides a secret gratification for it—or at least the pleasure of humility. . . . These are all dangerous feelings, and it's better not even to speak of them. Thank you for remembering me, and I hope with all my heart that your stay in Revel will be pleasurable.

I'll say a few words about myself. In the first place, I received the news from Petersburg that my passport has been issued—and I'm leaving Russia around the 20th of next month, so we'll still have time to exchange letters. I hope that our correspondence won't cease while I'm abroad. The permission to travel abroad pleases me . . . but at the same time I can't help admitting that it would be better for me not to go. To go abroad at my age means to fix my course permanently on a gypsy life and to abandon all thoughts of a family life. But what can be done? Obviously, such is my fate. But that's easily said: people without firmness of character love to make up a "fate" for themselves; that relieves them of the necessity of having their own will and of taking responsibility for themselves. In any event, *le vin est tiré—il faut le boire.*

I have no manor house here; I had one, but it burned down; I live in one old wing. But there's a large, fine orchard, just neighbor ladies—and I'm hardly an Onegin!

The hunting season hasn't yet begun. Oh yes, there's something else I should tell you: the anecdote I told you about a woman with whom I had dinner and who unintentionally disillusioned me has nothing to do with the woman about whom you write. . . .

You write Russian very nicely—do you know that? And not a single mistake, even in spelling! Nonetheless, write me in French. For one still observes a certain effort in your selection of phrase— and it's as if you translate mentally from French. It'll be easier for you to write French—and you'll write more eagerly.

---

1. Countess Elizaveta Egorovna Lambert, née Kankrina (1821-83), the wife of I. K. Lambert. An educated woman of great refinement, she and Turgenev conducted a lively, lengthy correspondence.

It pleases me to think that we'll be exchanging ideas and feelings, even if only occasionally; it's even more pleasant to think that there will come a time, God willing, when we'll see each other again and—I dare to hope—become firm friends. In the life of a man, just as in the life of a woman, there comes a time when one values calm, stable relationships more than anything else. Bright autumn days are the most beautiful days in the year. I hope that I'll be able to persuade you then not to be afraid to read Pushkin and others. Are you still afraid of "alarm"?

I no longer hope for happiness for myself, i.e., happiness in the same *alarming* sense in which it's currently understood by young hearts: there's no point in thinking about flowers when the time for blossoming has passed. God grant that there may at least be some sort of fruit—and those vain backward impulses can only hinder its ripening. One must learn from nature's correct, tranquil movement and her humility. . . . But when it comes to words, we're all wise men; let the first ridiculous passing fancy come our way, though, and we up and chase after it.

When I glance back at my life, all I seem to have done is chase after ridiculous things. Don Quixote at least believed in the beauty of his Dulcinea, but in our era Don Quixotes see that their Dulcineas are ugly and keep running after them anyway.

We have no ideal—that's why all this happens. Yet an ideal comes only from a strong civic environment, art (or science), and religion. But not everyone is born an Athenian or an Englishman, an artist or scientist—and religion isn't granted to everyone immediately. We'll wait and believe—and know that for the time being we're behaving foolishly. That realization may nevertheless be useful.

But I seem to have gotten carried away with philosophizing. And therefore—with your permission (remember, you said that I could)—I clasp your hand respectfully and cordially, I wish you all the best, and remain

Your sincerely devoted
Ivan Turgenev.

P.S. My sincere regards to your husband.

Letter to L. N. Tolstoy

Courtavenel (near Paris).
September 13, 1856.

Your letter reached me rather late, dear Lev Nikolaevich—I'd gone to England and found it here upon my return. I'll begin with the fact that I'm very grateful for what you wrote and for your having sent it to me; I'll never cease loving you and treasuring your friendship, although—and this is probably my fault—for a long time, each of us will feel a certain awkwardness in the presence of the other. I'm certain that we'll see each other again and will see each other often; when I was leaving, I told your sister that I wouldn't have the time to visit you at Iasnaia—but she understood my words quite differently. I think that you yourself understand the source of the awkwardness that I just mentioned. You're the only person with whom I've had such misunderstandings; that's happened precisely because I didn't want to limit myself merely to simple friendly relations with you—I wanted to go further and deeper; but I did that incautiously, I upset you, I alarmed you, and when I noticed my mistake, I backed away, perhaps too hurriedly; that's the reason this "ravine" has formed between us. But this awkwardness is only a *physical* impression and nothing more; and if, on meeting you, I act upset again, it really won't be because I'm a bad person. I assure you that there's no reason to think up a different explanation. Perhaps just to add that I'm much older than you and have traveled a different road. Aside from our own so-called literary interests—I'm convinced of this—we have few points of contact; your whole life has been aimed at the future, all mine has been built on the past. For me to follow you is impossible; for you to follow me is just as impossible; you're too remote from me, besides which, you stand too firmly on your own feet to become anyone's disciple. I can assure you that I never thought you were malicious, and I never suspected literary envy in you. I assumed (excuse me for saying this) that there was a great deal of confusion in you, but never anything bad; and you yourself are too perspicacious not to know that if one of us should envy the other, then it won't be me. In a word, I doubt that we'll ever be friends in Rousseau's sense of the word; but each of us will love the other, rejoice at his successes, and, when you calm down, I'm certain that we'll offer each other our hands just as happily and freely as we did on the day I first met you in Petersburg.

But enough about this. It's better that you tell me what you've been doing. Have you written anything? What about *Youth?* What about the Caucasus tale? And your brother's notes—have you published them and sent them to Petersburg? And can he really be planning to remain in the Caucasus? If he returns to the province of Tula, give him my regards. Where do you intend to spend the winter? All of this interests me very much. As for myself, I won't get to Spasskoe before next June. I haven't done anything here yet, but when I move to Paris (in about three weeks), I'll get down to work. I'm very happy here; I'm with people whom I sincerely love—and who love me. My tale will be in the October issue of *The Contemporary*—tell me whether you like it. My address for the time being is: Paris, poste restante. Fet is in Paris—he sends his regards—and I received a letter from Nekrasov in Berlin. *The Contemporary* will somehow manage without him.

Farewell, be well. I clasp your hand firmly.

Your Ivan Turgenev.

P.S. I'm writing to you in a letter to your sister. My regards to your aunt. By the way, if it's a matter of the 28th day of the month, I, too, was born on the 28th.

Rudin

I

It was a tranquil summer morning. The sun had already risen quite high in the clear sky, but the fields were still sparkling with dew, a fragrant, fresh breeze was wafting across the recently awakened valleys, and birds were merrily pouring forth their morning song in the forest, which was still damp and hushed. A small village was visible on the ridge of a gentle hill covered from top to bottom with blossoming rye. A young woman wearing a white muslin dress and a round straw hat, carrying a parasol in her hand, was walking along a narrow country road toward this small village. A servant boy was following her at a distance.

She was proceeding unhurriedly, as though enjoying the walk. The high, flexible stalks of rye swayed in long, softly rustling rows all around her, taking on a silvery green hue in some places and a trace of red in others. The larks were trilling overhead. The young woman had come from her own estate, which was located not more than a verst from the village toward which she was walking. Her name was Aleksandra Pavlovna Lipina. She was a childless widow who was fairly well off and lived with her brother, a retired cavalry officer named Sergei Pavlych Volyntsev. He was unmarried and supervised the management of her property.

Aleksandra Pavlovna reached the village and then, stopping in front of the farthest hut, a very old, low one, she summoned the boy and told him to go in and inquire about its mistress's health. He returned quickly, accompanied by a decrepit, elderly peasant with a white beard.

"Well, how is she?" asked Aleksandra Pavlovna.

"Well, she's still alive ...," began the old man.

"May I go in?"

"Why not? Yes."

Aleksandra Pavlovna entered the hut. It was crowded, stuffy, and smoky inside. Someone stirred on the stove that constituted the bed and began to moan. Aleksandra Pavlovna looked around in the semidarkness and discerned an elderly woman's jaundiced, wrinkled face wrapped in a checked kerchief. Covered up to her very chin by a heavy overcoat, she was having difficulty breathing and her wasted hands were twitching.

Aleksandra Pavlovna approached the elderly woman and laid her fingers on the woman's forehead. It was burning hot.

"How do you feel, Matrena?" she asked, bending over the bed.

"O—oh!" groaned the elderly woman, trying to see her visitor clearly. "Bad, very bad, my dear! My final hour has come, my darling!"

"God is merciful, Matrena, so perhaps you'll get better soon. Did you take the medicine I sent you?"

The elderly woman moaned painfully and didn't answer. She'd barely heard the question.

"She's taken it," declared the elderly man, who was standing at the door.

Aleksandra Pavlovna turned to him.

"Does anyone stay with her besides you?" she inquired.

"There's a girl, her granddaughter, but she keeps running away. She won't stay with her for long—she's such a flighty thing. It's too much trouble for her to give the old woman a drink of water. And I'm old—what use can I be?"

"Shouldn't she be taken to my estate, to the hospital?"

"No! Why take her to the hospital? She'd die just the same. She's lived out her life. It's God's will now, it seems. She'll never get up again. How could she go to the hospital? If they tried to lift her, she'd die."

"Oh!" groaned the sick woman. "My pretty lady, don't abandon my little orphan. Our masters are far away, but you. . . . "

She couldn't go on. She'd used up all her strength saying as much as she had.

"Don't worry," replied Aleksandra Pavlovna. "Everything will be taken care of. Here's some tea and sugar I've brought for you. If you can manage, you should drink some. Do you have a samovar, I wonder?" she added, glancing at the elderly man.

"A samovar? We don't have a samovar, but we could get one."

"Then get one, or else I'll send you one. And tell your grand-daughter not to leave her like this. Tell her it's not right."

The elderly man didn't reply, merely grasping the parcel of tea and sugar with both hands.

"Well, goodbye, Matrena!" said Aleksandra Pavlovna. "I'll come and see you again, but you mustn't lose heart. And take your medicine regularly."

The elderly woman raised her head and leaned slightly toward Aleksandra Pavlovna.

"Give me your little hand, dear lady," she murmured.

Aleksandra Pavlovna didn't extend her hand, but bent over and kissed her on the forehead instead.

"Now be sure to give her the medicine regularly," she said to the elderly man as she went out, "the way it's written down, and give her some tea to drink."

Once again, the elderly man didn't reply, but merely bowed.

Aleksandra Pavlovna breathed more easily when she emerged into the fresh air. She put up her parasol and was about to start for home when a man of about thirty suddenly appeared from around the corner of a little hut driving a low racing carriage, wearing an old overcoat made of gray linen and a cap of the same material. When he caught sight of Aleksandra Pavlovna, he immediately stopped his horse and turned toward her. His broad, pale face, with its small, light-gray eyes and nearly white moustache, almost matched the color of his clothes.

"Good morning!" he began, with a lazy smile. "What are you doing here, if I may ask?"

"I've been visiting a sick woman. . . . And where have you come here from, Mikhailo Mikhailych?"

The man addressed as Mikhailo Mikhailych looked into her eyes and smiled again.

"You're doing a good deed," he went on, "when you visit the sick, but wouldn't it be better for you to take her to the hospital?"

"She's too weak. It's impossible to move her."

"But you don't intend to close your hospital?"

"Close it? Why?"

"Just because."

"What a strange notion! Whatever put such an idea in your head?"

"Oh, you're always spending time with Daria Mikhailovna Lasunskaia now, you know. You seem to be under her influence.

And, in her words, hospitals, schools, and all those sorts of things are mere trifles—useless fads. Philanthropy ought to be entirely personal, and education as well, since this is all a matter of the soul.... That's how she puts it, I believe. From whom did she adopt that opinion, I wonder?"

Aleksandra Pavlovna laughed.

"Daria Mikhailovna is an intelligent woman. I like her, and I respect her very much, but even she can make mistakes, and I don't believe everything she says."

"And it's a very good thing you don't," Mikhailo Mikhailych responded, remaining seated in his carriage, "since she barely believes what she says herself. I'm very glad I ran into you."

"Why?"

"That's a fine question! As though it weren't always delightful to run into you. Today you look as bright and fresh as the morning itself."

Aleksandra Pavlovna laughed again.

"Why are you laughing?"

"Why, indeed! If you could see what a cold, indifferent expression you had on your face as you paid me your compliment! I'm surprised you didn't yawn as you uttered the last word!"

"A cold expression.... You always want fire, but a fire is no good at all. It flares up and smokes and goes out."

"And warms," put in Aleksandra Pavlovna.

"Yes . . . and burns."

"Well, what if it does burn? There's no great harm in that, either! Anyway, it's better than.... "

"Well, I'll see what you say when you get truly burned one day," Mikhailo Mikhailych interrupted her irritably, and he slapped his horse's back with the reins. "Goodbye."

"Mikhailo Mikhailych, wait a minute," cried Aleksandra Pavlovna. "When are you coming to visit us?"

"Tomorrow. Give my regards to your brother."

And the carriage rolled away.

Aleksandra Pavlovna watched Mikhailo Mikhailych leave.

"What a sack!" she thought. Sitting all huddled up, covered with dust, his cap pushed to the back of his head and tufts of blond hair straggling from beneath it, he did strikingly resemble a huge sack of flour.

Aleksandra Pavlovna calmly turned back onto the road homeward. She walked along with downcast eyes. The clop of a horse nearby made her stop and raise her head. . . . Her brother had ridden out on horseback to meet her; a young man of medium height wearing a light, unbuttoned coat, a light tie, and a light-gray hat, carrying a cane in his hand, was walking beside him. He'd been smiling at Aleksandra Pavlovna for a long while, even though he'd seen that she was absorbed in thought and wasn't noticing anything. As soon as she stopped, he went up to her and joyfully, almost tenderly, cried out:

"Good morning, Aleksandra Pavlovna, good morning!"

"Ah! Konstantin Diomidych! Good morning!" she replied. "Have you come from Daria Mikhailovna's?"

"Precisely, precisely," the young man responded with a radiant expression on his face. "From Daria Mikhailovna's. Daria Mikhailovna sent me to see you. I preferred to walk. . . . It's such a glorious morning, and it's only four versts from here. When I arrived, you weren't at home. Your brother told me you'd gone to Semenovka. He was just going out to the fields, and so I came with him to meet you. Yes, indeed. How very delightful this is!"

The young man spoke Russian clearly and accurately but with a foreign accent, although it was difficult to tell exactly what kind of accent it was. There was something Asiatic in his features: his long aquiline nose, large prominent eyes, thick red lips, retreating forehead, and jet-black hair—everything about him suggested Eastern extraction. But the young man said that his surname was Pandalevskii and referred to Odessa as his birthplace, even though he'd been brought up somewhere in Belorussia by a rich, benevolent widow. Another widow had obtained a government post for him. Middle-aged ladies in general eagerly befriended Konstantin Diomidych; he knew how to seek them out and find them. At this very moment, he was living with a wealthy lady landowner, Daria Mikhailovna Lasunskaia, in a capacity somewhere between that of a guest and a dependent. He was very polite and obliging, full of sensibilities, and secretly inclined to sensuality; he had a pleasant voice, played the piano sufficiently well, and had a habit of gazing intently into the eyes of anyone he was speaking to. He dressed very neatly, kept the same clothes for an extremely long time, shaved his broad chin very carefully, and arranged his hair curl by curl.

Aleksandra Pavlovna listened to his entire speech and then turned toward her brother.

"I keep running into people today. I've just been chatting with Lezhnev."

"Ah, Lezhnev! Was he going somewhere?"

"Yes, and can you imagine, he was driving a racing carriage and wearing a sort of linen sack, all covered with dust. . . . What an eccentric man he is!"

"Maybe so, but he's an outstanding individual."

"Who? Mr. Lezhnev?" Pandalevskii asked as though in surprise.

"Yes, Mikhailo Mikhailych Lezhnev," insisted Volyntsev. "Well, goodbye, sister. It's time for me to go to the fields—they're sowing your buckwheat. Mr. Pandalevskii will escort you home." And Volyntsev rode off at a trot.

"With the greatest of pleasure!" cried Konstantin Diomidych, offering Aleksandra Pavlovna his arm.

She took it and they both turned along the path to her house.

Walking with Aleksandra Pavlovna on his arm evidently afforded Konstantin Diomidych great delight: he proceeded with short, buoyant steps and smiled incessantly, while his exotic eyes began to glisten with a slight moisture. This was no rare occurrence, however: it didn't cost Konstantin Diomidych much to become emotional and dissolve into tears. And who wouldn't have been pleased to escort a pretty, graceful young woman? The entire district was unanimous in declaring Aleksandra Pavlovna charming—and the district wasn't wrong. Her straight, ever so slightly tilted little nose alone would have been enough to drive any mortal man out of his senses, to say nothing of her velvety dark eyes, her golden brown hair, the dimples in her smoothly curved cheeks, and her other attractions. But best of all was the sweet expression on her face: confiding, kindly, and gentle, it soothed and appealed at the same time. Aleksandra Pavlovna had the gaze and smile of a child; other women found her a bit simple. . . . Who could desire anything more?

"Daria Mikhailovna sent you to see me, you say?" she asked Pandalevskii.

"Yes, they sent me," he replied, pronouncing the letter *s* somewhat like the English *th*. "They'd particularly appreciate it if you'd be so good as to dine with them today, and told me to beg you to come most urgently." (Pandalevskii strongly preferred the plural when speaking in the third person, especially in reference to ladies.) "They're expecting a new guest whom they'd particularly like you to meet."

"Who's that?"

"Someone named Baron Muffel, a chamberlain from Petersburg.

Daria Mikhailovna recently made his acquaintance at Prince Garin's, and extols him as an amiable, cultivated young man. The baron is also interested in literature or, more strictly speaking—Ah! What an exquisite butterfly! Please look at it!—more strictly speaking, in political economics. He's written an article about some very interesting issue and wants to get Daria Mikhailovna's opinion."

"On an article about political economics?"

"From the linguistic point of view, Aleksandra Pavlovna, from the linguistic point of view. You're well aware, I presume, that Daria Mikhailovna is an authority in that area. Zhukovskii used to ask her for advice, and my benefactor in Odessa, that benevolent old gentleman, Roksolan Mediarovich Ksandryka.... You undoubtedly recognize the name of this eminent personage?"

"No, I've never heard of him."

"You've never heard of such a man? Amazing! I was going to say that Roksolan Mediarovich always had the very highest opinion of Daria Mikhailovna's knowledge of Russian."

"Is this baron a teacher, then?" asked Aleksandra Pavlovna.

"Not in the least. Daria Mikhailovna says, on the contrary, one can immediately see that he belongs to the best social circles. He once spoke about Beethoven so eloquently that even the old prince was enraptured by it. That, I admit, I wish I'd heard. You know that music is one of my passions. Allow me to offer you this lovely wildflower."

Aleksandra Pavlovna accepted the flower and, when she'd walked a few steps farther, let it fall to the ground. They weren't more than two hundred feet from her house. It had been built and whitewashed recently, and its wide, bright windows gleamed hospitably amid the thick foliage of old lime and maple trees.

"And so what message do you want me to give Daria Mikhailovna?" Pandalevskii began, slightly offended by the fate of the flower he'd given her. "Will you come for dinner? Your brother is invited, too."

"Yes, we'll most certainly come. And how is Natasha?"

"Natalia Alekseevna is well, thank God. But we've already passed the road that turns off toward Daria Mikhailovna's. Allow me to bid you farewell."

Aleksandra Pavlovna stopped. "But won't you come in?" she inquired in an indecisive tone of voice.

"I'd be deeply delighted, but I'm afraid it's late. Daria Mikhailovna wishes to hear a new étude by Thalberg, so I have to practice in order to get it ready. Besides, I must confess, I doubt that my visit would afford you any pleasure."

"Oh, no! Why on earth . . . ?"

Pandalevskii sighed and lowered his gaze expressively.

"Goodbye, Aleksandra Pavlovna!" he said after a slight pause, and then bowed and took a step backward.

Aleksandra Pavlovna turned away from him and headed toward her house.

Konstantin Diomidych headed homeward as well. All the amicability instantly vanished from his face, and a self-confident, almost severe expression appeared on it. Even his stride changed: his steps became farther apart and heavier. He'd walked for about two versts, casually swinging his cane, when he suddenly began to smile again: he'd caught sight of a young, rather pretty peasant girl by the roadside who was driving some calves out of an oatfield. Konstantin Diomidych approached the girl as warily as a cat and began to speak to her. She didn't say anything at first, merely blushing and laughing, but she eventually hid her face behind her sleeve, turned her back toward him, and murmured, "Go away, sir, truly. . . ."

Konstantin Diomidych shook his finger at her and told her to bring him some cornflowers.

"What do you want with cornflowers? Are you going to make a wreath?" retorted the girl. "There now, go away, master, truly. . . ."

"Listen, my pretty little sweet . . . ," Konstantin Diomidych began.

"There now, go away," the girl interrupted him. "The young gentlemen are coming."

Konstantin Diomidych looked around. Vania and Petia, Daria Mikhailovna's sons, were indeed running down the road; their tutor, Basistov, was walking behind them. A twenty-two-year-old young man who'd just finished his studies, Basistov was a full-grown youth with a simple face, a large nose, thick lips, and small piglike eyes; he was plain and awkward, but he was also kind, honest, and forthright. He dressed untidily and wore his hair long—not as an affectation, but out of laziness. He liked to eat and he liked to sleep, but he also liked a good book and an earnest conversation, and he hated Pandalevskii with all his heart.

Daria Mikhailovna's children worshiped Basistov and yet weren't the least bit afraid of him. He was on friendly terms with the rest of the household as well, a fact not altogether pleasing to its mistress, although she was fond of declaring that, as far as she was concerned, social prejudices didn't exist.

"Good morning, my dears," began Konstantin Diomidych. "How early you've come for your walk today! I myself have been out for quite a while already," he added, turning to Basistov. "It's a passion of mine—enjoying nature."

"We saw how you were enjoying nature," muttered Basistov.

"You're a materialist. God knows what you're imagining! I know you." When Pandalevskii spoke to Basistov or people like Basistov, he grew slightly irritated and pronounced the letter *s* quite clearly, even hissing slightly.

"Why, were you asking that girl for directions, in fact?" Basistov queried, his eyes darting from right to left.

He felt Pandalevskii staring straight at his face, which was exceedingly unpleasant for Basistov.

"I repeat, you're a materialist and nothing more. You doubtlessly prefer to observe solely the prosaic side...."

"Boys!" Basistov suddenly shouted. "See that willow tree in the meadow? Let's see who can get to it first. One! Two! Three!"

The boys ran off toward the willow at full speed. Basistov raced after them.

"What a peasant!" thought Pandalevskii. "He's spoiling those boys. An absolute peasant!"

And glancing with satisfaction at his own neat, elegant figure, Konstantin Diomidych brushed his open hand across his coat sleeve twice, pulled up his collar, and went on his way. When he reached his own room, he donned an old robe and sat down at the piano with an anxious expression on his face.

II

Daria Mikhailovna's house was considered virtually the preeminent one in the entire province. It was a huge stone edifice that had been constructed according to plans drawn up by Rastrelli in the style of the preceding century and stood in a commanding position on the summit of a hill at whose base flowed one of central Russia's principal rivers. Daria Mikhailovna herself was a wealthy, distinguished lady, the widow of a privy councillor. Although Pandalevskii repeatedly declared that she knew all of Europe and all of Europe knew her, Europe actually didn't know her very well. She hadn't even played a very prominent role in Petersburg, but everyone in Moscow did know her and exchanged visits with her. She moved in the highest social circles there, and was described as a somewhat eccentric woman who wasn't wholly good-natured but was exceedingly intelligent. She'd been very pretty in her youth. Poets had written verses to her; young men had been in love with her; distinguished men had pursued her. But twenty-five or thirty years had passed since then, and no trace of her former charms remained. Everyone who saw her for the first time at this point impulsively asked themselves whether this thin, sharp-nosed, sallow-complexioned, not-yet-old woman could possibly have ever been a beauty. Could she really be the same woman who'd been the inspiration of poets?. . . And everyone marveled inwardly at the mutability of all earthly things. It's true, as Pandalevskii discovered, that Daria Mikhailovna had preserved her magnificent eyes amazingly well—but this is the same Pandalevskii who maintained that all of Europe knew her.

Daria Mikhailovna moved to her country estate every summer, accompanied by her children (she had three: a seventeen-year-old daughter, Natalia, and two sons, aged nine and ten). She kept an open house in the countryside, that is, she received visits from men, especially unmarried ones—she couldn't endure provincial ladies. But what treatment she received from those ladies in return! According to them, Daria Mikhailovna was a haughty, immoral, insufferable tyrant, and worst of all, she allowed herself to take such liberties in conversation—it was simply shocking! Daria Mikhailovna certainly didn't like to constrain herself in the countryside, and a hint of the contempt of the social lioness from the capital for the petty, obscure creatures who surrounded her could be observed in the spontaneous directness of her manners. She treated her city acquaintances in quite relaxed and even sarcastic fashion, but that hint of contempt wasn't there.

By the way, reader, have you noticed that someone who behaves quite casually toward his inferiors never behaves casually toward his superiors? Why is that? But then again, such questions lead nowhere.

When Konstantin Diomidych, having finally learned the Thalberg étude by heart, descended from his tidy, cheerful room to the drawing room, he found that the entire household had already assembled; the salon had already begun. The lady of the house was reposing on a wide couch, her feet curled up beneath her and a new French pamphlet in her hand; Daria Mikhailovna's daughter was sitting behind an embroidery frame on one side of the window; Mlle. Boncourt, the governess, was sitting on the other side. She was a dried-up old maid of about sixty who wore fake black curls under a multicolored cap and cotton wool in her ears. Basistov had settled down in the corner near the door and was reading a newspaper; Petia and Vania were playing checkers near him. And bending toward the fire, his hands clasped behind his back, stood a short gentleman with a swarthy complexion, bristling gray hair, and evasive dark eyes, a certain Afrikan Semenych Pigasov.

This Pigasov was a strange person. Brimming with antagonism toward everything and everyone—especially women—he complained from morning to night, sometimes quite legitimately, sometimes rather pointlessly, but always with gusto. His irritability almost approached petulance. His laugh, the sound of his voice, his entire being seemed steeped in venom. Daria Mikhailovna always gave Pigasov a cordial reception, since he amused her with his sallies, which were certainly funny enough. He had an endless passion for exaggeration. For example, if he were informed of any disaster—that a village had been struck by lightning, or that a mill had been carried away by floods, or that a peasant had cut off his hand with an axe—he invariably asked, with concentrated bitterness, "And what's her name?" By this he meant: what's the name of the woman responsible for this misfortune? For he was convinced that a woman was the cause of every misfortune, if only you looked into the matter deeply enough. Once he went down on his knees before a lady he hardly knew at all, who'd been pressing her hospitality upon him, and tearfully—but with hostility written all over his face—begged her to have mercy on him, saying that he'd never done her any harm and promising that he wouldn't come to see her in the future. When a horse had bolted on a hill while one of Daria Mikhailovna's maids was riding it, had thrown her into a ditch, and had nearly killed her, from that day on, Pigasov always referred to that horse as the "good, good horse," and he even came to regard that hill and that ditch as particularly picturesque spots.

Pigasov hadn't been lucky in life—he'd reduced himself to this ludicrous position. He came from a poor family: his father had served in various minor positions, could barely read or write, and hadn't worried about his son's education; he'd fed and clothed him, but nothing more. His mother had spoiled him, but died while he was still young. Pigasov had educated himself, sent himself to the district school and then to high school, taught himself French,

German, even Latin, and, after finishing high school with a cer-
tificate of excellence, had gone to the University of Dorpat, where
he'd waged a ceaseless struggle with poverty but had managed to
complete a three-year course.

Pigasov's talents didn't surpass the level of the ordinary. Patience
and perseverance were his strengths, but the most powerful force
driving him was ambition, which manifested itself in the desire to
be accepted into good society, not to be inferior to others, to defy
fate. This ambition had led him to study diligently and to attend
the University of Dorpat. Poverty had exasperated him, and had
rendered him suspicious and cunning. He expressed himself with
originality: from his youth onward, he'd cultivated a distinctive
sort of acrimonious, provocative eloquence. His ideas didn't rise
above the common level, but his manner of speaking made him
seem not merely an intelligent but an extremely bright man.

Upon receiving his degree as a doctoral candidate, Pigasov decided to devote himself to the scholarly profession—he understood
that in no other career could he possibly be viewed as the equal
of his colleagues. (He tried to select them from a higher social
stratum, since he knew how to win their approval, and even tried
to flatter them, although he always criticized them behind their
backs.) But, to tell the truth, he didn't have enough raw material
to succeed. Having educated himself without any love for schol-
arship, Pigasov in essence knew too little. He'd failed horribly in
a public debate, whereas another student who'd shared a room with
him and had constantly been the object of his ridicule, a man of
very limited abilities but the recipient of a proper, solid education,
had thoroughly triumphed.

Pigasov was infuriated by this failure. He threw all his books
and manuscripts into the fire and entered government service. At
first, he didn't do too badly: he made a fair official—not a very
active one and yet an extremely self-confident, bold one. But he
wanted to advance more quickly, made a mistake, got into trouble,
and was forced to retire. He spent three years on a piece of property
he'd bought for himself and suddenly married a wealthy, semi-
educated woman who was captivated by his unceremonious, sarcastic manners. But Pigasov's character had become so sour and
irritable that domestic life was intolerable to him. After residing
with him for a few years, his wife sneaked off to Moscow and sold
her estate to an enterprising speculator, even though Pigasov had
just finished building a house on it. Utterly crushed by this final

blow, Pigasov initiated a lawsuit against his wife, but nothing came
of it. . . . After that, he lived in solitude, paying regular visits to
his neighbors, whom he criticized behind their backs and even to
their faces, who welcomed him with some sort of nervous half-
laugh, although he didn't fill them with any serious dread. He
never picked up a book. He owned about a hundred serfs; his
peasants weren't impoverished.

"Ah! *Constantin!*" Daria Mikhailovna exclaimed, as soon as Pandalevskii entered the drawing room, "Is *Alexandrine* coming?"

"Aleksandra Pavlovna asked me to thank you and to say that
they'll be extremely delighted to come," Konstantin Diomidych
replied, bowing affably in all directions and running his plump,
white hand with its trimmed, triangular nails through his perfectly
arranged hair.

"Is Volyntsev coming, too?"

"Yes."

"So, in your opinion, Afrikan Semenych," Daria Mikhailovna
continued, turning toward Pigasov, "all young ladies are artificial?"

Pigasov's mouth twitched, and he plucked nervously at his sleeve.

"I'm speaking," he began in an unhurried voice—during his
most intense bouts of exasperation he always spoke slowly and
precisely—"I'm speaking about young ladies in general. I'll remain
silent about the present company, naturally."

"But that doesn't prevent you from thinking about them," interjected Daria Mikhailovna.

"I'll remain silent about them," repeated Pigasov. "All young
ladies in general are artificial to the highest degree—artificial in the
expression of their feelings. If a young lady is frightened, for instance, or delighted, or saddened by something, she's sure to strike
some elegant pose first" (Pigasov twisted his body into an awkward
stance and spread out his arms), "and then she'll shriek 'Ah!'—
or laugh, or cry. Once" (here Pigasov smiled complacently), "I
did manage to elicit a genuine, unfeigned expression of emotion
from a remarkably artificial young lady!"

"How did you do that?"

Pigasov's eyes sparkled.

"I poked her in the side from behind with an aspen pole. She
really did shriek then, and I said to her, 'Bravo, bravo! That's the
voice of nature! That was a genuine shriek! Always behave like
that in the future!'"

Everyone in the room laughed.

"What nonsense you spout, Afrikan Semenych!" exclaimed Daria Mikhailovna. "Am I to believe that you'd actually poke a young woman in the side with a pole?"

"Yes, indeed, with a really big pole, like the ones used in the defense of a fort."

"*Mais c'est un horreur ce que vous dites là, Monsieur,*" cried Mlle. Boncourt, looking angrily at the boys, who were convulsed with laughter.

"Oh, you musn't believe him," said Daria Mikhailovna. "Don't you know better?"

But the indignant Frenchwoman couldn't be pacified for a long while, and kept muttering something to herself.

"You needn't believe me," Pigasov continued coolly, "but I assure you that I've told you the simple truth. Who would know it better than I? After this, perhaps you won't believe that our neighbor, Elena Antonovna Chepuzova, told me herself—notice, herself—that she'd murdered her nephew?"

"Another invention!"

"Wait a minute, wait a minute! Listen and judge for yourselves. To be sure, I don't want to slander her. I even like her, as far as one can like a woman. She doesn't have a single book in her house except a calendar. She can only read out loud, an exercise that leads her to perspire violently, and then she complains that her eyes are bursting out of her head. . . . In short, she's a fine woman, and her servant girls get fat. Why should I slander her?"

"You see," remarked Daria Mikhailovna, "Afrikan Semenych has gotten on his high horse, and now he won't get off it all night."

"My high horse! But women have at least three high horses, which they never get off except, perhaps, when they're asleep."

"What are those three?"

"Reproof, reproach, and recrimination."

"Do you know, Afrikan Semenych," began Daria Mikhailovna, "you can't be so bitter toward women for no reason at all. Some woman or other must have. . . . "

"Injured me, you mean?" Pigasov interrupted.

Daria Mikhailovna became somewhat embarrassed. She recalled Pigasov's unfortunate marriage, and just nodded.

"One woman certainly did injure me," said Pigasov, "although she was very, very kind."

"Who was that?"

"My mother," said Pigasov, lowering his voice.

"Your mother? How could she have injured you?"

"She brought me into the world."

Daria Mikhailovna frowned.

"Our conversation seems to have taken a gloomy turn," she said. "*Constantin*, play us Thalberg's new étude. I trust that the sound of the music will soothe Afrikan Semenych. Orpheus soothed the savage beasts."

Konstantin Diomidych took a seat at the piano and played the étude quite well. Natalia Alekseevna listened attentively at first, then bent over her embroidery again.

"*Merci, c'est charmant*," commented Daria Mikhailovna. "I love Thalberg. *Il est si distingué*. What are you thinking about, Afrikan Semenych?"

"I was thinking," Afrikan Semenych began slowly, "that there are three types of egoists: the egoists who live themselves and let others live, the egoists who live themselves and don't let others live, and the egoists who don't live themselves and don't let others live. Women, for the most part, belong to the third type."

"That's very flattering! I'm only surprised at one thing, Afrikan Semenych—what confidence you have in your opinions. Of course, you can never be mistaken."

"Who says so? I make mistakes—a man may be mistaken. But do you know the difference between a man's mistakes and a woman's? You don't? Well, here it is: a man may say, for example, that two times two equals five, or three and a half, not four, but a woman will say that two times two equals a wax candle."

"I think I've heard you say that before. But permit me to ask what connection your notion about the three types of egoists has to the music you've just been listening to?"

"None at all—but I wasn't listening to the music."

"Well, I see that you're incurable, your honor, no matter what," Daria Mikhailovna responded, slightly altering Griboedov's line. "What do you like, since you don't like music? Literature?"

"I like literature, but not contemporary literature."

"Why not?"

"I'll tell you why not. I recently crossed the Oka in a ferryboat with some gentleman. The ferry got stuck in a narrow place and they had to drag everything on board to shore by hand. This gentleman had a very heavy carriage. While the ferrymen were struggling to drag his carriage onto the bank, the gentleman standing on the ferry groaned so loudly that one felt quite sorry for him. . . . Well, I thought, here's a fresh application of the system of the division of labor! That's just like contemporary literature: other people do the work, and it does the groaning."

Daria Mikhailovna smiled.

"And it's called the representation of modern existence," Pigasov continued indefatigably, "by displaying profound sensitivity toward social questions, and so forth. . . . Oh, how I hate those grandiloquent words!"

"Well, the women you attack so fiercely—at least they don't use grandiloquent words."

Pigasov shrugged his shoulders.

"They don't use them because they don't understand them."

Daria Mikhailovna flushed slightly.

"You're beginning to be impertinent, Afrikan Semenych!" she remarked with a forced smile.

Everything in the room grew quiet.

"Where's Zolotonosha?" one of the boys suddenly asked Basistov.

"In the province of Poltava, my dear boy," replied Pigasov, "in the center of the Ukraine." (He was pleased to have an opportunity to change the subject.) "We were speaking about literature," he continued. "If I had money to spare, I'd immediately become a Ukrainian poet."

"What next? A fine poet you'd make!" retorted Daria Mikhailovna. "Do you know Ukrainian?"

"Not at all, but it's not necessary."

"It's not necessary?"

"Oh no, it's not necessary. You just have to take a sheet of paper and write 'A Ballad' at the top, then begin like this: 'Oh, alas, my destiny!' or 'The Cossack Nalivaiko was sitting on a hill,' and then add, 'On the mountain, ho, in a green tree, ho, the birds are singing, grae, grae, voropae, gop, gop!' or something of that sort. And the deed is done. Print it and publish it. The Ukrainian will read it, put his hand to his cheek, and invariably burst into tears— he's such a sensitive soul!"

"For heaven's sake!" exclaimed Basistov. "What are you saying? That's too absurd for words. I've lived in the Ukraine—I love it, and I know the language. . . . 'Grae, grae, voropae' is sheer nonsense."

"That may be, but the Ukrainian will weep all the same. You refer to the 'language.' . . . But does a Ukrainian language really exist? I once asked some local inhabitant to render in Ukrainian the first phrase that came to mind, which was the following: 'Grammar is the art of reading and writing correctly.' Do you know how he rendered it? 'Hrammur es the vaurt of roide and wroite corroictly.'... Is that a language, in your opinion? An independent language? I'd rather crush my best friend in a mortar than agree to that."

Basistov was on the verge of responding.

"Leave him alone," said Daria Mikhailovna. "You know that you'll get nothing but paradoxes from him."

Pigasov smiled cynically. A servant came in and announced the arrival of Aleksandra Pavlovna and her brother.

Daria Mikhailovna rose to greet her guests.

"How do you do, *Alexandrine?*" she began, walking over to welcome her. "How clever of you to come!... How are you, Sergei Pavlych?"

Volyntsev shook hands with Daria Mikhailovna and went up to Natalia Alekseevna.

"But what about that baron, your new acquaintance? Is he coming today?" asked Pigasov.

"Yes, he's coming."

"He's an eminent philosopher, they say. He's probably just brimming over with Hegel."

Daria Mikhailovna didn't reply. She made Aleksandra Pavlovna sit down on the sofa, and settled herself nearby.

"Philosophy," continued Pigasov, "constitutes an elevated point of view! There's another object of my contempt—those elevated points of view. What can you see from up above? For heaven's sake, if you want to buy a horse, you don't look at it from a steeple!"

"This baron was going to bring you some article?" inquired Aleksandra Pavlovna.

"Yes, an article," Daria Mikhailovna replied with exaggerated indifference, "one on the relationship of commerce to manufacturing in Russia.... But don't be afraid: we won't read it here.... I didn't invite you because of that. *Le baron est aussi aimable que savant.* And he speaks Russian beautifully! *C'est un vrai torrent...il vous entraîne.*"

"He speaks Russian so beautifully," grumbled Pigasov, "that he merits praise in French."

"You may grumble as much as you please, Afrikan Semenych.... It's in keeping with your tousled hairstyle.... I wonder why he hasn't come, though. Do you know what, *messieurs et mesdames?*" Daria Mikhailovna added, looking around. "Let's go into the garden. There's still nearly an hour before dinnertime and the weather is glorious."

The entire group arose and went out into the garden.

Daria Mikhailovna's garden extended all the way down to the river. It had numerous paths lined by old lime trees; it was filled with sunlight and shade and fragrance, offering glimpses of emerald green at the ends of its paths, as well as arbors of acacias and lilacs.

Volyntsev turned toward the lushest part of the garden with Natalia and Mlle. Boncourt. He walked beside Natalia in silence, while Mlle. Boncourt followed a little way behind.

"What have you been doing today?" Volyntsev eventually asked, pulling at the ends of his handsome, dark-brown moustache.

His facial features bore a striking resemblance to his sister's, but there was less animation in his expression, and his soft, beautiful eyes seemed somehow sad.

"Oh, nothing," answered Natalia. "I've been listening to Pigasov's excesses, I've done some embroidery on canvas, and I've been reading."

"And what have you been reading?"

"I've been reading . . . a history of the Crusades," Natalia responded after a slight hesitation.

Volyntsev looked at her.

"Ah!" he remarked at last. "That must be interesting."

He picked up a twig and began to twirl it in the air. They strolled another twenty feet.

"Who is this baron that your mother has gotten acquainted with?" Volyntsev began again.

"A chamberlain, a newcomer to the area. *Maman* speaks very highly of him."

"Your mother is readily attracted to people."

"That proves she's still young at heart," observed Natalia.

"True. I'll bring you your mare soon. She's almost broken in now. I want to teach her to gallop, and I'll accomplish that soon."

"*Merci!* . . . But I feel guilty. You're breaking her in yourself . . . and they say that's so difficult!"

"To give you the slightest pleasure, Natalia Alekseevna, you know that I'm ready to . . . I . . . and not in such small matters. . . . "

Volyntsev started to get embarrassed.

Natalia looked at him in a friendly manner and said "*Merci*" once more.

"You know," Sergei Pavlych continued after a long pause, "this isn't the kind of thing. . . . But why am I saying all this? You already know everything."

At that moment, a bell rang in the house.

"Ah! *La cloche du diner!*" cried Mlle. Boncourt. "*Rentrons.*"

"*Quel dommage!*" the elderly Frenchwoman thought to herself as she mounted the balcony steps behind Volyntsev and Natalia. "*Quel dommage que ce charmant garçon ait si peu de ressources dans la conversation,*" which might be translated thus: "You're a nice person, my dear boy, but you're a bit inept."

The baron hadn't arrived by dinnertime. They waited for him for half an hour. Conversation at the table flagged. Sergei Pavlych did nothing but gaze at Natalia, next to whom he was sitting, and assiduously fill her water glass. Pandalevskii tried in vain to entertain his neighbor, Aleksandra Pavlovna. He was bubbling over with amicability, but she could barely refrain from yawning. Basistov kept rolling up pellets of bread, not thinking about anything at all. Even Pigasov kept silent, and when Daria Mikhailovna remarked to him that he hadn't been very polite that day, he replied crossly, "When am I ever polite? That's not my custom." Smiling grimly, he added, "Have a little patience. I'm only kvass, you know, *du simple* Russian kvass, but your chamberlain. . . ."

"Bravo!" cried Daria Mikhailovna, "Pigasov is jealous—he's jealous in advance!"

But Pigasov didn't respond to her, and merely gave her a sullen look.

The clock struck seven, and everyone reassembled in the drawing room.

"He's not coming, evidently," said Daria Mikhailovna.

But just then the rumble of a carriage became audible, a small equipage drove into the courtyard, and a servant entered the drawing room a few moments later and handed Daria Mikhailovna a note on a silver tray. She glanced at it, and, turning to the servant, inquired, "But where's the gentleman who delivered this letter?"

"He's sitting in his carriage. Shall I invite him to come in?"

"Ask him to do so."

The servant went out.

"Imagine, how annoying!" continued Daria Mikhailovna. "The baron has been ordered to return to Petersburg at once. He's sent his article with a certain Mr. Rudin, a friend of his. The baron wanted to introduce him to me—he speaks very highly of him.

But this is so annoying! I'd hoped the baron would stay here for some time."

"Dmitrii Nikolaevich Rudin," announced the servant.

III

A man of about thirty-five came in. He was tall and somewhat stooped, with curly hair and a swarthy complexion. He had an asymmetrical but expressive, intelligent face, a straight, broad nose, and handsomely curved lips; a limpid brilliance shone in his lively dark-blue eyes. His clothes weren't new and were a bit tight on him, as though he'd outgrown them.

He quickly walked up to Daria Mikhailovna and, making a slight bow, told her that he'd desired the honor of an introduction to her for a long time, and that his friend the baron greatly regretted he couldn't say goodbye to her in person.

The thin sound of Rudin's voice seemed inappropriate to his tall stature and broad chest.

"Kindly sit down.... I'm very pleased," Daria Mikhailovna murmured and, after introducing him to the rest of the assemblage, she asked him whether he came from that area or was a visitor to it.

"My estate is located in the province of T——," Rudin replied, holding his hat on his knees. "I haven't been here very long. I came on business and stayed in your district's principal town for a while."

"With whom?"

"With the doctor. He's an old friend of mine from the university."

"Ah! The doctor. He's highly regarded—he knows his business, they say. And have you known the baron for a long time?"

"I met him in Moscow last winter, and I've just spent about a week with him."

"He's a very intelligent man, the baron."

"Yes."

Daria Mikhailovna sniffed at a little wadded-up handkerchief steeped in eau de cologne.

"Are you in government service?" she asked.

"Who? I?"

"Yes."

"No. I left."

A brief pause ensued. The general conversation then resumed.

"If you'll permit me to be inquisitive," Pigasov began, turning to Rudin, "are you familiar with the contents of the article which His Excellency the baron has sent?"

"Yes, I am."

"This article treats the relationship of commerce—or no, of manufacturing to commerce in our country. . . . I believe that was how you put it, Daria Mikhailovna?"

"Yes, it treats that subject," Daria Mikhailovna assented, pressing her hand to her forehead.

"I'm a poor judge in such matters, of course," continued Pigasov, "but I must confess that even the title of the article strikes me as excessively . . . (how can I put it delicately?) . . . excessively obscure and complex."

"Why does it strike you that way?"

Pigasov smiled and looked across at Daria Mikhailovna.

"Is it clear to you?" he inquired, turning his foxlike face toward Rudin again.

"To me? Yes."

"Hmm. No doubt you know better."

"Does your head ache?" Aleksandra Pavlovna asked Daria Mikhailovna.

"No. This happens to me—*c'est nerveux.*"

"Allow me to indulge my curiosity," Pigasov began again in his nasal voice. "Your friend, His Excellency Baron Muffel—I believe that's his name?"

"Just so."

"Does His Excellency Baron Muffel specialize in political economics, or does he merely devote the hours of leisure left over from his social engagements and official duties to that interesting subject?"

Rudin stared steadily at Pigasov.

"The baron is a dilettante in this field," he replied, blushing slightly, "but a good deal of his article is reasonable and stimulating."

"I can't argue with you, not having read the article. But I'll venture to ask—this work by your friend, Baron Muffel, is undoubtedly based more on general theories than on facts?"

"It contains both facts and theories based on the facts."

"Yes, yes. I must tell you that, in my opinion . . . and I have the right to give my opinion upon occasion, since I spent three years at Dorpat . . . all these so-called general theories, hypotheses, and

systems—forgive me, I'm a provincial, I speak the truth bluntly—
are absolutely worthless. They're all mere intellectualizations, intended solely to mislead people. Present us with the facts, gentlemen, and that's enough!"

"Really?" retorted Rudin. "But isn't one obligated to convey the
meaning of the facts?"

"General theories!" continued Pigasov. "They'll be the death of
me, these general theories, these propositions, these conclusions.
They're all based on so-called convictions. Everyone talks about
their convictions, and demands respect for them, and prides themselves on them. . . . Ah!"

And Pigasov shook his fist in the air. Pandalevskii laughed.

"Excellent!" exclaimed Rudin. "It follows that convictions don't
exist, in your opinion?"

"No, they don't exist."

"Is that your conviction?"

"Yes."

"Then how can you say that they don't exist? You've just asserted
one at the first opportunity."

Everyone in the room smiled and exchanged glances.

"Wait a moment, wait a moment, however," Pigasov began.

But Daria Mikhailovna clapped her hands, crying, "Bravo,
bravo! Pigasov has been defeated, he's been defeated!" and she
quietly took Rudin's hat out of his hand.

"Defer your delight for a bit, madam. There's plenty of time!"
Pigasov declared with annoyance. "It's not sufficient to utter a
witticism with an air of superiority. You must prove, you must
refute. . . . We've wandered away from the subject of our argument."

"If you'll allow me," Rudin remarked coolly, "the issue is very
simple. You don't believe in the value of general theories, you don't
believe in convictions. . . . "

"I don't believe in them. I don't believe in anything!"

"Very well. You're a skeptic."

"I see no need to use such a learned word. However. . . . "

"Don't interrupt!" interjected Daria Mikhailovna.

"Tsk, tsk, tsk!" Pandalevskii said to himself at the same moment,
and he smiled broadly.

"That word expresses my meaning," continued Rudin. "You
understand it, so why not use it? You don't believe in anything. . . .
Why do you believe in facts?"

"Why? That's a good one! Facts are matters of experience—everyone knows what facts are. I judge them by my experience, by my own senses."

"But can't your senses deceive you? Your senses tell you that the sun revolves around the earth . . . but perhaps you don't agree with Copernicus? Don't you even believe in him?"

A smile passed across everyone's face again and all eyes fastened on Rudin. "He's by no means unintelligent," everyone thought to themselves.

"You permit yourself to keep making jokes," said Pigasov. "Of course, that's very original, but it's not to the point."

"In what I've said up to now," responded Rudin, "there's much too little that's original, unfortunately. This has all been well established for a very long time, and has all been said a thousand times. That's not the issue. . . ."

"What is, then?" Pigasov inquired, not without insolence.

During arguments, first he'd always banter with his opponent, then he'd become rude, then finally he'd begin to sulk and would refuse to speak at all.

"This is the issue," continued Rudin. "I confess that I can't help feeling sincere regret when I hear sensible people attack . . ."

"Systems?" interrupted Pigasov.

"Yes, if you will, even systems. Why does that word frighten you so much? Every system is founded upon a knowledge of fundamental laws and the basic elements of life. . . ."

"But it's impossible to know them, to discover them . . . for heaven's sake!"

"I beg to differ. Of course, they aren't accessible to everyone, and to err is human. However, surely you'll agree with me that Newton, for instance, discovered at least some of those fundamental laws. He was a genius, we grant, but the greatness of discoveries by geniuses is that those discoveries become everyone's heritage. The effort to disclose universal principles amid the multiplicity of phenomena is one of the essential characteristics of human thought, and our entire culture. . . ."

"So that's what you're driving at!" Pigasov broke in with a strained voice. "I'm a practical man. I don't engage in all these metaphysical subtleties, and I don't want to."

"Very well! That's up to you. But notice that your very desire exclusively to be a practical man is itself a sort of system, a theory. . . ."

"You talk about culture!" blurted out Pigasov. "That's another impressive notion of yours! Much good it is, this vaunted culture! I wouldn't give a pittance for your culture!"

"But what a feeble argument, Afrikan Semenych!" Daria Mikhailovna observed, inwardly quite pleased by the self-possessed, elegant civility of her new acquaintance. "*C'est un homme comme il faut,*" she thought, looking at Rudin's face with benevolent scrutiny. "We should be nice to him." She mentally spoke those last words in Russian.

"I won't defend culture," Rudin continued after a short pause. "It doesn't require my defense. You don't like it . . . to each his own. Besides, that would take us too far afield. Allow me simply to remind you of the old saying, 'Jupiter, you're angry, therefore you're to blame.' I meant to say that all these attacks upon systems and general theories are particularly distressing because, in repudiating them, people repudiate knowledge in general, and science, and faith in science, and consequently faith in themselves as well, faith in their own abilities. But such faith is essential to human beings—they can't live in accordance with their sensations alone. They're wrong to fear ideas, not to trust them. Skepticism is always characterized by barrenness and impotence. . . . "

"Those are mere words!" muttered Pigasov.

"Maybe they are. But permit me to remind you that when we say 'Those are mere words!' we ourselves are often seeking to avoid saying something more than mere words."

"What?" Pigasov asked, blinking his eyes.

"You understood what I meant," Rudin retorted with involuntary, instantly repressed impatience. "I repeat, if someone has no strong principles in which he believes, no ground on which he can take a firm stand, how can he reasonably assess the needs, the values, or the future of his country? How can he know what he ought to do, if . . . "

"I surrender the field," Pigasov announced abruptly, and he turned away with a bow, not looking at anyone.

Rudin stared at him, smiled slightly, and fell silent.

"Aha! He's taken flight!" declared Daria Mikhailovna. "Never mind, Dmitrii. . . . I beg your pardon," she added with a cordial smile, "what's your patronymic?"

"Nikolaich."

"Never mind, my dear Dmitrii Nikolaich—he didn't deceive any of us. He's trying to pretend that he doesn't *want* to argue with you any more. . . . He actually senses that he *can't* argue with you. But you'd better come sit closer to us and chat a bit."

Rudin moved his chair forward.

"Why haven't we met until now?" continued Daria Mikhailovna. "That surprises me. Have you read this book? *C'est de Tocqueville, vous savez?*"

And Daria Mikhailovna held a French pamphlet out to Rudin.

Rudin took the thin volume in his hand, turned over a few pages, and, laying it down on the table, replied that he hadn't read this particular work by M. de Tocqueville, but that he'd often contemplated the question he addressed. A conversation sprang up. Rudin seemed uncertain and disinclined to speak freely at first, unable to find the right words, but he eventually became emboldened and began to hold forth. After a quarter of an hour, his voice was the only sound to be heard in the room. Everyone crowded around him in a circle. Only Pigasov remained aloof in a corner by the fireplace.

Rudin spoke intelligently and incisively, displaying broad learning and extensive reading. No one had expected to consider him remarkable—he was so shabbily dressed, and so little was known about him. Everyone found it strange and incomprehensible that such an intelligent man would have appeared among them out of nowhere, in the middle of the countryside. He thus seemed all the more surprising and, one could even say, fascinating to them all, beginning with Daria Mikhailovna. . . . She congratulated herself on having discovered him and was already envisioning how she would introduce Rudin to society; her first impressions were often almost childlike, in spite of her age. Aleksandra Pavlovna actually understood little of what Rudin said, but was highly impressed and pleased; her brother was impressed as well. Pandalevskii watched Daria Mikhailovna and grew envious. Pigasov thought, "If I have to pay five hundred rubles, I'll find a nightingale that can sing better than this!" But Basistov and Natalia were most impressed of all. Basistov barely breathed. He sat motionless the whole time, his mouth agape, eyes opened wide, and he listened— listened as he'd never listened to anyone in his life—while Natalia's face became flushed and her eyes, which were unwaveringly focused on Rudin, got darker and began to shine.

"What magnificent eyes he has!" Volyntsev whispered to her.

"Yes, they're very nice."

"It's just a shame that he has such big, red hands."

Natalia didn't respond.

Tea was served. The others began to converse, but the suddenness with which they fell silent as soon as Rudin opened his mouth disclosed the strength of the impression he'd produced. Daria Mikhailovna suddenly felt the urge to tease Pigasov. She went up to him and said in an undertone, "Why don't you speak up, instead of merely smiling sarcastically? Make the effort, challenge him again." And without waiting for him to reply, she beckoned to Rudin.

"There's one other thing you don't know about him," she said to Rudin, gesturing toward Pigasov. "He's a terrible woman-hater. He's always attacking them. Please lead him onto the path of righteousness."

Rudin looked down at Pigasov—unintentionally, since Pigasov's head just reached Rudin's shoulder. Pigasov nearly shriveled up in anger, and his peevish face went pale.

"Daria Mikhailovna is mistaken," he began in an unsteady voice. "I don't find fault with women. I'm not a great admirer of the human race as a whole."

"What could have given you such a low opinion of it?" asked Rudin.

Pigasov looked him straight in the face.

"Examining my own heart, no doubt, in which I find more and more that's vile every day. I judge others by comparison to myself. Perhaps this is unfair, and I'm far worse than other people, but what can I do? It's a habit!"

"I understand, and I sympathize with you," Rudin responded. "What noble soul hasn't experienced a yearning for self-abasement? But one shouldn't remain in that hopeless condition."

"I'm deeply grateful for the status of nobility you've conferred upon my soul," snapped Pigasov. "As for my condition, there's nothing very wrong with it, so that even if there were any hope for it, by God, I wouldn't look for it!"

"But that means—pardon the expression—you want to gratify your own pride more than you want to live and abide in the truth. . . . "

"Yes, indeed!" exclaimed Pigasov. "Pride—that's a word I understand, and you understand it, I expect, and everyone understands it, but the truth—what is the truth? Where is it, this truth?"

"I warn you, you're repeating yourself," remarked Daria Mikhailovna.

Pigasov shrugged his shoulders.

"Well, what difference does it make if I am? I ask you again—where is the truth? Even the philosophers don't know what it is. Kant says it's one thing, but Hegel says no, that's wrong, it's something else."

"Do you really know what Hegel says about it?" Rudin asked, without raising his voice.

"I repeat," Pigasov continued, becoming excited, "I can't understand how you define truth. In my opinion, it simply doesn't exist on earth—that is, the word exists, but not the thing itself."

"Shame on you! Shame on you!" cried Daria Mikhailovna. "You should be ashamed to say that, you old sinner! Truth doesn't exist? What on earth is there to live for, then?"

"Well, Daria Mikhailovna," Pigasov rejoined in an irritated tone, "I do believe, in any case, that it'd be much easier for you to live without truth than without your cook, Stepan, who's such an expert at making soup! And what do you want with the truth, tell me, please? You can't trim a bonnet with it!"

"A joke isn't an argument," observed Daria Mikhailovna, "especially when you stoop to slander...."

"I don't know much about the truth, but I see that it's hard to swallow," Pigasov muttered, and he turned away angrily.

Whereupon Rudin began to speak about pride—and he spoke admirably. He argued that a human being without pride is worthless, that pride is Archimedes's lever, by which the earth can be moved from its foundations, but at the same time, that only someone who knows how to control his pride the way a rider controls his horse, who offers his own individuality as a sacrifice to the general welfare, deserves to be called a human being....

"Egoism," he concluded, "is suicide. The egoist withers like a solitary, barren tree, but pride, manifest in the active pursuit of perfection, is the source of all great things.... Yes! A human being must eradicate the stubborn egoism of individuality in order to earn the right of self-expression."

"Can you lend me a pencil?" Pigasov inquired, turning to Basistov.

Basistov couldn't immediately grasp what Pigasov had said to him.

"What do you want a pencil for?" he finally asked.

"I want to write down Mr. Rudin's last sentence. If one doesn't write it down, one might forget it, I fear! But you yourself will agree that a sentence like that doesn't equal a grand slam in a game of whist."

"There are things that it's sinful to laugh at and make fun of, Afrikan Semenych!" Basistov asserted heatedly, turning his back on Pigasov.

In the meantime, Rudin had walked over to Natalia. She stood up, looking confused. Volyntsev, who was sitting next to her, also stood up.

"I see a piano," Rudin began with gentle courtesy, like a visiting prince. "Do you play?"

"Yes, I play," replied Natalia, "but not very well. Konstantin Diomidych here plays much better than I do."

Pandalevskii thrust his face forward and simpered. "You shouldn't say that, Natalia Alekseevna. Your playing is in no way inferior to mine."

"Do you know Schubert's *'Erlkönig'?*" asked Rudin.

"He knows it, he knows it!" interjected Daria Mikhailovna. "Take your place, *Constantin*. Do you like music, Dmitrii Nikolaich?"

Rudin merely nodded his head slightly and ran his hand through his hair, as though preparing to listen.... Pandalevskii began to play.

Natalia stood near the piano, directly across from Rudin. His face became transfigured by a beautiful expression at the first sound. His dark-blue eyes slowly traveled around the room, resting on Natalia from time to time. Pandalevskii finished playing.

Rudin said nothing, and walked up to the open window. A delicate mist lay over the garden like a soft shroud; a dreamy fragrance wafted from the nearby trees; the stars cast a gentle radiance. The summer night was tender—and made everything else seem tender as well. Rudin glanced at the dark garden and then turned around.

"This music and this evening," he began, "remind me of my student days in Germany—our gatherings, our serenades...."

"You've been to Germany, then?" queried Daria Mikhailovna.

"I spent a year in Heidelberg, and nearly a year in Berlin."

"And did you dress like a student? They say that students wear special costumes there."

"I wore high boots with spurs and a hussar's jacket decorated with braid, and I let my hair grow down to my shoulders in Heidelberg. In Berlin, students dress like everyone else."

"Tell us something about your student life," requested Aleksandra Pavlovna.

Rudin complied. His performance wasn't altogether successful—his descriptions lacked color. He didn't know how to entertain people. However, having described his adventures abroad, Rudin quickly turned to general observations on the value of education and science, elaborating on universities and university life as a whole. He sketched a vast, comprehensive picture in bold, broad strokes. Everyone listened to him with great care. He spoke in masterly fashion, compellingly if not altogether clearly . . . but even this lack of clarity added a special charm to his words.

The overabundance of his ideas hindered Rudin from expressing himself concretely and precisely. Image followed upon image; comparisons arose one after the other—some startlingly audacious, some strikingly apt. His impatient improvisation bespoke not the complacent efforts of the practiced speaker but the very essence of inspiration. He didn't search for words: they came to his lips obediently and spontaneously, each one seeming to flow straight from his soul, burning with all the fire of conviction. Rudin had learned perhaps the greatest secret of all—the music of eloquence. He knew how to strike one chord of the heart and thereby to set all the others faintly vibrating and echoing. Some of his listeners might not have understood exactly what he was talking about, but their bosoms heaved and they felt as though veils were being lifted before their eyes, as though something radiant were shimmering in the distance.

All Rudin's ideas appeared to be focused on the future, which lent him something of the impetuosity of youth. . . . Standing at the window, not looking at anyone in particular, he spoke at length, inspired by the universal sympathy and attention, the presence of young women, and the beauty of the night. Carried away upon the tide of his own emotions, he rose to the summit of eloquence, of poetry. . . . The very sound of his voice, intense and yet quiet, only increased his allure. It seemed as though some higher power, which even he hadn't expected, were speaking through his lips. . . . Rudin spoke about what lends eternal significance to the fleeting lives of human beings.

"I remember a Scandinavian legend," he said in conclusion, "in which a king and his warriors were sitting around a fire in a long, dark barn one winter night. Suddenly a little bird flew in through

an open door and out again through another. The king remarked
that this bird was like a human being on earth—it came in from
the darkness and went back out again, not remaining in the warmth
and light for long.... 'King,' replied the eldest warrior, 'even in
the dark, the bird didn't get lost. It found its nest.' Likewise, our
lives are brief and insignificant, yet every great accomplishment is
achieved by human beings. The awareness of being the instruments
of higher powers ought to outweigh all other joys for human beings.
Even in death, one finds life—one finds a nest."

Rudin stopped and lowered his eyes, smiling with involuntary
embarrassment.

"*Vous êtes un poète,*" Daria Mikhailovna commented under her
breath.

And everyone inwardly agreed with her—everyone except Pigasov. Without waiting for the end of Rudin's lengthy speech, he
quietly picked up his hat and, as he went out, maliciously whispered
to Pandalevskii, who was standing near the door: "No! I prefer
the company of fools."

No one tried to detain him, however, or even noticed his
departure.

The servants brought in some supper, and half an hour later,
everyone had said goodnight and gone home. Daria Mikhailovna
begged Rudin to spend the night. On the way home in the carriage
with her brother, Aleksandra Pavlovna repeatedly voiced her admiration for Rudin's extraordinary mind. Volyntsev agreed with
her, although he noted that Rudin occasionally expressed himself
somewhat obscurely, that is, not altogether intelligibly, he added—
no doubt wishing to make his own thoughts clear. But his face was
grim, and his eyes seemed more melancholy than ever as they stared
at a corner of the carriage.

Pandalevskii went to his room and, as he took off his delicately
embroidered suspenders, said aloud, "A very adroit fellow!" Then
he suddenly looked harshly at his servant and ordered him out
of the room. Basistov didn't sleep the whole night, nor did he
undress—he was working on a letter to a friend of his in Moscow
until dawn. And although she did get undressed and lie down on
her bed, Natalia didn't sleep at all, either—she never even closed
her eyes. With her head propped on her hand, she stared steadily
into the darkness; her veins were throbbing feverishly and she
periodically heaved a deep sigh.

IV

Rudin had just finished getting dressed the next morning when a servant brought him an invitation from Daria Mikhailovna to come and have tea with her in her study. Rudin found her alone. She greeted him most cordially, asked whether he'd spent a restful night, poured him a cup of tea with her own hands, inquired whether there was enough sugar in it, offered him a cigarette, and twice repeated that she was surprised she hadn't met him long ago. Rudin was about to sit down at a distance from her, but Daria Mikhailovna motioned him to an easy chair that was standing near hers and, leaning toward him slightly, began to ask him about his family, his plans, his preferences. Daria Mikhailovna spoke casually and listened with an air of distraction, but it was perfectly clear to Rudin that she was trying hard to please him, even to flatter him. She hadn't arranged this morning *tête-à-tête* and dressed so simply yet elegantly, *à la Madame Récamier*, for nothing! But Daria Mikhailovna soon ceased asking him questions. She began to tell him about herself, about her youth, and about the people she'd known. Rudin paid sympathetic attention to her stream of words, although—strangely enough—whatever personage Daria Mikhailovna might begin to talk about, she always ended up in the foreground by herself, and that personage somehow became effaced and disappeared. But to compensate for that, Rudin learned in great detail precisely what Daria Mikhailovna had said to a certain distinguished statesman and what influence she'd exercised over a certain celebrated poet. To judge from Daria Mikhailovna's accounts, one might think that all the distinguished men of the past twenty-five years had dreamed of nothing but making her acquaintance and winning her good graces. She spoke of them in simple terms, without particular enthusiasm or admiration, as though they were members of her household, labeling some of them eccentrics. As she talked about them, their names ranged themselves in a brilliant circlet around the principal name—that of Daria Mikhailovna—like an expensive setting fitted around a precious stone.

Rudin listened, smoking a cigarette, and kept still, except to insert an occasional, brief remark into the loquacious lady's speech. He was a good speaker and enjoyed speaking, but he wasn't good at carrying on a conversation, even though he was also a good listener. Everyone who wasn't simply intimidated by him from the start trustingly poured out their hearts in his presence, he followed the thread of someone else's narrative so readily and sympathetically. He was quite good-natured—good-natured in the way that people accustomed to considering themselves superior to others often are. In arguments, he seldom allowed his antagonist to complete his thoughts, crushing him with vehement, passionate dialectics.

Daria Mikhailovna expressed her thoughts in Russian. She prided herself on her knowledge of her native language, although French words and phrases often slipped out. She intentionally, albeit not always successfully, employed simple, popular figures of speech. Rudin's ear wasn't offended by the strange mixture of languages on Daria Mikhailovna's lips, though—indeed, he hardly heard it.

Daria Mikhailovna finally grew tired and, letting her head fall back against the cushions of her easy chair, fixed her gaze on Rudin as she fell silent.

"Now I understand," Rudin began, speaking slowly, "I understand why you come to the countryside every summer. This period of rest is essential for you. The quietude of the countryside refreshes and strengthens you after your hectic life in the capital. I'm sure you must be profoundly sensitive to the beauties of nature."

Daria Mikhailovna cast a sidelong glance at Rudin.

"Nature . . . yes . . . yes, of course. . . . I'm passionately fond of it. But you know, Dmitrii Nikolaich, one can't get along without other people, even in the countryside. And there's virtually no one here. Pigasov is the most intelligent person in the vicinity."

"The irascible old gentleman who was here last night?" asked Rudin.

"Yes, that one. Even he has his uses in the countryside, though— he occasionally makes one laugh."

"He's by no means stupid," Rudin replied, "but he's heading on a false course. I don't know whether you'll agree with me, Daria Mikhailovna, but salvation can't be found through rejection— absolute, universal rejection. Reject everything, and you'll readily appear to be an intellectual—it's a well-known trick. Amiable people are quite ready to conclude that you're worth more than whatever it is you reject. And that's often untrue. In the first place, you can pick holes in anything, and in the second, even if what you say is correct, it's still the worse for you. Engaged solely in rejection, your intellect becomes enfeebled and withers away. While you gratify your vanity, you deprive yourself of the true pleasures of contemplation. Life—the essence of life—evades your petty, jaundiced vision, and you end up merely ranting and looking ridiculous. Only the individual who can feel love has the right to criticize and condemn."

"*Voilà Monsieur Pigasov enterré,*" observed Daria Mikhailovna. "You're so gifted at analyzing people! But Pigasov probably wouldn't even have understood you. He loves nothing but his own individuality."

"And he criticizes himself in order to have the right to criticize others," Rudin stated further.

Daria Mikhailovna laughed.

"He judges the healthy—how does the saying go?—the healthy by comparison to the sick. By the way, what do you think of the baron?"

"The baron? He's a fine man with a kind heart and an active mind . . . but he has no character . . . and he'll remain half a scholar and half a man of the world, that is, a dilettante—that is, speaking plainly, neither one thing nor the other—all his life. . . . But it's a shame!"

"I share your opinion," declared Daria Mikhailovna. "I've read his article. . . . *Entre nous . . . cela a assez peu de fond.*"

"Who else comes to visit you here?" Rudin inquired after a pause.

Daria Mikhailovna knocked the ash off her cigarette with her little finger.

"Oh, hardly anyone else. There's Aleksandra Pavlovna Lipina, whom you met yesterday. She's very sweet, but that's all. Her brother is a fine person as well—*un parfait honnête homme.* Prince Garin you know. That's all. There are two or three other neighbors, but they're complete nonentities. They either show off—they're horribly pretentious—or they're antisocial, or else quite inappropriately informal. As you know, I don't exchange visits with ladies. There's one other neighbor who's said to be a highly cultured and even learned man, but who's a dreadful eccentric—a dreamer. *Alexandrine* knows him, and isn't indifferent to him, I suspect. . . . You ought to talk to her, Dmitrii Nikolaich. She's such a sweet creature. She merely requires a bit of cultivation—it's absolutely necessary to cultivate her."

"She's very nice," remarked Rudin.

"She's a perfect child, Dmitrii Nikolaich, an absolute infant. She was married, *mais c'est tout comme.* . . . If I were a man, I'd only fall in love with women like that."

"Really?"

"Certainly. At least such women are unspoiled, and freshness can't be feigned."

"But everything else can be?" Rudin asked, and he laughed— a thing he rarely did. When he laughed, his face became strange, almost old-looking—his eyes disappeared, his nose crinkled up. . . . "And who's this eccentric, as you call him, to whom Mrs. Lipin isn't indifferent?" he went on.

"A certain Mikhailo Mikhailych Lezhnev, a landowner here."

Rudin looked astonished; he raised his head.

"Lezhnev—Mikhailo Mikhailych?" he repeated. "Is he a neighbor of yours?"

"Yes. Do you know him?"

Rudin didn't speak for a minute.

"I used to know him a long time ago. He's wealthy, I presume?" he queried, tugging at the fringe on his chair.

"Yes, he's wealthy, although he dresses horribly and drives a racing carriage, like a bailiff. I've tried to get him to visit me here. He's reputed to be intelligent, and I have some business to conduct with him. . . . You know that I manage my estate myself."

Rudin nodded his head.

"Yes, I manage it myself," Daria Mikhailovna continued. "I haven't resorted to any foreign fads. I prefer what's our own, what's Russian, and, as you see, things don't seem to be going too badly," she concluded with a wave of her hand.

"I've long been convinced," Rudin remarked politely, "of the absolute injustice of those people who refuse to acknowledge the practical intelligence of women."

Daria Mikhailovna smiled affably.

"You're very generous," she commented. "But what was I going to say? What were we talking about? Oh, yes, Lezhnev. I have some differences with him over a boundary line. I've invited him here several times, and I'm even expecting him today, but there's no way of knowing whether he'll come. . . . He's such an eccentric!"

The curtain in front of the door quietly moved aside, and the steward came in. He was a tall man with thinning gray hair, wearing a black coat, a white tie, and a white vest.

"What is it?" Daria Mikhailovna inquired, and turning slightly toward Rudin, she added in a low voice, *"N'est ce pas, comme il ressemble à Canning?"*

"Mikhailo Mikhailych Lezhnev has arrived," announced the steward. "Do you wish to see him?"

"My God!" exclaimed Daria Mikhailovna. "Speak of the devil.... Invite him in."

The steward went out.

"He's such an eccentric. He's finally come, but at the wrong moment. He's interrupted our conversation." Rudin rose from his chair, but Daria Mikhailovna stopped him. "Where are you going? We can discuss this matter in front of you. And I want you to analyze him as well, the way you analyzed Pigasov. When you speak, *vous gravez comme avec un burin*. Please stay." Rudin started to say something, but after momentary reflection, he sat down again.

Mikhailo Mikhailych, with whom the reader is already familiar, entered the room. He wore the same gray overcoat and carried the same old cap in his sunburned hands. He bowed tranquilly to Daria Mikhailovna and walked over to the tea table.

"You've finally favored me with a visit, Monsieur Lezhnev!" began Daria Mikhailovna. "Please sit down. You're already acquainted, I understand," she noted, gesturing in Rudin's direction.

Lezhnev looked at Rudin and smiled somewhat strangely.

"I know Mr. Rudin," he acknowledged with a slight bow.

"We attended the university together," Rudin concurred in a subdued voice, lowering his eyes.

"And we also met later on," Lezhnev remarked coldly.

Daria Mikhailovna looked at each of them with some perplexity, and then invited Lezhnev to sit down. He did so.

"You wanted to see me," he began, "about the boundary line?"

"Yes, the boundary line. But I also wanted to meet you in any case. We're close neighbors, you know, and all but relatives."

"I'm most grateful to you," replied Lezhnev. "As regards that boundary line, I've completely settled the matter with your steward. I've agreed to all his proposals."

"I knew that."

"But he told me that the contract couldn't be signed without a private meeting with you."

"Yes, that's a rule I have. By the way, if you'll permit me to ask, do all your peasants pay rent?"

"Quite so."

"And you concern yourself with their boundary lines! That's very noble."

Lezhnev was silent for a moment.

"Well, I've come for a private meeting," he finally observed.

Daria Mikhailovna smiled.

"I see that you've come. You say that in a tone of such.... You mustn't have been very anxious to come and see me."

"I don't go anywhere," Lezhnev responded phlegmatically.

"Nowhere? But you go to see Aleksandra Pavlovna."

"I'm an old friend of her brother."

"Her brother! However, I never seek to force anyone.... But forgive me, Mikhailo Mikhailych, I'm older than you are, and I may be permitted to give you advice. Why are you so eager to pursue such an isolated way of life? Or is *my* house particularly distasteful to you? Do you dislike me?"

"I don't know you, Daria Mikhailovna, and therefore I can't dislike you. You have a wonderful house, but I frankly admit that I don't like to constrain myself. I don't have a respectable suit, I don't have any gloves, and I don't belong to your social circle."

"You belong to it by birth, by education, Mikhailo Mikhailych! *Vous êtes des nôtres.*"

"Birth and education are all well and good, Daria Mikhailovna, but that's not the issue...."

"A person ought to enjoy the companionship of other people, Mikhailo Mikhailych! What pleasure is there in sitting like Diogenes in his barrel?"

"Well, to begin with, he was very contented there, and besides, how do you know that I don't enjoy the companionship of other people?"

Daria Mikhailovna bit her lip.

"That's a different matter! It merely remains for me to express my regret that I'm not worthy of the honor of being included among your friends."

"Monsieur Lezhnev," interjected Rudin, "seems to carry a laudable sentiment—the love of freedom—to excess."

Lezhnev didn't respond; he simply glanced at Rudin. A brief silence ensued.

"And so," Lezhnev began again, getting up, "I may consider our business concluded and tell your steward to send me the papers?"

"You may ... although I must confess, you've been so ungracious ... I really ought to refuse."

"But you know that this readjustment of the boundary line is far more advantageous to you than to me."

Daria Mikhailovna shrugged her shoulders.

"You won't even have some midday refreshment here?" she asked.

"Thank you, but I never eat at midday, and I'm in a hurry to get home."

Daria Mikhailovna stood up.

"I won't detain you," she declared, moving toward the window.

"I wouldn't dream of detaining you."

Lezhnev began to depart.

"Goodbye, Monsieur Lezhnev! Pardon me for having disturbed you."

"Oh, not at all!" Lezhnev replied, and he went out.

"Well, what do you make of him?" Daria Mikhailovna asked Rudin. "I'd heard he was eccentric, but that was really beyond all imagining!"

"He suffers from the same disease as Pigasov," Rudin asserted, "the desire to be original. The one pretends to be Mephistopheles, the other, a cynic. There's a lot of egoism, a lot of vanity, in all that, but there isn't much truth, there isn't much love. Indeed, there's even a kind of calculation to it. A man dons a mask of indifference and indolence so that someone will be sure to think, 'Look at that man. What talents he's wasted.' But if you examine him more carefully, you discover that he has no talents whatsoever."

"*Et de deux!*" Daria Mikhailovna affirmed. "The way you see through people is frightening. One can hide nothing from you."

"Do you think so?" responded Rudin. "However that may be," he continued, "I really shouldn't say anything about Lezhnev. I loved him, I loved him as a friend . . . but later on, through various misunderstandings. . . ."

"You quarreled?"

"No. But we went our separate ways and, it seems, we did so forever."

"Ah, I noticed that you weren't quite yourself during his entire visit. . . . Nonetheless, I'm deeply indebted to you for this morning. The time passed extremely pleasantly. But one must know when to stop. I'll release you until noontime, and I'll go look after my business affairs. My secretary, you met him—*Constantin, c'est lui qui est mon secrétaire*—must be waiting for me now. I commend him to you—he's an excellent, obliging young man who's utterly ecstatic about you. Until later, *cher* Dmitrii Nikolaich! How grateful I am to the baron for having enabled us to become acquainted!"

And Daria Mikhailovna held out her hand to Rudin. He first

clasped it, then raised it to his lips. He subsequently descended
to the drawing room and from there went out to the terrace. On
the terrace, he encountered Natalia.

V

Daria Mikhailovna's daughter, Natalia Alekseevna, might not have
appealed to everyone at first glance. She wasn't fully mature yet;
she was thin, dark, and slightly round-shouldered. But her features
were handsome and regular, albeit too large for a girl of seventeen.
Her clear, smooth forehead, rising above delicate eyebrows that
looked broken in the middle, was particularly handsome. She said
little, but listened and observed closely, almost intensely, as though
forming her own conclusions. She'd often stand motionless, her
hands by her sides, deep in thought. At such moments, her face
would reveal that her mind was hard at work. . . . A barely perceptible smile would suddenly cross her lips and vanish again, then
she'd slowly raise her large, dark eyes. . . . *"Qu'avez-vous?"* Mlle.
Boncourt would ask her, and then would begin to scold her, maintaining that it was improper for a young girl to think so hard and
look so absent-minded. But Natalia wasn't absent-minded; on the
contrary, she studied diligently, and read and worked with avidity.
Her emotions ran strong and deep, but only in secret. She seldom
cried, even as a child, and now she seldom even sighed, merely
paling slightly whenever anything distressed her. Her mother considered her a sensible, good-tempered girl, jocularly calling her
"mon honnête homme de fille," but didn't have a particularly high
opinion of her intellectual abilities. "My Natasha, fortunately, has
a cool temperament," she'd say, "not like me—and it's better that
way. She'll be happy." Daria Mikhailovna was mistaken. But then,
few mothers understand their daughters.

Natalia loved Daria Mikhailovna, but she didn't completely trust
her.

"You don't have anything to hide from me," Daria Mikhailova
remarked to her once, "otherwise you'd be quite secretive. You're
rather intellectually withdrawn. . . ."

Natalia looked her mother in the face and thought, "Why
shouldn't I be withdrawn?"

When Rudin found her on the terrace, she was just going to her
room with Mlle. Boncourt to put on her hat and take a stroll in the
garden, having finished her morning tasks. Natalia wasn't treated
like a little girl any more—Mlle. Boncourt hadn't given her lessons

in mythology and geography for a long time—but she was still required to read history books, travelogues, or other instructive works every morning in Mlle. Boncourt's company. Daria Mikhailovna ostensibly selected these works according to a special system of hers. In reality, she simply gave Natalia everything a French bookseller forwarded to her from Petersburg, except for the novels of *Dumas fils* and Co., naturally—Daria Mikhailovna read those novels herself. Mlle. Boncourt looked especially severe and sour behind her glasses when Natalia read history books. To the elderly Frenchwoman's way of thinking, history was filled with all sorts of impermissible things, although for some reason, of all the great men of antiquity, she herself knew about only one—Cambyses—and of those of modernity—only Louis XIV and Napoleon, whom she couldn't endure. But Natalia also read books whose existence Mlle. Boncourt didn't suspect: Natalia knew all of Pushkin by heart. . . .

Natalia flushed slightly upon encountering Rudin.

"Are you going for a walk?" he asked her.

"Yes. We're going into the garden."

"May I come with you?"

Natalia looked at Mlle. Boncourt.

"*Mais certainement, monsieur, avec plaisir,*" the old maid promptly replied.

Rudin picked up his hat and proceeded alongside them.

At first, Natalia was a bit uncomfortable walking next to Rudin on the same little path, but she gradually grew more at ease. He began to ask her about her studies, about how she liked the countryside. She replied not without timidity, but without the nervous bashfulness that is so often substituted and taken for modesty. Her heart was beating fast.

"You aren't bored in the countryside?" Rudin inquired, casting a sidelong glance at her.

"How can one be bored in the countryside? I'm very glad we're here. I'm very happy here."

"You're happy—that's a glorious word. However, it's understandable—you're young."

Rudin uttered this last word rather strangely—either he envied Natalia or else he felt sorry for her.

"Yes! Youth!" he exclaimed. "The entire goal of science is to achieve methodically what is bestowed upon youth as a gift."

Natalia looked at Rudin attentively. She didn't understand him.

"I've been conversing with your mother all morning," he continued. "She's an extraordinary woman. I understand why all our poets have prized her friendship. Do you like poetry?" he added after a pause.

"He's giving me an examination," Natalia thought as she said aloud, "Yes, I like it very much."

"Poetry is the language of the gods. I myself love poems. But poetry doesn't occur solely in poems. It's manifest everywhere, it's all around us. Look at those trees, at that sky—we can feel the breath of beauty and life on all sides, and wherever one finds beauty and life, one finds poetry as well."

"Let's sit down here on this bench," he suggested. "That's good. I somehow think that when you've gotten to know me a little better" (and he smiled as he looked her straight in the face), "we'll be friends, you and I. What do you think?"

"He's treating me like a little girl," Natalia thought again, and, not knowing what to say, she asked him whether he intended to remain in the countryside for long.

"All summer and fall, and perhaps through the winter as well. I'm a very poor man, you know. My business affairs are in a shambles, and besides, I'm tired of wandering from place to place. It's time to rest."

Natalia was surprised.

"Do you really think that it's time for you to rest?" she asked him timidly.

Rudin turned to face Natalia.

"What do you mean by that?"

"I mean," she replied with some embarrassment, "that other people can rest, but you . . . you should work, you should strive to be useful. Who else, if not you . . . ?"

"Thank you for your flattering remarks," Rudin interrupted her. "To be useful . . . is easy to say!" (He drew his hand across his face.) "To be useful!" he repeated. "Even if I had any firm convictions, how could I be useful? Even if I had faith in my own powers, where is it possible to find sincere, kindred souls?"

Rudin dropped his hand so despondently and let his head sink so sadly that Natalia involuntarily asked herself whether those had really been his rhapsodic words, those words exuding hope, that she'd heard the evening before.

"But no," he declared suddenly, pushing back his lionlike mane of hair, "that's all foolishness, and you're right. I thank you,

Natalia Alekseevna, I sincerely thank you." (Natalia didn't have the slightest idea what he was thanking her for.) "One word from you has recalled me to my duty, has pointed out my path for me. . . . Yes, I must act. I shouldn't suppress my talents, if I have any, I shouldn't squander my strength on talk alone—empty, useless talk—on mere words. . . ."

And his words poured forth in a torrent. He spoke exquisitely, ardently, convincingly, about the sins of cowardice and indolence, about the necessity for action. He lavished reproaches on himself, maintaining that discussing what you intend to do beforehand is as unwise as pricking swollen fruit with a pin—it's just a pointless waste of effort and sap. He proclaimed that there's no noble idea incapable of gaining sympathy, that the only people who have remained misunderstood are either those who didn't know what they wanted themselves or those who didn't deserve to be understood. He spoke at some length, and concluded by thanking Natalia Alekseevna once more and utterly unexpectedly squeezing her hand, exclaiming, "You're a wonderful, noble creature!"

This liberty horrified Mlle. Boncourt, who in spite of forty years' residence in Russia, understood Russian with difficulty and was simply amazed at the forceful rapidity and flow of words that came from Rudin's lips. He was some sort of virtuoso or artist in her eyes, and it was impossible to demand strict adherence to propriety from people of that sort, according to her notions.

She stood up and straightened her dress abruptly, remarking to Natalia that it was time to go in, especially since Monsieur Volinsoff (as she referred to Volyntsev) was coming to dine with them.

"And here he is," she added, glancing down one of the paths that led to the house. Indeed, Volyntsev had just come into view nearby.

He approached them diffidently, greeted everyone from a distance, then turned to Natalia with a sickly expression on his face and said, "Oh, have you been taking a stroll?"

"Yes," replied Natalia. "We were just going home."

"Ah!" Volyntsev responded. "Well, then, shall we go?" And they all walked toward the house.

"How is your sister?" Rudin asked Volyntsev in an especially cordial tone. He'd also been very gracious to him the evening before.

"She's very well, thank you. Perhaps she'll come over here later today. . . . I believe you were discussing something when I came up?"

"Yes, I was conversing with Natalia Alekseevna. She said a word to me that deeply affected me...."

Volyntsev didn't inquire which word that was, and they all returned to Daria Mikhailovna's house in profound silence. Before dining, the salon reassembled in the drawing room. Pigasov didn't attend, however. Rudin wasn't at his best: he did nothing but press Pandalevskii to play Beethoven. Volyntsev remained silent and stared at the floor. Natalia didn't leave her mother's side, periodically becoming lost in thought, then bending over her embroidery. Basistov didn't take his eyes off Rudin, staying constantly on the alert lest he say something intelligent. About three hours passed this way, rather monotonously. Aleksandra Pavlovna didn't come to dine, and afterward, when they arose from the table, Volyntsev immediately ordered his carriage to be brought to the door, and he slipped away without saying goodbye to anyone.

His heart was heavy. He'd been in love with Natalia for a long time and had repeatedly resolved to propose to her.... She admired him, but her heart remained unmoved—he saw that clearly. He had no hope of inspiring any more tender sentiments in her, and was only waiting for the moment when she'd become completely accustomed to him and felt close to him. What could have made him unhappy? What change had he noticed during these past two days? Natalia was behaving toward him exactly the same way as she had before....

Whether the thought had occurred to him that perhaps he didn't know Natalia's character at all—that she was more of a stranger to him than he'd realized—or whether jealousy had begun to act on him, or whether he had an ominous, dim presentiment... in any event, he was suffering, no matter how much he tried to reason with himself.

When he went into his sister's sitting room, Lezhnev was there with her.

"Why did you come back so early?" queried Aleksandra Pavlovna.

"Oh—I was bored."

"Was Rudin there?"

"Yes."

Volyntsev threw his cap on the floor and sat down. Aleksandra Pavlovna turned toward him animatedly.

"Please, Serezha, help me convince this obstinate man" (she pointed at Lezhnev) "that Rudin is extraordinarily intelligent and eloquent."

Volyntsev muttered something.

"But I don't disagree with you at all," Lezhnev began. "I don't dispute Mr. Rudin's intelligence and eloquence. I merely said that I don't like him."

"Have you seen him?" asked Volyntsev.

"I saw him this morning at Daria Mikhailovna's. You know *he's* her grand vizier now. The time will come when she'll part company with him—Pandalevskii's the only man she'll never part company with—but for now, Rudin reigns supreme. I saw him, indeed! He was sitting there and she showed me off to him: 'You see, my good friend, what sort of eccentrics live here!' But I'm not a prize horse to be trotted out and exhibited, so I got up and left."

"But why did you go there?"

"A dispute about a boundary line—but that was all nonsense. She simply wanted to get a look at my physiognomy. She's an elegant lady—that's reason enough!"

"His superiority offends you—that's what it is!" Aleksandra Pavlovna asserted heatedly. "That's what you can't forgive. But I'm convinced that he must have a generous heart in addition to his intelligence. You should see his eyes when he . . ."

"'Of exalted honor speaks,'" quoted Lezhnev.

"You'll make me angry and I'll start to cry. I'm truly sorry I didn't go to Daria Mikhailovna's and stayed here with you instead. You don't deserve it. Stop teasing me," she added in a plaintive voice. "You'd be better off telling me about his youth."

"Rudin's youth?"

"Yes, please. Didn't you tell me that you knew him well, and have known him for a long time?"

Lezhnev stood up and started to walk around the room.

"Yes," he began, "I do know him well. You want me to tell you about his youth? All right. He was born in T——, the son of a poor landowner who died shortly after he was born. He and his mother were left alone. She was an extremely kind woman, and she doted on him—she lived on nothing but oatmeal, and spent every bit of money she had on him. He was educated in Moscow with funds provided first by some uncle, then later, when he'd grown up and become independent, by a wealthy prince whose favor he'd curried . . . oh, I beg your pardon, I won't do that again . . . with whom he'd made friends. Then he entered the university. I got to know him there, and we became close friends. I'll tell you about our life during those days some other time—I can't do that now. Then he went abroad. . . ."

Lezhnev continued to walk around the room. Aleksandra Pavlovna's gaze followed him.

"While he was abroad," Lezhnev went on, "Rudin rarely wrote
to his mother, and visited her only once, for about ten days. . . .
The old woman died alone, in the care of strangers, but she never
took her eyes off his portrait until the moment of her death. I went
to see her once when I was staying in T——. She was a kind,
extremely hospitable woman—she used to feed me cherry jam. She
loved her Mitia with all her heart. People like Pechorin tell us that
we always love those who are least capable of feeling love themselves, but it's *my* belief that all mothers love their children, especially absent ones. I subsequently encountered Rudin abroad. A
lady there, one of our countrywomen, some sort of bluestocking
who was middle-aged and very plain, the way a bluestocking should
be, had become attached to him. He stayed with her for a fairly
long time, but he eventually broke off the relationship with her—
or no, I beg your pardon—she broke it off with him. It was then
that I broke off my relationship with him as well. That's all."

Lezhnev fell silent, wiped his hand across his forehead, and
dropped into a chair as if he were exhausted.

"You know, Mikhailo Mikhailych," began Aleksandra Pavlovna,
"you're an evil person. In fact, you're no better than Pigasov. I'm
sure that everything you told me is true, that you haven't made
anything up, and yet you've cast it all in such an unfavorable light!
That poor old mother, her devotion, her solitary death, and that
lady. . . . What does it all amount to? You know that it's easy to
portray the life of the best of men in the kind of colors—without
adding a thing, please note—that would shock anyone! But that's
also a form of slander!"

Lezhnev stood up and started to walk around the room again.

"I didn't mean to shock you in any way, Aleksandra Pavlovna,"
he said at last. "I'm not prone to slander. However," he added
after a moment's thought, "there's actually an element of truth in
what you say. I didn't intend to slander Rudin, but—who knows!
Maybe he's managed to change since those days. Maybe I'm being
unfair to him."

"Ah! You see. . . . So promise me you'll renew your acquaintance
with him, get to know him thoroughly, and then report your ultimate verdict on him to me."

"As you wish. . . . But why are you so quiet, Sergei Pavlych?"

Volyntsev shivered and raised his head, as though he'd just
woken up.

"What can I say? I don't know him. Besides, I've had a headache all day."

"Yes, you do look rather pale this evening," observed Aleksandra Pavlovna. "Are you ill?"

"I have a headache," Volyntsev repeated, and he left the room. Aleksandra Pavlovna and Lezhnev watched him leave and then exchanged glances, although they said nothing to one another. What was taking place in Volyntsev's heart was no mystery to either of them.

VI

More than two months passed. Rudin virtually never left Daria Mikhailovna's house during that entire time. She couldn't get along without him; talking to him about herself and listening to his observations became necessities to her. He wanted to leave at one point on the grounds that he'd spent all his money—she gave him five hundred rubles. He borrowed another two hundred rubles from Volyntsev. Pigasov visited Daria Mikhailovna much less frequently than before—Rudin's presence oppressed him. And indeed, Pigasov wasn't the only one who felt oppressed.

"I don't like that clever man," Pigasov would say. "He expresses himself so unnaturally, like the hero of some Russian romantic tale. If he utters the word 'I,' he pauses in admiration . . . 'I, yes, I!' . . . And the words he uses are all so long. If you sneeze, he immediately begins to explain to you precisely why you sneezed instead of coughed. If he praises you, it's just as though he were elevating you in rank. If he begins to criticize himself, he grinds himself into the dust. Well, one thinks, he'll never dare face the light of day after that. Not at all! It even cheers him up, as if he'd treated himself to a glass of vodka."

Pandalevskii was somewhat afraid of Rudin and cautiously tried to cultivate his good will. Volyntsev found himself on strange terms with Rudin. Rudin called him a knight-errant and sang his praises both to his face and behind his back, but Volyntsev couldn't bring himself to like Rudin, and involuntarily became impatient and irritated each time Rudin began expanding on Volyntsev's virtues in his presence. "Is that man making fun of me?" Volyntsev would wonder, feeling a throb of hostility in his heart. He tried to keep his emotions in check, but he was jealous of Natalia's interest in Rudin. And even though Rudin himself always welcomed Volyntsev effusively, even though he called Volyntsev a knight-errant and borrowed money from him, he wasn't altogether well-disposed toward Volyntsev. It would have been difficult to identify the feelings of these two men when they shook one another's hands like friends and looked into one another's eyes. . . . Basistov continued to worship Rudin and to hang on his every word. Rudin paid very little attention to him. Rudin did spend one whole morning with Basistov, discussing the weightiest questions and problems of the world, arousing Basistov's keenest enthusiasm, but after that Rudin ignored him. . . . Evidently Rudin sought pure, devoted souls in words alone. Rudin didn't enter into long conversations with Lezhnev, who had become a frequent visitor at the house, and even seemed to avoid him. Lezhnev likewise treated Rudin coldly. Lezhnev didn't disclose his ultimate verdict about Rudin, however—a fact that greatly confused Aleksandra Pavlovna. She was fascinated by Rudin, but she had confidence in Lezhnev.

Everyone in Daria Mikhailovna's house indulged Rudin's whims; his slightest wish was fulfilled. He made the plans for the day. No *partie de plaisir* was organized without him. He wasn't particularly fond of spontaneous excursions or picnics of any sort, however, and took part in them the way grown-ups take part in children's games, with indulgent but slightly bored benevolence. He was actively involved in everything else, however. He and Daria Mikhailovna discussed her plans for the estate, for the education of her children, for her domestic arrangements, and for her affairs in general. He listened to her ideas without getting bored by even the most petty details, in turn proposing reforms and making suggestions. Daria Mikhailovna acceded to them verbally—and that was all. In financial matters, she was actually guided by the advice of her bailiff—an elderly, one-eyed Ukrainian, a good-natured, crafty old rogue. "What's old is fat, what's new is thin," he'd say with a quiet smile, winking his solitary eye.

Next to Daria Mikhailovna, Natalia was the person to whom Rudin talked most often, at greatest length. He secretly gave her books, confided his plans to her, and read her the first pages of articles and essays. Natalia didn't always fully grasp their significance, but Rudin didn't seem to care very much whether or not she understood, as long as she listened to him. His intimacy with Natalia didn't altogether please Daria Mikhailovna. "However," she thought, "let her chatter away with him here in the countryside. She amuses him now, as a little girl. There's no great harm in it and, at any rate, it'll improve her mind. . . . I'll put a stop to it right away in Petersburg."

Daria Mikhailovna was mistaken; Natalia didn't chatter away to Rudin like a little girl. She eagerly drank in his words, she tried to ascertain their full significance, she submitted her convictions and her doubts to his judgment; he became her leader, her guide. Thus far, only her mind had been stimulated, but in the young, the mind isn't stimulated by itself for long. What sweet moments Natalia spent sitting in the garden on a bench in the transparent shade of an aspen tree as Rudin would undertake to read Goethe's *Faust*, or Hoffman, or Bettina's letters, or Novalis to her, repeatedly stopping and explaining whatever seemed unclear. Like almost all Russian young ladies, she spoke German badly, but she understood it well. Rudin was thoroughly imbued with German poetry, with the German romantic and philosophical traditions, and he drew her after him into these forbidden realms. Hitherto unimagined splendors were spread out before her appreciative gaze. The pages of the book Rudin held on his knee poured glorious visions and inspiring new ideas into her soul in mellifluous streams, and her heart, moved by the noble delight of exalted sensations, gradually ignited and burned with the divine spark of ecstasy. . . .

"Tell me, Dmitrii Nikolaich," she began one day, sitting by the window at her embroidery frame, "will you come to Petersburg this winter?"

"I don't know," Rudin answered as he let the book he'd been paging through fall into his lap. "If I can find the means, I'll come."

He spoke dejectedly. He was tired, and had done nothing all day.

"I think you're bound to find the means."

Rudin shook his head.

"You think so!"

And he looked away significantly.

Natalia was about to reply, but she stopped herself.

"Look outside," Rudin told her, gesturing toward the window. "Do you see that apple tree? Its branches have broken due to the abundance and weight of its own fruit. A perfect emblem of genius. . . ."

"They've broken because they didn't have any support," responded Natalia.

"I understand you, Natalia Alekseevna, but it isn't so easy for a human being to find such support."

"I'd think the sympathy of others . . . in any case, solitude. . . ."
Natalia became somewhat confused, and blushed.

"What will you do in the countryside during the winter?" she
added hurriedly.

"What will I do? I'll finish my long article—you know—the one
on the tragic in life and art. I outlined it for you the day before
yesterday, and I'll send it to you."

"And will you publish it?"

"No."

"No? For whose sake will you work on it, then?"

"Possibly for yours."

Natalia lowered her eyes.

"It would be far beyond me, Dmitrii Nikolaich!"

"What is the subject of the article, if I may ask?" Basistov
inquired shyly. He was sitting a short distance away.

"The tragic in life and art," repeated Rudin. "Mr. Basistov can
also read it. But I haven't quite settled on the fundamental concept.
I haven't as yet sufficiently clarified to myself the tragic significance
of love."

Rudin talked about love eagerly and often. At first, Mlle. Boncourt was startled by the word "love," and pricked up her ears
like an old warhorse at the sound of the trumpet, but she'd eventually gotten used to it, and now she merely pursed her lips and
took snuff at intervals.

"It seems to me," Natalia said timidly, "that what is tragic in
love is unrequited love."

"Not at all!" rejoined Rudin. "That's more the comic side of
love. . . . The question should be put altogether differently. . . . It
has to be probed more deeply. . . . Love!" he went on. "Everything
about love is a mystery—how it starts, how it develops, how it
disappears. Sometimes it arrives all at once, indubitably and joyfully. At other times, it smoulders like a spark under the ashes,
and only bursts into flame in the soul after everything has ended.
And sometimes it slips into the heart like a snake and then suddenly
slips out again. . . . Yes, yes—it's an important question. But who
really does love nowadays? Who dares to love?"

And Rudin became thoughtful.

"Why is it that we haven't seen Sergei Pavlych for so long?" he
asked suddenly.

Natalia blushed and bent her head over her embroidery frame.

"I don't know," she murmured.

"What a supremely good, noble person he is!" Rudin declared, standing up. "He's one of the best examples of contemporary Russian gentlemen. . . . "

Mlle. Boncourt cast a sidelong glance at him with her little French eyes.

Rudin paced up and down the room.

"Have you noticed," he inquired, turning around sharply on his heels, "that on an oak tree—and the oak's a strong tree—the old leaves only fall off when new leaves begin to grow?"

"Yes," Natalia answered slowly, "I've noticed."

"That's what happens to a former love in a steadfast heart—that love has already died, but it still holds sway. Only another, new love can drive it out."

Natalia didn't reply.

"What does that mean?" she wondered.

Rudin stopped, pushed back his hair, and walked away.

Natalia went to her room. Perplexed, she sat on her little bed for a long while, mulling over Rudin's final words. Suddenly she clasped her hands and began to sob bitterly. Why was she crying? God knows! She herself didn't know why her tears were falling so fast. She tried to dry them, but they flowed afresh, like water from a long-pent-up source.

Aleksandra Pavlovna had a discussion with Lezhnev about Rudin the same day. He withstood all her entreaties in silence at first, but she finally managed to make him talk.

"I see that you dislike Dmitrii Nikolaich as much as you did before," she said to him. "I've intentionally refrained from questioning you until this moment, but you've had enough time now to decide whether there's been any change in him. And I want to know why you dislike him."

"Very well," Lezhnev responded with his habitual composure, "since your patience has been exhausted. Just be sure you don't get angry."

"Well then, begin, begin."

"And you'll let me complete my story."

"Of course, of course. Begin."

"All right," Lezhnev agreed, collapsing lazily onto the sofa. "I admit that I really don't like Rudin. He's an intelligent person. . . . "

"Yes, indeed."

"He's a remarkably intelligent person, albeit essentially empty...."

"It's easy to say that!"

"Albeit essentially empty," repeated Lezhnev. "Still, there's no particular harm in that. We're all empty. I won't even blame him for being a tyrant at heart, as well as lazy and not very knowledgeable...."

Aleksandra Pavlovna threw up her hands.

"Rudin isn't very knowledgeable!" she cried.

"Not very knowledgeable," Lezhnev reiterated in precisely the same tone. "He likes to live off other people's money, to play roles and so forth—that's all natural enough. But what's wrong is that he's as cold as ice."

"He's cold? That fiery soul is cold?" interrupted Aleksandra Pavlovna.

"Yes, as cold as ice, and he knows it, and pretends to be fiery. What's wrong," Lezhnev continued, gradually warming to his subject, "is that he's playing a dangerous game—not dangerous for him, of course, since he doesn't risk a single thing on it. But other people stake their souls...."

"Whom and what are you talking about? I don't understand you," declared Aleksandra Pavlovna.

"What's wrong is that he isn't honest. He's an intelligent man, to be sure, so he ought to know the value of his own words, and yet he voices them as if they cost him something.... I don't deny that he's eloquent—but it's not Russian eloquence. And indeed, after all, elaborate speech is pardonable in a boy, but at his age it's disgraceful to take pleasure in the sound of one's own voice, it's disgraceful to show off!"

"I think that it's all the same to his listeners whether or not he's showing off, Mikhailo Mikhailych."

"Forgive me, Aleksandra Pavlovna, but it's not the same at all. One man says some word to me and it completely thrills me, another says the same word or an even better one—and I turn a deaf ear. Why is that?"

"*You* do, that is," interjected Aleksandra Pavlovna.

"I do," Lezhnev affirmed, "although maybe my ears are too big. The point is that Rudin's words seem to remain mere words and never become deeds—meanwhile, these very words may disturb a young heart, may even destroy it."

"But whom do you have in mind, Mikhailo Mikhailych?"

Lezhnev paused.

"You want to know whom I have in mind? Natalia Alekseevna."

Aleksandra Pavlovna was taken aback for a moment, but she promptly started to smile.

"For heaven's sake," she began, "what strange notions you always have! Natalia is still a child, and besides, if there were anything to what you say, do you suppose that Daria Mikhailovna . . . ?"

"Daria Mikhailovna is an egoist, in the first place, and lives only for herself. In the second, she's so confident of her ability to bring up her children that it doesn't even enter her head to worry about them. Bah! How is this possible? One nod, one majestic glance, and everything will fall into place again—that's what this lady imagines. She considers herself a female Maecenas, a learned woman, and God knows what else, but in fact she's nothing more than a silly old socialite. But Natalia isn't a child. Believe me, she thinks more—and more deeply—than you and I do. Why must her honorable, passionate, ardent soul be drawn to such an actor, to such a flirt? But, of course, that too is in the nature of things."

"He's a flirt! You're calling him a flirt?"

"Of course he is. You tell me yourself, Aleksandra Pavlovna—what is his role in Daria Mikhailovna's household? To be the idol, the oracle of the house, to become involved in all its domestic arrangements, in its gossip, in its squabbles—are those dignified things for a man to do?"

Aleksandra Pavlovna looked at Lezhnev in surprise.

"I don't recognize you, Mikhailo Mikhailych," she said. "You've gotten all flushed and excited. I suspect that something else must be hidden. . . ."

"Oh, so that's it! Tell a woman the truth, based on conviction, and she won't rest until she's invented some petty, peripheral motive that she claims is forcing you to speak precisely the way you did and no other."

Aleksandra Pavlovna started to get angry.

"Bravo, Monsieur Lezhnev! You're beginning to attack women as well as Mr. Pigasov does. But, whatever you say, however perceptive you may be, it's hard for me to believe that you can have determined all of this in such a short period of time. I think you're mistaken. According to you, Rudin is some sort of Tartuffe."

"No, the point is that he isn't even a Tartuffe. At least Tartuffe knew what he was striving for, but this man, for all his intelligence. . . ."

"Well, well, what about him? Finish your speech, you unjust, vile person!"

Lezhnev stood up.

"Listen to me, Aleksandra Pavlovna," he began. "It's you who is unjust, not I. You're annoyed with me for my harsh criticism of Rudin. I have the right to speak harshly about him! I've paid dearly enough for the privilege, perhaps. I know him well—I lived with him for a long time. You remember, I promised to tell you about our life in Moscow sometime. The time to do so has clearly come. But will you have the patience to hear me out?"

"Tell me, tell me!"

"Very well, then."

Lezhnev began to walk around the room with slow steps, occasionally coming to a standstill and inclining his head forward.

"Maybe you know," he began, "or maybe you don't, that I was orphaned at an early age, and that by the time I was seventeen no one exercised any authority over me. I lived at my aunt's home in Moscow and did whatever I wanted to. As a boy, I was rather foolish and conceited—I liked to brag and show off. Upon entering the university, I behaved like a schoolboy, and quickly got into trouble. I won't tell you about it all in detail—it's not worth it. But I lied about it, lied rather maliciously. Everything came out, and I was publicly humiliated. I lost my head and cried like a baby. This happened at a friend's apartment in front of a group of my fellow students. They all began to laugh at me, except for one student who, please note, had been angrier with me than anyone else as long as I'd stubbornly refused to confess that I'd lied. Maybe he took pity on me. Anyway, he held me by the arm and led me off to his apartment."

"Was that Rudin?" asked Aleksandra Pavlovna.

"No, it wasn't Rudin. . . . It was a man . . . who's dead now. . . . He was an unusual man. His name was Pokorskii. It's beyond my powers to describe him in a few words, but, having begun to talk about him, one doesn't want to talk about anyone else. He had an elevated, pure soul and an intelligence of a sort I've never encountered since. Pokorskii lived in a small, low-ceilinged room in the attic of an old wooden house. He was very poor, and supported himself somehow by tutoring. Sometimes he couldn't even offer his friends a cup of tea, and his only sofa was so wobbly that sitting on it was like being on board a ship. But in spite of these inconveniences, a great many people used to come and visit him.

Everyone loved him—he appealed to their hearts. You wouldn't believe how pleasant and cheerful it was to sit in his impoverished little room! It was in this room that I met Rudin. He'd already parted company with his prince at that time."

"What was so exceptional about this Pokorskii?" inquired Aleksandra Pavlovna.

"How can I explain it to you? Poetry and truth—that was what attracted us to him. For all his lucid, capacious intellect, he was as sweet and simple as a child. Even now I can hear his jubilant laugh ringing in my ears, and at the same time, he

> Burned his midnight lamp
> Before the holiness of truth....

as the dear, half-crazed poet of our group described him."

"And could he speak well?" Aleksandra Pavlovna inquired further.

"He spoke quite well when he was in the mood, but not remarkably. Even then, Rudin was twenty times as eloquent as he."

Lezhnev paused and folded his arms.

"Pokorskii and Rudin were very different—Rudin had far more brilliance and flair, a greater facility with words, and, possibly, greater enthusiasm. He appeared to be much more gifted than Pokorskii, yet in fact he was a poor specimen by comparison. Rudin superbly expounded upon any idea and was masterly in debate. But his ideas didn't originate in his own brain—he borrowed them from other people, especially from Pokorskii. Pokorskii was quiet and gentle, even physically weak. He loved women madly, loved to carouse, and never considered himself insulted by anyone. Rudin seemed to be full of fire, courage, and life, but at heart he was cold and almost timid until his vanity was offended—then he'd do anything. He constantly sought to win people's hearts, and he did win them in the name of general principles and ideas. In fact, he actually exerted a strong influence over many of those people. To tell you the truth, though, no one liked him—I was perhaps the only one who became attached to him. The others submitted to his yoke, but they all freely surrendered themselves to Pokorskii. Rudin never refused to argue or debate with anyone he met. He hadn't read many books, but he'd read far more than Pokorskii and all the rest of us, at any rate. Besides, he had a systematic mind and a prodigious memory, which has an enormous effect on young people! They require generalizations and conclusions, even if they're incorrect, but conclusions nonetheless! A perfectly sincere person can never satisfy them. Try to explain to young people that you can't tell them the complete truth because you yourself don't possess it . . . and they won't listen to you. But you can't deceive them, either. You yourself must at least half-believe you do possess the truth. That was why Rudin had such a powerful effect on all of us.

"I told you just now that he hadn't read very much—but he had read philosophy books, and his brain was so constituted that he immediately extracted all the general ideas from what he'd read, penetrated to the very heart of the matter, and then formulated brilliant, well-founded lines of thought that led in all directions, opening up new spiritual perspectives. Our group was composed of boys, it's only fair to say, and ill-informed ones at that. Philosophy, art, science, and even life itself were all mere words to us— abstractions, if you like—fascinating, magnificent concepts, but fragmentary, isolated ones. We knew nothing of and had had no contact with the universal bond among those abstractions—the fundamental law of the universe—although we discussed it vaguely and tried to form some notion of it for ourselves. As we listened to Rudin, we felt for the first time as if we'd finally grasped it, this universal bond, as if a veil had finally been lifted from our eyes! Even supposing that he wasn't expressing his own ideas— what of it! A graceful order had been imposed on everything we knew, everything that had been fragmentary suddenly became coherent, taking shape and rising before our eyes like an edifice. Everything became illuminated, and inspiration could be found everywhere. . . . Nothing appeared meaningless or accidental any longer—logical necessity and beauty seemed inherent in all things. Everything assumed a clear yet secret significance, each separate aspect of life fell into accord. And some sort of holy awe and reverence, some sweet trepidation, descended upon us, for we felt ourselves to be the living vessels of eternal truth, as it were, to be its instruments, destined for some great. . . . Doesn't this all seem completely ridiculous to you?"

"Not in the least!" Aleksandra Pavlovna replied slowly. "Why would you think so? I don't completely understand you, but I don't think it's ridiculous."

"We've managed to grow wiser since then, of course," Lezhnev continued. "All this may seem childish to us now. . . . But, I repeat, we all owed a great deal to Rudin at that time. Yet Pokorskii was incomparably nobler than he, there's no doubt about it. Pokorskii breathed fire and strength into all of us, but he frequently became depressed and fell silent. He was nervous and unhealthy, but when he did stretch his wings—my God, how he could fly! Into the infinite distance of the azure skies! Whereas Rudin, as handsome and stately as he might have been, was extremely petty—he adored gossip, he passionately enjoyed meddling in everything, defining and explicating everything. His capacity for interference was inexhaustible—he was a politician by nature. I'm describing him as I knew him then. But, unfortunately, he hasn't changed. To be sure, his ideals haven't changed, either . . . at thirty-five! It's not everyone who can say that about themselves!"

"Sit down," commanded Aleksandra Pavlovna. "Why do you keep moving back and forth like a pendulum?"

"I like it better," responded Lezhnev. "Well, after I'd joined Pokorskii's group, I must tell you, Aleksandra Pavlovna, I was utterly transformed. I became humble and anxious to learn, I studied, I rejoiced, I worshiped—in a word, I felt as though I'd just entered a holy temple. And in fact, when I recall our gatherings, I remember a great deal about them that was admirable and even touching, by God. Imagine a group of five or six young men sitting together around one tallow candle. The tea that was served would be terrible and the cake would be stale, very stale, but you should have seen our faces, you should have heard our discussions! Eyes sparkling with enthusiasm, cheeks flushed, and hearts pounding, we'd talk about God, about truth, about the future of humanity, about poetry. . . . What we'd say would often be absurd, and we'd become ecstatic over nonsense, but what's so bad about that? . . . Pokorskii would sit with his legs crossed, his pale cheek resting on his hand, his eyes aglow. Rudin would stand in the middle of the room and would speak, speak beautifully, for all the world like the young Demosthenes by the sea. Our poet, Subotin, his hair thoroughly disheveled, would periodically interject abrupt exclamations as though in his sleep, while Scheller, a forty-year-old student, the son of a German pastor, whom we considered a profound thinker thanks to his eternal, inviolable silence, would maintain that silence with more rapt solemnity than usual. Even the lively Shchitov, the Aristophanes of our gatherings, would be subdued and merely smile, while two or three newcomers would listen with ecstatic pleasure. . . . And the night would seem to fly by on wings. The gray of morning would already be visible when we'd depart—moved, joyful, serious, and sober (there was never any mention of wine at such times), with some sort of sweet languor in our souls. . . . I remember walking along the empty streets, completely at peace, even looking up at the stars with a kind of confidence, as though they'd become nearer and more accessible. . . . Ah! That was a glorious time, and I can't bear to believe that it was completely in vain! And indeed, it wasn't in vain—even for those whose lives became squalid later on. How often I've happened to run across one of these former college friends! You'd think he'd become a sheer brute, only to utter Pokorskii's name in his presence and observe every bit of nobility in him suddenly awakened, just as if a forgotten bottle of perfume had been uncorked in some dark, dirty room. . . ."

Lezhnev stopped. His normally colorless face was flushed.

"But why did you quarrel with Rudin, then?" Aleksandra Pavlovna asked, looking at Lezhnev in bewilderment.

"I didn't quarrel with him, but I broke off my relationship with him abroad, when I got to know him thoroughly. Still, I might have quarreled with him in Moscow—he played a dirty trick on me there."

"What was that?"

"I'll tell you. I—how can I say this? It doesn't accord very well with my appearance—I was always strongly inclined to fall in love."

"You?"

"Yes. It's strange, isn't it? But, in any event, it's true. Well, I fell in love at that time with a very pretty young girl. . . . But why are you looking at me like that? I could tell you something much more surprising than that about myself!"

"And what is that something, if I may ask?"

"Oh, just this. In those Moscow days, I used to have trysts at night . . . with whom, do you suppose? With a young lime tree at the far end of my garden. I used to embrace its slender, graceful trunk, feeling as though I were embracing all of nature—and my heart would melt and expand as though it really were absorbing all of nature. That's the sort of person I was then. And perhaps you think I'd never write poetry? Why, I even composed an entire drama modeled on *Manfred*. Among the characters was a ghost with blood on his breast—not his own blood, please note, but the blood of humanity in general. . . . Yes, yes, you shouldn't be surprised at that. . . . But I was beginning to tell you about my love affair. I met a girl. . . ."

"Did you stop having trysts with your lime tree?" Aleksandra Pavlovna inquired.

"Yes, I stopped. This girl was an extremely nice, kind creature who had bright, cheerful eyes and a melodious voice."

"You've given a fine description of her," Aleksandra Pavlovna commented with a smile.

"You're such a severe critic," Lezhnev retorted. "Well, this girl lived with her elderly father. . . . But I won't go into all the details, I'll simply tell you that this girl was so generous that if you asked her for just half a cup of tea, she'd give you a cup that was brimming over! I was wild about her two days after I first met her. By the seventh day, I couldn't contain myself any longer and confessed everything to Rudin. A young man in love can't help talking about it, and I bared my soul to him. I was totally under his influence at that time, and his influence, I frankly admit, was beneficial in many ways. He was the first person who didn't treat me with contempt, trying to guide me instead. I loved Pokorskii passionately and felt a certain awe at his purity of soul, but I was closer to Rudin. When he heard about my love, he lapsed into indescribable ecstasies, congratulated me, embraced me, and immediately began to elaborate upon the broad significance of my new condition. I reveled in it all. . . . Well, you know how he can talk. His words had an extraordinary effect on me. I promptly acquired a surprising respect for myself, adopted a serious demeanor, and refused to laugh. As I recall, I even started to walk more carefully at the time, as though I were carrying a sacred chalice filled with a priceless liquid inside of me, which I was afraid of spilling. . . . I was very happy, especially since she was evidently well-disposed toward me. Rudin wanted to meet my beloved, and I myself almost insisted on introducing him to her."

"Ah! I see, I see what the problem is now," interrupted Aleksandra Pavlovna. "Rudin stole your beloved away from you, and you've never been able to forgive him. . . . I'm ready to bet that I'm right!"

"You'd lose your bet, Aleksandra Pavlovna: you're wrong. Rudin didn't steal her away from me—he didn't even try to steal her away—but he destroyed my happiness all the same, although, viewing it objectively, I'm prepared to thank him for it now. But I nearly went out of my mind at the time. Rudin didn't want to do me the slightest harm—quite the contrary! But as a result of his accursed habit of isolating and examining every experience, both his own and other people's, like butterflies pinned in a case, he began explaining our relationship to us, telling us how we ought to behave. He despotically compelled us to assess our thoughts and feelings, he praised us, he chastised us, he even began to correspond with us—can you imagine! Well, he managed to derail us completely! I hardly would have married the young lady even then (I had that much common sense left), but we might at least have spent a few months as happily as the characters in *Paul et Virginie*. Instead, tensions and misunderstandings of every sort set in—in a word, we became ridiculous. It ended one fine morning, when Rudin reached the conclusion that it was his sacred duty as a friend to inform her father all about it—and did so."

"Really?" cried Aleksandra Pavlovna.

"Yes, and, please note, did so with my consent—that's what's amazing! . . . I remember to this day what chaos my brain was in. Everything was simply spinning, the way it does in a camera obscura—white seemed to be black and black to be white, falsehood was truth, and a whim was a duty. . . . Ah! Even now I'm ashamed at the memory of it! Rudin never lost heart—not in the least! He carried on through all sorts of misunderstandings and complications like a swallow flying over a pond."

"And so you ended your relationship with the girl?" Aleksandra Pavlovna asked, naively bending her head to one side and arching her eyebrows.

"I ended it . . . and it was a horrible ending—painful, awkward, and public, quite unnecessarily public. . . . I myself wept, she wept, and the devil knows what happened. . . . It seemed as though some sort of Gordian knot had been tied that had to be cut—but it was painful! However, everything on earth turns out for the best. She married an excellent man, and is well off now. . . ."

"But confess, you've never been able to forgive Rudin, all the same . . . ," Aleksandra Pavlova began.

"Not at all!" interrupted Lezhnev. "Why, I cried like a baby when he left to go abroad. Still, to tell you the truth, that seed was planted in my heart even then. And when I encountered him later on, abroad . . . well, by that time I'd gotten older. . . . Rudin was revealed to me in his true colors."

"What exactly was it that you saw in him?"

"Why, everything I've been telling you about for the past hour. But that's enough about him. Maybe everything will turn out all right. I only wanted to show you that if I do judge him severely,

it isn't because I don't know him.... As far as Natalia Alekseevna
is concerned, I won't say another word, but you should pay attention
to your brother."

"My brother! Why?"

"Just look at him. You really haven't noticed anything?"

Aleksandra Pavlovna lowered her gaze.

"You're right," she assented. "Certainly...my brother...
hasn't been himself for some time now....But do you really
think—"

"Ssh! I think he's coming," whispered Lezhnev. "And Natalia
isn't a child, believe me, although unfortunately, she's as inexperienced as a child. You'll see. That girl will astonish all of us."

"In what way?"

"Oh, something like this....Do you know that it's precisely
this type of girl who drowns herself, takes poison, and so forth?
Don't be misled by her tranquil demeanor. Her passions run strong,
and her character—oh, my!"

"Well, I think you're indulging in a flight of fancy now. To a
phlegmatic person like you, I suppose even I seem like a volcano?"

"Oh, no!" Lezhnev replied with a smile. "And as for character—
you have no character at all, thank God!"

"What fresh impertinence is this?"

"This? This is the highest compliment, believe me...."

Volyntsev came in and looked at Lezhnev and his sister suspiciously. He'd gotten thin of late. They both began to talk to him,
but he barely smiled in response to their efforts to entertain him,
looking like a miserable rabbit, as Pigasov had once described him.
But there's probably no man on earth who hasn't looked even worse
than that at some point during his life. Volyntsev sensed that Natalia
was drifting away from him and, as she did, it seemed like the
earth was giving way under his feet.

VII

The next day was Sunday, and Natalia got up late. She'd been
very quiet until sunset the evening before—she was secretly
ashamed of her tears, and had slept very badly. Sitting half-dressed
at her little piano, she played a few chords—barely audibly, for fear
of waking Mlle. Boncourt—and then let her forehead rest on the
cold keys, remaining motionless for a long while. She couldn't stop
thinking, not about Rudin himself, but about one word or another
that he'd uttered, and she became wholly immersed in those

thoughts. Volyntsev occasionally entered into them—she knew that he loved her. But she promptly abandoned that line of thinking. . . . She felt strangely agitated. She dressed hurriedly, went downstairs, and, after saying good morning to her mother, seized the first opportunity and walked out to the garden by herself. . . . It was a hot, bright, sunny day, in spite of occasional rain showers. Low, misty clouds were sailing smoothly across the clear sky without obscuring the sun, periodically releasing sheets of rain that suddenly and briefly fell in the fields. Then thickly falling raindrops, flashing like diamonds, swiftly hit the ground with a kind of dull thud; the sunshine glistened through their sparkling network; the grass, which had been rustling in the wind, grew still, thirstily drinking in the moisture; every leaf on the drenched trees gently trembled; the birds continued to sing all the while, and it was delightful to hear their sociable chirps mingling with the fresh hiss and murmur of the flowing rain. The dusty roads steamed, slightly pitted by the sharp blows of the thick drops. Then the clouds moved on, a light breeze sprang up, and the grass began to glisten in shades of emerald and gold. The leaves on the trees grew transparent as they clung together. An intense fragrance spread everywhere. . . .

The sky was nearly cloudless by the time Natalia went into the garden. It exuded freshness and peace—that soothing, blissful peace in which the human heart is aroused by the delicious languor of secret sympathies and inchoate desires. . . .

Natalia walked along a lengthy row of silver poplars beside the pond. Suddenly Rudin appeared in front of her, as if he'd arisen from the earth. She became embarrassed. He glanced at her face.

"Are you alone?" he asked.

"Yes, I'm alone," Natalia replied, "but I just came out for a moment. It's time for me to go back in."

"I'll go with you."

And he began to walk beside her.

"You seem sad," he said.

"I do? I was just going to remark that I thought you weren't in good spirits."

"Possibly . . . that often happens to me. It's more excusable in me than in you, though."

"Why? Do you think that I don't have anything to be sad about?"

"At your age, you ought to be enjoying life."

Natalia took several steps in silence.

"Dmitrii Nikolaich!" she said.

"What?"

"Do you remember . . . the comparison you made yesterday . . . you remember . . . regarding the oak tree?"

"Yes, I remember. What about it?"

Natalia stole a look at Rudin.

"Why did you . . . what did you mean by that comparison?"

Rudin bowed his head and gazed into the distance.

"Natalia Alekseevna!" he began with the characteristically intense, meaningful expression on his face that always made his listeners believe Rudin wasn't expressing even a tenth of what was contained in his heart. "Natalia Alekseevna! You may have noticed that I've said little about my past. There are some strands I don't touch upon at all. My heart . . . who needs to know what's taken place within it? To expose all that to view has always seemed sacrilegious to me. But I've been candid with you, since you've won my confidence. . . . I can't conceal from you the fact that I, too, have loved and have suffered, like all men. . . . When and how? It's pointless to discuss all that, but my heart has known a lot of joy and a lot of sorrow. . . ."

Rudin paused briefly.

"What I said to you yesterday," he went on, "might be applied to me in my present situation, to a certain extent. But then again, it's pointless to discuss this. That segment of life has already ended for me. It merely remains for me to continue a tedious journey from place to place in a jolting carriage along a parched and dusty road. . . . When I'll arrive, or whether I'll arrive at all—God knows. . . . Let's talk about you instead."

"Is it possible, Dmitrii Nikolaich," Natalia interrupted him, "that you expect nothing from life?"

"Oh, no! I expect a great deal, but not for myself. . . . I'll never renounce activity or the blessings that come from activity, but I've renounced happiness. My hopes, my dreams, and my own happiness have nothing in common. Love" (he shrugged his shoulders upon uttering this word) "love isn't for me—I'm not worthy of it. A woman who loves has a right to demand the whole of a man, and I can no longer give the whole of myself. Besides, it's for youths to win love—I'm too old. How could I turn anyone's head? God grant that I keep my own head on my shoulders."

"I understand," Natalia declared, "that a man who strives for a lofty goal mustn't think about himself, but isn't a woman capable of appreciating such a man? I would have thought, on the contrary, that a woman is more likely to be repelled by an egoist. . . . All young people—the youths to whom you refer—are egoists, they're all occupied with themselves alone, even when they're in love. Believe me, a woman isn't merely capable of appreciating self-sacrifice—she, too, can sacrifice herself."

Natalia's cheeks had become slightly flushed and her eyes were shining. Prior to her acquaintance with Rudin, she never would have managed to utter such an extended, impassioned speech.

"You've heard my views on the mission of women more than once," Rudin replied with a condescending smile. "You know that, in my opinion, Joan of Arc was the only person who could have saved France . . . but that's not the point. I want to talk about you. You're standing on the threshold of life. . . . Discussing your future is both pleasant and not unprofitable. . . . Listen. You know that I'm your friend and that I take practically a relative's interest in you, so I hope you won't find my question indiscreet. Tell me, has your heart remained perfectly at peace thus far?"

Natalia blushed deeply, and said nothing. Rudin halted; she halted as well.

"Are you angry with me?" he inquired.

"No," she responded, "but I didn't expect. . . ."

"However," he continued, "you don't need to answer me. I know your secret."

Natalia looked at him with near dismay.

"Yes, yes, I know who has won your heart. And I must say that you couldn't have made a better choice. He's a wonderful man, he knows how to appreciate you. He hasn't been crushed by life—he's simple and pure in spirit . . . he'll insure your happiness."

"To whom are you referring, Dmitrii Nikolaich?"

"Is it possible that you don't understand to whom I'm referring? To Volyntsev, of course. Well? Isn't it true?"

Natalia slightly turned away from Rudin. She was completely distraught.

"Do you think he doesn't love you? For heaven's sake! He never takes his eyes off you and follows your every movement. Indeed, can love ever be concealed? And aren't you yourself well-disposed toward him? As far as I can tell, your mother also likes him. . . . Your choice. . . ."

"Dmitrii Nikolaich," Natalia interrupted him, stretching out one hand toward a nearby bush in her distress, "it's really extremely difficult for me to talk about this, but I assure you ... you're mistaken."

"I'm mistaken?" echoed Rudin. "I don't think so. I haven't known you for very long, but I already know you quite well. What's the meaning of the change I can see in you? I can see it clearly. Are you just the same as when I first met you six weeks ago? No, Natalia Alekseevna, your heart isn't at peace."

"Perhaps not," Natalia responded, barely audibly, "but all the same, you're mistaken."

"How so?" asked Rudin.

"Let me go! Don't ask me!" Natalia exclaimed, and she set off swiftly toward the house.

She herself was frightened by everything she was suddenly feeling.

Rudin overtook her and brought her to a halt.

"Natalia Alekseevna," he said, "our conversation can't end like this. It's too important for me as well. . . . How should I understand you?"

"Let me go!" repeated Natalia.

"Natalia Alekseevna, for God's sake!"

Rudin's face betrayed his agitation. He grew pale.

"You understand everything—you'll have to understand me, too!" Natalia cried. She snatched her hand away and walked ahead without looking around.

"Just one more word!" Rudin called out after her.

She stopped, but didn't turn around.

"You asked me what I meant by that comparison yesterday. You know I don't want to deceive you. I was talking about myself, about my past—and about you."

"What? About me?"

"Yes, about you. I repeat, I don't want to deceive you. You now know what feeling, what new feeling I was speaking about then. . . . Until today, I never would have dared. . . ."

Natalia abruptly hid her face in her hands and ran toward the house.

She was so shaken by the unexpected conclusion of her conversation with Rudin that she ran past Volyntsev without even noticing him. He was standing still, leaning against a tree. He'd arrived at the house a quarter of an hour earlier, had found Daria Mikhailovna in the drawing room, and, after exchanging a few words, had escaped unobserved and gone looking for Natalia. Led by a lover's instinct, he'd proceeded straight to the garden and had come upon her and Rudin at the very moment she'd snatched her hand away from him. Darkness seemed to fall across his eyes at that point. His gaze following Natalia, he moved away from the tree and took two steps without knowing where or why. Rudin saw him as he came closer. Each looked the other in the eye, bowed, and walked past one another in silence.

"This won't be the end of it," each one thought.

Volyntsev headed for the very end of the garden. He felt sad and sick at heart. From time to time, his blood pulsed angrily through his veins. A gentle rain began to fall again. Rudin returned to his own room. He wasn't calm, either—his thoughts were in a whirl. Intimate, unexpected contact with a youthful, honest soul is disturbing to anyone.

Everything somehow seemed wrong at dinner. Natalia was dreadfully pale, could barely stay seated in her chair, and didn't raise her eyes once. Volyntsev sat next to her as usual, and spoke to her from time to time in a forced manner. Pigasov happened to be having dinner at Daria Mikhailovna's that day. He talked more than anyone else at the table. Among other things, he claimed that people, like dogs, can be divided into two groups—those with short tails and those with long tails. "Individuals who have short tails," he asserted, "get them either by birth or by their own misdeeds. Things always go badly for those with short tails—they never succeed at anything, they have no confidence in themselves. But the individual who has a long, bushy tail is happy. He may be smaller and weaker than individuals with short tails, but he believes in himself. He displays his tail and everyone admires it. And yet this should be surprising, for the tail is a perfectly useless part of the body, you must admit. What good is a tail? But everyone judges your merits by your tail. I myself," he concluded with a sigh, "belong to the group of individuals with short tails, and what's most annoying of all is that I cropped my tail myself."

"By which you mean to say," Rudin commented casually, "what La Rochefoucauld said long before you—believe in yourself, and others will believe in you. I don't understand why you brought in the tail."

"Let each person," Volyntsev spoke up sharply, his eyes flashing, "express himself any way he pleases. Speaking of despotism. . . . I think there's no despotism worse than that of so-called intelligent people, the devil take them!"

Everyone was astonished at this outburst from Volyntsev and fell silent. Rudin would have looked at him, but he couldn't control his gaze, and he turned away smiling, without opening his mouth.

"Aha! So you've lost your tail as well!" Pigasov thought, while Natalia's heart froze with terror. Daria Mikhailovna gave Volyntsev a long, puzzled stare, and eventually was the first to speak. She began to describe an extraordinary dog belonging to her close friend, Minister N. N——. . . .

Volyntsev left shortly after dinner. As he said goodbye to Natalia, he couldn't resist saying to her: "Why are you so embarrassed, as though you've done something wrong to someone? You can't have done anything wrong!"

Natalia didn't understand him at all, and merely stared at him as he left. Rudin came up to her before tea and, bending over the table as though he were examining the newspapers, whispered: "It's all like a dream, isn't it? I absolutely must see you alone— if only for a moment." He turned to Mlle Boncourt. "Here," he said to her, "this is the article you were looking for," and then, bending toward Natalia again, he added in a whisper, "Try to be by the terrace in the lilac arbor at about ten o'clock. I'll wait for you."

Pigasov was the hero of the evening; Rudin left him in possession of the battlefield. He amused Daria Mikhailovna highly: first he told a story about one of his neighbors who, having been henpecked by his wife for thirty years, had himself grown so old-womanish that one day, crossing a little puddle in Pigasov's presence, he'd reached out his hand and picked up the skirt of his coat the way women pick up their dresses. Then Pigasov turned to a gentleman dining with them who'd been a freemason at one time, then a melancholic, and then had decided to become a banker.

"How did you go about becoming a freemason, Philipp Stepanych?" Pigasov asked him.

"You know how—I let the nail on my little finger grow long."

But what amused Daria Mikhailovna most of all was when Pigasov embarked upon a lengthy discussion of love, avowing that some women had actually pined away for him, that one impassioned German woman had even called him her "appetizing little Afrikan" and her "hoarse little crow." Daria Mikhailovna laughed, but Pigasov was telling the truth—he really did have the right to boast about several conquests. He maintained that nothing was easier than making any woman you chose fall in love with you—you merely had to repeat to her that there was heaven on her lips and bliss in her eyes, and that all other women were simply rag dolls compared to her, for ten days in a row, and on the eleventh day she herself would be prepared to say that there was heaven on her lips and bliss in her eyes, and would be in love with you. Everything eventually comes to pass on earth, and so, who knows? Perhaps Pigasov was right.

At half past nine, Rudin had already reached the arbor. The stars had just come out in the pale, distant depths of the sky; a crimson glow still showed where the sun had set—the horizon seemed brighter and clearer there. A golden half-moon shone through the black network of branches on a birch tree. The other trees either stood like grim giants, their thousands of chinks resembling eyes, or else blended together into compressed masses of darkness. Not a single leaf was stirring; the top branches of the lilacs and acacias seemed to stretch upward in the warm air, as though they were listening for something. The house loomed darkly nearby; patches of reddish light showed where the tall windows were illuminated. It was a mild, quiet evening, but a restrained, passionate sigh could be discerned amid the quiet.

Rudin stood upright, his arms folded across his breast, listening intently. His heart was beating violently and he involuntarily held his breath. He finally caught the sound of light, hurried footsteps, and Natalia entered the arbor.

Rudin rushed up to her and took her hands. They were as cold as ice.

"Natalia Alekseevna!" he began in an agitated whisper. "I wanted to see you so much.... I couldn't wait until tomorrow. I have to tell you what I didn't suspect, what I didn't realize even this morning—I love you!"

Natalia's hands trembled weakly in his.

"I love you!" he repeated. "How could I have deceived myself for so long? Why didn't I guess long ago that I love you?... And you?... Natalia Alekseevna, tell me, do you..."

Natalia could barely breathe.

"You see that I've come here," she said at last.

"No, tell me—do you love me?"

"I think so—yes," she whispered.

Rudin pressed her hands even more tightly and tried to draw her toward him.

Natalia looked around quickly.

"Let me go, I'm frightened. . . . I think someone's listening to us. . . . For God's sake, be careful. Volyntsev suspects."

"Never mind him! You saw that I didn't even respond to him today. . . . Ah, Natalia Alekseevna, I'm so happy! Nothing can ever separate us now!"

Natalia glanced into his eyes.

"Let me go," she whispered. "It's time for me to go."

"One moment," Rudin began.

"No, let me go, let me go."

"You seem to be afraid of me."

"No, but it's time for me to go. . . ."

"Just repeat at least once more. . . ."

"You say that you're happy?" Natalia asked.

"I? No man in the world is happier than I am! Can you doubt it?"

Natalia raised her head. Her pale, noble, youthful, passionate face was quite beautiful in the mysterious shadows of the arbor under the faint light reflected from the evening sky.

"Know, then," she said, "that I will be yours."

"Oh, my God!" cried Rudin.

But Natalia eluded his grasp and disappeared.

Rudin stood motionless for a few moments, then slowly left the arbor. The moon clearly illuminated his face; a smile spread across his lips.

"I'm happy," he said in a half whisper. "Yes, I'm happy," he reiterated, as though trying to convince himself.

He straightened his tall form, pushed back his hair, and quickly walked into the garden with a cheerful flourish of his hand.

Meanwhile, the bushes of the lilac arbor separated and Panda-levskii appeared. He looked around warily, shook his head, pursed his lips, remarked meaningfully, "So that's how it is. This must be brought to Daria Mikhailovna's attention"—and vanished.

VIII

When he returned home, Volyntsev was so miserable and dejected, gave his sister such listless answers, and shut himself up in his room so quickly that she decided to send a message to Lezhnev.

She always turned to him in difficult situations. Lezhnev sent word
that he'd come over the next day.

Volyntsev was no more cheerful in the morning. He'd intended
to work on the estate after having some tea, but he stayed at home
instead, lay down on the sofa, and picked up a book—a thing he
rarely did. Volyntsev had no interest in literature, and poetry simply
terrified him. "This is as incomprehensible as poetry," he'd say,
and in confirmation of his words, he'd quote the following lines
from the Russian poet Aibulat:

> And until the end of his sad days,
> Neither reason nor proud experience
> Will crush with their hands
> The bloodied forget-me-nots of life.

Aleksandra Pavlovna kept glancing uneasily at her brother, but
she didn't disturb him with questions. A carriage drew up to the
steps.

"Ah!" she thought. "It's Lezhnev, thank God!"

A servant came in and announced the arrival of Rudin. Volyntsev
flung his book on the floor and raised his head. "Who's come?"
he asked.

"Rudin, Dmitrii Nikolaich," the servant repeated. Volyntsev
stood up.

"Invite him to come in," he said, "and please, sister," he added,
turning to Aleksandra Pavlovna, "let us talk alone."

"But why . . . ," she began.

"I have a good reason," he interrupted vehemently. "I beg you
to let us talk alone."

Rudin came in. Standing in the middle of the room, Volyntsev
welcomed him with a cool bow, without offering his hand.

"Confess that you didn't expect me," Rudin commenced, and
he laid his hat down on the window seat. His lips were twitching
slightly. He was ill at ease, but he tried to conceal his discomfort.

"I certainly didn't expect you," Volyntsev replied. "After yesterday, I was more inclined to expect someone with a special message from you."

"I understand what you mean," Rudin declared, taking a seat,
"and am very grateful for your frankness. It's much better that
way. I myself have come to see you, since you're a man of honor."

"Can't we dispense with the compliments?" requested Volyntsev.

"I want to explain to you why I've come."

"We're acquainted—why shouldn't you come? Besides, this isn't the first time you've honored me with a visit."

"I came to you as one man of honor to another," Rudin repeated, "and now I want to appeal to your sense of justice. . . . I have complete confidence in you. . . ."

"What's this all about?" asked Volyntsev, who'd remained standing in his original position the entire time, staring sullenly at Rudin and occasionally pulling at the ends of his moustache.

"If you'd kindly. . . . I came here to offer an explanation, of course, but all the same, I can't do so all at once."

"Why on earth not?"

"A third person is involved in this matter."

"What third person?"

"Sergei Pavlych, you understand me."

"Dmitrii Nikolaich, I don't understand you in the least."

"You prefer. . . ."

"I prefer that you speak plainly!" exclaimed Volyntsev.

He was beginning to get angry in earnest.

Rudin frowned.

"Please . . . we're alone . . . I must tell you—although you're probably already aware of it" (Volyntsev shrugged his shoulders impatiently), "I must tell you that I love Natalia Alekseevna, and I have the right to believe that she loves me."

Volyntsev turned pale, but didn't respond. He walked to the window and stood with his back turned.

"You understand, Sergei Pavlych," Rudin continued, "that if I weren't convinced. . . ."

"For heaven's sake!" interrupted Volyntsev. "I don't doubt it in the least. . . . What of it? Good luck to you! I only wonder what the devil induced you to bestow this news on me. . . . What do I have to do with it? What difference does it make to me whom you love, or who loves you? I simply can't comprehend this."

Volyntsev continued to stare out the window. His voice sounded hollow.

Rudin stood up.

"I'll tell you why I decided to come and see you, Sergei Pavlych, why I didn't think I even had the right to hide our . . . our mutual inclination from you. I respect you too profoundly—that's why I've come. I didn't want . . . neither of us wanted to enact a comedy in front of you. Your feelings for Natalia Alekseevna were clear to me. . . . Believe me, I know my own worth. I know how little I deserve to supplant you in her heart, but if this was fated to happen, is it really better to be hypocritical, to pretend, to deceive? Is it really better to expose ourselves to misunderstandings or even to the possibility of the kind of scene that took place yesterday at dinner? Sergei Pavlych, tell me yourself, is it really better?"

Volyntsev folded his arms across his chest, as though trying to hold himself back.

"Sergei Pavlych," Rudin continued, "I've caused you pain, I can feel that. . . . But please understand us . . . understand that we had no other means of demonstrating our respect for you, of demonstrating that we value your straightforward nobility. Candor, total candor would have been inappropriate with anyone else, but with you, it became an obligation. We're happy to think that our secret is in your hands. . . ."

Volyntsev gave a forced laugh.

"Many thanks for your confidence in me!" he exclaimed. "But please note that I neither wished to know your secret nor to tell you mine, although you treat it as if it were your property. But excuse me—you speak as though you were speaking for two. Does it follow that I should presume Natalia Alekseevna knows about your visit and its purpose?"

Rudin was slightly taken aback.

"No, I didn't convey my intentions to Natalia Alekseevna. But I know that she shares my views."

"That's all very nice," Volyntsev began after a short pause, drumming on the windowpane with his fingers, "even though I must confess it would have been far better if you'd had a little less respect for me. You and your respect can go to the devil, to tell you the truth—but what do you want from me now?"

"I don't want anything—or no! I do want one thing. I want you not to regard me as treacherous or hypocritical. I want you to understand me. . . . I hope that you can't doubt my sincerity now. . . . I want us to part as friends, Sergei Pavlych. . . . I want you to extend your hand to me the way you've done before."

And Rudin approached Volyntsev.

"Forgive me, my dear sir," Volyntsev demurred, turning around and stepping back a few paces. "I'm ready to do complete justice to your intentions. It's all lovely and even exalted, let's say, but we're simple people, we don't decorate our pastries. We aren't capable of following the flights of great minds like yours. . . . What you deem sincere, we regard as improper and indiscreet. . . . What's simple and clear to you is complex and obscure to us.... You boast about what we conceal.... How can we understand you? Forgive me, but I can neither regard you as a friend nor shake your hand.... This is petty, perhaps, but I myself am a petty person."

Rudin picked up his hat from the window seat.

"Goodbye, Sergei Pavlych!" he said sorrowfully. "I was mistaken in my expectations. My visit was admittedly a rather strange one, but I'd hoped that you...." (Volyntsev made an impatient gesture.) "Forgive me, I won't talk about this any more. In light of everything, I can see clearly that you're right, that you couldn't have acted otherwise. Goodbye, and allow me at least once more, for the last time, to assure you of the purity of my motives.... I'm confident of your discretion...."

"This is too much!" Volyntsev exclaimed, shaking with anger. "I never asked for your confidence, thus you have no right whatsoever to depend on my discretion!"

Rudin started to say something, but then merely waved his hand, bowed, and left, while Volyntsev flung himself on the sofa and turned his face to the wall.

"May I come in?" Aleksandra Pavlovna's voice was audible at the door.

Volyntsev didn't answer right away, furtively wiping his hand across his face. "No, Sasha," he said in a slightly altered voice, "wait a little while longer."

Aleksandra Pavlovna came back to the door half an hour later.

"Mikhailo Mikhailych is here," she said. "Do you want to see him?"

"Yes," Volyntsev replied. "Have them show him in here."

Lezhnev came in.

"What—are you sick?" he inquired, seating himself in a chair near the sofa.

Volyntsev sat up, leaned on his elbow, and gazed into his friend's face for a long time, then repeated his entire conversation with Rudin word for word. He'd never given Lezhnev a hint of his feelings toward Natalia before, although he'd guessed that they were no secret to Lezhnev.

"Well, my friend, you've surprised me!" Lezhnev declared as soon as Volyntsev had finished his narrative. "I'd expected many strange things from him, but this is.... Still, I can recognize his handiwork."

"For heaven's sake!" Volyntsev cried agitatedly. "It's pure insolence! Why, I almost threw him out the window. Did he want to boast to me, or was he afraid of something? What was the purpose of it all? How could he decide to come to someone . . . ?" Volyntsev clasped his hands above his head and fell silent.

"No, my friend, that's not it," Lezhnev responded tranquilly. "You won't believe me, but he really did it with good intentions. Yes, indeed. It was noble, you see, and candid, and, I grant, it provided him with an opportunity to make a speech, to display his eloquence, which, of course, is what he needs, what he can't live without. . . . Ah! His tongue is his enemy. Yet it's a good servant as well."

"You can't imagine the solemnity with which he entered and spoke!"

"Well, he can't do anything without it. He buttons his overcoat as though he were fulfilling a sacred duty. I'd like to set him on a deserted island and secretly watch to see how he'd behave there. And he repeatedly discourses on simplicity!"

"But tell me, my dear fellow, for God's sake," requested Volyntsev, "what is this? Philosophy?"

"How can I put it? On one hand, it's definitely philosophy, if you will, and on the other, something altogether different. It's not fair to attribute everything foolish to philosophy."

Volyntsev looked at him.

"Then he wasn't lying, you don't think?"

"No, my boy, he wasn't lying. But do you know what? We've talked about this enough. Let's light our pipes and invite Aleksandra Pavlovna in. It's easier to talk and easier to remain silent when she's with us. She can make us some tea."

"All right," replied Volyntsev. "Sasha, come in here," he cried loudly.

Aleksandra Pavlovna came in. He grasped her hand and warmly pressed it to his lips.

Rudin returned home in a strange, troubled frame of mind. He was annoyed with himself; he reproached himself for his unpardonable thoughtlessness, his boyish impulsiveness. Someone has rightly said that there's nothing more painful than the consciousness of having just done something stupid.

Rudin was consumed by regret.

"What devil drove me to visit that gentleman?" he muttered between his teeth. "What an absurd idea it was! Just to expose myself to rudeness! . . ."

Meanwhile, something unusual was occurring at Daria Mikhailovna's house. The lady herself didn't appear the entire morning
and didn't come down for dinner—she had a headache, announced
Pandalevskii, the only person who'd been permitted to see her.
Rudin barely got a glimpse of Natalia, either; she stayed in her
room with Mlle Boncourt. When she encountered him at the dinner
table, she looked at him so mournfully that his heart sank. Her
face had changed, as though some sorrow had befallen her since
the previous day. Rudin began to feel oppressed by a vague sense
of foreboding. In order to distract his mind in some way, he turned
his attention to Basistov, conversing with him at length and finding
him to be an ardent, eager young man filled with enthusiastic hopes
and as yet untarnished faith. That evening, Daria Mikhailovna
came down to the drawing room for about two hours. She was
polite to Rudin, but somehow kept him at a distance, speaking in
a nasal tone, smiling and frowning more obliquely than ever. Everything about her bespoke the wellborn lady. She'd seemed somewhat cooler toward Rudin recently. "What's the meaning of this
puzzle?" he wondered, casting a sidelong glance at her haughtily
uplifted head.

He didn't have to wait long to find out the solution to this puzzle.
As he was returning to his room along a dark corridor at midnight,
someone suddenly thrust a note into his hand. He looked around:
a young woman was hurrying away—Natalia's maid, he surmised.
He went into his room, dismissed his servant, opened the note,
and read the following lines written in Natalia's handwriting:

"Come to Avdiukhin Pond, beyond the grove of oak trees, tomor-
row morning at seven o'clock, no later. No other time is possible.
This will be our final encounter, everything will be over if. . . .
Come. It will be necessary to decide. . . .

"P.S. If I don't come, it means we won't ever see one another
again. I'll let you know in that case. . . ."

Rudin turned the note around in his hands, mulling it over, then
placed it under his pillow, undressed, and lay down. But he couldn't
fall asleep for a long time, and slept very lightly. It wasn't even
five o'clock yet when he woke up.

IX

Avdiukhin Pond, where Natalia had asked Rudin to meet her, had
long ceased to be a pond. It had overflowed its banks about thirty
years earlier, and had been empty ever since. Only the smooth,

flat surface of a hollow, once covered with slimy mud, and traces of the banks enabled one to guess that it had ever been a pond. A farmhouse had stood near it at one time, but had also disappeared long ago. Two huge pine trees preserved its memory; the wind eternally whispered and sullenly moaned in their tall, stark, green tops. Mysterious rumors circulated among the local people about a horrible crime allegedly committed at the pines' very roots. They also said that neither of these trees would fall without bringing death to someone, and that a third had formerly stood there, which had fallen during a storm, crushing a young girl. The entire area around the old pond was supposed to be haunted. It was barren, dark, and dreary, even on a sunny day, and it seemed even darker and drearier due to the proximity of an ancient forest of dead, withered oak trees. A few of those huge trees reared their gray shapes above the low undergrowth of bushes like weary ghosts. They were a sinister sight—it seemed as though wicked old men had gathered in order to plot some evil deed. A narrow, almost indiscernible path wound alongside the banks. No one went near Avdiukhin Pond without some special reason. Natalia had intentionally selected this solitary place, which was less than half a verst from Daria Mikhailovna's house.

The sun had already been up for some time when Rudin arrived at Avdiukhin Pond, but it wasn't a bright morning. Thick, milky clouds covered the whole sky and were being briskly driven by a whistling, swirling wind. Rudin began to pace up and down along one bank covered with clinging burdock and blackened nettles. He was nervous. These encounters, these new emotions, intrigued him, but they also disturbed him, especially after the note he'd received the previous night. He felt that the end was drawing near and was secretly perturbed in spirit, although no one would have guessed it upon seeing the focused determination with which he folded his arms across his chest and looked around. Pigasov had rightly said that Rudin was like the statue of a Chinese idol—his head was always throwing him off balance. But the head alone, however powerful it may be, can't enable someone to know for certain what is taking place, even within himself. . . . Rudin, intelligent, insightful Rudin, was incapable of stating definitively whether he loved Natalia, whether he was suffering, and whether he'd suffer in the future if he parted from her. Why, then, since he didn't have the slightest inclination to play the role of Lovelace—one has to give him that much credit—had he distracted the poor girl? Why was he awaiting her with concealed trepidation? There's only one answer to this: no one gets carried away as easily as dispassionate people.

He was pacing along the bank while Natalia was hurrying to meet him, running straight across the fields through the wet grass.

"Mistress! Mistress! You'll get your feet wet!" cried Masha, her maid, who was hardly able to keep up with her.

Natalia didn't listen to her and kept running without looking around.

"Ah, what if they're watching us!" Masha fretted. "Indeed, it's surprising we got out of the house . . . and what if ma'mselle wakes up. . . . It's a blessing it's not far. . . . Ah, the gentleman's already waiting," she added, suddenly catching sight of Rudin's stately form standing picturesquely on the bank. "But he shouldn't be standing on that mound—he should have gone into the hollow."

Natalia stopped.

"Wait here by the pines, Masha," she said, and proceeded toward the pond.

Rudin started to approach her and then stopped short in amazement. He'd never seen such an expression on her face before: her eyebrows were lowered, her lips were set, her eyes looked sternly straight ahead of her.

"Dmitrii Nikolaich," she began, "we have no time to lose. I've come for five minutes. I must tell you that my mother knows everything. Mr. Pandalevskii saw us the day before yesterday, and he told her about our encounter. He was always Mama's spy. She summoned me to her room yesterday."

"Good God!" exclaimed Rudin. "This is terrible. . . . What did your mother say?"

"She wasn't angry with me and she didn't chastise me, but she did reproach me for my frivolity."

"Only that?"

"Yes, and she declared she'd rather see me dead than be your wife!"

"Did she really say that?"

"Yes, she did, and she also said that you yourself didn't want to marry me at all, that you'd only been flirting with me because you were bored, and that she hadn't expected this of you, but that she herself was to blame for having allowed me to see so much of you . . . that she'd relied on my prudence, that I'd greatly surprised her. . . . I can't remember everything else she said to me."

Natalia uttered all of this in a flat, almost expressionless tone.

"And you, Natalia Alekseevna, what did you say?" asked Rudin.

"What did I say?" echoed Natalia. "What do *you* intend to do now?"

"Good God, good God!" replied Rudin. "This is cruel! So soon! . . . Such a sudden blow! . . . And is your mother extremely angry?"

"Yes . . . yes, she won't listen to a word on your behalf."

"That's terrible! You mean there's no hope?"

"None."

"Why do we have to be so unhappy? That abominable Pandalevskii! . . . Natalia Alekseevna, you ask me what I intend to do? My head is spinning—I can't grasp anything. . . . I'm amazed that you can retain such self-possession!"

"Do you think that it's easy for me?" Natalia responded.

Rudin began to pace along the bank again. Natalia didn't take her eyes off him.

"Did your mother ask you any questions?" he finally inquired.

"She asked me whether I love you."

"Well . . . and what did you say?"

Natalia was silent for a moment.

"I didn't lie."

Rudin took her hand.

"Always, in all things, you're generous and noble in spirit! Oh, the heart of a young woman is pure gold! But did your mother assert her opposition to our marriage absolutely?"

"Yes, absolutely. I've already told you, she's convinced that you yourself don't intend to marry me."

"Then she regards me as a fraud! What have I done to deserve this?" And Rudin clutched his head in his hands.

"Dmitrii Nikolaich!" said Natalia. "We're wasting time. Remember, I'm meeting you for the last time. I didn't come here to cry or to lament—you can see that I'm not crying—I came here for advice."

"But what advice can I give you, Natalia Alekseevna?"

"What advice? You're a man. I've learned to believe in you, and I'll believe in you to the end. Tell me—what are your intentions?"

"My intentions? Your mother will probably throw me out of the house."

"Possibly. She told me yesterday that she'll have to terminate her acquaintance with you. . . . But you're not answering my question."

"What question?"

"What do you think we should do now?"

"What should we do?" responded Rudin. "Naturally, we should submit."

"Submit," Natalia repeated slowly, and her lips turned pale.

"Submit to fate," Rudin continued. "What else can we do? I know too well how bitter, how painful, how unendurable this is. But judge for yourself, Natalia Alekseevna. I'm poor. It's true, I can work, but even if I were a rich man, could you endure a forced separation from your family, or your mother's anger?...No, Natalia Alekseevna, it's pointless even to think about it. It's obvious that we weren't fated to be together, that the happiness I dreamed of isn't for me!"

Natalia suddenly hid her face in her hands and started to cry. Rudin went up to her.

"Natalia Alekseevna! Dear Natalia!" he said warmly. "Don't cry, for God's sake, don't torture me. Calm down...."

Natalia raised her head.

"You tell me to calm down," she began, her eyes blazing through her tears. "I'm not crying for the reason you suppose....I'm not suffering because of that. I'm suffering because I was wrong about you....What? I come to you for advice at a moment like this, and your first word is 'submit'! Submit! So this is how you enact your theories about independence, about sacrifice, which...."

Her voice broke.

"But Natalia Alekseevna," Rudin interjected in confusion, "remember...I'm not disavowing my words...only...."

"You asked me," she continued with renewed energy, "how I replied to my mother when she declared she'd rather see me dead than married to you. I replied that I'd rather die than marry any other man....And you say 'submit!' She must be right. Not having anything to do, being bored, you must have been toying with me...."

"I swear to you, Natalia Alekseevna...I assure you...," asserted Rudin.

But she didn't listen to him.

"Why didn't you stop me? Why did you yourself...or didn't you count on any obstacles? I'm ashamed to talk about this...but I see that it's all over now."

"You need to calm down, Natalia Alekseevna," Rudin began. "We need to consider together what measures...."

"You've talked about self-sacrifice so often," she broke in, "but do you know that if you'd said to me today, right now, 'I love you, but I can't marry you, I can't be responsible for the future. Give me your hand and come with me,' do you know that I'd have come with you? Do you know that I'd have risked everything? But it's quite far from word to deed—and you're frightened now, just as you were frightened of Volyntsev the day before yesterday at dinner."

The color rushed to Rudin's face. Natalia's unexpected energy impressed him, but her last words wounded his pride.

"You're too angry now, Natalia Alekseevna," he declared, "you can't realize how cruelly you're hurting me. I hope that you'll do me justice in time, that you'll understand what it's cost me to renounce the happiness that, as you've said yourself, wouldn't have placed any obligations on me. Your peace of mind is dearer to me than anything else in the world, and so I'd have been the vilest of men if I'd resolved to take advantage...."

"Perhaps, perhaps," Natalia interrupted. "Perhaps you're right. I don't know what I'm saying. But up until this moment I'd believed in you, I'd believed every word you said.... In the future, please weigh your words—don't toss them around so lightly. When I said 'I love you,' I knew what those words meant, I was ready for anything.... Now it merely remains for me to thank you for my lesson, and to say goodbye."

"Stop, for God's sake, Natalia Alekseevna, I implore you. I don't deserve your contempt, I swear to you. Put yourself in my position. I'm responsible for you and for myself. If I didn't love you with the most devoted love—my God! I'd instantly have suggested that you run away with me.... Sooner or later, your mother would forgive us ... and then.... But before thinking about my own happiness...."

He stopped. Natalia's gaze, which was fastened upon him, embarrassed him.

"You're trying to convince me that you're an honorable man, Dmitrii Nikolaich," she said. "I don't doubt that. You aren't capable of acting in a calculated manner—but did I want to be convinced of that, did I come here for that?"

"Natalia Alekseevna, I didn't expect...."

"Aha! You've finally said it! Yes, you didn't expect all this—you didn't know me. Don't worry ... you don't love me, and I'll never force myself on anyone."

"I do love you!" cried Rudin.

Natalia straightened up.

"Perhaps—but in what way do you love me? I remember all your words, Dmitrii Nikolaich. Remember, you told me, 'There's no love without complete equality.'... You're too exalted for me, I'm not an appropriate match for you.... I've been duly punished. Activities that are more worthy of you lie ahead of you. I won't forget this day.... Goodbye."

"Natalia Alekseevna, are you leaving? Do we have to part like this?"

He stretched out his hand to her. She stopped. His supplicating voice seemed to make her waver.

"No," she said at last. "I sense that something inside me has shattered.... I came here and I've been talking to you as if I were delirious. I have to try to collect myself. This must not be—you yourself said that this will not be. Good God, when I came out here, I mentally said farewell to my home, to my past—and what's happened? Whom have I met here? A coward.... How do you know I couldn't endure separation from my family? 'Your mother won't consent.... It's terrible!' That was all I heard from you. Is this you, is this you, Rudin? No! Goodbye.... Ah! If you did love me, I'd have felt it now, at this moment.... No, no, goodbye!"

She turned swiftly and ran toward Masha, who'd started to get worried much earlier and had been signaling to her.

"*You* are the coward, not I!" Rudin shouted as Natalia left.

She no longer paid any attention to him, and rushed homeward across the fields. She successfully managed to return to her bedroom, but she'd barely crossed the threshold when her strength failed her and she fell into Masha's arms, unconscious.

Rudin remained standing on the bank for a long while. He shivered at long last, made his way to the little path, and walked along it with slow steps. He was deeply ashamed ... and hurt. "What sort of young woman is this?" he thought. "At eighteen! ... No, I didn't know her! ... She's a remarkable young woman. What strength of will! ... She's right—she does deserve a different love than the kind I felt for her.... Felt?" he asked himself. "Can it already be that I no longer feel any love for her? So this is how it all had to end! What a pitiful wretch I was in her eyes!"

The faint sound of a racing carriage made Rudin raise his head. Lezhnev was coming toward him, driving his customary trotting pony. Rudin bowed to him without speaking, and as though struck by a sudden thought, turned off the road and rapidly headed in the direction of Daria Mikhailovna's house.

Lezhnev let him go by, watched him walk away, and, after a moment's thought, he too turned his horse's head around and drove back to Volyntsev's, where he'd spent the night. Volyntsev was asleep. Giving orders not to wake him up, Lezhnev sat down on the terrace to wait for some tea, smoking his pipe.

X

Volyntsev arose at ten o'clock. He was quite surprised to hear that Lezhnev was sitting on the terrace and sent a servant to ask Lezhnev to come to his room.

"What's happened?" Volyntsev asked him. "I thought you wanted to go home."

"Yes, I did want to, but I happened to see Rudin. . . . He was wandering through a field with quite a distressed expression on his face. I promptly turned back."

"You turned back because you saw Rudin?"

"Actually, to tell you the truth, I don't know why I came back myself—probably because I was reminded of you. I wanted to be with you, and I have plenty of time to get home."

Volyntsev smiled bitterly.

"Yes, one can't think about Rudin now without thinking about me as well. . . . You, boy!" he called out loudly. "Bring us some tea."

The friends began to drink their tea. Lezhnev talked about agricultural matters, about a new method of roofing barns with paper. . . .

Suddenly Volyntsev jumped up from his chair and struck the table with such force that the cups and saucers clattered.

"No!" he cried. "I can't stand this any more. I'll challenge that clever man to a duel and let him shoot me. At least I can try to put a bullet through his learned brains!"

"What are you talking about, for heaven's sake?" grumbled Lezhnev. "How can you shout like that? I dropped my pipe. . . . What's the matter with you?"

"The matter is that I can't hear his name and stay calm. It makes my blood boil!"

"Hush, my friend, hush! Aren't you ashamed?" Lezhnev responded, picking his pipe up off the floor. "Let it go! Leave him alone!"

"He's insulted me," Volyntsev continued, striding up and down the room. "Yes! He's insulted me. You must admit that yourself. I wasn't sharp enough at first—he took me by surprise. And who could have anticipated this? But I'll show him that he can't make a fool out of me.... I'll shoot him like a partridge, the damned philosopher."

"Much good that'll do! I won't even mention your sister. I can see that you're overcome by passion—how could you think about your sister? But concerning one other individual—do you think that when you've killed the philosopher, you'll have improved your own chances?"

Volyntsev flung himself into a chair.

"Then I'll go away somewhere! As long as I stay here, my heart's simply being crushed by misery. Only I can't find anywhere to go."

"Going away . . . that's another matter! I can accept that. And you know what I suggest? Let's go together—to the Caucasus, or just to the Ukraine to eat dumplings. That's a wonderful idea, my dear fellow!"

"Yes, but who'll stay with my sister?"

"And why can't Aleksandra Pavlovna come with us? By God, it'll work out beautifully. As for the responsibility of looking after her, I'll take that upon myself! There'll be no problem in getting anything we want. If she likes, I'll arrange for a serenade under her window every night, I'll sprinkle the coachmen with eau de cologne, I'll strew flowers along the roads. And we'll both simply become new men, my friend. We'll enjoy ourselves so much, we'll come back so fat, that we'll be impervious to the darts of love!"

"You're always joking, Misha!"

"I'm not joking at all. It's a brilliant idea of yours."

"No! Nonsense!" Volyntsev shouted again. "I want to fight, I want to fight a duel with him!"

"Here we go again! What a bad mood you're in today!"

A servant entered with a letter in his hand.

"Who's it from?" inquired Lezhnev.

"From Dmitrii Nikolaich Rudin. Mrs. Lasunskii's servant brought it."

"From Rudin?" Volyntsev repeated. "For whom?"

"For you."

"For me. . . . Give it to me."

Volyntsev seized the letter, quickly tore it open, and began to read, while Lezhnev watched him closely. A strange, almost joyful look of amazement spread across Volyntsev's face, and he let his hands fall to his sides.

"What is it?" asked Lezhnev.

"Read it," Volyntsev said in a low voice and handed him the letter.

Lezhnev began to read. This is what Rudin had written:

My dear sir, Sergei Pavlovich!

I'm leaving Daria Mikhailovna's house today, leaving it forever. This will probably surprise you, especially after what happened yesterday. I can't explain to you precisely what is causing me to act in this fashion, but for some reason it seems to me that I ought to inform you of my departure. You don't like me, and even consider me a worthless person. I don't intend to justify myself—time will justify me. In my opinion, it's both undignified and useless for a man to try to prove to a prejudiced individual the injustice of his prejudice. Anyone who seeks to understand me will forgive me, and anyone who doesn't seek to understand me or who can't do so—that person's condemnation doesn't disturb me. I was mistaken about you. In my eyes you remain a noble and honorable man, as before, but I thought that you could rise above the circumstances in which you were brought up. I was mistaken. What can I do? It isn't the first time and it won't be the last. I repeat, I'm leaving. I wish you every happiness. You must agree that this wish is perfectly disinterested, and I hope that you'll be happy now. Perhaps you'll change your opinion of me over time. I don't know whether we'll ever meet again, but in any case, I respectfully remain yours sincerely,

D.R.

P.S. I'll send you the two hundred rubles I owe you as soon as I reach my estate in the province of T——. In addition, I beg you not to mention this letter in Daria Mikhailovna's presence.

P.P.S. One more final but important request: since I'm leaving, I hope you won't allude to my visit to your home in front of Natalia Alekseevna.

"Well, what do you say to that?" Volyntsev asked as soon as Lezhnev had finished the letter.

"What's there to say?" replied Lezhnev. "Cry 'Allah! Allah!' in Eastern fashion and sit open-mouthed in astonishment—that's all one can do. He's leaving.... Well, good riddance! But here's what's curious. You see, he thought it was his *duty* to write you this letter, and he came to see you from a sense of *duty*. . . . These gentlemen find some duty at every step. Everything's a duty . . . or a debt," Lezhnev added, pointing to the postscript with a smile.

"And what phrases he serves up!" Volyntsev exclaimed. "He was mistaken about me. He expected that I'd rise above my circumstances. . . . What rubbish! Good God! It's worse than poetry!"

Lezhnev didn't respond, but his eyes were smiling. Volyntsev stood up.

"I want to go to Daria Mikhailovna's," he announced. "I want to find out what it all means. . . . "

"Wait a little while, my friend. Give him time to get away. What's the point in encountering him again? He'll disappear, evidently. What more do you want? You'd better go lie down and get a little rest. You've been tossing and turning all night, I expect. But now everything will turn out all right for you."

"What leads you to that conclusion?"

"Oh, it just seems that way to me. Really, go have a nap. I'll go see your sister—I'll keep her company."

"I'm not sleepy at all. What's the point of my going to bed? I'd rather go out to the fields," Volyntsev declared, putting on his coat.

"Well, that's all right, too. Go along, my friend, go along and take a look at the fields. . . . "

And Lezhnev went off to Aleksandra Pavlovna's section of the house.

He found her in the drawing room. She welcomed him warmly. She was always pleased when he came, but her face looked sad nonetheless. She was worried about Rudin's visit of the previous day.

"Have you seen my brother?" she asked Lezhnev. "How is he today?"

"He's all right. He's gone out to the fields."

Aleksandra Pavlovna didn't say anything for a moment.

"Tell me, please," she began, earnestly gazing at the hem of her handkerchief, "do you know why. . . . "

"Rudin came here?" interjected Lezhnev. "I do. He came to say goodbye."

Aleksandra Pavlovna raised her head.

"What do you mean—to say goodbye?"

"Yes. Haven't you heard? He's leaving Daria Mikhailovna's."

"He's leaving?"

"Forever—or at least so he says."

"But, for heaven's sake, how do you explain this, after everything that's . . . ?"

"Oh, that's a different matter! It's impossible to explain, but it's true. Something must have happened over there. He pulled the string too tight—and it snapped."

"Mikhailo Mikhailych," Aleksandra Pavlovna began, "I don't understand. You're making fun of me, I fear. . . ."

"No, indeed, by God . . . he's leaving, I tell you, and he even informed his acquaintances about it by letter. It's just as well from a certain point of view, of course, but his departure has prevented one astonishing enterprise that I'd begun to discuss with your brother from being carried out."

"What do you mean? What enterprise?"

"Why, this one. I'd suggested to your brother that he and I go on a trip in order to distract him, and that we take you with us. I'd take personal responsibility for looking after you. . . ."

"That's wonderful!" cried Aleksandra Pavlovna. "I can imagine how well you'd look after me. Why, you'd let me die of hunger."

"You say that, Aleksandra Pavlovna, because you don't know me. You think that I'm a completely heartless old fool. Do you realize that I'm capable of melting like butter, of spending whole days on my knees?"

"I'd like to see that, I must say!"

Lezhnev stood up abruptly. "Well, marry me, Aleksandra Pavlovna, and you'll see all that and more."

Aleksandra Pavlovna blushed.

"What did you say, Mikhailo Mikhailych?" she murmured in confusion.

"I said," Lezhnev responded, "what's been on the tip of my tongue to say a thousand times for so very long. I've finally said it, and you should do what you think best. But I'll go now, so as not to be in your way. If you want to be my wife . . . I'll walk around outside. . . . If you don't dislike the idea, you merely have to send someone to call me. I'll understand. . . ."

Aleksandra Pavlovna tried to detain Lezhnev, but he went out hurriedly. Going into the garden without his cap, he leaned on a little gate and began staring off into the distance.

"Mikhailo Mikhailych!" the voice of a maid rang out behind him. "Please come in to see my mistress. She sent me to call you."

Mikhailo Mikhailych turned around, took the girl's head in both his hands—to her great astonishment—kissed her on the forehead, and went back to Aleksandra Pavlovna.

XI

On returning home after encountering Lezhnev, Rudin shut himself up in his room and wrote two letters—one to Volyntsev (as the reader already knows), and the other to Natalia. He took a lot of time over this second letter, erasing or changing a good deal of it, and, after copying it carefully onto a sheet of fine note paper, he folded it up as tightly as possible and put it in his pocket. He paced back and forth in his room several times with a sorrowful look on his face, and then sat down in a chair by the window, leaning on his arm. Tears slowly welled up in his eyes. . . . He stood up, buttoned his jacket, summoned a servant, and told him to ask Daria Mikhilovna if it would be possible for him to see her.

The servant returned shortly and informed him that Daria Mikhailovna would be delighted to visit with him. Rudin promptly went to see her.

She received him in her study, just as she had that first time, two months earlier. But now she wasn't alone: Pandalevskii, unassuming, neat, clean, and agreeable as ever, was there as well.

Daria Mikhailovna greeted Rudin politely, and Rudin bowed politely in return, but one glance at each of their smiling faces would have revealed to anyone with even the slightest worldly experience that something unpleasant had happened between them, even if it hadn't been articulated. Rudin knew that Daria Mikhailovna was angry with him; Daria Mikhailovna suspected that he was already well aware of this.

Pandalevskii's disclosure had greatly disturbed her—it aroused her social arrogance. Rudin, an impoverished individual lacking any professional status and thus far lacking any fame, had presumed to arrange a tryst with her daughter—the daughter of Daria Mikhailovna Lasunskaia.

"Even supposing that he's intelligent, that he's a genius," she said, "what does that prove? How could anyone could hope to be my son-in-law after all this?"

"I couldn't believe my eyes for a long time," interjected Pandalevskii. "I'm surprised that he'd fail to know his place!"

Daria Mikhailovna had been deeply distressed, and Natalia had had to suffer for it.

Daria Mikhailovna asked Rudin to sit down. He sat down, but

not like the old Rudin—virtually the master of the house—not even like an old friend, but like a guest, and not even a very frequent guest at that. All this took place in an instant. . . . Water likewise is suddenly transformed into solid ice.

"I've come to see you, Daria Mikhailovna," Rudin began, "to thank you for your hospitality. I've received some news from my small estate today, and it's absolutely necessary that I go there right away."

Daria Mikhailovna looked at Rudin intently.

"He's anticipated me, so he must have guessed," she thought. "He's sparing me a complicated explanation. So much the better. Ah! Here's to intelligent people!"

"Really?" she replied aloud. "Ah, how disappointing! Well, what can one do? I hope to see you in Moscow this winter. We'll be leaving here soon ourselves."

"I don't know whether I'll manage to get to Moscow, Daria Mikhailovna, but if I find a way to do so, I'll consider it a duty to visit you."

"Aha, my good sir," Pandalevskii reflected in turn, "it hasn't been long since you acted like the master here, and now this is how you have to express yourself!"

"Then I gather you've received unsatisfactory news from your estate?" he asked with his customary nonchalance.

"Yes," Rudin answered drily.

"Some crop failure, perhaps?"

"No . . . something else. . . . Believe me, Daria Mikhailovna," Rudin added, "I'll never forget the time I've spent in your house."

"And I'll always recall our acquaintance with you with pleasure, Dmitrii Nikolaich. . . . When are you leaving?"

"Today, after dinner."

"So soon! . . . Well, I hope you have a pleasant journey. If your affairs don't detain you, perhaps you'll drop in again on us here."

"I probably won't manage to do that," Rudin responded, rising. "Forgive me," he went on, "I can't repay my debt to you right now, but as soon as I reach my estate. . . ."

"Nonsense, Dmitrii Nikolaich!" Daria Mikhailovna cut him short. "You should be ashamed of yourself for mentioning it! . . . But what time is it?" she asked.

Pandalevskii drew a gold and enamel watch out of his pocket and looked at it, carefully resting his rosy cheek on his stiff, white collar.

"Thirty-three minutes past two," he announced.

"It's time for me to change clothes," Daria Mikhailovna observed. "Goodbye, Dmitrii Nikolaich!"

The entire conversation between Rudin and Daria Mikhailovna had displayed a special character. Actors repeat their parts that way; diplomats at conferences exchange their prearranged phrases that way. . . .

Rudin went out. He knew by now, from experience, that men and women of society don't throw out someone who isn't of further use to them—they simply let him drop like a glove after a dance, like a paper candy-wrapper, like a losing lottery ticket.

He packed quickly, and impatiently began to await the moment of his departure. Everyone in the house was quite surprised to hear of his intentions; even the servants looked at him in bewilderment. Basistov couldn't conceal his grief. Natalia was evidently avoiding Rudin; she tried not to let her eyes meet his. He did manage to slip his letter into her hand, however. After dinner, Daria Mikhailovna repeated once more that she hoped to see him before they left for Moscow, but Rudin didn't reply. Pandalevskii talked to him more than anyone else did. Rudin felt the urge several times to spring at him and slap his pink, healthy face. Mlle. Boncourt repeatedly glanced at Rudin with a sly, strange expression in her eyes—one occasionally observes the same expression in old, highly intelligent hunting dogs.

"Aha!" she seemed to be saying to herself. "So this is what's happened to you!"

Six o'clock finally struck, and Rudin's carriage was brought around to the door. He hastily began to say goodbye to everyone. There was a hideous feeling in his soul. He hadn't expected to leave this house this way—it seemed as though they were driving him out. . . . "How smoothly this was all accomplished! And what was the point of being in such a hurry? Still, it's better to end it once and for all." He thought this as he bowed in every direction with a forced smile. He looked at Natalia for the last time, and his heart throbbed. Her eyes were turned toward him in reproachful, sad farewell.

He quickly ran down the steps and jumped into his carriage. Basistov had offered to accompany him to the next way station, and took a seat beside Rudin.

"Do you remember," Rudin began as soon as the carriage had driven out of the courtyard into the broad country road bordered with fir trees, "do you remember what Don Quixote says to his squire as he's leaving the duchess's court? 'Freedom, my friend Sancho,' he says, 'is one of the most precious possessions a person has, and happy is the man to whom heaven has given a bit of bread, who doesn't have to be indebted to anyone!' What Don Quixote felt then, I feel now. . . . God grant that you, my dear Basistov, may experience this feeling someday as well!'"

Basistov squeezed Rudin's hand, and the honest youth's heart pounded in his breast. Rudin spoke about the dignity of humanity and the meaning of true independence until they reached the station. He spoke nobly, fervently, justly, and when the time came to separate, Basistov couldn't refrain from throwing his arms around Rudin's neck and sobbing. Rudin himself also shed tears, but he wasn't crying because he was parting from Basistov. His tears were tears of wounded pride.

Natalia went to her room, where she read Rudin's letter.

"Dear Natalia Alekseevna," he wrote,

> I've decided to depart. No other course is open to me. I've decided to depart before I'm plainly told to go. All our difficulties will be resolved by my departure, and hardly anyone will miss me. What else did I expect? . . . It always happens this way—but why am I writing to you?
>
> I'm probably saying goodbye to you forever, and it would be too painful to leave you with a harsher memory of me than I deserve. That's why I'm writing to you. I don't want either to justify myself or to blame anyone at all except myself. I want to explain myself, as far as possible. . . . The events of the past few days have happened so unexpectedly, so suddenly. . . .
>
> Our encounter today will serve as a memorable lesson for me. Yes, you're right—I didn't know you, although I thought I knew you! I've dealt with all kinds of people during the course of my existence. I've gotten to know many women and many girls, but in meeting you, I met an absolutely honest, upright soul for the first time in my life. I wasn't prepared for this, and I didn't know how to appreciate you. I felt an attraction to you from the very first day we met—you may have noticed it. I spent hour after hour with you without getting to know you. I hardly even tried to get to know you—and I could still imagine that I loved you! I've been punished now for this sin.
>
> I loved a woman once before, and she loved me. . . . My feelings for her were complex, as were hers for me, but since she wasn't simple herself, it was all the more appropriate. I wasn't told the truth then—and I didn't recognize it now, when it stood before me. . . . I've finally

recognized it, when it's too late.... The past can't be revisited....
Our lives might have been united—and now they'll never be united.
How can I prove to you that I could have loved you with a true love—
a love of the heart, not of the imagination—when I don't know myself
whether I'm capable of such love?

Nature has endowed me generously. I know this, and I won't belittle
myself in front of you, especially now, at such a bitter, humiliating
moment for me.... Yes, nature has endowed me generously, but I'll
die without accomplishing anything worthy of my powers, without
leaving any significant mark behind me. All my riches have been
spent in vain. I won't see any fruit from the seeds I sow. I lack
something.... I myself can't say exactly what it is that I lack.... I
probably lack that quality without which one can't stir people's hearts,
or win a woman's love. And ruling over people's minds alone is
precarious as well as useless. Mine is a strange, almost comic fate. I
want to give myself over to some cause eagerly and wholeheartedly—
and I can't give myself over to anything. I'll end up sacrificing myself
for some nonsense or other that I won't even believe in.... My God!
To be thirty-five and still be preparing to accomplish something!...

I've never talked about myself so openly to anyone before. This is
my confession.

But that's enough about me. I'd like to talk about you, to give you
some advice—I can be of no other use to you.... You're still young—
but always follow the impulses of your heart as long as you live. Don't
submit to your own intellect or to anyone else's. Believe me, the
simpler, the narrower the circle in which one's life is conducted, the
better. The most important thing isn't to seek out life's new experiences, it's to achieve perfection in all of life's experiences at their
proper time. "Blessed is he who's been young in his youth." But I
suspect that this advice applies far more to me than to you.

I confess, Natalia Alekseevna, that I'm extremely unhappy. I never
deceived myself in regard to the nature of the feelings I inspired in
Daria Mikhailovna, but I'd hoped that I'd found at least a temporary
home.... Now I have to wander the world again. What will replace
your conversation, your presence, your attentive, intelligent gaze for
me?... I myself am to blame, but you must admit that fate seems to
have mocked us on purpose. A week ago, I myself barely suspected
that I loved you. The day before yesterday, that evening in the garden,
I heard from your lips for the first time... but why remind you of
what you said then? And now I'm already leaving today, I'm going
away in disgrace, after a cruel conversation with you, taking no hope
away with me.... And you still don't know to what degree I've
wronged you.... I suffer from some sort of idiotic openness, some

sort of garrulousness.... But why talk about it? I'm going away forever!

(Rudin was about to describe his visit to Volyntsev at this point, but he reconsidered and erased it all, and then added the second postscript to his letter to Volyntsev.)

I'll remain alone on earth in order to devote myself to activities more appropriate to me, as you put it this morning with cruel irony. Alas! If only I really could devote myself to those activities, if I could finally conquer my inertia.... But no! I'll remain the incomplete creature I've always been up until now.... The first obstacle—and I completely collapse. What happened with you has shown me that. If I'd sacrificed my love to my future work, to my vocation, at any rate ... but I was simply frightened by the responsibility that had descended upon me, and therefore am utterly unworthy of you. I'm not worth your tearing yourself away from your world because of me.... And indeed, perhaps this is all for the best. Perhaps I'll become stronger and purer as a result of this experience.

I wish you every happiness. Farewell! Think of me sometimes. I hope that you'll still hear something about me.

Rudin

Natalia let Rudin's letter fall into her lap and sat without moving for a long while, staring at the floor. This letter proved to her more clearly than any possible argument that she'd been right that morning when, in saying goodbye to Rudin, she'd involuntarily exclaimed that he didn't love her! But that didn't make things any easier for her. She sat perfectly still; it seemed as though waves of darkness had soundlessly closed over her head and that she'd sunk to the depths of the sea, cold and mute. Initial disillusionment is painful for anyone, but for a sincere soul, one wholly averse to self-deception, one alien to frivolity and exaggeration, it's almost intolerable. Natalia recalled that in her childhood, when going for an evening stroll, she'd always tried to walk toward the bright horizon, where the sunset was glowing, and not toward the darkened half of the sky. The life ahead of her now loomed darkly, and she turned her back on the light....

Tears came to Natalia's eyes. Tears don't always bring relief. Some are comforting and therapeutic when, after being pent up in one's breast for a long time, they finally start to flow—violently at first, then more gently, more sweetly, and they wash away the mute agony of sorrow.... But some tears are cold, tears that flow sparingly, wrung from the heart drop by drop as a result of the heavy, immovable burden misery has laid upon it; these tears aren't comforting, and bring no relief. Poverty sheds such tears; the individual who hasn't shed them yet hasn't been unhappy. Natalia got to know them on that day.

Two hours passed. Natalia collected herself, got up, wiped her eyes, and, having lit a candle, burned up Rudin's letter in the flame and threw the ashes out the window. Then she opened a book by Pushkin at random and read the first lines that caught her eye. (She frequently foretold her future this way.) Here's what she found:

> Whoever has felt has known
> The torturing ghost of days that are no more,
> For him there are no more enchantments,
> He meets memory's serpent,
> Regret gnaws at him. . . .

She paused and looked at herself in the mirror with an icy smile, nodded her head slightly, and went down to the drawing room.

As soon as she saw Natalia, Daria Mikhailovna called her into the study, made her sit down beside her, and caressingly stroked her cheek. At the same time, she carefully, almost curiously, looked into Natalia's eyes. Daria Mikhailovna was secretly perplexed. It struck her for the first time that she didn't really know her daughter. When she'd learned about Natalia's tryst with Rudin from Pandalevskii, Daria Mikhailovna wasn't so much displeased as amazed that her sensible Natalia could have resolved to take such a step. But when she'd sent for Natalia and had begun to upbraid her— not at all the way one would have expected from a European lady, but quite loudly and inelegantly—the firmness of Natalia's replies, the decisiveness of her gaze and her movements, had confused and even intimidated Daria Mikhailovna.

Rudin's sudden departure, which wasn't wholly comprehensible either, had taken a great weight off her heart, but she'd expected tears and hysteria. . . . Natalia's outward composure disconcerted her once more.

"Well, child," Daria Mikhailovna began, "how are you today?" Natalia looked at her mother. "He's gone, you see . . . your beloved. Do you know why he decided to leave so quickly?"

"Mama!" Natalia said in a low voice. "I promise you that if you won't mention him again, you'll never hear another word about him from me."

"Then you admit that you've done something wrong?"

Natalia looked down and repeated, "You'll never hear another word about him from me."

"Well, make sure I don't," Daria Mikhailovna responded with a smile. "I believe you. But the day before yesterday, do you remember how . . . well, I won't go on. It's all over, dead and buried, isn't it? Now I know you again—but I was completely mystified before. Well, kiss me, my bright girl!"

Natalia lifted Daria Mikhailovna's hand to her lips, and Daria Mikhailovna kissed her bowed head.

"Always listen to my advice. Don't forget that you're a Lasunskii, and my daughter," she added, "and you'll be happy. Now you may go."

Natalia left in silence. Daria Mikhailovna watched her go and thought, "She's like me—she'll also let herself get carried away by her feelings, *mais elle aura moins d'abandon.*" And Daria Mikhailovna began to mull over memories of the past—the distant past. . . .

Then she summoned Mlle. Boncourt and remained closeted with her for a long while. When she'd dismissed her, she sent for Pandalevskii. She wanted to discover the true cause of Rudin's departure at all costs . . . but Pandalevskii succeeded in completely reassuring her. It was what he was there for.

Volyntsev and his sister came to dinner the next day. Daria Mikhailovna had always been most affable toward him, but this time she was especially cordial. Natalia felt unbearably miserable, but Volyntsev was so respectful and addressed her so timidly that she couldn't help being grateful to him. The day passed quietly, rather tediously, but as they said goodbye, they all felt that they'd lapsed into their former routine—and that means a great deal, a very great deal.

Yes, they'd all lapsed into their former routine—all except Natalia. When she finally managed to be alone, she dragged herself to her bed with difficulty, weary and wounded, then collapsed, burying her face in her pillow. Life seemed so bitter, so hateful, so sordid; she was so ashamed of herself, her love, and her sorrow, that she probably would have agreed to die at that moment. . . . Many painful days, sleepless nights, and torturous emotions were in store for her; but she was young—life had barely begun for her— and sooner or later, life asserts its claims. Whatever blows may befall someone, he still has to eat that day—forgive the coarseness of the expression—or at least the next, and that's the first step toward consolation. . . .

Natalia suffered terribly, she suffered for the first time. . . . But first suffering, like first love, is never repeated—thank God!

XII

About two years passed. The beginning of May arrived. Aleksandra Pavlovna, no longer Lipina but Lezhneva, was sitting on the balcony of her house. She'd married Mikhailo Mikhailych more than a year earlier. She was as charming as ever, and had recently grown just slightly plumper. A nursemaid was walking along in front of the balcony where steps led to the garden, holding a rosy-cheeked baby wearing a little white coat and a white cap on his head. Aleksandra Pavlovna continually gazed at him. The baby didn't cry—he gravely sucked his thumb and calmly looked around. He was already proving himself to be a worthy son of Mikhailo Mikhailych.

Our old friend Pigasov was sitting on the balcony near Aleksandra Pavlovna. He'd grown noticeably grayer since we last saw him, becoming thin and stooped, and lisping when he spoke—one of his front teeth had fallen out. This lisp added even greater asperity to his words. . . . His spitefulness hadn't decreased over the years, but his sallies were less lively and he repeated himself more frequently than before. Mikhailo Mikhailych wasn't home; they were expecting him in time for tea. The sun had already set. A pale lemon-colored streak of light stretched across the distant horizon where the sun had gone down, and two more streaks appeared at the opposite edge of the sky, a lower, light-blue one, and a higher, reddish-purple one. Thin clouds seemed to be melting overhead. Everything promised a stretch of good weather.

Suddenly Pigasov burst out laughing.

"What is it, Afrikan Semenych?" inquired Aleksandra Pavlovna.

"Oh, just that yesterday I heard a peasant say to his wife—she'd been chattering away—'Don't squeak!' I liked that immensely. 'Don't squeak!' And in fact, what can a woman have to say? I never speak about present company, you know. Our ancestors were wiser than we are. In their stories, the beautiful woman always sits by the window with a star on her forehead and never utters a syllable. That's how it ought to be. Judge for yourself—the day before yesterday, our marshal's wife nearly fired a pistol at my head! She tells me she doesn't like my *tendencies!* Tendencies! Well, wouldn't it be better for her and everyone else if by some beneficent decree of nature she were suddenly deprived of the use of her tongue?"

"Oh, you're always the same, Afrikan Semenych. You're always attacking us poor . . . . Do you know, it's a kind of misfortune, in fact. I'm sorry for you."

"A misfortune! Why do you permit yourself to say that? In the first place, there are only three misfortunes on earth in my opinion—living in a cold apartment in winter, wearing tight shoes in summer, and spending the night in a room where a baby you can't sprinkle with insecticide is crying. In the second place, I've become the most mild-mannered of men. Why, I'm virtually a model you could draw copies of! See how properly I behave!"

"How properly, indeed! Elena Antonovna was complaining to me about you just yesterday."

"How so? What did she say to you, if I may ask?"

"She told me that during one entire morning you answered all her questions only by saying, 'What? What?' and you kept using the same high-pitched voice."

Pigasov laughed.

"But you'll concede that it was a good idea, eh, Aleksandra Pavlovna?"

"It was an astonishing one! Can you really have behaved so rudely to a woman, Afrikan Semenych?"

"How's that? Do you consider Elena Antonovna a woman?"

"What do you consider her?"

"A drum, for heaven's sake, an ordinary drum, the kind they beat with sticks. . . . "

"Oh," Aleksandra Pavlovna interrupted him, anxious to change the subject, "they tell me that one may congratulate you."

"On what?"

"The end of your lawsuit. The Glinovskii meadows have remained yours."

"Yes, they're mine," Pigasov replied morosely.

"You've been trying to win this for so many years, and yet now you seem dissatisfied."

"I assure you, Aleksandra Pavlovna," Pigasov responded slowly, "nothing can be worse, or more offensive, than happiness that arrives too late. It can't give you satisfaction in any event, and it deprives you of the right—the precious right—of cursing and condemning fate. Yes, madam, it's a cruel, insulting thing—belated happiness."

Aleksandra Pavlovna merely shrugged her shoulders.

"Nurse," she began, "I think it's time to put Misha to bed. Give him to me."

While Aleksandra Pavlovna was occupying herself with her son, Pigasov walked to the other corner of the balcony, muttering.

Suddenly, Mikhailo Mikhailych appeared not far off, driving his racing carriage down the road that ran the length of the garden. Two huge house dogs ran in front of the horse, one yellow, the other gray, both obtained only recently. They fought incessantly and were inseparable companions. An old mongrel went out through the gate to meet them. It opened its mouth as if it were about to bark, but ended up yawning and turning around again with a friendly wag of its tail.

"Look, Sasha," Lezhnev shouted to his wife, "see whom I'm bringing to visit you. . . . "

Aleksandra Pavlovna didn't immediately recognize the man who was sitting behind her husband's back.

"Ah! Mr. Basistov!" she finally cried.

"It's he," Lezhnev confirmed, "and he's brought some glorious news. Wait a minute—you'll find out right away."

And he drove into the courtyard.

He came onto the balcony with Basistov a few moments later.

"Hurray!" he exclaimed, embracing his wife. "Serezha's going to get married."

"To whom?" Aleksandra Pavlovna asked agitatedly.

"To Natalia, naturally. Our friend has brought the news from Moscow, and there's a letter for you."

"Do you hear, Misha?" he went on, lifting his son up in his arms. "Your uncle's going to get married. What criminal indifference! He just blinks his eyes!"

"He's sleepy," remarked the nursemaid.

"Yes," Basistov said, walking up to Aleksandra Pavlovna. "I've come from Moscow today on business for Daria Mikhailovna—to go over the accounts for her estate. But here's the letter."

Aleksandra Pavlovna hastily opened her brother's letter. It consisted of merely a few lines. In his first transports of joy, he informed his sister that he'd proposed to Natalia and had received her consent, as well as Daria Mikhailovna's. He promised to write more in the next letter, and sent hugs and kisses to everyone. It was clear that he was writing in some sort of delirium.

Tea was served, and Basistov sat down. They showered him with questions. Everyone, even Pigasov, was delighted at the news he'd brought.

"Tell me something, please," Lezhnev requested in passing. "Rumors reached us about a certain Mr. Korchagin. That was all nonsense, I suppose?"

(This Korchagin was a handsome young man, a social lion who was excessively conceited and self-important—he behaved with extraordinary dignity, as though he weren't a live human being but a statue of himself, erected by public subscription.)

"Well, no, not total nonsense," Basistov replied with a smile. "Daria Mikhailovna was quite favorably inclined toward him, but Natalia Alekseevna wouldn't consider him."

"I know him," interjected Pigasov. "He's an appalling idiot, a noisy idiot . . . for heaven's sake! If people were all like that, it'd require large sums of money to induce anyone to agree to stay alive . . . for heaven's sake!"

"Perhaps," Basistov rejoined, "but he plays more than a minor role in society."

"Well, it doesn't matter!" cried Aleksandra Pavlovna. "Never mind him! Ah, I'm so happy for my brother! And is Natalia cheerful, is she happy?"

"Yes. She's as calm as ever—you know the way she always is—but she seems pleased."

The evening was spent in friendly, lively conversation. They eventually sat down to supper.

"Oh, by the way," Lezhnev asked Basistov as he poured him some wine, "do you know where Rudin is?"

"I don't know for certain now. He came to Moscow last winter for a short time, and then went to Simbirsk with some family. I corresponded with him for quite a while. He informed me in his last letter that he was leaving Simbirsk—he didn't say where he was going—and I haven't heard anything about him since then."

"He's all right!" insisted Pigasov. "He's hanging around somewhere, sermonizing. That gentleman will always find two or three adherents who'll listen to him open-mouthed and lend him money. You'll see, he'll end up dying in some out-of-the-way corner, in Tsarevokokshaiska or Chukhloma, in the arms of some old maid who wears a wig and considers him the greatest genius on earth. . . ."

"You're treating him quite harshly," Basistov remarked under his breath in a dissatisfied tone.

"Not a bit harshly," replied Pigasov, "on the contrary, perfectly fairly. In my opinion, he's simply nothing but a sycophant. I forgot to tell you," he continued, turning to Lezhnev, "that I met that Terlakhov, the one with whom Rudin traveled abroad. Yes! Yes! You can't imagine what he told me about Rudin—it's absolutely ludicrous! It's notable that all Rudin's friends and admirers become his enemies over time."

"I beg you not to count me among those friends!" Basistov interrupted heatedly.

"Oh, you—that's a different matter! I wasn't talking about you."

"But what did Terlakhov tell you?" asked Aleksandra Pavlovna.

"Oh, he told me a lot—it's impossible to remember it all. But the best bit of it was an anecdote about something that happened to Rudin. He was ceaselessly developing—these gentlemen always are developing. Other people simply sleep and eat, but these people do their sleeping and eating while developing—isn't that so, Mr. Basistov?" Basistov didn't reply. "Thus, while he was constantly developing, Rudin logically arrived at the philosophical conclusion that he ought to fall in love. He began to look around for an object worthy of such a surprising conclusion. Fortune smiled on him— he made the acquaintance of a very pretty French dressmaker. The incident occurred in a German town set on the Rhine, please note. He began to go and visit her, to take her various books, to talk to her about nature and Hegel. Can you imagine the dressmaker's situation? She thought he was an astronomer. However, he isn't a bad-looking young man, you know, and he was a foreigner, a Russian—so he appealed to her. Well, he finally invited her to go on an outing, a highly poetical outing, in a boat on the river. The Frenchwoman accepted, put on her best clothes, and went out in the boat with him. They floated around for about two hours. And how do you think he spent the entire time? He stroked the French-woman's hair, gazed thoughtfully at the sky, and repeated several times that he felt a fatherly affection for her. The Frenchwoman went home in a rage, and she herself told the whole story to Terlakhov afterward. That's the kind of gentleman he is!"

Pigasov burst into loud laughter.

"You old cynic!" Aleksandra Pavlovna observed with annoyance. "I'm more and more convinced that even those people who dislike Rudin can't find anything bad to say about him."

"Nothing bad! For heaven's sake! His perpetual living off other people's money, his borrowing. . . . Mikhailo Mikhailych, he borrowed from you as well, no doubt, didn't he?"

"Listen, Afrikan Semenych!" Lezhnev began, and his face took on a serious expression. "Listen. You and my wife both know that the last time I saw him I felt no special attachment to Rudin, and I even criticized him frequently. Nonetheless" (Lezhnev filled up the glasses with champagne), "here's what I suggest to you now. We've just drunk to the health of our dear brother and his future bride—I propose that next we drink to the health of Dmitrii Rudin!"

Aleksandra Pavlovna and Pigasov looked at Lezhnev in astonishment as Basistov sat up wide-eyed, blushing and trembling all over with delight.

"I know him well," Lezhnev continued. "I'm well aware of his faults. They're all the more conspicuous because he himself isn't an inconspicuous individual."

"Rudin has the temperament of a genius!" exclaimed Basistov.

"Genius he probably has," Lezhnev responded, "but as for his temperament . . . that's precisely his misfortune, that he has no particular temperament. . . . But that isn't the point. I want to talk about what's worthwhile, about what's rare in him. He has enthusiasm—and believe me, as a phlegmatic person, that's a most precious quality today. We've all become insufferably rational, dispassionate, and lethargic. We've gotten sleepy and cold, and should be grateful to anyone who'll wake us and warm us up, even for a moment! It's high time! Do you remember, Sasha, when I was talking to you about him once, I reproached him for being cold? I was right, and yet I was wrong then, too. This coldness is in his blood—that's not his fault—but it isn't in his head. He isn't an actor, as I called him, or a cheat, or a villain. He lives off other people's money not as a swindler would, but as a child would. . . . Yes, no doubt he'll die somewhere in poverty and neglect, but should we cast stones at him as a result? He'll never accomplish anything himself, precisely because he has no temperament, no hot blood—but who can truly say that he has never been or never will be of use? Who can say that his words haven't sowed fruitful seeds in the hearts of other young people whom nature hasn't denied the strength to act, the ability to enact their own ideas, the way it has denied him? Indeed, I myself, for one, experienced all that. . . . Sasha knows what Rudin did for me in my youth. As I recall, I also claimed that Rudin's words couldn't affect people, but then I was speaking about people like myself, at my present age, people who have already lived and have been tempered by life; one false note in a speech and all its harmony disappears for us. But, fortunately, a young person's ear isn't so refined, it isn't so spoiled. If the essence of what he hears seems beautiful to him, what does he care about the quality of the tone? He'll supply the quality himself!"

"Bravo, bravo!" cried Basistov. "How justly that was said! And as regards Rudin's influence, I swear to you that this man not only knew how to excite you, he got you upon your feet, he didn't let you stand still! He stirred you to the depths, he set you on fire!"

"Do you hear that?" Lezhnev continued, turning to Pigasov. "What further proof do you need? You attack philosophy—in talking about it, you can't find words that are sufficiently contemptuous. I myself am not excessively fond of it and understand it poorly, but our principal misfortunes don't arise from philosophy! A Russian will never be infected by philosophical hair-splitting and fantasizing—he has too much common sense for that—but we mustn't let every sincere quest for truth and knowledge be attacked as 'philosophy.' Rudin's misfortune is that he doesn't know Russia—and that's a great misfortune, to be sure. Russia can do without each of us, but none of us can do without it. Woe to the individual who thinks he can, and twice the woe to the individual who actually does do without it! Cosmopolitanism is rubbish—the cosmopolitan is a nonentity, or worse than a nonentity. Without nationality, there's no art, no truth, no life, there's nothing. You can't imagine an ideal face without a physiognomy—you can only envision a vulgar face. But, I say again, that's not Rudin's fault. It's his fate—a cruel, painful fate—for which we can't blame him. It'd take us too far afield if we tried to explain why Rudins appear among us. But let's be grateful to him for what's worthwhile in him. That's easier than being unfair to him, and we've been unfair to him. It isn't our task to punish him, and it isn't necessary— he's punished himself far more cruelly than he deserved. . . . God grant that his unhappiness may have blotted out the worst in him and left only the best! I drink to Rudin's health! I drink to the companion of my finest years. I drink to youth—to its hopes, its endeavors, its faith, and its integrity, to everything that made our hearts beat fast when we were twenty. We have never known and

will never know anything better than that in life.... I drink to
that golden time—I drink to Rudin's health!"
Everyone raised a glass to Lezhnev's. Basistov nearly cracked
his in his enthusiasm, and drained it in one swallow. Aleksandra
Pavlovna squeezed Lezhnev's hand.

"Why, Mikhailo Mikhailych, I never suspected you were so
eloquent," remarked Pigasov. "That was equal to Mr. Rudin
himself—even I was moved by it."

"I'm not the least bit eloquent," Lezhnev replied, not without
annoyance, "and in any case, it'd be hard to move you, I imagine.
But that's enough about Rudin. Let's talk about something else.
What about—what's his name—Pandalevskii? Is he still living at
Daria Mikhailovna's?" he added, turning to Basistov.

"Oh yes, he's still there. She's managed to find him a highly
profitable position."

Lezhnev smiled wryly.

"There's a man who won't die in poverty—you can count on
that."

Supper ended; the guests dispersed. When she was alone with
her husband, Aleksandra Pavlovna looked into his face with a smile.

"You were just wonderful this evening, Misha," she said, stroking
his forehead. "You spoke so wisely and nobly! But confess that
you exaggerated a bit to Rudin's advantage, just as you exaggerated
to his disadvantage earlier...."

"I can't let them hit a man when he's down. And I was afraid
at the time that you were becoming interested in him."

"No," Aleksandra Pavlovna replied simply, "he always seemed
too learned for me. I was afraid of him, and never knew what to
say in front of him. But do you concede that Pigasov ridiculed him
quite viciously today?"

"Pigasov?" Lezhnev responded. "I stood up for Rudin so vehemently precisely because Pigasov was here. He dares to call
Rudin a sycophant, indeed! Why, I consider the role that he plays—
Pigasov, I mean—a hundred times worse! He has an independent
income, he jeers at everyone, and yet he fawns all over wealthy or
famous people! Do you know that this Pigasov, who criticizes
everything and everyone with such scorn, who assails both philosophy and women, do you know that he took bribes when he was
in government service, and worse? Ah! That's the kind of man he
is!"

"Really?" cried Aleksandra Pavlovna. "I never would have expected that! Misha," she added after a short pause, "I want to ask you...."

"What?"

"Do you think my brother will be happy with Natalia?"

"How can I tell?... It's quite likely.... She'll be in charge... there's no reason to conceal that fact between us.... She's more intelligent than he is, but he's a wonderful person and he loves her with all his soul. What more could you want? We love one another and we're happy, aren't we?"

Aleksandra Pavlovna smiled and squeezed his hand.

On the same day during which everything we've described was taking place at Aleksandra Pavlovna's, a wretched little covered cart was being slowly drawn by three local horses in the sultry heat along the main road in one of the remote regions of Russia. A grizzled peasant wearing a ragged coat was perched on the front seat with his legs hanging sideways over the shaft. He kept flicking the reins, which were made of thin cord, and shaking his whip. A tall man in a cap and a dusty old coat was sitting on a narrow suitcase inside the cart. It was Rudin. He sat with his head lowered, the peak of his cap pulled over his eyes. The jolting of the cart threw him from side to side, but he seemed completely oblivious, as though he were asleep. Eventually he sat up straight.

"When do we come to a way station?" he asked the peasant sitting in the front.

"Just over the hill, your honor," the peasant said, and he shook the reins more forcefully. "About two versts farther as the crow flies, not more.... Hey there! Pay attention!... I'll teach you," he added in a shrill voice, starting to whip the horse on the right.

"You seem to drive very badly," observed Rudin. "We've been crawling along since early this morning, and we never seem to get there. You should have sung some song."

"Well, what do you want, your honor? The horses are underfed, as you can see for yourself... and then there's the heat. And I can't sing, I'm not a coachman.... Hey, you little sheep!" the peasant suddenly shouted, turning toward a man walking along wearing a brown shirt and woven shoes worn down at the heels. "Get out of the way!"

"Some driver!" muttered the man, who halted after they passed.

"You wretched Muscovite," he added in a voice full of contempt. Then he shook his head and limped onward.

"What are you up to?" the peasant called out at intervals, pulling at the shaft horse. "Ah, you sly thing! Yes, you're a sly one. . . ."

The exhausted horses somehow finally dragged themselves to the way station. Rudin climbed out of the cart, paid the peasant (who didn't bow to him and kept shaking the coins in the palm of his hand for a long while—evidently there wasn't much left for vodka), and carried his suitcase into the station's waiting room himself.

An acquaintance of mine who traveled around Russia a great deal in his day once made the observation that if the paintings hanging on the walls of a way station represent scenes from *The Prisoner of the Caucasus* or are portraits of Russian generals, then it's possible to get fresh horses quickly, but if the paintings depict the life of the well-known gambler George de Germann, then the traveler has no hope of leaving soon. He'll have plenty of time to admire the hair combed to a peak, the white unbuttoned vest, and the exceedingly short, narrow trousers of the gambler in his youth, as well as his frenzied physiognomy when, in his old age, he kills his son, waving a chair above his head in a cottage with a narrow staircase. It was precisely these paintings, from "Thirty Years, or the Life of a Gambler," that were hanging in the room Rudin entered. In response to his summons, the stationmaster appeared, having just woken up (by the way, has anyone ever seen a stationmaster who hadn't just woken up?), and without even waiting for Rudin to ask, informed him in a sleepy voice that there weren't any horses.

"How can you say that there aren't any horses," asked Rudin, "when you don't even know where I'm going? I came here with local horses."

"There aren't any horses that can go anywhere," replied the stationmaster. "But where are you going?"

"To Sk——."

"There aren't any horses," the stationmaster repeated, and he left.

Rudin went up to the window and threw his cap on a table in frustration. He hadn't changed very much, but his complexion had yellowed somewhat in the past two years. Silver threads gleamed here and there amid his curls, and his eyes, while still handsome, somehow seemed dimmer. Fine wrinkles, the traces of bitter, exhausting emotions, surrounded his lips and spread across his cheeks onto his temples. His clothes were old and shabby, and no sign of clean linen could be seen anywhere. His best days, evidently, were past—as gardeners say, he'd gone to seed.

He began to read the inscriptions on the walls—a well-known source of entertainment for tired travelers. Suddenly the door creaked and the stationmaster came in.

"There aren't any horses to go to Sk—— and there won't be any for a long time," he said, "but there are some ready to return to V——."

"To V——?" echoed Rudin. "For heaven's sake, that's not the direction I'm going in at all. I'm going to Penza, and V—— is located in the direction of Tambov, I believe."

"So what? You can go on from Tambov, and so you won't go out of your way at all."

Rudin thought for a moment.

"Well, all right," he finally said. "Tell them to harness the horses. It's all the same to me—I'll go to Tambov."

The horses were ready shortly. Rudin carried out his own suit-case, climbed into the cart, and took his seat, lowering his head as he had before. There was something helpless and pathetically submissive in his bowed form. . . . The three horses set off at a slow trot, their harness bells jangling discordantly.

Epilogue

Several more years passed.

It was a cold autumn day. A traveling carriage drew up to the steps of the central hotel in the regional capital of S——, and a gentleman stepped out of it, stretching and groaning slightly. He wasn't old, but he'd had time to acquire the fullness of figure that habitually commands respect. He walked up the steps to the main floor and stopped at the entrance to a wide corridor. Finding no one there, he loudly requested a room. A door creaked somewhere, then a tall attendant jumped out from behind a low screen and came toward him with rapid, sideways steps, his glossy back and rolled-up sleeves gleaming in the semidark corridor. The traveler entered the room he was given, immediately threw off his coat and scarf, sat down on the sofa, propped his fists on his knees, looked around as though he were hardly awake at first, and then asked that his servant be summoned. The hotel attendant bowed and disappeared. The traveler was none other than Lezhnev. He'd come from the countryside to S—— about some army recruitment matters.

Lezhnev's servant, a curly-haired, rosy-cheeked youth in a gray overcoat with a blue belt tied around his waist and soft felt shoes, entered the room.

"Well, my boy, we made it," Lezhnev declared, "and you were afraid that a wheel was going to come off the whole time."

"We made it," the boy responded, trying to smile above the high collar of his coat, "but the reason the wheel didn't come off...."

"Is someone here?" a voice rang out in the corridor.

Lezhnev was startled, and began to listen.

"Eh? Who's there?" repeated the voice.

Lezhnev stood up, walked over to the door, and abruptly threw it open.

A tall, stooped, almost completely gray-haired man wearing an old cloth coat with bronze buttons was standing in front of him.

"Rudin!" Lezhnev cried out excitedly.

Rudin turned around. He couldn't distinguish Lezhnev's features clearly, since Lezhnev was standing with his back to the light, and Rudin looked at him bewilderedly.

"Don't you recognize me?" asked Lezhnev.

"Mikhailo Mikhailych!" Rudin exclaimed, and held out his hand, but then he drew it back again in embarrassment.... Lezhnev hurriedly seized it in both of his.

"Come in, come in!" he urged Rudin, and led him into his room.

"How you've changed!" Lezhnev observed after a brief silence, unintentionally lowering his voice.

"Yes, so they say!" Rudin replied, his eyes straying around the room. "So many years... and you haven't changed at all. How's Aleksandra... your wife?"

"She's fine, thank you. But what act of fate has brought you here?"

"It's a long story. Strickly speaking, I came here by accident. I was looking for an acquaintance of mine. But I'm very glad...."

"Where are you going to have dinner?"

"Oh, I don't know. At some restaurant. I have to leave here today."

"Do you have to?"

Rudin smiled significantly.

"Yes, I do. They're sending me home to my estate."

"Have dinner with me."

Rudin looked Lezhnev straight in the face for the first time. "You're inviting me to have dinner with you?" he asked.

"Yes, Rudin, for the sake of old times and old friendship. Would you like to? I never expected to run into you here, and God only knows when we'll see each other again. I can't say goodbye to you like this!"

"If you want me to, then I accept."

Lezhnev shook Rudin's hand, and calling to his servant, ordered some dinner and told him to have a bottle of champagne put on ice.

In the course of their dinner, as though by agreement, Lezhnev and Rudin talked only about their student days, recalling numerous activities and numerous friends—both living and dead. Rudin spoke reluctantly at first, but he warmed up after he'd drunk a few glasses of wine. The waiter eventually took the final plate away. Lezhnev stood up, closed the door, and coming back to the table, sat down straight across from Rudin, gently resting his chin on his hands.

"Now, then," he began, "tell me everything that's happened to you since I saw you last."

Rudin looked at Lezhnev.

"Good God!" thought Lezhnev. "How he's changed, the poor man!"

Rudin's features hadn't changed much, particularly since we last saw him at the way station, although approaching old age had had time to set its mark on them—but their expression had been altered. His eyes regarded the world differently. His entire body, his every movement—slow one moment, sudden and erratic the next—and his frozen, defeated manner of speaking all betrayed sheer exhaustion and a quiet, secret dejection far different from the half-affected melancholy he'd flaunted periodically, the way young people generally do when they're filled with hope and self-confident pride.

"Tell you everything that's happened to me?" he replied. "It's impossible to tell you everything, and it isn't worthwhile. . . . I'm worn out. I've wandered a long way—in spirit as well as body. How many things, how many people I've lost faith in, by God! The kind of people I've grown close to! The kind of people!" Rudin reiterated, noticing that Lezhnev was looking him in the face with some sort of special sympathy. "How many times have my own words become repellent to me! I don't mean the words on my own lips, but those on the lips of people who'd adopted my opinions! How many times have I switched from the petulance of a child to the sluggish insensibility of a horse that no longer even lashes its tail when a whip strikes it. . . . How many times have I been happy and hopeful, and made enemies and humiliated myself for nothing! How many times have I taken flight like an eagle—only to return to earth like a snail whose shell has been crushed! . . . Where haven't I been? What roads haven't I traveled? . . . And the roads are often dirty," Rudin added, turning away slightly. "You know . . . ," he continued. . . .

"Listen," interrupted Lezhnev, "we used to use the familiar form of 'you' with one another. Let's revive the old custom. . . . Do you want to? Let's drink to *you!*"

Rudin shivered and straightened up, a gleam of something no words can express shining in his eyes.

"Yes, let's," he said. "Thank you, my friend. Let's drink."

Lezhnev and Rudin drained their glasses.

"*You* know," Rudin began again with a smile, stressing the familiar form of "you," "there's some kind of worm inside me that gnaws and tears at me, and will never let me be at peace until I die. It makes me come into conflict with people—first they fall under my influence, but then. . . ."

Rudin waved his hand in the air.

"Since I said goodbye to you, to *you*, I've seen and experienced a lot of things. . . . I've begun to live, I've embarked on something new twenty times or more—and here you see the results!"

"You didn't have any support," Lezhnev said, as though to himself.

"As you say, I didn't have any support. . . . I was never able to build anything, for it's difficult to build anything, my friend, when there isn't any ground under your feet, when you yourself have to establish your own foundation! I won't describe all my adventures to you—that is, to put it precisely, I'll describe two or three occasions . . . those occasions in my life when it seemed as if success were smiling on me, or rather, when I began to hope for success— which isn't altogether the same thing. . . ."

Rudin pushed back his thin gray hair with the same gesture he'd formerly used to brush back his thick dark curls.

"Well, listen," he commenced. "I came across a rather strange gentleman in Moscow. He was very wealthy and owned a number of extensive estates—he didn't work for a living. His chief, his sole passion was his love of science, science in general. To this day, I've never been able to ascertain why that passion manifested itself in him! It suited him about as well as a saddle suits a cow. He ascended mental heights only with difficulty, and he could barely speak—he merely rolled his eyes expressively and shook his head meaningfully. I've never encountered a less capable, less gifted nature than his. . . . There are places like that in the province of Smolensk—nothing but sand and a few tufts of grass no animal can eat. Nothing prospered at his hands—everything seemed to evade his grasp, and he was always determined to turn everything simple into something complicated. If it had depended on his wishes, the members of his household would have eaten their meals standing on their heads, I swear. He studied and read and wrote indefatigably. He devoted himself to science with a kind of stubborn perseverance, a terrible patience. His pride was immense, and he had a will of iron. He lived alone and had the reputation of being an eccentric. I became acquainted with him . . . and, well, he liked me. I must confess that I saw through him quickly enough, but his zeal attracted me. Besides, he commanded such great resources, so much good might have been accomplished through him, so many substantive achievements. . . . I moved into his house, and eventually went to the countryside with him. My plans were on a grand scale, my friend—I dreamed of various reforms, of innovations. . . . "

"Just like at Mrs. Lasunskii's, do you remember?" Lezhnev remarked with a good-natured smile.

"Ah, but then I knew in my heart that nothing would come of my words. This time . . . an altogether different field of endeavor lay before me. . . . I took books on agriculture with me . . . although, to tell you the truth, I didn't read any of them all the way through. . . . Well, I set to work. Things didn't progress as I'd expected at first, but then they did get going in a way. My new friend continually observed, without saying anything. He didn't interfere with me—at least he didn't interfere with me to any noticeable extent. He accepted my suggestions and carried them out, but he did so with a stubborn sullenness, a secret lack of faith— and he twisted everything to his own purposes. He surpassingly prized all his own ideas, and arduously strove to realize them, like a ladybug perched on a blade of grass, interminably sitting there as though pluming its wings and getting ready to take flight, then suddenly falling off and beginning to crawl again. . . . Don't be surprised at these comparisons—they were always being stirred up in my soul at that time."

"So I struggled along there for two years. The work went badly, in spite of all my efforts. I got tired of it, and my friend started to bore me—I began to sneer at him. He stifled me the way a down comforter does. His lack of faith turned into mute resentment, and a feeling of enmity crept over both of us. We couldn't talk about anything any more. He calmly but incessantly tried to prove to me that he wasn't under my influence—my orders were either set aside or utterly transformed. I eventually realized that I was playing the role of a court jester in the noble landowner's house by providing him with intellectual amusement. I became embittered at having wasted my time and energy for nothing, embittered at having deceived myself in my expectations again and again. I knew perfectly well what I was losing if I left, but I couldn't control myself, and one day, after witnessing a painful, revolting scene that placed my friend in a most disadvantageous light, I definitely quarreled with him and finally did leave, abandoning this newfangled pedant who was compounded of our native flour kneaded together with German molasses."

"That is, you gave up your source of daily bread," Lezhnev declared, laying both hands on Rudin's shoulders.

"Yes, and I was adrift once more, naked and penniless in an empty universe, to go wherever I chose. Ah! Let's drink!"

"To your health!" proposed Lezhnev, standing up and kissing Rudin on the forehead. "To your health, and to the memory of Pokorskii. He knew how to be poor as well."

"Well, that was my principal adventure," Rudin began again after a short pause. "Should I go on?"

"Please do go on."

"Ah! I have no desire to talk. I'm tired of talking, my friend. . . . However, so be it. After wandering from place to place. . . . By the way, I could tell you how I became the secretary of a benevolent dignitary and what resulted from that, but it'd take me too long. . . . After wandering from place to place, I finally resolved to become . . . don't smile, please . . . a practical businessman. A certain opportunity presented itself—I got to know . . . perhaps you've heard of him . . . a man named Kurbeev. . . . No?"

"No, I've never heard of him. But for heaven's sake, Rudin, with your intelligence, how could you fail to suspect that you had no business . . . forgive the pun . . . becoming a businessman?"

"I know I didn't, but then again, what does my business consist of? And if you'd seen Kurbeev! Please don't imagine that he was some empty windbag. They say that I used to be eloquent—I was simply nothing compared to him. He was an amazingly well-educated, knowledgeable man with a creative mind who had a head for business and commercial enterprises. His brain seemed to seethe with the most audacious, the most unexpected schemes. I joined forces with him and we decided to devote those forces to a project of social value...."

"What was it, may I ask?"

"You'll laugh at it."

"Why should I? No, I won't laugh."

"We decided to make a river in the province of K—— fit for navigation," Rudin acknowledged with an embarrassed smile.

"So that's it! This Kurbeev was a capitalist, then?"

"He was poorer than I was," Rudin responded, and his gray head quietly sank onto his breast.

Lezhnev began to laugh, but he suddenly stopped and took Rudin by the hand.

"Please forgive me, my friend," he said, "but I didn't expect that at all. Well, I presume that your enterprise remained only on paper?"

"Not completely. We made a start. We hired workers ... well, and began to work, but then we encountered various obstacles. In the first place, the mill owners didn't try to understand our project at all. Moreover, we couldn't turn the water from its course without machinery, and we didn't have enough money for machinery. We lived in mud huts for six months. Kurbeev lived on dry bread, and I didn't have much to eat, either. However, I won't complain about that—the scenery there is magnificent. We struggled and struggled, appealing to the merchants, writing letters and circulars. I ended up spending all my money on that project."

"Well," Lezhnev remarked, "I imagine that it wasn't hard to spend all your money."

"Precisely—it wasn't hard."

Rudin glanced out the window.

"But the project really wasn't a bad one, by God, and it might have been of immense service."

"And where did Kurbeev end up?" Lezhnev inquired.

"Oh, he's in Siberia now. He's become a gold trader. And you'll see, he'll make a living for himself, he'll get by."

"Maybe he will, but now you probably won't make a living for yourself."

"I won't? Well, that can't be helped! Besides, I know I was always a worthless creature in your eyes."

"You? That's enough, my friend. There certainly was a time when I focused on your defects, but now, believe me, I've learned to appreciate you. You won't make a living . . . and I love you for that . . . for heaven's sake."

Rudin smiled faintly.

"Really?"

"I respect you for it!" Lezhnev affirmed. "Do you understand me?"

Both men fell silent for a little while.

"Well, should I proceed to my third adventure?" asked Rudin.

"Please do."

"Very well. The third and last. I've just recently extricated myself from it. But haven't I bored you enough already?"

"Go on, go on."

"Well," Rudin began, "the idea occurred to me one day during some leisure moment . . . I've always had plenty of leisure moments . . . the idea occurred to me that I have a fair amount of knowledge and my intentions are good. . . . For even you won't deny that I have good intentions?"

"I should think not!"

"I'd more or less failed in every other regard. . . . Why shouldn't I become a pedagogue or, to put it simply, a teacher . . . instead of wasting my life?"

Rudin paused and sighed.

"Instead of wasting my life, wouldn't it be better for me to try to pass on what I know to others? Perhaps they could extract at least some benefit from my knowledge. I have above average abilities and, in any event, I can master my tongue. . . . So I decided to devote myself to this new activity. I had difficulty obtaining a job—I didn't want to give private lessons, and there was nothing I could do in the lower schools. I finally managed to get an appointment as a teacher in the high school here."

"A teacher of what?" queried Lezhnev.

"A teacher of Russian literature. I tell you, I never embarked on any task with such zeal as I did on this one. The thought of influencing young people inspired me. I spent three weeks composing my introductory lecture."

"Do you have it with you?" Lezhnev interrupted.

"No, I lost it somewhere. It didn't come out too badly, and was well received. I can see the faces of my listeners even now—decent, young faces wearing expressions of pure-souled attention and sympathy, even of astonishment. I mounted the platform and read my lecture feverishly. I thought that it'd take more than an hour, but I finished it in twenty minutes. The inspector was sitting there as well—a dessicated old man wearing silver-rimmed glasses and a short wig—he occasionally turned his head in my direction. When I'd finished, he jumped up from his seat and said to me, 'That was good, albeit somewhat exalted and obscure, and too little was said about the subject itself.' But the students gazed at me with respect in their eyes . . . they truly did. Ah, that's why youth is so precious! I gave a second lecture I'd written, then a third. . . . I began to improvise my lectures after that."

"Were you successful?" inquired Lezhnev.

"I was highly successful. Audiences crowded in. I transmitted everything that was in my soul to them. There were two or three really remarkable boys among them; the rest didn't understand me very well. I must confess, though, that even those who did understand me sometimes embarrassed me with their questions. Yet I didn't despair. They all loved me—I gave them all high scores on examinations. But then a conspiracy against me was formed . . . or no! It wasn't a conspiracy at all, it was simply that I didn't mind my own business. I got in other people's way, and they got in mine. I didn't lecture to the high school students as they were ordinarily lectured to—they took very little away from my lectures. . . . I myself didn't know the facts very well. Besides, I wasn't satisfied with the limited sphere of action allotted to me . . . . As you know, that's always been my weakness. I wanted radical reforms, and, I swear to you, those reforms were both sensible and easy to carry out. I'd hoped to carry them out with the help of the director, a kind, honorable man over whom I had some influence at first. His wife assisted me. I haven't met many women like her in my life. She was about forty, but she believed in goodness and loved all beautiful things with the enthusiasm of a girl of fifteen. She wasn't afraid to voice her convictions in front of anyone at all. I'll never forget her noble, pure spirit. Acting on her advice, I began to draw up a plan. . . . But then my influence was undermined—I became the object of slander. My chief enemy was the professor of mathematics, a small, bitter, bilious man who

didn't believe in anything, like Pigasov, but was more capable
than he was. . . . By the way, how is Pigasov? Is he still alive?"
  "Oh, yes, and if you can believe it, he's married to a peasant
woman who beats him, they say."
  "Serves him right! And is Natalia Alekseevna well?"
  "Yes."
  "Is she happy?"
  "Yes."
  Rudin fell silent for a moment.
  "What was I talking about? . . . Oh, yes! About the mathematics
teacher. He utterly detested me—he compared my lectures to
fireworks, he pounced on every phrase of mine that wasn't perfectly
clear, and once he even corrected me regarding some sixteenth-
century monument. . . . But the main thing was that he found my
intentions suspect—my last soap bubble landed on him as if he
were a spike, and it burst. The inspector, with whom I'd gotten
along badly from the outset, turned the director against me, and
a confrontation ensued. I wasn't ready to give in—I got angry. The
matter came to the attention of the authorities, and I was forced
to resign. I didn't stop there, though. I wanted to prove that they
couldn't behave like that. . . . But in fact, they could behave any
way they wanted toward me. . . . Now I have to leave here."
  A silence followed. Both men sat with their heads bowed.
  Rudin was the first to speak.
  "Yes, my friend," he began, "I can now say, in the words of
Koltsov, 'You've led me astray, my youth, until I have nowhere
left to guide my steps.' . . . And yet, is it possible that I was really
unsuited to anything, that there was really no work for me to do
on earth? I've often asked myself this question, and however much
I've tried to belittle myself in my own eyes, I couldn't help but
feel within me the presence of capabilities that aren't given to
everyone! Why have these capabilities remained unfulfilled? And
then there's this. You remember that, when I was abroad with you,
I was conceited and hypocritical. . . . In fact, at that time I didn't
clearly recognize what I wanted—I reveled in words and believed
in phantoms. But now, I swear to you, I can express to anyone
everything that I want. I have absolutely nothing to hide. I'm an
utterly well-intentioned man, in the truest sense of the term. I'm
resigned, I'm prepared to adapt myself to circumstances. I don't
want much. I want to achieve some modest goal, to be of even the
slightest use. But no! I'll never succeed. What does this mean?

What keeps me from living and working like other people? . . . I just dream about that now. But no sooner do I get into any concrete situation, no sooner do I pause at a certain point, than fate takes it all away from me. I've come to dread it—my fate. . . . What's the point of all this? Explain this enigma to me!"

"This enigma!" repeated Lezhnev. "Yes, that's right—you've always been an enigma to me. Even in our youth, after engaging in some minor prank, when you'd suddenly speak as though you were pierced to the heart and then you'd begin all over . . . well, you know what I mean . . . even then, I didn't understand you. That's why I became disenchanted with you. . . . You have such enormous capabilities, such indefatigable yearning for an ideal. . . . "

"Words, all words! There were no deeds!" Rudin broke in.

"No deeds! What deeds . . . ?"

"What deeds? Feeding an old blind woman and her entire family through one's own efforts, the way Priazhentsev did, do you remember? . . . There's a deed for you."

"Yes, but a kind word is also a deed."

Rudin looked at Lezhnev without speaking and quietly shook his head.

Lezhnev wanted to say something, and he wiped his hand across his face.

"So you're going to the countryside?" he finally asked.

"Yes."

"Then you still have some property left?"

"Something's left there—two and a half serfs. It's a corner to die in. Perhaps you're thinking this very minute: 'Even now he can't get along without fine phrases!' Fine phrases have surely been my downfall—they've consumed me, and I couldn't escape them until the end. But what I've said wasn't merely a fine phrase. This white hair, my friend, these wrinkles, these ragged elbows—they aren't merely fine phrases. You've always been severe toward me, and you were justified. But now isn't a time for severity, when everything's over, when there's no fuel left in the lamp, when the lamp itself is broken and the wick's barely smoldering. . . . Death, my friend, should finally reconcile. . . . "

Lezhnev leaped up.

"Rudin!" he cried. "Why are you talking to me like this? What have I done to deserve this from you? What sort of judge am I, and what sort of a man would I be, if at the sight of your hollow cheeks and your wrinkles, 'fine phrases' would come to my mind? Do you want to know what I think about you? Well, I think that here's an individual ... with his talents, what might he have accomplished, what worldly advantages might he have obtained by now, if he'd wanted to! ... And I find him hungry and homeless. ... "

"I arouse your compassion," Rudin murmured in a choked voice.

"No, you're wrong. You instill respect in me—that's what you do. Who prevented you from spending year after year at the home of that landowner, your friend who would have provided for you, I'm absolutely certain, if you'd merely been willing to humor him? Why couldn't you get along well at the high school? Whatever notions you may have had in embarking on such an undertaking, why have you—you strange man!—ended up sacrificing your personal interests every time, refusing to plant your roots in anything but good soil, however profitable it might have been to do otherwise?"

"I was born a rolling stone," Rudin interjected with a weary smile. "I can't stop."

"That's true, but it's not because a worm is gnawing at you, as you said to me earlier, that you can't stop. ... It's not a worm, not a spirit of idle restlessness—the fire of love for the truth burns inside you, and clearly, in spite of all your difficulties, it burns more intensely inside you than it does inside many people who don't consider themselves egoists and who probably dare to label you a manipulator. In your place, I, for one, would have managed to silence that worm in me a long time ago, and would have reconciled myself to everything, whereas you haven't even been embittered by it. You're ready today, right now, to take up a new task again like a boy, I'm sure of it."

"No, my friend, I'm tired now," Rudin replied. "I've had enough."

"Tired! Any other man would have been dead years ago. You say that death reconciles people, but don't you think that life reconciles them? An individual who's lived and hasn't become tolerant toward others doesn't deserve to receive tolerance himself. And who can say that he doesn't need tolerance? You've done what you could, you've struggled as long as you could. ... What else should you have done? Our paths separated. ... "

"You were utterly different from me, my friend," Rudin interrupted with a sigh.

"Our paths separated, perhaps," Lezhnev continued, "precisely because, thanks to my wealth, my cold blood, and other fortunate circumstances, nothing prevented me from staying at home and remaining a spectator with my hands folded, but you had to go out into the world, to roll up your shirtsleeves, to struggle, to work. Our paths separated . . . but see how close we are to one another. We speak virtually the same language, we understand one another with half a hint, we grew up on the same emotions. There aren't many of us left now, my friend, for we're the last of the Mohicans! We might have differed and even quarreled in the old days, when so much of life still remained ahead of us, but now, when our ranks are thinning, when the younger generation is forging past us with aims quite different from ours, we ought to hold on to one another tightly! Let's drink a toast and sing 'Gaudeamus igitur,' the way we used to!"

The friends toasted and sang the old student song with strained voices, thoroughly out of tune, in true Russian style.

"So now you're going to the countryside," Lezhnev began again. "I don't think you'll stay there for long, and I can't imagine where and how you'll end up. . . . But remember, whatever happens to you, you'll always have a place, a nest where you can hide yourself away. That's my home . . . do you hear, old fellow? Ideas have their invalids as well—they ought to have a home, too."

Rudin stood up.

"Thank you, my friend," he said, "thank you! I won't forget you for this. Only I don't deserve a home. I've wasted my life, I haven't served ideas the way I should have. . . ."

"Hush!" Lezhnev insisted. "Every individual remains what nature has made him, and it's impossible to ask more of him! You've called yourself the Wandering Jew. . . . But how do you know?— maybe you were meant to wander forever, maybe you're fulfilling a higher calling that way than you know. Popular wisdom says with good reason that we're all in God's hands. You're leaving," Lezhnev continued, seeing that Rudin was picking up his hat. "You won't spend the night?"

"Yes, I'm leaving! Goodbye. Thank you. . . . But I'll come to a bad end."

"God only knows. . . . You're determined to leave?"

"Yes, I'm leaving. Goodbye. Don't remember me unkindly."

"Well, don't remember me unkindly, either . . . and don't forget what I said to you. Goodbye. . . ."

The friends embraced one another. Rudin went out quickly. Lezhnev paced back and forth in his room for a long time, stopped by the window, thought for a moment, and murmured half out loud, "Poor man!" Then, sitting down at the table, he began to write a letter to his wife.

Meanwhile, the wind had arisen outside, nastily moaning and angrily shaking the rattling windowpanes. The long autumn night had set in. He who sits in the shelter of his home on such a night, he who has a warm little corner, is fortunate. . . . May the Lord help all homeless wanderers!

On a sultry afternoon in Paris, on the twenty-sixth of July in 1848, when the revolution of the *atelier nationaux* had already been nearly suppressed, a battalion of army troops ranged in rows was assaulting a barricade in one of the narrow alleys of the faubourg St. Antoine. A few gunshots had effectively vanquished the resistance. The surviving defenders had abandoned the barricade, thinking only of their own safety, when suddenly, at its very top, on the flimsy frame of an overturned omnibus, a tall man appeared wearing an old overcoat belted with a red sash and a straw hat on his gray, disheveled hair. He held a red flag in one hand, a blunt, curved saber in the other, and as he scrambled upward, he shouted something in a shrill, strained voice, waving his flag and his saber. A Vincennes marksman aimed at him . . . and fired. . . . The tall man dropped the flag—and toppled over like a sack, face downward, as though he were bowing at someone's feet. The bullet had passed right through his heart.

"*Tiens!*" one of the fleeing *insurgés* said to another. "*On vient de tuer le Polonais.*"

"*Bigre!*" responded the other, and they both ran into the cellar of a house whose shutters were all closed and whose walls were streaked with traces of gunpowder and bullets.

This "*Polonais*" was Dmitrii Rudin.

Letter to L. N. Tolstoy.

Paris.
January 3, 1857.

Dear Tolstoy,

I don't know whether my letters make you very happy, but yours comfort me. A change—a very good one—is obviously taking place in you. (Excuse me for seeming to pat you on the head: I'm a full ten years older than you, and in general I feel myself becoming an old prattler.) You're calming down, becoming serene, and— most importantly—you're growing free, free of your own views and prejudices. To take a look to the left is just as nice as to the right— there are no impediments, there are "perspectives" everywhere (Botkin stole that word from me)—all you have to do is open your eyes wide. God grant that your horizons widen with every passing day! The only people who treasure systems are those whom the whole truth evades, who want to catch it by the tail. A system is just like truth's tail, but the truth is like a lizard. It will leave the tail in your hand and escape; it knows that it will soon grow another tail. That comparison is somewhat bold, but the fact is that your letters comfort me. That's beyond doubt.

I received a very nice and rather lengthy letter from your sister. It made me very happy; I'm sincerely attached to her—and the news of her illness saddened me greatly. She also liked my "Faust." What a strange fate that piece has had! Some people find it not at all to their taste—by the way, and to my extreme regret, that includes Madame Viardot. Apropos, what absurd rumors are being spread among you back home! Her husband is as healthy as can be and I'm as far away from marriage as, for example, you are. But I love her more than ever, and more than anyone on earth. That's the truth.

Your "Childhood and Adolescence" is creating a furor among the Russian ladies here; the copy that I had sent to me is being read greedily, and I've already had to promise several people that I'll introduce them to you—they ask me for your autograph. In a word, you're in fashion—even more so than crinoline. I'm telling you this because no matter what you say, in your heart somewhere there's a little bump that such praise (moreover, any kind of praise) tickles pleasantly. And let it tickle—to your heart's content!

From the letters I receive from Petersburg I have to conclude that literary life there—and every other sort, too—is on the move. Sometimes I'm greatly vexed that I'm not with all of you at this

time, and I even think ("Man is egotistical") that I could be useful.
But I can't even think of leaving here before April—and therefore
I'm postponing all such fantasies until next winter. You write that
you won't even sit out this winter in Petersburg. Why on earth do
you have the idea of going to the Caucasus? It'd be better for you
to get your brother out of there.

Don't forget to send me everything that appears in *The Contemporary*.

Your acquaintance with Shakespeare—or more accurately, your
approaching it—makes me happy. He's like Nature: sometimes it
has such a vile physiognomy (just recall any of our lachrymose,
slimy October days in the steppe)—but even then there's necessity
and truth in it—and (prepare yourself: your hair will stand on end)
purpose. Get to know *Hamlet, Julius Caesar, Coriolanus, Henry IV,
Macbeth*, and *Othello* as well. Don't let superficial absurdities repel
you; dig down to the center, to the heart of the work—and you'll
be amazed at the harmony and profound truth in that great spirit.
Even from here I can see you smiling as you read these lines. But
just think—Turgenev *might* just be right. Stranger things have
happened.

I haven't been telling you about my acquaintances here; I've only
met one nice woman—and she's Russian—and one very intelligent
man—and he's a Jew. Frenchies don't attract me; they may be
superb soldiers and administrators, but all they have in all their
heads is the same little lane down which the same thoughts—always
the same—scurry along. Anything that isn't theirs seems wild and
stupid to them. "*Ah! le lecteur français ne saurait admettre cela!*"
And having pronounced those words, a Frenchman can't even imagine
that you might object in some way. The devil can take them!

Well, farewell, dear Tolstoy. Grow as broad as you've been growing
deep up to now—and in time we'll all sit under your shade
and praise its beauty and coolness.

                                                        Your
                                                        Ivan Turgenev.

Letter to V. P. Botkin.[1]

Paris.

February 17, 1857.

Dear Botkin, I'm not exaggerating when I say that I've started to write you ten times, but not once could I write more than half a page; maybe this time I'll be luckier. I won't bother to tell you about myself: I'm a bankrupt man—and that's that; there's no point in talking about it. I constantly feel like trash that someone forgot to sweep out—that's my *Stimmung*. Nevertheless, perhaps it will pass when I leave Paris. You know that Nekrasov was here and then suddenly took off for Rome; Tolstoy is here—he looks at everything in wide-eyed silence; he's gotten much smarter, but he still feels uncomfortable with himself—and that's why other people don't feel completely at ease around him. But I rejoice in seeing him: to tell the truth, he's our literature's single hope. As concerns me, I'll whisper this in your ear along with the request that you not spread it any further: besides the piece promised to Druzhinin, which I'm sending off only because I don't want a repeat of the Katkov incident—not a single line of *mine* will be published (or even written) before the end of the world. The day before yesterday I didn't burn them (because I was afraid of imitating Gogol), but I tore up and threw down the watercloset all my beginnings, plans, and so on. It's all nonsense. I don't have the sort of talent that has its own special physiognomy and integrity; there were some poetic strains—but they've resounded and died away. I don't feel like repeating myself—so time to retire! This is no flash of vexation, believe me—it's the expression or fruit of slowly ripening convictions. The failure of my tales (a fact related to me by very reliable sources, Kolbasin and others) came as nothing new to me. I'm removing myself from the scene; as a writer with tendencies, Mr. Shchedrin will replace me (the public now needs things that are piquant and coarse), and full, poetic natures such as Tolstoy will finish and present clearly and fully that at which I could only hint. All this is rather strange after "the obligatory invitation," *mais je m'en lave les mains.* Since I have a decent command of the Russian language, I'm planning to translate *Don Quixote*—if my health holds out. You'll probably think this is all an exaggeration—and you

1. Vasilii Petrovich Botkin (1810-69), author of articles on literature, the arts, and philosophy.

won't believe me. You'll see, I hope, that I've never spoken more seriously or sincerely.

Thank you for sending the article about Fet; the main idea is correct and sensible, and there are subtle and intelligent remarks generously sprinkled throughout. If I discover a talent for it, I wouldn't mind writing articles of that sort—and maybe I'll try myself. But as for writing fiction—no more! You know that I stopped writing poetry just as soon as I became convinced that I wasn't a poet; and my present conviction is that I'm as much a teller of tales as I was a poet.

I've met a lot of people, including Mérimée! I could be spending time very, very pleasantly if I weren't so miserable. When we see each other, I'll have lots of things to tell you—but I don't feel like writing them down.

Farewell, dear Botkin. I don't know whether you're in Petersburg or Moscow—and that's why I'm sending you this letter via Annenkov. Be healthy. I embrace you.

Your
Ivan Turgenev.

A Journey to Polesje

The First Day

The appearance of a huge pine forest that embraces the whole horizon, the appearance of "Polesje," resembles the appearance of the ocean. And the sensations it arouses are the same: the same primeval, untapped strength spreads out before the eyes of the observer in all its breadth and majesty. From the core of the eternal forests and from the source of the immortal waters comes the same voice: "I have nothing to do with you," nature says to man. "I reign supreme, while you worry about how to escape death." But the forest is sadder and more monotonous than the sea, especially the pine forest, which is always the same, always almost soundless. The ocean threatens, it caresses, it sparkles with every color, it speaks with every voice; it reflects the sky, from which also wafts the breath of eternity, but this is an eternity that doesn't seem alien to us. . . . The dark, unchanging pine forest maintains a sullen silence or is filled with a dull roar—and an awareness of human insignificance pierces the heart ever more deeply, ever more irrefutably, at the sight of it. It's hard for a human being—the creature of a day, born yesterday and doomed to die today—to bear the cold, unfeeling gaze of the eternal Isis when it's fixed upon him: not only are the daring hopes, the dreams of youth, humbled and extinguished within him, enfolded by the icy breath of the elements, but his entire soul sinks and falls. He senses that the last of his kind may vanish off the face of the earth and not one needle will quiver on those branches; he senses his isolation, his weakness, his gratuitousness—and in hurried, secret panic he turns to the petty cares and tasks of life. He's more at ease in the world he himself has created: there he's at home, there he still dares to believe in his own significance and his own power.

Such were the thoughts that came to my mind some years ago when, standing on the steps of a small inn perched on the bank of the marshy little stream Reseta, I first set eyes on Polesje. The bluish vastness of the coniferous forest lay before me in long, continuous ridges; here and there appeared the green patches of small birch groves. Everything up to the horizon was enveloped by the pine forest: nowhere was the white gleam of a church or the bright stretch of a meadow visible—there were only trees and more trees, the ragged edges of the treetops, and a dim, delicate mist, the eternal mist of Polesje, which hung over the trees in the distance. It wasn't mere idleness, this lack of living movement. No—it was the absence of life, it was something dead, albeit impressive, that reached out to me from every point on the horizon. I remember that big white clouds were slowly drifting past high in the sky, and that the hot summer day lay still across the silent earth. The reddish water of the stream glided among the thick reeds without a splash; round cushions of spiny moss were vaguely discernible at its bottom; its banks disappeared into the swampy mud at some points and sharply reappeared at others as white mounds of fine, crumbling sand.

Near the little inn ran a well-trodden highway. On this highway, directly opposite the steps, stood a cart loaded with boxes and baskets. Its owner, a thin, stooped, lame peddler with a hooked nose and mouselike eyes, was harnessing up his little nag, who was just as lame as he. He was a gingerbread salesman making his way to the fair at Karachev. Suddenly several people appeared on the road, and a few others straggled behind them . . . then a whole throng came trudging into sight. They all had walking sticks in their hands and knapsacks on their shoulders. From their tired, unsteady gait, as well as their sunburned faces, one could tell that they'd walked a long way. They were leatherworkers and ditch-diggers returning from a search for work. An elderly man of about seventy, whose hair was completely white, seemed to be their leader. From time to time, he turned around and calmly encouraged those who lagged behind. "Come on, come on, boys," he said, "co-ome on." The rest all walked without speaking, in some sort of solemn silence. Only one of them, a short man with an angry expression on his face, wearing an unbuttoned sheepskin coat and a lambswool cap pulled right down to his eyes, having reached the gingerbread salesman, suddenly inquired, "How much is the gingerbread, you fool?"

"Which gingerbread, good sir?" the surprised salesman replied in a reedy little voice. "Some pieces are a kopeck, and others are half a kopeck. Do you have half a kopeck in your pouch?"

"It'd probably grease my belly too much," retorted the sheepskin wearer, and he backed away from the cart.

"Hurry up, boys, hurry up," I heard the elderly man call out. "It's still a long way to our night's lodging."

"An ignorant bunch," the gingerbread salesman remarked, casting a sidelong glance at me as soon as the whole lot had filed past. "Is food such as this for the likes of them?"

And quickly harnessing his horse, he went down to the river, where a little wooden ferry could be seen. A peasant in a white felt "schlyk" (the standard Polesje headgear) came out of a low mud hut to meet him, and ferried him over to the opposite bank. The little cart began to creep along the trampled, deeply rutted road, one wheel creaking from time to time.

I fed my horses and then took the ferry across as well. After struggling through a boggy meadow for a couple of versts, I finally reached a narrow log roadway leading to a clearing in the forest. My carriage jolted unevenly over the road logs; I got out and proceeded on foot. The horses moved in unison, snorting and shaking their heads to get rid of the gnats and flies.

Polesje welcomed us into its bosom. On its outskirts, closest to the meadow, birch trees grew, along with aspens, limes, maples, and oaks. Then those trees appeared more rarely, and the dense firs closed around us in an unbroken wall. Farther on stood the red, bare trunks of pine trees, and then came a stretch where the various types were all mixed together, surrounded at their bases by hazelnut bushes, mountain ash, and brambles, as well as stout, vigorous weeds. The sun's rays cast a brilliant light on the treetops, reaching the ground here and there in pale streaks and patches, filtering through the branches. There was almost no sign of birds— they don't like large forests. Only the mournful, thrice-repeated call of a cuckoo and the angry screech of a nuthatch or jay resounded from time to time. A silent, solitary crow occasionally flew across some glade, its lovely feathers giving off flashes of gold and bright blue.

The trees grew farther apart in one place, the light broke through ahead of us, and the carriage entered a sandy clearing. Thin stalks of rye were growing in rows all across it, noiselessly nodding their pale tips. On one side stood a dark, dilapidated little chapel with a slanting cross suspended above a well. A hidden brook was murmuring peacefully, emitting lilting, musical tones, as though it were flowing into an empty bottle. Up ahead, the road was abruptly cut in half by a birch tree that had recently fallen, and the forest loomed around it, so old, so lofty, so dreamy, that the air itself seemed trapped within. The clearing lay under water in spots. On both sides extended a forest marsh, all verdant and dark, covered with reeds and tiny alder trees. Ducks flew up in pairs—and it was strange to see those water birds rapidly darting among the pines. "Ga, ga, ga, ga," their prolonged cry kept ringing out unexpectedly. Then a cowherd appeared, driving his cattle through the underbrush; one brown cow with short, pointed horns noisily broke through the bushes and then stood stock-still at the edge of the clearing, turning her big, dark eyes toward the dog running in front of me. A slight breeze conveyed the delicate, pungent odor of burned wood. In the distance, some white smoke was drifting through the pale-blue forest air in eddying rings, revealing that a peasant was burning coal for a glass factory or a foundry.

The farther we went, the darker and quieter it became all around us. It's always quiet in a pine forest—some sort of extended murmur, a subdued hum, continually reverberates in the treetops high overhead. . . . One goes on and on, but this eternal reverberation of the forest never ceases, and one's heart gradually begins to ache. One longs to come out into the open, into the daylight, as quickly as possible; one longs to draw a deep breath again—and is oppressed by the fragrant dampness and decay. . . .

We advanced primarily at a walking pace, rarely at a trot, for about fifteen versts. I wanted to get to Sviatoe, a village lying at the very heart of the forest, before sundown. Twice I encountered peasants transporting stripped bark or long logs on carts.

"Is it far to Sviatoe?" I asked one of them.

"No, not far."

"How far?"

"It's about three versts."

Another hour and a half passed. We went on and on. After a while, we heard the creak of yet another laden cart. A peasant was walking beside it.

"How far is it to Sviatoe, friend?"

"What?"

"How far to Sviatoe?"

"Eight versts."

The sun was already setting when I finally emerged from the forest and saw a little village in front of me. About twenty houses were tightly grouped around an old wooden church that had a single green cupola and tiny windows shining bright red in the evening's glow. This was Sviatoe. I reached its outskirts. A herd of livestock returning home overtook my cart and moved past my carriage, lowing, grunting, and bleating. Young girls and bustling peasant women came out to meet their animals. Blond boys ran after refractory pigs with gleeful shrieks. The dust swirled along the road in light clouds that turned crimson as they rose higher in the air.

I stopped at the house of the village elder, a crafty, intelligent Polesjan, one of those Polesjans who, they say, can see two yards into the ground. Early the next morning, accompanied by the village elder's son and another peasant called Egor, I set off in a little cart harnessed to a pair of pot-bellied peasant's horses in order to hunt woodcocks and moorhens. The forest formed a continuous blue ring around the rim of the sky. Not more than about two hundred acres of plowed land were said to surround Sviatoe, but one had to go some seven versts to find good places to hunt. The elder's son was named Kondrat. He was a flaxen-haired, rosy-cheeked, helpful, talkative young fellow with a good-natured, peaceable expression on his face. He drove the horses. Egor sat next to me. I want to say a few words about him.

He was considered the best hunter in the entire district. He'd covered every foot of ground for fifty versts in each direction over and over again. He seldom shot at a bird, due to a lack of gunpowder and ammunition, but he was content to flush out a moorhen or detect the track of a grouse. Egor had the reputation of being an honest man, as well as "the silent type." He didn't like to talk, and never exaggerated the number of birds he'd caught—a trait rare in a hunter. He was a thin man of medium height with a drawn, pale face and large, honest eyes. All his features, especially his straight, immobile lips, bespoke untroubled serenity. He smiled slightly and, as it were, inwardly—a gentle, very sweet smile—whenever he uttered a word. He never drank wine and worked industriously, but never prospered. His wife was always sick; none of his children ever survived; he grew poorer and poorer, never getting his affairs straightened out. And there's no denying that it isn't appropriate for a peasant to have a passion for hunting, and that anyone who "plays with a gun" is sure to be a bad farmer. Either from constantly being in the forest, face to face with the stern, melancholy scenery in that uninhabited realm, or else due to the particular cast of his personality, some sort of modest dignity and stateliness were noticeable in everything Egor did—it was stateliness, not mere pensiveness—the stateliness of a noble stag. He'd killed seven bears in his time, lying in wait for them amid the oatfields. He'd managed to shoot the last one only on the fourth night of his ambush; the bear had never turned sideways toward him, and he'd had just one bullet. Egor had killed it the day before my arrival. When Kondrat took me to see Egor, he was in his backyard, squatting on his heels next to the huge beast, trimming away the fat with a short, blunt knife.

"That's a fine specimen you've brought down there!" I observed.

Egor raised his head and looked first at me, then at the dog that accompanied me.

"If it's hunting you've come for, there are woodcocks at Moshnyi, three coveys of them, and five of moorhens," he remarked, and went back to work.

I set off in the cart the next day to hunt with Egor and Kondrat. We rolled rapidly across the open fields surrounding Sviatoe, but when we got to the forest, we slowed to a walking pace once more.

"Look, there's a wood pigeon," Kondrat suddenly declared, turning toward me. "It'd be good to knock it off!"

Egor looked in the direction Kondrat was pointing but didn't say anything. The wood pigeon was over a hundred feet away from us, and one can't kill it from forty feet away, because it has such resilient feathers.

A few more remarks were offered by the loquacious Kondrat, but the forest hush eventually exerted its influence even over him, and he fell silent. Exchanging a word or two only occasionally, looking straight ahead, listening to the puffing and snorting of the horses, we finally got to "Moshnyi"—that's the name given to an older pine forest, one scattered with an undergrowth of fir saplings. We got out; Kondrat guided the cart into the bushes so that the gnats wouldn't bite the horses. Egor examined the trigger of his gun and crossed himself; he never began to do anything without making the sign of the cross first.

The forest we'd entered was exceedingly old. I don't know whether the Tartars had wandered through it, but Russian thieves or Lithuanians may well have hidden in its recesses during periods of social upheaval. The mighty pines, with their slightly curved, massive, pale-yellow trunks, stood at a respectful distance from one another. Between them stood others that were somewhat younger, in single file. The ground was covered with greenish moss and sprinkled everywhere with dead pine needles. Blueberries grew in dense clumps; the berries' strong odor, like the smell of musk, stifled one's breathing. The sun couldn't pierce through the lofty network of pine branches, but it was suffocatingly hot in the forest nonetheless, and it wasn't dark. Heavy, transparent resin seeped out and slowly trickled down the coarse bark of the trees like large drops of sweat. The motionless air, devoid of sunbeams and shadows, made one's face tingle. Everything was silent; even our footsteps were inaudible—we walked on the moss as if it were a carpet. Egor in particular moved as soundlessly as a ghost; the brushwood didn't crackle under his feet. He walked without haste, from time to time blowing a shrill note on a whistle; a woodcock soon answered back, and darted into a thick fir tree before my very eyes. Egor pointed it out to me in vain: however intensely I strained my eyes, I couldn't see it. Egor finally had to take a shot at it. We also came across two coveys of moorhens; the birds flew up at a distance with an abrupt, muffled sound. We did manage to kill three young ones, however.

At one *maidan*,[1] Egor suddenly stopped and summoned me.

"A bear's been trying to get some water," he observed, pointing to a fresh, broad scratch mark in the very middle of a hole covered with fine moss.

"Is that its paw print?" I inquired.

"Yes. But the water's dried up. That's its mark on this pine tree, too. It's been climbing for honey. It's cut into the bark with its claws like a knife."

We went on making our way into the innermost depths of the forest. Egor looked upward only rarely, striding forward serenely and confidently. I caught sight of a tall, round rampart enclosed by a half-filled ditch.

"What's that? Another *maidan*?" I asked.

"No," replied Egor. "This is where a thieves' village stood."

"A long time ago?"

"A long time ago. Our grandfathers remember it. The thieves

---

1. *Maidan* is the name given to a place where tar was made.

buried their treasure here. And they took a lasting vow on human blood."

"We went another mile and a half. I began to get thirsty. "Sit down for a little while," said Egor. "I'll go get some water. There's a well not far from here."

He set off, and I remained by myself.

I sat down on a stump, leaned my elbows on my knees, and, after a long interval, raised my head and looked around. Oh, how quiet and somberly sad everything around me appeared—or no, not even sad, but mute and cold and menacing at the same time! My heart sank. At that instant, on that spot, I felt the breath of death, I felt that I could almost touch its ceaseless proximity. If only one sound had reverberated or one momentary rustle had arisen in the overwhelming stillness of the pine forest that hemmed me in on all sides! I lowered my head again, almost in terror. It was as though I'd looked someplace where no human being ought to look. . . . I put my hand over my eyes—and suddenly, as though obeying some mysterious command, I began to review my entire existence. . . .

My childhood flashed before me as both noisy and quiet, frolicsome and benign, with its transient joys and swift sorrows; then my youth arose as dim, strange, and prideful, with all its mistakes and false starts, its disorganized exertions and uneasy idleness. . . . The comrades who'd shared my early aspirations came to mind . . . then a few bright memories gleamed like lightning bolts at night . . . then shadows began to grow and bear down upon me . . . it got darker and darker all around me. The monotonous years ran by ever more emptily and silently—and dejection weighed down my heart like a stone.

I sat without stirring and stared, stared with effort and amazement, as though I were seeing my whole life before me, as though scales had fallen from my eyes. "Oh, what have I done?" my lips involuntarily murmured in a bitter whisper. "Oh, life, life, where, how have you gone by without a trace? How can you have slipped through my clenched fingers? Did you deceive me, or didn't I know how to make use of your gifts? Is that possible? Is this morsel, this scant handful of dust and ashes, all that's left of you? Is this cold, stagnant, needless entity—is it I, the same 'I' as before? How can this be? My soul was athirst for such perfect happiness; it rejected everything small, everything inadequate, with such scorn; it kept on waiting. Soon happiness would burst upon it in a torrent—and hasn't even one drop moistened its parched lips? Oh, my golden strings that once quivered so delicately, so sweetly— I never heard your music, it seems. . . . You'd only just begun to vibrate when you were broken. Or maybe happiness, the unmitigated happiness of my entire life, passed nearby, smiled a radiant smile at me—and I failed to recognize its divine countenance. Or did it actually visit me and sit at my bedside, but I forgot it, like a dream? Like a dream," I repeated disconsolately.

Elusive images roamed through my soul, awakening something between sorrow and bewilderment. . . . "You dear, familiar, long-lost faces thronging around me in this lifeless solitude," I thought, "why are you so profoundly, sadly silent? From what abyss have you arisen? How should I interpret your enigmatic gazes? Are you greeting me, or bidding me farewell? Oh, is it possible that there's no hope, no turning back? Why are these large, belated tears trickling from my eyes? Oh, my heart, to what end, why are you still grieving? Try to forget, if you want peace, try to reconcile yourself to a final parting, to the bitter words 'goodbye' and 'forever.' Don't look behind you, don't reminisce, don't strive to reach a place where it's light, where youth laughs, where hope is decked with the flowers of spring, where dovelike delight soars on azure wings, where love glows with ecstatic tears like dew in the sunrise. Don't look where bliss and faith and strength abide—that isn't the place for us!"

"Here's your water," I heard Egor's melodious voice ring out behind me. "Drink it with God's blessing."

I shuddered involuntarily. The sound of live speech startled me and sent a joyful tremor through my entire being. It was as though I'd fallen into some dark, unknown depths, where everything around me was hushed and nothing was audible except the soft, persistent moan of some eternal grief. . . . I felt faint, I couldn't struggle . . . then suddenly a friendly voice floated down to me and some mighty hand drew me up into the light of day with a single heave. I looked around, and caught sight of the serene, honest face of my guide with inexpressible pleasure. He was standing in front of me casually and gracefully, holding out a wet flask full of a clear liquid, wearing his habitual smile. . . . I stood up.

"Let's go. Lead the way," I said eagerly.

We set off and wandered around for a long while, until evening. As soon as the noonday heat "burned out," it became cold and dark in the forest so quickly that one had no desire to remain within it.

"Go away, restless mortals," it seemed to whisper sullenly from behind each pine tree. We left that spot, but we couldn't find Kondrat right away. We shouted, we called to him, but he didn't answer. All of a sudden, in the profound stillness, we distinctly heard him crying out from a nearby ravine. . . . The wind, which had suddenly sprung up and just as suddenly subsided again, had prevented him from hearing our calls. Traces of its onslaught were visible only in the trees that stood some distance away: many of their leaves had been turned upside down and remained that way, which gave a mottled look to the motionless foliage. We got into the cart and rode home. I sat swaying to and fro, slowly inhaling the damp, somewhat biting air. All my recent memories and regrets were drowned in the single sensation of drowsiness and fatigue, in the single desire to return to the shelter of a warm house as soon as possible, to have a cup of tea with thick cream, to nestle into the soft, loose hay, and to sleep, sleep, sleep. . . .

The Second Day

The three of us set off again the next morning, heading for the "Charred Wood." Ten years earlier, several thousand acres of Polesje had burned down, and they still hadn't grown back again; young firs and pines were shooting up in a few places, but for the most part the ground was covered with nothing but moss and ashes. All sorts of berries grow in massive profusion in this Charred Wood, which is calculated to be about twelve versts from Sviatoe, and grouse, which eagerly consume strawberries and blueberries, congregate there.

We were riding along in silence when Kondrat suddenly raised his head.

"Ah!" he exclaimed. "Why, that's Efrem standing over there. Greetings, Aleksandrych," he added, raising his voice and waving his cap.

A short peasant wearing a black shirt belted with a cord came out from behind a tree and approached the cart.

"Well, have they let you go?" asked Kondrat.

"How could they not?" replied the peasant, grinning. "You won't catch them holding onto the likes of me."

"And Petr Filippych didn't mind?"

"That Filippov? Oh, sure, he didn't mind."

"You don't say! Why, Aleksandrych, I thought . . . well, friend, thought I, now the goose has to lie down in the frying pan!"

"On account of Petr Filippov, eh? You must be joking! We've seen plenty like him. He tries to pass for a wolf and then slinks off like a dog. Going hunting, master, eh?" the peasant abruptly inquired, quickly turning his squinty little eyes toward me and immediately turning them away again.

"Yes."

"Whereabouts, more or less?"

"We're going to the Charred Wood," said Kondrat.

"You're going to the Charred Wood? Don't get caught in the fire."

"What?"

"I've seen a lot of woodcocks," the peasant went on, seeming to laugh the whole time and failing to answer Kondrat. "But you'll never get there. It's about twenty versts as the crow flies. Why, even Egor here—there's no doubt he's as much at home in the forest as in his own yard—but even he won't make his way there. Greetings, Egor, you honest child of God!" he shouted suddenly.

"Greetings, Efrem," Egor replied slowly.

I looked at this Efrem with curiosity. I hadn't seen such a strange face for a long time. He had a long, sharp nose, thick lips, and a scanty beard. His little blue eyes danced impishly. He stood in a casual pose, his hands on his hips, without removing his cap.

"Going home for a quick visit, eh?" Kondrat asked him.

"Go on! For a visit! It's not the weather for that right now, friend. It's the time for me to move around. It's all open wide, friend, yes it is. You can lie on the stove all winter and not have to move an inch. When I was in town, the clerk said, 'Let us alone, Leksandrych,' says he. 'You just get out of the district. We'll give you a passport, a first-class one. . . .' But then I'd feel sorry for you Sviatoe folks. You'd never get another thief like me."

Kondrat laughed.

"You're a joker, uncle, a real joker," he declared, and shook the reins. The horses started up.

"Whoa," said Efrem. The horses stopped.

Kondrat didn't like this joke.

"That's enough of your nonsense, Aleksandrych," he remarked in a low voice. "Don't you see we're with a gentleman? You watch out, or he'll get angry."

"Hey there, you seagull! What's he got to be angry about? He's a kind master. You see, he'll give me some vodka. Hey, master, give a poor scoundrel a little swallow! Won't I gulp it down!" he added, raising his shoulders up to his ears and grinding his teeth.

I couldn't help smiling, gave him a copper coin, and told Kondrat to go ahead.

"Much obliged, your honor," Efrem shouted after us in formal fashion. "And you, Kondrat, in the future you'll know whose manners to study. A faint heart always fails, but a bold one always triumphs. When you come back, drop by my place—do you hear? There'll be drinking going on for three days at home, there'll be some necks broken. My wife's a devil of a woman. Our house sits on the side of a hill.... Hey, magpie, have a good time until your tail gets pinched." And with a piercing whistle, Efrem plunged into the bushes.

"What sort of person is he?" I asked Kondrat, who was sitting in front and kept shaking his head, as though debating with himself.

"That fellow?" Kondrat responded, and he looked down. "That fellow?" he repeated.

"Yes. Is he from your village?"

"Yes, he's from Sviatoe. He's such a.... You won't find anyone like him if you search for a hundred versts in any direction. What a thief and a swindler—my God! Another man's property simply catches his eye, so to speak. You could bury something underground and you couldn't hide it from him—and as for money, you could be sitting on it and he'd get it out from under you without your noticing it."

"How bold he is!"

"Bold? Yes, he isn't afraid of anyone. But just look at him—his physiognomy makes it plain that he's a rogue. You can tell by his nose." (Kondrat frequently went on trips with gentlemen and had spent time in the provincial capital, so he liked to show off upon occasion.) "There's absolutely nothing to be done with him. How many times has he been taken to town to be put in prison? But it's simply not worthwhile. They start to tie him up and he says: 'Come on, why don't you fasten this leg? Fasten that one a little tighter, too. I'll sleep a bit in the meantime, and I'll get home before your guards do.' And you look around, and sure enough, he's back again, yes, he's back again, by God! Well, even though all of us locals know the forest, having gotten familiar with it in childhood, we're no match for him. Last summer he came straight from Altukhin to Sviatoe at night, when no one had ever been known to do that on foot—it's over forty versts. And he steals honey, too. He's better than anyone at doing that—and the bees don't sting him. There isn't a hive he hasn't plundered."

"I assume he doesn't spare the wild bees, either?"

"Well, no—why make a false charge against him? That sin's never been observed in him. A wild bees' hive is something sacred for us. An ordinary hive's enclosed by fences and is guarded. If you get any honey, you're in luck. But a wild bee is God's creature and its hive isn't guarded. Only a bear can touch it."

"That's why it's a bear," remarked Egor.

"Is Efrem married?"

"Of course. He also has a son. And he'll be a thief too, that son! He completely takes after his father. Efrem's training him even now. The other day Efrem took a pot with some old coins in it that he'd stolen somewhere, no doubt, and went and buried it in a clearing in the forest. Then he went home and sent his son to the clearing. 'Until you find that pot,' says Efrem, 'I won't give you anything to eat or let you come back home.' His son spent the whole day in the forest, and spent the night there, too, but he found the pot. Yes, he's a wise man, that Efrem. When he's at home, he's quite courteous. He treats everyone well—you can eat and drink as much as you want, and there'll be dancing and all sorts of festivities at his place. And when he comes to one of our meetings—we have parish meetings in our village, you know—well, no one makes more sense than he does. He'll come up from behind you, he'll listen, say a word as if it were chopped off, then leave again. And a weighty word it'll be, too. But when he's loose in the forest—well, that means trouble! We have to watch out for mischief, although, I must say, he doesn't touch his own people unless he's in a tight spot. If he meets anyone from Sviatoe, he'll shout, 'Go around me, friend,' from a long way away. 'The forest spirit's gotten into me. I'll kill you!' It's too bad!"

"What are all of you concerned about? A whole district can't even handle one man?"

"Well, that's just how it is."

"Is he a sorcerer, then?"

"Who knows? Just a few days ago, he crept over to a nearby deacon's one night to get some honey, and the deacon himself was guarding the hive. Well, the deacon caught him and gave him a good beating in the dark. When he'd finished, Efrem says to him:

'But do you know who it is you've been beating?' When the deacon recognized Efrem by his voice, he was amazed. 'Well, friend,' says Efrem, 'you won't get off so easily for this.' The deacon collapsed at his feet. 'Take what you want,' says he. 'No,' says Efrem, 'I'll take something from you in my own time, any way I like.' What do you think of that? Since that day, the deacon acts as though he'd been scalded. He wanders around like a ghost. 'He's wrung all the heart out of me,' says he. 'It was an awfully powerful curse the robber placed on me, to be sure.' That's what happened to the deacon."

"This deacon must be a fool," I observed.

"A fool? Well, but what do you make of this? Once an order was issued to seize this fellow, Efrem. We had a district policeman then who was a clever fellow. And so about ten men went into the forest to catch Efrem. They look around, and he's coming to meet them. . . . One of them shouts, 'Here he is, here he is, grab him, tie him up!' But Efrem slips into the forest and cuts himself a branch two fingers' thick, like this, then he leaps out into the road again, looking quite wild, quite frightening, and gives orders like a general at a military inspection: 'On your knees!' And all of them virtually fall down. 'Who here shouted, "Grab him, tie him up!"?' says he. 'You, Serega?' That fellow simply jumps up and runs away. . . . And Efrem goes after him, swinging the branch at his heels. . . . He lashed at him for nearly a verst. Afterward, he kept expressing regret. 'Ah,' he'd say, 'it's annoying—I didn't keep him out of the confessional.' For it was just before St. Philip's Day. Well, they replaced the policeman right after that, but it all would have ended the same way."

"But why did everyone submit to him?"

"Why? Well, there's something. . . ."

"He's intimidated all of you, and now he does what he wants with you."

"Intimidated, yes. . . . He'd intimidate anyone you can name. And he's extremely resourceful, by God! I came across him in the forest once. A heavy rain was falling, and I wanted to go back. . . . But he looked at me and beckoned to me with his hand, like this. 'Come here,' says he, 'don't be afraid, Kondrat. Let me show you how to live in the forest and keep dry in the rain.' I went up to him, and he sat down under a fir tree and made a fire out of damp twigs. The smoke gathered in the fir tree and kept the rain from dripping through. I was astonished. And I'll tell you what he thought up another time." (Kondrat laughed.) "He really did do a funny thing. They'd been threshing oats in the threshing barn, and they hadn't finished—they hadn't had time to rake up the last heap of oats. Well, they'd put two watchmen—who weren't the bravest sort, either—beside it for the night. Well, they were sitting there gossiping, and Efrem stuffs his shirtsleeves full of straw, ties up the wrists, and pulls the shirt over his head. And so he sneaks up to the threshing barn in that shape, then pops out around a corner and gives them a glimpse of his horns. One of the men says to the other: 'Did you see that?' 'Yes,' says the other, then he up and shrieks all of a sudden . . . and nothing more could be heard except the gates outside creaking. Efrem shoveled the oats into a bag and dragged it home. He told the story afterward himself. He put them to shame, those men . . . he really did!"

Kondrat laughed again. Even Egor smiled. "So the gates outside creaked and that was all?" he asked.

"That's all there was," Kondrat affirmed. "They were simply gone in a flash."

We all fell silent again. Suddenly Kondrat shivered and sat up straight.

"Eh, merciful heavens!" he exclaimed. "That must be a fire!"

"Where, where?" we asked.

"Over there, see, up ahead, where we're going. . . . That *is* a fire! Efrem, that Efrem—why, he foretold it! If it's his doing, that accursed soul. . . ."

I glanced in the direction Kondrat was pointing. Two or three miles ahead of us, there really was a thick column of dark-blue smoke rising slowly from the ground behind a green strip of low fir saplings, gradually twisting and coiling into a cap-shaped cloud. To the right and left of it, other smaller, whiter clouds were visible.

A flushed, perspiring peasant wearing nothing but a long shirt, his tousled hair hanging down on either side of his frightened face, galloped straight toward us and only brought his hastily bridled horse to a stop with difficulty.

"Friends," he began breathlessly, "you haven't seen the foresters, have you?"

"No, we haven't. What is it? Is the forest on fire?"

"Yes. We've got to get the inhabitants out or else, if it makes it to Trosnoe. . . ."

The peasant pumped his elbows and pounded his heels on the horse's sides. . . . It galloped off.

Kondrat likewise urged on his pair of horses. We went straight toward the smoke, which was spreading wider and wider; it suddenly turned black in places and floated aloft. The nearer we came to it, the more indistinct its outlines grew. Soon the whole sky became clouded over, a strong smell of something burning filled the air, and the first pale-red tongues of flame flickered here and there between the trees, quivering strangely and ominously in the sunshine.

"Well, thank God," Kondrat remarked, "it seems to be an above-ground fire."

"What's that?"

"An above-ground fire? One that runs above the ground. An underground fire, now, is much more difficult to deal with. What can you do when the earth's on fire two feet deep? There's only one hope—digging ditches—and do you suppose that's easy? But an above-ground fire's nothing. It just scorches the grass and burns off the dry leaves! The forest should be all the better for it. Still, merciful heavens, see how it's flaring up."

We proceeded almost to the edge of the fire. I got out and walked toward it, which was neither dangerous nor difficult. The fire was running through the thinly wooded pine forest against the wind; it moved in an uneven line, or, to put it more accurately, in a thick, jagged wall of curved flames. The smoke was being carried away by the wind. Kondrat had been right: it really was an above-ground fire that merely scorched the grass and passed by without finishing its work, leaving a black, smoking, yet not even smoldering trail behind it. Occasionally, it's true, when the fire reached a hole filled with dry wood and twigs, it suddenly rose up in long, tremulous flames with a certain distinctive, somewhat malevolent roar, but it quickly subsided again and ran along as it had before, slightly hissing and crackling. I even noticed several oak bushes with dry, dangling leaves that were surrounded and yet untouched by the fire except where their bases were mildly singed. I must confess that I couldn't understand why the dry leaves hadn't caught on fire. Kondrat explained to me that this was because the fire was an above-ground one, "which is to say, not angry." "But it's still a fire," I protested. "An above-ground fire," Kondrat reiterated. However, above-ground though it was, the fire nonetheless produced its effects: hares raced back and forth in some disorder, needlessly running into the range of the fire; birds flew down into the smoke, then circled in confusion; the horses looked around and neighed;

the forest itself seemingly groaned—and one grew uncomfortable from the heat unexpectedly beating against one's face. . . .

"What's there to look at?" Egor suddenly inquired from behind me. "Let's go."

"But where should we go?" asked Kondrat.

"Go to the left, across the dry bog. We'll get through."

We turned to the left and did get through, although it was difficult at times for both the horses and the cart.

We wandered around the Charred Wood the whole day. In the evening—the sunset hadn't begun to redden the sky, but the long, motionless shadows of the trees were already stretched across the ground, and one could feel the chill that spreads through the grass before the dew falls—I lay down by the roadside near the cart, to which Kondrat was placidly harnessing the horses after they'd been fed. I recalled my cheerless musings of the previous day. Everything around me was as quiet as it had been the evening before, but there was no forest to stifle and oppress the spirit. The pure, gentle, fading light of the setting sun shone on the dry moss, on the lilac-colored grass, on the finely ground dust in the road, on the slender stems and clean little leaves of the young birch trees. Everything was at rest, immersed in soothing coolness; nothing was asleep yet, but everything was ready for the restorative slumber of evening and night. Everything was seemingly saying to each human being: "Be at peace, brother of ours. Breathe easily, and don't grieve at the sleep that awaits you."

I raised my head and saw one of those large flies with an emerald head, a long body, and four transparent wings—which the coquettish French call "maidens," whereas our artless people have named them "bucket yokes"—sitting at the very end of a delicate twig. For a long while, for more than an hour, I didn't take my eyes off it. Soaked with sunshine through and through, it didn't stir, merely turning its head from side to side occasionally and shifting its elevated wings . . . that was all. Looking at it, I suddenly felt as though I understood existence in nature, as though I understood its clear, unmistakable significance, although it was still mysterious to many people. Tempered, gradual animation, the methodical restraint of sensations and energies, the equilibrium of sickness and health in each creature—this is nature's essence, its immutable law, this is what it's based on and what it adheres to. Everything that upsets this elemental balance—whether by going too high or too low doesn't matter—nature casts off as worthless.

Many insects die as soon as they know the joys of love, which destroy life's equilibrium. A sick animal plunges into a thicket and dies alone there; it seems to feel it no longer has the right to see the sun that shines on everyone, or to breathe the open air—it doesn't have the right to live. And the individual who has fared badly on earth, whether due to his own faults or the faults of others, at least ought to know how to remain silent.

"Well, Egor!" Kondrat suddenly shouted. He'd already gotten settled on the box of the cart and was fidgeting with the reins. "Come and sit down. Why have you turned so thoughtful? Still thinking about that cow?"

"About that cow? What cow?" I repeated, and glanced at Egor. As calm and dignified as ever, he certainly did seem thoughtful, gazing off into the distance toward the fields, which were already beginning to grow dark.

"Don't you know?" replied Kondrat. "His last cow died last night. He has bad luck. What can you do?..."

Egor sat down on the box without speaking, and we set off. "This man knows how to live without complaint," I thought.

Letter to A. N. Apukhtin.[1]

Village of Spasskoe.
September 29, 1858.

What a gloomy letter you wrote me, dear Alexei Nikolaevich! I sympathize with you very much because, as you correctly observed, I myself ran along the same path. But I have less sympathy for your melancholy; that melancholy is the inevitable companion of youth, which exerts itself so greatly precisely because it's in no condition to master its own wealth. That's in the nature of things; but to give in to that melancholy too much is harmful, and the voice of a forty-year-old person may be helpful in this situation.

Why are you so depressed? Is it because you don't know whether you have talent? Give it time to mature; and even if it turns out not to be there, is it really essential for a person to have precisely a *poetic* talent in order to live and function? The surrounding *milieu* weighs upon you? But, in the first place, it seems to me that you dwell on the surface of phenomena, and in the second place, if you're depressed and in despair now, in 1858, what would you have done if you'd been eighteen years old in 1838, when everything ahead was so dark—and has remained that way?

There's neither time nor reason for you to grieve now; you're faced with a great obligation to yourself: you must make *yourself*, make a person out of yourself—and as for what will become of you, where your life will lead you—you should leave that to your nature. You'll be justified before your own conscience. Think less about your personality and about your sufferings and joys; look at your personality as a form that needs to be filled with good, sensible content; work, study, sow seeds—they'll grow up in their time and place. Remember that many people like you all over the face of Russia are laboring and striving; you're not alone—what more do you need? Why despair and sit idly? If others do the same thing, what will be the result? You have a moral obligation to your comrades (many of whom you don't know) not to sit idly.

As regards the two poems that you sent me, they could just as easily be the youthful works of a genuine poet as youthful ones of a skillful dilettante. As of yet, they have no physiognomy, and without it, there can be no poetry—especially lyric poetry. But don't worry about that, or be distressed by it. Allow me to offer

1. Alexei Nikolaevich Apukhtin (1840-93), one of the more popular Russian poets of the late nineteenth century.

myself as an example: my physiognomy made itself felt when I was just under thirty—but, unfortunately, I didn't start writing at thirty!

And so, *coraggio*, Santo Padre! *Coraggio* Signore Alexis! Work steadily, calmly, without impatience: any land gives forth only that fruit of which it is capable. Continue to write poetry—who knows? Perhaps your calling is to be a poet—but don't publish it, and don't succumb to the *torpor of melancholy*: it's onanism, and just as harmful as the physical kind.

I don't know whether you'll be pleased by this letter—but it's dictated by my sincere concern for you. I'll be in Petersburg around the 10th of November, and I hope to see you often in the winter. Until then, be well. I clasp your hand cordially and remain

Your devoted
Iv. Turgenev.

A Nest of Gentry

I

A bright spring day was fading into evening. High overhead in the clear sky, small pink clouds were barely moving, seeming almost to be sinking into its azure depths. It was 1842. In a handsome house on one of the outlying streets in the provincial town of O——, two women were sitting at an open window—one was about fifty, the other was an elderly lady of seventy.

The former was named Maria Dmitrievna Kalitina. Her husband, a shrewd, decisive man with a stubborn, bilious temperament, had been dead for ten years. He'd been a provincial public prosecutor, noted in his day as a successful businessman. He'd received a good elementary education and had attended the university, but, having been born into impoverished circumstances, had recognized early on in life the necessity of making his own way in the world and earning money. Maria Dmitrievna had married for love. He was reasonably attractive, he was intelligent, and he could be very agreeable when he chose to be. Maria Dmitrievna Pestova—that was her maiden name—had been orphaned in childhood. She'd spent several years at a boarding school in Moscow and, after leaving school, had lived on the family estate of Pokrovskoe, about fifty versts from O——, with her aunt and an older brother. This brother had moved to Petersburg to work shortly thereafter and had sent back a meager allowance for his aunt and sister until his sudden death cut short his career. Maria Dmitrievna had inherited Pokrovskoe, but she hadn't lived there for long. Two years after her marriage to Kalitin, who'd managed to win her heart within a few days, Pokrovskoe had been exchanged for another estate, which yielded a much larger income but was utterly unattractive and had no manor house. At the same time, Kalitin had purchased a house in the town of O——, where he and his wife had settled permanently. A large garden surrounded the house, one side of which faced the open fields beyond the town. "And so," declared Kalitin, who greatly disliked the peace and quiet of rural life, "we won't need to drag ourselves off to the countryside."

In her heart, Maria Dmitrievna had regretted more than once the loss of her pretty Pokrovskoe, with its babbling brook, its wide meadows, and its green groves, but she'd never opposed her husband in any way, having had the deepest respect for his wisdom and knowledge of the world. When he'd died after fifteen years of marriage, leaving her with a son and two daughters, Maria Dmitrievna had grown so accustomed to her house and to life in town that she herself had no inclination to leave O——.

In her youth, Maria Dmitrievna had enjoyed the reputation of being an adorable blonde, and at fifty, her features hadn't lost all their charm, although they'd become somewhat puffy and less delicate. She was more sentimental than kindhearted, and even at a mature age, she'd retained the manners of a boarding-school girl. She was self-indulgent, easily annoyed, and even cried when any of her habits were disrupted. She was quite sweet and amiable, however, when all her wishes were carried out and no one opposed her. Her house was among the most pleasant in town. She possessed a considerable fortune, amassed not so much from her inheritance as from her husband's savings. Her two daughters lived with her; her son was being educated at one of the best government schools in Petersburg.

The elderly lady sitting at the window with Maria Dmitrievna was her father's sister, the same aunt with whom she'd once spent several solitary years at Pokrovskoe. Her name was Marfa Timofeevna Pestova. She had a reputation for eccentricity, since she was a woman of independent character who told everyone the truth straight to their faces and behaved just as if she had a fortune at her disposal, even in the most constrained financial circumstances. She couldn't stand Kalitin, and as soon as her niece had married him, she'd moved to her own small estate, where she'd lived in a smoky peasant's hut for ten whole years. Maria Dmitrievna was somewhat intimidated by her. A small, sharp-nosed woman with dark hair and eyes that had remained keen even in old age, Marfa

Timofeevna walked briskly, held herself absolutely erect, and spoke quickly and clearly in a sharp, ringing voice. She always wore a white cap and white blouse.

"What's the matter with you?" she asked Maria Dmitrievna suddenly. "What are you sighing about, for heaven's sake?"

"Nothing much," replied the latter. "What exquisite clouds!"

"Do you feel sorry for them or something?"

Maria Dmitrievna didn't respond.

"Why hasn't Gedeonovskii come?" Marfa Timofeevna remarked, knitting rapidly (she was making a large wool scarf). "He'd have sighed right along with you—or at least he'd have had something scandalous to tell you."

"You're always so hard on him! Sergei Petrovich is a respectable man."

"Respectable!" the elderly woman echoed scornfully.

"And he was so devoted to my poor husband!" Maria Dmitrievna observed. "He can't recall him without emotion to this very day."

"And no wonder! It was your husband who picked him up out of the mud," Marfa Timofeevna muttered, knitting more rapidly than ever.

"He looks so mild-mannered," she began again, "with all his gray hair, but no sooner does he open his mouth than out comes some lie or a bit of slander. And to think that he achieved the rank of councillor! In fact, though, he's merely a village priest's son."

"Who has no faults, Aunt? That's his weakness, certainly. Sergei Petrovich never received much of an education, of course, and he doesn't speak French, but still, say what you like, he's a nice man."

"Yes, he's always ready to kiss your hand. He doesn't speak French—that's no great loss. I'm not overly fluent in the French 'dialect' myself. It'd be better if he couldn't speak any language at all—then he wouldn't tell lies. But here he is—speak of the devil," added Marfa Timofeevna, glancing down the street. "Here comes your nice man now, striding along briskly. What a lanky creature he is—just like a stork!"

Maria Dmitrievna began to arrange her curls. Marfa Timofeevna looked at her amusedly.

"What's that—not a gray hair, surely? You must speak to your maid Palashka. What can she be thinking of?"

"Really, Aunt, you're always so . . . ," Maria Dmitrievna murmured irritably, drumming her fingertips on the arm of her chair.

"Sergei Petrovich Gedeonovskii!" announced a rosy-cheeked young servant in a shrill, piping voice, as he appeared in the doorway.

II

A tall man entered wearing a trim coat, rather short trousers, gray suede gloves, and two neckties—a black one on the outside and a white one underneath it. Everything about him had an air of decorum and propriety, from his well-shaped face and smoothly brushed hair to his low-heeled, soft boots. He bowed first to the lady of the house, then to Marfa Timofeevna, and, slowly removing his gloves, he advanced to take Maria Dmitrievna's hand in his own. After respectfully kissing it twice, he unhurriedly sat down in an armchair and, rubbing the very tips of his fingers together, asked with a smile:

"Is Elizaveta Mikhailovna quite well?"

"Yes," replied Maria Dmitrievna, "she's in the garden."

"And Elena Mikhailovna?"

"Lenochka's in the garden, too. Is there any news?"

"There is indeed, there is indeed!" responded the visitor, slowly blinking his eyes and pursing his lips. "Hmm!... Yes, if you please, there's one item of news, and very surprising news at that. Lavretskii—Fedor Ivanych—has arrived."

"Fedia?" cried Marfa Timofeevna. "Are you sure you're not making this up, my good man?"

"No, indeed, I saw him myself."

"Well, that still doesn't prove anything."

"He looks much healthier," Gedeonovskii continued, pretending not to have heard Marfa Timofeevna's last remark. "His shoulders are broader, and his cheeks have color in them."

"He looks healthier," said Maria Dmitrievna, dwelling on each syllable. "I'd have thought there wasn't much to make him look healthier."

"Yes, indeed," rejoined Gedeonovskii. "Any other man in his position would have hesitated to appear in society."

"Why so?" interjected Marfa Timofeevna. "What nonsense! The man has returned to his native country—where else would you have expected him to go? And has he been to blame, I'd like to know?"

"The husband is always to blame, madam, I venture to assure you, when a wife behaves badly."

"You say that, my good sir, because you've never been married yourself."

Gedeonovskii smiled stiffly.

"If I may be so inquisitive," he asked after a short pause, "for whom is that pretty scarf intended?"

Marfa Timofeevna cast a quick look at him.

"It's intended," she replied, "for a man who doesn't spread scandal, or use guile, or tell lies, if such a man can be found on earth. I know Fedia very well—he was only to blame in being too good to his wife. To be sure, he married for love, and no good ever comes of those types of marriages," the elderly woman added, with a sidelong glance at Maria Dmitrievna as she stood up. "And now, my good sir, you may sink your teeth into anyone you like— even me, if you choose. I'm leaving, so I won't hinder you." And Marfa Timofeevna walked away.

"She's always like that," Maria Dmitrievna declared, watching her aunt depart.

"We have to remember your aunt's age. . . . There's nothing else we can do!" Gedeonovskii responded. "She referred to someone who's guileless. But who isn't guileful nowadays? It's the age we live in. One of my acquaintances, a highly respected man of no low status, I assure you, used to say that nowadays even hens can't pick up a grain of corn without guile—they're always trying to approach it from one side. But when I look at you, dear lady, your nature is so truly angelic—let me kiss your little snow-white hand!"

Maria Dmitrievna held out her plump hand to him with a faint smile, her little finger held apart from the rest, and he pressed his lips to it. Then she drew her chair closer to his and, bending toward him slightly, asked in an undertone:

"So you saw him? Was he really—all right? Quite healthy and cheerful?"

"Yes, he was cheerful," Gedeonovskii replied in a whisper.

"You haven't heard where his wife is now?"

"She was in Paris recently. Now she's moved to some place in Italy, I've heard."

"It's terrible, really—Fedia's position. I wonder how he can endure it. Everyone occasionally has problems, naturally, but he, one may say, has become the talk of all Europe."

Gedeonovskii sighed.

"Yes, indeed, yes, indeed. They do say, you know, that she associates with artists and musicians and, as the saying goes, with all sorts of strange beasts. She's completely lost any sense of shame. . . ."

"I'm deeply, deeply grieved," Maria Dmitrievna observed, "because of our relationship. You know, Sergei Petrovich, that he's my cousin several times removed."

"Of course, of course. Don't I know about everything that concerns your family, for pity's sake?"

"Will he come to see us—what do you think?"

"One would suppose so, although they say that he intends to go to his house in the country."

Maria Dmitrievna raised her eyes skyward.

"Ah, Sergei Petrovich, Sergei Petrovich, how often I think about how carefully we women have to behave!"

"There are women and there are women, Maria Dmitrievna. There are certain ones, unfortunately . . . of questionable character . . . and of a certain age, too, who weren't brought up to have the proper principles." (Sergei Petrovich drew a blue checkered handkerchief out of his pocket and began to unfold it.) "Such women exist, of course." (Sergei Petrovich applied a corner of his handkerchief first to one eye and then to the other.) "But, generally speaking, if one takes into consideration, I mean. . . . The dust in town is really extraordinary today," he concluded.

"*Maman, maman,*" cried a pretty little girl of eleven, running into the room, "Vladimir Nikolaich is coming to see us on horseback!"

Maria Dmitrievna stood up. Sergei Petrovich stood up as well and bowed. "Our humble respects to Elena Mikhailovna," he remarked, and turning aside toward a corner out of good manners, he began to blow his long, straight nose.

"He has a wonderful horse!" continued the little girl. "He was just at the gate, and he told Liza and me he'd dismount at the steps."

The sound of hoofbeats became audible, and a graceful young man riding a beautiful bay horse appeared in the street. He came to a halt at the open window.

III

"How do you do, Maria Dmitrievna?" the young man cried in a pleasant, melodious voice. "How do you like my new purchase?"

Maria Dmitrievna went up to the window.

"How do you do, *Woldemar?* Ah, what a handsome horse! From whom did you buy it?"

"I bought it from an army contractor. . . . He made me pay for it, too—the thief!"

"What's its name?"

"Orlando. . . . But that's a stupid name. I want to change it. . . . *Eh bien, eh bien, mon garçon.* . . . What a restless beast!"

The horse snorted, pawed the ground, and shook its foam-flecked head.

"Lenochka, you can pat his nose—don't be afraid."

The little girl stretched her hand out the window, but Orlando suddenly reared and jumped to one side. Maintaining perfect self-possession, the rider gave the horse a cut with his whip across its neck, and keeping a tight grip with his legs, forced it to stand still again at the window in spite of its opposition.

"*Prenez garde, prenez garde,*" Maria Dmitrievna kept repeating.

"Go on and pet him, Lenochka," urged the young man. "I won't let him hurt you."

The little girl stretched out her hand again and timidly patted the horse's quivering nostrils as it continued to stir uneasily and champ at the bit.

"Bravo!" cried Maria Dmitrievna. "But now get down and come in."

The rider adroitly turned his horse around, touched it with his spur, and galloping down the street, shortly entered the yard. He ran into the drawing room a minute later through the door from the hallway, flourishing his whip; at the same moment, a tall, slender, dark-haired young woman of nineteen appeared in another doorway. This was Maria Dmitrievna's elder daughter, Liza.

IV

The name of the young man we've just introduced to the reader was Vladimir Nikolaich Panshin. He served on special commissions in Petersburg for the Ministry of the Interior. He'd come to the town of O—— to carry out some temporary government assignments, and was at the disposal of the regional governor, General Zonnenberg, to whom he happened to be distantly related. Panshin's father, a retired cavalry officer and a notorious gambler, had had gentle eyes, a mottled complexion, and a nervous tic near his mouth. He'd spent his entire life in aristocratic society, frequenting the English clubs in both Petersburg and Moscow, and had enjoyed a reputation as an attractive, somewhat unreliable, but very nice, good-natured fellow. In spite of his attractiveness, he'd almost always been on the brink of financial ruin, and the estate he'd left his only son was small and heavily encumbered. To make up for that, however, he'd exerted himself, in his own fashion, with respect to his son's education. Vladimir Nikolaich spoke French beautifully, English well, and German badly. This was as it should be: fashionable people would be ashamed to speak German well, but to utter an occasional—generally humorous—phrase in German is quite correct, *c'est même très chic*, as the Parisians of Petersburg put it.

By the time he was fifteen, Vladimir Nikolaich knew how to enter any drawing room without embarrassment, how to circulate around it gracefully, and how to leave it at the appropriate moment. Panshin's father had made numerous connections for his son. He'd never missed an opportunity, while shuffling the cards between two rubbers of bridge or playing a successful trump, to drop a hint about his Volodka to any important personage who was a devotee of cards. And during his stay at the university, which he left without receiving a particularly impressive degree, Vladimir Nikolaich for his part made the acquaintance of several notable young men and became a regular guest at the best houses. He was cordially welcomed everywhere: he was very good-looking, carefree, amusing, always in good health, and ready for anything. He was deferential when he had to be, insolent when he dared to be, excellent company, *un charmant garçon*. The promised land lay before him. Panshin had quickly grasped the secret of success in the world: he knew how to yield to its decrees with genuine respect; he knew how to treat trivial matters with semi-sarcastic seriousness, and to appear to regard everything serious as trivial; he danced to perfection; he dressed in the English style. In short order, he gained the reputation of being one of the nicest, most attractive young men in Petersburg.

In fact, Panshin was very attractive, no less so than his father; moreover, he was also very talented. He did everything well: he sang charmingly, sketched with spirit, wrote verses, and was a perfectly decent actor. He was only twenty-eight, and was already a *Kammerjunker* at a fairly high rank. Panshin had absolute confidence in himself, in his own intelligence, in his own perspicacity. He proceeded with light-hearted assurance, and everything went smoothly for him. He grew accustomed to being liked by everyone, young and old, and imagined that he understood people, especially women—he certainly did understand their ordinary weaknesses. As a man of artistic inclinations, he was sensitive to his own capacity for ardor, for getting somewhat carried away, for enthusiasm. Consequently, he permitted himself various irregularities: he went carousing, associated with certain people who didn't belong to good society, and generally conducted himself freely and easily. But at heart he was cold and calculating, and even during the most boisterous revelry, his sharp brown eyes were always on the alert, observing everything. This bold, independent young man could never forget himself and get completely carried away. To his credit, it must be said that he never boasted about his triumphs. He'd found his way to Maria Dmitrievna's house immediately upon arriving in O—— and quickly became thoroughly at home there. Maria Dmitrievna absolutely adored him.

Panshin exchanged courteous greetings with everyone in the room: he shook hands with Maria Dmitrievna and Lizaveta Mikhailovna, patted Gedeonovskii lightly on the shoulder, and, turning around on his heels, put his hand on Lenochka's head and kissed her on the forehead.

"Aren't you afraid to ride such a vicious horse?" Maria Dmitrievna asked him.

"I assure you that he's quite tame. But I'll tell you what I am afraid of—I'm afraid of playing cards with Sergei Petrovich. Yesterday he cleaned me out at the Belenitsyns'."

Gedeonovskii uttered a thin, sympathetic little laugh—he was anxious to get into the good graces of this brilliant young official from Petersburg, the governor's favorite. In conversations with Maria Dmitrievna, he often alluded to Panshin's remarkable abilities. Indeed, he argued, "How could anyone help admiring him? He's a young man advancing into the highest spheres, he's an exemplary official, and he isn't the slightest bit proud." In fact, Panshin was considered a capable official even in Petersburg; he accomplished a great deal of work; he spoke about it jocularly, as befits a man of the world who doesn't attach any special importance to his labors, but he always carried out orders. Superiors like such subordinates; he himself had no doubt that, if he chose, he could become a minister in the course of time.

"You're kind enough to say that I cleaned you out," Gedeonovskii replied, "but who was it that won twelve rubles and more off me last week . . . ?"

"You're a malicious person," Panshin interrupted him, with a genial but slightly contemptuous casualness, and paying no further attention to him, he went up to Liza.

"I can't get the overture to *Oberon* here," he began. "Mrs. Belenitsyn was bragging when she said she had every piece of classical music. In fact, she doesn't have anything except polkas and waltzes, but I've already written to Moscow and you'll receive the overture within a week. By the way," he continued, "I wrote the music to a new song yesterday, and the words, too. Would you like me to sing it? I don't know whether it came out well. Mrs. Belenitsyn thought it was very pretty, but her words don't mean a thing. I'd like to know what you think of it. Perhaps, though, it'd be better to wait until later on."

"Why later on?" interjected Maria Dmitrievna, "Why not now?"

"I obey," Panshin replied with a certain vibrant, sweet smile that often suddenly came and went on his face. He pushed a chair up to the piano with his knee, sat down, and, striking a few chords, began to sing the following song, articulating the words clearly:

> The moon floats high above the earth
> Amid pale clouds;
> Its magic light moves like the waves of the sea
> From on high.

> The sea of my soul has found
> Its moon in you,
> It's moved to joy and sorrow
> Only by you.

> My soul is full of love's cruel anguish,
> The anguish of vain longing;
> I am sad, but you know no suffering,
> Like that moon.

Panshin sung the second stanza with particular force and expressivity; the sound of waves could be heard in the stormy accompaniment. After the words "vain longing," he sighed softly, lowered his eyes, and let his voice gradually die away, *morendo*. When he'd finished, Liza praised the melody, Maria Dmitrievna cried, "Charming!" and Gedeonovskii went so far as to exclaim, "Ravishing poetry, and equally ravishing music!" Lenochka gazed at the singer with childish reverence. In short, everyone present was delighted with the young dilettante's composition—except for an elderly man who'd just come in. He was standing at the door leading into the drawing room from the hallway and, to judge by the expression on his downcast face and the shrug of his shoulders, he was by no means pleased with Panshin's song, pretty as it was. After waiting a moment and flicking the dust off his boots with a coarse handkerchief, this man suddenly narrowed his eyes, grimly compressed his lips, bent his already stooped body further forward, and slowly entered the drawing room.

"Ah! Khristofor Fedorych, how are you?" Panshin exclaimed before any of the others could speak, quickly jumping up from his seat. "I didn't suspect that you were here. Nothing could have induced me to sing my song in front of you. I know that you don't care for light music."

"I did not hear it," the newcomer declared in very bad Russian, and after exchanging greetings with everyone, he paused awkwardly in the middle of the room.

"Are you here, Monsieur Lemm, to give Liza her music lesson?" asked Maria Dmitrievna.

"No, not Lizaveta Mikhailovna, Elena Mikhailovna."

"Oh! Very well. Lenochka, go upstairs with Mr. Lemm."

The elderly man started to follow the little girl, but Panshin stopped him.

"Don't leave after the lesson, Khristofor Fedorych," he said. "Lizaveta Mikhailovna and I are going to play a Beethoven sonata as a duet."

Lemm just muttered something to himself, while Panshin continued in German, mispronouncing the words: "Lizaveta Mikhailovna showed me the religious cantata you dedicated to her—it's a beautiful piece! Please don't suppose that I can't appreciate serious music—quite the contrary. It's tedious at times, but it's very elevating, for all that."

The elderly man blushed deeply and, casting a sidelong look at Liza, hurriedly left the room.

Maria Dmitrievna asked Panshin to sing his song again, but he protested that he didn't want to torture the ears of the knowledgeable German, and suggested to Liza that they try the Beethoven sonata. Then Maria Dmitrievna heaved a sigh and in turn suggested a walk in the garden to Gedeonovskii. "I'd like to chat a bit more," she said, "and consult with you about our poor Fedia." Gedeonovskii bowed with a smirk and, using two fingers, picked up his hat, on whose brim his gloves had been tidily laid, then went off with Maria Dmitrievna. Panshin and Liza remained alone in the room. She got out the sonata and opened it; they both seated themselves at the piano in silence. The faint sounds of scales being played by Lenochka's uncertain fingers could be heard overhead.

V

Christopher Theodore Gottlieb Lemm was born in 1786 in the town of Chemnitz, in Saxony. His parents had been poor musicians: his father had played the French horn, his mother the harp. He himself was practicing on three different instruments by the time he was five. At the age of eight, he'd become an orphan, and at ten he'd begun to earn his living by performing. He'd led an itinerant life for many years, playing everywhere: restaurants, fairs, peasants' weddings, and balls. Eventually he'd joined an orchestra and, having been steadily promoted in it, he'd reached the position of conductor. He was a rather weak performer, but he understood music thoroughly. At twenty-eight, he'd emigrated to Russia at the invitation of a wealthy nobleman who didn't care for music himself but kept an orchestra to impress other people. Lemm had lived at his home for about seven years in the capacity of orchestra leader and had left there without anything to show for it. The nobleman had lost his fortune and had intended to give Lemm a promissory note, but had ultimately refused to give him even that—in short, he hadn't paid Lemm a thing. Lemm was advised to go home, but was unwilling to return from Russia—great Russia, that gold mine for artists—in poverty. He'd decided to remain and try his luck.

The poor German had been trying his luck for twenty years: he'd lived in various gentlemen's houses in Moscow as well as provincial towns, had suffered and withstood a great deal, had faced privation—had generally struggled like a fish on dry land. The thought of returning to his own country had never left him; among all the hardships he'd endured, it was this thought alone that had sustained him. But fate hadn't seen fit to grant him this alpha and omega of happiness. At fifty, in poor health and prematurely aged, he'd drifted to the town of O—— and had remained there for good, having abandoned once and for all any hope of leaving Russia, which he detested, earning a meager livelihood somehow by giving music lessons.

Lemm's appearance didn't work to his advantage: he was short and stooped, with crooked shoulders, a concave stomach, large, flat feet, and bluish-white nails on the gnarled, bony fingers of his sinewy, red hands. He had a wrinkled face, sunken cheeks, and compressed lips, which he was incessantly contorting and biting; this, together with his habitual taciturnity, created an almost sinister impression. His gray hair hung in tufts over his low forehead; his small, motionless eyes glowed dimly, like smoldering embers. He moved laboriously, swinging his ungainly body forward at every step. Some of his movements recalled the clumsy actions of an owl in a cage when it senses that it's being looked at but itself can hardly see out of its large, yellow eyes as it blinks fearfully and yet drowsily.

Pitiless, prolonged sorrow had laid its indelible stamp on the poor musician, distorting and deforming his body, which was by no means attractive to begin with. But anyone who was able to get beyond first impressions would have discerned something decent, honest, and out of the ordinary in this half-shattered creature. A devoted admirer of Bach and Handel, a master of his art, gifted with a lively mind and the boldness of imagination bestowed solely upon the German race, in time—who knows?—Lemm might have joined the ranks of the great composers of his fatherland, had his life been different—but he was born under an unlucky star! He'd written a good deal of music in his day, but he hadn't been destined to see even one of his compositions performed. He didn't know how to go about things in the right way, how to ingratiate himself in the right places, how to assert himself at the right moment. A long, long while earlier, his one friend and admirer, who was also German and also poor, had published two of Lemm's sonatas at his own expense, but the entire edition had remained on the shelves of the music shops; they'd subsequently disappeared without a trace, as though they'd been thrown into a river at night.

Lemm finally renounced all his hopes, and the years did their work as well: his mind grew as calloused and stiff as his fingers. He lived alone in a little cottage located not far from the Kalitins' house, attended by an elderly cook he'd found in an almshouse (he'd never married). He took long walks; he read the Bible, plus the Protestant version of the Psalms, and Shakespeare in Schlegel's translation. He hadn't composed anything for a long time, but apparently Liza, his best pupil, had been able to inspire him: he'd written a cantata for her, the one to which Panshin had referred. He'd borrowed the words for this cantata from his collection of psalms, to which he'd added a few verses of his own. It was supposed to be sung by two choruses—a chorus of the happy and a chorus of the unhappy. The two came into harmony at the end in order to sing together: "Merciful God, have pity on us sinners, and deliver us from all evil thoughts and earthly hopes." On the title page, an inscription had been extremely carefully printed and even illuminated: "Only the righteous are just. A religious cantata. Composed and dedicated to Miss Elizaveta Kalitina, his dear pupil, by her teacher, C. T. G. Lemm." The words "Only the righteous are just" and "Elizaveta Kalitina" had been encircled by rays of light. Below them was written: "For you alone, *für Sie allein.*" That's why Lemm had blushed and glanced at Liza reproachfully— he'd been deeply wounded when Panshin had made reference to the cantata in front of him.

VI

Panshin, who was going to play the bass part, struck the first chords of the sonata loudly and decisively, but Liza didn't begin her part. He stopped and looked at her. Liza's eyes were fastened directly on him, expressing displeasure. There was no smile on her lips; her whole face looked serious, almost sad.

"What's the matter?" he asked.

"Why didn't you keep your promise?" she responded. "I showed you Khristofor Fedorych's cantata on the explicit condition that you wouldn't say anything to him about it."

"I beg your pardon, Lizaveta Mikhailovna—the words just slipped out."

"You've hurt his feelings, and mine as well. Now he won't trust even me."

"How could I help it, Lizaveta Mikhailovna? Ever since I was a little boy, I couldn't see a German without wanting to tease him."

"How can you say that, Vladimir Nikolaich? This German is a poor, lonely, ruined man. Don't you have any sympathy for him? How can you want to tease him?"

Panshin was slightly taken aback.

"You're right, Lizaveta Mikhailovna," he declared. "It's my eternal thoughtlessness that's to blame. No, don't contradict me— I know myself too well. So much damage has been done to me because of this thoughtlessness. As a result of it, I'm considered an egotist."

Panshin paused. Whatever subject he began a conversation with, he usually ended up talking about himself, changing the subject so easily, so smoothly, so sincerely, that it seemed unintentional.

"In your household, for instance," he continued, "your mother certainly wishes me well—she's so kind. You . . . well, I don't know your opinion of me. But it's clear that your aunt simply can't stand me. I must have offended her, too, by some thoughtless, stupid remark. You know that I'm not a favorite of hers, am I?"

"No," Liza admitted with some reluctance, "she doesn't like you."

Panshin swiftly ran his fingers over the keys, and a barely perceptible smile glided across his lips.

"Well, and what about you?" he inquired. "Do you also think I'm an egotist?"

"I don't know you very well," Liza replied, "but I don't consider you an egotist. On the contrary, I can't help feeling grateful to you."

"I know, I know what you mean to say," Panshin interrupted, and ran his fingers over the keys again. "You're grateful to me for the music and books I bring you, for the wretched sketches with which I adorn your album, and so forth. I might do all that—and be an egotist all the same. I venture to think that you don't find me boring, and don't consider me a bad person, but you still suspect that I—what's the saying?—I'd sacrifice a friend or my father for the sake of a witticism."

"You're careless and forgetful, like all men of the world," observed Liza, "that's all."

Panshin frowned a bit.

"I tell you what," he said, "let's not talk about me any more—let's play our sonata. There's just one thing I must beg of you," he added, smoothing out the pages of the book on the music stand. "Think whatever you like about me, even call me an egotist—so be it! But don't call me a man of the world. I find that term intolerable. . . . *Anch'io sono pittore.* I'm also an artist, albeit a bad one, and I'll prove *that*—I mean, that I'm a bad artist—right now. Let's begin."

"All right, let's begin," said Liza.

The first adagio was fairly successful, although Panshin hit more than one wrong note. He played his own compositions, and anything else he'd practiced thoroughly, very nicely, but he sight-read badly. Thus the second part of the sonata—a rather quick allegro—

broke down completely. At the twentieth bar, Panshin, who was two bars behind, gave up and pushed back his chair, laughing.

"No!" he cried. "I can't play today. It's a good thing Lemm didn't hear us—he would have fainted."

Liza stood up, shut the piano, and turned to face Panshin.

"What are we going to do now?" she asked.

"That's just like you, that question! You can't ever sit with your hands in your lap. Well, if you like, let's sketch, since it's not quite dark yet. Perhaps the other muse, the muse of painting—what's her name? I've forgotten—will be better disposed toward me. Where's your album? I remember that the landscape I was drawing there isn't finished."

Liza went into another room to fetch the album, and Panshin, once he was alone, pulled a cambric handkerchief out of his pocket, buffed his nails with it, and looked at his hands seemingly critically. He had beautiful white hands and wore a spiral gold ring on the second finger of his left one. Liza came back; Panshin sat down by the window and opened the album.

"Ah!" he exclaimed. "I see that you've begun to copy my landscape—very well, too. This is excellent! Except right here—give me a pencil—the shadows aren't strong enough. Look."

And Panshin added a few long strokes with a flourish. He always drew precisely the same landscape: large, unkempt trees stood in the foreground, a stretch of meadow lay in the background, and jagged mountains appeared on the horizon. Liza watched him work over his shoulder.

"In drawing, just as in life as a whole," Panshin remarked, tilting his head first to the right and then to the left, "agility and daring—these are the great things."

At that moment, Lemm entered the room and then started to leave again after bowing stiffly, but Panshin, throwing aside the album and drawing pencils, placed himself in Lemm's way.

"Where are you going, dear Khristofor Fedorych? Aren't you going to stay and have some tea with us?"

"I am going home," Lemm responded sullenly. "I have a headache."

"Oh, what nonsense! Do stay. We'll argue about Shakespeare."

"I have a headache," repeated the elderly man.

"We started to work on the Beethoven sonata without you," Panshin continued, embracing him affectionately around the waist and smiling brightly, "but we couldn't get anywhere at all. Just think, I couldn't play two notes in a row correctly."

"You would have been better off singing your song again," Lemm retorted, moving Panshin's hands away and walking out. Liza ran after him. She overtook him on the stairs.

"Khristofor Fedorych, please," she said to him in German, accompanying him across the short green grass of the yard to the gate, "I owe you an apology—forgive me."

Lemm didn't respond.

"I showed Vladimir Nikolaich your cantata. I was sure he'd appreciate it—and he did like it very much, truly."

Lemm stopped.

"It is nothing," he said in Russian, and then added in his own language, "but he cannot understand anything. How can you fail to see that? He is a dilettante—and that is all there is to it!"

"You're being unfair to him," Liza replied. "He understands everything, and he can do almost anything himself."

"Yes, anything second-rate, cheap, and slipshod. That is always admired, and he is admired, and he is glad that this is the case—so much the better. I am not angry. That cantata and I—we are a pair of old fools. I am a little ashamed, but it is nothing."

"Forgive me, Khristofor Fedorych," Liza said again.

"It is nothing," he repeated once more in Russian. "You are a good girl . . . but here is someone who is coming to see you. Goodbye. You are a very good girl."

And Lemm walked with quickened steps toward the gate, through which some gentleman he didn't recognize had just entered wearing a gray coat and a wide straw hat. Bowing politely to him (Lemm always greeted every new personage in the town of O——, whereas he always turned away from his acquaintances on the street—that was the rule he'd made for himself), Lemm passed him and disappeared beyond the fence. The stranger watched him go in surprise, and then, after looking at Liza intently, walked right up to her.

VII

"You don't recognize me," he said, taking off his hat, "but I recognize you, in spite of its being eight years since I last saw you. You were a child then. I'm Lavretskii. Is your mother at home? May I see her?"

"Mama will be glad to see you," replied Liza. "She'd heard about your arrival."

"Let me see, your name is Elizaveta, I think?" Lavretskii remarked as he went up the stairs.

"Yes."

"I remember you very well—even then you had a face one doesn't forget. I used to bring you candy in those days."

Liza blushed and thought how strange this man was. Lavretskii paused in the hallway for a moment. Liza went into the drawing room, where Panshin's voice and laugh were audible—he'd been repeating some town gossip to Maria Dmitrievna and Gedeonovskii, who'd come in from the garden by this time, and he himself was laughing aloud at the story he was telling. Upon hearing Lavretskii's name, Maria Dmitrievna became quite agitated, turned pale, and went out to greet him.

"How do you do, how do you do, my dear *cousin?*" she cried in a plaintive, almost tearful voice. "I'm so glad to see you!"

"How are you, my dear cousin?" Lavretskii replied with a friendly clasp of her outstretched hand. "How has Providence been treating you?"

"Sit down, sit down, my dear Fedor Ivanych. Ah, I'm so glad to see you! But let me present my daughter Liza to you."

"I've already introduced myself to Lizaveta Mikhailovna," Lavretskii interjected.

"Monsieur Panshin . . . Sergei Petrovich Gedeonovskii. . . . Please sit down. When I look at you, I can hardly believe my eyes. How are you?"

"As you see, I'm flourishing. And you are, too, cousin—knock on wood!—you haven't grown any thinner these past eight years."

"To think how long it's been since we last saw one another!" Maria Dmitrievna observed dreamily. "Where have you just come from? Where did you leave . . . that is, I meant to say," she put in hastily, "I meant to say, are you going to be with us for a long time?"

"I've just come from Berlin," Lavretskii responded, "and I'm going to the countryside tomorrow—probably for a long while."

"You're going to live at Lavriki, I presume?"

"No, not at Lavriki. I have a little place that's twenty-five versts or so from here. I'm going there."

"Is that the little estate you inherited from Glafira Petrovna?"

"Yes."

"For heaven's sake, Fedor Ivanych! You have such a magnificent house at Lavriki."

Lavretskii frowned slightly.

"Yes . . . but there's a small lodge on this little estate, and I don't need anything more for the time being. That place is the most convenient one for me right now."

Maria Dmitrievna was thrown into such an agitated state once more that she became quite stiff, her arms hanging limply by her sides. Panshin came to her assistance by entering into conversation with Lavretskii. Maria Dmitrievna gradually regained her composure, leaned back in her armchair, and occasionally put in a word. But she looked at her guest with such sympathy, sighed so significantly, and shook her head so mournfully the entire time that the latter finally lost his patience and asked her rather sharply whether she was unwell.

"Thank God, no," replied Maria Dmitrievna. "Why do you ask?"

"Oh, it seemed to me you weren't quite yourself."

Maria Dmitrievna assumed a dignified, somewhat offended expression. "If that's how it is," she thought, "it's absolutely all the same to me. I see, my dear man, that it's all like water off a duck's back to you. Anyone else would have wasted away with sorrow, but you've gotten fat on it." Maria Dmitrievna didn't mince words in her private thoughts; she expressed herself with more discretion aloud.

Lavretskii certainly didn't look like a victim of fate. His ruddy, typical Russian face, with its large white forehead, fairly thick nose, and wide, straight lips, exuded the vitality, the vigorous, elemental energy of the steppes. He had a well-formed body, and his fair, curly hair stood up on his head like a boy's. It was only in his blue, protruding, rather immobile eyes that one could detect an expression somewhere between melancholy and exhaustion, and his voice had somewhat too measured a cadence.

Meanwhile, Panshin continued to keep up the conversation. He turned it to a discussion of the profits to be earned in sugar-making, a subject on which he'd recently read two French pamphlets. He undertook to expound upon their contents with modest composure, without mentioning a single word as to the source of his information, however.

"Why, it's Fedia!" the voice of Marfa Timofeevna suddenly rang out from the next room through the half-opened door, "Fedia himself!" And the elderly woman rushed into the room. Lavretskii didn't even manage to get up from his chair before she'd embraced him. "Let me have a look at you," she said, holding him back at arm's length. "Ah! What a handsome fellow you are! You've gotten a little older, but haven't changed a bit for the worse, in fact! But why are you kissing my hands? Kiss my face, if you aren't put off by my wrinkled cheeks. You never asked about me—whether your aunt was alive—I swear, and you were in my arms the minute you were born, you rascal! Well, that doesn't matter to you, I suppose. Why should you remember me? It was still a good idea of yours to come here. Only tell me, my good woman," she added, turning to Maria Dmitrievna, "have you offered him something to eat?"

"I don't want anything," Lavretskii hastened to declare.

"Come, now, at least you have to have some tea, my dear. Lord almighty! He's arrived from I don't know where, and they don't even give him a cup of tea! Liza, run and stir them up in the kitchen—and hurry. I remember, he was terribly greedy when he was a little boy, and I'll bet he likes to eat even now."

"My respects, Marfa Timofeevna," Panshin remarked, approaching the excited elderly woman from one side with a low bow.

"Pardon me, sir," replied Marfa Timofeevna, "for not noticing you in my delight. You've grown up to look like your mother, the poor darling," she went on, turning back to Lavretskii, "but your nose was always your father's, and it's remained your father's. Well, are you going to be with us for long?"

"I'm leaving tomorrow, Aunt."

"To go where?"

"Home to Vasilevskoe."

"Tomorrow?"

"Yes, tomorrow."

"Well, if it must be tomorrow, it must be tomorrow. God bless you—you know best. Only make sure you come and say goodbye." The elderly woman patted his cheek. "I didn't think I'd be here to see you. Not that I've made up my mind to die yet—I'll last another ten years, I expect. All we Pestovs live long—your late grandfather used to say that we had two lives. But, you see, there was no telling how much longer you were going to waste your time abroad. Well, you're a sturdy boy, a very sturdy boy. Can you lift twenty pounds with one hand the way you used to, eh? Your late father was foolish in some ways, if I may say so, but he did well to hire that man from Switzerland to bring you up. Do you

remember how you used to have boxing matches with him?—
gymnastics, wasn't that what they called it? But there, why am I
babbling away like this? I've merely been preventing Mr. Pan*shin*
(she never pronounced his name the correct way, *Pan*shin) from
holding forth. Besides, we'd better go and have some tea. Yes, let's
go out onto the terrace, my boy, and drink it there. We have
wonderful cream—not like what you get in your Londons and
Parises. Come along, come along, and you, Fediusha, give me your
arm. And oh, what a thick arm it is! There's no danger of my
stumbling while I'm with you!"

Everyone stood up and went out onto the terrace except Gedeonovskii, who departed quietly. During the whole of Lavretskii's
conversation with Maria Dmitrievna, Panshin, and Marfa Timofeevna, he'd sat in one corner, blinking attentively, gaping with
childish curiosity. Now he was in a hurry to spread the news of
the recent arrival all over town.

At eleven o'clock in the evening of the same day, here's what
was happening in Mrs. Kalitin's house: downstairs, seizing a favorable moment, Vladimir Nikolaich was saying goodbye to Liza
at the drawing-room door and declaring to her as he held her hand:
"You know who it is that attracts me here, you know why I constantly come to your house. What need is there for words when
everything is clear the way it is?" Liza didn't respond, gazing at
the ground without smiling, her eyebrows slightly raised and her
cheeks flushed, but she didn't withdraw her hand. Meanwhile,
upstairs in Marfa Timofeevna's room, by the light of a little lamp
hanging before some tarnished, ancient icons, Lavretskii was sitting
in a low chair, his elbows on his knees and his face buried in his
hands. The elderly woman, who was standing in front of him,
silently stroked his hair now and then. He spent more than an
hour with her after saying goodbye to his hostess. He barely said
anything to his kind old friend, and she didn't ask him any
questions. . . . Indeed, what reason was there to speak, what was
there to ask? She understood everything without doing so, and
sympathized with everything that filled his heart.

VIII

Fedor Ivanych Lavretskii (we must beg the reader's permission to
break off the thread of our story for a while) came from an ancient
noble family. The founder of the Lavretskii line had emigrated

from Prussia during the reign of Vasilii the Blind and had been granted two hundred chetverts of land in Bezhetsk. Many of his descendants had filled government positions, serving under princes and other eminent individuals in outlying districts, but none of them had risen above the rank of an inspector of the imperial table or had acquired any significant fortune.

Fedor Ivanych's great-grandfather, Andrei, a cruel, daring, intelligent, and crafty man, was the richest and most remarkable of all the Lavretskiis. To this very day, stories linger on about his tyranny, his savage temper, his reckless extravagance, and his insatiable greed. He was quite tall and stout, went beardless, and had a swarthy complexion. He spoke in a husky voice and often seemed to be half-asleep, but the more quietly he spoke, the more the people around him trembled. He'd managed to find a wife who was an appropriate mate for him. She was a gypsy by birth with bulging eyes, a hawk nose, and a round, sallow face. Hot-tempered and vindictive, she never deferred in any way to her husband, although he'd nearly killed her. She didn't live long after his death, although she'd constantly quarreled with him.

Andrei's son, Petr, Fedor's grandfather, didn't take after his father. He was a typical landowner of the steppes: somewhat unpredictable, loud, slow, coarse, but not ill-natured, very hospitable, and fond of hunting with dogs. He was over thirty when his father left him an estate in excellent condition, with two thousand serfs on it, but he quickly spent his wealth, partially mortgaged the estate, and spoiled the serfs. All sorts of disreputable people—both acquainted and unacquainted with him—came crawling into his spacious, warm, unkempt halls from all sides, like cockroaches. These people ate anything that was given to them, but always had their fill, drank until they got drunk, and carried off whatever they could, praising and blessing their genial host. And their host, when he was in a bad mood, blessed his guests in turn—as a pack of sponging parasites—but he got bored without them.

Petr Andreich's wife was a meek creature; he'd selected her from a neighboring family, in accordance with his father's orders. Her name was Anna Pavlovna. She never interfered in anything, cordially welcomed all guests, and readily paid visits herself, even though wearing a powdered wig, she repeatedly declared, would be the death of her. "They'd put a fox's tail on your head," she used to say in her old age, "comb all the hair up over it, smear it with grease and dust it with flour, then fasten it on with iron pins. You couldn't wash the powder off afterward. But going on visits without a powdered wig was utterly impossible—people would be offended. Ah, it was torture!" She liked being driven in carriages with fast-trotting horses, and was ready to play cards from morning until night, always keeping the record of how much money she'd won or lost hidden under her hand when her husband came near the card table. She'd put her whole dowry, her entire fortune, completely at his disposal. She bore him two children: a son, Ivan, Fedor's father, and a daughter, Glafira.

Ivan wasn't brought up at home, living instead with a rich old maiden aunt, Princess Kubenskaia. She'd chosen him to be her heir (otherwise his father wouldn't have let him go). She dressed Ivan up like a doll, hired all kinds of teachers for him, and put him under the charge of a tutor, a Frenchman who'd formerly been an abbé and a pupil of Jean-Jacques Rousseau, a Monsieur Courtin de Vaucelles, a subtle, wily intriguer—the very *fine fleur*, as she put it, of emigration. She ended up marrying this "*fine fleur*" at the age of almost seventy. Soon afterward, covered with rouge and redolent of perfume *à la Richelieu*, surrounded by African boys, delicate-legged greyhounds, and shrieking parrots, she died on a curved, silken divan built during the era of Louis XV, holding an enameled snuffbox of Petitot's workmanship in her hand. She died having been deserted by her husband: the ingratiating Monsieur Courtin had preferred to betake himself to Paris with her money.

Ivan had just turned twenty when this unexpected blow (we mean the princess's marriage, not her death) fell upon him. He didn't want to stay in his aunt's house, where he found himself suddenly transformed from a wealthy heir into a poor relation; the Petersburg social circles in which he'd grown up were now closed to him; he was disinclined to enter government service in the lower ranks, with nothing but hard work and obscurity ahead of him (this was at the very beginning of Emperor Alexander's reign). He was thus reluctantly obliged to return to the countryside, to his father's house. How squalid, poor, and wretched his parental domicile seemed to him! The stagnation and sordidness of country life offended him at every turn; he was consumed by boredom. Moreover, everyone in the house except his mother looked upon him with unfriendly eyes. His father didn't like his citified manners, his dress coats, his frilly shirts, his books, his flute, his fastidious habits, in all of which his father detected—not incorrectly—a disgust for his surroundings. Petr Andreich constantly criticized and complained about his son.

"Nothing here suits him," his father often noted. "He fusses at the table and doesn't eat; he can't bear the odor and stuffiness of the room; the sight of people getting drunk upsets him; one doesn't dare beat anyone in front of him, either; he doesn't want to enter government service—he's unhealthy, you see. Shame on him, the big baby! And it's all because he's got a head full of Voltaire." The old man had a particular dislike for Voltaire, as well as the "fanatic" Diderot, although he hadn't read a word of their works—reading wasn't his strong suit.

Petr Andreich wasn't mistaken: his son's head actually was full of both Diderot and Voltaire, and not only of them, but of Rousseau as well, and Helvetius, and many other writers of the same ilk—but they were only in his head. The retired abbé and encyclopedist who'd been Ivan Petrovich's tutor had taken great delight in pouring all the wisdom of the eighteenth century into his pupil, who was simply brimming over with it as a result. Thus it was all there inside him, but it didn't mix with his blood, or penetrate into his soul, or shape itself into any firm convictions.... But then, could one expect to find convictions in a young man living fifty years ago, when we haven't succeeded in attaining them today?

The guests who frequented his father's house were likewise oppressed by Ivan Petrovich's presence. He loathed them, and they were afraid of him. And he didn't get along at all with his sister Glafira, who was twelve years older than he. This Glafira was a strange creature: she was ugly, hunchbacked, and terribly thin, with large, stern eyes and narrow, compressed lips. She took after her grandmother the gypsy, Andrei's wife, in her face, her voice, and her swift, angular movements. Stubborn and enamored of power, she wouldn't even consider marriage. Ivan Petrovich's return didn't accord with her plans: as long as Princess Kubenskaia had kept him with her, Glafira had hoped to receive at least half of her father's estate—she took after her grandmother in her avarice, too. Besides, Glafira envied her brother: he was so well-educated, and spoke such good French in a Parisian accent, whereas she could barely pronounce the words *bonjour* or *comment vous portez-vous*. To be sure, her parents didn't know any French either, but that was no comfort to her.

Ivan Petrovich didn't know what to do with himself in his misery and boredom. He spent only a year in the countryside, but that year seemed like ten to him. The sole consolation he could find was in talking to his mother, and he'd sit for hours on end in her low-pitched room, listening to the kindly woman's simple-hearted prattle and eating sweets. It so happened that among Anna Pavlovna's maids was one very pretty girl named Malania, a shy, intelligent creature who had clear, gentle eyes and refined features. She attracted him at first sight, and he fell in love with her—he fell in love with her timid movements, her bashful replies, her quiet voice, and her quiet smile; she seemed more appealing to him every day. She, in turn, became devoted to Ivan Petrovich with all the strength of her soul, as only a Russian girl can be devoted—and she gave herself to him. Nothing can be kept secret for long in a large household on a country estate. Everyone soon found out about the love affair between the young master and Malania; the gossip finally even reached the ears of Petr Andreich himself. Under other circumstances, he probably wouldn't have paid any attention to a matter of so little import, but he'd held a grudge against his son for so long that he was delighted at the opportunity to humiliate the Petersburg wit and dandy. An uproarious tumult ensued: Malania was locked in the pantry, Ivan Petrovich was summoned to his father's presence. Anna Pavlovna also appeared in the midst of all the commotion. She tried to pacify her husband, but Petr Andreich wouldn't listen to a word. He pounced on his son like a hawk, reproaching him with immorality, atheism, and hypocrisy. He took the opportunity to vent all the wrath against Princess Kubenskaia that had been boiling up inside him as well, and lavished abusive epithets on his son.

At first, Ivan Petrovich kept silent and restrained himself, but when his father decided to threaten him with some shameful punishment, he couldn't endure it any longer. "Ah," he thought, "the fanatic Diderot has been brought into the act again, so I'll make good use of him and astonish you all." Then and there, in a calm, even voice, although inwardly quaking in every limb, Ivan Petrovich declared to his father that it was unnecessary to reproach him with immorality, that, even though he didn't intend to justify it, he was ready to make amends for his behavior, the more willingly in that he considered himself superior to every kind of prejudice, and in fact—was ready to marry Malania. In uttering these words, Ivan Petrovich undoubtedly attained his goal: he so astonished Petr Andreich that the latter simply stood there, wide-eyed and dumbstruck, for a moment. But he instantaneously recovered, and, dressed just as he was, in a robe with a squirrel-fur border and slippers on his bare feet, he launched himself at Ivan Petrovich,

fists flying. The latter, as though by design, had arranged his hair
à la Titus that morning and had put on a new, blue English coat,
high boots with small tassels, and very tight, modish buckskin
trousers. Anna Pavlovna shrieked with all her might and covered
her face with her hands, while her son set off running through the
entire house, dashed out into the courtyard, rushed across the
kitchen garden and the grounds, flew into the road, and kept on
running without looking behind him, until he finally stopped hearing the heavy tramp of his father's footsteps and the labored panting
between his father's shouts. "Stop, you villain!" his father kept
exclaiming. "Stop, or I'll curse you!"

Ivan Petrovich took refuge with a neighbor, a small landowner.
Petr Andreich returned home worn out and wet with perspiration.
Without taking a breath, he announced that he was going to deprive
his son of his paternal blessing and inheritance, then gave orders
to burn all his son's foolish books and to send the girl Malania to
a distant village at once. Some kindhearted people found Ivan
Petrovich and informed him of all this. Humiliated and enraged,
he swore that he'd get revenge on his father. That same night, he
lay in wait for the peasant's cart in which Malania was being taken
away, seized her by force, galloped off with her to the nearest town,
and married her. He'd been supplied with money by the neighbor,
a good-natured retired sailor and confirmed drunkard who took
immense pleasure in every kind of—as he put it—romantic tale.
Ivan Petrovich wrote a polite but stingingly cold letter to Petr
Andreich the next day, and set off for the village where his second
cousin, Dmitrii Pestov, lived with his sister, who's already been
introduced to the reader: Marfa Timofeevna. Ivan related everything, declared his intention to go to Petersburg in hope of finding
work there, and begged them to give his wife a home, at least for
a while. At the word "wife" he shed tears, and despite his urban
upbringing and philosophy, he prostrated himself at his relatives'
feet in humble, supplicatory Russian fashion, even touching his
forehead to the floor. The Pestovs, who were kind, compassionate
people, readily agreed to his request. He stayed with them for
three weeks, secretly expecting a reply from his father; but no
reply came—and none would be forthcoming. Upon hearing of his
son's marriage, Petr Andreich took to his bed and forbade Ivan
Petrovich's name to be mentioned in his presence. But his wife,
without her husband's knowledge, borrowed five hundred rubles
from the rector and sent them to her son's wife, along with a small

icon. She was afraid to write a letter, but conveyed a message to Ivan Petrovich through a lean peasant who could walk sixty versts a day, saying that he shouldn't be overly discouraged, that, with God's grace, everything would work out and his father's wrath would be transformed into benevolence, that she, too, would have preferred a different daughter-in-law, but evidently it was God's will, and that she sent Malania Sergeevna her maternal blessing. The lean peasant received a ruble, asked permission to see the new young mistress, whose godfather he happened to be, kissed her hand, and ran away as fast as he could.

Meanwhile, Ivan Petrovich left for Petersburg with a light heart. An unknown future was awaiting him, poverty was potentially threatening him, but he'd escaped the country life he detested, and, above all, he hadn't betrayed his teachers—he'd actually put the doctrines of Rousseau, Diderot, and *la Déclaration des droits de l'homme* into practice. A sense of having done his duty, of triumphant pride, filled his soul. The separation from his wife didn't upset him much—he would have been more distressed by constantly having to be with her. That deed was done, and now he wanted to start doing other deeds. In Petersburg, contrary to his own expectations, he had some luck: Princess Kubenskaia, whom Monsieur Courtin had deserted by then but who was still alive, in order to make up to her nephew in some way for having wronged him, commended him to all her friends and presented him with five thousand rubles—almost all her remaining money—as well as a Lepikovskii watch with his monogram encircled by cupids. Less than three months later, he obtained a job at the Russian Embassy in London, and he set out across the sea on the first English vessel that sailed (steamships hadn't even been envisioned at that time).

A few months after that, he received a letter from Pestov. The kindly landowner congratulated Ivan Petrovich on the birth of a son, who'd been born in the village of Pokrovskoe on the twentieth of August 1807 and named Fedor, in honor of the holy martyr Fedor Stratilat. Malania Sergeevna had added only a few lines, due to her extreme weakness, but even these few lines were a surprise, for Ivan Petrovich hadn't known that Marfa Timofeevna was teaching his wife to read and write. Ivan Petrovich didn't abandon himself to any sweet surge of parental feeling for long: he was dancing attendance on some notorious Phryne or Laïs of the day (classical names were still in vogue then), the Peace of Tilsit had just been concluded, the whole world was chasing after pleasure

in a giddy whirl of dissipation, and he'd been captivated by the
dark eyes of some flirtatious beauty. He didn't have much money,
but he was lucky at cards, readily made acquaintances, and took
part in every social event. He was, so to speak, in the swim.

IX

The elder Lavretskii couldn't forgive his son for getting married
for a long time. If Ivan Petrovich had come to him six months
later with a penitent face and thrown himself at his feet, Petr
Andreich would most likely have pardoned him, after giving him
a fairly severe scolding and a tap with his cane by way of intim-
idation. But Ivan Petrovich went on living abroad and apparently
wasn't the least bit repentant.

"Silence! Don't you dare refer to him," Petr Andreich said to
his wife every time she tried to urge him to be merciful. "The
puppy, he ought to thank God that I haven't cursed him for all
time. My father would have killed him with his own hands, the
good-for-nothing, and he would have been right, too." Anna
Pavlovna could only cross herself in secret after such terrible
pronouncements.

As for Ivan Petrovich's wife, Petr Andreich couldn't even stand
to hear her name at first, and in response to a letter from Pestov
in which his daughter-in-law was mentioned, he went so far as to
send Pestov word that he knew nothing about any daughter-in-law,
and that it was forbidden by law to harbor runaway girls, a fact
of which he considered it his duty to remind Pestov. But he was
mollified later on when he learned about the birth of a grandson,
and secretly gave orders to inquire as to the health of the mother.
He also anonymously sent her a little money.

Fedia was less than a year old when Anna Pavlovna developed
a fatal illness. A few days before her death, when she could no
longer leave her bed, she informed her husband in the presence
of a priest, with timid tears in her swiftly-dimming eyes, that she
wanted to see her daughter-in-law in order to bid her farewell, and
wanted to give her grandchild her blessing. The heartbroken old
man calmed her down and immediately sent his own carriage to
fetch his daughter-in-law, referring to her formally as Malania Sergeevna for the first time. Malania came with her son and Marfa
Timofeevna, who wouldn't permit her to go alone under any circumstances, being unwilling to expose her to possible indignity.
Half dead with fright, Malania Sergeevna went into Petr Andreich's

room. A nurse followed her, carrying Fedia. Petr Andreich looked at her without speaking. She went up to take his hand; her trembling lips were barely able to touch it with a silent kiss. "Well, my fresh lady," he finally began, "how do you do? Let's go and see the mistress." He stood up and bent over Fedia. The baby smiled and stretched his little white hands out toward him. This changed the elderly man's mood. "Ah," he said, "poor little one, you were pleading on behalf of your father. I won't abandon you, little bird."

As soon as Malania Sergeevna entered Anna Pavlovna's bedroom, she fell to her knees near the door. Anna Pavlovna motioned to her to approach the bedside, embraced her, and blessed her son. Then, turning a face cruelly contorted by suffering toward her husband, she attempted to speak.

"I know, I know what you want to say," declared Petr Andreich. "Don't worry. She can stay with us, and I'll forgive Vanka for her sake."

Anna Pavlovna strained to grasp her husband's hand and pressed it to her lips. She breathed her last that very evening.

Petr Andreich kept his word. He informed his son that, in accordance with his mother's dying wish and for the sake of little Fedor, he was sending Ivan Petrovich his blessing and was allowing Malania Sergeevna to remain at his house. Two rooms on the ground floor were allotted to her; he presented her to his most honored guests, the one-eyed brigadier Skurekhin and his wife, and assigned her two maids plus a servant to run errands. Marfa Timofeevna said goodbye to her—she detested Glafira, having argued with her three times in the course of a single day.

The situation was painful and embarrassing for poor Malania at first, but she learned to bear it after a while, and gradually grew accustomed to her father-in-law. He also grew accustomed to her and actually became fond of her, although he hardly ever spoke to her and some sort of involuntary contempt was perceptible even in his gestures of affection toward her. Malania Sergeevna suffered the most at the hands of her sister-in-law. During her mother's lifetime, Glafira had gradually succeeded in getting the entire household under her control—everyone, from her father on down, submitted to her rule. Not a single lump of sugar was distributed without her permission; she'd rather have died than share her authority with another mistress—and a mistress like this! Her brother's marriage had incensed her even more than Petr Andreich. She decided to teach the upstart a lesson, and Malania Sergeevna became her slave from the very first hour. And, indeed, how could Malania have contended against the masterful, haughty Glafira, as submissive, constantly confused, frightened, and sickly as she was? Not a day went by without Glafira reminding her of her former social status and praising her for not forgetting her past. Malania Sergeevna could readily have reconciled herself to these reminders and praises, however painful they might have been—but Fedia was taken away from her, and that crushed her. On the pretext that she wasn't capable of overseeing his upbringing, she was barely allowed to see him at all. Glafira undertook that task: the child was put completely in her charge.

In her distress, Malania Sergeevna began to beseech Ivan Petrovich in her letters to return home soon. Petr Andreich wanted to see his son himself, but Ivan Petrovich did nothing except write back. He thanked his father for the kindness to his wife and for the money he'd sent, promised to return soon—and didn't come. Only the year 1812 finally brought him home from abroad. When they met again after six years' separation, the father embraced his son without making a single allusion to their former differences. It wasn't the time for that, then: all of Russia was rising up against its enemy, and both of them felt that they had Russian blood in their veins. Petr Andreich equipped a whole regiment of volunteers at his own expense. But the war came to an end; the danger passed. Ivan Petrovich began to get bored again, and again was drawn to distant parts, to the world in which he'd grown up, where he felt at home. Malania Sergeevna couldn't restrain him—she meant too little to him. Even her fondest hopes were dashed: her husband found it much more suitable to leave Fedia's education to Glafira.

Ivan Petrovich's poor wife couldn't bear this blow—she couldn't endure a second separation. After a few days, without a murmur, she quietly died. She'd never been able to oppose anything in her entire life, and she didn't struggle against her illness. When she could no longer speak, when the shadows of death already lay across her face, her features expressed bewildered resignation and steadfast, uncomplaining humility, as they always had. She gazed at Glafira with her customary mute submissiveness and, just the way Anna Pavlovna had kissed her husband's hand on her deathbed, Malania kissed Glafira's, entrusting her only son to her, to Glafira. Thus ended the earthly existence of this kindly, gentle creature, torn like a tree uprooted from its natural soil, God only knows why, and suddenly thrown down with its roots in the air. She wasted away and disappeared, leaving no trace, and no one mourned her. Malania Sergeevna's maids did miss her—and so did Petr Andreich. The old man felt the loss of her silent presence. "Forgive me. Farewell, my meek one!" he whispered as he said goodbye to her in church for the last time. He wept as he threw a handful of earth on her grave.

He didn't survive her for long, not more than five years. In the winter of 1819, he died peacefully in Moscow, where he'd moved with Glafira and his grandson, having left instructions that he should be buried beside Anna Pavlovna and "Malasha." Ivan Petrovich was entertaining himself in Paris at that time; he'd retired from government service shortly after 1815. When he learned of his father's death, he decided to return to Russia. It was necessary to make arrangements concerning the management of the estate. Moreover, Fedia had reached the age of twelve, according to Glafira's letter, and the time had come to begin his education in earnest.

X

Ivan Petrovich returned to Russia a confirmed Anglomaniac. His short-cropped hair, his starched shirt, his long pea-green overcoat with multiple collars, his sour facial expression, his somehow simultaneously intense and indifferent manner, his habit of speaking through his teeth, his abrupt, wooden laugh, his lack of a smile, his exclusively political or political-economic conversation, his passion for roast beef and port wine—everything about him radiated Great Britain, so to speak. But, amazingly, at the very time he'd been transformed into an Anglomaniac, Ivan Petrovich had also become a patriot. At least he called himself a patriot, although he didn't know Russia well, hadn't retained a single Russian habit, and expressed himself in Russian rather oddly: in ordinary conversation, his statements were awkward, verbose, and liberally sprinkled with Gallicisms. Whenever the discussion touched on important subjects, Ivan Petrovich promptly invoked such phrases as "engendering new experiments in self-discipline," "these do not conform to the essential nature of the circumstances," and so forth.

Ivan Petrovich brought back a few manuscripts relating to the administration and reform of government. He was highly displeased with everything he saw; the lack of any systematic organization particularly aroused his ire. Upon being reunited with his sister, he immediately announced to her that he was determined to introduce radical reforms, that henceforth everything having to do with him would be done according to a different system. Glafira Petrovna didn't reply to Ivan Petrovich—she merely ground her teeth and thought to herself, "Where can I go to escape?" After she returned to the countryside with her brother and nephew, however, her fears were quickly laid to rest. Some changes were made in the house, to be sure: the parasites and malingerers were summarily dismissed. Two old women among them particularly suffered—one was blind, another paralyzed—as well as a decrepit major from the era of Catherine the Great who, due to his truly abnormal appetite, had been fed on nothing but black bread and lentils. Orders were issued not to admit any of the previous guests; they were replaced by a distant neighbor, some blond, scrofulous baron, who was a very well-educated and very stupid man. New furniture was transported from Moscow; spittoons and bells and washstands were introduced; breakfast began to be served differently; imported wines replaced vodka and sweet syrups; the servants were given new uniforms; a motto was added to the family arms: *in recto virtus*.

In reality, though, Glafira's power was in no way diminished; the purchase and distribution of household supplies still depended on her. The Alsatian steward who'd been hired from abroad tried to combat her—and lost his job, despite the master's efforts to protect him. As for the management of the house and administration of the estate (Glafira Petrovna had assumed these duties as well), notwithstanding Ivan Petrovich's intention—voiced more than once—to breathe new life into this chaos, everything remained the way it had been before: rent was merely raised in a few places, the mistress was stricter, and the peasants were forbidden to speak directly to Ivan Petrovich. The patriot had already acquired a profound contempt for his fellow-countrymen. Ivan Petrovich's system was applied in full force only to Fedia. His education really did undergo a "radical reformation"; his father exclusively devoted himself to it.

XI

Until Ivan Petrovich's return from abroad, Fedia, as has already been noted, was in Glafira Petrovna's hands. He was almost eight years old when his mother died; he hadn't seen her every day, but he'd loved her passionately. The image of her—her pale, gentle face, her sorrowful gaze, her timid embrace—was forever imprinted in his memory. Still, he'd vaguely understood her position in the house, and had felt that a barrier existed between them, one she didn't have either the courage or the capacity to break down. He was shy around his father; Ivan Petrovich, for his part, never caressed him. His grandfather patted him on the head sometimes and gave him one hand to kiss, but considered him worthless and called him a little fool.

After Malania Sergeevna's death, his aunt finally got him totally under her control. Fedia was afraid of her: he was afraid of her bright, sharp eyes and harsh voice; he didn't dare utter a sound in her presence. Frequently, when he'd just shift a bit in his chair, she'd instantly hiss: "What are you doing? Sit still!" On Sundays, after church, he was allowed to play, that is, he was given a thick, mysterious book, the creation of a certain Maksimovich-Ambodik, entitled *Symbols and Emblems*. This book was a compilation of approximately a thousand often highly enigmatic pictures, and equally as many enigmatic interpretations of them, in five languages. Cupid, portrayed with a naked, very puffy body, played a leading role in the illustrations. One of them, under the heading "Saffron and the Rainbow," had the appended interpretation, "The influence of this is vast." Opposite another, entitled "A heron flying with a violet in its beak," stood the inscription, "They are all well known to you." "Cupid and a bear licking its fur" was labeled "Little by little." Fedia used to pore over these pictures; he knew them all down to the most minute details. Some of them, always the same ones, used to set him daydreaming, awakening his imagination; he had no other sources of amusement. When the time came to teach him foreign languages and music, for next to nothing Glafira Petrovna engaged an old maid, a Swedish woman with eyes like a rabbit's, who spoke French and German, making mistakes in every other word, played the piano after a fashion, and above all, salted cucumbers to perfection.

Fedia spent four long years in the company of this governess, his aunt, and an elderly maid, Vasilevna. He often sat in the corner with his *Emblems*—he'd sit there endlessly. The scent of geraniums would fill the low-ceilinged room, a solitary candle would burn dimly, a lone cricket would chirp monotonously, as though it were tired, a little clock on the wall would tick away steadily, a mouse would scratch stealthily and gnaw at the wallpaper, and the three old women, like the Fates, would swiftly and silently ply their knitting needles. The shadows would race after their hands, quivering strangely in the semi-darkness, and strange, semi-dark ideas would swarm in the child's brain.

No one would have called Fedia an interesting child: he was somewhat pale, fat, awkwardly built, and clumsy—a thorough peasant, as Glafira Petrovna would say. The pallor would soon have disappeared from his cheeks if he'd been allowed to go out in the fresh air more often. He was a fairly quick learner, although he was generally lazy. He never cried, but he was occasionally overcome by a fit of savage obstinacy—then no one could control him. Fedia didn't love any of the people around him.... Sad is the heart that hasn't loved in youth!

Ivan Petrovich found him in this condition, and, losing no time, he set to work to apply his system to Fedia.

"First and foremost, I want to make a man of him, *un homme*," he told Glafira Petrovna, "and not just a man, but a Spartan." Ivan Petrovich began to carry out his intentions by dressing his son in a Scottish kilt; the twelve-year-old boy had to walk around with bare knees and a feather stuck in his Scottish cap. The Swedish lady was replaced by a young Swiss tutor who was an expert in gymnastics. Music was discarded as a pursuit unworthy of a man. The natural sciences, international law, mathematics, carpentry (in accordance with Jean-Jacques Rousseau's precepts), and heraldry— to encourage chivalrous feelings—were what the future "man" was required to study. He was awakened at four o'clock in the morning, immediately splashed with cold water, and made to run around a high pole holding onto a cord; he was given just one meal a day consisting of a single course; he rode on horseback and shot with a crossbow; at every convenient opportunity, he was trained to exercise firmness of will, following his parent's example; every evening he had to inscribe an account of the day, along with his impressions of it, in a special book. Ivan Petrovich, for his part, wrote him instructions in French in which he referred to Fedia as *mon fils* and addressed him as *vous*. In Russian, Fedia addressed his father using the familiar form of "you," but he didn't dare sit down in his father's presence.

The "system" dazed the boy, confusing and stifling his intellect, but his health, by contrast, benefited from the new way of life. He came down with a fever at first, but recovered quickly and began to grow tall and strong. His father was proud of him and called him, in his strange jargon, "a child of nature, my creation." When

Fedia reached the age of sixteen, Ivan Petrovich decided that it was his fatherly duty to instill a contempt for the female sex in his son ahead of time. Hence the young Spartan, with shyness in his heart and the first signs of a beard on his lip, full of sap and vigor and youthful blood, nonetheless tried to seem indifferent, cold, and rude.

Meanwhile, time was passing. Ivan Petrovich spent the greater part of the year at Lavriki (that was the name of the principal estate he'd inherited from his ancestors). But he used to go to Moscow by himself in the winter; he stayed at an inn there, diligently visiting his club, making speeches, and articulating his plans in drawing rooms. He behaved more than ever like an Anglomaniac, grumbling and groaning about politics. But the year 1825 arrived, and brought much sorrow with it. Intimate friends and acquaintances of Ivan Petrovich underwent painful experiences. Ivan Petrovich hurriedly withdrew to the countryside and shut himself up in his house. Another year passed, and Ivan Petrovich suddenly became enfeebled and sickly, as his health began to deteriorate. He, the freethinker, began to go to church and have prayers said for him; he, the European, began to sit in steambaths, to have dinner at two o'clock and to go to bed at nine, dozing off to the chatter of the old steward; he, the man of political convictions, burned all his plans and all his correspondence, trembling before the governor and growing uneasy at the sight of the police captain; he, the man of iron will, whimpered and complained when he developed a sore or when they gave him a bowl of cold soup. Glafira Petrovna took control of everything in the house once more: the overseers, bailiffs, and ordinary peasants began to come to the back stairs again to speak to "the old witch," as the servants dubbed her.

The change in Ivan Petrovich made a powerful impression on his son. Fedia had just turned nineteen and had begun to think for himself, becoming emancipated from the authority that had pressed down on him like a weight. Even prior to this, he'd observed a certain discrepancy between his father's words and his deeds, between his broad, liberal theories and his harsh, petty despotism, but Fedia hadn't anticipated such a total breakdown. The confirmed egotist now completely revealed himself.

The young Lavretskii was preparing to go to Moscow in order to enter the university when a new, unexpected calamity overtook Ivan Petrovich: he went blind, hopelessly blind, in a single day. Having no confidence in the skills of Russian doctors, he tried to

obtain permission to go abroad. It was refused. Then he gathered
up his son, and for three whole years they wandered across Russia,
going from one doctor to another, incessantly moving from town
to town, while he drove his physicians, his son, and his servants
to despair with his impatience and cowardice. He returned to Lavriki a complete wreck, a tearful, capricious child. Bitter days
followed; everyone had to put up with a great deal from him. Ivan
Petrovich was only quiet when he was eating—he'd never been so
greedy and eaten so much. The rest of the time he gave himself
as well as everyone else no peace. He prayed; he cursed his fate;
he heaped abuse upon himself, upon politics, upon his system,
upon everything he'd bragged about and been proud of, upon
everything he'd formerly held up to his son as a model; he announced that he believed in nothing and then began to pray again;
he couldn't bear a single moment of solitude and expected the
members of his household to sit by his chair continually, day and
night, entertaining him with stories, which he repeatedly interrupted with such exclamations as "You're always lying!" and
"That's sheer nonsense!"

Glafira Petrovna was particularly essential to him. He absolutely
couldn't manage without her—she carried out every one of the sick
man's whims up to the very end, although sometimes she couldn't
bring herself to respond to him right away, for fear the sound of
her voice would betray her profound hostility. He languished in
this condition for two years, and finally died at the beginning of
May, after he'd been carried out on the balcony into the sun.
"Glasha, Glashka! Soup, soup, old foo...," his halting tongue
had mumbled; before he could fully articulate the last word, it fell
silent forever. Glafira Petrovna, who'd just taken a cup of soup
from the steward's hands, stopped, looked at her brother's face,
slowly made a large sign of the cross, and silently turned away.
His son, who happened to be there, didn't say anything either; he
leaned on the railing of the balcony and gazed for a long while at
the garden, which was so fragrant and green as it basked in the
rays of the golden spring sunshine. He was twenty-three years old.
How horribly, how imperceptibly swiftly those twenty-three years
had passed!... Life was opening up before him.

XII

After burying his father and entrusting the management of his
estate and the supervision of his bailiffs to the unfailing Glafira

Petrovna, the young Lavretskii went off to Moscow, where he was drawn by a vague but strong attraction. He recognized the defects in his education and resolved to regain lost ground as best he could. In the past five years, he'd read many books and seen a few things; many ideas had passed through his head; any professor might have envied a portion of his knowledge; at the same time, he didn't know some things that any schoolboy would have learned long ago. Lavretskii was conscious of his limitations; he secretly considered himself an eccentric. The Anglomaniac had played a poor joke on his son—the whimsical education had borne its fruits. He'd submitted to his father unquestioningly for many long years. By the time he'd begun to see through his father, the damage had already been done—his habits were deeply rooted. He didn't know how to associate with people; at the age of twenty-three, with an unquenchable thirst for love in his shy heart, he still hadn't dared to look any woman in the face. Given his lucid, sound, but somewhat ponderous intellect, coupled with his tendencies toward stubbornness, contemplativeness, and indolence, he should have been thrown into the mainstream of life from his earliest years on, but instead he'd been kept in artificial seclusion. Now the magic circle had been broken, but he continued to remain inside it, wrapped up and imprisoned within himself. At his age, it was ridiculous for him to put on a student's uniform—but he wasn't afraid of ridicule; his Spartan education had at least had the beneficial effect of fostering in him a contempt for other peoples' opinions, and he donned an academic uniform without embarrassment. He enrolled in the department of applied mathematics. Robust, red-cheeked, bearded, and taciturn, he produced a strange impression on his classmates; they didn't suspect that this austere man, who came to lectures so punctually in a wide, rural carriage drawn by a pair of horses, was virtually a child inside. He seemed like some sort of peculiar pedant to them. They didn't have any use for him and made no overtures toward him; he in turn avoided them. During the first two years he spent at the university, he only grew close to one student, from whom he took Latin lessons. This student, named Mikhalevich, was an enthusiast and poet who sincerely loved Lavretskii and accidently became the means of bringing about a crucial change in Lavretskii's destiny.

One time at the theater—Mochalov was at the height of his fame then, and Lavretskii never missed a performance—he caught sight of a young woman in a box in the front tier, and although no woman had ever come near his grim figure without making his heart pound, never had it pounded so hard before. The young woman was sitting perfectly still, leaning her elbows on the velvet rim of the box. Sensitive, youthful animation played across every feature of her dark-complexioned, lovely oval face; refined intelligence was reflected in her beautiful eyes, which gazed benignly and attentively from under delicate brows, as well as in the swift smile on her expressive lips and in the very shape of her head, her hands, her neck. She was exquisitely dressed. Beside her sat a woman of about forty-five with sallow, wrinkled skin, wearing a low-cut dress and a black toque, a toothless smile fixed on her distracted, vacuous face; an elderly man in a large dress suit and high collar was visible in the inner recesses of the box. He had small eyes filled with an expression of mindless self-importance and some sort of obsequious distrustfulness, a dyed moustache and sideburns, a large, undistinguished forehead, and wrinkled cheeks. By all indications, he was a retired general. Lavretskii didn't take his eyes off the young woman who'd made such an impression on him. Suddenly, the door of the box opened and Mikhalevich entered. The appearance of this man, virtually his sole acquaintance in all of Moscow, in the company of the young woman who was absorbing all his attention struck him as strange and significant. Continuing to stare at the box, he noted that everyone in it treated Mikhalevich like an old friend. The performance on the stage ceased to interest Lavretskii; even though Mochalov was in his "finest form" that evening, he didn't make the usual impression on Lavretskii. At one extremely pathetic moment, Lavretskii involuntarily looked at his beauty: she was bending forward and her cheeks were glowing. Under the influence of his persistent gaze, her eyes, which had been fixed on the stage, slowly turned and rested on him. He was haunted by those eyes all night; the skillfully constructed barriers had finally been broken down. He was atremble, he was on fire—and the next day he went to see Mikhalevich.

He learned from him that the name of this beauty was Varvara Pavlovna Korobina, that the elderly people sitting in the box with her were her father and mother, and that he, Mikhalevich, had become acquainted with them a year earlier, while he'd been staying at the home of Count N——, near Moscow, in the capacity of a tutor. The enthusiast voiced ecstatic praise for Varvara Pavlovna. "My dear fellow," he exclaimed with the impetuous tone in his voice distinctive to him, "this young woman is a marvelous creature, a genius, an artist in the true sense of the word—and she's supremely virtuous, too." Deducing from his inquiries the impression Varvara Pavlovna had made on Lavretskii, Mikhalevich himself proposed to introduce Lavretskii to her, adding that they treated him like one of the family, that the general wasn't the least bit proud, and that the mother was so foolish she wouldn't say "boo" to a goose. Lavretskii blushed, muttered something unintelligible, and fled. He struggled with his shyness for five whole days. On the sixth, the young Spartan put on a new uniform and placed himself at Mikhalevich's disposal. The latter, being his own valet, confined himself to combing his hair—and they set off together for the Korobins'.

XIII

Varvara Pavlovna's father, Pavel Petrovich Korobin, a retired major-general, had spent his entire term of government service in Petersburg. In his youth, he'd enjoyed the reputation of being a good dancer and a good soldier. Due to his poverty, he'd served as an adjutant to two or three undistinguished generals, and had married the daughter of one of them, who possessed a dowry of about twenty-five thousand rubles. He'd mastered all the intricacies of military discipline and maneuvers and had steadily advanced until finally, after twenty years of service, he'd been awarded the rank of general and the command of a regiment. At that point, he might have relaxed and quietly secured his financial position. Indeed, this was what he'd counted on doing, but he'd managed things somewhat incautiously. He'd devised a new method of investing public funds—the method seemed to be an excellent one in itself—but he'd neglected to distribute bribes in the right places and was consequently exposed; a highly unpleasant, ugly scandal had ensued. The general had gotten out of the affair somehow, but his career had been ruined, and he was advised to retire from active duty. He'd lingered in Petersburg for two more years, hoping to discover some snug berth in the civil service, but no such berth had come his way. His daughter had left school, his expenses were increasing every day. . . . Resigning himself to his fate, he'd decided to move to Moscow because of the lower cost of living there, had rented a tiny, low-pitched house on Old Stables Road that displayed a coat of arms seven feet long on the roof, and had begun to live the life of a retired general on an income of 2,750 rubles a year.

Moscow is a hospitable city, ready to welcome all stray newcomers, especially generals. Pavel Petrovich's bulky figure—which wasn't without martial dignity, however—soon began to be seen in the best drawing rooms of Moscow. His bald head with its tufts of dyed hair, as well as the soiled ribbon bearing the Order of St. Anne that he wore over a tie the color of a raven's wing, became familiar to all the pale, listless young men who sulkily hang around the card tables while the dancing is going on. Pavel Petrovich knew how to gain a foothold in society: he spoke little, but from long-standing habit, he spoke condescendingly—except when he was speaking to individuals of a rank higher than his own, of course. He played cards carefully and ate moderately at home, but consumed enough for six at parties. Hardly anything needs to be said about his wife. Her name was Kalliopa Karlovna. There was always a tear in her left eye, on the strength of which Kalliopa Karlovna (she was, one must add, of German extraction) considered herself a woman of great sensibility. She was constantly frightened of something, looked as though she were badly nourished, and wore tight velvet dresses, toques, and tarnished hollow bracelets. Pavel Petrovich and Kalliopa Karlovna's only daughter, Varvara Pavlovna, had just turned seventeen when she left boarding school, where she'd been considered, if not the prettiest, at least the brightest student and the best musician, and where she'd won a prize. She wasn't quite nineteen when Lavretskii saw her for the first time.

XIV

The young Spartan's legs were shaking under him as Mikhalevich conducted him into the Korobins' rather shabbily furnished drawing room and introduced him to them. But Lavretskii's overwhelming feeling of shyness swiftly disappeared. The affability innate in all Russians was intensified in the general by that special kind of friendliness peculiar to everyone who's been disgraced; most people somehow ignored the general's wife; as for Varvara Pavlovna, she was so calm and self-assuredly cordial that everyone immediately felt at home in her presence. Besides, her entire fascinating body—her smiling eyes, her innocently sloping shoulders and pale pink arms, her light yet seemingly languid movements, the very sound of her slow, sweet voice—all exuded an impalpable, subtle charm, like a faint perfume, a mild, albeit still modest allure. It was something that's hard to convey in words, but it was something that stirred and aroused—and what it aroused wasn't shyness. Lavretskii turned the conversation to the theater, to the perform-

ance of the preceding day; she herself promptly began to discuss
Mochalov, not merely confining herself to sighs and exclamations,
but offering several accurate observations filled with feminine insight in regard to his acting. Mikhalevich spoke about music; she
sat down at the piano without any ado and played some of Chopin's
mazurkas, which were just coming into fashion, quite adeptly.
Dinnertime came. Lavretskii would have left then, but they made
him stay. At dinner, the general regaled him with excellent Lafitte,
which the general's servant had hastened to fetch in a sleigh from
Dupré's.

Lavretskii returned home late that evening. He sat for a long
while without undressing, in a daze of enchantment, covering his
face with his hands. It seemed as though only at that moment did
he understand what made life worth living. All his previous as-
sumptions, all his plans, all that stuff and nonsense had disappeared
in an instant. His entire soul became absorbed in one feeling, one
desire—the desire to obtain happiness through love, sweet feminine
love. From that day onward, he began to visit the Korobins on a
regular basis. Six months later he presented himself to Varvara
Pavlovna and asked her to marry him. His offer of marriage was
accepted; much earlier, virtually on the eve of Lavretskii's first
visit, the general had inquired of Mikhalevich how many serfs
Lavretskii owned. Indeed, Varvara Pavlovna, who'd preserved her
customary composure and clarity of mind throughout the young
man's courtship, even at the very moment of his declaration of
love, was also perfectly well aware that her suitor was a wealthy
man. Kalliopa Karlovna thought, "*Meine Tochter macht eine schöne
Partie,*" and bought herself a new toque.

XV

Thus his offer of marriage was accepted, but on certain conditions.
In the first place, Lavretskii had to quit the university at once.
Who would want to be married to a student, and what a strange
idea in any case—how could a landowner, a rich man, take lessons
like a schoolboy when he was twenty-six years old? In the second
place, Varvara Pavlovna took upon herself the task of ordering and
purchasing her trousseau, and even of choosing her present from
the bridegroom. She had a lot of common sense, a great deal of
taste, and a very great love of comfort, along with a remarkable
ability to obtain that comfort for herself. Lavretskii was especially
struck by this ability when, immediately after their wedding, he'd

gone to Lavriki alone with his wife in the comfortable carriage she'd bought. How carefully everything with which he was surrounded had been considered, anticipated, and arranged in advance by Varvara Pavlovna! What charming traveling knickknacks appeared in various snug corners, what fascinating toilet cases and coffeepots accompanied them—and how delightfully Varvara Pavlovna herself made the coffee in the morning! Lavretskii wasn't inclined to be observant at that time, however. He was blissful, he was drunk with happiness—he gave himself over to it like a child. Indeed, he was as innocent as a child, this young Hercules. His young wife's entire being didn't exude charm in vain, nor was her sensuous promise of the mysterious luxury of untold pleasure in vain, either—the fulfillment was richer than the promise.

When she reached Lavriki at the very height of summer, she found the house dark and dirty, the servants inept and old-fashioned, but she didn't deem it necessary even to hint at this to her husband. If she'd intended to remain at Lavriki permanently, she would have changed everything there, beginning with the house, of course, but the idea of staying in that out-of-the-way corner of the steppes never entered her head for an instant. She lived there as if she were living in a tent, good-naturedly putting up with all its inconveniences and indulgently joking about them. Marfa Timofeevna came to pay a visit to her former charge, and Varvara Pavlovna liked her very much—but she didn't like Varvara Pavlovna. The new mistress didn't get along well with Glafira Petrovna, either. She would have left Glafira in peace, but old Korobin wanted to have a hand in the management of his son-in-law's affairs. To superintend the property of such a close relative, he said, wasn't beneath the dignity even of a general. One should add that Pavel Petrovich wouldn't have considered himself above managing the property even of a total stranger.

Varvara Pavlovna conducted her attack very skillfully, without disclosing her aim in advance. Apparently completely absorbed in the bliss of the honeymoon, in the peace of country life, in music and reading, she gradually drove Glafira to such a state that one morning the latter rushed into Lavretskii's study like someone possessed and, throwing a bunch of keys on the table, declared that she no longer had the strength to manage the household and didn't want to remain in the countryside. Having been suitably prepared beforehand, Lavretskii immediately agreed to her departure. Glafira Petrovna hadn't anticipated this. "Very well," she said, and her eyes darkened. "I can see that I'm not wanted here! I know who's forcing me out of my ancestral home. Just you mark my words, nephew. You'll never find yourself a home anywhere— you'll be a wanderer forever. These are my final words to you." She went off to her own little estate the same day, and General Korobin was installed a week later. With a mild melancholy in his gaze and manner, he took the responsibility for supervising the entire estate into his own hands.

In September, Varvara Pavlovna took her husband away to Petersburg. She spent two winters in Petersburg (she went to stay at Tsarskoe Selo for the summer), living in a handsome, well-lit, artistically furnished flat. They made many acquaintances from the middle and even upper ranks of society, paid many visits, and entertained at home a great deal, giving the most charming dances and musical evenings. Varvara Pavlovna attracted guests the way a flame attracts moths.

Fedor Ivanych didn't altogether like such a frivolous life. His wife advised him to accept some government position, but in respect for his father's memory—and also in accordance with his own views—he refused to enter government service. Nonetheless, he remained in Petersburg to please Varvara Pavlovna. He shortly discovered that no one prevented him from going off by himself, however, that it wasn't by accident he had the quietest, most comfortable study in all of Petersburg, that his ever-considerate wife was even ready to help him go off by himself—and from this time forth, everything went well. He applied himself once more to what he considered his own unfinished education: he began to read again, and even to learn English. It was a strange sight to see his powerful, broad-shouldered figure constantly bent over his desk, his full-bearded, ruddy face half-buried in the pages of a dictionary or notebook. Every morning he set to work, then had an excellent dinner (Varvara Pavlovna was unrivaled as a housekeeper), and in the evenings, he entered an enchanted world of light and perfume inhabited by cheerful young people—and the center of this world was that very same adept housekeeper, his wife. She brought him more joy with the birth of a son, but the poor child didn't live for long. It died in the spring; and that summer, on the advice of the doctors, Lavretskii took his wife abroad to some mineral springs. Distraction was essential for her after such a misfortune, in addition to which, her health required a warm climate. They spent the summer and autumn in Germany and Switzerland; then, as one would naturally expect, they went to Paris for the winter.

Varvara Pavlovna blossomed like a rose in Paris, managing to make herself a little nest as quickly and cleverly as she had in Petersburg. She found a very pretty apartment in one of the quiet but fashionable streets of Paris, embroidered a robe for her husband such as he'd never worn before, engaged a coquettish maid, an excellent cook, and an agile butler, procured a marvelous carriage, and purchased an exquisite piano. Before a week had passed, she was crossing the street, wearing her shawl, opening her parasol, and putting on her gloves in a manner equal to that of a true Parisienne. She soon cultivated acquaintances. At first, only Russians visited her; subsequently, Frenchmen began to visit her, too— very polite, attentive, unmarried ones with superb manners and euphonious names. They all talked readily and rapidly, bowed casually, and smiled agreeably, their white teeth flashing between their rosy lips. How they could smile! All of them brought their friends, and *la belle Madame de Lavretskii* soon became known from the chaussée d'Antin to the rue de Lille. In those days—it was 1836—the tribe of journalists and reporters who now swarm on all sides like ants in an anthill hadn't yet begun to flourish, but even then a Monsieur Jules could be seen in Varvara Pavlovna's salon, a gentleman of unprepossessing appearance with a scandalous reputation, who was insolent and mean-spirited, like all duelists and other people who have suffered some defeat. Varvara Pavlovna felt a deep aversion to this Monsieur Jules, but she received him because he wrote for various journals and was incessantly mentioning her, one time referring to her as *Madame de L——tzki*, another as *Madame de . . .*, *cette grande dame russe si distinguée, qui demeure rue de P——*, and telling all the world—that is, the several hundred subscribers who had nothing to do with *Madame de L——tzki*—how charming and amiable this lady was: a true Frenchwoman in spirit (*une vraie française par l'esprit*)— Frenchmen can offer no higher praise than this—an extraordinary musician, and a marvelous dancer (Varvara Pavlovna did waltz so wonderfully, in fact, that she attracted all eyes to the hem of her gauzy, twirling skirt). In sum, he spread her fame throughout the world, and that, whatever one may say, is always pleasant. Mademoiselle Mars had already retired from the stage and Mademoiselle Rachel hadn't yet made her appearance, but Varvara Pavlovna nevertheless attended the theater assiduously. She rhapso-dized over Italian music, yawned decorously at the Comédie Fran-çaise, and wept at the performance of Madame Dorval in some ultraromantic melodrama. Best of all, Liszt played in her home twice, and was so kind, so unpretentious—it was a sheer delight! The winter was passed in enjoyable activities like these, at the end of which time Varvara Pavlovna was even presented at the royal court.

Fedor Ivanych, for his part, wasn't bored, although his life pe-riodically weighed rather heavily on him—because it was empty. He read the newspapers, listened to lectures at the Sorbonne and the Collège de France, followed political debates in the Chambers, and began to work on a translation of a well-known scientific treatise on irrigation. "I'm not wasting my time," he thought. "This is all useful. But I have to return to Russia next winter without fail, and set to work." It's hard to say whether he had any clear, precise notion of what this work would entail, and God knows whether he would have succeeded in returning to Russia that winter. In the meantime, he was preparing to go to Baden with his wife....An unexpected occurrence destroyed all his plans.

XVI

Going by chance into Varvara Pavlovna's boudoir one day in her absence, Lavretskii caught sight of a carefully folded piece of paper lying on the floor. He mechanically picked it up, unfolded it, and read the following note, written in French:

> Sweet angel Betsy! (I never can make myself call you Barbe or Varvara!) I waited for you in vain at the corner of the boulevard. Come to our little room at half-past one tomorrow. Your fat, good-natured husband [*ton gros bonhomme de mari*] is usually buried in his books by that time. We'll sing the song by your poet *Pouskine* [*de votre poète Pouskine*] that you taught me: 'Old husband, cruel hus-band!' A thousand kisses on your little hands and feet. I'm waiting for you.
>
> Ernest.

Lavretskii didn't immediately comprehend what he'd read. He read it a second time—then his head began to swim, and the ground began to sway under his feet like the deck of a ship on a rolling sea. He started to shout and gasp and cry all at the same moment. He was utterly overwhelmed. He'd trusted his wife so blindly that no possibility of deception or betrayal had ever entered his mind. This Ernest, his wife's lover, was an attractive, twenty-three-year-old blond youth with a small snub nose and a refined little moustache, virtually the least significant of all her acquaintances. A few minutes passed, half an hour passed—Lavretskii remained standing in the same place, crushing the fatal note in his hands and gazing mindlessly at the floor. Pale forms seemed to swirl around him in some sort of tempestuous haze; his heart was numb with anguish. He seemed to be falling, falling, falling—and there was no bottom. The familiar light rustle of a silk dress roused him from his stupor: Varvara Pavlovna was hurriedly returning from her walk, wearing her hat and shawl. Lavretskii trembled all over and started to flee from the room. He felt he was capable at that moment of tearing her to pieces, of beating her half to death as a peasant might, of strangling her with his bare hands. In amazement, Varvara Pavlovna tried to stop him; he could only whisper "Betsy," and run out of the house.

Lavretskii hired a carriage and ordered the driver to take him outside of town. He wandered around on foot for the remainder of the day and the entire night, repeatedly stopping short and clasping his hands. One moment he was furious, the next, he seemed amused, even happy in a way. By morning, he'd grown calm with exhaustion and went into a wretched tavern on the outskirts of town. He asked for a room, and sat down on a chair by the window. He was suddenly overwhelmed by a fit of convulsive yawning. He could barely stand upright—his whole body was worn out—and yet he didn't even feel fatigued, although fatigue had begun to do its work. He sat and stared without comprehending anything: he didn't comprehend what had happened to him, or why he found himself alone in an empty, unfamiliar room with stiff limbs, a bitter taste in his mouth, and a weight on his heart; he didn't comprehend what had impelled her, his Varia, to give herself to this Frenchman, or how, knowing herself to be unfaithful, she could go on being just as calm, just as affectionate, just as intimate with him as before! "I can't understand any of it!" his parched lips whispered. "Who can guarantee that even then, in Petersburg . . . ?" And he didn't finish the question; he just yawned again, shivering all over.

Memories—both happy and sad—tormented him equally. Suddenly it crossed his mind that, several days earlier, she'd sat down at the piano and sung the song "Old husband, cruel husband!"

for him and Ernest. He recalled the expression on her face, the strange light in her eyes, the color in her cheeks—and he rose from his chair. He would have liked to go to them and tell them, "You made a mistake to toy with me. My great-grandfather used to hang peasants up by their arms, and my grandfather himself was a peasant," and kill them both. Then, suddenly, it seemed to him that everything happening to him was a dream, or not even a dream, but just some kind of absurd joke, that he merely needed to shake himself and look around.... He looked around—and like a hawk clutching its captured prey, anguish pierced his heart more and more deeply. On top of everything else, Lavretskii had been hoping to become a father in a few months.... His past, his future, his entire existence had been poisoned. He finally went back to Paris, registered at a hotel, and sent Ernest's note to Varvara Pavlovna accompanied by the following letter:

> The enclosed piece of paper will explain everything to you. Let me tell you, by the way, that I'm surprised at you—surprised that you, who are always so careful, would leave such valuable papers lying around. (Poor Lavretskii had spent hours preparing and congratulating himself on this phrase.) I can't see you again, and I suspect that you'd hardly desire an encounter with me, either. I'm assigning you 15,000 francs a year—I can't give you any more. Send your address to the estate office. Do what you please. Live where you please. I wish you happiness. No reply is necessary.

Lavretskii told his wife that no reply was necessary . . . but he awaited, he thirsted for a reply, for some explanation of this incredible, inconceivable development. Varvara Pavlovna wrote him a long letter in French the same day. It was the final blow. His last doubts vanished—and he began to be ashamed that he'd still harbored any doubts. Varvara Pavlovna didn't attempt to defend herself; her sole desire was to see him. She begged him not to condemn her irrevocably. The letter was cold and constrained, even though traces of tears were visible here and there. Lavretskii smiled bitterly and sent a messenger to say everything was fine as it was.

Three days later, he'd already left Paris. But he hadn't gone back to Russia—he'd gone to Italy. He himself didn't know why he'd chosen Italy; he hadn't really cared where he'd gone, as long as it wasn't home. He mailed instructions to his steward regarding his wife's allowance, and at the same time told him to take control of his estate completely out of General Korobin's hands right away, without waiting for him to draw up any account, and to arrange for his excellency's departure from Lavriki. He could vividly picture the dispossessed general's confusion, his futile self-importance, and Lavretskii felt a certain malevolent satisfaction in the midst of all his sorrow. Next, he sent Glafira Petrovna a letter asking her to return to Lavriki, and drew up a deed authorizing her to take possession of it. But Glafira Petrovna didn't return to Lavriki, and had it announced in the newspapers that the deed had been canceled, although this was perfectly unnecessary for her to do.

Lavretskii stayed out of sight in some small Italian town, but he couldn't help keeping track of his wife's movements for a long while. He learned from the newspapers that she'd gone from Paris to Baden, as she'd intended—and her name soon appeared in an article written by Monsieur Jules. There was a sort of sympathetic condolence beneath the habitual playfulness of this article. A deep sense of disgust spread throughout Fedor Ivanych's soul as he read the article. Later, he learned that his daughter had been born; two months after that, he was informed by his steward that Varvara Pavlovna had asked for the first third of her allowance. Then worse and worse rumors began to reach him. A tragicomic story, in which his wife played an unenviable role, was eventually enthusiastically reported in all the papers. It was the final blow: Varvara Pavlovna had become "notorious."

Lavretskii quickly ceased to follow her movements, but he couldn't gain control of himself as quickly. Sometimes he was overcome by such a longing for his wife that he would have forsaken everything, he thought perhaps he even . . . could have forgiven her, just to hear her caressing voice again, to feel her hand in his again. Time didn't pass in vain, however. He wasn't born to be a victim; his healthy nature reasserted itself. A great deal became clear to him, and even the blow that had struck him no longer appeared to him to have been utterly unforeseen. He came to understand his wife—we can only fully understand those who are close to us when we're far away from them. He could take up his studies, he could work again, albeit with nothing like his former zeal. Skepticism, already half-embedded by his experiences and his education, took complete possession of his heart. He became indifferent to everything. Four years passed, and he decided that he was strong enough to return to his own country, to encounter his relatives. Without stopping in either Petersburg or Moscow, he went straight to the town of O——, where we parted from him, and where we'll now ask the indulgent reader to return with us.

XVII

The morning after the day we've described, at about ten o'clock, Lavretskii was climbing the steps of the Kalitins' house. As he did, he encountered Liza, who was coming out of the house wearing her hat and gloves.

"Where are you going?" he asked her.

"To church services. It's Sunday."

"Why, do you attend church regularly?"

Liza looked at him in silent amazement.

"I beg your pardon," Lavretskii continued. "I didn't mean to say that. I've come to say goodbye to you. I'm leaving for my estate in an hour."

"Is it far from here?" Liza inquired.

"About twenty-five versts."

Lenochka appeared in the doorway, escorted by a maid.

"Be sure you don't forget us," Liza remarked as she went down the steps.

"And don't you forget me. By the way," he added, "since you're going to church, while you're there, pray for me, too."

Liza stopped short and turned around toward him. "Certainly," she replied, looking him straight in the eye. "I'll pray for you, too. Come on, Lenochka."

Lavretskii found Maria Dmitrievna alone in the drawing room. She exuded the fragrances of eau de cologne and mint. She had a headache, she said, and had passed a restless night. She received him with her usual languid graciousness and gradually fell into conversation with him.

"Vladimir Nikolaich is really a delightful young man, don't you think?" she queried.

"Which Vladimir Nikolaich?"

"Panshin, of course. The one who was here yesterday. He liked you tremendously. I'll tell you a secret, *mon cher cousin:* he's simply wild about my Liza. Well, he comes from a good family, he has an excellent position in the government, and he's an intelligent man, a *Kammerjunker.* And if it's God's will to unite them, I, for my part, as a mother, will be extremely pleased. Of course, my responsibility is immense—the happiness of children depends on parents, no matter what they say. Up until now, for better or worse, I've done everything, I've been everywhere with them alone, that is to say, I've raised my children and taught them everything myself. . . . Indeed, I've just written to request a French governess from Madame Boluce."

Maria Dmitrievna launched into a description of her cares, her miseries, and her maternal sentiments. Lavretskii listened in silence, turning his hat around in his hands. His cold, serious gaze embarrassed the loquacious lady.

"And do you like Liza?" she asked.

"Lizaveta Mikhailovna is a very fine young woman," Lavretskii replied. He stood up, said goodbye, and went off to find Marfa Timofeevna. Displeased, Maria Dmitrievna watched him go, thinking: "What a dolt—a regular peasant! Well, now I understand why his wife couldn't remain faithful to him."

Marfa Timofeevna was sitting in her room, surrounded by her small entourage. It consisted of five creatures, each of which was almost equally dear to her heart: a trained bullfinch with a big beak, which she'd taken a liking to after it stopped whistling and sipping water on cue; a very timid, gentle little dog, Roska; an ill-tempered cat, Matross; a dark-complexioned, agile little girl about nine years old with big eyes and a sharp nose named Shurochka; and an elderly woman of approximately fifty-five wearing a white cap and a short, cinnamon-colored jacket over a dark skirt, who was named Nastasia Karpovna Ogarkova. Shurochka was an orphan whose parents had belonged to the merchant class. Marfa Timofeevna had taken her to her heart out of compassion, like Roska: she'd found both the little dog and the little girl in the street; both were thin and hungry; both were being drenched by the autumn rain; no one had come in search of Roska, and Shurochka was handed over to Marfa Timofeevna with positive alacrity by her uncle, a drunken shoemaker who didn't get enough to eat himself, and didn't feed his niece, either, but did beat her over the head with his belt. Marfa Timofeevna had made the acquaintance of Nastasia Karpovna on a pilgrimage to a monastery. She'd gone up to her in a church (Marfa Timofeevna had been drawn to her because, as Marfa Timofeevna put it, Nastasia Karpovna had said her prayers so nicely), had begun a conversation with her, and then had invited her to have a cup of tea. From that day on, Marfa Timofeevna had never parted from her. Nastasia Karpovna was a woman of the most cheerful, meek disposition, a childless widow from an impoverished noble family. She had a round head, gray hair, soft white hands, and a soft face with large, kindly features and a rather comical turned-up nose. She stood in awe of Marfa Timofeevna, who was very fond of her, although she laughed at the widow's tenderheartedness. Nastasia Karpovna had an affinity for all young people, and couldn't help blushing like a girl at the most innocent joke. Her entire fortune consisted of a mere 1,200 rubles. She lived at Marfa Timofeevna's expense, but on an equal footing with her—Marfa Timofeevna wouldn't have tolerated any servility.

"Ah, Fedia!" she began as soon as she saw him. "Last night you didn't get to meet my family. You have to admire them—we've all gathered together for tea. This is our second one, our holiday tea. You can give them all a kiss, except that Shurochka won't let you, and the cat'll scratch you. Are you leaving today?"

"Yes." Lavretskii sat down on a low little seat. "I've just said goodbye to Maria Dmitrievna. I saw Lizaveta Mikhailovna, too."

"Call her Liza, my dear boy. There's no need for Mikhailovna with you! But sit still, or you'll break Shurochka's chair."

"She's gone to church," Lavretskii continued. "Is she religious?"

"Yes, Fedia, very much so. More than you and I, Fedia."

"Aren't you religious, then?" lisped Nastasia Karpovna. "You haven't been to the early service today, but you're going to the late one."

"No, not at all. You'll have to go alone. I've gotten too lazy, my dear," replied Marfa Timofeevna. "I'm already indulging myself with tea." She addressed Nastasia Karpovna familiarly, as she would a child, even though she treated her as an equal. She wasn't a Pestov for nothing: three Pestovs had been included on the execution list of Ivan the Terrible, and Marfa Timofeevna was well aware of that fact.

"Tell me, please," Lavretskii began again, "Maria Dmitrievna has just been telling me about this—what's his name?—Panshin. What sort of a man is he?"

"What a chatterbox she is, the Lord preserve us!" Marfa Timofeevna muttered. "She told you in confidence, I presume, that he's turned up as a suitor. She might have whispered it to her priest's son, but no, he's not important enough for her, it seems. And so far there's nothing to tell, thank God! But she's already gossiping about it."

"Why thank God?" asked Lavretskii.

"Because I don't like that fine young gentleman—so why should I rejoice over him?"

"You don't like him?"

"No, he can't fascinate absolutely everyone. He'll have to be satisfied with the fact that Nastasia Karpovna is in love with him."

The poor widow was utterly horrified. "How can you say that, Marfa Timofeevna? You have no fear of God!" she cried, and a crimson flush instantly spread across her face and neck.

"And he certainly knows it, the rogue," Marfa Timofeevna interrupted her. "He knows how to captivate her—he gave her a snuffbox. Fedia, ask her for a pinch of snuff. You'll see what a marvelous snuffbox it is—it has a hussar on horseback on the lid. You can't deny it, my dear."

Nastasia Karpovna only threw up her hands.

"Well, and as for Liza," Lavretskii inquired, "is she attracted to him?"

"She seems to like him, but then, God knows! The heart of another human being, you know, is like a dark forest, and a girl's heart is more like that than any other. Shurochka's heart, for instance—I defy you to understand it! What makes her hide and not come out ever since you arrived?"

Shurochka choked with suppressed laughter and skipped out of the room. Lavretskii rose from his seat.

"Yes," he said in a halting voice, "you can't decipher a girl's heart."

He began to say goodbye.

"Well, will we see you again soon?" asked Marfa Timofeevna.

"Probably, Aunt. It's not far away, you know."

"Yes, to be sure, you're going to Vasilevskoe, you don't want to stay at Lavriki. Well, that's your own business, only make sure you go and say a prayer at your mother's grave, and your grandmother's, too, incidentally. Out there, in those foreign parts, you've picked up all kinds of ideas—but who knows? Perhaps they'll feel that you've come to see them, even in their coffins. And Fedia, don't forget to have a service sung for Glafira Petrovna as well. Here's a silver ruble for you. Take it, take it—I want to pay for a service for her. I didn't like her during her lifetime, but all the same, there's no denying that she was a woman of character. She was an intelligent creature, and a good friend to you. Now go before I wear you out, and God be with you."

And Marfa Timofeevna embraced her nephew.

"But Liza isn't going to marry Panshin, don't you worry. That's not the sort of husband she deserves."

"Oh, I'm not the least bit worried," Lavretskii responded, and he left.

XVIII

Four hours later, he set off for home. His carriage quickly rolled along the soft road. There hadn't been any rain for two weeks; a fine, milky mist had diffused throughout the air and was obscuring a distant forest; the smell of burning fires was coming from there. A multitude of darkish clouds with blurred edges were creeping across the pale-blue sky; a fairly strong breeze was blowing in a dry, steady stream without dispelling the heat. Leaning his head back on a cushion and folding his arms across his breast, Lavretskii gazed at the furrowed fields unfolding like a fan before his eyes, at the willow bushes as they slowly came into sight, at the slow-witted ravens and crows that glanced sideways at the approaching carriage with mute suspicion, and at the long ditches overgrown with ragweed, wormwood, and mountain ash. As he gazed, the fresh, fertile, remote solitude of this steppe wilderness, the verdure, the rolling slopes, the valleys filled with stunted oak bushes, the gray little villages, the scant birch trees—the entire Russian landscape, which he hadn't seen for so long, stirred emotions that were gratifying yet almost painful to his heart at the same time, and he felt a kind of pleasant pressure weighing down his chest. His thoughts wandered slowly; their outlines were as vague and indistinct as the outlines of the clouds that seemed to be randomly wandering overhead. He recalled his childhood and his mother; he recalled her death, how they'd carried him in to see her and how, as she'd feebly clasped his head to her bosom, she'd begun to weep over him, then had glanced at Glafira Petrovna—and had checked herself. He recalled his father, who'd been so vigorous at first, stridently voicing his dissatisfaction with everything, and then later had become blind and lachrymose, with an unkempt gray beard; he recalled how, after drinking too much wine at dinner and spilling gravy on his napkin one day, his father had burst out laughing and begun to recount his amorous conquests, growing red in the face and blinking his sightless eyes; he recalled Varvara Pavlovna—and involuntarily shuddered, the way a man shudders

from a sudden internal pain, then shook his head. Next his thoughts
came to rest on Liza.

"There," he thought, "is a new creature, one just embarking
on life. A fine young woman—what will her future hold? She's
good-looking, too, with a pale, fresh face, a very serious mouth,
serious eyes, and an honest, innocent gaze. Unfortunately, she
seems a bit intense. She has a lovely figure, a light step, and a
soft voice. I really like the way she suddenly pauses, listens carefully, without smiling, then grows thoughtful and pushes her hair
back. I agree that Panshin isn't good enough for her. What's wrong
with him, anyway? And yet, what business is it of mine? She'll
follow the same road as all the rest. I'd better go to sleep." And
Lavretskii closed his eyes.

He couldn't sleep, but he sank into the drowsy numbness caused
by travel. Images from the past slowly rose again, as they had
before, and floated into his soul, getting confused and entangled
with other images. God knows why, Lavretskii began to think about
Robert Peel . . . about French history . . . about how he'd win a battle if he were a general . . . he imagined the shots and the cries. . . .
His head slipped to one side, and he opened his eyes. The same
fields were there, the same steppe scenery; the polished shoes of
the horses gleamed alternately amid the blowing dust; the coachman's yellow-and-red-striped shirt was being puffed out by the
wind. . . . "I was right to come home!" flashed through Lavretskii's
mind, and he shouted, "Keep going!" wrapping his coat around
him more tightly and pressing himself deeper into the cushions.
The carriage jolted. Lavretskii sat up and opened his eyes wide.
A little village was stretched out on the slope in front of him; a
small, ancient manor house with closed shutters and a winding
flight of stairs was visible slightly to the right; green nettles as
thick as hemp were growing across the wide courtyard up to its
very gates; a strong oak storage shed was standing in the middle
of the courtyard. This was Vasilevskoe.

The coachman drove as far as the gates and stopped the horse.
Lavretskii's groom stood up on the box and called out, "Hey!" as
though preparing to jump down. There was a sleepy, muffled sound
of barking, but no dog appeared. The groom prepared to jump
again and called out, "Hey!" once more. The feeble barking was
repeated, and a moment later a man dressed in a cloth coat, his
hair as white as snow, ran into the courtyard from some unseen
quarter. He stared at the carriage, shading his eyes against the sun.

Suddenly, he slapped his thighs with both hands, fidgeted in place a bit, and then rushed to open the gates. The carriage rolled into the courtyard, crushing the nettles beneath its wheels, and came to a halt at the stairs. The white-haired man, who seemed very alert, was already standing on the bottom step, his legs bent and spread wide apart. He unfastened the door of the carriage, pulling its strap handle back with a jerk and helping his master alight, then he kissed Lavretskii's hand.

"How do you do, how do you do, friend?" began Lavretskii. "Your name is Anton, I believe? You're still alive?" The old man bowed without speaking and ran off to get the keys. While he was gone, the coachman remained motionless, sitting sideways and staring at the closed door; Lavretskii's groom remained where he'd leaped down, standing in a picturesque pose with one hand thrown across the driver's box. The old man brought out the keys, and, quite needlessly twisting like a snake, his elbows raised high, he opened the front door, stood to one side, and bowed down to the ground again.

"So here I am, at home. Here I am, back again," Lavretskii thought, as he walked into the small entryway while, one after another, the shutters were being opened with much creaking and banging, and the light of day began to pour into the deserted rooms.

XIX

The small manor house to which Lavretskii had come and in which, two years earlier, Glafira Petrovna had drawn her last breath, had been built from solid pinewood during the preceding century. It looked ancient, but it was still strong enough to stand for another fifty years or more. Lavretskii toured all the rooms and, to the discomfiture of the aged, sluggish flies that had settled under the lintels, which were covered with white dust, he ordered all the windows to be opened—they hadn't been open since Glafira Petrovna's death. Everything in the house had remained the way it was: the thin-legged, white miniature couches in the drawing room, so tattered and rickety, covered with glossy gray material, vividly recalled the days of Catherine the Great; the mistress's favorite armchair with the high, straight back that she never leaned against, even in her old age, also stood in the drawing room. A very old portrait of Fedor's great-grandfather, Andrei Lavretskii, hung on one long wall: his dark, sallow face was barely distinguishable from the warped, blackened background; his small, cruel eyes looked out grimly from beneath eyelids that drooped as if they were swollen; his dark, unpowdered hair bristled above his stern, pockmarked forehead. In the corner of the portrait hung a wreath of dusty dried flowers. "Glafira Petrovna herself made that," Anton announced. A narrow bed under a canopy of old-fashioned, high-quality striped material stood in the bedroom; a heap of faded cushions and a thin, quilted coverlet lay on the bed; at its head hung a picture of the Presentation of the Holy Mother of God in the Temple. It was this very picture that the elderly woman, dying alone, forgotten by everyone, had pressed to her lips for the last time as they grew cold. A small dressing table made of inlaid wood, with brass fittings and a warped mirror in a tarnished frame, sat by the window. Next to the bedroom was a little icon room whose walls were bare; it contained a heavy stand covered with icons in one corner; a threadbare rug spotted with wax lay on the floor— Glafira Petrovna used to pray while kneeling on it, bowing down to the ground.

Anton went off with Lavretskii's groom to unlock the stable and the carriage house. An old woman of about Anton's age, wearing a kerchief tied around her head that came down to her very eyebrows, appeared in his place. Her head shook and her eyes were dim, but they expressed eagerness to please—the habit of years of submissive service—and, at the same time, some sort of respectful commiseration. She kissed Lavretskii's hand and then stood in the doorway, awaiting his orders. He absolutely couldn't remember her name and didn't even remember whether he'd ever seen her before. Her name, it turned out, was Aprakseia. Forty years earlier, Glafira Petrovna had thrown her out of the manor house and ordered her to be put in charge of the poultry. In any event, she didn't say much. She seemed to have lost her senses in her old age; she merely gazed at him obsequiously. In addition to these two elderly creatures and three pudgy children in long tunics—Anton's great-grandchildren— a one-armed peasant exempt from servitude also lived in the manor house. He grumbled endlessly and was of no use whatsoever. The decrepit dog who'd greeted Lavretskii's return by barking wasn't much better—for ten years, it had been tethered to a chain, bought at Glafira Petrovna's command, that was so heavy the dog could barely move.

Having looked around the house, Lavretskii went into the garden, which greatly pleased him. It was overgrown with tall grass, burdock, and gooseberry and raspberry bushes, but there was plenty of shade cast by numerous old lime trees remarkable for their immense size and unusually shaped branches: they'd been planted too close together, and at one time or another—some hundred years earlier—they'd been cut back. A small, clear pool bordered by high, reddish rushes lay at the end of the garden. Traces of human life pass very quickly: Glafira Petrovna's estate hadn't had time to become completely wild, but it already seemed to be submerged in the quiet slumber that everything on earth enjoys when the infection of human restlessness doesn't intrude.

Fedor Ivanych also walked through the peasants' village. The women stared at him from the doorways of their huts, their cheeks resting on their hands, while the men greeted him from a distance, the children ran away, and the dogs barked indifferently. He finally began to feel hungry, but he didn't expect his servants or his cook until evening and the wagons of provisions from Lavriki hadn't arrived yet. Thus he had to resort to Anton. Anton promptly arranged everything: he caught, killed, and plucked an old hen, then Aprakseia gave it a thorough rubbing and cleaning, washing it like linen before putting it into a stewpan. When it was finally cooked, Anton spread a cloth and set the table, placing a three-legged saltshaker made of tarnished silver and a cut-glass decanter with a round stopper and a narrow neck beside the knife and fork. He then announced to Lavretskii in a singsong voice that the meal was ready, and took his stand behind Lavretskii's chair with a napkin twisted around his right fist that emitted an odd, strong, ancient odor resembling that of a cypress tree. Lavretskii tried the soup, and picked up the hen: its skin was covered with large blisters, a tough tendon ran down each leg, and the meat tasted like wood and soda water.

When he'd finished dinner, Lavretskii said that he'd drink a cup of tea if. . . . "I'll bring it this minute, sir," the old man interrupted. And he kept his word. A pinch of tea twisted up in a piece of red paper materialized; a small but very active, loudly hissing samovar also appeared, as well as small lumps of sugar that looked as though they were melting. Lavretskii drank his tea out of a large cup. He remembered this cup from childhood: there were playing cards painted on it, and only visitors used to drink out of it—now here he was, drinking out of it like a visitor.

His servants arrived that evening. Lavretskii didn't want to sleep in his aunt's bed, so he ordered them to set up a bed for him in the dining room. After extinguishing his candle, he stared at the room around him for a long while, then lapsed into cheerless reflections. He experienced the feeling familiar to everyone fated to spend the night in someplace long uninhabited: it seemed to him that the darkness surrounding him on all sides couldn't become accustomed to the new resident, that the very walls of the house seemed disconcerted. He finally sighed, drew a blanket up around him, and fell asleep.

Anton stayed up later than all the other members of the household. He gossiped with Aprakseia at length, periodically sighing quietly and crossing himself twice. Neither of them had expected that their master would settle down with them at Vasilevskoe when he owned such a magnificent estate nearby with such a well-built house on it. They didn't suspect that this very house was hateful to Lavretskii, that it stirred up painful memories for him. Having gossiped to his heart's content, Anton took a stick and struck the night watchman's board, which had hung silent for so many years, then lay down to sleep in the courtyard without any covering over his white head. The May night was mild and calm, and the old man slept peacefully.

XX

Lavretskii got up fairly early the next day, had a chat with the village bailiff, visited the threshing barn, ordered the yard dog to be unchained—it merely barked a little, but didn't even come out of its kennel—and, returning home, sank into some sort of peaceful torpor from which he didn't escape all day.

"Here I am, at the very bottom of the river," he told himself more than once. He sat at the window without stirring and listened to the current, as it were, of the quiet life surrounding him, listened to the occasional sounds in the country solitude: something from somewhere behind the nettles would chirp in a very shrill little voice, and a mosquito would seem to answer it; then the chirping would cease, but the mosquito would still continue to whine; the hum of a big bee repeatedly hitting its head against the ceiling would vibrate amid the amicable, persistent, annoying buzz of the flies; a rooster would crow in the street, hoarsely prolonging its last note; a cart would rattle; a gate in the village would creak. Then the jarring voice of a peasant woman would suddenly ring out: "What?" "Hey, you, my sweetheart," Anton would croon to the little two-year-old girl he was holding in his arms. "Fetch the kvass," the same woman's voice would repeat, and then a deathly silence would suddenly set in; nothing would make a noise, nothing would move; the wind wouldn't stir a leaf; the swallows would soundlessly fly one after another above the earth, and sadness would oppress the heart at their silent flight.

"Here I am, at the very bottom of the river," Lavretskii thought again. "And always, at all times, life here is quiet and tranquil," he mused. "Whoever comes within its circle must submit to it. There's nothing here to upset anyone, nothing to harass anyone. It's only possible to survive here by proceeding slowly, the way a plowman cuts a furrow with his plow. What vigor, what health abounds in this static place! Right here, under the window, the sturdy burdock is creeping out of the thick grass, the lovage is extending its juicy stems above it, and the blossoms of Virgin's tears are flinging their pink tendrils even higher; farther off, in the fields, the silky rye is growing, the oats are already in bloom, and every leaf on every tree, every blade of grass on every stalk, is spreading out to its fullest width.

"My best years have been spent in love with a woman," Lavretskii went on thinking. "Let me be sobered by the monotony of life here. Let me be soothed and healed, so that I may learn in time to do my duty." And he began listening to the silence again, expecting nothing—and at the same time, seemingly endlessly expecting something. The silence enfolded him on all sides. The sun calmly proceeded across the peaceful blue sky while the clouds calmly floated across it; they seemed to know why and where they were floating. At this very moment, in other places on earth, life was seething, bustling, roaring; here, life was slipping by noiselessly, like water over marshy grass. Lavretskii couldn't tear himself away from the contemplation of this ebb and flow of life until evening. Sorrow over the past was melting in his soul like snow in the spring, and—strangely enough—never had feelings for his native land coursed through him so deeply and strongly.

XXI

During the following two weeks, Fedor Ivanych put Glafira Petrovna's little house in order and cleared out the courtyard and the garden. Comfortable furniture was sent to him from Lavriki; wine, books, and newspapers were delivered from town; horses appeared in the stables. In sum, Fedor Ivanych provided himself with everything he needed, and he began to live—neither precisely the life of a country landowner nor precisely the life of a hermit. His days passed monotonously, but he wasn't bored, although he had no visitors. He set to work farming his estate diligently and carefully, went riding around the neighboring areas, and did some reading. He didn't read much, however—he found it more pleasant to listen to old Anton's tales. Lavretskii often sat at the window holding a pipe and a cup of cold tea while Anton stood by the door, his arms crossed behind him, and told his long, drawn-out stories about olden times, about those incredible times when oats and rye weren't sold by the measure but in large sacks at a trifling price per sack, when there were impassable forests and virgin steppes extending everywhere, even close to town. "But now," complained the old man, whose eightieth birthday had already passed, "there's been so much ground cleared, so much plowing everywhere, that there's nowhere you can go."

Anton also used to tell numerous stories about his mistress, Glafira Petrovna—how prudent and thrifty she'd been; how a certain gentleman, a young neighbor, had courted her and would often ride over to see her; how she'd even put on her best cap with the salmon-colored ribbons and a yellow dress of *tru-tru lévantine* for him; but how, later on, she'd gotten angry with this gentleman for making an unseemly inquiry—"How large, madam, might your fortune be, if you please?"—and had ordered them not to let him enter the house; how she'd subsequently given orders that, after her demise, everything down to the last rag should go to Fedor Ivanych. And indeed, Lavretskii found all his aunt's household goods intact, including her best cap with the salmon-colored ribbons and the yellow dress of *tru-tru lévantine*. There seemed to be no trace of any old papers or interesting documents, which Lavretskii had looked forward to finding, except for one old book in which his grandfather, Petr Andreich, had written, "Celebration of the peace concluded with the Turkish empire by His Excellency Prince Aleksandr Aleksandrovich Prozorovskii in the city of Saint Petersburg" in one place, and a prescription for a pectoral decoction in another place, along with the comment, "This prescription was given to the general's wife, Praskovia Fedorovna Saltykova, by the chief priest of the Church of the Life-giving Trinity, Fedor Avksentevich." A bit of political news was recorded in yet another place: "Somewhat less talk about the French tigers." Elsewhere appeared this entry: "The *Moscow Gazette* ran an announcement of the death of First-Major

Mikhail Petrovich Kolychev. Isn't this the son of Petr Vasilevich Kolychev?"

Lavretskii also found some old calendars and books interpreting dreams, as well as the mysterious work of Ambodik; many memories were awakened by the well-known but long-forgotten *Symbols and Emblems*. Lavretskii found a small packet tied up with a black ribbon, sealed with black sealing wax, and thrust into the most remote corner of a drawer in Glafira Petrovna's little dressing table. In this packet lay a pastel portrait of his father in his youth, showing soft curls straying over his brow, almond-shaped, languid eyes, and parted lips. It was lying face to face with an almost completely faded portrait of a pale woman in a white dress with a white rose in her hand—his mother. Glafira Petrovna had never allowed a portrait of herself to be painted.

"I myself, master, Fedor Ivanych," Anton told Lavretskii, "can still remember your great-grandfather, Andrei Afanasevich, even though I didn't live in the manor house then, seeing that I'd just turned eighteen when he died. I met him once, in the garden, and my knees were knocking together with fright, to be sure, but he didn't do anything except ask me my name and send me to his room to get his handkerchief. He was a master—how shall I say it?—who didn't consider anyone better than he was. For your great-grandfather had a magic amulet, I swear to you. A monk from Mount Athos gave him this amulet as a present. And he told him, this monk did, 'It's because of your kindness, your lordship, that I give you this. Wear it, and you won't need to fear any punishment.' Well, then again, your honor, we know what those times were like—whatever the master wanted to do, he did. Sometimes, if even a gentleman decided to oppose him in any way, he'd just stare at that gentleman and say, 'You swim in shallow water'—that was his favorite saying. And he, your great-grandfather of blessed memory, lived in a small wooden manor house. What goods he left behind him, what silver, what collections of all kinds! All the storehouses were filled to overflowing. He knew how to run a household. That very decanter you were pleased to admire was his—he used to drink vodka out of it. But then again, your grandfather, Petr Andreich, built himself a palace of stone, yet he never saved anything. Everything went badly for him, and he lived in far worse fashion than his father, getting no pleasure for himself, spending all his money. And now there's nothing to remember him by—not a single silver spoon has come down from him. We have Glafira Petrovna's careful management to thank for everything that's been saved."

"But is it true," Lavretskii interrupted him, "that they called her an old witch?"

"What sort of people called her that, I'd like to know?" Anton replied with a disgruntled air.

"And master," the old man found the courage to ask one day, "what about our mistress? Where is she making her residence?"

"I'm separated from my wife," Lavretskii answered with an effort. "Please don't ask any questions about her."

"Yes, sir," the old man responded mournfully.

After three weeks had passed, Lavretskii rode into O—— to visit the Kalitins, and spent an evening with them. Lemm was there, and Lavretskii took a great liking to him. Although Lavretskii played no instrument, thanks to his father, he loved music, true classical music, with a passion. Panshin wasn't at the Kalitins' that evening—the governor had sent him someplace out of town. Liza played the piano alone, quite competently. Lemm grew very lively, and even got so excited that he twisted a piece of paper into a baton and conducted. Maria Dmitrievna at first laughed as she looked at him. Later on, she went off to bed because, as she put it, Beethoven was too upsetting to her nerves. At midnight, Lavretskii accompanied Lemm to his lodgings and stayed there with him until three o'clock in the morning. Lemm talked a great deal; his bent figure became erect, his eyes opened wide and flashed with fire, his hair even stood up over his forehead. It'd been so long since anyone had given him sympathy, and Lavretskii was obviously interested in him, plying him with solicitous, probing questions. This touched the old man; he ultimately showed the visitor his music, playing and even singing excerpts from his compositions—including Schiller's ballad *Fridolin*, which he'd set to music—in a worn-out voice. Lavretskii admired it, made him repeat some passages, and, as he left, invited Lemm to visit him for a few days. Lemm immediately agreed as he accompanied him to the street and shook his hand warmly, but when Lemm was standing alone in the fresh, damp air as the sun was beginning to rise, he looked around, shuddered, shrank back, and crept up to his little room with a guilty air. "*Ich bin wohl nicht klug*" (I must be out of my senses), he muttered as he lay down on his hard, short bed. A few days later, he tried to say that he was sick when Lavretskii rode over to fetch him in an open carriage, but Fedor Ivanych went up to his room and managed to persuade him to come. What produced the most powerful effect on Lemm was the fact that Lavretskii had ordered a piano to be sent from town to the countryside expressly for him.

They went to the Kalitins' together and spent the evening with them, but not as pleasantly as they had the previous time. Panshin was there; he talked about his recent trip a great deal, most amusingly describing and mimicking the rural inhabitants he'd seen. Lavretskii laughed, but Lemm wouldn't come out of his corner and sat in silence, gently trembling all over like a spider, looking sullen and bored. He only revived when Lavretskii began to say goodbye. Even when seated in the carriage, the elderly man remained reticent and shy, but the warm, soft air, the light breeze, the transparent shadows, the scent of the grass and the buds on the birch trees, the peaceful glow of the starlit, moonless night, the pleasant tramp and snorting of the horses—all the enchantment of the road, the spring, and the night sank into the poor German's soul, and he himself initiated a conversation with Lavretskii.

XXII

He began to talk about music, about Liza, then about music again. He seemed to enunciate his words more slowly when he talked about Liza. Lavretskii turned the conversation to Lemm's compositions and, half in jest, offered to write him a libretto.

"Hmm, a libretto," Lemm replied. "No, that is not for me. I no longer have the energy, the play of imagination, that is required for an opera. I have lost too much of my strength. . . . But if I were still able to do something, I would be content with a song. Of course, I would like it to have beautiful words. . . ."

He stopped speaking and sat motionless for a long while, his eyes directed toward the sky.

"For instance," he finally said, "something like this—'Oh stars, pure stars!'"

Lavretskii turned toward him slightly and began to gaze at him.

"'Oh stars, pure stars,'" Lemm repeated. . . . "'You look down upon the virtuous and the sinful alike . . . but only the pure in heart'—or something like that—'comprehend you'—that is, no—'love you.' But I am not a poet. I am not equal to it! Something of that sort, though—something lofty."

Lemm pushed his hat to the back of his head. His face looked paler and younger in the dim glow of the clear night.

"'And you, too,'" Lemm continued, his voice gradually becoming lower, "'you know who loves, and who can love, because you, pure ones, you alone can comfort...' No, that is not it at all! I am not a poet," he said, "but it would be something of that sort."

"I'm sorry I'm not a poet," Lavretskii remarked.

"Vain dreams!" Lemm rejoined, and he retreated into a corner of the carriage. He closed his eyes, as though he was preparing to go to sleep.

A few moments passed.... Lavretskii listened.... "Stars, pure stars, love," muttered the elderly man.

"Love," Lavretskii repeated to himself. He sank into thought—and his heart grew heavy.

"That's beautiful music you've set to *Fridolin*, Khristofor Fedorych," he said aloud, "but what do you suppose Fridolin did after the Count had presented him to his wife.... Did he become her lover, eh?"

"You imagine that," Lemm replied, "because experience probably...." He suddenly stopped and turned away in embarrassment. Lavretskii laughed constrainedly, turning away as well, and began to gaze at the road.

The stars had grown paler and the sky had turned gray by the time the carriage drove up to the steps of the little house at Vasilevskoe. Lavretskii conducted his guest to the room that had been prepared for him, returned to his study, and sat down by the window. A nightingale in the garden was singing its last song before dawn. Lavretskii recalled that a nightingale had sung in the garden at the Kalitins'. He also recalled the gentle movement of Liza's eyes as they turned toward the dark window at its first notes. He began to think about her, and his heart became tranquil again. "Pure maiden," he murmured half-aloud. "Pure stars," he added with a smile, and quietly went to bed.

But Lemm sat on his bed for a long while, holding a music notebook on his lap. He felt as though a lovely, previously unheard melody was preparing to visit him. He was already thoroughly awake and aglow, he already felt the languor and sweetness of its proximity... but he couldn't reach it.

"Neither poet nor musician!" he finally murmured.... And his tired head sank heavily onto the pillows.

XXIII

The next morning, the master of the house and his guest drank tea in the garden under an old lime tree.

"Maestro," Lavretskii said in the course of their conversation, "you'll have to compose a triumphal cantata soon."

"Upon what occasion?"

"For the wedding of Mr. Panshin to Liza. Did you notice how much attention he paid to her yesterday? It seemed as though things have already gone pretty far with them."

"This will never be!" cried Lemm.

"Why not?"

"Because it is impossible. Although, in fact," he added after a short pause, "everything is possible on earth. Especially here among you Russians."

"Let's leave the Russians aside for the moment. What do you find wrong with this match?"

"Everything is wrong—everything. Lizaveta Mikhailovna is a fair-minded, serious young woman with elevated emotions, whereas he . . . he is a dilettante, in a word."

"But suppose she loves him?"

Lemm got up from his seat.

"No, she does not love him, that is to say, she is very pure in heart, and does not know herself what this means . . . love. Madame von Kalitin tells her that he is a fine young man, and she obeys Madame von Kalitin because she is still quite a child, even though she is nineteen. She says her prayers in the morning and in the evening—and that is all very well—but she does not love him. She can only love what is beautiful, and he is not—that is, his soul is not beautiful."

Lemm uttered this entire speech firmly, even forcefully, walking back and forth with short strides in front of the tea table while scanning the ground.

"Dearest maestro," Lavretskii cried suddenly, "it strikes me that you're in love with my cousin yourself."

Lemm stopped short.

"Please," he began in an uncertain voice, "do not mock me like that. I am not crazy. I am looking toward a dark grave, not toward a rosy future."

Lavretskii felt sorry for the German, and begged his pardon. After they finished their tea, Lemm played him his cantata, and after dinner, at Lavretskii's instigation, they began to talk about Liza again. Lavretskii listened to him closely, with curiosity.

"What do you think, Khristofor Fedorych?" he eventually said. "You see that everything here seems to be in order now, and the garden's in full bloom. Shouldn't we invite her to visit for a day along with her mother and my old aunt . . . eh? Would you like that?"

Lemm bent his head over his plate.

"Invite her," he murmured, barely audibly.

"And is Panshin required?"

"No, he is not required," the elderly man replied with an almost childlike smile.

Two days later, Fedor Ivanych set off for town to see the Kalitins.

XXIV

He found them all at home, but he didn't disclose his plan to them right away—he wanted to discuss it with Liza by herself first. Fortune favored him: they were left alone in the drawing room. They chatted a bit; she'd had time to get used to him by now—and she wasn't shy around anyone, as a rule. He listened to her, studied her face, and mentally repeated Lemm's words, agreeing with them. It occasionally happens that two people who have become acquainted but aren't close to one another become close in the course of a few moments, all of a sudden—and awareness of this increased closeness is immediately expressed in their eyes, in their quiet, affectionate smiles, in their very gestures. This was exactly what happened to Lavretskii and Liza. "So he's like this," she thought as she turned a friendly gaze toward him. "So you're like that," he thought in turn. Thus he wasn't overly surprised when she informed him, not without hesitating slightly, however, that she'd wanted to say something to him for a long time, but was afraid of offending him.

"Don't be afraid. Tell me," he replied, and stood still, facing her.

Liza raised her clear eyes to him.

"You're so kind," she began, and at the same time she thought, "Yes, he really is kind. . . ." "Please forgive me, I shouldn't speak to you about this . . . but how could you . . . why did you separate from your wife?"

Lavretskii shuddered. He glanced at Liza, and sat down beside her.

"My child," he began, "I beg you not to probe that wound. Your hands are tender, but it hurts me all the same."

"I know," Liza continued, as though she hadn't heard him, "she's wronged you. I don't want to defend her—but how can you put asunder what God has joined together?"

"Our convictions on that subject are too different, Lizaveta Mikhailovna," Lavretskii remarked rather sharply. "We can't understand one another."

Liza grew paler. Her whole body was trembling slightly, but she didn't desist.

"You must forgive," she murmured softly, "if you wish to be forgiven."

"Forgive!" interjected Lavretskii. "Shouldn't you first find out for whom you're interceding? Forgive that woman and take her back into my home, that empty, heartless creature! And who says that she wants to come back to me? She's perfectly satisfied with her present situation, I assure you. . . . But what a subject to discuss here! Her name should never be uttered by you. You're too pure— you aren't capable of comprehending such a creature."

"Why do you revile her this way?" Liza inquired with an effort. The trembling of her hands was perceptible now. "You yourself left her, Fedor Ivanych."

"But I've told you," Lavretskii rejoined with an involuntary burst of impatience, "you don't know what kind of creature that woman is!"

"Then why did you marry her?" Liza whispered, lowering her eyes.

Lavretskii abruptly rose from his seat.

"Why did I marry her? I was young and inexperienced then. I was deceived, I got carried away by a beautiful exterior. I didn't know any women. I didn't know anything. God grant that you have a happier marriage! But, believe me, you can't be sure of anything."

"I might be unhappy too," Liza conceded (her voice had grown unsteady), "but then I ought to reconcile myself to that. I don't know how to say this, but if we don't reconcile ourselves. . . ."

Lavretskii clenched his hands and stamped his foot.

"Don't be angry—please forgive me," Liza hurriedly begged him.

At that instant, Maria Dmitrievna came in. Liza stood up and started to leave.

"Wait a minute," Lavretskii called out to her unexpectedly. "I have a great favor to ask you and your mother. Please come and visit me in my new abode. You know I've had a piano delivered. Lemm's staying with me, the lilacs are in bloom now, you'll get a breath of country air—and you can return the same day. Will you agree to come?" Liza looked at her mother. Maria Dmitrievna was donning a long-suffering expression, but Lavretskii didn't give her time to open her mouth—he promptly kissed both her hands. Maria Dmitrievna, who was always susceptible to demonstrations of feeling and in no way expected such effusiveness from the "dolt," was won over and gave her consent. While she was deciding which day to come, Lavretskii, still greatly moved, went up to Liza and whispered to her alone: "Thank you. You're very kind. I owe you an apology," whereupon her pale face glowed with a bright, shy smile. Her eyes smiled as well—until that moment, she'd been afraid she'd offended him.

"Can Vladimir Nikolaich come with us?" inquired Maria Dmitrievna.

"Of course," Lavretskii replied, "but wouldn't it be better just to have the family?"

"Well, you know, it seems . . . ," began Maria Dmitrievna. "But do as you please," she added.

They decided to take Lenochka and Shurochka, but Marfa Timofeevna refused to join the expedition.

"It's hard for me," she said, "to give my old bones such a shaking, my dear. And there's nowhere for me to sleep at your house. Besides, I can't sleep in a strange bed. Let the young people do the frolicking."

Lavretskii didn't manage to speak to Liza in private again, but he looked at her in a way that made her feel good, and a little ashamed, and quite sorry for him. He clasped her hand warmly as he left. Once she was alone, Liza lapsed into thought.

XXV

When Lavretskii reached home, a tall, thin man wearing a threadbare blue coat, with a wrinkled yet lively face, a disheveled gray beard, a long straight nose, and small bloodshot eyes met him at the drawing-room doorway. It was Mikhalevich, his friend from the university. Lavretskii didn't recognize him at first, but embraced him warmly as soon as Mikhalevich mentioned his name. They hadn't seen one another since their Moscow days. Torrents of exclamations and questions followed; long-buried memories were revived. Rapidly smoking pipe after pipe, drinking cups of tea at a gulp, and gesturing energetically with his long arms, Mikhalevich recounted his adventures to Lavretskii. There was nothing very cheerful about them—he couldn't boast of any particular success in his various endeavors—but he repeatedly lapsed into hoarse, nervous laughter. A month earlier, he'd gotten a job in the private office of a wealthy liquor-tax collector who lived about three hundred versts from the town of O——, and learning that Lavretskii had returned from abroad, Mikhalevich had gone out of his way to see his old friend. He spoke as impetuously as he had in his youth, and was as loud and ebullient as ever. Lavretskii started to explain his situation, but Mikhalevich interrupted him, muttering hurriedly, "I've heard, my friend, I've heard—who could have predicted it?" and immediately turned the conversation to general topics.

"I have to leave tomorrow, my friend," he remarked, "so tonight, if you don't mind, we'll stay up late. Above all, I want to know what you're like, what your opinions and convictions are, what you've become, what life has taught you." (Mikhalevich still relied on the phraseology of the 1830s.) "As for me, I've changed in many ways. The waves of life have broken over my breast—who said that?—although I haven't changed in the important, essential ways. I still believe in goodness and truth. But I don't merely believe in them, now I have faith—yes, I have faith, I have faith. Listen, you know that I write verses. There's no poetry in them, but there is truth. Let me read my most recent poem aloud to you—I've expressed my deepest convictions in it. Listen." Mikhalevich began to read his poem. It was rather long, and ended with the following lines:

I gave myself over to new feelings with all my heart,
My soul became childlike.
And I've burned everything I once worshiped,
And now worship everything I once burned.

As he uttered the two last lines, Mikhalevich nearly started to weep. A slight spasm—the sign of deep emotion—crossed his wide mouth, and his unattractive face lit up. Lavretskii listened to him at length . . . and a spirit of antagonism arose within him. He was irritated by the unquenchable enthusiasm of the Moscow student, which was ever ready to burst forth. Before a quarter of an hour had elapsed, a heated argument had broken out between them, one of those endless arguments only Russians engage in. After many years' separation, living in two different worlds, lacking a clear understanding of one another's ideas or even of their own, groping for words and speaking in incomplete phrases, they argued about the most abstract issues—and they argued as though it were a matter of life and death for them both. They exclaimed and shouted so vehemently that everyone in the house was disturbed, and poor Lemm, who'd shut himself up in his room shortly after Mikhalevich's arrival, became thoroughly bewildered, and even began to feel vaguely alarmed.

"What are you then, after all this? Disillusioned?" Mikhalevich demanded to know at one o'clock in the morning.

"Do disillusioned people usually look like this?" Lavretskii replied. "They're usually quite pale and sickly. Would you like me to pick you up with one hand?"

"Well, if you aren't disillusioned, you're a *skepteek*, which is even worse." (Mikhalevich's speech retained a strong flavor of his motherland, the Ukraine.) "And what right do you have to be a *skepteek?* You've had some bad luck in life, we'll concede—but that wasn't your fault. You were born with an ardent, loving heart, and you were unnaturally isolated from women. The first woman you came across was bound to deceive you."

"She deceived you, too," Lavretskii observed grimly.

"Granted, granted. I was the tool of destiny in that. . . . What nonsense I'm uttering, though! There's no such thing as destiny. It's an old habit of mine to express things imprecisely. But what does that prove?"

"It proves this, that they psychologically deformed me from childhood on."

"Well, it's up to you to straighten yourself out! What's the good of your being a human being, a man? And in any event, is it possible, is it permissible to convert a personal experience, so to speak, into a general law, into an infallible principle?"

"What principle?" interrupted Lavretskii. "I don't acknowledge—"

"No, it's a principle—your principle," Mikhalevich interrupted in turn.

"You're an egotist, that's what it is!" he thundered an hour later. "You wanted self-gratification, you wanted pleasure in life, you wanted to live for yourself alone. . . ."

"What do you mean by self-gratification?"

"And everything deceived you—everything crumbled away beneath your feet."

"What do you mean by self-gratification, I ask you?"

"And it was bound to crumble. Either you sought support where it couldn't be found, or you built your house on shifting sands, or...."

"Speak more plainly, without the metaphors, *or* I won't understand you."

"Or—go ahead, laugh—or you had no faith, no strength of spirit. You had intellect, nothing but a modicum of intellect.... You're simply a pitiful, antiquated Voltairean, that's what you are!"

"I'm a Voltairean?"

"Yes, just like your father—and you yourself don't even suspect it."

"After all this," exclaimed Lavretskii, "I claim the right to call you a fanatic!"

"Alas," Mikhalevich responded with a contrite air, "I've done nothing thus far to deserve such an exalted title, unfortunately."

"I've finally figured out what to call you," Mikhalevich cried at three o'clock in the morning. "You aren't a skeptic, or a disillusioned man, or a Voltairean, you're an idler, idle on purpose—not a naive lazybones. Naive lazybones lie on their backs and don't do anything because they don't know how to do anything—and they don't think about anything, either. But you're a man of ideas—and yet you lie on your back. You could do something—and you don't do anything. You lie on your back with a full stomach, looking around superciliously and saying, 'It's better to lie on one's back like this, because everything people do is worthless and leads nowhere.'"

"From what, precisely, do you infer that I lie on my back?" Lavretskii protested stoutly. "Why do you attribute such views to me?"

"And besides that, you're all erudite idlers, the whole lot of you," Mikhalevich continued. "You know which leg the German limps on, you know what's wrong with the English and the French. And your pitiful erudition makes it worse—your shameful laziness, your abominable inactivity is justified by it. Some of you are even proud of it! 'I'm such a clever fellow,' you say. 'I do nothing, while these fools make such a fuss.' Yes! And there are gentlemen among us—I don't say this about you in particular—who reduce their entire lives to some sort of morass of boredom, who get used to it and live in it like—like a mushroom in white sauce," Mikhalevich added abruptly, and then laughed at his own simile. "Oh, this morass of boredom is the ruin of the Russian people. The abhorrent idler spends a whole lifetime preparing to work...."

"But what's the point of all this hostility?" Lavretskii exclaimed in turn. "Working.... Doing.... You'd be better off telling me what to do instead of condemning me, Demosthenes of Poltava!" "What a thing to say! I can't tell you that, my friend. Everyone should figure that out for themselves," retorted this Demosthenes ironically. "A landowner, a nobleman—and you don't know what to do? You have no faith, or else you'd know—no faith, and no inspiration."

"At least give me time to breathe. Give me time to look around," Lavretskii pleaded with him.

"Not for a minute, not for a second!" Mikhalevich replied, with an imperious wave of his hand. "Not for one second. Death doesn't delay, and life shouldn't delay, either."

"And when was it, where was it that human beings invented idleness?" he cried at four o'clock, in a voice finally betraying signs of weariness. "Among us! Right now, in Russia, where each separate individual has a responsibility resting upon his shoulders, a solemn obligation to God, to the people, to himself! We're asleep, and time is passing. We're asleep...."

"Permit me to observe," Lavretskii remarked, "that we aren't asleep at present, but are preventing others from sleeping instead. We're straining our throats like roosters—listen! One's crowing for the third time."

This sally made Mikhalevich laugh and calmed him down. "Until tomorrow, then," he said with a smile, and thrust his pipe into his pouch.

"Until tomorrow," Lavretskii echoed him. But the friends went on talking for more than an hour. Their voices were no longer raised, however, and their conversation was quiet, subdued, and affectionate.

Mikhalevich left the next day, despite all Lavretskii's efforts to restrain him. Fedor Ivanych couldn't persuade his friend to remain, but he'd talked to Mikhalevich to his heart's content. It appeared that Mikhalevich didn't have any money at all. The evening before, Lavretskii had noticed regretfully all the signs, all the habits, of years of poverty: Mikhalevich's boots were shabby, a button was missing from one side of his coat, his hands were unaccustomed to gloves, and his hair needed brushing. Upon arriving, he hadn't even thought of asking to get cleaned up, and at supper he'd eaten like a shark, tearing his meat apart with his fingers and crunching the bones with strong, blackened teeth. It further appeared that he hadn't saved anything from his previous job and was placing all his hopes on the tax collector, who'd hired him solely in order to have an "educated man" in his office. In spite of all that, Mikhalevich hadn't become discouraged, but had remained an idealist and a poet, living on a crust of bread, sincerely rejoicing and grieving over the fate of humanity and his own mission in life, worrying very little about how to avoid dying of hunger. Mikhalevich wasn't married, but he'd been in love countless times and had written poems to all the objects of his adoration; he'd sung the praises of a mysterious, dark-haired "noble Polish lady" with special fervor. There were rumors that this "noble Polish lady" was a plain Jewish woman well known to a goodly number of cavalry officers, it's true . . . but, after all, what do you think—does that really make any difference?

Mikhalevich didn't become very friendly with Lemm. His loud speeches and brusque manners frightened the German, who was unaccustomed to such behavior. One unfortunate person instantly, instinctively detects another, but in old age they rarely develop a friendship; and that's hardly surprising—they have nothing to share, not even hopes.

Mikhalevich had another long talk with Lavretskii before leaving, foretelling Lavretskii's ruin if he didn't see the error of his ways, urging Lavretskii to devote himself seriously to the welfare of his peasants. Mikhalevich pointed to himself as an example, saying that he'd been purified in the crucible of suffering. In the same breath, he called himself a happy man several times, comparing himself with the birds of the air and the lilies of the field.

"A black lily, though," Lavretskii commented.

"Ah, my friend, don't be a snob!" Mikhalevich retorted genially. "Just thank God instead that honest, plebeian blood runs in your veins, too. But I can see that you want some pure, heavenly creature to pull you out of your apathy."

"Thank you, my friend," Lavretskii responded. "I've had quite enough of those heavenly creatures."

"Silence, seeneek!" cried Mikhalevich.

"Cynic," Lavretskii corrected him.

"Just so, seeneek," Mikhalevich repeated, unabashed.

Even after he'd taken his seat in the carriage, to which his flat, yellow, strangely lightweight trunk had been carried, he kept on talking. (He was wrapped up in some sort of Spanish cape with a collar that was brown with age and a clasp made of two lion's paws.) He continued to expound his views on the destiny of Russia and to wave his swarthy hands in the air as though he were sowing the seeds of its future prosperity. The horses finally started. "Remember my three final words," he shouted, thrusting his whole body out of the carriage and standing on the step. "Religion, progress, humanity! . . . Goodbye!"

His head, covered by a cap pulled down to the level of his eyes, disappeared. Lavretskii remained standing alone on the steps, and he gazed steadily along the road into the distance until the carriage disappeared. "Maybe he's right, after all," Lavretskii thought as he went back into the house. "Maybe I am idle on purpose." Many of Mikhalevich's words had irrevocably penetrated his soul, even though he'd argued and disagreed with Mikhalevich. As long as someone has a good heart, no one can resist him.

XXVI

Two days later, Maria Dmitrievna visited Vasilevskoe as she'd promised, accompanied by all the young people. The little girls immediately ran into the garden, while Maria Dmitrievna languidly walked though every room and languidly admired everything. She regarded her visit to Lavretskii as an act of great condescension, as virtually a charitable deed. She smiled graciously when Anton and Aprakseia kissed her hand in the traditional house-servants' style, and requested some tea in a weak, nasal voice. To the great vexation of Anton, who'd donned white knit gloves just for the occasion, tea was served to the elegant lady visitor not by him, but by Lavretskii's hired valet, who, as the old man put it, had no notion of what was proper. To compensate for this, Anton asserted his rights at dinner: he took up a firm stance behind Maria Dmitrievna's chair and wouldn't surrender his place to anyone. The appearance of guests at Vasilevskoe after so long an interval both distressed and delighted the old man; he was certainly pleased to see that his master was acquainted with such refined people. He wasn't the only one who was agitated that day, however—Lemm was agitated as well. He'd put on a rather short, light-brown formal coat, tied his necktie stiffly, and kept coughing politely and stepping aside with a cordial, welcoming expression on his face. Lavretskii noticed with pleasure that his own relationship with Liza had become warmer: she'd held out her hand to him affectionately as soon as she'd come in.

After dinner, Lemm drew a small roll of music paper out of his coat pocket, in which he'd incessantly been fumbling, and compressing his lips, he laid it on the piano without saying a word. It was a song he'd composed the evening before, to which some old-fashioned German words had been set that made reference to stars. Liza sat down at the piano and played the song by sight.... Alas! The music turned out to be complex and painfully contrived. It was clear that the composer had striven to convey something passionate and profound, but he hadn't succeeded; the effort had remained merely an effort. Lavretskii and Liza both sensed this, and Lemm understood it. Without uttering a single word, he put his song back into his pocket, and in response to Liza's offer to play it again, he just shook his head, saying significantly, "No— that is enough!" and then, withdrawing into himself, he turned away.

Toward evening, the entire group went fishing. The pond beyond the garden was well stocked with carp and groundlings. Maria Dmitrievna settled into an armchair in the shade near the bank with a rug under her feet and was given the best fishing rod. Anton, as an old, experienced fisherman, offered her his services. He zealously put the worms on the hook, clapping his hand over them and spitting on them, and then threw the line in with a graceful forward movement of his whole body. Maria Dmitrievna spoke to Fedor Ivanych about Anton that very day, using her boarding-school French: "*Il n'y a plus maintenant de ces gens comme ça, comme autrefois.*" Lemm and the two little girls went farther off, to the pond's dam, and Lavretskii occupied a position near Liza. The fish were continually biting; the carp flashed their gold and silver scales in the air as they were reeled in. The little girls' cries of pleasure never ceased, and Maria Dmitrievna even uttered a brief, feminine shriek on two occasions. Lavretskii and Liza caught the fewest fish, probably because they paid less attention to the fishing than the others did, allowing their floats to drift right up to the bank. The high, reddish reeds rustled tranquilly all around them; the still water glimmered tranquilly in front of them; their conversation proceeded tranquilly as well. Liza stood on a small pier while Lavretskii sat on the curved trunk of a willow tree. She was wearing a white dress fastened at the waist by a broad white ribbon. Her straw hat was dangling from one hand, and she was holding a crooked fishing rod in the other with some effort. Lavretskii gazed at her well-defined, somewhat severe profile, at her hair pulled back behind her ears, at her soft cheeks glowing like a small child's, and thought, "Oh, how appealingly you stand next to my pond!" Liza wasn't turned toward him, but was looking at the water, half frowning and half smiling. The shadow of a nearby lime tree fell across both of them.

"Do you know," Lavretskii began, "I've been thinking about our last conversation a great deal and have come to the conclusion that you're an exceedingly kind person."

"That wasn't at all my intention in...," Liza started to reply, and then was overcome with embarrassment.

"You're a kind person," Lavretskii repeated. "I'm an obtuse individual, but I suspect that everyone must love you. Take Lemm, for instance. He's simply in love with you."

Liza didn't exactly frown, but she lowered her eyebrows slightly— that always happened when she heard something unpleasant.

"I was very sorry for him today," Lavretskii added, "sorry that his song failed. Being young and not to be capable of doing something is bearable, but being old and not having the ability to do something is hard to endure. And how mortifying it is not to know when your abilities are deserting you! It's difficult for an elderly man to withstand such blows!... Watch out, you have a fish about to bite.... They say," Lavretskii added after a short pause, "that Vladimir Nikolaich has written a very pretty song."

"Yes," Liza replied. "It's a mere trifle, but it's not bad."

"And what do you think?" inquired Lavretskii. "Is he a good musician?"

"I think he has a great gift for music, but thus far he hasn't worked at it the way he should."

"Ah! And is he a good person?"

Liza laughed and glanced swiftly at Fedor Ivanych.

"What a strange question!" she exclaimed, pulling in her line and throwing it out again farther off.

"Why is it strange? I'm asking you about him the way someone who's recently arrived here would, the way a relative would."

"A relative?"

"Yes. It seems I'm some sort of uncle of yours."

"Vladimir Nikolaich has a kind heart," Liza declared, "and he's intelligent. *Maman* likes him very much."

"And do you like him?"

"He's a good person. Why shouldn't I like him?"

"Ah!" Lavretskii responded, and fell silent. A half-sad, half-amused expression passed across his face. His steadfast gaze embarrassed Liza, but she went on smiling. "Well, God grant them happiness!" he eventually muttered, as though to himself, and turned his head away.

Liza blushed.

"You're mistaken, Fedor Ivanych," she said. "You're wrong to think.... But don't you like Vladimir Nikolaich?" she asked suddenly.

"No, I don't."

"Why not?"

"I don't think he has a heart."

The smile left Liza's face.

"You've gotten accustomed to judging people severely," she observed after a long silence.

"I don't think so. What right do I have to judge others severely, for heaven's sake, when I myself require leniency? Or have you forgotten that I'm a laughingstock to everyone who isn't too indifferent to laugh.... By the way," he added, "did you keep your promise?"

"What promise?"

"Did you pray for me?"

"Yes, I did pray for you—I pray for you every day. But please don't refer to that lightly."

Lavretskii began to assure Liza that the thought of doing so had never entered his mind, that he had the deepest respect for every conviction. Then he embarked upon a discourse on religion, on its significance in the history of mankind, and on the significance of Christianity....

"One must be a Christian," Liza remarked, not without some effort, "not in order to comprehend the divine...and the...earthly, but because every person has to die."

Lavretskii raised his eyes to look at Liza in involuntary astonishment, and met her gaze.

"What a strange phrase you've just uttered!" he said.

"It's not my phrase," she responded.

"Not yours.... But why did you mention death?"

"I don't know. I think about it often."

"Often?"

"Yes."

"One wouldn't have guessed that, looking at you now—you have such a bright, happy face, you're smiling...."

"Yes, I'm very happy right now," Liza replied simply.

Lavretskii would have liked to grasp both her hands and squeeze them tightly. . . .

"Liza! Liza!" cried Maria Dmitrievna. "Come here and see what a fine carp I've caught."

"One minute, *Maman*," Liza called out, and she moved toward her mother, but Lavretskii remained sitting on his willow tree. "I speak to her just as if life weren't over for me," he thought. As she went off, Liza hung her hat on a twig. Lavretskii regarded the hat and its long, rather crumpled ribbons with a strange, almost tender feeling. Liza came back shortly and took up her position on the pier again.

"What makes you think that Vladimir Nikolaich doesn't have a heart?" she inquired a few moments later.

"I've already said that I may be mistaken. Time will tell, however."

Liza grew thoughtful. Lavretskii began to tell her about his daily life at Vasilevskoe, about Mikhalevich, and about Anton. He felt the need to talk to Liza, to share everything that was occurring in his soul with her. She listened so sweetly, so attentively, and her occasional replies and observations seemed so simple and so intelligent to him. He even told her that.

Liza was surprised.

"Really?" she responded. "I thought I was like my maid, Nastia—that I had no words of my own. She said to her sweetheart one day, 'You must be bored with me. You always speak to me so elegantly, but I have no words of my own.'"

"Thank God for that!" thought Lavretskii.

XXVII

Meanwhile, evening arrived, and Maria Dmitrievna expressed a desire to return home. The little girls reluctantly left the pond and prepared for the journey. Lavretskii announced that he'd escort his guests halfway home, and ordered his horse saddled. As he was assisting Maria Dmitrievna into the carriage, he looked around for Lemm, but the elderly man was nowhere to be found; he'd disappeared as soon as the fishing had ended. With remarkable energy for his years, Anton slammed the doors shut and called out sharply, "Proceed, coachman!" The carriage started. Maria Dmitrievna and Liza were sitting in the back seat, the children and their maid in the front. The evening was calm and warm, and the windows on both sides were open. Lavretskii had his horse trot near the carriage on Liza's side, resting his hand on the door—he'd thrown the reins over the neck of the smoothly striding animal—and he occasionally exchanged a few words with Liza. The sunset's glow was disappearing, and night was setting in, yet the air seemed to grow even warmer. Maria Dmitrievna quickly fell asleep; the little girls and the maid soon fell asleep as well. The carriage rolled along swiftly and evenly.

Liza leaned forward; she was happy. The rising moon was shining on her face while the fragrant nocturnal breeze wafted over her eyes and cheeks. Her hand rested on the carriage door near Lavretskii's. He was happy, too. Borne along through the peaceful warmth of the night, never taking his eyes off that innocent young face, listening to that young voice, which was melodious even when it whispered, as it spoke about simple, decent subjects, he didn't even notice that he'd gone more than halfway. Not wanting to wake Maria Dmitrievna, he just pressed Liza's hand lightly and said, "I think we've become friends now, haven't we?" She nodded. He stopped his horse, and the carriage rolled away, gently rocking back and forth.

Lavretskii turned his horse homeward at a walking pace. The enchantment of the summer night enfolded him: everything around him suddenly seemed so strange yet so well known, so wonderfully familiar, at the same time. Everything near and far—and one could see quite far, although one couldn't clearly recognize much of what could be seen—was at peace. Youthful, blossoming life was almost palpable in this profound peace. Lavretskii's horse strode briskly, swaying rhythmically to the right and the left; its large black shadow moved along beside it. There was something unexpectedly enjoyable in the tramp of its hoofs, something uplifting and miraculous in the ringing cry of the quails. The stars had disappeared in some sort of bright mist; the moon, which wasn't full, shone with a steady brilliance; its light cast an azure stream across the sky and fell in patches of smoky gold on the thin clouds that drifted past. The fresh air brought a slight moisture to his eyes, tenderly embraced all his limbs, and freely flowed into his lungs. Lavretskii rejoiced in it all, and was pleased at his own rejoicing. "So we're still alive," he thought. "We haven't been completely destroyed by. . . ." He didn't say by what or by whom. Then he began to contemplate the fact that Liza couldn't really love Panshin; that if he'd met her under different circumstances—God knows what might have happened; that he understood what Lemm meant, even though Liza had no "words of her own." But this wasn't true, he concluded—she did have words of her own. "Don't refer to that lightly" came back to Lavretskii's mind. He rode a long way with his head bowed, and then, straightening up, he slowly repeated aloud:

And I've burned everything I once worshiped,
And now worship everything I once burned.

He prodded his horse with his whip and galloped all the way home. Dismounting from his horse, he looked around one final time with an involuntary smile of gratitude. The night, the silent, benevolent night, lay over the hills and valleys. From a distance, out of the fragrant depths—God knows whether those of the sky or the earth—rose a soft, mild warmth. Lavretskii bid Liza a final good night, and ran up the steps.

The next day passed rather monotonously; rain fell from early morning on. Lemm wore a scowl and kept compressing his lips more and more tightly, as though he'd sworn never to open them again. When Lavretskii retired to his room, he took up to bed with him a whole bundle of French newspapers and journals that had been lying unopened on his desk for more than two weeks. He began to tear open their wrappers indifferently and glance hastily through the newspaper columns—in which there was nothing new, however. He was just about to throw them aside—and suddenly leaped out of bed as if he'd been stung. In an article in one of the newspapers, Monsieur Jules, whom we've already met, communicated to his readers "a mournful bit of information. That charming and fascinating Muscovite," he wrote, "one of the queens of fashion who adorned Parisian salons, *Madame de Lavretskii*, had died quite suddenly, and this information, which was unfortunately only too well-founded," had just reached him, Monsieur Jules. He was, "one might say," so he continued, "a friend of the deceased."

Lavretskii got dressed, went out into the garden, and walked up and down the same path until morning.

XXVIII

The next morning, over tea, Lemm asked Lavretskii to let him have the horses in order for him to return to town. "It is time for me to get to work, that is, to my lessons," remarked the elderly man. "Besides, I am just wasting time here." Lavretskii didn't reply immediately—he seemed distracted. "All right," he finally said. "I'll come with you myself." Unaided by the servants, groaning angrily, Lemm packed his small suitcase, and tore up and burned a few sheets of music. The horses were harnessed. As he came out of his own room, Lavretskii put the newspaper he'd read the previous night into his pocket. During the entire journey, Lemm and Lavretskii said little to one another. Each was occupied with his own thoughts, and each was glad that the other didn't disturb him. They parted rather coolly, which is often the custom among friends in Russia, however: Lavretskii escorted the elderly man to his little house; Lemm got out, picked up his suitcase, and without holding out his hand to his friend (he was holding his suitcase in both arms against his chest), without even looking at him, merely said goodbye to him in Russian. "Goodbye," Lavretskii echoed, and ordered the coachman to drive to his lodgings—he'd rented living quarters in the town of O—— for occasional use. . . . After writing a few letters and dining hurriedly, Lavretskii went to the Kalitins'.

He found only Panshin in the drawing room. Panshin informed Lavretskii that Maria Dmitrievna would be coming in shortly, and promptly started to converse with him in engagingly cordial fashion. Until that day, Panshin had always treated Lavretskii, if not exactly haughtily, at least condescendingly. But in describing her expedition of the previous day to Panshin, Liza had spoken of Lavretskii as an admirable, intelligent man, and that was sufficient—Panshin had to make a conquest of the "admirable man." He began by complimenting Lavretskii in describing the rapture with which, according to him, Maria Dmitrievna's whole family had spoken about Vasilevskoe. Then, as was his custom, Panshin adroitly turned the conversation to himself and began to talk about his pursuits, about his opinions on life, the world, and government service, including a remark or two upon the future of Russia and the duty of rulers to maintain strict control over the country. At this point, he laughed lightheartedly at his own expense, adding that, among other things, he'd been entrusted in Petersburg with the duty *de populariser l'idée du cadastre*. He spoke at some length, dismissing any and all difficulties with nonchalant self-confidence and tossing around the weightiest administrative and political questions the way a juggler tosses balls in the air. Expressions such as "that's what I'd do if I were in the government," and "you, as an intelligent man, will immediately agree with me," were constantly on his lips. Lavretskii listened to Panshin's chatter coldly. He didn't like this handsome, intelligent, casually elegant young man who had such a bright smile, affable voice, and inquisitive eyes. With his characteristically swift insight into other people's feelings, Panshin quickly guessed that he wasn't giving his companion any special satisfaction and made some plausible excuse to leave the room, inwardly concluding that Lavretskii might indeed be "admirable," but that he was nonetheless unattractive, *aigri*, and, *en somme*, rather laughable.

Maria Dmitrievna soon appeared, escorted by Gedeonovskii. Marfa Timofeevna and Liza came in next, followed by the other members of the household. Then Mrs. Belenitsyn, the music lover, arrived. She was a small, thinnish lady with a listless, pretty, almost childish little face, wearing a rustling black dress and heavy gold bracelets, carrying a striped fan. Her husband, a fat, red-faced man with large hands and feet, white eyelashes, and an unvarying smile on his thick lips, had come with her. His wife never spoke to him in public, but at home, during moments of tenderness, she'd call him her little suckling pig. Panshin returned; the room became quite crowded and noisy. Such a crowd wasn't to Lavretskii's liking, and he was particularly irritated by Mrs. Belenitsyn, who kept staring at him through her lorgnette. He would have left at once, except for Liza. He wanted to say a few words to her in private, but he couldn't find a convenient moment for a long time, and had to content himself with watching her in secret delight; her face had never seemed lovelier and nobler to him. She gained a great deal in his eyes from being near Mrs. Belenitsyn. The latter was constantly fidgeting in her chair, shrugging her narrow little shoulders, emitting girlish little giggles, squinting, and then opening her eyes wide. Liza sat quietly, looking directly at everyone, without laughing at all.

Mrs. Kalitin sat down for a game of cards with Marfa Timofeevna, Mrs. Belenitsyn, and Gedeonovskii, who played very slowly, constantly making mistakes, then frowning and wiping his face with his handkerchief. Panshin adopted a melancholy air and expressed himself in brief, meaningful, gloomy phrases, performing the role of unappreciated genius to perfection. In spite of repeated requests by Mrs. Belenitsyn, who behaved quite coquettishly toward him, he wouldn't consent to sing his song; Lavretskii's presence constrained him. Fedor Ivanych also said little. The peculiar expression on his face had struck Liza as soon as he'd entered the room. She immediately sensed that he had something to tell her, and although she herself couldn't have said why, she was afraid to ask him what it was. Finally, as she was going into the next room to pour tea, she involuntarily turned her head in his direction. He promptly followed her.

"What's the matter?" she inquired, setting the teapot on top of the samovar.

"Why, have you noticed something?" he responded.

"You don't seem the same today as you were before." Lavretskii bent over the table.

"I wanted to tell you some news," he began, "but it's impossible right now. However, read what's marked in pencil in this article," he added, handing her the newspaper he'd brought with him. "Please keep this a secret. I'll come back tomorrow morning."

Liza was extremely puzzled. Panshin appeared in the doorway; she put the newspaper in her pocket.

"Have you read *Obermann*, Lizaveta Mikhailovna?" Panshin asked her pensively.

Liza made some reply in passing, left the room, and went up the stairs. Lavretskii returned to the drawing room and approached the card table. Flinging back the ribbons of her cap and flushing with annoyance, Marfa Timofeevna started to complain about her partner, Gedeonovskii, who, in her words, couldn't even begin to play.

"Playing cards, as you see," she said, "isn't as easy as spreading gossip."

The latter repeatedly blinked and wiped his face. Liza came into the drawing room and sat down in a corner. Lavretskii looked at her and she looked at him; both felt that the situation was intolerable. He read bewilderment and a sort of secret reproachfulness in her face. He couldn't talk to her the way he would have liked to, and to remain in the same room with her, a guest among other guests, was too painful. He decided to leave. As he said goodbye to her, he managed to repeat that he'd come tomorrow, and added that he counted on her friendship.

"Do come tomorrow," she responded with lingering bewilderment on her face.

Panshin brightened up at Lavretskii's departure; he began to give advice to Gedeonovskii, paid jocular attention to Mrs. Belenitsyn, and eventually sang his song. But when he addressed Liza, he consistently spoke and looked at her the way he had before, significantly and somewhat mournfully.

Lavretskii didn't sleep that night either. He wasn't sad, he wasn't upset, he was quite calm—but he couldn't sleep. He didn't summon up the past, he simply contemplated his life; his heart beat slowly and evenly. The hours glided by, but he didn't even think of sleep. At times, the thought would flash through his brain, "But it isn't true, it's all nonsense"—and he'd stop, bow his head, and then begin to ponder his life anew.

XXIX

Maria Dmitrievna didn't give Lavretskii an overly cordial welcome when he appeared the following day. "It seems like he's always coming and going," she thought. She didn't like him very much; moreover, Panshin, under whose influence she'd fallen, had praised him most offhandedly and insidiously the evening before. Since she didn't regard Lavretskii as a visitor, and didn't consider it necessary to entertain a relative, almost a member of the family, it turned out that, in less than half an hour, he found himself walking along a path in the garden with Liza. Lenochka and Shurochka were playing among the flowers a few feet away from them.

Liza was as calm as ever, but paler than usual. She took the piece of newspaper out of her pocket all folded up, and gave it to Lavretskii.

"That's terrible!" she said.

Lavretskii didn't reply.

"Perhaps it isn't true, though," Liza added.

"That's why I asked you not to mention it to anyone."

Liza walked a little farther.

"Tell me," she began, "aren't you saddened by this? Not at all?"

"I myself don't know how I feel," Lavretskii replied.

"But you loved her?"

"I did."

"Very much?"

"Very much."

"And you're not saddened at her death?"

"She's been dead to me for a long time."

"It's sinful to say that. Don't be angry with me. You call me your friend—a friend may say anything. To me, it's truly terrible. . . . Yesterday there was an evil look on your face. . . . Do you remember how you complained about her recently? And perhaps, at that very moment, she was dead. It's terrible. This has been sent to you as a punishment."

Lavretskii smiled bitterly.

"Do you think so? At least now I'm free."

Liza shuddered slightly.

"That's enough, don't talk like that. What good is your freedom to you? You shouldn't be thinking about that now, but about forgiveness."

"I forgave her long ago," Lavretskii interjected with a wave of his hand.

"No, that's not it," Liza responded, blushing. "You misunderstood me. You should be seeking to be forgiven."

"To be forgiven by whom?"

"By whom? By God. Who else can forgive us except God?"

Lavretskii seized her hand.

"Ah, Lizaveta Mikhailovna, believe me," he cried, "I've been punished enough as it is. I've atoned for everything already, believe me."

"You can't know that for certain," Liza murmured in an undertone. "You've forgotten—just a little while ago, when you were talking to me, you didn't want to forgive her."

She walked along the path in silence.

"And what about your daughter?" Liza asked, suddenly stopping short.

Lavretskii shivered.

"Oh, don't worry! I've already sent out letters of inquiry all over. The future of my daughter, as you call . . . as you put it, is assured. Don't worry."

Liza smiled sadly.

"But you're right," Lavretskii continued. "What can I do with my freedom? What good is it to me?"

"When did you receive that newspaper?" Liza inquired, without replying to his question.

"The day after your visit."

"Is it possible that you didn't even shed tears?"

"No, I didn't. I was thunderstruck—but where should the tears have come from? Should I have wept over the past? It's utterly extinct for me! Her crime itself didn't destroy my happiness, it merely showed me that it'd never existed at all. What was there to cry about now? Although, indeed, who knows? I might have been sadder, perhaps, if I'd gotten this news two weeks earlier."

"Two weeks earlier?" repeated Liza. "But whatever has happened in the past two weeks?"

Lavretskii didn't answer, and Liza suddenly blushed even more deeply than before.

"Yes, yes, you've guessed why," Lavretskii cried out suddenly. "In the course of these two weeks, I've gotten to know a pure woman's heart, and my past seems more remote from me than ever."

Liza became thoroughly embarrassed, and quietly walked off through the garden toward Lenochka and Shurochka.

"But I'm glad I showed you that newspaper," Lavretskii said, following behind her. "I've already gotten into the habit of not concealing anything from you, and I hope you'll repay me with the same trust."

"Do you think I will?" Liza asked, pausing. "In that case, I ought to . . . but no! That's impossible."

"What is it? Tell me, tell me."

"Really, I don't believe I should. . . . But, then again," Liza added, turning to Lavretskii with a smile, "what's the use of half-hearted trust? Do you know what? I received a letter today."

"From Panshin?"

"Yes. How did you know?"

"He's asking you to marry him?"

"Yes," Liza replied, looking straight at Lavretskii with a serious expression on her face.

Lavretskii looked at Liza seriously in return.

"Well, and what answer have you given him?" he finally managed to ask.

"I don't know what answer to give him," Liza responded, letting her clasped hands fall.

"Why not? Do you love him?"

"Yes, I like him. He seems to be a good man."

"You said the very same thing, in the very same words, four days ago. I want to know whether you love him with the intense, passionate feeling that we customarily call love?"

"As you define it—no."

"You're not in love with him?"

"No. But is that necessary?"

"What do you mean?"

"Mama likes him," Liza went on, "he's kind, and I have nothing against him."

"You're hesitating nonetheless?"

"Yes . . . and perhaps you, or your words, are the cause. Do you remember what you said three days ago? But this is weakness."

"Oh, my child!" Lavretskii exclaimed suddenly, and his voice was shaking. "Don't cheat yourself with rationalizations, don't dismiss as weakness that cry of your heart, which isn't ready to give itself to someone else without love. Don't assume such a fearful responsibility toward this man, whom you don't love and yet to whom you're prepared to belong."

"I'm just obeying—I'm not assuming any responsibility," Liza murmured.

"Obey your heart. It alone will tell you the truth," Lavretskii interrupted her. "Experience, prudence—that's all meaningless! Don't deprive yourself of the best, the sole happiness on earth."

"How can you say that, Fedor Ivanych? You yourself married for love. Were you happy?"

Lavretskii threw up his hands.

"Ah, don't talk about me! You can't begin to understand everything that a young, inexperienced, poorly brought-up boy may mistake for love! Still, after all, why should I be unfair to myself? I just told you that I hadn't been happy. . . . No! I was happy!"

"It seems to me, Fedor Ivanych," Liza declared in a low voice (when she didn't agree with the person to whom she was speaking, she always lowered her voice, and now she was deeply moved as well), "that happiness on earth doesn't depend on us."

"It does depend on us, on us alone, believe me." He seized both her hands. Liza grew pale and looked at him almost fearfully, yet intently. "If only we wouldn't ruin our own lives! For some people, marrying for love may bring unhappiness, but not for you, not with your tranquil temperament and pure soul. I implore you, don't marry without love, out of a sense of duty or self-sacrifice or anything else. . . . That's also infidelity, that's also calculation—and even worse. Believe me, I have the right to say so. I've paid dearly for that right. And if your God. . . . "

At that instant, Lavretskii noticed that Lenochka and Shurochka were standing near Liza and staring at him in mute astonishment. He dropped Liza's hands, saying hurriedly, "I beg your pardon," and turned toward the house.

"I ask just one thing of you," he added, turning back toward Liza again. "Don't decide right away. Wait a little while, and think about what I've said to you. Even if you don't believe me, even if you do decide on a marriage of prudence—even in that case, you shouldn't marry Panshin. He can't be your husband. Promise me that you won't do anything in a hurry, all right?"

Liza wanted to answer Lavretskii, but she didn't utter a word—not because she'd resolved to do something "in a hurry," but because her heart was beating too intensely, and a feeling akin to terror had taken her breath away.

XXX

As he was leaving the Kalitins', Lavretskii ran into Panshin; they bowed to one another coldly. Lavretskii went to his lodgings and locked himself in. He was experiencing emotions that he'd virtually never experienced before. How long was it since he'd been in a state of "peaceful petrification"? How long was it since he'd felt, as he'd put it, as though he were at the very bottom of the river? How had his situation changed? What had brought him up into the light? The most ordinary and inevitable—albeit always unexpected—event: death? Yes, that was it. But he wasn't thinking as much about his wife's death and his own freedom as about a question—what reply would Liza give Panshin? He felt that in the course of the last three days he'd come to view her with different eyes. He remembered how, after returning home, when he'd thought about her in the nocturnal silence, he'd said to himself, "If only . . . !" That "if only," by which he'd referred to the past, to the impossible, had become possible, although not in the way he'd imagined it. But his freedom by itself was insufficient. "She'll obey her mother," he thought. "She'll marry Panshin. But even if she refuses him, wouldn't it be all the same as far as I'm concerned?" Going up to the mirror, he minutely scrutinized his own face in every detail, and shrugged his shoulders.

The day passed quickly in such meditations, and evening arrived. Lavretskii went to the Kalitins'. He walked there swiftly, but his pace slackened as he drew near the house. Panshin's light carriage was standing in front of the steps. "Oh, well," thought Lavretskii, "I won't be an egotist"—and he entered the house. He didn't encounter anyone in the hallway, and there was no noise coming from the drawing room. He opened the door and saw Maria Dmitrievna playing cards with Panshin. Panshin bowed to him without speaking as the lady of the house exclaimed, "My, this is unexpected!" and frowned slightly. Lavretskii sat down near her and began to look at her cards.

"Do you know how to play piquet?" she asked him with a certain suppressed annoyance, and immediately declared that she'd incorrectly discarded a card.

Panshin counted to ninety and then began calmly and confidently taking tricks, maintaining a severe, dignified expression on his face. It befits diplomats to play this way—it was undoubtedly the way he played with some influential dignitary in Petersburg whom he wished to impress with his solidity and maturity. "A hundred and one, a hundred and two, hearts, a hundred and three," his voice rang out in measured tones, and Lavretskii couldn't decide whether it contained a note of reproach or of self-satisfaction.

"May I see Marfa Timofeevna?" he inquired, observing that Panshin was beginning to shuffle the cards with still greater dignity. No trace of the artist was detectable in him at that moment.

"I believe you may. She's at home, upstairs," replied Maria Dmitrievna. "Ask for her."

Lavretskii went upstairs. He found Marfa Timofeevna playing cards as well: she was playing Old Maid with Nastasia Karpovna. Roska barked at him, but both of the elderly women cordially welcomed him. Marfa Timofeevna seemed to be in particularly fine spirits.

"Ah, Fedia! Welcome!" she cried. "Please sit down, my dear. We're just finishing our game. Would you like some jam? Shurochka, bring him a serving of the strawberry. You don't want any? Well, sit right there—only please don't smoke. I can't bear the smell of your tobacco, and it makes Matross sneeze."

Lavretskii hastened to assure her that he didn't have the slightest desire to smoke.

"Have you been downstairs?" the elderly lady continued. "Whom did you see there? Is Panshin still on display? Did you see Liza? No? She was meaning to come up here. And here she is—speak of the angels. . . . "

Liza came into the room, and upon seeing Lavretskii, she blushed.

"I just came in for a minute, Marfa Timofeevna," she began.

"Why just for a minute?" interjected the elderly lady. "Why are you always in such a hurry, all you young women? You see that I have a visitor. Talk to him a little—entertain him."

Liza sat down on the edge of a chair. She raised her eyes to look at Lavretskii—and felt that it was impossible for her not to let him know how her exchange with Panshin had ended. But how could she do that? She felt both awkward and ashamed. She hadn't known him for very long—this man who so rarely went to church and who took his wife's death so calmly—yet here she was, confiding all her secrets to him. . . . It was true that he took an interest in her, that she herself trusted him and was drawn to him, but she was ashamed nonetheless, as though a strange man had entered her pure, maidenly bower.

Marfa Timofeevna came to her assistance.

"Well, if you won't entertain him," she said, "who will, the poor man? I'm too old for him, he's too intelligent for me, and he's too old for Nastasia Karpovna. She'll only pay attention to very young men."

"How can I entertain Fedor Ivanych?" Liza asked. "If he likes, I could play him something on the piano," she added irresolutely.

"That's an excellent idea. You're my bright girl," responded Marfa Timofeevna. "Go downstairs, my dears, and come back when you've finished. I've been made the Old Maid, and I don't like it. I want to exact my revenge."

Liza stood up. Lavretskii followed her. As she went down the staircase, Liza paused.

"It's right to say," she began, "that people's hearts are full of contradictions. Your example ought to frighten me, it ought to make me distrust marrying for love, but I. . . ."

"Have you rejected his proposal?" interrupted Lavretskii.

"No, but I haven't accepted it, either. I told him everything, everything that I felt, and I asked him to wait a little while. Are you pleased with me?" she added with a swift smile—and lightly resting her hand on the banister, she ran down the stairs.

"What shall I play for you?" she inquired, opening the piano.

"Whatever you like," Lavretskii answered, sitting so that he could look at her.

Liza began to play, and she didn't turn her eyes away from her fingers for a long time. When she finally glanced at Lavretskii, she stopped short. His face seemed strangely transfigured to her.

"What's the matter?" she asked.

"Nothing," he replied. "I'm perfectly fine. I'm happy to be with you. I'm happy to see you—go on."

"It seems to me," Liza said a few moments later, "that if he'd really loved me, he wouldn't have written that letter. He should have sensed that I couldn't give him an answer right now."

"That isn't important," observed Lavretskii. "What's important is that you don't love him."

"Stop it. How can we talk like this? I keep thinking about your deceased wife. You're frightening me."

"*Woldemar*, don't you think that my *Lizette* plays charmingly?" Maria Dmitrievna was saying to Panshin at that very moment.

"Yes," responded Panshin, "quite charmingly."

Maria Dmitrievna looked at her young partner tenderly, while he assumed an even more dignified, careworn expression, and bid fourteen kings.

XXXI

Lavretskii wasn't a young man; he couldn't delude himself for long as to the nature of the feelings Liza inspired in him—that very day, he arrived at the definite conclusion that he loved her. This conclusion didn't bring him any great joy. "Do I really have nothing better to do at the age of thirty-five," he thought, "than to put my soul into a woman's keeping again? But Liza isn't like *her*: she wouldn't demand degrading sacrifices from me, she wouldn't tempt me away from my responsibilities. She herself would encourage me to do honest, hard work, and we'd set off together toward a noble goal. Yes," he wound up his reflections, "that's all very fine. But the worst of it is that she doesn't want to set off with me in the least. She meant it when she said that I frightened her. But she doesn't love Panshin, either—though that's poor consolation!"

Lavretskii went back to Vasilevskoe, but he couldn't make it through four days there—he got so bored. He was also in an agony of suspense: the news from Monsieur Jules required confirmation, and he hadn't received any such letters. He returned to town and spent another evening at the Kalitins'. He could easily see that Maria Dmitrievna had turned against him, but he managed to mollify her a bit by losing fifteen rubles to her at piquet, and he spent nearly half an hour virtually alone with Liza, in spite of the fact that the previous evening her mother had advised her not to become too familiar with a man "*qui a un si grand ridicule.*" He noticed a change in her—she'd become more pensive, as it were. She reproached him for his absence and asked him whether he was going to church tomorrow. (The next day was Sunday.)

"Do go," she said, before he had time to answer. "We'll pray together for the repose of *her* soul." Then she added that she didn't know whether she had the right to make Panshin wait any longer for her decision.

"Why is that?" Lavretskii inquired.

"Because," she replied, "I'm beginning to suspect what that decision will be."

She declared that she had a headache and went off to her room upstairs after diffidently extending her fingertips to Lavretskii. Lavretskii attended the church services the next day. Liza was already inside the church when he came in. She noticed him, although she didn't turn toward him. She was praying fervently; her eyes were shining as she quietly bowed her head and raised it again. He sensed that she was praying for him, too, and his soul was filled with a wondrous tenderness. He felt both pleased and a little guilty. The people who were reverently standing there, the homely faces, the harmonious singing, the odor of incense, the long, slanting rays of light from the windows, the darkness of the walls and arched roofs, all spoke to his heart. He hadn't been to church for a long time; he hadn't turned to God for a long time. Even now, he uttered no words of prayer—he didn't even pray without words—but at least for a moment, mentally if not physically, he humbly bowed down to earth. He remembered that during his childhood he'd always prayed in church until he'd felt a cool touch, as it were, on his brow. "My guardian angel is acknowledging me," he used to think, "laying the seal of grace on me." He glanced at Liza. "You brought me here," he thought now. "Touch me, touch my soul." She was still praying quietly. Her face seemed so joyful to him; he was moved once more. He prayed for another soul's peace, and for his own forgiveness. . . .

They met on the porch. She greeted him with cheerful dignity. The sun brightly illuminated the grass in the churchyard and the striped dresses and kerchiefs the women were wearing. The bells of the nearby churches were ringing, and the crows were cawing among the hedges. Lavretskii stood with his head uncovered, a smile on his lips; a gentle breeze tossed his hair and the ribbons on Liza's hat. He put Liza and Lenochka, who'd come with her, into their carriage, divided all his money among the poor, and serenely strolled home.

XXXII

Difficult days followed for Fedor Ivanych. He found himself in a continual state of unrest. He went to the post office every morning and tore open his letters and newspapers agitatedly, but nowhere did he find anything that could confirm or disprove the fateful rumor. Sometimes he considered himself disgusting. "What am I doing," he thought, "waiting for definitive word of my wife's death, like a vulture waiting for blood?" He went to the Kalitins' every day, but things hadn't become any easier for him there: the lady of the house was obviously annoyed with him and treated him quite condescendingly; Panshin spoke to him with exaggerated politeness; Lemm had immersed himself in his misanthropy and barely bowed to him; worst of all, Liza seemed to be avoiding him. Whenever she happened to be alone with him, in place of her former openness, she now betrayed visible constraint. She didn't know what to say to him—and he felt constrained as well. In the space of a few days, Liza had begun to behave quite differently from the way she'd behaved as he'd gotten to know her: her movements, her voice, her very laugh now held a secret tremor, an unevenness that had never been there before. Maria Dmitrievna, like a true egotist, didn't suspect anything, but Marfa Timofeevna began to keep an eye on her favorite. Lavretskii reproached himself more than once for having shown Liza the newspaper he'd received. He couldn't help realizing that, to a pure nature, there was something revolting about his spiritual condition. He also realized that the change in Liza was the result of her inner conflict, her doubts about what answer to give Panshin. One day she brought Lavretskii a book, a novel by Walter Scott, which she herself had asked him for.

"Have you read it?" he inquired.

"No. I can't bring myself to read right now," she replied, and started to walk away.

"Wait a minute. It's been so long since I've been alone with you. You seem to be afraid of me."

"Yes, I am."

"Why is that, for heaven's sake?"

"I don't know."

Lavretskii fell silent.

"Tell me," he began again, "have you decided yet?"

"What do you mean?" she asked, without raising her eyes.

"You know what I mean."

Liza suddenly flushed crimson.

"Don't ask me about anything!" she burst out heatedly. "I don't know anything, I don't know myself." And she left immediately.

The following day, Lavretskii arrived at the Kalitins' after dinner and found them preparing to hold a special evening service. Small icons in gold frames decorated with tarnished jewels had already been arranged in one corner of the dining room, leaning up against the wall on a square table covered with a clean cloth. The old servant, wearing a gray suitcoat and gray shoes, was moving all around the room quietly and calmly; he set two wax candles in the slim candlesticks placed before the icons, crossed himself, bowed, and slowly went out. The dark drawing room was empty. Lavretskii went into the dining room and asked if it was someone's birthday. In a whisper, they told him that it wasn't, but that an evening service had been set up at Lizaveta Mikhailovna and Marfa Timofeevna's request, that they'd expected a miracle-working icon to have been brought there, but that it'd been taken thirty versts away to help some sick person. The priest arrived shortly thereafter, accompanied by the deacons. He was a middle-aged man with a large, bald head. He coughed loudly in the hallway; the ladies promptly filed out of the study and walked over to receive his blessing. Lavretskii bowed to them in silence, and in equal silence they bowed back to him. The priest stood still for a little while, coughed once more, and then asked in a bass undertone, "Do you want me to begin?"

"Please begin, Father," replied Maria Dmitrievna.

He started to put on his robes; a deacon in a surplice obsequiously requested a hot ember; the odor of incense began to spread. The maids and menservants came in from the hallway and stood huddled together by the door. Roska, who ordinarily never came down from upstairs, suddenly ran into the dining room. They began to chase her out; she got scared, doubled back into the room, and sat down. A servant picked her up and carried her away.

The service began. Lavretskii squeezed himself into a corner. His sensations were strange, almost sad; he himself couldn't clearly determine what he was feeling. Maria Dmitrievna stood in front of everyone else, next to the chairs. She crossed herself with languid carelessness, like a grande dame, and repeatedly looked around to the sides, then suddenly raised her eyes to the ceiling—she was bored. Marfa Timofeevna seemed worried. Nastasia Karpovna bowed down to the ground and rose again with a kind of discreet, subdued rustle. Liza remained standing motionless in place. From the look of concentration on her face, it was evident that she was praying continuously and fervently. Having bowed to the cross at the end of the service, she also kissed the priest's large, ruddy hand. Maria Dmitrievna invited him to have some tea. He took off his vestment, assumed a somewhat more worldly air, and went into the drawing room with the ladies. Conversation—albeit not lively conversation—began. The priest drank four cups of tea, repeatedly wiping his bald spot with his handkerchief. Among other things, he told them that the merchant Avoshnikov was subscribing seven hundred rubles to gild the church "cumpola," and gave them a guaranteed remedy for freckles. Lavretskii tried to sit near Liza, but her manner was severe, almost stern, and she didn't glance at him even once. She appeared to be ignoring him intentionally; some sort of cold, somber, exalted spirit seemed to have taken possession of her. For one reason or another, Lavretskii tried to smile and say something amusing, but at heart he was confused, and he finally left in silent bewilderment. . . . He felt that there was something in Liza he could never comprehend.

Another time, Lavretskii was sitting in the drawing room listening to the witty but tedious gossip of Gedeonovskii when suddenly, without knowing why himself, he turned around and caught a profound, observant, inquisitive look in Liza's eyes. . . . This inquisitive look was directed toward him. Lavretskii thought about it the whole night long. His love wasn't like a boy's: he didn't indulge in sighs and torments, and Liza herself didn't inspire that kind of passion. But love has its miseries at any age—and he was spared none of them.

XXXIII

One day Lavretskii went to the Kalitins', as was his custom. After a miserably hot day, such a lovely evening had set in that Maria Dmitrievna, in spite of her aversion to drafts, ordered all the windows and doors to the garden to be thrown open, and declared that she wouldn't play cards, that it was a sin to play cards in such weather, and that they should enjoy nature. Panshin was the sole guest. He was moved by the beauty of the evening and experienced a flood of artistic sensations, but he didn't care to sing in front of Lavretskii, so he began to read poetry aloud. He read a few poems by Lermontov (Pushkin hadn't come back into fashion as yet) quite well, but performed too self-consciously, with unwarranted refinement. Then suddenly, as though ashamed of his enthusiasm, apropos of the well-known poem "Reveries," he began to criticize the younger generation. In so doing, he availed himself of the opportunity to explain how he'd rearrange everything according to his own views, if he had the power.

"Russia," he said, "has fallen behind Europe, and has to catch up with it. It's been said that we're young—that's nonsense. However, we have no resourcefulness. Khomiakov himself admits that we haven't even invented mousetraps. Consequently, whether we want to or not, we have to borrow from others. We're sick, Lermontov says, and I agree with him. But we're sick because we've become only half European. The more damage we've done to ourselves, the greater is our obligation to save ourselves" (*"le cadastre,"* thought Lavretskii). "The best minds, *les meilleures têtes,* among us," he continued, "have long been convinced of this. All nations are essentially the same. Simply introduce proper institutions, and the deed is done. Of course, adaptations to fit the specific circumstances of a given nation may be required, and that's our affair— the affair of the official" (he almost said ruling) "class. But in case of an emergency, have no fear. The institutions will transform those very circumstances."

Maria Dmitrievna most heartily concurred with everything Panshin said. "What an intelligent man is holding forth in my drawing room!" she thought. Liza sat in silence, leaning back against the window. Lavretskii also kept silent. Marfa Timofeevna, playing cards with her old friend in the corner, muttered something to herself. Panshin paced up and down the room, speaking eloquently, yet with suppressed exasperation. It seemed as if he were criticizing not an entire generation, but a few select people he knew.

A nightingale had built its nest in a large lilac bush in the Kalitins' garden, and its early evening notes filled in the pauses of the elaborate speech. The first stars were just beginning to shine in the rosy sky over the motionless tops of the lime trees. Lavretskii stood up and started to respond to Panshin; an argument sprang up. Lavretskii championed Russian youth and autonomy. He was prepared to condemn himself and his generation, but he defended the new Russians and their convictions, their desires. Panshin replied sharply and irritably, maintaining that intelligent people were obliged to change everything. He eventually even got to the point of forgetting his status as a *Kammerjunker* and his position as a government official, calling Lavretskii an antiquated conservative and even hinting—quite obliquely, to be sure—at Lavretskii's dubious position in society.

Lavretskii didn't lose his temper. He didn't raise his voice (he recalled that Mikhalevich had also called him antiquated, albeit an antiquated Voltairean) and calmly proceeded to refute Panshin on every point. He proved to him the impracticability of sudden shifts and reforms imposed from the heights of officialdom that were justified neither by knowledge of the native land nor by any genuine faith in any ideal, even a negative one. He adduced his own education as an example, and, above all, demanded recognition of the people's truth and submission to it, without which even the most courageous battle against falsehood is impossible. Finally, he accepted the reproach—which was well deserved, in his opinion—for his reckless waste of time and energy.

"That's all very fine!" Panshin finally cried, getting angry. "You've just returned to Russia—what do you intend to do?"

"Cultivate the soil," responded Lavretskii, "and try to cultivate it as well as possible."

"That's highly praiseworthy, no doubt," Panshin retorted, "and I've been told that you've already had great success along those lines, but you must admit that everyone isn't fit for pursuits of that kind."

"*Une nature poétique*," observed Maria Dmitrievna, "can't cultivate, of course . . . *et puis*, it's your destiny, Vladimir Nikolaich, to do everything *en grand*."

This was too much, even for Panshin. He fell silent, and then changed the subject. He tried to turn it to the beauty of the starlit sky, to the music of Schubert, but somehow nothing took hold. He ended up proposing a game of piquet to Maria Dmitrievna.

"What? On such an evening?" she replied feebly. Nevertheless, she ordered the cards to be brought out.

Panshin opened a new deck of cards with a loud smack, while both Liza and Lavretskii stood up, as if by agreement, and went over to sit down near Marfa Timofeevna. They both suddenly felt so happy that they were even a little afraid of being alone together, and, at the same time, they both felt that the embarrassment they'd been conscious of for the past few days had vanished, never to return. The elderly woman stealthily patted Lavretskii on the cheek, squinted slyly, and shook her head once or twice, adding in a whisper, "You've silenced that bright young man. Many thanks." Everything became hushed in the room; the only sounds were the faint crackling of the wax candles, the occasional tap of someone's hand on the table, an exclamation or the calculation of points by the card players, and the rich torrent of the nightingale's powerfully,

piercingly sweet song, which poured in at the window along with
the dewy freshness of the night.

XXXIV

Liza hadn't uttered a single word during the course of the dispute
between Lavretskii and Panshin, but she'd followed it closely and
was completely on Lavretskii's side. Politics interested her very
little, but the supercilious tone adopted by the worldly official (he'd
never delivered his opinions in that manner before) repelled her,
and his contempt for Russia wounded her. It had never occurred
to Liza that she was a patriot, but she felt an affinity with the
common Russian people, and the Russian turn of mind delighted
her. She'd talk to the peasant overseer of her mother's property
without any constraint whatsoever for hours on end when he came
to town, speaking to him as she would to an equal, without displaying the slightest condescension of a social superior. Lavretskii
perceived all this; he wouldn't have taken the trouble to respond
to Panshin if he'd been alone—he'd spoken solely for Liza's sake.
They hadn't said anything to one another, their eyes had seldom
even met. But they both realized that they'd become much closer
that evening; they realized that they liked and disliked the same
things. They differed on only one point—but Liza secretly hoped
to convert him to God.

They sat near Marfa Timofeevna and appeared to be watching
her play—indeed, they really were watching her—but in the meantime, their hearts were swelling in their breasts, and nothing was
lost on them. It was for them that the nightingale was singing and
the stars were shining and the trees were murmuring gently, lulled
to sleep by the summer's warmth and mildness. Lavretskii was
completely carried away, surrendering himself wholly to his passion, rejoicing in it. But no words can express what was happening
in Liza's pure heart—it was a mystery to her as well. And may it
remain a mystery to everyone. No one knows, no one has ever
seen or will ever see how the seed destined for life and growth
bursts open and ripens in the bosom of the earth.

The clock struck ten. Marfa Timofeevna went upstairs to her
own room with Nastasia Karpovna. Lavretskii and Liza walked
across the drawing room, paused at the door opened to the garden,
glanced out into the dark distance and then at one another, and
smiled. They could have clasped each other's hands, it seemed,

and talked to their hearts' content. But they returned to Maria
Dmitrievna and Panshin, whose game of piquet was still dragging
on. The last king was finally played and the lady of the house,
sighing and groaning, rose from her well-cushioned easy chair.
Panshin picked up his hat, kissed Maria Dmitrievna's hand, remarking that nothing hindered some fortunate people from going
to sleep now, but that he had to stay up working on some stupid
papers until morning, and departed, bowing coldly to Liza (he
hadn't expected that she'd ask him to wait so long for a reply to
his proposal, and he was therefore annoyed with her). Lavretskii
followed him. They said good night at the gate. Panshin awakened
his driver by poking him in the neck with the end of his cane,
took a seat in his carriage, and rolled off.

Lavretskii didn't want to go home. He walked away from town
toward the open countryside. The night was calm and bright,
although there was no moon. Lavretskii rambled over the dewy
grass for a long while. He came across a narrow little path and set
off along it. It led him up to a long fence, then to a little gate.
Without knowing why, he pushed on it. The gate opened with a
faint creak, as though it'd been awaiting the touch of his hand.
Lavretskii went into a garden. After going a few paces along a path
lined by lime trees, he stopped short in amazement: he recognized
the Kalitins' garden.

He promptly stepped into a dark patch of shade cast by a thick
hazel bush and stood in that spot for a long time, shrugging his
shoulders in astonishment.

"This can't have happened by accident," he thought.

Everything around him was hushed. No sound reached him from
the direction of the house. He moved forward cautiously. At a bend
in the path, the entire house suddenly revealed its dark face; a
light was shining only in two upstairs windows. A candle was
burning behind a white curtain in Liza's room, and a lamp with
a red flame was glowing in front of the icon in Marfa Timofeevna's
bedroom and was being reflected by the gold frame with an equal
glow. Downstairs, the door onto the balcony was standing wide
open. Lavretskii sat down on a wooden garden bench, leaned on
his hand, and began to watch this door, as well as Liza's window.
It struck midnight in town, and a little clock in the house also
shrilly chimed twelve as the night watchman echoed it with short
strokes on a hollow board. Lavretskii was thinking of nothing,

expecting nothing. It was delightful for him just to feel that he was near Liza, to sit in her garden on a bench where she herself had sat more than once.

The light in Liza's room vanished.

"Sleep well, my dear girl," Lavretskii whispered, continuing to sit motionless, his eyes fastened on the darkened window.

Suddenly, a light appeared in one of the windows on the ground floor, then moved into another window, and then a third. . . . Someone was walking through the rooms carrying a candle. "Could it be Liza? It couldn't be." Lavretskii stood up. . . . He caught a glimpse of a familiar face—Liza had walked into the drawing room. Wearing a white robe, her hair hanging loose around her shoulders, she quietly went up to the table, bent over it, put down the candle, and began to look for something. Then, turning around to face the garden, she approached the open door and paused on the threshold, a delicate, slender figure all in white. A tremor ran through Lavretskii.

"Liza!" broke from his lips, barely audibly.

She shivered, and began to peer into the darkness.

"Liza!" Lavretskii repeated more loudly, and he stepped out of the shadows onto the path.

Liza raised her head in alarm and shrank back—she'd recognized him. He called to her a third time and stretched out his arms toward her. She moved away from the door into the garden.

"Is that you?" she asked. "You're here?"

"I—I—listen to me," Lavretskii whispered, and seizing her hand, he led her to the bench.

She followed him without resistance, her pale face, her immobile eyes, and all her movements expressing unutterable bewilderment. Lavretskii made her sit down, and stood facing her.

"I didn't mean to come here," he began. "Something led me. . . . I—I love you," he announced with involuntary horror.

Liza slowly looked at him. It seemed as though only at that very instant did she know where she was and what was happening. She tried to stand up but couldn't, and she covered her face with her hands.

"Liza," Lavretskii murmured. "Liza," he repeated, and knelt at her feet.

Her shoulders began to heave slightly; the fingers of her pale hands pressed against her face more firmly.

"What is it?" Lavretskii asked, and caught the sound of a subdued sob. His heart stood still. . . . He grasped the meaning of those tears. "Can it be that you love me?" he whispered, caressing her knees.

"Get up," he heard her voice say. "Get up, Fedor Ivanych. What are we doing?"

He stood up and sat down beside her on the bench. She wasn't crying any more, and she gazed at him steadily with moist eyes. "This frightens me. What are we doing?" she reiterated.

"I love you," he told her again. "I'm ready to devote my entire existence to you."

She shivered again, as though she'd been stung by something, and raised her eyes toward the sky.

"All that is in God's hands," she asserted.

"But do you love me, Liza? Will we be happy?" She lowered her eyes. He gently drew her toward him, and her head sank onto his shoulder. . . . He bent his head a little and touched her pale lips.

Half an hour later, Lavretskii was standing in front of the little garden gate. He found it locked, and had to climb over the fence. He returned to town and walked along the slumbering streets. A sense of immense, unhoped-for happiness was filling his soul; all his doubts had faded away. "Vanish, dark phantom of the past!" he thought. "She loves me, she'll be mine." Suddenly, it seemed to him that strains of divine, triumphant music were floating in the air above his head. He stopped. The sounds reverberated with even greater splendor. They streamed forth in a powerful flood— and it seemed that all his bliss was voiced, was singing in those sounds. He looked around; the music was floating down from the two upper windows of a small house.

"Lemm!" Lavretskii cried as he ran toward the house. "Lemm! Lemm!" he cried more loudly.

The sounds died away and the figure of the elderly man appeared at the window. He was in a robe, his chest bare, his hair disheveled.

"Aha!" he exclaimed with dignity. "Is it you?"

"Khristofor Fedorych, what marvelous music! For heaven's sake, let me in."

Not uttering a word, the elderly man threw the key to the street door out of the window with a majestic flourish of his arm.

Lavretskii ran upstairs, went into Lemm's room, and started to rush up to the German, but the latter imperiously motioned him to a chair, saying abruptly in Russian, "Sit down and listen," seated himself at the piano, looked around proudly and sternly, and began to play. It had been a long time since Lavretskii had heard anything like this. The lovely, passionate melody seized his heart from the very first note: it glowed and ached with inspiration, joy, and beauty; it swelled and melted away; it evoked everything precious, mysterious, and sacred on earth. It bespoke immortal sadness and mounted to the sky, dying away. Lavretskii straightened up and arose, cold and pale with ecstasy. The music seemed to clutch at his very soul, so recently shaken by the raptures of love—the music was ablaze with love, too. "Play it again," he whispered as soon as the final chord resounded. Lemm threw him a sharp glance, struck his hand against his chest, and, saying deliberately in his own language, "I did this, for I am a great musician," he played his marvelous composition once more.

There was no candle in the room; the light of the rising moon slanted through the window; the mild air vibrated with sound. The poor little room seemed to have become a shrine. The elderly man's head was outlined in the silvery half-light, appearing noble and inspired. Lavretskii went up and embraced him. At first, Lemm didn't respond to Lavretskii's embrace, and even pushed him away with one elbow. He maintained the same stern, almost morose, expression on his face, without moving a muscle for a long time, merely growling, "Aha!" twice. But his transfigured face finally relaxed and looked calmer. He first smiled a little in response to Lavretskii's hearty congratulations, then burst into tears and sobbed weakly, like a child.

"It is incredible that you have arrived at this very moment," he said, "but I know, I know everything."

"You know everything?" Lavretskii echoed him in amazement.

"You heard me," replied Lemm. "Have you not understood that I know everything?"

Lavretskii couldn't fall asleep until daybreak; he sat up on his bed all night. Liza didn't sleep, either—she was praying.

XXXV

The reader knows how Lavretskii was reared and molded; now we'll say a few words about Liza's upbringing. Her father had died when she was ten, but he'd never overly concerned himself about her. Burdened with business affairs, ever anxious to increase his property, bilious, sharp-tongued, and impatient, he unsparingly spent money on teachers, governesses, clothes, and the other things his children required, but he couldn't bear "to play nursemaid to squalling brats," as he put it, and, indeed, he didn't have time to play nursemaid. He worked for hours on end, slept little, occasionally played cards, and worked some more. He periodically compared himself to a horse harnessed to a threshing machine. "My life has slipped by so quickly," was his sole comment on his deathbed, as a bitter smile spread across his parched lips. Maria Dmitrievna hadn't really worried about Liza any more than her husband had, even though she'd boasted to Lavretskii that she'd brought up her children by herself. She'd dressed Liza like a doll, stroked her on the head in front of visitors, called her a bright child and a little darling to her face—and that was all. Any kind of continuous activity was too exhausting for the indolent lady.

During her father's lifetime, Liza was put in the care of a governess from Paris, Mademoiselle Moreau; after his death, she passed into the care of Marfa Timofeevna, whom the reader already knows. Mademoiselle Moreau was a tiny, wrinkled creature with birdlike manners and a birdlike intellect. She'd led a highly dissipated life in her youth, but she'd retained only two passions in her old age—eating and cards. When she'd eaten her fill and was neither playing cards nor chatting, her face assumed an almost deathlike expression. She'd sit in a chair, look around, and breathe—yet it was clear that there wasn't a single idea in her head. One couldn't even call her good-natured—birds aren't good-natured. As a result of either her frivolous youth or the Parisian air she'd inhaled since childhood, a kind of cheap, generalized skepticism had insinuated itself into her mind, which was usually expressed by the words *tout ça c'est des bêtises*. She spoke ungrammatically but in a pure Parisian dialect, didn't spread gossip, and had no special idiosyncrasies—what more can one desire in a governess? She exerted little influence over Liza; hence, all the stronger was the influence her nursemaid, Agafia Vlasevna, did exert over her.

This woman's story was remarkable. She came from a peasant family. She married a peasant laborer at the age of sixteen, but she was strikingly different from other peasant girls. Her father had been an overseer for twenty years, had made a good deal of money, and had spoiled her. She was exceptionally beautiful—the best-dressed girl in the entire district—as well as intelligent, articulate, and spirited. Her master, Dmitrii Pestov, Maria Dmitrievna's father, a shy, gentle individual, saw her in the threshing barn one day, talked to her, and fell passionately in love with her. She was widowed shortly thereafter. Even though he was a married man, Pestov had her moved into his house and clothed like a lady. Agafia immediately adapted to her new situation, just as if she'd never lived any differently during her entire life. She grew paler and plumper; her arms became as "floury-white" as a merchant's wife's under her muslin sleeves. The samovar never left her table, she wore nothing but silk or velvet, and she slept on well-stuffed feather beds.

This blissful existence lasted for five years, but then Dmitrii Pestov died. His widow, a kindhearted woman, in regard for the memory of the deceased, didn't wish to treat her rival unfairly, all the more so because Agafia had never forgotten her status in the widow's presence. She married Agafia off to a cowherd, however, and sent her a long way away. Three years passed. Then, one hot summer day, in riding past, her mistress happened to stop at the cattleyard. Agafia served her such delicious, cool cream, behaved so modestly, and was so neat, so cheerful, so contented with everything, that her mistress indicated her forgiveness and allowed Agafia to return to the house. Within six months she'd become so attached to Agafia that she promoted her to housekeeper and entrusted the management of the entire household to her. Agafia returned to power once again, and once again grew plump and pale. Her mistress placed the utmost confidence in her.

Thus passed five more years, and then another misfortune overtook Agafia. Her husband, whom she'd promoted to the position of footman, began to drink, periodically vanishing from the house, and ended up stealing six of the mistress's silver spoons and hiding them in a box belonging to his wife until a favorable moment might arrive to take them away. The box was opened. He was sent to work as a cowherd again, and Agafia fell into disfavor. She wasn't thrown out of the house, but she was demoted from housekeeper to sewing-woman and was ordered to wear a kerchief on her head instead of a cap. To everyone's astonishment, Agafia bore the blow that had fallen upon her with humble resignation. She was about thirty at the time; all her children were dead, and her husband didn't live much longer. The time had come for her to reflect—and reflect she did. She became quite silent and devout, never missing a single morning or Sunday church service, and giving away all her fancy clothes. She spent fifteen years quietly, sub-missively, and sedately, never quarreling with anyone, deferring to everyone. If someone criticized her, she merely bowed to them and thanked them for the admonition. Her mistress had forgiven Agafia long ago, restoring her to favor and presenting her with one of her own caps. But Agafia herself was unwilling to give up her kerchief, and always wore a dark dress. After her mistress's death, she became even more quiet and submissive. Russians readily feel fear and affection, but it's hard to gain their respect: it's neither given quickly nor to just anyone. But everyone in the household had great respect for Agafia; no one even remembered her earlier sins, as though they'd been buried along with the old master.

When Kalitin became Maria Dmitrievna's husband, he wanted to entrust the care of the house to Agafia, but she refused, "for fear of temptation." He chastised her, but she just bowed meekly and left the room. Kalitin was adept at understanding people; he understood Agafia, and didn't forget her. When he moved to town, he assigned Agafia—with her consent—the position of nursemaid to Liza, who'd recently turned five years old.

Liza was initially frightened by the austere, serious face of her new nursemaid, but she quickly became accustomed to Agafia and began to love her. Liza herself was a serious child. Her features resembled Kalitin's—well-defined and regular—but her eyes were not her father's: they shone with a quiet concentration and a goodness rare in children. She didn't like to play with dolls, never laughed loudly or for long, and behaved with remarkable decorum. She didn't often become thoughtful, but when she did, it was almost always for a good reason; after a brief silence, she'd usually turn to some adult with a question that showed she'd been contemplating some new impression. She outgrew a childish lisp early on, and by the time she was four years old spoke perfectly clearly. She was afraid of her father; her feelings toward her mother were somewhat undefined—Liza wasn't afraid of her, but neither was she affectionate toward her; then again, she wasn't even affectionate toward Agafia, although this was the only person Liza loved.

Agafia never left her side. It was odd to see them together. Dressed all in black with a dark kerchief on her head, her thin face as transparent as wax but still beautiful, still expressive, Agafia would sit up straight, knitting a stocking; Liza would sit at her feet in a little chair, also occupied with some kind of handiwork or, gravely raising her bright eyes, listening to what Agafia was telling her. Agafia wouldn't tell her stories—in even, measured tones, she'd narrate the life of the Holy Virgin, as well as the lives of hermits, saints, and holy martyrs. She'd tell Liza how the martyrs had lived in deserts, how they'd been saved, how they'd suffered from hunger and deprivation and hadn't feared kings, but had confessed their belief in Christ, how the birds of the air had brought them food and the wild beasts had obeyed them, and how flowers had sprung up in the places where their blood had been spilled. "Water lilies?" Liza asked one day—she was very fond of flowers. . . . Agafia spoke to Liza solemnly and yet humbly, as though she deemed herself unworthy to utter such exalted, sacred words. As Liza listened to her, the image of a ubiquitous, omniscient God lodged in her very soul with some sort of pleasing power, filling it with pure, reverent awe. Christ, by contrast, became somehow close and familiar, almost related to her.

Agafia also taught her to pray. Sometimes she'd awaken Liza early, at daybreak, dress her hurriedly, and secretly take her to the morning service. Liza would follow her on tiptoe, almost holding her breath. The cold half-light of the early morning, the cleanliness and emptiness of the church, the very secrecy of these unexpected expeditions, the cautious return home to her little bed—all these mingled impressions of the forbidden, the strange, and the holy made a strong impression on the little girl and penetrated to the very innermost depths of her being.

Agafia never criticized anyone, and never scolded Liza for misbehaving. When Agafia was displeased with anything, she merely fell silent. And Liza understood this silence; with a child's perspicacity, she also knew perfectly well when Agafia was displeased with other people, including Maria Dmitrievna or Kalitin himself. Agafia was Liza's nursemaid for a little over three years, then Mademoiselle Moreau replaced her. But the frivolous Frenchwoman, with her icy demeanor and her exclamation "*tout ça c'est des bêtises*," could never dislodge this beloved being from Liza's heart—the seeds that had been sown in it had become too deeply rooted. Besides, even though Agafia was no longer Liza's nursemaid, she remained in the house and frequently saw her charge, who had as much faith in Agafia as before.

Agafia didn't get along very well with Marfa Timofeevna when she came to live at the Kalitins' house, however. Such gravity and dignity on the part of someone who'd once worn the motley skirt of a peasant girl annoyed the impatient, self-willed elderly woman. Agafia subsequently asked permission to go on a pilgrimage, and never came back. Dark rumors circulated that she'd entered a convent run by schismatics. But the impression she'd made on Liza's soul was never obliterated. Liza went to services just as she had before, as though she were going to a festival; she prayed with rapture, with a kind of restrained, embarrassed transport at which Maria Dmitrievna secretly quite marveled. Even Marfa Timofeevna, although she never restricted Liza in any way, tried to temper her zeal, and wouldn't let her bow too often during her prayers—it wasn't a ladylike habit, Marfa Timofeevna declared.

Liza was a good student, that is to say, a persevering one. She wasn't blessed with especially brilliant talents or an expansive intellect; she couldn't achieve anything effortlessly. She played the piano well, but only Lemm knew what that had cost her. She'd read fairly little, she didn't have any "words of her own"—but she did have her own ideas, and she went her own way. It wasn't a mere accident that she resembled her father—he'd never asked other people what he should do, either. So she'd grown up tranquilly and unhurriedly until she'd reached the age of nineteen. She was very attractive without being aware of it herself. Her every movement was full of spontaneous, somewhat artless grace; her voice had the silvery ring of innocent youth; the slightest feeling of pleasure brought an enchanting smile to her lips and added a deep luster and some sort of veiled tenderness to her shining eyes. Pervaded through and through by a sense of duty, by a dread of hurting anyone at all, endowed with a generous, compassionate heart, she loved everyone—and no one in particular. God alone she loved passionately, timidly, and tenderly. Lavretskii was the first person to intrude upon her peaceful inner life.

This was Liza.

XXXVI

At twelve noon on the following day, Lavretskii set off for the Kalitins'. On the way, he saw Panshin galloping past him on horseback, his hat pulled down to his very eyebrows. Lavretskii wasn't invited into the Kalitins' for the first time since he'd renewed his acquaintance with them. Maria Dmitrievna was "resting," a servant informed him—her ladyship had a headache; Marfa Timofeevna and Lizaveta Mikhailovna weren't home. Lavretskii walked around to the garden in the faint hope of finding Liza, but he didn't see anyone. He came back two hours later and met with the same reception, accompanied by a somewhat dubious look from the servant. Lavretskii considered it unseemly to drop by for a third time the same day, and he decided to go to Vasilevskoe, where he had some business to take care of, in any event. Along the way, he made various plans for the future, each one better than the last, but he was overcome by sadness when he reached his aunt's little estate. He lapsed into conversation with Anton; as if on purpose, the old servant seemed full of morbid ideas. He told Lavretskii how, at the moment of her death, Glafira Petrovna had bitten her own arm. Then, after a brief pause, he added with a sigh: "Everyone, dear master, is destined to devour himself."

It was late when Lavretskii left to go back to town. He was haunted by the music of the previous day, and Liza's image returned to him in all its appealing clarity. He lingered with melting tenderness over the thought that she loved him, and reached his little residence soothed and happy.

The first thing that struck him as he walked into the hallway was an odor of patchouli, which had always been repellent to him. There were some tall traveling trunks standing there. The expression on the face of the servant who ran out when he arrived looked strange to him. Not stopping to analyze these impressions, he crossed the threshold into the drawing room. . . . Upon his entrance, a lady wearing a black silk dress with flounces on it rose from the sofa, lifting a cambric handkerchief to her pale face. She took a few steps forward, bent her carefully coifed, perfumed head, and knelt at his feet. . . . Then, only then, did he recognize her: this lady was his wife!

He caught his breath. . . . He leaned against the wall.

"*Théodore*, don't drive me away!" she said in French, and her voice cut to his heart like a knife.

He looked at her vacantly, and yet he instantly, involuntarily noticed that she'd gotten both paler and fleshier.

"*Théodore!*" she repeated, raising her eyes from time to time and discreetly wringing her marvelously beautiful hands, with their rosy, polished fingernails. "*Théodore*, I've wronged you, wronged you terribly. I'll say more—I've committed a crime. But listen to me—I'm tortured by remorse. I've become hateful to myself, I couldn't endure my situation any longer. How many times I've thought of returning to you, but I feared your anger. I've resolved to break every tie with the past. . . . *Puis, j'ai été si malade.* . . . I've been so ill," she added, drawing her hand across her forehead and cheek. "I took advantage of the widespread rumor of my death— I forsook everything. I hurried here without stopping day or night.

I hesitated for a long while before appearing before you, my judge . . . *paraître devant vous, mon juge.* But, remembering your constant goodness, I finally decided to come to your home—I found out your address in Moscow. Believe me," she continued, slowly getting up from the floor and sitting on the very edge of an armchair, "I've often thought about death, and would have found enough courage to take my own life. . . . Ah! Life's an unbearable burden for me now! . . . But the thought of my daughter, my little Ada, stopped me. She's here, she's asleep in the next room, the poor child! She's tired—you'll see her soon. At least she hasn't wronged you. But I'm so unhappy, so unhappy!" exclaimed Mrs. Lavretskii, and she dissolved into tears.

Lavretskii finally collected himself. He moved away from the wall and turned toward the door.

"You're leaving?" his wife cried in a despairing voice. "Oh, that's cruel! Without saying a single word to me—not even a reproach. . . . This contempt will kill me, it's so terrible!"

Lavretskii halted.

"What do you want to hear from me?" he asked in an expressionless tone.

"Nothing, nothing," she replied quickly. "I know that I have no right to expect anything. I'm not insane, believe me—I don't hope, I don't dare to hope for your forgiveness. I only dare to beg you to tell me what I should do, where I should live. I'll fulfill all your commands, whatever they may be, like a slave."

"I have no commands to give you," Lavretskii replied in the same expressionless tone of voice. "You know that everything's over between us . . . and now more so than ever. You can live anywhere you like, and if your allowance is too small. . . ."

"Ah, don't say such dreadful things," Varvara Pavlovna interrupted him. "Spare me, if only . . . if only for the sake of this angel." As she uttered these words, Varvara Pavlovna impulsively ran into the next room and promptly returned with a small, very elegantly dressed little girl in her arms. Thick, light-brown curls fell across her pretty, rosy little face and onto her large, sleepy, dark eyes. She smiled and blinked her eyes at the light, laying a chubby little hand on her mother's neck.

"*Ada, vois, c'est ton père,*" said Varvara Pavlovna, pushing the curls away from her daughter's eyes and kissing her vigorously. "*Prie le avec moi.*"

"*C'est ça papa?*" stammered the little girl, lisping.

"Oui, mon enfant, n'est-çe pas que tu l'aimes?"

But this was more than Lavretskii could bear.

"Which melodrama is it that contains a scene just like this one?" he muttered, and walked out of the room.

Varvara Pavlovna stood in the same place for some time, then shrugged her shoulders slightly, carried the little girl into the next room, undressed her, and put her to bed. Next she picked up a book, sat down near a lamp, and, after waiting for about an hour, went to bed herself.

"Eh bien, madame?" queried her maid, a Frenchwoman whom she'd brought from Paris, as she helped Varvara Pavlovna undress.

"Eh bien, Justine," she replied. "He's much older, but I imagine that he's just as good-natured as ever. Give me my gloves for the night, get out my gray, high-necked dress for tomorrow, and don't forget the mutton cutlets for Ada. . . . I suppose it'll be difficult to get them here, but we have to try."

"A la guerre comme à la guerre," Justine responded, as she put out the candle.

XXXVII

Lavretskii wandered around the town streets for more than two hours; he recalled the night he'd spent in the outskirts of Paris. His heart was throbbing, and the same dark, incoherent, vile thoughts kept recurring in his stunned, senseless brain. "She's alive, she's here," he repeated with ever-increasing amazement. He realized that he'd lost Liza, and anger choked him—this blow had fallen on him too suddenly. How could he so readily have believed the nonsensical gossip in a newspaper, a wretched scrap of rag? "Well, if I hadn't believed it," he thought, "what would have been the difference? I wouldn't have known that Liza loved me. She wouldn't have known it herself." He couldn't rid himself of his wife's image, her voice, her eyes . . . and he cursed himself, he cursed everything on earth.

Toward morning, exhausted, he finally went to Lemm's. For a long while, he couldn't make anyone hear him. The elderly man's head eventually appeared at a window, adorned with a nightcap. His face looked sour, wrinkled, and utterly unlike the inspired, austere visage that had regally gazed at Lavretskii with all the hauteur of artistic majesty twenty-four hours earlier.

"What do you want?" asked Lemm. "I cannot play for you every night. I have taken some medicine for a cold." But Lavretskii's face evidently struck him as quite strange. The elderly man shaded his eyes with his hand, took a second look at his nocturnal visitor, and let him in.

Lavretskii went into Lemm's room and sank into a chair. Lemm stood facing him, wrapping his shabby, striped robe around himself, contorting his mouth and chewing on his lips.

"My wife has arrived," Lavretskii blurted out. He raised his head and suddenly burst into involuntary laughter.

Lemm's face expressed bewilderment; he didn't even smile. He merely wrapped himself more tightly in his robe.

"Of course, you don't know," Lavretskii continued. "I'd imagined . . . I'd read in a newspaper that she was dead."

"O-oh. Had you read that recently?" asked Lemm.

"Yes, quite recently."

"O-oh," the elderly man repeated, raising his eyebrows. "And she has arrived?"

"Yes. She's at my house now, and I . . . I'm an unhappy man." He laughed again.

"You are an unhappy man," Lemm echoed slowly.

"Khristofor Fedorych," Lavretskii began, "would you be willing to deliver a note for me?"

"Hmm. May I know to whom?"

"Lizavet. . . ."

"Ah . . . yes, yes, I understand. Very well. And when must the note be delivered?"

"Tomorrow, as early as possible."

"Hmm. I can send Katrine, my cook. No, I will go myself."

"And will you bring me a reply?"

"Yes, I will bring a reply."

Lemm sighed.

"Yes, my poor young friend—you certainly are an unhappy young man."

Lavretskii wrote a few words to Liza. He informed her of his wife's arrival, begged her to arrange to meet him, and then flung himself on the narrow sofa with his face turned to the wall. The elderly man lay down on the bed and muttered to himself for a long time, coughing and drinking his medicine in gulps.

Morning came; they both got up. They looked at one another with strange gazes. At that moment, Lavretskii longed to kill himself. The cook, Katrine, brought them some horrible coffee. The clock struck eight. Lemm put on his hat, and saying that he was supposed to give a lesson at the Kalitins' at ten but could find a suitable pretext for going there now, he set off. Lavretskii flung himself back onto the little sofa, and bitter laughter arose from the depths of his soul once more. He thought about how his wife had driven him out of his own house; he imagined Liza's situation, covered his eyes, and then clasped his hands behind his head. Lemm finally returned, bringing a scrap of paper on which Liza had scribbled the following words in pencil: "We can't see one another today. Perhaps tomorrow evening. Goodbye." Lavretskii thanked Lemm briefly and distractedly, then went home.

He found his wife having breakfast. Ada, wearing curlers and a little white dress decorated with blue ribbons, was eating her mutton cutlet. Varvara Pavlovna stood up as soon as Lavretskii entered the room and walked toward him with a humble expression on her face. He asked her to follow him into the study, shut the door behind them, and began to pace back and forth. She sat down, discreetly laying one hand over the other, following his movements with her eyes, which were still beautiful, although their lids had been lightly outlined with a pencil.

Lavretskii couldn't speak for some time—he sensed that he couldn't control himself. He could clearly see that Varvara Pavlovna wasn't the least bit afraid of him, but was trying to appear to be on the verge of fainting.

"Listen, madam," he finally began, breathing with difficulty and periodically gritting his teeth, "it's useless for us to pretend to one another. I don't believe in your repentance. And even if it were sincere, it'd be impossible for me to be on intimate terms with you again, or to live with you."

Varvara Pavlovna bit her lips and half closed her eyes. "This is aversion," she thought. "It's all over. I'm not even a woman in his eyes."

"It'd be impossible," Lavretskii repeated, fastening the top buttons of his coat. "I don't know what induced you to come here. I suppose you've used up all your money."

"Ah! You hurt me!" whispered Varvara Pavlovna.

"However that may be, nonetheless you're my wife, unfortunately. I can't drive you away . . . and so this is what I propose to you. If you want, you may go to Lavriki at once and live there. There's a good house there, as you know. You'll have everything you need, in addition to your allowance. . . . Is that acceptable?"

Varvara Pavlovna lifted an embroidered handkerchief to her face.

"I've already told you," she replied, her lips twitching nervously, "that I'll agree to whatever you see fit to do with me. At present, it merely remains for me to ask you—will you at least allow me to thank you for your magnanimity?"

"Don't thank me, I beg you—it's better without any of that," Lavretskii hurriedly responded. "So, then," he continued, approaching the door, "I may depend on...."

"I'll be at Lavriki by tomorrow," Varvara Pavlovna declared, respectfully rising from her chair. "But Fedor Ivanych...." (She no longer called him *Théodore*.)

"What do you want?"

"I know I haven't gained any right to forgiveness yet. May I at least hope that in time...."

"Ah, Varvara Pavlovna," Lavretskii interrupted her, "you're an intelligent woman—but I'm no fool, either. I know that you don't want my forgiveness at all. And in any event, I forgave you long ago—but there's always been a vast gulf between us."

"I know how to submit to circumstances," Varvara Pavlovna replied, bowing her head. "I haven't forgotten my sin. I wouldn't have been surprised to learn that you'd even rejoiced at the news of my death," she added quietly, gesturing slightly toward his copy of the newspaper, which Lavretskii had forgotten was lying on the table.

Fedor Ivanych shuddered; the item in question had been marked in pencil. Varvara Pavlovna gazed at him even more humbly. She was superb at that moment: her gray Parisian gown clung gracefully to her supple, almost girlish figure; her slender, soft neck was encircled by a white collar; her bosom gently stirred as she breathed evenly; her hands were devoid of bracelets and rings—her entire form, from her shining hair to the tip of her barely visible little shoe, was so elegant....

Lavretskii took it all in with a vicious glance. He could barely refrain from shouting "Bravo!" and knocking her down with a blow of his fist to her shapely head. He turned on his heel. An hour later, he'd already left for Vasilevskoe. Two hours later, Varvara Pavlovna had commandeered the best carriage in town, donned a simple straw hat with a black veil and a modest mantilla, placed Ada in Justine's care, and set off for the Kalitins'. From inquiries she'd made among the servants, she'd learned that her husband went to see them every day.

XXXVIII

The day Lavretskii's wife had arrived in the town of O——, a miserable day for him, had been a difficult day for Liza as well.

She hadn't even gone downstairs and said good morning to her mother yet when the tramp of hooves sounded outside the window. With secret dismay, she saw Panshin riding into the courtyard. "He's come this early for a final answer," she thought—and she wasn't mistaken. After a brief conversation in the drawing room, he invited her to go into the garden with him, and then asked her for her decision regarding his fate. Liza summoned up all her courage and told him that she couldn't be his wife. He heard her out, standing at an angle to her and pulling his hat down over his forehead. Then courteously, but in an altered voice, he asked her whether this was her final word—had he given her any grounds for such a change in her way of thinking? He pressed his hand to his eyes, sighed softly and brokenly, and removed his hand from his face again.

"I didn't want to follow the beaten path," he said huskily. "I wanted to choose a wife according to the dictates of my heart—but it seems that this wasn't meant to be. Farewell, fond dream!" He bowed deeply to Liza and went back into the house.

She hoped that he'd leave immediately, but he went into Maria Dmitrievna's study and remained with her for nearly an hour. As he came out, he told Liza, "*Votre mère vous appelle. Adieu à jamais,*" then mounted his horse and set off at a full gallop from the very steps. Liza went to see Maria Dmitrievna and found her in tears. Panshin had informed her of his unhappiness.

"Do you want to be the death of me? Do you want to be the death of me?" the disconsolate widow began her lamentations. "Whom do you want? Wasn't he good enough for you? A *Kammerjunker* wasn't appealing! He could have married any aristocrat in Petersburg he liked. And I—I'd so hoped for it! Has it been a long while since you changed your mind about him? How did this cloud come over us? It can't have come of its own accord! Is it that dolt of a cousin's fault? A fine person you've picked to advise you!"

"And Panshin, the poor dear," Maria Dmitrievna went on, "how respectful he is, how attentive, even in his sorrow! He's promised not to desert me. Ah, I could never bear that! Oh, my head aches so much it's splitting! Get me Palashka. You'll be the death of me if you don't reconsider, do you hear?" And twice calling her an ungrateful girl, Maria Dmitrievna sent her away.

Liza went to her own room. But she didn't even have time to recover from her encounters with Panshin and her mother before another storm broke over her head, and this time from a quarter where she would have least expected it. Marfa Timofeevna came into her room and promptly slammed the door behind her. The elderly woman's face was pale, her cap was awry, her eyes were flashing, and her hands and lips were trembling. Liza was astonished—she'd never seen her intelligent, reasonable aunt in such a state before.

"This is fine, my lady," Marfa Timofeevna began in a shaky, broken whisper, "just fine! Who taught you such behavior, miss, I'd like to know? . . . Give me some water. I can't talk."

"Calm down, Aunt—what's the matter?" Liza responded, handing her a glass of water. "Why, I thought you didn't much care for Mr. Panshin yourself."

Marfa Timofeevna pushed the glass away. "I can't drink—I'll knock my last teeth out if I try. What's Panshin got to do with it? Why bring Panshin in? You'd better tell me who taught you to arrange trysts at night—eh, miss?"

Liza paled slightly.

"Now please don't try to deny it," continued Marfa Timofeevna. "Shurochka herself saw everything and told me. I've had to forbid her to repeat idle chatter, but she isn't a liar."

"I don't deny it, Aunt," Liza replied, barely audibly.

"Aha! That's it, is it, miss—you arranged a tryst with that old sinner who seems so meek?"

"No."

"How did it happen, then?"

"I went down to the drawing room to look for a book. He was in the garden—and he called out to me."

"And you went? That's fine! So you love him, eh?"

"I do love him," Liza answered softly.

"Merciful heavens! She loves him!" Marfa Timofeevna snatched off her cap. "She loves a married man! Ah! She loves him."

"He told me . . . ," Liza began.

"What has he told you, the villain, eh?"

"He told me that his wife had died."

Marfa Timofeevna crossed herself. "May she rest in peace," she whispered. "She was a vain creature, God forgive her. So, then, he's a widower, I suppose. And he's losing no time, I see. He's buried one wife and now he's after another. What sort of a person does that? Just let me tell you one thing, niece. In my day, when I was young, harm came to girls from such goings-on. Don't be angry with me, miss—only fools get angry at the truth. I've given orders not to invite him in today. I love him, but I'll never forgive him for this. And so he's a widower! Give me some water. But as to your sending Panshin about his business—I think you're a brave girl for doing that. Only don't you go sitting around with men or any animals of that sort at night. Don't break an old woman's heart, or else you'll see that I'm not all caresses—I can bite, too. . . . A widower!"

Marfa Timofeevna left; Liza sat down in a corner and began to cry. Bitterness stirred in her soul—she hadn't deserved such humiliation. Love had brought her no happiness: she was crying for a second time since the previous evening. This new, unexpected feeling had just arisen in her heart—and what a heavy price she'd already had to pay for it, how roughly other people's hands had touched her sacred secret! She felt ashamed and embittered and ill, but she had no doubts, no dread—and Lavretskii was dearer to her than ever. She'd hesitated as long as she didn't understand herself, but after that encounter, after that kiss—she couldn't hesitate any longer. She knew that she was in love, that she was now truly, seriously in love, that she was firmly attached for the rest of her life—and she didn't fear any threat. She felt that this bond couldn't be broken by force.

XXXIX

Maria Dmitrievna became greatly agitated when she was informed that Varvara Pavlovna Lavretskaia had arrived. She didn't even know whether to invite her in—she was afraid of offending Fedor Ivanych. Curiosity finally prevailed. "Why not?" she concluded. "She's a relative, too." Seating herself in an armchair, she told the servant, "Show her in." A few moments passed, the door opened, and Varvara Pavlovna approached Maria Dmitrievna swiftly, with barely audible steps. Not allowing Maria Dmitrievna to rise from her chair, Varvara Pavlovna almost went down on her knees before her.

"Thank you, dear Aunt," she began in a soft, emotion-laden voice, speaking Russian. "Thank you. I didn't hope for such indulgence on your part. You're an angel of goodness."

As she uttered these words, Varvara Pavlovna quite unexpectedly took hold of one of Maria Dmitrievna's hands, and pressing it lightly between her pale lavender gloves, raised it to her full, rosy lips in an abject manner. Maria Dmitrievna became completely flustered, seeing such a handsome, charmingly dressed woman virtually at her feet. She didn't know how to behave toward Varvara

Pavlovna. She tried to withdraw her hand, while at the same time endeavoring to make her sit down and to say something affectionate to her. She ended up by helping Varvara Pavlovna rise again and then kissing her on her smooth, perfumed forehead. Varvara Pavlovna was thoroughly overwhelmed by this kiss.

"Hello, *bonjour,*" said Maria Dmitrievna. "Of course, I didn't expect . . . but, of course, I'm delighted to see you. You understand, my dear, it's not for me to judge between a husband and wife. . . ."

"My husband is absolutely in the right," Varvara Pavlovna interjected. "I alone am to blame."

"That's a highly praiseworthy sentiment," responded Maria Dmitrievna, "highly praiseworthy. Have you been here long? Have you seen him? But sit down, please."

"I arrived yesterday," Varvara Pavlovna answered, meekly sitting down. "I've seen Fedor Ivanych, and I've spoken with him."

"Ah! Well, how did he seem?"

"I was afraid that my sudden arrival would provoke his anger," Varvara Pavlovna continued, "but he didn't refuse to see me."

"That's to say, he didn't. . . . Yes, yes, I understand," remarked Maria Dmitrievna. "He's just a bit rough on the surface, but he has a soft heart."

"Fedor Ivanych hasn't forgiven me—he wouldn't hear me out. But he was kind enough to grant me Lavriki as a place of residence."

"Ah! A splendid estate!"

"I'm going there tomorrow in fulfillment of his wishes, but I considered it my duty to visit you first."

"I'm very, very grateful to you, my dear. Relatives should never forget one another. And you know, I'm surprised at how well you speak Russian. *C'est étonnant.*"

Varvara Pavlovna sighed.

"I've been abroad for too long, Maria Dmitrievna, I know that. But my heart has always been Russian, and I haven't forgotten my native land."

"Yes, yes, that's the most important thing. Fedor Ivanych didn't expect you at all, however. Yes, trust my experience—*la patrie avant tout.* Ah, show this to me, please. What a charming mantilla you have!"

"Do you like it?" Varvara Pavlovna quickly slipped it off her shoulders. "It's a very simple little item from Madame Baudran's."

"One can see that at once. From Madame Baudran's? How lovely, and what good taste! I'm sure you've brought a number of exquisite things with you. If only I could see them!"

"All my things are at your service, dearest Aunt. If you'll permit me, I can show some patterns to your maid. I have a servant from Paris with me—a wonderfully clever dressmaker."

"You're very kind, my dear. But, really, I'm ashamed...."

"Ashamed!" Varvara Pavlovna repeated reproachfully. "If you want to make me happy, dispose of me as if I were your personal property."

Maria Dmitrievna was utterly enchanted.

"*Vous êtes charmante*," she declared. "But why don't you take off your hat and gloves?"

"What? Will you permit me to?" Varvara Pavlovna asked, slightly clasping her hands, as though she were moved.

"Of course you'll dine with us, I hope. I—I'll introduce you to my daughter." Maria Dmitrievna became a bit embarrassed. "Well! It's too late now!" she thought. "She's not very well today."

"*O ma tante*, you're too kind!" Varvara Pavlovna exclaimed, and she lifted her handkerchief to her eyes.

A servant announced Gedeonovskii's arrival. The old gossip entered bowing and smiling. Maria Dmitrievna introduced him to her visitor. He was thrown into confusion at first, but Varvara Pavlovna treated him with such coquettish respectfulness that his ears tingled, and gossip, slander, and compliments began to drip from his lips like honey. Varvara Pavlovna listened to him with a restrained smile and gradually began to converse herself. She spoke modestly about Paris, about her travels, about Baden. She made Maria Dmitrievna laugh twice, slightly sighing afterward each time, as if reproaching herself inwardly for misplaced levity. She obtained permission to bring Ada to visit. Taking off her gloves, she used her smooth hands, which were redolent of soap *à la guimauve*, to show how and where flounces, ruches, lace, and rosettes were being worn. She promised to bring over a bottle of the new English perfume, Victoria's Essence, and was happy as a child when Maria Dmitrievna consented to accept it as a gift. She was moved to tears by the memory of the feeling she'd experienced when she heard Russian bells for the first time. "They pierced my heart so deeply," she explained.

At this moment, Liza came in.

Ever since that morning, ever since the very instant when she'd read Lavretskii's note, frozen with horror, Liza had been prepar-

ing herself to meet his wife; she had a presentiment that she'd
see her. Liza resolved not to avoid her, as punishment for her
sinful hopes, as she called them. The sudden crucial turn in her
destiny had shaken Liza to the core; her face had grown thinner
in just over two hours. But she didn't shed a single tear. "It's
what I deserve!" she said to herself, laboriously, agitatedly suppressing some sort of bitter, evil impulses in her soul that frightened her. "Well, I have to go!" she thought as soon as she learned
of Mrs. Lavretskii's arrival—and she went downstairs. . . .
     She stood at the drawing-room door for a long while before she
could summon up the courage to open it. Telling herself, "I've
wronged her," Liza crossed the threshold and forced herself to look
at her, forced herself to smile. Varvara Pavlovna went over to meet
her as soon as she caught sight of Liza, and slightly but still
respectfully bowed to her. "Allow me to introduce myself," she
began in an insinuating voice. "Your *maman* has been so indulgent
toward me that I hope you'll also be . . . kind." Varvara Pavlovna's
expression as she uttered these last words, her simultaneously cold
and benign gaze, her hypocritical smile, the movements of her
hands, her shoulders, her very dress—her entire being aroused such
revulsion in Liza that she couldn't reply to her, and merely made
herself hold out her hand. "This young lady despises me," Varvara
Pavlovna thought, warmly grasping Liza's cold fingers, and, turning to Maria Dmitrievna, she remarked in an undertone, "*Mais
elle est délicieuse!*" Liza flushed faintly; she recognized the ridicule,
the insult inherent in this exclamation. But she decided not to trust
her first impressions and sat down by the window at her embroidery
frame.
     Varvara Pavlovna didn't leave her in peace even there. She began
to admire her taste, her skill. . . . Liza's heart throbbed intensely
and painfully. She could barely restrain herself, she could barely
remain in her chair. It seemed to her that Varvara Pavlovna knew
everything, and was mocking her in secret triumph. To her relief,
Gedeonovskii began to talk to Varvara Pavlovna, thereby distracting
her. Liza bent over the embroidery frame and surreptitiously
watched her. "*He* loved that woman," she reflected. But she immediately drove away the very thought of Lavretskii. She was afraid
of losing her self-control—she felt that her head was spinning. Maria
Dmitrievna began to talk about music.
     "I've heard, my dear," she began, "that you're a wonderful
performer."

"It's been a long time since I've played," Varvara Pavlovna replied, seating herself at the piano without delay and confidently running her fingers over the keys. "Would you like me to?"

"If you'd be so kind."

Varvara Pavlovna played a brilliant, difficult étude by Hertz like a master. She displayed a great deal of power and expressivity.

"A *sylphide!*" cried Gedeonovskii.

"Marvelous!" Maria Dmitrievna chimed in. "Well, Varvara Pavlovna, I confess that you astonish me," she declared, addressing her by name for the first time. "You could give concerts. We h a musician here, an old German who's quite eccentric, but a v knowledgeable musician. He gives Liza piano lessons. He'll simply go crazy over you."

"Is Lizaveta Mikhailovna also a musician?" Varvara Pavlovna inquired, turning her head slightly toward Liza.

"Yes, she plays fairly well and loves music—but what is that compared to you? There's one other young man here with whom we must acquaint you. He's an artist at heart, and composes most charmingly. Only he will be able to appreciate you fully."

"A young man?" interjected Varvara Pavlovna. "Who is he? Some impoverished person or other?"

"Heavens, no. He's our most eligible bachelor. And not only among us—*et à Petersbourg.* A *Kammerjunker* who's welcomed in the best social circles. You must have heard of him: Vladimir Nikolaich Panshin. He's here on a government commission . . . a future minister, for heaven's sake!"

"And an artist?"

"He's an artist at heart, and so polite. You'll see him—recently, he's visited my home quite frequently, and I've invited him here this evening. I *hope* that he'll come," Maria Dmitrievna added with a gentle sigh and an oblique, bitter smile.

Liza understood the meaning of this smile, but it didn't matter to her now.

"And he's young?" Varvara Pavlovna repeated, shifting to a slightly lower key.

"He's twenty-eight, and has a most attractive appearance. *Un jeune homme accompli*, indeed."

"An exemplary young man, one may say," remarked Gedeonovskii. Varvara Pavlovna suddenly started to play a lively waltz by Strauss, beginning it with such a loud, rapid trill that Gedeonovskii was quite startled. In the very middle of the waltz, she suddenly switched to a sad melody, and concluded with an aria from *Lucia*, "*Fra poco.*"... She'd realized that cheerful music was inappropriate to her situation. The aria from *Lucia*, with emphasis on the sentimental passages, deeply moved Maria Dmitrievna. "What a soul!" she observed to Gedeonovskii in an undertone. "A *sylphide!*" Gedeonovskii reiterated, raising his eyes toward heaven.

The dinner hour arrived. Marfa Timofeevna came down from upstairs when the soup had already been served. She addressed Varvara Pavlovna very drily, replying to her civilities in half-sentences without looking at her. Varvara Pavlovna herself quickly realized that there was nothing to be gained from this elderly woman, and gave up trying to talk to her. To make up for this, Maria Dmitrievna became even more cordial to her guest—her aunt's rudeness irritated her. Marfa Timofeevna not only refused to look at Varvara Pavlovna, however—she wouldn't look at Liza, either, although Liza's eyes were glistening with tears and she was sitting as though she were made of stone, her face sallow and pale, her lips compressed, eating nothing. Liza did seem calm—and in fact, her heart was more at ease. A strange apathy, the apathy of the condemned, had descended upon her. At dinner, Varvara Pavlovna said little. She seemed to have grown shy again, and her face wore an expression of modest melancholy. Gedeonovskii alone enlivened the conversation with his stories, although he repeatedly glanced toward Marfa Timofeevna and coughed—he was always overtaken by a fit of coughing when he was about to tell a lie in her presence— but she didn't hinder him with any interruptions. After dinner, it came out that Varvara Pavlovna was truly devoted to the card game of preference. Maria Dmitrievna was so elated by this that she was completely won over, and thought to herself, "But what a fool Fedor Ivanych must be, if he couldn't appreciate a woman like this!"

She sat down to play cards with Varvara Pavlovna and Gedeonovskii, while Marfa Timofeevna led Liza upstairs with her, saying that Liza looked dreadful and probably had a headache.

"Yes, she has a terrible headache," Maria Dmitrievna affirmed, turning to Varvara Pavlovna and rolling her eyes. "I myself often have just such migraine headaches."

"You don't say!" responded Varvara Pavlovna.

Liza went into her aunt's room and helplessly sank into a chair. Marfa Timofeevna silently gazed at her for a long while, slowly knelt down in front of her—and silently began to kiss her hands. Liza bent forward, blushing—and burst into tears. But she didn't make Marfa Timofeevna stand up; she didn't take her hands away. Liza felt that she didn't have the right to take them away, that she didn't have the right to prevent the elderly woman from expressing her remorse and her sympathy, from begging Liza's forgiveness for what had happened the day before. And Marfa Timofeevna couldn't kiss those poor, pale, helpless hands enough; mute tears flowed from her eyes as well as Liza's. Meanwhile, the cat Matross was purring in a wide armchair amid balls of knitting yarn, and the tall flame of the little lamp was faintly flickering before the icon. In the next room, Nastasia Karpovna was standing behind the door, and she, too, was furtively wiping her eyes with a checkered handkerchief she'd rolled up into a ball.

XL

All the while, the game of preference was merrily being played in the drawing room downstairs. Maria Dmitrievna was winning, and thus was in an extremely good mood. A servant came in and announced that Panshin had arrived.

Maria Dmitrievna put down her cards and shifted expectantly in her armchair. Varvara Pavlovna looked at her with a half-smile, then turned her eyes toward the door. Panshin appeared, wearing a black coat buttoned up to the throat and a high English collar. "It was hard for me to do so, but, as you see, I've come"—this was the message his unsmiling, freshly shaven face conveyed.

"For heaven's sake, *Woldemar*," cried Maria Dmitrievna, "you used to come in unannounced!"

Panshin's sole reply to Maria Dmitrievna was a glance. He bowed to her courteously, but didn't kiss her hand. She introduced him to Varvara Pavlovna. He stepped back a pace, bowed to her with the same courtesy but with even greater elegance and respect, and took a seat near the card table. The game of preference ended shortly. Panshin inquired about Lizaveta Mikhailovna, learned that she wasn't feeling very well, and expressed his regret. Then he began to talk to Varvara Pavlovna, diplomatically weighing and underscoring each word, politely listening to her answers. But the seriousness of his diplomatic tone didn't impress Varvara Pavlovna, and she didn't adopt it. On the contrary, she looked him straight in the face with cheerful interest and chatted casually, while her delicate nostrils quivered as though she were suppressing laughter. Maria Dmitrievna began to rhapsodize over Varavara Pavlovna's artistic talent. Panshin graciously nodded his head to the extent that his collar would allow, declared that he'd "been sure of this in advance," and nearly turned the conversation to the subject of Metternich himself. Varvara Pavlovna half closed her velvety eyes, said in a low voice, "Why, you're also an artist, *un confrère*," and added still lower, "*Venez!*" with a nod toward the piano. As soon as it was thrown at him, the single word "*venez*" instantly changed Panshin's entire appearance as if by magic. His preoccupied manner disappeared, he smiled and became quite animated, unbuttoning his coat and repeating the words, "A poor artist, alas! Now you, I understand, are the true artist." He followed Varvara Pavlovna to the piano. . . .

"Make him sing his song 'How the Moon Floats,'" cried Maria Dmitrievna.

"Do you sing?" Varvara Pavlovna inquired, encompassing him in a swift, radiant glance. "Sit down."

Panshin began to make excuses.

"Sit down," she repeated insistently, tapping on a chair behind him. He sat down, cleared his throat, straightened his collar, and sang his song.

"*Charmant*," declared Varvara Pavlovna. "You sing very well, *vous avez du style*. Sing it again."

She walked around the piano and stood directly facing Panshin. He sang his song again, enhancing the melodramatic tremor in his voice. Varvara Pavlovna stared at him steadily, leaning her elbows on the piano and holding her white hands level with her lips. Panshin finished the song.

"*Charmant, charmante idée*," she repeated with the calm self-confidence of a connoisseur. "Tell me, have you composed anything for a woman's voice, for a mezzo-soprano?"

"I hardly compose at all," replied Panshin. "That was merely tossed off at odd moments . . . but do you sing?"

"Yes, I do."

"Oh! Sing something for us," urged Maria Dmitrievna.

Varvara Pavlovna pushed her hair away from her glowing cheeks and gave her head a little shake.

"Our voices should go well together," she observed, turning to

Panshin. "Let's sing a duet. Do you know '*Son geloso*,' or '*La ci darem*,' or '*Mira la bianca luna*'?"

"I used to sing '*Mira la bianca luna*' at one time," Panshin answered, "but that was a long while ago. I've forgotten it." "Never mind, we'll rehearse it quietly. Allow me." Varvara Pavlovna sat down at the piano, and Panshin stood next to her. They sang through the duet in an undertone, and Varvara Pavlovna corrected him several times as they did so. Then they sang it aloud, and subsequently twice repeated their performance of "*Mira la bianca lu-u-una*." Varvara Pavlovna's voice had lost its freshness, but she controlled it with great skill. Panshin was hesitant at first, and slightly off-key, but then he warmed up, and if his singing wasn't thoroughly beyond reproach, at least he twisted his shoulders, swayed his entire body, and lifted his hand from time to time like a real performer. Varvara Pavlovna went on to play two or three short pieces by Thalberg, then coquettishly rendered a brief French ballad. Maria Dmitrievna no longer knew how to express her delight; she wanted to send for Liza several times. Gedeonovskii was at a loss for words as well, and could only nod his head—but he suddenly yawned unexpectedly and barely had time to cover his mouth with his hand. This yawn didn't escape Varvara Pavlovna's notice: she promptly turned her back on the piano, remarking, "*Assez de musique comme ça*. Let's converse," and folded her arms. "*Oui, assez de musique*," Panshin echoed her cheerily, and he immediately lapsed into lively, offhand conversation in French. "Just like the best Parisian salons," Maria Dmitrievna thought as she listened to their fluent, witty repartee. Panshin was experiencing the sensation of sheer satisfaction—his eyes were shining and he was smiling contentedly. Early on, he'd run his hand across his face, lowered his eyebrows, and sighed spasmodically whenever he happened to encounter Maria Dmitrievna's eyes. But he gradually forgot her altogether, and utterly surrendered himself to the pleasure of half-worldly, half-artistic conversation.

Varvara Pavlovna revealed herself to be a great philosopher—she had an immediate response to everything, never hesitating, never displaying doubts about anything. It was obvious that she'd often conversed at length with intelligent people of various sorts. All her ideas, all her feelings revolved around Paris. Panshin turned the conversation to literature—it turned out that, like him, she read only French books. She was exasperated by George Sand; she respected Balzac, although he exhausted her; she discerned pro-

found knowledge of human nature in Sue and Scribe; she adored
Dumas and Féval. In her heart of hearts, she preferred Paul de
Kock to all of these, but naturally, she didn't even mention his
name. To tell the truth, literature held no great attraction for her.
Varvara Pavlovna very skillfully avoided anything that could even
remotely remind anyone of her situation. She never referred to love
in her remarks; on the contrary, they tended to express severity, disillusionment, and resignation regarding the allure of passion. Panshin argued with her. She didn't agree with him . . . but strangely
enough . . . at the very moment when critical—often highly critical—
words were issuing from her lips, those words had a soft, caressing
sound, and her eyes bespoke. . . . Precisely what those lovely eyes
bespoke was hard to define, but whatever it was, it wasn't stern,
it wasn't clear—and it was very appealing.

Panshin tried to decipher that cryptic message and to make his
own eyes speak in return, but he didn't succeed. He realized that
Varvara Pavlovna, who qualified as an authentic social lioness
from abroad, towered over him, as a result of which he couldn't
maintain complete self-mastery. During conversations, Varvara
Pavlovna had a habit of lightly touching the sleeve of the person
she was talking to, and these momentary contacts greatly dis-
quieted Vladimir Nikolaich. Varvara Pavlovna possessed the ability to get along easily with anyone, and before two hours had
passed, it seemed to Panshin that he'd known her for ages, and
that Liza, the same Liza whom he still loved, to whom he'd proposed marriage the evening before, had vanished in the haze, as
it were.

Tea was served; the conversation became even livelier. Maria
Dmitrievna summoned a servant and gave orders to tell Liza to
come down if her headache was better. On hearing Liza's name,
Panshin began to discuss the concept of self-sacrifice and the question of who was more capable of such sacrifice—a man or a woman.
Maria Dmitrievna immediately got excited, began to affirm that a
woman is more capable of self-sacrifice, declared that she'd prove
it in a few words, became confused, and ended up making some
sort of fairly inept comparison. Varvara Pavlovna picked up a book
of music and, half-hiding behind it, bending toward Panshin, she
observed in a whisper as she nibbled on a biscuit with a serene
smile on her lips and in her eyes, "*Elle n'a pas inventé la poudre,
la bonne dame.*" Panshin was slightly taken aback and rather surprised at Varvara Pavlovna's audacity, but he didn't realize how

much contempt for him was contained in this unexpected observation, and forgetting Maria Dmitrievna's kindness and affection,
forgetting the dinners she'd given for him and the money she'd
loaned him, he replied (the wretch!) with the same smile, in the
same tone, "*Je crois bien,*" and not even "*Je crois bien,*" but "*J'crois
ben!*"

Varvara Pavlovna cast a friendly glance at him and stood up.
Liza came in; Marfa Timofeevna had vainly tried to stop her—
Liza was determined to endure her suffering to the fullest. Varvara
Pavlovna went up to greet her, accompanied by Panshin, on whose
face the former diplomatic expression had reappeared.

"How are you?" he asked Liza.

"I'm better now, thank you," she replied.

"We've been enjoying a little music here. It's a pity you didn't
get to hear Varvara Pavlovna—she sings superbly, *en artiste con-
sommée.*"

"Come here, *ma chère,*" rang out Maria Dmitrievna's voice.

Varvara Pavlovna went over to her at once with the submissiveness
of a child, and sat down on a little stool by her feet. Maria Dmitrievna had called Varvara Pavlovna over in order to leave her
daughter alone with Panshin, if only for a moment—she was still
secretly hoping that Liza would relent. Besides, an idea had entered
her head that she was anxious to impart immediately.

"You know," she whispered to Varvara Pavlovna, "I want to
attempt to reconcile you and your husband. I won't promise to
succeed, but I'll make the effort. He has great respect for me, you
know."

Varvara Pavlovna slowly raised her eyes to look at Maria Dmitrievna and expressively clasped her hands.

"You'd be my savior, *ma tante,*" she responded mournfully. "I
don't know how to thank you for all your kindness. But I've
wronged Fedor Ivanych too deeply—he can't forgive me."

"But did you . . . in fact . . . ," Maria Dmitrievna began inquisitively.

"Don't question me," Varvara Pavlovna interrupted her, and she
lowered her gaze. "I was young and frivolous then. But I don't
want to justify myself."

"Well, anyway, why not try? Don't despair," Maria Dmitrievna
replied. She was about to pat Varvara Pavlovna on the cheek, but
after glancing at her, she didn't have the courage. "She's humble,
very humble," Maria Dmitrievna thought, "but still truly a social
lioness."

"Are you ill?" Panshin was saying to Liza in the meantime.

"Yes, I'm not well."

"I understand you," he declared after a rather protracted silence.

"Yes, I understand you."

"What?"

"I understand you," Panshin repeated significantly. He actually didn't know what to say.

Liza became embarrassed, and then concluded, "So be it!" Panshin donned a mysterious expression and fell silent, looking away severely.

"It seems that it's after eleven, though," observed Maria Dmitrievna.

Her guests took the hint and began to say goodbye. Varvara Pavlovna had to promise that she'd come for dinner the following day and bring Ada. Gedeonovskii, who'd all but fallen asleep sitting in his corner, offered to escort her home. Panshin solemnly said goodbye to everyone, but on the steps, as he helped Varvara Pavlovna into her carriage, he shook her hand and cried out, "*Au revoir!*" as she left. Gedeonovskii sat beside her all the way home. She amused herself by pressing the tip of her little foot against his leg as if by accident. He became totally confused, and began to pay her compliments. She giggled and batted her eyelashes at him whenever the light of a street lamp illuminated the carriage interior. The waltz she'd played was ringing in her head, exciting her. Whatever circumstances she might find herself in, she merely needed to imagine lanterns, a ballroom, rapid whirling to strains of music—and her spirit would ignite, her eyes would glitter strangely, a smile would play across her lips, and a sort of bacchanalian grace would spread throughout her entire body. When she arrived home, Varvara Pavlovna lightly bounded out of the carriage—only actual lionesses know how to bound like that—and, turning around to say goodbye to Gedeonovskii, she suddenly burst into ringing laughter right in his face.

"An attractive person," thought the councillor of state as he made his way to his lodgings, where a servant was awaiting him with a glass of brandy. "It's a good thing I'm a sober-minded individual. But what was she laughing at?"

Marfa Timofeevna spent the whole night sitting beside Liza's bed.

XLI

Lavretskii spent a day and a half at Vasilevskoe, passing most of that time wandering around the countryside—he couldn't stay in one place for long. He was devoured by anguish; he was unremittingly tortured by futile, violent impulses. He recalled the feeling that had taken possession of him the day after his arrival in the countryside; he recalled the plans that he'd made then—and became intensely irritated with himself. What had been able to tear him away from what he'd acknowledged to be his duty, to be the sole task of his future? The thirst for happiness—once again, that same old thirst for happiness.

"It seems that Mikhalevich was right," he thought. "You wanted to taste happiness in life for a second time," he said to himself. "You forgot that happiness is a luxury, that it's an undeserved blessing, even if it comes to a man only once. It wasn't complete, it wasn't genuine, you say—but prove that you have the right to complete, genuine happiness! Look around you and see who's happy, who's enjoying life? Look at that peasant on the way to his mowing—is he contented with his fate? . . . What? Would you like to change places with him? Remember your mother—how infinitely little she asked of life, and how she was destined to live. You were only bragging, evidently, when you told Panshin that you'd come back to Russia to cultivate the soil—you came back to pursue young girls in your old age. As soon as the news of your freedom arrived, you forsook everything, you forgot about everything, you ran like a boy chasing a butterfly. . . ."

The image of Liza constantly intruded upon his musings. He strove to drive it away, along with another importunate image and its serenely calculating, beautiful, detested features. Old Anton noticed that his master was out of sorts. After sighing several times outside the door and several more times in the doorway, he made up his mind to go in, and advised him to drink something hot. Lavretskii shouted at him and ordered him to get out; later on, Lavretskii begged his pardon, but that only made Anton even sadder. Lavretskii couldn't stay in the drawing room; it seemed to him that his great-grandfather Andrei was contemptuously regarding his feeble descendant from his canvas. "Bah! You swim in shallow water," the distorted lips seemed to be saying. "Is it possible," Lavretskii thought, "that I can't get hold of myself, that I'm going to give in to this . . . nonsense?" (People who have been badly wounded in war always call their wounds "nonsense." If human beings didn't deceive themselves, they couldn't survive on this earth.) "Am I a mere boy? Ah, well, I saw the possibility of happiness to last a lifetime up so close, I could nearly hold it in my hands. Then it suddenly disappeared. It's just like the lottery—turn the wheel a little farther and a beggar might become a rich man. If it doesn't happen, then it doesn't—and it's all over. I'll set to work with my teeth clenched, and I'll make myself keep silent. It's just as well—this isn't the first time I've had to take myself in hand. And why have I run away, why am I staying here sticking my head in the sand like an ostrich? Is it such a horrible thing to face disaster? Nonsense! Anton," he called out aloud, "order the carriage prepared immediately. Yes," he thought again, "I have to make myself keep silent, I have to take myself firmly in hand. . . ."

Lavretskii tried to ease his pain with these rationalizations, but that pain was deep and strong, and Apraksia, who survived not so much on intellect as on emotion, shook her head and watched him sadly as he took his seat in the carriage for the ride to town. The horses set off at a gallop. He sat upright and motionless, staring at the road in front of him.

XLII

Liza had written to Lavretskii the day before, telling him to come and see her the next evening, but he went back to his lodgings first. He found neither his wife nor his daughter at home. He learned from the servants that she'd taken the child to the Kalitins'. This news astonished and infuriated him. "Varvara Pavlovna has evidently decided not to let me live at all," he thought with a burst of hatred in his heart. He began to pace back and forth, his hands and feet constantly bumping into children's toys and books, as well as various feminine items. He summoned Justine and told her to remove all the "trash." "*Oui, monsieur*," she replied with a grimace, and began to straighten up the room, bending over gracefully and letting Lavretskii know with her every movement that she considered him an uncivilized bear. He gazed hostilely at her pale yet still "piquante," cynical Parisian face, at her white elbow sleeves, silk apron, and dainty cap. He finally sent her away, and after hesitating for a long while (since Varvara Pavlovna hadn't returned), he decided to go to the Kalitins', not to see Maria Dmitrievna (he wouldn't have entered that drawing room—the room where his wife was—for anything in the world), but to see Marfa Timofeevna. He remembered that the back staircase by the servants' entrance led straight to her section of the house. He acted on this plan, and fortune favored him: he ran into Shurochka in the courtyard, and she escorted him up to Marfa Timofeevna's sitting room. Contrary to her usual custom, she was alone when he came in. She was sitting in a corner, not wearing a cap, bent over, her arms folded across her chest. The elderly woman became quite agitated when she saw Lavretskii. She quickly stood up and started to walk around the room as if she were looking for her cap.

"Ah, it's you," she began, bustling about and avoiding his gaze. "Well, how are you? Well, well, what's to be done? Where were you yesterday? Well, she's come, well, yes. Well, so it must . . . one way or another."

Lavretskii sank into a chair.

"Well, sit down, sit down," the elderly woman continued. "Did you come straight upstairs? Well, yes, naturally. So . . . you came to see me? Thanks."

She fell silent for a moment. Lavretskii didn't know what to say to her, but she understood him.

"Liza . . . yes, Liza was here just now," Marfa Timofeevna continued, tying and untying the tassels on a small workbag. "She wasn't altogether well. Shurochka, where are you? Come here, miss. Why can't you sit still for a minute? I have a headache, too. It must be the effect of all that singing and playing music."

"What singing, Aunt?"

"Why, we've been having those—let's see, what do you call them?—duets here. All in Italian—*chi-chi* and *cha-cha*. They sound just like magpies with their long, drawn-out notes, as if they wanted to extract your very soul. It's that Panshin, as well as your wife. And how quickly everything was arranged, as though they were all relatives, without any formalities. However, they say that even a dog will try to find a home, and won't remain a stray as long as people won't drive it away."

"Still, I confess, I didn't expect that," Lavretskii responded. "It must take great courage to do that."

"No, my dear, it isn't courage, it's calculation. May God forgive her! They say you're sending her off to Lavriki. Is it true?"

"Yes, I'm giving that estate to Varvara Pavlovna."

"Has she asked you for any money?"

"Not yet."

"Well, that request won't be deferred for long. But I've just gotten a good look at you now. Are you all right?"

"Yes."

"Shurochka!" Marfa Timofeevna cried suddenly. "Run and tell Lizaveta Mikhailovna—that is, no, ask her. . . . Is she downstairs?"

"Yes."

"Well, then, ask her where she put my book. She'll know."

"All right."

The elderly woman began to bustle about again, opening drawers in a chest. Lavretskii sat in his chair without stirring.

Suddenly, light footsteps on the stairs became audible—and Liza came in.

Lavretskii stood up and bowed; Liza remained standing in the doorway.

"Liza, Liza, darling," Marfa Timofeevna began fussily, "where's my book? Where did you put my book?"

"Which book, Aunt?"

"Why, my lord, that book! But I didn't call you, though. . . . Well, it doesn't matter. What are all of you doing downstairs? You see, Fedor Ivanych has come. How's your headache?"

"It's nothing."

"You keep saying that it's nothing. What's going on downstairs—more music?"

"No, they're playing cards."

"Well, she's ready for anything. Shurochka, I can see that you want to play in the garden. Run along."

"Oh, no, Marfa Timofeevna."

"Don't argue, please—just run along. Nastasia Karpovna has gone out into the garden all by herself. You can keep her company. You must treat the elderly with respect." Shurochka left. "But where's my cap? Where's it gone?"

"Let me look for it," Liza offered.

"Sit down, sit down. I still have the use of my legs. It must be in my bedroom."

And casting a sidelong glance in Lavretskii's direction, Marfa Timofeevna went out. She left the door open, but then she suddenly came back and shut it.

Liza leaned back against her chair and quietly covered her face with her hands. Lavretskii stayed where he was.

"So this is how we had to see one another again!" he uttered at last.

Liza took her hands away from her face.

"Yes," she said hollowly. "We've been swiftly punished."

"Punished?" Lavretskii responded. "What have you done to deserve being punished?"

Liza turned her eyes toward him. Neither sorrow nor distress was reflected in them; they seemed smaller and dimmer. Her face was pale, as were her slightly parted lips.

Lavretskii's heart shuddered with pity and love.

"You wrote to me that it's all over," he whispered. "Yes, it's all over—before it began."

"We have to forget it all," Liza asserted. "I'm glad that you've come. I wanted to write to you, but it's better this way. Only we should hurry up and take advantage of these few moments. It merely remains for us both to do our duty. Fedor Ivanych, you have to reconcile with your wife."

"Liza!"

"I beg you to do this. That's the only way we can atone for . . . everything that's happened. You'll think this over—and you won't refuse me."

"Liza, for God's sake, you're asking the impossible. I'm prepared to do everything that you require—but to reconcile with her *now!* . . . I consent to everything, I've forgotten everything, but I can't force my heart. . . . Have some pity—this is cruel!"

"I'm not asking you to . . . what you say. Don't live with her if you can't, but do reconcile," Liza replied, and she hid her face in her hands again. "Remember your little girl. Do it for my sake."

"All right," Lavretskii muttered between his teeth, "I'll do it. I suppose that I'll do my duty this way. Whereas you—what does your duty consist in?"

"Only I know that."

Lavretskii suddenly shivered.

"You can't have made up your mind to marry Panshin?" he asked.

Liza gave an almost imperceptible smile.

"Oh, no!" she stated firmly.

"Ah, Liza, Liza!" exclaimed Lavretskii. "How happy we might have been!"

Liza looked at him again.

"Now you see yourself, Fedor Ivanych, that happiness doesn't depend on us, but on God."

"Yes, because you. . . . "

The door to the adjoining room opened abruptly and Marfa Timofeevna entered, carrying her cap in her hand.

"I've finally found it," she said, standing between Lavretskii and Liza. "I'd put it away myself. That's what age does to you, alas, even though youth's not much better. Well, are you yourself going to Lavriki with your wife?" she added, turning to Lavretskii.

"To Lavriki with her? I don't know," he answered after a moment's hesitation.

"You're not going downstairs?"

"Today—no, I'm not."

"Well, well, you know best—but Liza, you ought to go down, I think. Ah, merciful heavens, I've forgotten to feed my bullfinch. There, wait a minute, I'll be right...." And Marfa Timofeevna hurried away without putting on her cap.

Lavretskii quickly went up to Liza.

"Liza," he began in a pleading voice, "we're saying goodbye forever, my heart's being torn apart. At least let me shake your hand in farewell."

Liza raised her head. Her exhausted eyes, their light almost extinguished, rested on him.... "No," she declared, and drew back the hand she'd held out. "No, Lavretskii" (it was the first time she'd used this name), "I won't shake your hand. What purpose would be served? Go away, I beseech you. You know that I love you ... yes, I love you," she added with an effort, "but no ... no."

She pressed her handkerchief to her lips.

"At least give me that handkerchief."

The door creaked ... the handkerchief slid onto Liza's lap. Lavretskii seized it before it had time to fall to the floor, swiftly thrust it into his side pocket, and turning around, met Marfa Timofeevna's eyes.

"Liza, darling, I think your mother's calling you," the elderly woman announced.

Liza immediately stood up and went out.

Marfa Timofeevna sat down again in her corner. Lavretskii began to say goodbye to her.

"Fedia," she said suddenly.

"What is it?"

"Are you an honorable man?"

"What?"

"I'm asking you—are you an honorable man?"

"I hope so."

"Hmm. But give me your word of honor that you're an honorable man."

"If you want. But why?"

"I surely know why. And if you think about it enough, my dear friend—you're no fool—you'll understand why I'm asking you this. And now goodbye, my boy. Thanks for your visit. Remember that you've given me your word, Fedia, and kiss me. Oh, my love, it's hard for you, I know, but then, it isn't easy for anyone. I used to envy the flies once—I thought that those are the ones for whom it's good to be alive on this earth. But one night I heard a fly moaning in a spider's web. . . . I decided that they have their troubles, too. There's nothing we can do, Fedia—but remember your promise, all the same. Now go."

Lavretskii went down the back staircase and had reached the gate when a servant overtook him.

"Maria Dmitrievna sent me to invite you to come in and see her," he told Lavretskii.

"Please tell her that I can't right now . . . ," Fedor Ivanych began.

"I was told to invite you most particularly," continued the servant. "I was told to say that she was alone."

"Have the visitors really left?" Lavretskii asked.

"Certainly, sir," the servant replied with a grin.

Lavretskii shrugged his shoulders and followed him in.

XLIII

Maria Dmitrievna was sitting by herself in her study in an easy chair, sniffing eau de cologne; a glass of orange-flavored water was standing on a little table next to her. She was agitated, and seemed frightened.

Lavretskii came in.

"You wanted to see me," he said, bowing coldly.

"Yes," Maria Dmitrievna replied, and she sipped a little water. "I found out that you'd gone straight to see my aunt, and I gave orders to ask you to come here. I wanted to have a little chat with you. Sit down, please." Maria Dmitrievna took a deep breath. "You know," she continued, "that your wife has arrived."

"I'm aware of it," Lavretskii responded.

"Well, yes, that is, I wanted to say, she came to my home, and I invited her in. That's what I wanted to explain to you, Fedor Ivanych. I may say, I've gained universal respect, thank God, and for no reason on earth would I do anything improper. Even though I foresaw that it might displease you, I still couldn't resolve to send her away, Fedor Ivanych. She's a relative of mine—through you.

Put yourself in my position. What right did I have to send her away? Don't you agree?"

"You're needlessly concerning yourself, Maria Dmitrievna," Lavretskii asserted. "You've done nothing wrong—I'm not the least bit angry. I have no intention whatsoever of depriving Varvara Pavlovna of an opportunity to see her acquaintances. I didn't come in to visit you today simply because I didn't want to run into her—that was all."

"Ah, I'm so glad to hear you say that, Fedor Ivanych," cried Maria Dmitrievna, "but I expected no less of you, with your noble sentiments. As for my being concerned, that's not surprising—I'm a woman and a mother. And as for your wife . . . of course, I can't take sides between the two of you, as I said to her herself. But she's such an amiable woman that she can provide nothing but pleasure."

Lavretskii gave a short laugh and toyed with his hat.

"And I wanted to say something more to you, Fedor Ivanych," Maria Dmitrievna went on, moving slightly closer to him. "If you'd seen how humbly she behaved, how respectful she was! Really, it's quite touching. And if you'd heard the way she spoke about you! I'm completely at fault, she said. I didn't know how to appreciate him, she said. He's an angel, not a man, she said. Really, that's just what she said—an angel. Her penitence is so. . . . My Lord, I've never seen such penitence!"

"Well, Maria Dmitrievna," Lavretskii remarked, "if I may be so inquisitive, I'm told that Varvara Pavlovna has been singing in your drawing room. Did she sing in the midst of her penitence, or . . . ?"

"Ah, you should be ashamed to talk like that! She sang and played the piano only to give me pleasure, because I absolutely begged and virtually commanded her to do so. I saw that she was unhappy, so unhappy, I was trying to distract her—and I'd heard that she had such marvelous talent! I assure you, Fedor Ivanych, she's utterly crushed. Just ask Sergei Petrovich. She's a broken-hearted woman *tout à fait*. Can't you see that?"

Lavretskii merely shrugged his shoulders.

"And what a little angel that Adochka of yours is—what a darling! How sweet she is, and what a bright little thing. She speaks French, and understands Russian, too—she called me 'aunt' in Russian. And you know, as for shyness—almost all children are shy at her age—there's not a trace of it. She looks so much like you that it's amazing, Fedor Ivanych. Her eyes, her forehead—well, it's you all over again. I'm not particularly fond of little children, I must confess, but I simply lost my heart to your little girl."

"Maria Dmitrievna," Lavretskii blurted out suddenly, "permit me to ask—why are you speaking to me like this?"

"Why?" Maria Dmitrievna sniffed her eau de cologne again and took another sip of water. "Well, I'm speaking to you, Fedor Ivanych, because . . . I'm a relative of yours, and so I take the most sincere interest in you. I know that you're supremely kindhearted. Listen to me, *mon cousin*—I'm a woman of experience, at any rate, and I don't speak idly. Forgive her, forgive your wife." Maria Dmitrievna's eyes suddenly filled with tears. "Just think of her youth, her inexperience . . . and who knows, perhaps she had bad examples. She didn't have the sort of mother who could bring her up properly. Forgive her, Fedor Ivanych—she's been punished enough."

The tears were trickling down Maria Dmitrievna's cheeks, and she didn't wipe them away—she liked to cry. Lavretskii sat as if he were on thorns. "My God," he thought, "what torture this is! What a day I've had to endure today!"

"You're not responding," Maria Dmitrievna began again. "How should I interpret this? Can you really be so cruel? No, I can't believe it. I sense that my words have influenced you, Fedor Ivanych. May God reward you for your goodness—and now take back your wife from my arms. . . . "

Lavretskii involuntarily leaped up from his chair. Maria Dmitrievna stood up as well, and quickly moving behind a screen, led out Varvara Pavlovna. Pale, passive, her eyes downcast, she seemed to have abandoned all her own thoughts, all her own will—to have utterly surrendered herself to Maria Dmitrievna.

Lavretskii stepped back a pace.

"You've been here all the time!" he exclaimed.

"Don't blame her," Maria Dmitrievna hurriedly replied. "She was extremely unwilling to stay, but I insisted, I put her behind the screen. She assured me that this would only make you angrier, but I wouldn't even listen to her—I know you better than she does. And so take back your wife from my arms. Go on, Varia, don't be afraid. Fall at your husband's feet" (she tugged at Varvara Pavlovna's arm) "and receive my blessing. . . . "

"Wait a minute, Maria Dmitrievna," Lavretskii interrupted her in a low but startlingly impressive voice. "You probably love touching scenes." (Lavretskii was right: Maria Dmitrievna still retained a schoolgirl's passion for certain theatrical effects.) "They may amuse you, and yet they may be unpleasant for other people. But I won't address you any further—you aren't the principal character in *this* scene. What do *you* want to get from me, madam?" he inquired, turning to his wife. "Haven't I done everything I could for you? Don't tell me you didn't contrive this interview. I won't believe you—and you know that I can't possibly believe you. What is it that you want? You're intelligent—you don't do anything without a purpose. You must realize that I can't live with you the way I did before, not because I'm angry with you, but because I've become a different person. I told you so the day after you returned, and you yourself agreed with me in your heart at that moment. But you want to reestablish yourself in public opinion. It's not enough for you to live in my house—you want to live under the same roof with me, is that it?"

"I want your forgiveness," Varvara Pavlovna declared without raising her eyes.

"She wants your forgiveness," echoed Maria Dmitrievna.

"Not even for my sake, but for Ada's," murmured Varvara Pavlovna.

"Not even for her sake, but for your Ada's," echoed Maria Dmitrievna.

"All right. Is that really what you want?" Lavretskii asked with an effort. "If it is, then I consent to that, too."

Varvara Pavlovna cast a swift glance at him, while Maria Dmitrievna cried, "Well, thank God!" and drew Varvara Pavlovna forward by the arm again. "Take her back from me now...."

"Wait a minute, I tell you," Lavretskii interrupted her. "I agree to live with you, Varvara Pavlovna," he continued, "that is to say, I'll take you to Lavriki, and I'll live there with you as long as I can stand it, then I'll go away—and I'll come back again. You see, I don't want to deceive you. But don't demand anything more. You yourself would laugh if I were to carry out the desire of our respected cousin, if I were to press you to my breast and begin to assure you that... that the past hadn't occurred, that a fallen tree can sprout leaves again. But I see that I have to resign myself to this. You won't understand that phrase... but it doesn't matter. I repeat, I'll live with you... or, no, I can't promise that... I'll reestablish a relationship with you, I'll consider you my wife once more."

"At least shake her hand," urged Maria Dmitrievna, whose tears had long since dried up.

"I've never deceived Varvara Pavlovna before," Lavretskii responded. "She'll believe me as it is. I'll take her to Lavriki—and remember, Varvara Pavlovna, our agreement will be broken as soon as you leave there. And now permit me to say goodbye."

He bowed to both ladies and left hurriedly.

"Aren't you going to take her with you?" Maria Dmitrievna cried. . . . "Let him go," Varvara Pavlovna whispered to her. She promptly embraced Maria Dmitrievna and began to thank her, kissing her hands and calling her a savior.

Maria Dmitrievna accepted her caresses indulgently, but at heart she was dissatisfied with Lavretskii, with Varvara Pavlovna, and with the entire scene she'd staged. Too little sentimentality had resulted from it; in her opinion, Varvara Pavlovna ought to have flung herself at her husband's feet.

"How could you have failed to understand me?" she queried. "I kept saying 'get down.'"

"It's better the way it was, dear Aunt. Don't worry, everything's fine," Varvara Pavlovna assured her.

"Well, he's as cold as ice, anyway," Maria Dmitrievna commented. "You didn't cry, it's true, but I wept floods of tears right in front of him. He wants to imprison you at Lavriki. Why, you won't even be able to come and see me. All men are unfeeling," she concluded with a meaningful shake of her head.

"Then it's women who can appreciate kindness and nobility," Varvara Pavlovna responded, and gently dropping to her knees before Maria Dmitrievna, she flung her arms around Maria Dmitrievna's plump body and pressed her face against it. That face wore a sly smile, but Maria Dmitrievna's tears began to flow once again.

When Lavretskii returned home, he locked himself in his servant's room, flung himself on a sofa, and lay like that until morning.

XLIV

The following day was Sunday. The sound of bells ringing for the early church service didn't awaken Lavretskii—he hadn't closed his eyes all night—but it reminded him of another Sunday when, at Liza's request, he'd gone to church. He got up hastily, for a secret voice told him that he'd see her there today as well. He left the house without a sound, giving orders to tell Varvara Pavlovna, who was still asleep, that he'd be back for dinner, and strode in the direction the monotonous, mournful bells were summoning him. He arrived early—there was hardly anyone inside the church. The deacon was reading the service in the chancel; his voice droned on—occasionally interrupted by a cough—rising and falling at regular intervals. Lavretskii stationed himself near the entrance. Worshipers entered one by one, all stopping, crossing themselves, and bowing in every direction. Their footsteps reverberated distinctly under the arched roof of the empty, silent church. A poor, decrepit little old woman wearing a worn-out cloak with a hood was kneeling near Lavretskii, praying assiduously. Her toothless, yellowed, wrinkled face betrayed intense emotion; her bloodshot eyes gazed steadily upward at the icons on the icon stand; her bony hand kept emerging from under her cloak and slowly, earnestly making a broad sign of the cross. An unkempt peasant with a bushy beard and a surly face came into the church, immediately fell to his knees, and hurriedly began bowing and crossing himself, tilting his head back and shaking it after each bow. Such bitter grief was expressed in his face and all his motions that Lavretskii decided to approach him and ask what was wrong. The startled peasant recoiled, then looked up at him grimly.... "My son died," he declared rapidly, and began bowing down to the ground again. "What could ever replace the consolations of the Church for these people?" Lavretskii wondered. He tried to pray himself, but his heart had hardened and grown heavy, and his thoughts were far away. He kept expecting Liza, but she didn't come. The church began to fill up with people; she still hadn't arrived. The service commenced. The deacon had already read from the Gospel; the bells began to ring for one of the prayers. Lavretskii moved forward slightly—and suddenly caught sight of Liza. She'd gotten there before he had, but he hadn't noticed her. She'd secluded herself in a recess between the wall and the chancel, and hadn't moved, hadn't looked around. Lavretskii didn't take his eyes off her until the very end of the service—he was saying goodbye to her. The worshipers started to disperse, but she stayed behind. It seemed as though she were waiting for Lavretskii to leave. She eventually crossed herself for the last time and went out—no one but a maid had accompanied her—without turning around. Lavretskii left the church after she did, and overtook her in the street. She was walking quite rapidly with her head bowed and a veil pulled down over her face.

"Good morning, Lizaveta Mikhailovna," he said aloud with feigned casualness. "May I accompany you?"

She didn't reply; he began to walk beside her.

"Are you pleased with me?" he asked her, lowering his voice. "Have you heard what happened yesterday?"

"Yes, yes," she answered in a whisper, "that was very good." And she walked even more rapidly.

"Are you pleased?"

Liza merely nodded her head in assent.

"Fedor Ivanych," she began in a calm but feeble voice, "I want to ask you not to come see us any more. Go away as soon as possible. We may see one another again later—sometime—in a year. But now, do this for me—fulfill my request, for God's sake."

"I'm prepared to obey you in every way, Lizaveta Mikhailovna— but do we really have to part like this? Won't you say even a single word to me?"

"Fedor Ivanych, you're walking beside me right now. . . . But you're already so very far away from me. And not just you, but. . . ."

"Speak plainly, I implore you!" cried Lavretskii. "What do you mean?"

"You'll hear, perhaps. . . . But whatever may happen, forget . . . no, don't forget me, remember me."

"Could I forget you . . . ?"

"That's enough. Goodbye. Don't follow me."

"Liza," Lavretskii began. . . .

"Goodbye, goodbye!" she repeated, pulling her veil down farther and practically running forward. Lavretskii watched her go, and then turned back along the street with his head lowered. He bumped into Lemm, who was also walking with his eyes trained on the ground, his hat angled close to his nose.

They looked at one another without speaking.

"Well, what do you have to say?" Lavretskii finally inquired.

"What do I have to say?" Lemm replied gloomily. "I have nothing to say. Everything is dead, and we are dead—*Alles ist todt, und wir sind todt*. So you are turning to the right here, are you?"

"Yes."

"And I to the left. Goodbye."

The following morning, Fedor Ivanych set off for Lavriki with his wife. She went first in one carriage, along with Ada and Justine; he followed them in another carriage. The pretty little girl didn't turn away from the window during the entire journey. She was amazed at everything: the peasant men and women, the huts, the wells, the yokes over the horses' heads, the bells, and the flocks of crows; Justine shared her amazement. Varvara Pavlovna laughed at their comments and exclamations—she was in excellent spirits. Before their departure from town, she'd reached an understanding with her husband.

"I comprehend your situation," she said to him, and from the look in her intelligent eyes, he inferred that she did fully comprehend his situation. "But you must at least do me this much justice— I'm easy to live with. I won't tie you down or constrain you in any way. I wanted to secure Ada's future. I don't need anything else."

"Well, you've achieved your goal," observed Fedor Ivanych.

"I dream of only one thing now—of burying myself in seclusion forever. I'll always remember your kindness. . . . "

"That's enough of that," he interrupted.

"And I'll be careful to respect your independence and your peace of mind," she continued, completing the phrases she'd prepared.

Lavretskii bowed deeply to her. Varvara Pavlovna understood that her husband was thanking her in his heart.

They reached Lavriki the evening of the following day. A week later, Lavretskii set off for Moscow, leaving his wife five thousand rubles for her household expenses. The day after Lavretskii's departure, Panshin appeared—Varvara Pavlovna had begged him not to forget her in her solitude. She gave him the nicest possible reception; the lofty rooms of the house and even the garden echoed and reechoed with the sounds of piano music, singing, and lively French conversation until late that night. Panshin remained at Varvara Pavlovna's for three days. When he said goodbye to her, warmly pressing her lovely hands, he promised to come back very soon—and he kept his word.

XLV

Liza had a room to herself on the second floor of her mother's house. It was a small, clean, sunlit room with a little white bed, flowerpots in the corners and in front of the windows, a small desk, a bookcase, and a crucifix on the wall. It had always been called the nursery; Liza had been born in it. When she returned from church after seeing Lavretskii, she put all the things in her room in order more carefully than usual, dusted everywhere, reread all her notebooks and letters from girlfriends and then retied them with ribbons, locked all the drawers, and watered the flowers, caressing each blossom with her hand. She did everything calmly and noiselessly, with some sort of rapt, gentle concern on her face. She finally stopped in the middle of the room, looked around slowly, and then, going up to the desk, above which the crucifix was hanging, she fell to her knees, rested her head on her clasped hands, and remained motionless.

Marfa Timofeevna came in and found her in this position. Liza didn't notice her aunt's entrance. The elderly woman tiptoed outside the door and coughed loudly several times. Liza rose quickly and wiped her eyes, which were glistening with unshed tears.

"Ah, I see you've been straightening up your little cell again," Marfa Timofeevna remarked as she bent over a young rose tree in a pot. "That smells so lovely!"

Liza looked at her aunt thoughtfully.

"How odd that you should use that particular word!" she murmured.

"Which word, eh?" the elderly woman responded alertly. "What do you mean? This is horrible," she declared, suddenly pulling off her cap and sitting down on Liza's little bed. "It's more than I can bear! This is the fourth day that I've been virtually seething inside. I can't pretend not to notice any longer. I can't stand to see you getting pale, withering away, and weeping, I can't, I can't!"

"Why, what's the matter, Aunt?" asked Liza. "It's nothing...."

"Nothing!" cried Marfa Timofeevna. "You may say that to other people, but not to me. Nothing! Who was on her knees just now? And whose eyelashes are still wet with tears? Nothing, indeed! Why, look at yourself—what have you done to your face, what's happened to your eyes? Nothing! Don't I know everything?"

"This will pass, Aunt. Give it time."

"This will pass—but when? Good God! Merciful Savior! Can you have loved him so much? Why, he's an old man, Liza darling. Now, I don't deny that he's a good person, that there's no harm in him, but what of it? We're all good people. The world isn't so small—there'll always be plenty of that commodity."

"I tell you, this will all pass—it's all already passed."

"Listen to what I'm going to say to you, Liza darling," Marfa Timofeevna suddenly commanded, making Liza sit down beside her and straightening Liza's hair and kerchief. "It seems to you now, in the midst of the worst of it, that nothing can ever remedy your sorrow. Ah, my darling, the only thing that can't be cured is death. You just have to say to yourself right now, 'I won't give in to this—so there!' and you'll be surprised yourself at how soon, how easily this will pass. Just be patient."

"Aunt," Liza replied, "it's already passed. Everything has passed."

"Already passed! In what sense has it passed? Why, your poor little nose has been growing thinner, and you say it's passed. This is a fine way of passing!"

"Yes, it's passed, Aunt—if you'll only try to help me," Liza asserted with sudden spirit, and she flung her arms around Marfa Timofeevna's neck. "Dear Aunt, be my friend, help me. Don't be angry, try to understand me...."

"Why, what is it, what is it, miss? Don't scare me, please—I'm going to scream in another minute. Don't look at me like that. Just tell me quickly—what is it?"

"I—I want...." Liza hid her face on Marfa Timofeevna's bosom. "I want to enter a convent," she announced hollowly.

The elderly woman almost leaped off the bed.

"Cross yourself, my dear girl, Liza darling. Think about what you're saying. Where did you get such an idea? God have mercy on you!" she murmured at last. "Lie down, my dove, and sleep a little bit. All this comes from exhaustion, my sweetheart."

Liza raised her head; her cheeks were glowing.

"No, Aunt," she responded, "don't say that. I've made up my mind. I've prayed, I've asked God for guidance. Everything's over, my life with you is over. This lesson wasn't taught to me for nothing, and this isn't the first time I've thought of it. I wasn't intended for happiness—even when I had hopes of happiness, my heart was always aching. I'm aware of all my own sins, as well as those of others, and of how Papa made our fortune. I know everything. There has to be some atonement, some atonement for all of that. I'm sorry for you, sorry for Mama and Lenochka, but there's nothing else I can do. I sense that there's no future life for me here. I've said goodbye to everything, I've spoken to everything in the house for the last time. Something is calling out to me. I'm sick at heart, I want to hide myself away forever. Don't stand in my way, don't try to dissuade me. Help me, or else I'll have to go away by myself...."

Marfa Timofeevna listened to her niece with horror.

"She's ill, she's delirious," Marfa Timofeevna thought. "We have to send for a doctor—but which one? Gedeonovskii was praising one the other day. He always tells lies, and yet maybe this time he was telling the truth." But when she was convinced that Liza wasn't ill and wasn't delirious, when Liza kept giving the same responses to all her objections, Marfa Timofeevna became alarmed and unhappy in earnest. "But, my dove," she tried to reason with Liza, "you don't know what life is like in those convents! Why, they'll feed you on green hemp oil, my pet, and put you in the coarsest of coarse linen, and make you walk around in the cold. You'd never be able to bear all that, Liza darling. This is all Agafia's doing—she's the one who led you astray. But then, you know, she began by living for her own pleasure, and continued that way—you have to live, too. At least let me die in peace, then do as you please. And who's ever heard of such a thing! To enter a convent for the sake of such a—for the sake of an old goat, God forgive me! Why, if you're so sick at heart, go on a pilgrimage, offer prayers to some saint, have a service sung—but don't put a black hood on your head, my dear creature, my sweet girl. . . ."

And Marfa Timofeevna bitterly burst into tears.

Liza comforted her, wiped away her tears, and cried herself, but she remained adamant. In her despair, Marfa Timofeevna threatened to tell Liza's mother all about it . . . but that was of no avail, either. Liza agreed to defer carrying out her plan for six months only after the elderly woman's most urgent entreaties. Marfa Timofeevna had to promise in return that if Liza hadn't changed her mind after six months, she herself would help Liza, and do all that she could to win Maria Dmitrievna's consent.

In spite of Varvara Pavlovna's promise to bury herself in seclusion, at the first sign of cold weather, having provided herself with sufficient funds, she moved to Petersburg, where she rented a modest but charming apartment that Panshin, who'd left the district of O—— a bit earlier, had found for her. During the latter part of his stay in O——, he'd completely forsaken Maria Dmitrievna's good graces. He'd suddenly stopped visiting her, and hardly ever left Lavriki. Varvara Pavlovna had enslaved him, literally enslaved him—no other word can describe her boundless, irresistible, unassailable power over him.

Lavretskii spent the winter in Moscow, and in the spring of the following year, the news reached him that Liza had become a nun in the B—— convent, which was located in one of the most remote regions of Russia.

Epilogue

Eight years passed. Spring arrived once again. . . . But let's say a few words first about the fates of Mikhalevich, Panshin, and Mrs. Lavretskii—and then say goodbye to them. After extensive wandering, Mikhalevich has finally settled into a suitable job: he's obtained the position of senior superintendent in a government school. He's eminently satisfied with his fate, and his students adore him, although they mimic him as well. Panshin has significantly advanced in rank, and is already aspiring to a position of leadership. He walks with a slight stoop, no doubt caused by the weight around his neck of the Vladimir Cross that was conferred on him. The official in him has finally gained ascendancy over the artist—his still youngish face has grown sallow, and his hair has gotten thinner; he neither sings nor sketches now—but he does secretly apply himself to literature. He's written a comedy in the style of a "proverb," and since all writers nowadays have to depict a "portrait" of someone or something, he's depicted the "portrait" of a coquette in it, and has read it in private to two or three ladies who are well disposed toward him. He hasn't entered into matrimony, however, although numerous excellent opportunities to do so have presented themselves—Varvara Pavlovna is responsible for this.

As for her, she lives in Paris full-time, as she did before. Fedor Ivanych has given her a promissory note for a large sum, thereby protecting himself against the possibility of her unexpectedly descending upon him a second time. She's grown somewhat older and plumper, but is as charming and elegant as ever. Everyone has an ideal, and Varvara Pavlovna has found hers in the dramatic works of Dumas *fils*. She diligently frequents the theater when consumptive, sentimental *dames aux camélias* are brought out onto the stage. Being Madame Doche seems to her to be the height of human bliss—she once declared that she couldn't desire a better fate for her own daughter. One must hope that fate will spare Mademoiselle Ada such happiness: she's changed from a rosy-cheeked, chubby child into a pallid, frail girl, and her nerves are already strained. The quantity of Varvara Pavlovna's admirers has diminished, but she still retains a certain number of them; she'll probably keep a few until the end of her days. The most ardent of them recently is a retired guardsman, a certain Zakurdalo-Skubyrnikov, who's a full-bearded, thirty-eight-year-old man with an exceptionally powerful physique. The French *habitués* of Mrs. Lavretskii's salon have dubbed him *le gros taureau de l'Ukraine*.

Varvara Pavlovna never invites him to her fashionable evening gatherings, but he fully enjoys her favor.

And so—eight years passed. The breezes of spring were gloriously wafting from the sky once again; spring was smiling upon the earth and its inhabitants once again; under its caresses, everything was beginning to blossom, to radiate affection, to sing, once again. The town of O—— had undergone few changes in the course of these eight years, but Maria Dmitrievna's house seemed to have grown younger. Its freshly painted white walls offered a cheerful welcome and the panes of its open windows shone crimson in the setting sun. Vibrant, joyful sounds of resonant young voices and continual laughter floated into the street through those windows; the entire house seemed to be astir with life, to be brimming over with merriment. The lady of the house herself had long since gone to her grave: Maria Dmitrievna had died two years after Liza became a nun, and Marfa Timofeevna hadn't survived her niece for much longer—they lay side by side in the town cemetery. Nastasia Karpovna was no longer alive, either. For several years, the faithful old woman had gone to say a prayer over her friend's ashes every week. . . . Her time had come, and now her bones also lay in the damp ground. But Maria Dmitrievna's house hadn't passed into strangers' hands, it hadn't left the family—the nest hadn't been destroyed. In residence were Lenochka, who'd been transformed into a slim, beautiful young woman, and her fiancé, a blond officer of the hussars; Maria Dmitrievna's son, who'd just gotten married in Petersburg and had come to O—— with his young wife for the spring; his wife's sister, a schoolgirl of sixteen with glowing cheeks and shining eyes; and Shurochka, who'd also grown up and was also very attractive. They comprised the youthful household whose laughter and conversation made the walls of the Kalitin house reverberate.

Everything in the house had changed; everything had become suited to its new inhabitants. Beardless servant boys who grinned and joked had replaced the sober, elderly servants of former days. Two setters raced around wildly, cavorting on the sofas where the fat Roska had once waddled in solemn dignity. The stables were filled with slender walking horses, spirited carriage horses, fiery spare horses with braided manes, and saddle horses from the Don region. Breakfast, dinner, and supper hours were all confused and intermingled. As the neighbors put it, "unheard-of arrangements" had been made.

On the evening about which we're speaking, the residents of the

Kalitin house (the eldest of them, Lenochka's fiancé, was only twenty-four) were engaged in a game that, although it wasn't very complicated, was exceedingly enjoyable to them, to judge from their companionable laughter: they were running from room to room chasing one another. The dogs were running alongside and barking, and the canaries hanging in cages above the windows were straining their throats, adding to the general uproar with the piercing trills of their furious chirps. At the very height of these deafening festivities, a mud-spattered carriage pulled up to the gate. A man of about forty-five wearing a traveling suit stepped out and paused in astonishment. He stood still for a moment, studying the house with a careful gaze. Then he went through the little gate into the yard and slowly mounted the steps. He found no one in the hallway, but a door was suddenly thrown open and Shurochka rushed through it, her face completely flushed. She was immediately followed by all the other young people, who were pursuing her with ringing shouts. They stopped short and abruptly fell silent at the sight of a stranger, but the clear eyes directed at him all wore the same friendly expression, and their fresh faces continued to smile as Maria Dmitrievna's son went up to the visitor and asked him cordially what he could do for him.

"I'm Lavretskii," replied the visitor.

He was answered by a friendly cry, not because these young people were so greatly delighted at the arrival of a distant, nearly forgotten relative, but simply because they were ready to be delighted and to make noise at any convenient opportunity. They promptly surrounded Lavretskii. Lenochka, as an old acquaintance, was the first to mention her own name, assuring him that she definitely would have recognized him in another moment. She introduced him to the rest of the group, addressing each one, even her fiancé, by a nickname. They all trooped through the dining room into the drawing room. The walls of both rooms had been repapered, but the furniture was still the same—Lavretskii recognized the piano. Even the embroidery frame in the window was just the same, placed in just the same position and, it seemed, holding just the same unfinished piece of embroidery on it as it had eight years ago. They made him sit down in a comfortable armchair, and they all politely sat down in a circle around him. Questions, exclamations, and stories vied with one another.

"It's been a long time since we've seen you," Lenochka remarked simply, "and we haven't seen Varvara Pavlovna, either."

"Well, no wonder!" her brother hastened to interject. "I took you off to Petersburg, and Fedor Ivanych has been living in the countryside the whole time."

"Yes, and Mama died shortly after that."

"And Marfa Timofeevna," observed Shurochka.

"And Nastasia Karpovna," added Lenochka, "and Monsieur Lemm."

"What? Is Lemm dead, too?" asked Lavretskii.

"Yes," replied young Kalitin. "He left here to go to Odessa. They say that someone lured him there, and then he died."

"You don't happen to know... whether he left any music behind?"

"I don't know. It's not very likely."

Everyone fell silent and exchanged glances. A slight cloud of melancholy flitted across all the young faces.

"But Matross is alive," Lenochka announced suddenly.

"And Gedeonovskii," added her brother.

At the mention of Gedeonovskii's name, friendly laughter instantly erupted.

"Yes, he's alive, and as big a liar as ever," Maria Dmitrievna's son continued. "Just imagine, yesterday this madcap child"—pointing to the schoolgirl, his wife's sister—"put some pepper in his snuffbox."

"He sneezed so hard!" Lenochka exclaimed, and another burst of unrestrained laughter ensued.

"We've had some news about Liza recently," young Kalitin noted, and a hush fell over everyone again. "She's all right—she's feeling somewhat better now."

"Is she still in the same convent?" Lavretskii inquired, not without some effort.

"Yes, still the same one."

"Does she write to you?"

"No, never. But we get news through other people." A sudden, profound silence set in. "A good angel is passing by," everyone thought.

"Wouldn't you like to go out into the garden?" Kalitin asked, turning to Lavretskii. "It's very nice right now, although we've let it run a bit wild."

Lavretskii went out into the garden, and the first thing that met his eyes was the very bench on which he'd once spent a few blissful, never-to-be-repeated moments with Liza. It had gotten dark and warped, but he recognized it, and his soul was filled with a feeling unequaled for both its pleasure and its pain—a feeling of keen sorrow for youth that has vanished, for happiness that was once treasured. He strolled along the paths, accompanied by the young people. The lime trees hardly looked any older or taller after eight years, but their shade was thicker. By contrast, all the shrubbery had grown higher, the raspberry bushes had spread profusely, and the hazels had become a tangled thicket; the fresh scent of trees, grass, and lilacs arose on all sides.

"This would be a good place to play Puss-in-the-Corner," Lenochka suddenly cried, as they came upon a small patch of green lawn surrounded by lime trees. "And there are exactly five of us, too."

"Have you forgotten Fedor Ivanych?" responded her brother. "Or didn't you count yourself?"

Lenochka blushed slightly.

"But would Fedor Ivanych, at his age . . . ," she began.

"Please, play your game," Lavretskii hurriedly interjected. "Don't pay any attention to me. I'll be happier knowing I'm not in your way. And there's no need for you to entertain me. We old people have something to occupy us about which you know nothing yet, which no game can replace—our memories."

The young people listened to Lavretskii with polite, slightly amused respectfulness—as though a teacher were giving them a lesson—then they all suddenly dispersed and ran to the patch of lawn. Four of them stood near trees, one stood in the middle, and the game began.

In the meantime, Lavretskii went back to the house, into the dining room. He approached the piano and touched one of the keys. It emitted a faint but clear sound that secretly echoed in his heart: that note had begun the inspired melody with which Lemm, the deceased Lemm, had moved him to such transports on that supremely happy night long ago. Then Lavretskii went into the drawing room, and didn't leave it for a long while; in the room where he'd seen Liza so often, her image rose before him the most vividly; he seemed to feel traces of her presence around him. His grief for her was the oppressive kind, the kind that wasn't easy to bear—it had none of the peace that comes with death, for Liza was still alive somewhere, hidden far away. He thought of her as alive, but he didn't recognize the young woman he'd once loved in that dim, pale phantom cloaked in a nun's habit, encircled by smoky clouds of incense.

Lavretskii wouldn't have recognized himself, if he could have seen himself as he mentally saw Liza. In the course of these eight years, he'd passed the turning point in life that many people never pass—but without passing this point, no one can remain a decent person up to the end: he'd truly ceased to think about his own happiness, about his personal goals. He'd become tranquil and—why hide the truth?—he'd grown old, not just in face and body, but in spirit. To keep your heart young until old age, some say, is both difficult and almost ludicrous; the individual who hasn't lost faith in goodness, steadfastness of will, and the desire to work may well be satisfied. Lavretskii had the right to be satisfied: he'd actually become an excellent farmer, he'd actually learned to cultivate the soil, and he hadn't labored solely for himself—to the best of his abilities, he'd insured the welfare of his peasants.

Lavretskii went out of the house into the garden and sat down on the familiar bench. And on this beloved spot, facing the house where he'd vainly stretched out his hand one last time toward the enchanted cup that bubbled and sparkled with the golden wine of delight, he, a solitary, homeless wanderer, reviewed his life, while the joyous shouts of the younger generation already replacing him floated across the garden toward him. His heart was sad, but neither overburdened nor embittered: he had much to regret, but nothing to be ashamed of.

"Go on playing, vigorous youth! Be happy! Grow strong!" he thought, and there was no resentment in his thinking. "Your life is ahead of you, and life will be easier for you. You won't have to seek out a path for yourselves, or to struggle, to fall, and to rise again in the dark, as we did. We had to worry about surviving— and how many of us didn't survive?—but you merely have to do your duty, to work hard, and the blessings of the older generation will be upon you. After today, after undergoing these sensations, it just remains for me to bid you a final farewell, and sadly but unenviously, without any feeling of antagonism, to say in sight of the end, in sight of God, who awaits me, 'Welcome, lonely old age! Burn out, useless life!'"

Lavretskii quietly stood up and quietly left; no one noticed him, no one detained him. The joyous cries resounded ever more vigorously in the garden behind the thick green wall of the tall lime trees. He took his seat in the carriage, ordering the coachman to drive home and not to rush the horses.

"And the end?" the dissatisfied reader will possibly inquire. "What happened to Lavretskii after that, and to Liza?" But what can one say about people who, even though they're still alive, have withdrawn from the battlefield of life? Why return to them? It's said that Lavretskii visited the remote convent where Liza had hidden herself away, and saw her. Crossing from chancel to chancel, she walked close by him, proceeding with the even, hurried, but humble steps of a nun—and didn't glance at him. The lashes of the eye turned toward him merely quivered slightly, she merely lowered her emaciated face—and pressed together even more tightly the fingers of her clasped hands that were holding a rosary. What were they both thinking? What were they both feeling? Who knows? Who can say? There are some moments in life, some feelings. . . . One can only point to them—and pass by.

Letter to E. E. Lambert.

Village of Spasskoe.

March 27, 1859.

I arrived here yesterday, and I'm writing to you today, dear Countess. I'm not saying that in order to boast, but to prove to you that thoughts of you come to my mind before anything else. I found everything here as it had been, only to my genuine grief, in my absence, death has carried off almost our only neighbor, a very nice, kind young man by the name of Karateev.... My former attendant, an old man of about sixty-five, also died.... Death isn't selective when it takes people. We're all in its debt, and debtors can't tell a creditor with whom he should begin to collect....

But let's leave these sad meditations aside. I found winter here (that's sad, too, but what can be done about it?). Five days or so ago, there was such an enormous snowfall that I had trouble making it home, but let's hope that all this will soon change. In a few days, I'm going to Orel to be present, if possible, at the committee's meetings, but by April 5th, i.e., by the time the woodcocks arrive, I'll be home again. On the 23d, you remember, you're having tea at my place in Petersburg.

I'm now busy formulating the plan and so on for a new story: it's rather exhausting—all the more so as it doesn't leave any *visible* traces: you lie on the couch or pace around the room while turning over in your mind some character or situation—you look, and three or four hours have passed—but you seem to have made little headway. Frankly speaking, there's rather little pleasure in our craft— but that's as things should be: everyone, even artists, even wealthy people, ought to live by the sweat of their brow.... And so much the worse for anyone whose brow isn't sweaty: his heart is either ill or withering up. During all these days, I've often been recalling the little room on Furshtatskaia Street and the evenings that I spent there.... These recollections turn out to be the best thing that I brought away from Petersburg life. I'm very glad that I didn't yield to the desire to take advantage of my novel's success and didn't make forays all over the place—besides exhaustion and perhaps the sinful pleasure of the petty, worthless feeling of vanity, it wouldn't have provided me with anything. I've become convinced that every person should treat himself strictly and even rudely and distrustfully; it's difficult to tame the beast in oneself. It sometimes happens that you don't yield to coarse, stupid flattery and think, "What a fine person I am!" but if they served you the same flattery with tastier seasoning—you'd begin to swallow it like oysters. I don't know why I'm indulging in these thoughts; since I left I haven't succumbed to the slightest temptation of flattery; obviously something was sitting inside me that needed to find its way out.

Please write me at the following address: Orel Province, City of Mtsensk. Give my regards to your husband and all the residents and guests of your home on Furshtatskaia. By the way, I forgot to give you the 75 rubles (do you remember for what use?). Please use that sum of money as you see fit and I'll return it to you in Petersburg.

Be well and don't be depressed—that's the main thing—and don't forget me: that's the main thing for me. I wish you all the best and kiss your hands. You remember our agreement: write me in French.

> Your sincerely devoted
> Iv. Turgenev.

Letter to I. A. Goncharov.[1]

Spasskoe.
April 7, 1859.

I can't conceal the fact, dear Ivan Aleksandrovich, that, contrary to custom, this time it's with little pleasure that I take pen in hand to reply to you, because what pleasure is there in writing to a person who considers you the appropriator of others' ideas (*plagiare*), a liar (you suspect that there's craftiness again in my new tale, that I only intend to divert your attention), and a chatterbox (you suppose that I told Annenkov about our conversation). You have to agree that whatever my "diplomacy," it's difficult to smile and be diffident when you receive such bitter pills. You must also agree that in response to half—what am I saying!—the tenth part of similar accusations, you would have grown completely furious. But I—call this what you please in me, weakness or dissimulation— I only wondered, "Does he have a good opinion of me?" and was only surprised that you still found something in me that you could like. Thanks even for that! It's without any false humility that I tell you that I agree completely with what "the teacher" said about my *Nest of Gentry*. But what would you have me do? I can't repeat *A Sportsman's Sketches* ad infinitum! Nor do I feel like giving up writing either. All I can do is compose the sort of tale in which, without making any claims to the integrity or strength of the characters, or to profound, multifaceted penetration into life, I might express what comes into my head. There will be torn spots sewn up with white thread, and so on. But what can I do about that? Whoever needs a novel in the epic meaning of that word has no need of me; but I think of writing a novel as often as I do about walking on my head: no matter what I write, the result is a series of sketches. *E sempre bene!* But even in this confession you'll see diplomacy: Tolstoy thinks that I sneeze, drink, and sleep—all for the sake of a phrase. Take me as I am or don't take me at all; but don't demand that I remake myself, and most importantly, don't consider me such a Talleyrand!

1. Ivan Aleksandrovich Goncharov (1812-91), the author of *A Common Story* and *Oblomov*, among other works. Goncharov was consumed by the notion that Turgenev had taken ideas for *A Nest of Gentry* and *On the Eve* from Goncharov's *The Precipice*, a work then in progress. By 1860, rumors of Turgenev's "plagiarism" were so rife in Petersburg that Turgenev turned the matter over to a court of arbitration, which ruled that any similarities between Turgenev's and Goncharov's works were purely coincidental.

But enough about that. All this fuss leads to nothing: we'll all die and stink after death.

Spring has arrived here, almost all the snow has melted, but it's rather ugly and lifeless. The days are wet, cold, and gray; the fields are naked and deathly yellow. The grass is already coming up in the woods, though. There's little wild fowl. I hope to finish up everything here by the 20th; I'll be in Petersburg on the 24th (on the 29th, you know, I'm leaving to go abroad). We'll see each other in Petersburg and perhaps abroad as well, although they'll probably recommend different waters for me than for you. I hope that your stay in Marienbad will be as beneficial in all respects as it was in '57. Give my regards to all our good acquaintances and to dear Maikova. I learned of Bosio's death today and felt very bad for her. I saw her on the day of her last performance: she was playing "*Traviata*"; she had no idea then, while she was playing a dying person, that she'd soon have to perform that role in real life. Everything earthly is dust and decay and falsehood.

Goodbye, unjust person! I clasp your hand.

I forgot the most important thing: the letter to Count Kushelev about Solianikov's translation. I'll write to him tomorrow, but to tell the truth, I haven't the least bit of faith in that Mitrofanushka-Maecena.

Letter to E. E. Lambert.

Village of Spasskoe.
October 14, 1859.

Why do you tell me sweet things, my dear Countess? After all, I don't tell you sweet things. However, I console myself with the thought that in sending me the excerpt from the letter you wrote about me, you were moved not so much by the desire to say sweet things to me as by the intention to reproach me indirectly for the insignificance and paleness of my last letters. But a person who, like me, wrote you a few days ago what was practically an eclogue, can calmly cross his arms on his chest and await the sentence of dispassionate fate or your sentence—which aren't quite the same things.

But all the same, don't write me sweet things. Man is so made that he's always ready to stuff himself with fruit preserves, even if he knows that they're bad for him and that the preserves, properly speaking, don't even belong to him. But women love to stroke your head, especially after they've scratched you—and they call *that* kindness.

But I'm nevertheless happy that your skeptical, mistrustful mood has been replaced by a melancholy, sad one. A skeptic is dissatisfied with others and with himself, but a melancholic only with himself, which is much easier and better.

I'm sitting here like a crayfish on the riverbottom—I don't even show my nose outside the room. I can't speak—I cough, but I'm working hard. The weather here is warm—I passionately adore such autumn days, but I'm forced to admire them through double windows. It's not fun, but, as I was once asked by Count Bludov (the secretary to the Ambassador in London), who was amazed to see me hurrying to the train station: "Can there really be anything on earth for which it's worth hurrying?" That's just the way I sometimes think: isn't it all the same where one is? Can there really be anything worth desiring?

As soon as I wrote these words, I realized that I'd written nonsense. Too bad! I know of many things that I passionately desire that will probably never be granted to me. In your letter, you already commented on one of my wishes and used a terrible phrase that I don't want to repeat, which made me shudder. But besides *that* single, main wish, I have many others whose realization would make me very happy: for instance, I'd like to be healthy and sitting with you in your little room on Furshtatskaia; I'd like my novel to be a success; I'd like . . . but I can't even list them all. There's a Russian saying: "Even as a man dies, he jerks his foot."

It recently occurred to me that there's something tragic in the fate of almost every person—it's just that the tragic is often concealed from a person by the banal surface of life. One who remains on the surface (and there are many of them) often fails to suspect that he's the hero of a tragedy. A woman will complain of indigestion and not even know that what she means is that her whole life has been shattered. For example: all around me here there are peaceful, quiet existences, yet if you take a close look—you see something tragic in each of them, something either their own, or imposed on them by history, by the development of the nation. And besides that, we're all fated to die. . . . What more tragic thing could one want?

I don't know what brought on this attack of philosophizing. But when I write you, I never know what I'll end up saying, nor do I want to know. I do know that I'll never under any circumstances write that I don't love you. Farewell, dear Countess, be cheerful, give my regards to your husband and all our friends. I kiss your hands.

Your Iv. Turgenev

P.S. Why do you send your letters registered? As a result, they take an extra day to reach me.

First Love

Dedicated to P. V. Annenkov

The guests had departed long ago. The clock struck half-past twelve. The host remained in the drawing room alone with Sergei Nikolaevich and Vladimir Petrovich.

The host rang for a servant and had the remains of supper cleared away.

"And so it's settled," he remarked, settling back deeper in his easy chair and lighting up a cigar. "Each of us will recount the story of his first love. It's your turn, Sergei Nikolaevich."

Sergei Nikolaevich, a rotund little man with a plump face and a fair complexion, first looked at his host and then turned his eyes toward the ceiling.

"I didn't have a first love," he finally said. "I began with the second."

"How did that happen?"

"It was very simple. I was eighteen when I embarked upon my first flirtation with a charming young lady, but I flirted with her as though it were nothing new to me, just as I flirted with others later on. Accurately speaking, the first and last time I fell in love was with my nursemaid when I was six years old, but that's way in the past. The details of our relationship have escaped my memory—and even if I remembered them, whom could they possibly interest?"

"Then how shall we proceed?" asked the host. "There was nothing much of interest about my first love, either. I never fell in love with anyone until I met Anna Nikolaevna, who's now my wife, and everything went as smoothly as possible for us. Our parents arranged the match, we quickly came to love one another, and got

486

married in no time. My story can be told in a couple of lines. I must confess, gentlemen, that in bringing up the subject of first love, I was counting on you—I won't say old, but no longer young—bachelors. Can't you entertain us somehow, Vladimir Petrovich?"

"My first love actually didn't belong to the ranks of the completely ordinary," Vladimir Petrovich responded with some reluctance. He was a man of about forty whose dark hair was turning gray.

"Ah!" cried the host and Sergei Nikolaevich with a single voice. "So much the better.... Tell us about it."

"If you wish ... or no, I won't tell you the story. I'm no good at telling a story—I either make it brief and dry, or elaborate and affected. But if you'll permit me, I'll write down everything I remember and read it to you."

His friends wouldn't agree at first, but Vladimir Petrovich insisted on getting his own way. They reassembled two weeks later, and Vladimir Petrovich kept his word.

His manuscript contained the following story.

I

I was sixteen at the time. This happened in the summer of 1833.

I was living in Moscow with my parents. They'd rented a house in the country for the summer near the Kaluga gate, across from the Neskuchnii gardens. I was preparing for the university, but I wasn't working a lot—I was in no hurry.

No one interfered with my freedom. I did whatever I liked, especially after the departure of my last tutor, a Frenchman who'd never been able to get used to the idea that he'd fallen into Russia "like a bomb" (*comme une bombe*), and would lie in bed lethargically with an embittered expression on his face for days at a time. My father treated me with offhand affection; my mother barely paid any attention to me, although I was her only child—other cares thoroughly absorbed her. My father, who was still young and very handsome, had married her out of financial considerations—she was ten years older than he. My mother led a sad life: she was incessantly agitated, jealous, and angry, albeit not in my father's presence. She was truly afraid of him; his behavior toward her was severe, cold, and distant.... I've never encountered anyone more overtly serene, self-confident, and self-controlled.

I'll never forget the first weeks I spent at the country house. The weather was magnificent; we'd left town on the ninth of May, on

St. Nicholas's Day. I used to go for strolls either in our own garden or the Neskuchnii gardens, or else beyond the town gates. I'd take some book or other—Kaidanov's history, for instance—but I rarely opened it, preferring to declaim verses out loud, many of which I knew by heart. My blood was on fire and my heart was aching—ever so sweetly and foolishly. I was all anticipation, a little intimidated by something and full of wonder at everything, on the edge of expectation. My imagination kept rapidly revolving around the same fancies, like martins circling a bell tower at dawn. I dreamed, I mourned, I even wept; but through the tears, through the sadness, when inspired by a lyrical verse or the beauty of evening, a joyous sense of young, effervescent life burst forth like the grass in springtime.

I had a horse to ride; I used to saddle it and go somewhere far off by myself. I'd break into a fast gallop and imagine I was a knight at a tournament. How cheerfully the wind whistled in my ears! Or turning my face toward the sky, I'd sit absorbing its shining radiance and azure blue into my soul, which opened wide to welcome it.

As I recall, the image of a woman, the vision of a woman's love, rarely took definite shape in my mind at that time. But in all I thought and all I felt lay hidden a semiconscious, embarrassed presentiment of something new and unutterably sweet, something feminine....

This presentiment, this expectation, permeated my entire being; I breathed it in, it coursed through my veins with every drop of blood.... It was destined soon to be fulfilled.

Our country residence consisted of a wooden manor house decorated with columns plus two small lodges. In the lodge on the left, there was a small factory that manufactured cheap wallpaper.... I'd strolled that way more than once to look at about a dozen thin, unkempt boys with greasy aprons and emaciated faces who were perpetually jumping onto wooden levers that forced down the square blocks of a press in order to imprint variegated patterns on the wallpaper with the weight of their feeble bodies. The lodge on the right stood empty and was for rent. One day—three weeks after the ninth of May—the blinds in the windows of this lodge were raised, and women's faces appeared inside: some family had installed itself in it. I remember that the same day, at dinner, my mother asked the butler who our new neighbors were, and hearing the name Princess Zasekina, she first reacted with some respect, "Ah! A princess!..." and then added, "A poor one, I presume."

"They arrived in three rented carriages," the butler observed, as he deferentially served a dish. "They don't keep their own carriage, and the furniture's of the lowest quality."

"Ah," my mother replied, "so much the better."

My father cast an icy glance at her; she fell silent.

Certainly Princess Zasekina couldn't have been a rich woman— the lodge she'd rented was so dilapidated, small, and low-pitched that anyone even modestly well-off in the world would hardly have consented to occupy it. At the time, however, all this went in one ear and out the other. The royal title had very little effect on me— I'd just been reading Schiller's *The Robbers*.

II

I was in the habit of wandering around in our garden every evening with a gun, on the lookout for crows—I'd long cherished a hatred for those wary, sly, rapacious birds. On the day I've been speaking about, I went into the garden as usual, and after patrolling all the walks unsuccessfully (the crows recognized me, and merely cawed spasmodically at a distance), I happened to approach the low fence that separated our house from a narrow, elongated strip of garden belonging to the lodge on the right. I was walking along, my eyes trained on the ground. Suddenly, I heard a voice; I looked across the fence and froze....I was confronted by a strange spectacle.

A few steps away from me, on a grassy spot among some green raspberry bushes, stood a tall, slender young woman in a pink striped dress with a white kerchief on her head; four young men were gathered around her, and she was striking each of them in turn on the forehead with those small gray flowers whose name I don't know, although they're well known to children: the flowers form little bags and burst open with a snap when you hit them against anything hard. The young men presented their foreheads so eagerly, and the gestures of the young woman (I saw her in profile) betokened something so fascinating, imperious, caressing, mocking, and endearing, that I almost cried out with surprise and delight, and would instantly, I thought, have given anything in the world just to have had those charming fingers strike me on the forehead as well. My gun slipped to the grass, I forgot everything; my eyes devoured that graceful shape and neck, and those lovely arms, and the slightly disheveled fair hair under the white kerchief, and the half-closed, intelligent eye, and its eyelashes, and the soft cheek beneath them. . . .

"Young man, hey, young man," a voice near me abruptly called out, "is it polite to stare at young ladies you don't know that way?"

I was startled and struck speechless. . . . Close by me, on the other side of the fence, a man with short, dark hair was standing regarding me sarcastically. At the same moment, the young woman also turned toward me. . . . I caught a glimpse of big gray eyes in an energetic, animated face that suddenly quivered and laughed, a flash of white teeth, and somehow amusedly elevated eyebrows. . . . I blushed, snatched my gun off the ground, and, pursued by musical but not ill-natured laughter, I fled to my room, flung myself on the bed, and hid my face in my hands. My heart was virtually leaping; I was intensely ashamed and overjoyed at the same time; I felt an excitement I'd never known before.

After resting for a while, I brushed my hair, washed my face, and went downstairs to have tea. The image of the young woman floated before me; my heart was no longer leaping, but was somehow delightfully subdued.

"What's the matter?" my father asked me suddenly. "Have you killed a crow?"

I was about to tell him all about it, but I stopped and merely smiled to myself. As I was going to bed, I rotated three times on one leg—I don't know why—pomaded my hair, got into bed, and slept like a top all night. I woke up for a moment before dawn, raised my head, looked around in ecstasy, and fell asleep again.

III

"How can I meet her?" was my first thought when I woke up the next morning. I went out into the garden before morning tea, but I didn't go too close to the fence and didn't see anyone. After having some tea, I walked up and down the street in front of the house several times and looked into the windows from a distance. . . . I imagined that I saw *her* face behind a curtain, and hurried away in alarm.

"I have to meet her, though," I thought, distractedly pacing around a sandy field that stretched in front of the Neskuchnii gardens, "but how? That's the question." I reviewed the smallest details of our encounter yesterday; for some reason or other, I had a particularly vivid memory of the way she'd laughed at me. . . .

But while I racked my brains and formulated various plans, fate had already taken care of me.

In my absence, my mother had received a letter from her new neighbor on gray paper, sealed with brown wax of a sort used only on notices from the post office or the corks of cheap winebottles. In this letter, which was written in illiterate language and slovenly script, the princess begged my mother to exercise her powerful influence on the princess's behalf; according to the princess, my mother was well acquainted with prominent people upon whom the princess's fate and that of her children depended, since she was engaged in some very important legal matters. "I address myself to you," she wrote, "like one gentlewoman at another gentlewoman, and for thus reason are glad to avail of the opportunity." In conclusion, she begged my mother's permission to visit her. I found my mother in a disagreeable frame of mind; my father wasn't at home, and she didn't have anyone else to ask for advice. Not to reply to a "gentlewoman," and a princess at that, was unthinkable, yet my mother was unsure how to reply. To write a note in French struck her as inappropriate, but Russian spelling wasn't one of my mother's strong points, either; she was aware of this, and didn't like to compromise herself. She was overjoyed when I appeared, and promptly told me to go over to the princess's and explain to her orally that my mother would always be glad to do Her Excellency any service within her powers, and begged her to come for a visit at one o'clock. This unexpectedly rapid fulfillment of my secret desires both thrilled and terrified me. I gave no indication of the emotions that possessed me, however, and in preparation for the visit, I went to my own room to put on a new tie and a suit coat—at home, I still wore short jackets and flat collars, much as I detested them.

IV

Upon entering the narrow, untidy hallway of the lodge, involuntarily trembling in every limb, I was received by an elderly grayhaired servant with a dark, copper-colored face, surly little piglike eyes, and deeper wrinkles on his forehead and temples than any I'd ever beheld before. He was carrying a plate containing the remains of a half-eaten herring, and, shutting the door to the drawing room with his foot, he blurted out, "What do you want?"

"Is Princess Zasekina at home?" I inquired.

"Vonifatii!" a jarring female voice shouted from behind the door.

The servant turned his back on me without a word, exhibiting as he did so the extremely threadbare rear side of his uniform, which had a solitary reddish heraldic button on it. He put the plate down on the floor and walked away.

"Did you go to the police station?" the same female voice called out again. The servant muttered something in reply. "Eh? . . . Has someone arrived?" I subsequently heard: "The young gentleman from next door? Well, ask him in."

"Will you come into the drawing room?" the servant requested, reappearing and picking the plate up off the floor. I made an effort to control my emotions and entered the drawing room.

I found myself in a small, not overly clean room containing some meager furniture that looked as if it'd hurriedly been placed where it stood. A bareheaded, ugly woman of about fifty, wearing an old green dress and a striped worsted scarf around her neck, was sitting at the window in an easy chair with a broken armrest. Her small black eyes pierced me like pins.

I went up to her and bowed.

"Do I have the honor of addressing Princess Zasekina?"

"I'm Princess Zasekina—and you're the son of Mr. V——?"

"Yes. I've come with a message for you from my mother."

"Sit down, please. Vonifatii, where are my keys? Have you seen them?"

I conveyed my mother's reply to Princess Zasekina's note. She heard me out, drumming on the windowsill with her fat red fingers, and when I'd finished, she stared at me again.

"Very well, I'll come without fail," she eventually remarked. "You're so young! How old are you, may I ask?"

"Sixteen," I answered with an involuntary stammer.

The princess pulled some greasy papers covered with writing out of her pocket, raised them right up to her nose, and began to read through them.

"A good age," she suddenly declared, shifting restlessly in her chair. "And please don't stand on ceremony—I keep a simple establishment."

"Too simple," I thought, scanning her unprepossessing figure with instinctive disgust.

At that moment, another door flew open abruptly, and the young woman I'd seen in the garden the previous evening appeared in the doorway. She raised her hand, and a mocking smile flashed across her face.

"Here's my daughter," the princess observed, gesturing with her elbow. "Zinochka, this is the son of our neighbor, Mr. V——. What's your name, may I ask?"

"Vladimir," I replied, standing up and stuttering in my excitement.

"And your patronymic?"

"Petrovich."

"Ah! I used to know a commissioner of police whose name was Vladimir Petrovich, too. Vonifatii! Don't look for my keys—the keys are in my pocket."

The young woman kept gazing at me with the same smile on her face, fluttering her eyelashes slightly and tilting her head a little to one side.

"I've seen Monsieur Voldemar before," she began. (The silvery sound of her voice made some sort of delicious shiver run right through me.) "May I call you that?"

"Oh, please do," I faltered.

"Where was that?" the elder princess inquired.

The younger princess didn't answer her mother.

"Do you have anything to do now?" she asked, not taking her eyes off me.

"Oh, no."

"Would you like to help me wind some wool? Come in here, into my room."

She nodded to me and left the drawing room. I followed her.

The furniture was of somewhat better quality in the room we entered, and was arranged with more taste. To be sure, I was barely capable of noticing anything at that moment. I moved as if in a dream, sensing some sort of intense blissfulness verging on imbecility course throughout my entire being.

The younger princess sat down, took out a skein of red wool, and, motioning me to a chair opposite her, she carefully untied the skein and laid it across my hands. She did all this in silence, with some sort of amused deliberation, the same bright, sly smile spread across her slightly parted lips. She began to wind the wool onto a twisted card, and then suddenly dazzled me with such a brilliant, rapid glance that I couldn't help lowering my eyes. When her eyes, which were generally half closed, opened to their full extent, her face was completely transfigured: it was as though it were flooded with light.

"What did you think of me yesterday, Monsieur Voldemar?" she asked after a brief pause. "You thought badly of me, I suppose?"

"I . . . Princess . . . I didn't think anything. . . . How could I? . . ." I responded in embarrassment.

"Listen to me," she rejoined, "you don't know me yet. I'm a very strange person—I always like to be told the truth. You're sixteen, I've just heard, and I'm twenty-one. So you see, I'm a lot older than you, and thus you should always tell me the truth . . . and do what I tell you," she added. "Look at me. Why won't you look at me?"

I became even more embarrassed; however, I raised my eyes to her face. She reacted not with her earlier smile but with a smile of approbation. "Look at me," she urged, lowering her voice caressingly. "That's not unpleasant to me . . . I like your face. I have a presentiment that we're going to be friends. But do you like me?" she added craftily.

"Princess . . . ," I began.

"In the first place, you should call me Zinaida Aleksandrovna, and in the second place, it's a bad habit for children" (she corrected herself) "for young people not to express precisely what they feel. That's all right for adults. You like me, don't you?"

Although I was extremely pleased that she'd spoken to me so freely, I was still a little hurt. I wanted to show her that she wasn't dealing with a mere boy, and adopting as sophisticated and serious an expression as I could, I remarked, "Of course, I like you very much, Zinaida Aleksandrovna. I have no desire to conceal it."

She nodded her head emphatically. "Do you have a tutor?" she inquired abruptly.

"No, I haven't had a tutor in a long, long time."

I was telling a lie: it was less than a month since I'd said goodbye to my Frenchman.

"Oh! I see, then—you're all grown up."

She tapped me lightly on the fingers. "Hold your hands out straight!" And she busily devoted herself to winding the ball of yarn.

While she was looking down, I seized the opportunity to examine her, stealthily at first, then more and more boldly. Her face struck me as even more charming than it had the previous evening: every feature of it was so delicate, so intelligent, so appealing. She was sitting with her back to a window that was covered by a white curtain; the sunshine streaming in through the curtain cast a soft light across her fluffy golden curls, her innocent neck, her sloping shoulders, and her tender, tranquil bosom. I gazed at her—how near and dear she'd already become to me! It seemed to me that I'd known her for ages, and had never known anything or lived at all before I met her. . . . She was wearing a dark, rather shabby dress and an apron; I felt that I gladly would have caressed every fold of that dress and that apron. The tips of her little shoes peeped out from under her dress; I could have bowed down to those shoes in worship. . . . "And here I am, sitting across from her," I thought. "I've gotten acquainted with her. . . . My God, what happiness!" I could hardly keep from leaping out of my chair in ecstasy, but I merely swung my legs a little, like a small child who's just been given some candy.

I was as happy as a fish in water, and could have stayed in that room forever, never budging from that spot.

She raised her eyelids calmly, her radiant eyes sparkled affectionately at me again—and she smiled again.

"You're staring at me!" she remarked slowly, and she shook her finger at me in reproach.

I blushed. . . . The thought, "She sees it all, she understands it all," flashed through my mind. "And how could she fail to see and understand it all?"

Suddenly a sound came from the next room—the clink of a saber.

"Zina!" the elder princess shrieked in the drawing room. "Belovzorov's brought you a kitten."

"A kitten!" Zinaida cried, and jumping up from her chair impetuously, she flung the ball of wool in my lap and ran out.

I got up as well and, laying the skein and ball on the windowsill, I went into the drawing room and then paused in bewilderment. A tabby kitten was lying in the middle of the room with its paws outstretched, and Zinaida was kneeling in front of it, cautiously lifting up its little face. A blond, curly-haired young man, a hussar with a ruddy complexion and protruding eyes, was standing near the elder princess, occupying virtually the entire space between the two windows.

"What a funny little thing!" Zinaida was affirming. "And its eyes aren't gray, they're green. What big ears! Thank you, Viktor Egorych! You're very kind."

The hussar, whom I recognized as one of the young men I'd seen the evening before, smiled, then bowed with a clink of his spurs and a jingle of the chain on his saber.

"You were pleased to mention yesterday that you wanted to have a tabby kitten with big ears . . . and so I obtained one. Your word is law." He bowed again.

The kitten mewed weakly and began to sniff the ground.

"It's hungry!" Zinaida exclaimed. "Vonifatii, Sonia! Bring it some milk."

A maid wearing an old yellow dress and a faded kerchief around her neck came in carrying a saucer of milk and set it down in front of the kitten. The kitten shivered, blinked, and started to lap it up.

"What a pink little tongue it has!" Zinaida noted, lowering her head almost to the ground and peering at it sideways under its very nose.

The kitten, having had its fill, began to purr and knead its paws gingerly. Zinaida stood up, and turning to the maid, said indifferently, "Take it away."

"In return for the kitten—your little hand," the hussar requested with a smile, bending forward his entire, powerful body, which was tightly buttoned up in a new uniform.

"Both," Zinaida replied, and she held out her hands to him. While he was kissing them, she looked at me over his shoulder.

I remained motionless in the same spot, not knowing whether to laugh, to say something, or to keep silent. Suddenly, I caught sight of our footman, Fedor, through the open door to the hallway. He was signaling to me. I mechanically walked out to speak to him.

"What do you want?" I asked.

"Your mama sent me to get you," he whispered. "She's angry that you haven't come back with an answer."

"Why, have I been here a long time?"

"Over an hour."

"Over an hour!" I repeated involuntarily, and returning to the drawing room, I began to bow, scraping my heels.

"Where are you off to?" the younger princess inquired, glancing at me from behind the hussar.

"I have to go home. So should I say," I added, addressing the elder princess, "that you'll come to visit us at two?"

"Please say so, my good sir."

The elder princess hastily pulled out her snuffbox and inhaled some snuff so loudly that I actually jumped. "Please say so," she repeated, blinking tearfully and sneezing.

I bowed one more time, turned, and walked out of the room with the sensation of awkwardness in my spine that a very young man gets when he knows he's being watched from behind. "Be sure you come to see us again, Monsieur Voldemar," Zinaida called out, and she laughed once more.

"Why is she always laughing?" I wondered as I went back home escorted by Fedor, who said nothing but followed behind me with an air of disapprobation. My mother scolded me and asked whatever had I been doing at the princess's for so long. I didn't answer her and went off to my own room. I suddenly felt very sad. . . . I tried hard not to cry. . . . I was jealous of the hussar.

V

The elder princess called on my mother as she'd promised, and didn't make a good impression. I wasn't present at their encounter, but my mother told my father at dinner that this Princess Zasekina struck her as a *femme très vulgaire*, that she'd completely worn my mother out begging her to engage Prince Sergei on her behalf, that she seemed to be involved in innumerable lawsuits and business dealings—*de vilaines affaires d'argent*—and must be a highly litigious person. My mother added that she'd nonetheless invited the princess and her daughter to dinner the next day (hearing the word "daughter," I pressed my nose to my plate), since she was a neighbor, after all, and did have a title. At this announcement, my father informed my mother that he now remembered who this lady was, and that in his youth he'd known Prince Zasekin, subsequently deceased, a very well-bred, albeit frivolous and foolish person, who'd been nicknamed "*le Parisien*" by his social set because he'd lived in Paris for many years, who'd been very rich but had gambled away his entire fortune, who for some unknown reason, probably for money—although, if this was so, he might have chosen better, my father noted with a cold smile—had married the daughter of some steward, and who, after his marriage, had engaged in speculation and had utterly ruined himself.

"If only she doesn't try to borrow money," my mother remarked.

"That's extremely likely," my father responded tranquilly. "Does she speak French?"

"Very badly."

"Hmm. It doesn't matter, anyway. I think you said you'd invited the daughter, too. Someone was telling me that she's a very charming, cultivated young woman."

"Ah! Then she can't take after her mother."

"Or her father, either," my father rejoined. "He was cultivated as well, but was still a fool."

My mother sighed and lapsed into thought; my father fell silent. I was very uncomfortable during the course of this conversation.

After dinner, I went out into the garden, but I didn't bring my gun. I swore to myself that I wouldn't go near the "Zasekin garden," but an irresistible force drew me there—and not in vain. I'd barely reached the fence when I caught sight of Zinaida. This time she was alone. She was holding a book in her hands, walking slowly along the path. She didn't notice me.

I almost let her pass by, but I suddenly changed my mind and coughed.

She turned around but didn't stop, pushed back the broad blue ribbon of her round straw hat with one hand, looked at me, smiled slowly, and directed her eyes back to her book.

I took off my cap and, after hesitating for a moment, walked away with a heavy heart. "*Que suis-je pour elle?*" I thought (God knows why) in French.

I heard familiar footsteps coming up behind me and looked around—my father was approaching me with his light, rapid stride.

"Is that the younger princess?" he asked me.

"Yes."

"Do you actually know her?"

"I saw her this morning at the elder princess's."

My father stopped and, turning sharply on his heel, went back. When he drew even with Zinaida, he bowed to her courteously. She bowed to him in return, not without some astonishment on her face, and dropped her book. I saw her gaze follow him as he left. My father was always dressed simply and elegantly, in a style all his own, but his figure had never struck me as more graceful, his gray hat had never sat more becomingly on his curls, which weren't much thinner than they'd ever been.

I started to move toward Zinaida, but she didn't even glance at me. She picked up her book again and walked away.

VI

I spent that whole evening and the following morning in some sort of dejected stupor. As I recall, I tried to work, and turned to Kaidanov, but my eyes passed over the boldly printed lines and pages of the famous textbook to no effect—I read the words "Julius

Caesar was distinguished by warlike courage" ten times in a row.
I didn't comprehend a thing, and tossed the book aside. Before
dinner I put pomade on my hair and donned my suit coat and tie
again.

"What's all this for?" my mother demanded. "You aren't a
university student yet, and God knows whether you'll pass the
entrance examination. And you've just gotten a new jacket—you
can't throw it away!"

"We're having visitors," I murmured, almost in despair.

"That's nonsense! What sort of visitors are these?"

I had no choice but to submit. I exchanged my coat for a short
jacket, but I didn't take off my tie. The princess and her daughter
arrived half an hour before dinnertime. The elderly lady had put
on a yellow shawl and an old-fashioned cap adorned with flame-
colored ribbons in addition to the green dress I was already
acquainted with. She immediately began to discuss her financial
difficulties, repeatedly sighing, complaining about her poverty, and
begging for assistance. But she wasn't the least bit embarrassed
by any of that: she took snuff as noisily and fussed and fidgeted
in her chair as unconstrainedly as ever. It was as if it had never
entered her mind that she was a princess. Zinaida's demeanor, by
contrast, was stiff, almost haughty—she was every inch a princess.
Icy immobility and dignity had appeared on her face. I wouldn't
have recognized her; I wouldn't have recognized her smile or her
gaze, although I found her equally lovely in this new incarnation.
She wore a light, gauzy dress with pale-blue flowers embroidered
across it; her hair fell in long curls down her cheeks in the English
fashion, a style that went well with the cold expression on her face.
My father sat beside her during dinner and entertained his neighbor
with his characteristically elegant, serene courtesy. He glanced at
her from time to time, and she glanced back at him, albeit quite
strangely, almost with hostility. Their conversation was conducted
in French; I remember being surprised at the purity of Zinaida's
accent. During dinner, as before, the elder princess didn't observe
any of the niceties: she ate a great deal and praised all the food.
My mother was obviously bored by her, and responded to her
remarks with some sort of sorrowful disdain; my father faintly
frowned now and then. My mother didn't like Zinaida, either.

"That's a conceited minx," she declared the next day. "And if
you think about it, what does she have to be conceited about, *avec
sa mine de grisette?*"

"It's obvious that you've never seen any grisettes," my father observed to her.

"Thank God I haven't!"

"Thank God, to be sure. . . . But how can you form an opinion about them, then?"

Zinaida paid no attention to me whatsoever. The elder princess got up to leave shortly after dinner.

"I'll rely on your patronage, Maria Nikolaevna and Petr Vasilich," she told my mother and father in a doleful, singsong voice. "What can I do? There were some fine times, but they're all gone. Here I am, a titled personage," she added with an unpleasant laugh, "but what good is such an honor when there's nothing to eat?"

My father bowed to her respectfully and escorted her to the door in the hallway. I was standing there in my short jacket, staring at the floor like a man condemned to death. Zinaida's behavior toward me had utterly crushed me. Thus, how great was my astonishment when, as she walked past me, she whispered quickly, with the earlier, affectionate expression in her eyes, "Come over to visit at eight o'clock, do you hear, without fail. . . ." I simply threw up my hands, but she'd already left, flinging a white scarf over her head.

VII

At precisely eight o'clock, wearing my suit coat, my hair brushed up into a tuft on top of my head, I entered the hallway of the lodge where the elder princess lived. The old servant looked at me crossly and rose uneagerly from his bench. The sound of cheerful voices rang out from the drawing room. I opened the door and stepped back in amazement. The younger princess was standing on a chair in the middle of the room, holding a man's hat out in front of her; five men were crowded around the chair. They were trying to put their hands into the hat as she held it above their heads and shook it vigorously. On catching sight of me, she cried, "Wait, wait, here's another guest. He has to have a ticket, too," and lightly jumping down from the chair, she grasped the cuff of my coat. "Come on," she said, "why are you just standing there? *Messieurs*, let me introduce you—this is Monsieur Voldemar, our neighbor's son. And these men," she continued, addressing me and indicating her guests in turn, "are Count Malevskii, Dr. Lushin, Maidanov the poet, retired captain Nirmatskii, and Belovzorov the hussar, whom you've already met. I hope you'll become good friends."

I was so confused that I didn't even bow to anyone. I recognized in Dr. Lushin the dark-complexioned man who'd so mercilessly embarrassed me in the garden; the others were unfamiliar to me. "Count," Zinaida went on, "make Monsieur Voldemar a ticket." "That's not fair," the count objected in a slight Polish accent. He was a very handsome, fashionably dressed man with brown hair, expressive brown eyes, a narrow little white nose, and a delicate little moustache above a tiny mouth. "This gentleman hasn't been playing forfeits with us."

"It's unfair," Belovzorov repeated in unison with the gentleman described as a retired captain, a man of about forty who was hideously pockmarked, as curly-haired as an Arab, round-shouldered and bowlegged, attired in a military coat without epaulets, which he'd unbuttoned.

"Make him a ticket, I tell you," the princess reiterated. "What's this mutiny? Monsieur Voldemar's joining us for the first time, so there aren't any rules for him today. There's no point in grumbling—make one, since I want you to."

The count shrugged his shoulders but bowed submissively, picked up a pen in his white, ring-bedecked fingers, tore off a scrap of paper, and wrote on it.

"Let's at least explain to Mr. Voldemar what we're doing," Lushin began in a sarcastic voice, "or else he'll be quite lost. Do you see, young man, that we're playing forfeits? The princess has to pay a penalty this time, and whoever draws the lucky ticket will obtain the privilege of kissing her hand. Do you understand what I've told you?"

I merely glanced at him, continuing to stand utterly still, as if in a fog, while the princess jumped back up on the chair and began to shake the hat again. They all stretched their hands up toward her, and I imitated them.

"Maidanov," the princess said to a tall young man with a thin face, small dull eyes, and exceedingly long dark hair, "as a poet, you ought to be magnanimous and give your ticket to Monsieur Voldemar, so that he'll have two chances instead of one."

But Maidanov shook his head in refusal and tossed his hair. I put my hand into the hat after everyone else and unfolded my ticket. . . . Good Lord! How I reacted when I saw the word "kiss" on it!

"Kiss!" I couldn't help shouting out loud.

"Bravo! He's won," the princess affirmed. "I'm so glad!" She

got down from the chair and gave me such a direct, delicious look
that my heart throbbed. "Are you glad?" she asked me.

"Me . . . ?" I faltered.

"Sell me your ticket," Belovzorov growled suddenly, right in my
ear. "I'll give you a hundred rubles."

I responded to the hussar with such an indignant glare that
Zinaida clapped her hands and Lushin cried, "Good for you!"

"But as the master of ceremonies," he went on, "it's my duty
to see that all the rules are obeyed. Monsieur Voldemar, get down
on one knee. That's how we do this."

Zinaida stood in front of me, leaning her head a little to one
side as though trying to get a better look at me; she held out her
hand to me in a dignified manner. A mist spread before my eyes;
I meant to drop to one knee but sank onto both instead, and pressed
my lips to Zinaida's fingers so awkwardly that I scratched myself
slightly on the tip of her nail.

"Well done!" Lushin exclaimed, and he helped me up.

The game of forfeits continued. Zinaida sat me down beside her.
She invented all sorts of extraordinary penalties! Among other
things, she had to represent a "statue," and she chose the hideous
Nirmatskii as a pedestal, ordering him to bend over in an arch
and to bow his head down to his breast. The laughter never subsided
for a moment. For me, an only child somberly reared in a sedate
manor house, all this noise and commotion, this unceremonious,
almost riotous merriment, these unusual activities with unfamiliar
people, were simply intoxicating. My head was spinning, as though
I'd drunk too much wine. I began to laugh and talk more loudly
than anyone else, to such an extent that the elder princess, who
was sitting in the next room with some clerk from the Iverskii gate
whom she'd asked to consult about her business affairs, came in
to look at me. But I was so happy that I didn't give two hoots, as
they say, about anyone's laughter or dubious looks. Zinaida continued to show a preference for me and kept me by her side. For
one penalty, I had to sit next to her while we both hid under one
silk scarf; I was supposed to tell her *my secret*. I remember our
two heads suddenly being surrounded by a warm, fragrant semi-
darkness, I remember her eyes shining in the dark, so close and
soft, and her breath burning between her parted lips, and her teeth
gleaming, and the ends of her hair tickling me, making me feel
as though I were on fire. I kept silent. She smiled slyly and mys-

teriously, and finally whispered to me, "Well, what is it?" But I merely blushed, laughed, and turned away, barely able to catch my breath. We got tired of forfeits; we began to play a game with a piece of string. My God! What ecstasy I experienced when I received a sharp, vigorous slap on my fingers from her for not paying attention, and how I subsequently tried to pretend that I wasn't paying attention—but thereafter she only teased me, and wouldn't touch the hands I held out to her!

What didn't we do during the course of that evening! We played the piano, and sang, and danced, and recreated a gypsy camp. Nirmatskii had to dress up like a bear and drink salt water. Count Malevskii showed us several sorts of card tricks, and ended up by dealing himself all the trump cards at whist after shuffling the deck, for which Lushin "had the honor to congratulate him." Maidanov recited portions of his poem "The Murderer" (romanticism was at its height at this time), which he intended to publish in a black cover with the title printed in blood-red letters. They stole the clerk's cap off his knee and made him perform a Cossack dance in order to ransom it; they dressed up old Vonifatii in a woman's cap, and the young princess put on a man's hat. . . . I couldn't possibly recount everything we did. Belovzorov alone kept retreating more and more into the background, scowling and angry. . . . Sometimes his eyes would grow bloodshot, he'd become totally flushed, and it'd seem as though he were about to charge at us any minute and scatter us in all directions like wood shavings. But the princess would look over and shake her finger at him, and he'd retreat into his corner once more.

We finally got completely worn out. Even the elder princess, although she was ready for anything, as she expressed it, and no sort of noise disturbed her, eventually felt weary and wanted to get some rest. At midnight, a supper was served that consisted of a hunk of stale, dry cheese plus some cold turnovers filled with minced ham, which seemed more delicious to me than any pastries I'd ever tasted. There was only one bottle of wine, and it was a strange one: it was a dark-colored bottle with a wide neck that contained pink wine. No one drank it, however. Exhausted and faint with happiness, I left the lodge; in saying goodbye, Zinaida shook my hand warmly and smiled mysteriously again.

The night air felt heavy and damp against my flushed face; a storm seemed to be gathering. Black clouds developed and crept across the sky, their misty outlines visibly changing. A light wind restlessly shook the dark trees and, somewhere on the horizon, muffled thunder muttered angrily, as if to itself. I went up to my room by the back stairs. My old servant was asleep on the floor, and I had to step over him. He woke up, saw me, and told me that my mother had gotten very angry with me and had wanted to send him to find me again, but that my father had prevented her. (I'd never gone to bed without saying good night to my mother and asking for her blessing.) I couldn't do anything about that now!

I told my servant that I'd get undressed and go to bed by myself, and I extinguished the candle. But I didn't get undressed and I didn't go to bed.

I sat down on a chair and remained there for a long while, as though spellbound. What I was feeling was so new, so sweet. . . . I barely looked around, not moving, breathing slowly. I only laughed silently at some memory from time to time, or turned cold inside at the thought that I was in love, that this was it, this was love. Zinaida's face quietly floated before my eyes in the darkness— it floated there, and didn't float away: her lips maintained the same enigmatic smile, her eyes gazed at me slightly from the side with an inquisitive, thoughtful, tender look . . . just as they had at the moment when I'd said goodbye to her. I finally stood up, tiptoed to my bed and, without undressing, laid my head carefully on the pillow, as though afraid to disturb the emotions with which I was overflowing by any sudden movement. . . .

I lay down, but I didn't even close my eyes. Before long, I noticed that some faint glimmers of light kept coming into the room. . . . I sat up and looked at the window. The window frame was clearly distinguishable from the mysterious, dimly lit panes. "It's a storm," I thought—and, indeed, it was a storm, but it was raging so very far away that its thunder couldn't be heard. Faint, elongated, seemingly branched bolts of lightning continuously flashed across the sky; they actually didn't flash so much as shiver and tremble like the wing of a dying bird. I got up, went over to the window, and stood there until morning. . . . The lightning never halted for a second; it was what the peasants call a "sparrow's night." I gazed at the silent, sandy field, at the dark mass of the Neskuchnii gardens, at the yellowish facades of distant buildings, which also seemed to shiver at each weak flash. . . . I gazed, unable to turn away: those mute flashes of lightning, those restrained gleams, seemed to mirror the secret, mute impulses flaring up inside me. Morning began to dawn; the sky became flushed with patches of crimson. As the sun drew nearer, the lightning gradually got paler and briefer; the quivering gleams grew fewer and fewer and finally vanished altogether, engulfed by the sobering, inexorable light of the coming day. . . .

And my lightning vanished as well. I felt a sense of great weariness and calm . . . but Zinaida's image still floated triumphantly in my soul. Yet even this image itself seemed more tranquil: like a swan rising up from the reeds of a marsh, it stood out among the other indistinguishable figures surrounding it, and as I fell asleep, I prostrated myself before it in loyal, parting adoration. . . .

Oh, tender feelings, gentle sounds, the goodness and peace of an uplifted soul, the melting bliss of love's first raptures—where are you, where are you?

VIII

The next morning, when I came down for breakfast, my mother scolded me—albeit less severely than I'd expected—and made me tell her what I'd done the previous evening. I answered her in a few words, omitting many details and trying to make everything appear in the most innocent light possible.

"Nonetheless, these people aren't *comme il faut*," my mother remarked, "and you've got no business wasting time over there instead of preparing for your examination by studying."

Since I knew that my mother's concern about my studies was confined to these few words, I didn't deem it necessary to offer any opposition. After breakfast was over, my father took me by the arm and, walking out into the garden with me, made me tell him everything I'd seen at the Zasekins'.

My father had a strange influence over me—the relationship between us was equally strange. He took virtually no interest in my upbringing, but he never hurt my feelings; he respected my freedom; he treated me—if I may put it this way—with courtesy . . . only he never let me get really close to him. I loved him, I admired him, he was my ideal of a man—and, my God, how passionately devoted I'd have been to him if I hadn't continually been aware that he was keeping me at a distance! But whenever he wanted, he could almost instantaneously evoke my unlimited trust in him with a single word, a single gesture. My soul would open up—I'd chatter away to him as if he were a wise friend, an indulgent teacher.... Then, just as suddenly, he'd rebuff me and set me at a distance again, gently and affectionately, but still at a distance.

Sometimes, when he was in a particularly good mood, he was ready to romp and frolic with me like a boy (he liked every sort of strenuous physical activity); once—it never happened a second time!—he caressed me with such tenderness that I almost burst into tears.... But his cheerfulness and tenderness alike would vanish without a trace, and what had occurred between us gave me no hope for the future—it was as though I'd dreamed it all. Sometimes I'd scrutinize his intelligent, handsome, animated face.... My heart would throb, and my entire being would reach out to him.... He'd seem to realize what was going on inside me, would give me a pat on the cheek in passing, and would go away or become involved in some work or suddenly completely freeze, as only he knew how to freeze, and I'd immediately withdraw into myself and turn cold as well. His rare bursts of affection toward me were never occasioned by my silent but intelligible entreaties; they always took place unexpectedly. Thinking over my father's character later on, I came to the conclusion that he had no energy to spare for me or for family life; his heart was invested in something else, and he found complete satisfaction in that. "Take what you can for yourself, and don't be controlled by others. Belonging to oneself—the whole essence of life lies in that," he told me one day. Another time, I, as a young democrat, began to air my views on freedom (he was "kind," as I used to call it, that day, and I could talk to him as much as I liked on such days).

"Freedom," he repeated."Do you know what gives someone freedom?"

"What?"

"Will, one's own will. It also gives power, which is better than freedom. Know how to want and you'll be free, and will lead others."

My father wanted to live, first and foremost, and he did live.... Perhaps he foresaw that he wouldn't have long to enjoy the "essence" of life: he died at the age of forty-two.

I described my evening at the Zasekins' to my father in detail. He listened to me half attentively, half abstractedly, sitting on a garden bench and tracing a design in the sand with the tip of his cane. He laughed from time to time, threw me cheerful, amused glances, and urged me on with brief questions and comments. At first, I couldn't bring myself even to utter Zinaida's name, but I couldn't restrain myself for long, and I began to sing her praises. My father laughed some more, then he became thoughtful, stretched, and stood up.

I remembered that as he'd come out of the house, he'd ordered his horse to be saddled. He was an excellent rider and, long before Mr. Rarey, knew how to break the wildest horses.

"May I come with you, Papa?" I asked.

"No," he answered, and his face resumed its normal expression of friendly indifference. "Go alone, if you like. Tell the coachman I'm not going."

He turned his back on me and walked away rapidly. I watched him go; he disappeared through the gates. I saw his hat moving alongside the fence; he entered the Zasekins' lodge.

He stayed there for less than an hour, then immediately went into town and didn't return home until evening.

After dinner, I myself went over to the Zasekins'. I found the elder princess alone in the drawing room. Upon seeing me, she scratched her head beneath her cap with a knitting needle and suddenly asked me whether I could copy a petition for her.

"With pleasure," I replied, sitting down on the edge of a chair.

"Just be sure that you make the letters bigger," the princess directed, handing me a dirty sheet of paper. "Could you do it today, my good sir?"

"I can do it right away."

The door to the next room was opened a crack, and through this crack I caught a glimpse of Zinaida's pale, pensive face, her hair having been carelessly pushed back. She regarded me with big, cold eyes, and quietly closed the door.

"Zina, Zina!" the elderly lady called out.

Zinaida didn't respond. I took the elderly lady's petition home and spent the whole evening working on it.

IX

My "passion" dated from that day. At the time, as I recall, I felt something like what a man must feel when embarking upon government service—I'd now ceased to be merely a young boy. I'd fallen in love. I've said that my passion dated from that day; I might have added that my sufferings also dated from the same day. When I was apart from Zinaida, I languished; I couldn't study; everything went wrong for me; I spent entire days thinking about her intensely. . . . I languished when we were apart . . . but I was no better off in her presence. I was jealous, I was conscious of my own insignificance, I was absurdly sulky or absurdly servile—and nonetheless, an irresistible force attracted me to her, and I felt an involuntary shiver of delight whenever I stepped across the threshold of her room. Zinaida promptly guessed that I was in love with her, and indeed, I never even considered concealing it. She amused herself with my passion; she teased, petted, and tormented me. There's a certain pleasure in being the sole source, the despotic and unassailable cause, of the greatest joy and the deepest sorrow in another human being—and I was like wax in Zinaida's hands.

To be sure, I wasn't the only one in love with her: all the men who visited the house were crazy about her, and she kept them all on a string, at her feet. It amused her to arouse their hopes and then their fears, to twist them around her little finger (she used to call it knocking their heads together). They never dreamed of offering any resistance, and eagerly submitted to her. Her entire being, so full of life and beauty, possessed some especially bewitching mixture of craftiness and ingenuousness, of artificiality and simplicity, of composure and playfulness. Everything she did or said, every movement she made, conveyed a delicate, refined charm in which a unique, vibrant strength manifested itself. Her face, which was constantly changing, was also vibrant: it expressed mockery, thoughtfulness, and passion almost simultaneously. The most varied emotions, as insubstantial and fleeting as the shadows of clouds on a windy sunny day, continually chased one another across her lips and eyes.

Each of her worshipers was important to her. Belovzorov, whom she sometimes called "my wild beast" and sometimes simply "mine," would gladly have flung himself into the fire for her sake. Without making reference to his intellectual abilities and other virtues, he repeatedly proposed marriage to her, hinting that the others were merely big talkers. Maidanov corresponded to the poetic strands of her nature: a relatively cold individual, like almost all writers, he exerted himself to assure her—and perhaps himself as well—that he adored her, sang her praises in endless verses, and read them to her with a sort of ecstasy that was at once affected and sincere. She sympathized with him, and she made fun of him a little at the same time. She didn't believe most of what he said, and she'd make him read Pushkin after listening to his outpourings, in order to clear the air, as she put it. Lushin, the derisive doctor whose words were always so cynical, knew her better and loved her more than the rest, although he criticized her both to her face and behind her back. She respected him but didn't spare him, and periodically, with special, malicious pleasure, made him feel that he, too, was at her mercy. "I'm a flirt, I'm heartless, I'm an actress by nature," she said to him one day in my presence. "So be it! Give me your hand, then. I'll stick this pin into it, you'll be ashamed of this young man's seeing it, and it'll hurt you, but you'll laugh anyway, Mr. Righteous Man." Lushin blushed slightly, turned away, and bit his lip, but ended up presenting his hand. She pricked it, and he actually did begin to laugh. . . . She laughed as well, inserting the pin quite deeply and peering into his eyes, which he vainly strove to avert. . . .

Least of all did I understand the relationship that existed between Zinaida and Count Malevskii. He was handsome, intelligent, and suave, but there was something dubious, something false about him that was apparent even to me, a boy of sixteen, and I was surprised that Zinaida didn't notice it. But perhaps she did notice this element of falsity, and simply wasn't repelled by it. Her irregular upbringing, her strange acquaintances and habits, the constant presence of her mother, the poverty and disorder of their household—everything, beginning with the very freedom this young woman enjoyed, along with the consciousness of her superiority to the people around her, had developed some sort of half-contemptuous nonchalance and a lack of fastidiousness in her. Anything might happen at any time— Vonifatii might announce that there was no sugar, or some revolting item of gossip might reach her ears, or her guests would begin to quarrel among themselves—she'd merely shake her curls and say, "That's trivia!" refusing to worry about it.

But my blood would occasionally boil with indignation when Malevskii would approach her with a sly maneuver, like a fox, lean gracefully on the back of her chair, and begin to whisper in her ear with a self-satisfied, ingratiating little smile, while she'd fold her arms across her chest, gaze at him intently, smile herself, and nod her head.

"Why do you welcome Count Malevskii so eagerly?" I asked her one day.

"He has such a wonderful moustache," she answered. "But that's none of your business."

"You shouldn't think that I love him," she told me another time. "No, I can't love people I have to look down on. I have to have someone who can master me. . . . But, merciful God, I hope I never run across someone like that! I don't want to get caught in anyone else's claws—oh, no!"

"You'll never be in love, then?"

"And what about you? Don't I love you?" she replied, and flicked me on the nose with the tip of her glove.

Yes, Zinaida amused herself hugely at my expense. I saw her every day for three weeks—and what, oh what, didn't she make me do! She rarely came to see us, and I didn't regret that; she was transformed into a young lady, a young princess, in our house, and I was overawed by her. I was afraid of betraying myself in front of my mother—she'd taken a great dislike to Zinaida and kept a hostile eye on us. I wasn't as frightened of my father; he didn't seem to notice me. He didn't talk to her very much, but somehow always did so with particular intelligence and meaning. I gave up working and reading entirely; I even gave up walking around the neighborhood and riding my horse. Like a beetle tied by the leg, I continually circled around my favorite little lodge. I'd gladly have stayed there forever, it seemed . . . but that was impossible. My mother scolded me, and sometimes Zinaida herself drove me away. Then I used to shut myself up in my room, or go down to the very end of the garden, and, climbing into the remaining ruins of a tall stone greenhouse, I'd sit for hours with my legs dangling over a wall that faced the road, gazing and gazing and seeing nothing. White butterflies would lazily flit past me above the dusty nettles; a saucy sparrow would perch nearby on half-crumbling red brickwork and twitter irritably, ceaselessly twisting its whole body around and turning and preening its tailfeathers; the ever-mistrustful crows would caw now and then, sitting up high on the bare top of a birch tree as the sun and wind would tranquilly play across its pliant branches; the tinkle of the bells from the Donskoi monastery would float over to me from time to time, sounding so peaceful and sad; meanwhile I'd sit there, gazing and listening, filled with a nameless sensation that contained everything: sorrow, and joy, and foreboding about the future, and desire, and fear of life. But I didn't understand any of this at that time and couldn't have given a name to everything I was experiencing, or I would have called it all by one name—the name Zinaida.

Zinaida continued to play cat and mouse with me. At one moment she'd flirt with me and I'd get all excited and ardent, then she'd suddenly thrust me away and I didn't dare go near her, didn't dare look at her.

I remember that once she was very cold to me for several days in a row. I was completely crushed, and, timidly creeping over to their lodge, I tried to keep close to the elder princess, regardless of the fact that she was complaining and shouting a great deal at that particular time: her financial affairs had been going badly, and she'd already had two interviews with police officials.

I was strolling in the garden beside the familiar fence one day and caught sight of Zinaida; holding her head in her hands, she was sitting on the grass without moving a muscle. I was cautiously about to go away, but she suddenly raised her head and imperiously summoned me. I froze in place; I didn't understand her at first. She repeated her signal. I promptly jumped over the fence and joyfully ran up to her, but she brought me to a halt with a single look and motioned me to the path two feet away from her. In confusion, not knowing what to do, I fell to my knees at the edge of the path. She was so pale, and such bitter suffering, such intense weariness was expressed in every feature of her face that it made my heart ache, and I instinctively murmured, "What's the matter?"

Zinaida stretched out her hand, picked up a blade of grass, sucked on it, and flung it away from her.

"You love me very much, don't you?" she finally asked. "Yes?"

I didn't answer—indeed, what reason was there for me to answer?

"Yes," she reiterated, looking at me the way she had before. "That's right. The same eyes," she added, sinking into thought, and she hid her face in her hands. "Everything's become repugnant to me," she whispered. "I'd rather have gone to the ends of the earth first—I can't bear this, I can't adjust.... And what awaits me in the future?...Ah, I'm so miserable...my God, so miserable!"

"Why?" I inquired shyly.

Zinaida didn't reply, simply shrugging her shoulders. I stayed on my knees, looking at her with intense sadness. Every word she uttered simply cut me to the heart. At that instant, I felt that I cheerfully would have sacrificed my life if only she'd stop being unhappy. I looked at her—and even though I couldn't understand why she was so miserable, I vividly pictured to myself how, in a fit of insupportable anguish, she'd suddenly come out into the garden and sunk to ground as though mown down by a scythe. Everything was sunlit and verdant all around her; the wind was whispering in the leaves of the trees, occasionally stirring one long branch of a raspberry bush above Zinaida's head. Doves were

cooing somewhere, and bees were humming as they flew low across
the sparse grass. The sky was radiantly blue overhead—and I was
so sad. . . .

"Read me some poetry," Zinaida requested in a low voice, propping herself on her elbow. "I like it when you read poetry. You
read in a singsong voice, but that doesn't matter—it comes from
being young. Read me 'On the Hills of Georgia.' Only sit down
first."

I sat down and read "On the Hills of Georgia."

"'That the heart cannot help but love,'" Zinaida repeated.
"That's why poetry is so good: it tells us what doesn't exist, and
what's not only better than what does exist, but is much closer to
the truth. It 'cannot help but love'—it might not want to, but it
can't help it." She fell silent again, then she suddenly shivered and
stood up. "Let's go. Maidanov's inside with Mama—he brought
me his poem, but I deserted him. His feelings are hurt now,
too. . . . I can't help that! You'll understand it all someday. . . . Just
don't be angry at me!"

Zinaida hastily squeezed my hand and ran on ahead. We went
back into the lodge. Maidanov started to read us his poem "The
Murderer," which had just been published, but I didn't listen to
him. He half-shouted, half-sang his four-foot iambic lines, the
alternating rhythms jangling like noisy, hollow little bells. I continued to gaze at Zinaida and tried to grasp the import of her final
words.

> Perhaps some secret rival
> Has surprised and conquered you?

Maidanov nasally cried out all of a sudden—and my eyes met
Zinaida's. She looked down, blushing faintly. I saw her blush, and
grew cold with terror. I'd been jealous before, but only at that
moment did the idea that she'd fallen in love flash through my
mind: "My God! She's in love!"

X

My real torments began from that moment. I racked my brains,
changed my mind, changed it back again, and kept an unremitting,
albeit as far as possible secret, watch over Zinaida. A change had
come over her—that much was obvious. She began to go for walks,
long walks, by herself. Sometimes she wouldn't admit any visitors;
she'd sit by herself in her room for hours on end. This had never

been a custom of hers until now. I suddenly became—or imagined that I'd become—extraordinarily perceptive.

"Is he the one? Or is he?" I asked myself, anxiously considering one of her admirers after another. Count Malevskii secretly struck me as more dangerous than the others (although, for Zinaida's sake, I was ashamed to acknowledge it).

My watchfulness didn't extend beyond the end of my nose, and my secrecy probably didn't deceive anyone; at least Dr. Lushin quickly saw through me. But he, too, had changed recently: he'd gotten thinner, and even though he laughed as often as before, his laughter seemed more empty, more spiteful, and more abrupt; an involuntary, nervous irritability had replaced his former offhand sarcasm and supercilious cynicism.

"Why are you constantly hanging around here, young man?" he said to me one day when we'd been left alone together in the Zasekins' drawing room. (The younger princess hadn't come home from a walk yet, and the elder princess's shrill voice was audible on the stairway—she was scolding the maid.) "You ought to be studying and working while you're young—but what are you doing instead?"

"You can't tell whether or not I work at home," I retorted, not without haughtiness, but not without embarrassment as well.

"What kind of work do you do? That isn't what's on your mind. Well, I won't argue with you. . . . At your age, this is in the natural order of things. But your choice of diversions is extremely unfortunate. Don't you see what kind of a house this is?"

"I don't understand you," I remarked.

"You don't understand me? So much the worse for you. I consider it my duty to warn you. Old bachelors like myself can come here— what harm can it do us? We're tough, nothing can hurt us. But your skin is still tender, this air is bad for you. Believe me—you may be infected by it."

"How so?"

"Why, are you healthy now? Are you in a normal state? Is what you're feeling valuable to you, is it good for you?"

"Why, what am I feeling?" I rejoined, even though I knew in my heart that the doctor was right.

"Ah, young man, young man," the doctor continued with an expression on his face suggesting that something highly insulting to me was contained in those two words, "what's the use of your being devious when, thank God, what's in your heart is still reflected on

your face? But, then again, what's the use of talking? I wouldn't
come here myself if ..." (the doctor compressed his lips) "if I
weren't such an eccentric person. There's only one thing that surprises me: how can it be that you, with all your intelligence, don't
see what's going on around you?"

"What's going on, then?" I interjected, thoroughly on my guard.
The doctor looked at me with some sort of amused compassion.
"That was nice of me," he murmured, seemingly to himself.
"As if he really needs to know anything about it. In a word," he
added, raising his voice, "I tell you again, the atmosphere here
isn't good for you. You like being here, but what does that mean?
It's delightfully fragrant in a greenhouse—and yet you can't live in
one. No, indeed! Do as I tell you—go back to your Kaidanov."

The elder princess came in and began complaining to the doctor
about a toothache. Then Zinaida appeared.

"Now," the elder princess went on, "you have to scold her,
doctor. She drinks ice water all day long. Can that be good for
her, with her delicate constitution?"

"Why do you do that?" Lushin queried.

"Why, what could happen?"

"What could happen? You could catch cold and die."

"Really? Do you mean it? Oh, well—so much the better."

"So that's how it is!" the doctor muttered. The elder princess
had left.

"Yes, that's how it is," Zinaida repeated. "Is life so enjoyable?
Just look around you.... What is this—something good? Or do
you think that I don't understand what this is, that I don't perceive
any of this? Drinking ice water gives me pleasure—and can you
assure me in all seriousness that a life like this is worth too much
to be risked for a moment of pleasure? I won't even mention
happiness."

"Oh, all right," Lushin responded. "Caprice and independence ... those two words sum you up—your entire nature is captured in those two words."

Zinaida laughed nervously.

"You've missed the mail delivery, my dear doctor. You didn't
watch carefully—you're too late. Put on your glasses. I'm not capricious now. Making fools of you, making a fool of myself ...
what pleasure is there in that? And as for independence.... Monsieur Voldemar," Zinaida added suddenly, stamping her foot, "wipe

that melancholy expression off your face. I can't stand it when people feel sorry for me." She abruptly left the room.

"This atmosphere is very, very bad for you, young man," Lushin told me once more.

XI

On the evening of the same day, the usual guests assembled at the Zasekins'; I was among them. The conversation turned to Maidanov's poem. Zinaida expressed genuine admiration for it. "But you know what?" she said to him. "If I were a poet, I'd choose very different subjects. Maybe it's all nonsense, but strange ideas come into my head sometimes, especially when I wake up early in the morning just as the sky is beginning to turn both pink and gray. For instance, I'd.... You won't laugh at me?"

"No, no!" we all cried in unison.

"I'd describe a whole group of young girls," she continued, folding her arms across her breast and looking away, "sailing on a silent river at night in a large boat. The moon is shining, and they're dressed all in white, wearing garlands of white flowers, and singing, you know, something like a hymn."

"I see, I see. Go on," Maidanov interjected meaningfully and dreamily.

"All of a sudden, there are sounds, laughter, torches, and tambourines on the shore.... There's a troop of Bacchantes dancing there, accompanied by songs and cries. It's up to you to paint the picture, Mr. Poet ... only I'd like the torches to be red and give off a lot of smoke, and the Bacchantes' eyes to gleam under their wreaths, which should be dark. Don't forget the tiger skins, either, and the goblets—and gold, lots of gold."

"Where should the gold be?" Maidanov inquired, tossing his sleek head and flaring his nostrils.

"Where? On their shoulders, their arms, their legs—everywhere. They say that women wore golden rings on their ankles in ancient times. The Bacchantes summon the girls in the boat to join them. The girls have stopped singing their hymn—they can't continue it—but they don't move. The river carries them to the bank. And suddenly one of them quietly rises.... You have to describe carefully how quietly she stands up in the moonlight, and how frightened her companions are.... She steps over the edge of the boat, the Bacchantes surround her and whisk her away into the night, into the darkness. . . . Put in clouds of smoke here, and make everything get confused. Nothing more can be heard but the sound of their shrill cries—and her wreath is left lying on the bank."

Zinaida stopped. ("Oh! She's in love!" I thought again.)

"And that's the end?" Maidanov asked.

"That's the end."

"This can't be the subject of a whole poem," he declared pompously, "but I'll use your idea for a lyrical fragment."

"In the romantic style?" Malevskii queried.

"Of course, in the romantic style—the Byronic."

"Well, in my opinion, Hugo is better than Byron," the young count remarked nonchalantly. "He's more interesting."

"Hugo is a first-class writer," Maidanov replied. "And my friend, Tonkosheev, in his Spanish romance *El trovador*. . . ."

"Ah! Is that the book with the upside-down question marks?" Zinaida interrupted.

"Yes—that's the Spanish custom. I was about to observe that Tonkosheev. . . ."

"Wait! You're going to argue about classicism and romanticism again," Zinaida interrupted him a second time. "We'd be better off playing. . . ."

"Forfeits?" Lushin suggested.

"No, forfeits are boring. Let's play comparisons." (Zinaida had invented this game herself: some object was mentioned, everyone tried to compare it with something, and the one who offered the best comparison got a prize.)

She went up to the window. The sun was just setting; large, reddish clouds were drifting high across the sky.

"What do those clouds look like?" Zinaida asked, and without waiting for our answer, she said, "I think they look like the purple sails of the golden ship Cleopatra sailed on when she went to meet Antony. Remember, Maidanov, you were telling me about that recently?"

All of us, like Polonius in *Hamlet*, decided that the clouds didn't resemble anything else as much as they did those sails, and that none of us could invent a better comparison.

"Just how old was Antony at that time?" Zinaida inquired.

"He was a young man, no doubt," asserted Malevskii.

"Yes, a young man," Maidanov chimed in affirmatively.

"I beg your pardon," Lushin cried. "He was over forty."

"Over forty," Zinaida echoed, casting a rapid glance at him. I went home shortly. "She's in love," my lips involuntarily repeated. "But with whom?"

XII

The days went by. Zinaida grew stranger and stranger, more and more incomprehensible. I went over to her lodge one day and found her sitting in a straw chair, her head pressed against the sharp edge of a table. She straightened up. . . . Her face was covered with tears.

"Ah, it's you!" she observed with a cruel smile. "Come here." I walked up to her. She put her hand on my head and, suddenly grabbing hold of my hair, she began to pull it.

"That hurts," I finally confessed.

"Ah! Does it? Do you think nothing hurts me?" she replied.

"Ooh!" she cried abruptly, realizing that she'd pulled out a small tuft of hair. "What have I done? Poor Monsieur Voldemar!"

She carefully smoothed the hair she'd torn out, laid it on her finger, and twisted it into a ring.

"I'll put your hair in a locket and wear it around my neck," she promised, tears still glittering in her eyes. "That might console you a bit . . . and now goodbye."

I went back home, and found an unpleasant situation there. My mother was having an argument with my father; she was reproaching him for something while he maintained a polite, chilly silence, as usual, and left shortly thereafter. I couldn't hear what my mother was saying—and indeed, I wasn't interested in any of it. I just remember that when the argument was over, she summoned me to her room and expressed extreme displeasure at the frequent visits I paid to the elder princess, who was, in her words, *une femme capable de tout*. I kissed her hand (which was what I always did when I wanted to cut a conversation short), and went off to my own room. Zinaida's tears had utterly confused me; I didn't know what in the world to think, and was ready to cry myself; I was still a child, after all, despite my sixteen years. I no longer suspected Malevskii, although Belovzorov did, becoming more and more threatening every day and glaring at the wily count like a wolf at a sheep; I didn't suspect anything or anyone. I got lost in fantasies, and kept seeking out solitary seclusion. I was especially fond of the deserted greenhouse. I'd climb up on the high wall, perch there, and sit still, such an unhappy, lonely, miserable youth that

I felt sorry for myself—and how much consolation I found in those sad sensations, how I reveled in them!...

One day, I was sitting on the wall, gazing into the distance and listening to the bells ring.... Suddenly, something wafted up to me—not a breath of wind, not a motion, but something like a whiff of fragrance, like a sense of someone's proximity.... I looked down. Zinaida was rapidly walking along the path below me, wearing a light, grayish dress, resting a pink parasol on her shoulder. She caught sight of me, stopped, and, pushing back the brim of her straw hat, raised her velvety eyes to me. "What are you doing up there so high?" she asked me, with a rather strange smile. "Well, then," she went on, "you always swear that you love me. If you really love me, jump down here to the road."

Zinaida had hardly uttered those words when I came flying down, just as though someone had given me a violent shove from behind. The wall was about fourteen feet high. I hit the ground on my feet, but the shock of landing was so great that I couldn't keep my footing; I fell down and lost consciousness for a moment. When I came to, without opening my eyes, I felt Zinaida kneeling beside me. "My dear boy," she was saying as she bent over me, and there was a note of alarmed tenderness in her voice, "how could you do that, how could you obey me?... You know I love you.... Get up."

Her breast was heaving beside me, her hands were caressing my head, and suddenly—what I underwent at that moment!—her soft, moist lips began to cover my face with kisses ... they touched my lips.... But then Zinaida evidently deduced from the expression on my face that I'd regained consciousness, although I still kept my eyes closed, and rising rapidly to her feet, she said: "Come on, get up, you naughty, crazy boy. Why are you lying in the dust?" I got up. "Get me my parasol," Zinaida commanded. "I threw it down somewhere. And don't look at me like that.... What foolishness is this? You aren't hurt, are you? You were stung by the nettles, I suppose. Don't look at me, I tell you.... But he doesn't understand anything, he can't respond," she added, as though to herself.... "Go home, Monsieur Voldemar, brush yourself off, and don't you dare follow me, or I'll get angry, and I won't ever...."

She didn't finish her sentence and walked away swiftly, while I sat down by the side of the road.... My legs wouldn't support me.

The nettles had stung my hands, my back was aching, and my head was spinning, but the feeling of rapture I experienced at that moment has never, ever recurred. It turned into a delectable pain that ran throughout my body and ultimately found expression in ecstatic hops, skips, and shouts. Yes, I was still a child.

XIII

I was so proud and happy that entire day, I so vividly retained the impression of Zinaida's kisses on my face, I so joyously recalled every word she'd uttered, I so cherished my unexpected happiness, that I even got frightened, I even became unwilling to see her— the individual responsible for these new sensations. It seemed to me that I could ask nothing more of fate, that now I ought to "take a deep, final breath, and die." But the next day when I went over to the lodge, I felt a flood of embarrassment, which I vainly tried to conceal beneath a display of quiet sophistication befitting a man who wants to demonstrate that he knows how to keep a secret. Zinaida welcome me quite simply, without any show of emotion. She merely shook her finger at me and asked me whether I was black and blue. All my quiet sophistication and secrecy vanished instantaneously, and my embarrassment went with them. Of course, I hadn't expected anything in particular, but Zinaida's composure made me feel like a bucket of cold water had been thrown over me. I realized that I was only a child in her eyes— and I became utterly miserable again! Zinaida paced up and down the room, giving me a brief smile whenever she caught my eye, but her thoughts were far away, I could see that clearly. . . . "Should I mention what happened yesterday myself?" I wondered. "Should I ask her where she was going so fast, in order to find out once and for all . . . ?" But, with a wave of my hand, I just went and sat down in a corner.

Belovzorov came in; I was relieved to see him.

"I haven't been able to find you a sufficiently tame horse to ride," he stated sulkily. "Freitag has guaranteed me one, but I'm not sure. I'm afraid."

"What are you afraid of," Zinaida inquired, "if you'll permit me to ask?"

"What am I afraid of? Why, you don't know know how to ride. God knows what might happen! How do you explain this whim that's come over you all of a sudden?"

"Well, it's my business, Monsieur Wild Animal. In that case,

I'll ask Petr Vasilevich. . . . " (My father's name was Petr Vasilevich. I was surprised at her mentioning his name so freely and easily, as though certain he'd be willing to do her a favor.)

"Oh, so that's how it is," Belovzorov retorted. "You intend to go out riding with him, then?"

"With him or with someone else—it doesn't matter as far as you're concerned. Only not with you, anyway."

"As you wish," Belovzorov echoed. "However you want. What can I do? I'll find you a horse."

"Yes—just be sure you don't send me some old cow. I warn you, I want to gallop."

"Gallop away, by all means. . . . With whom are you going to ride, then—with Malevskii?"

"And why not with him, warrior? Well, calm down," she added, "and don't glare. I'll take you, too. You know that now I find Malevskii—ugh!" She shook her head.

"You're saying that to console me," Belovzorov growled.

Zinaida half-closed her eyes. "Does that console you? Oh . . . oh . . . you . . . you warrior!" she finally cried, as though she could find no other word. "And what about you, Monsieur Voldemar? Would you like to come with us?"

"I don't want to . . . in a large group," I muttered, without raising my eyes.

"You prefer a *tête-à-tête*? . . . Well, to each his own," she remarked with a sigh. "Go away, Belovzorov, and make yourself useful. I have to have a horse to ride tomorrow."

"Oh, and where's the money going to come from?" asked the elder princess.

Zinaida scowled.

"I won't ask you for it. Belovzorov will trust me."

"He'll trust you, will he . . . ?" the elder princess mumbled, and then she suddenly screeched at the top of her voice, "Duniashka!"

"*Maman*, I've given you a bell to ring," Zinaida reminded her.

"Duniashka!" the elderly lady screeched again.

Belovzorov departed; I went out with him. Zinaida didn't try to detain me.

XIV

I got up early the next morning, cut myself a long stick, and set off on a walk beyond the town gates—I thought I could walk away my sadness. It was a lovely, clear day, and not too hot; a refreshing, cheerful breeze wafted above the ground—it whispered softly and playfully, touching everything yet disturbing nothing. I wandered among the hills and trees for a long time. I didn't feel happy; I'd left home with every intention of giving myself over to dejection. But youth, the exquisite weather, the fresh air, the pleasure of rapid motion, the delight of lying on the thick grass in solitude, all gained the upper hand; the memory of those never-to-be-forgotten words, those kisses, arose in my soul once more. It was gratifying for me to think that, in any event, Zinaida couldn't fail to acknowledge my courage, my heroism.... "The others may seem better suited to her than I am," I mused. "So be it! But the others only talk about what they'd do for her, whereas I've done something. And what else wouldn't I be willing to do for her?" My imagination went to work: I began picturing to myself how I'd save her from the hands of her enemies, how, covered with blood, I'd forcibly rescue her from prison and expire at her feet. I recalled a painting hanging in our drawing room—Malek-Adel carrying off Matilda—but at this point, my attention was absorbed by the appearance of a speckled woodpecker that busily climbed up the slender stem of a birch tree and uneasily peeped out from behind it, first to the right, then to the left, like a musician behind a double bass.

After that, I started to sing "Not the white snows," shifting from this song to a then-famous one, "I await you when the zephyr blows." Next, I began to read aloud Ermak's speech to the stars in Khomiakov's tragedy. I tried to compose something sentimental myself, and came up with the line that would conclude each verse: "O Zinaida, Zinaida!" but couldn't get any further than that. Meanwhile, it was getting close to dinnertime. I went down into a valley; a narrow, sandy path winding through it led to town. I proceeded along this path.... The dull thud of horses' hooves became audible behind me. I looked around, instinctively stopped, and took off my cap. I caught sight of my father and Zinaida, riding side by side. My father was saying something to her, bending over toward her, his hand propped on her horse's neck; he was smiling. Zinaida was listening to him silently, her eyes severely cast down and her lips tightly compressed. At first, I saw only them, but a few moments later, Belovzorov also came into view around a bend in the valley. He was wearing a hussar's uniform complete with cape, riding a sweat-drenched black horse. The gallant steed tossed its head, snorted, and pranced from side to side; its rider was restraining it and spurring it on at the same time. I stood aside. My father gathered up his reins and moved away from Zinaida. She slowly raised her eyes to meet his, and they both galloped off. . . . Belovzorov flew after them, his saber clattering behind him. "He's as red as a crab," I reflected, "while she's. . . . Why is she so pale? She's been out riding the whole morning—and yet she's pale?"

I redoubled my pace and got home just in time for dinner. My father, having freshly bathed and changed clothes, was already sitting by my mother's chair; he was reading her an article from the *Journal des Débats* in his measured, mellifluous voice. My mother was listening to him distractedly, and when she saw me, she asked where I'd been all day long, adding that she didn't like all this gadding about, God knows where, God knows with whom. "Except that I've been out walking by myself," I was on the verge of replying—but then I looked at my father, and for some reason or other, I held my tongue.

XV

I barely saw Zinaida for the next five or six days; she said she was ill, a fact that didn't prevent all the usual visitors from dropping in at the lodge, however, to do their duty, as they put it—all except Maidanov, that is, who promptly got bored and depressed when he wasn't given the opportunity to appear ecstatic. Belovzorov sullenly sat in one corner, his face flushed, his coat buttoned up to the throat. An evil smile flickered across Malevskii's refined face—he'd truly fallen out of favor with Zinaida, and cultivated the elder princess with special assiduity, even escorting her to call on the governor-general in a hired carriage. This expedition turned out to be unsuccessful, though, and even led to an unpleasant incident for Malevskii: he was reminded of some sort of scandal in connection with some sort of officer from the Engineers' regiment, and was forced to plead his youth and inexperience then as an excuse. Lushin came twice a day, but didn't stay for long. I was somewhat afraid of him after our previous conversation—and felt genuinely attracted to him at the same time. He went for a walk with me in the Neskuchnii gardens one day and was very genial and kind, telling me the names and properties of various plants and flowers. Suddenly, for no good reason, as they say, hitting himself on the forehead, he cried out, "And I, fool that I am, thought she was a flirt! It's clear that self-sacrifice is sweet—for some people!"

"What do you mean by that?" I asked.

"I don't mean anything by it," Lushin retorted abruptly.

Zinaida avoided me; my presence—I couldn't help noticing—had an unpleasant effect on her. She instinctively turned away from me . . . instinctively—that was what was so bitter, that was what crushed me! But there was nothing I could do about it, and so I tried not to cross her path, merely watching over her from a distance, although I wasn't always able to do so. Once again, something that I didn't understand was happening to her; her face looked different, she looked completely different. One warm, quiet evening, I was especially struck by the change that had taken place in her. I was sitting on a low garden bench under a spreading honeysuckle. I was fond of that recess; I could see the window of Zinaida's room from there. As I sat, a little bird was busily hopping amid the darkness of the leaves over my head; a gray cat, having stretched itself out to its full length first, was warily creeping around the garden; some beetles were droning heavily as they flew through the air, which was still clear even though it was no longer light. I sat gazing at the window, waiting to see whether it would open. It did open, and Zinaida appeared at it. She was wearing a white dress—and she was white herself, so pale were her face, shoulders, and arms. She stood still for a long time, staring straight ahead of her, her brow furrowed. I'd never seen the look that was on her face. Then she clasped her hands very tightly, raised them to her lips, to her forehead—and suddenly pulling her fingers apart, she pushed her hair back behind her ears, tossed her head, nodded with some sort of resolve, and slammed the window shut.

Three days later, she ran into me in the garden. I started to turn away, but she stopped me herself.

"Give me your hand," she said to me with her old warmth. "It's been a long time since we've chatted."

I glanced at her: her eyes were filled with a soft light, and her face looked as though it were smiling through a haze.

"Are you still sick?" I asked her.

"No, that's all over now," she answered, and she plucked a small, red rose. "I'm a little tired, but that will pass, too."

"And will you be the way you used to be again?" I queried.

Zinaida lifted the rose up to her face, and it seemed as if the reflection of its bright petals had fallen on her cheeks. "Why, have I changed?" she inquired.

"Yes, you've changed," I responded in a low voice.

"I've been cold to you, I know," Zinaida observed, "but you shouldn't pay any attention to that. . . . I couldn't help it. . . . But then, why talk about it?"

"You don't want me to love you—that's what it is!" I exclaimed morosely, in an involuntary outburst.

"No, do love me—but not the way you did."

"How, then?"

"Let's be friends—that's how!" Zinaida gave me the rose to sniff. "Listen, you know that I'm much older than you. I could be your aunt, in fact, or, well, not your aunt, but an older sister. And you. . . ."

"You think of me as a child," I interrupted.

"Well, yes, as a child, but an adorable, nice, intelligent child whom I love very much. Do you know what? From this day forth, I confer on you the position of my page—and don't you forget that pages are obligated to stay close to their ladies. Here's a token of your new status," she added, sticking the rose in the buttonhole of my jacket, "the token of my favor."

"I used to receive other favors from you," I murmured.

"Ah!" Zinaida responded, and she gave me a sidelong look. "What a memory he has! Well? I'm ready right now. . . ." And bending toward me, she bestowed an innocent, calm kiss on my forehead.

I simply stared at her while she turned away, saying, "Follow me, my page," and walked off toward the lodge. I followed her—utterly bewildered. "Can this gentle, reasonable young woman," I thought, "be the same Zinaida I used to know?" It seemed to me that even her walk was more sedate, that her whole form was more stately and graceful. . . .

And, my God, with what fresh force did love flare up within me!

XVI

After dinner, the usual guests assembled at the lodge once more, and the younger princess came out to greet them. Everyone was there in full force, just as they'd been on my first, unforgettable evening—even Nirmatskii had limped over to see her. Maidanov came the earliest this time, bringing some new verses. The games of forfeits began again, but without the strange pranks, the practical jokes, and the noise—the gypsy element had vanished. Zinaida imparted a different mood to the proceedings. I sat beside her by

virtue of my position as page. Among other things, she proposed
that anyone who had to pay a forfeit should relate one of his dreams,
but this didn't work very well. The dreams were either uninteresting
(Belovzorov had dreamed that he'd fed carp to his mare, and that
she'd had a wooden head) or artifically composed. Maidanov regaled us with a full-length story: there were crypts and angels with
lyres and talking flowers and sounds wafting from afar. Zinaida
didn't let him finish. "If we have to listen to compositions," she
said, "then everyone should tell us something they've made up,
without any pretense." The first one who had to speak after that
was Belovzorov again.

The young hussar became embarrassed. "I can't make anything
up!" he cried.

"What nonsense!" Zinaida retorted. "Well, for instance, imagine
that you're married, and tell us how you'd treat your wife. Would
you lock her up?"

"Yes, I'd lock her up."

"And would you stay with her yourself?"

"Yes, I'd definitely stay with her myself."

"That's fine. Well, what if she got sick of that and betrayed
you?"

"I'd kill her."

"And if she ran away?"

"I'd catch up with her and kill her anyway."

"Oh. And suppose that I were your wife—what would you do
then?"

Belovzorov was silent for a minute. "I'd kill myself. . . ."

Zinaida laughed. "I can see that your story isn't a long one."

The next forfeit was Zinaida's. She gazed at the ceiling and lapsed
into thought.

"Well, then, listen," she eventually began, "here's what I've
imagined. . . . Picture to yourselves a magnificent palace, a summer
night, and a marvelous ball. This ball is being given by a young
queen. Gold, marble, crystal, silk, torches, diamonds, flowers, per-
fumes, every form of luxury, can be seen everywhere."

"Do you love luxury?" Lushin interrupted.

"Luxury is beautiful," she responded. "I love everything that's
beautiful."

"More than everything that's good?" he inquired.

"Somehow that's a clever question, which I don't understand.
Don't interrupt me. In any event, the ball is magnificent. There

are crowds of guests, all of whom are young, handsome, brave, and madly in love with the queen."

"Are there no women among the guests?" Malevskii asked.

"No—or wait a minute—yes, there are a few."

"Are they all ugly?"

"No, they're charming. But all the men are in love with the queen. She's tall and graceful. She's wearing a little gold diadem in her black hair."

I looked at Zinaida, and at that moment she seemed to me to be so superior to all of us, to exude so much lively intelligence and so much power from her white forehead and unruffled eyebrows, that I thought, "You yourself are that queen!"

"They all throng around her," Zinaida continued, "and lavish the most flattering compliments upon her."

"And she likes flattery?" Lushin interjected.

"What an intolerable person! He keeps interrupting. . . . Who doesn't like flattery?"

"One more, final question," Malevskii remarked. "Does the queen have a husband?"

"I hadn't thought about that. No—why should she have a husband?"

"Of course," Malevskii affirmed, "why should she have a husband?"

"*Silence!*" Maidanov cried in French, which he spoke very badly.

"*Merci!*" Zinaida said to him. "And so the queen listens to their compliments, and listens to the music, but doesn't look at any of the guests. Six windows are open from top to bottom, from floor to ceiling, and beyond them one can see a dark sky full of big stars, and a dark garden with big trees. The queen gazes out into the garden. Out there, among the trees, stands a fountain. It glows white in the darkness, and looms tall, as though it were an apparition. The queen hears the soft splash of its water amid the conversation and the music. She gazes into the darkness and thinks: 'You, gentlemen, are all noble, intelligent, and wealthy. You crowd around me, you treasure every word I utter, you're all prepared to die at my feet. I hold you in my power. . . . But out there, by the fountain, near that splashing water, the man I love, the man who holds me in his power, stands and waits. He has neither rich attire nor precious stones, he has no position in society, but he awaits me, certain that I'll come—and I will come, and there's no power that can stop me when I want to go to him, to stay with him, to disappear with him out there, in the darkness of the garden, amid the whispering of the trees and the splashing of the fountain...."'

Zinaida fell silent.

"Is that an imaginary story?" Malevskii inquired slyly. Zinaida didn't even look at him.

"And what would we have done, gentlemen," Lushin spoke up suddenly, "if we'd been among the guests, and had known about the lucky man at the fountain?"

"Wait a minute, wait a minute," Zinaida interrupted. "I'll tell you myself what each of you would have done. You, Belovzorov, would have challenged him to a duel. You, Maidanov, would have written an epigram about him.... But, no, you can't write epigrams—you would have made up a long poem about him in the style of Barbier and published your work in the *Telegraph*. You, Nirmatskii, would have borrowed...no, you would have loaned him money at a high rate of interest. You, doctor...." She stopped. "Then again, I don't really know what you would have done...."

"In my capacity as court physician," Lushin replied, "I would have advised the queen not to give balls when she wasn't in the mood to entertain her guests...."

"Perhaps you would have been right. And you, Count...."

"And I?" Malevskii echoed with his wicked smile....

"You would have offered him a piece of poisoned candy."

Malevskii's face changed slightly, assuming a threatening expression for an instant, but he immediately laughed.

"And as for you, Voldemar...," Zinaida went on, "however, that's enough. Let's play another game."

"Monsieur Voldemar, as the queen's page, would have carried her train when she ran into the garden," Malevskii remarked maliciously.

I flared up angrily, but Zinaida hurriedly laid a hand on my shoulder and, standing up, said in a slightly shaky voice, "I've never given Your Excellency the right to be rude, and I therefore ask you to leave." She pointed to the door.

"I beg your pardon, Princess," Malevskii muttered, and he turned extremely pale.

"The princess is right," Belovzorov cried, and he stood up as well.

"Good God, I didn't expect this at all," Malevskii continued. "There was nothing in my words, I thought, that could...I had no intention of offending you.... Forgive me."

Zinaida cast a cold look at him and smiled coldly. "Then stay, if you wish," she said with a casual wave of her hand. "Monsieur Voldemar and I were needlessly incensed. You like to annoy people. . . . May you prosper by it."

"Forgive me," Malevskii repeated once more, while I, recalling Zinaida's wave of the hand, thought to myself that no real queen could have shown a presumptuous subject the door with greater dignity.

The game of forfeits continued for a short time after this little scene. Everyone felt a bit ill at ease, not so much because of the scene itself, but because of some other, not quite defined and yet oppressive feeling. No one referred to it, but everyone was conscious of it in themselves and the others. Maidanov read us his verses, and Malevskii praised them with exaggerated warmth. "Now he wants to show how kind he can be," Lushin whispered to me. We departed shortly thereafter. A pensive mood seemed to have come over Zinaida; the elder princess informed us that she had a headache; Nirmatskii had complained about his rheumatism. . . .

I lay down, but I couldn't fall asleep for a long time—I was struck by Zinaida's story. "Can there possibly have been a hint in it?" I asked myself. "And at whom, at what was she hinting? If there really is anything to hint at . . . how can I find out? No, no, there can't be," I whispered, turning over from one burning cheek onto the other. . . . But I remembered the expression on Zinaida's face as she'd told her story. . . . I remembered the exclamation Lushin had uttered in the Neskuchnii gardens, the sudden change in her behavior toward me—and I became lost in conjectures. "Who is he?" These three words seemed to dangle before my eyes as though they'd been traced upon the darkness. It was as if a low, malevolent cloud were hanging over me; I felt its oppressiveness, and was waiting for it to burst any second. I'd gotten used to many things in recent days; I'd seen many things at the Zasekins'—the messiness, the meager tallow candle-ends, the broken knives and forks, Vonifatii's gloominess, the maids' shabbiness, the elder princess's manners—and their entire, strange mode of existence no longer amazed me. . . . But I could never get used to what I was now dimly discerning in Zinaida. . . . "An adventuress!" my mother had called her one day. An adventuress—she, my idol, my goddess? This accusation tormented me, and I tried to escape it by burying my face in my pillow. I was indignant—and at the same time, what wouldn't I have agreed to, what wouldn't I have given, just to be that lucky man at the fountain!...

My blood was on fire, raging inside me. "The garden...the fountain...," I mused. "I'll go down to the garden." I swiftly got dressed and slipped out of the house. The night was dark, and the trees were barely stirring; a soft, cool breeze drifted from the sky; the smell of fennel wafted over from the kitchen garden. I walked along the different paths, and the faint sound of my own footsteps both startled and emboldened me. I stopped, stood still, and listened to my heart beating loudly and fast. I finally went up to the fence and leaned against the thin railing. Suddenly—or was it my imagination?—a female form glimmered a few steps away from me....I strained my eyes in the darkness and held my breath. What was that sound? Did I hear steps, or was it my heart beating again? "Who's there?" I faltered, barely audibly. Was that the sound again? A smothered laugh...or the rustling of the leaves... or a sigh right by my ear? I got scared...."Who's there?" I repeated even more softly.

The breeze gusted for an instant, and a streak of flame flashed across the sky: a star was falling. "Zinaida?" I wanted to call out, but her name died away on my lips. And suddenly everything became profoundly silent, as often happens in the middle of the night....Even the cicadas stopped chirping in the trees—only a window rattled somewhere. I stood there for a long time, and then went back to my room, to my cool bed. I felt strangely agitated, as though I'd gone out expecting to have a tryst but had ended up alone, having passed close by someone else's happiness.

XVII

I got only a fleeting glimpse of Zinaida the following day, when she was going off somewhere with the elder princess in a rented carriage. But I did see Lushin—who barely greeted me, however— as well as Malevskii. The young count grinned and began affably chatting with me. Of all those who visited the lodge, he alone had succeeded in gaining admission to our house and had favorably impressed my mother. My father didn't like him, and treated him with a courtesy bordering on the insulting.

"Ah, *monsieur le page*," Malevskii began, "I'm delighted to see you. What's your lovely queen doing?"

His fresh, handsome face was so repugnant to me at that moment, and he looked at me with such contemptuous amusement, that I refused to answer him at all.

"Are you still angry?" he went on. "You have no reason to be. It wasn't I who called you a page, you know, and pages do primarily wait on queens. But permit me to observe that you're performing your duties very badly."

"How so?"

"Pages ought to be inseparable from their mistresses, pages ought to know everything they do. Pages even ought to keep watch over them," he added, lowering his voice, "day and night."

"What do you mean?"

"What do I mean? I believe I've expressed myself quite clearly. Day and night. By day, it's not so important—it's light, and there are people around during the daytime—but at night, beware of disaster. I advise you not to sleep at night, and to keep watch, to keep watch with all your might. Remember, in the garden, at night, by the fountain—that's where you need to stand guard. You'll thank me."

Malevskii laughed and turned his back on me. He probably attached no great importance to what he'd said to me; he had a reputation for thoroughly mystifying people and was noted for his ability to fool people at masquerades, an ability that was greatly enhanced by the almost unconscious mendacity his whole nature was steeped in.... He merely wanted to tease me, but every word he uttered ran through my veins like poison. The blood rushed to my head. "Ah! So that's it!" I said to myself. "Good! So my forebodings of yesterday were justified! I wasn't drawn to the garden in vain! This can't be!" I cried aloud, and struck myself on the chest with my fist, although I myself didn't know precisely what it was that couldn't be. "Whether Malevskii himself goes into the garden" (I thought perhaps he was bragging—he was insolent enough for that) "or someone else" (our garden fence was quite low, so it wasn't difficult to climb over), "if anyone falls into my hands, so much the worse for him! I don't advise anyone to risk an encounter with me! I'll prove to the entire world and to her in particular, the traitress" (I actually used the word "traitress"), "that I can get revenge!"

I returned to my room, took an English knife I'd recently bought out of the desk, felt its sharp edge, and, knitting my brows with an air of cold, concentrated determination, thrust it into my pocket, as though doing such things were nothing unusual for me, as though

I weren't doing this for the first time. My heart throbbed angrily and felt as heavy as a stone. I kept scowling all day long, keeping my lips tightly compressed, and I continually paced up and down with my hand in my pocket, clutching the knife, which grew warm from my grasp, while I prepared myself in advance for something terrible. These new, unusual sensations so occupied and even elated me that I hardly thought about Zinaida herself. I was incessantly haunted by the image of Pushkin's Aleko, the young gypsy— "Where are you going, handsome young man? Lie still," and then "You are covered with blood.... Oh, what did you do?... Nothing!" What a cruel smile I wore as I repeated that "Nothing!" My father wasn't home, but my mother, who'd been in an almost constant state of suppressed irritation for some time now, noticed my fatalistic attitude and asked me at supper, "Why are you sulking?" I merely smiled condescendingly in reply and thought, "If they only knew!" It struck eleven. I went to my room, but didn't get undressed. I waited for midnight, and it finally struck. "It's time!" I muttered between my teeth, and buttoning my jacket up to the throat, even rolling up my sleeves, I went into the garden.

I'd already selected the best spot to stand guard. At the end of the garden, where the fence separating our residence from the Zasekins' joined a shared wall, there was a solitary pine tree. Standing under its low, thick branches, I could see whatever might happen quite well, at least to the extent that the dark night permitted. A winding path ran right by there that had always seemed mysterious to me: it coiled like a snake under the fence, which at that point bore traces of having been climbed over, and led to a round arbor formed by thick acacias. I made my way to the pine tree, leaned my back against its trunk, and began my watch.

The night was as silent as the night before had been, but there were fewer clouds in the sky, and the outlines of bushes, even of tall flowers, could be seen more distinctly. The first moments of waiting were torturous, almost horrifying. I'd made up my mind to go to any extreme. I merely debated how to proceed, whether to thunder: "Where are you going? Stop! Identify yourself—or die!" or simply to strike.... Every sound, every whisper, every rustle seemed unusual and portentous to me.... I braced myself.... I leaned forward.... But half an hour passed, an hour passed; my blood grew calmer and cooler. The sense that I was doing all this for nothing, that I was even being somewhat ridiculous, that Malevskii had just been making fun of me, began to steal over me. I abandoned my hiding place and walked around the entire garden. As if on purpose, there wasn't a sound to be heard anywhere; everything was at rest. Even our dog was asleep, curled up in a ball by the gate. I climbed up into the deserted greenhouse, saw the distant field in front of me, recalled my encounter with Zinaida, and began to ponder....

I suddenly shivered.... I thought I heard the creak of a door opening, then the faint crack of a broken twig. I got down from the greenhouse in two bounds, and froze in place. Rapid and light but cautious footsteps echoed distinctly throughout the garden. They were coming in my direction. "Here he is ... here he is at last!" the thought pierced me to the heart. I convulsively pulled the knife out of my pocket and convulsively opened it. Red flashes were whirling before my eyes, my hair was standing on end in my fear and fury.... The steps were coming straight toward me—I leaned forward, I stretched myself out.... A man appeared.... My God! It was my father!

I instantly recognized him, even though he was completely wrapped up in a dark cloak and had his hat pulled down low on his face. He walked past on tiptoe. He didn't notice me: nothing concealed me, but I'd leaned so far forward that I seemed to be almost flat on the ground. The jealous Othello, ready to murder someone, was promptly transformed into a schoolboy.... I was so taken aback by my father's unexpected appearance that I didn't notice at first where he'd come from or where he'd gone. I merely straightened up and thought, "Why is my father walking in the garden at night?" after everything had grown silent again. In my shock, I'd dropped my knife in the grass, but I didn't even try to find it. I was terribly ashamed of myself. I completely calmed down all at once. On my way home, however, I went to my seat under the honeysuckle tree and looked up at Zinaida's little window. The small, slightly convex panes of that little window shone dimly in the faint light cast on them by the nocturnal sky. Suddenly, their color began to change.... Behind them—I saw this, saw it distinctly—quietly and cautiously, a whitish curtain was lowered down to the window frame—and then remained motionless.

"What is all this?" I asked myself aloud, almost involuntarily, when I returned to my room. "A dream, a coincidence, or...." The ideas abruptly entering my mind were so new and strange that I didn't dare to articulate them.

XVIII

I got up the next morning with a headache. My emotional upheaval of the previous day had vanished. It'd been replaced by a dreary perplexity and some sort of sadness I'd never known until that day, as though something in me had died.

"Why are you walking around looking like a rabbit with half its brain removed?" Lushin inquired upon encountering me. At lunch, I stole a look first at my father, then at my mother: he was composed, as usual; she was secretly irritated, as usual. I waited to see whether my father would make some friendly remark to me, as he occasionally did. . . . But he didn't even give me his usual cool caress. "Should I tell Zinaida everything?" I wondered. . . . "It doesn't matter, anyway. It's all over between us." I went to see her, but didn't tell her anything, and indeed, I couldn't have managed to speak to her privately even if I'd wanted to. The elder princess's son, a twelve-year-old cadet in a military school, had arrived from Petersburg for his vacation. Zinaida immediately handed her brother over to me.

"Here, my dear Volodia"—it was the first time she'd ever called me that—"is a companion for you," she announced. "His name is Volodia, too. Please be nice to him. He's still shy, but he has a kind heart. Show him the Neskuchnii gardens, go for walks with him, take him under your wing. You'll do that, won't you? You're so kind, too!"

She affectionately laid both her hands on my shoulders, and I became utterly bewildered. The presence of this boy transformed me into a boy as well. I silently regarded the cadet, who stared back at me just as silently. Zinaida laughed and pushed us toward each other. "Embrace one another, children!" We embraced. "Would you like me to show you our garden?" I asked the cadet. "If you don't mind," he replied in a cadet's hoarse voice.

Zinaida laughed again. . . . I noticed that her face had more exquisite color in it than I'd ever seen before. I went off with the cadet. There was an old-fashioned swing in our garden. I put him on its narrow wooden seat and began to swing him. He sat perfectly still in his new little uniform, which was made of thick cloth and had broad gold braiding, holding onto the cords tightly. "You might want to unbutton your collar," I said to him.

"It's all right. We're used to it," he replied, and cleared his throat.

He looked like his sister—his eyes particularly resembled hers. I enjoyed being nice to him, and at the same time felt an aching sadness gnawing at my heart. "Now I'm just like a child," I thought, "but yesterday...." I remembered where I'd dropped my knife the night before, and went to find it. The cadet asked me to give it to him, picked a thick stalk of wild parsley, made a pipe out of it, and began to whistle on it. Othello whistled, too.

But that evening, how he wept in Zinaida's arms, this Othello, when she found him in a corner of the garden and asked him why he was so sad. My tears flowed with such force that she got frightened. "What's wrong with you? What is it, Volodia?" she kept repeating, and when I didn't answer and didn't stop crying, she decided to kiss my wet cheek. But I turned away from her and whispered through my sobs: "I know everything. Why did you toy with me?...What did you need my love for?"

"I've treated you badly, Volodia...," Zinaida declared. "I've treated you terribly...," she added, wringing her hands. "There's so much that's ugly and dark and sinful in me!... But I'm not toying with you now. I do love you—you don't even suspect how much or why.... But what is it that you know?"

What could I tell her? She stood facing me, gazing at me—and I wholly belonged to her, from head to toe, as soon as she gazed at me.... A quarter of an hour later, I was running races with Zinaida and the cadet. I was no longer crying, I was laughing, although a tear or two leaked from my swollen eyelids as I laughed. I was wearing one of Zinaida's ribbons around my neck as a tie, and I shouted with joy whenever I managed to catch her by the waist. She did whatever she liked with me.

XIX

I'd have great difficulty if I were forced to describe exactly what went on inside me during the week after my unsuccessful midnight expedition. It was a strange, feverish period, a somehow chaotic one, in which the most profoundly opposed emotions, ideas, suspicions, hopes, joys, and torments whirled together in a kind of cyclone. I was afraid to look deeply within myself, if a boy of sixteen can ever look deeply within himself; I was afraid to explain anything to myself; I simply hurried to live through each day until evening, and then I slept at night.... The lightheartedness of childhood came to my rescue. I didn't want to know whether I was loved, and I didn't want to admit to myself that I wasn't loved. I avoided my father—but I couldn't avoid Zinaida.... I felt as if I were on fire in her presence ... but why did I need to know what kind of fire it was that made me burn and melt? It was delectable for me to melt and burn. I gave myself over to every passing sensation, deceiving myself, ignoring my memories, and closing my eyes to what I suspected lay before me.... This languid condition probably wouldn't have lasted long in any case ... but a thunderbolt cut it short in a single clap and hurled me in an entirely new direction.

Coming back for dinner after a fairly long walk one day, I was surprised to learn that I'd be dining alone—my father had gone out and my mother didn't feel well, didn't want any dinner, and had locked herself in her bedroom. I surmised from the expressions on the servants' faces that something unusual had occurred.... I didn't dare to interrogate them, but was on good terms with one young cook, Philipp, who was passionately fond of poetry and played the guitar. I resorted to him, and learned that a terrible scene had taken place between my father and mother (every word of which had been overheard in the maid's room; much of it had been in French, but Masha, her personal maid, had lived with a dressmaker from Paris for five years and understood it all), that my mother had accused my father of infidelity, of having an intimate relationship with the young lady next door, that my father had defended himself at first, but then had lost his temper and said something cruel "in reference to her age," which had made my mother cry. Philipp also noted that my mother had alluded to some loan that had evidently been made to the elder princess, and had spoken about her and the young lady as well in highly negative terms, and that my father had threatened her then and there.

"And all this trouble," Philipp continued, "resulted from an anonymous letter. No one knows who wrote it, and otherwise there wouldn't have been any reason whatsoever for these matters to have come out."

"But was there really anything to it?" I asked with difficulty, as my hands and feet went cold and something shuddered in the depths of my chest.

Philipp winked meaningfully. "There was. You can't conceal those things, although your father was careful this time—but he still would have had to rent a carriage or something, for instance ... and you can't get anywhere without servants, either."

I sent Philipp away and collapsed onto my bed. I didn't sob, I

didn't give myself over to despair. I didn't ask myself when and
how all this had happened. I didn't wonder how I'd failed to guess
this earlier, long ago—I didn't even rage against my father. . . .
What I'd learned was more than I could bear; this sudden revelation
had stunned me. . . . Everything was over. All my beautiful flowers
had been torn up by their roots at the same moment and lay all
around me, strewn on the ground and trampled underfoot.

XX

The next day, my mother declared her intention to return to town.
Later that morning, my father went into her bedroom and remained
alone with her for quite a while. No one overheard what he said
to her, but my mother didn't cry any more. She regained her
composure and asked for something to eat, but didn't come out of
her room or change her plans. As I recall, I wandered around all
day, but didn't go into the garden, and didn't glance at the lodge
even once. That evening, I witnessed a surprising event: I saw my
father lead Count Malevskii by the arm through the dining room
into the hallway and, in the presence of a servant, say to him icily,
"A few days ago your excellency was shown out of a certain house.
I won't engage in any further discussion with you at this time, but
I have the honor of informing you that if you ever visit my home
again, I'll throw you out the window. I don't care for your handwriting." The count bowed, compressed his lips, slunk away, and
vanished.

The preparations for our return to town, to the Arbat district
where we owned a house, got underway. My father himself probably
didn't want to stay at the country house any longer, but he'd
apparently succeeded in persuading my mother not to create a
public scandal. Everything was done calmly, without visible haste;
my mother even sent her regards to the elder princess and expressed regret that, due to illness, she'd be unable to see her
again before our departure. I wandered around like someone possessed, longing for only one thing, for it all to be over as soon
as possible. One thought wouldn't leave my head: how could she,
a young woman—and a princess, at that—take such a step, knowing
that my father wasn't free, and having the opportunity to marry
anyone—Belovzorov, for instance? What had she hoped for? Why
wasn't she afraid of ruining her entire future? Yes, I thought, this
is love, this is passion, this is devotion . . . and Lushin's words came
back to me: for some people, self-sacrifice is sweet. I somehow

happened to catch sight of a white blur in one of the windows in the lodge.... "Could that be Zinaida's face?" I thought.... Yes, it definitely was her face. I couldn't restrain myself—I couldn't part from her without saying a final goodbye. I seized a convenient moment and went over to the lodge.

The elder princess met me in the drawing room with her typically uncouth, casual greeting.

"Why is it, my good man, that you people are going off in such a hurry?" she queried, inserting some snuff into her nose.

I looked at her, and a load was lifted from my heart. The word "loan," which Philip had mentioned, had been torturing me. She didn't suspect anything . . . or so I thought then, at least. Zinaida came in from the next room; she was pale, dressed all in black, and her hair was hanging loose. She took me by the hand without a word and led me away with her.

"I heard your voice," she began, "and came in right away. Was it so easy for you to desert us, you bad boy?"

"I've come to say goodbye to you, princess," I replied, "probably forever. Perhaps you've heard that we're leaving."

Zinaida looked at me intently.

"Yes, I've heard. Thank you for coming. I was beginning to think I'd never see you again. Don't remember me unkindly. I've tormented you sometimes, but I'm not what you think I am, all the same."

She turned away and leaned against the window.

"Really, I'm not like that. I know that you have a bad opinion of me."

"I do?"

"Yes, you do . . . you do."

"I do?" I echoed mournfully, and my heart throbbed just as it once had under the influence of her irresistible, indescribable fascination. "I? Believe me, Zinaida Aleksandrovna, whatever you've done, however you've tormented me, I'll love and adore you to the end of my days."

She quickly turned toward me, and spreading her arms wide, hugged me and gave me a deep, passionate kiss. God knows whom that prolonged farewell kiss was seeking, but I eagerly drank in its sweetness. I knew that it would never be repeated. "Goodbye, goodbye," I kept saying. . . .

She tore herself away and went out; I then left. I can't put into words the feeling I had when I left. I wouldn't ever want to

experience that feeling again, but I'd consider myself unfortunate
if I'd never experienced it.

We moved back to town. I didn't forsake the past quickly; I
didn't get back to work soon. My wounds began to heal slowly—
but I didn't nourish any negative feelings toward my father. On
the contrary, he'd grown in my eyes, as it were.... Let psychologists explain this contradiction as best they can. One day I was
walking along a boulevard and, to my indescribable delight, I ran
into Lushin. I'd always liked him for his straightforward, unhypo-
critical character, and besides, I valued him because of the memories he awakened in me. I ran up to him.

"Aha!" he said, frowning. "So it's you, young man. Let me
take a look at you. You're still as sallow as ever, but at least you
don't have that shiftless gaze anymore. You look like a man, not
a lapdog. That's good. Well, what are you doing? Working?"

I sighed. I didn't want to lie, but I was ashamed to tell him the
truth.

"Well, never mind," Lushin continued. "Don't be embarrassed.
The main thing is to lead a normal life and not let yourself get
distracted. What's the point? Wherever the tide carries you—it's
always bad. Everyone has to stand on a rock, on their own two
feet. I've got a cough ... and Belovzorov—have you heard anything
about him?"

"No. What's happened?"

"He's dropped out of sight, and there's no news of him. It's
rumored that he's gone off to the Caucasus. Let that be a lesson
to you, young man. And it all comes from not knowing how to
extricate oneself in time, how to break out of the net. You seem
to have escaped quite well. Make sure you don't fall into the same
trap again. Goodbye."

"I won't ...," I thought. "I'll never see her again." But I was
destined to see Zinaida one more time.

XXI

My father used to go horseback riding every day. He had a magnificent English mare, a chestnut piebald with a long, slender neck
and long legs, an untiring, vicious beast. Her name was Electric.
No one could ride her except my father. He walked up to me one
day in a good mood, a condition I hadn't seen him in for a long
time; he was getting ready for his ride, and had already put on his
spurs. I began begging him to take me with him.

"We'd be much better off playing a game of leapfrog," my father replied. "You'll never keep up with me on your pony."

"Yes, I will. I'll put on spurs, too."

"All right, then, come on."

We started off. I had a shaggy little black horse, a strong, fairly spirited one. It's true, it had to gallop as hard as it could when Electric went at a fast trot; still, I didn't get left behind. I've never seen anyone ride like my father: he sat with such attractive, casual grace that it seemed as though the horse beneath him was conscious of it, and proud of its rider. We rode along various boulevards, passed through Maidens Field, jumped several fences (I'd been afraid to jump at first, but my father despised cowards, and I quickly stopped being afraid), and crossed the Moscow River twice. I was under the impression that we were on our way home, especially since my father himself had remarked that my horse was tired, when he suddenly veered away from me at the Crimean Ford and galloped along the riverbank. I rode after him. When he reached a tall pile of old logs, he abruptly slid off Electric, told me to dismount, and, handing me his horse's reins, told me to wait for him there, at the log pile. He walked off toward a small street and disappeared. I began pacing up and down the riverbank, leading the horses and scolding Electric, who kept pulling, shaking her head, snorting, and neighing as we walked, and never ceased pawing the ground, whinnying, and biting my pony on the neck whenever we stood still. In fact, she behaved like a spoiled thoroughbred.

My father didn't come back soon. A damp, unpleasant mist was rising from the river; a fine rain gently began to fall, making tiny dark flecks on the idiotic gray log pile, which I continued to walk past and had become thoroughly sick of. I got horribly bored, and my father still didn't come back. Some sort of sentry, a Finn who looked gray all over, like the logs, wearing a huge, old-fashioned shako resembling a pot on his head, carrying a halberd (what was a sentry doing on the banks of the Moscow River, anyway?), approached me and, turning his wrinkled, old-womanish face toward me, inquired: "What are you doing here with these horses, young master? Let me hold them."

I didn't answer him. He asked me for some tobacco. To get rid of him (I was tortured by impatience), I took a few steps in the direction my father had gone, then proceeded to walk along the little street to the end, turned the corner, and stopped. Forty feet away from me, my father was standing in the street at the open window of a small wooden house, his back turned toward me. He was leaning his chest against the windowsill, while inside the house, half hidden by a curtain, a woman in a dark dress sat talking to my father. The woman was Zinaida.

I was stunned. I confess that I hadn't expected this at all. My first impulse was to run away. "My father will look around," I thought, "and I'm doomed...." But a strange feeling—a feeling stronger than curiosity, even stronger than jealousy, stronger than fear—kept me there. I began to watch; I strove to hear. It seemed my father was insisting on something; Zinaida wouldn't consent. I can see her face to this day: sad, serious, and beautiful, wearing an unutterable expression that combined devotion, grief, love, and some sort of despair—I can't find any other words for it. She spoke in monosyllables without raising her eyes, merely smiling—submissively yet stubbornly. I'd have recognized my former Zinaida by that smile alone. My father shrugged his shoulders and straightened his hat on his head, which always served as a sign of impatience with him.... Then I caught the words: "*Vous devez vous séparer de cette....*" Zinaida sat up and stretched out her arm.... Suddenly, before my very eyes, the impossible happened: my father abruptly raised the whip with which he'd been brushing the dust off his coat and struck a sharp blow on that arm, which was bare to the elbow. I could hardly keep from crying out as Zinaida shuddered, looked at my father without a word, and then, slowly lifting her arm to her lips, kissed the streak of red that had appeared upon it. My father flung the whip away from him and, hastily running up the steps, dashed into the house.... Zinaida turned around, and with her arms outstretched and her head bowed, she moved away from the window as well.

My heart sank with panic and some sort of horrified bewilderment. I stumbled backward, and running down the lane, almost losing hold of Electric, I returned to the riverbank. I couldn't think clearly. I knew that my cold, reserved father was sometimes seized by fits of fury, but nonetheless, I could in no way comprehend what I'd just seen.... At the same time, I felt that, however long I lived, I could never forget Zinaida's gesture and look and smile; I felt that her image, this new image so unexpectedly manifested before me, had been imprinted on my memory forever. I stared vacantly at the river, never noticing that tears were streaming down my face. "She's being beaten," I kept thinking, "beaten... beaten...."

"Hey, there! What are you doing? Give me my horse!" I heard my father's voice call out behind me.

I mechanically handed him the reins. He leaped onto Electric. . . . The mare, who'd gotten cold from standing still, reared back on her haunches and promptly sprang ten feet forward . . . but my father settled her down quickly, drove his spurs into her sides, and struck her on the neck with his fist. . . . "Ah, I don't have my whip," he muttered.

I recalled the recent swish and fall of that very whip, and shuddered.

"Where did you put it?" I asked my father after a brief pause.

My father didn't answer me, and galloped on ahead. I overtook him—I desperately wanted to see his face.

"Were you bored waiting for me?" he muttered through his teeth.

"A little. Where did you drop your whip?" I asked again.

My father swiftly glanced at me. "I didn't drop it," he replied. "I threw it away." He sank into thought, and lowered his head. . . . Then, for the first and almost last time, I saw how much tenderness and pity his stern features were capable of expressing.

He galloped ahead again, and this time I couldn't overtake him; I got home a quarter of an hour after he did.

"This is love," I said to myself again that night as I sat at my desk, on which books and notepads had begun to appear. "This is passion! . . . Imagine not objecting, imagine enduring a blow from anyone, no matter whom . . . even from the most beloved hand! But, evidently, it's possible, if you love. . . . Yet I . . . I imagined. . . . "

I'd grown much older during the preceding month—and now my love, all its transports and torments notwithstanding, struck me myself as something so small and childish and pitiful beside this other, unknown phenomenon, which I could barely comprehend and which frightened me, like an unfamiliar, beautiful, but menacing face that can't be clearly discerned in the semi-darkness. . . .

I had a strange, terrible dream that very night. I dreamed that I went into a low, dark room. . . . My father was standing there holding a whip in his hand, stamping his foot; Zinaida was crouching in one corner, and a streak of red ran not across her arm but across her forehead . . . while Belovzorov, covered with blood, towered behind both of them; he was spreading his pale lips wide and angrily threatening my father.

I entered the university two months later, and within six months my father died of a stroke in Petersburg, where he'd just moved with my mother and me. A few days before his death, he'd received a letter from Moscow that had greatly upset him. . . . He'd gone to my mother to beg her for some favor, and, I was told, he'd even burst into tears—he, my father! On the very morning of the day he'd had the stroke, he'd begun a letter to me in French. "My son," he wrote to me, "fear a woman's love, fear that bliss, that poison. . . ." After his death, my mother sent a considerable sum of money to Moscow.

XXII

Four years passed. I'd just graduated from the university and didn't know exactly what to do with myself, which door to knock on; I was relaxing for a while without doing anything. One beautiful evening, I ran into Maidanov at the theater. He'd gotten married and had entered the civil service, but I found him otherwise unchanged. He just as needlessly became ecstatic, and then just as suddenly became depressed.

"You know, by the way," he said to me, "that Mrs. Dolskii's here."

"What Mrs. Dolskii?"

"Can you have forgotten her? The former Princess Zasekina, with whom we were all in love, including you. Remember, at the country house near the Neskuchnii gardens?"

"She married someone named Dolskii?"

"Yes."

"And she's here, at the theater?"

"No, but she's in Petersburg. She came here a few days ago. She's going abroad."

"What sort of person is her husband?" I asked.

"A wonderful man, with property. He's a colleague of mine in Moscow. You can understand—after that scandal . . . which you must know all about . . ." (Maidanov smiled significantly), "it wasn't easy for her to find a suitable spouse. There were consequences . . . but with her intelligence, anything's possible. Go and see her—she'll be delighted to see you. She's prettier than ever."

Maidanov gave me Zinaida's address. She was staying at the Hotel Demuth. Old memories were stirred up inside me. . . . I promised myself I'd go and visit my former "passion" the very next day. But some sort of business matters turned up; a week passed, then another; when I finally went to the Hotel Demuth and asked for Mrs. Dolskii, I learned that she'd died four days earlier, quite suddenly, in childbirth.

It was as if something had stabbed me in the heart. The thought that I might have seen her, hadn't seen her, and now would never see her—that bitter thought struck me with all the force of an overwhelming reproach. "She's dead!" I repeated, staring blankly at the hall porter. I slowly found my way back to the street and set off without knowing myself where I was going. Everything that had gone on in the past instantly surfaced and rose up before me. So this was the conclusion, this was the goal toward which that young, ardent, glorious life had striven so hurriedly and anxiously! I contemplated this, I pictured to myself those precious features, those eyes, those curls, in a narrow box amid the damp darkness underground, lying here, not far away from me—and, perhaps, a few feet away from my father—while I was still alive. . . . I thought about all this, I strained my imagination, and yet at the same time the lines

> From indifferent lips I learned of her death,
> And indifferently I acknowledged it.

were echoing in my heart.

Oh youth, youth! You don't worry about anything; you seem to possess all the treasures of the universe—even sorrow gives you pleasure, even grief suits you. You're self-confident and arrogant, you say, "I alone am alive—look!" But your days fly by and vanish without a trace, without an accounting; every bit of you melts like wax in the sun, like snow. . . . And perhaps the whole secret of your charm lies not in your ability to do everything, but in your ability to think that you will do everything; it lies precisely in the fact that you cast to the four winds powers you couldn't otherwise use; it lies in the fact that each of us seriously regards himself as a prodigy, seriously imagines that he's justified in saying, "Oh, what I might have done, if only I hadn't wasted my time!"

Now I . . . what did I hope for, what did I expect, what rich future did I foresee, when the phantom of my first love, rising up for an instant, had barely evoked a single sigh, a solitary mournful sensation?

And what's come of all I'd hoped for? Now, when the shadows of evening are beginning to steal across my life, what do I have left that are fresher, that are more precious, than the memories of that early-morning, quickly passing spring storm?

But I do myself an injustice. Even then, in those lighthearted, youthful days, I wasn't deaf to the voice of sorrow when it addressed me in solemn strains that came floating to me from beyond the grave. I remember that, a few days after I learned of Zinaida's death, due to some special, irresistible impulse, I was present at the death of a poor old woman who lived in the same house we did. Covered with rags, lying on hard boards, a sack beneath her head, she died slowly and painfully. Her entire life had been spent in a bitter struggle with daily privation—she hadn't known any joy, hadn't tasted the honey of happiness. One would have thought that she'd have rejoiced at death, at her deliverance, her final rest. But nonetheless, as long as her decrepit body survived, as long as her breast still heaved in agony under the icy hand weighing upon it, as long as her last ounce of strength didn't desert her, the old woman kept crossing herself and kept whispering, "Lord, forgive my sins"—and the look of fear and horror at the approaching end vanished from her eyes only with the last spark of consciousness. And I remember that there, by the deathbed of that poor old woman, I grew frightened for Zinaida, and I wanted to pray for her, for my father—and for myself.

Letter to K. N. Leontiev.[1]

Courtavenel.
October 3, 1860.

I'm writing to you, dear Konstantin Nikolaevich, from a village located fifty versts from Paris, or more accurately, from a château that belongs to good friends of mine. I received your kind letter two weeks ago, and I thank you for remembering me and for your interest. Unfortunately, I can't return to Russia this year; I say unfortunately because, due to family obligations, I'll have to spend the winter in Paris, which I find loathsome. If the case were otherwise, I'd definitely come to see you and take a look at how you live. I've rented an apartment in Paris on rue de Rivoli, 210; write me at that address and tell me which capital you settle in; I'd like it to be Petersburg. God grant that you move on firm legs down the literary road, which you haven't yet properly set foot on. But that shouldn't depress you; talents, like fruits, don't mature at the same time or in the same season of the year. Fall fruits are sometimes sweeter than summer ones. Your weakness lies (as is always the case) just where your strength is: your devices are too subtle and exquisitely clever, often to the point of obscurity. A poet must be a psychologist, but a secret one: he should know and feel the roots of phenomena but present only the phenomena themselves—in full bloom or as they fade away. I took the liberty of eliminating several superfluous psychological bits from your tale that was published in *Library for Reading*, and I hope that you weren't irritated with me for that. And I expect many good things from your *Podlipki*—just finish it soon, don't spend too long on it. You read it to Dudyshkin, and he sang its praises to me—and he's a good judge. It's obvious from what he said, however, that your novel ought to be shortened.

Everything you write about Baron Rozen's family interests me very much. I don't know whether I'll ever manage to meet his wife in person; life brings some people into constant contact with each other and seems to keep others apart; God only knows, for instance, when you and I will see each other. Give my regards to both of them if you write them or see them.

I enjoyed reading your opinion of "First Love." For people like me, a veteran on the eve of full retirement, it's hard to change; what we did badly can't be corrected; what was successful can't

1. Konstantin Nikolaevich Leontiev (1831-91), one of the most colorful figures in nineteenth-century Russian literature.

be repeated. We have only one thing left that we should think about: *being able to fall silent in time.* Meanwhile, work isn't yet over; now I've planned a rather long piece. And there's nothing surprising in the fact that, as you say, I've recently grown sad: I'll soon be forty-two, and I haven't made a nest for myself or secured any place for myself on this earth; there's little cause for merriment in that.

While awaiting a reply from you, I wish you all the best and clasp your hand cordially. Mrs. Markovich (Marko Vovchok), about whom you want to write an article, is here in Paris: she's a wonderful woman. But do you really like "The King of Hearts"? It strikes me that this particular story is the least successful of all her stories, though the basic idea in it is true to life, as is always the case with Marko Vovchok.

Your devoted
Iv. Turgenev

P.S. To insure more accurate delivery, I don't frank my letters.

Hamlet and Don Quixote

(A speech delivered on January 10, 1860, at a public reading to benefit the Society for the Aid of Needy Writers and Scholars)

Ladies and Gentlemen!

The first edition of Shakespeare's tragedy *Hamlet* and the first part of Cervantes's *Don Quixote* appeared in the very same year, at the beginning of the seventeenth century.

This coincidence strikes us as remarkable; indeed, the nearly simultaneous appearance of these two works has led us to an entire sequence of thoughts. We beg your permission to share these thoughts with you, and we rely on your indulgence in advance. "He who wishes to understand a poet must enter into his realm of thought," said Goethe. An author of prose has no right to make such a request, but at least he can hope that his readers—or listeners—are willing to travel with him on his voyages, to partake of his quests.

Perhaps some of our views will surprise you by their singularity, ladies and gentlemen, but the special power of great artistic works lies in the fact that the interpretations of them, like those of life in general, can be endlessly varied, even diametrically opposed—and at the same time equally correct. How many commentaries have already been written on *Hamlet*, and how many are yet to appear in the future! How many different conclusions has the study of this essentially inexhaustible work reached! *Don Quixote*, by the very nature of its task, by the truly magnificent clarity of its narrative—as if it were illuminated by the southern sun—offers less basis for discussion. Unfortunately, we Russians do not have a good translation of *Don Quixote;* the greater part of us retain a fairly vague impression of it. By the term "Don Quixote" we often simply mean "a joke";

the word "quixoticism" in Russian is equivalent to the word "absurdity," although it would actually be appropriate for us to use the term "quixoticism" to acknowledge the lofty principle of self-sacrifice, even if this principle is viewed from a comic perspective. A good translation of *Don Quixote* would constitute a true service to our public, and general gratitude awaits the writer who transmits this singular work to us in all its beauty. But let us return to the subject of our discussion.

We have said that the almost simultaneous appearance of *Don Quixote* and *Hamlet* strikes us as remarkable because it seems to us that two fundamental, and fundamentally opposed, qualities of human nature are presented in the two character types portrayed—the two poles of the axis on which that nature turns. It seems to us that every individual more or less belongs to one of these two types, that virtually every one of us inclines either toward Don Quixote or toward Hamlet. To be sure, there are far more Hamlets than Don Quixotes in our time, but there is never a lack of Don Quixotes either.

Let us explain.

All people live—consciously or unconsciously—on the strength of their commitment to their principles, to their ideals—that is, to what they consider the true, the beautiful, the good. Many people receive their ideals already perfectly formed, in delimited, historically determined shape; they live, envisioning their lives in terms of these ideals, occasionally departing from them under the influence of passion or accident, but never evaluating them, never doubting them. Others, by contrast, subject their ideals to the analysis of their own intellects. However that may be, it seems that we are not wholly mistaken if we say that, for all of us, these ideals, which provide the foundations and goals of existence, are to be found either within ourselves or outside ourselves. In other words, these ideals, which are of paramount importance for each of us, are rooted either inside us, in each individual ego, or else outside us, in something we acknowledge to be higher. One could reply to us that actuality does not permit such narrow distinctions, that both types of ideals can coexist and can even converge to a certain degree in one and the same living being. But we do not intend to allege the impossibility of variation and contradiction in human nature. We merely want to suggest two different ways in which people derive their ideals—and we shall now try to represent how, as we understand it, these two different ways of deriving them are embodied in the two character types we have identified.

Let us begin with Don Quixote.

What qualities does Don Quixote embody? Let us not consider him with the patient gaze that lingers over superficialities and petty details. We shall look at Don Quixote not simply as the knight of the sad countenance, as a figure created in order to poke fun at ancient courtly novels. It is well known that this character's significance was greatly enhanced by the distinctive hand of his immortal creator, and that the Don Quixote of the novel's second part, the gracious interlocutor of the duke and duchess, is no longer the Don Quixote of the novel's first part—especially not the one at the beginning—is no longer that strange, silly eccentric on whom blows so generously fall. But we must therefore seek to penetrate to the very heart of the matter. We repeat: what qualities does Don Quixote embody? Faith, above all, faith in something eternal and immutable—in a word, in truth, in the truth that exists outside the individual but is easily discovered by him, the truth that demands service and sacrifice, but is worthy of constant service and profound sacrifice.

Don Quixote is utterly imbued with a commitment to ideals for which he is ready to go to all possible extremes, even to sacrifice his life. He only values this life to the extent that it can serve as a means of promulgating those ideals, of securing truth and justice on earth. It has been said to us that his disturbed mind derived his ideals from the fantastical world of courtly novels. We agree—and this is what constitutes the comic side of Don Quixote. But the ideals themselves endure in all their untainted purity. To live for oneself, to care only for oneself—Don Quixote would have deemed this cowardly. He lived (if one may use that term) wholly outside himself, on behalf of others, on behalf of his fellow human beings, dedicated to the eradication of evil, to the opposition of the forces ranged against humanity—magicians and giants—which is to say, oppressors. There is not the slightest trace of egoism in him; he does not worry about himself; he is all self-sacrifice—treasure that word! He believes, and believes strongly, without reservation. As a result, he is patient and long-suffering, he accepts the most meager food, the most shabby clothing—he is indifferent to such things. Simple of heart, he is great and bold of spirit; his benign resignation does not constrain his freedom. Foreign to vanity, he has no doubts about himself, about his purpose, even about his physical prowess; his will is an unbending will. Constant striving toward one and the same goal imparts a certain singularity to his thoughts, a one-sidedness to his mind; he knows little—but then, he does not need to know much. He knows what matters to him, he knows why he is alive on earth—and this is the most important knowledge of all.

Don Quixote can occasionally seem utterly insane, because the most indubitable physical phenomenon disappears before his eyes, melted like a wax candle by his enthusiasm (he really sees live Moors in wood puppets and knights in sheep). He can occasionally seem limited, because he can neither lightly sympathize with anyone nor lightly enjoy anything. But, like an ancient tree, he has dug his roots deeply into the soil, and he is inherently incapable of betraying his convictions or of transferring them from one object to another. The strength of his moral composition (notice that this mad, wandering knight is the most moral element in his universe) gives special power and majesty to all his judgments and speeches, to his entire persona, despite the comic and humiliating situations into which he repeatedly lapses. . . . Don Quixote is an enthusiast, the servant of an idea, and is therefore encompassed by its aura.

What qualities does Hamlet embody?

Analysis above all, and egoism—hence disbelief. He lives completely for himself; he is truly an egoist. And an egoist cannot even believe in himself—he can only believe in that which is outside of and superior to any individual. But this ego, in which he cannot believe, is precious to Hamlet. It is a point of departure to which he constantly returns, because he cannot find anything in the entire world to which his soul can cling. He is a skeptic—and he eternally struggles with himself. He is incessantly occupied with his own condition, not with his obligations. Doubting everything, Hamlet understandably does not spare even himself; his mind is too well-developed to be satisfied with what he finds within himself. He is conscious of his own weaknesses, but all self-consciousness makes for strength—thence proceeds his sarcasm, the opposite of Don Quixote's enthusiasm. Hamlet excessively enjoys berating himself, endlessly enjoys observing himself, eternally enjoys looking within himself. He knows all his inadequacies down to the finest detail. He loathes them, he loathes himself—and at the same time, he thrives on this loathing; one may say, he feeds upon it. He does not believe in himself—and he is vain; he does not know what he wants or why he is alive—and he is attached to life. . . .

Thus, in the second scene of the first act, Hamlet exclaims:

O that this too too sullied flesh would melt,
Thaw, and resolve itself into a dew!
Or that the Everlasting had not fix'd
His canon 'gainst self-slaughter! O God, God,
How weary, stale, flat, and unprofitable
Seem to me all the uses of this world!

But he does not forsake this flat and unprofitable life. He dreams of suicide only until his father's ghost appears, until he embarks upon the dangerous mission that definitively demolishes his already broken will—but he does not kill himself. Love of life is expressed in those very dreams of ending it. Every eighteen-year-old youth is familiar with such feelings: "Now the blood boils, now energy overflows." But we shall not be too hard on Hamlet. He suffers— and his sufferings are more painful and more piercing than Don Quixote's sufferings. The crude shepherds and criminals that Don Quixote frees beat him, whereas Hamlet inflicts his own wounds; Hamlet tears himself to pieces. He also carries a sword in his hands: the double-edged sword of analysis.

Don Quixote, we must concede, is thoroughly ridiculous. His figure comes close to being the most comical figure ever portrayed in literature. His name has become a comic sobriquet even in the mouths of Russian peasants—we have heard his name used this way with our own ears. The mere mention of the name arouses in one's imagination the vision of an emaciated, angular, hook-nosed figure dressed in outlandish armor, borne on the sunken skeleton of a pathetic horse, that poor, eternally hungry and wretched Rosinante, to whom it is impossible to deny some half-jocular, half-heartfelt sympathy. Don Quixote is comical . . . but there is conciliatory, redemptive power in his comicality. And if it is not said in vain, "What you laugh at is what you serve," then one can add that whomever you laugh at you have already forgiven, and have even begun to love.

Hamlet, by contrast, has an attractive appearance. His melancholy and pale, if not thin, visage (his mother remarks of him, "Our son is fat"), his black velvet clothes, the pen in his hat, his elegant manners, the indubitable poetry of his speeches, his unwavering sense of absolute superiority over others in conjunction with his piercing, sarcastic self-deprecation—all of these attributes are pleasing, all of them are captivating. It is flattering to someone to be taken for Hamlet; no one would want to deserve the appel-

lation Don Quixote. "Hamlet Baratynskii," Pushkin called one
friend of his. No one even thinks of laughing at Hamlet—and this
is precisely his curse: it is virtually impossible to like him. Only
such people as Horatio are drawn to Hamlet—we shall speak about
them later. Everyone sympathizes with Hamlet, and this is understandable: almost everyone finds characteristics of their own in
him. But it is impossible to like him, we repeat, because he does
not like himself.

Let us continue our comparison. Hamlet is the son of a king
who was killed by his own brother, a pretender to the throne; his
father comes to Hamlet from the grave, from "the jaws of hell,"
in order to command Hamlet to avenge him, but Hamlet hesitates,
he rationalizes, he takes pleasure in criticizing himself, and he
ultimately kills his stepfather by accident. This is a profound psychological portrait, for which many highly intelligent but myopic
people have dared to condemn Shakespeare! Whereas Don Quixote,
who is impoverished—is nearly a beggar, lacking any wealth or
connections—old and isolated, takes it upon himself to punish evil,
to aid distressed individuals (completely unknown to him) throughout the entire world. What difference does it make that his first
attempt to free the innocent from their oppressors brings down a
double misfortune on the head of the most innocent? (We are
thinking of the scene in which Don Quixote rescues a boy from a
beating by his master, who, after the rescuer's departure, punishes
the poor lad ten times more severely.) What difference does it make
that, thinking he is confronting dangerous giants, Don Quixote
attacks windmills? . . . The comic exterior of these images need not
direct our eyes away from the meaning concealed behind them. He
who, in preparing to sacrifice himself, would first decide to enu-
merate and weigh all the consequences, all the probabilities of the
success of his behavior, is hardly capable of self-sacrifice.

Nothing like this could happen to Hamlet. Could he, with his
insightful, acute, skeptical mind, make such a crude mistake? No—
he would not tilt at windmills. He does not believe in giants . . .
but he would not attack them even if they actually did exist. Hamlet
would not begin to affirm, as Don Quixote does when he shows
the barber's basin to everyone, that this is actually Mambrino's
magic helmet. But we suggest that if the truth were set forth before
his very eyes, in person, Hamlet would not allow himself to believe
that this was really it, really the truth. . . . For, who knows? Perhaps
there is no truth, just as there are no giants. We laugh at Don

Quixote . . . but, ladies and gentlemen, who among us, if we examine ourselves, our past and present convictions, can confidently affirm with a clear conscience that in every instance he can always distinguish and has always distinguished a barber's tin basin from a magic golden helmet? Thus it seems to us that any and all significance lies in the sincerity and strength of one's convictions . . . with the result that one's fate rests in one's own hands. Those convictions alone can show us whether we have struggled with phantoms or with real enemies, they alone can reveal with what shield we have covered our heads. . . . Our task is to arm ourselves, and to do battle.

The attitudes of the people, the so-called masses, toward Hamlet and Don Quixote are also noteworthy.

Polonius represents the masses to Hamlet; Sancho Panza represents the masses to Don Quixote. Polonius is a businesslike, practical, healthy-minded, although at the same time limited and loquacious old man. He is an excellent administrator, a model father: remember his advice to his son Laertes prior to Laertes's departure abroad, advice that can be compared in wisdom to the famous decrees of Governor Sancho Panza on the island of Barataria. For Polonius, Hamlet is not so much mad as he is a child, and if Hamlet were not the king's son, Polonius would despise him for his fundamental uselessness, for the impossibility of any affirmative, constructive application of Hamlet's ideas. The famous scene in which Hamlet and Polonius discuss the clouds—the scene in which Hamlet decides to make a fool of the old man—clearly underscores our interpretation. . . . We shall permit ourselves to remind you of it:

> *Polonius.* My lord, the queen would speak
>   with you, and presently.
> *Hamlet.* Do you see yonder cloud that's almost
>   in shape of a camel?
> *Polonius.* By th' mass and 'tis, like a camel
>   indeed.
> *Hamlet.* Methinks it is like a weasel.
> *Polonius.* It is backed like a weasel.
> *Hamlet.* Or like a whale.
> *Polonius.* Very like a whale.
> *Hamlet.* Then I will come to my mother by and by.

Is it not clear in this scene that Polonius is simultaneously the courtier humoring a prince and the adult not wishing to contradict a sick, capricious child? Polonius does not believe Hamlet one bit—and Polonius is right. With all his typical, circumscribed self-assurance, he attributes Hamlet's capriciousness to a love for Ophelia. In this, of course, Polonius is mistaken, but he is not mistaken in his assessment of Hamlet's character. Hamlets are indeed useless to the masses; Hamlets do nothing for the masses; Hamlets lead them nowhere, because Hamlets themselves go nowhere. Just so, for how can one lead without knowing whether there is ground under one's feet? Moreover, Hamlet despises the masses—who can respect someone failing to return that respect? And is it even worth worrying about the masses? They are so vulgar and dirty; Hamlet, by contrast, is an aristocrat, and not by birth alone.

Sancho Panza presents a completely different spectacle. For he laughs at Don Quixote—he knows very well that Don Quixote is mad. Nonetheless, Sancho Panza leaves his native land, his home, his wife, and his daughter in order to accompany this madman three times. He follows Don Quixote everywhere, undergoes every sort of unpleasantness, is dedicated to him unto death itself, believes in him, is proud of him, and sobs worshipfully at the pitiful bed where his former master lies dying. It is impossible to ascribe this devotion to the expectation of gain or personal profit. Sancho Panza has too much good sense; he knows perfectly well that, aside from beatings, the squire of the wandering knight has virtually nothing to hope for. It is necessary to search deeper for the cause of this devotion. It is rooted, if one may express it thus, in arguably the best qualities of the masses: their capacity for felicitous, honorable blindness (other types of blindness are also well known to it, alas!), in their capacity for unmitigated enthusiasm, and in their hatred of direct personal profit, a hatred that is almost as strong in a poor individual as is the hatred for plain bread. These are great, universal qualities!

The masses always end up wholeheartedly believing and following those individuals whom they themselves mock, individuals whom they even curse and persecute, but individuals who, not fearing their curses or their persecution, not fearing even their laughter, continue steadily forward, having fastened a spiritual gaze on the only goal such individuals can see. Those individuals go forth, they fall, they rise, and at last they find . . . but, in fact, only he who follows his heart ever finds anything. "Great thoughts come from the heart," said Vauvenargues. But Hamlets find nothing, invent nothing, and leave no trace of themselves, except the trace of their own personalities. They leave no deeds behind them. They do not love, they do not believe—what can they possibly find? Even in chemistry (not to mention organic nature), in order for a third object to occur, it is necessary to unite two others. But Hamlets are always occupied solely with themselves; they are solitary, hence they are barren.

But someone will ask us: "What about Ophelia? Doesn't Hamlet love her?"

Let us speak about her—and also about Dulcinea. There is also much that is noteworthy regarding these two types of women.

Don Quixote loves Dulcinea, a nonexistent woman, and is ready to die for her. (Remember his words when, having been conquered, ground into the dust, he speaks to his conqueror after surrendering his lance to him: "Dulcinea del Toboso is the most beautiful woman in the world. I am the most unfortunate knight on earth, and it is not right that my weakness should diminish this truth. Stab me with your lance, knight, and deprive me of my life, since you have deprived me of my honor.") He loves purely, ideally—so ideally that he does not even suspect the object of his passion in no way exists; he loves so purely that, when Dulcinea appears before him in the form of a coarse, dirty peasant woman, he does not believe the evidence of his own eyes, and assumes that she has been transformed by an evil magician.

In our own time, in our travels, we ourselves have seen people die for an equally nonexistent Dulcinea, or for something coarse and often dirty, in which they have caught sight of their ideal, the transformation of which they also attribute to the influence of evil— we almost said "magicians"—evil incidents and evil individuals. We have seen such people—and when they pass away, may the book of history close on them forever! There will be nothing of interest to read. Don Quixote does not have the slightest trace of sensuality; all his dreams are shy and innocent; not even in the innermost recesses of his heart does he hope for an eventual union with Dulcinea—nor does he even desire that union!

But doesn't Hamlet love? Didn't his own ironic creator, the deepest prober of the human heart, decide to bestow a loving, devoted heart upon the egoist, the skeptic wholly permeated by the corrupting poison of analysis? Shakespeare did not admit this contradiction. It does not cost the observant reader much effort to become convinced that Hamlet is a sensual and even secretly vo-

luptuous person (the courtier Rosencrantz does not smile silently
for no reason at all when Hamlet says in his presence that he is
sick of women). Hamlet does not love; he merely pretends to love,
and does so offhandedly at that. We have the testimony of Shakespeare himself on this subject. In the first scene of the third act,
Hamlet says to Ophelia:

> *Hamlet.* . . . I did love you once.
> *Ophelia.* Indeed, my lord, you made me believe so.
> *Hamlet.* You should not have believ'd me. . . .
>   I loved you not.

In uttering these final words, Hamlet is much closer to the truth
than he suspects. His feelings toward Ophelia, an innocent creature
pure to the point of saintliness, are either cynical (remember his
words, his double entendre, during the scene of the theatrical performance, when he asks her permission to lie . . . at her feet) or
histrionic (note the scene between Hamlet and Laertes when Hamlet leaps into Ophelia's grave and utters a speech worthy of a
Bramarbas or Captain Pistol: "Forty thousand brothers / Could not
with all their quantity of love / Make up my sum. . . . let them
throw / Millions of acres on us . . . " and so forth). All his encounters with Ophelia have likewise been nothing more for him
than expressions of his self-absorption. And in his exclamation,
"Nymph, in thy orisons / Be all my sins remembered," we see
merely the profound consciousness of his own sickly impotence—
his inability to love—as it almost superstitiously worships before
"sacred purity."

But we have spoken enough about the darker aspects of the
Hamletic type, precisely those aspects which annoy us the most,
in the sense that they are closer and more comprehensible to us.
Now we shall try to elucidate what is valuable and therefore eternal
in him. A core of negativity is lodged in him, the very core that
another great poet, distinguishing it from all that is purely human,
presented to us in the image of Mephistopheles. Hamlet is also a
Mephistopheles, but a Mephistopheles incorporated within the live
realm of human nature. As a result, his negativity is not evil—it
is itself directed against evil. Hamlet's negativity doubts goodness,
but it does not doubt evil and enters into a fierce battle with it. It
doubts goodness—that is, it suspects its truth and sincerity—and
attacks it, not as evil, but as false goodness, under the guise of
which evil and falsity, its age-old enemies, are still hidden. Hamlet

does not laugh the demonic, merciless laugh of Mephistopheles; there is an element of dejection in his ever-so-bitter smile that bespeaks his sufferings, and therefore reconciles us with him.

Moreover, Hamlet's skepticism does not bespeak indifference, and his significance, his worth, consists in this fact: he does not collapse good and evil, truth and falsehood, beauty and ugliness, into one random, mute, meaningless, nameless entity. Hamlet's skepticism, his disbelief in the contemporary realization of truth, so to speak, implacably battles with falsehood and, by means of that battle, becomes one of the main combatants on behalf of the truth in which he cannot completely believe. But in negation, as in fire, there is a destructive force—and it is difficult to know how to contain that force within limits, how to direct it, or precisely where to stop it, when that which it must destroy and that which it must defend often conflate, often seamlessly join. This is what so often appears to us to be the remarkably tragic side of human life: both will and thought are required for action, but will and thought are separated, and with each passing day they separate further. "And thus the native hue of resolution / Is sicklied o'er by the pale cast of thought," Shakespeare says to us through Hamlet's lips. And so, on the one side stand Hamlets as rational, deliberate, often perceptive individuals, but often also as useless individuals condemned to inaction; on the other side—half-mad Don Quixotes, who can only bestir and thus are only of use to people who see and know a single goal, which frequently does not even exist in the form they perceive it. Questions instinctively arise: Is it necessary to be mad in order to believe in truth? Does the mind that has controlled itself deprive itself of all its strength in so doing?

Even a superficial discussion of these questions would take us far afield. We shall confine ourselves to the observation that in this separation, in the duality we have observed, we must acknowledge an elemental law of all human life: this life, in sum, is nothing more than the eternal reconciliation and eternal opposition of two ceaselessly separating and ceaselessly converging cores. If we were not afraid to offend your ears with philosophical terms, we would permit ourselves to say that Hamlets constitute the expression of the elemental centripetal force of nature, according to which every living thing considers itself the center of creation and considers all else to be things that exist solely in order to benefit this center. (Thus the mosquito, having landed on the forehead of Alexander of Macedonia, sucked his blood as its appropriate food, calmly convinced of its right to do so. Exactly thus does Hamlet—although he despises himself as the mosquito does not, for it has not risen to this height—exactly thus does Hamlet, we say, constantly relate everything to himself.) Without this centripetal force (the force of egoism), nature itself could not exist, just as it could not exist without another, centrifugal force, according to which everything that exists does so in order to benefit something else. (This force, this principle of devotion and sacrifice, illuminated, as we have already said, in a comic light—so as not to strike too close to home— is represented by Don Quixote.) These two forces—of inertia and of motion, of conservation and of progress—constitute the fundamental forces of all that exists. They explain the growth of flowers to us, and they even enable us to comprehend the development of the most powerful nations.

We hasten to move beyond these potentially inappropriate speculations to some considerations more appropriate for us to discuss.

It is well known that, of all Shakespeare's works, *Hamlet* is quite possibly the most popular. This tragedy belongs to the group of plays that unfailingly fill theaters every time. The contemporary condition of our society, its striving for self-awareness and self-comprehension, its doubts about itself and its youth, all make this phenomenon understandable. But, even without discussing the beauties with which this perhaps most distinguished product of an innovative spirit is overflowing, it is impossible not to be amazed at the genius who, being himself in many ways akin to Hamlet, distinguished himself from Hamlet by the free exercise of creative power—and set forth Hamlet's image for the eternal study of generations to come. The spirit that gave rise to this image is the spirit of a northern individual, a spirit of reflection and analysis, a ponderous, gloomy spirit, one deficient in harmony and bright colors, a spirit not surrounded by elegant, often subtle, forms, but a deep, strong, multifaceted, independent, commanding spirit nonetheless. This spirit extracted the essence of the Hamletic type from the very core of its own being. And in so doing, it demonstrated that in the realm of literature, as in other realms of national life, the parent is superior to its offspring, because the former completely comprehends the latter.

The spirit of the southern individual determined the composition of Don Quixote. It is a bright, cheerful, naive, receptive spirit, one not plumbing the depths of life, not subsuming, but rather reflecting all its phenomena. We cannot resist the temptation here, if not to draw a parallel between Shakespeare and Cervantes, merely to indicate several points of similarity and difference between them. Some may ask, what sort of comparison can there be between Shakespeare and Cervantes? Shakespeare is a giant, a demigod.... Yes, but Cervantes is not a pygmy in comparison to the giant who composed *King Lear.* Cervantes is a human being, a complete human being—and a human being has the right to stand on his feet even before a demigod. Shakespeare unquestionably overwhelms Cervantes—and not only Cervantes—in the wealth and power of his imagination, in the brilliance of his finest poetry, in the depth and breadth of his enormous intellect. But you will not find in Cervantes's novel the strained witticisms, the unnatural similes, or the artificial conceits you find in Shakespeare. Nor will you find on Cervantes's pages the severed heads, the ripped-out eyes, all those torrents of blood, all that implacable, blatant cruelty—the vast heritage of the Middle Ages—the barbarism that took longer to disappear in stubborn, northern natures. To be sure, Cervantes, like Shakespeare, was alive during St. Bartholomew's Night; heretics were still burned and blood was spilled long after that—and indeed, when will it cease to be spilled?

The Middle Ages are expressed in *Don Quixote* by the gleam of Provençal poetry, by the fabled references to those very novels at which Cervantes laughed so good-naturedly and to which he himself paid a final tribute in *Persiles and Sigismunda.* (It is well known that the courtly novel *Persiles and Sigismunda* appeared *after* the first part of *Don Quixote.*) Shakespeare takes his images from everywhere— from the heavens, from the earth; nothing is barred to him, nothing can evade his all-penetrating gaze. He grasps everything with irresistible strength, with the strength of an eagle seizing its prey. Cervantes gently displays his few images before his readers the way a father displays his children. He portrays only what is close to him—but how well he knows what is close to him! Everything human seems subject to the powerful genius of the English poet; Cervantes draws his wealth from his spirit alone, a spirit that is pure, and sweet, and rich with life experience, but not embittered by it. In the course of a terrible seven-year captivity, Cervantes did not study the science of patience, as he himself put it, in vain. The circle he encompasses is narrower than Shakespeare's, but within it, as within every separate living being, is manifested all that is human. Cervantes does not blind you with the lightning flash of a word; he does not astonish you with the titanic strength of his triumphant inspiration. His poetry is not the Shakespearean, sometimes murky, sea; it is a deep river, calmly flowing between varied shores—and his reader, gradually distracted, charmed on all sides by its transparent waves, gladly gives himself over to the truly epic silence and smoothness of its flow.

The imagination eagerly summons before itself the images of both these poet-contemporaries, who died on the very same day, April 26, 1616. Cervantes probably knew nothing of Shakespeare, but the great tragedian, in the quietude of the Stratfordshire home where he retreated three years before his death, could have read the remarkable novel, which had already been translated into English at that time. . . . The image is worthy of the hand of a painter-intellectual: Shakespeare reading *Don Quixote!* Happy are the countries in which such individuals, teachers of contemporary and future generations, arise! The everlasting laurel wreaths by which great human beings are crowned also lie on the brows of their nations.

Concluding our far from complete study, we beg permission to convey a few more specific observations to you.

In our presence once, an English lord (a fine judge in these matters) cast Don Quixote in the image of a true gentleman. In fact, if simplicity and sedateness of manner serve as reliable signs of such a so-called decent individual, Don Quixote has a perfect right to this appellation. He is a true hidalgo, a hidalgo even when the duke's amused servants wash his face all over. The simplicity of his manner proceeds from the absence of what we have decided to call not self-love but self-respect. Don Quixote is not self-absorbed, and yet he has respect for himself and others. He does not dream of showing off, whereas Hamlet, it seems to us, amid all his elegant surroundings, has the airs—excuse the French expression—of a parvenu; he is morose, sometimes to the point of rudeness; he poses; he mocks. To be sure, he is endowed with the virtue of uniquely keen verbal expressiveness, a virtue typical of every thinking, self-cultivating individual—a virtue therefore utterly inappropriate to Don Quixote. Hamlet's analytical depth and subtlety, in addition to his broad education (one must not forget that he studied at the University of Wittenberg), bestowed upon him almost infallible taste. He is a superlative critic; his advice to the actors is astoundingly astute and apropos; the feel for refinement in him is almost as strong as the feel for duty in Don Quixote.

Don Quixote deeply respects all existing institutions, religions, monarchs, and dukes; at the same time, he is free, and acknowledges the freedom of others. Hamlet scorns kings and courtiers—and is in essence oppressive and intolerant. Don Quixote barely knows grammar; Hamlet probably kept a diary. Don Quixote, for all his ignorance, has a defined concept of governance, of administration; Hamlet never studies such things, and never has any reason to.

Many have protested against the endless battles with which Cervantes burdened Don Quixote, and we have noted in this regard that no one beats the poor knight any longer in the second part of the novel. But we shall add that, without these battles, he would have been less pleasing to children, who read about his exploits with such avidity—and he would not have appeared in his true light even to us adults, but would have seemed somehow cold and arrogant, which would have contradicted his character. We have just said that no one beats him any longer in the second part, but at its very end—after the Knight of the Moon's decisive defeat of Don Quixote, when he has dressed anew as a student—after his recantation of knighthood, not long before his death, a herd of swine tramples his legs. We have had occasion to hear reproaches directed toward Cervantes on this account more than once—why did he include this scene, as if he were merely repeating old, shopworn jokes? But here Cervantes was ruled by the instinct of genius—and beneath the very ugliness of this adventure lies a profound truth. In the lives of Don Quixotes, swine trample their legs all the time—especially just before those lives end. This is the final tribute such individuals must pay to coarse randomness, to indifferent, insolent incomprehension.... This is the scorn of the Pharisees.... Then Don Quixotes can die. They have passed through all the fires of the crucible. They have won immortality for themselves—and it opens up before them....

Upon occasion, Hamlet is crafty and even cruel. Remember the death he planned for the king's two courtiers who were sent to England; remember his speech about Polonius after killing him. Again we see here, as we have already noted, an expression of the Middle Ages, which had ended not long before. We are obliged to underscore the contrasting inclination to semiconscious, semi-innocuous deceit, to self-delusion, in the honorable, righteous Don Quixote—an inclination almost always attendant upon the fantasies of the enthusiast. He clearly invents his story about what he saw in the cave of Montesinos, and does not deceive the clever, simple Sancho Panza.

Hamlet's spirit often flags, and he complains at the least lack of success, whereas Don Quixote, beaten black and blue by rows of criminals until he cannot move, entertains not the slightest doubt in the success of his undertaking. Thus, they say, for the course of many years Fourier went out every day hoping to meet an Englishman whom he had summoned in the newspapers by promising to pay him a million francs for bringing Fourier's plans to fulfillment but who, understandably, never appeared. This is undoubtedly very funny, but here is what comes to mind: the ancients called their gods envious—and in time of need considered it useful to mollify them with voluntary sacrifices (remember the ring thrown into the sea by Policrates). Why shouldn't we consider it one of the requisite duties of a comic author to add to the deeds—to the very character—of a people summoned to perform some great new action by offering a gift, a soothing sacrifice to the envious gods? For without those comic Don Quixotes, without those eccentric explorers, humanity would not move forward—and Hamlets would have nothing to contemplate.

Yes, we repeat: Don Quixotes explore—Hamlets exploit. But how, they ask us, can Hamlets exploit anything, when they doubt everything and don't believe in anything? To this we reply that, according to the sagacious arrangement of nature, pure Hamlets, just like pure Don Quixotes, do not exist: these are only the extreme expressions of two tendencies, markers placed by poets on two different paths. Life strives toward them, but never reaches them. One must not forget that, just as the principle of analysis is turned into tragedy in Hamlet, so the principle of enthusiasm is likewise turned into comedy in Don Quixote. But in life, the purely comic and the purely tragic are rarely encountered.

Hamlet gains much in our eyes from Horatio's attachment to him. This type of character is charming, appearing fairly often in our time—to the credit of our time. In Horatio, we recognize the character of the follower, the student in the best sense of the term. With a stoic, forthright temperament, an ardent heart, and a somewhat limited intellect, he senses his inadequacies and is therefore humble, as infrequently occurs with limited people. He thirsts for instruction, for direction, and reveres the intelligent Hamlet as a result, devoting himself to Hamlet with all the strength of his honorable spirit, not even requiring reciprocity. Horatio submits to Hamlet not because Hamlet is a prince but because he is a leader. One of the most important virtues of Hamlets lies in the fact that they mold and stimulate individuals like Horatio, individuals who, having obtained the seeds of thought from them, fertilize those seeds in their hearts and then distribute them throughout the world. The words by which Hamlet acknowledges Horatio's significance do honor to Hamlet himself. For he expresses in them his own sense of the exalted value of the individual, as well as the noble aspirations he himself harbors, which no skepticism can diminish in strength. "Dost thou hear?" he says to Horatio:

> Since my dear soul was mistress of her choice
> And could of men distinguish her election,
> S'hath sealed thee for herself, for thou hast been
> As one in suff'ring all that suffers nothing,
> A man that Fortune's buffets and rewards
> Hast ta'en with equal thanks; and blest are those
> Whose blood and judgment are so well commeddled
> That they are not a pipe for Fortune's finger
> To sound what stop she please. Give me that man
> That is not passion's slave, and I will wear him
> In my heart's core, ay, in my heart of hearts,
> As I do thee.

The honorable skeptic always respects the stoic. When the ancient world—and every epoch like that epoch—fell apart, the best people were saved by stoicism, as the sole refuge in which it was still possible to preserve human dignity. The skeptics, if they did not have the strength to die, "set off for that country from which no traveler returns"—they made themselves into Epicureans! A phenomenon that is comprehensible, and sad, and all too familiar to us!

Both Hamlet and Don Quixote die touchingly, but how different are their deaths! The last words of Hamlet are superb. He grows calm and quiet, commands Horatio to live, lends his dying voice in support of young Fortinbras, the wholly untarnished representative of the right of inheritance . . . but the gaze of Hamlet does not turn forward. . . . "The rest is silence," says the dying skeptic— and he is indeed silenced forever. The death of Don Quixote casts an unspoken pall over the spirit. In that moment, the total, vast significance of this character becomes apparent to everyone. When his former squire, wishing to comfort him, tells him that they will soon depart again on a knightly expedition, the dying man replies: "Let us go gradually, for there are no birds today in the nests of yesterday. I was mad, but now I am sane. I was Don Quixote de la Mancha, but I am now Alonso Quixano the Good, as I have said. With your mercy, may my repentance and honesty return me to the estimation in which you once held me."

This admission is astonishing; the mention of this appellation, for the first and last time, shocks the reader. Yes, this admission alone still has significance in the face of death. Everything will pass, everything will disappear—the most noble rank, the most supreme power, the most all-encompassing genius—everything will scatter into dust. . . .

> Everything of earthly greatness
> Will float away, like smoke. . . .

But good deeds do not float away like smoke; they are more enduring than the most shining beauty. "Everything changes," said the Apostle. "Only love remains."

There is nothing for us to add after these words. We shall consider ourselves fortunate if, by the mention of these two elemental tendencies of the human spirit, we have awakened some ideas in you—even if they are ideas that perhaps do not accord with our own—fortunate if we have thereby fulfilled our task, albeit approximately, and if we have not overly taxed your kind attention.

Letter to M. N. Katkov.[1]

Paris.

Oct. 30, 1861.

Dear Mikhail Nikiforovich, I recently wrote to you, but after receiving your letter yesterday, I consider it necessary to reply to you briefly. I agree with your remarks—with almost all of them—especially regarding Pavel Petrovich and Bazarov himself. As for Odintsova, the vague impression produced by that character shows me that I still need to work a little on her, too. (By the way, the *argument* between P.P. and Bazarov has been completely redone and shortened.) It's obvious that the tale, by reason of present circumstances, and as a result of its internal lack of finish, must be put aside—*for the time being*—with which you too will agree. I'm very sorry that things have turned out this way, but with such a subject, one must appear before the reader as fully armed as possible. I want to look over all of it at leisure and replow it. I presume that all the difficulties—internal and external—that *now* exist will disappear by the time I return to Russia, i.e., by spring (by April)—and I'll finally succeed in letting this child out into the world.

There's one thing with which I can't agree: Mrs. Odintsov shouldn't be mocking, nor should the peasant stand above Bazarov, even if he himself is empty and sterile.... Perhaps my view of Russia is more misanthropic than you suppose: he—in my eyes—is really a hero of our time. "What a hero and what a time," you'll say.... But that's the way it is.

I repeat my request about keeping my work under lock and key. I clasp your hand firmly and remain

Your devoted
Iv. Turgenev.

---

1. Mikhail Nikiforovich Katkov (1818-87), editor of *The Russian Messenger.*

Fathers and Sons

Dedicated to the memory of Vissarion Grigorevich Belinskii

I

"Well, Petr, no sight of him yet?" asked a gentleman about forty years old wearing a short, dusty coat and checkered trousers, standing hatless on the low steps of an inn on the *** road. It was the twentieth of May 1859. He was addressing his servant, a round-cheeked young man with whitish down on his chin and small, lackluster eyes.

The servant, whose turquoise earring, variegated hair plastered with grease, and refined movements all betokened a man belonging to the newest, most advanced generation, glanced down the road condescendingly, and replied: "No, sir, no sight of him at all."

"No sight of him?" repeated his master.

"No, sir," the servant responded a second time.

His master sighed and sat down on a little bench. Let's introduce him to the reader while he sits looking around thoughtfully, his feet tucked up underneath him.

His name is Nikolai Petrovich Kirsanov. He owns a fine estate located fifteen versts from the inn that has two hundred serfs or, as he puts it—ever since he arranged to share his land with the peasants—"a farm" of nearly five thousand acres. His father, an army general who served during 1812, was a coarse, half-educated, but not villainous Russian. He worked hard all his life, first commanding a brigade, then a division, and lived continually in the provinces where, by virtue of his rank, he played a fairly important role. Nikolai Petrovich was born in the south of Russia, as was his elder brother, Pavel, of whom more later. He was educated at home until he was fourteen, surrounded by underpaid tutors and casually obsequious adjutants, in addition to all the usual regimental and staff personnel. His mother, a member of the Koliazin family, was called Agathe as a girl but Agafokleia Kuzminishna Kirsanova as a general's wife. She was one of those "mother-commanders" who wore elaborate caps and rustling silk dresses. In church, she was the first to advance to kiss the cross; she talked a great deal in a loud voice; she let her children kiss her hand in the morning and gave them her blessing at night—in a word, she conducted her life just as she pleased.

As a general's son, Nikolai Petrovich was expected, like his brother Pavel, to enter the army, although he not only lacked courage but even deserved to be called a little coward. He broke his leg on the very day that word of his commission arrived, however, and had to lie in bed for two months, staying "gimpy" to the end of his days. His father gave up on him and let him pursue civilian life. He took Nikolai Petrovich to Petersburg as soon as his son was eighteen and enrolled him in the university. Pavel happened to have been made an officer in the Guards at about the same time. The young men started to live together in one apartment under the distant supervision of a cousin on their mother's side, Ilia Koliazin, a high-ranking official. Their father returned to his division and his wife, and every once in a while just sent his sons large gray sheets of paper with a military clerk's handwriting scrawled across them. At the bottom of these sheets, carefully encircled by a scroll design, were inscribed the words, "Petr Kirsanov, General-Major." In 1835, Nikolai Petrovich graduated from the university; General Kirsanov retired the same year after an unsuccessful review, and brought his wife to live in Petersburg. He was about to rent a house in the Tavricheskii garden and join the English Club when he suddenly died of a stroke. Agafokleia Kuzminishna died shortly thereafter—she couldn't ever accustom herself to the dull life of the capital; she was consumed by the emptiness of existence away from the regiment.

Meanwhile, before his parents' death and somewhat to their chagrin, Nikolai Petrovich had managed to fall in love with the daughter of his former landlord, a minor official named Prepolovenskii. She was a pretty and, as they say, advanced young woman; she used to read serious articles in the "Science" column of journals. He married her as soon as the mourning period for his parents was over. Having left the civil service, in which his father had procured him a position through his connections, Nikolai Petrovich lived with his Masha in perfect bliss, first in a country villa near the Lesnii Institute, then in a pretty little apartment in town that had a clean staircase and a chilly drawing room, and after that in the countryside, where he finally settled down and where within a short time his son, Arkadii, was born. The young couple lived quite happily and tranquilly. They were hardly ever apart; they read books together, they sang and played duets together on the piano. She tended her flowers and looked after the poultry-yard; he occasionally went hunting and busied himself with the estate. Arkadii grew up just as happily and tranquilly.

Ten years passed like a dream. In 1847, Kirsanov's wife died. He almost succumbed to this blow—his hair turned gray in the space of just a few weeks. He got ready to go abroad in order to distract his mind a bit...but then came the year 1848. He unwillingly returned to the countryside, and after a rather prolonged period of inactivity, he began to take an interest in improving the management of his estate. In 1855, he took his son to the university; he spent three winters with him in Petersburg, hardly going out anywhere and trying to make friends with Arkadii's youthful companions. He hadn't been able to go the previous winter—and thus we see him in May of 1859, already completely gray, somewhat stout, and slightly stooped. He was waiting for his son, who'd just graduated, as he'd once done himself.

The servant, motivated by a sense of propriety, and possibly not eager to remain under his master's eye anyway, had gone beyond the gate and was smoking a pipe. Nikolai Petrovich bowed his head and began to stare at the crumbling steps. A large, mottled hen walked toward him sedately, treading firmly on its long yellow legs; a muddy cat gave him an unfriendly look, coyly twisting itself around a railing. The sun was scorching; the odor of hot rye bread drifted out from the semidark passage of the inn. Nikolai Petrovich lapsed into daydreams. The words "my son...a graduate... Arkasha..." continually revolved in his head. He tried to think about something else, but the same thoughts kept recurring. He recalled his deceased wife.... "She didn't live to see this!" he murmured sadly. A plump, dark-blue pigeon flew into the road and hastily took a drink from a puddle near the well. Nikolai Petrovich began to watch it, but his ear had already caught the sound of approaching wheels.

"It seems that they're coming, sir," the servant announced, returning from the gateway.

Nikolai Petrovich jumped up and directed his gaze along the road. An open carriage with three horses harnessed abreast appeared; he caught a glimpse of the blue band of a student's cap and the familiar outline of a beloved face inside the carriage. "Arkasha! Arkasha!" Kirsanov cried and ran forward, waving his arms. . . . A few moments later, his lips were pressed against the beardless, dusty, sunburned cheek of the young graduate.

II

"Let me dust myself off first, Papa," Arkadii said in a voice that was tired from the journey but boyish and clear as a bell, as he cheerily responded to his father's caresses. "I'll get you all dirty."

"It's nothing, it's nothing," Nikolai Petrovich assured him, smiling tenderly and slapping the collar of his son's coat as well as his own twice with his hand. "Let me take a look at you, let me take a look at you," he added, stepping back from him; then he immediately hurried toward the courtyard of the inn, calling out, "This way, this way, and bring the horses at once."

Nikolai Petrovich seemed to be much more agitated than his son; it was as if he were a little lost, and a little shy. Arkadii stopped him.

"Papa," he said, "let me introduce you to my good friend, Bazarov, about whom I've written to you so often. He's been kind enough to promise to stay with us."

Nikolai Petrovich promptly turned around and, walking up to a tall man wearing a long, loose coat with tassels who'd just gotten out of the carriage, he warmly shook that man's bare, reddened hand, which hadn't been extended to him immediately.

"I'm extremely pleased," he began, "and grateful for your kind willingness to visit us. . . . May I ask your first name and patronymic?"

"Evgenii Vasilich," Bazarov answered in a lazy but powerful voice and, turning down the collar of his coat, revealed his entire face to Nikolai Petrovich. It was long and thin, with a broad forehead, a nose that was flat at the base and sharp at the tip, large greenish eyes, and drooping, sandy-colored sideburns. His face was illuminated by a calm smile, radiating self-assurance and intelligence.

"I hope you won't find it too boring at our home, dear Evgenii Vasilich," continued Nikolai Petrovich.

Bazarov's thin lips moved almost imperceptibly. He made no

formal reply and merely took off his cap. His long, thick, dark-blond hair couldn't conceal some large protuberances on his capacious head.

"Well then, Arkadii," Nikolai Petrovich began again, turning to his son, "should the horses be harnessed right away, or would you like to rest?"

"We'll rest at home, Papa. Tell them to harness the horses."

"Right away, right away," his father assented. "Hey, Petr, do you hear? Get everything ready, my boy—hurry now."

Petr, as an up-to-date servant, hadn't kissed the young master's hand but had merely bowed to him from a distance. He vanished through the gateway again.

"I came here with our carriage, but there are three horses for your carriage, too," Nikolai Petrovich remarked fussily, while Arkadii drank some water from an iron dipper the innkeeper brought to him and Bazarov began to smoke a pipe as he walked up to the coachman who was unharnessing the horses.

"It's only a two-seated carriage, and I don't know how your friend. . . ."

"He'll go in the open carriage," Arkadii interrupted in an undertone. "You mustn't stand on ceremony with him, please. He's a wonderful person, and utterly unpretentious—you'll see."

Nikolai Petrovich's driver brought out the fresh horses.

"Well, hurry up, bushy beard!" Bazarov urged, addressing the coachman.

"Do you hear what the gentleman called you, Mitiukha?" interjected another coachman who was standing nearby, his arms thrust behind him through a slit in his sheepskin coat. "It's a bushy beard you have, too."

Mitiukha merely tugged at his cap and pulled the reins off a sweaty shaft-horse.

"Faster, faster, boys, lend a hand," cried Nikolai Petrovich. "There'll be some vodka for you!"

The horses were harnessed within a few minutes; father and son were installed in the two-seated carriage; Petr climbed up onto its box; Bazarov jumped into the open carriage and nestled his head against a leather cushion—and both vehicles rolled away.

III

"So here you are, a university graduate at last, and you've come home," Nikolai Petrovich said, repeatedly touching Arkadii, first on the shoulder and then on the knee. "At last!"

"And how's my uncle? Is he well?" asked Arkadii. In spite of the genuine, almost childlike delight filling his heart, he wanted to shift the conversation from an emotional to an everyday tone as soon as possible.

"Quite well. He was considering coming with me to meet you, but for some reason or other he gave up on the idea."

"How long have you been waiting for me?" Arkadii inquired.

"Oh, about five hours."

"Dear old Papa!"

Arkadii energetically turned toward his father and planted a noisy kiss on his cheek. Nikolai Petrovich chuckled softly.

"I've got such a marvelous horse for you!" he began. "You'll see. And your room's been freshly wallpapered."

"But is there a room for Bazarov?"

"We'll find one for him, too."

"Please, Papa, make a fuss over him. I can't tell you how much I prize his friendship."

"Have you gotten to know him recently?"

"Yes, quite recently."

"Ah, that's why I didn't see him last winter. What's he's studying?"

"His main subject is the natural sciences. But he knows everything. Next year he wants to get a physician's diploma."

"Ah! He's in the department of medicine," Nikolai Petrovich observed, and he fell silent for a moment. "Petr," he began again, stretching out his hand, "aren't those our peasants going past?"

Petr looked where his master was pointing. Some carts harnessed with unbridled horses were rapidly rolling along a narrow side road. There were one or two peasants wearing unbuttoned sheepskin coats in each cart.

"Yes indeed, sir," Petr replied.

"Where are they going—to town?"

"To town, I should think. To the tavern," he added contemptuously, turning toward the driver slightly, as though appealing to him for reinforcement. But the latter didn't move a muscle; he was an old-fashioned individual, and didn't share the newest attitudes.

"I've had a lot of trouble with the peasants this year," Nikolai Petrovich continued, addressing his son. "They won't pay their rent. What can one do?"

"But are you satisfied with your hired laborers?"

"Yes," Nikolai Petrovich said between clenched teeth. "They're being turned against me, that's the problem—and they don't really try very hard. They spoil the tools. But they've tilled the land fairly well. When things have settled down a bit, it'll be all right. Are you interested in farming now?"

"You don't have any shade. That's a pity," remarked Arkadii, without answering the last question.

"I've had a large awning put up on the north side, above the balcony," Nikolai Petrovich noted. "Now we can even have dinner outside."

"That'd be too much like a summer dacha somehow.... Still, this is all trivial. What wonderful air there is here, though! How delicious it smells! Really, it seems to me there's no place on earth as fragrant as the regions around here! And the sky here...."

Arkadii suddenly stopped short, cast a stealthy glance behind him, and fell silent.

"Of course," Nikolai Petrovich observed, "you were born here, and so everything's bound to strike you in a special...."

"Come on, Papa, it doesn't matter where a person was born."

"But...."

"No, it doesn't matter at all."

Nikolai Petrovich gave his son a sidelong glance. The carriage traveled half a verst farther before the conversation between them was renewed.

"I don't recall whether I wrote to you," Nikolai Petrovich began, "that Egorovna, your old nursemaid, died."

"Really? Poor old woman! Is Prokofich still alive?"

"Yes, and he hasn't changed a bit—grumbles as much as ever. In fact, you won't find many changes at Marino."

"Do you still have the same bailiff?"

"Well, in fact, I've made a change there. I decided not to keep any emancipated serfs with me who'd been house servants, or at least not to entrust them with responsibilities of any significance." (Arkadii glanced toward Petr.) "*Il est libre, en effet*," Nikolai Petrovich commented under his breath, "but, you see, he's only a valet. So now I have a bailiff from town who seems to be a sensible person. I pay him two hundred and fifty rubles a year. But," Nikolai Petrovich added, rubbing his forehead and eyebrows with his hand, which always indicated some inner turmoil, "I just told you that you wouldn't find changes at Marino.... That's not quite true. I consider it my duty to warn you, although...."

He hesitated for an instant, and then continued in French.

"A strict moralist would regard my candor as improper, but, in the first place, this can't be concealed and, in the second, you're aware that I've always had unique ideas regarding the relationship between parent and child. Yet, of course, you'd be justified in condemning me. At my age.... In short, that ... that young woman about whom you've probably already heard...."

"Fenechka?" Arkadii asked casually.

Nikolai Petrovich blushed. "Please don't mention her name out loud.... Well ... she's living with me now. I've installed her in the house ... in two little rooms there. But that can all be changed."

"For heaven's sake, Papa, why?"

"Your friend's going to stay with us.... It might be awkward...."

"Please don't worry on Bazarov's account. He's above all that."

"Well, there's you, too," Nikolai Petrovich added. "The little lodge is so awful—that's the problem."

"For heaven's sake, Papa," Arkadii interjected, "it's as though you were apologizing. You ought to be ashamed."

"Of course I ought to be ashamed," Nikolai Petrovich responded, becoming more and more flushed.

"That's enough, Papa, that's enough. Please don't!" Arkadii smiled affectionately. "What a thing to apologize for!" he thought to himself, and his soul was filled with a feeling of condescending tenderness toward his kind, gentle father that was mixed with some sort of veiled sense of superiority. "Please stop," he insisted once more, instinctively reveling in the consciousness of his own progressiveness and freedom from prejudice.

Nikolai Petrovich glanced at him from behind the hand with which he was still rubbing his forehead, and felt a pang in his heart.... But he instantly blamed that on himself.

"Here are our fields at last," he observed after a long silence.

"And that's our forest ahead of us, isn't it?" Arkadii asked.

"Yes. Only I've sold it. They're going to cut it down this year."

"Why did you sell it?"

"We needed the money. Besides, that land will go to the peasants."

"The ones who don't pay you their rent?"

"That's their business. Anyway, they'll pay it someday."

"I'm sorry about the forest," Arkadii remarked, and he began to look around.

The countryside through which they were driving couldn't be

called picturesque. Field upon field stretched all the way to the very horizon, gently sloping upward in some spots, then slanting downward again in others; small forests were visible here and there; ravines covered with low, scanty bushes, reminiscent of their representations on ancient maps from the era of Catherine the Great, wound through the terrain. The travelers came across shallow streams with barren banks; tiny lakes with narrow dams; little villages with huts under dark, often decrepit roofs, rickety barns with woven brushwood walls and gaping doorways next to neglected threshing sheds; churches, some of which were brick, their plaster peeling off in patches, others of which were wood, their crosses hanging askew and their graveyards overgrown. Arkadii's heart slowly sank.

To complete the picture, the peasants they encountered were all shabbily dressed, riding the sorriest little ponies; the willows near the road, whose trunks had been stripped of bark and whose branches had been snapped, stood along the roadside like ragged beggars; emaciated, shaggy cows, pinched with hunger, were greedily tearing at the grass along the ditches—they looked as though they'd just been snatched from the murderous clutches of some hideous monster. The piteous aspect of the broken-down beasts in the midst of the lovely spring day evoked the white phantom of endless, dismal winter, with its storms, frosts, and snows. . . . "No," thought Arkadii, "this isn't a wealthy region, it doesn't impress one by its abundance of resources or its industry. It mustn't, it mustn't remain like this. Reforms are absolutely necessary . . . but how can one carry them out—how can one start . . . ?"

Such were Arkadii's reflections . . . yet even as he reflected, the springtime began to take hold of him. Everything all around him was golden-green, everything—trees, bushes, and grass—was shimmering, gently stirring in wide ripples under the soft breath of the warm breeze; the endless trilling of larks poured forth from all sides; peewits either called out as they hovered over the low-lying meadows or silently ran across the mounds of grass; crows strutted among the half-grown spring corn, standing out darkly against its tender verdure, and disappeared in the rye that had already turned slightly white, occasionally sticking their heads out from amid its hazy waves. Arkadii gazed steadily, his reflections gradually becoming less focused and fading away. . . . He flung off his coat and turned toward Nikolai Petrovich with a face so bright and boyish that his father gave him another hug.

"We're not far away now," Nikolai Petrovich remarked. "We

just have to go up this hill, and the house will be in sight. We'll get along beautifully together, Arkasha. You'll help me farm the estate, if that isn't too boring for you. We have to grow close to one another now, and get to know one another really well, don't we?"

"Of course," replied Arkadii. "But what a marvelous day it is today!"

"It's in honor of your arrival, my dear boy. Yes, it's spring in all its loveliness. Although I agree with Pushkin—do you remember, in *Eugene Onegin*:

> To me, how sad your advent is,
> Spring, spring, the time of love!
> What. . . .

"Arkadii," Bazarov's voice called out from his carriage, "pass me a match. I don't have anything to light my pipe with."

Nikolai Petrovich fell silent, while Arkadii, who'd begun to listen to him not without surprise, albeit not without sympathy either, hastily pulled a silver matchbox out of his pocket and passed it to Petr to transmit.

"Do you want a cigar?" Bazarov shouted out again.

"All right," Arkadii answered.

Petr returned to the carriage and handed him a thick black cigar along with the matchbox. Arkadii promptly began to smoke, diffusing such a strong, pungent odor of cheap tobacco that Nikolai Petrovich, who'd never smoked, was forced to turn his head away as imperceptibly as he could, for fear of offending his son.

A quarter of an hour later, the two vehicles came to a stop before the steps of a new, gray, wooden house with a red iron roof. This was Marino, also known as New Village or, as the peasants had nicknamed it, Poverty Farm.

IV

No crowd of house serfs ran out onto the steps to greet the gentlemen; no one but a little twelve-year-old girl appeared. Following behind her, a young man closely resembling Petr emerged from the house dressed in gray livery with white military buttons; he was Pavel Petrovich Kirsanov's personal servant. Without speaking, he opened the door of the two-seated carriage and unfastened the latch of the open carriage. Nikolai Petrovich accompanied his son and Bazarov down a dark, almost empty hall. They caught a glimpse of a young woman's face from behind a door before they entered a drawing room furnished in the most contemporary style.

"Here we are, at home," Nikolai Petrovich declared, taking off his cap and pushing his hair away from his forehead. "The most important thing now is to have some supper and to rest."

"Having something to eat wouldn't be a bad idea, in fact," Bazarov remarked, stretching his limbs and then sinking onto a sofa.

"Yes, yes, let's have supper, let's have supper as soon as possible." For no apparent reason, Nikolai Petrovich stamped his foot. "And here comes Prokofich just at the right moment."

A white-haired, thin, dark-complexioned man about sixty years old entered the room wearing a cinnamon-colored dress coat with brass buttons and a pink scarf around his neck. He beamed, went up to kiss Arkadii's hand, and then, bowing to the guest, retreated to the doorway and put his hands behind his back.

"Here he is, Prokofich," began Nikolai Petrovich. "He's come back to us at last. . . . Well, how does he look to you?"

"Never better, sir," responded the elderly man, beaming again, but he quickly knitted his bushy eyebrows. "Do you wish supper to be served?" he inquired impressively.

"Yes, yes, please. But wouldn't you like to go to your room first, Evgenii Vasilich?"

"No, thanks, I don't need to. Just have my little suitcase taken to it, along with this garment," he added, taking off his overcoat.

"Certainly. Prokofich, take the gentleman's coat." (Prokofich, as if bewildered, picked up Bazarov's "garment" in both hands and, holding it high above his head, retreated on tiptoe.) "And you, Arkadii, are you going to your room for a minute?"

"Yes, I want to wash up," Arkadii replied, and started to move toward the door, but at that instant a man of medium height, dressed in a dark English suit, a modishly short tie, and kid leather shoes, came into the drawing room. It was Pavel Petrovich Kirsanov. He appeared to be about forty-five; his short, gray hair shone with a dark luster, like new silver; his face was sallow but free of wrinkles, exceptionally even and fine-featured, as though carved by a light, delicate chisel, and contained traces of remarkable beauty; his clear, dark, almond-shaped eyes were especially attractive. In its aristocratic elegance, his entire body had preserved the gracefulness of youth and the impression of buoyancy, of the defiance of gravity, that's usually lost after one's twenties.

Pavel Petrovich extracted one of his exquisite hands with its long pink fingernails from his trouser pocket—a hand that seemed even more exquisite thanks to the snowy whiteness of the shirt cuff surrounding it, which was fastened by a single, large, opal cuff link—and offered it to his nephew. After a preliminary handshake in the European style, he kissed him three times in Russian fashion—that is to say, he touched Arkadii's cheek with his perfumed moustache three times—and said, "Welcome home."

Nikolai Petrovich introduced him to Bazarov. Pavel Petrovich greeted him with a slight inclination of his supple figure and a slight smile, but he didn't hold out his hand to Bazarov, and even put it back in his pocket.

"I'd begun to think you weren't coming today," he announced in a pleasing voice, nodding genially and shrugging his shoulders as he displayed his handsome white teeth. "Did anything happen on the road?"

"Nothing happened," Arkadii responded. "We just proceeded rather slowly. But we're as hungry as wolves now. Make Prokofich hurry, papa, and I'll come back right away."

"Wait, I'm coming with you," Bazarov cried, suddenly pulling himself up from the sofa. Both young men went out.

"Who is he?" asked Pavel Petrovich.

"A friend of Arkasha—according to him, an intelligent young man."

"Is he going to stay with us?"

"Yes."

"That long-haired creature?"

"Why, yes."

Pavel Petrovich drummed his fingertips on the table. "I imagine Arkadii *s'est dégourdi,*" he observed. "I'm glad he's come back."

At supper, there was little conversation. Bazarov in particular said almost nothing, but he ate a great deal. Nikolai Petrovich recounted various incidents in what he termed his career as a farmer, talked about impending government measures, committees, deputations, the necessity of introducing machinery, and so forth. Pavel Petrovich slowly paced up and down the dining room (he never ate supper), periodically sipping a glass of red wine and occasionally uttering some remark, or rather exclamation, of the sort "Ah! Aha! Hmm!" Arkadii conveyed some news from Petersburg, but he felt a slight sense of discomfort, the discomfort that frequently overcomes a young man when he's just ceased to be a child and then returns to a place where people are accustomed to consider him a child. He made his sentences unnecessarily long, avoided the word "Papa," and sometimes even replaced it with the word "Father"— mumbled between his teeth, it's true. With exaggerated carelessness, he poured far more wine into his glass than he really wanted, and drank it all up. Prokofich, continually chewing on his lips, didn't take his eyes off Arkadii. After supper, everyone promptly separated.

"Your uncle's rather eccentric," Bazarov said to Arkadii, as he sat by Arkadii's bedside in his robe, smoking a small pipe. "Can you imagine such dandyism in the countryside! His fingernails, now, his fingernails—you ought to send them to an exhibition!"

"Well, of course, you don't know about him," Arkadii replied. "He was a social lion in his own day. I'll tell you about his past sometime. He was very handsome, you know, and used to attract lots of women."

"Oh, so that's it, is it? He keeps it up as a memorial to the past. It's a pity that there's no one for him to fascinate here, though. I kept staring at his amazing collars—they're like marble—and his chin was shaved to perfection. Come on, Arkadii Nikolaich, isn't that ridiculous?"

"Probably, and yet he's really a decent person."

"He's an archaic phenomenon! But your father's a fine man. He wastes his time reading poetry and he doesn't know much about farming, but he's a good soul."

"My father's worth his weight in gold."

"Did you notice that he seemed shy?"

Arkadii nodded his head as though he himself weren't shy.

"It's astonishing," Bazarov continued. "These old romantics— they continuously refine their nervous systems until those systems break down ... so that their equanimity is destroyed. And now, good night. There's an English washstand in my room, but the door won't lock. Still, that ought to be encouraged—an English washstand means progress!"

Bazarov left, and a joyous feeling swept over Arkadii. It's lovely to fall asleep in one's own home, in a familiar bed, under a blanket stitched together by loving hands—perhaps by a former nursemaid's hands—those affectionate, kindly, untiring hands. Arkadii recalled Egorovna, sighed, and wished her peace in heaven. ... He didn't pray for himself.

Both he and Bazarov fell asleep soon, but other inhabitants of the

house remained awake for a long while. His son's return had agitated
Nikolai Petrovich. He got into bed but didn't put out the candles,
and, propping his head on his hand, he lapsed into prolonged musing. His brother stayed in his study until well after midnight, sitting
in a wide armchair before the fireplace, in which some embers were
faintly smoldering. Pavel Petrovich hadn't undressed—he'd merely
replaced the leather shoes on his feet with some red Chinese slippers. He held the most recent issue of *Galignani* in his hands, but
he wasn't reading; he was steadily gazing at the fireplace, where a
bluish flame flickered, dying down and then flaring up again. . . .
God knows where his thoughts were wandering, but they weren't
wandering solely in the past: the expression on his face was focused
and grim, which isn't the case when someone is wholly absorbed in
memories. And in a small back room, a young woman wearing a
blue jacket and a white kerchief thrown over her dark hair was sitting on a large chest—this was Fenechka. She was half alert, half
dozing, repeatedly looking toward an open door, through which a
child's cradle was visible and the regular breathing of a slumbering
infant could be heard.

V

The next morning, Bazarov got up earlier than anyone else and went
out of the house. "Ah," he thought, looking around him, "this little
place isn't much to brag about!" When Nikolai Petrovich had
divided his land with the peasants, he'd had to build a new residence on four acres of perfectly flat, barren fields. He'd constructed
a house, offices, and a farmyard, laid out a garden, dug a pond, and
sunk two wells. But the young trees hadn't thrived, very little water
had collected in the pond, and the water in the wells tasted brackish.
Only one arbor consisting of lilac and acacia bushes had done fairly
well; the brothers occasionally had tea or ate dinner in it. Within a
few minutes, Bazarov had traversed every one of the little garden
paths, had visited the cattleyard and the stable, had sought out two
farm boys, whom he promptly befriended, and had set off with
them toward a small swamp about a verst from the house to find
frogs.

"What do you want frogs for, master?" one of the boys asked
him.

"I'll tell you what for," responded Bazarov, who possessed the
special faculty of inspiring confidence in him among people of a
lower social class, although he never tried to win them over, and

treated them quite casually. "I'll cut a frog open and see what's going on inside, and then, because you and I are a lot like frogs, except that we walk on legs, I'll know what's going on inside us, too."

"And what do you want to know that for?"

"So as not to make a mistake if you get sick and I have to cure you."

"Are you a doctor, then?"

"Yes."

"Vaska, do you hear—the gentleman says you and I are the same as frogs. Weird!"

"I'm scared of frogs," remarked Vaska, a boy of about seven with hair as white as flax and bare feet, dressed in a long gray shirt with a stand-up collar.

"What's there to be scared about? Do they bite?"

"Come on, paddle into the water, philosophers," commanded Bazarov.

Meanwhile, Nikolai Petrovich had also woken up and gone to see Arkadii, whom he found already dressed. Father and son went out onto the terrace under the shelter of the awning; the samovar was already boiling on a table near the railing, amid large bouquets of lilacs. A little girl appeared, the same one who'd been the first to meet them at the steps upon their arrival the evening before. She announced in a shrill voice, "Fedosia Nikolaevna isn't feeling well—she can't come. She told me to ask you if you'd be so kind as to pour the tea yourself or if should she send Duniasha."

"I'll pour it myself, I'll do it," Nikolai Petrovich interjected hurriedly. "Arkadii, how do you drink your tea, with cream or with lemon?"

"With cream," Arkadii answered. After a brief silence, he tentatively said: "Papa?"

Nikolai Petrovich looked at his son disconcertedly.

"What?" he asked.

Arkadii lowered his eyes.

"Forgive me if my question seems inappropriate to you, Papa," he began, "but by your candor yesterday you yourself encourage me to be candid.... You won't get angry...?"

"Go on."

"You give me the courage to ask you.... Isn't the reason Fen... isn't the reason she won't come out here to pour the tea the fact that I'm here?"

Nikolai Petrovich turned away slightly.

"Perhaps," he eventually acknowledged. "She supposes....
She's ashamed...."

Arkadii cast a rapid glance at his father.

"She shouldn't be ashamed. In the first place, you're aware of
my view of the matter" (it was highly pleasing to Arkadii to utter
these words), "and in the second, would I want to constrain your
life, your habits, the slightest bit? Besides, I'm sure you couldn't
make a bad choice. If you've allowed her to live under the same
roof with you, she must deserve it. In any case, a son can't judge
his father—least of all me, and least of all a father like you, who's
never constrained my freedom in any way."

Arkadii's voice was shaky at the beginning; he felt that he was
being magnanimous, although at the same time he realized that he
was delivering something in the nature of a lecture to his father.
But the sound of his own voice has a powerful effect on any man,
and Arkadii pronounced his concluding words resolutely, even
emphatically.

"Thank you, Arkasha," Nikolai Petrovich replied hollowly, and
his fingers strayed across his eyebrows and forehead once more.
"Your suppositions are in fact correct. Of course, if this young
woman hadn't deserved.... This isn't some frivolous caprice. It's
awkward for me to talk to you about this, but you understand that
it'd be difficult for her to come out here in your presence, especially
the first day after you've returned home."

"In that case, I'll go and see her," Arkadii cried with a fresh
burst of magnanimity, and he jumped up from his chair. "I'll
explain to her that she doesn't need to be ashamed around me."

Nikolai Petrovich stood up as well.

"Arkadii," he began, "please ... how can ... there ... I haven't
told you yet...."

But Arkadii didn't listen to him and ran off the terrace. Nikolai
Petrovich watched him go, and then sank back into his chair,
overwhelmed by embarrassment. His heart began to pound....
At that moment, was he envisioning the inevitable strangeness
about to be introduced into the relationship between himself and
his son? Was he acknowledging that Arkadii might have shown
him greater respect by never touching on this subject at all? Was
he reproaching himself for weakness? It's hard to say; all these
feelings were occurring inside him, but only as sensations—vague

sensations. Meanwhile, the flush on his face didn't subside, and his heart continued to pound.

The sound of hurrying footsteps became audible, and Arkadii came back out onto the terrace. "We've gotten acquainted, Father!" he exclaimed with some sort of affectionate, good-natured, triumphant expression on his face. "Fedosia Nikolaevna really isn't feeling well today, and she'll come out a little later. But why didn't you tell me I had a brother? I would have kissed him last night the way I just kissed him now."

Nikolai Petrovich tried to say something, tried to stand up and embrace his son. . . . Arkadii flung his arms around his father's neck.

"What's this? Embracing again?" the voice of Pavel Petrovich rang out from behind them.

Father and son were equally pleased by his appearance at that moment: there are genuinely touching situations from which one longs to escape as quickly as possible.

"Why should you be so surprised at that?" Nikolai Petrovich retorted cheerfully. "Think how many ages I've been waiting for Arkasha. . . . I haven't had a chance to get a good look at him since yesterday."

"I'm not the least bit surprised," remarked Pavel Petrovich. "I'm not opposed to embracing him myself."

Arkadii went up to his uncle and felt his cheeks caressed again by that perfumed moustache. Pavel Petrovich sat down at the table. He was wearing an elegant, English-style morning suit; a little fez adorned his head. This fez and his carelessly tied short tie betokened the informality of country life, but the stiff collar on his shirt—which wasn't white, of course, but striped, as is correct for morning attire—stood up as inexorably as ever under his well-shaved chin.

"Where's your new friend?" he asked Arkadii.

"He isn't inside the house. He usually gets up early and goes off somewhere. The important thing is not to pay any attention to him. He doesn't like formality."

"Yes, that's obvious." Pavel Petrovich began methodically spreading butter on his bread. "Is he going to stay with us for a long time?"

"Possibly. He came here on the way to his father's."

"And where does his father live?"

"In our district, about eighty versts from here. He has a small estate there. He used to be an army doctor."

"Hmm. So that's why I kept asking myself, 'Where have I heard that name, Bazarov?' Nikolai, do you remember, wasn't there a surgeon named Bazarov in our father's division?"

"I believe there was."

"Yes, yes, indeed. So that surgeon was his father. Hmm!" Pavel Petrovich stroked his moustache. "Well, and precisely what sort of person is Mr. Bazarov himself?" he asked in measured tones.

"What sort of person is Bazarov?" Arkadii smiled. "Would you like me to tell you precisely what sort of person he is, Uncle?"

"If you'd be so kind, Nephew."

"He's a nihilist."

"What?" responded Nikolai Petrovich, while Pavel Petrovich suspended his knife in the air, a small piece of butter on its tip, and held still.

"He's a nihilist," repeated Arkadii.

"A nihilist," echoed Nikolai Petrovich. "That's from the Latin, *nihil*, 'nothing,' as far as I can judge. The word must mean someone who . . . who doesn't believe in anything?"

"Say, 'who doesn't respect anything,'" interjected Pavel Petrovich, and he began to spread his butter again.

"Who regards everything from a critical point of view," observed Arkadii.

"Isn't it all the same?" inquired Pavel Petrovich.

"No, it's not all the same. A nihilist is someone who doesn't bow down to any authority, who doesn't accept any principle on faith, no matter how revered that principle may be."

"Well, is this a good thing?" Pavel Petrovich interrupted.

"That depends, Uncle. For some people it's good, but for others it's very bad."

"Indeed. Well, I see that it's not our sort of thing—we're old-fashioned people. We imagine that without principles" (Pavel Petrovich uttered this word softly, the French way, whereas Arkadii pronounced it forcefully, with the accent on the first syllable), "without principles accepted on faith, as you put it, no one can take a single step, no one can breathe. *Vous avez changé tout cela.* May God grant you good health and a general's rank, while we'll merely sit back and marvel at your worthy . . . what was the word?"

"Nihilists," Arkadii declared distinctly.

"Yes. There used to be Hegelians, and now there are nihilists.

We'll see how you'll survive in isolation, in a vacuum. But now please call a servant, brother Nikolai Petrovich. It's time for my cocoa."

Nikolai Petrovich rang a bell and called out, "Duniasha!" But instead of Duniasha, Fenechka herself walked out onto the terrace. She was a young woman of about twenty-three, with white, soft skin, dark hair and eyes, red, childishly pouting lips, and gentle little hands. She wore a tidy print dress; a new blue scarf lay lightly across her plump shoulders. She was carrying a large cup of cocoa, and, setting it down in front of Pavel Petrovich, she was engulfed by shame: her pulsing blood sent a crimson wave across the delicate skin of her lovely face. She lowered her eyes and stood next to the table, leaning forward slightly on the very tips of her toes. It seemed that she felt guilty about having come there, and at the same time felt that she had a right to come there.

Pavel Petrovich furrowed his brow severely, and Nikolai Petrovich became embarrassed.

"Good morning, Fenechka," he muttered through his teeth.

"Good morning," she replied in a soft but resonant voice, and, casting a sidelong glance at Arkadii, who gave her a friendly smile, she left quietly. She had a slightly rolling gait, which suited her.

Silence reigned on the terrace for several moments. Pavel Petrovich sipped his cocoa. Suddenly he raised his head. "Here's Mr. Nihilist coming toward us," he observed under his breath.

Bazarov was indeed walking through the garden, stepping over the flower beds. His linen coat and trousers were smeared with mud; clinging marsh weeds were twined around the crown of his old, round-shaped hat; in his right hand, he was holding a small bag that had something alive moving in it. He rapidly approached the terrace and said with a nod: "Good morning, gentlemen. Sorry I was late for my tea. I'll be back in a minute. I just have to put these captives away."

"What do you have there—leeches?" queried Pavel Petrovich.

"No, frogs."

"Do you eat them—or take them apart?"

"For experiments," Bazarov stated matter-of-factly, and he went off into the house.

"So he's going to cut them up," remarked Pavel Petrovich. "He doesn't believe in principles, but he believes in frogs."

Arkadii looked at his uncle compassionately. Nikolai Petrovich stealthily shrugged his shoulders. Pavel Petrovich himself sensed

that his witticism hadn't gone over well, and he began to talk about
husbandry, then about the new bailiff who'd come to him the
evening before to complain that a certain laborer, Foma, was "de-
boshed," and completely out of control. "He's such an Aesop,"
the bailiff had said, among other things. "He goes around everywhere declaring that he's a worthless human being—he gets away
with anything as a result."

VI

Bazarov returned, sat down at the table, and hastily began to drink
tea. The two brothers gazed at him in silence, while Arkadii furtively looked first at his father and then at his uncle.

"Did you go far from here?" Nikolai Petrovich eventually
inquired.

"Where you've got a little swamp, near the aspen grove. I startled
five snipe or so. You could shoot them, Arkadii."

"Aren't you a hunter, then?"

"No."

"Is your particular field of study medical science?" Pavel Petrovich inquired in his turn.

"Medical science, yes, and the natural sciences in general."

"They say that the Teutons have recently made great advances
in that area."

"Yes, the Germans are our instructors in this," Bazarov responded offhandedly.

Pavel Petrovich had used the word "Teutons" instead of the word
"Germans" for ironic effect, which no one noticed, however.

"Do you have such a high opinion of the Germans?" Pavel Petrovich asked with exaggerated courtesy. He was secretly beginning to
feel irritated. His aristocratic nature was revolted by Bazarov's
thoroughgoing nonchalance. This surgeon's son not only wasn't intimidated, he replied to questions laconically, even dismissively, and
there was something churlish, almost insolent, in his tone of voice.

"The scientists there are sensible people."

"Ah, I see. You probably don't have such high regard for Russian
scientists?"

"I suppose that's so."

"That's most praiseworthy self-abnegation," Pavel Petrovich
commented, straightening up and tossing his head back. "But why

was Arkadii Nikolaich just telling us that you don't acknowledge any authorities? Don't you believe in *them?*"

"Why should I acknowledge any? And what should I believe in? They tell me the truth, and I agree—that's all."

"Do Germans always tell the truth?" rejoined Pavel Petrovich, and his face assumed an extremely austere, remote expression, as though he'd mentally withdrawn to some height above the clouds.

"Not all of them," Bazarov replied with a brief yawn. He obviously didn't want to continue this war of words.

Pavel Petrovich glanced at Arkadii, as if to say to him, "Your friend is certainly polite, isn't he?"

"For my part," he began again, not without some effort, "I'm so unregenerate as to dislike Germans. I'm not referring to Russian Germans now—we all know what sort of creatures they are. But even German Germans aren't much to my taste. There were a few in earlier times, here and there. Then they had—well, Schiller, I suppose, and Goethe. . . . My brother especially prefers them. . . . But now they've all turned into chemists and materialists. . . ."

"A good chemist is twenty times as useful as any poet," Bazarov interjected.

"Oh, indeed," retorted Pavel Petrovich, and he faintly raised his eyebrows, as though he were falling asleep. "Then you don't believe in art, I gather?"

"The art of making money or of curing hemorrhoids!" Bazarov cried with a contemptuous laugh.

"Yes, yes. You enjoy making jokes, I see. You reject all that, no doubt? Granted. Then you believe solely in science?"

"I've already explained to you that I don't believe in anything. And what is science—science in the abstract? There are sciences, just as there are trades and crafts, but science in the abstract doesn't exist at all."

"That's very nice. Well, do you maintain the same negative attitude in regard to all the other traditions governing the conduct of human affairs?"

"What is this, an examination?" asked Bazarov.

Pavel Petrovich turned slightly pale. . . . Nikolai Petrovich decided that he was obligated to intervene in the conversation.

"We'll discuss this subject with you in more detail some other day, dear Evgenii Vasilich. We'll find out about your views and express our own. For my part, I'm heartily glad that you're study-

ing the natural sciences. I've heard that Liebig has made some
wonderful discoveries regarding the improvement of soils. You can
help me in my agricultural labors—you can give me some useful
advice."

"I'm at your service, Nikolai Petrovich, but Liebig is way over
our heads! One has to learn the alphabet before beginning to read,
and we haven't set our eyes on the letter 'a' yet."

"You certainly are a nihilist, I can see that," thought Nikolai
Petrovich. "Nonetheless, permit me to turn to you occasionally,"
he added aloud. "And now, Brother, I believe it's time for us to
have a little chat with the bailiff."

Pavel Petrovich got up from his chair.

"Yes," he said, without looking at anyone. "It's unfortunate to
live in the countryside like this for five years or so, at such a
distance from mighty intellects! You promptly turn into a fool. You
may try not to forget what you've been taught, but then—just like
that!—they'll prove it's all nonsense, tell you that sensible men
don't concern themselves with such trifles any more and that you,
if you please, are an antiquated old fogey. What can one do? Young
people are evidently much smarter than we are!"

Pavel Petrovich slowly turned on his heel and slowly walked
away; Nikolai Petrovich followed him.

"Is he always like that around you?" Bazarov asked Arkadii coolly
as soon as the door had closed behind the two brothers.

"Listen, Evgenii, you dealt with him too sharply," Arkadii asserted. "You've hurt his feelings."

"Well, should I coddle them, these provincial aristocrats? Why,
it's all pride, it's fashionable custom, it's foppishness. He should
have continued to pursue his career in Petersburg, if that was his
inclination. Anyway, the hell with him! I've found a rather rare
species of water-beetle, *Dytiscus marginatus*. Do you know it? I'll
show it to you."

"I promised to tell you about his past," Arkadii began.

"The beetle's past?"

"Come on, Evgenii, that's enough. My uncle's past. You'll see
that he's not the sort of person you think he is. He deserves more
pity than scorn."

"I don't deny it—but why are you so concerned about him?"

"One should be fair, Evgenii."

"How does that follow?"

"No, listen. . . ."

And Arkadii told him about his uncle's past. The reader will find the gist of it in the next chapter.

VII

Pavel Petrovich Kirsanov was educated first at home, like his younger brother, and subsequently in the Corps of Pages. From childhood on, he'd been distinguished by remarkable beauty; moreover, he was self-confident, slightly cynical, and had a rather cutting sense of humor—he couldn't fail to please. As soon as he'd received his officer's commission, he began to go everywhere. He was greatly admired in society, and indulged every whim, committed every folly, affecting a supercilious air—but even that was attractive in him. Women went out of their minds over him; men called him a dandy and secretly envied him. As has already been mentioned, he lived in the same apartment as his brother, whom he sincerely loved, although he didn't resemble him in the least. Nikolai Petrovich was slightly lame, had diminutive, pleasant, somewhat melancholy features, small, dark eyes, and thin, fine hair; he liked indolence, but he also liked to read, and he feared all social activities. Pavel Petrovich never spent a single evening at home, prided himself on his agility and daring (he was just introducing gymnastics to fashionable young men), and had read a total of five or six French books. At the age of twenty-eight, he was already a captain; a brilliant career awaited him. Suddenly everything changed.

At that time, a woman occasionally appeared in Petersburg society who hasn't been forgotten to this day, Princess R——. She had a well-bred, well-mannered, but rather stupid husband, and was childless. She used to go abroad suddenly, and just as suddenly return to Russia, generally leading a strange life. She had the reputation of being a frivolous coquette; she eagerly abandoned herself to every form of pleasure, danced to the point of exhaustion, and laughed and joked with the young people she entertained in her half-lit drawing room prior to dinner. But, at night, she wept and prayed, found no source of solace anywhere, and often paced around her room until morning, wringing her hands in anguish, or sat reading a psalter, pale and cold. Day would come, and she'd transform herself into a great lady once again; she'd go out once again, laughing, chattering, and seemingly flinging herself headlong into anything that could afford her the slightest distraction. She had a wonderful figure; her hair was the color of gold and hung down to her knees, as heavy as gold; but no one would have called

her a beauty. Her only good facial features were her eyes, and not
even her eyes themselves—they were small and gray—but their gaze,
which was alert and deep, unconcerned to the point of audacity,
and thoughtful to the point of melancholy—an enigmatic gaze. Some
extraordinary light shone in that gaze, even while her tongue was
lisping the most inane speeches. She dressed with elaborate care.

Pavel Petrovich met her at a ball, danced the mazurka with her—
in the course of which she didn't utter a single significant word—
and fell passionately in love with her. Accustomed to making romantic conquests, he quickly attained his object in this instance as
well, but the ease of his success didn't dampen his ardor. On the
contrary, he found himself in ever-increasing torment, in ever-
increasing bondage to this woman who, even at the very moment
when she wholly surrendered herself, always seemed to remain
somehow mysterious and unfathomable, somehow unattainable.
What lay hidden in that soul—God knows! It was as though she
were in the grips of some sort of secret forces incomprehensible
even to her—they played on her at will, and her intellect wasn't
strong enough to tame their caprices. All her actions were characterized by inconsistency; she wrote the only letters that could
have awakened her husband's legitimate suspicions to a man who
was a virtual stranger to her. Her love always incorporated an
element of sorrow: she ceased to laugh and joke with a man she'd
chosen as a lover, listening to him and gazing at him with a bewildered look on her face. Sometimes, typically all of a sudden,
this bewilderment would turn to icy horror: her face would assume
a wild, deathlike expression; she'd lock herself up in her bedroom;
her maid, putting one ear to the keyhole, could hear her smothered
sobs. More than once, as he was going home after an intimate
tryst, Kirsanov experienced the heartrending, bitter frustration that
follows upon total failure.

"What more do I want?" he asked himself, as his heart ceaselessly ached. One day he gave her a ring with a sphinx engraved
on the stone.

"What's this?" she asked. "A sphinx?"

"Yes," he answered, "and this sphinx is you."

"I?" she queried, slowly turning her enigmatic gaze toward him.
"Do you know that this is very flattering?" she added with a
meaningless smile, her eyes retaining the same strange look.

Pavel Petrovich suffered even while Princess R—— loved him,
but when she cooled toward him—which happened fairly soon—

he nearly lost his mind. He was in agony; he was jealous; he gave her no peace, following her everywhere. She got tired of his relentless pursuit and went abroad. He resigned his commission, despite the entreaties of his friends and the exhortations of his superiors, and set off after the princess; he spent some four years in foreign countries, at times seeking her out, at other times intentionally losing sight of her. He was ashamed of himself, he was disgusted at his own lack of spirit...but nothing availed. Her image, that incomprehensible, almost senseless, but bewitching image, was deeply rooted in his soul. In Baden, he somehow regained his former status with her once more; it seemed as though she'd never loved him so passionately...but it was all over in a month—the flame flared up for the final time and went out forever. Foreseeing an inevitable separation, he at least wanted to remain her friend, as though friendship with such a woman were possible.... She left Baden in secret, and from that time onward, she steadily avoided Kirsanov.

He returned to Russia and tried to resume his former life, but he couldn't get back into the old groove. He wandered from place to place like someone who'd been drugged. He still frequented society, maintaining the habits of a man of the world; he could boast of two or three fresh conquests; but he no longer expected anything much of himself or of anyone else, and he didn't undertake any new activity. He grew old and gray. Spending all his evenings at his club, where he became jaundiced and bored, he found dispassionately arguing in bachelor company ever more essential to him—a bad sign, as we all know. He didn't even consider marriage, understandably.

Ten years passed this way, colorlessly, fruitlessly, and quickly—terribly quickly. In no other country does time fly as fast as it does in Russia; in prison, they say, it flies even faster. One day during dinner at his club, Pavel Petrovich learned of Princess R——'s death. She'd died in Paris in a condition bordering on insanity. He got up from the table and walked around the rooms of the club for a long while, pausing to stand near the cardplayers as though carved in stone—but he didn't go home any earlier than usual. Days later, he received a packet addressed to him; it contained the ring he'd given the princess. She'd drawn lines above the sphinx in the shape of a cross and ordered the messenger to tell him that the solution to the enigma was—the cross.

This happened at the beginning of 1848, at the very time when

Nikolai Petrovich came to Petersburg after losing his wife. Pavel Petrovich had hardly seen his brother since the latter had settled down in the countryside; Nikolai Petrovich's marriage had coincided with the very beginning of Pavel Petrovich's acquaintance with the princess. When Pavel Petrovich had returned from abroad, he'd gone to visit Nikolai Petrovich, intending to stay with him for a couple of months to admire his happiness, but he'd only managed to endure a week: the difference between the two brothers' situations had been too great. By 1848, this difference had diminished: Nikolai Petrovich had lost his wife and Pavel Petrovich had lost his memories—after the princess's death, he tried not to think about her. But Nikolai still possessed the sense of a well-spent life and a son growing up before his eyes; Pavel, by contrast, was a solitary bachelor entering upon that indefinite twilight period of regrets that are akin to hopes and hopes that are akin to regrets, when youth is over but old age still hasn't arrived. And this period was harder for Pavel Petrovich than for other men: in losing his past, he'd lost everything.

"I won't invite you to Marino just now," Nikolai Petrovich told him one day (he'd named his estate that in honor of his wife). "You were bored there while my beloved wife was alive, and now I think you'd die of boredom."

"I was still foolish and fretful then," responded Pavel Petrovich. "Since that time, I've gotten calmer, if not wiser. On the contrary, if you'll let me, now I'm ready to settle down with you for good."

In place of an answer, Nikolai Petrovich just hugged him. But a year and a half passed after this conversation occurred before Pavel Petrovich decided to carry out his plan. Once he did settle down in the countryside, however, he didn't leave it, even during the three winters Nikolai Petrovich spent in Petersburg with his son. He began to read, chiefly in English; he arranged his entire life in English fashion, generally speaking; he rarely visited neighbors, and only attended local elections, where he typically remained silent, just occasionally making liberal sallies that annoyed and alarmed the old-fashioned landowners, while refusing to associate with representatives of the new generation. Both sides considered him arrogant, and both sides respected him. They respected him for his refined, aristocratic manners; for his reputation for amorous conquests; for the fact that he was dressed handsomely and always stayed in the best room of the best hotel; for the fact that he ordinarily dined well, and had once even dined with Wellington at Louis Philippe's residence; for the fact that he brought a real silver toiletry case and a portable bathtub with him everywhere; for the fact that he always wore some exceptionally "noble" fragrance; for the fact that he played whist in masterly fashion and always lost. Lastly, they respected him for his incorruptible honesty. Ladies found him enchantingly melancholic, but he didn't cultivate the acquaintance of ladies. . . .

"So you see, Evgenii," Arkadii observed as he finished his narrative, "how unfairly you've judged my uncle! To say nothing of his having gotten my father out of trouble more than once, and having given my father all his money—the estate wasn't divided, as perhaps you don't know. He's happy to help anyone, and, among other things, he always sticks up for the peasants. It's true that he frowns and sniffs eau de cologne when he talks to them. . . ."

"His nerves, no doubt," Bazarov interjected.

"Maybe, but he has the kindest of hearts. And he's far from stupid. He's given me such useful advice . . . especially . . . especially in regard to relationships with women."

"Aha! A scalded dog fears water, we know that!"

"In short," Arkadii concluded, "he's profoundly unhappy, believe me. It's a sin to despise him."

"Who despises him?" Bazarov retorted. "Still, I must say that a man who stakes his whole life on one card—a woman's love—and turns sour when that card loses, letting himself deteriorate until he's incapable of accomplishing anything, isn't a man, he's an animal. You say that he's unhappy—you know best—but he hasn't gotten rid of all his faults. I'm convinced that he seriously considers himself a useful individual because he reads *Galignani* and once a month saves a peasant from being flogged."

"But remember his upbringing, and the times in which he lived," Arkadii remarked.

"His upbringing?" Bazarov cried. "Every person has to bring himself up, like I've done, for instance. . . . And as for the times, why should I depend on them? Let them depend on me instead. No, my friend, that's all inanity and indiscipline! And what's all this about mysterious relationships between men and women? We physiologists know what these relationships are. You study the anatomy of the eye: where does that enigmatic gaze, as you put it, come from? The rest is all romanticism, nonsense, aesthetic garbage. We'd be much better off going and looking at the beetle."

And the two friends went to Bazarov's room, which was already permeated by some sort of medicinal-surgical odor mingled with the smell of cheap tobacco.

VIII

Pavel Petrovich didn't stay for long at his brother's chat with the bailiff, a tall, thin man with a sickly sweet voice and devious eyes who responded, "Certainly, sir," to all Nikolai Petrovich's remarks and characterized all the peasants as thieves and drunkards. The estate had recently been put under a new system and was creaking like an ungreased wheel, warping and cracking like homemade furniture carved out of unseasoned wood. Nikolai Petrovich wasn't ready to give up, but he frequently sighed and became pensive; he felt that the enterprise couldn't go any further without more money, and his money was almost all gone. Arkadii had told the truth: Pavel Petrovich had helped his brother out more than once; more than once, seeing Nikolai Petrovich struggling and racking his brains, not knowing which way to turn, Pavel Petrovich had slowly moved to the window, his hands thrust into his pockets, had muttered between his teeth, "*Mais je puis vous donner de l'argent,*" and had given him some money. But he had none himself at the moment, and preferred to withdraw. The petty details of agricultural management bored him to tears; besides, it repeatedly occurred to him that Nikolai Petrovich, all his industry and zeal notwithstanding, wasn't handling things the right way, although he couldn't have indicated precisely where Nikolai Petrovich's mistakes lay. "My brother isn't sufficiently practical," Pavel Petrovich concluded to himself. "People deceive him." Nikolai Petrovich, by contrast, had the highest possible regard for Pavel Petrovich's practicality and always asked his advice. "I'm a mild, weak-willed sort of person. I've spent my entire life in a remote area," he'd say, "whereas you haven't lived in society so long for nothing. You see through people—you have an eagle eye." In response, Pavel Petrovich would merely turn away—but he never contradicted his brother.

Leaving Nikolai Petrovich in the study, he walked along the corridor that separated the front part of the house from the back. When he reached a low door, he paused in thought, and then, stroking his moustache, he knocked on it.

"Who's there? Come in," Fenechka's voice called out.

"It's I," Pavel Petrovich announced, and he opened the door.

Fenechka jumped up from the chair she was sitting in while

holding her baby, and, thrusting him into the arms of a girl who promptly carried him out of the room, she hastily straightened her scarf.

"Pardon me if I'm disturbing you," Pavel Petrovich began, without looking at her. "I just wanted to ask you.... They're sending someone into town today, I think.... Please have that person buy me some green tea."

"Certainly," Fenechka replied. "How much do you want him to buy?"

"Oh, half a pound will be enough, I imagine. You've made some changes here, I see," he added, casting a quick glance around the room that glided across Fenechka's face as well. "These curtains," he explained, noticing that she didn't comprehend his remark.

"Oh, yes, the curtains. Nikolai Petrovich gave them to us as a present. But they've been up for a long while now."

"Yes, and it's been a long while since I've come to visit you. It's very nice in here now."

"Thanks to Nikolai Petrovich's kindness," Fenechka murmured.

"Are you more comfortable here than you were in the little lodge?" Pavel Petrovich inquired courteously, but without the slightest trace of a smile.

"Of course, this is better."

"Who's moved into that place now?"

"The laundry maids are there now."

"Ah!"

Pavel Petrovich fell silent. "Now he's going to leave," Fenechka thought. But he didn't leave, and she stood facing him as though rooted to the spot, feebly entwining her fingers.

"Why did you send your little one away?" Pavel Petrovich inquired at last. "I love children. Let me see him."

Fenechka blushed deeply with embarrassment and delight. She was afraid of Pavel Petrovich; he hardly ever spoke to her.

"Duniasha," she called out, "will you bring Mitia here, please?" (Fenechka addressed everyone in the house politely.) "But wait a minute. He should be wearing something nice," Fenechka declared as she moved toward the door.

"That doesn't matter," Pavel Petrovich remarked.

"I'll be right back," Fenechka responded, and she went out quickly.

Having been left alone, Pavel Petrovich looked around again, this time quite carefully. The small, low-ceilinged room in which he found himself was very clean and cozy. It smelled of the fresh paint on the floor and of chamomile. Chairs with lyre-shaped backs, purchased by the late general during his campaign in Poland, were lined up along the walls; a little bedstead under a muslin canopy stood in one corner beside an ironbound chest with a convex lid. A small lamp was burning in the opposite corner before a large, dark icon of Saint Nikolai the miracle-worker; a tiny porcelain egg hung down to the saint's breast on a red ribbon attached to a protruding gold halo. Carefully sealed, greenish glass jars filled with last year's jam were lined up by the windows; Fenechka herself had written "Gooseberry" in big letters on their paper labels— Nikolai Petrovich was especially fond of that flavor. A cage with a short-tailed finch in it hung on a long cord attached to the ceiling; the finch incessantly chirped and hopped around, as a result of which the cage constantly shook and swayed, and hemp seeds kept falling onto the floor with a light tapping sound. On the wall just above a small chest of drawers hung some rather poor photographs of Nikolai Petrovich in various poses that had been taken by an itinerant photographer. A photograph of Fenechka herself that was an absolute failure also hung there in a dingy frame: it displayed some eyeless face wearing a forced smile, and nothing more. And above Fenechka hung a portrait of General Ermolov wearing a Circassian cloak as he scowled menacingly toward the Caucasian mountains in the distance from beneath a little silk–shoe pincushion that fell right to his forehead.

Five minutes passed; bustling and whispering were audible from the next room. Pavel Petrovich picked up an old book off the chest of drawers, an odd volume of Masalskii's *Musketeers*, and turned a few pages. . . . The door opened and Fenechka came in, carrying Mitia. She'd dressed him in a little red smock with an embroidered collar, and had combed his hair and washed his face. He was breathing laboriously, his whole body was wriggling, and he was waving his little hands in the air, the way all healthy babies do, but his fancy smock had obviously impressed him—every part of his plump little body expressed delight. Fenechka had also combed her own hair and rearranged her scarf, but she might as well have stayed the way she was. For, in fact, is there anything on earth more appealing than a beautiful young mother with a healthy baby in her arms?

"What a chubby little boy!" Pavel Petrovich remarked graciously, and he tickled Mitia's small double chin with the tapered nail of his forefinger. The baby stared at the finch and giggled.

"That's your uncle," Fenechka told him, tilting her face toward Mitia and rocking him slightly, while Duniasha quietly set a smoldering perfumed candle in the window and placed a coin underneath it.

"How many months old is he?" Pavel Petrovich asked.

"Six months. It'll be seven soon, on the eleventh."

"Isn't it eight, Fedosia Nikolaevna?" Duniasha interjected, not without shyness.

"No, seven. How is that possible?" The baby giggled again, stared at the chest of drawers, and suddenly caught hold of his mother's nose and mouth with all five of the fingers on one of his hands. "Saucy little rascal," Fenechka commented, without drawing her face away.

"He looks like my brother," observed Pavel Petrovich.

"Who else would he look like?" Fenechka thought.

"Yes," Pavel Petrovich continued, as though speaking to himself, "there's an unmistakable likeness." He looked at Fenechka intently, almost sadly.

"That's your uncle," she repeated, this time in a whisper.

"Ah! Pavel! So you're in here!" Nikolai Petrovich's voice suddenly rang out.

Pavel Petrovich hurriedly turned around, frowning, but his brother gazed at him with such delight and such gratitude that Pavel Petrovich couldn't help responding to his brother's smile.

"You've got a handsome little cherub," he declared, and looked at his watch. "I came in here to inquire about some tea."

And assuming a nonchalant expression, Pavel Petrovich immediately left the room.

"Did he come by himself?" Nikolai Petrovich asked Fenechka.

"Yes, he knocked and came in."

"Has Arkasha been to see you again?"

"No. Shouldn't I move into the lodge, Nikolai Petrovich?"

"Why?"

"I wonder whether it wouldn't be better, if only at first."

"N-no," Nikolai Petrovich concluded hesitantly, rubbing his forehead. "We should have done it before.... How are you, pudgy?" he added, suddenly perking up, and going over to the baby, he kissed him on the cheek. Then he bent down slightly and pressed his lips to Fenechka's hand, which was lying on Mitia's little red smock, as white as milk.

"Nikolai Petrovich! What are you doing?" she whispered, lowering her eyes, then slowly raising them again. The expression in her eyes when she gazed at him a bit mistrustfully, while smiling tenderly and a little foolishly, was charming.

Nikolai Petrovich had met Fenechka in the following way. Once, three years earlier, he'd happened to stay overnight at an inn in a remote district town. He was pleasantly surprised by the cleanliness of the room allotted to him, as well as the freshness of its bed linen. "The lady of the house must be German," he concluded. But she turned out to be Russian, a woman of about fifty who dressed neatly and had an attractive, intelligent countenance, along with a discreet manner of speaking. He entered into conversation with her over tea; he liked her very much. Nikolai Petrovich had just moved into his new residence at that time, and, not wanting to keep serfs in the house, was searching for paid servants. The mistress of the inn, for her part, complained about the small number of visitors passing through town and the hard times. He invited her to come to his new residence in the capacity of housekeeper; she consented. Her husband had died long ago, leaving her an only daughter, Fenechka. Within a forthnight, Arina Savishna (that was the new housekeeper's name) arrived at Marino with her daughter and installed herself in the little lodge.

Nikolai Petrovich's choice proved to be a successful one—Arina imposed order on the entire household. As for Fenechka, who was seventeen at the time, no one ever mentioned her, and hardly anyone ever saw her; she led a quiet, sedate life; Nikolai Petrovich merely noticed the delicate profile of her pale face in church on Sundays, somewhere off to one side. More than a year passed this way.

One morning, Arina came into his study and, bowing deeply as usual, asked him if he could do anything to help her daughter, who'd gotten a cinder in her eye from the stove. Nikolai Petrovich, like all people who largely stay at home, had studied various remedies, and had even compiled a homeopathic guide. He immediately told Arina to bring the patient to see him. Fenechka became quite frightened when she heard that the master had sent for her, but she followed her mother to the study. Nikolai Petrovich led her up to the window and took her head in his hands. After thoroughly examining her red, swollen eye, he prescribed an eyewash, which he himself promptly concocted, and tearing his handkerchief into pieces, he showed her how it had to be applied. Fenechka listened to everything he said, and then wanted to leave.

"Kiss the master's hand, silly girl," Arina told her.

Nikolai Petrovich didn't offer her his hand; instead, in confusion, he himself kissed her bowed head on the part in her hair.

Fenechka's eye healed quickly, but the impression she'd made on Nikolai Petrovich didn't pass as quickly. He was constantly haunted by that pure, delicate, timidly raised face; he kept feeling that soft hair on the palms of his hands and kept seeing those innocent, slightly parted lips between which pearly teeth gleamed with moist brilliance in the sunshine. He began to watch her with greater attention in church, and tried to engage her in conversation. She stayed away from him at first, and one day, as evening was approaching, upon encountering him in a narrow footpath running through a field of rye, she fled into the tall, thick stalks, which were overgrown with cornflowers and wormwood, in order to avoid meeting him face to face. He caught sight of her small head through a golden network of ears of rye, from which she was peeping out like a little wild animal, and hailed her affectionately: "Hello, Fenechka! I don't bite."

"Hello," she whispered, refusing to come out of her hiding place.

She was gradually becoming more accustomed to him, but still behaving diffidently in his presence, when her mother, Arina, suddenly died of cholera. What was to become of Fenechka? She'd inherited her mother's love of order, sobriety, and respectability—but she was so young, so alone. Nikolai Petrovich himself was so kind, so unpretentious.... There's no need to describe the rest....

"So my brother came in to see you?" Nikolai Petrovich asked her. "He knocked and came in?"

"Yes."

"Well, that's nice. Let me give Mitia a swing."

And Nikolai Petrovich began tossing him nearly up to the ceiling, to the huge delight of the baby and the considerable concern of the mother, who stretched out her arms toward his bare little legs each time he flew upward.

Pavel Petrovich went back to his elegant study, whose walls were covered with handsome, bluish-gray wallpaper. Various weapons hung on a multicolored Persian rug nailed to one wall; the room contained walnut furniture upholstered in dark-green velveteen, a Renaissance bookcase made of old, dark oak, bronze statuettes arrayed on a magnificent desk, and a fireplace. He threw himself down on the sofa, clasped his hands behind his head, and lay still, gazing at the ceiling almost in despair. Whether he wanted to hide what was reflected in his face from the very walls—or for some other reason—he got up, closed the heavy window curtains against the light, and threw himself back down on the sofa.

IX

Bazarov made Fenechka's acquaintance the same day. He was strolling in the garden with Arkadii, explaining to him why some of the trees, especially the oaks, weren't doing very well.

"They should have planted silver poplars here, as well as spruce firs and possibly lime trees, and given them some loam. That arbor over there has done well," he added, "because it's full of acacia and lilac bushes. They're easy-going types—they don't require much care. But there's someone there."

Fenechka was sitting in the arbor with Duniasha and Mitia. Bazarov paused, and Arkadii nodded to Fenechka like an old friend.

"Who's that?" Bazarov asked him as soon as they'd walked past the arbor. "What a pretty girl!"

"Whom are you referring to?"

"It's obvious—only one of them was pretty."

Not without embarrassment, Arkadii briefly explained to him who Fenechka was.

"Aha!" Bazarov responded. "Your father's got good taste, one can see that. I like your father, yes, I do! He's done well. We have to get acquainted, though," he added, and turned back toward the arbor.

"Evgenii!" Arkadii cried after him in dismay. "Be careful, for God's sake."

"Don't worry," Bazarov replied. "I know how to behave around most people—I'm no fool."

Approaching Fenechka, he took off his cap.

"Allow me to introduce myself," he began with a polite bow. "I'm a harmless person and a friend of Arkadii Nikolaevich."

Fenechka got up from the garden bench and gazed at him without speaking.

"What a handsome child!" Bazarov continued. "Don't be concerned—my compliments have never brought anyone bad luck yet. Why are his cheeks so flushed? Is he cutting his teeth?"

"Yes," Fenechka answered, "he's already cut four teeth, and now his gums are swollen again."

"Show me . . . and don't be afraid. I'm a doctor."

Bazarov picked the baby up in his arms and, to both Fenechka's and Duniasha's astonishment, the child offered no resistance—he wasn't frightened.

"I see, I see. . . . It's nothing, everything's in order. He'll have a good set of teeth. If anything goes wrong, let me know. And are you in good health yourself?"

"I'm quite well, thank God."

"Thank God, indeed—that's the most important thing of all. And you?" he added, turning to Duniasha.

Duniasha was a very prim girl inside the master's house, but a giddy one beyond its gates, and she merely giggled in reply.

"Well, that's fine. Here's your gallant warrior."

Fenechka took the baby back in her arms.

"How well-behaved he was with you!" she commented in an undertone.

"Children are always well behaved around me," Bazarov responded. "I have a way with them."

"Children know who loves them," Duniasha remarked.

"Yes, they certainly do," Fenechka agreed. "Why, Mitia here won't let some people hold him for anything."

"Will he let me?" inquired Arkadii, who, after standing at a distance for some time, had approached the arbor.

He tried to entice Mitia into his arms, but Mitia threw his head back and screamed, to Fenechka's great embarrassment.

"Another day, when he's had time to get used to me," Arkadii said indulgently, and the two friends walked away.

"What's her name?" asked Bazarov.

"Fenechka . . . Fedosia," answered Arkadii.

"And her patronymic? One should know that, too."

"Nikolaevna."

"*Bene*. What I like about her is that she isn't overly constrained. Some people would think badly of her for that, I suppose. What nonsense! Why should she be constrained? She's a mother—she has rights."

"She has rights," Arkadii observed, "but my father. . . ."

"He has rights, too," Bazarov interrupted.

"Well, no, I don't think so."

"Evidently the existence of an extra heir doesn't thrill you?"

"You should be ashamed of yourself for attributing ideas like that to me!" Arkadii cried heatedly. "I don't consider my father wrong from that point of view—I think he ought to marry her."

"Aha!" Bazarov responded tranquilly. "What magnanimous people we are! You still attach significance to marriage—I didn't expect that of you."

The friends proceeded a few steps in silence.

"I've seen your father's entire establishment," Bazarov began again. "The cattle are inferior and the horses are worn out. The buildings aren't in good condition, either, and the workmen look like confirmed loafers, while the bailiff is an idiot or a thief—I haven't quite figured out which one yet."

"You're quite hard on everything today, Evgenii Vasilevich."

"And the kind-hearted peasants are definitely swindling your father. You know the proverb, 'A Russian peasant will cheat God Himself.'"

"I'm beginning to agree with my uncle," Arkadii remarked. "You certainly do have a poor opinion of Russians."

"As though that mattered! The only good thing about a Russian is that he has the lowest possible opinion about himself. What matters is that two times two makes four—all the rest is trivial."

"And is nature trivial?" Arkadii inquired, looking meditatively into the distance at the brightly colored fields beautifully and softly illuminated by the setting sun.

"Nature is also trivial in the sense that you mean it. Nature isn't a temple—it's a workshop, and a human being is the worker in it."

At that instant, the long, drawn-out notes of a cello floated across to them from the house. Someone was playing Schubert's "Expectation" with great feeling, albeit with an untrained hand, and the sweet melody flowed through the air like honey.

"What's that?" Bazarov asked in astonishment.

"It's my father."

"Your father plays the cello?"

"Yes."

"How old is your father?"

"Forty-four."

Bazarov suddenly burst into a roar of laughter.

"What are you laughing at?"

"For heaven's sake, a man of forty-four, a paterfamilias in the district of ★★★, playing the cello!"

Bazarov went on laughing, but, as much as he revered his teacher, this time Arkadii didn't even smile.

X

About two weeks passed. Life at Marino continued to flow on its customary course. Arkadii relaxed and enjoyed himself while Bazarov worked. Everyone in the house had gotten used to Bazarov, to his casual manners and his curt, fragmentary way of speaking. Fenechka in particular had become so comfortable with him that one night she'd had a servant awaken him: Mitia had had convulsions. Bazarov had agreed to come, half joking and half yawning as usual, had stayed with her for two hours, and had assisted the child. By contrast, Pavel Petrovich had grown to detest Bazarov with all the strength of his soul: he considered Bazarov proud, insolent, cynical, and vulgar; he suspected that Bazarov didn't respect him, indeed, that he all but despised him—him, Pavel Kirsanov! Nikolai Petrovich was somewhat frightened of the young "nihilist" and doubted whether his influence over Arkadii was all to the good, yet he eagerly listened to Bazarov, eagerly attended his medical and chemical experiments—Bazarov had brought a microscope with him and occupied himself with it for hours on end. The servants also took to Bazarov, even though he made fun of them; they nonetheless felt that he was one of them, not one of the gentry. Duniasha loved to giggle at him, and cast meaningful glances at him whenever she ran past him "like a little quail." Petr, an extremely vain, unintelligent man who constantly furrowed his brow affectedly, whose entire worth consisted in the fact that he acted civilized, could spell out words, and diligently brushed his coat—even he grinned and livened up whenever Bazarov paid any attention to him. The boys on the farm simply ran after the "doctor" like puppies. Old Prokofich was the only one who didn't like him: he served Bazarov food at meals with a surly expression on his face, called him a "butcher" and an "upstart," and declared that Bazarov's sideburns made him look like a pig in a sty. In his own way, Prokofich was just as much of an aristocrat as Pavel Petrovich.

The best days of the year arrived—the first days of June. The weather was wonderful; some distance from there, it's true, another outbreak of cholera was threatening, but the inhabitants of that district had managed to become accustomed to its visits. Bazarov got up very early every day and walked for two or three versts, not on a stroll—he couldn't bear walking without an aim—but to collect plant and insect specimens. Sometimes he took Arkadii with him. On the way home, an argument usually sprang up and Arkadii was usually vanquished, although he talked more than his companion did.

One day they'd lingered rather late for some reason; Nikolai Petrovich went out to the garden to look for them, and as he reached the arbor, he suddenly heard the rapid footsteps and the voices of the two young men. They were walking on the other side of the arbor and couldn't see him.

"You don't know my father well enough," Arkadii was saying.

Nikolai Petrovich kept silent.

"Your father's a kind man," Bazarov declared, "but he's behind the times. His day is done."

Nikolai Petrovich listened intently.... Arkadii didn't respond.

The man who was "behind the times" stood still for about two minutes, and then slowly made his way home.

"The day before yesterday, I saw him reading Pushkin," Bazarov continued in the meantime. "Please explain to him that that's no use whatsoever. He's not a boy, you know—it's time to give up that rubbish. And the desire to be a romantic at the present moment! Give him something sensible to read."

"What should I give him?" asked Arkadii.

"Oh, Büchner's *Stoff und Kraft*, I suppose, to begin with."

"I think so too," Arkadii remarked approvingly. "*Stoff und Kraft* is written in popular language...."

"So, it seems," Nikolai Petrovich said to his brother that same day after dinner, as he sat in the latter's study, "you and I have fallen behind the times, and our day is done. Oh, well. Maybe Bazarov is right. But one thing is painful to me, I must confess— I did so hope to develop a close, friendly relationship with Arkadii now, and it turns out that I've fallen behind, whereas he's gone ahead, and we can't understand one another."

"In what sense has he gone ahead? And in what way is he so superior to us?" Pavel Petrovich cried impatiently. "It's that high and mighty gentleman, that nihilist, who's crammed all this into his head. I hate that medical man—in my opinion, he's nothing but a charlatan. I'm convinced that, for all his tadpoles, he hasn't gotten very far even in medicine."

"No, Brother, you can't say that—Bazarov's intelligent, and he knows his subject."

"And his conceit is absolutely revolting," Pavel Petrovich interrupted again.

"Yes," Nikolai Petrovich observed, "he is conceited. But one can't get anywhere without that, it seems—only that's what I didn't take into account. I thought I was doing everything to keep up with the times. I've provided for the peasants, and I've started a model farm, as a result of which they go so far as to call me a 'red radical' all over the district. I read, I study, I try to keep abreast of contemporary issues in general—and they say that my day is done. And, I'm beginning to think that it is, Brother."

"Why so?"

"I'll tell you why. This morning I was sitting and reading Pushkin.... I remember, it happened to be *The Gypsies*.... All of a sudden, Arkadii came up to me and, without uttering a word, with the most affectionate compassion on his face, as gently as if I were a child, he took the book away from me, laid another one in front of me, a German book... smiled, and went away, taking Pushkin with him."

"So that's it! What book did he give you?"

"This one."

And Nikolai Petrovich extracted the ninth edition of Büchner's famous treatise out of his back pocket.

Pavel Petrovich turned it over in his hands. "Hmm!" he growled. "Arkadii Nikolaevich is taking your education in hand. And so, did you try to read it?"

"Yes, I tried."

"Well, what did you think of it?"

"Either I'm stupid or it's all—nonsense. I must be stupid, I suppose."

"You haven't forgotten your German?" inquired Pavel Petrovich.

"Oh no, I understand the German."

Pavel Petrovich turned the book over in his hands again and glanced at his brother mistrustfully. Both fell silent.

"Oh, by the way," Nikolai Petrovich began again, obviously seeking to change the subject, "I've gotten a letter from Koliazin."

"Matvei Ilich?"

"Yes. He's come to *** on an inspection tour of the district. He's quite an important personage now and writes to me that he'd like to see us again, since we're relatives, so he's invited you and Arkadii and me to town."

"Will you go?" asked Pavel Petrovich.

"No. Will you?"

"No, I won't go either. What point would there be in dragging oneself across fifty versts on a wild-goose chase? *Mathieu* wants to display himself in all his glory, the devil take him! He'll have the entire district paying homage to him—he can get along without the likes of us. A great dignitary indeed, a privy councillor! If I'd stayed in military service, if I'd continued to slave away in that stupid harness, I'd have been a general-adjutant by now. Besides, you and I are behind the times, you know."

"Yes, brother, it seems that it's time to order a coffin and fold one's arms across one's breast," Nikolai Petrovich observed with a sigh.

"Well, I'm not going to surrender quite so fast," muttered his brother. "I've got a skirmish coming with that medical man, I predict."

The skirmish occurred that very evening, over tea. Pavel Petrovich came into the drawing room already prepared for the fray, irritable and determined. He was merely awaiting an excuse to attack the enemy, but an excuse didn't present itself for a long while. As a rule, Bazarov said little in the presence of the "old Kirsanovs" (that was how he referred to the brothers), and that evening he was in a bad mood, drinking cup after cup of tea without saying a word. Pavel Petrovich was aflame with impatience; his desires were eventually fulfilled.

The conversation turned to one of the neighboring landowners. "Rotten aristocratic snob," Bazarov remarked matter-of-factly. He'd met the man in Petersburg.

"Permit me to inquire," began Pavel Petrovich, whose lips were trembling, "according to your views, do the words 'rotten' and 'aristocrat' mean the same thing?"

"I said 'aristocratic snob,'" Bazarov replied, lazily swallowing a sip of tea.

"Quite so, but I assume that you hold the same opinion of aristocrats as you do of aristocratic snobs. I consider it my duty to inform you that I don't share this opinion. I venture to say that everyone knows me to be a man of liberal ideas, one devoted to progress, but precisely because of that I respect aristocrats—real aristocrats. Be so good, my dear sir" (at these words, Bazarov raised his eyes and looked at Pavel Petrovich), "my dear sir," he repeated acrimoniously, "be so good as to recall the English aristocracy. They don't sacrifice one iota of their rights, and for that reason they respect the rights of others. They insist on the fulfillment of obligations to themselves, and for that reason they fulfill their own obligations to others. The aristocracy has given England her freedom, and maintains it for her."

"We've heard that song sung many times," Bazarov rejoined, "but what are you trying to prove by this?"

"What I'm trying to prove by *thifs*, my dear sir" (when Pavel Petrovich was angry, he intentionally said "thifs" and "thefse" instead of "this" and "these," although he knew very well that such forms aren't strictly correct. A vestige of the customs of the Alexandrine era was discernible in this fashionable mannerism. On the rare occasions when the nobility of that era spoke their own language, they employed either "thifs" or "thiks," as if to say, "Of course, we're native-born Russians, and, at the same time, we're worldly people who are free to disregard scholastic rules"), "what I'm trying to prove by *thifs* is that without a sense of personal dignity, without self-respect—and these two sentiments are highly developed in the aristocrat—there's no secure basis for the social . . . *bien public* . . . the social welfare. Individual character, my dear sir—that's the main thing. Individual character must be as solid as a rock, since everything is built upon it. I'm perfectly well aware, for instance, that you consider my habits, my clothes, and my various refinements ridiculous, but all of that proceeds from a sense of self-respect, from a sense of duty—yes indeed, of duty. I live in the countryside, in a remote area, but I won't demean myself. I respect the human being in myself."

"Let me ask you this, Pavel Petrovich," Bazarov commenced. "You respect yourself so much and sit with your hands folded. What sort of benefit does that provide the *bien public*? If you didn't respect yourself, you'd behave exactly the same way."

Pavel Petrovich turned pale. "That's a completely different question. It's absolutely unnecessary for me to explain to you now why I sit with my hands folded, as you put it. I merely want to say that aristocratism is a principle, and in our times no one but immoral or vapid people can live without principles. I said that to Arkadii the day after he came home, and I repeat it now. Isn't that so, Nikolai?"

Nikolai Petrovich nodded his head.

"Aristocratism, liberalism, progress, principles," Bazarov was saying in the meantime. "If you think about it, what a lot of foreign—and useless—words! To a Russian, they're utterly unnecessary."

"What *is* necessary to a Russian, in your opinion? If we listen to you, we'll find ourselves beyond all humanity, beyond its laws. For heaven's sake—the logic of history demands...."

"But what difference does that logic make to us? We can get along without that, too."

"What do you mean?"

"Why, just this. You don't need logic, I trust, to put a piece of bread in your mouth when you're hungry. Where do all these abstractions get us?"

Pavel Petrovich raised his hands in horror.

"I don't understand you when you say that. You insult the Russian people. I don't understand how it's possible not to accept principles, rules! What gives you the strength to act, then?"

"I've already told you that we don't accept any authorities, Uncle," Arkadii interjected.

"We act on the strength of what we recognize to be useful," Bazarov declared. "At the present time, the most useful thing of all is negation—hence we negate."

"Everything?"

"Everything!"

"What? Not just art and poetry . . . but even . . . it's too horrible to say. . . ."

"Everything," Bazarov repeated with inexpressible composure.

Pavel Petrovich stared at him—he hadn't expected this—while Arkadii fairly blushed with delight.

"Allow me to observe, though," began Nikolai Petrovich, "you negate everything, or, to put it more precisely, you destroy everything. . . . But one has to construct something too, you know."

"That isn't our task right now. . . . The ground needs clearing first."

"The present condition of the people demands it," Arkadii added with dignity. "We're obligated to meet these demands. We have no right to indulge in the satisfaction of our personal egoism."

This last phrase evidently displeased Bazarov: it had a hint of philosophy—that is to say, romanticism, for Bazarov also called philosophy romanticism—about it. But he didn't deem it necessary to correct his young disciple.

"No, no!" Pavel Petrovich cried with sudden energy. "I'm not willing to believe that you gentlemen really know the Russian people, that you're the representatives of their demands or their aspirations! No! The Russian people aren't what you believe them to be. They hold tradition sacred. They're patriarchal people—they can't live without faith...."

"I won't dispute this," Bazarov interrupted. "I'm even prepared to agree that, in *this*, you're right."

"But if I'm right...."

"All the same, this proves nothing."

"This proves absolutely nothing," Arkadii repeated, with the confidence of an experienced chess-player who's foreseen an apparently dangerous move on the part of an adversary and hence isn't the least bit disturbed by it.

"How can this prove nothing?" Pavel Petrovich muttered in amazement. "Are you opposed to your own people, then?"

"And what if we are?" shouted Bazarov. "The people imagine when it thunders that the prophet Ilia is riding across the sky in his chariot. What then? Should I agree with them? Besides, the people are Russian, and aren't I Russian as well?"

"No, you aren't Russian after everything you've just said! I can't acknowledge you to be Russian."

"My grandfather plowed the land," Bazarov responded with haughty pride. "Ask any of your peasants which one of us—you or me—he'd more readily acknowledge to be a compatriot. You don't even know how to talk to him."

"Whereas you talk to him and hold him in contempt at the same time."

"Well, suppose he deserves contempt! You criticize my attitude—but how do you know that I've developed it at random, that it isn't a product of the very national spirit in whose name you're arguing so vehemently?"

"Indeed! How worthwhile nihilists are!"

"Whether they're worthwhile or not isn't for us to decide. Why, even you don't consider yourself a useless person."

"Gentlemen, gentlemen, please, nothing personal!" Nikolai Petrovich exclaimed, standing up.

Pavel Petrovich smiled and, laying his hand on his brother's shoulder, forced him to sit down again.

"Don't worry," he said. "I won't forget myself, precisely by virtue of that sense of dignity our Mr. ... Mr. Doctor mocks so mercilessly. Allow me to ask you this," he resumed, turning back to Bazarov. "Can you possibly suppose that your doctrine is new? You're sadly mistaken. The materialism you advocate has already been in vogue more than once, and has always proved to be insufficient...."

"Another foreign word!" interjected Bazarov. He was beginning to get angry, and his face assumed a sort of coarse, coppery hue. "In the first place, we advocate nothing—that's not among our customs...."

"What *do* you do, then?"

"I'll tell you what we do. Not long ago, we used to say that our officials took bribes, that we had no roads, no commerce, no real justice...."

"Oh, I see. You're reformers—that's what this is called, I believe. Even I would agree with many of your reforms, but...."

"Then we realized that talk—and nothing but talk—about our social ills isn't worth the effort, that it merely leads to banality and pedantry. We saw that our most intelligent individuals, the so-called leaders and reformers, are useless. We saw that we devote ourselves to absurdities, that we debate about art, unconscious creativity, parliamentarianism, trial by jury, and the devil knows what else, when the issue is getting enough bread to eat, when we're stifling under the grossest superstitions, when all our financial enterprises go bankrupt simply because there aren't enough honest people to run them, when the very emancipation our government has been fussing about will hardly do any good because our peasants are happy to rob even themselves in order to get drunk at the local tavern."

"Granted," Pavel Petrovich interrupted. "So—you became convinced of all this and decided not to undertake anything seriously yourselves."

"We decided not to undertake anything," Bazarov repeated grimly. He suddenly got annoyed with himself for having so extensively exposed his ideas before this gentleman.

"And to confine yourselves to criticism?"

"To confine ourselves to criticism."

"And that's called nihilism?"

"And that's called nihilism," Bazarov echoed, this time with particular insolence.

Pavel Petrovich squinted slightly. "So that's it!" he declared in a strangely composed voice. "Nihilism will cure all our woes, and you—you'll be our heroes and saviors. But why do you revile everyone else, even those reformers? Don't you do as much talking as everyone else?"

"Whatever our sins may be, that isn't one of them," Bazarov muttered between his teeth.

"What, then? Are you people of action? Are you preparing to act?"

Bazarov didn't answer. Pavel Petrovich seemed to tremble, but instantly regained control of himself.

"Hmm!...Action, destruction...," he continued. "But how can you destroy without even knowing why?"

"We destroy because we're a force," Arkadii asserted.

Pavel Petrovich looked at his nephew and laughed.

"Yes, a force, which doesn't have to account for itself," Arkadii maintained, straightening up.

"Unhappy boy!" Pavel Petrovich lamented, utterly incapable of restraining himself any longer. "If only you realized what it is about Russia that you're affirming with your banal sententiousness. No—it's enough to try the patience of an angel! A force! There's a force in the savage Kalmuck, in the Mongolian—but what does that have to do with us? What's precious to us is civilization. Yes, yes, my dear sir, its fruits are the ones that are precious to us. And don't tell me that those fruits are worthless. The poorest dabbler in art, *un barbouilleur*, the man who plays dance music for five kopecks an evening, are all more useful than you are, because they're representatives of civilization and not of brute Mongolian force! You consider yourselves leaders, and all the while you're only fit for a Kalmuck's hovel! A force! And then remember, you forceful gentlemen, that you're a total of four and a half men, whereas there are millions of others who won't let you trample their most sacred beliefs under foot, who'll crush you instead!"

"If we're crushed, it'll serve us right," Bazarov observed. "But that still remains to be seen. We aren't as few as you suppose."

"What? Do you seriously think that you can convert an entire people?"

"All Moscow was burned down by a cheap candle, you know," responded Bazarov.

"Yes, yes. First almost satanic pride, then mockery. This, this is what attracts the young, this is what wins over the inexperienced hearts of little boys! Here's one of them sitting beside you, ready to worship the ground you walk on. Look at him!" (Arkadii turned away and frowned.) "And this plague has already spread far and wide. I've been told that, when in Rome, our artists never set foot in the Vatican. They regard Raphael as virtually a fool because he's an authority, if you please, whereas they're all disgustingly sterile and inept beings whose imaginations don't rise above 'A Girl at a Fountain,' however hard they try! And even that girl is drawn incredibly poorly. In your view, they're courageous individuals, aren't they?"

"In my view," Bazarov retorted, "Raphael isn't worth a thing, and they're no better than he was."

"Bravo! Bravo! Listen, Arkadii . . . this is how youths of today have to express themselves! And if you think about it—how could they fail to follow you? In earlier times, young people had to study—they didn't want to be taken for ignoramuses, so they had to work hard whether they liked it or not. But now one just has to say, 'Everything on earth is absurd!' and the deed is done—young people are overjoyed. In fact, they were simply dolts before, whereas now they've suddenly become nihilists."

"Your praiseworthy sense of personal dignity has failed you," Bazarov remarked phlegmatically, even as Arkadii became thoroughly angry and his eyes began to flash. "Our argument has gone too far—it's better to break it off, I think. I'll be quite prepared to agree with you," he added as he stood up, "when you can name one single institution existing in our contemporary culture, either familial or societal, that doesn't merit complete, merciless destruction."

"I can name millions of such institutions," Pavel Petrovich averred, "millions! Take the commune, for instance."

An icy smile curved across Bazarov's lips. "Well, as regards the commune," he returned, "you'd better speak to your brother. I suspect that he's seen by now what the commune actually is—what its reciprocal guarantees, its sobriety, and other features of that kind actually mean."

"The family, then—the family as it exists among our peasants!" cried Pavel Petrovich.

"I believe that you yourselves had better not explore this question in detail, either. Perhaps you've heard about the privileges the head of the family enjoys in choosing his daughters-in-law? Take my advice, Pavel Petrovich, and give yourself two days to mull it over—you probably won't find anything right away. Consider all our social classes, and think about each one carefully, while Arkadii and I will...."

"Continue to subject everything to ridicule," interjected Pavel Petrovich.

"No, continue to dissect frogs. Let's go, Arkadii. Goodbye, gentlemen!"

The two friends walked off. The brothers were left alone, and merely exchanged glances at first.

"So," Pavel Petrovich finally began, "that's what today's youths are like! They're our successors!"

"Our successors!" Nikolai Petrovich repeated with a dejected sigh. He'd been sitting as if he were on thorns throughout the argument, and had done nothing but stealthily glance at Arkadii with an aching heart. "Do you know what I was reminded of, brother? Once I had a disagreement with our poor mother. She was shouting and wouldn't listen to me. Ultimately, I said to her: 'Of course, you can't understand me. We belong to two different generations.' She was terribly offended, but I thought: 'What can one do? It's a bitter pill, but she has to swallow it.' Now our turn has come, you see, and our successors can say to us: 'You don't belong to our generation. Swallow your pill.'"

"You're much too generous and humble," replied Pavel Petrovich. "On the contrary, I'm convinced that you and I are far more in the right than these young gentlemen, even though perhaps we do express ourselves in somewhat old-fashioned language, *vieilli*, and don't have the same arrogant conceit.... Young people nowadays are so pretentious! You ask one of them, 'Do you want red wine or white?' 'I customarily prefer red!' he answers in a deep bass voice, with a face as solemn as if the whole universe were watching him at that instant...."

"Would you care for any more tea?" Fenechka inquired, sticking her head through the doorway. She hadn't dared to enter the drawing room while the sound of voices arguing in there was audible.

"No. You can tell them to take the samovar away," Nikolai Petrovich responded, and he rose to greet her. Pavel Petrovich abruptly said "*Bon soir*" to him and went off to his study.

XI

Half an hour later, Nikolai Petrovich went out to his favorite arbor in the garden. A wave of unhappy thoughts washed over him. For the first time, he clearly perceived the gulf between himself and his son; he foresaw that it would grow wider and wider with every passing day. In vain, then, had he spent whole days reading the latest books during the winters in Petersburg; in vain had he listened to the conversations of young people; in vain had he rejoiced when he'd managed to interject his own ideas into their heated discussions. "My brother says we're right," he thought, "and, all vanity aside, I myself do believe that they're farther from the truth than we are, although at the same time I do feel that there's something inside them we haven't got, some form of superiority over us. . . . Is it youth? No, it's not just youth. Doesn't their superiority consist in their having fewer traces of the landowner in them than we have in us?"

Nikolai Petrovich's head sank despondently, and he rubbed his hand across his face.

"But to renounce poetry?" he thought further. "To have no feeling for art, for nature . . . ?" And he looked around him, as though trying to understand how it was possible to have no feeling for nature.

It was already evening; the sun was hidden behind a small aspen grove that lay half a verst from the garden; its shadow stretched across the motionless fields. A peasant on a little white horse was trotting along a dark, narrow path right next to the grove; his entire figure was clearly visible, right down to the patch on his shoulder, despite the fact that he was in the shade; his horse's hoofs flashed along in a smooth rhythm. The sun's rays fell across the grove from the far side, piercing its thickets to throw such a warm light over the aspens' trunks that they looked like pine trees, turning their leaves almost dark-blue, while a pale-blue sky faintly tinged by the glow of sunset spread above them. Swallows were flying high overhead; the wind had completely died away; some dilatory bees were humming lazily and drowsily among the lilac blossoms; a swarm of midges was hanging like a cloud over a lone branch delineated against the sky.

"My God, how beautiful!" Nikolai Petrovich marveled, and his favorite verses began to come to his lips—when he remembered Arkadii's *Stoff und Kraft* and fell silent. But he continued to sit there, he continued to give himself over to the sad and yet comforting play of solitary reflections. He liked to daydream, and his life in the countryside had enhanced this tendency in him. How recently had he been daydreaming like this, waiting for his son at the inn—and what a change had occurred since that day! Their relationship, then still undefined, was defined now—and defined in what way! His deceased wife came to his mind's eye, not as he'd known her for so many years, not as the thrifty, kind housewife, but as a young girl with a slim figure, innocently inquiring eyes, and a tight coil of hair fastened at her childlike neck. He recalled the first time he'd seen her—he was still a student then. He'd encountered her on the staircase of his lodgings, and jostling against her by accident, he'd wanted to apologize, but could only mutter, "*Pardon, monsieur,*" while she'd bowed, smiled, then had suddenly seemed frightened and had run away, although at a bend in the staircase she'd glanced at him quickly, donned a serious expression, and blushed. Afterward had come the first shy visits, the half-words and half-smiles, the embarrassment, the melancholy, the yearnings, and finally, that breathless rapture.... Where had it all gone? She'd become his wife, he'd been happy as few people on earth are happy....

"But," he wondered, "why couldn't one live an eternal, immortal life in those first, sweet moments?"

He didn't try to clarify his idea to himself, but he sensed that he longed to regain that blissful time through something stronger than memory; he longed to feel his Maria near him again, to feel her warmth, her breath—and after a little while, it seemed as if he could envision over his head....

"Nikolai Petrovich," Fenechka's voice rang out nearby. "Where are you?"

He was startled. He wasn't upset or ashamed.... He'd never even considered the possibility of comparing his wife and Fenechka—but he regretted the fact that she'd decided to come and look for him. Her voice instantly reminded him of his gray hair, his age, his present....

The enchanted world into which he'd just stepped, which had risen out of the dim mists of the past, shimmered—and vanished.

"I'm here," he answered, "I'm coming. Run along. There they are, the traces of the landowner," the thought flashed through his mind. Fenechka silently glanced toward him in the arbor, then disappeared, and he noticed with astonishment that night had fallen while he'd been daydreaming. Everything around him was dark and hushed; Fenechka's face, ever so pale and small, had gleamed as she went past him. He stood up and started to go back to the house. But the emotions that had been stirred up in his heart couldn't be soothed all at once, and he began to walk slowly around the garden, at times staring at the ground beneath his feet, at other times raising his eyes skyward, where masses of stars were twinkling. He walked for a long while, until he was nearly exhausted, but the restlessness within him—some sort of searching, vague, mournful restlessness—still wasn't assuaged. Oh, how Bazarov would have laughed at him if he'd known what was going on inside Nikolai Petrovich at that moment! Even Arkadii would have condemned him. He, a forty-four-year-old man, an agriculturist and farmer, was shedding tears, groundless tears; this was a hundred times worse than the cello.

Nikolai Petrovich went on walking, unable to decide to go into the house, into the snug, peaceful nest that regarded him so hospitably from all its lighted windows; he didn't have the strength to tear himself away from the darkness, from the garden, from the sensation of fresh air on his face, or from that melancholy, that restless craving. . . .

At a turn in the path, he ran into Pavel Petrovich. "What's the matter with you?" he asked Nikolai Petrovich. "You're as white as a ghost. You must not feel well. Why don't you go to bed?"

Nikolai Petrovich briefly described his spiritual condition to his brother and walked away. Pavel Petrovich went to the end of the garden, where he also grew pensive and also raised his eyes skyward. But nothing was reflected in his handsome, dark eyes except the light of the stars. He hadn't been born a romantic, and his fastidiously dry, serious soul, with its inclination toward French' misanthropy, wasn't capable of daydreaming. . . .

"Do you know what?" Bazarov said to Arkadii the same night. "I've got a magnificent idea. Your father was saying today that he'd received an invitation to visit your illustrious relative. Your father's not going—so let's head for *** ourselves, since this gentleman invited you, too. You see what fine weather it is. We'll stroll around and take a look at the town. We'll enjoy ourselves for five or six days, and that's enough."

"Then you'll come back here again?"

"No, I have to go to my father's. You know that he lives about thirty versts from ***. I haven't seen him, or my mother either, in a long time. I should cheer the old folks up. They've been good to me, especially my father—he's priceless. I'm their only son, too."

"Will you stay with them for a long time?"

"I don't think so. It'll be boring, I suspect."

"And you'll drop in here on your way back?"

"I don't know. . . . I'll see. Well, what do you say? Do we go?"

"If you like," Arkadii replied languidly. In his heart, he was highly delighted at his friend's suggestion, but he considered it his duty to conceal his feelings. He wasn't a nihilist for nothing! The next day he and Bazarov set off for ***. The younger members of the household at Marino were saddened by their departure— Duniasha even cried . . . but the older inhabitants breathed more easily.

XII

The town of ***, to which our friends headed, was under the jurisdiction of a young governor who was both a progressive and a despot, as is often the case in Russia. By the end of his first year of governance, he'd managed to quarrel not only with the marshal of the nobility, a retired officer of the Guards who entertained frequently and bred horses, but even with his own subordinates. The difficulties that ensued as a result eventually assumed such proportions that the ministry in Petersburg had deemed it necessary to send out some trusted representative, accompanied by a commission, to investigate the entire matter on the spot. By choice of the authorities, the job fell to Matvei Ilich Koliazin, son of the Koliazin under whose protection the Kirsanov brothers had found themselves at one time. He was also a "young man," that is to say, he'd recently turned forty, but he was already well on the way to becoming a statesman, and wore a star on each side of his chest— one of them was foreign, it's true, and not of the highest rank. Like the governor whom he'd come to pass judgment on, he was considered progressive. Even though he was already an important personage, he didn't resemble the majority of important personages. He had the highest possible opinion of himself—his vanity knew no bounds—but he behaved simply, gazed at people affably, listened indulgently, and laughed so good-naturedly that on first acquaintance he might even be taken for "a marvelous man." On important occasions, however, he knew how to make his authority felt, as they say. "Energy is essential," he used to declare at those times, "*l'énergie est la première qualité d'un homme d'état.*" Despite all that, he was readily deceived, and any moderately experienced official could twist him around his little finger. Matvei Ilich spoke

of Guizot with great respect, and strove to impress upon everyone
that he didn't belong to the category of *routiniers* and backward
bureaucrats, that not one significant social event escaped his notice. . . . All such phrases were well known to him. He even followed
developments in contemporary literature, albeit with dignified indifference, the same way that an adult who encounters a procession
of small boys marching down the street will occasionally walk along
behind it. In reality, Matvei Ilich hadn't progressed very far beyond
those government officials of the Alexandrine era who used to
prepare for an evening party at Mrs. Svechin's (she was living in
Petersburg at that time) by reading a page of Condillac. But his
methods were different, more modern. He was an adroit courtier,
an expert conniver—and nothing more; he had no special aptitude
for business, and no intellectual gifts. But he knew how to conduct
his own affairs successfully—no one could get the better of him
there—and that's the most important thing, after all.

Matvei Ilich welcomed Arkadii with the good cheer—we might
even call it playfulness—characteristic of the enlightened high-
ranking official. He was astonished, however, when he learned that
the cousins he'd invited had stayed at home in the countryside.
"Your papa always was an eccentric," he remarked, toying with
the tassels on his magnificent velvet dressing gown. Then, suddenly
turning to a young official wearing a discreetly buttoned-up uniform, he cried, "What?" with an air of concern. The young man,
whose lips had become glued together from prolonged silence, stood
up and looked perplexedly at his chief. But, having disconcerted
his subordinate, Matvei Ilich paid no further attention to him. As
a rule, our high-ranking officials are fond of disconcerting their
subordinates, and the means to which they resort in order to attain
this goal vary widely. The following means, among others, are
widely employed, "are quite a favorite," as the English say: a high-
ranking official suddenly ceases to understand even the simplest
words, feigning total deafness.

He'll ask, for instance, "What day is today?"

He's respectfully informed, "Today's Friday, your Ex-x-x-x-
lency."

"Eh? What? What's that? What are you saying?" the official
repeats tensely.

"Today's Friday, your Ex-x-x-x-lency."

"Eh? What? What's Friday? Which Friday?"

"Friday, your Ex-x-x-x-lency, the day of the week."

"Well, well, so you dare to instruct me, eh?"

Matvei Ilich was precisely this sort of official, even though he was considered a liberal.

"I advise you to go and visit the governor, my dear boy," he said to Arkadii. "You realize that I don't advise you do so because I subscribe to the old-fashioned belief in the necessity of paying one's respects to the authorities, but simply because the governor is a very decent fellow. Besides, you probably want to meet the prominent members of society here.... You aren't antisocial, I trust? And he's giving a large ball the day after tomorrow."

"Will you be at the ball?" Arkadii inquired.

"He's giving it in my honor," Matvei Ilich responded almost pityingly. "Do you know how to dance?"

"Yes, I do, but not very well."

"That's a shame! There are some pretty girls here, and it's disgraceful for a young man not to be able to dance. Again, I don't say that because of any old-fashioned ideas—I don't believe for a moment that a man's wit lies in his feet. But Byronism is ridiculous—*il a fait son temps.*"

"But, uncle, it's not at all because of Byronism that I...."

"I'll introduce you to the ladies here—I'll take you under my wing," Matvei Ilich interrupted, and he laughed complacently. "You'll find it warm enough there, eh?"

A servant entered and announced the arrival of the superintendent of public lands, a mild-looking elderly man with deep creases around his mouth who was extremely fond of nature, especially on a summer day when, in his words, "every busy little bee takes a little bribe from every little flower." Arkadii departed.

He found Bazarov at the inn in which they were staying; it took him a long time to persuade his friend to go to the governor's. "Well, there's no other choice," Bazarov finally said. "It's no good doing something halfway. We came to look at the townspeople— let's go and look at them!"

The governor welcomed the young men cordially enough, but he neither asked them to sit down nor sat down himself. He was constantly in a hurry; he donned a tight uniform and an extremely stiff tie each morning; he never ate or drank too much; he was always organizing things. They called him Burdalieu around the district, hinting not at the famous French prophet but at the word *"burda,"* an indecisive person. He invited Kirsanov and Bazarov to his ball and, within a few minutes, invited them a second time, regarding them as brothers and calling them both Kirsanov.

They were on their way home from the governor's when a short man in a Slavophile overcoat suddenly leapt out of a passing carriage, crying, "Evgenii Vasilich!" and dashed up to Bazarov.

"Ah! It's you, Herr Sitnikov," Bazarov observed, continuing along the pavement. "What brought you here?"

"Can you imagine, I'm here completely by accident," he replied. Then, returning to the carriage, he waved his hand several times and shouted, "Follow us, follow us! My father had some business here," he continued, hopping across a ditch, "and so he invited me.... I heard about your arrival today, and I've already been to see you...." (On returning to their room, the friends did, in fact, find a card with turned-down corners that bore the name of Sitnikov, in French on one side, in Cyrillic characters on the other.) "You aren't coming from the governor's, I hope?"

"It's no use hoping—we've come straight from there."

"Ah! In that case, I'll visit him, too.... Evgenii Vasilich, introduce me to your ... to the...."

"Sitnikov, Kirsanov," Bazarov mumbled, without stopping.

"I'm most honored," Sitnikov began, walking sideways and smirking as he hurriedly pulled off his extremely elegant gloves. "I've heard so much.... I'm an old acquaintance of Evgenii Vasilich and, I may say—his disciple. I'm indebted to him for my regeneration...."

Arkadii looked at Bazarov's disciple. A combined expression of anxiety and stupidity was imprinted on the small but pleasant features of his sleek face; his little eyes, which seemed too close together, had a fixed, worried look, and his laugh—a sort of short, wooden laugh—was worried as well.

"Would you believe it," he continued, "when Evgenii Vasilich said for the first time in my presence that it wasn't right to accept any authorities, I experienced such ecstasy ... as though I'd been blind and had recovered my sight! Now, I thought, I've finally found an authentic human being! By the way, Evgenii Vasilich, you absolutely must get to know a lady here who's really capable of understanding you, and for whom a visit from you would be a real treat. You've heard of her, I presume?"

"Who is it?" Bazarov asked reluctantly.

"Kukshina, *Eudoxie*, Evdoksia Kukshina. She has a remarkable nature, *émancipée* in the true sense of the word—an advanced woman. Do you know what? Let's all go together to visit her right now. She lives a mere two steps from here. We'll have a meal there. Have you eaten yet?"

"No, not yet."

"Well, that's excellent. She's separated from her husband, you understand. She isn't dependent on anyone."

"Is she pretty?" Bazarov interrupted him.

"N-no, you couldn't say that."

"Then what the devil are you asking us to go and see her for?"

"Oh, you jokester, you. . . . She'll give us a bottle of champagne."

"So that's it. The practical person is now in evidence. By the way, is your father still in the gin business?"

"Yes," Sitnikov hurriedly replied, and he laughed shrilly. "Well? Will you come?"

"I really don't know."

"You wanted to look at people. Go ahead," Arkadii remarked under his breath.

"And what do *you* say, Mr. Kirsanov?" Sitnikov interjected. "You have to come, too. We can't go without you."

"But how can we all burst in on her at the same time?"

"That's no problem. Kukshina's a marvelous person!"

"There'll be a bottle of champagne?" Bazarov queried.

"Three!" Sitnikov exclaimed. "I'll swear to that."

"By what?"

"My own head."

"Your father's wallet would be better. However, let's go."

XIII

The small, nobleman's house designed in the Moscow style inhabited by Avdotia Nikitishna—otherwise known as Evdoksia Kukshina—was located in one of the sections of *** that had recently burned down; it's well known that our provincial towns catch on fire every five years. By the door there was a bell–rope hanging above a visiting card nailed askew, and in the entryway the visitors were met by some woman, neither exactly a servant nor a companion, wearing a cap—these were unmistakable tokens of the progressive tendencies of the lady of the house. Sitnikov asked whether Avdotia Nikitishna was at home.

"Is that you, *Victor?*" piped a thin voice from the adjoining room. "Come in."

The woman in the cap promptly disappeared.

"I'm not alone," Sitnikov responded, casting a sharp glance at Arkadii and Bazarov as he briskly pulled off his overcoat, beneath which appeared something in the nature of a coachman's long velvet jacket.

"It doesn't matter," answered the voice. "*Entrez.*"

The young men went in. The room into which they walked was more like an office than a drawing room. Sheets of paper, letters, and thick issues of Russian journals, their pages for the most part uncut, were strewn across dusty tables; white cigarette butts lay scattered in every direction. A fairly young lady was semi-reclining on a leather sofa. Her blond hair was somewhat disheveled; she was wearing a silk, not perfectly spotless dress, heavy bracelets on her short arms, and a lace scarf on her head. She rose from the sofa, casually drawing a velvet cape trimmed with yellowish ermine around her shoulders, languidly said, "Good morning, *Victor*," and shook Sitnikov's hand.

"Bazarov, Kirsanov," he announced abruptly, in imitation of Bazarov.

"Pleased to meet you," Mrs. Kukshin responded, staring at Bazarov with a pair of round eyes, between which stood a small, forlorn, turned-up red nose. "I know you," she added, shaking his hand as well.

Bazarov scowled. There was nothing repulsive about the plain little figure of this emancipated woman, but her facial expression produced an unpleasant effect on the observer. One involuntarily felt compelled to ask her, "What's the matter? Are you hungry? Or bored? Or shy? Why are you so edgy?" Like Sitnikov, she was always perturbed in spirit. Her manner of speaking and moving was quite unconstrained and yet awkward at the same time. She obviously regarded herself as a good-natured, simple creature, and nonetheless, whatever she did, it always seemed that this was precisely what she didn't want to do; everything associated with her appeared to be done on purpose, as children say—that is, not simply, not naturally.

"Yes, yes, I know you, Bazarov," she repeated. (She had the habit peculiar to many provincial and Moscow ladies of calling men by their last names from the very first day of her acquaintance with them.) "Would you like a cigar?"

"A cigar's all well and good," interjected Sitnikov, who by now was lolling in an armchair, his legs dangling in the air, "but give us something to eat—we're awfully hungry. And tell them to bring us a little bottle of champagne."

"Sybarite," Evdoksia retorted, and she laughed. (Whenever she laughed, the gums above her upper teeth showed.) "Isn't it true that he's a sybarite, Bazarov?"

"I like comfort in life," Sitnikov affirmed self-importantly. "That doesn't prevent me from being a liberal."

"Yes, it does, it does prevent you!" Evdoksia cried. She gave instructions to her maid, however, regarding both the food and the champagne.

"What do you think about it?" she added, turning to Bazarov. "I'm confident that you share my opinion."

"Well, no," Bazarov demurred. "A piece of meat is better than a piece of bread, even from the chemical point of view."

"Are you studying chemistry? That's my passion. I've actually invented a new sort of compound myself."

"A compound? You?"

"Yes. And do you know what for? To make dolls' heads unbreakable. I'm practical as well, you see. But everything isn't quite ready yet—I still have to read Liebig. By the way, have you read Kisliakov's article on female labor in the *Moscow Gazette*? Read it, please. You're interested in the woman's question, I presume? And in the schools, too? What does your friend do? What's his name?"

Mrs. Kukshin let her questions fall one after another with affected nonchalance, without waiting for any reply. Spoiled children talk to their nursemaids that way.

"My name's Arkadii Nikolaich Kirsanov," Arkadii answered, "and I don't do anything."

Evdoksia giggled. "How charming! What, don't you smoke? You know, *Victor*, I'm very angry with you."

"What for?"

"They tell me you've begun to sing the praises of George Sand again. She's a retrograde woman, and nothing more! How can people compare her with Emerson? She doesn't have any ideas on education, or physiology, or anything. She's never heard of embryology, I'm sure, and these days—where can you get without that?" (Evdoksia even threw up her hands.) "Ah, what a wonderful article Elisevich has written on that subject! He's a gentleman of genius." (Evdoksia regularly employed the word "gentleman" instead of the word "person.") "Bazarov, come and sit by me on the sofa. Perhaps you don't know that I'm horribly afraid of you."

"Why so, if you'll permit me to inquire?"

"You're a dangerous gentleman—you're such a critic. Good God! Why, how ridiculous—I'm talking like some countrified landowner. I really am a landowner, though—I manage my estate myself. And can you imagine, my bailiff Erofei is a wonderful type—just like Cooper's Pathfinder. There's something so spontaneous about him! I've finally settled down here. It's an intolerable town, isn't it? But what can one do?"

"One town's like another," Bazarov remarked coolly.

"All its activities are such petty ones—that's what's so awful! I used to spend the winter in Moscow . . . but now my lawful spouse, Mr. Kukshin, is residing there. And besides, Moscow nowadays . . . I don't know . . . it's not the same as it used to be. I'm considering going abroad. I was on the verge of setting off last year."

"To Paris, I presume?" Bazarov asked.

"To Paris and Heidelberg."

"Why Heidelberg?"

"For heaven's sake—Bunsen's there!"

Bazarov could find no reply to make to this.

"*Pierre* Sapozhnikov . . . do you know him?"

"No, I don't."

"For heaven's sake, *Pierre* Sapozhnikov. . . . He's always at Lidia Khostatova's."

"I don't know her, either."

"Well, it was he who undertook to escort me. Thank God, I'm independent—I don't have any children. . . . What did I say? *Thank God!* It doesn't matter, though."

Evdoksia rolled a cigarette between her fingers, which were brown with tobacco stains, raised it to her tongue, licked it, and began to smoke. The maid came in carrying a tray.

"Ah, here's our meal! Would you like an appetizer first? *Victor,* open the bottle—that's your forte."

"Yes, that's my forte," Sitnikov grumbled, and then he laughed shrilly again.

"Are there any pretty women here?" Bazarov inquired as he drank a third glass of champagne.

"Yes, there are," Evdoksia replied, "but they're all such empty-headed creatures. *Mon amie* Mrs. Odintsov, for example, isn't bad-looking. It's a pity she has a certain reputation. . . . This wouldn't matter, however, except that she has no independence of thought, no breadth, nothing . . . like that. The entire system of education needs changing. I've thought about this a great deal—our women are very badly educated."

"You can't get anywhere with them," Sitnikov averred. "One ought to despise them, and I do despise them, utterly and absolutely!" (The opportunity to feel and express contempt was most gratifying to Sitnikov. He attacked women in particular, never suspecting that he was fated to be cringing before his wife a few months later merely because she'd been born Princess Durdoleosova.) "Not one of them would be capable of understanding our conversation, not one of them deserves to be mentioned by serious men like us!"

"But there's no need whatsoever for them to understand our conversation," observed Bazarov.

"Whom do you mean?" Evdoksia inquired.

"Pretty women."

"What? Do you share Proudhon's views, then?"

Bazarov straightened up haughtily. "I don't share anyone's views—I have my own."

"Damn all authorities!" Sitnikov shouted, delighted to have a chance to express himself forcefully in front of the man he slavishly admired.

"But even Macaulay . . . ," began Mrs. Kukshin.

"Damn Macaulay," thundered Sitnikov. "Are you going to stick up for mindless hussies?"

"For mindless hussies, no, but for the rights of women, which I've sworn to defend to the last drop of my blood."

"Damn . . . ," here Sitnikov stopped. "But I don't deny them," he asserted.

"No—I can see that you're a Slavophile."

"No, I'm not a Slavophile, although, of course. . . ."

"No, no, no! You're a Slavophile. You're an advocate of the patriarchal despotism espoused by the *Domostroi*. You'd like to have a whip in your hand!"

"A whip's an excellent thing," Bazarov remarked, "but we've gotten to the last drop. . . ."

"Of what?" Evdoksia interrupted.

"Of champagne, most honored Avdotia Nikitishna, of champagne—not of your blood."

"I can never listen calmly when women are attacked," Evdoksia continued. "It's awful, just awful. Instead of attacking them, you'd be better off reading Michelet's book *De l'amour*. It's marvelous!

Gentlemen, let's talk about love," Evdoksia added, letting her arm languorously fall onto a rumpled sofa cushion.

A sudden silence ensued.

"No—why should we talk about love?" asked Bazarov. "But you just mentioned a Mrs. Odintsov . . . that was what you called her, I believe. Who is this lady?"

"She's charming, charming!" Sitnikov piped up. "I'll introduce you. She's intelligent, wealthy, and a widow. Unfortunately, she isn't sufficiently advanced yet. She ought to get to know our Evdoksia better. I drink to your health, *Eudoxie*! Let's toast! *Et toc, et toc, et tin-tin-tin! Et toc, et toc, et tin-tin-tin*!!!"

"*Victor*, you're a naughty boy."

The meal continued for a long while. The first bottle of champagne was foliowed by another, then a third, and even a fourth. . . . Evdoksia chattered away without pausing; Sitnikov aided and abetted her. They had a long discussion about whether marriage is a prejudice or a crime, whether all human beings are born equal or not, and precisely what constitutes individuality. Things finally got to the point where Evdoksia, flushed from the wine she'd drunk, tapping her flat fingertips on the keys of a badly tuned piano, began to sing in a hoarse voice, first gypsy songs and then Seymour Schiff's ballad "Granada lies slumbering," while Sitnikov tied a scarf around his head and enacted the role of the dying lover at the words:

And your lips with mine
In a burning kiss entwine.

Finally, Arkadii couldn't stand it. "Ladies and gentlemen, it's getting to be like Bedlam in here," he stated out loud. Bazarov, who'd inserted an amused remark into the conversation at rare intervals—he'd paid more attention to the champagne—yawned loudly, stood up, and without saying goodbye to their hostess, left with Arkadii. Sitnikov jumped up and followed them.

"Well, well, what do you think of her?" he inquired, obsequiously skipping from the right to the left of them. "Didn't I tell you she's a remarkable individual? If only we had more women like that! In her own way, she's a manifestation of the highest morality."

"And is the establishment that your father owns also a manifestation of morality?" Bazarov queried, pointing to a tavern they were passing at that moment.

Sitnikov gave another shrill laugh. He was deeply ashamed of his origins, and didn't know whether to feel flattered or offended by Bazarov's unexpected familiarity.

XIV

A few days later, the ball at the governor's residence took place. Matvei Ilich was truly "the hero of the hour." The marshal of the nobility declared to one and all that he'd come purely out of respect for Matvei Ilich; meanwhile, even at the ball, even as he stood absolutely still, the governor kept on "organizing things." The geniality of Matvei Ilich's manner was equaled only by its stateliness. He was gracious to everyone—in some cases with a hint of disgust, in others with a hint of respect; he was all bows and smiles, *"en vrai chevalier français"* toward the ladies, and frequently burst into the hearty, sonorous laughter befitting a high-ranking official. He slapped Arkadii on the back and loudly called him "nephew"; he graced Bazarov, who was attired in a somewhat aged dress coat, with a sidelong glance in passing—a distracted but indulgent one—and with an indistinct but affable grunt, in which nothing could be distinguished but the words "I" and "very much"; he gave Sitnikov one finger to shake, accompanied by a smile, although his head was already averted; he even said *"Enchanté"* to Mrs. Kukshin, who appeared at the ball wearing dirty gloves, a dress with no crinoline, and a bird of paradise decoration in her hair.

There were scads of people, and no lack of men who could dance; the civilians for the most part crowded up against the walls, but the officers danced assiduously, especially one of them who'd spent six weeks in Paris, where he'd mastered various reckless interjections such as *"Zut,"* *"Ah fichtrrre,"* *"Pst, pst, mon bibi,"* and so forth. He pronounced them to perfection, with genuine Parisian *chic*, and yet said, *"si j'aurais"* for *"si j'avais,"* *"absolument"* in the sense of "essentially"—in sum, employing that Russo-French dialect the French so ridicule when they needlessly assure us that we speak French like angels, *"comme des anges."*

Arkadii, as we already know, danced badly, and Bazarov didn't dance at all; they both took up positions in a little corner; Sitnikov attached himself to them. Exhibiting contemptuous scorn on his face, giving vent to spiteful comments, he kept looking around insolently, and sincerely seemed to be enjoying himself. Suddenly, his expression changed, and, turning toward Arkadii as if embarrassed, he announced, "Mrs. Odintsov's here!"

Arkadii glanced around and caught sight of a tall woman wearing a black dress who was standing in the doorway to the room. He was struck by the dignity of her bearing. Her uncovered arms gracefully rested beside her slender waist; some delicate sprays of fuchsia gracefully hung from her gleaming hair down to her sloping shoulders; her bright eyes looked out tranquilly and intelligently beneath a somewhat protruding white forehead—her look was definitely tranquil, not pensive—and her lips curved in a barely perceptible smile. Some sort of compassionate, gentle strength shone in her face.

"Are you acquainted with her?" Arkadii asked Sitnikov.

"Intimately. Would you like me to introduce you?"

"Please . . . after this quadrille."

Bazarov likewise directed his attention toward Mrs. Odintsov.

"Who's that with the striking figure?" he inquired. "She doesn't look like the other females."

Having waited until the end of the quadrille, Sitnikov led Arkadii up to Mrs. Odintsov, but he hardly seemed to be intimately acquainted with her: he muddled his sentences, and she gazed at him with some surprise.

But her face assumed a pleased expression when she heard Arkadii's last name—she asked him whether he was the son of Nikolai Petrovich Kirsanov.

"Yes, indeed."

"I've met your father twice and have heard a great deal about him," she continued. "I'm very glad to meet you."

At that instant, some adjutant rushed up to her and begged her to dance a quadrille. She consented.

"Do you dance, then?" Arkadii asked respectfully.

"Yes, I do. Why would you suppose that I don't dance? Do you think I'm too old?"

"For heaven's sake, how could I possibly. . . ? But, in that case, let me ask you to join me for a mazurka."

Mrs. Odintsov smiled kindly. "Certainly," she said, and looked at Arkadii not exactly disdainfully, but the way married sisters look at very young brothers.

Mrs. Odintsov was a little older than Arkadii—she was almost twenty-nine—but he felt like a schoolboy, a young student, in her presence, as if their age difference were much greater. Matvei Ilich approached her with a majestic air and ingratiating remarks. Arkadii moved away, but he continued to watch her; he didn't take his eyes off her, even during the quadrille. She spoke with equal ease to her partner and to the official, quietly turning her head and eyes from one to the other, and quietly laughing twice. Her nose—like almost all Russian noses—was a bit thick, and her complexion wasn't perfectly clear; despite this, Arkadii concluded that he'd never met such an attractive woman before. He couldn't get the sound of her voice out of his ears; the very folds of her dress seemed to hang differently on her than on all the other women—more flatteringly and amply—and her movements were distinguished by both a special fluidity and naturalness.

Arkadii secretly felt somewhat shy when, at the first sounds of the mazurka, he began to sit out the dance beside his partner—he'd expected to embark upon a conversation with her, but he merely ran his hand through his hair without finding a single word to say. His shyness and discomfort didn't last long, however; Mrs. Odintsov's tranquillity communicated itself to him as well, and before a quarter of an hour had passed, he was talking to her freely about his father, his uncle, his life in Petersburg and in the countryside. Mrs. Odintsov listened to him with courteous attention, opening and closing her fan slightly; his chatter was interrupted when other partners sought her out—Sitnikov, among others, invited her to dance twice. She came back, sat down again, and picked up her fan, not even breathing more rapidly, as Arkadii began to chatter away again, filled by the happiness of being near her, of talking to her, of gazing at her eyes, her handsome forehead, her entire lovely, dignified, intelligent face. She herself said little, but her words reflected a knowledge of life; from some of her observations, Arkadii gathered that this young woman had already experienced and thought about a great deal. . . .

"Whom were you standing with," she asked him, "when Mr. Sitnikov brought you over to meet me?"

"Did you notice him?" Arkadii asked in turn. "He has an impressive face, doesn't he? That's my friend Bazarov."

Arkadii started to discuss his "friend." He spoke of him in such detail, with such enthusiasm, that Mrs. Odintsov turned toward Bazarov and looked at him intently. Meanwhile, the mazurka was drawing to a close. Arkadii grew sorry to say goodbye to his partner—he'd spent nearly an hour with her so enjoyably! During the whole time, it's true, he'd continually felt as though she were condescending to him, as though he ought to be grateful to her . . . but young hearts aren't weighed down by feelings like that. The music stopped.

"*Merci*," Mrs. Odintsov remarked, standing up. "You've promised to come and visit me—bring your friend with you. I'd be very curious to meet someone who has the courage to believe in nothing." The governor walked up to Mrs. Odintsov, announced that supper was ready, and offered her his arm with a careworn expression on his face. As she moved away, she turned to bestow a final smile and bow on Arkadii. He bowed low in return, watched her walk off (how graceful her figure seemed to him, draped in the grayish luster of black silk!), thinking, "She's forgotten my existence this very instant," and felt some sort of exquisite humility enter his soul. . . .

"Well?" Bazarov questioned Arkadii as soon as he'd rejoined his friend in the corner. "Did you have a good time? A gentleman has just been telling me that this lady is 'oi-oi-oi,' but I gather that this gentleman is a fool. What do you think—is she really 'oi-oi-oi'?"

"I don't quite understand what that means," Arkadii replied.

"Oh my! What innocence!"

"In this case, I don't understand the gentleman you're referring to. Mrs. Odintsov is very nice—no doubt about it—but she behaves so coldly and strictly that. . . ."

"Still waters . . . as you know!" interjected Bazarov. "You say she's cold—that's just what adds a special flavor. Besides, you like ice cream, don't you?"

"Possibly," Arkadii muttered. "I can't decide about that. She wants to meet you, and asked me to bring you to visit her."

"I can imagine how you've described me! But you've done very well. Take me. Whatever she may be—whether she's simply a provincial social lioness or an 'emancipated woman' like Mrs. Kukshin—in any case, she's got a pair of shoulders of a sort I haven't seen in a long time."

Arkadii was offended by Bazarov's cynicism, but—as often happens—he didn't directly reproach his friend for what he didn't like about him. . . .

"Why are you unwilling to accept freedom of thought in women?" he inquired in a low voice.

"Because, my friend, as far as I can see, the only women who think freely are monsters."

Their conversation was cut short at this point. Both young men left immediately after supper, followed by Mrs. Kukshin's nervously hostile but not unconstrained laughter; her vanity had been deeply wounded by the fact that neither of them had paid any attention to her. She stayed at the ball later than anyone else, and at four o'clock in the morning, she was dancing a polka-mazurka in Parisian style with Sitnikov. This edifying spectacle constituted the final event of the governor's ball.

XV

"Let's see what species of mammal this specimen belongs to," Bazarov said to Arkadii the following day as they mounted the staircase of the hotel in which Mrs. Odintsov was staying. "I smell something wrong here."

"I'm surprised at you!" Arkadii cried. "What? You, Bazarov, clinging to the narrow morality that...."

"What an odd person you are!" Bazarov cut him off casually. "Don't you know that 'something wrong' means 'something right' in our dialect, to our sort? It's a virtue, of course. Didn't you yourself tell me this morning that she'd made a strange marriage—although, in my opinion, marrying a wealthy old man is by no means a strange thing to do. On the contrary, it makes perfect sense. I don't believe the town gossip, but I'd like to think that it's justified, as our learned governor says."

Arkadii didn't respond and knocked on the door of the suite. A young servant dressed in livery conducted the two friends into a large room, which was badly furnished, like all rooms in Russian hotels, but was filled with flowers. Mrs. Odintsov herself appeared shortly, wearing a simple morning dress. She looked even younger in the spring sunlight. Arkadii introduced Bazarov, noticing with concealed amazement that he seemed ill at ease, whereas Mrs. Odintsov remained perfectly tranquil, just as she'd been the previous day. Bazarov himself was aware of being ill at ease, and became irritated. "Here we go—frightened of a female!" he thought and, lolling in an armchair no less informally than Sitnikov, began to speak with undue familiarity, while Mrs. Odintsov kept her clear eyes trained on him.

Anna Sergeevna Odintsova was the daughter of Sergei Nikolaevich Loktev, a man renowned for his handsome appearance, his schemes, and his gambling, who, after holding on and making a sensation in Petersburg and Moscow for fifteen years, had ended

up completely ruining himself at cards and being forced to retire
to the countryside, where he'd died shortly thereafter, leaving a
small estate to his two daughters—Anna, a young woman of twenty,
and Katerina, a child of twelve. Their mother—who was descended
from an impoverished line of princes, the Kh——s—had died in
Petersburg while her husband was still in his prime.

Anna's situation after her father's death had been very difficult.
The brilliant education she'd received in Petersburg hadn't prepared her to cope with the cares of managing a household, or with
a lonely existence in an out-of-the-way place. She'd known absolutely no one in the entire district, and she'd had no one to
consult. Her father had tried to avoid all contact with the neighbors;
he'd despised them in his way, and they'd despised him in theirs.
She hadn't lost her self-possession, though, and had promptly sent
for her mother's sister, Princess Avdotia Stepanovna Kh——, a
spiteful, arrogant old lady who, upon installing herself in her niece's
house, appropriated all the best rooms for her personal use, criticized and complained from morning to night, and wouldn't even
take a walk in the garden without being accompanied by her one
serf, a surly servant who wore a threadbare, pea-green suit of livery
with light-blue trim and a three-cornered hat.

Anna had patiently put up with all her aunt's caprices, gradually
proceeded with her sister's education, and seemed to have reconciled herself to the idea of wasting away in a remote area. . . . But
destiny had decreed another fate for her. She happened to have
been noticed by a certain Odintsov, a very wealthy man of about
forty-six, who was an eccentric and a hypochondriac. Stout, morbid, and embittered, but not stupid and not evil, he'd fallen in
love with her and had asked her to marry him. She'd consented
to become his wife; he'd lived with her for six years and, upon
his death, had left all his property to her. Anna Sergeevna had
remained in the countryside for nearly a year after his death. After
that, she'd gone abroad to travel with her sister, but had just spent
time in Germany—she'd gotten bored, and had come back to live
at her beloved Nikolskoe, which was located nearly forty versts
from the town of ***. She owned a magnificent, wonderfully furnished house with a beautiful garden and conservatories there; her
late husband had spared no expense to gratify his desires.

Anna Sergeevna very rarely went to town—generally only on
business—and then she didn't stay long. She wasn't well liked in
the district; there had been a fearful outcry at her marriage to

Odintsov. All sorts of fictitious stories were told about her: it was alleged that she'd helped her father in his cardsharping activities, and even that she'd gone abroad for good reason, that it had been necessary to conceal the lamentable consequences.... "You understand why?" the indignant gossips would wind up. "She's gone through fire," they said of her, to which a noted local wit usually added, "and through the other elements as well." All this talk eventually reached her ears, but she ignored it; there was a good deal of independence and determination in her character.

Mrs. Odintsov leaned back in her armchair and listened to Bazarov with her hands folded. Contrary to his custom, he was talking a lot, and was obviously trying to engage her interest—which surprised Arkadii again. He couldn't decide whether Bazarov was achieving his goal, though. It was difficult to guess what impression was being made on Anna Sergeevna from her face: it constantly retained the same cordial, refined expression; her beautiful eyes glowed with attentiveness, but it was serene attentiveness. She was unpleasantly affected by Bazarov's artificial manner during the first minutes of the visit, as by a bad odor or a discordant sound, but she quickly gathered that he was ill at ease, and this actually flattered her. Nothing was repulsive to her but vulgarity, and no one could have accused Bazarov of vulgarity.

Arkadii was repeatedly forced to encounter surprises that day. He'd expected that Bazarov would talk to an intelligent woman like Mrs. Odintsov about his ideas and opinions—she herself had expressed a desire to listen to the man "who has the courage to believe in nothing"—but instead of that, Bazarov talked about medicine, about homeopathy, and about botany. It turned out that Mrs. Odintsov hadn't wasted her time in solitude: she'd read a number of excellent books and spoke perfectly correct Russian. She turned the conversation to music, but noticing that Bazarov didn't appreciate art, she subtly brought it back to botany, even though Arkadii was just launching into a discourse upon the significance of folk melodies. Mrs. Odintsov continued to treat him as though he were her younger brother; she seemed to appreciate his goodness and youthful simplicity—and that was all. Their lively, unhurried conversation went on for more than three hours, ranging freely over various subjects.

The friends finally stood up and began to say goodbye. Anna Sergeevna looked at them cordially, held out her beautiful, white hand to each one and, after a moment's thought, said with an uncertain but attractive smile, "If you aren't afraid of getting bored, gentlemen, come and see me at Nikolskoe."

"For heaven's sake, Anna Sergeevna," Arkadii cried, "I'd consider it a particular pleasure...."

"And you, Monsieur Bazarov?"

Bazarov merely bowed—and a final surprise was in store for Arkadii: he noticed that his friend was blushing.

"Well?" Arkadii said to him on the street. "Do you still maintain your previous opinion of her—that she's 'oi-oi-oi'...?"

"Who knows? You see how icy she is!" Bazarov retorted, and after a brief pause he added: "She's a grand duchess, a royal personage. She just needs a train trailing behind her and a crown on her head."

"Our grand duchesses don't speak Russian like that," Arkadii remarked.

"She's seen some ups and downs, my dear boy—she's eaten some of our bread!"

"Anyway, she's charming," Arkadii responded.

"What a magnificent body!" Bazarov continued. "If only I could see it on a dissection table now."

"Stop it, for God's sake, Evgenii! That's going too far."

"Well, don't get angry, you big baby. I just meant that it's of superior quality. We'll have to go and stay with her."

"When?"

"Well, why not the day after tomorrow? What's there for us to do here? Drink champagne with Mrs. Kukshin? Listen to your cousin, the liberal official?... Let's head out the day after tomorrow. By the way—my father's little place isn't far from there. Isn't this Nikolskoe on the S—— road?"

"Yes."

"Optime. Why hesitate? Leave that to fools—and intellectuals. I tell you, that's a magnificent body!"

Three days later, the two friends were driving along the road to Nikolskoe. The day was bright but not too hot, and the sleek horses trotted along merrily, lightly switching their bound, braided tails. Arkadii looked at the road, and without knowing why, he smiled.

"Congratulate me!" Bazarov suddenly exclaimed. "Today's the twenty-second of June, my guardian angel's day. Let's see whether he'll help me out somehow. They're expecting me home today," he added, lowering his voice. . . . "Well, they can go on expecting me a little longer. What difference does it make?"

XVI

The estate inhabited by Anna Sergeevna stood on an exposed hill not far from a yellow stone church that had a green roof and white columns, with a fresco representing the resurrection of Christ painted in the "Italian" style over the main entrance. A swarthy warrior especially conspicuous for his rotund contours, wearing a helmet, was stretched out in the fresco's foreground. Beyond the church extended a village arranged in two long rows of houses whose chimneys peeped out here and there above the thatched roofs. The estate's manor house was built in the same style as the church, that known among us as the Alexandrine style: the house was also painted yellow and had a green roof and white columns, as well as a pediment with an escutcheon on it. The regional architect had designed both buildings with the approval of the late Odintsov, who couldn't stand—as he put it—any sort of pointless, arbitrary innovations. The house was sheltered on both sides by the dark trees of an old garden; an avenue of sculpted pines led up to the entrance.

Our friends were met in the hallway by two tall servants dressed in livery; one of them immediately ran to fetch the steward. That steward, a stout man in a black dress coat, promptly appeared and led the visitors up a staircase covered with rugs to a special room in which two beds had already been prepared for them, along with all the necessary toiletries. It was clear that order reigned supreme in the household: everything was clean, and the air was permeated with some sort of pleasant fragrance reminiscent of the reception rooms of government ministers.

"Anna Sergeevna requests that you join her in half an hour," the steward announced. "Do you have any orders to give in the meantime?"

"There won't be any orders, most respected sir," replied Bazarov. "Perhaps you'd be so kind as to bring me a glass of vodka."

"Yes, sir," the steward responded, not without perplexity, and he withdrew, his boots creaking as he walked.

"What *grande genre!*" Bazarov observed. "That's what it's called by your sort, isn't it? She's a duchess, and that's all there is to it."

"A nice duchess," Arkadii retorted. "At our very first encounter, she invited prominent aristocrats like you and me to visit her."

"Especially me, a future doctor, a doctor's son, and a village sexton's grandson. . . . I presume you know that I'm the grandson of a sexton? Like Speranskii," Bazarov added after a brief pause, compressing his lips. "At any rate, she indulges herself—oh, how she indulges herself, this lady! Shouldn't we put on evening clothes?"

Arkadii merely shrugged his shoulders . . . but even he felt a little uncomfortable.

Half an hour later, Bazarov and Arkadii entered the drawing room. It was a large, lofty room furnished rather luxuriously, but not in particularly good taste. Heavy, expensive furniture stood in a conventionally stiff arrangement along the walls, which were covered by cinnamon-colored paper with gold flowers on it; Odintsov had ordered the furniture from Moscow through a friend and agent of his, a wine merchant. Above a sofa centered against one wall hung a portrait of a flabby, blond-haired man who seemed to be regarding the visitors in unfriendly fashion. "It must be the great man himself," Bazarov whispered to Arkadii, and wrinkling his nose he added, "Hadn't we better run for it . . . ?" But at that moment, the lady of the house came in. She wore a light, gauzy dress; her hair, which was smoothly combed back behind her ears, gave a girlish look to her clean, fresh face.

"Thank you for keeping your promise," she began. "You'll have to stay with me for a little while—it really isn't too bad here. I'll introduce you to my sister. She plays the piano well, which is a matter of indifference to you, Monsieur Bazarov, but you, Monsieur Kirsanov, like music, I believe. Besides my sister, an elderly aunt of mine lives with me, and one of our neighbors drops by occasionally to play cards. That comprises our entire social circle. And now let's sit down."

Mrs. Odintsov delivered this little speech with notable precision, as though she'd learned it by heart. Then she turned toward Arkadii: it appeared that her mother had known Arkadii's mother, and had even been the latter's confidante regarding her love for Nikolai Petrovich. Arkadii began to talk about his deceased mother with great warmth, while Bazarov started to leaf through picture albums. "What a tame beast I've become!" he thought to himself.

A beautiful greyhound wearing a blue collar ran into the drawing room, its nails tapping on the floor, followed by a dark-haired, dark-complexioned girl of about eighteen, who had a somewhat round but appealing face and small, dark eyes. She was holding a basket filled with flowers in her hands.

"This is my Katia," Mrs. Odintsov declared, gesturing toward her with a nod of the head. Katia made a slight curtsey, sat down beside her sister, and began picking through the flowers. The greyhound, whose name was Fifi, went up to each of the visitors in turn, wagging her tail and thrusting her cold nose into his hands.

"Did you pick all those yourself?" asked Mrs. Odintsov.

"Yes," answered Katia.

"Is our aunt coming to have tea?"

"Yes."

When Katia spoke, she smiled quite sweetly, shyly and naively, somehow looking up from under her eyebrows with comical severity. Everything about her was still young and immature: her voice, the rosy color that spread across her whole face, her pink hands with their whitish palms, and her slightly rounded shoulders. . . . She was constantly becoming flushed and out of breath.

Mrs. Odintsov turned to Bazarov. "You're looking at those pictures out of politeness, Evgenii Vasilich," she began. "That doesn't interest you. You'd better come over here by us and we'll argue a little about something."

Bazarov moved closer. "What subject do you have in mind?" he inquired.

"Any one you like. I warn you, I'm terribly argumentative."

"You?"

"Yes—that seems to surprise you. Why?"

"Because, as far as I can judge, you have a calm, cool temperament, and one has to get carried away to be argumentative."

"How could you have managed to comprehend me so quickly? In the first place, I'm impatient and obstinate—you should ask Katia—and, in the second, I get carried away very easily."

Bazarov looked at Anna Sergeevna. "Possibly. You'd know better than I. And so you're in the mood for an argument—by all means. I was looking at pictures of the Saxon mountains in your album, and you remarked that those couldn't interest me. You said so because you assume that I have no feeling for art—and in fact, I really don't have any. But those views might interest me from a geological standpoint—regarding the formation of the mountains, for instance."

"I beg your pardon. But as a geologist, you'd be more likely to resort to a book, to a specialized work on the subject, than to a drawing."

"The drawing shows me at glance what would be spread over ten pages in a book."

Anna Sergeevna fell silent for a moment.

"So you don't have the tiniest drop of artistic feeling?" she queried, putting her elbow on the table and by that very motion bringing her face closer to Bazarov's. "How can you get along without it?"

"And what do I need it for, may I ask?"

"Well, at least in order to study and comprehend people."

Bazarov smiled.

"In the first place, life experience takes care of that, and in the second, I assure you, studying separate individuals isn't worth the trouble. All human beings resemble one another, in soul as well as body. Each of us has an identically constructed brain, spleen, heart, and set of lungs. And the so-called moral qualities are also the same in everyone—the slight variations don't mean a thing. A single human specimen is sufficient to judge every other one by. People are like trees in a forest—no botanist would think of studying each individual birch tree."

Katia, who was arranging the flowers one at a time in leisurely fashion, raised her eyes to regard Bazarov quizzically, and upon encountering his quick, careless glance, she blushed all over. Anna Sergeevna shook her head.

"The trees in a forest," she repeated. "Then, in your view, there's no difference between a stupid person and an intelligent one, between a good one and an evil one?"

"No, there is a difference, just as there is between a sick one and a healthy one. The lungs of a tubercular patient aren't in the same condition as yours and mine, although they're constructed the same way. We more or less know where physical diseases come from. Moral diseases come from bad education, from all the inanities people's heads are stuffed with from childhood onward—from the defective state of society, in short. Reform society, and there won't be any diseases."

Bazarov uttered all this as though thinking to himself the entire time, "Believe me or not—it's all the same to me!" He slowly ran his long fingers through his sideburns while his eyes strayed around the room.

"And so," Anna Sergeevna said, "you conclude that when society has been reformed, there won't be either stupid or evil people?"

"At any rate, given the proper organization of society, it won't matter in the least whether someone is stupid or intelligent, evil or good."

"Yes, I understand. They'll all have the same spleen."

"Just so, madam."

Mrs. Odintsov turned to Arkadii. "And what's your opinion on his matter, Arkadii Nikolaevich?"

"I agree with Evgenii," he responded.

Katia looked at him mistrustfully.

"You surprise me, gentlemen," commented Mrs. Odintsov, "but we'll discuss this together further. Right now, I hear my aunt coming in to have tea. We should spare her ears."

Anna Sergeevna's aunt, Princess Kh——, a thin little woman with a pinched face and malevolent eyes staring out beneath a gray wig, came in and, barely bowing to the guests, lowered herself into a wide, velvet-covered armchair that no one was allowed to sit in except her. Katia put a footstool under her feet; the elderly lady didn't thank her, didn't even look at her, but merely shifted her hands under the yellow shawl that nearly covered her feeble body. The princess liked yellow: her cap had bright-yellow ribbons on it as well.

"How did you sleep, Aunt?" Mrs. Odintsov inquired, raising her voice.

"That dog is in here again," the elderly lady muttered in reply, and noticing that Fifi had taken two hesitant steps in her direction, she cried, "Shoo . . . shoo!"

Katia summoned Fifi and opened the door for her.

Fifi rushed out in delight, hoping to be taken for a walk, but when she was left alone outside the door, she began scratching on it and whining. The princess scowled. Katia started to go out. . . .

"I expect that the tea is ready," Mrs. Odintsov observed. "Let's go into the other room, gentlemen. Aunt, will you come and have some tea?"

The princess got up from her chair without speaking and led the way out of the drawing room. They all followed her into the dining room. An armchair covered with cushions, devoted to the princess's use, was drawn back from the table with a scraping noise by a young servant wearing livery; she sank into it. Katia, pouring the tea, handed her a cup emblazoned with a heraldic crest first of all. The elderly lady put some honey in the cup (she considered it both sinful and extravagant to drink tea with sugar in it, although she herself never spent any money on anything) and suddenly asked in a hoarse voice, "So what does Prince Ivan have to say?"

No one replied. Bazarov and Arkadii quickly realized that no one paid any attention to her, even though everyone addressed her respectfully.

"They keep her for the sake of status, because of her noble lineage . . . ," thought Bazarov.

After tea, Anna Sergeevna suggested that they go out for a walk, but it began to drizzle, and the entire group, with the exception of the princess, returned to the drawing room. The neighbor, a dedicated cardplayer, arrived; his name was Porfirii Platonych. He was a stoutish, grayish man with short, spindly legs who was highly polite and amusing. Anna Sergeevna, still conversing primarily with Bazarov, asked whether he'd like to play the card game of preference with them in the old-fashioned way. Bazarov assented, declaring that he ought to prepare himself in advance for the duties awaiting him as a country doctor.

"You'll have to be careful," Anna Sergeevna warned. "Porfirii Platonych and I will beat you. As for you, Katia," she added, "play something for Arkadii Nikolaevich. He likes music, and we can listen, too."

Katia reluctantly went over to the piano, and Arkadii, although he really did like music, reluctantly followed her—it seemed to him that Mrs. Odintsov was sending him away. Like every young man at his age, he was already experiencing some sort of vague, oppressive sensation that resembled a presentiment of love welling up in his heart. Katia raised the top of the piano and asked in a low voice, without looking at Arkadii, "What should I play for you?"

"Whatever you want," Arkadii responded indifferently.

"What sort of music do you like the best?" Katia inquired, without changing her position.

"Classical," Arkadii replied in the same tone of voice.

"Do you like Mozart?"

"Yes, I like Mozart."

Katia pulled out Mozart's Sonata-Fantasia in C minor. She played very well, albeit somewhat stiffy and unemotionally. She sat upright and immobile, her eyes fixed on the notes and her lips tightly compressed. Only at the conclusion of the sonata did her face begin to glow and her hair come loose, a little lock of it falling onto her dark forehead.

Arkadii was particularly affected by the last part of the sonata, the part in which, amid the bewitching gaiety of the carefree melody, sonorities of mournful, almost tragic, suffering suddenly intrude.... But the thoughts Mozart's music prompted in him had no connection to Katia. Looking at her, he simply thought, "Well, this young lady doesn't play badly—and she isn't bad-looking, either."

When she'd finished the sonata, without taking her hands off the keys, Katia asked, "Is that enough?" Arkadii declared that he wouldn't dare to trouble her further and began to chat about Mozart with her; he asked her whether she'd chosen that sonata herself or someone had recommended it to her. But Katia answered him in monosyllables; she withdrew into herself; she *hid*. Whenever this happened to her, she didn't come out of herself again very quickly; her face assumed an obstinate, almost obtuse expression at such times. She wasn't exactly shy, but she was mistrustful, and rather overawed by her sister, who'd brought her up and had no suspicion of that fact, naturally. Arkadii was finally forced to summon the reappearing Fifi and pat her on the head with an affable smile in order to make himself seem to be at ease. Katia began to arrange her flowers again.

Bazarov, meanwhile, kept losing—Anna Sergeevna played cards in masterly fashion, and Porfirii Platonych could hold his own at this game as well. Bazarov lost a sum that, although trifling in itself, wasn't altogether comfortable for him to lose. At supper, Anna Sergeevna once again turned the conversation to botany.

"Let's go for a walk tomorrow morning," she said to him. "I want you to teach me the Latin names and species of the wildflowers."

"What good are the Latin names to you?" Bazarov inquired.

"Order is essential in everything," she replied.

"What an exquisite woman Anna Sergeevna is!" Arkadii exclaimed when he was alone with his friend in the room allotted to them.

"Yes," Bazarov responded, "a female with brains. And she's seen something of life, too."

"In what sense do you mean that, Evgenii Vasilich?"

"In a good sense, a good sense, my dear friend, Arkadii Nikolaich! I'm sure that she manages her estate superbly, too. But she isn't what's wonderful—it's her sister."

"What, that dark little thing?"

"Yes, that dark little thing. She's the one who's fresh and untouched, and shy, and reticent, and everything you could want. She's someone worth devoting yourself to. You could make whatever you like out of her. But the other one—she's a stale loaf."

Arkadii didn't reply to Bazarov, and each of them got into bed with unaccustomed thoughts in his head.

Anna Sergeevna thought about her guests in turn that evening. She liked Bazarov for his lack of flirtatiousness, and even for his sharply defined views. She saw something new in him, something she'd never happened to encounter before, and it aroused her curiosity.

Anna Sergeevna was a rather strange creature. Having no prejudices of any kind, or even strong convictions, she never retreated for any reason or went out of her way for anything. She'd seen many things quite clearly, and was interested in many things, but nothing had totally satisfied her; then again, she hardly desired total satisfaction. Her intellect was at once probing and impartial; her doubts were never assuaged to the point of oblivion, and they never became strong enough to alarm her. If she hadn't been wealthy and independent, perhaps she would have thrown herself into some battle, would have discovered some passion. . . . But life was easy for her, although she got bored at times, and she continued to spend day after day without haste, only rarely becoming agitated. Dreams did occasionally burst into rainbow colors before her eyes, but she breathed more freely when they faded away, and she didn't regret their passing. Her imagination periodically overstepped the bounds of that which is deemed permissible by conventional morality, but even then her blood flowed as quietly as ever through her intriguingly graceful, tranquil body. Once in a while, emerging from a fragrant bath, thoroughly warm and enervated, she'd begin to muse on the insignificance of life, on its sorrows, its toil, its evil. . . . Her soul would become filled with sudden courage and would swell with noble ardor, but a draft would blow through a half-opened window, Anna Sergeevna would shrink back, feeling plaintive and almost angry, and only one thing would matter to her at that moment—to escape from that horrid draft.

Like all women who haven't truly been in love, she wanted something without knowing herself precisely what it was. Strictly speaking, she didn't want anything—but it seemed to her that she wanted everything. She'd barely been able to endure the late Odintsov (she'd married him out of calculation, although she probably wouldn't have agreed to become his wife if she hadn't believed he was a kind man), and had conceived a secret repugnance for all men, whom she could envision as nothing other than slovenly, ponderous, drowsy, and feebly importunate creatures. Once, somewhere abroad, she'd met a handsome young Swede with a chivalrous expression on his face and honest blue eyes under a broad forehead. He'd made a strong impression on her—but it hadn't prevented her from returning to Russia.

"What a strange person this doctor is!" she thought as she lay on the lace pillows of her magnificent bed under a light silk coverlet. . . . Anna Sergeevna had inherited a little of her father's inclination toward luxury. She'd loved her sinful but good-natured father dearly, and he'd adored her, had joked with her in friendly terms, as though she were an equal, and had confided in her fully, often asking her advice. She barely remembered her mother.

"What a strange person this doctor is!" she repeated to herself. She stretched, smiled, clasped her hands behind her head, then ran her eyes over two pages of a frivolous French novel, dropped the book—and fell asleep, perfectly clean and cool amid her clean, fragrant linen.

The following morning, Anna Sergeevna went off botanizing with Bazarov immediately after breakfast and returned just before midday. Arkadii didn't go anywhere and spent about an hour with Katia. He wasn't bored in her company—she herself offered to repeat the sonata of the day before—but when Mrs. Odintsov finally came back, when he caught sight of her, his heart momentarily contracted. She walked through the garden with somewhat tired steps; her cheeks were glowing and her eyes were shining more brightly than usual beneath her round straw hat. She was twirling the thin stalk of a wildflower in her fingers, a light mantilla had slipped down to her elbows, and the wide gray ribbons of her hat were clinging to her bosom. Bazarov walked behind her, as self-confident and casual as always, but the expression on his face, however cheerful and even friendly it was, didn't please Arkadii. Muttering "Good morning!" between his teeth, Bazarov went off to his room, while Mrs. Odintsov shook Arkadii's hand abstractedly and also walked past him.

"Good morning!" thought Arkadii.... "As though we hadn't already seen one another today!"

XVII

Time, as is well known, sometimes flies like a bird and sometimes crawls like a worm, but human beings are generally particularly happy when they don't notice whether it's passing quickly or slowly. That was the condition in which Arkadii and Bazarov spent two weeks at Mrs. Odintsov's. The regimen she'd instituted in her household and her daily life partially made this possible. She strictly adhered to this regimen herself, and forced others to submit to it as well. Everything during the day was done at a fixed time: in the morning, precisely at eight o'clock, the whole group assembled to have tea; from that morning tea until noontime, everyone did whatever they pleased—the hostess herself was closeted with her bailiff (the estate was run on the rent system), her steward, and her head housekeeper; before dinner, the group reassembled to converse or read; the evening was devoted to strolls, cards, and music; at half past ten, Anna Sergeevna retired to her room, gave her orders for the following day, and went to bed.

Bazarov didn't like this measured, somewhat ceremonious punctuality in daily life—"like riding on rails," he averred; the livery-clad servants and the decorous stewards offended his democratic sensibilities. He declared that if one went this far, one might as well dine in the English style, wearing white tie and tails. He expressed his views on the subject to Anna Sergeevna one day. Her manner was such that no one ever hesitated to speak freely in front of her. She heard him out and then commented, "From your point of view, you're right—perhaps, in that respect, I truly am a noble-woman. But one can't live in the country without order—one would be consumed by boredom." And she continued to do things her way. Bazarov grumbled, but life was as easy as it was at Mrs. Odintsov's for him and Arkadii precisely because everything in the house "rode on rails."

Nonetheless, a change had taken place in both young men since the first days of their stay at Nikolskoe. Bazarov, whom Anna Sergeevna obviously favored, although she seldom agreed with him, had begun to show signs of unprecedented perturbation: he was easily irritated, reluctant to talk, he gazed around angrily, and couldn't sit still in one place, as though he were being swept away by some irresistible force; Arkadii, who'd definitely decided that he was in love with Mrs. Odintsov, had begun to yield to a gentle melancholy. This melancholy didn't hinder him from becoming better acquainted with Katia, however—it even impelled him to pursue a friendly, warm relationship with her. "*She* doesn't appreciate me! So be it! . . . But here's a gentle creature who won't turn away from me," he thought, and his heart tasted the sweetness of magnanimous sensations once more. Katia vaguely realized that he was seeking some sort of consolation in her company and didn't deny either him or herself the innocent pleasure of a half-shy, half-confiding friendship. They didn't converse with one another in Anna Sergeevna's presence; Katia always withdrew into herself under her sister's sharp gaze, and Arkadii, as befits a man in love, couldn't pay attention to anything else when he was near the object of his desire—but he was happy when he was alone with Katia. He sensed that he didn't possess the power to interest Mrs. Odintsov; he was intimidated and confused when he was alone with her. She didn't know what to say to him, either—he was too young for her. With Katia, by contrast, Arkadii felt at home; he treated her indulgently, encouraged her to express the impressions made on her by music, fiction, poetry, and other such trifles, without noticing or admitting that those trifles interested him as well. Katia, for her part, didn't try to dispel his melancholy.

Arkadii was comfortable with Katia, as Mrs. Odintsov was with Bazarov, and thus it usually worked out that the two couples, after being together for a little while, went their separate ways, especially during strolls. Katia adored nature, and Arkadii loved it too, although he didn't dare to admit it; Mrs. Odintsov was relatively indifferent to the beauties of nature, like Bazarov. The nearly continual separation of the two friends wasn't without its consequences: their relationship began to change. Bazarov ceased to talk to Arkadii about Mrs. Odintsov, even ceasing to criticize her "aristocratic ways." It's true that he praised Katia as much as before, merely recommending that her sentimental tendencies be restrained, but his praises were hasty, his advice was dry, and he generally spoke to Arkadii less than before. . . . He seemed to be avoiding Arkadii, as if he were ashamed of his friend. . . .

Arkadii observed all this, but he kept his observations to himself.

The real cause of this "change" was the feeling Mrs. Odintsov inspired in Bazarov, a feeling that tortured and maddened him, one that he would have instantly denied with scornful laughter and cynical derision if anyone had even remotely hinted at the possibility that it existed inside him. Bazarov was a great admirer of women and of female beauty, but love in the ideal or, as he put it, romantic sense he termed lunacy, unpardonable imbecility. He regarded chivalrous sentiments as something on the order of a deformity or disease, and had more than once expressed his surprise that Toggenburg hadn't been put into an insane asylum, along with all minnesingers and troubadours. "If you like a woman," he'd say, "try to achieve your goal. But if you can't, well, then turn your back on her—there are lots of fish in the sea."

He liked Mrs. Odintsov; the widespread rumors about her, the freedom and independence of her ideas, as well as her unmistakable inclination toward him—everything seemed to be in his favor. Still, he quickly saw that he wouldn't "achieve his goal" with her, and yet, to his own bewilderment, he found that it was beyond his strength to turn his back on her. His blood took fire as soon as he thought about her. He could have easily mastered his blood, but something else was taking hold of him, something he'd never accepted in any way, at which he'd always jeered, at which every bit of his pride revolted. In his conversations with Anna Sergeevna, he expressed his calm contempt for everything romantic more firmly than ever; when he was alone, though, he indignantly perceived the romantic in himself. Then he'd set off for the forest and tramp through it with long strides, smashing the twigs that got in his way and cursing both her and himself under his breath. Otherwise, he'd climb into the hayloft in the barn and, obstinately closing his eyes, he'd try to force himself to sleep—although he didn't always succeed, of course. He'd suddenly imagine those chaste arms entwining around his neck someday, and those proud lips responding to his kisses, and those intelligent eyes resting with tenderness— yes, tenderness—on his. Then his head would begin to spin and he'd lose consciousness for an instant, until indignation would boil up inside him again. He caught himself having all sorts of "shameful" thoughts, as though some devil were mocking him. Sometimes it seemed to him that a change was taking place in Mrs. Odintsov as well, that something special had appeared in the expression on her face, that maybe . . . but at this point, he'd stamp his foot or grit his teeth, and clench his fists.

In fact, Bazarov wasn't altogether mistaken. He'd stirred Mrs. Odintsov's imagination, he'd intrigued her—she thought about him a great deal. She wasn't bored in his absence, she didn't wait for him, but she always became more animated upon his arrival; she liked to be left alone with him and she liked to talk to him, even when he made her angry or offended her tastes, her refined habits. She was seemingly eager both to test him and to examine herself. One day, walking in the garden with her, he suddenly announced in a sullen voice that he intended to leave shortly for the village his father lived in.... She turned pale, as though something had stabbed her in the heart, stabbed her so hard that she was taken aback, and she wondered for a long while afterward what the significance of this feeling could be. Bazarov had informed her of his departure with no thought of testing her, of seeing what would come of it; he never "fabricated" anything. That morning he'd had a visit from his father's bailiff, Timofeich, who'd taken care of him when he was a child. This Timofeich, an experienced, astute little old man with faded blond hair, a weather-beaten, ruddy face, and tiny teardrops in his shrunken eyes, had unexpectedly presented himself to Bazarov wearing a short overcoat made of thick grayish-blue cloth belted with a strip of leather, and tar-covered boots.

"Hello, old man, how are you?" Bazarov cried.

"Hello, Evgenii Vasilich," began the little old man, and he smiled delightedly, as a result of which his whole face was suddenly covered with wrinkles.

"Why have you come? They've sent for me, is that it?"

"For heaven's sake, sir, how could they do that?" Timofeich mumbled. (He remembered the strict instructions he'd received from his master as he was leaving.) "I was sent to town on the master's business, and I heard that your honor was here, so I turned off along the way—to have a look at your honor, so to speak.... As if I'd ever want to disturb you!"

"Come on, don't tell lies!" Bazarov interrupted him. "Is this the road you take to town?"

Timofeich hesitated, and didn't answer.

"Is my father well?"

"Yes, thank God."

"And my mother?"

"Arina Vlasevna is well, too, praise be to God."

"They're expecting me, I suppose?"

The little old man leaned his small head to one side.

"Ah, Evgenii Vasilich, how could they not expect you? It makes my heart ache to look at your parents, I swear to God."

"All right, all right! Don't elaborate! Tell them I'll be there soon."

"Yes, sir," Timofeich replied with a sigh.

As he walked out of the house, he pulled his cap down on his head with both hands, clambered into a wretched-looking lightweight carriage he'd left by the gate, and set off at a trot—but not in the direction of town.

The evening of that same day, Mrs. Odintsov was ensconced in her study with Bazarov, while Arkadii paced around the main hall listening to Katia play the piano. The princess had gone upstairs to her room; she couldn't bear guests as a rule, especially this "new riffraff," as she dubbed them. She merely sulked in public; but she made up for it in private by bursting into such coarse language in front of her maid that the cap and wig on her head fairly danced. Mrs. Odintsov was well aware of all this.

"Why is it that you're preparing to leave?" she began. "What about your promise?"

Bazarov shivered. "Which one?"

"Have you forgotten? You were going to give me some chemistry lessons."

"What can I do? My father is expecting me—I can't loiter any longer. However, you can read Pelouse and Frémy's *Notions générales de chimie*. It's a good book, quite clearly written. You'll find everything you need in it."

"But don't you remember, you assured me that a book can't replace . . . I've forgotten how you put it, but you know what I mean. . . . Don't you remember?"

"What can I do?" Bazarov repeated.

"Why leave?" Mrs. Odintsov asked, lowering her voice.

He glanced at her. She'd tilted her head toward the back of her easy chair and had folded her arms, which were bare to the elbow, across her chest. She seemed paler by the light of a single lamp covered with a perforated paper shade. A full white gown completely enfolded her; even the tips of her feet, which she'd also crossed, were barely visible.

"Why stay?" Bazarov responded.

Mrs. Odintsov turned her head slightly. "How can you ask why? Haven't you enjoyed yourself with me? Or do you think you won't be missed here?"

"I'm sure of it."

Mrs. Odintsov fell silent for a moment. "You're wrong in thinking that. But I don't believe you. You couldn't say that in all seriousness." Bazarov remained motionless. "Evgenii Vasilich, why don't you say something?"

"What should I say to you? People generally aren't worth missing, and I less than most."

"Why so?"

"I'm a pragmatic, uninteresting person. I don't know how to talk."

"You're fishing for compliments, Evgenii Vasilich."

"That's not a custom of mine. Don't you yourself recognize that I've got nothing in common with the elegant side of life, the side you prize so highly?"

Mrs. Odintsov nibbled the corner of her handkerchief.

"You may think what you like, but I'll be bored when you go away."

"Arkadii will stay," Bazarov observed.

Mrs. Odintsov shrugged her shoulders slightly. "I'll be bored," she repeated.

"Really? In any case, you won't be bored for long."

"What makes you think that?"

"Because you yourself told me that you're only bored when your regimen is disrupted. You've organized your life with such impeccable regularity that there can't be any room in it for either boredom or sadness . . . for any unpleasant emotions."

"And do you find that I'm so impeccable . . . that is, that I've organized my life so regularly?"

"Absolutely! Here's an example—in a few minutes, the clock will strike ten, and I know in advance that you'll send me away."

"No, I won't send you away, Evgenii Vasilich. You may stay. Open that window. . . . It seems stuffy to me somehow."

Bazarov rose and pushed on the window. It flew open with a bang. . . . He hadn't expected it to open so easily—besides which, his hands were shaking. The mild, dark night seemed to fill the room with its nearly black sky, its faintly rustling trees, and the fresh fragrance of its pure, flowing air.

"Draw the blinds and sit down," Mrs. Odintsov told him. "I want to chat with you before you go away. Tell me something about yourself—you never talk about yourself."

"I try to discuss useful subjects with you, Anna Sergeevna."

"You're very modest. . . . But I'd like to know something about you, about your family—about your father, for whom you're forsaking us."

"Why is she saying these things?" Bazarov wondered.

"None of that is the least bit interesting," he said aloud, "especially for you. We aren't prominent people."

"And I'm an aristocrat, in your opinion?"

Bazarov raised his eyes to look at Mrs. Odintsov.

"Yes," he said with exaggerated sharpness.

She smiled. "I see that you don't know me very well, although you maintain that all people are alike. I'll tell you about my life sometime.... but, first, tell me about yours."

"I don't know you very well," Bazarov reiterated. "Maybe you're right—maybe everyone really is a riddle. You, for instance. You avoid society, you're oppressed by it—and you've invited two students to visit you. What makes you live in the countryside, with your intellect, with your beauty?"

"What? What was that you said?" Mrs. Odintsov interjected eagerly. "With my ... beauty?"

Bazarov scowled. "It doesn't matter," he muttered. "I meant to say that I don't fully understand why you've settled down in the countryside."

"You don't understand it.... But do you nevertheless explain it to yourself somehow?"

"Yes.... I assume that you constantly remain in the same place because you've spoiled yourself, because you're quite fond of comfort and convenience and quite indifferent to everything else."

Mrs. Odintsov smiled again. "You absolutely refuse to believe that I'm capable of being carried away by anything?"

Bazarov glanced at her mistrustfully. "By curiosity, possibly, but not by anything else."

"Really? Well, now I understand why we've become such good friends—you're just the same as I am, you see."

"We've become such good friends...," Bazarov uttered in a choked voice.

"Yes! ... Why, I'd forgotten that you want to leave."

Bazarov stood up. The lamp was burning dimly in the middle of the dark, luxurious, isolated room; from time to time, the bitingly fresh night air wafted through the swaying blinds with its mysterious whispers. Mrs. Odintsov didn't move a muscle, but she was gradually being seized by secret agitation.... It communicated itself to Bazarov. He suddenly realized that he was alone with a beautiful young woman....

"Where are you going?" she asked slowly.

He didn't reply, and sank into a chair.

"So you consider me to be a placid, coddled, spoiled creature," she continued in the same voice, never taking her eyes off the window, "whereas I know that I'm very unhappy."

"You're unhappy? Why? Surely you can't attach any importance to idle gossip?"

Mrs. Odintsov frowned. It annoyed her that he'd interpreted her words that way.

"Such gossip can't possibly affect me, Evgenii Vasilevich, and I'm too proud to allow it to disturb me. I'm unhappy because . . . I have no desires, no appetite for life. You look at me incredulously— you think that this is being said by an 'aristocrat' who's dressed all in lace, sitting in a velvet armchair. I don't conceal the fact that I love what you call comfort, and at the same time, I have little desire to live. Explain that contradiction any way you can. But this is all romanticism in your eyes."

Bazarov shook his head. "You're healthy, independent, and rich. What else could you possess? What do you want?"

"What do I want?" echoed Mrs. Odintsov, and she sighed. "I'm very tired, I'm old—I feel as if I've lived for a very long time. Yes, I'm old," she added, gently drawing the ends of her lace mantilla over her bare arms. Her eyes met Bazarov's, and she blushed faintly. "I already have so many memories—my life in Petersburg, wealth, then poverty, then my father's death, then marriage, then the inevitable trip abroad. . . . So many memories, yet nothing to remember. And in the future that's ahead of me— there's a long, long road, but no goal. . . . I have no desire to go on."

"Are you so disillusioned?" asked Bazarov.

"No," Mrs. Odintsov replied with emphasis, "but I'm not satisfied. I think that if I could firmly attach myself to something. . . ."

"You want to fall in love," Bazarov interrupted her, "but you can't fall in love—therein lies your misfortune."

Mrs. Odintsov began to examine the edges of her mantilla.

"Is it true that I can't fall in love?" she inquired.

"Hardly! Only I was wrong in labeling that a misfortune. On the contrary, someone is more deserving of disdain than pity when such a thing occurs."

"When what occurs?"

"Falling in love."

"And how do you know that?"

"Hearsay," Bazarov responded angrily.

"You're flirting," he thought. "You're bored, and you're teasing me from the lack of anything better to do, while I . . . ." His heart actually felt as though it were being torn to pieces.

"Besides, maybe you're too demanding," he suggested, bending his entire body forward and playing with the fringe of the chair.

"Maybe. In my opinion, it's all or nothing. A life for a life— take mine, give up yours, and do so without regret, without turning back. Nothing else will suffice."

"So?" Bazarov rejoined. "Those are fair terms, and I'm surprised that thus far you . . . haven't found what you wanted."

"But do you think it'd be easy to surrender oneself completely to something, whatever that might be?"

"It isn't easy, if you begin to think, to wait, and to attach value to yourself, to prize yourself, I mean. But to surrender yourself to something without thinking is very easy."

"How can one help prizing oneself? If I have no value, who'd need my devotion?"

"That isn't my business—it's someone else's business to discover what my value is. The main thing is to be able to surrender yourself."

Mrs. Odintsov leaned forward in her chair. "You speak," she began, "as though you'd had experience with all this."

"It happened to come up, Anna Sergeevna. As you know, all this isn't my sort of thing."

"But could you surrender yourself?"

"I don't know. I don't want to boast."

Mrs. Odintsov didn't respond, and Bazarov fell silent. The sounds of the piano floated up to them from the drawing room.

"Why is Katia playing so late?" Mrs. Odintsov wondered.

Bazarov stood up. "Yes, it really is late now. It's time for you to go to bed."

"Wait a bit. Where are you rushing off to? . . . I want to say a word to you."

"What is it?"

"Wait a bit," Mrs. Odintsov whispered.

Her eyes rested on Bazarov. It seemed as though she were examining him closely.

He walked across the room, then suddenly went up to her, hurriedly said, "Goodbye," squeezed her hand so hard she almost screamed, and left. She raised her crushed fingers to her lips, blew on them, and then suddenly, impulsively rising from her low chair, she moved toward the door with rapid steps, as though she wanted to bring Bazarov back.... A maid entered the room, carrying a decanter on a silver tray. Mrs. Odintsov stopped, told her to leave, sat down again, and sank into thought once more. Her hair came unbound and fell to her shoulders in a dark coil. The lamp burned in Anna Sergeevna's room for a long time, and she remained motionless for a long time, just occasionally chafing her hands, which ached slightly from the night's coolness.

Bazarov went back to his bedroom two hours later, disheveled and morose, his boots wet with dew. He found Arkadii seated at the desk holding a book in his hands, his coat buttoned up to the throat.

"You haven't gone to bed yet?" Bazarov asked, as if annoyed.

"You stayed with Anna Sergeevna for a long while this evening," Arkadii remarked, without answering his question.

"Yes, I stayed with her the whole time you were playing the piano with Katia Sergeevna."

"I wasn't playing...," Arkadii began, and then stopped. He felt tears coming to his eyes, and he didn't want to cry in front of his sarcastic friend.

XVIII

The following morning, when Mrs. Odintsov came down to have some tea, Bazarov, who was sitting still, bending over his teacup, suddenly glanced up at her.... She turned toward him as though he'd struck her, and he thought that her face had become slightly paler since the previous night. She went back to her own room shortly thereafter and didn't reappear until noontime. It had been raining from early morning on; there was no possibility of going for a walk. The entire group assembled in the drawing room. Arkadii picked up the most recent issue of some journal and began to read it out loud. Typically, the princess first looked amazed, as though he were doing something improper, and then glared at him angrily, but he paid no attention to her.

"Evgenii Vasilevich," Anna Sergeevna said, "let's go to my study.... I want to ask you.... You mentioned a reference book yesterday...."

She stood up and went to the door. The princess turned around with an expression that seemed to say, "Look, look at how shocked I am!" and glared at Arkadii again. But he raised his voice, exchanging glances with Katia, by whom he was sitting, and went on reading.

Mrs. Odintsov walked to her study with rapid steps. Bazarov followed her quickly without raising his eyes, merely catching the sound of her silk dress delicately swishing and rustling as it glided ahead of him. Mrs. Odintsov sank into the same easy chair she'd sat in the previous evening, and Bazarov took his former place.

"What was the name of that book?" she began after a brief silence.

"Pelouse and Frémy, *Notions générales*," Bazarov replied. "However, I might also recommend Ganot's *Traité élémentaire de physique expérimentale*. The illustrations in that book are clearer, and it's generally...."

Mrs. Odintsov stretched out her hand. "Evgenii Vasilich, I beg your pardon, but I didn't invite you here to discuss textbooks. I wanted to continue our conversation of last night. You went away so suddenly.... Will it bore you?"

"I'm at your service, Anna Sergeevna. But what were we talking about last night?"

Mrs. Odintsov cast a sidelong glance at Bazarov.

"We were talking about happiness, I believe. I told you about myself. By the way, I mentioned the word 'happiness.' Tell me why it is that even when we're enjoying music, for instance, or a lovely evening, or a conversation with sympathetic people, it all seems like an intimation of some immeasurable happiness existing somewhere else, rather than actual happiness, that is, the kind we ourselves possess. Why is that? Or perhaps you've never experienced a sensation like this?"

"You know the old saying, 'Happiness is to be found wherever we are not,'" Bazarov replied. "Besides, you told me yesterday that you're not satisfied. Such thoughts have certainly never entered my mind."

"Maybe they seem ridiculous to you?"

"No, but they haven't entered my mind."

"Really? You know, I'd very much like to know what you do think about."

"What? I don't understand."

"Listen to me. I've wanted to speak openly with you for a long time. There's no need to tell you—you're aware of it yourself—that you aren't an ordinary person. You're still young—all of life lies before you. What are you preparing yourself for? What sort of future is awaiting you? I mean to say—what goal do you want to attain? What are you heading toward? What's in your soul? In short, who are you? What are you?"

"You surprise me, Anna Sergeevna. You're well aware that I'm studying the natural sciences, and who I...."

"Well, who are you?"

"I've already explained to you that I'm going to become a district doctor."

Anna Sergeevna made an impatient gesture. "Why do you say that? You yourself don't believe it. Arkadii might answer me that way, but not you."

"Why, in what way is Arkadii...."

"Stop! Is it possible that you could content yourself with such a humble career, and aren't you yourself always maintaining that you don't believe in medicine? You—with your pride—a district doctor! You answer me that way to keep me at arm's length, because you have no confidence in me. But you know, Evgenii Vasilich, I could understand you. I myself have been poor and proud, like you. Perhaps I've been through the same trials as you have."

"That's all very well, Anna Sergeevna, but you have to excuse me.... As a rule, I'm not used to talking about myself freely, and there's such a gulf between you and me...."

"What sort of gulf? You mean to tell me again that I'm an aristocrat? That's enough of that, Evgenii Vasilich. I thought I'd proved to you...."

"Even apart from that," Bazarov interrupted, "what could induce anyone to talk and think about the future, which for the most part is beyond our control? If an opportunity to do something turns up, so much the better, and if it doesn't turn up—at least you'll be glad that you didn't idly chatter about it beforehand."

"You call a friendly conversation idle chatter? Or perhaps you don't consider me, a woman, worthy of your confidence? For you despise us all."

"I don't despise you, Anna Sergeevna, and you know that."

"No, I don't know anything... but let's assume this is so. I understand your disinclination to talk about your future career. But as to what's taking place inside you now...."

"Taking place!" Bazarov repeated. "As though I were some sort of government body or social group! In any case, it's utterly uninteresting—and besides, can someone always speak out loud about everything that's 'taking place' inside him?"

"But I don't see why you can't express everything contained in your soul."

"Can *you?*" Bazarov asked.

"Yes," Anna Sergeevna answered after a brief hesitation.

Bazarov bowed his head. "You're more fortunate than I am." Anna Sergeevna looked at him inquiringly. "If you say so," she continued. "But still, something tells me that we haven't gotten acquainted for nothing, that we'll be close friends. I'm sure that this—what should I call it?—constraint, this reticence in you will eventually vanish."

"So you've noticed reticence . . . or how did you put it . . . constraint?"

"Yes."

Bazarov stood up and went to the window. "Would you like to know the reason for this reticence? Would you like to know what's taking place inside me?"

"Yes," Mrs. Odintsov repeated with a sort of dread she didn't understand at that moment.

"And you won't be angry?"

"No."

"No?" Bazarov was standing with his back toward her. "Let me tell you, then, that I love you absurdly, madly. . . . There, you've dragged it out of me."

Mrs. Odintsov extended both hands in front of her, while Bazarov leaned his forehead against the windowpane. He was breathing hard; his whole body was visibly trembling. But it wasn't the trembling of youthful timidity or the sweet alarm that follows an initial declaration of love that possessed him; it was passion struggling inside him, fierce, painful passion—not unlike hatred, and possibly akin to it. . . . Mrs. Odintsov became both frightened and sorry for him.

"Evgenii Vasilich," she began, and there was a ring of involuntary tenderness in her voice.

He quickly turned around, threw her a ravenous look—and, grasping both her hands, suddenly drew her to his breast.

She didn't immediately free herself from his embrace, but a moment later, she was already standing far away in a corner, gazing at Bazarov from there. He rushed toward her. . . .

"You've misunderstood me," she whispered hurriedly, in alarm. It seemed that if he'd taken another step, she would have screamed. . . . Bazarov bit his lip and left.

Half an hour later, a maid gave Anna Sergeevna a note from Bazarov. It simply consisted of one line: "Should I go away today, or can I stay until tomorrow?"

"Why should you go? I didn't understand you—you didn't understand me," Anna Sergeevna wrote him in reply; she thought to herself, "I didn't understand myself, either."

She didn't appear until dinnertime. She continually paced back and forth in her room, pausing sometimes at the window, sometimes at the mirror, slowly rubbing her handkerchief across her neck, where she seemed to feel a burning sensation. She asked herself what had induced her to "drag out" his confession, in Bazarov's words, and whether she'd suspected anything. . . . "I'm to blame," she declared aloud, "but I couldn't have foreseen this." She became pensive and then blushed, remembering Bazarov's almost bestial expression as he'd rushed toward her. . . .

"Or . . . ?" she suddenly wondered, stopping short and shaking her curls. . . . She caught sight of herself in the mirror: her head was thrown back, and a mysterious smile shining in her half-closed eyes and spreading across her half-parted lips at that moment told her something about which she herself was embarrassed, it seemed. . . .

"No," she finally decided. "God knows what it might lead to. One mustn't joke about this—after all, tranquillity is the best thing on earth."

Her tranquillity hadn't been disrupted, but she felt sad, and even shed a few tears at one juncture without knowing why—certainly not because of the insult paid to her. She didn't feel insulted; she was more inclined to feel guilty. Under the influence of various vague emotions, a sense of life passing by, and a desire for novelty, she'd forced herself to go up to a certain point, had forced herself to look ahead of her—and had seen ahead of her not even an abyss, but emptiness . . . or chaos.

XIX

As great as her self-control was, and as superior as she was to every kind of prejudice, Mrs. Odintsov felt awkward when she went into the dining room for dinner. The meal proceeded fairly pleasantly, however. Porfirii Platonych arrived and related various anecdotes; he'd just come back from town. Among other things, he informed them that the governor, Burdalieu, had ordered the officials on his special commissions to wear spurs so that they could go faster on horseback in case he sent them off anywhere. Arkadii talked to Katia in an undertone and diplomatically waited on the princess; Bazarov maintained a grim, obstinate silence. Mrs. Odintsov looked at him twice, not obliquely but straight in the face, which was bilious and forbidding, his eyes downcast, contemptuous determination stamped on every feature, and she thought, "No . . . no . . . no. . . ." After dinner, she strolled out into the garden with the entire group, and, realizing that Bazarov wanted to speak to her, she took a few steps to one side and stopped. He went up to her—but even then he didn't raise his eyes—and declared hollowly, "I owe you an apology, Anna Sergeevna. You can't fail to be furious with me."

"No, I'm not angry with you, Evgenii Vasilich," Mrs. Odintsov responded, "but I'm disappointed."

"So much the worse. In any event, I've been sufficiently punished. My situation is utterly idiotic, as you'll probably grant. You wrote a note to me that said, 'Why go away?' But I can't stay, and don't want to. Tomorrow I'll no longer be here."

"Evgenii Vasilich, why are you . . . ?"

"Why am I going away?"

"No, I wasn't going to say that."

"You can't return to the past, Anna Sergeevna . . . and this was bound to happen sooner or later—hence I should go. I can only conceive of one circumstance in which I could remain, but that circumstance will never exist. Excuse my impertinence—but you don't love me and never will love me, I presume?"

Bazarov's eyes glittered for an instant under their dark brows.

Anna Sergeevna didn't reply to him. The thought, "I'm afraid of this man," flashed through her brain.

"Goodbye, then," Bazarov concluded, as though he'd divined her thought, and he went back into the house.

Anna Sergeevna followed him slowly and, summoning Katia, took her arm, not leaving her side until that evening. She didn't play cards and laughed more than usual, which didn't accord in the slightest with her pale, troubled face. Arkadii was bewildered, and looked at her the way all young people do—that is, as if he were constantly asking himself, "What does all this mean?" Bazarov locked himself in his room; he came back down for tea, however. Anna Sergeevna longed to say some kind word to him, but she didn't know how to initiate a conversation with him. . . .

An unexpected event relieved her of her discomfort: the steward announced the arrival of Sitnikov.

It's difficult to convey in words how birdlike the young apostle of progress seemed as he fluttered into the room. Even though his characteristic impudence had led him to decide to travel to the countryside to visit a woman he hardly knew, who'd never invited him to come but with whom, according to some information he'd gathered, such intelligent, intimate friends of his were staying, he was nevertheless trembling to the very marrow of his bones. Instead of making the apologies and paying the compliments he'd memorized ahead of time, he muttered some inanity about Evdoksia Kukshina having sent him to inquire after Anna Sergeevna's health, and after Arkadii Nikolaevich's, too, having always referred to him in the highest terms.... At this point he faltered, losing his presence of mind so completely that he sat down on his own hat. However, since no one sent him away and Anna Sergeevna even introduced him to her aunt and her sister, he quickly recovered himself and began to chatter volubly. The appearance of the banal is often useful during the course of life: it relieves excessive tension and tempers overly self-confident or self-sacrificing impulses by recalling the close kinship it has with them. Upon Sitnikov's arrival, everything became somehow duller—and simpler; they all even ate more supper and went to bed half an hour earlier than usual.

"I might repeat to you now," Arkadii said to Bazarov, who was getting undressed as Arkadii lay down in bed, "what you once said to me: 'Why are you so sad? One would think you'd fulfilled some sacred duty.'" For some time now, the two young men had been carrying on a sort of pseudocasual bantering, which is always a sign of secret displeasure or unspoken suspicions.

"I'm leaving for my father's tomorrow," Bazarov announced.

Arkadii raised himself up and leaned on his elbow. He felt both surprised and, for some reason, pleased. "Ah!" he responded. "And is that why you're sad?"

Bazarov yawned. "You'll get old if you know too much."

"And Anna Sergeevna?" Arkadii persisted.

"What about Anna Sergeevna?"

"I mean, will she let you go?"

"I'm not her hired help."

Arkadii fell into thought as Bazarov lay down and turned his face to the wall.

Several minutes went by in silence. "Evgenii!" Arkadii suddenly cried.

"What?"

"I'll leave with you tomorrow as well."

Bazarov didn't reply.

"Only I'll go home," Arkadii continued. "We'll travel together as far as Khokhlovskii, where you can get some horses at Fedot's. I'd be delighted to meet your family, but I'm afraid of being in their way and yours. You're coming back to visit us later, aren't you?"

"I've left all my things with you," Bazarov pointed out, without turning over.

"Why doesn't he ask me why I'm going just as suddenly as he is?" Arkadii wondered. "In fact, why am I going, and why is he going?" he reflected further. He couldn't find any satisfactory answers to his own questions, and his heart became filled with some bitter feeling. He sensed that it might be hard to say goodbye to this life, to which he'd grown so accustomed, but that it'd be somehow odd for him to stay by himself. "Something's happened between them," he reasoned to himself. "What good would it do me to hang around after he's gone? She's utterly sick of me, and I'll lose the last bit of respect she has for me." He began to picture Anna Sergeevna to himself; then other features gradually eclipsed the lovely image of the young widow.

"I'm sorry to leave Katia, too!" Arkadii whispered to his pillow, on which a tear had already fallen. . . . Suddenly he tossed his head and said aloud, "What the devil made that fool Sitnikov turn up here?"

Bazarov first stirred in bed a bit, then uttered the following rejoinder: "You're a fool, too, my friend, I can see that. Sitnikovs are indispensable to us. I—do you understand?—I need dolts like him. In reality, it's not up to gods to bake bricks! . . . "

"Aha!" Arkadii thought to himself, and only then did the fathomless depths of Bazarov's pride dawn on him in a flash. "Are you and I gods? At least, you're a god—but am I a dolt, then?"

"Yes," Bazarov affirmed morosely, "you're a fool, too."

Mrs. Odintsov expressed no particular surprise the next day when Arkadii told her that he was leaving with Bazarov; she seemed tired and distracted. Katia looked at him silently and seriously; the princess actually crossed herself under her shawl in a way he couldn't help noticing. Sitnikov, by contrast, was utterly disconcerted. He'd just come in to eat wearing a fashionable new outfit not, on this occasion, in the Slavophile style; the evening before, he'd astonished the servant who'd been told to wait on him by the quantity of linen he'd brought with him—and now his comrades were suddenly deserting him! He took a few tiny steps, doubled back like a hunted rabbit at the edge of a forest, and abruptly, almost with dismay, almost with a wail, announced that he proposed to leave as well. Mrs. Odintsov didn't attempt to detain him.

"I have a very comfortable carriage," added the unfortunate young man, turning to Arkadii. "I can take you, and Evgenii Vasilich can take your carriage, so it'll be even more convenient."

"For heaven's sake, it's not on your way at all, and it's quite far to where I live."

"That's nothing, that's nothing. I've got plenty of time, and besides, I've got business in that direction."

"Selling gin?" Arkadii inquired, somewhat too contemptuously.

But Sitnikov was in such despair that he didn't even laugh the way he usually did. "I assure you, my carriage is exceedingly comfortable," he mumbled, "and there'll be room for everyone."

"Don't disappoint Monsieur Sitnikov by refusing," urged Anna Sergeevna.

Arkadii glanced at her, and nodded his head significantly.

The visitors left right after they'd eaten. As she said goodbye to Bazarov, Mrs. Odintsov held out her hand to him and remarked, "We'll see one another again, won't we?"

"That's for you to decide," Bazarov replied.

"In that case, we will."

Arkadii descended the steps first and got into Sitnikov's carriage. A servant tucked him in respectfully, but Arkadii could have cheerfully punched him or burst into tears. Bazarov took a seat in the other carriage. When they reached Khokhlovskii, Arkadii waited until Fedot, the innkeeper, had harnessed the horses and then, going up to Bazarov's carriage, said with his old smile, "Evgenii, take me with you. I want to go to your house."

"Get in," Bazarov muttered through his teeth.

Sitnikov, who'd been walking around the wheels of his equipage whistling briskly, could merely gape when he heard these words, while Arkadii coolly pulled his luggage out of Sitnikov's carriage, took his seat beside Bazarov, and, after bowing politely to his former traveling companion, called out, "Go ahead!" Their carriage rolled away and quickly disappeared from sight. . . . Utterly confused,

Sitnikov looked at his coachman, but the latter was flicking his whip above the trace horse's tail. Sitnikov proceeded to jump into his own carriage, and growling at two passing peasants, "Put your caps on, you idiots!" he rode back to town, where he arrived very late and where, the next day at Mrs. Kukshin's, he verbally dispensed with the "two disgusting, stuck-up boors."

When seated in the carriage beside Bazarov, Arkadii shook his hand warmly and said nothing for a long while. It seemed as though Bazarov understood and appreciated both the handshake and the silence. He hadn't slept the entire previous night, hadn't smoked, and hadn't eaten much of anything for several days. His narrow profile stood out gloomily and sharply under his cap, which was pulled down to his eyebrows.

"Well, my friend," he finally said, "give me a cigarette. But look at me—I wonder, is my tongue yellow?"

"Yes, it is," Arkadii confirmed.

"Hmm . . . and the cigarette doesn't taste good. The machine's out of order."

"You've definitely looked different lately," Arkadii observed.

"It's nothing! I'll be all right soon. One thing's a bore—my mother is so tenderhearted, if you don't grow a big belly and eat ten times a day, she gets all upset. My father's all right—he's been everywhere and has known both feast and famine. No, I can't smoke," he added, and he flung the cigarette into the dust of the road.

"Is it twenty-five versts to your house?" Arkadii inquired.

"Yes. But you should ask this sage here." He pointed at the peasant sitting on the carriage box, a laborer from Fedot's.

But the sage merely replied, "Who can tell—versts aren't measured hereabouts," and he proceeded to swear at the shaft horse under his breath for "kicking with her head-piece," that is, for pulling with her head down.

"Yes, yes," Bazarov began, "let it be a lesson to you, an instructive example, my young friend. The devil knows what nonsense it all is! All human beings hang by a thread, an abyss may open under their feet at any moment, and yet they have to go and invent all sorts of difficulties for themselves and spoil their lives."

"What are you hinting at?" Arkadii asked.

"I'm not hinting at anything. I'm saying straight out that we've both behaved quite stupidly. What's the point of analyzing it? Still,

I've noticed in hospital clinics that the man who's furious at his illness will invariably get over it."

"I don't completely understand you," Arkadii remarked. "I'd have thought you didn't have anything to complain about."

"Since you don't completely understand me, I'll tell you this—in my opinion, it's better to break stones on the highway than to let a woman control even the tip of one's little finger. All that is . . ." Bazarov was about to utter his favorite word, "romanticism," but he checked himself and said, "nonsense. You don't believe me now, but I tell you this—you and I found ourselves in female society, and it was very pleasant for us. But forsaking that society is just like taking a dip in cold water on a hot day. A man doesn't have the time to devote himself to such trivia—a man should remain untamed, as an excellent Spanish proverb says. Now you, I suppose," he added, turning to the peasant sitting on the box, "you're a smart man—have you got a wife?"

The peasant turned his flat face and dull eyes toward the two friends.

"A wife? I do. Who doesn't have a wife?"

"Do you beat her?"

"My wife? Everything happens sometimes. I don't beat her without a reason."

"That's fine. Well, does she beat you?"

The peasant tugged on the reins. "That's a funny thing you've said, master. It's all a joke to you. . . ." He was obviously offended.

"Do you hear, Arkadii Nikolaevich? But we've taken a beating. . . . That's what comes of being educated people."

Arkadii gave a forced laugh. Bazarov turned away and didn't open his mouth again during the entire journey.

The twenty-five versts seemed like at least fifty to Arkadii. But eventually, the small hamlet where Bazarov's parents lived appeared on the gentle slope of a hill. Next to it, a small house with a thatched roof was visible amid a young birch grove. Two peasants wearing hats were standing beside the closest hut, exchanging insults.

"You're a huge sow," said one, "and uglier than a little suckling pig."

"Your wife's a witch," returned the other.

"From their unconstrained behavior," Bazarov remarked to Arkadii, "and their playful retorts, you can deduce that my father's peasants aren't overly oppressed. Why, there he is himself, coming out on the steps of his house. He must have heard the bells on the harness. It's he, it's he—I recognize his shape. Aha! He's gotten so gray, though, the poor man!"

XX

Bazarov leaned out of the carriage, and Arkadii thrust his head out behind his companion's back, thereby catching sight of a tall, thinnish man with disheveled hair and a narrow aquiline nose, dressed in an old, unbuttoned military coat, standing on the steps of the small manor house. His legs spread wide apart, he was smoking a long pipe and squinting to keep the sun out of his eyes.

The horses came to a stop.

"You've arrived at last," Bazarov's father remarked, continuing to smoke, although the pipe was nearly leaping up and down between his fingers. "Well, get out, get out and let me hug you!" He embraced his son. . . .

"Eniusha, Eniusha," rang out a tremulous female voice. The door flew open, and a plump little old woman in a white cap and a short striped jacket appeared in the doorway. She gasped, staggered, and probably would have fallen if Bazarov hadn't reached out to support her. Her plump little arms instantly entwined around his neck, her head pressed against his breast, and a hush fell over everything. The only sound to be heard was that of her broken sobs.

The elder Bazarov inhaled deeply and squinted harder than ever.

"There now, that's enough, that's enough, Arisha! Stop it," he urged, exchanging glances with Arkadii, who remained standing next to the carriage, while even the peasant on its box turned his head away. "That's not the least bit necessary. Please stop it."

"Ah, Vasilii Ivanych," faltered the elderly woman, "how many ages, my treasure, my darling, Eniusha . . . ," and without unclasping her hands, she drew back her wrinkled face, which was wet with tears while exuding tenderness, and gazed at Bazarov with somehow blissful, foolish eyes, then collapsed against him again.

"Well, now, to be sure, this is all in the nature of things," Vasilii Ivanych declared, "only we'd better go inside. Here's a visitor who's come with Evgenii. You must excuse us," he added, turning toward Arkadii and shuffling his feet slightly. "You understand— a woman's weakness, and, well, a mother's heart. . . ."

His own lips and eyebrows were twitching, and his beard was

quivering ... but he was obviously trying to control himself and appear almost nonchalant. Arkadii bowed.

"Let's go inside, Mother, really," Bazarov said, and he led the overwrought elderly woman into the house. Settling her into a comfortable armchair, he hurriedly embraced his father once more and introduced Arkadii to him.

"I'm extremely happy to make your acquaintance," Vasilii Ivanovich affirmed, "but you mustn't expect great things. Here in my house everything's done in a plain way, on a military footing. Arina Vlasevna, calm down, I beg of you. What is this weakness? Our gentleman guest will think badly of you."

"My dear sir," the elderly woman spoke up through her tears, "I don't have the honor of knowing your first name and patronymic...."

"Arkadii Nikolaich," Vasilii Ivanych reported solemnly, in a low voice.

"Please excuse a silly woman like me." Arina Vlasevna blew her nose and, bending her head first to the right and then to the left, she carefully wiped one eye after the other. "Please excuse me. You see, I thought I'd die without living long enough to see my da-a-arling."

"Well, you see, we've lived long enough after all, my lady," interjected Vasilii Ivanovich. "Taniushka," he continued, turning to a bare-legged little girl of about thirteen wearing a bright red cotton dress, who was timidly peering in at the door, "bring your mistress a glass of water—on a tray, do you hear? And you, gentlemen," he added with some sort of old-fashioned joviality, "let me invite you into the study of a retired veteran."

"Just let me embrace you once more, Eniusha," moaned Arina Vlasevna. Bazarov bent down toward her. "Why, what a handsome fellow you've become!"

"Well, handsome or not," Vasilii Ivanovich observed, "he's a man, as the saying goes, *ommfay*. And now I hope that, having satisfied your maternal heart, Arina Vlasevna, you'll turn your thoughts to satisfying the appetites of our dear guests, because, as the saying goes, even nightingales can't be fed on fairy tales."

The elderly woman got up from her chair. "The table will be set this very minute, Vasilii Ivanovich. I myself will run to the kitchen and have the samovar brought in. Everything will be taken care of, everything. Why, I haven't seen him, I haven't given him anything to eat or drink these past three years. Is that easy?"

"Well, then, good mother, start bustling, don't embarrass us. Meanwhile, gentlemen, I beg you to follow me. Here Timofeich comes to pay his respects to you, Evgenii. He's delighted too, I'll wager, the old dog. Eh, aren't you delighted, you old dog? Be so kind as to follow me."

And Vasilii Ivanovich fussily led the way, shuffling and flapping the slippers he was wearing, which were worn down at the heel. His whole house consisted of six tiny rooms. One of them—the one to which he led our friends—was called the study. A thick-legged table littered with papers darkened from an accumulation of ancient dust, as though they'd been preserved by smoke, occupied the entire space between the two windows; on the walls hung Turkish firearms, whips, a saber, two maps, some anatomical diagrams, a portrait of Hoffland, a sampler woven from horsehair in a dark frame, and a diploma under glass. A leather sofa, the cushions of which were worn into hollows and torn in places, was situated between two huge birchwood cupboards, on whose shelves books, boxes, stuffed birds, jars, and phials were jumbled together at random; in one corner stood a broken electric generator.

"I warned you, my dear Arkadii Nikolaich," Vasilii Ivanych began, "that we live on bivouac, so to speak. . . ."

"Now stop that. What are you apologizing for?" Bazarov interrupted. "Kirsanov knows very well that we're not Croesuses, and that you don't have a butler. Where are we going to put him?— that's the question."

"For heaven's sake, Evgenii, I have a fine room out in the little lodge. He'll be very comfortable there."

"So you've had a lodge built?"

"Why, yes, where the bathhouse is," Timofeich put in.

"That is, next to the bathhouse," Vasilii Ivanych added hurriedly. "It's summer now. . . . I'll run right over there and arrange everything. Meanwhile, Timofeich, you bring in their things. Naturally, I'll offer you my study, Evgenii. *Suum cuique.*"

"There you have it! A most amusing old fellow, and extremely good-natured," Bazarov remarked as soon as Vasilii Ivanych had gone out. "Just as much of an eccentric as yours, only in a different way. He chatters too much."

"And your mother seems to be an awfully nice woman," Arkadii commented.

"Yes, there isn't anything artificial about her. You'll see what a dinner she'll give us."

"They didn't expect you today, sir—they haven't gotten any beef," said Timofeich, who'd just dragged in Bazarov's suitcase. "We'll get along perfectly well without beef—there's no use asking for the stars. Poverty is no vice, they say."

"How many serfs does your father have?" Arkadii suddenly inquired.

"The estate isn't his, it's my mother's. There are fifteen serfs, as I recall."

"Twenty-two in all," Timofeich noted with an air of displeasure.

The flapping of slippers became audible, and Vasilii Ivanovich reappeared. "Your room will be ready to receive you in a few minutes," he cried triumphantly. "Arkadii . . . Nikolaich? That's correct, isn't it? And here's a servant for you," he added, pointing at a short-haired boy who'd entered with him, wearing a blue caftan that had ragged elbows and a pair of boots that didn't belong to him. "His name is Fedka. Again, I must repeat, even though my son tells me not to, that you shouldn't expect much. He knows how to fill a pipe, though. You smoke, of course?"

"I generally smoke cigars," Arkadii replied.

"And you do so very sensibly. I myself prefer cigars, but it's exceedingly difficult to obtain them in these isolated parts."

"There, now, that's enough humble pie," Bazarov interrupted again. "It'd be much better for you to sit down here on the sofa and let us have a look at you."

Vasilii Ivanovich laughed and sat down. His face was quite similar to his son's, except that his forehead was lower and narrower and his mouth somewhat wider. He was constantly in motion, shifting his shoulders as though his jacket were cutting him under the armpits, blinking, clearing his throat, and gesticulating with his fingers, whereas his son was distinguished by a kind of nonchalant immobility.

"Humble pie!" echoed Vasilii Ivanovich. "Evgenii, you mustn't think that I want to appeal to our guest's sympathies, so to speak, by suggesting that we live in such a godforsaken place. Quite the contrary—I maintain that for anyone who thinks, no place is godforsaken. At least I try as hard as I can not to get rusty, as they say, not to fall behind the times."

Vasilii Ivanovich drew a new yellow silk handkerchief out of his pocket, one he'd managed to snatch up on his way to Arkadii's room, and flourishing it in the air, he proceeded: "I'm not alluding to the fact that, not without considerable sacrifice to myself, for example, I've put my peasants on the rent system and have given my land to them in return for half the profits—I regarded that as my duty. Common sense itself reigns in such circumstances, although other landowners don't even dream about doing so. I'm alluding to the sciences, to education."

"Yes, I see that you have *The Friend of Health* from 1855 here," Bazarov remarked.

"It was sent to me by an old comrade, out of friendship," Vasilii Ivanovich hastened to respond, "but we even have some idea of phrenology, for instance," he added, addressing himself principally to Arkadii, however, pointing to a small plaster model of a head divided into numbered squares standing on one of the cupboards. "We aren't even unacquainted with Schenlein and Rademacher."

"Why, do people still believe in Rademacher in this province?" asked Bazarov.

Vasilii Ivanovich cleared his throat. "In this province.... Of course, gentlemen, you know far better. How could we keep up with you? For you've come to take our places. In my day, too, there was some sort of humoralist named Hoffmann, and someone named Brown, with his vitalism—they seemed quite ridiculous to us, but they'd also made a lot of noise at one time or another, of course. Someone new has replaced Rademacher for you—you look up to that man—but in another twenty years, it'll probably be his turn to be laughed at."

"For your consolation," Bazarov interjected, "I'll tell you that nowadays we laugh at medicine in general, and don't look up to anyone."

"How can that be? Why, you still want to be a doctor, don't you?"

"Yes, but the one doesn't preclude the other."

Vasilii Ivanovich poked his third finger into his pipe, where a bit of smoldering ash remained. "Well, perhaps, perhaps—I'm not going to argue. After all, what am I? A retired army doctor, *volatu*. Now I've taken to farming. I served in your grandfather's brigade," he addressed Arkadii again. "Yes, sir, yes, sir, I've seen many sights in my day. And I've been thrown into all quarters of society, I've come into contact with all sorts of people! I myself, the man you see before you now, have felt the pulse of Prince Wittgenstein, and of Zhukovskii! They were in the southern army, in the fourteenth, you understand." (Vasilii Ivanovich compressed his lips significantly at this point.) "I knew each and every one of them. Still, all in all, my business was on the sidelines. I knew my lancet, and that was enough! Your grandfather was a very honorable man, a real soldier."

"Come on, confess that he was a typical blockhead," Bazarov countered lazily.

"Ah, Evgenii, how can you use such an expression? Have some respect. . . . Of course, General Kirsanov wasn't one of the. . . ."

"Well, now, drop the subject," Bazarov interrupted. "I was pleased to see your birch grove as I was arriving here. It's spread out gloriously."

Vasilii Ivanovich brightened up. "And you have to see what a little garden I've got now! I planted every tree myself. There are fruit trees, as well as berries, and all kinds of medicinal herbs. However clever you young gentlemen may be, old Paracelsus spoke the sacred truth: *in herbis, verbis et lapidibus*. . . . For I've retired from practice, you know, but two or three times a week it happens that I'm recalled to my old duties. They come for advice—I can't drive them away. Sometimes the poor turn to me for help. And indeed, there aren't any doctors around here anyway. One of the local inhabitants, a retired major, also tries to cure people, if you can imagine that. I ask the question, 'Has he studied medicine?' and they tell me, 'No, he hasn't. He does it more out of philanthropy.' . . . Ha! Ha! Ha! Out of philanthropy! What do you think of that? Ha! Ha! Ha!"

"Fedka, fill me a pipe!" Bazarov demanded rudely.

"And there's another doctor here who'd just reached a patient once," Vasilii Ivanovich persisted with some sort of desperation, "when the patient had already gone *ad patres*. The servant didn't let the doctor in. 'You're no longer needed,' he told him. The doctor hadn't expected this, got confused, and asked, 'Well, did your master hiccup before he died?' 'Yes.' 'Did he hiccup a lot?' 'Yes.' 'Ah, well, that's good,'—and off he went again. Ha! Ha! Ha!"

The elderly man was the only one to laugh; Arkadii forced himself to smile, and Bazarov merely stretched. The conversation continued this way for about an hour. Arkadii had time to go and see his room, which turned out to be an anteroom attached to the bathhouse but was very snug and clean. Taniusha finally came in and announced that dinner was ready.

Vasilii Ivanovich stood up first. "Let's go, gentlemen. Please be magnanimous and pardon me if I've bored you. I'm certain that my capable wife will satisfy you better."

The dinner, although prepared in haste, turned out to be very good, and even abundant. Only the wine wasn't quite up to the mark, as they say—it was some nearly black sherry purchased by Timofeich in town at a well-known merchant's, which had a faintly coppery, resinous flavor—and the flies were a terrible nuisance. On ordinary days, a young serf drove them away with a large green branch, but Vasilii Ivanych had dismissed him on this occasion for fear of being criticized by the younger generation. Arina Vlasevna had had time to change clothes: she'd put on a tall cap with silk ribbons and a pale-blue flowered shawl. She burst into tears again as soon as she caught sight of her Eniusha, but her husband didn't need to admonish her; she herself hurriedly wiped away her tears in order to avoid getting spots on her shawl.

Only the young men ate anything; the master and mistress of the house had dined much earlier. Fedka waited on the table, obviously encumbered by the unusual requirement that he wear boots; he was assisted by a woman with a masculine cast of face and only one eye whose name was Anfisushka; she performed the duties of housekeeper, poultrywoman, and laundress. Vasilii Ivanovich paced back and forth all during dinner, talking about the deep-seated anxiety he felt over Napoleonic politics and the intricacies of the Italian question with a perfectly happy, even beatific countenance. Arina Vlasevna paid no attention to Arkadii; she didn't even urge him to eat. She leaned her round face—to which full, cherry-colored lips, as well as little moles on her cheeks and above her eyebrows, imparted a highly good-natured expression— on her closed little fist and didn't take her eyes off her son. She sighed repeatedly; Arina Vlasevna was dying to know how long he intended to stay but was afraid to ask him. "What if he says for two days?" she thought, and her heart sank.

After the main course had been consumed, Vasilii Ivanovich disappeared for a moment and returned with an opened half-bottle of champagne. "You see," he cried, "even though we live in a remote area, we do have something to celebrate with on festive occasions!" He filled three champagne glasses and a little wineglass, proposed the health of "our inestimable guests," and downed his glass all at once, in military fashion; he also made Arina Vlasevna drain her glass to the last drop. When the time came for dessert, although he couldn't bear anything sweet, Arkadii nonetheless deemed it his duty to taste four different kinds of preserves that had been freshly made, the more so since Bazarov flatly refused to have any and immediately began to smoke a cigarette. Tea subsequently appeared, along with cream, butter, and cookies. Then Vasilii Ivanovich led everyone out into the garden to admire the beauty of the evening. As they passed a garden bench, he whispered to Arkadii: "I love to contemplate philosophy in this spot as I watch the sunset—it suits a recluse like me. Over there, a little farther off, I've planted some of the trees beloved by Horace."

"What trees?" Bazarov asked, overhearing this.

"Oh . . . acacias."

Bazarov began to yawn. "I suspect that it's time our travelers were in the arms of Morpheus," observed Vasilii Ivanovich.

"That is, it's time for bed," Bazarov added. "That's a fair conclusion. It's definitely time."

Bidding good night to his mother, he kissed her on the forehead; she embraced him, and stealthily, behind his back, made the sign of the cross over him three times. Vasilii Ivanovich conducted Arkadii to his room and wished him "as refreshing a repose as I enjoyed at your delightful age." And Arkadii did in fact sleep extremely well in his bathhouse; it smelled of mint, and two crickets behind the fireplace exchanged soporific chirps with one another. Vasilii Ivanovich went from Arkadii's room to his study, and, perching on the sofa at his son's feet, was about to begin to chat with him. But Bazarov promptly sent his father away, saying that he was sleepy—yet he didn't fall asleep until dawn. His eyes wide open, he angrily stared into the darkness; childhood memories had no power over him, and besides, he still hadn't had time to efface his recent, bitter impressions. Arina Vlasevna first prayed to her heart's content, then had a long, long conversation with Anfisushka, who stood stock-still facing her mistress, fixing her single eye upon her, and conveyed all her observations and conclusions about Evgenii Vasilevich in a secretive whisper. The elderly woman's head was spinning from happiness and wine and cigar smoke; her husband tried to talk to her, but he gave up with a wave of his hand.

Arina Vlasevna was an authentic Russian gentlewoman of a bygone era; she ought to have lived about two centuries earlier, in the days of old Moscow. She was deeply devout and quite sensitive; she believed in fortune-telling, charms, dreams, and omens of every possible type; she believed in holy wanderers, in house-goblins, in wood-goblins, in unlucky encounters, in the evil eye, in folk remedies; she ate specially prepared salt on Holy Thursday; she believed that the end of the world was at hand, that if the candles didn't go out at vespers on Easter Sunday, then there'd be a good crop of buckwheat, and that a mushroom won't grow after it's been seen by a human eye; she believed that the devil likes to be wherever there's water, and that all Jews have a bloodstained patch on their chests. She was afraid of mice, snakes, frogs, sparrows, leeches, thunder, cold water, drafts, horses, goats, red-haired people, and black cats; she regarded crickets and dogs as unclean beasts; she never ate veal, doves, crayfish, cheese, asparagus, artichokes, rabbits, or watermelons, because a sliced-open watermelon recalled the head of John the Baptist; she couldn't speak about oysters without a shudder; she was fond of eating—and rigorously fasted; she slept ten hours out of every twenty-four—and never went to bed at all if Vasilii Ivanovich even had a headache; she'd never read a single book except *Alexis, or the Cottage in the Forest;* she wrote one or two letters a year at most, but was adept at keeping house, preserving fruits, and making jam, even though she never touched a thing with her own hands and was generally disinclined to get up from her chair.

Arina Vlasevna was very kind and, in her own way, not at all stupid. She knew that the world is divided into gentry, whose duty it is to give orders, and plain people, whose duty it is to obey them—and thus she felt no repugnance toward servility or submissive bows. But she treated her servants gently and affectionately, never let a single beggar go away empty-handed, and never spoke ill of anyone, although she did occasionally indulge in gossip. In her youth, she'd been quite pretty, had played the clavichord, and had spoken a little French; but in the course of many years of traveling with her husband, whom she'd married against her will, she'd grown stout, and had forgotten what music and French she knew. She loved and feared her son beyond words; she'd handed the management of her estate over to Vasilii Ivanovich and no longer interfered in anything; she'd simply groan, wave her handkerchief, and raise her eyebrows higher and higher with horror when her elderly husband began to discuss impending government reforms and his own plans. She was apprehensive, constantly expecting some dire misfortune, and began to cry as soon as she recollected anything sad. . . . Such women aren't common nowadays—God knows whether we ought to rejoice!

XXI

When he arose, Arkadii opened the window—and the first object that met his view was Vasilii Ivanovich. Attired in a Bokharan robe fastened around the waist with a scarf, he was industriously digging away in the garden. He noticed his young visitor, and leaning on his spade, he called out: "The best of health to you! How did you sleep?"

"Wonderfully," Arkadii replied.

"Here I am, as you see, like some Cincinnatus, marking out a bed for the late turnips. The time has now come—and thank God that it has!—when everyone is obligated to produce their food with their own hands. There's no point in relying on other people—one must perform the labor oneself. And it turns out that Jean-Jacques Rousseau was right. Half an hour ago, my dear young man, you would have seen me in an entirely different situation. A peasant woman arrived who was complaining of looseness—that's how they put it, or, as we put it, dysentery—and I . . . how can I best express this? I administered opium to her. And I extracted a tooth for someone else. I offered that woman an anesthetic . . . but she wouldn't consent. I do all that *gratis—anamater.* Nevertheless, I'm thoroughly used to it. You see, I'm a plebeian, *homo novus*—I don't come from high society, like my good wife. . . . But wouldn't you like to join me out here, in the shade, to inhale the fresh morning air before we have some tea?"

Arkadii went outside.

"Welcome once again," Vasilii Ivanovich declared, raising his hand in military fashion to the dirty skullcap that covered his head. "You're accustomed to luxury and various comforts, I know, but even the luminaries of this world don't object to spending a brief period of time under a cottage roof."

"Good heavens!" Arkadii protested. "As though I were one of the luminaries of this world! And I'm not accustomed to luxury."

"Pardon me, pardon me," Vasilii Ivanovich rejoined with a polite simper. "Although I've been relegated to the archives at this point, I've seen something of the world, too—I can tell a bird by its flight. I'm also a psychologist in my own way, as well as a physiognomist. If I hadn't been endowed with those gifts, I venture to say, I'd have fallen by the wayside long ago—I wouldn't have stood a chance, a poor man like me. I must tell you, without the least bit of flattery, that I'm sincerely delighted by the friendship I observe between you and my son. I've just seen him. He got up very early, as he usually does—no doubt you're well aware of that—and went rambling around the neighborhood. Permit me to inquire—have you known my son long?"

"Since last winter."

"Indeed. And permit me to ask further—but hadn't we better sit down? Permit me, as a father, to ask with complete candor—what's your opinion of my Evgenii?"

"Your son is one of the most remarkable men I've ever met," Arkadii responded emphatically.

Vasilii Ivanovich's eyes suddenly opened wide, and his cheeks became faintly flushed. The spade dropped out of his hand.

"And so you expect . . . ," he began.

"I'm convinced," Arkadii interjected, "that your son has a great future in store for him—that he'll bring honor to your name. I've been certain of that ever since I first met him."

"How . . . how did that happen?" Vasilii Ivanovich inquired with an effort. His wide mouth had spread into a triumphant smile that wouldn't dissolve.

"Would you like me to tell you how we met?"

"Yes . . . and generally. . . ."

Arkadii began to tell him that story, speaking about Bazarov with even greater warmth, with even greater enthusiasm, than he'd displayed the evening he'd spent the mazurka with Mrs. Odintsov.

Vasilii Ivanovich listened intently, blinking repeatedly, rolling his handkerchief up into a ball with both hands, clearing his throat, and running his hands through his hair, until he finally couldn't restrain himself any longer—he leaned over toward Arkadii and kissed him on the shoulder.

"You've made me perfectly happy," he announced, never ceasing to smile. "I ought to tell you that I . . . idolize my son. I won't even speak about my wife—we all know what mothers are like!—but I don't dare to express my feelings around him, because he doesn't like it. He's averse to any display of emotion. Many individuals even criticize him for such firmness of character, regarding it as a sign of pride or indifference, but people like him shouldn't be judged by ordinary standards, should they? Right here, for example, many others in his place would have been a constant burden on their parents, but he—would you believe it?—has never taken a kopeck more than he could help, by God, from the day he was born!"

"He's an unselfish, honorable man," Arkadii observed.

"Just so—he's unselfish. Not only do I idolize him, Arkadii Nikolaich, I'm proud of him, and the height of my ambition is that the following lines will appear in his biography someday: 'The son of a simple army doctor who nonetheless was capable of divining his greatness early on and spared nothing for his education. . . .'" The elderly man's voice broke.

Arkadii squeezed his hand.

"What do you think," Vasilii Ivanovich inquired after a brief silence, "will it be in the field of medicine that he attains the celebrity you predict for him?"

"Probably not in medicine, even though he'll be one of the leading scientists in that field."

"Then in which field, Arkadii Nikolaich?"

"It's hard to say right now—but he'll be famous."

"He'll be famous!" the elderly man echoed, and he sank into thought.

"Arina Vlasevna sent me to invite you inside for tea," Anfisushka informed them, walking up carrying a huge dish of ripe raspberries.

Vasilii Ivanovich was startled. "Will there be chilled cream for the raspberries?"

"Yes."

"Make sure it's chilled! Don't stand on ceremony, Arkadii Nikolaich—take some more. Why hasn't Evgenii come back?"

"I'm in here," Bazarov's voice rang out from Arkadii's room.

Vasilii Ivanovich turned around quickly. "Aha! You wanted to pay a visit to your friend, but you were too late, *amice*, and we've already had a long conversation with him. Now we have to go and drink some tea—your mother is calling us. By the way, I want to have a brief talk with you."

"About what?"

"There's a little peasant here who's suffering from icterus. . . ."

"You mean jaundice?"

"Yes, a chronic, quite obstinate case of icterus. I've prescribed centaury and St. John's wort for him, ordered him to eat carrots, and given him baking soda, but those are all merely palliative measures. We need some more efficacious treatment. Even though you laugh at medicine, I'm certain you can give me some useful advice. But we'll talk about that later. Now come in for tea."

Vasilii Ivanovich briskly jumped up from the garden seat and hummed a few bars from *Robert le Diable:*

> The rule, the rule, the rule we set ourselves,
> To live . . . to live . . . to live for joy!

"Remarkable vitality!" Bazarov commented, stepping back from the window.

Midday arrived. The sun was shining fiercely behind a thin veil of unbroken whitish clouds. Everything was hushed; there was no sound in the village except that of cocks irritably crowing at one another, which produced a strange sensation of drowsiness and boredom in everyone who heard them; somewhere, high up in the treetops, the incessant, plaintive peep of a young hawk could be heard. Arkadii and Bazarov were lying in the shade of a small haystack, having placed two armfuls of dry and rustling but still green, fragrant grass beneath them.

"This aspen tree," Bazarov began, "reminds me of my childhood. It's growing at the edge of the hole where a brick barn once stood, and in those days, I firmly believed that this hole and this aspen tree possessed special, talismanic powers—I was never bored when I was near them. At the time, I didn't realize that I wasn't bored because I was a child. Well, now I've grown up, and the talisman has lost its power."

"How long did you live here in all?" Arkadii inquired.

"Two years in a row. Then we started to move around. We led an itinerant life for the most part, drifting from town to town."

"And was this house built a long time ago?"

"Yes. My grandfather built it—my mother's father."

"Who was your grandfather?"

"The devil knows. Some sort of major. He served with Suvorov, and was always telling stories about crossing the Alps—lies, probably."

"There's a portrait of Suvorov hanging in your drawing room. I like these little houses like yours—they're so warm and old-fashioned, and they always have some special sort of odor."

"The smell of lamp oil and clover," Bazarov noted, yawning. "And the flies in these lovely little houses . . . ugh!"

"Tell me," Arkadii requested after a brief pause, "did they discipline you much when you were a child?"

"You can see what my parents are like. They aren't the strict type."

"Do you love them, Evgenii?"

"I do, Arkadii."

"They love you so much!"

Bazarov fell silent for a while. "Do you know what I'm thinking about?" he eventually asked, clasping his hands behind his head.

"No, what?"

"I'm thinking that my parents have a good life. At the age of sixty, my father is bustling around, talking about 'palliative' measures, ministering to people, playing the role of bountiful master to the peasants—having the time of his life, in sum. And my mother's well off, too—her day is so filled to the brim with all sorts of activities, and sighs, and groans, that she doesn't even have time to consider herself, whereas I...."

"Whereas you...?"

"Whereas I think: I'm lying here by a haystack.... The tiny space I occupy is so infinitesimal in comparison with the rest of space, which I don't occupy and which has no relation to me. And the period of time in which I'm fated to live is so insignificant beside the eternity in which I haven't existed and won't exist.... And yet in this atom, this mathematical point, blood is circulating, a brain is working, desiring something.... What chaos! What a farce!"

"Allow me to observe that what you're saying applies to everyone...."

"You're right," Bazarov broke in. "I was going to say that they— my parents, I mean—are busy, and don't worry about their own insignificance. It doesn't sicken them ... whereas I ... I experience nothing but boredom and anger."

"Anger? Why anger?"

"Why? How can you ask why? Have you forgotten?"

"I remember everything—but I still don't concede that you have any right to be angry. You're unhappy, I'll admit, but...."

"Hah! Then I can see that you, Arkadii Nikolaevich, regard love the way all modern young men do—you summon the hen, cluck, cluck, cluck, but if the hen comes near you, you pray to God you can get away. I'm not that type. But enough of this. What can't be helped shouldn't be discussed." He turned over on his side.

"Aha! There goes a valiant ant dragging off a half-dead fly. Take her away, friend, take her away! Don't pay any attention to her resistance. It's your privilege as an animal to ignore the feeling of compassion—not like us self-damaging humans!"

"You shouldn't say that, Evgenii! When have you ever damaged yourself?"

Bazarov raised his head. "That's the only thing I pride myself on. I haven't damaged myself, so a woman can't damage me. Amen! It's all over! You won't hear another word about it from me."

Both friends lay in silence for some time.

"Yes," Bazarov began again, "human beings are strange animals. When you get a distant, oblique view of the solitary lives our 'fathers' lead here, you think, 'What could be better?' You eat and drink and know that you're acting in the most reasonable, the most correct manner possible. But no—you're consumed by boredom. One wants to come into contact with people, if only to criticize them, but at least to come into contact with them."

"One ought to organize one's life so that every moment in it is significant," Arkadii stated reflectively.

"Who says so? Significance is enjoyable however illusory—but one could even make one's peace with what's insignificant. Whereas pettiness, pettiness . . . that's the trouble."

"Pettiness doesn't exist for people as long as they refuse to acknowledge it."

"Hmm . . . what you've just said is the antithesis of a trite phrase."

"What? What do you mean by that expression?"

"I'll tell you. To say that education is beneficial, for instance, is to employ a trite phrase, but to say that education is harmful is to employ the antithesis of a trite phrase. It has more style to it, as it were, but essentially it's all the same."

"And where's the truth—on which side?"

"Where? Like an echo I'll reply, 'Where?'"

"You're in a melancholy mood today, Evgenii."

"Really? The sun must have softened my brain, I suppose—and I shouldn't eat so many raspberries, either."

"In that case, a nap wouldn't hurt," Arkadii suggested.

"Probably not—only don't look at me. Everyone's face looks silly when they're asleep."

"But do you care what people think about you?"

"I don't know what to say to you. A real person shouldn't care.

A real person is someone there's no point in thinking about, someone you have to either defer to or detest."

"It's strange! I don't detest anybody," Arkadii remarked after a
moment's thought.

"And I detest so many people. You're a tender soul, a softie—
how could you detest anyone? . . . You get intimidated. You don't
have much confidence in yourself. . . . "

"And you?" Arkadii interrupted. "Do you have confidence in
yourself? Do you have a high opinion of yourself?"

Bazarov paused. "When I meet someone who isn't inferior to
me," he said, dwelling on each syllable, "then I'll change my
opinion of myself. I know what it means to detest someone! You
said today, for instance, as we walked past our bailiff Filipp's
cottage—the one that's so nice and clean—there, you said, Russia
will achieve perfection when the poorest peasant has a place like
that, and each of us ought to strive to make this happen. . . .
Whereas I've come to detest this poor peasant, this Filipp or Sidor,
for whom I'm supposed to be ready to jump out of my skin, who
won't even thank me for doing so . . . and why should he thank
me? Well, suppose he'll be living in a clean house while the nettle
plants are growing out of me—well, what then?"

"Hush, Evgenii. . . . Listening to you today, one would be driven
to agree with those who reproach us for a lack of principles."

"You talk like your uncle. There are no general principles—
haven't you even figured that out yet? There are only products of
the senses. Everything depends on them."

"How so?"

"Why, for instance, I take negative positions because of the products of my senses. It's pleasurable for me to negate—my brain's made
that way—and that's that! Why do I like chemistry? Why do you like
apples? Because of the products of my senses. It's all the same thing.
Human beings will never get any deeper than that. Not everyone will
tell you this, and in fact I won't tell you this a second time."

"What? Is even honesty a product of the senses?"

"Absolutely!"

"Evgenii," Arkadii began in a dejected voice.

"Well, what? Isn't all this to your liking?" Bazarov interrupted
him. "No, my friend. If you've decided to mow everything down,
don't spare your own legs. But we've done enough philosophizing.
'Nature breathes the silence of sleep,' as Pushkin said."

"He never said anything of the sort," Arkadii protested.

"Well, if he didn't, he could and should have said it, as a poet. By the way, he must have served in the military."

"Pushkin was never in the military!"

"For heaven's sake, on every page he writes, 'To arms! To arms! For Russia's honor!'"

"What stories you invent! This is sheer calumny."

"Calumny? That's a weighty matter! What a word he's found to frighten me with! Whatever calumny you may utter against someone, you can be sure he actually deserves twenty times worse than that."

"We'd better go to sleep," Arkadii recommended in frustration.

"With the greatest of pleasure," Bazarov responded.

But neither of them went to sleep. A feeling of near enmity crept over both young men. Five minutes later, they opened their eyes and silently exchanged glances.

"Look," Arkadii said suddenly, "a dry maple leaf has become detached and is falling to the ground. Its movement looks exactly like a butterfly's flight. Isn't that strange? The most sad and lifeless phenomenon so resembles the most cheerful and vital."

"Oh, my friend, Arkadii Nikolaich!" Bazarov cried. "I beg one thing of you—don't speak eloquently."

"I speak the best way I can. . . . And this is the ultimate despotism. An idea came into my head—why shouldn't I express it?"

"Fair enough—but why shouldn't I express my ideas as well? I think that eloquent speech is—indecent."

"And what's decent? Swearing?"

"Ha! Ha! I see that you really do intend to follow in your uncle's footsteps. How pleased that idiot would be if he could hear you!"

"What did you call Pavel Petrovich?"

"I called him an idiot, quite appropriately."

"But this is intolerable!" Arkadii exclaimed.

"Aha! Family feeling revealed itself there," Bazarov commented coolly. "I've noticed how stubbornly it clings to people. Someone is ready to forsake everything and abandon every prejudice, but to admit, for instance, that his brother who steals handkerchiefs is a thief—that's beyond his strength. For, in fact, he thinks, it's *my* brother, *mine*—and he's no genius. . . . Is this possible?"

"It was a simple sense of justice in me that revealed itself, not family feeling in the least," Arkadii asserted vehemently. "But since that's a feeling you don't understand—since you don't have that *product of the senses*—you can't appreciate it."

"In other words, Arkadii Kirsanov is too exalted for my comprehension. I'll bow down to him and say no more."

"Don't go on, Evgenii, please. We'll really quarrel in the end."

"Ah, Arkadii! Do me a favor—let's quarrel for once in earnest, to the limit, to the point of exhaustion."

"But then perhaps we'd wind up by...."

"Fighting?" Bazarov put in. "So what? Here, on the hay, in these idyllic surroundings, far from civilized society and people's eyes, it wouldn't matter. But you couldn't handle me. I'd have a hold of you by the throat in no time...."

Bazarov spread out his long, cruel fingers.... Arkadii turned around and, as though in jest, prepared to resist.... But his friend's face struck him as so sinister, such grave menace seemed to manifest itself both in the smile that distorted Bazarov's lips and in his glittering eyes, that Arkadii instinctively felt apprehensive....

"Ah! So this is where you've betaken yourselves!" the voice of Vasilii Ivanovich rang out at that moment, and the old army doctor appeared before the young men wearing a homemade linen jacket and a straw hat, also homemade, on his head. "I've been looking for you everywhere.... Well, you've picked out a wonderful place, and you're extremely well employed. Lying on 'earth,' gazing up at 'heaven.' You know, there's some sort of special significance in that!"

"I never gaze up at heaven except when I want to sneeze," Bazarov growled, and turning to Arkadii, he added in an undertone, "It's a shame he interrupted us."

"Come on, now, that's enough!" Arkadii whispered, and he furtively grasped his friend's hand. But no friendship can withstand such blows for long.

"I look at you, my youthful interlocutors," Vasilii Ivanovich was saying in the meantime, nodding his head and leaning his folded arms on a rather cleverly bent stick he himself had carved that had the figure of a Turk for a knob, "I look at you, and I can't refrain from admiring you. You have such strength, such blooming youth, such abilities, such talents! Simply ... Castor and Pollux!"

"There you go again—spouting mythology!" Bazarov observed. "You can immediately see that he was a great Latinist in his day! Why, I seem to remember that you won a silver medal for composition, didn't you?"

"The Dioscuri, the Dioscuri!" Vasilii Ivanovich reiterated.

"Now that's enough, father. Don't show off."

"Surely it's permissible, once in a while," murmured the elderly man. "However, I haven't been looking for you to pay you compliments, gentlemen, but, in the first place, to inform you that we'll be having dinner soon, and, in the second, to prepare you, Evgenii. . . . You're an intelligent person, you know what people are like, you know women—and consequently, you'll forgive. . . . Your mother wanted to have a service of thanksgiving sung upon the occasion of your arrival. Don't imagine that I'm asking you to attend this service—indeed, it's already over. But Father Aleksei. . . ."

"The village priest?"

"Well, yes, the priest. He . . . is going to eat . . . with us. . . . I didn't expect this, and didn't even recommend it . . . but somehow it happened. . . . He didn't understand me. . . . And, well, Arina Vlasevna. . . . Besides, he's a very decent, sensible man."

"He won't eat my share of dinner, I presume?" Bazarov queried.

Vasilii Ivanovich laughed. "For heaven's sake, what an idea!"

"Well, that's all I ask. I'm prepared to sit down at the dinner table with anyone."

Vasilii Ivanovich straightened his hat. "I was certain before I spoke," he said, "that you were superior to any kind of prejudice. Here I am, an old man of sixty-two, and I have none." (Vasilii Ivanovich didn't dare to confess that he himself had desired the service. . . . He was no less religious than his wife.) "And Father Aleksei very much wanted to meet you. You'll like him, you'll see. He doesn't even object to playing cards, and he occasionally—but this is between us—smokes a pipe."

"That's all right. We'll play a round of whist after dinner, and I'll clean him out."

"Ha! Ha! Ha! We shall see what we shall see!"

"Well, aren't you a past master?" Bazarov remarked with particular emphasis.

Vasilii Ivanovich's tanned cheeks became faintly flushed.

"Shame on you, Evgenii. . . . What's done is done. Ah, well, I'm prepared to admit in front of this gentleman that I had precisely that passion in my youth—and I paid for it, too! It's so hot, though! Let me sit down by you. I won't be in your way, I trust?"

"No, not at all," Arkadii replied.

Sighing, Vasilii Ivanovich lowered himself on the hay. "Your present quarters, my dear sirs," he began, "remind me of my military life in bivouacs, of the aid stations we set up somewhere like this, near a haystack, and we thanked God even for that." He sighed. "I've experienced many, many things in my day. For example, if you'll allow me, I'll tell you about an unusual episode involving the plague in Bessarabia."

"For which you received the Vladimir Cross?" interjected Bazarov. "We know, we know. . . . By the way, why aren't you wearing it?"

"Why, I told you that I don't have any prejudices," Vasilii Ivanovich muttered (he'd had the red ribbon taken off his coat just the previous evening), and he proceeded to relate that episode. "Why, he's fallen asleep," Vasilii Ivanovich suddenly whispered to Arkadii, pointing at Bazarov and winking good-naturedly. "Evgenii! Get up!" he added loudly. "Let's go in and have dinner."

Father Aleksei, an attractive, stout man with thick, carefully combed hair and an embroidered belt tied around his lilac silk cassock, turned out to be someone of great wit and tact. He hastened to be the first to offer his hand to Arkadii and Bazarov, as though realizing in advance that they didn't want his blessing, and he generally behaved quite informally. He neither compromised his own dignity nor gave any offense to anyone else's; he laughed a bit at seminary Latin in passing and stood up for his bishop; he drank two small glasses of wine but refused a third; he accepted a cigar from Arkadii but didn't proceed to smoke it, saying he'd take it home with him. The only thing that wasn't altogether appealing about him was a habit he had of slowly and carefully raising his hand from time to time to catch flies as they landed on his face and then occasionally crushing them. He took his seat at the card table with a mild expresson of satisfaction, and ended up winning two and a half rubles in paper money from Bazarov—they never considered betting with silver in Arina Vlasevna's house. . . .

She was sitting near her son, as before (she didn't play cards), her cheek propped on her little fist, as before; she only got up to give orders for some new treat to be served. She was afraid to caress Bazarov, and he gave her no encouragement; he never invited her caresses. Besides, Vasilii Ivanovich had advised her not to "worry" him too much. "Young people aren't fond of that sort of thing," he assured her. (It's unnecessary to describe what the dinner was like that day: Timofeich had personally galloped off at the crack of dawn for special Circassian beef; the bailiff had headed in another direction for turbot, perch, and crayfish; forty-two copper kopecks had been paid to peasant women for mushrooms alone.) Arina Vlasevna's eyes, steadfastly trained on Bazarov, expressed not only devotion and tenderness: sorrow was visible in them as well, mingled with awe and curiosity; some sort of humble reproach could also be discerned.

Bazarov, however, was in no mood to analyze the precise expression in his mother's eyes; he seldom turned toward her, and then only with some brief question. Once he asked to hold her hand "for luck"; she gently laid her soft little hand on top of his rough, broad palm.

"Well," she asked, after waiting a bit, "did it help?"

"Worse luck than ever," he replied with a careless laugh.

"He plays too rashly," Father Aleksei declared with seeming compassion, and he stroked his handsome beard.

"Napoleon's rule, good father, Napoleon's rule," interjected Vasilii Ivanovich, leading an ace.

"It brought him to St. Helena, though," Father Aleksei observed as he trumped the ace.

"Would you like some currant tea, Eniusha?" Arina Vlasevna inquired.

Bazarov merely shrugged his shoulders.

"No!" he said to Arkadii the next day. "I'm leaving here tomorrow. I'm bored. I want to work, but that's impossible here. I'll go back to your place in the countryside—I've left all my equipment there, anyway. At least at your house it's possible to lock myself up, whereas here my father always says to me, 'My study's at your disposal—nobody will interfere with you,' but he himself never moves even a step away from me. And I feel so guilty somehow if I shut myself off from him. It's the same thing with my mother, too. I hear her sighing on the other side of the wall, yet if I go in to see her, I can't find anything to say."

"She'll be bitterly disappointed," Arkadii observed, "and so will he."

"I'll come back to see them again."

"When?"

"Well, on my way to Petersburg."

"I feel particularly sorry for your mother."

"Why's that? Has she won you over with her berries, or what?"

Arkadii lowered his eyes. "You don't understand your mother, Evgenii. She's not only an extremely nice woman, she's very intelligent, really. This morning she talked to me quite sensibly and interestingly for half an hour."

"She was probably holding forth about me the whole time, wasn't she?"

"We didn't just talk about you."

"Maybe. You see better from the outside. If a woman can keep up a conversation for half an hour, that's always a good sign. But I'm leaving, all the same."

"It won't be very easy for you to break the news to them. They keep discussing what we're going to do two weeks from now."

"No, it won't be easy. Some demon drove me to tease my father today. He had one of his rent-paying peasants flogged the other day, and did so quite rightly, too—yes, yes, don't look at me with such horror—he did so quite rightly, because this peasant is a terrible thief as well as a drunkard. Only my father had no idea that I was cognizant of the facts, as they say. He got very embarrassed, and now I'll have to distress him even more. . . . Never mind! He'll get over it!"

Bazarov had said, "Never mind," but a whole day went by before he could bring himself to inform Vasilii Ivanovich of his intentions. Finally, just as he was saying goodnight to his father in the study, he remarked with a feigned yawn, "Oh . . . I almost forgot to tell you. . . . Send someone to Fedot's for our horses tomorrow."

Vasilii Ivanovich was dumbfounded. "Is Mr. Kirsanov leaving us, then?"

"Yes. And I'm going with him."

Vasilii Ivanovich virtually reeled. "You're leaving?"

"Yes . . . I have to go. Please make the arrangements about the horses."

"All right . . . ," faltered the old man, "to Fedot's . . . all right. . . . Only . . . only. . . . Why are you doing this?"

"I have to go and stay with him for a little while. I'll come back here again later."

"Ah! For a little while. . . . All right." Vasilii Ivanovich drew out his handkerchief, and, blowing his nose, bent over nearly to the ground. "Oh, well . . . everything will be arranged. I thought you were going to be with us . . . a little longer. Three days. . . . After three years, it's not very much—it's not very much, Evgenii!"

"But I'll come back soon, I tell you. I'm obligated to go."

"Obligated. . . . Oh, well! One must do one's duty before anything else. So I should send for the horses? All right. Arina and I didn't expect this, of course. She's just asked a neighbor for some flowers—she wanted to decorate your room." (Vasilii Ivanovich didn't mention the fact that every morning, just after dawn, he conferred with Timofeich, standing with his bare feet in slippers, pulling out one dog-eared ruble note after another with trembling fingers and ordering him to make various purchases, with special emphasis on good things to eat and red wine, which, as far as he could tell, the young men liked very much.) "Freedom—that's the main thing. That's my rule. . . . I don't want to constrain you . . . not. . . . "

He suddenly stopped talking and made for the door.

"We'll see each other again soon, Father, honestly."

But Vasilii Ivanovich merely waved his hand without turning around, and went out. When he got back to his bedroom, he found his wife in bed, and began saying his prayers in a whisper to avoid waking her up. She did wake up, however. "Is that you, Vasilii Ivanovich?" she asked.

"Yes, Mother."

"Have you just left Eniusha? You know, I'm afraid that he isn't comfortable sleeping on that sofa. I told Anfisushka to give him your portable mattress and the new pillows. I would have given him our featherbed, but I seem to remember he doesn't like too soft a bed. . . . "

"Never mind, Mother, don't worry. He's all right. Lord, have mercy on me, a sinner," he went on praying under his breath. Vasilii Ivanovich felt sorry for his elderly wife—he didn't intend to tell her that night what sorrow lay in store for her.

Bazarov and Arkadii set off the next day. From early morning on, dejection reigned throughout the house; Anfisushka let dishes slip out of her hands; even Fedka was distressed, and ended up taking off his boots. Vasilii Ivanovich bustled around more than ever—he was obviously trying to put up a good front, talking loudly and stamping his feet, but his face looked haggard and his gaze studiously avoided his son. Arina Vlasevna was crying quietly; she would have utterly broken down and couldn't have controlled herself at all if her husband hadn't spent two whole hours early that morning exhorting her to do so. When, after repeated promises to come back in not more than a month, Bazarov had finally torn himself from the embraces detaining him and taken his seat in the carriage; when the horses had set off, the harness bells ringing and the wheels turning, and it no longer did any good to try to see them; when the dust had settled and Timofeich, stooped over and walking unsteadily, had crept back to his little room; when the elderly couple had been left alone in their little house, which suddenly seemed to have grown smaller and more decrepit—only then did Vasilii Ivanovich, after a few more moments of heartily waving his handkerchief from the porch steps, sink into a chair and let his head slump onto his breast.

"He's forsaken us, he's forsaken us," he murmured. "He's forsaken us. He got bored with us. We're alone, all alone!" he repeated several times, holding the index finger of one hand out in front of him. After a while, Arina Vlasevna went up to him and, leaning her gray head against his gray head, said: "There's nothing we can do, Vasia! A son is a separate piece of us that's been cut off. He's like the falcon that flies home and flies away again as he chooses, while you and I are like mushrooms in the hollow of a tree—we sit side by side and never stir from our place. Only I remain eternally constant to you, as you remain to me."

Vasilii Ivanovich took his hands away from his face and embraced his wife, his friend, more warmly than he'd ever embraced her in his youth—she comforted him in his sorrow.

XXII

Our friends traveled as far as Fedot's mostly in silence, rarely exchanging a few insignificant words. Bazarov wasn't altogether pleased with himself—and Arkadii was definitely displeased with him. He was also feeling the baseless melancholy known only to very young people. The coachman changed the horses, and, climbing up onto the box, he inquired, "Do we go right or left?"

Arkadii was startled. The road to the right led to town, and from there to his home; the road to the left led to Mrs. Odintsov's.

He looked at Bazarov.

"To the left, Evgenii?" he asked.

Bazarov turned away. "What foolishness is this?" he muttered.

"I know that it's foolishness," Arkadii replied. "But what difference does that make? It isn't the first time."

Bazarov pulled his cap down over his forehead.

"Whatever you decide," he finally said.

"Turn to the left," Arkadii shouted.

The carriage rolled off in the direction of Nikolskoe. But having resolved to pursue this foolishness, the friends became more obstinately silent than before, and even seemed to be angry.

As soon as the steward met them on the steps of Mrs. Odintsov's house, the friends could tell that they'd acted imprudently in yielding to such a sudden passing impulse. They obviously hadn't been expected; they sat in the drawing room for a fairly long while, looking fairly silly. Mrs. Odintsov finally came in to greet them. She addressed them with her customary politeness, but was surprised at their hasty return and, as far as one could judge from the deliberateness of her gestures and words, wasn't terribly pleased by it. They hastened to announce that they'd merely dropped in along their way, and had to proceed to town within four hours. She confined herself to a slight exclamation, begged Arkadii to remember her to his father, and sent for her aunt. The princess made her entrance looking very sleepy, which gave her wrinkled old face a more malicious expression than ever. Katia wasn't feeling well, and didn't leave her room. Arkadii suddenly realized that he was at least as eager to see Katia as to see Anna Sergeevna herself. The four hours passed in trivial discussions of one thing or another; Anna Sergeevna both listened and spoke without smiling. It was only at the very moment they were departing that her former friendliness seemed to revive, as it were.

"I'm suffering from a bout of depression right now," she said, "but you mustn't pay any attention to that, and must come again— I say this to you both—before very long."

Bazarov and Arkadii each responded with a silent bow, took a seat in the carriage, and, without stopping again anywhere, went straight to Marino, where they arrived safely the evening of the following day. During the course of the entire journey, neither one even mentioned Mrs. Odintsov's name. Bazarov in particular hardly opened his mouth and kept staring off to the side, away from the road, with some sort of fierce tension in his face.

Everyone at Marino was exceedingly pleased to see them. His son's prolonged absence had begun to worry Nikolai Petrovich; he uttered a cry of delight and jumped for joy, kicking his feet up, when Fenechka ran in to find him and with sparkling eyes informed him of the arrival of the "young gentlemen." Even Pavel Petrovich was conscious of a certain degree of pleasurable excitement, and smiled condescendingly as he shook hands with the returning wanderers. Conversation and questions followed; Arkadii talked the most, especially at supper, which lasted until long after midnight. Nikolai Petrovich ordered some bottles of ale that had just been sent from Moscow to be served, and partook of the festive beverage until his cheeks turned crimson; he kept producing a half-childish, half-nervous laugh. The servants were infected by the general exhilaration as well: Duniasha ran back and forth like someone possessed, slamming doors, while Petr, even at three o'clock in the morning, kept attempting to strum a cossack melody on the guitar. The strings emitted a sweet, plaintive sound in the still air, but, with the exception of a brief preliminary flourish, nothing came of the cultured valet's efforts—nature had given no more musical talent to him than to anyone else.

Meanwhile, things weren't going too smoothly at Marino, and poor Nikolai Petrovich was having a hard time. Difficulties on the farm were springing up every day—pointless, depressing difficulties. The troubles with the hired laborers had become intolerable—some asked for their wages to be paid in full or for a raise, while others ran off with the wages they'd received in advance; the horses got sick; a harness fell to pieces as though it'd been set on fire; work was done carelessly; one threshing machine that had been ordered from Moscow turned out to be useless because of its vast weight, and another broke down the first time it was used; half the cattle sheds burned to the ground when one of the house servants, a blind old woman, went out with a burning torch in windy weather to fumigate her cow. . . . To be sure, the old woman maintained that the entire disaster was due to the master's plan to begin production of newfangled cheeses and milk products. The overseer suddenly got lazy and even began to grow fat, the way all Russians grow fat when they obtain a "snug berth." When he caught sight of Nikolai Petrovich in the distance, he'd fling a stick at a passing pig or threaten some half-naked urchin, but he generally slept the rest of the time. The peasants who'd been put on the rent system didn't bring their money on time and stole the forest lumber; the watchmen caught some peasants' horses in the farm meadows almost every night and sometimes forcibly rounded them up. Then Nikolai Petrovich would assess a monetary fine for the damages, but after the horses had been kept for a day or two, eating the master's fodder, these incidents usually concluded with the return of the horses to their owners.

To cap it all off, the peasants began to quarrel among themselves: brothers asked for their property to be divided because their wives couldn't get along together in the same house; suddenly, as though at a given signal, a squabble would boil up, and everyone in the village would come running to the office steps at the same time, often drunk, their faces battered, crowding in to see the master, demanding justice and retribution; a great hue and cry would arise, the women's shrill wails mingling with the men's curses. Then he had to question the opposing parties and shout himself hoarse, knowing all the while that he could never arrive at a fair verdict anyway.... There weren't enough workers to gather the harvest; one neighboring landowner with a most benevolent countenance had contracted to supply him with reapers for a commission of two rubles an acre and had cheated him in the most shameless fashion; his own peasant women demanded unheard-of sums, and in the meantime, the grain spoiled; now they weren't proceeding with the mowing, and the Council of Guardians was threatening him, demanding prompt, non-negotiable payment of a percentage....

"It's beyond my strength!" Nikolai Petrovich cried in despair more than once. "I can't flog them myself. And my principles don't permit me to call in the police captain—yet it's impossible to accomplish anything without the fear of punishment!"

"*Du calme, du calme,*" Pavel Petrovich would remark in response to all this, but even he would mutter to himself, knit his eyebrows, and tug at his moustache.

Bazarov held himself aloof from these "trivial" matters—and indeed, as a guest, it wasn't appropriate for him to meddle in other people's business. The day after his arrival at Marino, he went to work on his frogs, his amoebae, and his chemical experiments, keeping constantly occupied with them. By contrast, Arkadii considered it his duty, if not to help his father, at least to appear to be prepared to help him. He provided a patient audience, and once even offered him some advice, not with any notion of its being followed but to demonstrate his interest. The prospect of managing a farm didn't arouse any aversion in him—he'd even dreamed about agronomical work with pleasure—but his brain was swarming with other ideas at this point in time. To his own astonishment, Arkadii incessantly thought about Nikolskoe. Formerly he just would have shrugged his shoulders if anyone had told him that he could ever be bored while living under the same roof as Bazarov—and the roof was his father's! Yet he actually was bored, and yearned to escape. He tried going for long walks to wear himself out, but that didn't help.

In a conversation with his father one day, he learned that Nikolai Petrovich had several rather interesting letters written by Mrs. Odintsov's mother to his wife in his possession, and Arkadii gave his father no rest until he got hold of the letters, for which Nikolai Petrovich had to rummage through twenty different drawers and boxes. Having obtained possession of these half-crumbling pieces of paper, Arkadii felt calmer, as it were, as though he'd caught a glimpse of the goal toward which he ought to proceed. "I say this to you both," he constantly whispered—she'd added that herself! "I'll go, I'll go, the devil take it!" Only then he'd recall the last visit, the cold reception, his former discomfort, and timidity would get the better of him.

But the "adventurousness" of youth, the secret desire to try his luck, to test his abilities on his own, without anyone's protection, finally won out. Before ten days had elapsed after his return to Marino, on the pretext of studying how Sunday schools work, he took a carriage to town, and from there to Nikolskoe. Ceaselessly urging the driver on, he flew along like a young officer riding to battle; he felt both terrified and lighthearted, and was breathless with impatience. "The main thing is not to think," he kept repeating to himself. His driver happened to be an intrepid individual; he halted before every inn, inquiring, "Do we want a drink or not?" But to make up for that, having had something to drink, he didn't spare his horses.

At last, the lofty roof of the familiar house came into sight. . . . The thought, "What am I doing?" flashed through Arkadii's mind. "Well, there's no turning back now!" The three horses galloped in unison; the driver whooped and whistled at them. Now the bridge was groaning under the hoofs and wheels, and now the avenue of sculpted pines seemed to be coming forward to meet them. . . . A woman's pink dress glimmered amid the dark green, a young face peeped out from under the delicate fringe of a parasol. . . . He recognized Katia, and she recognized him. Arkadii told the driver to stop the galloping horses, leaped out of the carriage, and walked up to her. "It's you!" she cried, a deep blush gradually spreading across her face. "Let's go find my sister—she's out here in the garden. She'll be pleased to see you."

Katia led Arkadii into the garden. His encountering her struck him as a particularly favorable omen; he was as delighted to see her as though she were a relative of his. Everything had turned out so well: no steward, no formal entrance. At a turn in the path, he caught sight of Anna Sergeevna. She was standing with her back to him. Hearing footsteps, she slowly turned around.

Arkadii started to grow uncomfortable again, but her first words immediately put him at ease. "Welcome back, runaway!" she said in her measured, caressing voice, and walked over to him, smiling and frowning at the same time to keep the sun and wind out of her eyes. "Where did you find him, Katia?"

"I've brought you something, Anna Sergeevna," he began, "that you in no way expect...."

"You've brought yourself—that's the best thing of all."

XXIII

Having seen Arkadii off with amused compassion, and having made it clear that he wasn't the least bit deceived as to the real object of Arkadii's journey, Bazarov went into total seclusion; he was overwhelmed by a feverish desire to work. He no longer argued with Pavel Petrovich, especially since the latter regularly assumed an extremely aristocratic demeanor in Bazarov's presence and expressed his opinions more in inarticulate sounds than in words. Only once did Pavel Petrovich begin a debate with the "nihilist" on the issue—much discussed at that time—of the rights of the nobility in the Baltic provinces, but he suddenly stopped of his own accord, remarking with icy politeness, "However, we can't understand one another. Or at least, I don't have the honor of understanding you."

"Of course not!" Bazarov cried. "Someone's capable of understanding anything—how the atmosphere vibrates and what occurs on the sun—but he's incapable of understanding how other people can blow their noses differently than he does."

"Oh—is that witty?" Pavel Petrovich remarked quizzically, and he walked away.

Nonetheless, he occasionally requested permission to attend Bazarov's experiments, and once even lowered his fragrant face, cleansed with the very finest soap, to the microscope to see how a transparent amoeba swallowed a green speck and busily gulped it down by means of two very rapidly moving sorts of rods located in its throat. Nikolai Petrovich visited Bazarov much oftener than his brother; he would have come every day "to study," as he put it, if his difficulties with the farm hadn't distracted him. He didn't hinder the young scientific researcher; he'd sit down somewhere in a corner of the room and watch attentively, occasionally permitting himself a discreet question. During mealtimes, he often tried to turn the conversation to physics, geology, or chemistry, since all other topics, even agriculture—to say nothing of politics— might lead, if not to conflict, at least to mutual dissatisfaction.

Nikolai Petrovich suspected that his brother's hatred of Bazarov hadn't diminished in the slightest. One minor incident, among many others, confirmed his suspicions. Cholera began to appear in some places around the region, and even "carried off" two people at Marino itself. One night Pavel Petrovich happened to have a rather severe attack. He was in pain until morning, but didn't avail himself of Bazarov's skills. And when he encountered Bazarov the following day, still quite pale but scrupulously groomed and shaven, in reply to Bazarov's inquiry as to why he hadn't sent for him, Pavel Petrovich observed, "But I seem to recall that you yourself said you didn't believe in medicine."

Thus the days went by. Bazarov stubbornly and grimly continued to work.... Meanwhile, there was one creature in Nikolai Petrovich's house to whom, if Bazarov didn't open his soul, he was at least eager to talk.... This creature was Fenechka.

He'd encounter her for the most part early in the morning, in the garden or the courtyard; he never went to her room to see her, and she'd only come to his door once, to ask whether she ought to let Mitia have his bath or not. It wasn't just that she trusted him, that she wasn't afraid of him; she was more relaxed, more informal around him than around Nikolai Petrovich himself. It's hard to say why this had happened—perhaps it was because she unconsciously sensed in Bazarov the absence of all the gentility, all the superiority, that both attracts and overawes. In her eyes, he was at once an excellent doctor and an ordinary man. She cared for her baby without any constraint in his presence; one day, when she suddenly felt dizzy and had a headache, she accepted a spoonful of medicine from his hand. In front of Nikolai Petrovich, she kept her distance from Bazarov, as it were; she didn't behave this way out of cunning, but out of some sort of feeling of propriety. She feared Pavel Petrovich more than ever; he'd been watching her for some time, and would appear all of a sudden, as though he'd sprung up out of the earth behind her back, wearing his English suit, his face alert but immobile, his hands in his pockets. "It's like having a bucket of cold water thrown on you," Fenechka complained to Duniasha. The latter sighed in response and thought about another "unfeeling" man: without the slightest suspicion of the fact, Bazarov had become the "cruel tyrant" of her heart.

Fenechka liked Bazarov; he liked her, too. His face was actually transformed when he talked to her—it assumed a radiant, almost kindly expression—and his habitual nonchalance was replaced by some sort of jocular attentiveness. Fenechka was getting prettier every day. There's a time in the lives of young women when they suddenly begin to grow and bloom like summer roses; this time had arrived for Fenechka. Everything contributed to this, even the July heat that was then prevailing. Wearing a delicate white dress, she herself seemed whiter and more delicate; she wasn't tanned by the sun, but the heat, from which she couldn't shield herself, spread a slight flush across her cheeks and ears, diffusing a tranquil indolence throughout her entire body that was reflected by a dreamy languor in her lovely eyes. She was virtually incapable of working; her hands seemed to fall naturally into her lap. She barely moved around at all, and was constantly sighing and complaining with comical helplessness.

"You should go swimming more often," Nikolai Petrovich told her. He'd created a large pool covered by an awning in the one of the farm's ponds that hadn't quite disappeared yet.

"Oh, Nikolai Petrovich! By the time you get to the pond, you could die, and coming back you could die again. You see, there isn't any shade in the garden."

"That's true, there isn't any shade," Nikolai Petrovich replied, rubbing his forehead.

One day, as he was returning from a walk at about seven o'clock in the morning, Bazarov came across Fenechka in the lilac arbor, which had long since blossomed but was still thick and green. She was sitting on a bench and had thrown a white kerchief over her head as usual; near her lay a whole pile of red and white roses that were still wet with dew. He said good morning to her.

"Ah! Evgenii Vasilich!" she responded, lifting the edge of her kerchief slightly to look at him; in doing so, her arm was bared to the elbow.

"What are you doing here?" Bazarov inquired, sitting down beside her. "Are you making a bouquet?"

"Yes—for the table at noon. Nikolai Petrovich likes that."

"But it's still a long while until noon. What a mass of flowers!"

"I gathered them now because it'll be hot then, and you can't go out. Now is the only time you can breathe. I've gotten so weak from the heat—I'm already afraid that I might get sick."

"What an idea! Let me feel your pulse." Bazarov took her hand, found the rhythmically beating pulse, and didn't even begin to count its throbs. "You'll live for a hundred years!" he declared, releasing her hand.

"Ah, God forbid!" she exclaimed.

"Why? Don't you want to live a long time?"

"Well, yes—but a hundred years! There was an old woman living near us who was eighty-five years old—and what a martyr she was! Gray, deaf, stooped, and coughing all the time. She was nothing but a burden to herself. What sort of life is that?"

"So it's better to be young?"

"Well, isn't it?"

"But how is it better? Tell me!"

"How can you ask how? Why, here I am now, I'm young, I can do everything—come and go and carry things, without needing to ask anyone for anything.... What could be better?"

"Whereas it's all the same to me whether I'm young or old."

"What do you mean—it's all the same? What you say isn't possible."

"Well, judge for yourself, Fedosia Nikolaevna—what good is my youth to me? I live alone, a poor bachelor...."

"That's entirely your own fault."

"It isn't my fault at all! If only someone would take pity on me."

Fenechka cast a sidelong glance at Bazarov, but said nothing. "What's this book you have?" she inquired after a short pause.

"This one? This is a scientific book, a very difficult one."

"Are you still studying? And don't you get bored? You already know everything, I'd say."

"Not everything, evidently. Try to read a little."

"But I won't understand any of it. Is it Russian?" Fenechka asked, picking up the heavily bound book with both hands. "It's so thick!"

"Yes, it's Russian."

"All the same, I won't understand anything."

"Well, I didn't give it to you for you to understand. I wanted to look at you while you were reading. When you read, the tip of your little nose moves so prettily."

Fenechka, who'd quietly begun to try to read through an article on "creosote" that she'd happened to select, laughed and put the book down.... It slipped from the bench onto the ground.

"I also like it when you laugh," Bazarov observed.

"That's enough of that!"

"I like it when you talk. It's just like a little brook babbling."

Fenechka turned her head away. "What a silly thing to say!" she remarked, separating the flowers with her fingers. "And how can you like to listen to me? You've had conversations with such intelligent ladies."

"Ah, Fedosia Nikolaevna! Believe me, all the intelligent ladies in the world aren't worth your little elbow."

"Well now, that's something else you've made up!" Fenechka murmured, clasping her hands.

Bazarov picked the book up off the ground.

"That's a medical book—why are you throwing it away?"

"It's medical?" Fenechka echoed, and she turned toward him again. "Do you know what? Ever since you gave me those drops—do you remember?—Mitia has slept so well! I truly can't imagine how to thank you. You're so kind, really."

"But these days you have to pay doctors," Bazarov commented with a smile. "Doctors, as you yourself know, are greedy people."

Fenechka raised her eyes, which looked even darker than usual in contrast to the whitish reflection the kerchief cast on the upper part of her face, and gazed at Bazarov. She didn't know whether he was joking or not.

"If you like, we'll be delighted. . . . I'll have to ask Nikolai Petrovich. . . ."

"Why, do you think I want money?" Bazarov interrupted her. "No, I don't want money from you."

"What, then?" Fenechka asked.

"What?" Bazarov repeated. "Guess!"

"I'm no good at guessing!"

"Then I'll tell you. I want . . . one of those roses."

Fenechka laughed again and even clapped her hands, so amusing did Bazarov's request seem to her. She laughed, and at the same time felt flattered. Bazarov looked at her intently.

"By all means," she finally said, and bending over the bench, she began to pick through the roses. "Which do you want—a red one or a white one?"

"Red—and not too large."

She straightened up again. "Here, take this one," she suggested, but instantly drew back her outstretched hand, glanced toward the entrance of the arbor, biting her lips, and started to listen.

"What is it?" Bazarov inquired. "Nikolai Petrovich?"

"No. . . . He's gone out to the fields. . . . Besides, I'm not afraid of him . . . but Pavel Petrovich . . . I thought. . . ."

"What?"

"I thought that *he* was coming here. No . . . no one's there. Take this." Fenechka gave Bazarov the rose.

"What reason do you have to be afraid of Pavel Petrovich?"

"He always scares me. Most people talk readily—he doesn't talk, he just looks around knowingly. And even you don't like him. You remember, you always used to quarrel with him. I don't know what you were quarreling about, but I could see you twisting him around this way and that."

Fenechka demonstrated with her hands the way Bazarov twisted Pavel Petrovich around, in her opinion.

Bazarov smiled. "But if he started to give me a beating," he probed, "would you come to my defense?"

"How could I come to your defense? But no—no one could get the better of you."

"Do you think so? I know a hand that could conquer me with one finger if it wanted to."

"Which hand is that?"

"Why, don't you really know? Smell the delicious fragrance of this rose you gave me."

Fenechka stretched her little neck forward and put her face close to the flower. . . . The kerchief slipped off her head onto her shoulders; the soft masses of her dark, shining, slightly ruffled hair became visible.

"Wait—I want to smell it with you," Bazarov declared. He bent over and kissed her firmly on her parted lips.

She flinched and put both hands on his chest to push him back, but only pushed weakly, so that he was able to renew and prolong his kiss.

A dry cough sounded behind the lilac bushes. Fenechka instantly moved to the other end of the bench. Pavel Petrovich appeared, made a slight bow, and, remarking with some sort of hostile dejection "You're here," he retreated. Fenechka immediately gathered up all her roses and left the arbor. "That was sinful of you, Evgenii Vasilevich," she whispered as she was leaving. There was a note of genuine reproach in her whisper.

Bazarov recalled another recent scene, and felt both ashamed and contemptuously annoyed. But he promptly shook his head, sarcastically congratulated himself "on his formal assumption of the role of Lothario," and went off to his own room.

Pavel Petrovich left the garden and made his way to the forest with deliberate strides. He stayed there for a fairly long while, and when he returned at noon, Nikolai Petrovich anxiously asked whether he was quite well—his face had gotten so dark.

"You know I sometimes suffer from a liver ailment," Pavel Petrovich responded tranquilly.

XXIV

Two hours later, Pavel Petrovich knocked on Bazarov's door.

"I must apologize for interrupting your scientific pursuits," he began, seating himself on a chair by the window and resting both hands on a handsome cane with an ivory handle (he ordinarily walked without a cane), "but I'm forced to beg you to spare me five minutes of your time . . . no more."

"My time is completely at your disposal," Bazarov replied. Some unusual expression had flashed across his face as soon as Pavel Petrovich had crossed the threshold.

"Five minutes will suffice for me. I've come to ask you a single question."

"A question? What's it about?"

"I'll tell you, if you'll be so kind as to hear me out. Early on during your stay in my brother's house, before I'd deprived myself of the pleasure of conversing with you, I had the opportunity to hear your opinions about many subjects. But, if memory serves, we never discussed the subject of single combat or dueling in general, nor did you ever discuss it in my presence. May I inquire what your opinion on that subject is?"

Bazarov, who'd risen to greet Pavel Petrovich, sat down on the edge of a table and crossed his arms.

"My opinion," he said, "is that, from a theoretical point of view, dueling's absurd. From a practical point of view, however—it's a different proposition."

"That is, you mean to say—if I understand you correctly—whatever your theoretical view of dueling might be, in practice, you wouldn't allow yourself to be insulted without demanding satisfaction?"

"You've thoroughly grasped my meaning."

"Excellent. I'm very glad to hear you say so. Your words relieve me of uncertainty. . . . "

"Of indecision, you mean to say."

"It's all the same. I express myself so as to be understood— I . . . I'm not a creature of the seminary. Your words save me from a certain regrettable necessity. I've decided to fight a duel with you."

Bazarov's eyes opened wide. "With me?"

"Indubitably."

"But why, for heaven's sake?"

"I could explain the reason to you," Pavel Petrovich began, "but I'd prefer to remain silent about it. To my way of thinking, your presence here is an imposition. I can't endure you. I despise you. And if that isn't enough for you. . . ."

Pavel Petrovich's eyes glittered. . . . Bazarov's were also flashing.

"All right," he assented. "There's no need for further explanations. You've conceived a whim to test your sense of chivalry out on me. I might deny you this pleasure, but—so be it!"

"I'm deeply obliged to you," Pavel Petrovich replied. "May I then rely upon your acceptance of my challenge without my being compelled to resort to violent measures?"

"I take it you're alluding to that cane, to speak nonmetaphorically?" Bazarov remarked coolly. "You're perfectly correct—it's quite unnecessary for you to insult me. Indeed, it wouldn't be altogether safe. You can remain a gentleman. . . . And I accept your challenge in equally gentlemanly fashion."

"That's excellent," Pavel Petrovich responded, depositing his cane in a corner. "We'll say a few words about the conditions of our duel in a moment, but I'd like to ascertain first whether you deem it necessary to resort to the formality of some trifling dispute that might serve as a pretext for my challenge?"

"No. It's better without any formalities."

"I think so myself. I presume that it's also inappropriate to delve into the actual basis of our dispute. We can't abide one another. What more could be required?"

"What more, indeed?" Bazarov repeated sarcastically.

"In regard to the conditions of the encounter itself, seeing that we won't have any seconds—for where could we get them?"

"Just so—where could we get them?"

"I therefore have the honor to present the following proposal to you: the duel should take place early tomorrow morning, at six, let's say, beyond the grove, with pistols, at a distance of ten paces. . . ."

"Ten paces? That will do—we hate one another at that distance."

"We might make it eight," Pavel Petrovich noted.

"We might."

"Each of us will fire twice, and in order to be prepared for any eventuality, let's each put a brief letter in one of his pockets that blames himself for his own demise."

"Now, I don't approve of that at all," Bazarov declared. "That's like something out of a French novel, something quite implausible."

"Perhaps. You do agree, however, that it might be unpleasant to incur the suspicion of having committed murder?"

"I agree on that. But there's a way to avoid such a lamentable accusation. We won't have any seconds, but we can have a witness."

"Who, if you'll allow me to inquire?"

"Why, Petr."

"Which Petr?"

"Your brother's valet. He's a man who's scaled the heights of contemporary culture, and will perform his part with all the *comilfo* required in such circumstances."

"It seems to me that you're joking, my dear sir."

"Not in the slightest. If you think my suggestion over, you'll become convinced that it's full of common sense and simplicity. You can't make a silk purse out of a sow's ear, but I'll endeavor to prepare Petr in a suitable manner and bring him to the field of battle."

"You persist in joking," Pavel Petrovich commented, rising from his chair. "But after the courteous cooperation you've given me, I have no right to hold this against you.... And so, everything's been arranged.... By the way, do you have any pistols?"

"Where would I get any pistols, Pavel Petrovich? I'm not in the army."

"In that case, let me offer you mine. You may rest assured that it's been five years since I've fired one."

"That's a very consoling piece of information."

Pavel Petrovich picked up his cane.... "And now, my dear sir, it merely remains for me to thank you and leave you to your studies. I have the honor to bid you good day."

"Until we have the pleasure of meeting again, my dear sir," Bazarov responded, conducting his visitor to the door.

Pavel Petrovich went out. Bazarov remained standing in front of the door for a minute, then suddenly exclaimed: "What the devil! How refined—and how idiotic! What a farce we've enacted! Like trained dogs dancing on their hind legs. But refusing was out of the question. Why, for all I know, he'd have struck me, and then...." (Bazarov turned pale at the very thought; his pride was instantly aroused.) "At that point, it might have come to my strangling him like a kitten." He went back to his microscope, but his heart was pounding, and the composure needed to make scientific observations had vanished. "He saw us today," Bazarov thought, "but would he really behave like this on his brother's behalf? And how important is a kiss? There must be something else to it. Bah! Maybe he's in love with her himself. Of course, he's in love—it's as clear as day. What a development!... It's a bad business!" he finally concluded. "It's a bad business, whichever way you look at it. In the first place, it'll be necessary to risk having a bullet put through my brains and then, in any case, to go away. In the second, there's Arkadii ... and that dear, innocent lamb, Nikolai Petrovich. It's a bad, bad business."

The day passed in some sort of special quietude and languor. Fenechka seemed to have disappeared from the face of the earth; she sat in her little room like a mouse in its hole. Nikolai Petrovich looked preoccupied—he'd just learned that blight had begun to invade his wheat, upon which he'd particularly rested his hopes. Pavel Petrovich overwhelmed everyone, even Prokofich, with his icy courtesy. Bazarov began a letter to his father, but tore it up and threw it under the table.

"If I die," he thought, "they'll find out—but I'm not going to die. No, I'll struggle along on this planet for a good while yet." He ordered Petr to come and see him about important business the next morning, as soon as it was light; Petr imagined that Bazarov wanted to take him along to Petersburg. Bazarov went to bed late, and was tormented by chaotic dreams all night long.... Mrs. Odintsov kept appearing in them: first she was his mother, followed by a kitten with black whiskers, which turned out to be Fenechka; then Pavel Petrovich took the shape of a huge forest, with which he nonetheless had to fight. Petr awakened Bazarov at four o'clock; he promptly got dressed and went outside with Petr.

It was a lovely, fresh morning; tiny striped clouds hovered overhead like little curls of fleece in the pale, clear blue sky; fine drops of dew lay on the leaves and grass, sparkling on spiders' webs like silver; the damp, dark earth still seemed to retain traces of the rosy dawn; larks' songs came pouring from every corner of the sky. Bazarov walked as far as the grove, sat down in the shade at its edge, and only then disclosed to Petr the nature of the service required of him. The cultured valet became mortally frightened, but Bazarov calmed Petr down by assuring him that he wouldn't have to do anything except stand at a distance and observe, that he wouldn't incur any sort of responsibility. "And in the meantime," Bazarov added, "just think what an important role you have to play!" Petr gestured helplessly, lowered his gaze, and leaned against a birch tree, turning green with terror.

The road from Marino skirted the grove; light dust lay across the road, which hadn't been disturbed by wheel or foot since the previous day. Bazarov involuntarily stared along this road, then pulled and sucked on a blade of grass while he kept repeating to himself, "What stupidity!" The early morning chill made him shiver twice. . . . Petr looked at him dejectedly, but Bazarov merely smiled—he wasn't afraid.

The tramp of horses' hoofs on the road became audible. . . . A peasant came into sight from behind the trees. He was driving two horses that had been hobbled together ahead of him, and, as he passed Bazarov, he looked at him somewhat strangely, without touching his cap, which evidently struck Petr as an bad omen. "There's someone else who's up early," Bazarov mused, "but at least he's gotten up for work, whereas we. . . ."

"It seems the gentleman's coming," Petr suddenly whispered.

Bazarov raised his head and saw Pavel Petrovich. Dressed in a light checked jacket and snow-white trousers, he was rapidly walking down the road carrying a box wrapped in green cloth under his arm.

"I beg your pardon—I believe I've kept you waiting," he began, bowing first to Bazarov and then to Petr, whom he treated with respect at that moment as something like a second. "I didn't want to awaken my valet."

"It doesn't matter," Bazarov responded. "We've just arrived ourselves."

"Ah! So much the better!" Pavel Petrovich took a look around. "There's no one in sight—no one will hinder us. Can we proceed?"

"Yes, let's proceed."

"You don't require any fresh explanation, I presume?"

"No, I don't."

"Would you like to load these?" Pavel Petrovich inquired, taking the pistols out of the box.

"No, you load them, and I'll measure out the paces. My legs are longer," Bazarov added with a smile. "One, two, three. . . ."

"Evgenii Vasilevich," Petr mumbled with an effort (he was trembling as though he had a fever), "no matter what you say, I'm going farther away."

"Four . . . five. . . . Go ahead, my friend, go ahead. You can even get behind a tree and cover your ears—just don't shut your eyes. And if anyone falls, run and pick him up. Six . . . seven . . . eight. . . ." Bazarov stopped. "Is that enough?" he asked, turning toward Pavel Petrovich, "or should I add two more paces?"

"It's up to you," replied the latter, inserting a second bullet.

"Well, let's make it two more." Bazarov drew a line on the ground with the toe of his boot. "There's the barrier, then. By the way, how many paces may each of us step back from the barrier? That's an important question, too. The issue wasn't discussed yesterday."

"I'd think ten," Pavel Petrovich answered, handing Bazarov both pistols. "Will you be so good as to choose?"

"I will. But you must admit, Pavel Petrovich, that our duel is unusual to the point of absurdity. Just look at the countenance of our second."

"You're inclined to laugh at everything," Pavel Petrovich retorted. "I don't deny that our duel is strange, but I consider it my duty to warn you that I intend to duel in earnest. *A bon entendeur, salut!*"

"Oh! I don't doubt that we've made up our minds to annihilate one another, but why not laugh, too, and unite *utile dulci*? So you speak French to me, whereas I speak Latin to you."

"I'm going to duel in earnest," Pavel Petrovich repeated, and he walked over to his position. Bazarov, for his part, counted off ten paces from the barrier and stood still.

"Are you ready?" asked Pavel Petrovich.

"Perfectly."

"Then we can approach one another."

Bazarov moved forward slowly, and Pavel Petrovich, his left hand thrust into his pocket, advanced toward him, gradually raising the muzzle of his pistol. . . . "He's aiming straight at my nose," Bazarov observed to himself, "and he's aiming carefully, the villain! This isn't a pleasant sensation, though. I'm going to look at his watch chain."

Something suddenly whizzed right past his ear, and at the same instant, the sound of a shot rang out. The thought, "I heard it, so it must be all right," had time to flash through Bazarov's brain. He took one more step and, without aiming, pulled the trigger.

Pavel Petrovich shuddered slightly and clutched at his thigh. A stream of blood began to trickle down his white trousers.

Bazarov flung his pistol aside and went over to his antagonist. "Are you wounded?" he queried.

"You had the right to summon me to the barrier," Pavel Petrovich declared, "but that's of no consequence. According to our agreement, each of us has one more shot."

"Well, forgive me, but that can occur another time," Bazarov replied, seizing hold of Pavel Petrovich, who was beginning to turn pale. "Now I'm not a duelist, I'm a doctor, and I have to take a look at your wound before anything else occurs. Petr! Come here, Petr! Where are you hiding?"

"That's all nonsense. . . . I don't need anyone's assistance," Pavel Petrovich affirmed jerkily, "and . . . we must . . . again. . . ." He tried to tug at his moustache, but his hand went limp, his eyes grew dim, and he lost consciousness.

"Here's a new twist! A fainting fit! What next?" Bazarov involuntarily exclaimed as he laid Pavel Petrovich on the grass. "Let's have a look and see what's wrong." He pulled out a handkerchief, wiped away the blood, and began feeling around the wound. . . . "The bone hasn't been broken," he muttered through his teeth. "The bullet didn't go deep—one muscle, *vastus externus*, was grazed. He'll be dancing in three weeks! . . . And he faints! Oh, I'm so sick of these high-strung types! My, what delicate skin!"

"Is he dead?" Petr's tremulous voice inquired from behind Bazarov's back.

Bazarov looked around. "Go get some water as quickly as you can, my friend, and he'll outlive us all."

But the modern servant didn't seem to comprehend his words, and didn't move. Pavel Petrovich slowly opened his eyes. "He's dying!" Petr whispered, and he began crossing himself.

"You're right. . . . What a foolish countenance!" the wounded gentleman remarked with a forced smile.

"Well, go get some water, you devil!" Bazarov shouted.

"There's no need. . . . It was momentary *vertige*. . . . Help me sit up . . . there, that's right. . . . I just need something to bind this scratch, and I can go home on foot, or else you can send a cart for me. If it's all right with you, the duel won't be renewed. You've behaved honorably . . . today, I emphasize, today."

"There's no need to recall the past," Bazarov rejoined, "and as for the future, it isn't worth it for you to trouble your head about that, either, because I intend to head out without delay. Let me bandage your leg now—your wound isn't serious, but it's always best to stop any bleeding. I have to bring this mortal to his senses first, though."

Bazarov shook Petr by the collar and sent him to fetch a cart.

"Be sure that you don't frighten my brother," Pavel Petrovich told him. "Don't you dream of informing him about this."

Petr raced off, and while he hastily sought a cart, the two antagonists sat on the ground without speaking. Pavel Petrovich tried not to look at Bazarov; he still didn't want to become reconciled with him. He was ashamed of his own haughtiness and of his failure; he was ashamed of the whole situation he'd created, even though he felt that it couldn't have ended in a more fortuitous manner. "At any rate, there won't be any scandal," he consoled himself, "and I'm grateful for that." The silence was prolonged, awkward, and distressing; both of them were uncomfortable. Each was aware that the other understood what he was feeling. This awareness is always pleasant for friends, and always most unpleasant for those who aren't friends, especially when it's impossible either to confront one another or to go separate ways.

"Have I bound your leg too tightly?" Bazarov finally inquired.

"No, not at all, it's fine," Pavel Petrovich answered, and, after a brief pause, he added, "We won't be able to deceive my brother. We'll have to tell him that we quarreled about politics."

"That's fine," Bazarov assented. "You can say I insulted all Anglomaniacs."

"That will do beautifully. What do you suppose this man thinks about us now?" Pavel Petrovich continued, pointing to the same peasant who'd driven the hobbled horses past Bazarov a few minutes prior to the duel, who now, returning along the road, took off his cap at the sight of the "gentry."

"Who on earth knows?" Bazarov responded. "Most likely, he doesn't think anything. The Russian peasant is the mysterious unknown that Mrs. Radcliffe once analyzed at such length. Who can understand him? He doesn't understand himself!"

"Ah! So that's your attitude!" Pavel Petrovich began, and then he suddenly cried, "Look what your fool Petr has done! Here comes my brother galloping out to find us!"

Bazarov turned around and caught sight of the pale face of Nikolai Petrovich, who was sitting in the cart. He jumped out of it well before it stopped and rushed up to his brother.

"What does this mean?" he asked in an agitated voice. "Evgenii Vasilich, for heaven's sake—what is all this?"

"It's nothing," answered Pavel Petrovich. "They've alarmed you in vain. I had a minor dispute with Mr. Bazarov, and I've had to pay for it a little bit."

"But why did all this happen, for God's sake?"

"What can I tell you? Mr. Bazarov alluded to Sir Robert Peel disrespectfully. I must hasten to add that I'm the only person to blame in all this, while Mr. Bazarov has behaved most honorably. I challenged him."

"But you're all covered with blood, for heaven's sake!"

"Well, did you suppose I had water in my veins? But this bloodletting is actually beneficial to me. Isn't that so, doctor? Help me get into the cart, and don't succumb to melancholy. I'll be perfectly well tomorrow. There, that's fine. Go ahead, driver."

Nikolai Petrovich walked behind the cart; Bazarov was going to stay where he was. . . .

"I have to ask you to look after my brother," Nikolai Petrovich said to him, "until we get another doctor from town."

Bazarov silently nodded his head. Within an hour's time, Pavel Petrovich was lying in bed with a skillfully bandaged leg. The entire household was upset; Fenechka felt sick. Nikolai Petrovich kept stealthily wringing his hands, while Pavel Petrovich laughed and joked, especially with Bazarov. Pavel Petrovich put on a delicate cambric nightshirt and an elegant morning robe, as well as a fez, didn't allow the blinds to be drawn, and humorously complained about the need to be deprived of food.

Toward nightfall, however, he grew feverish; his head started to ache. The doctor arrived from town. (Nikolai Petrovich wouldn't listen to his brother, and indeed, Bazarov himself didn't want him to. Bazarov had spent the whole day in his room, looking jaundiced and malevolent, and had only stopped in to see the patient for the briefest possible periods; he'd happened to run into Fenechka twice, but she'd shrunk away from him in horror.) The new doctor advised a diet of cool foods; he confirmed Bazarov's assessment that there was no danger, however. Nikolai Petrovich told him that his brother had wounded himself by accident, to which the doctor responded, "Hmm!" But after twenty-five silver rubles were slipped into his hand on the spot, he remarked, "You don't say so! Well, that often happens, to be sure."

No one in the house went to bed, or even undressed. Nikolai Petrovich kept tiptoeing in to look at his brother and tiptoeing out again; Pavel Petrovich dozed, groaned slightly, told him in French, *"Couchez-vous,"* and asked for something to drink. Nikolai Petrovich sent Fenechka to bring him a glass of lemonade; Pavel Petrovich gazed at her intently and downed the liquid to the last drop. Toward morning, the fever increased a bit; a slight delirium developed. Pavel Petrovich uttered incoherent words at first; then he suddenly opened his eyes, and, seeing his brother standing close to his bed, anxiously bending over him, he said, "Nikolai, don't you think that Fenechka looks somewhat like Nellie?"

"Which Nellie is that, Pavel dear?"

"How can you ask? Princess R——. Especially in the upper part of the face. *C'est de la même famille.*"

Nikolai Petrovich didn't reply, but he marveled inwardly at the persistence of youthful passions in human beings. "It's at times like these when they come to the surface," he thought.

"Ah, how I love that hollow creature!" Pavel Petrovich moaned, drearily clasping his hands behind his head. "I can't stand the thought that any insolent upstart would dare to touch . . . ," he whispered a few moments later.

Nikolai Petrovich merely sighed; he didn't in the least suspect to whom those words referred.

Bazarov presented himself to Nikolai Petrovich at eight o'clock the next morning. He'd already managed to pack and to set all his frogs, insects, and birds free.

"Have you come to say goodbye to me?" Nikolai Petrovich inquired, standing up as Bazarov came in.

"Just so."

"I understand what you're doing, and fully approve. My poor brother is to blame, of course, and he's been punished for it. He himself told me that he made it impossible for you to act otherwise. I believe that you couldn't have avoided this duel, which . . . which is explained alone to some extent by the almost constant antagonism of your respective views." (Nikolai Petrovich was getting his words slightly mixed up.) "My brother is a man of the old school, he's hot-tempered and stubborn. . . . Thank God it's ended the way it has. I've taken every precaution to avoid all public attention. . . ."

"I'm leaving you my address, in case there's any trouble," Bazarov remarked nonchalantly.

"I hope there won't be any sort of trouble, Evgenii Vasilich. . . .

I'm very sorry that your stay in my house should have come to such a . . . such an end. It's all the more distressing to me that Arkadii. . . ."

"I'll probably be seeing him," Bazarov observed—"explanations" and "protestations" of every sort always made him impatient. "In case I don't, I beg you to say goodbye to him for me, and to accept the expression of my regret."

"And I beg . . . ," Nikolai Petrovich responded with a bow. But Bazarov went out without waiting for the end of his sentence.

When he learned of Bazarov's intended departure, Pavel Petrovich expressed a desire to see him, and shook his hand. But Bazarov remained as cold as ice even then—he realized that Pavel Petrovich wanted to play the role of the magnanimous nobleman. He didn't manage to say goodbye to Fenechka; he merely exchanged glances with her through one window. Her face looked sad to him. "She'll probably have some hard times," he said to himself. . . . "But she'll pull through somehow!" Petr was so overwhelmed by emotion that he wept on Bazarov's shoulder until Bazarov stifled him by asking whether he had an endless supply of moisture in his eyes; Duniasha was forced to run off into the grove to hide her distress. The man guilty of causing all this misery got into a carriage, lit a cigar, and at a bend in the road after the fourth verst, where the Kirsanovs' farm buildings and new house were visible in a long row, he merely spat, muttering, "Damned snobs!" and wrapped himself more tightly in his coat.

Pavel Petrovich began to improve shortly thereafter, but he had to stay in bed for about a week. He bore his captivity, as he called it, quite patiently, merely taking great pains with his toilette and having everything scented with eau de cologne. Nikolai Petrovich read him journals; Fenechka waited on him as usual, bringing him soup, lemonade, hard-boiled eggs, and tea, but she was filled with concealed dread whenever she went into his room. Pavel Petrovich's unexpected actions had alarmed everyone in the house—and her more than anyone else. Prokofich was the only person who wasn't concerned; he discoursed upon the way in which gentlemen in his day used to fight duels, albeit "only with real gentlemen. They used to have low curs like that horsewhipped at the stables for their insolence."

Fenechka's conscience barely reproached her, but she was periodically tormented by the thought of the true cause of the dispute.

And Pavel Petrovich looked at her so strangely . . . in such a way that she could feel his eyes on her even when her back was turned. She grew thinner from the ceaseless inner agitation and, as so often happens, became even lovelier as a result.

One day—this incident occurred in the morning—Pavel Petrovich felt better and moved from his bed to the sofa, while Nikolai Petrovich, having assured himself that his brother really was better, went off to the threshing barn. Fenechka brought Pavel Petrovich a cup of tea, and setting it down on a little table, was about to withdraw. He detained her.

"Where are you going in such a hurry, Fedosia Nikolaevna?" he began. "Are you busy?"

"No, sir . . . yes, sir . . . I have to pour the tea."

"Duniasha will do that without you. Sit here for a little while with a poor invalid. Anyway, I want to have a chat with you."

Fenechka silently sat down on the edge of an easy chair.

"Listen," Pavel Petrovich said, tugging at his moustache, "I've wanted to ask you something for a long time. Are you afraid of me for some reason?"

"Me?"

"Yes, you. You never look at me—as though your conscience weren't clear."

Fenechka was starting to blush, but she glanced at Pavel Petrovich. He seemed somewhat strange to her, and her heart began to throb quietly.

"Is your conscience clear?" he inquired.

"Why shouldn't it be clear?" she faltered.

"Goodness knows why! Besides, whom could you have wronged? Me? That's not likely. Anyone else in the house here? That's also improbable. Could it be my brother? But you love him, don't you?"

"I do love him."

"With all your soul, with all your heart?"

"I love Nikolai Petrovich with all my heart."

"Truly? Look at me, Fenechka." (It was the first time that he'd used this name.) "You know, it's a terrible sin to lie!"

"I'm not lying, Pavel Petrovich. If I were to stop loving Nikolai Petrovich—I wouldn't want to live after that."

"And you'll never forsake him for anyone else?"

"For whom would I forsake him?"

"For whom, indeed! Well, how about that gentleman who's just left here?"

Fenechka stood up. "My God, Pavel Petrovich, why are you torturing me? What have I done to you? How can you say such things?"

"Fenechka," Pavel Petrovich addressed her in a sorrowful voice, "you know that I saw...."

"What did you see?"

"Out there ... in the arbor."

Fenechka blushed to the roots of her hair. "How was I to blame for that?" she inquired with an effort.

Pavel Petrovich lifted himself up. "You weren't to blame? No? Not at all?"

"I love Nikolai Petrovich and no one else in the world, and I'll always love him!" Fenechka exclaimed with sudden force, and her throat seemed to be nearly bursting with sobs. "As for what you saw, I'll declare on the final day of judgment that I'm not to blame and wasn't to blame for it, and I'd rather die right now than have people suspect me of doing anything to hurt my benefactor, Nikolai Petrovich...."

Her voice broke at this point, and at the same point, she felt Pavel Petrovich grasping and squeezing her hand.... She looked at him and became almost petrified. He'd turned even paler than before; his eyes were shining and, most surprising of all, a large, solitary tear was rolling down his cheek.

"Fenechka," he said in some sort of wonderful whisper, "love him—love my brother! He's such a kind, decent man! Don't forsake him for anyone in the world! Don't listen to anyone else! Think about it—what can be more terrible than to love and not to be loved? Never leave my poor Nikolai!"

Fenechka's eyes dried and her terror subsided, so great was her astonishment. But even greater was her astonishment when Pavel Petrovich, Pavel Petrovich himself, put her hand to his lips and seemed to pierce it without kissing it, merely heaving convulsive sighs from time to time....

"My Lord," she thought, "is he having some kind of attack?"

At that instant, his entire ruined life was crumbling inside him.

The staircase creaked under rapidly approaching footsteps.... He pushed her hand away from him and let his head fall back on the pillow. The door opened and Nikolai Petrovich entered, looking cheerful, refreshed, and ruddy. Mitia, as refreshed and ruddy as his father, wearing nothing but a light shirt, was frisking on Nikolai Petrovich's shoulder, catching his little bare toes on the big buttons of his father's coarse country coat.

Fenechka virtually flung herself at Nikolai Petrovich, and clasping him and her son together in her arms, she let her head fall against his shoulder. Nikolai Petrovich was surprised: Fenechka, the reserved, shy Fenechka, had never embraced him in the presence of a third party.

"What's the matter?" he asked, and glancing at his brother, he handed Mitia to her. "Do you feel worse?" he asked next, approaching Pavel Petrovich.

Pavel Petrovich buried his face in a cambric handkerchief. "No . . . not at all. . . . On the contrary, I feel much better."

"You were in too much of a rush to move to the sofa. Where are you going?" Nikolai Petrovich added, turning around to address Fenechka. She'd already closed the door behind her, however. "I was bringing my young hero in to show you—he's been missing his uncle. Why has she taken him away? What's wrong with you, though? Has anything happened between the two of you, eh?"

"Brother!" Pavel Petrovich began solemnly.

Nikolai Petrovich flinched. He felt dismayed, although he himself couldn't have said why.

"Brother," Pavel Petrovich repeated, "give me your word that you'll carry out my sole request."

"What request? Tell me."

"It's very important—the happiness of your entire life depends on it, in my opinion. I've been thinking a great deal this whole time about what I want to say to you now. . . . Brother, do your duty, the duty of an honorable, generous man. Put an end to the scandal and the bad example you're setting—you, the best of men!"

"What do you mean, Pavel?"

"Marry Fenechka. She loves you. She's the mother of your son."

Nikolai Petrovich retreated a step and threw up his hands. "Is it you who's saying this, Pavel? You, whom I've always regarded as the most steadfast opponent of such marriages! You're saying this? Don't you know that it's been purely out of respect for you that I haven't done what you so rightly call my duty?"

"You were wrong to respect me, in that case," Pavel Petrovich responded with a weary smile. "I'm beginning to think that Bazarov was right in accusing me of aristocratism. No, my dear brother, let's not worry about the world's opinion anymore. We're

old, humble people now—it's time we set aside all sorts of vanity.
Let's just do our duty, as you say, and you'll see—we'll obtain
happiness in the bargain."

Nikolai Petrovich rushed over to hug his brother.

"You've finally opened my eyes!" he cried. "I was right in always
affirming that you are the most intelligent, kindhearted person in
the world, and now I see that you're just as wise as you are
generous."

"Gently, gently," Pavel Petrovich interrupted him. "Don't hurt
the leg of your wise brother who, at the age of nearly fifty, fought
a duel like an ensign. So then, it's settled. Fenechka will become
my . . . *belle soeur.*"

"My dearest Pavel! But what will Arkadii say?"

"Arkadii? He'll be ecstatic, for heaven's sake! Marriage is against
his principles, but then again, his sense of equality will be gratified.
And, after all, what significance do class distinctions have *au dix-
neuvième siècle?*"

"Ah, Pavel, Pavel! Let me kiss you once more! Don't be afraid—
I'll be careful."

The brothers embraced one another.

"What do you think—shouldn't you inform her of your intentions
right away?" Pavel Petrovich inquired.

"Why hurry?" Nikolai Petrovich responded. "Has there been
any sort of discussion between the two of you?"

"A discussion between us? *Quelle idée!*"

"Well, that's all right, then. First of all, you have to get well,
and meanwhile, there's plenty of time. We should think it through
carefully, and consider. . . ."

"But your mind's made up, I trust?"

"Of course my mind's made up, and I thank you from the bottom
of my heart. I'll leave you now—you should rest. Any excitement
is bad for you. . . . But we'll talk it over again later. Sleep well,
dear one, and God bless you!"

"Why is he thanking me so much?" Pavel Petrovich wondered
when he'd been left alone. "As though it didn't depend on him!
I'll go away as soon as he gets married, somewhere far away—
Dresden or Florence—and I'll live there until I die."

Pavel Petrovich moistened his forehead with eau de cologne and
closed his eyes. Illuminated by the bright light of day, his handsome, emaciated head lay on the white pillow like the head of a
dead man . . . and, indeed, he was a dead man.

XXV

At Nikolskoe, Katia and Arkadii were sitting in the garden on a sod bench beneath the shade of a tall ash tree. Fifi had settled herself on the ground near them, arranging her slender body in that graceful position known among dog fanciers as "the hare curve." Both Arkadii and Katia were silent; he was holding a book half-open in his hands, while she was picking out the few crumbs of bread left in a basket and throwing them to a small family of sparrows who, with their typical cowardly impudence, were hopping and chirping right at her feet. A faint breeze stirring the ash tree's leaves slowly scattered pale-gold flecks of sunshine up and down across the path and over Fifi's tawny back. A patch of unbroken shade covered Arkadii and Katia; from time to time, a bright streak of light gleamed on her hair. Both were silent, but the very way in which they were silent, the way in which they were sitting together, bespoke trustful intimacy; both of them seemed utterly unaware of any companion, while secretly rejoicing in one another's presence. Even their faces had changed since we last saw them: Arkadii's looked more tranquil, Katia's, more animated and bold.

"Don't you think," Arkadii began, "that the ash has been quite aptly named *iasen*[1] in Russian? No other tree is as delicate and 'transparent' in the air as it is."

Katia raised her eyes upward and said, "Yes," while Arkadii thought, "Well, she doesn't reproach me for speaking eloquently."

"I don't like Heine," Katia declared, glancing toward the book Arkadii was holding in his hands, "when he either laughs or cries. I like him when he's pensive and mournful."

"Whereas I like him when he laughs," Arkadii remarked.

"Those are the remnants of your satirical tendencies. . . ." ("The remnants!" Arkadii thought. "If only Bazarov could hear that!")

"Wait a little while—we'll transform you."

"Who'll transform me? You?"

"Who? My sister. Porfirii Platonovich, with whom you no longer quarrel. My aunt, whom you escorted to church the day before yesterday."

"Well, I couldn't refuse! And as for Anna Sergeevna, she agreed with Evgenii about many things—do you remember?"

"My sister was under his influence then, just as you were."

---

[1] The adjective *iasnyi* means "clear" or "transparent."

"Just as I was? Do you really think that I'm free of his influence now?"

Katia didn't say anything.

"I know," Arkadii continued, "that you never liked him."

"I can't form an opinion about him."

"Do you know, Katerina Sergeevna, that whenever I hear this reply, I distrust it. . . . There's no one about whom each of us couldn't form an opinion! That's simply an evasion."

"Well, then, I'll admit that I don't. . . . It's not exactly that I don't like him—but I sense that he's different from me, and that I'm different from him . . . and that you're different from him as well."

"How so?"

"What can I say to you?. . . He's a wild animal, whereas you and I are tame."

"Even I'm tame?"

Katia nodded.

Arkadii scratched his ear. "Let me tell you, Katerina Sergeevna, that this is deeply insulting."

"Why, would you like to be wild?"

"Not wild, but strong, energetic."

"It's pointless to want to be that. . . . Your friend doesn't want to be that, you see, but it's inside him all the same."

"Hmm! So you believe he wielded a great deal of influence over Anna Sergeevna?"

"Yes. But no one can maintain the upper hand over her for long," Katia added under her breath.

"Why do you think that?"

"She's very proud. . . . I didn't mean that. . . . She highly prizes her independence."

"Who doesn't prize it?" Arkadii asked, but the thought flashed through his mind: "What good is it?" "What good is it?" Katia wondered as well. When young people frequently spend time together in friendly fashion, they constantly stumble onto the same ideas.

Arkadii smiled, and drawing slightly closer to Katia, he said in a whisper, "Confess that you're a little bit afraid of *her*."

"Of whom?"

"*Her*," Arkadii repeated meaningfully.

"And what about you?" Katia asked in turn.

"I am, too. Notice that I said, 'I am, *too*.'"

Katia shook her finger at him. "I'm surprised at that," she

observed. "My sister's never been as well-disposed toward you as she's recently been—much more so than when you first came."

"Really?"

"Why, haven't you noticed? Aren't you glad?"

Arkadii grew thoughtful.

"How have I managed to earn Anna Sergeevna's good opinion? Was it because I brought her your mother's letters?"

"Both because of that and other reasons, which I won't tell you."

"Why not?"

"I won't say."

"Oh! I know that you're extremely stubborn."

"Yes, I am."

"And observant."

Katia gave Arkadii a sidelong look. "Maybe so. Does that irritate you? What are you thinking about?"

"I'm wondering how you've gotten to be as observant as you actually are. You're so shy, so reserved. You keep everyone at a distance. . . ."

"I've lived alone a great deal—that forces one to become contemplative involuntarily. But do I really keep everyone at a distance?"

Arkadii threw a grateful glance at Katia. "That's all very well," he continued, "but people in your situation—I mean, in your financial circumstances—don't often possess that gift. It's as hard for them to reach the truth as it is for tsars."

"But I'm not rich, you see."

Arkadii was taken aback, and didn't immediately understand what Katia meant. The thought, "Why, of course—the property all belongs to her sister!" suddenly struck him. This thought didn't displease him. "You said that so well!" he commented.

"What?"

"You said that well—simply, without either being ashamed or bragging. By the way, I believe that there must always be something special, some unique sort of pride, in the emotional state of individuals who know they're poor, and say so."

"I've never experienced anything of that sort, thanks to my sister. I merely referred to my financial circumstances now because the subject happened to come up."

"True, but you must admit that you have a portion of the pride I just mentioned."

"How so, for instance?"

"For instance, you—please forgive the question—you wouldn't marry a rich man, would you?"

"If I loved him very much. . . . No, I think that I wouldn't marry him even then."

"There! You see!" Arkadii cried. And after a short pause, he added, "And why wouldn't you marry him?"

"Because of what's said in ballads about unequal matches."

"Maybe you want to have control, or. . . ."

"Oh, no! Why would I? On the contrary, I'm ready to obey someone. But inequality is oppressive. To respect oneself and obey someone else—that I can understand, that's happiness. But a subordinate existence. . . . No, I've had enough of that as it is."

"You've had enough of that as it is," Arkadii echoed Katia's words. "Yes, yes," he continued, "you're not Anna Sergeevna's sister for nothing. You're just as independent as she is, but you're more reserved. I'm sure that you aren't the one to express this feeling first, however intense and sacred it might be. . . ."

"Well, what would you expect?" Katia inquired.

"You're equally intelligent, and you've got as much strength of character, if not more than she. . . ."

"Please don't compare me to my sister," Katia hurriedly interrupted him. "It works too much to my disadvantage. You seem to have forgotten that my sister is beautiful and intelligent and. . . . You in particular, Arkadii Nikolaevich, shouldn't say such things—with such a serious face, moreover."

"What do you mean by 'you in particular'—and what makes you suppose I'm joking?"

"Of course you're joking."

"Do you think so? But what if I'm convinced of what I say? What if I believe I still haven't put it strongly enough?"

"I don't understand what you mean."

"Really? Well, now I see—I clearly took you to be more observant than you are."

"How so?"

Arkadii didn't reply. He turned away, while Katia sought out a few more crumbs in the basket and started to throw them to the sparrows. But she moved her arm too vigorously, and they flew away without stopping to pick up the crumbs.

"Katerina Sergeevna!" Arkadii began suddenly. "It's probably of no consequence to you, but let me tell you that I wouldn't trade you, not only for your sister, but for anyone else on earth."

He stood up and left quickly, as though frightened by the words that had fallen from his lips.

Katia let her hands drop into her lap alongside the basket and stared for a long while at the path Arkadii had taken, her head bowed. A faint crimson flush gradually spread across her cheeks, but her lips didn't smile, and her dark eyes filled with a look of perplexity, as well as some other, still undefined emotion.

"Are you alone?" she heard the voice of Anna Sergeevna speaking next to her. "I thought you came into the garden with Arkadii."

Katia slowly raised her eyes to look at her sister (she was standing in the path, elegantly, even elaborately dressed, tickling Fifi's ears with the tip of her open parasol), and slowly replied, "Yes, I'm alone."

"So I see," Anna Sergeevna responded with a smile. "I suppose he's gone back to his room?"

"Yes."

"Were you reading together?"

"Yes."

Anna Sergeevna put her hand under Katia's chin and tilted her sister's face upward.

"You haven't been quarreling, I hope?"

"No," Katia said, and she calmly moved her sister's hand away.

"How solemnly you reply! I expected to find him here, and meant to suggest that he come for a walk with me—he's always asking to do that. They've sent you some shoes from town—go try them on. I just noticed yesterday that your old ones are quite shabby. You never think enough about such things, and you have such charming little feet! Your hands are nice, too . . . only they're quite large. So you have to make the most of your little feet. But you're not a coquette."

Anna Sergeevna proceeded further along the path with a quiet rustle of her beautiful dress. Katia rose from the bench and left as well, taking Heine with her—but not to try on her shoes.

"Charming little feet!" she thought as she slowly and lightly mounted the stone steps of the terrace, which were hot from the sun's rays. "Charming little feet, you say. . . . Well, he's going to end up falling at them."

But she suddenly felt ashamed, and swiftly ran upstairs.

Arkadii had started down a corridor toward his room when the steward overtook him and announced that Mr. Bazarov was waiting for him.

"Evgenii!" Arkadii murmured almost in dismay. "Did he arrive a long time ago?"

"Mr. Bazarov just arrived this minute, sir, and gave orders not to announce his arrival to Anna Sergeevna, but to take him straight up to your room."

"Can something bad have happened at home?" Arkadii wondered, and hurriedly running up the stairs, he threw open the door to his room. Bazarov's expression immediately reassured him, although a more experienced eye might well have discerned signs of inner agitation in the gaunt, albeit still energetic, form of his unexpected visitor. With a dusty coat thrown round his shoulders and a cap on his head, he was sitting at the window; he didn't even stand up when Arkadii flung his arms around his visitor's neck, voicing loud exclamations.

"This is so unexpected! What good fortune has brought you here?" he kept repeating, bustling around the room like someone who imagines—and wishes to demonstrate—that he's delighted. "I presume that everything's all right at home—they're all well, aren't they?"

"Everything's all right, but they're not all well," Bazarov replied. "Stop chattering. Send for some kvass for me, sit down, and listen while I tell you all about it in a few but, I hope, fairly impressive sentences."

Arkadii fell silent as Bazarov described his duel with Pavel Petrovich. Arkadii was quite surprised and even saddened, but didn't deem it necessary to reveal this. He merely asked whether his uncle's wound truly wasn't serious, and upon receiving the response that it was extremely interesting, though not from a medical point of view, he gave a forced smile. At heart, however, he felt both horrified and somehow ashamed. Bazarov seemed to understand him.

"Yes, my friend," he remarked, "that's what comes of residing with feudal types—you end up becoming a feudal type yourself and find yourself taking part in knightly tournaments. Well, so I set off for my parent's house," Bazarov wound up, "and I've stopped here along the way . . . to tell you all this, I'd say, if I didn't consider a useless lie tantamount to stupidity. No, I stopped here—the devil knows why. You see, sometimes it's a good thing for a man to seize himself by the scruff of the neck and pull himself up, the way you pull a radish up out of its soil. That's what I've been doing lately. . . . But I wanted to have one more look at what I'm parting from—at the soil where I was planted."

"I hope those words don't refer to me," Arkadii interjected agitatedly. "I hope you aren't thinking of parting from *me*."

Bazarov turned an intense, almost piercing gaze on him.

"Would that distress you so much? It strikes me that *you* have already parted from me. You look so fresh and clean. . . . Your dealings with Anna Sergeevna must be going very well."

"Which dealings with Anna Sergeevna?"

"Why, didn't you come here from town on her account, little bird? By the way, how are those Sunday schools progressing? Do you mean to tell me you aren't in love with her? Or have you already reached the stage of being discreet?"

"Evgenii, you know that I've always been open with you. I can assure you—I swear to you—you're mistaken."

"Hmm! That's a new word," Bazarov remarked in an undertone. "But you don't need to get excited—it's a matter of absolute indifference to me. A romantic would say, 'I feel that our paths are beginning to diverge,' but I'll simply say that we've gotten tired of one another."

"Evgenii. . . ."

"My dear friend, that's no real disaster—one gets tired of much more than that on earth. And now I suppose we'd better say goodbye, hadn't we? I've felt absolutely vile ever since I got here, just as though I'd been reading Gogol's letters to the wife of the governor of Kaluga. In any event, I didn't tell them to unharness the horses."

"For heaven's sake, this is beyond belief!"

"Why?"

"I won't say anything more about myself, but this would be the ultimate discourtesy to Anna Sergeevna, who'll definitely want to see you."

"Oh, you're mistaken there."

"On the contrary, I'm sure I'm right," Arkadii retorted. "And what are you pretending for? If it gets down to that, haven't you come here on her account yourself?"

"That may be true—and yet you're mistaken nonetheless."

But Arkadii was right. Anna Sergeevna did want to see Bazarov and sent the steward to ask him to come and chat with her. Bazarov changed his clothes before doing so—it turned out that he'd packed his new suit in order to be able to get it out easily.

Mrs. Odintsov met him not in the room where he'd so unexpectedly told her he loved her, but in the drawing room. She cordially extended her fingertips to him, and yet her face betrayed involuntary tension.

"Anna Sergeevna," Bazarov hastened to say, "before anything else transpires, I should set your mind at ease. In front of you stands a poor mortal who came to his senses long ago and hopes that other people have also forgotten his foolish behavior. I'm going away for a long while, and even though I'm not a particularly sensitive creature, as you'll agree, it'd be hard for me to carry away the thought that you remember me with distaste."

Anna Sergeevna heaved a deep sigh, like someone who's just climbed a high mountain, and her face brightened with a smile. She held out her hand to Bazarov a second time, and returned the pressure of his.

"Let's let bygones be bygones," she said, "all the more so because my conscience tells me that I was to blame then, too, for flirtatiousness—or for something else. In a word, let's be friends the way we were before. The rest was a dream, wasn't it? And who ever remembers dreams?"

"Who remembers them? And besides, love . . . is a purely contrived feeling, you know."

"Really? I'm very pleased to hear that."

Thus spoke Anna Sergeevna and thus spoke Bazarov; they both believed that they were speaking the truth. Was there truth, absolute truth, in their words? They themselves didn't know, nor does the author. But their conversation continued precisely as though they thoroughly believed one another.

Anna Sergeevna asked Bazarov, among other things, what he'd been doing at the Kirsanovs'. He was on the verge of telling her about his duel with Pavel Petrovich, but he checked himself with the thought that she might conclude he was trying to make himself appear interesting, and replied that he'd been working the entire time.

"Whereas I had a bout of depression at first," Anna Sergeevna observed. "God only knows why. I even made plans to go abroad, if you can imagine that! . . . Then the depression went away, your friend Arkadii Nikolaich arrived, and I lapsed back into my old routine. I assumed my present role again."

"Which role is that, may I ask?"

"The role of aunt, guardian, mother—call it whatever you like. By the way, do you know, I didn't understand your close friendship with Arkadii Nikolaich very well before—I considered him somewhat undistinguished. But now I've gotten to know him better and have become convinced he's quite intelligent.... And he's young, he's young ... that's the main thing ... not like you and me, Evgenii Vasilich."

"Is he still as shy as ever in your company?" Bazarov inquired.

"Why, was he ...?" Anna Sergeevna began, and after a brief pause, she added, "He's become more trusting now—he talks to me, whereas he used to avoid me. Of course, I didn't seek out his companionship, either. He's friendlier with Katia."

Bazarov got annoyed. "A woman can't help being devious!" he thought. "You say he used to avoid you," Bazarov remarked aloud with an icy smile, "but has it remained a secret to you that he was in love with you?"

"What? He was too?" fell from Anna Sergeevna's lips.

"He was too," Bazarov repeated with a submissive bow. "Is it possible that you didn't know this, that I've told you something new?"

Anna Sergeevna lowered her eyes. "You're mistaken, Evgenii Vasilich."

"I don't think so. But maybe I shouldn't have mentioned it."

"Just don't try to be devious in the future," he added to himself.

"Why not? Yet I imagine that you're attributing too much importance to a passing impression in this matter as well. I begin to suspect that you're inclined to exaggeration."

"We'd better not talk about it, Anna Sergeevna."

"Oh, why not?" she responded, but she herself turned the conversation in another direction. She was still uncomfortable with Bazarov, even though she'd told him and had assured herself that everything had been forgotten. While she was exchanging the simplest sentences with him, even while she was joking with him, she felt a faint undercurrent of dread. Thus do people sailing on a steamship converse and laugh carelessly, precisely as though they were on dry land, but should the slightest untoward incident occur, should the least sign of anything out of the ordinary arise, then an expression of special alarm betraying the constant awareness of constant danger immediately appears on every face.

Anna Sergeevna's conversation with Bazarov didn't last long. She became absorbed in thought, replied abstractedly, and finally suggested that they go into the main hall, where they found the princess and Katia. "But where's Arkadii Nikolaich?" inquired the lady of the house, and upon learning that he hadn't been seen for more than an hour, she sent for him. He couldn't be found right away; he'd betaken himself to the very densest part of the garden where, with his chin propped on his folded hands, he was sitting lost in meditation. It was deep, serious, but not mournful meditation. He knew that Anna Sergeevna was alone with Bazarov and yet he didn't feel jealous, the way he once had; on the contrary, his face slowly brightened. He seemed to be simultaneously surprised and joyful, and to have made up his mind about something.

XXVI

The deceased Odintsov hadn't liked innovations, but he'd tolerated "the fine arts within certain limits," and had consequently erected an edifice that resembled a Greek portico, made of Russian brick, in the garden between the greenhouse and the pond. Along the blank rear wall of this portico, or gallery, were niches for six statues, which Odintsov had intended to order from abroad. These statues were supposed to represent Solitude, Silence, Contemplation, Melancholy, Modesty, and Sensitivity. One of them, the goddess of Silence, her finger on her lips, had been received and set up, but some of the boys on the estate had broken off her nose that very same day. And even though a local plasterer had attempted to make her a new nose "twice as good as the old one," Odintsov had nonetheless ordered her to be removed, and she'd ended up in a corner of the threshing barn, where she'd stood for many years, a source of superstitious terror to the peasant women. The front section of the portico had become overgrown by thick vegetation long ago; only the capitals of the columns could be seen above the dense verdure. It was cool beneath the portico itself, even at midday. Anna Sergeevna hadn't liked to visit this spot ever since she'd seen a snake there, but Katia often came and sat on a wide stone seat under one of the niches. Here, in the midst of the shade and the coolness, she read or studied or gave herself over to the sensation of perfect peace that's probably familiar to each of us, the charm of which consists in the barely conscious, silent recognition of life's vast current constantly flowing both around and inside us.

The day after Bazarov's arrival, Katia was sitting on her beloved stone seat, and Arkadii was sitting beside her once more. He'd asked her to come to the portico with him.

There was about an hour to go before their midday meal; the dewy morning had already given way to a sultry day. Arkadii's face had retained the expression of the preceding day; Katia's had a preoccupied look. Immediately after having had their morning tea, her sister had summoned Katia to her study, and after some preliminary caresses, which always scared Katia a little, she'd advised Katia to be more guarded in her behavior toward Arkadii, and in particular to avoid solitary conversations with him, since they were likely to attract the attention of their aunt, as well as the rest of the household. Moreover, Anna Sergeevna hadn't been in a good mood the previous evening, and Katia herself had been uncomfortable, as though she'd felt guilty for having done something wrong. In acceding to Arkadii's request, she told herself that it was for the last time.

"Katerina Sergeevna," he began with some sort of bashful familiarity, "while I've had the pleasure of living in the same house with you, I've discussed many things with you, but there's still one question that's very important . . . for me, which I haven't touched on until now. You remarked yesterday that I've been changed during my stay here," he went on, at once noticing and avoiding the inquiring gaze Katia turned toward him. "I've definitely changed a great deal, and you know that better than anyone else—you're in essence the one to whom I owe this change."

"I? . . . To me? . . . " Katia responded.

"I'm no longer the conceited boy that I was when I came here," Arkadii continued. "I haven't reached the age of twenty-three for nothing. I want to be useful, just as I did before; I want to devote all my energies to the pursuit of truth. But I no longer look for my ideals where I did before—they've presented themselves to me . . . much closer to hand. Up until now, I didn't understand myself, I set myself tasks that were beyond my strength. . . . My eyes have been opened recently, thanks to one feeling. . . . I'm not expressing myself entirely clearly, but I hope that you'll understand me. . . . "

Katia didn't reply, but she stopped looking at Arkadii.

"I believe," he began again, this time in a more agitated voice, while a finch lightheartedly sang its song among the leaves of a birch tree above his head, "I believe that it's the duty of every honorable person to be completely open with those . . . with those people who . . . in a word, with those who are close to him, and so I . . . I intend. . . . "

But at this point Arkadii's eloquence deserted him; he lost his train of thought, got confused, and was forced to fall silent for a moment. Katia still didn't raise her eyes. It seemed as though she didn't understand what he was leading up to by all of this, and was waiting for something.

"I foresee that I'm going to surprise you," Arkadii began once more, pulling himself together with an effort, "especially since this feeling relates in a certain way . . . in a certain way, please note . . . to you. You reproached me yesterday, if you remember, for a lack of seriousness." Arkadii continued like a man who's stepped into a bog and senses that he's sinking deeper and deeper at every step, yet hurries onward in hope of crossing it as soon as possible. "This reproach is often aimed . . . often falls . . . on young men even when they cease to deserve it. And if I had more self-confidence. . . . " ("Oh, help me, help me!" Arkadii was thinking in desperation, but Katia still didn't turn her head.) "If I could only hope. . . . "

"If I could only be sure of what you're saying," Anna Sergeevna's clear voice resounded at that moment.

Arkadii instantly fell silent, and Katia turned pale. A little path ran past the bushes that screened the portico; Anna Sergeevna was walking along it, escorted by Bazarov. Katia and Arkadii couldn't see them but could hear their every word, the rustle of their clothes, their very breathing. The two walked a few steps farther and, as though on purpose, stopped directly opposite the portico.

"You see," Anna Sergeevna continued, "you and I made a mistake. We're both past our early youth—I in particular. We've experienced life, we're tired. We're both—why pretend otherwise?—intelligent. At first we piqued one another's interest, our curiosity was aroused . . . and then. . . . "

"And then I got stale," Bazarov interjected.

"You know that this wasn't the cause of our misunderstanding. But, be that as it may, we didn't need one another—that's the main thing. There was too much in us . . . how shall I put it? . . . that was alike. We didn't realize it right away. By contrast, Arkadii. . . . "

"Do you need him?" Bazarov inquired.

"Hush, Evgenii Vasilich. You say that he isn't indifferent to me, and it always seemed to me that he liked me. I know that I could easily be his aunt, but I don't want to conceal from you that I've begun to think about him more often. There's some sort of charm in such youthful, fresh emotions. . . . "

"The word 'fascination' is more often employed in such instances," Bazarov interrupted, splenetic anger audible in his hollow if steady voice. "Arkadii was concealing something from me yesterday, and didn't refer either to you or to your sister. . . . That's a telling symptom."

"He's just like a brother to Katia," Anna Sergeevna commented, "and I like that in him, although perhaps I shouldn't have allowed such intimacy to develop between them."

"Is that thought prompted by . . . your feelings as a sister?" Bazarov drawled.

"Naturally . . . but why are we standing still? Let's go on. What a strange conversation we're having, aren't we? I never would have believed I'd be talking to you like this. You know that I'm afraid of you . . . and at the same time, I trust you, because you're fundamentally so kind."

"In the first place, I'm not the least bit kind. And in the second place, I no longer mean anything to you, and yet you tell me that I'm kind. . . . It's like laying a wreath of flowers on the head of a corpse."

"Evgenii Vasilich, we don't control . . . ," Anna Sergeevna began, but a gust of wind blew by, setting the leaves rustling and carrying away her words. "Of course, you're free," Bazarov declared after a brief pause. Nothing more could be distinguished; the footsteps retreated. . . . Everything became still.

Arkadii turned to Katia. She was sitting in the same position, but her head was bowed even lower. "Katerina Sergeevna," he said in a trembling voice, clasping his hands together tightly, "I love you infinitely and irrevocably, and I love no one but you. I wanted to tell you this, to find out what you think about me, and to ask you if you'll marry me, since I'm not rich, and I'm prepared to sacrifice everything. . . . Won't you answer me? Don't you believe me? Do you think I'm speaking lightly? But remember these last few days! Surely you must have realized for a long while now that everything—do you understand?—everything else vanished long ago without a trace? Look at me, say one word to me . . . I love . . . I love you. . . . Please believe me!"

Katia cast a radiant yet serious glance at Arkadii, and after lengthy pause, just barely smiling, she said, "Yes."

Arkadii leaped up from the stone seat. "Yes! You said 'yes,' Katerina Sergeevna! What does that word mean? Only that I do love you, that you believe me . . . or . . . or . . . . I can't go on. . . ."

"Yes," Katia repeated, and this time he understood what she meant. He grasped her large, beautiful hands and, breathless with rapture, pressed them to his heart. He could hardly stand upright, and could only whisper, "Katia, Katia . . . ," while she innocently began to weep, quietly laughing at her own tears. He who hasn't seen such tears in the eyes of his beloved still doesn't know to what extent someone who's faint with embarrassment and gratitude may be happy on this earth.

The next day, early in the morning, Anna Sergeevna summoned Bazarov to her study and, with a forced laugh, handed him a folded piece of notepaper. It was a letter from Arkadii; in it, he asked for permission to marry her sister.

Bazarov quickly scanned the letter and made an effort to control himself in order to conceal the malicious feeling that momentarily flared up in his breast.

"So that's how it is," he responded. "And only yesterday, it seems, you assumed that he loved Katerina Sergeevna like a brother. What do you intend to do now?"

"What do you advise me to do?" Anna Sergeevna inquired, still laughing.

"Well," Bazarov replied, laughing as well, although he felt anything but cheerful, and was no more inclined to laugh than she was, "I suppose that you ought to give the young people your permission. It's a good marriage in every respect—Kirsanov's financial circumstances are passable, he's the only son, and his father's such a good-natured man that he won't try to thwart him."

Mrs. Odintsov paced around the room. Her face alternately flushed and paled. "Do you think so?" she mused. "Well, I see no obstacles. . . . I'm happy for Katia . . . and for Arkadii Nikolaevich, too. Of course, I'll wait for his father's response—I'll send him in person to see his father. But, you see, it turns out that I was right yesterday when I told you we were both old people. . . . How was it that I didn't see anything? That's what surprises me!" Anna Sergeevna laughed again, and quickly turned her head away.

"Today's youth has gotten awfully devious," Bazarov remarked, and he laughed, too. "Goodbye," he spoke up again after a short silence. "I hope you'll bring this matter to a most satisfactory conclusion. I'll rejoice from a distance."

Mrs. Odintsov quickly turned toward him again. "You aren't going away? Why shouldn't you stay *now*? Stay. . . . It's enjoyable talking to you. . . . One seems to be walking on the edge of a precipice. One's intimidated at first, but one becomes braver as one goes forward. Do stay."

"Thank you for the invitation, Anna Sergeevna, and for your flattering estimation of my conversational talents. But I think I've already been moving in a sphere that isn't my own for too long. Flying fish can stay aloft for a while, but sooner or later they have to splash back into the water. Allow me to swim in my own element, too."

Mrs. Odintsov looked at Bazarov. His pale face was distorted by an embittered smile. "This man did love me!" she thought, feeling sorry for him, and she held out her hand to him in sympathy.

But he also understood her. "No!" he said, stepping back a pace. "I'm a poor man, but I've never taken charity thus far. Goodbye. Be well."

"I'm certain we aren't seeing one another for the last time," Anna Sergeevna declared with an impulsive gesture.

"Anything can happen on this earth!" Bazarov responded with a bow, and left.

"So you're considering building yourself a nest?" he said to Arkadii as he packed his suitcase the same day, crouching on the floor. "Well, it's a good thing. But you didn't need to be so cunning. I expected something completely different from you. Or maybe it took you yourself by surprise?"

"I certainly didn't expect this when I said goodbye to you," Arkadii replied, "but you're being cunning yourself, saying 'a good thing'—as though I didn't know your opinion of marriage."

"Ah, my dear friend," Bazarov cried, "the way you express yourself! Do you see what I'm doing? There's turned out to be an empty space in the suitcase, and I'm putting hay in it. That's how we treat the suitcases of our lives—we'd rather stuff them with something than accept a void. Please don't be offended—you'll undoubtedly remember what my opinion of Katerina Sergeevna has always been. Many young ladies are considered intelligent simply because they can sigh intelligently, but yours can hold her own, and, in fact, she'll do it so well that she'll get you under her thumb—indeed, that's just how it should be." He slammed the suitcase lid shut and got up from the floor.

"And now I'll say goodbye again, for it's pointless to deceive ourselves—we're saying goodbye forever, and you realize that yourself. . . . You've acted wisely. You aren't cut out for our bitter, rough, lonely existence. There's no insolence in you, no animosity, although there's youthful courage and youthful ardor. You aren't suited to our task. Your sort, the gentry, can never get beyond noble resignation or noble indignation, and they're worthless. For instance, you won't fight—and yet you consider yourselves gallant men. But we want to fight. Oh, well! Our dust would get in your eyes, our mud would spatter you. You aren't up to our level yet. You involuntarily admire yourselves, and you like to criticize yourselves, but we're sick of that—give us other people to deal with! We need other people to crush! You're a fine man, but you're a weak, liberal snob for all that—*e volatu*, as my estimable father likes to say."

"You're saying goodbye to me forever, Evgenii," Arkadii responded sadly, "and you have no other words for me?"

Bazarov scratched the back of his head. "Yes, Arkadii, I do have other words for you, but I'm not going to say them, because that's romanticism—that's sickeningly sweet. Still, get married as soon as you can, and build your nest, and have as many children as possible. They'll be smart ones, because they'll have been born at the right time, not like you and me. Aha! I see that the horses are ready. It's time to go. I've said goodbye to everyone else. . . . Well, what now? Should we embrace?"

Arkadii flung his arms around the neck of his former mentor and friend, and the tears virtually gushed from his eyes.

"That's what it means to be young!" Bazarov observed calmly. "But I have faith in Katerina Sergeevna. You'll see how quickly she'll console you! Goodbye, my friend!" he said to Arkadii when he'd gotten into the carriage. And pointing to a pair of crows sitting side by side on the stable roof, he added, "Those are for you! Study them."

"What does that mean?" Arkadii asked.

"What? Are you so weak in natural history, or have you forgotten that the crow is a most respectable family bird? They're an example for you! . . . Goodbye, señor!"

The carriage creaked and rolled away.

Bazarov had spoken the truth. Talking with Katia that evening, Arkadii completely forgot about his mentor. He'd already begun to defer to her; Katia was aware of this, and wasn't surprised by it. He was going to set off for Marino to see Nikolai Petrovich the next day. Anna Sergeevna wasn't inclined to put any constraints on the young people, and didn't leave them alone together too long merely for the sake of propriety. Magnanimously, she kept the princess out of their way; the latter had been reduced to a tearful frenzy by the news of the forthcoming marriage. At first, Anna Sergeevna was afraid that the sight of their happiness might prove somewhat distressing, but it turned out to be quite the opposite: this sight not only didn't distress her, it intrigued her; in the end, it even moved her. Anna Sergeevna was both pleased and saddened by this. "Evidently Bazarov was right," she thought. "It was curiosity, nothing but curiosity, and love of tranquillity, and egotism...."

"Children," she said aloud, "what do you think—is love a purely contrived feeling?"

But neither Katia nor Arkadii understood what she meant. They were shy around her; the fragment of conversation they'd unintentionally overheard haunted their memories. But Anna Sergeevna soon set their minds at ease, which wasn't difficult for her—she'd set her own mind at ease.

XXVII

Bazarov's elderly parents were overjoyed by their son's arrival, all the more because it was utterly unexpected. Arina Vlasevna got so excited and started to run around the house so energetically that Vasilii Ivanovich compared her to a "female partridge"—the tail of her short jacket actually did lend her a somewhat birdlike appearance. He himself merely mumbled, gnawed on the amber mouthpiece of his pipe, and, clutching his neck with his fingers, turned his head around as though checking to see whether it was properly attached, then suddenly opened his mouth wide and lapsed into completely noiseless laughter.

"I've come to stay with you for six whole weeks, old man," Bazarov told him. "I want to work, so please don't disturb me now."

"You'll totally forget my face—that's how much I'll disturb you!" Vasilii Ivanovich promised him.

He kept his promise. After installing his son in his study, as he had before, he nearly hid from Bazarov, and restrained his wife from any excessive displays of tenderness. "During Eniusha's first visit, my dear," he said to her, "we bothered him a little bit. We should be more prudent this time." Arina Vlasevna agreed with her husband, but that didn't matter very much, since she only saw her son at meals and had become thoroughly frightened of speaking to him. "Eniushenka," she'd occasionally say, but before he had

time to look around, she'd nervously finger the tassels of her workbag and murmur, "Never mind, never mind, I only...." Then
she'd go to find Vasilii Ivanovich and, resting her cheek on her
hand, would say to him: "Could you find out what Eniusha would
like for dinner today, darling—cabbage soup or borscht?" "But
why didn't you ask him yourself?" "Oh, he'll get tired of me!"

Bazarov soon ceased to isolate himself, however; his feverish
desire to work dissipated, and was replaced by dismal boredom
and vague restlessness. A strange fatigue manifested itself in all
his movements; even his firm, confidently bold stride changed. He
gave up walking in solitude and began to seek out company; he
drank tea in the drawing room, strolled around the kitchen garden
with Vasilii Ivanovich, and smoked with him in silence; once, he
even inquired about Father Aleksei.

Vasilii Ivanovich rejoiced over this change at first, but his joy
wasn't long-lived. "Eniusha's breaking my heart," he complained
to his wife in private. "It's not that he's dissatisfied or angry—that
wouldn't mean anything. But he's depressed, he's sad—that's what's
so terrible. He's always silent—if only he'd criticize us. He's getting
thin, and the color of his face is so bad." "Lord, Lord!" whispered
the old woman. "I'd hang an amulet around his neck, but you
know he wouldn't let me." Vasilii Ivanovich attempted to question
Bazarov several times in the most circumspect manner about his
work, about his health, about Arkadii.... But Bazarov replied reluctantly and offhandedly; one day, noticing that his father was
gradually trying to lead up to something in conversation, Bazarov
said with annoyance: "Why do you always seem to be walking
around me on tiptoe? That's even worse than the old way."

"There, there, I didn't mean any harm!" poor Vasilii Ivanovich
responded hurriedly. Thus his politic hints remained fruitless. He
hoped to engage his son's interest one day by beginning to talk
about progress in regard to the approaching emancipation of the
serfs, but Bazarov observed indifferently: "Yesterday I was walking
past the fence and I heard the peasant boys here bawling out a
popular song, 'The right time is coming, love is touching my heart,'
instead of singing some old ballad. That's progress for you."

Sometimes Bazarov went to the village and embarked upon a
conversation with some peasant in his usual bantering tone. "Well
now," he'd say to the peasant, "set forth your views on life to me,
my friend. You see, they say that the entire strength and future of

Russia lies in your hands, that you'll begin a new epoch in history-
that you'll give us our true language and our laws."

The peasant would either fail to reply at all, or would utter a
few words like this: "Well, we can . . . also, because, it means . . .
we've taken such a position, approximately. . . ."

"Explain to me what you think the world is," Bazarov would
interrupt, "and tell me—is it the same world that's said to rest on
three fishes?"

"It's the earth that rests on three fishes, your worship," the
peasant would explain soothingly in a patriarchal, kindly, singsong
tone, "whereas opposite ours, that is, our world, it's well known,
there's God's will, which is why you're our superiors. And the
stricter the master is, the better for the peasant."

After listening to such a reply one day, Bazarov shrugged his
shoulders contemptuously and turned away, whereupon the peasant
slowly sauntered homeward.

"What was he talking about?" inquired another middle-aged
peasant with a surly countenance who'd been listening to the conversation with Bazarov from a distance, at the door of his hut.
"Unpaid debts, eh?"

"Unpaid debts? No indeed, my friend!" answered the first peasant. There was no longer any trace of a patriarchal singsong tone
in his voice; on the contrary, some sort of disdainful gruffness
could be heard in it. "Oh, he babbled away about something or
other. He wanted to exercise his tongue a bit. Of course, he's a
gentleman—what does he understand?"

"What could he understand?" rejoined the other peasant, and
then, shoving back their caps and pushing down their belts, they
proceeded to discuss their concerns and their needs. Alas! Bazarov,
who shrugged his shoulders contemptuously, who knew how to
talk to peasants (as he'd boasted during one argument with Pavel
Petrovich), this self-confident Bazarov in no way suspected that in
their eyes he was something on the order of a buffoon. . . .

He finally found an activity to occupy him, though. One day,
Vasilii Ivanovich was bandaging a peasant's wounded leg in his
presence, but the elderly man's hands were shaking, and he couldn't
tie the bandages properly; his son helped him, and from that point
on, Bazarov began to participate in his father's practice, although
at the same time he repeatedly sneered both at the remedies he
himself advised and at his father, who hastened to make use of

them. But Bazarov's sneering didn't perturb Vasilii Ivanovich in the least; it actually comforted him. Holding his greasy robe closed across his stomach with two fingers and smoking his pipe, he listened to Bazarov with great pleasure; the more malicious his son's sallies, the more good-naturedly did the delighted father chuckle, displaying all of his blackened teeth. He'd even repeat these sometimes flat or pointless remarks for several days, constantly reiterating without rhyme or reason, for instance, "That's not a matter of major importance!" simply because his son, upon learning that Vasilii Ivanovich was going to matins, had used this expression. "Thank God! He's stopped moping!" Vasilii Ivanovich whispered to his wife. "He really gave it to me today—it was wonderful!" Moreover, the idea of having such an assistant overjoyed him, filling him with pride. "Yes, yes," he'd say to some peasant woman wearing a man's coat and a cap shaped like a horn, as he handed her a bottle of Goulard's extract or a jar of white ointment, "you ought to be thanking God every minute, my good woman, that my son's staying with me. Now you'll be treated according to the most scientific, the most modern methods. Do you know what that means? Even the French emperor, Napoleon, has no better doctor." And the peasant woman, who'd come to complain that she felt sort of odd all over (she herself wasn't able to explain the precise meaning of these words, however), merely bowed and rummaged around her bodice, where four eggs lay tied up in the corner of a piece of cloth.

Once Bazarov even extracted a tooth for a passing cloth peddler, and despite the fact that this tooth was an average specimen, Vasilii Ivanovich preserved it as a rarity, and incessantly repeated as he showed it to Father Aleksei, "Just look—what a fang! The strength Evgenii has! The peddler virtually leaped into the air. If it'd been an oak tree, it seems, he'd have uprooted it!"

"Most impressive!" Father Aleksei eventually commented, not knowing what response to make or how to get rid of the ecstatic old man.

One day, a peasant from a neighboring village brought his brother who had typhus to see Vasilii Ivanovich. The unfortunate man, lying flat on a pile of straw, was dying: his body was covered with dark spots, and he'd long since lost consciousness. Vasilii Ivanovich expressed regret that no one had thought of obtaining medical assistance any sooner, then declared that there was no hope. And in fact, the peasant didn't make it back to his brother's home—he died in their cart.

Three days later, Bazarov came into his father's room and asked him if he had a cauterizing stone.

"Yes. What do you want it for?"

"I need it . . . to burn a cut."

"For whom?"

"For myself."

"What—for yourself? Why's that? What sort of a cut? Where is it?"

"Here, on my finger. I went to the village today, you know, where they'd taken that peasant who had typhus. They were just about to cut open the body for some reason or other, and I haven't had any practice at that sort of thing for a long time."

"And so?"

"And so I asked the district doctor for permission, and I dissected it."

Vasilii Ivanovich suddenly turned completely pale, and without uttering a word, he rushed to his study, from which he immediately returned with a piece of cauterizing stone in his hand. Bazarov wanted to take it and leave.

"For God's own sake," Vasilii Ivanovich pleaded, "let me do it myself."

Bazarov smiled. "What a dedicated practitioner!"

"Please don't make jokes. Show me your finger. The cut isn't a large one. Does this hurt?"

"Press harder—don't be afraid."

Vasilii Ivanovich stopped. "What do you think, Evgenii— wouldn't it be better to burn it with a hot iron?"

"That should have been done sooner. Even the cauterizing stone is useless at this point, actually. If I've been infected, it's too late now."

"How . . . too late . . . ?" Vasilii Ivanovich could hardly pronounce the words.

"Yes, indeed! It's been more than four hours."

Vasilii Ivanovich seared the cut a little more. "But didn't the district doctor have a cauterizing stone?"

"No."

"How could that be? My God! He's a doctor—and he doesn't have as indispensable a thing as that!"

"You should have seen his lancets," Bazarov commented as he walked out.

Up until late that evening and the entire following day, Vasilii Ivanovich seized every possible opportunity to go into his son's room. Although he didn't refer to the cut, and even tried to talk about the most unrelated subjects, he peered into his son's eyes so persistently and regarded him so anxiously that Bazarov lost his patience and threatened to leave. Vasilii Ivanovich promised not to bother him, all the more readily since Arina Vlasevna, from whom he kept everything secret, naturally, was beginning to pester him about why he couldn't sleep and what had come over him. He restrained himself for two whole days, although he didn't like the way his son looked at all; he kept watching him stealthily . . . but by the third day, at dinner, he couldn't bear it any longer. Bazarov was sitting with his eyes downcast, without touching his food.

"Why aren't you eating, Evgenii?" he inquired, donning a thoroughly nonchalant expression. "The food has been prepared quite nicely, I think."

"I don't want anything, so I'm not eating."

"Don't you have any appetite? How's your head?" Vasilii Ivanovich added timidly. "Does it ache?"

"Yes, it does. Why shouldn't it ache?"

Arina Vlasevna sat up and became alert.

"Please don't be angry, Evgenii," Vasilii Ivanovich continued, "but won't you let me feel your pulse?"

Bazarov stood up. "I can tell you without feeling my pulse that I have a fever."

"Have you been shivering?"

"Yes, I've been shivering, too. I'll go lie down, and you can have someone bring me some lime tea. I must have caught a cold."

"Indeed, I heard you coughing last night," Arina Vlasevna observed.

"I've caught a cold," Bazarov reiterated, and he went out.

Arina Vlasevna busied herself preparing the lime tea, while Vasilii Ivanovich went into the next room and silently clutched at his hair.

Bazarov didn't get up again that day and spent the whole night in a heavy, semiconscious torpor. At about one in the morning, opening his eyes with an effort, he saw his father's pale face bending over him in the lamplight and told him to go away. The elderly man begged his pardon and left, but quickly came back on tiptoe and, half-hidden by the cupboard door, steadily gazed at his son. Arina Vlasevna didn't go to bed either, and leaving the study door slightly ajar, she kept coming up to it to hear "how Eniusha was breathing" and to look at Vasilii Ivanovich. She couldn't see anything except his motionless, stooped back, but even that afforded her some consolation.

The next morning, Bazarov tried to get up; his head began to spin and his nose began to bleed; he lay down again. Vasilii Ivanovich attended to him in silence; Arina Vlasevna went in to see him and asked him how he was feeling. He answered, "Better"— and turned toward the wall. Vasilii Ivanovich waved his wife away with both hands; she bit her lip in order not to cry, and went out.

The whole house suddenly seemed dark; everyone's face looked drawn; a strange hush set in; one noisy rooster was moved from the yard to the village, unable to comprehend why he was being treated that way. Bazarov continued to lie still with his face turned toward the wall. Vasilii Ivanovich tried to pose various questions to him, but they exhausted Bazarov, and the elderly man sank into his armchair, merely cracking his knuckles every now and then. He went into the garden for a few moments and stood there like a statue, as though overwhelmed by inexpressible bewilderment (an astonished expression almost never left his face), then returned to his son, trying to avoid his wife's inquiries. She finally grasped him by the arm and passionately, almost menacingly, asked: "What's wrong with him?" Then he collected himself and forced himself to try to smile in reply, but to his own horror, instead of smiling, he found himself somehow overcome by a fit of laughter.

He sent for a doctor at daybreak. He deemed it necessary to inform his son of this fact, for fear he'd get angry. Bazarov suddenly rolled over on the sofa, trained a fixed, vacant gaze on his father, and asked for something to drink. Vasilii Ivanovich gave him some water and, as he did so, felt his son's forehead. It seemed to be on fire.

"Old man," Bazarov began in a slow, drowsy voice, "I'm in terrible shape. I've been infected, and you'll have to bury me in a few days."

Vasilii Ivanovich staggered as though someone had struck a blow at his legs.

"Evgenii," he faltered, "what are you saying? . . . God have mercy on you! You've caught a cold. . . . "

"That's enough of that!" Bazarov interrupted him deliberately. "A doctor isn't allowed to talk like that. I have all the symptoms of infection—you know that yourself."

"Where are the symptoms ... of an infection, Evgenii? ... For heaven's sake!"

"And what's this?" Bazarov asked, pulling up his shirt sleeve and showing his father the ominous red patches that were appearing on his arm.

Vasilii Ivanovich shuddered and grew cold with terror.

"Supposing," he finally said, "even supposing ... even if there's something like ... an infection...."

"Pyemia," interjected his son.

"Well, yes ... something ... like the epidemic...."

"Pyemia," Bazarov repeated abruptly and distinctly. "Have you forgotten your textbooks?"

"Well, yes—whatever you want.... In any event, we'll cure you."

"Come on—that's out of the question. But that isn't the point. I didn't expect to die so soon. It's a very unpleasant development, to tell you the truth. You and mother ought to make the most of your deep religious faith—now's the time to put it to the test." He drank a little water. "I want to ask you about one thing ... while my mind is still under my control. Tomorrow or the next day my brain will submit its resignation, you know. I'm not even quite certain whether I'm expressing myself clearly right now. As I've been lying here, I've kept thinking that red dogs were running around me and that you were making them point at me as if I were a woodcock. It's like I was drunk. Can you understand me all right?"

"For heaven's sake, Evgenii, you're speaking perfectly coherently."

"All the better. You told me you'd sent for the doctor.... You did that to comfort yourself.... To comfort me as well, send a messenger...."

"To Arkadii Nikolaich?" interjected the elderly man.

"Who's Arkadii Nikolaich?" Bazarov asked, as though in doubt.... "Oh, yes! That little bird! No, leave him alone—he's turned into a crow now. Don't be alarmed—that's not delirium yet. Send a messenger to Mrs. Odintsov, to Anna Sergeevna. She's a lady with an estate.... Do you know her?" (Vasilii Ivanovich nodded.) "Say that Evgenii Bazarov sends his regards and sends word that he's dying. Will you do that?"

"Yes, I will. . . . But is it possible that you could be dying, Evgenii? . . . Just think! How could there be any justice after that?" "I don't know anything about that—just send the messenger." "I'll send one this minute, and I'll write a letter myself." "No—what for? Say that I send my regards—nothing else is required. And now I'll go back to my dogs. It's strange! I want to focus my thoughts on death, and nothing happens. I see some sort of blur . . . and nothing more."

He laboriously turned back to the wall again, while Vasilii Ivanovich left the study and, struggling as far as his wife's bedroom, helplessly dropped to his knees in front of the icons.

"Pray, Arina, pray!" he moaned. "Our son is dying."

The doctor arrived, the same district doctor who hadn't had a cauterizing stone, and after examining the patient, he advised them to continue the palliative treatments, saying a few words at that point about the possibility of recovery.

"Have you ever seen people in my condition *not* set off for Elysium?" Bazarov inquired, and suddenly grabbing the leg of a heavy table that stood near his sofa, he shook the table and pushed it out of place. "There's strength here, there's strength," he murmured. "Everything's still here, but I have to die! . . . An old man at least has time to divorce himself from life, but I . . . . Well, go try to negate death. Death will negate you, and that's all! Who's crying there?" he added after a short pause. "Mother? Poor thing! Whom will she feed her exquisite borscht to now? And you, Vasilii Ivanovich, are you whimpering, too? Well, if Christianity can't help you, be a philosopher, a Stoic, or whatever! Didn't you boast that you were a philosopher?"

"Me, a philosopher!" Vasilii Ivanovich wailed as the tears simply streamed down his cheeks.

Bazarov grew worse with every passing hour; the disease progressed rapidly, as is typical in cases of surgical poisoning. He still hadn't lost consciousness, though, and could understand what was said to him; he was still struggling. "I don't want to start raving," he'd whisper, clenching his fists. "What nonsense this is!" And then he'd say, "How much is eight minus ten?" Vasilii Ivanovich wandered around like someone possessed, proposing first one remedy, then another, and ended up doing nothing but covering his son's feet. "Try a cold pack . . . an emetic . . . mustard plasters on the stomach . . . bleeding," he'd suggest tensely. The doctor, whom he'd begged to remain, agreed with him, ordered the patient to drink lemonade, and requested a pipe, as well as something "warming and strengthening"—that is, vodka—for himself. Arina Vlasevna sat on a low stool near the door and only left from time to time to pray. A few days earlier, a mirror had slipped out of her hands and broken, and she'd always considered this an evil omen; Anfisushka herself couldn't say anything to console her. Timofeich had gone to Mrs. Odintsov's.

Bazarov had a bad night. . . . He was in agony from the high fever. Toward morning, he became a little more comfortable. He asked Arina Vlasevna to comb his hair, kissed her hand, and drank two sips of tea. Vasilii Ivanovich perked up a bit. "Thank God!" he declared. "The crisis has come. . . . The crisis has passed."

"There, just think what a word can do!" Bazarov observed. "He's found one—he's said 'crisis'—and he feels better. It's astonishing how an individual can still believe in words. If someone tells him he's a fool, for instance, even though he doesn't suffer physically as a result, he'll be miserable. Call him an intelligent person and he'll be pleased, even if you go off without paying him."

This little speech by Bazarov, reminiscent of his former "sallies," greatly moved Vasilii Ivanovich.

"Bravo! Well said! Very good!" he exclaimed, pretending to clap his hands.

Bazarov smiled sadly.

"So what do you think," he asked, "has the crisis passed, or has it just begun?"

"You're better, that's what I see—that's what delights me," Vasilii Ivanovich replied.

"Well, that's good. Delight is never a bad thing. And that lady—did you remember to send someone to see her?"

"Of course I did."

The change for the better didn't last long. The disease resumed its onslaught. Vasilii Ivanovich remained sitting beside Bazarov. It seemed as though the elderly man were being tormented by some special anguish. He was on the verge of speaking several times—and couldn't.

"Evgenii," he began at last, "my son, my precious, adored son!"

This unfamiliar endearment had its effect on Bazarov. Turning his head somewhat and obviously trying to fight against the leaden weight of oblivion pressing down upon him, he asked, "What is it, Father?"

"Evgenii," Vasilii Ivanovich continued, and fell on his knees in front of Bazarov, although the latter had closed his eyes and couldn't see him. "Evgenii, you're getting better now. God grant that you'll get well. But make use of this time, comfort your mother and me— perform the duty of a Christian! What causes me to say this to you is horrible, but it's even more horrible... forever and ever, Evgenii.... Think a bit about what...."

The elderly man's voice broke, and a strange look passed across his son's face, although he lay still and kept his eyes closed.

"I won't refuse, if that can bring you any comfort," Bazarov finally declared, "but it seems to me that there's no need to rush. You yourself say that I'm getting better."

"Oh, yes, Evgenii, you're better, you're better—but who knows? It's all in God's hands, and in doing the duty...."

"No, I'll wait a little while," Bazarov interrupted him. "I agree with you that the crisis has come. And if we're wrong, what about it? They also give the sacrament to people who are unconscious, you know."

"Evgenii, for heaven's sake...."

"I'll wait a little while. Now I want to go to sleep. Don't disturb me." And he turned his head back to its previous position.

The elderly man rose from his knees, sat down in the armchair, and clutching his beard, began biting his nails....

The sound of a carriage bouncing on springs, a sound that's particularly impressive in the depths of the countryside, suddenly reached his ears. The slender wheels rolled nearer and nearer; the neighing of horses became audible.... Vasilii Ivanovich jumped up and ran to the little window. A two-seated carriage with four horses harnessed to it entered the yard in front of his house. Without stopping to consider what this meant, with a burst of some sort of mindless joy, he ran out onto the steps.... A groom in livery was opening the carriage doors; a lady wearing a black veil and a black mantilla was getting out of it....

"I'm Mrs. Odintsov," she announced. "Is Evgenii Vasilich still alive? Are you his father? I've brought a doctor with me."

"You're nobility itself!" Vasilii Ivanovich cried, and clasping her hand, he convulsively pressed it to his lips, while the doctor Anna Sergeevna had brought, a little man with glasses who had Germanic features, slowly stepped out of the carriage. "He's still alive, my Evgenii's alive, and now he'll be saved! Wife! Wife!... An angel from heaven has come to see us...."

"What does this mean? Oh, Lord!" quavered the elderly woman, running out of the drawing room without comprehending anything. She fell at Anna Sergeevna's feet there in the hallway and began to kiss her dress like a madwoman.

"What are you doing? What are you doing?" Anna Sergeevna protested, but Arina Vlasevna didn't listen to her, while Vasilii Ivanovich could only repeat, "An angel! An angel!"

"*Wo ist der Kranke?* And where is the patient?" the doctor finally inquired, not without a certain impatience.

Vasilii Ivanovich recovered himself. "Here, here, follow me, *wertester Herr Collega,*" he added, drawing upon old memories.

"Ah!" grunted the German, grinning sourly.

Vasilii Ivanovich led him into the study. "A doctor engaged by Anna Sergeevna Odintsova is here," he said, bending down to his son's very ear, "and she's here herself."

Bazarov suddenly opened his eyes. "What did you say?"

"I said that Anna Sergeevna's here, and has brought this gentleman, a doctor, to see you."

Bazarov looked around. "She's here.... I want to see her."

"You can see her, Evgenii, but first we have to have a little chat with the doctor. I'll tell him the entire history of your illness, since Sidor Sidorych" (that was the district doctor's name) "has left, and we'll have a short consultation."

Bazarov glanced at the German.

"Well, consult quickly, but not in Latin—you see, I know what *jam moritur* means."

"*Der Herr scheint des Deutschen mächtig zu sein,*" began the new follower of Aesculapius, turning toward Vasilii Ivanovich.

"*Ich . . . gabe. . . .* We'd better speak Russian," suggested the elderly man.

"Ah, hah! So that's how it is.... If you prefer...." And the consultation began.

Half an hour later, Vasilii Ivanovich led Anna Sergeevna into the study. The doctor had managed to whisper to her that there was no hope of the patient's recovery.

She glanced at Bazarov . . . and stopped in the doorway, so greatly was she struck by his flushed and yet deathlike face, whose lack-luster eyes were fastened upon her. She was overcome by some sort of icy, suffocating fear; the thought that she wouldn't have felt like this if she'd really loved him instantaneously flashed through her mind.

"Thank you," he said laboriously. "I didn't expect this. You're doing a good deed. So we're seeing one another again, as you promised."

"Anna Sergeevna was so kind . . . ," Vasilii Ivanovich began.

"Father, leave us alone. Anna Sergeevna, will you mind? Now, it seems. . . ." With a motion of his head, he indicated his prostrate, helpless body.

Vasilii Ivanovich went out.

"Well, thank you," Bazarov repeated. "This is regal of you. Tsars also visit the dying, they say."

"Evgenii Vasilich, I hope. . . ."

"Ah, Anna Sergeevna, let's concede the truth. It's all over for me—I've fallen under the wheel. So it turns out that there was no reason to think about the future at all. Death's an old joke, but each individual encounters it anew. So far I'm not afraid . . . but unconsciousness will arrive soon, and then *pffft!*" (He waved his hand feebly.) "Well, what can I say to you? . . . I loved you! There was no point in that before, and there's less than ever now. Love requires a form, and my own form is already decomposing. I'd rather talk about how lovely you are! And right now you're standing here, so beautiful. . . ."

Anna Sergeevna involuntarily shuddered.

"Never mind, don't be distressed. . . . Sit down over there. . . . Don't come close to me—you know that my illness is contagious."

Anna Sergeevna crossed the room swiftly and sat down in the armchair near the sofa on which Bazarov was lying.

"Noble-hearted!" he whispered. "Oh, how close—and so young, and fresh, and pure . . . in this loathsome room! . . . Well, goodbye! Live a long while—that's the best thing of all—and make the most of your life while you have time. You see what a hideous spectacle I am—a worm that's half-crushed but still writhing. And, after all, I did think that I'd overcome so many things, that I wouldn't die— why should I? There are problems to solve, and I'm a giant! And now the whole problem for the giant is how to die decently, although that doesn't matter to anyone, either. . . . Don't worry—I'm not going to break down."

Bazarov fell silent and groped for his glass with one hand. Anna Sergeevna helped him take a sip without removing her glove, drawing her breath timidly.

"You'll forget me," he began again. "The dead are no companions for the living. My father will tell you what a man Russia is losing. . . . That's ridiculous, but don't contradict the old man.

Whatever toy will comfort a child . . . you know. And be kind to my mother. People like them can't be found in your elegant world if you search high and low. . . . I'm necessary to Russia. . . . No, it's clear that I'm not necessary. And who is necessary? The shoemaker is necessary, the tailor is necessary, the butcher . . . gives us meat . . . the butcher . . . wait a minute, I'm getting confused. . . . There's a forest here. . . ."

Bazarov put his hand on his forehead.

Anna Sergeevna bent over him. "Evgenii Vasilich, I'm here. . . ."

He immediately took his hand away and raised himself up.

"Goodbye," he said with sudden strength, and his eyes gleamed with their last light. "Goodbye. . . . Listen. . . . You know, I didn't kiss you then. . . . Blow on the dying lamp, and let it go out. . . ."

Anna Sergeevna touched her lips to his forehead.

"That's enough!" he murmured, and fell back onto the pillow. "Now . . . darkness. . . ."

Anna Sergeevna went out quietly. "Well?" Vasilii Ivanovich asked her in a whisper.

"He's fallen asleep," she replied, barely audibly.

Bazarov wasn't fated to awaken again. He sank into complete unconsciousness toward evening, and he died the following day. Father Aleksei had performed the last rites over him. When they'd anointed him in extreme unction, when the holy oil had touched his breast, one of his eyes had opened, and it seemed as though the sight of the priest in his vestments, the smoking censers, and the candles before the icon had caused something like a shudder of horror fleetingly to cross his death-stricken face.

When he'd finally drawn his last breath, and lamentation had arisen throughout the house, Vasilii Ivanovich was seized by a sudden frenzy. "I said that I'd rebel," he shrieked hoarsely, his face inflamed and distorted, shaking his fist in the air as though threatening someone, "and I rebel—I rebel!" But Arina Vlasevna, who'd dissolved in tears, threw her arms around his neck, and they fell to their knees on the ground together. "Side by side," Anfisushka reported afterward in the servants' quarters, "they bowed their poor heads like lambs in the noonday heat. . . ."

But the noonday heat passes, evening comes, and then nighttime, when it's possible to return to some quiet refuge where it's sweet for the tortured and the weary to sleep. . . .

XXVIII

Six months went past. Deepest winter had set in, accompanied by its cruelly still, cloudless frosts, thick, crisp snow, rosy rime on the trees, pale emerald sky, wreaths of smoke above the chimneys, puffs of steam rushing out doors when they're opened for an instant, people's frostbitten faces, and briskly trotting, chilly horses. A January day was drawing to its close; the evening cold was keener than ever in the motionless air, and a brilliant red sunset was rapidly fading away. Lights were burning in the windows of the house at Marino; Prokofich, wearing a black dress coat and white gloves, had set the table for seven with special solemnity. A week earlier, two weddings had taken place quietly, almost without witnesses, in the small parish church—Arkadii's to Katia, and Nikolai Petrovich's to Fenechka—and this evening, Nikolai Petrovich was giving a farewell dinner for his brother, who was leaving for Moscow on business. Anna Sergeevna had also left for there as soon as the ceremony was over, after giving the young couple some very handsome presents.

They all gathered around the table at precisely three o'clock. Mitia had been brought in, too; a nurse in a glossy brocade cap appeared along with him. Pavel Petrovich took a seat between Katia and Fenechka; the husbands took their places beside their wives. Our friends had changed recently: they all seemed to have grown bigger and handsomer; only Pavel Petrovich had gotten thinner, which gave an even more elegant, "grand seigneurial" aspect to his expressive features. . . . Fenechka also looked different. Wearing a fresh silk dress, a wide velvet cap on her hair, and a gold chain around her neck, she sat perfectly still, exuding both self-respect and respect for everything surrounding her, and smiling as though she wanted to say, "I beg your pardon, I'm not to blame." And she wasn't alone—the others all smiled and seemed apologetic as well; they all felt a little awkward, a little sad, and essentially very happy. They served one another with comical courtesy, as though they'd all agreed to enact some sort of innocent farce. Katia was the calmest of all; she gazed around her confidently, and it was evident that Nikolai Petrovich already loved her deeply. At the end of dinner, he stood up, and taking his glass in his hand, he turned to Pavel Petrovich.

"You're leaving us . . . you're leaving us, my dear brother," he began. "Not for long, of course, but still, I can't help expressing to you what I . . . what we . . . how much I . . . how much we. . . . Now, the worst of it is that we don't know how to make speeches. Arkadii, you say something."

"No, Papa, I haven't prepared anything."

"As though I were so well prepared! Well, brother, let me simply hug you, wish you good luck, and tell you to return to us as soon as you can!"

Pavel Petrovich exchanged kisses with everyone, not excluding Mitia, of course. Moreover, he kissed Fenechka's hand, which she hadn't learned to offer properly yet, and draining the glass that had been refilled, he said with a deep sigh, "Be happy, my friends! *Farewell!*" The fact that he spoke this final word in English passed unnoticed, but everyone was touched.

"To the memory of Bazarov," Katia whispered in her husband's ear as she touched her glass against his. Arkadii pressed her hand warmly in return, but he didn't dare propose this toast out loud.

Would it appear that this is the end? But perhaps one of our readers would like to know what each of the characters we've introduced is doing now, right now. We're prepared to satisfy that reader.

Anna Sergeevna has recently gotten married, not out of love but out of prudence, to one of the future leaders of Russia, a very intelligent man—a lawyer with a vigorous, practical mind, a strong will, and remarkable verbal skills—a still young, good-natured man who's as cold as ice. They're living together in great harmony, and will live long enough, perhaps, to attain happiness . . . perhaps, to attain love. The Princess Kh—— is dead, having been forgotten the very day of her death.

The Kirsanovs, both father and son, have settled down at Marino; their situation is beginning to improve. Arkadii has become a zealous landowner, and the "farm" is now yielding a fairly good income. Nikolai Petrovich has ended up as one of the mediators appointed to carry out the emancipation reforms, and labors with all his might: he constantly travels throughout his district, delivering long speeches (he maintains the view that the peasants ought to be "brought around," that is, they ought to be reduced to a state of quiescence by the constant repetition of the same words). And yet, to tell the truth, he doesn't completely satisfy either the refined gentry, who at times stylishly and at times sadly speak about the "mancipation" (pronouncing the syllable "an" through their noses), or the unrefined gentry, who unceremoniously curse "the damned 'muncipation.'" He's too soft-hearted for either side. Katerina Sergeevna has had a son, little Nikolai; Mitia now runs around brashly and chatters fluently. Next to her husband and Mitia, Fenechka—Fedosia Nikolaevna—adores no one more than her daughter-in-law, and when Katia is sitting at the piano, Fenechka would gladly spend the whole day by her side. A brief word about Petr: he's become completely ossified with stupidity and self-importance, pronouncing all his *e*'s like *u*'s, but he's married, too, having received a respectable dowry from his bride, the daughter of a town greengrocer who'd refused two perfectly good suitors only because neither of them had a watch, whereas Petr not only had a watch—he had a pair of patent leather shoes.

On the Brühl Terrace in Dresden between two and four in the afternoon—the most fashionable time for strolling—you may encounter a man of about fifty who's quite gray and looks as though he suffers from gout, but is still handsome, elegantly dressed, and has the special air exhibited only by those who spend a lot of time amid the highest strata of society. This is Pavel Petrovich. Having left Moscow, he went abroad for the sake of his health and settled permanently in Dresden, where he associates mostly with English residents and Russian travelers. He behaves simply, almost modestly, but not without dignity toward the English; they find him somewhat boring, but respect him for being, as they say, "a perfect gentleman." He's more casual with the Russians, venting his spleen and making fun of himself and them. But he does all this with great amiability, nonchalance, and propriety. He holds Slavophile views—it's well known that this is considered *très distingué* in the highest social circles. He never reads anything Russian, but he keeps a silver ashtray shaped like a peasant's woven shoe on his desk. He's much sought after by our tourists; Matvei Ilich Koliazin, finding himself "in temporary opposition," graced him with a visit on the way to a Bohemian spa. The native inhabitants, with whom, incidentally, he associates quite rarely, virtually grovel at his feet. No one can obtain a ticket for the court chapel, the theater, and so forth, as easily and quickly as *der Herr Baron von Kirsanoff.* He does everything as genially as he can; he still makes a little bit of noise in the world—it isn't for nothing that he was once a social lion—but life is hard for him . . . harder than he himself suspects. One merely has to glance at him in the Russian church when, leaning against a wall to one side, he sinks into thought and remains motionless for long stretches of time, bitterly compressing his lips, then suddenly collects himself and almost imperceptibly begins to cross himself. . . .

Mrs. Kukshin also went abroad. She's in Heidelberg now, studying not the natural sciences but rather architecture, in which, according to her, she's discovered new laws. She still fraternizes with students, especially the young Russian physicists and chemists Heidelberg is filled with, who, at first astounding the naive German professors by their sound views of things, later astound the same professors by their utter inefficiency and absolute laziness. Sitnikov roams St. Petersburg in the company of two or three such chemists, who can't tell oxygen from nitrogen but are full of skepticism and conceit—and the great Elisevich. Sitnikov is likewise preparing to become great and, according to his own assurances, is continuing the "work" of Bazarov. They say that someone recently beat him up, but he got his revenge: in an obscure little article hidden in an obscure little journal, he hinted that the man who beat him up was a coward. He calls this irony. His father bullies him as much as ever, while his wife considers him a fool . . . and a man of letters.

There's a small village graveyard in one of the remote corners of Russia. Like almost all of our graveyards, it has a wretched appearance: the ditches surrounding it were overgrown long ago; the gray, wooden crosses have fallen over and lie rotting under their once-painted little roofs; the stone slabs are all tilted, as though someone had pushed them from behind; the two or three bare trees provide hardly any shade; sheep wander amid the graves unchecked. . . . But among those graves is one that no one touches and no animal tramples—only the birds perch on it and sing at daybreak. An iron railing runs around it; two young fir trees have been planted at each end. Evgenii Bazarov is buried in this grave.

Two quite feeble elderly people often come from the little village not far off to visit it—husband and wife. Holding one another up, they walk with heavy steps; they approach the railing, kneel down, and remain on their knees, crying long and bitterly, looking long and intently at the mute stone under which their son is lying; they exchange a brief word, wipe the dust off the stone, straighten the branch of a fir tree, and pray again, unable to tear themselves away from this spot, where they seem to be closer to their son, closer to their memories of him. . . . Can it be that their prayers, their tears, are fruitless? Can it be that love, sacred, devoted love, isn't omnipotent? Oh, no! However passionate, sinful, and rebellious the heart hidden in that grave may have been, the flowers growing on it gaze serenely at us with their innocent eyes. They speak to us not only of eternal peace, of that glorious peace of "indifferent" nature; they also speak to us of eternal reconciliation and life everlasting. . . .

Letter to F. M. Dostoevsky.

Paris.

March 18, 1862.

Dear Fedor Mikhailovich, I need hardly tell you how happy your reaction to *Fathers and Sons* made me. It's not a question of satisfying any vanity, but rather of convincing yourself that you didn't make a mistake and haven't completely blundered—and that your work didn't go for naught. That was all the more important to me inasmuch as people whom I trust very much (I don't mean Kolbasin) seriously advised me to throw my work into the fire—and just a few days ago Pisemskii (just between us) wrote me that the character of Bazarov was a complete failure. How could I thus not have doubts and be puzzled? It's difficult for an author to sense *immediately* to what extent his idea has been embodied—and whether it's accurate—and whether he's mastered it, and so on. It's as though he were lost in the woods in his own work.

You've probably experienced this often yourself. And therefore thanks again. You grasped so completely and keenly what I wanted to express in Bazarov that I could only spread my arms in amazement—and pleasure. It's as if you had entered my soul and felt even those things that I didn't consider it necessary to say. May God grant that this shows not just the subtle perspicacity of a master, but the simple understanding of a reader as well—that is, God grant that everyone see at least a part of what you did! I'm now calm as regards the fate of my tale: it has done its work—and I have no reason to repent.

Here's one more proof for you of the extent to which you understood that character: in Arkadii's meeting with Bazarov where, as you say, there's something missing, Bazarov, in telling him about the duel, made fun of *knights*, and Arkadii listened to him with secret horror and so on. I threw that out—and now I'm sorry that I did so. In general, I made many changes and redid a lot of things under the influence of unfavorable comments—and that may be the reason for the drawn-out quality which you remarked.

I received a nice letter from Maikov and I'll answer him. People will rebuke me strongly—but I just need to sit that out, as one does a summer rain.

I'd be very sorry if I didn't find you in Petersburg. I'm leaving here at the end of this April, i.e., in a month. Now I can tell you *for certain* that I'll bring you my work in final form—it's not only going along well, but coming to an end. It will be about three signatures long. It's turning out to be a strange piece. It's the very same "Phantoms" as a result of which Katkov and I quarreled several years ago—I don't know whether you remember that. I was about to start on another piece—but suddenly latched onto this one and worked on it for several days with enthusiasm. Now all that's left is to finish off a few pages.

I'm happy for *Time's* success. It's vexing that you can't arrange proper delivery of the journal. I'm not saying this so much out of personal interest—after all, I'll be returning soon—but for your profit. *The Russian Messenger* is delivered here properly. (I still haven't received the February issue, though.)

Again I clasp your hand very, very firmly and say thank you. Give my sincere regards to your wife and be well.

Your devoted
Iv. Turgenev

Letter to K. K. Sluchevskii.[1]

Paris.

April 14, 1862.

I hasten to reply to your letter, for which I'm very grateful, dear Sluchevskii. One can't help but value the opinion of young people; in any event I'd very much like for there to be no misunderstandings about my intentions. I'll answer point by point.

(1) The first reproach reminds me of the accusation made to Gogol and others as to why *good* people weren't presented along with the others. Bazarov nevertheless overwhelms all the other characters in the novel (Katkov thought that I'd presented an apotheosis of *The Contemporary* in him). The qualities attributed to him are not accidental. I wanted to make a tragic character out of him; there was no room in this case for gentleness. He's honest, truthful, and a democrat through and through—and you don't find any *good* sides to him? He recommends *Stoff und Kraft* precisely because it's a *popular*, i.e., an empty book; the duel with Pavel Petrovich is introduced specifically as a visual demonstration of the emptiness of elegant gentry chivalry—it's presented in an almost exaggeratedly comic way—how could he decline? After all, Pavel Petrovich would have clubbed him. It seems to me that Bazarov constantly crushes Pavel Petrovich, and not vice versa; and if he is called a nihilist, then that ought to read "revolutionary."

(2) What was said about Arkadii, about the rehabilitation of the fathers, and so on, only shows—I'm sorry to say!—that I haven't been understood. *My entire tale is directed against the gentry as a progressive class.* Take a close look at the characters of Nikolai Petrovich, Pavel Petrovich, and Arkadii. Weakness and flabbiness or limitations. Aesthetic considerations made me take specifically *good* representatives of the gentry so as to prove my point all the more surely; if the cream is good, what does that imply about the milk? Taking bureaucrats, generals, bandits, and so on would be crude, *le pont aux ânes*—and completely inaccurate. Every true *negator* that I've known (Belinsky, Bakunin, Herzen, Dobroliubov, Speshnev, and so on) came, without exception, from relatively good, honest parents. And therein is contained a notion of great significance: this takes away from the *activists*, from the negators, even

---

1. Konstantin Konstantinovich Sluchevskii (1837-1904), a poet whom Turgenev supported and helped early in the former's career. After 1866, Turgenev's attitude toward Sluchevskii cooled considerably.

the slightest shade of *personal* indignation or irritability. They follow along their own path only because they're more sensitive to the demands of the nation's life. Countess Salias is wrong in saying that characters like Nikolai Petrovich and Pavel Petrovich are our grandfathers. Nikolai Petrovich is me, Ogarev, and thousands of others; Pavel Petrovich is Stolypin, Esakov, Rosset—also our contemporaries. They're the best of the gentry—and that's precisely why I chose them, in order to demonstrate their bankruptcy. To present bribe-takers on the one hand, and on the other—an ideal youth—that's a picture that I'll let others draw.... I wanted something larger. At one point (I threw it out because of censorship), I had Bazarov say to Arkadii, to that same Arkadii in whom your Heidelberg comrades see a *more successful character*: "Your father is a fine, decent fellow; but even if he were the worst bribe-taker imaginable—you still wouldn't get any further than well-born meekness or rage, because you're a nice little gentry lad."

(3) Good Lord! Mrs. Kukshin, that caricature, is the *most successful* of all in your view! I can't even reply to that. Mrs. Odintsov is as little *in love* with Arkadii as with Bazarov—how can you fail to see that?—she's the same sort of representative of our idle, dreamy, curious, and cold epicurean gentry ladies. Countess Salias understood *that* character perfectly. She'd first like to stroke a wolf's fur (Bazarov), as long as he doesn't bite—and then a little boy's curls—and continue lying on velvet, freshly bathed.

(4) Bazarov's death (which Countess Salias calls *heroic* and therefore criticizes) ought, in my opinion, to have put the final mark on his tragic figure. But you young people even find his death accidental! I'll finish with the following remarks: if the reader doesn't come to love Bazarov, with all his coarseness, callousness, pitiless dryness and harshness—I repeat—if he doesn't come to love him, then I'm at fault and have missed the mark. But I didn't want to "oversweeten things," to use his words, though by doing so I'd probably have had the young people on my side immediately. I didn't want to solicit popularity with concessions of that sort. It's better to lose a battle (and I seem to have lost it) than to win it by a ruse. I imagined a gloomy, wild, large figure, half grown out of the soil, strong, spiteful, honest—and nonetheless doomed to perish—because that figure is still in the anteroom of the future—I had imagined some sort of strange *pendant* to Pugachev and so on—but my young contemporaries shake their heads and tell me: "Hey, friend, you made a mistake and even offended us. Arkadii

came off better—too bad you didn't work on him even a little more." All I can do is "remove my cap and make a low bow," as in the gypsy song. Up until now Bazarov has been understood, i.e., my intentions have been understood, completely by only two people—Dostoevsky and Botkin. I'll try to send you a copy of my tale. And now enough about that.

Your poems, unfortunately, were rejected by *The Russian Messenger.* That's unfair; your poems are at least ten times better than those by Messrs. Shcherbina and others that are published in *The Russian Messenger.* If you'll allow me, I'll take them and have them published in *Time.* Write me a couple of words about this. Don't worry about your name—it won't be printed.

I haven't yet received a letter from Natalia Nikolaevna, but I have news of her via Annenkov, whose acquaintance she's made. I won't be traveling through Heidelberg—but I'd like to have a look at the young Russians there. Give them my regards, even though they consider me backward. . . . Tell them that I ask them to wait a while yet before they pronounce the final verdict. You can convey the contents of this letter to anyone you like.

I clasp your hand firmly and wish you all the best. Work, work— and don't be in a hurry to draw conclusions.

Your devoted
Iv. Turgenev

Letter to E. E. Lambert.

Paris.

Rue de Rivoli, 210.

October 28, 1862.

Dear Countess, I hasten to thank you for your letter and, without further explanations or justifications, to renew our correspondence. Besides, what's the point of them, these justifications, between people who, like you and me, have long since known and, I make so bold as to add, come to love each other? We'll take advantage of the unhappy fact that we ended up on this planet at all—but we ended up here at the same time—and we won't let each other out of our sight; everyone needs help from everyone else—from the first day of life to the last.

By the way, I've mentioned the first day of life. Today, October 28, was precisely that first day for me forty-four years ago. Almost my entire life is already behind me—and I can't tell you precisely with what feeling it is that I glance at the past. I'm not exactly sorry or vexed, and I don't think that I could have lived it better if . . . ! I'm not afraid to look ahead—it's just that I recognize the power that eternal, invariable, but deaf and dumb laws have over me—and the tiny squeal of my consciousness means just as little as if I took it into my head to babble "I, I, I" on the shore of an ocean flowing away inexorably. A fly still buzzes, but in another instant—and thirty or forty years are also an instant—it will no longer buzz. Instead, the same fly, but with a different nose, will start buzzing—and so on until the end of time. The spray and foam of the river of time! But that's enough of that sort of philosophizing—and the more so as these comparisons and so on will hardly be to your liking.

What you tell me about yourself touches me and makes me happy: I see that you have reached that tranquil self-negation which is just as blessed and salutary as the tranquillity of egoism is sterile and arid. To desire and expect nothing for oneself—and to have profound sympathy for others—is genuine holiness. I don't mean to say that you've reached it, but you're on the way, and that's already a great accomplishment. I hope that you'll understand that when I say "not to desire anything for oneself," I don't for a second mean to deny your concern for your soul: loving one's soul and loving oneself are two different things. You mention the "beneficial effect" that I once had on you; if I really was such a great person, then allow me to demand my reward—namely, that you should never entertain the idea of indifference when you speak of my feelings toward you.

You don't write anything about your health—I hope that it's no worse than last year's. It was very nice to hear about your husband. As for Count Karl, one can't help feeling very sorry for him—and I imagine that this is severe punishment for his uncompromising soul. Why do you imagine that Pauline (who sends you warm greetings) doesn't go to church? Not only have I "not taken God away from her," but I go to church with her myself. I wouldn't allow myself such an encroachment on her freedom. And if I'm not a Christian, that's my personal affair—and perhaps my personal misfortune. Pauline, on the contrary, is very religious.

Farewell, dear Countess; I clasp your hand firmly and cordially and remain

Your devoted
Iv. Turgenev.

Enough

A Fragment from the Notes of a Dead Artist

I

. . . .

II

. . . .

III

"Enough," I said to myself as I walked with halting steps along a steep mountainside down toward a quiet little stream. "Enough," I repeated as I drank in a pine grove's resinous fragrance, especially strong and pungent in the freshness of the oncoming evening. "Enough," I said once again as I sat on a mossy knoll just above the little stream and gazed into its dark, slowly flowing waters, above which sturdy reeds thrust their pale green blades.... "Enough!" No more struggle, no more strain. Time to withdraw, time to grasp one's head in both hands and bid one's heart be silent. No more brooding over the voluptuous delight of vague, seductive sensations, no more chasing after each new form of beauty, no more clinging to every tremor of its delicate yet strong wings. Everything has been experienced, everything has been foreseen many times ... I'm tired. What do I care that at this moment the sunset is flooding the heavens, as though aflame with some sort of triumphant passion, more broadly, more vibrantly than ever? What's it to me that, amid the peace and comfort and glow of evening, suddenly, two steps away from me, in a thick bush's dewy stillness, a nightingale has begun to sing in such magical tones, as though no nightingale had existed on earth before this one and it were the first to sing the first song of first love? This has all happened, this has all taken place before, has been repeated and will be repeated a thousand times—and to think that it will continue this way for all eternity, as though decreed, as though ordained, even makes one annoyed! Yes... annoyed!

IV

Ah, I've gotten old! Such thoughts would never have come to mind before—in those former, happy days, when I too was aflame like the sunset and sang like the nightingale. I have to confess: everything's faded all around me, all of life has paled. The light that gives it color and meaning and strength—the light that comes from the hearts of human beings—has been extinguished within me.... No, it hasn't been extinguished yet—it's just barely smoldering, emitting no light, no warmth. Once, late at night in Moscow, I remember that I went up to the lattice window of an old church and leaned against its uneven frame. It was dark under the low arched roof; a little lantern shed a dim, red light upon an ancient icon—only the severe, sorrowful lips of the sacred face could vaguely be discerned. The sullen darkness loomed around it, seemingly ready to crush the feeble ray of impotent light under its hollow weight.... The same light and the same darkness are now in my heart.

V

I write this to you—to you, my sole, unforgettable friend, to you, my dear friend, whom I've forsaken forever but won't cease to love until the end of my life.... Alas! You know what parted us. But I don't want to discuss that now. I've forsaken you... but even here, in this remote place, in this distant exile, I'm completely transfixed by you, I'm as much in your power as I was before, I feel the delectable burden of your hand on my bowed head as I did before!

One last time, I'm dragging myself out of the grave of silence in which I'm now lying. I'm casting a tender, affectionate gaze across my entire past... our entire past.... There's no hope and no return, but there's no bitterness in my heart, and no regret, either—and beautiful memories, clearer than the azure of heaven, purer than the first snow on the mountain tops, rise up before me like the forms of deceased gods.... They don't come thronging in

crowds, they follow one another in a tranquil procession, like those
robed Athenian figures we admired so much—do you remember?—
on the ancient bas-reliefs in the Vatican. . . .

VI

I've already mentioned the light that comes from the human heart
and illuminates everything surrounding it. . . . I long to talk to you
about that blessed time when my heart burned bright with this
light. Listen . . . and I'll imagine you sitting across from me, gazing
at me with your fond and yet almost stern, attentive eyes. Oh,
never-to-be-forgotten eyes! On whom, on what are they fastened
now? Who is enfolding your gaze in his soul, the gaze that seems
to flow from unknown depths so similar to mysterious springs—
like you, both clear and dark—that gush in the very core of narrow
ravines under overhanging cliffs. . . . Listen.

VII

At the end of March, before Annunciation, shortly after I'd seen
you for the first time, not yet suspecting what you'd become to me
but already having silently, secretly, taken you into my heart, I
had to cross one of the great rivers of Russia. The ice on it hadn't
broken up yet, but looked swollen and dark; it was the fourth day
of a thaw. The snow was melting everywhere, quickly yet quietly;
water was dripping on all sides; a noiseless wind wafted through
the mild air. Earth and sky alike were flooded by a single, unvarying, milky hue; there was neither fog nor bright light; not one
object stood out clearly amid the general whiteness; everything
looked both close and indistinct. Having left my carriage far behind, I walked swiftly across the ice of the river, and, except for
the muffled thud of my own footsteps, I didn't hear a sound. I went
on, enfolded on all sides by the first breath, the first tremor of early
spring. . . . And gradually, gaining strength with every stride, with
every movement forward, some sort of joyous, incomprehensible
excitement arose and spread within me. . . . It drew me on, it impelled me onward, and so strong were its transports that I finally
stopped in astonishment and looked around me inquisitively, as if
seeking some external cause for my ecstatic condition. . . . Everything was still, white, slumbering. I raised my eyes: a flock of
migrating birds was winging past high in the sky. . . . "Spring!
Welcome, spring!" I shouted aloud. "Welcome, life, and love, and
happiness!" And at that instant, with a delightfully disturbing

power, your image suddenly blossomed inside me like a cactus flower, blossomed and grew, enchantingly beautiful and radiant, and I knew that I loved you, and you alone, that I was completely overflowing with you. . . .

VIII

I think about you . . . and many other memories, other pictures arise before me—and you're everywhere, I encounter you on all the paths of my life. At times, I see an old Russian garden on the slope of a hillside, bathed in the last rays of the summer sun. The wooden roof of a manor house peeps out from behind some silver poplars, a thin curl of reddish smoke rising above its white chimney, and a little gate stands slightly ajar in its fence, as though someone had closed it with an uncertain hand. I stand still and wait, gazing at that gate and at the sand on the garden path. I'm amazed and moved: everything I behold seems new and unusual, everything is enveloped by some sort of bright, tender mystery, and I can already hear the swift patter of footsteps. I stand there, as tense and alert as a bird that's just folded its wings, ready to take flight anew— and my heart glows and trembles with joyous fear of the nearby, approaching happiness. . . .

IX

At times, I see an ancient cathedral in a beautiful, far-off land. Tightly packed groups of people kneel in rows; a devout chill, somehow grave and melancholy, wafts from the high, bare roof and the huge, branching columns. You're standing at my side, silent and detached, as though you didn't know me. Each fold of your dark cloak hangs motionless, as if carved in stone; motionless, too, are the bright patches on the worn tiles at your feet cast by the stained-glass windows. Then, forcefully stirring the incense-clouded air, stirring us up inside, the notes of an organ pour forth in a mighty torrent . . . and you grow pale and rigid. Your glance slides across me, glides higher, and rises heavenward—it seems to me that only an immortal soul could gaze like that, with such eyes. . . .

X

At times, another image recurs to me. No ancient temple oppresses us with its stern magnificence—the low walls of a small, snug room shut us off from the whole world. What am I saying? We're alone, alone in the whole world. Except for the two of us, nothing is alive;

outside these friendly walls are darkness and death and emptiness. It isn't the wind that howls, it isn't the rain that falls in streams; it's Chaos that wails and moans, it's his sightless eyes that are weeping. But inside, it's peaceful and bright, warm and welcoming; something amusing, something childishly innocent, like a butterfly—isn't this true?—flutters around us. We nestle close to one another, we lean our heads together and read the same good book. I feel a delicate vein beating in your soft forehead; I hear that you're alive, you hear that I'm alive; your smile is born on my face before it appears on yours; you give a mute answer to my mute question; your thoughts and my thoughts are like the two wings of a single bird disappearing into the infinite sky.... The final barriers have fallen—and our love is so calm, so deep, any division has vanished so utterly that we don't even need to exchange a word or a look.... Just to breathe, to breathe together is all we desire, just to live together, to be together ... and not even to be aware that we're together....

XI

Or, last of all, I see before me that bright September morning when we walked through the deserted yet blooming garden of an abandoned palace on the bank of a great river—not a Russian one— under the benign brilliance of a cloudless sky. Oh, how can I convey those sensations? The eternally flowing river, the solitude, the serenity, the bliss, and some sort of intoxicating sorrow, the surges of happiness, the unfamiliar, ordinary town, the autumn cries of the crows in the high, sunlit treetops, the affectionate words and smiles, the long, soft looks penetrating to the very depths of one's soul, and the beauty, the beauty within ourselves and all around us, everywhere—that's all simply beyond words. Oh, the bench on which we sat in silence with our heads bowed from an excess of emotion—I won't forget all that until the hour I die! How charming were those few strangers who walked by with brief greetings and kind faces, as were the large, quiet boats floating past (in one—do you remember?—a horse stood pensively gazing at the water gliding by under its nose), as were the innocent murmurs of the tiny ripples on the bank and the barks of faraway dogs that carried across the surface of the water and the shouts of a fat officer off to one side, drilling red-faced recruits with their elbows protruding and knees bent like grasshoppers! ... We both felt that nothing on earth had ever been or would ever be better for us than those moments, that everything else. . . . But what good are comparisons? Enough . . . enough. . . . Alas! Yes—enough.

XII

I've given myself over to those memories for the last time, and I'm bidding them farewell forever. This is the way a miser, gloating one last time over his hoard, his gold, his bright treasure, buries it in the damp, gray earth. This is the way the wick of a smoldering lantern, having flared up in a final bright burst of flame, sinks into cold ashes. The wild animal has looked out from its lair for the last time at the velvet grass, at the friendly sun, at the caressing blue water—then has retreated to the very depths of its cave, curled up, and gone to sleep. Will it have glimpses, even in its sleep, of the grass and the friendly sun and the caressing blue water? . . .

. . . .
. . . .
. . . .

XIII

Sternly, remorselessly, fate guides each of us; only at the beginning, when we're absorbed in details, in all sorts of nonsense, in ourselves, are we unaware of its harsh hand. As long as one can deceive oneself and isn't ashamed to lie, one can survive, and isn't ashamed to hope. Truth—not the full truth, which may not really exist— but even that bit of truth we can attain immediately seals our lips, binds our hands, and leads us on toward "nothingness." Then there's only one way for an individual to remain upright, not to fall to pieces, not to sink into the mire of self-oblivion . . . or self-contempt. That's calmly to turn away from everything, to say, "Enough!" and, folding one's useless arms across one's empty breast, to retain the ultimate, the sole attainable virtue, the virtue of recognizing one's own insignificance—the virtue at which Pascal hints when, calling a human being a thinking reed, he says that if the whole universe crushed it, it, that reed, would still be superior to the universe, because it'd know the universe was crushing it, whereas the universe wouldn't know that. A meager virtue! A sorry consolation! However you may try to be imbued by it, to have faith in it—whoever you may be, my poor fellow human being—you can't refute those ominous words of the poet:

> Life's but a walking shadow, a poor player,
> That struts and frets his hour upon the stage

And then is heard no more: it is a tale
Told by an idiot, full of sound and fury
Signifying nothing.

I quoted these lines from *Macbeth*, and its witches, phantoms, and apparitions came to mind. . . . Alas! It isn't apparitions, it isn't fantastic, unearthly powers that are terrible; there are no terrors in the world of Hoffmann, no matter what guise they appear in. . . . What's terrible is that there's nothing terrible, that the very essence of life is petty, uninteresting, and degradingly trite. Once one is permeated through and through with *that* knowledge, once one has tasted *that* bitterness, honey no longer seems sweet, and even the highest, sweetest joy, the joy of love, of perfect intimacy, of irrevocable devotion—even that loses all its enchantment; all its worth is destroyed by its own pettiness, by its brevity. Yes: someone has loved, has burned with passion, has murmured about eternal bliss and undying raptures; then you look, and any trace of the very worm that devoured the last remnant of his withered tongue has disappeared long ago. Likewise, on a frosty day in late autumn, when everything is lifeless and mute in the grayish grass on the bare forest's edge, if the sun breaks through the fog for an instant and casts a bright light on the frozen ground, gnats immediately swarm up on all sides: they cavort in the warm rays, they buzz to and fro, they flutter up and down, they circle around one another. . . . The sun disappears again, the gnats fall down in a feeble shower—and that's the end of their momentary existence.

XIV

But aren't there any great visions, any great words of consolation: patriotism, justice, freedom, humanity, art? Yes, those words exist, and many people live by them, on their behalf. And yet it seems to me that if Shakespeare could be reborn, he'd have no cause to retract his Hamlet, his Lear. His searching gaze would discover nothing new in human life: the same motley and essentially uncomplicated picture would unfold before him in all its terrifying monotony. The same credulity and the same cruelty, the same lust for blood, for gold, and for filth, the same vulgar pleasures, the same senseless torments in the name of . . . why, in the name of the very same absurdities that Aristophanes jeered at two thousand years ago, the same rude traps in which the many-headed beast, the human multitude, is so readily caught, the same grasping for

power, the same traditions of slavishness, the same natural acceptance of falsehood—in a word, the same busy leaps of a squirrel
turning the same old unreplaced wheel. . . . Shakespeare would have
made Lear repeat his cruel statement, "None doth offend," which
in other words means, "None fails to offend," and he, too, would
have said, "Enough!" He, too, would have turned away. There
may be only one hope: perhaps, by contrast to the gloomy, tragic
tyrant Richard, the great poet's ironic genius would have wanted
to depict another, more contemporary type of tyrant, one who's
almost ready to believe in his own decency and sleeps well at night,
or finds fault with too sumptuous a dinner at the very moment
when his half-crushed victims are trying to find some comfort in
imagining him, like Richard III, haunted by the phantoms of the
people he's destroyed. . . .
But why?
Why try to prove—even by selecting and weighing one's words,
by smoothing and rounding off one's phrases—why try to prove to
gnats that they're really gnats?

XV

But what about art? . . . beauty? . . . Yes, these are powerful words;
indeed, they're more powerful than those I've already used. The
Venus de Milo is quite possibly more real than Roman law or the
principles of 1789. It may be objected—how many times have these
objections been heard!—that beauty itself is relative, that it's envisioned completely differently by the Chinese than by the Euro-
peans. . . . But it isn't the relativity of art that disturbs me: the
brevity of it, once again the brevity of it, the dust and ashes of
it—that's what robs me of courage and faith. Art at any given
moment is quite possibly more powerful than nature, for no sym-
phony by Beethoven, no painting by Ruysdäel, no poem by Goethe
occurs in nature, and only dim-witted pedants or disingenuous
babblers can continue to insist that art is an imitation of nature.
But in the end, nature is inexorable: it has no reason to hurry,
and, sooner or later, it takes what belongs to it. Unconsciously and
inflexibly obedient to its own laws, it doesn't know art, just as it
doesn't know freedom, just as it doesn't know goodness. Enduring
from century to century, adapting from century to century, it allows
nothing to become immortal, nothing to remain unchanged. . . .
Human beings are its children, but that which is human—art—is
inimical to nature, precisely because art strives to be immortal and

unchanging. Human beings are the children of nature, but nature is the universal mother and has no preferences; everything that exists in its bosom has arisen only at the cost of something else, and in time must yield its place to something else. Nature creates while destroying, and doesn't care whether it creates or destroys—as long as life isn't extinguished, as long as death doesn't lose its rights. . . . Hence it covers the divine countenance of Phidias's Jupiter with mold just as serenely as it covers the simplest pebble, and gives the vilest worm the most precious verses of Sophocles as food. To be sure, human beings jealously aid nature in its destructive labors, but isn't this the same elemental force, the force of nature, that expresses itself in the fist of the barbarian who recklessly smashes the radiant brow of Apollo, in the savage yells he utters as he hurls the portrait of Apelles into the fire? How can we poor humans, poor artists, be a match for this deaf, mute, blind force, which doesn't even triumph in its conquests, but proceeds onward, ever onward, consuming all things? How can we hold our ground against those crude, massive waves endlessly and indefatigably advancing? How, in the end, can we believe in the meaning and value of those fleeting images that we shape out of dust for an instant, in the dark, on the edge of the abyss?

XVI

All this is so . . . but only the transient is beautiful, said Schiller, and nature itself, in the incessant play of its emerging and disappearing forms, isn't averse to beauty. Doesn't it carefully decorate the most transitory of its children—the petals of flowers, the wings of butterflies—in the most attractive hues, doesn't it give them the most exquisite markings? Beauty doesn't need to live forever to be eternal—one instant is sufficient. Yes, that's probably true—but only where there isn't any individuality, where there aren't any human beings, where there isn't any freedom. A withered wing on a butterfly appears again and again over a thousand years as the same wing on the same butterfly; thus necessity completes its circle sternly, fairly, and impersonally. . . . But human beings aren't repeated like butterflies, and the work of their hands, their art, their spontaneous creation, once destroyed, is lost forever. . . . To them alone is it given to "create" . . . but it's strange and horrifying to declare that we're creators . . . for an hour—as there once was a caliph for an hour, they say. In this lies our preeminence—and our curse: each and every individual "creator" by himself, precisely that one and no other, precisely this "I" is seemingly constructed with an intention, a design. Each individual is more or less dimly aware of his significance, is aware that he's something innately superior, something eternal—and lives, is obligated to live, in the moment and for the moment.* We sit in the mud, my good man, and reach for the stars! The greatest among us are precisely those who have acknowledged this elemental contradiction more deeply than anyone else. But in that case, it may be asked, are such words as "greatest" and "great" appropriate?

XVII

What, then, can be said about those to whom, every good intention notwithstanding, one can't apply such terms, even in the sense imparted to them by the frail tongue of a human being? What can be said about the ordinary, sturdy, second-rate, third-rate toilers, whoever they may be—statesmen, scientists, artists—especially artists? How can one force them to shake off their mute indolence, their despondent stupor? How can one draw them back into the field of battle once the concept of the futility of everything human, of every sort of effort that sets a higher aim for itself than merely obtaining their daily bread, has insinuated itself into their brains? By what crowns can they be lured, those for whom laurel wreaths and thorns are equally insignificant? For what purpose will they once again face the laughter of "the unfeeling crowd" or "the judgment of the fool"—the old fool who can't forgive them for abandoning former idols, or the young fool who demands that they immediately kneel with him in order to grovel at the feet of new, recently discovered idols? Why should they reenter that jostling realm of phantoms, that marketplace where seller and buyer cheat one another equally, where everything is noisy and loud, where everything is so paltry and worthless? Why, "worn to the bone," should they continue to struggle in a world such as this, where the masses, like peasant boys on a holiday, wallow in the mud for a handful of empty nutshells, or gape with open mouths in front of cheap, tinsel-draped pictures, in a world such as this, where only that which has no right to live is living, where each

* One can't help recalling here Mephistopheles's words to Faust:

Er (Gott) findet sich in einem ew'gen Glanze,
Uns hat er in die Finsterniss gebracht—
Und euch taugt einzig Tag und Nacht.

individual, deafening himself with his own shouting, hurries feverishly toward an unknown, incomprehensible goal? No . . . no. . . . Enough . . . enough . . . enough!

XVIII

. . . The rest is silence . . . .
. . . .

Letter to P. V. Annenkov.[1]

Baden-Baden.
Wednesday, February 14, 1868.

Your letter found me still here, dear Pavel Vasilevich! I was detained in Baden by Viardot's very serious illness, which only two days ago took a decisive turn for the better. . . . On Sunday, if everything works out, I'll leave for Paris for about eight days. But before that, I want to have a chat with you. First of all, please give Korsh the enclosed letter and ask him to publish it in *The Petersburg News*. I began to feel sorry for that poor unfortunate fellow whom they're kicking even after his death. Second, I read both Tolstoy's novel and your article about it. I'm not trying to flatter you when I tell you that it's been a long time since you wrote anything more intelligent or sensible; the whole piece testifies to its author's acute, subtle critical perception, and only in two or three phrases is there any vagueness or any sort of awkwardness of expression. The novel itself aroused my lively interest: there are dozens of pages that are entirely remarkable, first-class—all the scenes of everyday life and the descriptive ones (hunting, sleighing at night, and so on); but the historical passages, which are the real reason for our readers' delight, are puppet theater and charlatanism. Just as Voroshilov in *Smoke* throws dust in people's eyes by citing the latest words of science (without knowing either the first or second ones, which the conscientious Germans can't even imagine), so Tolstoy strikes the reader with the tip of Aleksander's boot or Speranskii's laugh, making him think that if he's even gotten down to these minor details, then he knows *everything* about it—when in fact he knows only the minor details. It's a trick, nothing more—but that's just what the public has fallen for. And one could say a great deal in regard to Tolstoy's so-called psychology: there's no real development in a single character (which you noted very well), but there's the old habit of conveying the vacillations and vibrations of one and the same emotion or state, which he places so mercilessly in the mouths and consciousnesses of each of his heroes: I love, but really I hate, and so on and so forth. Oh, how tired and fed up I am with these quasi-subtle reflections and thoughts, these observations of one's feelings! Tolstoy either doesn't seem to know any other

1. Pavel Vasilevich Annenkov (1812–87), critic and memoirist, was one of Turgenev's closest friends. A major part of Turgenev's correspondence is with Annenkov, and *First Love* is dedicated to him.

psychology or he purposely ignores it. And how painful are these premeditated, obstinate repetitions of one and the same trait—the little moustache on Princess Bolkonskaia's upper lip, and so on. But alongside all that, there are things in the novel that no one in all of Europe but Tolstoy could write and that aroused the chill and fever of delight in me.

I've already written you that I've received all the journals safely, but the copies of the translation of Du Camp's novel still haven't turned up!!

Two articles by Mérimée about Pushkin were published in two issues of *Moniteur* around January 15th, New Style, definitely between the 10th and the 20th. I clasp your hand cordially and remain

Your devoted
Iv. Turgenev.

Letter to Ludwig Pietsch.[1]

Carlsruhe.
Hotel Crown Prince.
Tuesday, December 1, 1868.

My dear friend,

A million thanks for the really marvelous photograph! I'll have it framed and from now on it will adorn my room.

Yes, my friend, I'm fifty years old—or, as you express it so euphemistically—I've lived the first half of my century, but I have no hope of seeing the end of the coming quarter. By the way, I know the year of my death quite accurately: 1881. My mother predicted it to me in a dream—the same numerals as the year of my birth, 1818—but reversed. Oh, yes: I'll definitely die in 1881, if it doesn't happen sooner—or later. But fifty is a foul number! One must resign oneself.

Madame Viardot has taken a beautiful apartment—Lange Strasse, 235—with a large salon in which music sounds marvelous. She's already sung once at a soirée at our *friend* Pohl's—songs by Schubert and Schumann (one of them especially, "Longing," you have to hear!). Lessing was there—he looked like a retired Austrian major. Such a severe, robust, upright figure—and such a flabby, limp, wan talent! There was a painter there—Mr. von Breuer—who spoke a great deal of Riefstahl and other Berlin artists, but who seems himself to be rather superficial and a not very genuine Hurluberlu. Do you know him? I haven't yet met Woltmann—but I'll receive him with open arms, of course, just as I will Riefstahl. Didie is working very zealously; for my birthday she made me a "Removal from the Cross"—an absolute miracle! That child has more imagination in her head than ten Lessings! All in all, everything is fine, but poor Viardot is aging greatly. Fortunately, Berthe stayed in Baden!

I'm going to translate my gloomy and ugly story; my friends in Petersburg liked it.

I'm very happy for your Weimar success; watch out—or you'll earn a noble title and the White Eagle, First Class.

I was upset by the sad news of your wife's poor health; let's hope that she'll soon improve!

---

1. Ludwig Pietsch (1824-1911), German artist, illustrator, and writer. The original of this letter is in German.

Aglaia will be on tour here in December—she's living in Berlin now, you know. If they stage *The Huguenots*, be sure to go see it! Write me here poste restante and give my regards to all my good friends—Menzel, especially Jul. Schmidt and his wife, the Eckerts (I hope that you see them often, although you don't mention them), Begas, and the others.

I thank you once again and clasp your hand most intimately.

Your I. Turgéneff

A Strange History

A Story

About fifteen years ago, began Kh——, official duties compelled me to spend a few days in the capital of the province of T——. I stayed at a decent hotel built six months before my arrival by a Jewish tailor who'd gotten rich. I'm told that it didn't flourish for long, as is often the case in our country, but I encountered it while it was in full flower: at night, the new furniture emitted sounds like pistol shots, the bed linen, tablecloths, and napkins all smelled soapy, and the painted floors reeked of olive oil, which, according to the waiter, an exceedingly elegant but not altogether clean individual, tended to deter the spread of insects. This waiter, a former valet to Prince G——, was distinguished by his informal manners and self-assurance. He invariably wore a secondhand coat and shoes with worn-down heels, carried a table napkin under his arm, and had a multitude of pimples on his cheeks. Gesturing freely with his sweaty hands, he made numerous brief but suggestive observations. He displayed a certain patronizing interest in me as someone capable of appreciating his culture and knowledge of the world; he regarded his own lot in life with a rather disillusioned eye. "No doubt about it," he said to me one day. "What sort of condition are we in nowadays? Might be sent packing any day!" His name was Ardalion.

I had to pay a few visits to various officials in the town. Ardalion found me a carriage and a servant, both equally shabby and loose in the joints, but the servant did wear a uniform, and the carriage was adorned with a heraldic crest. After making all my official visits, I went to see a certain gentleman, an old friend of my father, who'd been living in this town for a long time. . . . I hadn't seen him for twenty years; he'd managed in the meantime to get married, to establish the usual family, to be left a widower, and to have made a fortune. His business was farming, that is to say, he made loans to investors at a high rate of interest so that they could purchase farms.... "There's always honor in risk," it's said, although, in fact, the risk was quite small.

In the course of our conversation, a delicate-looking, slender young woman of about seventeen came into the room with hesitant steps, as quietly as though she were on tiptoe. "This is my eldest daughter, Sophie," said my acquaintance. "I'm pleased to introduce her to you. She's taken my poor wife's place, looks after the house, and cares for her brothers and sisters." I bowed a second time to the young woman who'd just come in (meanwhile, she'd abruptly sat down in a chair without saying a word), and thought to myself that she didn't look much like a housekeeper or a governess. Her face was quite childish and round, with small, attractive, but immobile features; her blue eyes, under high, equally immobile irregular eyebrows, had an attentive, almost astonished look in them, as though they'd just witnessed something unexpected; her full little mouth, its upper lip raised slightly, not only didn't smile, but appeared as though it never indulged in such a practice; a rosy flush spread beneath the soft skin of her cheeks in broad, even strips that neither diminished nor deepened; her fluffy, fair hair hung in light clusters on each side of her small head. Her bosom breathed calmly, and her arms were pressed against her narrow waist somewhat awkwardly and rigidly. Her blue dress hung without folds—like a child's—down to her little feet. The general impression this young woman made on me wasn't that of something sickly, but of something enigmatic. I saw before me not simply a shy, provincial young lady but a creature of a special type that I couldn't define. This type neither attracted nor repelled me; I didn't fully comprehend it. I merely felt that I'd never come across a more sincere soul. Pity ... yes! Pity was the feeling that arose within me at the sight of this young, serious, keenly alert life—God knows why! "Not of this earth" was the thought that came to me, although there was nothing particularly "ideal" in the expression on her face, and although Mademoiselle Sophie had obviously come into the room to fulfill the role of the lady of the house to which her father had referred.

He began to talk about life in the town of T——, about the social diversions and advantages it afforded.

"It's very quiet here," he observed. "The governor's a melancholy man, and the marshal of the province is a bachelor. But there's going to be a large ball in the Hall of Nobility the day after tomorrow. I urge you to go—there are some young women here who aren't without beauty. And you'll see all our intelligentsia, too."

My acquaintance, as a man with a university education, was fond of using learned expressions. He uttered them ironically yet respectfully. It's well known that moneylending develops a certain profundity in people, as well as respectability.

"May I ask whether you'll be at the ball?" I said, turning to my friend's daughter. I wanted to hear the sound of her voice.

"Papa intends to go," she answered, "and I expect to go with him."

Her voice turned out to be soft and deliberate, and she articulated every syllable carefully, as though bewildered by the question.

"In that case, allow me to accompany you in the first quadrille."

She nodded her head in assent, but didn't smile even then.

I left shortly thereafter, and I remember that the expression in her eyes as they gazed steadily at me struck me as so strange that I involuntarily looked over my shoulder to see whether she was looking at someone or something behind me.

I returned to the hotel, and after dining on the invariable *soupe-julienne*, cutlets, green peas, and grouse cooked to a blackened crisp, I sat down on a sofa and gave myself over to contemplation. The subject of my contemplation was Sophie, this enigmatic daughter of my acquaintance, but Ardalion, who was clearing the table, accounted for my pensiveness his own way: he attributed it to boredom.

"There are very few forms of entertainment for visitors in our town," he began in his normal, casually condescending fashion, while he slapped the backs of the chairs with a dirty dinner napkin at the same time—a practice, as is well known, that's typical of servants with higher education. "Very few!" He paused, and the huge clock on the wall, which had a lilac rose on its white face, seemed to echo his words with its monotonous, sleepy tick: "Very! Ve-ry!" "No concerts, no theaters," Ardalion continued. (He'd traveled abroad with his master and had nearly stayed in Paris. He knew better than to pronounce the word "theater" the way peasants do, "kijater.") "There are no dances, for instance, or evening recep-

tions among the nobility and gentry—nothing of that sort occurs."
(He paused for a moment, probably to allow me to observe the
precision of his diction.) "They rarely visit one another. Everyone
sits like a pigeon on its perch. And so it ends up that visitors have
absolutely nowhere to go."

Ardalion stole a sidelong glance at me.

"But there's one possibility," he went on, speaking with a drawl,
"in case you'd be so inclined. . . ."

He glanced at me a second time and even grinned, but evidently
didn't observe any signs of the requisite inclination in me.

The elegant waiter went toward the door, thought for a moment,
came back, and after uneasily fidgeting a bit, bent down to my
ear and said with a playful smile, "Would you like to behold the
dead?"

I stared at him in bewilderment.

"Yes," he continued in a whisper, "there's a man like that here.
He's a simple artisan, and can't even read or write, but he performs
miracles. If, for example, you go to him and want to see one of
your departed friends, he'll show you that person without fail."

"How does he do that?"

"That's his secret. For even though he's an uneducated man—
to put it bluntly, he's illiterate—he's very great in godliness! He's
highly respected by all the merchants!"

"Does everyone in town know about this?"

"Those who need to know do, but, of course, one must guard
against the police. Because, whatever you may say, such activities
are forbidden. They're a temptation for the common people—the
common people, the masses, as we all know, quickly lapse into
quarrels."

"Has he shown you the dead?" I asked Ardalion. I had trouble
bringing myself to be on more familiar terms with such an educated
being.

Ardalion nodded. "He has. He presented my father before my
eyes as if my father were alive."

I stared at Ardalion. He laughed, toying with his dinner napkin,
and condescendingly but unflinchingly gazed at me.

"This is all very odd!" I finally cried. "Couldn't I meet this
artisan?"

"You can't go straight to him by yourself, but you can approach
him through his mother. She's a respectable old woman who sells
pickled apples on the bridge. If you'd like, I'll ask her."

"Please do."

Ardalion coughed behind his hand. "And some gratuity, whatever sum you consider appropriate—nothing much, of course—should also be given to her, to the old lady. For my part, I'll make her understand that she has nothing to fear from you, since you're a visitor here, a gentleman, and you can understand that this is a secret, naturally, and won't get her into trouble, in any case."

Ardalion picked up the tray in one hand and, gracefully swinging both the tray and his body around, turned toward the door.

"So I can depend on you?" I shouted after him.

"You can count on me!" I heard his self-assured voice reply. "We'll talk to the old woman, and transmit her answer to you with the utmost precision."

I won't dwell on the thoughts awakened in me by Ardalion's report of such an extraordinary phenomenon, but I'm willing to admit that I awaited the promised reply impatiently. Late that evening, Ardalion came to my room and announced that, to his annoyance, he couldn't find the old woman. By way of encouragement, however, I handed him a three-ruble note. The next morning he reappeared in my room with a beaming countenance: the old woman had consented to see me.

"Hey! Boy!" Ardalion shouted into the corridor. "Hey! You, apprentice! Come here!" A boy of about six came in, completely covered with soot, like a kitten. His head was shorn, and totally bald in spots; he was wearing a torn striped shirt and huge galoshes on his bare feet. "You take the gentleman you-know-where," Ardalion said, addressing the "apprentice" and pointing to me. "And you, sir, when you arrive, ask for Mastridia Karpovna."

The boy gave a hoarse grunt, and we set off.

We walked for quite a while along the unpaved streets of T——. Finally, my guide stopped in one of them, virtually the most deserted and desolate of all, in front of an old, two-story wooden house, and wiping his nose on his shirtsleeve, he declared: "This is it. Go to the right." I walked across the porch into an outer passageway and stumbled to my right. A low door creaked on rusty hinges, and I saw a stout old woman wearing a brown jacket lined with rabbit fur, a multicolored kerchief on her head, standing in front of me.

"Mastridia Karpovna?" I inquired.

"The same, at your service," the old woman replied in a reedy voice. "Please come in. Won't you sit down?"

The room into which the old woman led me was so littered with all sorts of rubbish—rags, pillows, blankets, bags—that I could barely turn around in it. The sunlight straggled in through two dusty little windows. In one corner, feeble whimpering and wailing was coming from behind a heap of boxes piled on top of one another. . . . It wasn't clear what was making the noise: possibly a sick baby, possibly a puppy. I sat down on a chair, and the old woman stood directly across from me. Her face was yellow and semitransparent, like wax; her lips had collapsed so completely that they formed a single, straight line amid a multitude of wrinkles; a tuft of white hair hung down below the kerchief on her head. Nonetheless, her sunken gray eyes peered out alertly and intelligently from under a bony, protruding forehead, and her sharp little nose stuck out like a spindle, sniffing the air as if to say, "I'm too smart for you!" "Well, you're no foolish old woman!" I thought. All the same, she did smell of vodka.

I explained the purpose of my visit to her, which I realized she must have already known, however. She listened to the explanation, though, blinking her eyes rapidly and raising her nose so that it stuck out even more sharply, as if she were getting ready to peck at something with it.

"To be sure, to be sure," she finally said. "Ardalion Matveich did mention something, certainly. It's my son Vasenka's art you were wanting to see. . . . But we can't be sure, my dear sir. . . ."

"Oh, why not?" I interrupted. "You may rest perfectly easy in regard to me. . . . I'm not an informer."

"Oh, your honor," the old woman broke in hurriedly, "what do you mean? How could we dare think such a thing about your worship! And on what grounds could anyone inform against us? Do you suppose ours is some sinful business? No, sir, my son's not the sort to agree to anything wicked . . . or indulge in any sort of witchcraft. . . . God forbid, indeed, holy mother of heaven!" (The old woman crossed herself three times.) "He's the leader of the whole province in prayer and fasting, the leader, your honor, truly he is! And that's just it—great grace has been bestowed upon him. Yes, indeed. It's not the work of his hands. It's from on high, my dear, yes it is."

"So you agree?" I asked. "When can I see your son?"

The old woman blinked again and shifted a balled-up handkerchief from one sleeve to the other.

"Oh, well, sir—well, sir, I can't say. . . ."

"Allow me to give you this, Mastridia Karpovna," I interrupted, and I handed her a ten-ruble note.

The old woman immediately clutched it in her fat, crooked fingers, which were reminiscent of an owl's fleshy claws, quickly slipped it into her sleeve, thought for a moment, and, as though she'd suddenly reached a decision, slapped her thighs with her palms.

"Come here this evening at about eight o'clock," she said, not in her previous tone, but in a different, more solemn and subdued one. "Only not to this room. Please go straight up to the floor above us. You'll find a door on your left, and you'll open that door, and you'll go into an empty room, your honor, and you'll see a chair in that room. Sit down on that chair and wait. And whatever you see, don't utter a word and don't move. And please don't speak to my son, either. He's still young, and he suffers from fainting fits. He gets scared very easily—he'll tremble and shake like some sort of chicken. . . . It's a sad sight!"

I looked at Mastridia. "You say he's young, but since he's your son. . . ."

"In spirit, sir, in spirit! Many's the orphan I've taken under my wing!" she added, nodding her head toward the corner the plaintive whimpering was coming from. "O—Oh God Almighty, holy mother of God! And you, your honor, before you come here, think carefully about which of your deceased relations or friends—the kingdom of heaven be theirs!—you'd like to see. Consider all your deceased friends, and whichever one you select, keep him in mind, keep him in mind every minute until my son comes!"

"But shouldn't I tell your son whom . . . ?"

"Not a word, sir, not a single word. He'll find out what he needs to know about your thoughts by himself. You just have to keep your friend firmly in mind, and at your dinner, drink a drop of wine—just two or three little glasses. Wine never disrupts anything." The old woman laughed, licked her lips, rubbed one hand across her mouth, and sighed.

"So, at seven-thirty?" I remarked, getting up from my chair.

"At seven-thirty, your honor, at seven-thirty," Mastridia Karpovna responded reassuringly.

I said goodbye to the old woman and went back to the hotel. I had no doubt that they were going to make a fool of me—but how? That's what aroused my curiosity. I didn't exchange more than two or three words with Ardalion. "Did she see you?" he asked me, frowning, and at my affirmative reply, he exclaimed, "That old woman's as good as any ministry official!"

I set to work, in accordance with the "ministry official's" advice, to consider all my deceased friends. After fairly prolonged hesitation, I finally decided to focus on an elderly man who'd been dead for many years, a Frenchman who'd been my tutor at one time. I selected him not because he had any special significance for me, but because his appearance had been unique, so unlike the appearance of any contemporary individual, that it'd be utterly impossible to imitate it. He'd had an enormous head, fluffy white hair brushed straight back, thick black eyebrows, a hooked nose, and two large, lilac-colored warts in the middle of his forehead. He used to wear a green coat with smooth brass buttons, a striped vest with a stand-up collar, a jabot, and lace cuffs. "If he shows me my old Dessaire," I thought, "well, I'll have to admit he's a sorcerer!"

At dinner, I followed the old woman's advice and drank a bottle of the best Lafitte—so Ardalion averred, although it had a very strong flavor of burned cork, and a thick sediment formed at the bottom of each glass.

At exactly seven-thirty, I stood in front of the house where I'd conversed with the worthy Mastridia Karpovna. All the window shutters were closed, but the door was open. I went into the house, climbed the shaky staircase up to the next floor, and, opening a door on the left, found myself, as the old woman had said I would, in a completely empty, rather large room. A tallow candle placed on the windowsill cast a dim light over the room. A wicker-bottomed chair stood against the wall opposite the door. I trimmed the candle, which had already been burning long enough to form a smoldering wick, sat down on the chair, and began to wait.

The first ten minutes passed rather quickly. There was absolutely nothing in the room itself that could divert my attention, but I listened intently to every rustle, gazed intently at the closed door. . . . My heart was pounding. Another ten minutes followed the first ten, then half an hour, three-quarters of an hour, and no movement of any kind occurred anywhere! I coughed several times in order to make my presence known. I began to get bored and angry: I hadn't envisioned being made a fool of in precisely this manner. I was about to get up from my chair, take the candle from the windowsill, and go downstairs. . . . I looked at it—the wick needed trimming again. But as I turned from the window to the door, I involuntarily shuddered: a man was standing there, leaning his back against the door. He'd entered so quickly and noiselessly that I hadn't heard a thing.

He wore a plain blue shirt; he was of medium height and was rather stocky. He stared at me, holding his hands behind his back and keeping his head down. I couldn't discern his features clearly in the dim candlelight: I could only see a shaggy mane of matted hair falling onto his forehead, thick, somewhat twisted lips, and whitish eyes. I wanted to speak to him, but I recalled Mastridia's injunction and bit my lip. The man who'd come in kept on staring at me. I stared back at him and, strangely enough, I began to feel something like fear at the same time. Then, as though on command, I promptly started thinking about my old tutor. *He* remained standing by the door, breathing heavily, as though he'd been climbing a mountain or lifting weights, while his eyes seemed to expand, seemed to move closer to me—and I grew uncomfortable under their obstinate, oppressive, menacing gaze. Those eyes periodically glowed with a malevolent inner fire, the kind of fire I've seen in the eyes of a hunting dog when it "points" at a rabbit. And like a hunting dog, *he* intently kept *his* eyes on mine when I tried to "double back," that is, when I tried to avert my eyes.

I don't know how much time passed this way—maybe a minute, maybe a quarter of an hour. He kept on staring at me, and I kept on feeling a certain discomfort and alarm, and kept on thinking about the Frenchman. I tried to say to myself a couple of times, "What nonsense! What a farce!" I tried to smile, to shrug my shoulders . . . but it was no use! All my decisiveness had instantaneously "frozen up" inside me—I can't find any other way to describe it. Some sort of numbness engulfed me. I suddenly noticed that *he* had moved away from the door and was standing a step or two closer to me. Then he almost leaped up in the air, keeping both feet together, and came even closer. . . . Then again . . . and again, while his menacing eyes remained unwaveringly fastened on my face, and his hands stayed behind his back, his broad chest heaving painfully. These leaps struck me as ridiculous, but I was frightened as well—and, although I couldn't understand how it happened, a feeling of drowsiness suddenly began to come over me. My eyelids drooped shut. . . . The shaggy figure with the whitish eyes in the blue shirt seemed to duplicate itself right in front of me, and then suddenly vanished altogether! . . . I shook myself— he was standing between the door and me again, but now he was much closer. . . . Then he vanished again—as if a mist had descended over him—then he reappeared . . . vanished again . . . and reappeared, ever closer and closer. . . . His laborious, almost desperate breathing touched me now. . . . The mist descended once more, and all of a sudden, out of this mist, the head of old Dessaire began to take distinct shape, beginning with the white hair brushed straight back! Yes: there were his warts, his black eyebrows, his hooked nose! There were his green coat with its brass buttons and his striped vest and his jabot. . . . I shrieked, I jumped up. . . . The elderly man vanished, and I saw the man in the blue shirt again in his place. He staggered to the wall, leaned his head and both arms against it, gasping for air like an overburdened horse, and demanded, "Tea!" in a husky voice. Mastridia Karpovna—I can't say where she came from—rushed up to him, saying, "Vasenka! Vasenka!" and began anxiously wiping away the sweat that was simply streaming down his face and hair. I was about to approach her, but she cried out, "Your honor! Merciful gentleman! Have pity on us! Go away, for Christ's sake!" so insistently, in such a heartrending voice, that I obeyed; she then turned back to her son. "My sustenance, my darling," she murmured soothingly, "you'll get your tea right away, right away. And you, sir, you'd better have a cup of tea at home as well!" she shouted as I left.

When I got home, I did as Mastridia had suggested and ordered some tea. I felt tired—even weak. "Well? Were you there?" Ardalion asked. "Did you see anything?"

"He certainly did show me something . . . which, I confess, I hadn't expected," I replied.

"He's a man of great wisdom," Ardalion observed, carrying out the samovar. "He's highly respected by the merchants."

After I went to bed and reflected at length on the incident that had occurred, I finally concluded that I'd found an explanation. The man indubitably possessed considerable magnetic power. Acting on my nerves by some method I didn't understand, of course, he'd evoked the image of the old man about whom I was thinking so vividly, so specifically, that I finally imagined I saw him before my very eyes. . . . Such "metastases," such transferences of sensation, are well known to science. This was all fine—but the force capable of producing such effects still appeared to be amazing and mysterious. "Whatever one may say," I thought, "I saw my dead tutor—I saw him with my own eyes."

The ball in the Hall of Nobility took place the next day. Sophie's father came to see me and reminded me of the invitation I'd extended to his daughter. At ten o'clock, I was standing by her side in the center of a ballroom illuminated by a number of bronze lamps, preparing to execute the relatively simple steps of the French quadrille to the thunderous blare of a military orchestra. There were crowds of people present. The ladies were especially numerous and very pretty, but my partner certainly would have been considered the prettiest, if it hadn't been for the somewhat strange, even somewhat wild, look in her eyes. I noticed that she hardly ever blinked; the unmistakable expression of sincerity in her eyes didn't account for what was extraordinary about them. But she had a charming figure and moved gracefully, if shyly. When she bent her slender neck toward her right shoulder as she waltzed, pulling herself back a little, as though she wanted to withdraw from her partner, it was impossible to imagine anything more touchingly youthful and innocent. She was dressed all in white, with a turquoise cross on a black ribbon tied around her neck.

I asked her to dance a mazurka, and tried to talk to her. But her answers were brief and reluctant, although she listened attentively, with the same expression of thoughtful absorption that had struck me when I first met her. She didn't display the slightest trace of desire to please, despite her age and appearance. I noticed only the absence of a smile and those eyes, which were continually directed straight into the eyes of her interlocutor, although they seemed to be seeing something else, to be concerned with something different, at the same time. . . . What a strange creature! Not really knowing how to entertain her, it occurred to me to tell her about my adventure of the previous day.

She listened to the whole story with evident interest, but wasn't surprised at what I told her, as I'd expected, and merely asked whether *he* was named Vasilii. I remembered that the old woman had called him "Vasenka."

"Yes, his name's Vasilii," I replied. "Do you know him?"

"There's a saintly man living here named Vasilii," she noted. "I wondered whether it was he."

"Saintliness has nothing to do with this," I remarked. "It's simply the action of magnetism—a phenomenon of interest to doctors and students of science."

I proceeded to set forth my views on the special force called magnetism, on the possibility of one man's will being brought under the influence of another's, and so on, but my explanations—which were somewhat confused, I grant—seemed to make no impression on her. Sophie listened to me, resting her clasped hands on her knees while holding a fan motionless in them. She didn't play with it—she didn't move her fingers at all—and I sensed that my words were falling on deaf ears, as though she were a stone statue. She understood them, but she evidently had her own convictions, which nothing could shake or eradicate.

"You can hardly accept the possibility of miracles!" I cried.

"Of course I accept the possibility," she responded calmly. "How can one fail to accept it? Aren't we told in the gospel that even he who has a grain of faith as big as a mustard seed can move mountains? One just needs to have faith—the miracles will come!"

"Evidently there isn't much faith nowadays," I observed. "Somehow one doesn't hear much about miracles."

"And yet there are miracles—you've seen one yourself. No, faith isn't dead nowadays, and the beginning of faith. . . ."

"The fear of God is the beginning of wisdom," I interrupted.

"The beginning of faith," Sophie continued, in no way daunted, "is self-abasement . . . humiliation."

"Even humiliation?" I asked.

"Yes. Human pride, haughtiness, arrogance—these are what must be utterly uprooted. You mentioned the will—it must be broken."

I ran my eyes up and down the figure of the young woman who was making such assertions. . . . "And this child isn't joking, either," I thought. I glanced at the people on both sides of us in the mazurka; they glanced back at me, and I detected that my astonishment amused them. One of them even smiled at me sympathetically, as though to say: "Well, what do you think of our eccentric young lady? Everyone here knows what she's like."

"Have you tried to break your own will?" I inquired, turning back to Sophie.

"Everyone is obligated to do what they think is right," she replied in a somewhat dogmatic tone.

"Let me ask you," I began after a brief silence, "do you believe in the possibility of calling up the dead?"

Sophie quietly shook her head.

"There are no dead."

"What?"

"There are no dead souls. They're immortal, and can always appear when they want to. . . . They always surround us."

"What do you mean? Do you suppose, for instance, that an

immortal soul may be hovering near that garrison major with the red nose at this very moment?"

"Why not? The sunlight shines on him and his nose, and doesn't the sunlight, like all light, come from God? And what difference does external appearance make? To the pure, nothing is impure! If one could just find a teacher, a leader!"

"But wait a moment, wait a moment," I interjected, not without a certain malicious pleasure, I must confess. "You want a leader . . . but what about a priest?"

Sophie looked at me coldly.

"You're trying to make fun of me, apparently. My priest tells me what I should do, but what I want is a leader who'd show me by his actions how to sacrifice myself!"

She turned her eyes toward the ceiling. With her childlike face and that expression of concentrated thoughtfulness, of secret, continual astonishment, she reminded me of Pre-Raphaelite Madonnas. . . .

"I've read somewhere," she went on, without turning toward me, barely moving her lips, "about a nobleman who gave orders to bury him under a church porch so that all the people who came to worship would walk on top of him and trample him. . . . That's what one ought to do in life. . . ."

"Boom! Boom! Ta-ra-ra!" thundered the orchestra drums. . . . I must confess that having a conversation like this at a ball struck me as extremely eccentric—and the ideas instinctively kindled within me were anything but religious. I took advantage of someone else inviting my partner to dance one of the sections of the mazurka to avoid renewing our quasi-theological discussion.

A quarter of an hour later, I escorted Mademoiselle Sophie over to her father, and I left the town of T—— two days after that. The image of the young woman with the childlike face and the soul as impenetrable as stone quickly faded from my memory.

Two years passed, and this image came to be resurrected before me. It happened thus: I was talking to a colleague who'd just returned from a trip to southern Russia. He'd spent some time in the town of T——, and told me various bits of news about the neighborhood. "By the way," he cried, "you know V.G.B—— quite well, I think, don't you?"

"Of course I know him."

"And his daughter Sophie, do you know her?"

"I've seen her twice."

"Well, imagine this—she's run away!"

"How can that be?"

"That's all I know. She disappeared three months ago, and they haven't heard a word about her. And the surprising thing is that no one knows whom she's run away with. Imagine, they don't have the least idea—not the slightest suspicion! She'd refused all the suitors who'd proposed to her, and her behavior was always absolutely impeccable. Ah, these quiet, religious young women are the unpredictable ones! It's created an awful scandal all over the province! B—— is in despair. . . . Why did she have to run away? Her father fulfilled all her wishes. The most incomprehensible part is that all the Lovelaces of the province are right there—not one of them is missing."

"And they haven't found her yet?"

"I tell you, she might as well be at the bottom of the sea! It's one less rich heiress in the world—that's the worst of it."

This piece of news greatly surprised me. It didn't seem to fit at all with the recollection I had of Sophie B——. But then, anything can happen!

In the fall of that same year, fate brought me to the province of S——, which, as everyone knows, is right next to the province of T——, on official business. The weather was cold and rainy, the exhausted horses could barely drag my lightweight carriage through the soggy black turf on the road. I remember that one day was particularly difficult: we ended up "sitting" in mud up to the axles of the wheels three times. My coachman, grunting and groaning, kept abandoning one track and shifting to another, only to find things no better there. As a result, I'd gotten so exhausted by evening that, upon reaching a way station, I decided to spend the night at the inn there. I was given a room with a broken-down wooden sofa, a sloping floor, and torn wallpaper; it reeked of kvass, straw matting, onions, and even turpentine, and had swarms of flies sitting on everything. But at least I was sheltered from the weather there—and the rain had settled down, as they say, for the whole day. I asked for a samovar to be brought in, and, seated on the sofa, I gave myself over to those cheerless roadside reflections so familiar to travelers in Russia.

They were interrupted by the sound of heavy knocking coming from the public rooms, which were separated from my room by a wooden partition. This knocking was accompanied by an intermittent metallic jingle, like the clanking of chains. A coarse male voice boomed out suddenly: "The blessing of God on all who live within this house. The blessing of God! The blessing of God! Amen! Amen! Scatter His enemies!" the voice repeated, somehow incoherently and savagely drawing out the last syllable of each word. . . . A loud sigh followed, and a heavy body sank onto a bench with the same jingling sound.

"Akulina! Servant of God! Come here!" the voice started up again. "Behold! Clothed in rags and blessed! . . . Ha-ha-ha! Bah! My lord God, my lord God, my lord God!" the voice droned on like the deacon of a choir. "My lord God, creator of my body, behold my iniquity. . . . O-ho-ho! Ha-ha! . . . Bah! Bring all abundance to this house in the seventh hour!"

"Who's that?" I asked the hospitable landlady when she brought the samovar.

"That, your honor," she answered me in a hasty whisper, "is a blessed holy wanderer. He's appeared in our region recently, and he's been gracious enough to visit us here now. In such weather! The water's simply pouring off him in streams, the poor dear man! And you should see the chains on him. It's awful!"

"The blessing of God! The blessing of God!" the voice rang out again. "Akulina! Hey, Akulina! Akulinushka—my friend! Where is our paradise? Our heavenly paradise? Our paradise is in the wilderness . . . paradise. . . . And to this house, from the beginning of time, bring great happiness . . . oh . . . oh . . . oh. . . ." The voice muttered something inarticulate and, after a protracted yawn, suddenly emitted another hoarse laugh. This laugh seemed to burst out unintentionally each time, and was followed each time by vigorous spitting.

"Dear me! Stepanych isn't here! That's the worst thing!" the landlady said as if to herself, standing at the door, obviously listening with extreme care. "He'll say some word of salvation and I may not hear it, foolish woman that I am!"

She went out quickly.

There was a chink in the partition; I put my eye up to it. The holy wanderer was sitting on a bench with his back to me. I could see only his shaggy head, as huge as a beer keg, and his broad, bowed back covered by a patched, wet shirt. A frail-looking woman was kneeling in front of him on the earthen floor, wearing the kind of jacket worn by women belonging to the artisan class—an old one that was also wet—and a dark kerchief pulled down almost over her eyes. She was trying to pull off the holy wanderer's boots, but her fingers kept sliding down the greasy, slippery leather. The landlady was standing nearby with her arms folded across her chest, gazing reverently at the "man of God." He was mumbling inarticulately again.

The woman finally managed to pull off the boots. She almost fell backward, but recovered her balance and began unwinding the strips of rags that were wrapped around the man's legs. He had a wound on the sole of his foot. . . . I turned away.

"Wouldn't you like me to get you a cup of tea, my dear?" I heard the landlady saying in an obsequious voice.

"What an idea!" responded the holy wanderer. "To indulge the sinful body. . . . O-ho-ho! Break all the bones in it . . . but she thinks about tea! Oh, oh, worthy old woman, Satan is mighty within us. . . . Fight him with hunger, fight him with cold, with the heavenly hordes, with the pouring, penetrating rain, and he remains unharmed—he is still alive! Remember the day of the Intercession of the Mother of God! You will receive, you will receive in abundance!"

The landlady faintly gasped in surprise.

"Just listen to me! Give all you have, give your food, give your clothes! If they do not ask, give nonetheless! For God is all-seeing! Is it hard for Him to destroy your roof? He has given you bread in His mercy, and so you bake it in the oven! He sees all! See-e-s! Whose eye is in the triangle? Tell me, whose?"

The landlady stealthily crossed herself under her shawl.

"The old enemy is adamant! A-da-mant! A-da-mant!" The holy wanderer repeated the word several times, gnashing his teeth. "The old serpent! But God will arise! Yes, God will arise and scatter His enemies! I will call up all the dead! I will go forth against His enemy. . . . Ha-ha-ha! Bah!"

"Do you have any oil?" inquired another, barely audible voice. "Let me put some on the wound. . . . I have a clean rag."

I peeped through the chink again; the woman in the jacket was still attending the holy wanderer's sore foot. . . . "A Magdalene!" I thought.

"I'll get it right away, right away, my dear," replied the landlady, and coming into my room, she took a spoonful of oil from the lamp burning in front of the icon.

"Who's the woman waiting on him?" I asked.

"We don't know who she is, sir. I suppose she's seeking salvation, too, atoning for her sins. But what a saintly man he is!"

"Akulinushka, my sweet child, my dear daughter," the holy wanderer kept repeating, and then he suddenly burst into tears. The woman kneeling in front of him raised her eyes to look at him. . . . My God, where had I seen those eyes? The landlady went up to her with the spoonful of oil. She finished her task, and getting up from the floor, she asked if the inn had a clean loft with a little hay. . . . "Vasilii Nikitich likes to sleep on hay," she added.

"Of course there is. Come this way," answered the woman. "Come this way, my dear," she turned to the holy wanderer, "and dry yourself off, and rest." The man coughed, got up slowly from the bench—his chains clanked again—and turning around toward me, looked for the room's icons, and began to cross himself with broad gestures.

I instantly recognized him: it was the very same Vasilii, the artisan who'd once shown me my dead tutor!

His features hadn't changed much, except that their expression had become even more extraordinary, even more horrifying. . . . An unkempt beard had grown all over the lower part of his swollen face. Tattered, filthy, and wild-looking, he inspired more repugnance than fear in me. He stopped crossing himself, but his gaze still wandered aimlessly around the corners of the room and the floor, as though he were waiting for something. . . .

"Vasilii Nikitich, please follow me," the woman in the jacket requested, bowing. He suddenly straightened up and turned around, but stumbled and tottered. . . . His companion immediately ran up to him and supported him under the arm. To judge by her voice and figure, she seemed young; it was impossible to see her face.

"Akulinushka, my friend!" the man repeated once more in some sort of startling voice, and opening his mouth wide and striking himself on the breast with his fist, he uttered a deep groan that seemed to come from the very depths of his soul. Both of them followed the landlady out of the room.

I lay down on my hard sofa and mused on what I'd seen for a long time. My mesmerizer had ultimately become a holy wanderer. This was the state he'd been brought to by the power one couldn't fail to acknowledge in him!

The next morning, I got ready to continue my trip. The rain was falling as hard as it had the day before, but I couldn't delay any longer. As he brought me some water to bathe with, my servant had a special smile on his face, a smile of restrained mockery. I

knew this smile quite well: it meant that my servant had heard
something unfavorable or even shocking about some member of
the upper classes. He was obviously burning with impatience to
tell it to me.

"Well, what is it?" I finally asked him.

"Did your honor see the holy wanderer yesterday?" my servant
promptly responded.

"Yes. Why?"

"And did you see his companion, too?"

"Yes, I saw her."

"She's a young lady from a noble family."

"What?"

"I'm telling you the truth. Some merchants from T—— arrived
here this morning, and they recognized her. They even told me
her name, but I've forgotten it. . . . "

This struck me like a flash of lightning. "Is that holy wanderer
still here?" I inquired.

"I don't think he's left yet. He's been sitting at the gate for a
long time, making so much noise that it's impossible to get past
him. He's amusing himself with this nonsense. He's found that it
pays, no doubt."

My servant belonged to the same class of cultivated servants as
Ardalion.

"And is the lady with him?"

"Yes. She's attending to him."

I went out onto the steps and caught sight of the holy wanderer.
He was sitting on a bench at the gate, bent way over, shaking his
lowered head back and forth with both his palms pressed against
it, looking exactly like a wild beast in a cage. His thick mane of
curly hair covered his eyes and swung from side to side, as did his
pendulous lips. . . . A strange, almost inhuman muttering came from
those lips. His companion had just finished washing her hands and
face with water from a pitcher that was hanging on a pole, and
not yet having replaced her kerchief on her head, she was making
her way back to the gate along a narrow plank laid across the dark
puddles of the filthy yard. I glanced at her head, which was now
entirely uncovered, and impulsively threw up my hands in astonishment: before me was Sophie B——!

She turned around quickly and fastened her blue eyes—which
were as immobile as ever—on me. She'd gotten a lot thinner, her
skin looked coarser and had a yellowish-red tinge of sunburn, her

nose was sharper, and the line of her lips was more severe—but she was no less attractive. Only now, another expression was added to her former one of thoughtful amazement—a resolute, almost bold, intensely exalted expression. There wasn't a trace of childishness left in her face now.

I went up to her. "Sofia Vladimirovna," I cried, "can it be you? In this dress . . . with such company . . . ?"

She shuddered, gazed at me even more intently, as though trying to ascertain who was speaking to her, and, without saying a word to me, rushed up to her companion.

"Akulinushka," he faltered with a heavy sigh, "our sins, sins. . . ."

"Vasilii Nikitich, let's go right now! Do you hear, right now, right now," she urged, pulling her kerchief onto her head with one hand while she supported the holy wanderer under the elbow with the other. "Let's go, Vasilii Nikitich. There's danger here."

"I'm coming, my good girl, I'm coming," the man responded obediently, and inclining his whole body forward, he got up from the bench. "There's just one chain I have to fasten. . . ."

I approached Sophie once more and told her my name. I began begging her to listen to me, to say just one word to me. I pointed to the rain, which was coming down in torrents. I implored her to take care of her own health and the health of her companion. I mentioned her father. . . . But she seemed possessed by a sort of evil, implacable drive. Without paying any attention to me, clenching her teeth and breathing hard, she encouraged the distracted man in a low voice with short, insistent words, put his belt around him, fastened his chains, pulled a child's cloth cap with a broken peak over his hair, thrust a walking stick into his hand, flung a knapsack over her own shoulder, and went out of the gate into the street with him. . . . I didn't have the right to stop her physically, and it wouldn't have done any good. She didn't even turn around in response to my last, despairing cry. Supporting the "man of God" under his arm, she rapidly walked through the black mud in the street, and after a few moments, I caught a final glimpse of the two figures, the holy wanderer and Sophie, through the dim mist of the foggy morning, amid the thick network of falling raindrops. . . . They turned past the corner of a protruding hut, and vanished forever.

I went back to my room and lapsed into thought. I couldn't understand it: I couldn't understand how such a wealthy young woman who'd been so well brought up could forsake everything and everyone, her own home, her family, her friends, how she could abandon all her customs, all the comforts of life—and for what? To follow a half-crazed vagrant, to become his servant! I couldn't possibly even for a moment entertain the notion that the motive for such a step arose from any romantic inclination, from love or passion, however depraved. . . . One merely needed to glance at the repulsive figure of the "man of God" to dismiss such a notion entirely! No, Sophie had remained pure—and, as she'd once told me, nothing was impure in her eyes. I couldn't understand what Sophie had done, but I didn't blame her, just as I didn't blame other young women later on who likewise sacrificed everything for what *they* considered to be the truth, for what *they* took to be their vocation. I couldn't help regretting that Sophie had chosen precisely *that* path, but neither could I deny her respect, even admiration. She hadn't spoken in vain about self-abasement, about humiliation. . . . In *her*, words weren't opposed to deeds. She'd sought a leader, a guide, and had found him . . . my God, in whom!

Yes, she'd lain down to be trampled, to be trodden underfoot. . . .

In time, a rumor reached me that her family had finally managed to find its lost sheep and bring her home. But she didn't survive at home for long—she died like a nun who'd taken a vow of silence, without having spoken a word to anyone.

May peace be granted to your heart, you poor, enigmatic creature! Vasilii Nikitich is probably still wandering—the resilient health of such people is truly amazing. Or perhaps epilepsy has defeated him.

Letter to P. V. Annenkov.

Baden-Baden.
Thiergartenstrasse, 3.
January 10, 1870.

I'm writing you while still under the influence of sad news, dear Annenkov: about an hour ago I learned that Herzen is dead. I couldn't restrain myself from tears.

No matter what the differences were in our opinions, no matter what conflicts occurred between us, still and all, an old comrade, an old friend has disappeared—our ranks are thinning, thinning! Moreover, as ill luck would have it, I saw him in Paris no more than a week ago, had breakfast with him (after a seven-year separation), and never was he more merry, talkative, even noisy. That was last *Friday*; he fell ill that evening, and the next day I saw him in bed with a high fever and pneumonia; up until my departure, last Wednesday, I visited his family every day, but I couldn't see him anymore—the doctor wouldn't allow it; and when I left I already knew that his case was hopeless. His illness consumed him horribly quickly. I couldn't stay in Paris any longer; but it's almost with horror that I think of what will become of his family. His son still hasn't had time to arrive from Florence. His elder daughter Natalia—a wonderful, charming creature—was out of her head for six weeks as a result of some strange misunderstandings, and has just barely recovered now. . . . This death may again jolt her sanity.

Everyone in Russia will probably say that Herzen ought to have died earlier, that he outlived himself; but what do those words mean, what does our so-called activity mean in the face of that mute abyss that swallows us all? As though to live and continue living weren't the most important thing for a person? Death especially nauseates me, inasmuch as a few days ago I had the quite unexpected chance to smell my fill of it, specifically, I received an invitation (in Paris) via a friend to be present not only at Troppmann's execution, but at the announcement of the death sentence to him, at his *toilette*, and so on. There were eight of us in all. I won't ever forget that terrible night, during which "I have supp'd my full of horrors" and conceived a decisive loathing for capital punishment in general, the way that it's carried out in France in particular. I've already begun a letter to you in which I relate all of this in detail and which, if you want, you may then publish in *The St. Petersburg News*. I'll just say one thing for now—that I couldn't even imagine such courage, such contempt for death, as there was in Troppmann. But the whole thing is horrible ... horrible.

By the way, did you receive my letter about Polonskii, and did you have it placed in the journal? He's wailing *like a gull* about this and assures me in his letters that he's so unfortunate that he's certain of the article's nonappearance. Please prove to him that the opposite is the case, although my article, alas, can't grant him any special *good fortune*.

So long, my friend. Be well. I send my regards to your wife and clasp your hand.

Your Iv. Turgenev

P.S. I'm not moving to Weimar until February 7.

The Execution of Troppmann

I

In January of the current year (1870), while dining in Paris at the house of an old friend of mine, I received from Du Camp, the well-known writer and expert on the statistics of Paris, an utterly unex-pected invitation to be present at the execution of Troppmann—and not only at his execution: it was proposed that I should be admitted to the prison itself, together with a small number of other privileged persons. The terrible crime committed by Troppmann still has not been forgotten, but at that time Paris was as interested in him and his impending execution, if not more, than it was in the recent ap-pointment of the pseudo-parliamentarian ministry of Olivier or the murder of Victor Noir, who fell at the hand of the afterward sur-prisingly acquitted Prince Pierre Bonaparte. All the windows of the photographers' and stationers' shops exhibited whole rows of photographs showing a young fellow with a large forehead, dark eyes, and puffy lips, the "famous" Pantin murderer (de l'illustre assassin de Pantin), and for several evenings in a row, thousands of workmen had already been gathering in the environs of Roquette Prison in hopes of seeing the erection of the guillotine, dispersing only after midnight. Taken by surprise at Du Camp's proposal, I accepted, without giving it much thought. And having promised to arrive at the place fixed for our meeting—the statue of Prince Eugene on the boulevard of the same name, at eleven o'clock in the evening—I did not want to go back on my word. False pride prevented my doing so. . . . And what if they should think that I was a coward? As a punishment to myself—and as a lesson to others—I should now like to recount everything I saw. I intend to revive in my memory all the painful impressions of that night. It

will not be only the reader's curiosity that is satisfied: he may
derive some benefit from my story.

II

A small crowd of people was already waiting for Du Camp and
me at the prince's statue. Among them was Monsieur Claude, the
police commissioner of Paris (*chef de la police de sûreté*), to whom
Du Camp introduced me. The others were privileged visitors like
myself, journalists, reporters, etc. Du Camp had warned me that
we would probably have to spend a sleepless night in the office of
the prison warden. The execution of condemned criminals takes
place during the winter at seven o'clock in the morning; but one
had to be at the prison before midnight or one might not be able
to push one's way through the crowd. It is only about half a mile
from the statue of Prince Eugene to Roquette Prison, but so far I
could see nothing in any way out of the ordinary. There were just
a few more people on the boulevard than usual. One could not
help noting one thing, though: almost all the people were going—
and some, especially women, running—in the same direction; in
addition, all the cafés and taverns were ablaze with lights, which
is very rare in the remote quarters of Paris, especially so late at
night. The night was not foggy, but was dismal, damp without
rain, and cold without frost—a typical French January night. Claude
said that it was time to go, and off we went. He preserved the
imperturbable cheerfulness of a practical man in whom such events
did not arouse any feelings, except perhaps the desire to dispose
of his sad duty as soon as possible.

Claude was a thickset, broad-shouldered man of about fifty, of medium height, with a round, closely cropped head and small, almost
minute, features—only his forehead, chin, and the back of his head
were at all broad. Relentless energy was evident in his dry, even
voice, his pale-gray eyes, his short, strong fingers, his muscular
legs, and all his unhurried but decisive movements. He was said to
be an expert at his profession, inspiring mortal terror in all thieves
and murderers; political crimes were not part of his responsibilities.
His assistant, Monsieur J——, whom Du Camp also admired,
looked like a kindly, almost sentimental man, and his manners were
much more refined. With the exception of these two gentlemen and
perhaps Du Camp, we all felt a little awkward—or did it only seem
that way to me?—and a little ashamed, too, although we walked
along jauntily, as though on a hunting expedition.

The nearer we came to the prison, the more crowded the streets became, even though there were no real crowds as yet. No shouts could be heard, or even any overly loud conversations; it was evident that the "performance" had not yet commenced. Only the street urchins were already weaving around us; their hands thrust in the pockets of their trousers and the peaks of their caps pulled down to their eyes, they sauntered along with that special insolent, rollicking gait that can only be seen in Paris and that can be converted into agile running and jumping like that of a monkey in the twinkling of an eye.

"There he is—there he is—it's him!" a few voices shouted around us.

"Why," Du Camp suddenly said to me, "you've been mistaken for the executioner!"

"A lovely beginning!" I thought.

The Paris executioner, Monsieur de Paris, whose acquaintance I made that same night, is as tall and gray as I am.

But soon we came to a long, not terribly wide square bounded on two sides by barracklike buildings with grimy facades and crude architecture: that was Roquette Square. On the left was the prison for young criminals (*prison des jeunes détenus*) and on the right— the building for condemned prisoners (*maison de dépôt pour les condamnés*), or Roquette Prison.

III

A squad of soldiers was drawn up four deep right across the square, and about two hundred feet from it, another squad was also drawn up four deep. As a rule, no soldiers are present at an execution, but in this case, in view of Troppmann's "reputation" and the present state of public opinion, excited by Noir's murder, the government thought it necessary to take special measures and not to leave the preservation of law and order to the police alone. The main gates of Roquette Prison were exactly in the center of the empty space closed in by the soldiers. A few police sergeants walked slowly up and down before the gates; a young, rather fat police officer in an unusually richly embroidered cap (evidently the chief inspector of that quarter of the city) swooped down on our group so peremptorily that it reminded me of the good old days in my beloved country; but upon recognizing his superiors, he became calmer. They let us into a small guardroom beside the gates with immense caution, barely opening the gates, and—after a preliminary examination and interrogation—led us across two inner court-yards, one large and another small, to the warden's lodgings.

The warden, a tall, stalwart man with a gray moustache and goatee, had the typical face of a French infantry officer: an aquiline nose, immobile, rapacious eyes, and a tiny skull. He received us very politely and benignly; but even without his being aware of it, his every gesture, his every word, at once showed that he was "a reliable fellow" (*un gaillard solide*), an utterly loyal servant, who would not hesitate to carry out any order given by his master. Indeed, he had proved his zeal in action: on the night of the coup d'état of December second, he and his battalion had occupied the printing works of the *Moniteur*.

Like a true gentleman, he put the whole of his apartment at our disposal. It was on the second floor of the main building and con-sisted of four fairly well-furnished rooms; in two of them, a fire was lit in the fireplace. A small Italian greyhound with a dislocated leg and a mournful expression in its eyes, as though it, too, felt like a prisoner, limped from one rug to another, wagging its tail. There were eight of us visitors; I recognized some from their photographs (Sardou, Albert Wolf), but I did not feel like talking to any of them. We all sat down on chairs in the drawing room. (Du Camp had gone out with Claude.)

It goes without saying that Troppmann became the subject of conversation and, as it were, the center of all our thoughts. The prison warden told us that he had been asleep since nine o'clock in the evening and was sleeping like a log; that he seemed to have guessed what had happened to his request for a reprieve; that he had implored him, the warden, to tell him the truth; that he kept stubbornly insisting that he had accomplices, whom he refused to name; that he would probably lose his nerve at the decisive moment, but that he ate with appetite, did not read books, etc., etc. For our part, some of us wondered whether one ought to give credence to the words of a criminal who had proved himself to be an in-veterate liar, went over the details of the murder, asked ourselves what phrenologists would make of Troppmann's skull, raised the question of capital punishment—but all this was so lifeless, so dull, so platitudinous, that even those who spoke did not feel like con-tinuing. To talk about something else was rather embarrassing, even impossible—impossible out of respect for death alone, for the man who was doomed to die. We were all overwhelmed by a feeling of irksome and tedious—yes, tedious—discomfort; no one was really bored, but this dreary feeling was a hundred times worse than boredom! It seemed as though there would be no end to the night! As for me, there was one thing I was sure of: namely, that I had no right to be where I was, that no psychological or philosophical considerations excused me. Claude came back and told us how the notorious Jude had slipped through his fingers and how he was still hoping to catch him, if he was still alive. But suddenly we heard the heavy clatter of wheels, and a few moments later we were informed that the guillotine had arrived. We all rushed out into the street—just as though we were pleased!

IV

Before the prison gates stood a huge, closed van, drawn by three horses harnessed one behind the other; another two-wheeled van, a small, low one, which looked like an oblong box and was drawn by one horse, had stopped a little farther off. (That one, as we learned later, was to transport the body of the executed man to the cemetery immediately after the execution.) A few workmen wearing short jackets were visible around the vans, and a tall man in a round hat and white necktie, with a light overcoat thrown across his shoulders, was giving orders in an undertone. . . . That was the executioner. All the authorities—the prison warden, Claude, the district police inspector, and so on—were surrounding and greeting him. "*Ah, Monsieur Indric! Bon soir, Monsieur Indric!*" (His real name is Heidenreich: he is an Alsatian.) Our group also walked up to him: for a moment *he* became the center of our attention. There was a certain strained but respectful familiarity in the way everyone treated him: "We don't look down upon you, for you are, after all, a person of importance!" Some of us, probably just to show off, even shook hands with him. (He had a pair of beautiful, remarkably white hands.) I recalled a line from Pushkin's *Poltava*:

> The executioner. . . .
> Playing with his white hands. . . .

Indric comported himself very simply, gently, and courteously, but not without a touch of patriarchal gravity. It seemed as though he felt we regarded him that night as second in importance only to Troppmann, and, so to speak, as his first minister.

The workmen opened the bigger van and began taking out all the component parts of the guillotine, which they had to put up within fifteen feet of the prison gates.* Two lanterns began to move back and forth just above the ground, illuminating the polished cobblestones of the roadway with small, bright circles of light. I looked at my watch—it was only half past twelve! It had grown darker and colder. There were already a large number of people present, and behind the rows of the soldiers bordering the empty space in front of the prison rose an uninterrupted, dim hubbub of human voices. I walked up to the soldiers: they stood motionless, having drawn a little closer together and thereby breaking the original symmetry of their ranks. Their faces expressed nothing but cold, patiently submissive boredom; even the faces I could discern behind the shakos and uniforms of the soldiers and behind the three-cornered hats and tunics of the policemen, the faces of the workmen and artisans, all expressed virtually the same thing, merely adding some sort of indefinable amusement. Up ahead, from behind the mass of the stirring, shoving crowd, one could hear exclamations like "*Ohé Troppmann! Ohé Lambert! Fallait pas qu'y aille!*" There were shouts and shrill whistles. One could clearly make out a noisy argument going on someplace; a fragment of some cynical song came creeping along like a snake—and there was a sudden burst of loud laughter that was instantly taken up by the crowd, ending with a roar of coarse guffaws. The "real business" had not yet begun; one could not hear the antidynastic shouts everyone expected, or the all-too-familiar menacing reverberations of the Marseillaise.

I went back to a spot near the slowly rising guillotine. A certain curly-haired, dark-complexioned gentleman in a soft, gray hat, probably a lawyer, was standing beside me haranguing two or three other gentlemen in tightly buttoned-up overcoats, waving the forefinger of his right hand forcefully up and down, trying to prove that Troppmann was not a murderer, but a maniac. "*Un maniaque! Je vais vous le prouver! Suivez mon raisonnement!*" he kept saying. "*Son mobile n'était pas l'assassinat, mais un orgueil que je nommerais volontier démesuré! Suivez mon raisonnement!*" The gentlemen in the overcoats "followed his reasoning," but to judge by their expressions, he hardly convinced them; the worker sitting on the platform

---

* I refer readers wishing to acquaint themselves not only with all the details of "executions" but with everything that precedes and follows them to the excellent article by Monsieur Ducain, "*La Prison de la Roquette,*" in *Revue des Deux Mondes,* no. 1, 1870.

of the guillotine looked at him with undisguised contempt. I returned to the prison warden's apartment.

V

A few of our "colleagues" had already gathered there. The courteous warden was regaling them with mulled wine. They started to discuss once more whether Troppmann was still asleep, what he ought to be feeling, whether he could hear the noise of the people despite the distance of his cell from the street, and so on. The warden showed us a whole pile of letters addressed to Troppmann, who, the warden assured us, refused to read them. Most of them seemed to be full of silly jokes, but there were also some that were serious, in which he was admonished to repent and confess everything; one Methodist clergyman sent a whole theological thesis of twenty pages; there were also short notes from ladies, some of whom enclosed flowers—daisies and chrysanthemums. The warden told us that Troppmann had tried to get some poison from the prison pharmacist and wrote a letter asking for it, which the pharmacist, of course, immediately forwarded to the authorities. I could not help feeling that our worthy host was rather at a loss to explain to himself the interest we took in a man like Troppmann who, in his opinion, was a savage, disgusting animal, and all but ascribed it to the casual curiosity of civilian men of the world, the "idle rich."

After a little more conversation, we just crawled off into different corners. During the whole of that night we wandered around like condemned souls—"*comme des âmes en peine*," as the French say—went into various rooms, sat down side by side on chairs in the drawing room, inquired about Troppmann, glanced at the clock, yawned, went downstairs into the yard and street again, came back, sat down again. . . . Some of us told off-color anecdotes, exchanged trivial personal news, touched lightly on politics, the theater, Noir's murder; others tried to crack jokes, to say something witty, but that evidently did not work at all, provoking some sort of unpleasant laughter, which was instantly cut short, some sort of false approbation. I found a tiny sofa in an anteroom and somehow or other managed to lie down on it. I tried to sleep, but did not succeed, of course—I did not doze off for one moment.

The distant, hollow noise of the crowd was getting louder, deeper, and more and more unbroken. By three o'clock, according to

Claude, who kept coming into the room, sitting down on a chair, falling asleep at once, then disappearing again, summoned by one of his subordinates, more than twenty-five thousand people had already gathered there. The noise astonished me with its resemblance to the distant roar of the sea: it was the same sort of unending Wagnerian crescendo, not rising continuously, but with huge intervals between the ebb and flow; the shrill notes of women's and children's voices rose in the air like thin spray over this enormous rumbling noise; in it was discernible the brutal power of some elemental force. It would grow quiet and die down for a moment; then the hubbub would restart, grow and swell, and in another moment would seem to be about to strike, as though wishing to tear everything down; and then it would retreat again, grow quiet, and swell once more—there seemed to be no end to it. And what, I could not help asking myself, did this noise signify? Impatience? Joy? Malice? No! It did not serve as an echo of any distinct human feeling. . . . It was simply the rumble, the roar of the elements.

VI

At about three o'clock in the morning, I must have gone out into the street for the tenth time. The guillotine was ready. Its two beams, separated by about two feet, connected by the slanting line of the blade, stood out dimly and strangely, rather than terribly, against the dark sky. For some reason, I imagined that those beams ought to be more distant from each other; their proximity lent the whole machine a sort of sinister shapeliness, the shapeliness of a long, carefully stretched out swan's neck. A large, dark-red wicker basket, looking like a suitcase, aroused a feeling of disgust in me. I knew that the executioners would throw the warm, still quivering dead body and the cut-off head into that basket. . . .

The mounted police (*garde municipale*), who had arrived a little earlier, took up their positions in a large semicircle before the façade of the prison; from time to time the horses neighed, champing at their bits and tossing their heads; large drops of white froth appeared on the pavement between their forelegs. The riders dozed somberly beneath their bearskin caps, which they had pulled down over their eyes. The lines of the soldiers cutting across the square and holding back the crowds had retreated farther: now there were not two hundred but three hundred feet of empty space before the prison.

I went up to one of those lines and gazed at the people crammed behind it for a long time; their shouting actually was elemental, that is, senseless. I still remember the face of a workman, a young fellow of about twenty: he stood there grinning, with his eyes trained on the ground, just as though he were thinking of something amusing, then he would suddenly throw back his head, open his mouth wide, and begin to shout in a drawn-out voice, without words, and then his head would sink again and he would start to grin again. What was going on inside that man? Why had he consigned himself to such a painfully sleepless night, to an almost eight-hour-long immobility?

My ears did not catch any snatches of conversation; occasionally, through the unceasing uproar, would come the piercing cry of a hawker selling a leaflet about Troppmann, his life, his execution, and even his "last words." . . . Or an argument would break out again somewhere far away, or there would be a hideous burst of laughter, or some women would start screaming. . . . This time I heard the Marseillaise, but it was sung by just five or six men, with interruptions, too, at that—the Marseillaise becomes significant only when thousands are singing it. "*A bas Pierre Bonaparte!*" someone shouted at the top of his voice. . . . "Oo-oo-ah-ah!" the crowd responded in an incoherent roar. In one place, the shouts assumed the measured rhythm of a polka: one-two-three-four! one-two-three-four! to the well-known tune *des lampions!*

A heavy, rank breath of alcoholic fumes came from the crowd. A great deal of wine had been consumed by all those bodies; there were a great many drunken men there. Not for nothing did the taverns glow with reddish lights in the general background of this scene. The night had grown pitch-dark; the sky had become totally overcast, turning black. There were small clumps on the sparse trees, which loomed indistinctly in the darkness, like phantoms: they were street urchins who had climbed the trees and were sitting among the branches, whistling and screeching like birds. One of them had fallen and, it is said, was fatally injured, having broken his spine; but he only aroused loud laughter, and only for a short time.

On my way back to the warden's apartment, I passed the guillotine and saw the executioner, surrounded by a small crowd of inquisitive people, on its platform. He was performing a "rehearsal" for them: he threw down the hinged plank to which the criminal was fastened and whose tip touched the semicircular slot between the beams as it fell; he released the knife, which came down heavily and smoothly with a rapid, hollow roar, and so forth. I did not stop to watch this "rehearsal," that is to say, I did not climb onto the platform; the feeling of having committed some unknown transgression, the sense of some secret shame, was growing stronger and stronger inside me.... Perhaps this feeling accounts for the fact that the horses harnessed to the vans, calmly chewing the oats in their nosebags, at that moment seemed to me to be the only innocent creatures among us all.

I went back to the solitude of my little sofa once more, and once more began to listen to the roar of the breakers on the seashore....

VII

Contrary to the general assumption, the *last* hour of waiting passes much more quickly than the first, and even more quickly than the second or third.... So it was now. We were surprised by the news that it had struck six, and that only one more hour remained to the moment of execution. We were supposed to go to Troppmann's cell in exactly half an hour, at half past six. All traces of sleep promptly disappeared from every face. I do not know what the others were feeling, but I felt terribly sick at heart. A new figure appeared: a short, gray-haired man with a thin little face, the priest, flashed by wearing his long, black cassock, along with the ribbon of the *Légion d'honneur* and a low, wide-brimmed hat. The warden had prepared a sort of breakfast for us, *une collation*; huge cups of chocolate appeared on the round table in the drawing room.... I did not even go near it, although our hospitable host advised me to fortify myself "because the morning air might be harmful." Eating food at that moment seemed to me ... disgusting. Good Lord—a feast at such a time! "I have no right," I said to myself for the hundredth time since the beginning of that night.

"Is *he* still asleep?" one of us asked, sipping his chocolate.

(They were all speaking about Troppmann without referring to him by name; there could be no question of any other *him*.)

"Yes, he's asleep," replied the warden.

"In spite of this terrible racket?"

(The noise had grown extraordinarily loud, in fact, turning into a kind of hoarse roar; the menacing chorus no longer rose in a crescendo—it rumbled victoriously, cheerfully.)

"His cell is behind three walls," the warden observed.

Claude, whom the warden clearly treated as the most important person among us, looked at his watch and said: "Twenty past six."

We all must have shuddered inwardly, I expect, but we just put on our hats and set off noisily after our guide.

"Where are you dining today?" a reporter asked in a loud voice. But that struck us all as a little too unnatural.

VIII

We went out into the large prison courtyard; there, in the corner on the right, a sort of roll call took place in front of a half-closed door; then we were shown into a tall, narrow, entirely empty room with a leather stool in the center.

"It is here that *la toilette du condamné* takes place," Du Camp whispered to me.

We did not all fit in: there were about ten of us, including the warden, the priest, Claude, and his assistant. During the next two or three minutes we spent in that room (some kind of official documents were being signed there), the thought that we had no right to do what we were doing, that by being present with an air of hypocritical solemnity at the killing of a fellow human being we were performing some odious, iniquitous farce—that thought flashed through my mind for the last time; as soon as we set off, following Claude again along the wide stone corridor dimly lit by two nightlights, I no longer felt anything except that now—now—this minute—this second.... We rapidly climbed two staircases, entered another corridor, walked through it, went down a narrow spiral staircase, and found ourselves before an iron door.... Here!

The warden unlocked the door cautiously. It opened quietly—and we all slowly and silently filed into a rather spacious room with yellow walls, a high barred window, and a crumpled bed on which no one was lying.... The steady glow of a large night-light illuminated all the objects in the room quite clearly.

I was standing a little behind the rest and, as I recall, I involuntarily squinted; however, I immediately saw a young, dark-haired, dark-eyed person diagonally opposite me, gazing at us all with huge, round eyes that moved slowly from left to right. It was Troppmann. He had woken up just before our arrival. He was standing in front of the table on which he had just written a farewell (albeit rather trivial) letter to his mother. Claude took off his hat and went up to him.

"Troppmann," he said in his dry, soft, but peremptory voice, "we have come to inform you that your appeal for a reprieve has been denied and that the hour of retribution has come for you."

Troppmann turned his eyes toward him, but they were no longer "huge"; he regarded him calmly, almost somnolently, and did not utter a word.

"My child," the priest exclaimed hollowly, going up to him from the other side, "*du courage!*"

Troppmann looked at him exactly as he had looked at Claude.

"I knew he wouldn't be afraid," Claude declared in a confident tone, addressing us all. "Now, when he has gotten over the first shock (*le premier choc*), I can count on him."

(Thus does a schoolmaster wishing to cajole his pupil tell him beforehand that he is "an intelligent fellow.")

"Oh, I'm not afraid (*Oh, je n'ai pas peur!*)," said Troppmann, addressing Claude again, "I'm not afraid!"

His voice, a pleasant, youthful baritone, was perfectly steady.

The priest took a small bottle out of his pocket.

"Won't you have a drop of wine, my child?"

"Thank you, no," Troppmann replied politely, with a slight bow.

Claude addressed him again.

"Do you insist that you are not guilty of the crime for which you've been condemned?"

"I did not strike the blow! (*Je n'ai pas frappé!*)"

"But . . . ?" the warden interjected.

"I did not strike the blow!"

(For some time, as everyone knows, contrary to his former depositions, Troppmann had asserted that he did take the Kink family to the place where they had been butchered, but that they were murdered by his accomplices, that even the injury to his hand was the result of his attempt to save one of the small children. However, he had told more lies during his trial than most criminals had done before him.)

"And do you still assert that you had accomplices?"

"Yes."

"You can't name them, can you?"

"I can't and I won't. I won't." Troppmann raised his voice, and his face became flushed. It seemed as though he were getting angry.

"Oh, all right, all right," Claude responded hurriedly, as though implying that he had put his questions only as a formality and that something else had to be done now. . . .

Troppmann had to undress.

Two guards went up to him and began taking off his prison straitjacket (*camisole de force*), a kind of blouse made of coarse bluish cloth that had belts and buckles in back and long, sewn-up sleeves, the ends of which had strong pieces of tape attached to the waist and the thighs. Troppmann stood sideways, within two feet of me. Nothing prevented me from closely scrutinizing his face. It could have been described as handsome except for the unpleasantly full lips, which made his mouth protrude a little too much and turn upward, funnel-like, similar to an animal's, and for the two rows of bad, sparse teeth fanned behind his lips. He had thick, slightly wavy dark hair, full eyebrows, expressive, bulging eyes, a broad, clear forehead, a regular, slightly aquiline nose, and little curls of dark down on his chin. . . . If you had happened to meet such a man outside the prison and not in such surroundings, he would doubtlessly have made a good impression on you. Hundreds of such faces could be seen among young factory workers, pupils in public institutions, etc. Troppmann was of medium height, and had a youthfully thin, slender build. He looked to me like an overgrown boy, and, indeed, he was not yet twenty. He had a natural, healthy, slightly rosy complexion; he did not turn pale even upon our entrance. . . .

There could be no doubt that he really had slept all night. He did not raise his eyes, and his breathing was regular and deep, like a man walking up a steep hill. He shook his hair once or twice, as though wishing to dismiss a troublesome thought, tossed back his head, threw a quick glance at the ceiling, and heaved a hardly perceptible sigh. With the exception of those almost instantaneous movements, nothing in him disclosed—I won't say fear, but even agitation or anxiety. We were all much paler and more agitated than he, I am sure. When his hands were released from the sewn-up sleeves of the straitjacket, he held this straitjacket up in front of him, by his chest, with a pleased smile while it was being undone at the back; little children behave like that when they are being undressed. Then he took his shirt off himself, put on another clean one, and carefully buttoned the neckband. . . . It was strange to see the free, sweeping movements of that naked body, to see those bare limbs against the yellowish background of the prison wall. . . .

Next he bent down and put on his boots, knocking the heels and soles loudly against the floor and the wall to make sure his feet got into them properly. He did all this cheerfully, without any sign of constraint—almost joyfully, as though he had just been invited to go for a walk. He was silent—and we were silent. We merely exchanged glances, unintentionally shrugging our shoulders in surprise. We were all struck by the simplicity of his movements, a simplicity which, like any other calm and natural manifestation of life, amounted almost to elegance. One member of our group, who met me by accident later that day, told me that all during our stay in Troppmann's cell he had kept imagining that it was not 1870 but 1794, that we were not ordinary citizens but Jacobins, and that we were taking to his execution not a common murderer but a marquis legitimist, *un ci-devant, un talon rouge, monsieur!*

It has been observed that when people sentenced to death have their sentences read to them, they either lapse into complete insensibility and, as it were, die and decompose beforehand, or show off and brazen it out, or else surrender themselves to despair, weeping, trembling, and begging for mercy.... Troppmann did not fall into any of these categories—and that was why he puzzled even Claude himself.

Let me say, by the way, that if Troppmann had begun to howl and weep, my nerves would certainly not have withstood it and I would have run away. But at the sight of that composure, that simplicity and seeming modesty, all the feelings in me—the feelings of disgust for a pitiless murderer, a monster who cut the throats of little children while they were crying *Maman! Maman!*, the feeling of compassion in the end for a man whom death was about to swallow up—disappeared and dissolved in a feeling of astonishment. What was sustaining Troppmann? Was it the fact that, although he did not show off, he did "cut a figure" before *spectators,* giving us his last performance? Or was it innate fearlessness or vanity aroused by Claude's words, the pride of the struggle that had to be waged to the end—or something else, some as yet undivined feeling? ... He took that secret to the grave with him. Some people are still convinced that Troppmann was not in his right mind. (I mentioned earlier the lawyer in the white hat, whom, incidentally, I never saw again.) The pointlessness—one might almost say the absurdity—of the annihilation of the entire Kink family serves to confirm that point of view to a certain extent.

IX

But presently he finished with his boots, straightened up, and shook himself—ready! They put the prison jacket on him *again.* Claude asked us to go out and leave Troppmann alone with the priest. We had to wait in the corridor for less than two minutes before his small figure appeared among us, his head fearlessly held high. His religious feelings were not very strong, and he probably carried out the last rite of confession, conducted by the priest to absolve his sins, merely as a formality. All of our group, with Troppmann in the center, immediately went up the narrow spiral staircase we had descended a quarter of an hour before, and—disappeared in pitch darkness: the night-light on the staircase had gone out. It was an awful moment. We all rushed upstairs: we could hear the rapid, harsh clatter of our feet on the iron steps; we trod on one another's heels; we bumped against one another's shoulders; one of us had his hat knocked off. Someone behind me angrily shouted: "*Mais sacré-dieu!* Light a candle! Let's have some light!" And there among us, together with us in the pitch darkness, was our victim, our prey, that unfortunate man—and which of those who were pushing and scrambling upstairs was he? Would it not occur to him to take advantage of the darkness and, given all his agility and the determination of despair, to escape—where? Anywhere—to some remote corner of the prison—and just smash his head against a wall there! At least he would have killed himself. . . .

I do not know whether these "apprehensions" occurred to anyone else. . . . But they appeared to be unfounded. Our whole group, with the small figure in the middle, emerged from the inner recess of the staircase into the corridor. Troppmann evidently belonged to the guillotine—and the procession set off toward it.

X

This procession could be called a flight. Troppmann walked in front of us with quick, resilient, almost bounding steps; he was obviously in a hurry, and we all hurried after him. Some of us, anxious to have a look at his face once more, even ran ahead to the right and left of him. So we rushed across the corridor and ran down the other staircase, Troppmann jumping two steps at a time, hastened across another corridor, leaped over a few steps, and finally found ourselves in the high-ceilinged room with the stool I have mentioned, on which "the toilette of the condemned man" was to be completed.

We entered through one door, and the executioner appeared in the other door, walking solemnly, wearing a white tie and a black "suit," looking for all the world like a diplomat or a Protestant pastor. He was followed by a short, fat old man in a black coat, his first assistant, the hangman of Beauvais. The old man held a small leather bag in his hand. Troppmann stopped at the stool. Everyone took up a position around him. The executioner and his old assistant stood to the right of him, the warden and Claude to the left. The old man unlocked the bag, took out a few white rawhide straps, some of them long, some short, and kneeling down behind Troppmann with difficulty, began to hobble his legs. Troppmann accidentally stepped on the end of one of these straps, and the old man, trying to pull it out, muttered twice, *"Pardon, monsieur,"* and at last touched Troppmann on the calf of the leg. Troppmann instantly turned around and, with his customary polite half-bow, raised his foot and freed the strap.

Meanwhile, the priest was softly reading prayers in French out of a small book. Two other assistants came up, quickly removed Troppmann's jacket, tied his hands behind him, and began to tie the straps around his whole body. The chief executioner gave orders, pointing here and there with a finger. It seemed that there were not enough holes in the straps for the tongues to go through—no doubt the man who made the holes had had a fatter man in mind. The old man first searched in his bag, then fumbled around in all his pockets, and having felt everything carefully, finally pulled out of one of them a small, crooked awl, with which he painfully began to bore holes in the straps; his clumsy fingers, swollen with gout, obeyed him poorly, and besides, the hide was new and thick. He would make a hole, try it out—the tongue would not go through; he had to bore a little more. The priest evidently realized that things were not as they should be, and glancing stealthily once or twice over his shoulder, began to draw out the words of the prayers so as to give the old man time to get things right. Eventually the operation, during which I was covered with cold sweat, I frankly confess, ended, and all the tongues were inserted where required.

But then another one started. Troppmann was asked to sit down on the stool before which he was standing, and the same gouty old man began cutting his hair. He took out a pair of small scissors and, curling his lips, carefully cut off the collar of Troppmann's shirt first, the shirt he had just put on and from which it would have been so easy to tear off the collar beforehand. But the cloth was coarse and tightly pleated, and it resisted the none-too-sharp blades. The chief executioner had a look and was dissatisfied: the space left by the severed piece was not big enough. He indicated with his hand how much more he wanted cut off, and the gouty old man set to work again cutting off another big piece of cloth.

The top of the back was uncovered—the shoulder blades became visible. Troppmann twitched them slightly; it was cold in the room. Then the old man started on the hair. Putting his puffy left hand on Troppmann's head, which promptly bent over obediently, he began cutting the hair with his right. Thick strands of wiry, dark-brown hair slid down the shoulders and fell onto the floor; one of them rolled right up to my boot. Troppmann kept his head bent in his continually obedient manner; the priest dragged out the words of the prayers even more slowly. I could not take my eyes off those hands, once stained with innocent blood but now lying so helplessly one on top of the other—and above all, that slender, youthful neck.... In my imagination, I could not help seeing a line cut straight across it.... There, I thought, a five-hundred-pound axe would pass in a few moments, smashing the vertebrae, cutting through the veins and muscles, and yet the body did not seem to expect anything of the kind: it was so smooth, so white, so healthy....

I could not help asking myself what that ever-so-obediently bent head was thinking about at that moment. Was it holding on stubbornly—as the saying goes, with clenched teeth—to one and the same thought: "I won't break down"? Were all sorts of memories of the past, probably quite unimportant ones, flashing through it at that moment? Was the memory of the face of one of the members of the Kink family, twisted in the agony of death, passing through it? Or was it—that head—simply trying not to think, merely repeating to itself, "That's nothing, that doesn't matter, we shall see, we shall see..."? And would it go on repeating this until death came crashing down upon it—and there would be nowhere to recoil from it?...

The little old man kept on cutting and cutting.... The hair crunched as it was caught up by the scissors.... At last this operation, too, came to an end. Troppmann stood up quickly, shook his head.... Ordinarily, the condemned prisoners who are still able to speak address the warden of the prison at this point with a last request, remind him of any money or debts they may be leaving behind, thank their guards, ask that a last note or a strand of hair be sent to their relatives, convey their regards for the last time—but Troppmann was evidently not an ordinary prisoner: he scorned such "sentimentalities" and did not utter a single word—he remained silent. He waited. A short tunic was thrown over his shoulders. The executioner grasped his elbow....

"Look here, Troppmann (*Voyons, Troppmann*)," Claude's voice resounded in the deathlike stillness, "soon, in another minute, everything will be at an end. Do you still persist in claiming that you had accomplices?"

"Yes, sir, I do persist (*Oui, monsieur, je persiste*)," Troppmann answered in the same pleasant, firm baritone voice, and he bent forward slightly, as though courteously apologizing and even regretting that he could not answer otherwise.

"*Eh bien! Allons!*" cried Claude, and we all set off. We went out into the large prison courtyard.

XI

It was five to seven, but the sky had barely grown any lighter, and the same dismal mist covered everything, concealing the contours of every object. The roar of the crowd encompassed us in an unbroken, earsplitting, thunderous wave as soon as we stepped across the threshold. Our little group, which had become thinner—for some of us had lagged behind, and I, too, although walking with the others, kept myself a little apart—moved rapidly over the cobbled pavement of the courtyard straight to the gates. Troppmann minced along nimbly, his shackles interfering with his stride. How small he looked to me then—almost like a child! Suddenly the two halves of the gates, like the immense mouth of some animal, slowly opened up before us—and all at once, seemingly accompanied by the enormous roar of the overjoyed crowd that had finally caught sight of what it had been waiting for, the monster of the guillotine stared at us with its two narrow black beams and its suspended axe.

I suddenly became cold, so cold that I almost felt sick; it seemed to me that this cold also rushed into the courtyard toward us through those gates; my legs gave way under me. However, I managed to cast another glance at Troppmann. He unexpectedly recoiled, tossing back his head and bending his knees, as though someone had hit him in the chest. "He's going to faint," someone whispered in my ear. . . . But he recovered himself immediately and proceeded forward with a firm step. Those of us who wanted to see how his head would roll off rushed past him into the street. . . . I did not have enough courage for that, and I stopped at the gates with a sinking heart. . . .

I saw the executioner rise suddenly like a black tower on the left side of the guillotine platform; I saw Troppmann, separated from the huddle of people below, scramble up the steps (there were ten of them—as many as ten!); I saw him stop and turn around; I heard him say: "*Dites à Monsieur Claude.* . . . "*; I saw him appear up above as two men pounced on him from the right and the left, like spiders on a fly; I saw him suddenly fall forward, his heels kicking. . . .

But at this point I turned away and began to wait, the ground slowly rising and falling under my feet. . . . And it seemed to me that I was waiting for a terribly long time.† I managed to notice that at Troppmann's appearance the roar of the crowd abruptly seemed to wind itself up—and a breathless hush fell over everything. . . . A sentry, a young red-cheeked fellow, was standing in front of me. . . . I had time to see him looking at me intently with perplexity and horror. . . . I even had time to think that this soldier probably hailed from some godforsaken village, probably came from a decent, law-abiding family, and—and the things he had to see now! At last I heard a light knock of wood on wood—that was the sound made by the top part of the yoke, with its slit for the passage of the knife, as it fell around the murderer's head and held it immobile. . . . Then something suddenly descended with a hollow growl and stopped with an abrupt thud . . . just as though a huge animal had retched. . . . I cannot think of any better comparison. I felt dizzy. Everything swam before my eyes. . . .

Someone seized me by the arm. I looked up; it was Claude's assistant, J——, whom my friend Du Camp, as I learned afterward, had asked to keep an eye on me.

"You are very pale," he remarked with a smile. "Would you like a drink of water?"

But I thanked him and went back to the prison courtyard, which seemed to me like a place of refuge from the horrors on the other side of the gates.

XII

Our group assembled in the guardhouse by the gates to say goodbye to the warden and wait for the crowds to disperse. I went in there

---

* I did not hear the rest of the sentence. His last words were: "*Dites à Monsieur Claude que je persiste,*" that is to say, tell Claude that I persist in claiming that I had accomplices. Troppmann did not want to deprive himself of this last pleasure, this last satisfaction—to leave the sting of doubt and reproach in the minds of his judges and the public.

† As a matter of fact, only *twenty* seconds passed between the time Troppmann put his foot on the first step of the guillotine and the moment when his dead body was flung into the prepared basket.

as well, and learned that, while lying on the plank, Troppmann
had suddenly thrown his head convulsively to the side, so that it
did not fit into the semicircular hole. The executioners were forced
to drag it there by the hair, and while they were doing so,
Troppmann bit the finger of one of them—the chief one. I also
heard that immediately after the execution, as the body, which had
been thrown into the van, was rapidly being taken away, two men
took advantage of the first moments of unavoidable confusion to
force their way through the lines of soldiers, and crawling under
the guillotine, they began wetting their handkerchiefs in the blood
that had dripped through the chinks of the planks. . . .

But I listened to that entire conversation as though in a dream.
I felt very tired—and I was not the only one to feel like that. They
all looked tired, although they all obviously felt relieved, as if a
load had been removed from their shoulders. But not one of us,
*absolutely no one looked like a man who realized that he had been
present at the performance of an act of social justice.* Everyone tried
to turn away in spirit and, as it were, shake off the responsibility
for this murder.

Du Camp and I said goodbye to the warden and went home. A
whole stream of human beings—men, women, and children—rolled
past us in disorderly, untidy waves. Almost all of them were silent;
only the laborers occasionally shouted to one another: "Where are
you off to? And you?" and the street urchins whistled at the "co-
quettes" who rode past. What drunken, morose, sleepy faces! What
looks of boredom, fatigue, dissatisfaction, disappointment—listless,
mindless disappointment! I did not see many drunks, though: they
had either already been picked up or had quieted down by themselves. The workaday life was receiving all these people into its
bosom once more—and why, for the sake of what sensations, had
they left its rut for a few hours? It is awful to contemplate what
is hidden there. . . .

About two hundred feet from the prison we hailed a cab, got
into it, and rode off.

On the way, Du Camp and I discussed what we had seen, about
which he had recently (in the January issue of *Revue des Deux
Mondes* previously quoted by me) said so many weighty, sensible
things. We spoke of the unnecessary, senseless barbarism of that
entire medieval procedure, thanks to which the criminal's agony
continued for half an hour (from twenty-eight minutes past six to
seven o'clock), of the hideousness of all those undressings, dress-

ings, hair-cutting, those journeys along corridors and up and down staircases. . . . By what right was all that done? How could such a shocking routine be allowed? And capital punishment itself—could it possibly be justified? We had seen the impression such a spectacle made on the common people; indeed, there was no trace whatsoever of a so-called instructive spectacle. Barely one-thousandth part of the crowd, no more than fifty or sixty people, could have seen anything in the semidarkness of early morning at a distance of 150 feet through the lines of soldiers and the rumps of the horses. And all the rest? What benefit, however small, could they have derived from that drunken, sleepless, idle, depraved night? I remembered the young laborer who had been shouting senselessly and whose face I had studied for several minutes. Would he start to work today as a man who hated vice and idleness more than before? And what about me? What did I get out of it? A feeling of involuntary astonishment at a murderer, a moral monster, who could show his contempt for death. Can the lawgiver desire such impressions? What "moral purpose" can one possibly allege after so many refutations, confirmed by experience?

But I am not going to indulge in arguments—they would lead me too far afield. And besides, who is not aware of the fact that the question of capital punishment is one of the most urgent questions that humanity has to solve at this moment? I will be content and excuse my own misplaced curiosity if my account supplies a few arguments to those who are in favor of the abolition of capital punishment or, at least, the abolition of public executions.

Weimar, 1870

Letter to M. A. Miliutina.[1]

Paris. 50, Rue de Douai.
Sunday, February 22, 1875.

What a task you've set me, dear Maria Ageevna! I doubt that any other writer has ever received such an assignment. To define my personal world view . . . what's more, in concise form, in a letter?! It would be easy and even natural to treat such a question either negatively or humorously . . . and would be no less natural or accurate to say "the Lord only knows!" But since I don't want to cause your son any trouble (though I confess frankly that I can't help but be amazed at the strange assignments the students of the Katkov Lycée are given), I'll say, in brief, that I'm predominantly a realist—and that more than anything else I'm interested in the living truth of human physiognomy; I'm indifferent to the supernatural, I don't believe in any absolutes or systems, more than anything else I love freedom—and, as far as I can tell, I'm receptive to poetry. Everything human is dear to me. Slavophilism is alien, just as is any orthodoxy. I think that I've said enough—and in essence, this is all just words. I don't know how to tell you anything more about myself.

I'll be very interested to read your son's composition on this topic.

Thank you for the news about yourself. We had our share of alarms and troubles, too, but apparently everything is back to normal now, *which is the best thing of all*. Oh, the blessed charm of uniformity and the similarity of today and yesterday! I thoroughly enjoy that charm. My gout is leaving me alone—for the time being; all my loved ones here are well, including the newly arrived little girl (my dear Claudie's daughter, Mme. Viardot's granddaughter)—so there's nothing more that one could wish for; to my great pleasure, I'm not working either.

I'm glad that Antokolskii has undertaken a statue of Pushkin, and I'm not surprised that the bust of your husband wasn't a success: portraits aren't in his line.

Apropos of portraits: the painter Kharlamov has done remarkable portraits of the Viardots—and now he's doing mine.

Give my cordial regards to all your loved ones and accept the assurance of the sincere attachment of

Your devoted Iv. Turgenev.

1. Maria Ageevna Miliutina, née Abaza (1834-1903), wife of Nikolai Alekseevich Miliutin.

Letter to V. L. Kign.[1]

Village of Spasskoe-Lutovinovo.
(Orel Province, City of Mtsensk.)
Wednesday, June 16, 1876.

I received your letter here, Vladimir Ludvigovich: it was forwarded to me by the editorial office of *The Messenger of Europe*. I regret that I didn't read your piece in *The Week*. I could have judged about your talents *de visu*. But people such as Skabichevskii and G. Uspenskii aren't about to talk nonsense: you can believe them. But you've set me a difficult task: how can I tell you in a short letter how I work, and how one ought to work in general, and what objective writing is, which you even go so far as to call epic! The figurative language in your Balzac quotation is not as murky as you suppose: he simply meant that it is sometimes amusing to think up a plot because a certain play of the imagination goes on there—but bringing it to fruition, getting it all down on paper, is difficult and bothersome. As for the question of whether there's objectivity in your talent, here's what I have to say: if the study of human physiognomy, of other people's lives, interests you *more* than the exposition of your own feelings and ideas; if, for example, you find it more pleasant to convey accurately and faithfully the external appearance not only of a person, but of a simple thing, than to express eloquently and passionately what you experience at the sight of that person or thing—then that means you are an objective writer and can take up a tale or a novel.

As for work, without it, without painstaking work, any writer or artist definitely remains a dilettante; there's no point in waiting for so-called blissful moments, for inspiration; if it comes, so much the better—but you keep working anyway. And you must not only work on your own piece, so that it expresses exactly what you wanted to express and exactly in the same way and form that you wanted; in addition, you must read and study ceaselessly. Try to penetrate everything around you, try to grasp life not only in all of its manifestations—but to understand it, to understand the laws that guide it and don't always come to the surface; you must go beyond the game of chance happenings to achieve types—and with all of that, remain ever-faithful to the truth, not be satisfied with superficial study, shun effects and deceitfulness. The objective writer takes a great burden upon himself: his muscles must be firm.

---

1. Vladimir Ludvigovich Kign (1856-1908), minor writer.

That's the way I used to work—even then, not always; now I've gotten lazy—and old.

Look at what a storm I've talked up—and in the final analysis, there's only one conclusion: if you have an objective talent, you have it. If you don't—you can't procure it. But in order to find out whether you have it, you need to put yourself to the test; then you'll be able to tell.

I wish you, my "literary grandson," all possible success and remain

Always at your service,
Iv. Turgenev.

Autobiography

Ivan Sergeevich Turgenev was born October 28, 1818, in the town of Orel, the son of Sergei Nikolaevich Turgenev and Varvara Petrovna Lutovinova. He was the second of three children; the oldest of them, Nikolai, is alive to this day; the youngest, Sergei, died at the age of sixteen. Ivan Sergeevich's father served in the Elisavetgradskii cuirassier regiment quartered in Orel. Retiring with the rank of colonel, he settled on his wife's estate, Spasskoe-Lutovinova, located ten versts from the town of Mtsensk, in the province of Orel. In 1822, he made a trip abroad with his entire family and their servants in two carriages plus a closed wagon— during the course of which I.S. nearly perished in the Swiss town of Bern. He had fallen through the railing surrounding a hole in which the town bears were kept, and his father barely managed to grab him by the leg.

Upon their return to Spasskoe, the Turgenev family took up the typical estate life—that gentrified, slow, broad, shallow life, the very memory of which has already been virtually effaced among the current generation—with the usual assemblage of governesses and tutors from Switzerland and Germany, as well as local domestic servants and peasant cooks.

At the beginning of 1827, the Turgenev family moved to Moscow, where they bought a house on the Samoteka, and in 1833, I.S., at the age of only fifteen, entered Moscow University in the department of "philology," as it was called at that time. Among his former teachers, I.S. recalls with gratitude D. N. Dubenskii, his Russian language teacher, P. N. Pogorelskii, his mathematics teacher, and I. P. Kliushnikov, then a rather famous writer who signed his verses with the letter "F." I.S. did not remain at Moscow University for long—only a year. He attended the lectures of Professors Pogodin and Pavlov, who was a follower of Schelling's philosophy, having studied physics by means of it, and in addition, old Pobedonostsev, who drilled students on Lomonosov's laudatory odes and forced them to employ "Greek rhetoric."

In 1834, I.S.'s father transferred him to Petersburg University so that he could share an apartment with his elder brother, who had entered the Gvardeiskii artillery corps. His father died that year. I.S. left the university in 1837, having received his degree, and, in 1838, he set out to complete his education in Berlin on the steamship *Nikolai I*, which caught fire in sight of the *Travemunda*. The quantity of knowledge he obtained at Petersburg University was not great: of all his professors, only P. A. Pletnev had any effect on his listeners. In Berlin, I.S. studied primarily Hegelian philosophy (with Werder), philology, and history. At that time, the University of Berlin could pride itself on the presence of Böch, Zumpt, Rank, Ritter, Hans, and many others. I.S. spent two semesters in Berlin; Granovskii and Stankevich attended lectures with him.

In 1840, after a brief stay in Russia and a trip to Italy, he returned to Berlin and remained there for about another year, sharing an apartment with the famous M. A. Bakunin, who was not engaged in political activity at that time. In 1841, he returned to Russia and began to work in the offices of the Ministry of the Interior under the direction of V. I. Dal. He performed quite carelessly and ineffectually, and he retired in 1843. In that same year, he embarked upon a literary career, publishing a short narrative poem, "Parasha," without leaving his estate, however, and he became acquainted with Belinskii. In the course of the next two years, he continued to write verses and even narrative poems, which neither received nor deserved any approbation.

Going abroad at the end of 1846, he decided either to cease altogether or to alter his sphere of activity; the success of a short sketch in prose entitled "Khor and Kalinych," which he had submitted to the editors of the recently revived journal *The Contemporary*, restored him to literary labors. He has not paused since then—and last year the fifth edition of his collected works appeared. An insignificant interruption of these labors occurred only in 1852, when, because of the publication of his article on the death of Gogol—or, more precisely speaking, as a result of the appearance of a separate edition of *A Sportsman's Sketches*—I.S. was imprisoned for a month in a police station, and then sent to live on his estate, from which he departed only in 1854. Since 1861, I.S. has lived for the most part abroad.

Letter to Ia. P. Polonskii.[1]

50, Rue de Douai.

Paris.

Thursday, Apr. 7, 1877.

Dear Iakov Petrovich:

Your poem, in which there are remarkable lines such as, for instance:

The damp haze of the whining night
Looks in through the window and floods the eyes.

produced a profound melancholy in me, so you might understand why I'm copying out a few lines from my diary for you: "*March* 5/17. *Midnight.* I'm sitting at my desk again; downstairs my poor friend is singing something in her quite cracked voice; and in my soul it's darker than a dark night. . . . It's as if the grave were hurrying to devour me: the days fly past like some mere moment, empty, aimless, colorless. You look: and it's time to flop into bed again. I have neither the right nor the urge to live; there's nothing more to do, nothing to expect, or even to desire. . . . "

I won't copy out any more: it's already melancholy enough. You forget that I'm fifty-eight, and she's fifty-five; not only can she not sing—but for the opening of the theater that you describe so eloquently, she, the singer who once upon a time created the role of Fidès in *Prophète*, wasn't even sent tickets: what would be the point? After all, there's been nothing to expect from her for a long time now. . . . And you speak of the "rays of fame" and "the charms of song. . . . " My friend, we're both two fragments of a vessel long since shattered. I, at least, feel like a retired chamber pot. . . .

You can now understand how your verses affected me. (I beg you, however, to destroy this letter.)

There's only one good thing in all of this, though you don't write anything about it: your awful illness has probably passed—and you're left with just your old complaints, which are truer than friends and don't abandon people.

The proximity of war doesn't help me to feel especially cheerful either. But we'll discuss all this in person shortly. We'll see each other in two weeks—since I'm leaving here soon—and until then I embrace you heartily and remain

Your devoted Iv. Turgenev.

1. Iakov Petrovich Polonskii (1819–98), minor poet.

The Dream

I was living with my mother at that time in a little seaside town. I was seventeen; my mother was almost thirty-five—she'd gotten married when she was very young. I was only seven years old when my father died, but I remember him quite well. My mother was a blond, fairly short woman with a charming but sad face, a quiet, languid voice, and restrained gestures. She'd been praised for her beauty in her youth, and remained lovely and appealing to the end of her days. I've never seen deeper, more tender, more mournful eyes, or finer, softer hair; I've never seen more elegant hands. I adored her, and she loved me. . . . But our existence wasn't a cheerful one—some hidden, hopeless, undeserved sorrow seemed to be constantly gnawing at the very roots of her being. This sorrow couldn't simply be attributed to the loss of my father, as great as that loss was to her, as passionately as my mother had loved him, and as devoutly as she cherished his memory. . . . No! Something else was hidden inside her, something I didn't understand but something I felt, dimly yet intensely, whenever I looked at those gentle, immobile eyes, at those beautiful, equally immobile lips, which, without being compressed in bitterness, were seemingly set in the same expression forever.

I've said that my mother loved me—but there were moments when she drove me away, when she found my presence unbearably oppressive. At such times, she seemingly felt an involuntary aversion to me—and was horrified afterward, tearfully reproached herself, and pressed me to her heart. I used to ascribe these momentary fits of antagonism to the deterioration of her health, to her unhappiness. . . . In fact, these antagonistic feelings might have been evoked to some extent by strange outbursts of malevolent, criminal impulses that periodically arose in me, although I myself couldn't comprehend them. . . . But these outbursts never coincided with those moments of aversion.

My mother always wore black, as though she were in mourning. We lived in fairly comfortable circumstances, but we socialized with almost no one.

II

My mother concentrated her every thought and care upon me. Her life was wrapped up in mine. That type of relationship between parents and children isn't always good for the children . . . it's more likely to be harmful to them. Besides, I was my mother's only son . . . and only children generally grow up in an abnormal way. In bringing them up, the parents think about themselves as much as they do about the children. . . . That's not the issue, though. I was neither spoiled nor embittered (one or the other often happens to only children), but my nerves were strained for a while. In addition, taking after my mother, whom I closely resembled in appearance, I didn't enjoy very good health. I avoided the companionship of boys my own age; I avoided people in general; I even spoke to my mother fairly little. Above all, I liked to read, to go on solitary walks—and to daydream, to daydream! It'd be hard to say what my daydreams were about: sometimes I seemed to be standing in front of a half-open door, beyond which lay untold mysteries. I seemed to stand there and wait, enthralled, without stepping over the threshold, continually pondering what lay beyond, and would go on waiting until I grew unconscious . . . or fell asleep. If there had been a vein of poetry in me, I probably would have started to write verses; if I'd had an inclination toward piety, maybe I'd have entered a monastery. But I had no tendencies of these sorts—and I continued to daydream . . . and to wait.

III

I've just mentioned that sometimes I used to fall asleep under the influence of vague thoughts and daydreams. I generally slept quite a bit, and the dreams I had while I was asleep played an important role in my life. I dreamed almost every night. I didn't forget my dreams—I attributed significance to them, I considered them portents, and tried to divine their concealed meaning. Some of them recurred from time to time, which always struck me as strange and surprising. I was particularly perplexed by one dream: I dreamed that I was in an old-fashioned town, walking along a narrow, badly paved street that ran between stone houses with multiple stories and pointed roofs. I was looking for my father, who wasn't dead but, for some reason or other, was hiding from us, living in one of those very houses. Then I went through a low, dark gateway, crossed a long courtyard filled with planks and beams, and finally made my way to a little room with two round windows. My father was standing in the middle of that room, wearing a robe and smoking a pipe. He didn't resemble my real father in any way: he was tall and thin, with black hair, an aquiline nose, and sullen, piercing eyes; he appeared to be about forty. He was displeased that I'd found him; I wasn't the least bit happy about encountering him either, and stood stock-still in bewilderment. He turned away slightly, beginning to mutter something while pacing back and forth with short strides. . . . Then he gradually moved farther away, never ceasing to mutter and repeatedly looking back over his shoulder. The room grew larger and became shrouded in fog. . . . I suddenly felt horrified at the idea that I was losing my father again and rushed after him, but I couldn't see him any more; I could only hear his angry muttering, which sounded like a bear growling. . . . My heart sank. I woke up and couldn't fall asleep again for a long while. . . . I thought about this dream all the next day and, of course, couldn't make any sense out of it.

IV

The month of June arrived. The town my mother and I were living in became exceptionally lively around that time. A number of ships were anchored in the harbor; a number of new faces appeared in the streets. I liked to wander along the embankment at such times, past cafés and hotels, staring at the various sailors and other people sitting at small white tables under linen awnings with pewter mugs of beer in front of them.

One day, as I was passing by a certain café, I caught sight of a man who instantly arrested my attention. Dressed in a long, black, loose-fitting coat and a straw hat pulled right down to his eyes, he was sitting perfectly still, his arms folded across his chest. Straggly curls of black hair fell almost to his nose; his thin lips clenched the mouthpiece of a short pipe. This man struck me as so familiar, each feature of his swarthy, bilious face and entire body was etched in my memory so unmistakably, that I couldn't help stopping short in front of him, I couldn't help asking myself, "Who is that man? Where have I seen him before?" Probably becoming aware of my intense stare, he raised his black, piercing eyes to look at me. . . . I instinctively gasped. . . .

This man was the father I'd been searching for, the father I'd seen in my dream!

There was no possibility of a mistake—the resemblance was too striking. Even the color and style of the very coat that enfolded his gaunt limbs in its lengths resembled the robe my father had worn in my dream.

"Am I asleep now?" I wondered. . . . No. . . . It was daytime, crowds of people were thronging around me, the sun was shining brightly in the blue sky, and this was no phantom—this was a living human being in front of me.

I went up to an empty table, asked for a mug of beer and a newspaper, and sat down a short distance from this mysterious figure.

V

Holding a sheet of the newspaper level with my face, I continued to devour the stranger with my eyes. He barely moved, merely raising his bowed head from time to time. He was obviously expecting someone. I watched without a pause. . . . Sometimes it seemed to me that I must have invented it all, that there really wasn't any resemblance, that I'd succumbed to a semi-involuntary trick of my imagination. . . . But then suddenly *he* would turn in his chair somewhat or raise his hand slightly—and I'd nearly cry out again, I'd see my "nocturnal" father before me once more!

He finally noticed my unwavering attention, and glancing in my direction first with surprise, then with annoyance, he started to get up, and in so doing, knocked over a small cane that he'd rested against the table. I instantly jumped to my feet, picked it up, and handed it to him. My heart was pounding.

He smiled tensely and thanked me, then, drawing his face close to mine, he raised his eyebrows and opened his mouth slightly, as though struck by something.

"You're very polite, young man," he suddenly began in a dry, acerbic, nasal voice. "That's rare nowadays. Let me congratulate you—you've been well brought up."

I don't remember precisely how I responded, but a conversation quickly sprang up between us. I learned that he was a fellow

countryman, that he'd recently returned from America, where he'd
spent many years, and that he was going back there shortly. He
called himself a baron . . . I couldn't hear his name clearly. Just
like my "nocturnal" father, he ended every remark with some sort
of indistinct mutter to himself. He wanted to know my last
name. . . . Upon hearing it, he seemed surprised again, asked me
if I'd lived in this town for a long time, and with whom I was
living. I told him that I was living with my mother.

"And your father?"

"My father died a long time ago."

He asked what my mother's first name was and immediately
laughed uneasily, but then apologized, saying that he'd picked up
some American manners, and was rather eccentric in general. He
subsequently inquired where our residence was located. I told him.

VI

The agitation that had overcome me at the beginning of our conversation gradually subsided; I found our encounter rather strange—
that was all. I didn't like the little smile the baron wore on his
face as he interrogated me; I didn't like the expression in his eyes
as he seemed to look right through me with them. . . . There was
something predatory in them, something supercilious . . . something
sinister. I hadn't seen those eyes in my dream. The baron's face
was so strange! It was pallid, fatigued, and young-looking at the
same time—unpleasantly young-looking! My "nocturnal" father
also hadn't had a deep scar that slanted straight across my new
acquaintance's forehead, which I hadn't noticed until I'd moved
closer to him.

I'd barely finished telling the baron the address of the house we
were living in when a tall Arab wrapped in a cloak up to his very
eyes approached him from behind and very gently tapped his
shoulder. The baron turned around, said, "Aha! At last!" and,
after giving me a slight nod, went into the café with the Arab. I
remained under the awning. I wanted to await the baron's return,
not so much to begin another conversation with him (I really didn't
know what to talk to him about), as to reconfirm my first impression. But half an hour passed, an hour passed. . . . The baron
didn't reappear. I went into the café, hurried through all the rooms,
but couldn't see the baron or the Arab anywhere. . . . They must
have both gone out through a back door.

I had a slight headache, so in order to get some fresh air, I walked along the seafront to a large park beyond the town that had been laid out two hundred years earlier. After strolling in the shade of the immense oak and elm trees for a couple of hours, I went back home.

VII

Our maid rushed up to me in great distress as soon as I appeared in the hallway. From the expression on her face, I immediately guessed that something bad had happened in our house during my absence. And, in fact, I learned that a terrible shriek had suddenly resounded in my mother's bedroom an hour prior to my return. The maid who'd run in had found her on the floor in a faint that had lasted for several minutes. My mother had finally regained consciousness, but had needed to lie down on her bed, looking frightened and strange. She hadn't uttered a single word, hadn't answered any questions, had done nothing but continually look around and shudder. The maid had sent the gardener to get a doctor. The doctor had come and prescribed a sedative, but my mother hadn't even wanted to talk to him. The gardener insisted that, a few moments after the shriek had come from my mother's room, he'd seen an unfamiliar man hastily running through the bushes in the garden toward the gate to the street. (We lived in a single-story house with windows that opened onto a largish garden.) The gardener hadn't had time to get a look at the man's face, but had observed that he was thin and was wearing a shallow straw hat and a long, loose coat. . . . The thought, "The baron's clothes!" immediately flashed through my mind. The gardener wouldn't have been able to overtake him, and besides, he'd immediately been called into the house and sent to get the doctor.

I went into my mother's room. She was lying on the bed, whiter than the pillow on which her head was resting. When she recognized me, she smiled faintly and held out her hand to me. I sat down beside her and began to ask her questions. At first, she said no to everything; however, she finally admitted that she'd seen something that had greatly frightened her.

"Did someone come in here?" I asked.

"No," she replied hurriedly, "no one came in. It seemed to me . . . I had a vision. . . ."

She fell silent and hid her face in her hands. I was about to tell her what I'd learned from the gardener and, incidentally, to describe my encounter with the baron . . . but, for some reason, the words died on my lips. I did venture to remark to my mother, however, that visions don't usually appear in the daytime. . . .

"Stop," she whispered. "Please, don't torture me now. You'll find out sometime. . . ."

She fell silent again. Her hands were cold, and her pulse was throbbing rapidly and unevenly. I gave her some medicine and moved slightly to the side in order not to disturb her. She didn't get up the entire day. She lay there, silent and inert, merely heaving a deep sigh now and then and timidly shielding her eyes. Everyone in the house was thoroughly bewildered.

VIII

My mother grew a bit feverish toward evening, and she sent me away. I didn't go to my own room, though—I lay down on the sofa in the next room. I got up every quarter of an hour, tiptoed to the door, and listened. . . . Everything was quiet—but my mother barely slept that night. When I went into her room early the next morning, her face looked hollow and her eyes shone with an unnatural brightness. She got a little better in the course of the day, but the feverishness increased again toward evening. Until then, she'd obstinately remained silent, but all of a sudden, she began to speak in a hurried, broken voice. She wasn't delirious; there was meaning in her words—but no sort of connection among them. Just before midnight, she suddenly raised herself up in bed with a convulsive movement (I was sitting beside her), and in the same hurried voice, repeatedly sipping water from a glass beside her, feebly gesticulating with her hands, and never once looking at me, she began to tell me the story. . . . She kept stopping, making an effort to control herself, and then continuing again. . . . It was all so strange, just as though she were doing everything in a dream, as though she herself weren't there and someone else were either speaking through her lips or forcing her to speak.

IX

"Listen to what I'm going to tell you," she began. "You're not a little boy any more—you ought to know everything. I had a good friend. . . . She married a man she loved with all her heart, and she and her husband were very happy. During the first year of their marriage, they went to the capital together to spend a few weeks there and enjoy themselves. They stayed at a fine hotel and frequently attended parties and the theater. My friend was very pretty—everyone noticed her. Lots of young men paid attention to her, but there was one of them . . . a military officer. He followed her incessantly, and everywhere she went, she saw his black, evil eyes. He'd never been introduced to her and had never spoken to her, he just perpetually stared at her—quite insolently and strangely. All the pleasures of the capital were spoiled by his presence. She persuaded her husband to hasten their departure, and they began to make the preparations necessary for the journey.

"One evening, her husband went out to a club—he'd been invited there by officers of the regiment to which that officer belonged— to play cards. . . . She was left alone for the very first time. Her husband didn't return for a long while. She dismissed her maid and went to bed. . . . All at once, she became very frightened, grow- ing terribly cold and beginning to shiver. She thought that she heard a slight noise on the other side of one wall, like a dog scratching—and she began to look at that wall. A lamp was burning in the corner; all the room's walls were covered with tapestries. . . . Suddenly something moved, rose up, revealed itself. . . . An elon- gated figure all in black emerged straight out of the wall—that awful man with the evil eyes! She wanted to scream, but couldn't. She became completely frozen with terror. He approached her rapidly, like a wild beast, flung something over her head, something stifling, heavy, white. . . . I don't remember what happened then . . . I don't remember! It was like death, like a murder. . . . When that horrible darkness was finally lifted, when I . . . when my friend came to, there was no one in the room. She still didn't have the strength to scream, and didn't for a long time. She did scream, eventually . . . then everything got confused again. . . .

"The next thing she saw was her husband at her side. He'd been detained at the club until two o'clock in the morning. . . . He looked distraught. He began to ask her questions, but she didn't tell him anything. . . . Then she fainted again. . . . I remember, though, that later, when she was alone in the room, she examined the place in the wall. . . . There turned out to be a secret door underneath the tapestry hangings. And her engagement ring had disappeared from her hand. This ring had an unusual design: seven little gold stars alternated with seven little silver stars; it was an old family heir- loom. Her husband asked her what had happened to the ring; she couldn't give him any answer. Her husband assumed that she'd dropped it somehow, and searched everywhere, but couldn't find it. He grew depressed; he decided to go home as soon as possible, and the moment the doctor allowed it, they left the capital. . . . But imagine! On the very day of their departure, they unexpectedly encountered a stretcher being carried along the street. . . . A man who'd just been killed lay on the stretcher with his head cut open—and imagine! This very man was the horrible nocturnal visitor with the evil eyes. . . . He'd been killed over some gambling dispute!

"My friend subsequently went back to the countryside . . . became a mother for the first time . . . and lived with her husband for several more years. He never found out anything—and indeed, what could she have told him? She herself didn't know anything.

"But her former happiness vanished. Gloom was cast over their lives, and that gloom never lifted again. . . . They had no other children, either before or after . . . and that son. . . ."

My mother trembled all over and hid her face in her hands. . . .

"But tell me now," she went on with redoubled energy, "was my friend at fault in any way? What did she have to reproach herself with? She was punished—but didn't she have the right to declare before God Himself that the punishment meted out to her was unjust? Then why is it that she, like a criminal tortured by pangs of conscience, why is it that she's been confronted by such a dreadful shape from the past, after so many years? Macbeth killed Banquo—so it's no wonder that he'd be haunted . . . but I. . . ."

At this point my mother's words became so mixed up that I ceased to comprehend her. . . . I no longer doubted that she was delirious.

X

Anyone could readily envision the tremendous impression my mother's narrative made on me! From her first words on, I guessed that she was talking about herself and not any friend of hers. Her slip of the tongue only confirmed my suspicions. It must be that this really was my father, whom I'd been seeking in my dream, whom I'd seen in broad daylight! He hadn't been killed, as my mother had supposed, but merely wounded. . . . He'd come to see her and then had run away, frightened off by her terror. I suddenly understood everything: the feeling of involuntary aversion to me that periodically arose in my mother, her perpetual sadness, and our secluded life. . . . I remember that my head seemed to start spinning, and I clutched it with both hands, as though to hold it in place. But one idea fastened it down, as it were: I firmly decided that, come what may, I had to find this man again! What for? To what end? I couldn't give myself a clear answer, but finding him . . . finding him—that became a matter of life and death to me! The next morning, my mother finally grew calmer . . . her fever abated . . . she fell asleep. Entrusting her to the care of the servants, I embarked on my quest.

XI

First of all, naturally, I made my way back to the café where I'd met the baron, but no one in the café knew him or had even noticed him; he'd been a random customer. The proprietors had noticed the Arab—his figure was so striking!—but no one knew who he was or where he was staying. Leaving my address at the café in any case, I began to walk along the streets and the embankments by the harbor, then along the boulevards, peering into every public establishment, but I couldn't find anyone resembling the baron or his companion anywhere! . . . Not having caught the baron's last name, I was deprived of the possibility of turning to the police; however, I spoke privately to two or three watchmen—who, I grant, stared at me in bewilderment and didn't completely believe me— and let them know that I'd liberally reward them if they managed to find any trace of the two individuals whose appearance I tried to describe as precisely as possible. After wandering around in this fashion until dinnertime, I returned home exhausted.

My mother had gotten out of bed, but something new, some sort of meditative perplexity that cut me to the heart like a knife, had been added to her usual sadness. I spent the evening with her. We hardly spoke at all; she played solitaire while I looked at her cards in silence. She never made the slightest reference to what she'd told me, or to what had happened the preceding evening. It was as though we'd made a secret pact not to touch on any of these harrowing, strange occurrences. . . . She seemed to be annoyed with herself, to be ashamed of what had involuntarily been wrung from her, even though perhaps she herself didn't altogether remember what she'd said in her semidelirious feverishness, and to be hoping that I'd spare her. . . . Indeed, I did spare her, and she felt it; she avoided my gaze, just as she had the previous day. I couldn't sleep at all that night.

Outside, a fearful storm suddenly arose. The wind howled and blew furiously, the windowpanes banged and rattled, despairing shrieks and groans rent the air, as though something were being torn to shreds overhead and were flying above the quaking houses with a frenzied wail. I finally dozed off just before dawn. . . . Suddenly it seemed to me that someone had come into my room and had called my name, speaking in a quiet yet resolute voice. I raised my head and didn't see anyone, but, strange to say, not only was I not afraid—I was glad. I suddenly became convinced that I'd definitely attain my goal now. I hurriedly got dressed and left the house.

XII

The storm had died down . . . but its final tremors were still perceptible. It was very early—there were no people in the streets. Many spots were strewn with bits of chimneys, tiles, pieces of demolished fences, and broken branches of trees. . . . "What must have gone on at sea last night!" I couldn't help thinking at the sight of the traces left by the storm. I'd intended to head for the harbor, but my legs, as though obeying some irresistible force, carried me in another direction. Less than ten minutes had passed when I found myself in a part of town I'd never visited until then. I didn't walk fast, but I didn't stop either, proceeding step by step with a strange sensation in my heart. I knew that I was expecting something extraordinary, something inconceivable, and yet I was absolutely certain that this extraordinary phenomenon would occur.

XIII

And then it did occur, this extraordinary phenomenon that I'd expected! Suddenly, twenty feet ahead of me, I saw the very Arab who'd addressed the baron in the café while I was there! Muffled in the same cloak I'd noticed on him then, he seemed to have sprung out of the earth, and having turned his back toward me, he was walking along the narrow pavement of the winding street with rapid strides. I promptly strove to overtake him, but he, too, redoubled his pace, although he didn't look in my direction, and he abruptly made a sharp turn around the corner of a house that jutted out into the street. I ran up to this corner, made the turn around it as quickly as the Arab had. . . . What miracle was this? A long, narrow, perfectly empty street stood before me. The morning fog filled this street with a leaden dullness, but my gaze reached to its very end—I could scan all the buildings on it . . . and not a single living creature was stirring anywhere! The tall Arab in the cloak had vanished as suddenly as he'd appeared! I was bewildered . . .

but only for a moment. Another feeling instantly took hold of me: this street, which stretched out before my eyes, totally mute and seemingly dead, was familiar to me! It was the street in my dream. I was startled; I shivered—the morning was quite cool—and immediately, without the slightest hesitation, with some sort of tremulous conviction, I went forward!

I began to search with my gaze. . . . Yes, here it was: here, on the right, standing at an angle to the street, was the house in my dream; here, too, was the old-fashioned gateway with the stone scrollwork on both sides. . . . It's true, the windows of the house were rectangular, not round . . . but that wasn't important. . . . I knocked on the gate two or three times, more and more loudly. . . . The gate slowly opened with a heavy groan, as though it were yawning. I was confronted by a young servant girl with disheveled hair and sleepy eyes. She'd apparently just woken up.

"Does the baron live here?" I asked, and took in the deep, narrow courtyard with a swift glance. . . . Yes, everything was right . . . there were the planks and boards I'd seen in my dream.

"No," the servant girl replied, "the baron doesn't live here."

"He doesn't? That's impossible!"

"He isn't here now. He left yesterday."

"Where did he go?"

"To America."

"To America!" I involuntarily echoed. "Is he coming back?"

The girl looked at me suspiciously.

"We don't know about that. Maybe he isn't coming back at all."

"Has he been living here for a long time?"

"Not for long—a week. He isn't here now."

"And what was his last name, this baron's?"

The girl stared at me. "You don't know his name? We simply called him the baron. Hey! Petr!" she shouted, noticing that I was intruding into the courtyard. "Come here. There's some stranger here who keeps asking questions."

The clumsy figure of a day laborer came out of the house.

"What is it? What do you want?" he asked in a sleepy voice, and, having listened to me sullenly, repeated what the girl had told me.

"But who does live here?" I inquired.

"Our master."

"And who's he?"

"A carpenter. They're all carpenters on this street."

"Can I see him?"

"You can't right now—he's asleep."

"But can't I go into the house?"

"No. Go away."

"Well, can I see your master later on?"

"Why not? Of course, you can always see him.... He's in business here. Only go away right now. It's so early in the morning, for heaven's sake."

"Well, but what about that Arab?" I asked suddenly.

The laborer looked first at me and then at the servant girl in bewilderment.

"What Arab?" he eventually queried. "Go away, sir. You can come back later. You can discuss it with the master."

I went out into the street. The gate promptly slammed behind me, sharply and heavily, this time without a groan.

I carefully noted the name of the street and the number of the house, and then left—but I didn't go home. I was experiencing something like disillusionment. Everything that had happened to me had been so strange, so extraordinary—and then had all ended so inanely! I'd been certain, I'd been convinced that I'd see the room I knew in that house, and see my father, the baron, in the middle of it, wearing a robe, holding a pipe.... But instead, the owner of the house was a carpenter, I could go and see him as often as I wanted—and probably order furniture from him.

Whereas my father had gone to America! What was left for me to do?... Tell my mother everything, or bury the very memory of that encounter forever? I simply couldn't resign myself to the idea that such a supernatural, mysterious beginning could have such a meaningless, ordinary conclusion!

I didn't want to return home, and I set off aimlessly walking away from town.

XIV

I walked with my head down, without thinking, almost without feeling, utterly withdrawn into myself. A rhythmic, hollow, angry noise aroused me from my torpor. I raised my head: it was the sea, roaring and moaning about fifty feet away from me. I realized that I was walking along the sand dunes. Roiled by the storm of the previous night, the sea was white with foam to the very horizon; the sharp crests of its vast, billowing waves were rolling forward one after another and breaking against the flat shore. I went closer to it, and walked along the line left by the ebb and flow of the tide on the yellow, furrowed sand, which was strewn with strands of trailing seaweed, broken shells, and snakelike ribbons of sea-grass. Gulls with pointed wings, gliding on the wind out of the remote depths of the sky, issued plaintive cries, soared upward, as white as snow against the gray clouds, swooped down abruptly, and flew off again, seeming to leap from wave to wave, disappearing from sight like gleams of silver in the streaks of frothy foam. I noticed that several of them were hovering persistently above one large rock, which stood alone amid the level plane of the sandy shore. Coarse sea-grass grew on one side of the rock in irregular clumps, and something black was visible where its matted tangles rose out of a yellow briny marsh, something that was longish, curved, and not very large.... I began to look intently.... Some dark object was lying there, lying motionless beside the rock.... This object became clearer and more defined the closer I got to it....

A distance of only thirty feet remained between me and the rock....

Why, it was the outline of a human form! It was a corpse; it was a drowned man tossed onto the shore by the sea! I walked right up to the rock.

This corpse was the baron, my father! I stopped short, as though I'd been turned to stone. Only then did I realize that I'd been guided by some unknown forces since early morning, that I was in their power—and for several moments my soul was emptied of everything except the endless crashing of the sea and mute horror at the fate that had overcome me....

XV

He lay on his back, tipped slightly to one side, his left arm bent behind his head ... the right one was twisted beneath his body. The toes of his feet, encased in high sailor's boots, had been sucked into the slimy mud; his short blue jacket, drenched with brine, was still buttoned tightly; a red scarf was tied in a knot around his neck. His swarthy face, turned toward the sky, looked as if it were laughing; his small, close-set teeth were visible under his elevated upper lip; the dim pupils of his half-closed eyes could barely be discerned in his darkened eyeballs; his matted hair, covered with bubbles of foam, spread across the ground, exposing his smooth forehead and the purple line of his scar; his narrow nose rose in a sharp white crest between his sunken cheeks. The previous night's storm had done its work.... He'd never see America! The man who'd humiliated my mother, who'd ruined her life, my father—yes, my father! I could have no doubt of that—lay pathetically outstretched in the mud at my feet. I experienced a gratifying feeling of revenge, as well as pity, revulsion, and above all, horror . . . a double horror— at what I saw and at what had happened. The evil, criminal impulses I mentioned earlier, those incomprehensible bursts of rage, arose within me . . . choking me. "Aha!" I thought. "So that's why I'm the way I am . . . this is how my bloodline expresses itself!"

I stood beside the corpse, staring and waiting. Wouldn't those dead eyes move, wouldn't those stiff lips quiver? No! Everything was still; the sea-grass itself seemed frozen where the breakers had flung it; even the gulls had flown away; there wasn't a single bit of debris anywhere, not a strip of wood or a broken piece of rigging. There was utter desolation on all sides . . . except for the two of us and, in the distance, the pounding sea. I glanced behind me; I saw the same desolation there: a ridge of lifeless hills on the horizon . . . and that was all!

My heart began to revolt against the idea of leaving this unfortunate wretch in this solitude, on the muddy slime of the seashore, to be devoured by fish and birds. An inner voice told me that I ought to find some other people, to summon them, if not to help—what help was possible now?—at least to pick him up, to carry him to some inhabited dwelling. . . . But an indescribable panic suddenly seized me. It seemed to me that this dead man knew I had come, that he himself had planned this final encounter. I even imagined that I heard the indistinct muttering I knew so well. . . . I started to run away . . . I looked back once more. . . . Something shiny caught my eye; it brought me to a halt. It was a gold band on the corpse's hand. . . . I recognized my mother's engagement ring. I remember that I forced myself to turn back, to approach the body, to bend down. . . . I remember the clammy touch of the cold fingers; I remember that I held my breath, half closed my eyes, and gritted my teeth in order to pull off the obstinate ring. . . .

It finally came off . . . and I started running, running away at full speed—and something rushed after me, on my heels, overtaking me.

XVI

Everything I'd been through and felt was probably written across my face when I got home. My mother straightened up abruptly as soon as I came into her room, and looked at me so urgently and inquisitively that, after an unsuccessful attempt to explain, I ended up silently holding the ring out to her. She turned horribly pale; her eyes opened extraordinarily wide and went dead, like *those* eyes. She uttered a faint cry, clasped the ring, reeled, collapsed against my breast, and virtually lost consciousness, her head falling back and her blank, wide-open eyes directed toward me. I put both my arms around her and, standing where I was, without moving, without hurrying, in a subdued voice, I told her everything, not concealing a single detail: my dream, the encounter, and so on and so on. . . . She heard me out to the end without uttering a single word, but her bosom heaved more and more deeply and her eyes suddenly came alive and turned away from me. Then she put the ring on her third finger and, retreating a few steps, began to put on her hat and scarf. I asked her where she intended to go. She glanced at me with surprise and tried to answer, but her voice failed her. She shuddered several times, rubbed her hands as though trying to warm them up, and finally said, "Let's go there right now."

"Where, mother?"

"Where his body is lying. . . . I want to see . . . I want to find out . . . I have to find out. . . ."

I endeavored to persuade her not to go, but she nearly lapsed into a nervous fit. I realized that it was impossible to oppose her wishes, and we set off.

XVII

And so I was walking along the sand again, but I wasn't alone this time—my mother was on my arm. The tide had ebbed, the sea had retreated even farther than before; it was calmer, but its roar, although weaker, was still menacing and ominous. The solitary rock finally appeared ahead of us, as did the sea-grass. I looked carefully, trying to discern that curved object lying on the ground— but I couldn't see anything. We went closer; I instinctively slackened my pace. But where was that black, motionless object? Only the dark clumps of sea-grass lay on the sand, which had dried by now. We went right up to the rock. . . . There was no corpse anywhere—there was just a hollow indentation where it had lain, and one could tell where the arms and legs had been. . . . The sea-grass all around there looked as if it'd been trampled, and the footprints of *one* man were visible. They crossed the dunes and then disappeared when they reached the stony ridge.

My mother and I exchanged glances, and were frightened at what we read in one another's faces. . . .

Surely he hadn't gotten up by himself and walked away?

"Are you sure that he was dead?" she asked in a whisper.

I could only nod my head in assent. Less than three hours had passed since I'd come across the baron's corpse. . . . Someone had discovered it and carried it away. I had to find out who had done this, and what had become of him.

But first I had to take care of my mother.

XVIII

While she'd been walking to the fatal spot, she'd been distraught, but she'd controlled herself. The disappearance of the dead body struck her as the final blow. She fell into a stupor; I feared for her sanity. I got her home with great difficulty. I made her lie down on her bed again; I sent for the doctor again. But as soon as my mother had recovered a bit, she immediately demanded that I set off without delay to find "that man." I obeyed. But, in spite of every possible effort, I couldn't find out anything. I went to the police several times, visited several villages in the vicinity, put several advertisements in the papers, collected information everywhere—and all in vain! In fact, I was informed that the corpse of a drowned man had been picked up in one of the seaside villages. . . . I rushed there immediately, but from all I could gather, the body bore no resemblance to the baron. I found out the name of the ship on which he'd set sail for America. At first, everyone was positive that this ship had sunk in the storm, but a few months later, rumors began to circulate that it'd been seen anchored in New York harbor. Not knowing what other steps to take, I tried to find the Arab I'd seen, offering him a considerable sum of money through the newspapers if he'd come to our house. Some tall Arab in a cloak did actually come once, in my absence. . . . But after questioning the maid, he departed abruptly and never came back again.

Thus all traces of my . . . my father disappeared; he irretrievably vanished into the mute darkness. My mother and I never spoke about him, except for one day, I remember, when she expressed surprise that I'd never told her about my strange dream, and added, "It must mean that he really . . . ," but then didn't complete her thought. My mother was ill for a long time, and even after her recovery, our former close relationship never revived. She felt awkward around me to the very day of her death . . . awkward—that was it precisely. And this is a type of sorrow for which there's no cure. Anything can be smoothed over—memories of even the most tragic family events gradually lose their intensity and bitterness—but if a feeling of awkwardness ever installs itself between two close-knit people, it can never be dislodged!

I never again had the dream that periodically had so distressed me; I no longer "search" for my father. But occasionally it seemed to me—and it seems to me even now—that I hear some distant wailing, some continuous, mournful lamentation, in my dreams; it seems to come from somewhere behind a high wall that can't be surmounted. It wrings my heart, and I weep with closed eyes, never able to tell what it is: is it the moan of a living person, or am I listening to the wild, drawn-out wail of the troubled sea? And then it subsides again into that savage muttering—and I fall asleep with anguish and horror in my soul.

Letter to V. P. Gaevskii.[1]

Moscow.
Prechistensky Boulevard,
Crown Office Building.
Thursday, Apr. 24, 1880.

Dear Viktor Pavlovich,

I haven't been able to write you anything about the Pushkin Commemoration until now because the program wasn't definitely arranged until yesterday. Here it is: on the 25th (the eve of the unveiling) in the morning—an open meeting of the Society of Admirers of Russian Letters, chaired by Iurev, with speeches. The morning of the 26th—the unveiling of the monument, then a grand dinner, chaired by Grot, for men of letters, delegates from the University, and so on, with separate short speeches (and toasts). Speeches will be given only by those people whose names will be on a list compiled by the committee, by which means any *undesirable elements* will be eliminated. Here are the people in Petersburg whom the Committee has invited to give these short speeches: Goncharov, Dostoevsky, Saltykov, Potekhin, Polonskii, Grigorovich, Pypin, Maikov. It goes without saying that, as the president of our Society, you'll receive an invitation, too, just as will universities, learned societies, the editorial committees of journals, and so on. It may be that some of the people mentioned by me won't want to attend and give talks—please try to persuade them (for instance, Goncharov, without whom a Pushkin Commemoration would be incomplete). In this connection we must lay aside all vanity, apprehensions, and extraneous considerations. I even assume that since we can be certain that no discordant voices à la Katkov will be there to hinder us, we ought to banish any thought of a separate Petersburg dinner, which would be like mustard after supper. Talk to Stasiulevich about this. Governor-General Dolgorukov will be among the guests and has promised not only every assistance, but the widest latitude in our speeches as well. The following people from Moscow will speak: Ostrovskii, Pisemskii, I. Aksakov, Bartenev, Tikhonravov, and others. I'll try to persuade Lev Tolstoy, whom I'll be seeing very soon. (I'm going to the country on Tuesday—but I'll be back here by the 23d.) On the 27th, a grand musical and theater evening will be held (the actor

---

1. Viktor Pavlovich Gaevskii (1826–88), literary historian and activist in Russian literary circles.

837

Samarin and N. Rubinstein have undertaken to arrange it)—and
if there's a great demand, it will be repeated on the following day.
It's greatly to be desired that all our literary lights gather together
for the Pushkin Commemoration.

I conclude with a request that concerns you personally, which I
forgot to convey to you during my stay in Petersburg. I have a
good friend in Paris, Mr. Commanville, who owns a large lumber
factory. He concluded a contract with Mr. Sollogub (the son) for
the purchase of large forests in the Caucasus and the delivery of
logs to Le Havre. Up until now everything has been going well:
but since Mr. Sollogub doesn't enjoy too reliable a reputation—Mr.
Commanville, in case of any vacillation, misunderstanding, or failure to deliver, would like to have a lawyer in Russia, *un homme de
loi*, to whom he could entrust the affair. Upon Stasiulevich's advice,
I suggested you to him, since, as it is, you're a lawyer for the
French Embassy. So, if Mr. Commanville should appeal to you for
advice and directions, you may be assured that he's a quite solid
person on whom you may rely, and for whom I can vouch. I hope
that you won't find anything in this that contradicts your interests
or the merits of your position.

Please accept, dear Viktor Pavlovich, the assurance of the complete respect and devotion

Of your Iv. Turgenev.

Speech Delivered at the Dedication of the Monument to A. S. Pushkin in Moscow

Ladies and Gentlemen!

We have assembled to hail the erection of a monument to Pushkin, a monument to which all of educated Russia has contributed, which all of educated Russia supports, and in celebration of which so many of our noblest citizens—representatives of agriculture, government, science, literature, and painting—have gathered. The erection of this monument strikes us as a tribute to the abiding love our society possesses for one of its most deserving members. We shall try to delineate the nature and import of this love in a few words.

Pushkin was the first Russian poet-artist. Art, if one employs this term in the broad sense that includes poetry within its realm, is an act of creation laden with ideals, located at the core of the life of a people, defining the spiritual and moral shape of that life. As such, art constitutes one of the elemental activities of human beings. Inspired and guided by nature itself, art—fine art—is, in fact, a form of imitation, but it takes on a spiritual aspect that identifies it as something distinctively human during the earliest period of a people's existence. The primitive man of the Stone Age who used the tip of a piece of flint to draw a bear's or an elk's head on a smoothed fragment of bone had already ceased to be primitive, had ceased to be an animal. But only when the creative powers of a few select individuals enable a people to achieve recognizably complete, unique expression of its fine art, of its poetry, only then can that people assert its definitive right to its own place in history, only then does it enter into brotherhood with the other peoples who acknowledge it. It is no accident that Greece calls itself the homeland of Homer, Germany the homeland of Goethe, and England the homeland of Shakespeare.

We would not think of denying the importance of artifacts created in religious, political, and other spheres as well to the life of a people—but the special creative powers we have just mentioned give a people its fine art, its poetry. And there is nothing surprising about this: a people's fine art embodies its living, individualized spirit, its thought, its language in the highest sense of the word. When fine art achieves its complete expression, it becomes the property of all humanity, even more than science does, precisely because fine art has a vibrant, human, conscious spirit—an immortal spirit, for it can survive the physical existence of its body, its people. What has been left to us of ancient Greece? Its spirit has been left to us! First religious forms, and then scientific ones, also outlive the peoples among which they have appeared, but these forms do so by virtue of what is general and eternal in them. Poetry, the fine arts—they outlive their peoples by virtue of what is particular and alive in them.

Pushkin was, we repeat, our first poet-artist. A poet who serves as the ultimate testimony to a people's existence unites two fundamental principles: the principle of receptivity and the principle of self-sufficiency—feminine and masculine principles, we dare to add. Among us Russians, who have entered into the circle of the European family later than others, both these elements take on a special coloration. Our receptivity is dual-edged, both for our own life and for the lives of other Western peoples, given all the riches receptivity has yielded and yet the bitter fruits it has periodically borne for us. Our self-sufficiency also assumes a certain peculiar, uneven, sporadic, and therefore sometimes brilliant power as it struggles both with external complications and with its own internal contradictions. Remember Peter the Great, ladies and gentlemen, whose nature is somehow akin to the nature of Pushkin himself. It is no accident that Pushkin nourished a particular feeling of loving gratitude toward him!

The dual-edged receptivity we have just mentioned was notably reflected in the life of our poet: by his birth in a noble family's manor house, by his foreign education in a lycée, and by the influence of the society of that time, which was permeated by principles imported from the outside—those of Voltaire, Byron, and the Great War of 1812; subsequently by his exile to the depths of Russia, his immersion in popular life and popular speech, and the reunion with his famous elderly nurse and her epic tales. . . . As for self-sufficiency, it was awakened early in Pushkin, and fast losing its searching, undefined character, it was transformed early on into a liberated creativity. He was not even eighteen when Batiushkov, having read Pushkin's elegy "The floating bank of clouds is thinning," exclaimed, "Villain! How can he have begun to write this way!"

Batiushkov was right: no one in Russia had ever begun to write *this way*. Perhaps in exclaiming "Villain!" Batiushkov secretly foresaw that a number of his own verses and epigrams would be called Pushkin's one day, even though they had appeared prior to Pushkin's. *"Le génie prend son bien partout où il le trouve,"* as the French proverb goes. Pushkin's self-sufficient genius—if one does not consider a few, insignificant exceptions—freed him from both the imitation of European images and the seductions of a falsely popular tone. For to employ a falsely popular tone—to cultivate popularity in general—is both inappropriate and useless, just as it is inappropriate and useless to submit to foreign authorities, the best proof of which is provided by Pushkin's fairy tales on the one hand, and *Ruslan and Liudmila* on the other, which are, as is well known, the weakest of all his works.

Everyone agrees, of course, as to the inappropriateness of imitating foreign authorities, but some will object, perhaps, that if, in his own labors, a poet does not constantly keep the people in mind and does not constantly make reaching the people an inherent goal, he will never become a poet, and the people, the common people, will never read him. But then again, ladies and gentlemen, what great poet is read by those whom we call the common people? The common German people do not read Goethe, the common French people do not read Molière, even the common English people do not read Shakespeare. The cultivated portions of their nations read these authors. Every work of art is an elevation of life to an ideal; rooted in the soil of mundane, quotidian life, the common people remain below that ideal level. This is a height that must be actively approached.

Nonetheless, Goethe, Molière, and Shakespeare are popular poets in the true meaning of the word, that is, they are national poets. Permit us a comparison: Beethoven and Mozart, for example, are undoubtedly national German classical composers, and their music is fundamentally German classical music. Yet in each of their works you will find not only traces of borrowing from popular music, the

music of the common people, but even of complete coincidence
with it, precisely because this popular, still rudimentary music was
transmitted to them in their flesh and blood; it was brought to life
and ingrained in them, as was the very theory of their art—the
same way the rules of grammar, for example, are ingrained and
then disappear in the living work of a writer. The very label
"popular" becomes meaningless in regard to other realms of fine
art that are even more distant from that quotidian soil, even more
self-contained. Thus there are national painters, such as Raphael
and Rembrandt; there are no popular painters. We shall note,
incidentally, that the ability to introduce an element of popular life
into painting, poetry, or literature is typical only of weak, immature
peoples, or of peoples in an enslaved, oppressed condition. To be
sure, their poetry must serve other, important goals—even the preservation of their very existence. Thank God, Russia does not find
itself in such circumstances; it is not weak or enslaved by another
people. It has no need to tremble for itself and jealously to preserve
its self-sufficiency. In the consciousness of its own strength, Russia
even embraces those who point out its defects.

Let us return to Pushkin. A question: can he be called a national
poet in the sense that Shakespeare, Goethe, and others are called
national poets? We shall leave this answer to be revealed later on.
But there is no doubt that he formulated our poetic, literary language, and that it merely remains for us and our descendants to
follow along the path forged by his genius. From what we have
said, you should have become convinced by now that we do not
share the opinion of those admittedly decent people who affirm
that a contemporary Russian literary language simply does not
exist, and that only the common people, in conjunction with certain
other redemptive entities, will give it to us. We, by contrast, find
all levels of expressivity encompassed within the language formulated by Pushkin; Russian creativity and Russian receptivity
have been gracefully combined in this magnificent language. And
Pushkin himself was a magnificent Russian artist.

Precisely—Russian! The very essence, the very uniqueness of his
poetry coincides with the uniqueness, the essence of our people.
We are not even referring to the manly strength, charm, and clarity
of his language, the unvarnished honesty, the absence of falsity
and artificial phrases, the simplicity, the openness and integrity of
the emotions expressed. All these honorable reflections of the hon-

orable Russian people in Pushkin's works amaze not only us, his compatriots, but those foreigners to whom he has become accessible. The judgments of those foreigners can be valuable—patriotic considerations do not subvert them. Mérimée, for example, the well-known French writer and admirer of Pushkin, without hesitation, virtually in the presence of Victor Hugo himself, called Pushkin the greatest poet of his era. Mérimée said to us one day, "Your poetry seeks truth above all, whereas beauty then appears by itself. Our poets, by contrast, proceed along a completely opposite path. They worry above all about the effect, the wit, the brilliance of their work, and if, in addition to all that, the opportunity to avoid violating verisimilitude presents itself to them, then they will take it into the bargain, if you will. In Pushkin," he added, "poetry blossoms in marvelous fashion, as if on its own, from the very sobriety of prose."

This same Mérimée repeatedly applied to Pushkin the familiar maxim: "*Proprie communia dicere,*" thereby acknowledging Pushkin's ability to transmit common truths in original fashion, which is the very essence of poetry, of that poetry in which the ideal and the real are reconciled. He also compared Pushkin to the ancient Greeks in the symmetry of his forms, in the contents of his images and themes, in the absence of any digressions or moral conclusions. I remember that, after Mérimée had read the final quatrain of "The Upas Tree" one day, he remarked, "No contemporary poet could have refrained from offering some commentary here." Mérimée also praised Pushkin's ability to begin immediately, *in medias res*— "to take the bull by the horns," as the French say—and he pointed to Pushkin's *Don Juan* as an example of such mastery.

Yes, Pushkin was a pivotal artist, someone who was able to approach the very core of Russian life. We must ascribe this ability of his to a mighty power to assimilate foreign forms in an original manner, an ability that foreigners themselves actually concede we possess by their somewhat condescending acknowledgment of our capacity for "accommodation." This capacity gave Pushkin the opportunity to compose the monologue in *The Covetous Knight*, for example, of which Shakespeare might proudly have claimed authorship. Equally amazing in Pushkin's poetic temperament is that special mixture of passion and calm, or, more correctly speaking, that objectivity inherent in his gift, whereby the subjectivity of his personality is expressed solely through an inner intensity and fire.

All this is true. . . . But are we correct to call Pushkin a national poet in the universal sense (these two terms are often synonymous), the way we call Shakespeare, Goethe, and Homer national poets?

Pushkin could not do everything. We must not forget that he had to perform by himself two tasks that are divided among the authors of an entire century and more in other countries: namely, to formulate a language and to establish a literature. Moreover, the cruel fate that pursues our select few artists with a near vicious persistence also bore down upon him. He was not even thirty-seven years old when he was taken from us. It is impossible to read the words he wrote in one of his letters several months before his death without profound sadness, without some secret, albeit pointless, indignation: "My spirit has expanded: I sense that I can create." Create! And the mindless bullet that would put an end to his blossoming creativity had already been cast. Perhaps it had been cast at the same time as that other bullet intended for the murder of that other poet, Pushkin's successor [M. Lermontov], who had begun his notable career with the famous, wrathful poem inspired by the death of his teacher. . . . But we shall not linger over these tragic accidents, the more tragic in that they were accidents. We shall turn away from this darkness toward the light: we shall return to Pushkin's poetry.

There is neither time nor space here to mention his individual works—others can do this better than we can. We shall confine ourselves to mentioning that in his compositions Pushkin left us a multitude of images and character types (still one of the indubitable signs of the gift of genius!), character types that were subsequently perfected in our literature. Merely recall the scene at the tavern in *Boris Godunov*, or "The History of the Village of Goriukhina," and so forth. Do not images such as those of Pimen or the main characters in *The Captain's Daughter* serve as proof that the past lived in him with the same vitality as did the present, as did the future he anticipated?

Pushkin did not escape the normal fate of a poet-artist who attempts to inaugurate a tradition. He endured the cooling of his contemporaries toward him. And the next generation distanced itself from him still further, ceasing to need him or to be educated by him. Only in recent times has a return to his poetry become perceptible. Pushkin himself foresaw this loss of popularity. As is well known, during the final years of his life, at the peak of his creativity, he shared almost nothing with his readers, leaving such works as "The Bronze Horseman" unpublished, sitting in his portfolio. How could he have failed to sense the antagonism of the public, which had learned to see in him some sort of sweet-tongued singer, a kind of nightingale. . . . And how can we blame him, remembering that as intelligent and insightful a person as Baratynskii, who, along with a few others summoned to go through Pushkin's private papers after his death, did not hesitate to exclaim in a letter addressed to an equally intelligent friend: "Can you imagine what most astounds me in all these poems? The abundance of thought! Pushkin—a thinker! Who would have expected it?"

Pushkin foresaw all of this. One famous sonnet ("To The Poet," July 1, 1830) is proof of that, which we beg permission to read before you, although, of course, each of you knows it by heart. . . . But we cannot resist the temptation to decorate our plain, prosaic speech with this poetic gold:

Poet, do not prize the love of the people!
The short-lived sound of ecstatic praise will
pass,
You will hear the judgment of fools and
the laughter of the cold crowd,
But you must remain firm, calm, and aloof.

You are a tsar; live on your own.
Go by the free road wherever your free mind takes
you,
Cultivating the fruits of beloved thoughts,
Not demanding any rewards for noble action.

Those are within you. You yourself are your
highest judge,
You can evaluate your work more severely than
anyone else.
Are you satisfied with it, exacting artist?

Are you satisfied? Then let the crowd attack it,
And spit upon the altar where your flame burns,
And shake your pedestal in childish jealousy.

Pushkin was not altogether correct here, though, especially in relation to the subsequent generation. The causes of this loss of popularity lay neither in "the judgment of fools" nor in "the laughter of the cold crowd." Those causes lay deeper. They are sufficiently well known; we need only mention them to you. They lay in the very fate of our society, in the course of its historical development, in the conditions under which it was newly born, shifting from a literary epoch to a political one. Unanticipated and yet legitimate goals, unprecedented and yet irrefutable demands emerged; questions it was impossible to answer arose.... No one was capable of producing poetry, or any other form of art, at that time. Only first-rate *literateurs*, whom the strong if dark waves of that new life merely flowed past, could *equally* praise *Dead Souls* and "The Bronze Horseman" or "Egyptian Nights." Pushkin's worldview seemed narrow; his burning sympathy for our occasional moments of official glory seemed old-fashioned; his classical feeling for measure and harmony seemed coldly anachronistic. The people abandoned the white marble tomb where the poet was a priest, where, it is true, a single flame still burned—a solitary stick of incense continued to smolder on the altar. They went instead to noisy festivities in order to find novelty, which was precisely what they required . . . and novelty they found. A poet-echo, as Pushkin put it—centripetal, drawn inward, affirmative, reflecting life at peace—was replaced by a poet-herald—centrifugal, drawn outward, negative, reflecting life in motion. Belinskii himself, the first and foremost commentator on Pushkin, was replaced by other critics who little valued poetry. We have pronounced the name Belinskii— and although no one's praise should resound alongside Pushkin's today, perhaps you will permit us to honor the memory of that remarkable individual with a sympathetic word when you learn that fate led him to die precisely on the twenty-sixth of May, the birth- day of the poet who was for him the ultimate embodiment of Russian genius!

Let us return to the development of our idea. After the voice of Lermontov had been cut off so early, when Gogol had already become the ruler of the people's ideas, the voice of "the poet of revenge and sadness" [N. Nekrasov] rang out next, then after him came others—and they led a growing generation after them. Fine art, winning the right of citizenship through Pushkin's works, asserting the indubitability of its existence, employing the language he formulated, began to serve other causes so necessary to social development. Many saw—and see up to this very moment—a simple social decline reflected by this change in the direction of art, but we shall permit ourselves to observe that only something dead can degenerate, only something inorganic can be utterly eradicated.

Something living is always renewed organically—by regeneration. And Russia is regenerating, not degenerating.

To be sure, anything that grows is inevitably attended by illnesses, by torturous crises, by the most baneful and at first glance inescapable contradictions. It is not necessary to prove this, it would seem. Not only history in general but the history of each individual also teaches us this. Science itself tells us about ineluctable diseases. But only old-fashioned or short-sighted people are disturbed by them, only people like that weep for some prior, albeit relative, state of tranquillity and try to return to it—and they try to return others to it as well, even if by force. In a period of a people's life that bears the designation "transitional," the task of a thinking individual, of a sincere citizen of his country, is to go forward, despite the dirt and difficulty of the path, to go forward without losing from view even for a moment those fundamental ideals on which the entire existence of the society to which he belongs is built.

Ten or fifteen years ago, the celebration that drew us all here today would have been welcomed as an act of justice, as a sign of social nobility. But perhaps the feeling of spiritual unity that now transfixes all of us without distinction as to education, occupation, or age would not have existed. We have already noted the happy fact that the youth are once again reading and studying Pushkin, but we must not forget that several generations in a row have gone past—generations for whom the very name of Pushkin was nothing but a mere name among a number of other names doomed to be forgotten. We shall not pause to criticize this generation too much, however; we have tried to explain briefly why this obliviousness was unavoidable. But neither can we fail to rejoice at this return to poetry.

We particularly rejoice at it because our youth are returning to it not as penitents who, having been disappointed in their hopes and overwhelmed by their own mistakes, seek shelter and calm in that which they had previously rejected. Instead, we see in this return a symptom of at least some authentic pleasure. We see evidence that at least a few of their goals—on behalf of which it was deemed not only permissible but even obligatory to reject everything not related to sacrifice, everything not facilitating the channeling of energy in a single direction—have clearly been achieved, and that the future promises the achievement of others.

Therefore, nothing any longer prevents poetry, the preeminent exemplars of which Pushkin provided, from assuming its rightful place among the other rightful institutions of social life. There was a time when belles lettres served as virtually the sole expression of that life. Then came a time when poetry completely left the stage. . . . The former realm was too broad for it, whereas the latter was narrow to the point of annihilation. But, having found its natural boundaries, poetry has become forever strong. Under the influence of an old but not yet outmoded teacher—we firmly believe this—the realm of art, the artistic enterprise itself, will stride forth again in all its might, and—who knows? Perhaps a new, still unknown, select individual will surpass his teacher and will completely deserve the label of national-universal poet that we do not permit ourselves to bestow upon Pushkin, although we do not dare to deprive him of it, either.

Be that as it may, Pushkin's service to Russia has been great, meriting national recognition. He gave definitive shape to our language, which is acknowledged even by foreign philologists to be second only to Greek in its richness, power, logic, and beauty of form. He summoned up representative images and immortal sounds to last the entire course of Russian life. Above all, his mighty hand raised high the banner of poetry throughout the Russian lands for the first time. And if the dust of battle stirred up after him darkened that bright banner for a time, now, when this dust has begun to settle, the victorious banner he raised is shining on high once again.

Shine, then, like this noble bronze face erected in the very heart of the ancient capital, and speak to the coming generation about its right to be called a great people because amid that people there was born, among a series of great men, *such* a great man! And as was said of Shakespeare—that every person who has newly learned to read inevitably becomes his new reader—we likewise hope that each of our descendants, pausing with love before the sculptured image of Pushkin and recalling the significance of this love, will prove through the conduct of his own life that he, like Pushkin, has become more Russian, will prove that he has become a more educated, more liberated human being! Do not let that word surprise you, ladies and gentlemen! For there is a liberating, everlasting moral force in poetry. We also hope that in the not-too-distant future even the children of our common people, who do not now read our poet, will come to comprehend what the name Pushkin means! And we hope that they will then deliberately repeat what we chanced to hear not long ago from some youthful, unintentionally lisping lips: "This is a monument to a teacher!"

Letter to M. G. Savina.[1]

Village of Spasskoe-Lutovinovo.
(Orel Province, City of Mtsensk.)
Monday, May 19, 1880.

Dear Maria Gavrilovna!

It's incredible. The weather has been divine for three days now, and from morning until evening I stroll around the park or sit on the terrace, trying to think—and I do think—about various subjects, but down there, somewhere at the bottom of my soul, a single note keeps sounding. I imagine that I'm meditating on the Pushkin Commemoration—and suddenly I notice that my lips are whispering: "What a night we would have spent.... And what would have happened afterward? The Lord only knows!" And immediately added to this is the realization that this can never be and that I'll end up departing for that "unknown land" without taking with me the recollection of something I'd never experienced. For some reason, it often seems to me that we'll never see each other again: I never did believe and still don't believe that your trip abroad will take place, I won't arrive in Petersburg for the winter—and you're just wasting your time in reproaching yourself by calling me "your sin." Alas, I'll never be that. And even if we do see each other in two or three years, I'll be an old man by then, you surely will have settled down for good—and nothing will remain of what was. For you that's not such a loss ... your whole life is ahead of you— mine is behind me—and the hour that we spent in the train car, when I almost felt like a twenty-year-old youth, was the last flare-up of the lamp. It's difficult for me even to explain to myself what feeling you inspired in me. I don't know whether I'm in love with you; that used to happen to me in quite a different way. This unquenchable desire for merging, for possession—and for surrendering oneself, where even sensuality is consumed by a delicate fire.... I'm surely talking nonsense—but I would have been unspeakably happy if ... if.... But now, when I know that this isn't to be, I'm not exactly unhappy, I don't even feel any special melancholy, but I'm profoundly sorry that that lovely night is really lost forever, without having touched me with its wing.... I'm sorry for myself and—I dare to add—for you as well, because I'm certain

---

1. Maria Gavrilovna Savina (1854–1915), one of the most distinguished actresses of her time.

that you too wouldn't have forgotten the happiness you would have given me.

I wouldn't be writing all of this to you if I didn't sense that this is a farewell letter. Not that our correspondence has ceased—oh, no!—I hope that we'll hear from one another often. But a door that was half open, that door behind which I seemed to glimpse something mysteriously wonderful, has slammed shut forever. . . . Now it's quite definite that *le verrou est tiré*. No matter what happens, I'll no longer be this way—nor will you.

Well, and now that's enough. What *was* . . . (or wasn't) is now gone—and forgotten. Which doesn't prevent me from wishing you all the best in the world and kissing your dear hands in my thoughts. You needn't answer this letter . . . but do answer the first one.

Your Iv. Turgenev

P.S. Please don't be alarmed for the future. You will never receive another letter *like this one*.

The Song of Triumphant Love

[MDXLII]

Dedicated to the Memory of Gustave Flaubert

"Wage Du su irren und su träumen!"
—Schiller

I once read the following in an old Italian manuscript:

I

Around the middle of the sixteenth century, in Ferrara (it was then flourishing under the scepter of its magnificent archdukes, patrons of the fine arts and poetry), there lived two young men named Fabio and Muzzio. They were the same age, came from closely related families, and were hardly ever apart: a heartfelt friendship had united them from early childhood on, and the similarity of their lives strengthened the bond between them. Both belonged to ancient families; both were wealthy, independent, and unmarried; both had the same tastes and inclinations. Muzzio was devoted to music; Fabio, to painting. All of Ferrara regarded them with pride, as ornaments of the court, the society, and the town. They did not look alike, however, although both were distinguished by a graceful, youthful beauty. Fabio was taller, with a fair complexion, light-brown hair, and blue eyes. Muzzio, by contrast, had a swarthy complexion and black hair; his dark-brown eyes did not shine with a merry light, and his lips did not display a genial smile, like Fabio's. His thick eyebrows protruded above narrow eyes, whereas Fabio's golden eyebrows formed refined half-circles on his clear, smooth forehead. Moreover, Muzzio was less animated in conversation than Fabio. Nonetheless, the two friends were viewed with

852

equal favor by all the ladies—they were not models of chivalrous gallantry and generosity for nothing.

At this same time, a girl named Valeria also lived in Ferrara. She was considered one of the greatest beauties in the town, although it was possible to see her only rarely, since she led a solitary life, and never left her house except to go to church or to take a stroll on major holidays. She lived with her mother, a widow who came from a noble though impoverished family and had no other children. Everyone Valeria met was filled with instinctive admiration and equally instinctive tenderness and respect, so modest was her demeanor and so little, it seemed, was she herself aware of the full power of her own charms. It is true that some found her a little pale; her eyes, which were almost always cast downward, expressed a certain shyness and even timidity; her lips rarely smiled, and then only faintly; her voice had almost never been heard by anyone. But it was rumored to be beautiful, and it was said that when she sat in her own room early in the morning, while everyone else in the town was still asleep, she loved to sing old songs to the sound of a lute she played herself. In spite of her pallor, Valeria was blooming with health, and when even elderly people looked at her, they could not help thinking, "Oh, how happy will be that young man for whom this pure maiden bud, now still enfolded in its petals, one day blossoms into full flower!"

II

Fabio and Muzzio saw Valeria for the first time at a magnificent public holiday celebrated by command of the archduke of Ferrara, Ercole, son of the celebrated Lucrezia Borgia, in honor of some illustrious grandees who had come from Paris at the invitation of the archduchess, daughter of the French king, Louis XII. Valeria was sitting beside her mother on an elegant platform, which had been built according to a design by Palladio in the principal square of Ferrara for the most respected ladies in the town. Both Fabio and Muzzio fell passionately in love with her that very day, and since they never kept any secrets from one another, each of them soon found out what was occurring in his friend's heart. They agreed that they would both try to get to know Valeria, and that if she should deign to choose one of them, the other would submit to her decision without a murmur. A few weeks later, thanks to the excellent reputations they so deservedly enjoyed, they managed to gain admission to the widow's house—as difficult as it was to obtain such an invitation, she invited them to visit her. From that point onward, they were able to see and converse with Valeria almost every day, and the passion that had been kindled in the hearts of both young men grew stronger and stronger with each passing day. Valeria showed no particular preference for either of them, however, although their company was obviously agreeable to her. She studied music with Muzzio, but she talked at greater length with Fabio—she was less shy with him. They finally resolved to learn their fate once and for all, and sent Valeria a letter in which they begged her to be candid with them and tell them which of them she intended to marry. Valeria showed this letter to her mother and informed her that she was prepared to remain unmarried, but that if her mother considered it time for her to embark upon matrimony, then she would marry whichever one her mother should choose. The excellent widow shed a few tears at the thought of parting from her beloved child, and yet there was no good reason for refusing the suitors; she considered each of them equally worthy of her daughter's hand. But she secretly preferred Fabio, and since she suspected that Valeria also liked him better, she selected him. The next day Fabio learned of his good fortune, while Muzzio was forced to keep his word and to acquiesce.

This he did—but to witness the triumph of his friend and rival was more than he could bear. He promptly sold most of his property, collecting several thousand ducats, and embarked on a lengthy journey to the East. Before he left, as he said goodbye to Fabio, Muzzio told him that he would not return until he was sure that the last traces of passion had vanished from his heart. It was painful for Fabio to part from the friend of his childhood and youth, but the joyous anticipation of his approaching bliss quickly overwhelmed all other emotions, and he wholly gave himself over to the transports of a victorious love.

Shortly thereafter, he celebrated his marriage to Valeria, and only then did he learn the full value of the treasure he had been fortunate enough to obtain. He owned a charming villa surrounded by a shady garden not far from Ferrara, and he moved there with his wife and her mother. A joyful period then began for them. Married life brought out all Valeria's perfections in a new, enchanting light. Fabio became an artist of distinction—no longer a mere amateur, but a real master. Valeria's mother rejoiced, thanking God as she looked upon the happy couple. Four years flew by imperceptibly, like a delicious dream. Only one thing was missing for the young couple, one that brought them sorrow: they had no children . . . but they had not given up hope. At the end of their fourth year together, though, they suffered a truly great loss: Valeria's mother died after a brief illness.

Valeria wept inconsolably, and could not adjust to this loss for a long time. But another year went by, life reasserted its sway and flowed along its former course. And then, one fine summer evening, without warning anyone in advance, Muzzio returned to Ferrara.

III

During the whole of the five years that had elapsed since his departure, no one had heard a thing about Muzzio. Even rumors about him had died away, as though he had vanished from the face of the earth. Thus when Fabio encountered his friend in one of the streets of Ferrara, he almost cried out, first in surprise, then in delight, and he promptly invited Muzzio to stay at his villa. A spacious pavilion separate from the house stood in Fabio's garden, and he invited his friend to move into this pavilion. Muzzio readily agreed, and moved there the same day, accompanied by his servant, a mute Malay—mute but not deaf—and indeed, to judge by the alertness of his expression, a very intelligent man. . . . His tongue had been cut out. Muzzio brought dozens of boxes with him, all filled with the various treasures he had collected in the course of his extended travels. Valeria was delighted at Muzzio's return, and he greeted her in friendly but calm fashion. His every action showed that he had kept his promise to Fabio. During that day, he arranged everything in the pavilion. Aided by the Malay, he unpacked his rare possessions: rugs, silk tapestries, velvet brocade clothing, weapons, goblets, enameled plates and bowls, gold and silver curios inlaid with pearl and turquoise, amber and ivory carved boxes, cut-glass bottles, spices, incense, the skins of wild beasts, the feathers of exotic birds, and a large number of other things whose purpose appeared mysterious, if not incomprehensible. Among all these precious items was an opulent pearl necklace bestowed upon Muzzio by the king of Persia as a reward for secretly performing some great service. He received Valeria's permission to put this necklace around her neck with his own hands. It seemed very heavy to her, and to have some sort of strange heat in it. . . . It was as though it adhered to her skin. Toward evening, they sat on the terrace by the oleanders and laurels, and Muzzio began to recount his adventures. He talked about what he had seen: the distant lands, the cloud-topped mountains, the arid deserts, and the rivers like seas. He described immense palaces and temples, thousand-year-old trees, birds and flowers the colors of the rainbow. He named the cities and the peoples he had visited—and their very names seemed to come from a fairy tale. The entire East was familiar to Muzzio: he had traversed Persia and Arabia, where the horses are nobler and more beautiful than any other living creatures; he had penetrated to the very heart of India, where one group of people grows as tall and straight as stately trees; he had reached the borders of China and Tibet, where the living god, called the Grand Lama, dwells on earth in the guise of a silent man with narrow eyes. His tales were marvelous! Both Fabio and Valeria listened to him as if enchanted.

In actuality Muzzio's appearance had not changed very much: his complexion, which had been swarthy in childhood, had grown even darker, burned under the rays of a hotter sun, and his eyes seemed more deeply set than before—that was all. But the expression on his face had definitely changed: it was now dignified and solemn. It did not get animated even when he retold the dangers he had encountered at night in forests that resounded with the roar of tigers, or during the day on solitary roads where savage fanatics lay in wait for travelers, hoping to slay them in honor of their stern goddess, who required human sacrifices. And Muzzio's voice had grown deeper, more controlled; the movements of his hands, of his whole body, had lost the expansiveness typical of Italians. With the aid of his servant, the obsequiously attentive Malay, he showed his hosts a few feats he had learned from the Indian Brahmans. Thus, for instance, having concealed himself behind a curtain, he suddenly appeared sitting cross-legged in the air, the tips of his fingers pressed lightly on a vertical bamboo cane, an act that greatly surprised Fabio and positively alarmed Valeria.... "Could he be a sorcerer?" she wondered. When he then proceeded to play on a little flute to summon some snakes out of a covered basket and they stuck their dark, flat heads out from under a colored cloth, flicking their tongues, Valeria became terrified, and begged Muzzio to put those loathsome creatures away as quickly as possible.

At supper, Muzzio treated his friends to a Shiraz wine in a long-necked flagon. The wine was a golden color tinged with green, had an extraordinary fragrance and texture, and gleamed mysteriously as it was poured into tiny jasper goblets. Its flavor was unlike that of European wines: it was very sweet and spicy, and, drunk slowly, in small sips, it produced a sensation of pleasant drowsiness in all one's limbs. Muzzio made both Fabio and Valeria drink a goblet of it, and he drank one himself. Bending over her goblet, he murmured something, his fingers shaking as he did so. Valeria noticed this, but since there was something foreign, something out of the ordinary in all Muzzio's actions, in all his manners, she merely thought, "Can he have adopted some new faith in India, or are these the customs there?" Then, after a short silence, she asked him whether he had continued to study music during his travels. In reply, Muzzio ordered the Malay to bring him his Indian violin. It resembled a contemporary one, but there were only three strings instead of four, its upper section was covered with bluish snakeskin, and its slender reed bow, shaped like a half-moon, had a pointed diamond glittering at its very tip.

First Muzzio played some mournful airs, which he told them were national songs, that struck an Italian ear as strange and even barbaric. The sound of the metallic strings was plaintive and feeble. But when Muzzio began his last song, this sound suddenly gained strength, and rang out mellifluously and forcefully; a passionate melody flowed from the strings under the broad sweeps of the bow. It flowed exquisitely, twisting and coiling like the snake whose skin covered the upper part of the violin, and such fire, such triumphant joy, glowed in this melody that Fabio and Valeria felt wrung to the heart, and tears came to their eyes . . . while Muzzio, his head bent, his pale cheek pressed close to the violin, his eyebrows drawn together in a single straight line, seemed even more dignified and solemn than before. The diamond at the end of the bow flashed sparks of light as it moved, as though it had been ignited by the fire of the glorious song. When Muzzio had finished, still holding the violin tightly between his chin and his shoulder, he let the hand that held the bow fall to his side. "What is that? What have you been playing for us?" Fabio cried. Valeria didn't utter a word— but her whole being seemed to echo her husband's question. Muzzio laid the violin on the table, and brushing his hair back slightly, he replied with a polite smile: "That? That is a melody . . . that is a song I once heard on the island of Ceylon. That song is known among the people there as the song of happy, gratified love." "Play it again," Fabio murmured. "No, it must not be played again," Muzzio replied. "Besides, it is too late now. Signora Valeria ought to rest, and it is time for me to rest, too . . . I am tired."

During that day, Muzzio had treated Valeria with respectful simplicity, as a very old friend would do, but as he went out, he clasped her hand very tightly, pressing his fingers against her palm and looking into her face so intently that, although she did not raise her eyes to look at him, she nevertheless felt his look on her suddenly flaming cheeks. She did not say anything to Muzzio, but she pulled her hand away, and after he left, she stared at the door through which he had passed. She remembered that even in the past she had been a little afraid of him ... and now she was overcome by bewilderment. Muzzio went off to his pavilion; the husband and wife retired to their bedroom.

IV

Valeria did not fall asleep right away. She sensed a mild, languid fever in her blood and a slight ringing in her ears ... from that strange wine, she supposed, and perhaps from Muzzio's stories, as well as his performance on the violin. . . . She finally fell asleep toward morning, and had an extraordinary dream.

She dreamed that she was entering a large room with a low ceiling. . . . She had never seen a room like this in her whole life. The walls were covered with tiny blue tiles streaked with gold; slender carved alabaster pillars supported the marble ceiling. The ceiling itself, as well as the pillars, seemed semitransparent. . . . A pale, rosy glow suffused the room, casting a mysterious, uniform light on all the objects in it. Brocade cushions lay on a narrow rug in the very middle of the floor, which was as smooth as a mirror. In the corners, lofty, nearly concealed containers of incense in the shape of monstrous beasts were giving off smoke. There were no windows anywhere. A small, dark door covered with a velvet curtain stood in a recess in the wall. Suddenly, the curtain stirred softly and was moved aside ... Muzzio entered. He bowed, spread his arms open wide, and laughed. . . . His hands fiercely clasped Valeria's waist, his burning lips scorched her all over. . . . She fell backward onto the cushions. . . .

Moaning with horror, after a protracted struggle, Valeria woke up. Not yet realizing where she was or what was happening to her, she lifted herself up on the bed and looked around. . . . A tremor ran through her whole body. . . . Fabio was lying beside her. He was asleep, but his face was as pale as a corpse's in the light of the brilliant full moon gazing in at the window. . . . It was sadder than the face of a dead man. Valeria awakened her husband, and

as soon as he looked at her, he exclaimed, "What is the matter?"
"I had—I had a terrible dream," she whispered, still trembling all
over. . . .

But at that instant, powerful sounds began to come from the
direction of the pavilion, and both Fabio and Valeria recognized
the melody Muzzio had played for them, which he had called the
song of gratified, triumphant love. Fabio looked at Valeria in
bewilderment. . . . She closed her eyes, turned away, and both of
them, holding their breath, listened to the song until it ended. As
the last note died away, the moon went behind a cloud; it suddenly
grew dark in the room. . . . Both young people let their heads sink
back on their pillows without exchanging a word, and neither of
them noticed when the other fell asleep.

V

The next morning, Muzzio came over for breakfast. He appeared
contented, and greeted Valeria cheerfully. She responded uncer-
tainly, stole a glance at him—and became frightened at the sight
of that contented, cheerful face and those piercing, inquisitive eyes.
Muzzio began to tell another story . . . but Fabio interrupted him
at the first word.

"You could not sleep in your new quarters, evidently. My wife
and I heard you playing last night's song."

"Yes? Did you hear it?" Muzzio inquired. "I did play it, it is
true, but I had been asleep before that, and had actually had a
wonderful dream."

Valeria grew tense.

"What sort of dream?" Fabio asked.

"I dreamed," Muzzio replied, not taking his eyes off Valeria,
"that I was entering a spacious room with a ceiling decorated in
Eastern fashion. Carved columns supported the roof, the walls were
covered with tiles, and even though there were neither windows
nor lamps, the entire room was filled with a rosy glow, just as
though it were all made of translucent stone. Chinese containers
of incense were giving off smoke in the corners, and brocade cushions lay on a narrow rug on the floor. I went in through a door
covered with a curtain, and a woman whom I had once loved
appeared at another door just opposite me. And she seemed so
beautiful to me that I became completely inflamed with my former
love. . . . "

Muzzio paused significantly. Valeria sat without moving; her face gradually turned white . . . and she breathed more slowly.

"Then," Muzzio continued, "I woke up and played that song."

"But who was the woman?" Fabio queried.

"Who was she? The wife of an Indian. I met her in the town of Delhi. . . . She is no longer among the living—she died."

"And her husband?" Fabio asked, not knowing himself why he was asking this question.

"Her husband also died, they say. I lost track of them both."

"It is strange!" Fabio remarked. "My wife also had an extraordinary dream last night"—Muzzio gazed intently at Valeria—"which she did not tell me about," Fabio added.

But at this point Valeria stood up and left the room. Immediately after breakfast, Muzzio left as well, explaining that he had to go to Ferrara on business and would not be back before evening.

VI

A few weeks before Muzzio's return, Fabio had begun a portrait of his wife, depicting her with the attributes of Saint Cecilia. He had made considerable progress in his art: the renowned Luini, a pupil of Leonardo da Vinci, used to visit him in Ferrara, and, while aiding Fabio with his own advice, also passed on the precepts of his great master. The portrait was almost completely finished— all that remained was to add a few strokes to the face—and Fabio could justly be proud of his creation. After seeing Muzzio off on his way to Ferrara, Fabio went to his studio, where Valeria was usually waiting for him, but he did not find her there. He called out to her—she did not respond. Fabio was gripped by a hidden anxiety, and he began to look for her. She was not in the house. Fabio ran into the garden and caught sight of Valeria in one of the more secluded paths. She was sitting on a bench, her head bowed to her chest and her hands folded on her knees, while behind her, peeping out amid the dark-green leaves of a cypress, a marble satyr was pressing his pouting lips against a reed pipe with a distorted, malicious grin on his face. Valeria was visibly relieved at her husband's appearance, and in response to his agitated questions, she said that she had a slight headache, but that it was of no consequence and that she was ready to come and sit for him. Fabio led her to the studio, positioned her properly, and picked up his brush, but, to his great annoyance, he could not finish the face satisfactorily. This was not because she was somewhat pale and looked exhausted . . . no. But he could not find the pure, saintly expression that he liked so much, which had given him the idea of painting Valeria as Saint Cecilia, in her face that day. He finally flung down the brush, told his wife that he was not in the mood to work and thus would not keep her from lying down, since she did not look very well, then placed the canvas with its face to the wall. Valeria agreed with him that she ought to rest, and repeating her complaint of a headache, she withdrew to the bedroom.

Fabio remained in the studio. He felt a strange, confused sensation incomprehensible even to him. Muzzio's stay under his roof, a stay that he, Fabio himself, had encouraged, was making him uncomfortable. Not that he was jealous—no one could have been jealous of Valeria!—but he did not recognize his former comrade in his friend. Everything alien, unfamiliar, and new that Muzzio had brought with him from those distant lands, that seemed to have permeated his very flesh and blood—all those magical feats, songs, strange drinks, that mute Malay, even the pungent fragrance wafting from Muzzio's garments, his hair, his breath—everything inspired a feeling akin to distrust, or perhaps more to apprehension, in Fabio. And why did that Malay stare at him with such unpleasant attentiveness when he was waiting on the table? Really, one might almost conclude that he understood Italian. Muzzio had said that this Malay had made a great sacrifice by losing his tongue and that, in return, he was now possessed of great powers. What sort of powers? And how could he have obtained them at the price of his tongue? All this was very strange! Utterly incomprehensible! Fabio went into his wife's room. She was lying on the bed, fully dressed; she was not asleep. Hearing his footsteps, she shivered, then again seemed delighted to see him, just as she had been in the garden. Fabio sat down by the bed, grasped Valeria's hand, and after a momentary silence, asked her to tell him about the extraordinary dream that had frightened her so much the previous night, and whether it was similar to the dream Muzzio had described.

Valeria blushed and said hurriedly: "Oh no! No! I saw . . . a sort of monster, which was trying to tear me to pieces."

"A monster? In the shape of a man?" Fabio inquired.

"No, a wild beast . . . a wild beast!"

Valeria turned away and hid her flushed face in the pillows. Fabio held his wife's hand for a while longer, then he silently raised it to his lips and withdrew.

Both young people spent that day unhappily. Something dark

seemed to be hanging over their heads . . . but they could not tell what it was. They wanted to be together, as though some danger were threatening them, but they did not know what to say to one another. Fabio tried to work on the portrait and to read Ariosto, whose epic poem had just appeared in Ferrara and was already creating a stir all over Italy, but nothing was any use. . . . Late in the evening, right before suppertime, Muzzio returned.

VII

He seemed calm and contented—but he did not tell them much. Instead he devoted himself to questioning Fabio about their common acquaintances, the German war, and the emperor Charles. He spoke about his own desire to visit Rome to see the new pope. He offered Valeria some more Shiraz wine and, when she refused, remarked as though to himself, "It is not necessary anymore."

After retiring to the bedroom with his wife, Fabio soon fell asleep. Waking up an hour later, he realized that no one was sharing his bed: Valeria was not beside him. He promptly got up, and at that very instant, he caught sight of his wife coming out of the garden into the bedroom wearing her nightgown. The moon was shining brightly, although a light rain had been falling not much earlier. With her eyes closed and an expression of secret horror on her immobile face, Valeria approached the bed, and feeling for it with her outstretched hands, she quickly, quietly lay down. Fabio turned to her and asked a question, but she did not answer—she seemed to be asleep. He touched her, and felt drops of rain on her clothes and hair; he noticed tiny grains of sand on the soles of her bare feet. Then he leapt up and ran into the garden through the half-open door. The moon's almost cruel brilliance flooded every object with light. Fabio looked around and caught sight of two pairs of footprints on the sand of the path—one pair of feet was bare—and the footprints led to a jasmine gazebo off to the side, between the pavilion and the house. He halted in confusion, and then suddenly heard the strains of that song he had heard the night before resounding again. Fabio shuddered and rushed into the pavilion. . . . Muzzio was standing in the middle of the room, playing the violin. Fabio ran up to him.

"Have you been in the garden? Have you gone out? Are your clothes wet from the rain?"

"No . . . I don't know . . . it seems . . . I haven't been out . . . ,"

Muzzio responded slowly, as if surprised at Fabio's entrance and his agitation.

Fabio seized him by the hand.

"And why are you playing that melody again? Have you had another dream?"

Muzzio glanced at Fabio with the same air of surprise, and remained silent.

"Answer me!"

> The moon rose high like a round shield.
> The river shines like a snake....
> The friend is awake, the foe is asleep....
> The hen is in the falcon's clutches.... Bring help!

Muzzio muttered in a singsong voice, as though unconsciously.

Fabio stepped back a few paces, stared at Muzzio, thought for a moment ... and went back to the house, to the bedroom.

Valeria's head was resting on her shoulder and her hands were dangling limply—she was sound asleep. He could not awaken her right away ... but as soon as she did wake up and see him, she flung her arms around his neck and embraced him convulsively. She was trembling all over.

"What is the matter, my precious? What is it?" Fabio kept repeating, trying to soothe her. But she merely clung to his breast.

"Ah, what horrible dreams I have!" she whispered, hiding her face against him.

Fabio would have asked her more questions ... but she just went on trembling.... The windowpanes were glowing with the first light of morning when she finally fell asleep in his arms.

VIII

The next day, Muzzio disappeared during the morning, and Valeria informed her husband that she intended to visit a neighboring monastery where her spiritual father lived. He was an elderly, austere monk in whom she had boundless confidence. In response to Fabio's inquiries, she replied that she wanted to go to confession in order to unburden her soul, which was weighed down by the extraordinary impressions of the last few days. Looking at Valeria's drawn face and listening to her weakened voice, Fabio himself approved of her plan: the worthy Father Lorenzo might give her valuable advice, might alleviate her doubts.... Escorted by four attendants, Valeria set off for the monastery, while Fabio remained at home and wandered around the garden, waiting for his wife's return, trying to comprehend what had happened to her, experiencing continual fear and anger, plus the pain of inchoate suspicions. . . . He went over to the pavilion more than once, but Muzzio had not returned. Each time, the Malay gazed at Fabio like a statue, obsequiously bowing his head, maintaining a distant—or so it seemed to Fabio—secretive smile on his bronze-colored face.

Meanwhile, Valeria told everything to her priest in confession, not so much with shame as with horror. The priest listened to her attentively, gave her his blessing, and absolved her from her unintentional sin, but thought to himself: "Sorcery, the arts of the devil. . . . The matter cannot be left like this. . . ." And he returned to the villa with Valeria, allegedly for the purpose of calming and reassuring her. At the sight of the priest, Fabio became somewhat upset, but the experienced old man had determined in advance how to proceed with him appropriately. When he was left alone with Fabio, he did not betray the secrets of the confessional, naturally, but he did advise him to get rid of the guest they had invited into their house if at all possible, because his stories, his songs, and his general behavior were all unsettling Valeria's imagination. Moreover, in the priest's opinion, since Muzzio formerly had not been overly firm in the faith, as he recalled, and had spent so much time in lands unenlightened by the truths of Christianity, he might well have brought back from there the contagion of false doctrine, might even have become conversant with secret, magic arts. Therefore, although long friendship indeed had its claims, wisdom and prudence nonetheless dictated the necessity of separation. Fabio fully agreed with the excellent monk, and Valeria was overjoyed when her husband conveyed the priest's advice to her. Sent on his way with the cordial good wishes of both spouses, and loaded down with costly gifts for the monastery and the poor, Father Lorenzo returned home.

Fabio intended to explain everything to Muzzio immediately after supper, but his strange guest did not return in time for supper. At that point, Fabio decided to defer his conversation with Muzzio until the following day, and both spouses went to bed.

IX

Valeria fell asleep quickly, but Fabio could not fall asleep at all. In the nocturnal stillness, everything he had seen, everything he had felt, presented itself more and more vividly. He kept insistently asking himself questions to which, as before, he could find no answers. Had Muzzio really become a sorcerer—and had he not already poisoned Valeria? She was ill . . . but with what illness? Resting his head on his hands, restraining his feverish breathing, he gave himself over to painful reflection. Meanwhile, the moon rose again in a cloudless sky, and together with the beams shining in through the semitransparent windowpanes, a breeze began to blow from the direction of the pavilion—or was it Fabio's imagination?—like a light, fragrant current. . . . Then an urgent, passionate murmur became audible . . . and at the same moment, he noticed that Valeria was beginning to stir faintly. He shivered, and started to watch: she arose, sliding first one foot, then the other, out of bed. Her unseeing eyes staring lifelessly ahead of her, her hands outstretched, she began to walk toward the garden like someone bewitched by the moon! Fabio immediately rushed out the other door of the room, and quickly running around the corner of the house, he bolted the door that led to the garden. . . . He had barely had time to grasp the bolt when he felt someone trying to open the door from the inside, pressing against it . . . again and again . . . and then the sound of piteous moans could be heard. . . .

The thought, "But Muzzio has not come back from town," flashed through Fabio's mind, and he hastened to the pavilion. . . .

What did he see then?

Muzzio was coming toward him along the path so brightly illuminated by the moon's rays, also walking like someone bewitched by the moon, his hands held out in front of him and his eyes open yet lifeless. . . . Fabio ran up to him, but Muzzio proceeded forward without noticing him, treading evenly, step by step, his immobile face smiling in the moonlight like the Malay's. Fabio would have called out to him by name . . . but at that instant he heard a window creak in the house behind him. . . . He looked around. . . .

In fact, the window of the bedroom had been opened from top to bottom, and Valeria was standing in it, putting one foot over the sill. . . . Her hands seemed to be searching for Muzzio. . . . She was extending her whole body toward him.

Unspeakable fury flooded Fabio's breast in a sudden overwhelming wave. "Damned sorcerer!" he shrieked furiously, and seizing Muzzio by the throat with one hand, he felt for the dagger in his belt with the other, then he plunged the blade into Muzzio's side up to the hilt.

Muzzio uttered a piercing scream, and clapping his hand to the wound, he rapidly staggered back to the pavilion. . . . At the very same moment that Fabio stabbed Muzzio, Valeria screamed just as piercingly, and fell to the ground like grass mowed down by a scythe.

Fabio ran over to her, picked her up, carried her back to bed, and began speaking to her. . . .

She lay motionless for a long time, but finally opened her eyes, heaved a deep, unsteady, joyful sigh, like someone who has just been rescued from imminent death, saw her husband, and, twining her arms around his neck, embraced him tightly.

"You, you—it is you," she faltered.

Gradually her arms relaxed their hold, her head sank back, and having murmured with a blissful smile, "Thank God, it is all over. . . . But how exhausted I am!" she lapsed into a sound yet not heavy sleep.

X

Fabio sat down beside her bed, never taking his eyes off her pale and thin but already calmer face, and began to consider what had happened . . . as well as what he ought to do now. What steps should he take? If he had killed Muzzio—and remembering how deeply the dagger had gone in, he could not doubt that he had—this fact could not be concealed. He would have to bring it to the attention of the archduke, the judges . . . but how could he explain, how could he portray such an incomprehensible action? He, Fabio, had killed his relative, his best friend, in his own house! They would ask, "Why? On what grounds?" . . . But what if Muzzio were not dead? Fabio could not bear to remain in uncertainty any longer, and after assuring himself that Valeria was asleep, he cautiously got up from his chair, went out of the house, and made his way to the pavilion. Everything was quiet; light was visible in only one window. He opened the outer door with a sinking heart (there were still blood-stained fingerprints on it, in addition to black drops of blood on the sand of the path), entered the first dark room . . . and stopped on the threshold, overwhelmed with astonishment.

Muzzio was lying in the middle of the room on a Persian rug, a brocade cushion under his head and all his limbs stretched out straight, covered by a broad red shawl with a black pattern on it. His face, yellow as wax, with closed eyes and bluish eyelids, was turned toward the ceiling. No breathing was discernible: he appeared to be a corpse. At his feet knelt the Malay, who was also wrapped in a red shawl. He was holding a branch of some unknown plant resembling a fern in his left hand and, bending forward slightly, was staring fixedly at his master. A small torch wedged in the floor burned with a greenish flame, providing the only light in the room; the flame neither flickered nor smoked. The Malay did not stir upon Fabio's entrance, but merely turned his eyes toward him and then trained them on Muzzio again. From time to time, he raised and lowered the branch and then waved it in the air while his mute lips slowly parted and moved, as though uttering soundless words. The dagger with which Fabio had stabbed his friend lay on the floor between the Malay and Muzzio; the Malay struck the bloodstained blade a single blow with the branch. One minute passed . . . then another. Fabio approached the Malay and, stooping down, asked him in an low voice, "Is he dead?" The Malay nodded his head up and down, and, disentangling his right hand from his shawl, he imperiously pointed to the door. Fabio would have reiterated his question, but the imperious hand repeated its gesture and Fabio went out, indignant and amazed, but obedient.

He found Valeria sleeping as before, with an even more tranquil expression on her face. He did not undress, but sat down instead by the window, propped his head on his hands, and sank into thought once more. The rising sun found him in that very position. Valeria had not awoken.

XI

Fabio had intended to wait until she awoke and then go to Ferrara, when suddenly someone lightly tapped on the bedroom door. Fabio went out and saw his old steward, Antonio. "Signore," the elderly man began, "the Malay has just informed me that Signore Muzzio has been taken ill and wishes to move to town with all his belongings. He begs you to let him have servants to assist in packing his things now, then, at dinnertime, to provide pack horses, saddle horses, and a few attendants for the journey. Do you agree to this?"

"The Malay informed you of this?" Fabio asked. "In what manner? After all, he is mute."

"Here is the paper on which he wrote all this out in our language, Signore—quite correctly, too."

"And Muzzio is ill, you say?"

"Yes, he is very ill, and cannot see anyone."

"Have they sent for a doctor?"

"No. The Malay forbade it."

"And was it the Malay who wrote this?"

"Yes, it was he."

Fabio was silent for a moment.

"Well, then, arrange it," he finally said. Antonio withdrew.

Bewildered, Fabio watched his servant leave. "Then he is not dead?" he thought . . . and he did not know whether to rejoice or be sorry. Muzzio is ill? But a few hours ago he had seen a corpse!

Fabio returned to Valeria. She woke up and raised her head. Husband and wife exchanged a long, meaningful look.

"Is he gone?" Valeria suddenly inquired.

Fabio shuddered.

"Gone . . . in what sense? Do you mean . . . ?"

"Has he gone away?" she continued.

A weight fell from Fabio's heart.

"Not yet, but he is going away today."

"And I will never, never see him again?"

"Never."

"And these dreams will not recur?"

"No."

Valeria heaved another sigh of relief, and a blissful smile reappeared on her lips. She held out both hands to her husband.

"And we will never speak about him, never, do you hear, my dear? And I will not leave my room until he is gone. So now send me my maids . . . but wait—take that thing away!"

She pointed at the pearl necklace lying on a little bedside table, the necklace Muzzio had given her.

"Throw it into our deepest well immediately. But first embrace me—I am your Valeria again. Don't come back to me until . . . he has gone."

Fabio took the necklace—he thought its pearls looked dull—and did as his wife had requested. Then he began to wander around the garden, watching the pavilion, where the bustle of preparations for departure was commencing, from a distance. Servants were carrying out boxes, loading up the horses . . . but the Malay was not among them.

An irresistible impulse to see what was going on in the pavilion once more drew Fabio in that direction. He remembered that there was a secret door in the rear by which he could reach the inner room where Muzzio had been lying that morning. He stole around to this door, found it unlocked, and, lifting the folds of a heavy curtain covering it, cast an uncertain glance around the room.

XII

Muzzio was no longer lying on the rug. Dressed for a journey, he was sitting in an armchair, but he still appeared to be a corpse, just as he had on Fabio's first visit. His head had fallen like a stone against the back of the chair, and his outstretched hands hung lifelessly by his knees, yellow and rigid. His breast did not rise and fall. Near the chair, on the floor that had been strewn with dried herbs, stood some flat bowls filled with a dark liquid that exuded a powerful, almost suffocating odor, the odor of musk; around each bowl coiled a small, bronze-colored snake whose golden eyes flashed from time to time. Just opposite Muzzio, two steps away from him, rose the tall figure of the Malay, wrapped in a cloak of multicolored brocade belted at the waist by a tiger's tail, wearing a tall hat in the shape of a pointed tiara. He was anything but motionless, however: at one moment, he bowed down reverently and appeared to be praying; at the next, he drew himself up to his full height, even stood on tiptoe; then, with a rhythmic motion, he threw open his arms and waved them insistently in Muzzio's direction, seeming to threaten or command him, frowning and stamping his foot. All these movements evidently cost him great effort, and even caused him pain: he was breathing heavily, and sweat was streaming down his face. Suddenly he sank to the ground and, drawing a deep breath, furrowing his brow, he drew his clenched hands toward him as though he were pulling on reins with them . . . and to Fabio's indescribable horror, Muzzio's head slowly moved away from the back of the chair and bent forward, following the Malay's hands. . . . The Malay let his hands drop, and Muzzio's head fell back heavily again; the Malay repeated his movements, and the obedient head followed them again. The dark liquid in the bowls began to boil, the bowls themselves began to ring with a faint bell-like tone, and the bronze-colored snakes undulated around each of them. The Malay next took a step forward, raising his eyebrows high and opening his eyes immensely wide, then lowered his head toward Muzzio . . . and the eyelids of the dead man quivered, opened unevenly, and eyeballs as dull as lead became visible underneath them. The Malay's face grew radiant with triumphant pride and delight, an almost malevolent delight. He opened his lips wide, and a prolonged howl forcefully burst from the depths of his chest. . . . Muzzio's lips opened, too, and a faint moan quivered on them in response to that inhuman sound. . . .

But Fabio could not endure it any longer at this point—he imagined that he was present at some satanic incantation! He uttered a shriek as well and rushed out, running homeward, homeward as fast as possible, without looking back, repeating prayers and crossing himself as he ran.

XIII

Three hours later, Antonio came to him to announce that everything was done, all the things had been packed, and Signore Muzzio was getting ready to start. Without a word in reply to his servant, Fabio went out onto the terrace, from where the pavilion was visible. A few pack horses were assembled before it, and a powerful black horse saddled for two riders was being led up to the very steps, where bare-headed servants were standing alongside armed attendants. The door of the pavilion opened, and Muzzio appeared, supported by the Malay, who again wore his ordinary attire. Muzzio's face was deathlike, and his hands hung like a dead man's— but he was walking . . . yes, definitely walking! And when seated on the horse, he sat upright, he felt for and found the reins. The Malay put Muzzio's feet in the stirrups, leaped up behind him on the saddle, put his arms around Muzzio's waist, and the whole group started off. The horses moved at a slow pace, and when they turned around in front of the house, Fabio thought that two spots of white gleamed in Muzzio's dark face. . . . Could it be that Muzzio had turned his eyes toward him? The Malay alone bowed to him . . . mockingly as usual.

Did Valeria see all of this? The blinds of the windows were drawn . . . but it is possible that she was standing behind them.

XIV

At dinnertime, she came into the dining room, and was very calm and affectionate; she still complained of weariness, however. But she displayed no internal agitation now, none of her former ceaseless confusion and secret dread. And the day after Muzzio's departure, when Fabio began to work on her portrait again, he found once more in her features that pure expression whose momentary absence had so troubled him . . . and his brush moved lightly and accurately across the canvas.

The husband and wife resumed their former way of life. Muzzio vanished as though he had never existed for them. It was as if Fabio and Valeria had agreed not to utter a word about him, not to learn anything about his subsequent fate—which remained a mystery to everyone, in any event. Muzzio actually did disappear as though he had sunk into the earth. Fabio decided one day that he was obligated to tell Valeria exactly what had taken place on that fatal night ... but she apparently divined his intention, and held her breath, half-shutting her eyes, as though expecting a blow. ... And Fabio understood her—he did not inflict that blow.

One fine autumn day, Fabio was putting the finishing touches on the picture of his Cecilia; Valeria sat at the organ, her fingers straying randomly over the keys. ... Suddenly, unintentionally, the first notes of the song of triumphant love that Muzzio had once played resounded beneath her fingers—and at the same instant, for the first time since her marriage, she felt the throb of a new life growing inside her. ... Valeria shivered, and stopped. ...

What did this mean? Could it be. ...

At this point, the manuscript ended.

Letter to L. N. Tolstoy.

(Seine-et-Oise.) Bougival.
Les Frênes.
Oct. 19, 1882.

Dear Lev Nikolaevich,

I received your letter and I thank you for your promise to send the piece. I'll be waiting for the arrival of Mrs. Olsufiev, with whom I think I'm already acquainted, by the way—if this is the same Mrs. Olsufiev I used to see in Paris at Mrs. Rakhmanov's. And there's no question but that I'll read your piece in just the way you desire. I know that it was written by a very intelligent, very talented, and very *sincere* person; I may disagree with him— but first of all I'll try to understand him, to put myself quite in his place.... That will be more instructive and interesting for me than measuring him by my own yardstick or seeking to find what comprises his differences with me. *To be angry*, however, is quite unthinkable—the only people who get angry are young people who imagine that they're the center of the universe...and I'll be sixty-four in a few days. A long life teaches one not to doubt everything (because doubting everything means to believe in oneself), but to doubt oneself, i.e., to believe in something else—and even to need it. That's the spirit in which I'll be reading you.

I'm very glad that you've built a nest for yourself and that things are so good for you and all your family. But the Lord only knows when I'll see you! My condition is most peculiar. A man is quite healthy...only he can't *stand*—or *walk*—or *ride* without unbearable pain in his left shoulder, as though from a rotten tooth. It's a thoroughly absurd situation, as a result of which I'm condemned to immobility. And how long this will go on—no one knows that either. I'm gradually growing accustomed to this idea—but it's difficult. Recently, however, I've set to work again.

How happy I'd be if I found out that you too had done that! You're right, of course: before anything else one needs to live *as one should;* but, after all, the one thing doesn't contradict the other.

In a few days I'll send you a very short story, "The Quail"— you remember, I promised to write it for your children's journal.

I'll remain here about a month.

I send my regards to all your family and clasp your hand firmly.

Your sincerely loving Iv. Turgenev

Poems in Prose

To the Reader

My dear reader, don't race through these poems in order. You'll probably get bored, and the book will fall from your hands. Instead, read them haphazardly—one today, another tomorrow—and perhaps something of them will slip into your soul.

The Dog

There are two of us in the room: my dog and I. . . . A terrible storm is howling outside.

My dog is sitting in front of me, looking me straight in the eye.

I'm looking back, straight into her eyes.

She seems to want to tell me something. She's mute, she has no words, she doesn't understand herself—but I understand her.

I understand that the same feeling exists within each of us at this moment, that there's no difference between us. We're the same; the same tremulous spark is burning and glowing in both of us.

Death will sweep down with a wave of its cold, broad wing. . . .

And that will be the end!

Then who will be able to tell precisely which was the spark that glowed in each of us?

No! This isn't an animal and a man exchanging glances. . . .

These are two pairs of identical eyes, riveted on one another.

And in each pair, the animal's and the man's, the same life presses closer to the other's in fear.

A Satisfied Man

A young man is skipping and bounding along a street in the capital. His movements are cheerful and bold; there's a sparkle in his eyes, a broad smile on his lips, a pleasant flush on his beaming face. . . . He's all satisfaction and delight.

What's happened to him? Has he received an inheritance? Has he been promoted? Is he rushing to meet his beloved? Or is it simply that he's had a good breakfast and that the sense of health, the sense of well-nourished strength, is coursing through his limbs? Surely they haven't hung your lovely eight-pointed cross, oh Polish King Stanislas, around his neck?

No. He'd invented a rumor about a friend, had assiduously spread it around, had then heard that very rumor from the lips of another friend—*and had believed it himself!*

Oh, how satisfied, indeed, how very gracious, is this amiable, promising young man at this moment!

The Sparrow

I was returning from hunting, walking along a path in the garden. My dog was running ahead of me.

Suddenly, he shortened his steps and began to slink along as though he were tracking game.

I looked down the path and noticed a young sparrow with a yellow band around its beak and tufts of down on its head. It had fallen out of its nest (the wind was briskly shaking the birch trees along the path) and was sitting there unable to move, helplessly flapping its barely-sprouted little wings.

My dog was slowly approaching it when, suddenly darting down from a nearby tree, an old, dark-breasted sparrow fell like a stone right in front of her nose. All fluffed up and terrified, emitting desperate, pitiful cheeps, it took two hops toward the open jaws and their shining teeth.

It had rushed to help, it had offered itself to protect its child . . . but its whole tiny body was shaking with horror; its little voice was harsh with the strain. Dying of fear, it was sacrificing itself!

What a huge monster the dog must have seemed to it! And yet it couldn't remain perched on its high branch, out of danger. . . . A force stronger than its own will had made it come down.

My Trésor stopped, and then retreated. . . . Evidently she also recognized this force.

I hurried forward to call off the bemused dog, and walked away full of reverence.

Yes, don't laugh. I felt reverence for that tiny heroic bird, for its loving impulse.

Love, I thought, is stronger than death, stronger than the fear of death. Only through it, through love, does life sustain itself and move forward.

The Skulls

A sumptuous, brilliantly illuminated hall is filled with a large number of ladies and gentlemen.

All the faces are animated, the talk is lively.... A noisy conversation about a famous singer is being conducted. They call her divine, immortal.... Oh, how admirably she rendered her final trill yesterday!

Then suddenly—as if by the wave of a magic wand—the delicate covering of skin slipped off every head and every face, and the deadly whiteness of skulls instantaneously appeared, along with the occasional leaden shimmer of bare jaws and gums.

I beheld with horror the shifting movements of those jaws and gums; I saw how the lumpy, bony spheres revolved in the joints, glistening in the light of the lamps and candles, and how other, smaller spheres, the spheres of mindless eyes, rolled amid them.

I didn't dare to touch my own face, didn't dare to look at myself in the mirror.

But the skulls turned from side to side the way they had before.... And as noisily as ever, their tongues rapidly fluttering between their grinning teeth like little red rags, they continued to babble about how marvelously, how inimitably the immortal—yes, immortal—singer had rendered her final trill!

The Rose

It was during the last days of August.... Autumn was already at hand.

The sun was setting. A sudden downpour of rain, without thunder or lightning, had just swiftly passed across our wide plain.

The garden in front of the house was steaming and glowing, flooded with the fire of the sunset as well as the deluge.

She was sitting at a table in the drawing room, pensively gazing through the half-open door into the garden.

I knew what was occurring in her soul then, I knew that at that instant, after a brief but agonizing struggle, she was surrendering herself to a feeling she could no longer master.

Suddenly she stood up, hastily went out to the garden, and disappeared.

An hour passed . . . then a second; she didn't return.

Eventually, I stood up, and going out of the house, I turned into the path along which—I had no doubt—she'd gone.

Everything had gotten dark; night had already fallen. But on the damp sand of the path, a roundish object was discernible even in the darkness, glowing bright red.

I stooped down. . . . It was a fresh, newly blossomed rose. I'd seen this very rose on her breast two hours earlier.

I carefully picked up the flower that had fallen in the dirt and, going back to the drawing room, I laid it on the table by her chair.

She finally came back, and walking across the length of the room with light footsteps, she sat down at the table.

Her face was both paler and more animated. Her swollen eyes, which looked smaller somehow, shifted rapidly from side to side in cheerful uncertainty.

She noticed the rose, seized it, glanced at its crushed, soiled petals, glanced at me—and her eyes, suddenly brought to a standstill, began to shine with tears.

"Why are you crying?" I inquired.

"Oh, because of this rose. Look what's happened to it."

Then I decided to utter a profound remark.

"Your tears will wash away the dirt," I declared impressively.

"Tears don't wash, they burn," she replied. And turning toward the fireplace, she flung the rose into the dying flames.

"Fire burns even better than tears," she exclaimed, not without an effort, and her lovely eyes, still bright with tears, laughed insolently and delightedly.

I saw that she, too, had been scorched.

To the Memory of Iu. P. Vrevskaia

On the dirt, on the stinking wet straw under the porch of a tumbledown barn hastily converted into a camp hospital in a devastated Bulgarian village, she lay for over two weeks, dying of typhus.

She was unconscious, and not a single doctor even looked at her. The sick soldiers, whom she'd tended as long as she could stand on her feet, took turns getting up from their contaminated cots to lift the shards of a broken pot containing a few drops of water to her parched lips.

She was young and beautiful; she was known in high social circles; even dignitaries had expressed interest in her. Ladies had envied her, men had danced attendance on her . . . two or three had been secretly, deeply in love with her. Life had smiled on her—but there are smiles that are worse than tears.

A soft, tender heart . . . and such strength, such thirst for sacrifice! To help those who needed help. . . . She didn't know any other form of happiness. . . . She didn't know any other, and had never known any other—all other forms of happiness had passed her by. But she'd accepted that long ago, and, aglow with the fire of an unquenchable faith, she'd completely given herself over to the service of her fellow human beings.

No one ever knew what hidden treasure she'd buried in the depths of her heart, in her most secret recesses—and now, of course, no one will ever know.

And, anyway, what for? Her sacrifice has been made . . . her work is done.

But it's sad to think that no one voiced any gratitude even to her corpse, although she herself was embarrassed by and foreign to all gratitude.

Thus may her dear shade not be offended by this belated little wreath that I'm daring to lay upon her grave!

The Threshold

I see a huge building.

A narrow door in its front wall is open wide. Inside the doorway looms a dank fog. A young woman is standing before its high threshold—a Russian young woman.

The impenetrable fog exudes icy streams of frost, and a slow, toneless voice is carried out from the depths of the building along with those streams.

"Oh you who wishes to cross this threshold—do you know what awaits you?"

"I know," the young woman answers.

"Cold, hunger, hatred, mockery, scorn, resentment, imprisonment, illness, and even death?"

"I know."

"Utter alienation, isolation?"

"I know. I'm ready. I'll bear all the suffering, all the blows."

"Not only from your enemies, but even from your relatives, your friends?"

"Yes . . . even from them."

"Very well. You are prepared for any sacrifice?"

"Yes."

"For anonymous sacrifice? You will perish, and no one . . . no one will even know whose memory to honor!"

"I don't need either gratitude or pity. I don't need a name."

"Are you prepared to commit a crime?"

The young woman bowed her head. . . .

"I'm even prepared to commit a crime."

The voice didn't immediately continue its questions.

"Do you know," it eventually spoke up again, "that you may cease to believe what you believe now, that you may realize you have deceived yourself and have destroyed your young life in vain?"

"I know this as well. Nonetheless, I want to enter."

"Then enter!"

The young woman crossed the threshold—and a heavy curtain fell behind her.

"Fool!" someone shrieked from behind it.

"Saint!" came from somewhere in reply.

The Visit

I was sitting at an open window. . . . It was morning, early morning, on the first of May.

The dawn hadn't broken yet, but the dark, warm night had already grown pale and cold at its approach.

No mist had arisen, no breeze was stirring, everything was the same color, everything was silent . . . but the nearness of awakening could be felt; the rarefied air smelled keen and was moist with dew.

Suddenly, with a light whirring rustle, a large bird flew into my room through the open window.

I was startled at first, then looked closely at it. . . . It wasn't a bird, it was a tiny winged woman dressed in a long, clinging robe that flowed to her feet.

She was light-gray all over, the color of mother-of-pearl; only the inside of her little wings glowed with the tender flush of a blossoming rose. A wreath of lilies of the valley wound through the curls scattered over her round little head, and two peacock feathers amusingly waved like a butterfly's antennae above her lovely curved forehead.

She flew around in a circle twice, near the ceiling. Her tiny face was laughing, as were her huge, clear, black eyes. The joyous playfulness of her capricious flight made them flash like diamonds.

In her hand she held the long stalk of a flower of the steppes—

"the tsar's scepter," as Russians call it, since it really does resemble a scepter.

Rapidly flying above my head, she touched it with the flower.

I rushed toward her.... But she'd already fluttered out through the window and darted away....

In the garden, in a thicket of lilac bushes, a wood dove greeted her with its first morning coo ... and the milk-white sky flushed a soft pink at the spot where she vanished.

I know you, goddess of fantasy! You visited me by accident; you flew on to seek out the young poets.

Oh poetry! Youth! Virginal feminine beauty! You can gleam for me just for a moment, in the early dawn of early spring!

Cabbage Soup

The only son of a widowed peasant woman, a young man of twenty, the best worker in the village, had just died.

The lady who owned this village, hearing of the woman's loss, went to visit her on the very day of the funeral.

She found the woman at home.

Standing in the middle of her hut in front of a table, without any haste, with a regular movement of her right arm (her left one was hanging limp at her side), she was scooping up weak cabbage soup from the bottom of a blackened pot and swallowing it, spoonful by spoonful.

The woman's face was pinched and somber; her eyes were red and swollen ... but she held herself erect as rigidly as she had in church.

"Good Lord!" thought the lady. "How can she eat at a time like this? ... However, they all have such coarse feelings!"

At this point, the lady recalled that a few years earlier, when she'd lost her little nine-month-old daughter, she'd refused to rent a lovely country house near Petersburg in her grief, and had spent the whole summer in town!

Meanwhile, the woman went on eating her cabbage soup.

The lady finally couldn't contain herself any longer.

"Tatiana!" she exclaimed.... "For heaven's sake! I'm surprised! Is it possible you didn't love your son? How can it be that you haven't lost your appetite? How can you eat that soup?"

"My Vasia's dead," the woman observed quietly, and tears of anguish ran down her hollow cheeks again. "So it's the end of me, too. It's tearing my heart out. But the soup still mustn't be wasted—there's salt in it."

The lady merely shrugged her shoulders and left. Salt didn't cost her very much.

The Reporter

Two friends were sitting at a table, drinking tea.

A sudden hubbub arose in the street. They heard pitiable groans, furious curses, and bursts of malignant laughter.

"They're beating someone up," observed one of the friends, glancing out the window.

"A criminal? A murderer?" inquired the other. "Listen, whatever he may be, we can't tolerate illegal violence. Let's go defend him."

"But it isn't a murderer they're beating up."

"It isn't a murderer? Is it a thief, then? It doesn't matter—let's go get him away from the crowd."

"It isn't a thief, either."

"It isn't a thief? Is it a cashier, a train conductor, an army contractor, a Russian art collector, a lawyer, a well-intentioned editor, a social reformer? . . . In any event, let's go help him!"

"No . . . it's a newspaper reporter they're beating up."

"A reporter? Well, in that case, I tell you what—let's finish our tea first."

The Sphinx

There's yellowish-gray sand, soft on top and hard below . . . sand without end, wherever you look.

And above this desert of sand, above this sea of dead dust, rises the immense head of the Egyptian sphinx.

What do they want to say, those thick, protruding lips, those motionless, distended, upturned nostrils, and those eyes—those elongated, half-drowsy, half-watchful eyes under the double arch of the high brows?

They definitely want to say something! They actually do speak, but only Oedipus can solve the riddle and comprehend their silent speech.

Wait! For I know those features. . . . There's nothing Egyptian about them. A white, low forehead, prominent cheekbones, a short, straight nose, a handsome mouth with white teeth, a soft moustache, a curly beard, small, wide-set eyes . . . and a cap of hair parted down the middle on its head. . . . It's you, Karp, Sidor,

Semen, a peasant from Iaroslav, from Riazan, my fellow countryman, Russian flesh and blood! Did you become one of the sphinxes
long ago?

Or do you want to say something, too? Yes, you're a sphinx
as well.

Your eyes—those colorless, deep eyes—also speak. . . . And their
speech is just as silent and enigmatic.

But where's your Oedipus?

Alas! It isn't enough to put on a peasant shirt in order to become
your Oedipus, oh all-Russian sphinx!

Nature

I dreamed that I'd entered an immense underground temple with
a lofty, arched roof. It was filled with some sort of underground,
steady light.

In the very center of the temple sat a majestic woman wearing
a flowing green robe. Her head was propped on her hand, and she
seemed to be deeply lost in thought.

I immediately realized that this woman was Nature herself, and
a sensation of reverent awe sent an instantaneous shiver through
my innermost soul.

I approached the seated woman and, making a respectful bow,
I cried: "Oh universal Mother of us all! What is the subject of
your meditation? Are you contemplating the future destiny of humanity? Or how it may attain the highest possible perfection and
happiness?"

The woman slowly turned her dark, menacing eyes toward me.
Her lips moved, and I heard a ringing voice that resembled the
clanging of iron.

"I'm thinking about how to give greater power to the leg muscles
of the flea, so that it may escape from its enemies more easily. The
balance between the ability to attack and the ability to defend has
been upset. . . . It must be restored."

"What?" I faltered in reply. "This is what you're thinking about?
But aren't we human beings your favorite children?"

The woman frowned slightly. "All creatures are my children,"
she declared. "I care for them all equally—and I destroy them all
equally."

"But what about goodness . . . reason . . . justice . . . ?" I faltered
again.

"Those are human words," I heard the iron voice proclaim. "I know neither good nor evil. . . . Reason is not a law unto me—and what is justice? I have given you life, and I will take it away and give it to others, to worms or to people . . . I don't care. . . . Meanwhile, fend for yourself, and don't disturb me!"

I wanted to respond . . . but the earth gave a hollow groan and shuddered—and I awoke.

What Will I Think? . . .

What will I think when the time comes for me to die, if I'm in any condition to think at that time?

Will I think about what poor use I've made of my life, how I've slept or dozed through it, how I've failed to enjoy its gifts?

"What? Is death here already? So soon? Impossible! Why, I haven't had time to do anything yet. . . . I've only been getting ready to do something!"

Will I review the past, and dwell on the few delightful moments I've experienced, on precious images and faces?

Will my bad deeds come to mind, and will my soul be filled with the burning anguish of belated remorse?

Will I think about what awaits me beyond the grave . . . if anything really does await me there?

No. . . . I suspect that I'll try not to think, and will force myself to become occupied with some triviality, simply in order to distract my attention from the menacing void darkly looming ahead of me.

I once saw a dying man who kept complaining that they wouldn't let him have any hazelnuts to chew on! . . . And only in the depths of his fast-dimming eyes was there something quivering and struggling, like the broken wing of a mortally wounded bird. . . .

Prayer

Whatever a person may pray for, that person prays for a miracle. Every prayer comes down to this: "Almighty God, grant that two times two not equal four."

Only a prayer like this is a real prayer, from someone to someone. To pray to a universal spirit, to a higher being, to a Kantian, Hegelian, impersonal, amorphous God, is impossible, unimaginable.

But can even a personified, living, concrete God make two times two not equal four?

Every believer is obligated to answer: *he can*—and is obligated to convince himself of this.

But if his reason revolts against such nonsense?

Then Shakespeare comes to his aid: "There are more things in heaven and earth, Horatio . . . ," etc.

And if someone else begins to object in the name of truth, he merely needs to repeat the famous question, "What is truth?"

Therefore, let's drink and be merry—and pray.

The Russian Language

In days of doubt, in days of dreary musings on my country's fate, you alone are my comfort and support, oh great, powerful, righteous, and free Russian language! Were it not for you, how could I fail to lapse into despair in view of all that's occurring at home? But it's impossible to believe that such a language wasn't given to a great people!

Letter to L. N. Tolstoy.

Bougival.

Les Frênes.

Chalet.

The beginning of July, Russian style

Bougival. 1883.

Dear Lev Nikolaevich!

I haven't written to you for a long time because, speaking frankly, I've been and *am* on my deathbed. I can't recover—there's no point in even thinking of that. I'm writing you, in fact, to tell you how glad I was to be your contemporary—and to convey to you my last, sincere request. My friend, return to literary activity! After all, that gift comes to you from where all else does, too. Oh, how happy I'd be if I could think that my request would have that effect on you!! I'm a doomed man—the doctors don't even know what to call my disease, *névralgie stomacale goutteuse.* I can't walk or eat or sleep or anything! It's boring even to repeat all this! My friend, great writer of the Russian land, heed my request! Let me know if you receive this note, and allow me once more to heartily, heartily embrace you, your wife, and all your family. I can't go on anymore, I'm tired.

About the Editor

Elizabeth Cheresh Allen is Associate Professor and Chair of the Department of Russian at Bryn Mawr College. She is the author of *Beyond Realism: Turgenev's Poetics of Secular Salvation.* She is also the editor, with Gary Saul Morson, of *Freedom and Responsibility in Russian Literature: Essays in Honor of Robert Louis Jackson,* published by Northwestern University Press.